KNIGHTS CORRUPTION COMPLETE SERIES

S. NELSON

AUTHOR NOTE:
These books touch on the subjects of rape, violence, and hard situations that may trigger bad memories for those who have been in similar situations.
Not suitable for anyone under 18.

MAREK

This book is dedicated to my husband. Thank you so much for being patient with me while I lock myself in the office, writing for countless hours on end. I love you!

PROLOGUE

Marek

TOO MANY VOICES SHOUTED DEMANDS, hands shoving me roughly forward until I was no longer standing on my own two feet. "Get on the ground!" was the one I heard the most. My knees hit hard off the gravel, my stomach kissing earth while my hands were jerked behind my back before I could utter a single word of protest. People in uniforms clambering to throw me and all my brothers down like we'd done something wrong. Don't make any mistake, we certainly weren't boy scouts, but the sudden invasion was most definitely unwarranted.

The DEA agent towering over me was none other than Sam Koritz, the most crooked motherfucker I knew, and that was saying a lot since I was the furthest from a straight arrow myself. He was forever trying to nail my club, even though it was because of us that his pockets were fattened to not only look the other way, but to forget we even existed.

Running my club, the Knights Corruption, was profitable but extremely dangerous. We were accountable for two-thirds of the cocaine supply smuggled into central California. The ports we utilized were run by us and people we paid handsomely to keep the profit high and the risk low. But every now and then, someone became greedy—hence Koritz busting in like he owned the joint.

Fuck him if he thought he was gonna get away with this shit. I'd put one of my boys on him just as soon as we were able to. Maybe pay a visit to his house, have a little chat, remind him who paid for his kid's private school.

While I sucked the dirt into my lungs, my arms aching from the tightly coiled position, I dreamed up ways of paying back exactly who I knew was responsible—besides Koritz, of course.

The Savage fucking Reapers.

Koritz was most likely in bed with them as well, and whoever paid more won out every time. I had no doubt Henry 'Psych' Brooks, the president of the Savage Reapers, had put the DEA agent up to it. And why not? Killing two birds with one stone. If they found what they were looking for—drugs, guns and money—they'd profit. And if not, they'd been able to send a message by allowing us to witness Koritz's betrayal.

The continual war between our two clubs was coming to a head very soon. We'd already had casualties, and it would be over my dead body if any more of us were gonna meet the Devil any time soon.

"Where the hell is it, Marek?" Koritz shouted, stomping his boot down on top of my neck. *I'm gonna kill this sonofabitch as soon as I get the chance.*

Trying my best not to give him the reaction he wanted, I spit the soil from my mouth and laughed. As soon as the sound burst forth, he kicked me in the ribs before I could change positions to protect myself. I should have known it was coming, but I was too preoccupied with pissing the bastard off.

A rush of air flew from my lips, a low groan escaping before I could stop it. "Touch my prez one more fuckin' time, and you'll be meetin' your maker real soon," my VP, Stone, yelled. We faced each other on the ground, and as soon as his eyes met mine, I shot him a warning look for him to shut his mouth and lock it up. His reddened face told me he was seconds away from exploding.

Luckily, he did as I'd silently cautioned.

Loyalty.

Plain and simple.

His mouth and hot-ass temper were gonna land us in more trouble if he kept going. While I appreciated his undying allegiance to me and to the club, we needed to let this all play out.

Koritz didn't even pay Stone's threat any attention, keeping his focus on me the entire time instead. I saw his foot leave the ground, cock back then swing forward. I braced myself that time, but it didn't do any good—the fucker came wearing shit-kickers, and my ribs certainly felt the brunt of it. I wouldn't be surprised if he'd broken a couple in his attempt to make me talk. But that's okay, because when the opportunity presented itself to pay him back, I'd make sure to return the favor.

"I'm not gonna ask you again, *Prez,*" he gritted, pacing back and forth, waiting for me to divulge the location of what they'd come here looking for—the product. But if he thought he would find it on our own goddamn compound, he was even stupider than I thought. We never kept that shit on site. The worst thing they would come across would be a few illegal handguns. That's it.

Lifting my head off the ground, I craned my neck to look up at him. Words fell from my lips, but he couldn't hear them. Which was done half on purpose, because I wanted him to squat down to my level. The other part was because I was having a hard time breathing. Finally, he did exactly what I wanted him to, leaning down so he could hear me.

"What was that, you piece of shit?" he yelled.

"Nothing," I replied, a drop of blood spraying from my mouth and hitting the dirt.

"What?" He was losing whatever patience he had left, and if I wasn't careful my ass was gonna really be hurtin' come morning.

He knew enough to make sure I was tied up and on the ground before he attacked me, otherwise, he'd have an up–close-and-personal relation-ship with my fists. He was no match for me, and the coward knew it. The man was in his late forties and ate too much garbage, the pot belly hanging over his belt proof of his overindulgences. His receding hairline was noticeable even though he tried to hide it with a laughable comb-over.

I was everything he wasn't and he knew it, so he exerted his authority, or whatever authority he thought he had. Once I found my opportunity, we'd see who the big man was then.

"Nothing," I said louder. "There's nothing here, so you assholes are wasting my precious tax dollars," I goaded.

"Tax dollars? As far as I'm aware, criminals don't pay taxes, or did that change? Oh, wait, I forgot all about the little strip club the Knights own," he chided. "Maybe that'll be our next stop. Maybe it accidently gets torched," he threatened, nodding as if he was truly pondering it.

I'd been venturing out to legal businesses, my main goal to turn my club legit. Simply put, the way we were doing things was way too danger-ous, and I was tired of it all. I was only twenty-eight years old, but most days I felt twice my age. Physically, I was as fit as could be, but mentally, I was drained. Stressed the fuck out. Sick of the bloodshed. I'd seen more in my short life than most men saw in their entire existence, and enough was enough. But there were debts which had to be repaid and vengeance that needed to be carried out before I called it legit for good. Once we went straight, we weren't gonna teeter back and forth between the two worlds, so we had to be sure everything was taken care of first.

Realizing Koritz wasn't gonna get anything out of us, he straightened up and yelled to his men, "Search it! Tear it apart if you have to. We have all night," he promised, his foot coming dangerously close to my face.

"Don't you need a warrant, asshole?" Ryder, my Sergeant-at-Arms, yelled, an outburst which earned him a swift blow to the stomach. He was fortunate—or unfortunate, depending on how one looked at it—to not be lying down. He was on his knees with his fingers interlocked and resting on the top of his head, his hands bound while one of the agents held him in place so he couldn't move. Cuffed or not, my men would run off at the mouth without a second's hesitation.

"Nope," Koritz's lapdog said, pulling back and sucker punching Ryder, that time in the face.

All these fuckers are goin' down.

After two very long hours, they finally deemed the compound all clear, only finding a few dime bags of weed. Nothing they were gonna waste their time over. They kept us locked in the same positions, my arms screaming in pain along with my possibly broken ribs. Koritz stalked my way, beyond pissed that he wasn't able to pin anything on me. For as crooked as he was, he wasn't stupid enough to plant evidence, though, probably out of fear of retaliation. Little did he know I was already plotting my revenge.

All in due time.

Reaching down, he took hold of my upper arm and pulled, but he was so weak he needed another man to help lift me. Once on my feet, I staggered a few steps, trying to find my footing all while doing my best to breathe. I masked the pain by clenching my teeth and trying to appear as pissed off as possible—which wasn't hard to do, given everything that'd happened.

"You lucked out this time, Marek," Koritz said, swiftly patting my side. The pain radiated through my entire body, and I held the air in my lungs, waiting to see what he was gonna do next. With my hands still cuffed behind my back, I knew I wasn't capable of doing shit until he released me. Roughly grabbing my wrists, he jerked them back, the muscles of my arms hollering in protest. "If you make a move on me or any of my men, I'll shoot you where you stand. You understand?" His putrid breath hit the side of my face, and I almost threw up.

When I nodded quickly, he withdrew the key to the restraints and popped them open. Normally, I would rub my wrists because of the tight pressure of the cuffs, but I simply flexed my fists at my sides, reminding myself that he would make good on his promise of killing me if I dared to strike back.

As soon as all my men were released, and all of the DEA agents left our compound, I vowed then and there to never be put into that situation ever again.

Everyone would feel the wrath of the Knights Corruption MC before we turned to the other side.

ONE

Sully

TURNING HIS HEAD IN MY direction, the man leading me down a dark, narrow hallway practically spit at me in anger. "If you don't hurry up, Sully, you're gonna regret being so goddamn slow." I knew that tone. I was petrified of that tone. But I was used to it and unfortunately, I was used to him and the way he treated me.

My tired legs tried to hurry, but I was extremely sluggish. Vex had woken me from a dead sleep, forced me to pleasure him, then tossed me out of bed. Throwing some dark-colored clothes at me, he ordered me to dress, hauled me from the compound and shoved me in the passenger side of a beat-up gray truck.

I didn't even need to ask where we were going. I already knew. Every now and again, he would drag me with him to be his lookout while he broke into people's homes and stole their drugs—cocaine, to be specific. He would snort as much of the nose candy as he could, then sell the rest to bring in a profit for our club, the Savage Reapers. Having a talent for bypassing even the most high-tech security systems, it was a shame he didn't put his talents to better use, but when it came right down to it, Vex Montale was a low-level criminal, never aspiring to be anything more than he was.

I took two more steps down the darkened space and ran smack-dab right into his back. He'd suddenly stopped, but I knew enough to keep my mouth shut instead of asking why. I learned long ago to know my place when it came to Vex, only speaking if he asked me a question. I was only fourteen years old when he claimed me from my father, Vex being all of eighteen himself. That was six years ago. At first, I was attracted to him, his sandy-brown hair and piercing green eyes were certainly head-turning.

His square jaw and perfectly proportionate nose only added to his good looks, even with the slight bump in the middle. He'd broken it during one of the many fights he'd incited, never bothering to have it set properly. His lean, muscular build had enticed my awakening young hormones, but that quickly changed the first time his fist connected with my face. No matter how good-looking he was on the outside, the ugliness inside him had pushed through and repulsed me from then on.

I wasn't stupid enough to believe he was faithful to me either, witnessing him having sex with other girls on a few occasions. But did he care when he'd been caught? No. The times I'd accidentally walked in on him rutting like some kind of animal, he leered at me and continued on until he roared out his disgusting release.

Vex snatched my arm and pulled me closer, snarling at me like some sort of rabid dog. Hell, even a sick dog was nicer than he was, especially when he'd been snorting that shit up his nose, which happened more and more lately. "His room is the last one on the right. We have to get in and grab what we can," he sniffed, pinching his nose between his thumb and forefinger before starting to move again. "Don't fuck this up. Do you hear me?" he asked, squeezing my arm tight.

"Yes," I whimpered. Even though he'd asked me a direct question—my cue to speak—he didn't like it when I talked too much.

He was the second dangerous man I knew, my father trumping him and taking the title for the worst human being alive. At least Vex didn't keep me locked in a closet for days without food or water when I'd done or said something he didn't like. Don't get me wrong, I lived in Hell every single day, praying for a quick death each and every time he struck, raped and choked me unconscious. But because I was still breathing air into my lungs, my destiny obviously hadn't been fulfilled yet.

When we reached the room we were supposed to enter, he stilled on the threshold, peering inside and listening for anything that would tell him we weren't alone. Although the information he'd received from one of the other brothers told him the owner was out for the night—leaving his place unattended for the likes of us—he'd been given erroneous tips before.

I detested being dragged into situations I wanted nothing to do with. But I had no choice, just like I had no choice in anything that happened in my life.

It was better to go along than resist.

I had the scars to prove it.

Moving slower than I thought was possible while he was coked out of his mind, he shoved me forward into the dark bedroom. "Look in the closet." He pinched his nose again, making a sound with his throat before mumbling to himself, "He told me it was here."

Without answering, I did as I was told and headed for the closet in the far corner of the large room. The only light I had was from a small keychain flashlight. Anything bigger would pull too much attention—at least, that's what Vex told me.

While I searched for the kilos of cocaine that were supposed to have been hidden somewhere in the bedroom, Vex rummaged through drawers, opening and closing them before moving on to other areas of the expansive room.

Whoever lived here certainly had money. Not only was the house huge, but the furnishings looked expensive. The small light of my keychain had allowed me to see the king-sized bed, which took up the middle of the space, with four carved pillars the focal point. Two matching dressers and nightstands completed the bedroom set, the wood a rich mahogany color I itched to run my fingers over.

Living at the clubhouse, which was unheard of for a female, we only had old, ratty furniture. Most of it was rigged somehow, and the pieces that weren't would splinter apart with the slightest force. I wasn't a materialistic person, not by any stretch of the imagination, but just once I would like to own something new.

"Did you find anything yet?" he gritted, his warm breath hitting the side of my face while he crowded my personal area inside the closet. Before I could answer, he shoved me back into the bedroom and rooted through the space himself, cursing me every time he came up short, like it was my fault he couldn't find what he was looking for.

My head hung low, the tiny light slowly faded in and out while I waited for him to finish his search. Uneasiness ate me up the longer we invaded the stranger's house, the hairs on the back of my neck sticking up with each tick of the clock. With every second that passed, we were that much closer to getting caught. And if were spotted, it was somehow going to be my fault, and I would pay dearly because of it. As it stood, Vex was probably going to punish me anyway, if for nothing other than the frustration that he couldn't find more product to feed his nasty habit. Either way, my night was going to be less than ideal. But what else was new?

Lost in my own head, I never heard him approaching.

I never saw the light flick on in the hallway.

I never saw his hand reach into the bedroom where we were standing and pause by the light switch.

I never saw him until the room was immersed in brightness, instantly blinding me until my eyes focused on the scene around me.

"What the hell, Sully? Turn off the light before I knock some sense into you."

I didn't pay any attention to his ramblings; instead, my eyes were trained on the man standing in front of me, his gun pointed directly at my chest.

At first glance, the stranger appeared to be civil, dressed in a finely pressed suit matched with the most expensive shoes I'd ever seen. The light from above shone off his cleanly shaved head, his neatly trimmed beard a lie as to how dangerous he really was.

I thought for sure fear and panic would have imprisoned me, but unfortunately, it wasn't the first time a gun had been aimed at me. Shit, it wasn't even the second or third time my life had been threatened in such a way. But a stranger, a man whose home we'd broken into, was the one pointing the weapon at me. I should have been scared. But instead, I was numb inside.

"What do we have here?" the stranger yelled, instantly gaining Vex's attention. Stepping from the closet, he came to stand behind me as soon as he saw the man had a weapon. It didn't shock me that he chose to use me as a shield in case the guy went nuts and started firing. Come to think of it, I prayed for that exact scenario; then I would be set free from the invisible chains which bound me to this dreadful life.

"Don't do anything crazy, man," Vex warned, his grip on my arms tightening the more he realized how dangerous our situation had become when the owner of the house stepped forward without an ounce of reservation.

"You break into my house, scour through my things looking for God knows what, and *you* tell *me* not to do anything crazy. Do you know who I am?" Silence danced around the room. "Well . . . Do you?" he roared, scratching his cheek with the barrel of his gun, a deranged look on his face the closer he stepped toward us.

I knew that look.

Vex *just* had it on his face.

Cocaine is a hell of a drug.

"Yes," Vex admitted. "Look, we didn't take anything. No harm, right?" His nervous laugh hit a nerve with me. He never took anything seriously because he thought he was protected by the club, doing anything he wanted, treating everyone like shit just because he thought he could get away with it simply because he was with the president's daughter. But what he didn't realize was that he was a liability and his brothers were tired of coming to his rescue. He had no idea, but I'd accidentally overheard a few of the members discussing his future, or lack thereof. I kept my mouth shut because I prayed they would make their move sooner rather than later. But until then, I had to bide my time.

"How the hell did you even get in here?" the man asked, stepping perilously closer. "You must be some sort of electronics wiz to bypass my security system. Is that it?"

He hit the nail on the head.

"Never mind, what's done is done." He grinned dangerously. "And while you may not have taken anything, it doesn't mean I won't." His statement confused me, until he lunged forward, seized my arm and pulled me against his large frame. "I think I'll have a little taste," he promised, his tongue snaking out and licking the side of my face as I twitched in his hold.

Even though Vex treated me like a piece of property, less than human, someone he kept around solely to do with as he saw fit, I was still his. And any threat to that was a direct insult to him.

The blast of a gun pierced the air, my eardrums feeling as though they'd exploded from the close proximity. One minute, the strange man held me close and the next he was on the ground, a pool of blood surrounding him where he lay.

"Fuckin' cocksucker," Vex grumbled, kicking the man to make sure he wasn't getting back up. Once he was satisfied he'd killed him, he continued searching the room as if he hadn't just ended the man. I was left to stand there dumbfounded, not so much by the corpse lying at my feet, but that Vex could have easily killed me instead. There hadn't been much space between us, and that he'd been able to achieve such a clean shot was mind-boggling.

Or was he hoping I would have perished right along with the man?

TWO

Sully

THE RIDE BACK HOME WAS in silence. I never did find out who the man was. The less I knew, the better.

Vex found what he'd been looking for hidden in a faulty floorboard, ten kilos of coke his prize for the evening. After snorting a few lines, he packed up everything in the duffel bag he'd brought and ushered us from the home, not a care in the world that he'd left a body behind to be discovered.

Once we were finally inside the clubhouse, I walked toward the kitchen, needing to grab a drink before I headed off to the room Vex and I shared. A strange male voice stopped me in my tracks. I knew better than to pay attention to the goings on inside the place I unfortunately called home, but an uneasiness gripped me.

My father, Henry Brooks—aka Psych, aka president of the Savage Reapers—rounded the corner, followed closely by a man I'd never seen before.

I would have crashed right into them had it not been for my quick reflexes.

"Sully," my father greeted, his tone dripping with an indication that he was up to no good. As usual.

"Father," I answered, apprehension wrapping around me like the coil of a dangerous snake. I never referred to my father as Dad or Daddy. Not since I was a toddler. The man hated me; it was the only excuse I could come up with for the way he treated me. So I decided long ago to bury any fleeting feelings I had toward him as my kin, disguising the need for his approval with formalities.

"Who do we have here?" the man standing behind my father asked.

Stepping to the side to allow his guest to feast his eyes on me, he answered, "My daughter, Sully."

"Sully," the man repeated, stepping closer until he was only a few feet away from me. My breath twitched in my throat, my heart picking up pace the more he continued to leer at me. His beady, soulless eyes roved over my body, and right then I was grateful for the dark, baggy clothes Vex had made me wear. "Is she taken?"

"Yeah, but you can have her if you want. I'll handle Vex, explain it's good business and all."

What the hell is he talking about?

As if being summoned, Vex appeared out of thin air, walking up behind my father and the strange man who'd suddenly become enthralled with me.

"What are you doing out of our room, Sully?" he yelled, stalking toward me and roughly gripping my neck. While his touch was painful, I welcomed the familiar feeling. Better Vex than the bastard standing in front of me.

"Vex, I was just telling Yanez here he can have a go at Sully. What do ya think?" Looking back and forth between the man who'd given me life and the man I belonged to, I was stunned to find out Vex wasn't going to put up a fight. Which was extremely odd. I was his property, and any threat to that was always met with sheer force. Sometimes even resulting in death, exactly like what had happened earlier.

While he didn't voice his refusal, his face said it all. But that didn't matter. My father's word was law, and if he was going to give me to this man, then there wasn't a damn thing either one of us could do.

I still tried, however.

Slowly backing away, I prayed I had enough time to make it to my room before any of them caught me. I'd lock myself inside and count the minutes until they left me alone.

I knew I was being delusional, but an escape inside my head was all I had.

"Don't even think about it," my father sneered, lurching forward and snagging my wrist. "Do you know who this man is?" I remained silent because I had no idea. Shaking me, he said, "This is Rico Yanez, right-hand man to Rafael Carrillo. The head of Los Zappas cartel. We've just finished some business, and if he wants to fuck you then you'll let him. Do you understand me?"

"Nooooo," I whimpered, his bruising hold making me wince in pain. "I won't do it."

"You don't have a choice. If you don't give it up, he'll just take it. Actually, I think he prefers it rough. Don't you?" he asked, turning to look at Yanez.

The man nodded and smirked.

I struggled to break free from my father, but it was no use. Being forced to have sex with someone I'd been with for years was one thing, but to be forced by a complete stranger was something entirely different.

Rape was rape, right?

Wrong.

Better the devil I knew and all that shit.

My father passed me off, his fingers freeing me as Yanez's trapped me. "Where can I take her?"

"In that room back there. You'll find a perfectly good sofa as well as a sturdy desk. Just don't make too much of a mess," he warned.

Without another word, I was dragged away, seconds from being thrust inside a smoke-filled office.

My father's office.

He'd given me up to seal the deal with the cartel.

A prize for doing business.

Once we were alone, I tried to reason with the man, praying there was something human residing inside him which would allow him to let me go.

"Please, don't do this," I pleaded, yanking free and putting as much allowable space between us as possible.

"Don't worry, sweetheart. You'll enjoy this, I promise." His gaze creepily raked over me, looking like he wanted to devour me whole. He approached, a lock of his dark, gray-streaked hair falling over his left eye. For a man who was as high up in the cartel, he was shabby-looking, a bushy mustache hiding his otherwise thin lips. He was as big as he was tall, his stomach hanging over the belt of his pants proving he didn't care about himself in the least.

His fat hands captured me again, pulling me so close I shivered in disgust. His breath enveloped my face, the smell of alcohol and cigarette smoke strong as he crashed his lips to mine. I tried to turn away, but he snatched my chin roughly to keep my head still. Licking at my mouth, he became frustrated when I wouldn't open for him.

"This is gonna happen whether you like it or not." His voice was sinister. He walked me backward until we were close to the edge of the desk, the gun in his waistband suddenly apparent and pressing into my side. "Take off your clothes," Yanez demanded, taking a step back and licking his thin lips while waiting for me to do as I was told.

"Please," I begged, holding my hands up in surrender, shaking in fear. The seriousness of my situation hit me like a sledgehammer, and I was terrified of what was about to happen.

"Don't speak again," he ordered.

I kept my mouth shut, my body unable to move and do as instructed.

"I'm not gonna ask you again. Take off your clothes!" he shouted. When I still refused to move, that's when he struck, pain radiating across my cheek before I could even think about protecting myself. I hadn't even seen it coming, but I should have expected it. Holding my face, tears instantly welled behind my eyes. I chastised myself for appearing weak, but I was shocked. And hurt.

"Refuse again and I'll use the butt of my gun next time. And trust me, sweetheart, the pain will be unbearable." He smirked, finding it amusing that he was tormenting me into submission. His fingers rested on the handle of his gun, prepared to extract it if necessary.

In all my years of abuse at the hands of my father, he'd never given me to another man—with the exception of Vex, of course. No, this was something new. Would he do it again, though? To whomever he deemed worthy of receiving a *gift* due to the nature of whatever shady deals he'd procured? Would I become *good business sense* again in the future?

My hands shook as I reached for the hem of my shirt, drawing it up my body, taking a few precious seconds before pulling it over my head. My long black hair fell forward, covering my face from his view for the briefest of moments, and I cherished not having to look at him.

"Now the pants."

I quickly pulled the dark jeans down my legs, kicking them to the side to stand in silence once again.

A low whistle sounded as he stared at my entire body. While I couldn't see him right then, I could feel his leer, goose bumps breaking across my skin in fear.

"You've certainly got some body on you, don't ya?" His question was rhetorical, of course. "Take it *all* off."

Pleading was pointless.

Refusing proved to be dangerous.

I had no other choice but to obey.

But for some reason, all sense of survival left me, the sudden need to flee overwhelming beyond any sense of security. My body reacted before my mind caught up, darting left before closing in on the door of the office. If I could only make it through, I'd run as fast as I could. Not to my room because they'd only haul me back to Yanez, most likely battered and bruised. No, I had to try and make it outside. Nature would protect me if I begged hard enough.

Our compound was in the middle of nowhere, surrounded by acres of nothing but trees and hidden streams. I tried to escape once before, but I had obviously failed, the mental scars of being tortured outweighing the permanent marks on my body.

My feet propelled me forward, my heart skipping a beat while I choked on the stifling tension surrounding me. Before I reached the door, however, I was ripped backward, a large hand clutching my throat and forcing out the remaining air from my lungs. My chest burned from lack of oxygen, my eyes bulging with the thought that this could be it. And there was something disappointing in the thought of dying at the hands of a stranger. If anything, I thought I'd recognize the eyes of my killer before I took my last breath.

He released me before I succumbed to the darkness, a raging coughing fit ensuing in order to draw air into my starved lungs.

"Where do you think you're goin'?" Yanez laughed, deliriously entertained with my need to protect myself. The man was cut from the same cloth as my father and Vex, their souls having been extinguished long ago.

Tossing me back toward the center of the room, he stood strong and blocked any further inclinations I had toward making it out of there before he'd had his fill of me.

"Strip."

I knew I was out of options so, with my head hung low, I finally complied.

My arms twisted behind my back and I slowly unhooked my bra, allowing it to slide off my shoulders before falling to the ground. I was tiny in stature; the only things out of proportion on my body were my breasts and my ass. Both attributes often drew unwanted attention from men, and I hated my body because of it.

His lust increased the more he stared, and it was only a matter of minutes until he would rip the last part of my soul from me. Hooking my fingers into the waistband of my panties, I drew them down my thighs until they were bunched at my feet. Stepping out of them, I moved to the side, brought my hands up and tried to cover myself.

"Drop your hands. Now," he commanded. I obeyed. Again. "Well, would you look at that?" He took a step closer. "Whose idea was it to have you shaved? No matter. All the better for me." Crossing the couple feet separating us, he turned me around and bent me over until my breasts hit the surface of the hard desk.

He didn't speak as he shoved my legs apart, unzipped his pants and pulled himself free. Of all the thoughts to race through my head, I was thinking how thankful I was that he left the rest of his clothes on, his massive gut something I most definitely didn't want to feel as it rubbed against me. Gripping my hip with his free hand, he shoved himself inside me with all the force he could muster. He wasn't small and, because I was completely dry, he tore through me, ripping me apart from the inside out. A cry erupted from my throat before I could stop it, my nails scouring the wood in agony.

Once he was fully sheathed, he rutted inside me, enjoying that he was fucking an unwilling participant. "Do you like that?" he panted. The only response I could muster was the frantic shaking of my head, tears soaking my cheeks and falling to the desk below.

If I remained still and let him get off then it would all be over with and I could return to my room. Hopefully, Vex would take pity on me and not beat me for allowing this man to rape me.

Yanez slowed his intrusion and without warning, fell from my body. I thought he was done so I tried to stand up, but he shoved me back down, pressing the side of my face against the hard surface.

"Not yet," he growled. "Gonna take that sweet ass." Before his words registered, he grabbed a fistful of my hair, yanking my head back until a cry tore from my lips. My anguish seduced him. He snatched my strands tighter, pain slicing through my poor head as he made me stand. "You know you want it," he threatened, pulling me so close my back hit his chest, his smoky breath making me sick.

"Put your hands on the desk." For a brief moment, there was no contact. He'd backed away, the chill of the room prickling my skin. But his absence was short-lived. Anchoring me to him, I heard him spit into his hand before he pressed himself against my tight, puckered hole. Instinct told me to struggle, but all that got me was an immobilizing grip to the neck, the sneer of his voice in my ear threatening to kill me if I resisted again.

Vex had repeatedly sodomized me, and for as many times as he forced himself there, it never felt any better. I braced myself, my paranoia pinning me in place. I tried desperately to mentally float off to a happier time, but I didn't have one. Yanez tangled his fingers in my hair once again, the pain of his grip shooting right through me.

"You're gonna love this," he rasped. Spreading my cheeks, he forced himself inside me, the unbearable pain causing my body to seize up. I stopped breathing, all while my heart slammed against my chest. Once he started to move, he ordered me to link my hands behind my back, releasing my hair to hold me in place by my wrists instead.

Fear and mortification flooded over me. Not only was this humiliating and degrading, the pain was indescribable.

My mind raced all over the place, pinging back and forth between the hell I was in and the hell I was going to find myself in once I returned to my room.

My wrists screamed under the weight of his pressure. I tried to wriggle them free, praying he was too distracted to notice. But he did. Instead of him yelling or gripping my hands tighter, he slammed his fist into the back of my head. Dots instantly invaded my vision, a searing pain slicing through my skull so fierce I almost passed out. Unfortunately for me, he hadn't hit me hard enough to knock me unconscious. At least then, I would have been saved from hearing him grunt out his release inside me.

When he finally finished, he withdrew from my body, zipped up his pants and disappeared from the room without a word.

I barely managed to clothe myself before I saw Vex striding straight toward me, the heat of rage dancing behind his eyes.

Realizing that bracing for his attack would only serve to piss him off even more, I stood there and waited for his punishment. He snatched my upper arm and dragged me from my father's office.

"You wait till I get you alone. You'll wish he'd killed you."

It was the last thing I remembered before darkness found me.

THREE

Marek

PICTURING KORITZ'S UGLY FACE WHILE I pummeled him to within an inch of his life made me smile. The thought of exacting my revenge made the cleanup somewhat bearable.

His men had trashed our clubhouse, and while some of the old ladies helped with the mess, they weren't allowed in the area where we met to talk private business. It was sacred, the one place we went to get away from it all, a separate suite inside the clubhouse.

Some clubs called it Church, but we called it Chambers. Mainly because it was where we talked about, then eventually delivered, justice.

The main room consisted of our meeting table and chairs, memorabilia plastered around the room for nostalgia. Off to the right was a bathroom linked to another room where the men chose to hide out if they were having issues with their women, or if they needed time to sort shit out that was rattling around inside their head. Since no one but the members were allowed in Chambers, they were safe for as long as it took for them to calm down enough to go back to their rooms, or any of the common areas.

"They sure made a mess, didn't they?" Stone grumbled, picking up pieces of broken glass from some of the dishes they tossed from the cupboards. *Really? What in the hell did they think we were hiding in there? Assholes.*

Stone and I had grown up together, and since the time we were young boys we knew someday we were going to run the KC. It was ingrained in us, our fathers pulling us into meetings early on to make sure we knew all the ins and outs of the club.

The politics.

The minute everyday details, from who was in our pockets to the best trade routes to what the dirt was on our biggest rival.

The fucking Savage Reapers.

Our clubs hated each other with a vengeance.

Their club was run with no rules, morals or consequences. They were heavily involved in human trafficking, selling women and children to the sickest, highest bidders. They beat and raped their own women, not a care in the world for another's life as long as they got what they wanted.

For all means and purposes, they certainly lived up to their name.

Savages.

And while we were no angels, exacting revenge when we felt it necessary, we at least lived by some sort of principle.

We didn't beat and rape our women, and we didn't kill innocent people. We ran drugs for the livelihood of the club, but they were forbidden to use. The strongest substances allowed at the compound were weed and alcohol. And although there had been many a time where some of the brothers went overboard and drank until they fell unconscious, they were easily controlled by the rest of us. All except for Ryder. When the club's Sergeant-at-Arms and head mechanic drank the hard shit, he was a mean motherfucker. Thank God he only partook when shit got bad, and since I'd taken over three years ago, I was able to control the shit that went down enough to ensure he'd only gotten out of pocket twice. Both times resulting in three of the brothers beating him into submission, locking him in his room until he finally calmed down.

Every man had his own room at the club, but they owned their own property away from the compound as well. I didn't require my men to stay together at all times, it mostly just worked out that way. Which was why most of them had problems in their relationships. But the women knew the life they were choosing when they shacked up with the guys, the men's first priority being the club above all else. Don't get me wrong, they loved their women and would kill to protect them and their families, but there was nothing like the brotherhood the club provided.

"Hey, Marek," Stone yelled across the room. "How about once we get shit right, we throw a ruckus?" That was code for an all-nighter, an 'anything goes' type of get-together. It also meant no wives or girlfriends allowed, only familiar party favors, aka club whores.

"Sure thing," I promised. "Get ahold of Zip and Hawke and tell them to make a liquor run. We're running low," I said, flipping the couch right-side up, cursing those DEA assholes with every flick of my eyes around the shambled room. "Then tell Ryder and Jagger to make their usual calls."

A ruckus was precisely what I needed right about then.

———◆———

THE CLUBHOUSE WAS A FLURRY of activity. Men chugging their favorite poison while barely clad women draped themselves around the member of their choice. Loud music and a cloud of smoke hung thick in the air while some snuck off to the back rooms for a quick fuck. It was exactly the kind of distraction I needed, and I welcomed it with open arms. I allowed my men to engage in a carefree night because, come tomorrow, we had to plan our revenge—on not only Koritz, but our biggest enemy.

The feud between the Knights Corruption and the Savage Reapers dated back to when I was a kid. But the real war began three years ago, and I was gonna be the president who finally put an end to those bastards, tearing them apart one by one. The reason for the battle was rooted in greed, mainly on the part of the Reapers, although my club wasn't innocent. We hadn't taken it to the extremes, however, killing off rival members solely for the purpose of getting rich.

No, they'd crossed the line.

Time and time again.

Swallowing the rest of my drink, I tapped the bar and signaled for Trigger to pour me another. "You sure you want to get shit-faced while there's plenty of pussy round here?" he teased, jerking his chin toward one of the wannabes walking straight for us. We referred to them as wannabes, amongst other things, because their ultimate agenda was to become someone's old lady. But the thing they didn't realize was there was no way a patched member was gonna make an honest woman out of someone who'd slept with half the club. The prospects, however, didn't know any better, until, of course, we explained the way things worked around here.

"Hi, Marek," Shelley cooed, kissing my cheek before whispering in my ear how she wanted to suck my dick until I shot my load down the back of her throat. She was attractive enough, her shoulder-length blonde hair cut into the latest trend, and a body made for a good time. Her tiny shirt showcased her perky tits and, although she wore a mini skirt, she was practically naked.

The attribute I liked most about Shelley was that, while I knew she wanted to be tied to me in the worst way, she didn't push too hard.

Knowing damn well I'd replace her with someone who was only going to give me what I wanted. Sex. Nothing more.

I tended to stick with one piece of ass at a time, having no tolerance in my world for jealous bitches who could turn a good ruckus into an all-out brawl. Once I had my fill, I released them to have sex with whomever they wanted, never to be touched by me again.

Downing the shot Trigger placed in front of me, the slow burn of the liquor clouded my thoughts, quieting all the shit rattling around inside my head. After another two shots, I rose from my seat, grabbed Shelley's hand and dragged her back to my room, the sound of her satisfied laughter following me down the long, darkened hallway.

Her whispers in the common room were enough incentive for me to unzip my pants and give her what she wanted. Pulling myself from my jeans, I pushed down on her shoulders. "On your knees, sweetheart," I demanded, leaning my head back against the wall while I waited for her to wrap her plump lips around my cock.

"Can't I have a kiss first, Marek?" she whispered, leaning in until her mouth was a little too close to mine.

"You know I don't kiss, Shelley." Putting more pressure on her shoulders, she finally obeyed and sank to her knees, pulling me into her mouth immediately, sucking me off quicker than she normally did. I wasn't stupid. I realized she was pissed that I still wouldn't give in and kiss her, so if she wanted to take out her anger on my dick, then so be it. As long as she didn't bite me, it was all good.

There was no mystery behind me not wanting to kiss any of the women I fucked. I didn't have some weird phobia or damaged reason why, I just didn't feel the need to be so intimate with someone I had no real connection with. I used them like they used me, and that was the long and short of it.

Deciding to give her something to cool her temper, I swiveled my hips and thrust into her mouth while blowing out a breath of pleasure. "Fuck, sweetheart," I gritted out. "I love that sweet little mouth of yours." Securing a chunk of her hair in my fist, I held her still while languidly sliding past her lips, her tongue swirling around the tip until I was pushing myself further down her throat. Thank God she didn't have a gag reflex or we'd have a big problem. "Love that cock, baby?" I growled, knowing damn well her mouth was too full to answer.

As soon as she brought her hand up to aid her mouth, I dropped away from her, pulled her off her knees and pushed her against the wall, flipping her barely there skirt over her ass. She didn't bother wearing anything underneath, and I was truly grateful for the small things. Snatching a condom off a nearby dresser, I quickly sheathed myself before spreading her legs.

"You ready for me to fuck you now?"

Plunging quickly inside her pussy before she could answer, I rocked my body into hers, taking her like I hadn't had it in weeks.

Bracing herself against the wall while I took her hard from behind, she purred while clinging to the wall for support. She was still relatively tight, and it was mere minutes before I charged down the path to explosion. Realizing I was close, I found her clit with my fingers, expertly rubbing her until her breathing picked up and she moaned my name over and over again. "That's it. Come for me," I coaxed, my own orgasm barreling down on me like a goddamn freight train.

As soon she threw her head back and screamed, I knew it was my turn. I may not kiss, but I certainly made sure they came before I did. Seizing her hips, I punished her body until I finally came inside her, the pleasure exploding from my body and leaving me in a haze of ecstasy for a few brief moments.

Then it was all over.

Discarding the condom in a nearby trash bin, I tucked myself away and zipped up my pants. Walking toward Shelley, I placed my hand on the small of her back to usher her from my room. There was no idle chitchat between us, even though I knew she was dying to engage me in some sort of conversation, hoping she could stay a little while longer. But once I came, I had no further use for her company. Never did. With any of them. She was invited to the clubhouse for one reason and one reason only, and she'd just fulfilled her duty for the evening.

Now it was time to go back out, drink some more and lose myself until I passed out, drunk off my ass.

As my hand circled the doorknob, I heard a shrill screech erupt from the front of the club. Pushing Shelley behind me, I snatched my gun from the end table and slowly opened the door. "Stay here," I instructed, pissed something was goin' down while I'd been too busy gettin' off.

Then I heard it again, the sound so ear piercing it cut right through me. The noise, which had me all amped up, was coming from a woman, and the more I ventured into the dark hallway, stealthily creeping forward, I realized a fight had erupted.

A cat fight.

FOUR

Marek

FUCKING WOMEN.

No doubt they were fighting over dick. It happened sometimes, especially when excessive drinking was involved. It seemed that was the time when people let go of all their sensibilities and overreacted to situations which would never have existed in the light of a sober day.

Retreating to my room, I escorted Shelley from my private area and forced her back out into the common area where all the action apparently was. She took a seat at the bar and watched on with curiosity. And, I had to admit, I was a bit inquisitive myself.

What I thought was a simple fight between two wannabes was anything but.

"I told you I'd cut a bitch the next time I found out," Hawke's woman, Edana, screamed so loud I thought glass was gonna shatter. Two prospects stood between her and the whore Hawke had apparently been fucking with, the look on the wannabe's face pure terror. Edana was a bit of a wild card, her temper notorious around our entire circle. Usually, Hawke could handle her, but there were times like this where she became uncontrollable. If fire could have shot from her eyes and disintegrated the wannabe on sight, it would have been less of a shock than what was about to happen.

How Hawke's woman even got in here was beyond me. She knew she wasn't supposed to show up, yet she chose to ignore club rules, which more than irked me, but I wanted to see how everything played out, so I was willing to let it go.

For now.

While the raving lunatic of a woman was focused on her man, the scared club whore grabbed her friend's hand and quickly headed toward the front entrance, realizing damn well that, if she stayed any longer, she was gonna regret it.

"Calm down, baby." Hawke laughed, his smile fueling the inferno that was Edana. He was clearly more than tipsy, and his brain wasn't registering the severity of what was about to pop off. He knew his woman better than anyone, and he of all people should have realized she was simply getting warmed up. They'd been together for years and their relationship had always been volatile. Sometimes they were lovin' on each other and other times . . . Well, other times were like this.

Full throttle all the way.

Simply because I craved a good show, I found an empty seat at the far end of the bar. Jerking my chin in Trigger's direction, for another drink, I swiveled around to watch.

"*Calm down?*" she shrieked, quickly tying back her long auburn hair, indicating she meant business. Reaching for the closest weapon she could find, which just so happened to be a switchblade someone had left lying around, she aimed directly for his face and hurled it through the air. "We'll see how pretty you are when you have a nice cut down the side of your face," she seethed, trying to push past Jagger, one of the prospects doing his best to hold her back. "See how many sluts want your ass when your face is all fucked up!" she screamed.

Edana was a small woman, but she was strong as fuck. I'd gotten in the midst of one of their wars one too many times, so I knew what a handful she was. But, for some reason, Hawke loved her and kept her around, despite everything.

Luckily, the part of the knife that made contact with him was only the butt of the blade. It hit him right in the forehead, to be exact. The look of shock on his face was amusing, although I had no idea why he was stunned. He knew what she was like—fuck, he had the scars to prove it.

"Are you crazy, woman?" he growled, the stun of the metal handle knocking him back into sobriety. Well, a little bit at least. "You could have cut me." Hawke's long black hair was secured on top of his head into some sort of man bun, he called it. At least his vision wasn't obstructed for what she chose to do next.

Before anyone realized what was happening, she grabbed one of the heavy blades Jagger kept on his waistband, stepped around the prospect and threw it with all her might at the man she supposedly loved more than life itself. His eyes went wide when he realized what she'd thrown, thankfully stepping out of the way in time to allow the knife to hit the wall directly behind him.

She'd missed him by an inch.

Okay, now shit just got real.

I jumped off my chair and rushed forward, closing the distance until I reached Hawke. His face showed his rage, and he looked like he was ready to tear her apart.

"You fucking cunt! I'm gonna kill you!" he threatened right before he dove forward, the crazy look in his eyes unnerving even me. Luckily, I was in the way, my large body stopping him from making contact. From the look of pure terror on her face, a quick change from the fury which had resided there not a minute before, she knew she'd crossed the line. Yet again.

Stone stepped into play, replacing the other prospect who was stuck in the middle of their craziness, and forced her backward. "You better get the hell out of here, sweetheart," he said, his teeth clenched as he spoke, realizing Hawke could have been seriously hurt, and all over a piece of ass.

Gone was the psycho bitch, her lip trembling in instant regret. She realized what she'd done was wrong, but when she was in the throes of her jealous fits, it was as if she shut off all reasoning and fell into the trap of temporary insanity. Hawke struggled to reach her and, if she didn't leave in the next two seconds, I would seriously consider letting him go. Teach her a lesson and all. I'd never tolerate him beating the shit out of her, but sometimes a harsh shake or a quick throat snatch was called for. Especially after she could have seriously maimed him—or worse, killed him where he stood.

When she still remained, I decided it was time for me to finally say something. "Edana, get the hell out of here," I roared, the authority in my voice booming in everyone's ears. "And don't you ever come here again when you're not supposed to," I added, before turning back to watch Hawke relax a little, the ferocity in his eyes lessening to a tolerable level.

I nodded toward Stone, indicating he needed to take her outside. He seized her arm and quickly walked toward the door, disappearing quicker than I thought either one of them could walk.

Fucking ruckus. Never fails.

FIVE

Marek

"PREZ!" I HEARD STONE SHOUT from outside the Chamber doors. I'd been leaning back in my chair, shit going over and over in my head as to how I was gonna handle what I knew was going to be an all-out war. My VP's intrusion was definitely welcome, pushing my bloodthirsty thoughts aside. At least for the time being. There was no way I would be able to escape them forever, though. A decision had to be made, and it had to be made soon. My men were constantly caught in the middle, struggling between the thin line of decency and a new *legal* way of life.

I was on my way to taking the club in a new direction, all legit and shit. I still had to get everyone on board, some of the older members quite stubborn when it came to cutting into their weekly profits.

But when it came down to it, I was dog tired of constantly having to look over my shoulder, not only for the law but for the other clubs vying for our territory. There'd been a lot of bloodshed over the past two years, and the war was continuing to wage on with no end in sight. The Savage Reapers ambushed some of our crew a few months back, killing two of my brothers and badly wounding two more. We would exact our revenge, but we had to be smart and not attack blindly.

The Reapers were growing in numbers, and while they weren't as large, our charters spreading wide across the country, they were proving to be a massive pain in our ass.

While they took anyone willing to kill and move their product, we had a much more stringent process for accepting new members. You had to either be related or have grown up with someone in the KC before you would even be considered. If the person *was* from outside our inner circle, he had to prove himself loyal, sometimes taking years to be fully patched in.

Throwing open the door, Stone burst in with a wild look dancing in his eyes. As soon as he saw me, he hurried in my direction, his six-foot-two frame striding toward me with dire purpose.

"Fuck," he exclaimed, his hands running through his disheveled dark blond hair. "Why the hell didn't you answer your phone?" he asked, finally coming to a stop when he entered my personal space.

Pushing back from the table, I stood next to him, our eyes connecting while we silently passed information to each other. I'd come to read his expressions very well, and I knew something had just gone down.

A little too close to home.

Shaking my head slowly, I prayed it wasn't something that called for us to spring into action, endangering us all before we had time to properly prepare for retaliation. Smaller clubs often gave us a problem here and there, but they were easily dealt with. Usually, it was one or two renegades who thought they were the shit, testing our power from time to time. And every time, we reminded them who the big dog was.

"What happened?" I grumbled, plopping back in my chair to better brace myself for what was gonna come flying out of his damn mouth. Taking his seat next to me, he spouted off the information he'd just been privy to, his words tripping over themselves he was speaking so fast.

"Mother fuckin' Savages!" he blurted, hitting the table hard with his fist. "A few of those bastards dared to enter our turf and threaten us!" he shouted, his voice becoming louder with each barely controlled word. His eyes were wild, and I knew it was only a matter of time before my VP demanded we end this once and for all. Exert our power over those godless fucks.

"What happened, Stone? Tell me exactly what you know."

"Some of 'em came into The Underground earlier tonight, threatening to take us down one by one. One of them was certainly fucked out of his mind. That's for sure. Not sure if it was some sort of drug or if the asshole is messed up in the head—crazy like." He swirled his finger around in a circle by his ear.

Anger cut across my face, strong enough to force Stone back in his chair, putting some distance between the two of us. The fact that some of our enemies dared to set foot into a bar we owned infuriated me. No, that was too calm an emotion. Rage coursed through my veins, my heart picking up pace the more I thought of the balls those fuckers had.

"Where are they now?" I roared, the vein in my neck bulging strong enough for me to feel as if it were gonna pop through my goddamn skin. "Who was there when they came in?"

Before Stone answered, I shot out of my seat and raced toward the door, heading into the common area before my next breath. "Breck and Cut were there," he responded, his voice closer as he quickly walked behind me to keep up. Purpose fueled my steps. I needed to have a full table, and I needed it now.

Whipping around to face Stone, I stepped closer and cocked my head slightly to the side. "Where the hell are they now?" His brow creased until he realized I was still asking about the men who dared to enter our bar.

"Our guys *detained* them in the back room."

"Then let's go," I commanded as I led the way. "Trig," I called out, walking past the bar. "Get everybody here pronto."

His response was a simple nod.

———◆———

"YOU SERIOUSLY THINK YOU CAN walk into KC territory and come out alive?" Breck yelled, punching one of the assholes right in the face. The guy he was wailing on looked like he'd been to Hell and back, the far-off look in his eyes telling me he wasn't all the way present. If I had to guess, I would say he was coked out of his mind. But then again, so were half of their crew.

Like I said, no rules.

The other two fucks were tied to a chair, the frightened look in their eyes telling me they had no idea what they'd walked into. They both looked to be no older than eighteen, probably following the guy Breck was beating on simply because they were trying to prove themselves. But they weren't prospects. They were both full-fledged members, their cuts proving as much.

"Breck," I called out, placing my hand on his shoulder to stop him from decimating the man's face any further. If he knocked him out, we wouldn't be getting any kind of information. The dark look in his eyes told me he wanted to kill the guy simply for breathing the same air as us. Breck was a bit of a wild card, following after his old man, Cutter. Both were loyal to a fault, but let them loose and they could cause a lot of damage. That's where their similarities ended. Looking at both of them no one would guess they were related. While Cutter's graying hair was cut close to his head, Breck wore his dark hair down to his shoulders, his shaggy beard a big contrast to his father's clean shaven face.

"Why don't we just shoot 'em, Prez?" Cutter asked, circling around the enemy to intimidate them more than they already were. Figures the Savage Reapers would send in three weak assholes, knowing damn well they were replaceable if and when we chose to kill them. The only good thing was that they would probably sing like canaries if we pushed them hard enough.

I guess we'll see.

We had the privacy of the office to deal with these guys, the bass of the music outside fueling my aggression.

"Why did you come in here tonight?" I asked calmly. A little *too* calmly, judging by the increased unease in their eyes. The guy Breck was messin' with snapped his head to face his buddies and yelled for them not to open their mouths.

Hmm . . . Interesting.

"Well, we already know you threatened to take us out one by one," I offered, leaning against the desk, crossing my ankles while my hands gripped the wood behind me. "So, tell me, how do you expect to do that? And why in the hell would you warn us about it first? Only thing I can figure is that you think we're dumb enough to fall for that shit. So, what?" I asked. "Did you expect to flee and have us chase you down? Only to lead us into some sort of ambush?"

One of the younger guys' eyes popped wide, and I realized I had my answer.

"Shut the fuck up!" their buddy yelled, louder this time to make sure there was no mistaking his instruction.

Nodding toward Breck, he curled his fist again and sent it crashing against the guy's jaw, blood splattering over the guy next to him. The other two appeared to be unharmed, which only meant they went willingly when my men had grabbed them.

Had the roles been reversed, my guys would have been tortured, reinforcing yet again that although we were all bad men, we were nothing like the Savage Reapers. I would at least give them a quick death; I didn't condone torturing unless it was absolutely necessary.

Pulling me back toward the corner of the room, Stone whispered in my ear, "What are we gonna do with 'em?" Glancing between all three of them, I came up blank. I had no idea what I was gonna do, but I knew it had to be swift.

"Guess it depends on what they tell us, right?" I asked, stepping around Stone and walking back toward all the action. Standing directly in front of the one I thought would break first, I leaned over and placed my hands on the arms of his chair. He kept his head down, twisted to the side, probably hoping I would move on to one of his friends.

"Look at me," I commanded, my face dangerously close to his. Shaking his chair, I spoke again. "If you don't look at me and answer my questions, I'm gonna let my buddy here gut you like a fish." Cutter stepped up behind me, twirling a large knife and smiling big. My threat was enough to make him obey, the soft quiver of his bottom lip telling me he would be a quick confessor.

Once his full attention was on me, I saw the guy Breck was beating shift in his chair. Just as he was about to open his mouth and say God knows what, my man snapped his head back with a powerful punch, knocking his ass out instantly.

"Now," I grumbled. "Why did you guys come in here tonight, spoutin' off at the mouth about taking down the KC?" Waiting not-so-patiently for his response, I pulled a switchblade from my pocket, snapped it open so the blade glistened bright and trailed it down the length of his thigh. His eyes followed my every movement, glancing up into mine before swallowing hard. No words left his lips, which only meant I had to show him I was serious. I hated doing this shit, but it had to be done.

Without further warning, I tapped his leg three times with the knife, then withdrew the weapon. His brows creased in confusion, but before his brain registered a response, I plunged the blade deep into his flesh.

The bellow which erupted from him was most expected from such a weak bastard. It was obvious there was no training on his part.

Never show weakness.

Never allow your enemy to see the threads inside you unraveling.

His breaths came in quick succession, his face paling the more he focused on the blade sticking out of his leg. I flicked the protruding handle and he screamed again, the pain agonizing enough for him to fall apart completely.

"Please," he begged. "I'll tell you whatever you want to know. Just . . . Don't."

"Don't what?" I played with him.

"Don't kill me," he pleaded. Tears of fear coursed down his face and even though there was a twinge of sympathy for the weak fucker, I knew I couldn't let him live. I knew his club had sent him, sent them all here, not expecting them to live. They knowingly sacrificed some of their members, and if they returned, it would be detrimental to my club.

Show no weakness.

Pulling the knife from his thigh, I leaned in close so there was no mistaking his fate. "I can't let you live, boy. But I *can* promise you a quick death if you tell me what you know." The glaze in his eyes told me he was petrified, but he should have known this was going to be the outcome, right? Didn't he know whose territory he was entering? Hadn't his club warned him?

He continued to beg for his life, the guy next to him joining in when they realized their clock was about to run out.

"Man up, you pussies!" Breck shouted, his irritation coloring his face a light shade of red. "Die with some sort of goddamn dignity."

Surprisingly, my man's words stopped the flow of theirs, although their faces continued to give way to their obvious fear, glancing back and forth between all of us, just waiting for the end.

"Let's try this again," I prompted, pushing back a strand of hair which had fallen over my eye. "Why did you come into our bar tonight?"

A few seconds passed before the injured one spoke up. "We were told to lure as many of you out of the bar as possible. We knew our threats were enough to entice you to chase us," he sputtered, looking over to Breck before reining in his trembling expression. It was almost as if he were trying to prove to us that he was manning up.

"Who gave you the order?"

I thought there would have been some sort of hesitation, at least to prolong the inevitable, but he gave up the answer before his next breath. "Our prez."

Psych's audacity surprised me, although it shouldn't have. His name said it all. He'd earned the road name simply because he was unpredictable, his psychotic tendencies ruling his daily existence. There was no code the snake lived by, but one would have thought he would have been a little less obvious with his plans. *Or did he honestly think we were dumb enough to fall for it?*

"Why?" I walked back toward the desk to put some distance between us.

The boy's face paled, the loss of blood seeping from his wound taking a quick toll on him. Or it could have been that he knew he was gonna meet his maker very soon.

"He said the war . . . The war between us and the Knights was gonna en-end soon," he stuttered, "The bl-blood of your men coating the streets would seal our position with the cartel once and for all."

"Fucking hell," I cursed, stalking forward. "This has to do with the trade with the cartel?" I asked the question although I already knew the answer. Our feud had everything to do with drugs, territory and money—for them. For us, it was about revenge for what they'd done to our men for all these years.

Little did they know I was trying to get us away from the drugs, but I guessed that didn't matter too much now.

"Cutter." I gestured with a quick jerk of my chin. "Help Breck dispose of these three, then drop them off in front of their club." Locking eyes with the boy I'd stabbed, I finished with, "And make sure they receive a quick death. After all, I did promise as much." The boy's head hung in defeat, his conscious buddy expelling his fear with short cries. The other man was out cold, and I guessed it was for the best. If one was going to their death, better to not see it coming, right?

SIX

Marek

I CONTEMPLATED MANY THINGS ON the ride back to the compound. Ways to make our enemies pay for all they'd done, focusing more on Psych and the men he kept close. The roar of my bike helped calm me while thoughts of murder danced inside my head. I'd like to say I wasn't a violent man by nature, but it was how I was conditioned all my life, although I wasn't like most leaders. I didn't *crave* the kill. I didn't *live* for it, allowing it to rule every fucking move I made.

I killed only when and if I needed to.

My men knew we were on our way back, so it was no surprise when the large metal gate which protected the compound swung open upon our arrival. Nodding at Jagger, one of our best prospects, my bike roared on through, followed by Stone, Cutter and Breck. Everyone else had been gathered and was anxiously waiting for us in Chambers.

This is gonna be a long night.

"WHY ARE WE WAITIN' SO long to attack?" Zip shouted, pounding his fist against the thick oak of our meeting table, rattling the gavel enough to jump and crash back down onto the wood surface. At just twenty years old, Zip had a fierce temper, one which should have only been warranted from someone who held a few more years of age and experience. From what I could gather, he'd had a pretty shitty upbringing, his father a KC rat who was disposed of after his deception had come to light. He'd been drugged out of his mind for years, hence the set-in-stone rule that none of my men were allowed to use. Couldn't ever trust a junkie. Zip's mother was a club whore who just got mixed up with the wrong guy. None of us really knew exactly what happened surrounding her death, but there were rumors that she was killed soon after her rat of a man. Even though she technically died in a car accident, there were thoughts it was simply a cover-up. My father had run the club during that time, and he never spoke about either one of them after they ceased to exist.

The club rules were a little different when my father was president, but when I took over, I made sure to ingrain in each and every one of the members that we were never to kill women or children, and we certainly didn't dispose of a fellow brother until we had irrefutable proof, which, thank God, wasn't an issue. All my guys were loyal to me and to their fellow brothers, Zip being right at the top of that list. I think he tried even harder than the rest because he didn't want anyone to think he was anything like his old man.

His dark hair was slicked away from his face, his green eyes glistening in anger and fueling a few of the other men's need for retaliation. His slight build became rigid while he waited for an answer.

"Zip," Stone warned, standing quickly and leaning over the table, his dark eyes threatening Zip where he sat. "Calm down and show some goddamn respect."

Raising his hands in a display of surrender, Zip turned his head toward me, breaking away from Stone's fierce gaze. "Sorry, Prez, I just wanna get those fuckers already. Enough is enough."

I didn't take any offense to his outburst—I had my VP for that. Relaxing in my chair, I nodded at Zip before turning my focus back on the men surrounding the large oblong table. I really did have a great group of fierce, take-a-bullet-for-you, crazy-ass motherfuckers.

"We have to wait until we hear they're all there together. You know damn well," I said, my eyes falling back onto Zip, "Psych and his VP, Rabid, are hardly at the same place at the same time. No, we have to take them both out so their club is left in shambles." Glancing back to Stone, a hard look set on his face, I finished my spiel. "We wait."

Killing those bastards was at the forefront of my agenda, but just in case we failed, I had another plan in place. A plan which was carefully being orchestrated with someone even more powerful than me.

All in due time.

Throwing down the gavel, I left no room for argument. Our meeting was done. My word was law, and even if a few of them didn't agree, they didn't show it. I welcomed everyone's input, but once I had my say, there was to be no more discussion on the topic.

"Let's go get us some pussy!" Hawke yelled, following Ryder and Trigger from the room. Lucky for him, and for all of us, Edana was two states away visiting her mother.

———◆———

A LOUD CRASH OUT FRONT drew all of our attention. We'd only been two hours into an impromptu ruckus when the shit started to go down. Men scattered, yelling and reaching for their closest weapon of choice. Running toward the secured entrance of the clubhouse, some of the men waited to be ordered outside to find out what the hell was going on. Stone followed behind me as I walked into our surveillance room, staring at all the cameras to find out who or what was behind the loud noise. Each screen turned up blank, no activity as the camera slowly turned from side to side. We saw our bikes all lined up in a row, the lot otherwise empty, the door of our garage pulled shut, and the large metal gate, which kept us securely inside. Something quickly moved past the gate, a dark shadow passing in front of the camera before we could identify it.

Everything was all clear except for the ghost we'd seen on camera.

Headlights illuminated the lot before backing up from the gate, something falling to the ground in front of the car before it sped off. Running toward the front door, I pushed past my VP and reached for the handle.

"Marek, NO!" he shouted, but his plea fell on deaf ears. A sinking feeling gutted me, but I had no idea why. I couldn't see who had crashed into our gate, nor the body who was dumped on our property. But I knew it wasn't good.

There was a lot of commotion surrounding me as I stalked toward the gate, the compound security lights suddenly flooding the area so we could all see better. With every step I took closer, my heart picked up its pace and rammed against my chest. My adrenaline pumped through my veins and my vision became cloudy. At first, I only saw a crumpled male body, but the closer I stepped the more I could make out. He was certainly one of ours, his cut showcasing our club's emblem of a skull with a sword slicing through it. His short hair was greased with blood, his head turned to the side so I couldn't see who he was.

Yet.

Quickly scanning the street to make sure we weren't gonna be ambushed, I shouted, "Open the fucking gate!"

The slow creak of the metal was infuriating, my pulse quickening the longer it took to reach the man who'd been dropped off as a warning. I knew by who, but had to make sure before I lost my shit once and for all.

Gurgling sounded from the bloody man's throat and I breathed a sigh of relief, although it was short-lived once I turned him on his back. His pulse was weak, and it was only a matter of time before he exhaled his last breath. There was so much blood it was hard for me to see where his wounds were.

"Let me take a look," I soothed, the tremor in my voice certainly betraying my faux calm tone. His arms fell away from his stomach, his hands hitting the pavement beside him with a heavy thud. I lifted his shirt and saw he'd been shot four times, the holes gaping and seeping blood faster than was safe, although being shot just once wasn't safe. He was gonna bleed out right in front of us, and I still couldn't identify him.

When I finally turned his head, familiar eyes met mine, and I about had a heart attack.

I knew him.

We all knew him, although we hadn't seen him in years.

The bloody man I was staring at was none other than Hawke's older brother, Tripp. He'd joined our nomad charter four years earlier. Not belonging to any one charter suited him just fine. A loner lifestyle was more his thing, even though he showed up every now and again to see not only his club brothers, but his blood brother as well. They were close, and I was waiting for shit to erupt as soon as Hawke realized his sibling was lying on the cold pavement, dying with each struggled breath.

"Who the hell is it, Marek?" Everyone crowded around while I tried to decide the best way to break the news to Hawke, while still doing my best to try and drag Tripp into the compound without further injuring him. I heard you weren't supposed to move someone who was hurt, but was that when they'd been shot? Or was that when they'd hurt their neck? Goddamn it! Too many thoughts plagued me and before I could decide on one course of action, I saw the dying man's younger brother approach, furrowing his brow the closer he came.

He stopped ten feet from us and looked shocked, his brain actively trying to compute just who he was staring at. The simple fact that he recognized his brother from that far away was amazing, seeing as how I had been up close and personal before I'd identified him.

When I finally lifted my head to meet Hawke's stare, I gave him a simple nod, my indication that what he thought was true. It was enough to force him out of his own head, his legs bringing him to an abrupt halt once he'd reached us.

"Fuck!" he yelled, gripping his hair in fear. "What the fuck? Tripp?" he whispered, falling to his knees so his brother could hear him, if he was even still conscious. By his labored breathing, I wasn't sure how much longer he was gonna last, and I sure as shit didn't want his death on my hands simply because I had no idea what I was doing.

I knew we couldn't act like normal people and take him to the emergency room. Because of the gunshot wounds, the police would be called right away, and there was no way we were willingly going to include those pigs in our business.

Hawke gripped his brother's hand and held it in his lap, all the while watching me to give direction on what the hell we were gonna do. Time seemed to slow, the men's shouts lessened to whispers with every agonizing second that passed. In reality, the action around me was a flutter of curses and shouts, people moving around us quickly to decide what the hell the best course of action was.

It was then, during my mini freak-out, that I remembered Trigger's niece was a nurse. She'd helped us out quite a few times before and had done a bang-up job. No pun intended, of course.

"Trig!" I shouted over all the noise, whipping my head around and scanning the growing crowd to try and locate the one man I needed right then.

Pushing past Stone and Ryder, Trigger stepped forward, stopping to stand directly beside me. "What do you need?" he asked, obvious panic dancing in his voice.

Quickly glancing down into Tripp's pale, ashen face, I whipped my eyes back to Trigger and mumbled, "You need to call your neice, man. Tell her it's an emergency." I inhaled a deep breath. "Tell her to get here now!"

A simple nod and he was hurrying back into the clubhouse, a few of the club whores, who'd come out to see what all the commotion was, following directly behind him. They knew enough to know that curiosity of club business would get them banned for life.

Kneeling on the ground and holding a lifeless brother's body was gut-wrenching. No matter how many times I'd seen death, or impending death, up close, it never got easier. I thought I would have become numb to our way of life, but there was always an undercurrent of life pulsing through my veins. A hope for something better for not only me but for my brothers.

For my club.

A half hour later, I heard someone call out, "She's here," right before two bright headlights blinded me. We'd managed to carefully drag Tripp further into the compound, locking ourselves inside in case whoever had dumped him decided to return.

Slamming her door, Trigger's niece, Adelaide, quickly walked toward us, the sight of the blood-soaked pavement never once making her falter. Although she wasn't a part of our way of life, she knew enough about it from her uncle, and her visits to help us, to know we lived dangerously. She gave no indication that she wanted to know more, and her uncle made damn sure she wasn't exposed more than she had to be.

Pulling her long blonde hair on top of her head in a messy bun, she knelt down beside us, placing her black bag on the ground next to Tripp's thigh. Sensing help had arrived, a guttural moan exploded from his throat, the sound putting us all on alert. While his groan reminded us of his dire situation—like we needed a reminder—his pain also gave us hope, seeing as how he hadn't moved or made any other noises in quite some time.

"What happened?" Adelaide asked, gently pushing up his blood-soaked shirt so she could get a better look at the damage. Her almond-shaped eyes widened when she realized the poor guy had been shot four times. "I need you to help me," she said, looking between me and Hawke, who'd been a permanent fixture next to his brother.

"With what?" I asked, scooting back a little as she moved closer on her knees. I heard a noise come from above me, but it wasn't until I jerked my head to the right that I realized it had come from my VP. He was watching Adelaide with such intensity it instantly put me on edge. In all the years we'd known each other, I'd never seen him react to a woman like this. It was weird, and it was freaking me out. Since he was still crowding my personal space, I jabbed my elbow into his shin, directing his attention on me and not on the woman who'd been called in to help a fellow brother. Widening my eyes and flaring my nostrils was enough to make him back up a step, averting his eyes from Adelaide in the process. Although not gazing upon her lovely face seemed to be distressing him.

"I need to gently roll him over to see if there are exit wounds. If there are, I think there is a good chance I can help him. Possibly," she contemplated, her brows furrowing in thought. "If not, if the bullets are still stuck inside, he's going to need surgery. And although I've assisted in many an operation, I don't have the experience or necessary instruments to take on such a task."

I hadn't even thought about that shit. Her words caused my chest to deflate, the last reserve of hope I had swirling around inside escaping through the long breath I pushed from my lips. What were the chances all four bullets shot clean through his body? The answer was slim.

Preparing for the worst, Hawke and I cautiously rolled his brother off his back, all the while cushioning him as best we could. Tripp groaned, his hands clenching into loose fists the more we moved his lifeless body. "It's okay, man," Hawke mumbled near Tripp's ear. "We're just trying to patch you up." The pain in his voice just about undid me. He was trying to remain strong, all the while shoving his panic way deep down inside.

When Tripp was finally resting on his side, Adelaide brought out a pair of scissors and cut the material from his body. Luckily, we'd been able to remove his cut before she'd arrived, otherwise, she would have tried to slice through that as well. Once his back was exposed, she gingerly felt around his skin with the tips of her delicate fingers.

Searching for holes in his flesh.

She reached into her bag and pulled out gauze, wiping away as much blood as she could so she could better assess the damage. "Well, it looks like three of the four bullets have gone straight through, but there's still one stuck in there. And it looks like it might be close to his heart." She looked over at me first, then met Hawke's eyes before subtly shaking her head. "He needs surgery, and he needs it quick or else I don't think he's going to make it."

Hawke's voice shattered the otherwise silent air. "Fuck!" he screamed, leaning over the body of his dying brother. He whispered something in Tripp's ear, words no one but his sibling heard. As soon as he gathered his resolve, he jumped to his feet, walked around Tripp and pulled Adelaide to her feet. Everything happened so fast I barely had time to react. But Stone filled in for me, taking the few necessary steps to brace Adelaide on her other side. "You have to fix my brother," Hawke gritted through clenched teeth. I knew he was doing his best to hold his shit together, but in the process he was scaring the hell out of Trigger's niece. She didn't ask to be dragged into our mess, and the mere fact that she'd dropped whatever the hell she was doing and raced over to the club said a lot about her character.

"Hawke," Stone warned, a rare gesture of possessiveness brimming just underneath the surface. "She already told you she can't perform the surgery, if that was where this shit was headed." He pulled her to the side, Hawke's grip loosening until his hand fell to his side. Unspoken threats were whispered between the two men while I decided what the hell we needed to do.

Adelaide eyed both men cautiously before gently pulling away from Stone, a strange look of hurt in his eyes when she moved. She smiled tightly before speaking again. "I think I may have another plan," she promised, pulling her cell phone from her purse and quickly punching the numbers. She took a few steps forward for some privacy, everyone watching after her in anticipation, the air suddenly thick with a mixture of hope and uneasiness.

SEVEN

Sully

A NOISE FROM THE HALLWAY jerked me awake—not that it took much, since I was an extremely light sleeper. I guess I'd been conditioned that way since I was a child, always wary of who was coming through my bedroom door. Sometimes it was my father, paying me one of his *special* visits, and other times it was Vex. Once my possessor declared me for himself, my father's visits ceased altogether, some kind of fucked-up code among club members.

There were some nights I wished whoever had walked through my door was there to do me in, to act in such a way which resulted in me taking my last breath.

To kill me.

Trust me, I realized it was morbid to put those kinds of wishes and dreams out into the universe, but if destiny proved anything thus far, it was that my life was not my own. Therefore, destiny was a goddamn liar. I had no control whatsoever over my own fate; I had to leave that in the hands of the men who surrounded me, stifling and suffocating me to the point I no longer saw any joy in the world. Granted, I hadn't seen much of it to begin with, but there were exceptions. Some days, at least. The soft song of a bird, the cool night breeze kissing my skin as the sun dipped below the horizon, the colors from the sunset embedding their awesomeness into my memory.

But the older I became, the less I saw these things as beauty, and the more I saw them as the universe's cruel joke at my expense. For as tempting as Mother Nature was, she spit in my face.

I could look but not touch.

I could feel but never experience.

While lost to the pity party for one, my bedroom door crashed open and slammed into the wall with such force I was convinced there was a gaping hole where there once was smooth plaster. One more distasteful thing to look at.

Vex rushed into the room, frantically searching for something he'd obviously hidden, but probably couldn't remember where. His eyes were as wide as saucers, his pupils dilated to an unhealthy level.

"What the hell are you looking at?" he yelled. His mood swings worsened the longer he snorted that poison. Thankfully, he didn't make me get high with him anymore. I hated every single second he forced the shit up my nose, but I didn't have a choice; it was either comply or endure some of the worst beatings of my young life. Truthfully, I think he stopped pressuring me because he'd become greedy. That and he was tired of hearing me complain, even though I gave in each and every time. Whatever the final reason was, I was grateful.

"Nothing," I muttered, quickly looking down at my trembling hands so as not to further aggravate him. Along with the mood swings, his paranoia heightened as well, forever accusing me of conspiring against him. As if I had anyone to even talk to, let alone plot against him with. Everyone in the club stayed clear of me, even the women. They knew Vex was unstable, and they chose not to have to deal with his crazy ass.

Normally, a young woman had her father to turn to for protection, but in my case my father was worse than Vex, simply because he held no love in his heart for me, which he proved over and over again. Rico Yanez being one such prime example. Never mind that he'd sanctioned the union between Vex and me when I was only fourteen years old, knowing damn well what a psychopath he was.

With the back of his hand, he swiped what few trinkets I'd been able to save over the years clear across the room. The glass from a snow globe shattered against the wall, tearing me apart because it was the last remaining item I had from my mother. Tears instantly welled behind my eyes, but I bit the inside of my cheek to distract myself from the pain building in my heart.

Vex knew exactly how much the trinket meant to me, and that it had not met with some sort of demise before was a miracle. For as cruel as he was, I thought there was a tiny piece inside him that wouldn't completely leave me with nothing.

But I was wrong. Of course I was wrong. What kind of stupid woman believed there was still some sort of humanity residing inside the likes of Vex, especially after all I had witnessed and experienced over the years?

"Fuck!" he shouted, walking quickly into the small closet we shared. Rooting through the mess, he yelled in frustration over and over again.

Even though my voice was not wanted, I needed to know what he was looking for. Maybe I'd seen the item, and the quicker he found it the quicker he would leave.

"What are you looking for?" I whispered, my voice loud enough for him to hear. He abruptly stopped all movement, turning on his heel so fast I thought he was going to trip over his own damn feet. Leering at me, he clenched his hands into tight fists, the craziness in his eyes coming out full force.

"You wanna know what I'm lookin' for?" he sneered. I remained quiet, silently berating myself for even opening my mouth to begin with. With every step he took closer, I braced myself, either for him to verbally berate me or for his fists to do the talkin'.

When I didn't respond, he reached for the book I'd left on a side table and whipped it at me. Thankfully, I'd been watching his every move and ducked at the very last second. Even if the book had hit me, it wouldn't have done much damage, seeing as it was a thin paperback. But still, any chance I could escape his wrath was a win, although it didn't happen often at all.

I knew it was in my best interest to answer him, even though my voice alone could cause him to fly off the handle even more. "Yes. I just . . . I just thought I could help you find it," I said dejectedly, looking back down at my lap.

"Well," he responded, "if you wanna help me so much, get off your lazy ass and help me look for my guns." He didn't wait for me to move before he tore the room apart, destroying the calm I'd tried so hard to create inside our bedroom. We didn't have much, but what we did have was neat and organized. I hated chaos. I couldn't stand a messy room, the scattered items instantly making me anxious. It's funny, I would give anything for a messy room to be my worst problem, but cleanliness was the only thing I could control, so I held on to it with everything I had still pumping inside me.

Knowing full well he was going to lash out at me if I didn't help him, I scrambled off the bed, the oversized T-shirt I had on falling down and hitting me mid-thigh. I had on boy shorts, but he couldn't see them under the shirt. I never purposely wore anything tight or revealing, mainly because I didn't wish to call any attention to myself, his possession of me casting over him in a near demonic way sometimes. Plus, the one time I wore clothing which actually fit me, he'd freaked out and accused me of wanting to have sex with every single one of his brothers.

It was the first time he'd raped me, but it certainly wasn't the last.

His eyes quickly grazed over my body before he resumed searching for his weapons. I breathed a sigh of relief that he wasn't focusing on me and helped him scour the small space.

Scrambling underneath the bed, I pulled out a small black duffel bag. Without looking inside, I called Vex's attention to me. "Is this what you're looking for?" I called out, taking a step back after placing the bag on top of the bed.

Whipping his head toward me, he eyed the bag before approaching. He was cautious not to appear thankful, or happy, or whatever emotion he thought would weaken him in front of me.

Pulling back the zipper, he peered inside, and I swore I saw a hint of a smirk trace over his lips before he closed the material. Without another word, he snatched the duffel and practically ran from the room, yelling for whoever was waiting for him.

A thin shield of fear enveloped me as soon as I was all alone. The only time Vex went in search of his extra guns was when they were preparing for a heavy defense or for retaliation.

And the only club we were truly at war with was the Knights Corruption. A club so vile they made ours sound like a walk in the park. At least that's what I'd been told my entire life. The fear of the devil had been drilled into me when it came to the KC MC. They were our most hated enemies and, although I was treated lower than the mud on their shoes, my club protected me from the outside world. Mainly, they protected me from the Knights. Contact with them in any way would prove detrimental to me. My father once told me he would rather see me dead than in the hands of the KC, threatening to pull the trigger himself if I ever found myself in such a predicament.

The biggest insult to the likes of our clubs was to be taken by the enemy. To be forced to live with them, to be integrated into their way of life and become one of them, for however long, was the worst kind of fate. Not only would my life be in ruins if the Knights ever got their hands on me, but I would no longer be accepted by the Savage Reapers.

They would hunt me down and kill me simply for breathing the same air as their nemesis.

EIGHT

Marek

FOUR DAYS HAD PASSED SINCE I'd found Tripp hanging on for dear life.

Four days of witnessing the touch-and-go status of a fellow brother, Hawke's actual blood brother.

Four days of planning our next move.

In our last meeting, I declared our retaliation would wait until we gathered enough intel, which would make our reprisal worth it. But things had since changed. They dared to spit at us, to taunt and harass us, jumping Tripp as he left The Underground. They knew enough not to go inside, the evidence of their last stupid mistake dumped in front of their club.

We had to move, and do it quickly, before anything else happened, or any more Knights' blood was spilled.

"That's it," I heard the soft tone of Adelaide say as I walked into Chambers. She was tending to Tripp with the utmost care, cleaning and re-dressing his many wounds, careful not to press too hard because of the amount of pain he was still reeling with. The call she'd made when we were in the thick of it was to a doctor friend of hers, someone she worked closely with at the hospital. She swore she trusted him but just in case, we put the fear of God into him as soon as he arrived. He looked none too pleased with the likes of us, his brows drawn and his face rigid, but luckily his features softened as soon as his eyes landed on Adelaide's face. And who could blame him? She was certainly the looker, her toned and tanned body nice and tight, her tits the perfect size with an ass that didn't quit. Her uncle had seen most of the men leering after her, and he'd made no qualms about threatening each of their lives if they even thought about touching her. A threat she found quite amusing, as was shown by the curvature of her full lips.

Our back room in Chambers had been turned into a makeshift operating room. Thankfully, the good doc, with the help of Adelaide, was able to remove the one remaining bullet from Tripp's chest. He'd given him a decent prognosis but warned us about infection, telling us the following twenty-four hours were going to be crucial.

My undying gratitude for Trigg's niece was not something I gave freely, but the woman was a miracle worker. Her gentleness with him was a welcome sight since we hardly witnessed such rare emotion in our lives. We lived hard, lived rough, so when an angel's touch was felt, it reminded me there was some good left in the world. Too bad I would never feel the effects of it. Not as far as I could see, at least.

"If you keep teasing me like that, sweetheart, you're gonna get a reaction you don't want," Tripp grumbled, his dry lips kicking up into a tiny smirk. His dark hair was clean, all the blood and dirt wiped from his face and body. She'd even given him a clean shave, ridding him of the slight stubble covering his jaw. He looked much better after she'd finished with him—pale, but much better. At least, that was what she proclaimed. Me? I could give two shits how my men looked. I only cared about how they acted.

Before Adelaide could respond, I spoke up, reminding him just who he was taunting. "Hey, buddy. You better watch yourself before Trigger comes in here and puts another bullet in you." I grinned, but he clearly looked confused. "Don't you know who you're hittin' on there?"

"My guardian angel." He chuckled, falling into a coughing fit and clutching his chest from the exertion.

"All right. All right. Let's not work him up too much. My patient has to rest, and I won't have the likes of you bothering him." She glanced back at me and smiled, not fearing me in the least. It was rare that someone spoke to me like she had, teasing or not. But my appreciation toward her gave her a pass; plus, I knew she meant nothing by it. She wasn't disrespecting me in any way and we both knew it, so I refused to make a big deal over it.

Another time and I'd throw the friendly warning at Tripp of just who his 'guardian angel' really was. I'd hate for the man not to be armed with the knowledge that she was a fellow brother's family, someone not to be messed with.

My demeanor changed as I approached them both. "Seriously, though, how is he doing?" I asked, stopping directly next to Adelaide and hovering over the recuperating form of our nomad member.

"He definitely has a hard road ahead of him, but I think he'll be fine. Luckily, none of the bullets did any major damage," she proclaimed, gripping his hand softly in hers. Tripp gave me a faint wink before drifting off to sleep. He was clearly exhausted, his body's fight to recover a tiresome one.

Once I was done checking up on Tripp, I thanked Adelaide once more and turned around to leave. It was then that I saw Stone hovering in the doorway. He looked unnerved, and I guessed it had something to do with one of the people behind me.

Walking closer so there was no mistaking my motive, I stopped two feet in front of him. His eyes instantly found mine and he relaxed a little. But there was some sort of fire burning in his eyes, and I had no idea why. As far as I was aware, there was no bad blood between my VP and the nomad. I couldn't pinpoint why he was so on edge until I heard her voice again, promising to care for Tripp until he was all better.

Then I saw it.

The tightening of his jaw.

His hands curling into fists.

His chest expanding and rigid.

His lips turning up into an unyielding sneer.

The look he shot their way was similar to the one he'd directed at Hawke when he put his hands on her while she was inspecting his brother.

It was an undying sign of possession. A rare emotion for Stone, for sure, but it was there nonetheless.

"Do we have a problem here, Stone?" I asked, preparing to physically remove him if I had to. The last thing we needed right then was a fight amongst brothers. I had enough to worry about with Trigger's threats for the men to stay away from his niece, never mind trying to figure out what the hell we were gonna do about payback. I didn't need to deal with Stone's weird reaction as well.

He looked past me when I spoke, so I shoved him back toward the threshold of the room. "Stone!" I shouted. As soon as his eyes found mine again, I repeated, "Do we have a problem here?"

His fiery gaze was his telltale sign that there was more going on than I knew. Countless tense seconds passed before he answered. Gritting his teeth, he unconvincingly said, "No. No problem here."

I obviously didn't believe him, but I wasn't gonna deal with whatever was up his ass right then. I had bigger issues to worry about. "Good. Now, go get everyone and tell them we're having an emergency meeting."

A fierce nod and he retreated from the room. When I looked behind me, I saw Adelaide's eyes following Stone, a strange look marring her features.

What the hell is going on with these two?

Sully

I HADN'T SEEN VEX SINCE the night he came storming into our bedroom. Having no idea where he'd gone, I'd kept to myself like I normally did. Women weren't allowed to wander the clubhouse unless they were called there for one particular reason—to be used and abused. Why most of them kept coming back for more was beyond me. They were free to live their lives outside of our MC, yet they craved the attention of the men. *Weird.*

I was the only exception to the rule simply because I was the president's daughter, although that didn't really mean much; they all knew how he treated me. But I was still allowed to wander the clubhouse at random, although I made sure to keep to the common areas, mainly because I knew Vex would accuse me of fucking someone if I wasn't in plain sight. Hell, he suspected it regardless, but I didn't want to encourage his paranoia any further than he already took it.

Pricking my ears toward a strange noise, I tried my best to listen for it again. Most of the men were retired to their rooms, only a few left to wander around the center room, drinking and laughing it up. It was a quiet night otherwise.

When all I heard were the sounds of the drunken club members, I resumed making myself a sandwich. The bread was but a whisper from my hungry lips when I heard what sounded like a car crash, the noise so explosive it drew the attention of the entire club. Men ran from their rooms in confusion, some of them tripping over items littered all over the common room floor. My need for cleanliness didn't expand past my bedroom.

"What the hell was that?" my father roared, appearing out of nowhere and zipping up his pants. Nancy, one of his many women, appeared but quickly hurried back inside the room he'd just come from.

His wild eyes found mine, his steps never faltering while he practically ran at me. "Get in your room, Sully. Lock and barricade the door and don't come out until I come and get you," he demanded, gripping my arm so tight I winced in pain. "Do you hear me?" he shouted.

"Yes," I whispered. He shoved me backward and once he saw me retreat down the long hallway toward my room, he ran for the front of the clubhouse, shouting for his men to get their guns ready.

There was so much commotion, so many people yelling indiscernible commands, it was hard to hear what was really going on. The only thing I knew was there was some kind of accident outside. It could have been deliberate or not. The men of our club were not the brightest bulbs, some of them downright stupid. While we were guarded by a tall, heavy fence, the men guarding it sometimes were so drunk off their asses, or coked out of their minds, they were utterly useless. On a sober day, they were ruthless and cunning, but get a little bit of poison in their veins and they were easy targets, making the entire place an easy target as well.

Once I'd successfully locked myself inside my room, I pushed a small dresser in front of the door. It was the only piece of furniture I could move myself, so I hoped it worked. I crouched in the corner, turning off the light so I was bathed in darkness. Shivering in fear of what was happening outside, I prayed to make it through unscathed. I was in mid-promise to God when I heard an endless spray of gunshots.

Reminding myself that I'd lived through this type of thing many times before, I tried my best to slow my thumping heart and calm myself with deep breaths, but nothing worked. Men continued to scream between unrelenting gunfire.

Minutes after bullets were discharged, I heard heavy footsteps coming down the hallway, commands being given to the men barreling toward my room. I didn't recognize their voices. They weren't coming from any of the evil beasts who normally resided behind our club walls. No, these deep, dark voices came from whoever had just invaded the Savage Reapers' lair.

And the only club daring enough to pull off such a thing was the Knights Corruption.

Our biggest enemy.

"Back here!" I heard one of them shout. I prayed they were looking for someone or something else, but my hopes were dashed when the handle to my bedroom jiggled. As soon as they realized it was locked, someone started pounding on the door, so hard it was a wonder they didn't split the wood down the middle.

More shouts.

More pounding.

All of a sudden, the frame splintered and a small sliver of light from the hallway filtered into the room. From where I was hiding, I couldn't see who was out there, but I could certainly hear them.

"She has to be in here," I heard one of the intruders yell. "There's no way they would leave her out of their sight." The second comment came from a different man, one whose voice was more gravelly and deeper than the first man. It was then I realized who they were talking about. They wouldn't be busting down the door for some common club whore.

No, they were coming for me.

Dreadful thoughts rampantly flitted through my mind. Thoughts of what they would do to me if they hauled me out of my room, and ugly thoughts of what my own club would do to me if they ever got me back.

Either way, I would be dead, but instead of welcoming the sweet lick of death to stroke my body, something I'd prayed for since I could remember, an innate need to survive kicked in from out of nowhere. Adrenaline pumped through me in waves, blurring my vision and hiccupping my breaths with each and every pound of the door, every shout directed toward and about me, and every gunshot that sliced through the thickening night air.

The room flooded with the hallway light, the door ripped from its hinges while I still tried to loose myself inside the small space. My room held no security for me, but as long as my ears were covered I could only hear muffled sounds, and stifled sounds were better than listening to what they were actually saying, what they had planned for me.

A loud crash jolted me back into the reality of the situation. I waited for more gunfire, but all that followed the toppling dresser was harsh, ragged breathing. I wasn't sure if the sounds were my own or from those who had just entered the room.

Then one of them spoke.

The man with the deep, gravelly voice. A voice which sent shivers of fear and fascination deep into my soul. The mixture of feelings confused me, but I had no time to delve into what they really meant. The only focus in the forefront of my disheveled mind was to figure out how to survive.

Would I beg for my life? Would I appear weak in the face of the enemy? I couldn't answer with certainty, and that alone was disarming. I had no idea what to do, what to say or how to feel.

Luckily, the decision was stolen from me the instant my eyes found him.

A tall, broad man stalked forward, every step closer deciding my fate. My head had instinctually risen so I could see who was coming for me, and what I saw stopped my heart. While my soon-to-be captor was covered in blood, no doubt from his up-close-and-personal bloodshed of my fellow Savages, his prowess shined through. His pale blue eyes pinned me defenseless, his hair short and cropped to his head, a trimmed beard covering his sharp jawline. Blood dripped from his cheeks, and I instantly wondered if he'd been hurt.

The man who had come to kidnap me was the most handsome man I'd ever laid eyes on. But I vowed then and there to never fall prey to his charms, if ever he decided to enchant me with them. Although I hated my club, my father and Vex, I wasn't a traitor. And falling for the enemy was the worst kind of sin to be committed in our ruthless, deadly world.

Shit, as far as I knew, he could be the Devil's nephew, just as brutal and evil as my father and Vex.

Reaching forward, his hand was suddenly thrust into my personal space. *Maybe if I close my eyes they'll all go away. Maybe it'll all be an awful dream, a nightmare I'll soon wake up from.* Shutting my lids tight, I squeezed my hands over my ears and drowned out the sounds in hope everything would return back to *normal.*

I'd never wished for my life more than I did right then, which was probably the saddest revelation I'd ever had.

While I rocked back and forth in my self-induced delirium, the man's hand gripped my wrist, the warmth of his skin setting me ablaze. My eyes flew open and before I could utter a single word, I was pulled to my feet so fast I tumbled forward. I would have fallen directly on my face had it not been for the man holding me upright.

His other hand shot to my side, stabilizing me so I wouldn't topple over and trip him up in the process, even though there was no way I would ever cause him to fall. His strength emanated off him in waves, and it was both frightening and intriguing. Caught in a whirlwind of unfamiliar emotions, I was utterly confused beyond my simple scope of reality. No words were exchanged between us. In fact, the other two men in the room never spoke either, watching intently to see what was going to take place between their fellow brother and the woman shaking in fear.

I started to tremble, cursing myself for being weak yet again. Luckily, my legs remained strong, and as soon as I found an opportunity I was going to put them to good use.

"Look at me," the man growled. I refused, keeping my head low. His impatience with me was evident, expletives falling freely from his lips as he shook me in frustration. "Fuckin' look at me," he repeated.

Very slowly, I found his eyes again, waiting for what he was going to do or say next.

"Are you the infamous daughter of the Savage Reapers?" His tone was mocking, the manner of his voice spurring me to defend myself, but I was indeed helpless. What could I do to protect myself? Fight? Argue with him? Plead for him to release me and pretend he'd never found me? I knew deep inside that whatever path I chose wouldn't matter. These men obviously had their minds made up, and the only thing I could do would be to follow suit. At least until I figured out my next move.

"Well, are you?" he gritted, his jaw pulsing with the weight of his impatience. It was then I reflected on his absurd question. *The infamous daughter of the Savage Reapers?* What an odd question. I was neither in-famous nor the proclaimed daughter of the entire club. Still reeling in my confusion, he wrenched me forward until I was flush with his blood-soaked chest. "Answer me, woman!" he shouted. "Are you fuckin' Psych's daughter?" *Now,* there's *a question which makes sense to me, even though I wish it wasn't true.*

"Yes," I whispered, although I wasn't sure why I hadn't chosen to lie. I should have denied it, declaring to be just another club whore. But then, why would a common whore be barricaded in one of the back rooms?

"She's even more beautiful up close," one of the men standing near the door announced.

"Sure is," the man in front of me assured, holding me tighter against him. Turning his head to face his men, he asked a question I was curious about myself. "Have you found her father yet? And that crazy-ass fucker who's always attached to her?"

Vex. They were talking about Vex. I almost offered up the detail that he was gone, had been gone for the past four days, but I forced my lips to stay closed, my confession resting heavy in my throat.

Even though I hated Vex with every fiber of my being, he was familiar to me.

He was the devil I'd been accustomed to.

"Not yet, but we will. Then we'll burn every last motherfucker in here," the tall, blond-haired man pronounced.

"Until then . . . ," my captor said, pulling me toward the other two men blocking the entrance to the room. I wasn't quite sure what happened, but all of a sudden I flew into a rage, years of feeling helpless finally unleashing their grip, unbridled strength spilling forth which I had no idea was even nestled inside me. His grip on my wrists wasn't tight, so I was able to shrug free of him rather easily. Taking a step back, I startled him when I threw my tiny fist in the air and connected with his jaw. The look on his stupidly handsome face was most telling. He was stunned . . . and pissed. Taking advantage of his shock, I ran around his looming body and fled toward the bathroom.

My escape was futile, though. A large arm wrapped around my waist and hoisted me into the air, all the breath pushed from my lungs from the force. Stars danced in my eyes as I tried to regain some kind of footing, but it was useless. He tossed me over his shoulder before I could recover and rushed from the room behind his two men.

Now what the hell am I going to do?

TEN

Marek

NEVER BEFORE HAD A WOMAN attempted to strike me, and that the first time it *did* happen was from the tiny spit-fire we'd abducted turned me inside out. Barging into her room hadn't prepared me for what or who I was going to find. Our main objective was to pay those fuckers back for all they'd done. Tripp was the final straw and we all knew it, even though I'd initially proclaimed I wanted to wait.

Well, four days was long enough this time around.

The goal was to destroy the Savage Reapers from the inside out, but because we weren't one hundred percent prepared, we'd only managed to wipe out half of the members present. Still a good hit, but it wasn't enough. We needed to wipe out Psych, take out his VP, Rabid, then destroy Vex, one of the most volatile members of the club. His crazy ass needed to be buried simply because he was one psychotic, soulless motherfucker.

I remembered hearing someone speak of Psych's daughter, her strange name something I'd never heard before. Her beauty was often whispered about, but then again I couldn't take stock in what a bunch of horny men said. Any pussy with a pair of tits and they would fall prey to their *beauty*.

There wasn't much information on her, always hidden away from the world, protected from the likes of rival clubs. To entice a woman from a rival club into your own was a big no-no. It was the epitome of insults to integrate them into your way of life, although it wasn't much different from their own, the biggest difference being the Savage Reapers were a den of devils. As far as dirty dealings, the Knights weren't much better, per se, but as far as morals and human decency went, we were ten times the men they were.

The ride back to the club was executed in silence. While I knew there was a chance of an extraction, I opted for taking the cage, aka van, instead of my bike, knowing full well I was gonna be the one escorting our *guest* back to our club. We only made it a habit of kidnapping people who needed to be reasoned with, and while this was a completely different turn of events, it couldn't be helped. We had to drive at least one nail into the SR's coffin, and stealing the president's daughter was the biggest 'fuck you' we could send.

Her hands and feet were bound tight enough so she couldn't wriggle free but not tight enough to cut into her lovely, creamy skin. Stone and Hawke were in the back with her, keeping an eye out just in case she chose to do something crazy. She'd already shocked the shit out of me once that day, and I wasn't taking any chances.

The rest of the men were in front of us, throwing the line of formation out of sorts with me and my VP riding behind everyone else. But the cage always held up the rear in case things jumped off and the riders fell into danger. There were enough weapons hidden behind secret panels to arm a small tribe, so it was up to whoever was riding in there to be sure we had our eyes peeled for anything. If we rode ahead of the others, we risked the lives of all the riding brothers in case they were ambushed.

A soft moan wafted through the otherwise silent vehicle. She'd drawn my attention immediately, and I couldn't help but inquire about her well-being. When I'd first laid eyes on her crouching in the corner of that small-ass, dingy room, I felt my chest constrict. A shiver of something foreign shot through me, and I had this inexplicable need to comfort her. To tell her that, although we wouldn't harm her, she had to come with us. But, of course, I never uttered any of those words, instead choosing to confront her like the man she probably believed me to be.

An intruder.

A killer.

An invader who was there to snatch her away from the only world she'd ever known.

And she was right. I was there to take her, to integrate her into our club and never allow her to see any of the Savage Reapers ever again.

"Is she all right?" I queried, never taking my eyes from the road while I impatiently waited for them to answer.

I counted two deep inhales of breath before one of my men's voices cut through the building tension.

"What the fuck?" Hawke yelped.

"What?" I shouted, tightening my grip on the steering wheel. When he didn't answer, I yelled again, more authority cutting my tone and letting him know how serious I was. "What's the problem, Hawke?"

"She fuckin' bit me," he grumbled, Stone chuckling beside him in amusement.

"Why the hell did she bite you, man? What were you doing to her?" I growled, the thought of him touching her inappropriately instantly angering me.

"You asked if she was okay, so I pushed her hair off her face to see her eyes, and my fingers fell too close to her mouth. Then she goddamn bit me," he repeated, his disgust apparent in his tone.

"Did she hurt you?"

"Hell yeah, that hurt," he complained.

"Good. Think of it as payback for the little escapade your woman subjected us to." The lilt of my voice told him I was messing with him, even though he totally deserved it for not getting Edana out of the clubhouse before she started throwing knives and shit.

"How is that my fault?"

"You need to control your woman better, brother." Stone was still laughing about his buddy cradling his hand in his lap, a gesture I could clearly see from the rearview mirror.

"Fuck you," he murmured. "Just because you don't feel any pain, ever, doesn't mean shit to the rest of us." My eyes flitted to the woman lying between the two men and saw a fleeting look of confusion pass over her lovely face. "This shit hurts," Hawke continued to gripe.

"Man up, pussy," I demanded from the front, relaxing my grip on the leather of the wheel.

Over the next few miles, I envisioned gazing on our new captive until my heart was content. It'd been dark in her room and, although I could see she was beautiful, I couldn't wait to see her in the light of my private space. Sprawled on my bed or washing in my shower.

Get it together before you fall into more trouble than you know how to dig yourself out of.

Luckily, the clubhouse was directly ahead of us, pushing me from whatever wayward thoughts had invaded my sanity.

Once the van came to a stop, I hurriedly threw it in park and made my way toward the back. Stone had opened the door and filed out directly behind Hawke, pushing his shoulder in jest and continuing to tease him about his fingers. Thankfully, Hawke wasn't feeling the initial effects of the incident, but when I grabbed his hand to see the supposed damage, I was shocked to see she'd actually broken skin.

She sure is a feisty one.

Leaning close to her ear, I warned, "Don't think about biting me, sweetheart, because I won't be held accountable for my reaction." I was serious, although I doubted I could ever lay a hand on her in anger. Sexually was a completely different story—one I hadn't yet written, of course.

Her eyes scanned my face, landing on my mouth for longer than was normal for someone in her situation. Finally, I guessed when her curiosity had been sated, she connected with my eyes, and it was in those beautiful dark brown orbs of hers that I saw her complicity. She was scared, of course, but something else hid behind her gaze. Unfortunately, I didn't have any time right then to figure out what it was.

Escorting her from the back of the vehicle, I made sure she was stable before bending down to cut the ties around her feet. "Don't think about running either. Nowhere for you to go," I promised. That time I didn't wait for her to acknowledge me, clipping the ties effortlessly before standing in front of her once more.

She was a tiny thing, my own six-foot-one frame towering over her. From what I could see in the darkened lot of the club, she was slim. A little too slim for my taste. She wore a large gray T-shirt, which fell to just above her knees, and from what I gathered when I flung her over my shoulder, she was wearing tiny-ass shorts underneath. An old pair of slip-on shoes adorned her small feet, a hole in the side of the left one making me furrow my brow in irritation. Her eyes followed mine, and when she realized I was staring at her shoes, she shifted her feet, hiding the damaged one behind the other.

Ushering her to walk in front of me, I placed my large hand on the small of her back, the heat from her skin powering through her thin shirt and hitting me right where it counted. My dick twitched in my pants and before things got too *hard* for me, I adjusted myself, grateful she was facing forward and didn't see me grab my crotch.

I had no idea why I worried about what she saw, or felt for that matter. I wasn't a heartless man. Ruthless when I needed to be, but not heartless. But I never cared what women thought of me or my club before. Plenty of them had thrown themselves at me ever since I could remember, and not once did I ever apologize for my actions or words, never caring one way or the other if I ever saw them again.

But she was . . . different.

I knew it in my soul.

I knew she was going to ruin me, yet I had no idea how.

ELEVEN

Sully

FUNNY HOW LIFE CHANGES AT the drop of a hat.

No warning.

No planning.

A simple prayer for my life as I knew it to cease . . . and in barged our biggest enemy.

Be careful what you wish for and all that shit. Isn't that the saying?

A sudden chill coursed through me. We were inside the Knights Corruption compound, leisurely walking toward what I assumed was their private bunker of sorts. The place they held meetings, threw wild parties and partook in unspeakable things. Well, if they were anything like my club, at least.

The only things I knew about the KC MC were what I'd heard over the years. So far, I hadn't witnessed any of their brutality. I certainly expected to be beaten after I'd attacked the man who snatched me from my room, then again when I bit the man with the long dark hair.

But nothing.

Neither one of them had laid a hand on me, which I found it very strange.

I was used to being punished for the simplest of things. Not having dinner ready on time, innocently glancing at one of the club members while they spoke, not cleaning up someone else's mess in a timely fashion. Those were the reasons I was punched and kicked. I couldn't even imagine what would have happened to me had I ever reacted and hit or bit Vex or my father, or anyone in the Reapers for that matter.

I would be dead. Of that, I was sure. So I was simply baffled why I'd chosen to react in such a manner with our most hated enemy.

Walking into what appeared to be a common room of sorts, I was instantly put on guard, ashamed of my appearance and what I looked like to the people suddenly swarming all around us. My hands were still restrained, my fingers interlocked and resting in front of me.

I quickly took in my surroundings, my eyes flitting over the beige-colored walls, neatly swept floor and array of various couches and chairs littered around the entire room. The area looked nothing like the common room back at my club. There were no dried bloodstains on the floor, no pile of used condoms strewn about and no liquor bottles cluttered into a massive mess in all four corners.

"Well, what do we have here, Prez?" an older man behind the bar asked as we continued to walk through. Keeping my head down, I heard the man who was guiding me speak up.

"We snagged us the SR princess," he responded. His voice was neither celebratory nor cocky; he was matter-of-fact, and it was even more unnerving than if he'd been boasting about his acquisition. We walked a few more paces before something dawned on me.

The man who'd stolen me from the only home I knew was the *president* of our enemies? How was that even possible? My father would never barge into enemy territory, instead choosing to send his foot soldiers to do his dirty work for him.

An abrupt growl sounded to my left, drawing my attention right away.

The large man with the blond hair stood a few feet from us, his attention on the one and only other woman in sight, a beautiful blonde-haired woman who looked extremely out of place. She carried a small black medical bag, one I'd seen many a time back home when some of the men needed patching up. She was unaware the man was staring at her and she continued forging ahead, her head down and reading something on her phone. It wasn't until she walked right into him that she looked up. They were close enough that I could hear their conversation. Hell, anyone paying attention could hear them.

"Stone," she cried out, "you startled me." A light blush crept over her cheeks as she continued to stare up at him. Endless tense seconds passed before she spoke again. "Did you all just get back?" She hadn't seen me; it was apparent in the innocent way she tried to engage that Stone character.

She certainly wasn't a club whore. She could have been the man's old lady, but I didn't think so. Maybe she was someone they simply called in to help out whenever someone was injured. I had no idea, but I knew she wasn't integrated wholly into their . . . *our* way of life.

"Back to tend to him again, Adelaide?" he asked, stepping back so he could gain some distance. His posture was rigid, and I saw his hands curl into tight fists. Thankfully having something other than my own uncertainty to feast on, I leaned in so I could hear them better.

"You know damn well I have to check on him, to make sure he's okay. You don't want him to die, do you?" she asked. She gripped her bag tighter and appeared as if she was fighting the urge to tell him off, knowing she was outmatched with all the men milling around the room. If I dared to ever ask such a question, I would have been reminded of my place, and quickly. I waited with bated anticipation to see how he was going to react, bracing myself to witness a deplorable act.

"You don't have to constantly touch him the way you do," he seethed. Although their talk was quiet, it drew the attention of the man behind the bar. He stepped around and quickly walked toward the two of them.

Glancing around, I noticed everyone's focus was on the scene unfolding in front of us—the president of the club, the man standing behind me, was no exception. I heard him sigh loudly, his warm breath cascading over my cheek and making me feel something. I wasn't sure what, but it wasn't terror.

Pinning my gaze back on the couple across the room, I pricked my ears to make sure I didn't miss a word.

"What's going on here?" the older man asked, reaching for the woman's arm. Was he her old man? When she didn't answer, he turned his gaze onto the blond man. "Are you angry with my niece for some reason, Stone?"

Oh . . . she's his niece.

Biting his lip, Stone stalled to find the right answer, I was sure. "I just don't know why she's always here. That's all, Trigger."

"She's here tending to a fellow brother. You know he's not out of the woods yet." Her uncle, this *Trigger*, looked pensive for a moment. "Wait . . . Are you jealous?" Before Stone could utter a complacent reply, the man cut him off. "No, that couldn't be possible," he gritted, "because that would mean you feel something for my niece, and you know better. You know better than to mess with my family, don't you?" He continued on as if he hadn't just asked him question after question. "You might not be able to feel pain, you fucker, but that doesn't mean I won't put a bullet in your ass if you touch one hair on her goddamn head." Stepping so close they were chest to chest, he practically spit in his face as he yelled, "Do you understand me?"

That's the second time someone made reference to this man not feeling pain. What the hell does that even mean?

"Uncle Trig," the woman interjected, "there's nothing going on between me and Stone. He's probably just pissy there's a woman constantly around, messing up the testosterone flow you all have going on up in here." She tried to joke to relieve some of the pulsating tension, but it was lost on her uncle. And on the irate man standing next to her.

The man behind me spoke up and his deep voice startled me. "Trig, Stone," he commanded. "Lock it up. Enough." His words were short and to the point. Both men glared at each other before moving aside. Stone gave the woman another hard leer before pushing past both of them, mumbling something incoherent under his breath.

At least the focus had been taken off me for a short time.

TWELVE

Marek

I SWEAR TO CHRIST! IF we didn't have enough shit to worry about, now I had to concern myself as to what the hell was goin' on with Stone and Adelaide . . . and Trigger, for fuck's sake. It wasn't enough that we'd just ambushed the Reapers' compound, kidnapped Psych's daughter, Vex's alleged woman, but then I had to worry about Trigger putting a bullet in my VP.

Can I not get one night of rest?

I ain't gonna lie. We were all intrigued to see what was gonna unfold between Stone and Adelaide, then Trigger stepping in, but I was tired and needed to get some sleep. But first, I had to take care of the woman still shackled in front of me.

My captive.

The newest permanent addition to the Knights Corruption.

Yeah, no way in hell I was releasing her back to them, no matter how much she begged, or how hard they came at us to retrieve her.

I ushered the tiny woman ahead, directing her down the hallway and to my room, which was the last one on the left. Turning the handle, I guided her inside and turned on the light so I could finally gaze at her uninterrupted.

Spinning her around to face me, she hung her head low so she didn't have to acknowledge her current situation. Well, fuck that—I wanted her to watch me as I watched her. Pulling my knife from my waistband, I cut the ties from her wrists. As they fell to the ground, I saw her chest expand with a heavy exhale. Little did she realize those ties falling loose meant nothing. Going forward, she was property of the KC. She was my prize for all of the wrongs her club had committed against ours.

She rubbed at her wrists even though I knew the restraints hadn't cut into her flesh or stopped the blood flow, although they did leave a slight red mark on her skin. It was while looking at the faint lines that I noticed a bruise higher up on her arm, then another . . . and another. Without warning, I reached for her chin and jerked her head upright so she had no choice but to look at me. A faded yellow contusion covered the right side of her cheekbone. If I had to guess, I would have said someone had clocked her about a week ago, judging from the color of the mark.

Something inside me snapped and before I realized what I was doing, I yanked her shirt up and over her head, tossing it to the ground before she could protest. Her hands instantly covered herself, but because her tits were so large she spilled over her tiny fingers. I had no idea she had all that hidden underneath the damn shirt. To say I was pleasantly surprised was an understatement. While she did her best to conceal herself from my view, I raked my eyes down the rest of her, stopping when I saw the first scar. It was four inches in length across her lower abdomen, jagged and raised. Then I saw another one just underneath where her left hand was currently covering her tit. That one was smaller, but just as rough. She was littered with marks, some dark and fresh, while others appeared faint, her body healing itself and discarding the evidence of obvious abuse.

The majority of her torture was on her torso, although there were a few marks on her thighs. As my eyes moved lower, they stopped on those tiny-ass black shorts she wore. Lower still, I took in the remainder of her front. For as small as she was, her legs were long and lean, her body trembling the longer the silence lingered between us. Making a circling motion with my finger, I silently told her to turn around. She shook her head no—it was subtle, but I saw it.

Gripping her shoulders, I forcefully turned her around so her back was facing me, a small gasp falling from her pouty lips and quickly distracting me. Ignoring her disbelief, I inspected her further and discovered what looked like two small burn marks on her lower back. Fury coursed through me that someone could do that to a fragile woman. Granted, I had no idea what kind of strength she possessed, but she was a woman nonetheless, no match for the likes of a man.

My gut told me that fucker Vex had something to do with the way she looked. His reputation preceded him, and I had no doubt he thought he owned her, marking her as he saw fit.

With my hands still resting on her trembling shoulders, I tried my best to calm the anger raging in my throat. I didn't want to scare her any more than she already was. "Sully, is it?" I asked, sure that was the odd name I'd heard was attached to the woman standing before me.

She nodded once.

"Who did these things to you?"

Silence.

I tried to remain calm, but the more she chose to ignore my question the more irate I became. Before I could stop myself, I yelled for her to answer me.

"Tell me right now who did this to you!" I whipped her back around so I could see her. Her lip quivered when her eyes landed on mine. She possessed the darkest brown eyes, the color so rich it was like nothing I'd ever seen. I knew she held back her tears, no doubt internally demanding she not cry in front of the big bad man, who'd stolen her. Her jet-black hair was long, a tangled mess from the night's events. She was a little dirty as well, definitely in need of a shower very soon.

If I didn't know any better, I would have thought she was homeless, had suffered from bouts of hunger and abuse at the hands of strangers on the street. The longer she stood before me, in all her pitiful beauty, the more she intrigued me. I longed to know her story but I also knew I had to keep my distance, my inner voice warning me about getting too close.

I shook her shoulders. "Tell me or so help me God . . ." I warned.

As her lips parted to speak, there was a loud knock on the door. "Prez, you better get out here!" Zip yelled from the hallway.

"Why?"

"Trigger and Stone are about to come to blows." *Fuck! I can't handle this shit right now.*

"Sully, you need to go take a shower. Everything you'll need is in the bathroom." Her body never moved, but her eyes followed me when I walked to my dresser and pulled out a pair of boxer shorts and a Knights T-shirt. "I know these are gonna be big on you, but it's all I have until I send someone to buy you a few things."

Zip banged on the door again. "Marek, you need to get out here. Now!" he hollered.

"Jesus Christ! I'm coming." I looked away from her sadness and opened the door, staring at Zip so harshly he backed up a step. "What the fuck?" I mumbled, pushing past him to walk down the hall.

When I entered the common area, I saw all the men huddling around a commotion. As I moved closer, I saw Trigger and Stone standing toe to toe, both of them looking as if they were gonna kill the other. Adelaide stood off to the side, desperately trying to convince her uncle to back away. Trigger had a good twenty years on both Stone and me, but the man had a right hook that had knocked out many a man. Stone, however, was not your typical opponent. The man was skilled in not only boxing but some mixed martial arts as well. What can I say? My VP was a badass, although I would never admit that to him. His head was already swollen enough.

Then there was the little thing about him never feeling any pain. It was true. I'd heard all sorts of rumors about him before, everything from he was immortal to he'd been shot a thousand times and never once flinched. All of it was bullshit, although there was *some* truth to the tales.

Stone had what was referred to as a congenital insensitivity to pain. The only reason I knew the medical term was because he'd told me, otherwise, I would've probably fallen into the trap of believing some of the rumors. The man had been in some nasty wrecks, his leg dangling behind him as he crawled off to the side of the road on one of those occasions, and he never even balked. Instead, he was pissed off because he knew he had to wear a cast and couldn't ride until he was completely healed. I'd also seen him take the brunt of a blade as well as a bullet—twice. Luckily never hitting any major organs. Although the man laughed it off when that shit happened, he could still die if the damage was extensive enough. Though sometimes, I thought he bought into his whole immortal bullshit himself.

"What the hell is going on?" I demanded, pushing through the crowd of men and coming to stand right next to the both of them.

"I saw your VP with his hands all over my niece," Trigger spit, shoving Stone as the last word left his angry mouth.

"Don't put your fuckin' hands on me, Trigger. You don't know what you saw, so just calm the hell down." The look in Stone's eyes was volatile, and I would surely have a mess to clean up if they decided to tear each other apart.

We should be fighting our enemies out there, not fighting each other in here.

"Uncle Trig, please . . . You don't understand. It's not what you think. Really," Adelaide cried, taking a step toward her family. "I tripped and Stone was simply holding me until I regained my balance." She tugged on his arm. "Please, don't do anything stupid."

"Is that right? Is she telling the truth?" Trigger asked Stone, careful not to back down until he confessed. Adelaide had given Stone an out, yet he hesitated to take it. The flaring of his nostrils and the tick in his jaw told me he was about to make a stupid mistake. But before he opened his mouth, a high-pitched yelp from down the hallway pulled all of our attention.

"*Now* what the hell?" I yelled.

Zip appeared out of nowhere, but instead of walking toward us like a normal fucking human being, he crawled along the floor, cursing and screaming with every slow inch of surface he covered. It was then I realized he'd come out of *my* room. The same room Sully was in, practically naked.

I swear to God, if he touched her, I'm gonna kill him.

Stalking toward him, I reached down and yanked him to his feet, his hands covering his crotch and continuing to double over in pain. Seething, I growled in his ear, "What did you do?"

"I . . . I didn't . . . do anything," he spurted, his breaths not fully carrying his words. They were short and choppy, probably because of the pain he was in. It didn't take a genius to see he'd obviously been kicked in the balls, but why? What had he done to warrant such a viscous attack? And I said vicious because it was one of the most excruciating, painful things to happen to a man. Although, getting shot was no walk in the park either.

"Well, you must have done something."

"I . . . I just . . . was trying to convince her to kiss me. That's all. I . . . I swear." Shoving him back down to the ground, I abruptly turned toward my entire club, most of the men still present after our little retaliation trip.

"Hear me now," I roared. "If anyone so much as touches a hair on Sully's head, you're gonna have to answer to me. And it won't be goddamn pretty. Trust me on that shit!"

Kicking Zip in the leg on my way back toward my room to check on her, I heard a few of the men grumble under their breaths. I didn't care if they thought she was gonna be passed around for their own amusement. She'd been through enough.

The evidence was scarred all over her body.

THIRTEEN

Sully

I HEARD SHOUTING IN THE hallway, and I thought I heard my name, but I'd shut the bathroom door soon after I'd defended myself against one of the club members. He wasn't doing anything different than any other man in my life had done—always wanting to touch me, to taste me—but, for some reason, I'd snapped. Again. The only explanation for my bouts of bravery must be that I was still in shock, not in my right frame of mind. Because if I were, I would have never done any of the things I had since I'd been kidnapped.

There was no way I was going to get away with fighting these men as much as I had been. Maybe they were gearing up for something awful, counting my insolent acts up to warrant the attack which was surely coming at me.

Maybe I'd finally fought back *because* I didn't know them. I had no frame of reference of how they would react, therefore leaving me to my own self-justified—or delusional—world of denial.

The bathroom I was now trapped in boasted nothing special. A cream color washed over the walls of the small room. There was a silver rack next to the toilet, a beige towel hanging haphazardly from it. A single vanity with an accompanying wooden mirror was set in the middle of the intimate space.

Like I said, nothing to write home about, but it was the most enticing room to me. It allowed me a sliver of solitude, and after being ripped from the only life I'd known, it was comforting to be alone.

Turning on the shower, I waited patiently while the water heated up, steam quickly fogging the small mirror. Stripping off my shorts, I slid the shower door open and stepped inside, instantly feeling a smidge better. The power of hot water cascading all over my tired, worn-out body was the best therapeutic release. All my demons were put to rest, all my self-loathing taking a backseat to the warmth I suddenly found myself enveloped in.

Reaching for the combined shampoo and conditioner bottle, I squeezed a healthy size into my palm before massaging it into my tangled hair. The soft repetition of my fingers on my scalp was quite relaxing, making me forget for a brief moment just where I was.

In the Knights Corruption's compound.

Naked in the president's shower.

My captor.

Once my long hair was rinsed free, I grabbed the shower gel and spread an ample amount on a washcloth, scrubbing my body clean. The masculine scent filled my nose and while it should have put me on guard, I noticed it had the reverse effect. The aroma calmed me. I'd smelled it before . . . on *him*. I first noticed it when he was standing behind me, guiding me toward his bedroom. Then again when he was inspecting my body, his hands holding me close to him as if he feared I was going to flee. And why shouldn't he think such a thing? Any normal person who'd been stolen away from her family—no matter how abusive and dysfunctional—would try and run given the opportunity to do so.

So, why wasn't I devising a plan to escape?

Focusing back on the task at hand, I almost didn't hear the bathroom door open, then close; the soft click of the handle was swallowed by the heavy flow of the water.

My head was immersed under the spray when I suddenly heard a gruff voice slice through the otherwise silent air.

"If you stay in there any longer you're gonna turn into a damn prune."

His deep voice startled me, my body's reaction completely involuntary. I jumped and slipped on the shower floor, my arms bracing myself against the tile so I didn't fall on my ass. Before I could reply, he quickly slid the door open and stood in front of me, a brief worried look passing over his handsome features.

I'm learning there's absolutely no sense of privacy when it comes to this man.

Reaching to take my hand, he pulled me toward the edge of the shower, keeping his eyes on my face and not my naked body. Not in the beginning, at least. His touch was soothing, but he also made me extremely self-conscious. Not simply because I was nude, but I felt he could see into the deepest parts of my soul. His blue eyes entranced me, blinking in slow motion as he seemed to memorize every aspect of my face. He stared so intently at my mouth that I could do nothing but lick my lips out of nervousness, biting down on the corner to sate my thumping heart. A low growl erupted from his throat, his hand tightening over mine as his gaze flew back up to meet my own.

Soon, he raked his eyes over the rest of me, being sure to take in his fill rather quickly.

"Are you all right?" he asked, licking his own lips while he waited for my answer. But I'd become mute all of a sudden. The chill of the room hardened my nipples, making them painfully erect. An ache shot through me while my heart pounded against my chest. But all I could focus on was his eyes . . . and that delectable mouth of his. He had the most perfect Cupid's bow, his lips full and inviting. A neatly trimmed beard coated his strong jaw, and the flare of his nostrils told me he was excited, although it was the only reaction which indicated so.

Instinctually, my fingers traced over the scar on my stomach, shielding the ugly, puckered skin from his view, in case he chanced a look down there again. But instead of hiding, he saw me—*all* of me—and it was quite unnerving.

"I still want answers," he demanded, quirking his brow while he continued to stand in the open doorway of the shower.

"About what?" I mumbled, knowing damn well what he was talking about.

Leaning closer, he said, "About who did that to you." He gestured toward my body with his finger. "I'll give you the night to settle in, seeing as how this is your home now. Then we'll talk, and you'll tell me everything I want to know. Got it?" he asked.

I remained silent, trying to process what I knew to be true, but it was somehow different when the words were spoken out loud. *This is your home now.* It couldn't be further from the truth, but I didn't know quite how to voice that without angering him. I'd been through such a whirlwind that evening; all I wanted to do was finish washing up and crawl into bed.

His bed.

But I didn't have another choice.

Did I?

His posture became rigid, as if he expected a fight, but I said nothing. I simply nodded, hoping he would close the door and leave me in peace.

Peace. What a funny word, one which had never pertained to me a day in my life.

Finally, after giving my body a once-over again, he closed the door and it was seconds before I heard another click, indicating he had vacated the one small room I wanted to spend the rest of my life in. I had no desire to ever see another person for as long as I could stand it, although the man who'd kidnapped me was different. I saw something in his eyes, a nature he tried his hardest to hide from people. Maybe it was because he was the leader of a notorious biker club, making sure no one questioned his power—hell, maybe even his sanity. Or maybe it was for a different reason altogether, but I knew I wasn't going to stick around long enough to find out.

While I had no set plan of escaping, I knew I had to do something eventually. I mean, who just gives up when kidnapped, complacent to remain with their captor, no questions asked?

Stepping from the shower, I dried my body before slipping on the shorts and T-shirt he'd given me earlier. Slowly opening the door, I stepped into his bedroom, but only once I deemed it safe . . . and abandoned. I crawled under the covers and pulled the material to my nose, strangely comforted by the scent which suddenly wrapped around me.

Drifting off to sleep, something I surely would have thought impossible, I envisioned a life where I wasn't a victim. Where I hadn't been snatched from my 'family.' Where I wasn't used as the most intricate part of a pawn played between two clubs who'd been at war for as long as I could remember.

My fantasies consisted of a life where I lived a simple existence, one which didn't involve constant fear and self-loathing.

At least you're away from your father and Vex, my inner voice screamed. The thing was I had no idea what kind of devil lurked in the darkened hallways of my new 'home.'

FOURTEEN

Marek

I HAD EVERY INTENTION OF leaving her alone, allowing her the night to herself, certain she was overwhelmed and probably scared out of her mind. Although, depending on the answer she gave me about who'd desecrated her body, she might be thankful to be away from the Savage Reapers.

Her family.

As I opened the door to my room to check on her before I left for the evening, I heard faint whimpers drift through the air. Stepping inside, I moved closer to the bed and noticed her spread out, jerking in her sleep and pushing at the air as if she were shoving someone away from her.

Who haunts your dreams?

While I made sure to remain as quiet as I could so as not to scare her, my eyes drifted down her body. She'd thrown the covers off and was lying in the clothes I'd given her, the sight of her in my shorts and top stirring up a possessiveness I'd never felt before. The bottom of the shirt rode up enough that I saw her stomach, the scar prevalent enough to fuel my anger all over again. Her full breasts pressed against the fabric, and it was everything I could do not to rip it from her body. My shorts, the ones she was wearing, hung so low on her hipbones that if they were any lower, I would see all of her. Not that I hadn't already, of course, but the slight tease of her pussy made my dick push against my jeans.

The longer I invaded her personal space the more she seemed to fight her nightmare, a scream suddenly erupting from her perfect mouth. Before I realized what I was doing, I rushed forward to wake her. For some reason, her thrashing around pierced my heart, but I had no time to dissect why I even cared.

She was the prize.

She was the enemy.

She's a game changer.

"Sully," I called out, gently shaking her shoulders to wake her. When she continued to cry out, I shook her harder. "Sully, wake up, damn it," I whispered harshly.

Her eyes popped open and looked directly at me, but she didn't see me. She saw whoever was in her dreams. "No . . . no . . . no," she whimpered, cowering toward the edge of the bed. Then suddenly, gone was the fear. Instead, a rage I knew all too well consumed her, her body lurching forward and connecting with mine. She raked her nails down my neck and, when I didn't back up quick enough, she clenched her hand into a fist and punched me, hitting me directly on the chin.

"Sully!" I roared, the sting of her nails settling over me in the oddest comfort. "What the hell!" Roughly pushing her back down on the mattress, I straddled her waist and held her flailing hands above her head, pinning her so she couldn't attack me again.

"Get off me!" she yelled, the vacant look on her face telling me she still wasn't present. Not mentally, at least.

Tightening my hold on her wrists, I dared to lean close so she could hear me. Restraining the anger in my voice, I tried to calm her down. "I'm not gonna hurt you." She continued to fight me. "What the hell? Why are you acting like this?"

Her legs bucked underneath me, trying her best to throw me off. But her efforts were completely wasted. She was no match for me and we both knew it. Well, she didn't know it, lost to whoever was tormenting her in her nightmare.

"You did nothing," she sobbed. "You just stood there while that bastard took me . . . and raped me." She took a few quick breaths. "I know you hate me, but why didn't you try to help? I'm supposed to belong to you"—she hiccupped—"but you let another man take me in the next room." Tears streamed down her flushed cheeks, and I didn't know what to do. She was obviously lashing out, but I had no idea if what she was saying was the truth or just a nightmare.

Not knowing what else to do to soothe her, I leaned closer still until my warm breath danced near her earlobe. "Sully, I'm not gonna hurt you. That man isn't here now. He can't hurt you. I'll protect you." My soothing words calmed her, her tears slowing while her breathing evened out.

Her warm body beneath me threw me into another world, one where I imagined us together, her looking at me adoringly, hungry for my touch each and every time her eyes fell on me.

What the hell is wrong with you, Marek?

She started to whisper something but I couldn't hear her, and it was driving me nuts. Was she revealing yet another piece of her story?

"What's that?" I questioned, careful to keep my tone calm so I wouldn't incite another episode.

"I tried to love you, but you hated me as soon as you claimed me." Her arms fell lax under my hold. "You hurt me so much. Every time you could, even when I didn't do anything to deserve it." Quick, terrified pants racked her body, tears still cascading down her cheeks as she said her final peace.

"I hate you, Vex."

As soon as that vile piece of shit's name fell from her lips, she drifted back to sleep. Hopefully, she would find the peace she craved, deep in the recesses of her damaged mind.

"TIME TO GET UP, SULLY," I called out, walking toward the bed and pulling the curtains open to allow the sun to shine through the room. "You slept half the day away." Still consumed with thoughts of the previous night, I refused to allow myself to go there while in her presence.

Groaning, she stretched her limbs and turned her attention to me. A shyness crept over her face, something I found oddly adorable.

I didn't think I'd ever used that word before, especially not when referring to a woman.

Pulling her shirt down so her skin was completely covered, she swung her legs over the edge of the bed and waited a few precious seconds before rising to her feet. She kept her head down as she moved past me and stumbled toward the bathroom. I waited impatiently while she finished her business.

When she finally emerged, I pointed toward the clothes I'd left for her. "One of the guys' wives brought those for you." She eyed the jeans and tank top, worry drifting off her in waves. Sighing loudly, I asked, "What's the matter?"

Her eyes found mine, and I swore she was about to break down right in front of me. "I don't think they'll fit," she mumbled.

"They'll be fine. Put 'em on." With that, I sauntered back toward the door. "And hurry up 'cause you're gonna help some of the women with the food." I left before she started spouting off questions which would only serve to irritate me.

I'd fallen under some kind of spell last night, sympathy drifting toward her because of her nightmare. But I had to snap out of that shit, had to remember she was the enemy, no matter how beautiful and enticing I may find her. She was brought here for one reason and one reason only—to become a permanent member of the Knights Corruption, essentially securing our advantage in the ongoing war with the Savage Reapers.

I hope she's up for what I have planned.

FIFTEEN

Sully

I'D SPENT FIVE LONG MINUTES just staring at the clothing he'd left on the chair for me. I knew what my hesitation was, but there was no way out of it. It'd been drilled into my damaged mind that I was worthless, so it was pointless to try and tempt other men with my body. At least that's what Vex had always told me, punishing me if I ever tried to wear 'sexy' clothes—or, in other words, clothes that were sized to my shape.

A light knock on the door yanked me from my recollections, the handle turning before I even made a move.

"Sully?" a soft female voice called out. There was something soothing about her tone, and I instantly relaxed. Adelaide peeked her head into the room, her long blonde hair falling over her shoulders in long waves. "Are you okay, hon?" she asked, stepping closer. "Do you need help with anything?"

Was it all a setup? The clothes, her coming to check on me? Were they waiting for me to make a mistake so they could finally punish me like I knew they were itching to do?

"I . . . I don't have any clothes . . . that hide me," I confessed, waving my hand back and forth over my form.

Adelaide's brow furrowed, glancing back and forth between my apprehensive face and the clothes on the chair. Reaching forward, she snatched them up and walked them over to me. "Here. These will fit just fine." She smiled but eyed me cautiously, clearly baffled as to what the problem was. "Do you not like them?"

"No. I mean yes, I like them, but they'll reveal too much," I all but whispered. "I'll be punished."

"Oh, honey. No, you won't. No one here is going to hurt you." She reached for my hand and gave a gentle squeeze. "Trust me." And for some reason, I did. "Now, hurry up and get ready. We need more help preparing food for the party." She smiled quickly, turned around and left me standing there, a million questions poised for her.

Looking at myself one more time, I deemed I was surely going to be punished, no matter how hard she tried to convince me otherwise. The jeans were dark and fit like a glove. The tag said they were skinny jeans, whatever that meant. I was very self-conscious about the red tank top. While the only exposed flesh was my neck and arms, I was wearing it sans bra, since I hadn't been wearing one when I was taken. My breasts weren't ginormous, but they were certainly too big to wear the shirt without being noticed.

Blowing out a nervous breath, I walked from the bedroom and made my way toward the common area. As soon as I was within view, I heard a few whistles, and at first I had no idea they were directed at me. That was until I found the man who'd taken me. I believed some of the men had called him Marek. He was in mid-conversation when I appeared, whatever he'd been talking about coming to an abrupt halt as soon as his eyes found mine.

I couldn't hear what he said, but I saw the angry look on his face, saw him mouth a few choice words. He was fast approaching, causing all of my muscles to lock up tight, fear coursing through me like a tidal wave. I prepared for his backlash, closing my eyes the closer he came, but it did nothing to stop my lip from trembling.

My body sensed when he was near because the hairs on the back of my neck stood up, goose bumps breaking out all over my skin as his presence overwhelmed me. When I finally opened my eyes, I saw he was staring at me, anger still prevalent in his stance but he was also . . . *intrigued?*

"Damn, Sully. What the hell?" he asked, but I had a feeling he really didn't want me to respond. His eyes lowered, skating his gaze over my practically exposed chest before focusing his attention back on my face. "You look beautiful," he offered, the rasp in his voice causing my body to shudder.

Did he really just say that? What the hell is going on?

I couldn't respond. Instead, a fierce flush washed over my skin.

"Nothing to be embarrassed about," he teased, grabbing my hand and pulling me through the crowd, past people I hadn't initially noticed. But as their faces came into view, I recognized a few of the men from the night before, and Adelaide of course. The rest of them, however, were complete strangers.

The majority of the men were drinking, some of them well on their way to becoming quite drunk, and as far as I knew it was still early in the day. There were plenty of women gathered as well, milling about the wide open space, laughing and carrying on as if it were the happiest day of their lives.

I wonder what it would be like to feel that free. I was jealous of my enemies, and I hated myself even more because of it.

Children ran through the throngs of people, laughing and screaming as they chased after each other. A few of them even knocked into me in their wild abandonment. I would have smiled but I was too focused on where Marek was leading me, the warmth of his hand on mine enough of a distraction as it was.

He directed us toward the bar, tapping on the counter to get the older man's attention—Trigger, I believe he'd called him. "Gimme two shots, Trig," he said, turning his head to look back at me. I met his focus briefly before lowering my head and breaking the connection. "Here," he commanded. "Drink this. You're gonna need it." He threw his drink back before I could deny his offering. Noticing I hadn't moved, he placed the shot glass in my hand and tipped it toward my mouth. "Drink it," he urged, his tone dripping in seriousness.

I placed the tip of the glass to my lips, counted to three then chugged it. I immediately started coughing, the amber liquid burning the back of my throat. Shit! I could feel the alcohol warming my chest the longer I stood there.

"Good, huh?" Trigger asked, strands of his graying hair falling from his ponytail as a wide smile spread across his face.

Again, I was at a loss for words, more so because I had no idea what to do. I shouldn't be engaging with the likes of the KC, let alone pretend as if I'd been with them for years. They didn't treat me badly, all things considered, but I was still waiting for the other shoe to drop.

"Come on," Marek urged, pulling me further into the room. People parted down the middle, flanking us on both sides. Curious eyes watched my every move. I heard them whispering as I passed. "Reapers' daughter" was the one comment I caught over and over. Feeling lightheaded all of a sudden, I reached for Marek's arm, the commotion of the room becoming too much for me to handle. All I wanted was to return to his bedroom and lock myself away from everyone. Especially him. He was making me think and feel things I shouldn't, and that wasn't sitting well with me.

"You okay?" he asked, turning around to catch me as I staggered forward. "You hungry? 'Cause we can get you somethin' to eat."

Tugging me forward a few short feet, he pushed open a door leading into their kitchen. Stepping inside, I noticed there were even more people back there, most of them women. They were laughing and telling stories, amusingly berating one of the men for stealing a piece of food from one of the trays.

Adelaide stepped around an older, dark-haired woman, and walked toward the both of us with a big smile on her face. "Sully," she greeted. "Don't you look pretty." Pulling me in for a momentary hug, she retreated, but not before eyeing Marek with a curious look. I was too concerned with not fainting to read too much into her glance, though.

"I was gonna have her help you all, but now it doesn't seem right," he pondered, tapping his finger on his lips and bringing all of my attention there. *Damn him.*

"Marek," Adelaide warned. "You better not. Not today of all days," she said, retying her apron behind her back, looking like she was ready to get back to it.

Curiosity got the better of me and before I could stop myself, I blurted out, "Why? What's so special about today?"

Marek turned around fully to face me, taking my other hand so both were encased in his strong, warm hold. Leaning in close, his breath licked across my suddenly dry lips. His eyes held mine, and I swore my heart skipped a damn beat. "Today is special, Sully," he promised. "Because today is the day you officially become a permanent member of the Knights Corruption." My heart skidded to a halt altogether. I tried to pull out of his grip, but it only tightened.

Arching a dangerous brow, he proclaimed, "Today's our wedding day."

SIXTEEN

Sully

TRIGGER MUST HAVE SURELY PUT something in the shot Marek practically forced me to drink. Something so powerful it caused me to hallucinate. A thin bead of sweat broke out on my hairline, my face and body suddenly feeling very overheated. The voices around me dimmed to an almost inaudible level, the women's movements distorted and blurred.

There was no way in hell he had just said what I thought he did.

Today is our wedding day?

Trying again to pry my hands from his, he tightened his hold once again and pulled me to him. His clenched jaw and steeled posture loomed over me with a power I'd never known before.

"Don't fight it, Sully. There's no way out of this, and it's useless to try and think of one." His scent tortured me, flicking on a light inside me I never even knew existed. Yet, he enraged me to the point that all I wanted to do was shield myself by lashing out at him. Hurt him like he was hurting me. Surely, he knew such a union was the same as signing my death warrant. He'd grown up in the same type of life I had, so he knew exactly what he was doing.

He was using me as a ploy to get back at the Savage Reapers for God knows what. But whatever it was, it must have been life-altering to be pulling a stunt like this.

Struggling with every ounce of energy I possessed, I wore myself out. And quickly. When he started walking forward, I dragged my feet and made it harder on him to move me. Or so I thought. My resistance was a mere annoyance, seeing as how he towered over me, no match for his sheer strength and will.

"No," I cried, but Marek trudged toward someone standing in the far corner of the room. The man's hands were clasped in front of him, an amused look on his face while he watched us approach.

"Yes," my captor sneered, whipping his head in my direction to show me how pissed he was. "Let's go." He jerked me forward so harshly I swear he almost ripped my arm out of its goddamn socket. There were fleeting moments when he showed me an ounce of compassion, and I'd been a fool to think he was being nice during those times. But he wasn't. He was playing me, just like everyone else in my life did, although he was the nicest man I'd ever encountered, which evidently wasn't saying much.

"I can't marry you!" I yelled, kicking my feet at the backs of his legs, struggling to dislodge his hold on me. But he was fierce, dragging me forward until we came to stand in front of the man with long gray hair, another club member who was obviously going to officiate the *marriage*.

Jerking his chin in the man's direction, he bit out, "Git on with it." Besides the fact that the bride-to-be was trying desperately to flee, everyone had a big fat smile plastered on their stupid faces. They all acted like what was transpiring was the most normal thing in the world. Then again, for all I knew, it was. Maybe they made a habit out of kidnapping other clubs' women and marrying them the following day.

What the hell did I know, anyway?

The man before us started speaking, but stopped briefly when someone entered the room, yelling and carrying on enough to disrupt the forced arrangement.

"Shit! Did I miss it?" the VP to the club yelled. He walked toward us, his brows arched and waiting for an answer.

"Sit down, Stone," Marek demanded. "We're just gettin' to it." I saw Marek wink at his second in command, and it pissed me off even more than I already was.

The one thing I was thankful for, however, was that Stone's unannounced interruption was the one thing which drew Marek's attention away for a split second. Enough time to loosen his hold on me. As soon as I felt the tension leave his hands, I yanked mine free, turned around and fled.

But I didn't get very far. Blinded by paranoia and fury, I wasn't paying attention to where I was going and instead of running toward safety, I ran right into the strong hold of the one man who'd just allowed me the opportunity to hightail it out of there.

Smacking right into his large frame, Stone's hands came up to hold me captive. "Whoa, sweetheart," he mocked. "Where do you think you're going? Don't you know what an honor it is to marry the president of the Knights Corruption? Fuck! I don't even think he's ever had a girlfriend before now," he said, looking directly over my head and straight at Marek, I was sure. Turning me around, he shoved me toward his friend, laughing at my back while I tried to find another way free.

But it was useless.

There were too many people present, blocking any plan of escape I could think of. I guessed there really was no way out of my new predicament. With drooped shoulders, I shuffled the few feet necessary to stand next to Marek, keeping my head down and away from his piercing eyes.

"Well, can we continue now?" the man presiding over our entanglement asked.

"Yes," Marek said curtly.

I tuned out most of what he said, until he came to the part about taking each other as husband and wife. Marek's simple answer when asked was, "Yeah." Not 'I do,' or even a standard 'Yes,' but what did I expect? That the man was in love with me? He was simply doing it to seal my fate, as well as his club's standing in the war between our two worlds. He didn't give a shit about me or what I wanted or needed; I was just a piece of property to him, just like I'd been to Vex and my father.

When it was my turn to respond, I picked my head up, looked Marek square in the eyes and said very loudly, "Hell no." I was hoping it was the loophole to get out of it, my blatant refusal a definite deal-breaker. Didn't he need my verbal consent?

Maybe outside of club life it would be enough, but not here.

"Don't need your agreement, darlin'," Marek condescended. "This is happening either way."

And it did.

He forcefully slid a ring onto my finger, and the president of our biggest enemy had just made me his wife.

SEVENTEEN

Marek

THE PLAN TO MARRY PSYCH Brooks's daughter had come to me *after* we'd taken her from them. Hell, I hadn't even planned on taking her when we breached their shitty compound, nothing but a few drunken assholes guarding the gate.

At first, we thought it was too easy, thinking it was a setup and they were gonna surprise us as soon as we stepped foot onto their grounds. But there were no Reapers hiding around the corner ready to attack.

It'd been quite easy, until we knocked down the door to their clubhouse. It was there we came face to face with the soulless men of our enemy. The ones who weren't drunk or high were extremely skilled in defending their territory, but in the end they were simply no match for me and my men.

Stone had shouted something about snatching Psych's daughter for the ultimate payback, and I'd readily agreed. When we came to the barricaded room, we knew instinctually she was hiding in there. Over the years, we heard stories of the woman who was kept hidden from the world, her beauty unmatched to any around her. Her hype was built up so much I half-expected to see a used, life-beaten-down woman when we broke down the door.

But as soon as I laid eyes on her, crouching in the corner of the dark room, I knew instantly the rumors were true. Not being able to fully take her all in until we arrived home was torture, but I'd seen enough to sate my curiosity. She was beyond beautiful, even with all the scars and marks, the sunken look of despair in her eyes. Hell, even with the mixture of awe and disgust she threw my way whenever she saw me.

We stood in silence in front of everyone after I shoved the ring on her finger, her defiance coming full force even though it was guarded. She still wasn't completely sure how I was gonna react to her outbursts. She'd flinch when I moved too quickly, surely from years of abuse at the hands of that psychopath, Vex. Shit, probably from her father as well.

Psych Brooks was the Devil incarnate.

Her fingers twirled the band, and I knew she was gonna try to remove it. I stopped her before she made the attempt. "Don't even think of taking that off." I gestured toward her ring. "You won't like my reaction if you do." I had to threaten her to do as I commanded, otherwise, things were gonna get out of hand.

Her hand dropped to her side, and she glared at me swiftly before lowering her head. I didn't blame her for not wanting to look at me, but there was no going back now.

We were married.

And no one was gonna change it, not even her.

A silence fell over the gathering, everyone curious as to what was gonna happen next. No one had found out about the impromptu wedding until a few hours prior. There were no questions asked. They all knew better.

My word was law, and it was never to be challenged.

"Kiss her!" someone shouted a few feet away. Sully's head jerked up and looked at me with wide eyes. *Fuck! She's beautiful.* I had no idea when I gave her those clothes how alluring she would look. Her tits were flawless, and don't get me started on that round, perfect ass of hers. It was a real shame our marriage was one of necessity, otherwise, I would have dragged her back to my room and fucked her long and hard. And each time she looked at me like she was now, I'd slam her against the wall, wrap her legs around my waist and sink inside her so fast she'd give up the breath in her lungs just to keep the connection.

I hadn't intended on kissing her, but I didn't let her in on the secret. I was bored, so I decided to play with her instead. Gripping her arms, I tugged her closer, licking my lips and throwing her a quick wink.

"Whatcha think, wife? Wanna give our guests a show?" She tried to pull away, her head shaking back and forth like she was having a goddamn convulsion. Her repulsion bothered me, even though I tried not to show it. My fingers dug into her soft skin and she winced. I hadn't meant to be so rough, but I couldn't help it. Yes, my face didn't show my annoyance, but my body had taken another directive. My jaw ticked and the mocking look on my face quickly disappeared, replaced by something I had yet to identify.

Every woman I knew would jump at the chance to have my mouth on them. But not her. No, she was freaking out, and it was all due to the thought of being kissed by me. My plan to tease her had just turned into the ultimate goal of planting one on her right there, in front of everyone to see.

I leaned in.

She pulled back.

I leaned in again, pulling her close so she had nowhere to go. She whimpered in my hold, but I didn't care; she was my wife now, and I would do whatever I wanted to her—within reason, of course.

I hadn't kissed a woman in years, but my need to make her comply drove me forward.

Slowly inching my hands upward, I rested them on the sides of her face, her body going still when she realized I was gonna go in for the kill. The closer our mouths came together, the more her body relaxed, which was quite odd. I would have thought it'd be the opposite.

Her demeanor softened slightly and I actually thought I might enjoy tasting her. I was but a breath away from her delectable lips when I heard someone close by whisper, "He's really gonna kiss her."

Women talked. I knew they did. Although club whores weren't allowed into the clubhouse unless a ruckus was going on, I knew their chatter spread to all the women of the club, old ladies alike. Everyone knew it was a steadfast rule of mine not to kiss. Again, no psychological reason why, I just didn't, not with the wannabes I fucked.

"You ready?" I whispered, my lips hovering over hers. I asked the question more to myself than to her, but it didn't really matter. As I was about to close the deal, Hawke barreled right into me, spilling his drink on the floor at my feet. He was half-drunk and already acting a fool.

Breaking the built-up tension between Sully and me, I backed up immediately and scowled at Hawke, his eyes glazed over as he mumbled an apology. He staggered away, bumping into people while he walked toward the bar to get another drink.

"Trigger!" I shouted. "Cut him off." I glared at Hawke, the priceless look of shock on his face almost worth me not tasting Sully's plump lips.

"Come on, Prez," he pleaded, slumping forward because he realized he wasn't gonna get another drop of liquor. Edana sidled up next to him, whispering something in his ear which made him smile. Taking her hand, he led her back toward his room, disappearing from sight before I could impose another punishment.

Movement in my periphery caused me to turn my head back toward Sully. She was shifting from one foot to the other, her obvious nervousness becoming quite annoying. She wouldn't say anything, however, choosing instead to just fidget next to me.

"What's the problem, Sully?" I growled, my patience evaporating into the air around me. The drawn look on her face almost made me correct my tone, but the fierce look in her eyes when she leered at me pushed that idiotic thought to the side.

"I want to go back to the room now." When I didn't answer, she added, "Please." I realized how hard it was for her to utter the word, but it did nothing to stop me from continuing to be difficult.

Strictly because I wanted to.

Nothing more.

"No. Everyone here came to celebrate our wedding. And, as my wife, you will entertain them." Flicking my wrist toward the crowd, I demanded, "Go mingle."

"Mingle?" She sounded shocked. "I'm not your wife. I'm your pris-oner," she angrily huffed.

"You *are* my wife. Everyone here is a witness. Now, go and play nice," I said, patting her ass and ushering her forward into the throngs of peo-ple gathered together. Catching Ryder's attention, I motioned for him to come over. Once he'd gotten close enough, I inspected whether or not he'd been drinking. Beer was fine, but if he'd been drinking hard liquor? Forget about it. I had enough shit to worry about; I didn't need to wrangle up a few of the brothers to watch his volatile ass.

"What's up?" he asked.

"You been drinking?"

"It's a celebration, isn't it?" He smirked. "Of course I'm drinking."

"What?"

"What . . . What?"

Frustration shot out of me. "What the hell are you drinking? Beer?"

"Yup. In fact, I'm about to get me another. Want one?" he asked, already preparing to retreat to the bar.

Grabbing hold of his arm to stop him, I laid a very important task on him. "Listen, Stone and I have to talk. I need you to watch Sully while we're in Chambers."

Knowing damn well he wouldn't refuse, he rolled his eyes before agreeing. "Where did she get off to?" he huffed, peering around the room to try and locate her.

"She's talking to Adelaide. Near the kitchen." As I walked past, I warned him, "Don't lose sight of her, Ryder. If anything happens to her, or if she takes off, I'm holding you personally responsible."

"I know, I know," he grumbled before snatching a beer from the bar and heading toward the two women engaged in conversation. Well, Adelaide was doing most of the talking, while Sully was propped against the wall with her arms folded tight across her chest.

I'm married.

I'm fucking married, and I have no idea who my wife is.

What the hell was I thinking taking it this far?

EIGHTEEN

Sully

I WAS BEYOND EXHAUSTED. THE day's surprise debacle took its toll on me, and I wanted nothing more than to crawl into bed and drift off into the darkness. But I would be sleeping in *his* bed. Again. *I don't have any other choice unless I want to sleep on the floor, which I just might consider depending on what happens when he retires for the evening.*

Did he expect me to have sex with him now that we were married?

Refusing to give in to my paranoia, I focused on what Adelaide was saying. We'd been talking the majority of the day. Thankfully, she'd saved me from having to talk to everyone else. Well, besides Ryder. The man had become my shadow and butted into our conversation every now and again, especially when Adelaide complained about men. I had a feeling she was talking about one man in particular, but she kept her comments generalized so as not to give anything away.

I was still very much a stranger to these people. Actually, 'prisoner' was more accurate. It was as if I were living in a parallel universe. I'd been taken from my home, forced to wed my enemy, yet no one hurt me. Besides the guy who tried to kiss me in Marek's room, no one had bothered with me. Adelaide was very sweet. Hell, Ryder was even pleasant, growing more so the more alcohol he consumed. Stone was a little rough around the edges, but even he was complacent around me. Granted, I'd only been there for a day, but a lot had transpired during that time.

A lifetime seemingly passed me by in a mere twenty-four hours.

Finding a brief reprieve in our conversation, I grabbed hold of the opportunity and ran with it. "Adelaide, do you think it would be all right if I went back to my room?" My hopeful eyes pinned hers while she contemplated my question.

"Don't you mean Marek's room?" Ryder chuckled. He was drunk and feeling no pain. At least he was a pleasant drunk, laughing and fully engaged, regaling us with stories of pranks he'd been a part of over the years. Leaning against the wall with one arm, his eyes took me in but he wasn't lecherous about it. It almost seemed like he was assessing the newest member to his club, friendliness and caution meshed together to form a whole new emotion.

"Well . . . Yes. I suppose so," I retorted, not sure if I should react defensively, coyly or shyly. I was completely out of my element but the two of them made me relax a little, the fear I'd held on to since I was abducted taking a step into the shadows. Not too far, though, because I would need to be on guard once out of their company.

I had a feeling I wasn't out of the woods. Not by the longest stretch of the imagination. And the majority of my fear had to do with the man who ruled the KC. The man who'd succeeded in snatching me right from under my father's nose. The man who'd forced me to join into a union with not only him but his club. The man who made me feel things I'd never experienced before, no matter how briefly they rattled my emotions.

My husband.

Saying my goodbyes, I moved past them and headed toward the back of the building, toward the one room where I could escape. The spray of the hot water beckoned me, and I found I couldn't move fast enough. Ryder was right on my heels, never once leaving me by myself. I guessed he was instructed to do so, and there was no way he was going to disobey Marek.

"I think I can handle it from here, Ryder." I shooed at him, but he kept on following.

"Not a chance. I'm not letting you out of my sight until Prez comes back."

Back? Where did he go?

Noticing the puzzled look, he answered before I uttered a single word. "He's in Chambers talkin' to Stone about club business. Should be around shortly," he explained, taking a long swig of his near empty beer.

I had no idea what he was talking about. Chambers? Was that the same thing my father and Vex referred to as Church?

Deciding not to inquire about the whereabouts of my new husband, I walked into the bedroom, turning around to close the door behind me. But Ryder stepped inside before I could shut him out.

"What are you doing?" I asked, backing up a few steps. He closed the door and sauntered forward.

"I told ya already. I'm not goin' anywhere." He swayed slightly on his feet. "I was told to babysit you, and that's what I'm doin'." Plopping on the small couch against the wall, he leaned back and rested his hands behind his head, looking at me as if he were seeing me for the very first time.

From what I gathered about Ryder, he was friendly, but he also seemed a bit reserved, if that made any sense. His dark eyes hid secrets—I knew because I saw those same shielded pupils when I looked in the mirror. Short, dark hair adorned his head, a faint shadow of hair prickling his jawline. He wore dark jeans and a white long-sleeved shirt under his cut.

He was attractive . . . for the enemy.

Actually, quite a few of the KC men were handsome, their ruggedness hiding any vulnerability they may have possessed. Their looks were disarming, their ability to blend into society a most definite attribute. I hadn't witnessed it thus far, but I was sure they had charm in spades whenever they felt it necessary.

His eyes glided over my body, a hint of appreciation for what I was wearing most definitely shining bright. "You're quite beautiful," he offered, finishing off his drink and tossing it aside.

The tone he used was sedate, but the longer I remained in his presence the more I feared he was going to *show* me how beautiful he thought me to be. Would he do such a thing? Did the men share each other's property? Their wives? If it was anything like my club, they didn't, although that was the only rule I knew of. A man didn't go after another man's old lady, not unless he wanted to die.

But the rules for the Knights Corruption might be different. I had no idea, and I didn't want to find out. It was enough that I was forced to become one of them; I didn't want to be passed around between brothers. Fending off his advances before he even offered them, I took a few steps back.

"I'm going to take a shower, then go to bed." I kept eye contact with him the entire time, preparing myself for any unexpected moves. "Are you going to be out here when I get done in there?" I asked, flicking my thumb toward the bathroom.

"Yup."

"Oh. . . ." In my uneasiness, I was instantly reminded that the only thing I had to wear to bed was the T-shirt and shorts Marek had given me the night before. At least the clothing was large enough to hide the majority of my body. With the simple realization, I turned my back on Ryder and hid away inside the comforts of the simple bathroom.

Once finished, I reentered the bedroom only to find a passed-out Ryder slumped back on the couch, his head lolled to the side. He was snoring, not too loud to be extremely distracting but loud enough to assure me he wasn't a threat.

Crawling into bed, I pulled the covers under my chin and prayed I would remain safe until morning. Being as defenseless as I was, I knew I would be no match for the likes of any of these men, and although my mind drifted off into imaginary scenarios, logically I had no cause for concern.

Not yet, at least.

NINETEEN

Marek

WE'D BEEN AT IT FOR three hours, and I was fucking exhausted. I tried to keep my brain focused on the task at hand, but I found it easily wandered to my new wife. It was useless. I couldn't get her out of my head and Stone knew I was distracted, repeating himself a few times throughout the meeting.

Hidden away in Chambers, we'd told everyone we weren't to be disturbed. We had some heavy shit to figure out for the club before it was too late. We had to make a move and do it quick, or our retaliation on the Savage Reapers would have been in vain. Well . . . sort of. I still had Psych's daughter.

And I'd be damned if I was ever giving her back.

No, she was mine now. No matter the consequences.

"Fuck, Marek!" Stone shouted, pounding his fist on the table. "Pay attention, man." Normally, if any other member had talked to me like that, they would have been facedown on the ground right then, but my VP was different. We'd grown up together. We were more like brothers than anything, and he knew he could get away with it. At least he only did it in private, making sure not to test my patience in front of everyone else. Otherwise, I would be forced to react in some way.

"What?" I feigned nonchalance. "I am. We have to set up a meeting with Los Zappas cartel—Rafael Carrillo, to be more specific. I'll call in my one favor, essentially cutting the Reapers off from the cartel's supply and crushing the entire club into the ground. They'll have nothing. Their supply will be dried up, and with it their money and livelihood as well. Yeah, they may be able to secure product from somewhere else, but it'll be shit, and their customers will eventually move on." I leaned in close to Stone. "Paying enough attention for you?"

"Fuck you." He smiled. "I'll set it up. Just be ready to ride in the next few days." He leaned back in his chair, his fingers tapping against the wood of the table while he studied me.

"The hell you lookin' at?" I grumbled, hating that he was inspecting me rather suspiciously.

"You're thinkin' about her, aren't you?" He rested his mouth on the lip of his bottle, waiting for my answer before allowing the cold liquid to fill his mouth.

I knew damn well who he was referring to, so I didn't bother to ask. Instead, I chose to lie. "No."

"Uh-huh," he replied unconvinced. Swallowing his beer, he gave me a cocky grin before rising from his seat. "You gonna fuck her tonight? She *is* your wife now, you know."

"I'm fully aware she's my wife. I was there, wasn't I?" Frustration laced my voice and there was no point in hiding it. I had no idea what the evening held once I entered my room and found her lying on my bed. My body certainly wanted to sink inside her but property, captive, wife or not, I wasn't going to force myself on her. I wasn't built that way, and neither were any of my men. I made sure of it. What was the point of forcing yourself on a woman when there was plenty of pussy available around the clock? All it took was a simple phone call, and we all knew it.

"Well, if you *do* fuck her, you have to tell me how she was. She's quite stunning. And that body of hers . . . Fuck, Marek." His words slurred the more he spoke, and it was only then that I realized he'd had quite a bit to drink. The more he talked the more he pissed me off, though, so I decided to return the favor. Finish him off so I wouldn't have to listen to him anymore.

"Actually, Adelaide is still here, so I think I'll see if she wants to have some fun. Trigger left for the night, so I won't have to deal with his cock-blockin' ass." Licking my lips I added, "Think she'll wanna fuck the prez?"

Stone's reaction was priceless . . . and expected. Kicking his chair behind him, it skidded across the floor, knocking against the wall before it finally stopped. His hands clenched into tight fists while his chest rose and fell with heavy rage. Sweat beaded on his brow and his face turned red. "Don't you dare go near her," he seethed, his warning telling me more than I wanted to be privy to. He'd given everything away with his response.

"Why do you care if I take her to bed, Stone?" I taunted, knowing damn well he was losing his mind.

"Because . . ."—he faltered—"you're married now . . . and off-limits." *Lame excuse.*

"What does me being married have to do with it? I'll continue to get pussy wherever I want. Sully won't put a stop to that." My pokes had begun for pure amusement, but the further we took it, the more I realized I was telling him how things would be for me going forward. Just because I had taken a wife, her of all people, didn't mean my life would change.

He took a step toward me, fury dancing in his eyes as he silently challenged me. "Just don't go near her, Marek," he gritted.

"Tell me why," I taunted. "If you don't give me a good reason, she's as good as riding my cock." My smirk challenged him right back.

All sense of protectiveness poured forth, the need to claim what was his too strong to back away from. "Because, motherfucker . . . She's mine!" he roared. "Don't you dare touch her or I'll kill you."

Wow!

Stone had never threatened me before. He was drunk, but that did nothing to excuse his outburst, and it was my job to remind him of that.

Snatching his throat, I slammed him against the wall, my grip tightening to show him how serious I was. "Don't you ever threaten me again, *friend*," I bit out. "I was just fucking with you. I know there's something going on with you two but didn't know how serious it was until right now." Pulling back my arm, I released him and he stumbled forward. Stone was trained to kill, more so than me, but it was my surprise attack which worked to my advantage.

His blond hair fell over his eyes and with a heavy hand, he pushed it back, flicking his stare in my direction before punching the wall, ripping the door open and staggering from the room. Most likely to search for Adelaide.

I didn't know the extent of their relationship, but I'd never seen Stone react like he just had toward any other woman before. Jealousy and possessiveness barreled from him like an unstoppable train.

I didn't blame him, though. Adelaide was quite beautiful, but no one was supposed to mess with a member of one of the men's family. It was an unwritten—or, in Trigger's case, a steadfast, written, spoken and threatened-about—rule. Never mind that she wasn't a part of our lifestyle. Sure, her uncle was, and she helped out from time to time when we needed her, but she wasn't involved with the way we lived.

She was a good girl. She was educated and had a good career. Her life was promising, but getting involved with Stone threatened all that. Everyone in the club knew the dangers of our business. The dangers of our mere existence.

It was one of the main reasons I chose never to get involved with anyone, even someone 'in the life.' Sure, I was married now, but I didn't love Sully. Hell, I didn't even know her, and I planned to keep it that way. For everyone's sake.

Letting Stone cool off a bit, I stayed in Chambers a few extra minutes before making my way back out to the common room. There were still plenty of people milling around, laughing and having a good ol' time. All of the kids had been sent home, as well as most of the old ladies, but some remained behind, helping clean up from the day's impromptu festivities.

Seeing Breck lounging on one of the sofas, a woman perched on each leg, I motioned him over. I didn't care that I interrupted his fun, and he knew it. Pushing the women off him, he streamlined straight for me, his pants already half-undone.

Adjusting himself, he jerked his chin and asked, "What's up, Prez?"

"You seen Ryder?" *That fucker better still be watching over Sully or so help me. . . .*

"Nope, not for some time. Last time I saw him, he was following your wife to your bedroom." He grinned when he said 'your wife,' not caring to hide his amusement about the whole thing.

I grunted because I simply had no words left for him. Turning around, I snatched a fresh beer from the bar, taking a moment before walking back to my room. The longer the seconds ticked by, the more heat shot through my body at the thought of the two of them alone, and in my room of all places. She looked at me like she hated me and to a point, I didn't blame her, but I saw the exchange she engaged in with Ryder when they'd all been talking earlier. She smiled at what he said, even going so far as to accept a drink from him, her fingers lingering on his hand a little too long for my liking. Maybe I was imagining the touching, but I sure as shit didn't imagine the way she'd talked to him. Her long black hair flowing freely around her, covering her tits until she flicked it behind her shoulders.

Why the hell didn't I take a closer look at the damn shirt before I gave it to her, or remembered she didn't even have a bra to wear? I saw the way the men leered after her, and who could blame them? She was gorgeous, but nonetheless I didn't like it.

"Then I'm leaving, you ass!" I heard someone shout from the back hallway. Adelaide stormed forward, looking like she was ready to kill someone. And, of course, Stone wasn't too far behind. They'd been arguing, but it ceased as soon as they were around everyone else.

She searched the room until her eyes fell on me. Breaching the tiny distance between us, she came to stand before me, her eyes glassy and looking like she was ready to let loose at any minute.

Steeling her resolve, she straightened and abruptly said good-bye. She'd always been polite, more so than was necessary, but it was how she was raised.

"I want to thank you for inviting me today, Marek." She touched my arm in a genuine gesture of appreciation, nothing more, but you wouldn't know it from the way Stone watched us. Then I'd remembered what I'd teased him about earlier and it made me smile, but Adelaide probably thought I was returning her politeness. "I really like Sully," she confessed. "If there is anything you need me to do for her—you know, to help her get adjusted to being with you crazy men—just let me know. Okay?"

Finding the perfect opportunity, I blurted out, "You could buy her a bra."

She looked stunned, apparently taken back from such an odd request.

"Okay. . . ." She stalled, not quite knowing why I'd said what I did.

"Well, she came with us so abruptly that she didn't have much with her. Actually, I would really appreciate it if you could pick up a few more things for her as well. Stop by tomorrow after work and I'll give you a list."

"Sounds like a plan." She smiled then leaned in to give me a quick hug, her innocent affection nothing new. When I glanced across the room, Stone looked like he was ready to go nuclear.

Adelaide walked right past him on her way out, completely ignoring him, even when he called after her time and time again. Disappearing from the clubhouse, I continued to hear him call her name, their voices swallowed up by the growing distance.

He was shit at hiding his feelings for Adelaide when she was around. Sooner or later, Trigger would find out for sure, and shit was gonna hit the fan in a big way.

He'd already threatened to put a bullet in my VP, and that was only when he'd *suspected* something was going on with Stone and Adelaide.

What would he do when he found out it was for real?

TWENTY

Sully

THE SOFT CLICK OF THE door woke me. At first, I was confused as to where I was, but I quickly heard the soft snore coming from the couch across the room. Ryder was still there with me. Turned out he wasn't much of a watch dog after all.

The noise from the club filtered into the room, along with the light from the hallway. A tall, broad form filled the doorway, frightening me enough to cower. Until I realized who it was.

Marek.

"Christ!" he growled, advancing toward a sleeping Ryder. "Good use you were, ya bastard." He nudged Ryder's leg with his foot but nothing happened, so he tried shoving at his arm. Still nothing. "What the fuck, Ryder," he grumbled, before smacking the man in the head. "Get. Up," Marek ordered.

That time, Ryder shifted awake, assuming a fighting stance because he had no idea where he was. I couldn't help it; I laughed, the sound so soft I didn't think either of them heard me. But Marek did, because he turned toward me.

The room was still bathed in darkness so I couldn't make out his expression, but I knew he was staring intently at me. My body just sensed it. Ryder rose off the couch and clumsily walked from the room, mumbling under his breath the entire time.

After closing the door, Marek flicked on a side light and instantly blinded me. I brought my hands up to my face to shield my eyes, allowing myself time to adjust to the brightness.

"I'm gonna take a shower," he announced, throwing his cut on the chair before grabbing the hem of his shirt and pulling it over his head.

Spreading my fingers over my eyes so I could see what he was doing, I inhaled a quick breath at the sight of his naked chest. Intricate designs wrapped around both arms, drifting over his shoulders and disappearing behind his back. A skull was inked in the center of his chest, flames shooting out from both sides, a large sword slicing through the middle of it. I'd seen that same design on the back of his cut, leading me to believe it was his club's emblem. Images of dark and light traced down his sides, the designs foreign to me because I was too far away to inspect them in any detail.

He was a walking work of art, and I'd never seen anything so beautiful before in my entire life. I'd seen men with tattoos before, but none that exuded such raw beauty like his.

His sun-kissed skin brought the artwork to life. Every twitch of his hard muscles moved the images, entrancing me the longer I watched him flit around the room. Before he said another word, he disappeared into the bathroom. I heard the running water and counted the minutes before he was standing before me again.

Is he going to sleep in here? Will he take the couch, or does he expect to sleep in the bed with me? My worry kept me occupied while the clock mocked me, time moving slow but fast all at the same time.

The bathroom door flung open and the steam from the shower billowed into the room, looking more like smog it was so heavy.

Marek sauntered into the room, and what I saw made me gasp out loud.

He was completely naked.

He busied himself running a towel through his wet hair, the fabric covering part of his face so he couldn't see me gawking at him. Maybe he forgot for a brief moment he wasn't alone. Or maybe he didn't. Maybe it was his way of telling me I didn't affect him, or his actions. He would continue to live his life just like he had, not caring at all that I was now involved.

Tossing the towel on the floor, an action which immediately irritated me since I liked the bedroom to be a place which was nice and neat, he stalked toward the bed.

Oh, my God! Is he going to get into bed with me naked? Does he expect to have sex? Is he going to force me?

I hadn't even realized my expression had changed, but it apparently had because he stopped walking and stood still. I couldn't help myself;

even in my frightened state, I blatantly admired his body. He was extremely fit, not an ounce of fat anywhere on him. His hardened muscles enticed me to touch, but I didn't dare. Running my eyes slowly down the length of him, I eventually came to the most intimate part of his body. Defined lower abdominal muscles in the form of a V encouraged my gaze to sink lower. It was then I saw all of him. His cock was flaccid . . . and very large. But the more my gaze tickled him, the more his body reacted, his thickness hardening right in front of me.

I licked my lips, both fear and desire dueling inside. When my eyes finally made their way back up to his face, my skin prickled at the way he watched me. A curl of his lip told me he liked the way I appreciated him.

My face flushed a bright red, my embarrassment at being caught ogling him beyond devastating.

"Are you done now, or do you wanna keep lookin'?"

I had no idea what to do or even say, so the only thing that came out of my mouth was a barely audible apology. "I'm sorry."

It was as if he was waiting to banter with me, his response so quick his deep voice actually startled me. "Don't apologize, sweetheart. Look all you want. I'm your husband now, so it's your right." Pulling the covers back, he added, "Just like it's now my right to look at you."

Scrambling toward the head of the bed, I gripped the covers tighter and watched him carefully while he situated himself on top of the mattress. He never made a move to grab me or to cover his nakedness, too busy basking in my uncertainty.

The longest minute passed between us before I finally broke the silence. "Are . . . Are you going to . . . ?" My ragged breaths stopped my voice altogether.

"Am I going to what?" he asked, raking his teeth over his bottom lip.

I swallowed hard, the sound piercing my ears and accelerating my panic. "Are you going to rape me?"

"Well, considering you're now my wife, isn't it your duty to give it up?" He chuckled, the sound both enticing and disarming.

"I-I . . . can't . . ." I stuttered.

Hopping off the bed, he grabbed a hunter-green T-shirt and some dark, loose-fitted jeans from his chest of drawers and quickly put them on. Pulling on his cut, he moved to the side of the bed I was lying on and leaned down so close his lips hovered above mine.

"Don't worry your pretty little head, Sully. When we finally do have sex, *you'll* be the one begging *me* for it." I balked at his audacity and the sheer madness of his statement. But I never said anything, too stunned to come back with a retort.

Walking across the room, he turned the handle on the door and pulled it open. Turning his head to the side, he gave me his parting words. "I'm gonna lock the door from the outside, but just in case you get creative in trying to escape, I always have a few men on duty walking around the compound." His voice became deeper all of a sudden. "Keeping out those we want *out* . . . and holding on to those we want *in*."

The last thing I saw was his back as he disappeared from the room, indeed locking me in with my own thoughts and fears.

TWENTY-ONE

Sully

HOT BREATH KISSED MY CHEEK.

Fingers trailed over my collarbone, latching around my neck before I could even open my eyes.

"You little cunt! Did you not think I'd find you?" the enraged voice seethed. "And here you are, in *his* bed." His grip tightened, cutting off any chance I had of taking breath into my starved lungs. "Did you let him fuck you?" Stars flashed behind my lids. "I bet you liked it too, you whore."

He straddled the bed, his thighs pinning my arms in place so I couldn't move. Opening my eyes, I saw Vex sitting on top of me, a large, sharp blade held in his free hand. His green eyes were darker than I'd ever seen them before, his square jaw ticking in an uncontrollable rage.

I tried to shake my head, but his grip was so tight I couldn't move. I tried to struggle underneath him, but he was no match for me.

I was completely immobilized.

I couldn't breathe to scream.

I couldn't move to escape.

I was going to die without the chance to defend myself—not that it would do much good anyway.

Just when I was falling into blackness from lack of air, he took his hand away from my throat, and sat back as if he was fascinated with what he'd done. I instantly started sucking in air and coughing uncontrollably. But I didn't scream. I couldn't. My throat burned from the pressure, bile threatening to spew forth if I wasn't able to control my response soon.

While I struggled with the scene unfolding in front of me, I dared to look up at his face, and what I saw had me closing my lids a few times just to refocus.

After the third time of opening and closing my eyes, I came to rest on the image of the man above me.

It was Marek, but he spoke with Vex's voice, his tone not as deep as my captor's.

"You're going to die now, Sully," he threatened, the blade glinting off the single beam of moonlight filtering in the room.

I tried again to scream but my vocal cords were paralyzed, my own body betraying me in my desperate time of need.

It was mere seconds before the sharp tip of the blade ripped open my skin, tearing through my chest and puncturing my heart. He pushed all of his weight down on the weapon, practically slicing me in two.

When he retracted the knife, he licked my blood from the metal, smiling insanely while he prepared to stab me again.

It was then that I found my voice and I let loose like never before, wailing loud enough for anyone to hear me. I prayed someone would come and save me, but the only person who showed up was my mother. She was standing in the corner of the room, bathed in white light, her arms outstretched to welcome me. I knew in that moment that I would be taking my final breaths, my pierced heart taking its final beats. My mother had been dead for years, and she was there to usher me home.

But I wasn't ready.

I fought it. I screamed and cried and begged for him to let me go.

His arms came down on my shoulders and he started shaking me. "Sully," he called out, his voice hard and unyielding. "Sully," he said once more. "Wake up," I heard, warm breath tickling my lips while my brain tried to understand what was going on.

Flickering my eyes open, I saw Marek's face suspended above me, a look of fear and anger pouring off him in waves. Letting out one final cry, my cheek burned from the connection of his hand on my face.

He'd slapped me.

I was hysterical and wouldn't calm down, but the shock of his hit balanced me in some small way. Focusing my gaze on the man above me, realization calmed me enough to stop my screaming.

I glanced around the room to see if there was anyone else there with us, and there was. Ryder and Stone stood by the door, watching on in confusion.

"Sully . . . It was just a dream," Marek soothed. "You're okay now." Backing off me so I could breathe, I pulled myself up into a sitting position, tucking my knees under my chin and rocking back and forth.

"It was so real," I confessed. "You . . . It was . . . It was you trying to kill me," I said, looking at him, not even knowing what to feel right then. "But it was Vex's voice. Your face but his voice," I mumbled, trying to make sense of the dream in the dawn of realization. "My mother . . . She was there too. I was dying, and she was there for me." I babbled on and on about my nightmare for the next two minutes, continuing to rock back and forth until I'd finally calmed.

Marek had no idea what to say or do. He was at a loss, so he just sat on the edge of the bed. Ryder and Stone had disappeared, leaving the two of us alone to hash things out.

"I thought you left," I said, my heartbeat finally falling back into a normal rhythm.

"I was just down the hall, staying in someone else's room."

For a split second, I thought he was referring to a woman, and a pang of jealousy ripped through me. My heart momentarily picked up its pace and my fingernails dug into the skin of my palm. Having no justification for the strange emotion, I shoved it aside and focused on his face instead. The way he looked at me was strange. He seemed annoyed that I'd woken him with my screams, yet compassion danced in his eyes. Or was that pity? I was still too unfocused to tell.

He rose from the bed. "Are you all right now?" he asked, shoving his fingers through his tousled dark hair.

"Yeah. I think I just need to wash up." Looking at the clock on the bedside table, it was only then I noticed it was six in the morning. Had it not been for the bright red numbers blaring at me, I would have no idea what time of day, or night, it was.

"Good, 'cause when you're done, we're gonna eat then I'll take you to my house. You can't stay here anymore. No females camp here," was his simple explanation. He took off before I could ask him any questions. What was going to come out of my mouth, I had no idea, but he didn't even give me time to think of something. He was always disappearing after he'd had his say.

Another minute and I was calm enough to scramble to my feet and walk toward the bathroom. A thick layer of sweat glistened on my skin and my clothes stuck to me, making me uncomfortable. I knew the hot water would work miracles for not only my body but my mind as well. I longed for the calming arms of peace to rain down over me, washing away my nightmare and helping to soothe the predicament of my new life.

My fingers trailed over my skin, the smell of Marek's body wash invading my senses and making me think only of him. An ache kicked up inside me, starting in my chest and traveling lower until my clit pulsed with a need I'd never experienced before.

I was aroused.

I'd explored my own body in the past, but I'd never felt such an explosive desire toward a man before.

A stranger.

An enemy.

Marek's handsome face appeared in front of my closed eyes. I'd seen him angry. I'd seen him cocky and condescending. And I'd also seen him concerned. Worried about me.

No one had ever been worried about my well-being before.

Not my father.

Not Vex.

It was astounding that the man who'd kidnapped me from my home would be the one to show me an ounce of compassion.

I palmed between my legs, trying my best to sate the need growing inside me. As I rubbed my finger over my clit, I remembered his promise from just hours before.

When we finally do have sex, you'll *be the one begging* me *for it.*

He sounded so sure of himself, his arrogance surprisingly quite a turn-on, although I would never voice such a thought. I never knew if he was testing me, or waiting for me to mess up so he could punish me. Usually, I kept quiet, minus the few outbursts which seemed out of my control at the time.

I pictured the way he licked his lips then bit down on the lower one while he'd stood naked in front of me. My own slickness allowed my finger to glide back and forth with ease, shooting bolts of desire through me, so pleasurable I never wanted to stop.

I recalled his large cock growing to life right before my eyes, how he seemed to love my appreciation for his glorious body, the way he remained still while I committed him to memory.

My back arched and I spread my legs, rubbing faster and faster until my body seized up. Balancing myself with one arm against the shower tile, I finished myself off, my orgasm tearing through me while I pictured the one man I shouldn't have.

My husband.

"Sully, Prez says to hurry the hell up." I was so involved with 'taking care of business' that I never even heard anyone enter the bathroom. *Oh, my God! Did he see me? Did he hear me? Was I even making any noises?* I was so wrapped up in my own head I had no idea if any sounds had escaped my lips.

I thought it was Ryder who'd scared the shit outta me, but I couldn't be sure. Shutting off the water, I slowly slid the shower door open to make sure no one was standing in the bathroom waiting for me.

The coast was clear.

I was almost done drying myself off when the door opened. I screamed out in surprise and quickly wrapped the towel around me. Marek stood in the doorway staring at me, his eyes narrowing the more he took me in.

"Why is your face all flushed?" He moved closer, the tension between us increasing with every step. "Were you playing with yourself in the shower?" His lips turned up in a sexy grin. "Were you thinkin' bout me?"

There was no way he could know, was there? Did he have cameras in there? My paranoia gave me away and he picked up on it. But I still tried to deny it.

"No," I whispered.

"No, you weren't playing with your pussy, or no, you weren't thinking about me?" He chuckled and moved even closer, the air suddenly extremely stifling.

"Uh . . . n-no . . . t-to both," I stammered. All I wanted was for him to leave, but then I knew once he did I'd miss his presence. He was nothing like I'd expected, and I found I craved his attention when he wasn't near me. But again, I would never let on to that because it was insane.

I should hate him.

I should cringe every time he came near me.

I should fear him.

But I didn't.

"Just say the word, Sully, and you could be riding my cock." He winked then walked from the room.

Again with the disappearing after he said shit like that.

TWENTY-TWO

Marek

WE PULLED UP OUTSIDE MY place, a half hour away from the club, when a thought occurred to me. Pulling out my phone once Sully had slid off the back of my bike and was stretching her legs from the ride, I dialed Jagger's number.

"Hey, I need you at my place in an hour. And bring shit with you for a few days." Ending the call, I swung my leg over the bike and planted my feet on the ground, rifling through my bag to find the keys.

"Let's go," I said, ushering my wife toward the front door. *My wife. Shit!* That was still such a fucked-up concept. It'd only been a couple days, but I didn't think I would ever get used to saying it.

Out loud or in my head.

Since I'd pushed the limits already by allowing Sully to stay at the clubhouse for more than a few hours, I knew it was best to set her up in my own personal residence. My house wasn't anything fancy, but it wasn't a rundown shack either. It was a nice log cabin I had built six years back, the wraparound porch one of my favorite features. What I loved most about it was that it sat on ten acres of solidarity, not a soul in sight, which was exactly how I liked it. I hated neighbors, and the less people I had to deal with the better in my book. Outsiders were judgmental, and could be quite dangerous if their curiosity got the better of them.

Pushing open the door, I guided her inside and set my bag down on the floor, walking toward the kitchen to grab a drink. I was thirsty, and the hot summer day only exacerbated my need for cool liquid. Twisting off the cap to a bottled water, I took a few long gulps then walked back over and handed it to Sully.

She frowned and looked as if I'd just handed her a dead kitten.

"What?"

"That's gross," she huffed, pushing the bottle away from her.

"What the hell are you talking about? It's just water."

"I don't want to drink after you. Why can't I have my own?" she asked before taking a step back. My expression probably put her on alert, although I didn't know why. I wasn't upset, just merely confused.

"What's the problem?" Shoving the bottle back in front of her, I said, "Just take it."

"Germs, bodily fluids . . . Should I go on?" Shocked she was speaking so freely, I crossed my arms over my chest and settled in. *This should be fun.* I stared at her so intently that she blushed and stopped talking.

"No, please continue."

"That's all," she whispered before lowering her head.

"Sully. Look at me." She raised her head and looked me directly in the eyes, her tongue sneaking out and wetting her bottom lip. My dick pulsed and pushed against the seam of my pants. Her dark eyes roved over me, leaving my face briefly before lowering them to take in the rest of my body. I didn't even think she realized she was checking me out, lost in a faraway place in that beautiful head of hers.

I cleared my throat, loving the unexpected back and forth between us, visually as well as spoken.

I was going to put our little conversation to bed. "As far as bodily fluids go, my spit will be the least of your worries." Reaching out, I grabbed hold of her wrist and pulled her to me. She didn't fight, which was a good sign, but I wasn't sure if she was shocked or if she was easing up around me. Lowering my mouth to her ear, I promised, "When I fuck that sweet pussy of yours, I'm gonna leave behind a reminder that I was inside you. So much of a reminder that it's gonna be dripping down those sexy-ass thighs of yours."

I heard her gasp and it made me smile. I had no idea why, but I loved toying with her. Maybe it was the innocent way she looked at me, trying her best to hide her desire for me. Maybe it was the pleasure of having someone who was all mine. Maybe I was trying too hard to show her she was safe in my club. Well, physically safe. Not so much sexually or emotionally.

Whatever the reason, I enjoyed getting a rise out of her.

She placed her tiny hands on my chest and tried to push me away, but I held steady. When I wouldn't budge, she lowered her arms to her sides, waiting for what would happen next.

Countless seconds passed, the only sounds our ragged breaths circling around us. I inhaled her scent before releasing her, smelling her hair like some kind of animal. But it was what she made me feel like when I was this close to her. Like some kind of beast that needed to claim her, mark her with my own scent so the others would know who she belonged to.

In reality, everyone knew she was mine, so they knew to stay clear of her—that was unless they wanted to deal with the repercussions of crossing me.

"Where's the bathroom?" she asked, avoiding any and all eye contact.

"Why? Do you need to play with yourself again?" I smirked when I saw the blush creep up her neck and explode across her cheeks. I'd been teasing her back at the club about it, but now I knew I'd hit the nail on the head. Her blatant reaction told me so.

"I have to go to the bathroom. I've had to go since we left." She shuffled back and forth, and I realized she was telling the truth, or she was a pretty good liar. Pointing down the hallway, I directed her to the second door on the left.

After checking my messages and staring into the refrigerator for a whole minute, trying to decide what we could eat, a loud knock on the door pulled my attention. As I moved toward the front of the house, Sully came walking down the hallway and headed toward the couch, sitting down and clicking the TV on, but only after asking my permission

It was gonna take her some time to get adjusted to living with me, but I was patient. Well . . . sometimes.

Cocking the gun at my side, I slowly opened the door. Jagger was standing on the front porch, looking put-out for having to rush right over, but so be it. He was a prospect, which meant he was the lowest man on the totem pole. Therefore, he would do whatever was asked of him, whether it was doing a pick-up run, cleaning up someone else's puke or babysitting my new wife.

As soon as he saw me, he straightened and gave me a smile. "What's up, Prez?" he asked, picking up his bag and waiting for me to invite him inside.

Jagger was all of twenty-two and was the fighter in our group. He'd competed in a few low-level MMA-type fights over the past year and won every one of them. He had a mean roundhouse kick as well as a lethal right hook. He and Stone had even gone toe-to-toe a few times, my VP showing him a few moves to make him even more of a contender. With his fighting skills, I trusted him to keep Sully safe while I wasn't around.

"I need you to watch over her while I'm not here," I told him, opening the door wider so he could enter. "I have business to attend to and will be gone for a few days."

It was all the explanation he needed. He placed his bag in the corner and stood near me, waiting for instructions. He didn't want to assume he was allowed to make himself at home, but seeing as how he was going to be staying there for a bit, I instructed him to relax.

And he did.

I didn't need two people with sticks up their asses keeping each other company.

Looking at my watch, I cursed out loud after realizing I needed to take care of a few things at the club before Stone and I headed out in the morning.

I walked around the couch until I stood in front of Sully, making sure she was paying attention to me before I spoke. "I have to leave now, but Jagger is gonna watch over you and make sure you don't try anything." She looked a little dejected. "Plus, he'll keep you safe. Just don't do anything stupid and you'll be fine."

Turning toward the prospect, I jerked my head toward the front door. "Walk me out," I demanded. As soon as we were outside, I laid down my strict list of rules. "You are not to leave her side. Where she goes, you go. If she goes to the bathroom, you follow and wait outside. If she's in the living room, then so are you. You two are not to leave this house, and the only other person allowed inside, besides you two, is Adelaide. She'll be dropping off some clothes for her." Handing him a key, I continued, "I had a new lock installed on my bedroom door yesterday, one you can lock from the outside. That's where she's to sleep. Make sure to lock her in, that way you can get some rest and not have to worry about whether she's gonna escape in the middle of the night." I grabbed him by the neck and pulled him close. "Sully is now my wife, Jagger, which means she's off-limits. Keep your distance . . . but keep her close. You feel me?" I growled.

Quickly nodding, he knew exactly what I was saying without having to spell it out. Jagger was a good-looking kid and he pulled down a lot of tail. I just didn't want him thinkin' he could fuck with my property.

TWENTY-THREE

Sully

"SO, HOW HAVE YOU BEEN getting along these past couple days?" Adelaide asked, cupping the hot mug of coffee between her hands, and blowing on the liquid before bringing it to her lips. She'd stopped by to bring me some underwear and clothes, the sizes she picked out being a perfect guess.

Eyeing me ever so precariously, I knew damn well she wasn't quite sure how I'd come to not only suddenly be part of the KC, but also ended up living in Marek's home.

I'd considered telling her the whole story about how he'd kidnapped me and taken me hostage, putting a guard on me every second of the day so there was no chance of escape, but for some reason I chose to keep my circumstances to myself. What good would it do? She was the niece to one of the club members. Even if she believed me, what was she going to do? Rat out her family for a complete stranger?

Plus, there was the tiny fact that I had nowhere to go. I was stuck and I knew it. Trying to escape and go back to the Savage Reapers was a suicide mission. They would never take me back. In fact, they were probably ordered to shoot me on sight.

No, thank you.

I refused to suffer one more second of their hatred toward me, and I sure as shit wasn't going to allow myself to die at their hands. Not when I had a choice.

Sort of.

It was funny. I used to pray for death . . . before I was stolen from my life. I lived only to exist. My days were gloomy, the only bright spot when I'd gotten my hands on a secondhand romance novel one of the club whores had left behind. I think some of them felt bad for me, witnessing how downtrodden I was, watching the way Vex and my father treated me. To be pitied by women who lived to have sex with as many men as possible was utterly pathetic. But it was my life, and I envied those women. Not for being used as nothing more than a place for any man to stick his dick, but for the freedom their lives held.

I was trapped.

Suffocating and slowly dying on the inside.

Then I was rescued.

I didn't see it that way when I was forced to leave with the enemy, but since I'd been in their company, I'd come to realize just how messed up my life had been. Not once since I'd been in the Knights' compound had a single person raised a hand to hurt me. Not once did someone say something to degrade me. Not once did they look upon me with disgust or go to the total opposite end of the spectrum and ignore me.

Ignore my cries.

Ignore my broken bones and bruises.

Ignore my broken spirit.

A breath of promise had been pumped back inside me, the vigor for life slowly coming back to me.

Eyeing Adelaide cautiously, I contemplated how to answer. I wanted to be truthful with her. She'd been the closest thing to a friend I'd ever had and I didn't want to jeopardize our budding relationship, but the fact remained that she was still a stranger, and I didn't know if I could trust her.

Tempting fate, I took a deep breath and opened my mouth. "I'm okay." *So much for a big revelation or confession.* Her kind eyes prompted me to keep speaking, which I decided was necessary, needing the banter to make me feel like a human being again. "It's weird being here, tucked away in this house with someone watching over me every second." I left out the part about Jagger locking me in Marek's bedroom when I slept.

"Well, that's how these men are. From what I gather, at least. They're very protective of their women, their families," she offered, smiling before she took another sip of her coffee. Shuffling closer, she propped her chin up with her hand, tipping her lips in curiosity. "So . . . How long have you known Marek, and how the hell did you tame that man?" She wiggled her brows in jest, but I knew she really wanted answers.

"I've only known him for a few days." I stopped talking and bit my lip in nervousness. I dropped my head from her glance but could feel her eyes burning through me. Thankfully, she didn't push, reading my body language and realizing I didn't wish to expand on my statement. For the next hour, we conversed about clothes and movies, two topics I had limited knowledge about, so I was happy she took the lead and did most of the talking.

Looking down at her watch, she made a face of disapproval and rose from her chair, carrying her cup to the sink. "Sorry, Sully, but I have to leave. My shift at the hospital starts soon, and I don't want to be late. I can stop by tomorrow. Do you want me to bring you anything else?"

"No, thank you. You've done enough."

"Okay, well, give me your number and I'll call you before coming over, just in case you change your mind." She pulled her phone from her purse and swiped the screen, lifting her head and waiting on me to give her my information.

"I don't have a phone," I mumbled.

Jagger walked into the kitchen just then, glancing back and forth between the two of us before heading to the fridge and snagging a beer. Twisting off the top, he took a long pull, the muscles of his throat working feverishly to allow the liquid to pass. He drank half the bottle before pulling it away from his lips.

"What?" he asked, frowning at the look Adelaide gave him.

"Is there a phone here? A landline?"

"Not that I know of. Why?"

"Because I'll be coming back again tomorrow, and I wanted to call Sully to see if she needs anything." Adelaide advanced on Jagger and he backed up a step, not quite sure what her agenda was.

She was forceful when she wanted to be, and I liked her even more because of it. "Give me your cell," she demanded.

"What for?" He truly looked baffled.

"Just give it to me, Jagger. Or I'll tell my uncle you tried to kiss me," she threatened, a slight tilt to her lips as she watched his eyes widen in fright.

"Fuck that!" he shouted. Pulling his phone from his back pocket, he handed it to her, shaking his head in disbelief. "You better not tell Trigger that shit. I mean it. Or my death will be on your hands."

"Oh, calm down, pretty boy. I'm just messing with you." She punched in her information then handed him the phone back, but only after she used it to call hers first. "There, now we have each other's numbers. I'll call you tomorrow before I come over," she said, looking at me while she spoke. "You let me know if you need anything, Sully. Anything at all."

Rising from the table, I breached the short distance between us and stood in front of her, not quite sure what to do next. I was still very awkward with interactions of any sort, slowly fumbling through with each passing day.

"Thank you so much for the clothes . . . and for visiting with me." Tears welled in my eyes before I could lock them up. I hated appearing weak in front of people, but unlike every other time during my life when tears meant sadness and pain, my emotion was a happy one. No one had ever taken the time to ask me how I was doing, let alone bring me a gift and purposely engage me in conversation.

"Don't think twice about it," she said, suddenly pulling me in for a quick hug. Awkwardly hugging her back, her sudden gesture of affection throwing me off, I stepped back and watched her move to the door.

Turning her head, she playfully threatened Jagger. "If you don't answer your phone when I call, you'll be gettin' a visit from Trigger." She laughed as she walked out the door.

Jagger didn't find it too amusing.

TWENTY-FOUR

Marek

TWO DAYS.

I'd left her alone for two days with one of our prospects. Jagger. A young, good-lookin' guy. A guy who looked like the boy next door, but with an edge. A guy who was probably jerking himself off every night just to the image of her.

Fuck! What the hell was I thinkin'? I should have made someone else watch over her, but my resources were limited. The other men in the club had better, more important things to take care of and couldn't be saddled with such a shit assignment. Though, they might have thought differently simply because they would have gotten the opportunity to be around her. All alone.

No matter who I picked to babysit her until I returned, I would have driven myself half-insane, so I guessed it didn't really matter.

Hitting the button on my phone, I frustratingly waited for the call to connect. *At least this will ease my mind for the time being.* "Hello," Jagger answered on the third ring, seemingly out of breath for someone who had the easiest job in the world.

"What are you doing?" My tone was downright accusatory and he knew it as soon as he heard the growl in my voice.

"Nothing, Prez. Just helping Adelaide with some of the groceries."

"What? Why is Adelaide there with food? I left the fridge and cupboards fully stocked." Running my hands through my hair, I flicked a glare at Stone, but he was too busy focusing on the name I'd mentioned. He was practically hovering over me and trying to listen to my conversation simply because he heard *his* woman's name.

Well, according to his prior reactions, Adelaide was his woman. But if Trigger ever found out something was going on between them, I'd be looking for a new VP.

"She's stopped by a few times, telling me she wanted to cook dinner for Sully, seeing as how she's still adjusting to being here." I heard the hesitation in his voice and instant jealousy raged deep within me, tearing through my throat and out of my mouth before I could filter my words.

"If I find out you touched one hair on her goddamn head, prospect, I'm going to tear you apart," I seethed. "Do you understand me?" Stone backed away as soon as he saw the volatile look on my face. *Smart move.*

"No! I haven't done any-anything," he stammered, but his quivering voice told another story. I wasn't sure what, but something was going on, and I couldn't wait until I was back home and could keep an eye on her myself.

Why I cared at all was probably the thing which was pissing me off the most. Never before had any woman affected me, twisting me up inside until I questioned my motives, thoughts and . . . dare I say feelings?

"Let me talk to her," I commanded. "Now!"

Hearing my heartbeat in my ears, I tried to take a few calming breaths, realizing I was more than likely blowing things out of proportion. But my mind only sped up my body's reactions, a small bead of sweat breaking out on my forehead, my heart beating even quicker inside my chest.

"H-hello." A soft voice sounded over the phone, and I'd instantly regretted leaving her. *What the hell is happening to me?*

Instead of asking her how she was, making sure she was settling in okay, what did I do? I freaked out on her and accused her of something I was almost positive was false.

"What the hell are you doing with Jagger? You lettin' him fuck you, Sully? Don't think for one second that I won't punish you both for going behind my motherfucking back! You think just because I'm not there I wouldn't find out? Huh?" I couldn't help myself. I kept going and going and when I was finally done, silence screamed in my ear. Tiny pants of breath came through the phone and made me even more infuriated.

Did her silence mean I'd hit the nail on the head? Or had I just scared the shit out of her for no reason?

Before I could start in on her again, another voice ripped through the line, her voice hysterical while her words crashed together as she spoke.

"What did you just say to her?" she cried, unease nestling deep in the timbre of her voice.

"None of your business, Adelaide. Now, put Sully back on the phone," I grated. I looked to my right and Stone was already headed my way, no doubt hearing her name fall from my lips again. I glared at him and he stopped mid-stride. "Don't even think about it," I threw at him.

"Then don't talk to her like that," he said, bracing himself for a fight.

"Mind your own goddamn business, Stone. I mean it," I warned, moving the phone away from my mouth while I continued to speak to him. "Just because I'm talking to your woman doesn't mean it has anything to do with you. Back off. I mean it."

Placing my cell back into position, I was ready to start arguing again when Adelaide's shrill voice barreled into my ear. "I'm not his woman, Marek! Don't start that rumor or else something bad is going to happen!"

"What's she sayin'?" Stone asked, forgetting himself and walking toward me again.

She was screaming in my ear while Stone continued to talk to me, the back-and-forth noise sending me off the deep end.

To hell with this!

"Give me your phone," I told my VP. When he looked confused, I hurried him along. "Give. Me. Your. Phone." Tossing me his cell, I made an even exchange, giving him the one with Adelaide ranting and raving on the other end.

Scrolling through his contact list, I found Adelaide's number, hitting the Call button while I shook my head. There was no reason whatsoever for him to have her number saved in his phone, unless they were fuckin' around. Her digits were another nail in his coffin if her uncle found out. But that was between the three of them. I had other shit I had to deal with.

I heard a brief silence from the other room, Stone's voice quieting long enough for Adelaide to answer her own phone.

"Hello?" she greeted, confusion evident in her voice.

"Where is she?" I grated. I swore if I were there in the room with her, I would have seen the disapproval written all over her face.

Another bout of silence passed before I heard her shift her phone to Sully.

"Hello?" I knew she had the cell pressed to her ear because I could hear her breathing. I hadn't meant to go off on her like that before, but my building jealousy had gotten the better of me, hurling unfounded accusations at her before I could reason with myself enough to calm down.

"I'm not doing anything wrong," she squeaked. I heard the tears in her voice and they instantly tore me apart. "I promise. He barely talks to me."

I believed her. It took me exploding, her fear, and then the sincerity in her voice to calm me down and realize I'd overreacted. I would never admit it, though. Not to anyone.

I never apologized.

Ever.

Choosing to ignore her words, I switched topics. "I'll be longer than I thought." I sighed, running my fingers over my face in utter frustration. "I'll call you in a couple more days and let you know." Stone came strolling out from the other room, a pissed-off look on his face, one I knew wasn't because of me, but instead because of the person he'd been talking to. Or the one who'd been shouting at him, to be more accurate.

"Okay. Did . . . Did you want to talk to Jagger again?"

"Yes." *Short and sweet.*

"I swear, Prez, I'm not doing nuthin' to her. I'm just watchin' over her like you told me to do," he started in, his words coming so fast I almost didn't understand him.

"Calm down. We'll be gone longer than anticipated. I'll call you soon when I know exactly when. And Jagger?" I waited for his acknowledgment. "Don't make me regret my decision to leave you at the house."

"You won't. I promise."

I hung up before he could say anything else.

I'd been staring down at the phone and hadn't realized Stone was scowling at me from across the room. I was too consumed with all the new feelings eating at me to pay much attention to anything else. Wrapped up in not only the image of Sully, but in what I'd just done to her, I clenched my jaw and fisted my hands. I was pissed at myself, but what was done was done.

"What was all that, Marek? Have you gone off the deep end?" My VP's voice startled me, and when I finally picked my head up to look at him, I saw true concern etched deep into every line of his face.

I was normally a pretty laid-back guy. Well . . . as laid-back as I could be running an entire MC. I wasn't known for blowing up at the drop of a hat, or acting irrational for no reason at all.

I wasn't sure if it was that Sully distracted me from my main goal, which was to remain unattached and focused solely on the club. Or if it was because she now belonged to me and another man being in her company, all alone, wasn't sitting right with me. Even if they weren't doing anything wrong.

But I'd been the one to make the decision to have Jagger watch over her in my absence, so I had to deal with the consequences. Like it or not.

"Nothin'," I promised. "All good." I thought if I tried to smile right then, he might've had me committed. Instead, I switched the subject. "Where we at with meeting with Carrillo?"

"I was gonna tell you before you went nuclear a few minutes ago, but he isn't coming. Some shit about too much heat and not being able to get away. Instead, he's sending his second in command, Yanez. He said we could finish things through him."

Rico Yanez was a lecherous man. No morals of any kind. Almost worse than the Reapers. Almost. I didn't like or trust him, but if he was who we had to deal with then so be it. The quicker we came to an agreement, the better.

Shrugging, Stone leaned against the wall opposite me. Tired and weary, the past couple days' events looked to have taken a toll on my dear friend. He had something going on with Adelaide, no matter how much he denied it. Then there was the added dangerous element of finalizing our end with Los Zappas cartel. Even though the head honcho, Rafael Carrillo, had given me his word he would release the KC from smuggling in and selling their product, there was always the chance he would go back on it, although I seriously doubted it.

He was a man who hated to be indebted to another, and it was exactly what he was to me. Not that I held it over him or anything, but I would use the opportunity to get what I needed, exploit the fact that I'd saved his life.

On a drug run last year, we were intercepted by a rival cartel. Gunfire thickened the air around us and we scarcely made it out alive. Rafael's men ran for cover, and he found himself without shelter. The look in his eyes reflected that he was prepared to die, although there was still hope underneath he would make it home to his wife and three kids that night.

I knew if I wanted to extract my club entirely from their grips, I had to make my move.

Save him from meeting his maker too soon.

If I knew anything about the man who hovered between life and death, it was his undying need to not owe anyone anything, and my saving his life would prompt him to do something in return.

My gesture paid off. In exchange for saving him, he agreed to let my club walk away, but only after they'd found another one to take our place.

He'd also agreed to cut all ties with the Savage Reapers, crippling them and cutting their legs out from beneath them.

But still, nothing was guaranteed until I heard the head of Los Zappas cartel tell me we were no longer in business with them.

"Well, when are we meetin' him then?"

"Tomorrow," he answered, walking toward the door and circling the handle with his fingers. "But tonight, we relax and have a good time. Right?" he shouted over his shoulder, pulling the door open and heading toward the common room.

We were staying at our Laredo charter. The guys there were most accommodating, pulling together a last-minute ruckus. Not that it was a problem by any means—any chance to overindulge in alcohol and pussy was certainly a most welcome event.

Later that evening, when I'd buried myself inside some woman whose name I never asked, I tried my best to push aside all thoughts of the woman waiting for me back home.

But it was useless.

With every thrust and moan, I imagined it was *her* I had pushed against the wall, my hand wrapped around *her* throat while I fucked *her* from behind. I envisioned it was *her* pussy clenching down on my cock as she rode out her orgasm.

Sully was the woman I pictured writhing in front of me, and it was the only thought in the past few days which helped soothe the rising inferno inside me.

TWENTY-FIVE

Sully

STILL TREMBLING FROM MAREK'S ACCUSATIONS, I excused myself from the room, quietly disappearing inside the bedroom I'd been staying in.

His bedroom.

Everywhere I looked, I was reminded of the man who'd forced me to marry him. His clothes hung in the closet, no order to the wardrobe whatsoever. His shoes littered the floor of the small space, strewn about as if he'd literally kicked them off his feet and left them wherever they fell. Crumpled receipts, along with a few watches and old Harley magazines covered the top of his dresser. Dirty laundry was piled up in the corner of his bathroom, even though an actual hamper stood right next to them. His beard trimmer, razors, and brushes littered the top of the small sink, and it was all I could do to take a deep breath and breathe through my anxiety.

Because of the way I preferred things, I began to tidy his room. All the clutter and mess didn't sit well with me. I tried to ignore it my first two nights, but since he'd told me he wouldn't be back anytime soon, there was no way I could continue to stay in a room so out of sorts.

A tidy room made me feel as if I had control over some aspect of my life. It gave me a sense of solace, no matter how false it may have been.

I didn't want to, but I couldn't help remembering our phone conversation, word for word. Every accusation he'd flung at me tore away a little bit more of my soul. I didn't trust the man, but he'd given me a sense of safety I'd never had before, only to rip it away with every word he spewed down the line. *What the hell are you doing with Jagger? You lettin' him fuck you, Sully? Don't think for one second that I won't punish you both for going behind my motherfucking back! You think just because I'm not there I wouldn't find out? Huh?*

I should have expected he was going to show his true colors sooner or later—apparently, it had been sooner. I was a fool to think he was any better than Vex or my father, but the way he'd looked at me, the way he'd tried to comfort me when I'd woken up screaming from my nightmares . . . It was all a façade.

Actually, he was worse than the men in my life because at least with them, I knew what I was in for. I knew exactly what they would do and say. But with Marek, I simply had no idea.

Finishing up the mess in the closet, I closed the door to the small space and headed toward the bathroom, but a soft rap on the bedroom door stopped me in my tracks.

"Sully," Adelaide called out. "Are you okay? Can I come in?"

I never answered, instead pulling the door open and giving her a faltering smile. I couldn't hide the hurt from my face or from my voice, even though I tried. The last thing I wanted to do was bring her into the mix of what was going on. I had no idea if she would be punished simply for interfering.

Crossing the room to sit on the edge of the bed, she leaned back on her hands and gazed at me, waiting to see if I would speak first. But I let her take the lead, as I did with most people.

"I'm so sorry for what he said to you, Sully." Her eyes pitied me, and I hated that she felt that way toward me. "Marek is usually pretty easygoing, all things considered. I'm not sure what's up his ass, but please don't take it personally," she pleaded.

"How do you know what he said to me?" I wasn't used to people interfering on my behalf or conversing with me about things which happened to me. My tone was more curt than I'd intended, but I didn't think she took any offense to it.

"I got the gist of it when I threatened Jagger."

"With your uncle again?" A small smile curved my mouth, mimicking her reaction.

"You know it. I can use that man as a threat any time I want to get my way." She laughed, pushing her hair behind her shoulder, continuing to hold my gaze until she knew I was okay.

"Don't pay him any mind. Seriously. Don't worry about it." Situating herself so she was sitting with her legs tucked underneath her, she continued to try and persuade me to talk. "What did he say when he called you on my phone?"

Playing with my hands in nervousness, I stood in front of her, not quite sure what I was allowed to reveal about my conversations with him, no matter how insignificant. I'd never had anyone to confide in before, and although it was an amazing feeling, it was also a bit frightening. I still wasn't quite sure who I could trust yet.

Patting the bed beside her, she widened her smile and put me at ease. Climbing next to her, I mirrored her and tucked my own legs under me, resting my hands on my thighs while I spoke. "He just told me he was going to be longer than expected and would call me in a couple days."

"Yeah, Stone told me that too."

Before I could filter myself, I blurted, "Are you and Stone together?"

Her eyes widened, her words suddenly caught in her throat. She appeared to be hiding something and wasn't sure if she should tell me the truth, probably not trusting me completely, much like I acted toward her.

But something inside her forced her to give me tidbits of information. "Can you keep a secret? And I mean from everyone, even Marek?" She looked pensive, but because I so wanted to know a private detail of someone else's life, I readily agreed. And meant every nod.

"Yes, I promise."

"We're not *together* together, but we've fooled around before. And, even though I really like him, we can't be together." Her expression turned, her sudden unhappiness pressing her lips into a frown while casting its veil over her eyes.

My intrigue forced me closer, all while continuing to give her the personal space she needed. "Why not?"

"It's complicated really." She hesitated for a brief moment before continuing. "I'm not part of your . . . their lifestyle, nor do I want to be. I love my uncle dearly, but I never wanted to grow up around what they do, how they ultimately handle themselves and their lives. And he didn't want that for me either. I'm more than happy to come by and help out when I can, like with Tripp, but other than that, I don't really want to be associated with the club. And Stone knows that." She looked dejected, as if she was reminded of a specific conversation she'd had with him.

"Would he ever leave the club? For you?" I knew I sounded like a twit, fantasizing and romanticizing her and Stone's complicated relationship, but I couldn't help myself. I'd read my share of romance novels and in those books, the main characters always found a way to work it out, their love conquering everything and all that happy stuff.

Looking at me as if I'd lost my mind, she shook her head and crushed my idiotic thoughts. "He grew up in this club, just like most of the men. He loves the KC, the men are his family. He'll never leave them for me, and I don't think I even want him to. He'd resent me if I made him make that choice." Throwing her head back so she was looking at the ceiling, she continued telling me her innermost secrets as she relaxed in my presence. "He keeps calling me, showing up at the hospital and begging me to be with him. Some days, I think I can be with him fully, give him what he wants . . . what *I* want, but then shit happens, like with Tripp, and I put that wall back up to protect myself. It kills me when I look at him, knowing he'll never truly be mine."

I was surprised when a lone tear streaked down her cheek, her thumb quickly brushing it away before her emotions became too much for her. She smiled lazily and straightened up on the bed. "Don't mind me, Sully. I think I'm getting my period." She laughed, the air of seriousness suddenly disappearing.

"Well, I think if you really want to be together, you'll find a way which will suit both of you. But from what I hear, your uncle won't be too pleased." I'd witnessed an encounter between Trigger and Stone, and even I was scared of the older man.

"Yeah, there's that too," she grimaced.

We finished our conversation and were about to move off the bed when Jagger came crashing into the room, stumbling over his feet and instantly putting us on alert. His dark golden hair stuck up in a few spots, his amber eyes wide in fright while he gave us time to collect ourselves.

"What the hell, Jagger? Where's the fire?" Adelaide threw at him.

"Funny you should ask," he rushed. "It's downstairs." If what had come out of his mouth hadn't been so serious, I would have laughed at the frenzied look on his face.

"Oh, shit!" she exclaimed. "My food." Scrambling off the bed, we all ran downstairs to assess the damage. Luckily, it was only smoke, but whatever Adelaide had been making was burnt to a crisp.

"Looks like pizza it is," Jagger announced, the two of them busting out into laughter while I stifled my amusement as best I could, a tiny sound escaping my lips to add to the surprise of the free-falling emotions.

TWENTY-SIX

Marek

"ARE YOU SURE THIS WILL be our last shipment," Stone asked, nervously shoving his messy hair off his face. The guy was pacing, mumbling to himself and making me tense just watching him.

"Yeah, Rafael gave me his word that after this next pickup, he's shifting his supply to the club in Vegas he's slowly been using, testing them for the past year to ensure they're the right fit." I was as nervous as my VP, but I played my concerns off as mere agitation, trying like hell to calm the air around us.

Stopping mid-stride, he hit me with yet another question. "Why do you really think he sent that asshole to meet with us then, instead of coming himself?"

"Not sure. I guess we'll find out soon enough." Rico Yanez called five minutes ago to let us know he would be arriving shortly. Normally, we didn't have meetings with anyone from Los Zappas cartel on club grounds, but there was too much heat on them nowadays to be seen out in public places meeting with the likes of two bikers. The three of us together would look way too suspicious. After making sure he wasn't being tailed, he'd arrive at the compound and disappear between the concealing metal gates.

Leaning forward with my arms resting on my thighs, a small bead of sweat gathered on my brow. The meeting Stone and I were about to have was of the utmost importance, our futures being decided in the next half hour.

Were we still gonna be in bed with the cartel, unwillingly going along with constantly risking not only prison, but death as well?

Or were we finally gonna be able to breathe the fresh air of legitimacy for the first time in over six decades? Having been on the wrong side of the law for at least that long.

We realized that, if we were indeed free after this last run, there would be initial blowback from our enemy. But once some time had passed and they were no longer strong enough to be a threat, we could start to really enjoy our lives.

Shit, I didn't even know what that would feel like.

A loud rapping on the Chambers door tore both Stone and me from our anxiousness. "He's here, Marek!" Salzer yelled from the hallway. He was one of the original members of the Laredo charter, old as hell with a mean streak to boot. If someone found themselves on his shit list, look out. His physical appearance was deceiving. A full head of white hair, a clean-shaven face and a dimple in his left cheek made him seem like someone's sweet old grandpa, though he was anything but. Most overlooked his temper because he was loyal as hell, willing to take a bullet for any one of his fellow brothers, home and charters alike. It didn't matter. And no one could ask for better than that.

My VP and I walked out toward the front entrance of the clubhouse just as Yanez and another man were ushered inside. It didn't surprise me one bit that he'd brought someone along with him, since I probably would have done the same thing had the roles been reversed. In our world, you couldn't trust a lot of people, especially virtual strangers.

A quick jerk of my head and the two men from Los Zappas followed us to a back room. The only people allowed to enter Chambers were actual club members, and although what we were going to discuss was technically club business, there was no way in Hell the likes of the cartel were going to be allowed inside those doors. Sacred shit and all that.

After we were all seated, I wasted no time in getting down to business. "So," I started. "I was hoping to meet with Carrillo face to face, but he assured me I could finalize through you." I eyed Yanez cautiously, his dark, beady eyes assessing me right back. His gaze flicked from me to Stone, and back to me again. I had no idea what he was expecting to happen, other than confirming the last run the Knights Corruption would make for Los Zappas.

"Pretend I'm him," he grumbled, obvious jealousy in his voice. The man was shit at hiding emotions, and I was sure right then that it was going to prove fatal for him in some future circumstance. I prided myself on reading people, and the man sitting across from me was a dangerous, soulless scum of the earth. Thankfully, it was probably the last time I'd ever have to lay eyes on him.

"Anyway," Stone interrupted, pulling Yanez's focus. "The final shipment for us is coming through in five days. We'll have guys there to pick it up and transport it across state lines, with the final payment meeting to be arranged in the next week."

The man who accompanied Yanez finally spoke up, his accent quite thick. While I had a hard time making out what he said, I understood three key components. Carrillo. Meet. Money. What the hell else was there to know?

Seeing we both struggled with his words, Yanez felt inclined to clarify what his man had just said. His thin lips parted, his lizard-like tongue sneaking out and wetting his bottom lip.

"Carrillo will get in touch with you to set up the final meet." No more words were exchanged as both Los Zappas men rose from their seats and headed toward the door.

Well, I guess that's the end of our meeting.

TWENTY-SEVEN

Sully

"NO, NO . . . NO!" he yelled. "Don't go in there!" The noise from the movie did nothing to drown out the worry in Jagger's voice. He was all caught up in the film, and while I'd been scared throughout the majority of it, witnessing his reaction did something to calm me. Seeing another respond so fiercely almost lightened the darkness of the movie for me. Almost.

It'd been five days since Marek had dropped me off at his house, and with a babysitter no less. And since there wasn't much to do, we'd taken to watching DVDs to help pass the time.

While I remained quiet around the prospect, he'd opened up rather quickly, although something nudged at me that it was simply his personality. He'd become borderline jovial over the passing days, and I soon realized people could discover a lot about one another in less than a week if they spent every waking moment of their time with them.

Now I, on the other hand, was a tightly sealed box of secrets. I gave him short and simple answers when he tried to politely interrogate me. Anyone trying to extract personal information was someone to be wary of. It was how I was raised, what was ingrained in my head over the years. But Jagger was slowly tearing away that notion, his simple curiosity making me start to rethink everything I'd ever been told. To a certain degree, of course.

A loud, crackling noise burst forth from the speakers of the television, so loud I literally jumped in my seat and practically ended up wrapping myself around Jagger. His body instantly tensed, the muscles of his arms rigid against my touch. I hadn't meant to react in such a way, but the damn movie he'd picked out was the newest horror movie. And it scared the hell out of me.

I'd quickly come to discover scary movies were not my thing. My life was enough of a fear-fest; I didn't need to watch that shit for entertainment. With my fingers splayed over my face, I was able to block out at least one of the senses, allowing me to continue with the movie.

"Is this too much for you, Sully?" Jagger asked, genuine concern in his voice. He had no idea what my life was like before Marek swooped into our clubhouse and kidnapped me.

Saved me.

The only information he knew was probably what he'd heard about the Savage Reapers, but why would any reasonable human being believe they would treat one of their own so badly? They wouldn't, so I kept it a secret. Only my new husband knew of such things, the evidence splayed all over my fragile stature.

"I'm okay," I answered. No sooner had I spoken than the sound of a chainsaw erupted on the screen, throwing me into yet another spasm of fear. He knew I'd obviously lied, and being the kind person I was learning he was, he reached across me and searched for the remote.

The warmth of his toned body helped to relax me, but stir me up as well, in a different way. A way I refused to acknowledge. While Jagger was extremely good-looking, and had a body to drool over—which I'd encountered when he'd walked into the kitchen in nothing but a towel—he didn't affect me like Marek did.

It just wasn't the same.

Any girl with a pair of eyes would be drawn to the prospect. His dark golden hair was a little longer on top than the sides, a style he kept pushed off his face at all times. Amber eyes looked back at me with growing friendship, his pupils dilating whenever he became excited about a specific topic, movies and music being the main two.

While I could admit I was attracted to the guy who'd become my shadow, he wasn't the man who consumed my thoughts day in and day out. I'd become somewhat comfortable enough with Jagger to actually enjoy his company with each passing day, and while I remained closed off about my life, my dreams were certainly up for discussion. Never having anyone to banter back and forth with before—besides the few interactions with Adelaide, of course—was something I never even knew I missed.

"That's okay," he reassured, clicking off the movie and choosing a home renovation show instead. "I can see horror movies aren't your favorite. How about a romantic comedy? Chicks love that shit, right?" He chuckled, staring at me as if he'd hit the nail on the head.

"I guess so, although I haven't seen many of them myself." I'd since moved back over to my side of the couch, embarrassed I'd basically ended up in his lap to begin with.

I watched intently as he rose from the couch and rummaged through the box of movies Adelaide had dropped off the other day, searching for something he thought I might like. To anyone else, it was a simple gesture, nothing to even think twice about. A normal everyday occurrence. But to me, it was huge. His actions spoke volumes, and my lips turned up at the thought that we were quickly becoming friends. His concern for me was touching.

Shaking a movie in front of me, he smiled wide as he opened the case. A strand of his hair fell forward and covered his left eye, and in the moment he reminded me of someone younger, someone innocent and not a part of the evil ways of the world yet. He was only two years older than me, all of twenty-two, but I knew he'd seen things most people would never witness their entire lives. Much like me.

When his eyes reconnected with mine, I saw something new, an emotion I couldn't quite pinpoint. Gone was the playfulness he'd displayed seconds before. His beautiful eyes quickly assessed me in a way he'd never done previously. Not while I'd been looking at him, at least. How he gazed at me when I wasn't paying attention, I couldn't say.

My breath lodged in my throat while I wondered what he was going to do or say next, the moment freezing us both in time, promising to shatter the second either one of us found our opportunity.

During my short life, I'd only been looked at as a means to an end, for some man to use and abuse as he saw fit. Never before had anyone stared at me in utter fascination. It was quite overwhelming and while I preferred it to being stared at like a piece of meat, my inner voice warned me to be careful. Of Jagger and of myself.

As if realizing he was staring a little too intently, he brushed his hair off his forehead, gave me a nervous laugh and turned around so his back was to me. I didn't want to do it, but I couldn't help but stare at his backside. His dark-washed jeans were baggy and hung low on his hips, but they did nothing to detract from the firm muscles of his ass I knew existed just beneath the fabric.

While I was learning to trust Jagger not to hurt me, I was now aware he desired me. And if I knew anything, I knew it was a very bad thing. For both of us. Even though I didn't return his affections, if Marek ever suspected his prospect harbored such feelings for his new wife, he'd probably kill him before confirming his suspicions.

Jagger sat down on the couch next to me, exactly where he was before getting up to change the movie, but for some reason it suddenly made me nervous. He wasn't doing anything differently, but because the air between us had changed, his close proximity shifted things between us.

Everything was unspoken, yet it lingered in the air just the same.

"Ready?" he asked, looking at me expectedly. His sharp jawline was clean-shaven, unlike most of his brothers. Beards were a common theme among the members, although each one varied in length.

"How did you get your road name, Jagger?" I asked, the question coming out of nowhere. I'd meant to simply nod when he asked if I was ready to watch the movie he'd picked out, but apparently my brain wanted to know more about the man who'd been put in charge of watching me in my husband's absence. Plus, I wanted to erase the tension-filled moment we'd just shared.

His expression shifted back to casual, his features softening while he leaned back on the couch.

"Well," he started. "Ryder and me got to talkin' about music one day and I mentioned how I loved the Stones. Long story short, he ended up nicknaming me Jagger." I had no idea who he was talking about. It was written all over my face, so he graciously elaborated. "Mick Jagger. He's the lead singer of the Rolling Stones. Only the best band in the world." He chuckled, turning his body fully toward me, his arm resting on the back of the couch. His fingertips accidentally brushed over my shoulder, and when I jerked involuntarily, he apologized with his eyes and righted himself so he was facing forward again. "I'll play you some of their music someday, if you want," he offered.

"I'd like that," I said truthfully. My life had been so sheltered I jumped at the opportunity to learn something new.

"Great. Now, what do you say we watch this movie?" He never waited for me to respond before he hit the Play button.

TWENTY-EIGHT

Marek

I LOVED MY BIKE AND reveled in the feel of the open road, but two days of continuous riding took its toll on me. Stone and I should have taken one of our trucks to Laredo, but like the dumbasses we were, we decided to ride instead, figuring the weather was nice enough to enjoy the trip. While the temperature had been favorable for the journey, my legs and arms were sore and my fucking balls ached. All I wanted to do was get home and take a long, hot shower. Preferably with some company.

I'd been successful in not thinking about Sully for the past hour, but there she was again, popping up in my head, knowing I'd missed her image. What could I say? My new wife was stunning, and the simple fact that she was now all mine made her even more enticing. I was fully aware of the way she watched me, especially when she thought I wasn't paying attention, her beautiful brown eyes roving all over my body. The funny part was she thought she was being inconspicuous. There were a few times when I'd been tempted to drag her to my bedroom so I could return the favor. But I never did, fearing if I pushed her too fast, she would shut down completely.

And the simple fact that I even cared about such things was quite irritating.

Stone and I waved to each other as we parted ways at the intersection, which was twenty minutes from the clubhouse. I went right and he went left. We were both headed home after a very long trip, which couldn't end soon enough.

When I'd finally made the turn toward my house, my tires kicking up the gravel of my driveway, I exhaled a long breath and smiled at the sight of my simple and welcoming home.

It was late, too late for anyone to still be awake, so I made sure to be as quiet as I could while unlocking the door and stepping inside. I soon came to realize there was no need for my thoughtful consideration when I saw the prospect and my wife cuddled together on my couch. Sleeping.

Slamming the door so hard I thought I broke a window, I cursed out loud in case the sudden noise hadn't been enough of a disturbance to wake them up.

Jagger was the first to stir, his eyes fluttering open before he realized who was standing ten feet away from him. At first, he looked calm, but as soon as he glanced to his left and noticed Sully's head resting on his shoulder, her legs tucked underneath her, his expression turned from serene to pure panic.

He jumped up so fast his sudden absence from Sully made her fall onto the cushion, her shoulder hitting the couch before she woke up. The nightshirt she wore barely covered her, riding up her thighs while she scrambled around on the couch.

"Jagger, what's the matter?" she groaned. The way she said his name made my blood boil, and it took everything in me not to shove my gun in his goddamn mouth.

Turning all of my focus back on the guy I wasn't sure if I was gonna kill yet, I clenched my jaw hard enough to keep me from freaking out. I opened my mouth to speak, but before a single word slipped out, he spoke so quickly he tripped over his words.

"Prez, w-we weren't doing n-nuthin'. I swear," he stammered. "We ju-just fell asleep watchin' a m-movie." All the color drained from his face, so much so it made me think he was actually guilty of something. Something that would get his life snatched from him. In other words, something that would cause me to put a bullet between his eyes. Before tonight, I'd actually liked Jagger.

Not anymore.

Sully had finally come around, her eyes wide and round as she sleepily rose to her feet. Taking a few precious steps toward me, she stopped suddenly when she saw the look of rage on my face. My nostrils flared from the sharp intake of air, my pulse kicking up a notch while I glared at the both of them. I was sure I probably looked like the Devil himself in the soft glow of the corner light.

"Marek," she whispered. "Jagger's tellin' the truth. We must have fallen asleep watching a movie." Her worried eyes pinned me. "I'm sorry.

It won't happen again."

"Did you fuck him?" I seethed.

"No!" she gasped. "We're just friends." Her head tilted down, her eyes staring at the ground as her long black hair covered half her face from me.

"Friends?" I sarcastically laughed, a sound that drew her attention immediately. Her eyes locked on mine again while I continued to mock her comment. "You think Jagger's your friend, sweetheart? No," I said, stepping away from the prospect and toward the one woman I couldn't stop thinking about. "He's not your fucking friend. He just wants to get into your pants. Don't let him fool you."

"No, he doesn't," she countered, fear and worry still dancing behind her dark brown eyes.

"Shut the hell up, Sully!" I yelled, running my hand through my hair in utter frustration. Too much shit was swimming around inside my head, and it was taking everything in me not to beat both their asses.

"Prez," he pleaded. "That's not true. I swear, we—"

I cut him off before he could finish his lame-ass argument. "Get outta here, Jagger, before you end up eatin' my gun."

Instead of hightailing it out of my house, however, he made a move which proved my goddamn point. He walked past me and stood in front of my wife, his stance protective, instantly giving everything away. *This fucker has feelings for her.*

"You're not gonna' do anything to her, are you?" His tone quivered, although he tried his hardest to appear strong and calculating. For some reason, I had the urge to assure him no harm would befall Sully, but as soon as I saw her hand touch his shoulder, I lost it. Gone was any shred of control I'd been holding on to. Gone was any sense of logic I had when first walking through the front door. Gone was the rationale to not overreact to a situation which was most likely innocent. Just like they both claimed.

Before I knew what was happening, I rushed forward and snatched Jagger by the throat, squeezing tightly before throwing him to the ground. His body hit the floor with a loud thud, his head smacking off the side of the table on his way down. His fingers rubbed at the side of his skull, covered in blood when he pulled them away. A grimace covered his face and in that moment, I knew I'd lost all control.

Not from realizing I'd hurt him, but for what I was about to do next.

TWENTY-NINE

Sully

MY BREATH STUCK IN MY throat while I waited to see what Marek was going to do next. Jagger and I hadn't been doing anything wrong, except for falling asleep after a very long day. I didn't even know Marek was due back that night, otherwise, I would have made sure not to be so comfortable around the prospect.

He and I were quickly becoming friends, something which was still a very new concept to me. Especially with a man. I found I was still reserved around him, but I allowed myself to laugh when he did or said something funny. I craved the genuineness he offered me, and now everything was being destroyed because I'd gone and fallen asleep next to him, laying my head on his shoulder while I rested. It was all my fault, and Jagger was going to pay the price for it.

And I would probably be next.

Marek reached down and grabbed him by the throat again, picking him up in one fluid motion and slamming him against the wall. The picture hanging above them fell to the ground, the frame splintering in two at their feet.

"Don't you ever question me again about my wife, *prospect*," Marek yelled. "You hear me?" He pulled Jagger toward his body before slamming him against the wall once again. "The only reason I don't kill you right now is because I don't feel like cleanin' up the mess. If you so much as look at Sully again, I won't think twice about snatching your life, though." He pulled him close. "Do you understand me?"

"Yes," Jagger croaked, his president's hand still wrapped tightly around his throat. When Marek finally released him, Jagger quickly walked toward the door, grabbing his keys from the side table. He disappeared from the house and true to his word, his eyes never once fell on me before he left.

My heartbeat picked up pace inside my chest. Fear shrouded me. I had no idea what Marek was capable of, especially in a state of rage, never mind that I was the only one left to deal with his rantings.

On top of being genuinely afraid, I was also sad because one of the few people I would have liked to call a friend was no longer allowed near me. Would he prohibit Adelaide from speaking to me as well?

It seemed as if he was going to make me revert back to the introvert I'd been my entire life. The small taste of freedom and budding friendships were glorious, but I guessed it was too good to be true.

Marek's back was to me, but I could tell by his posture he was struggling with not freaking out on me right then. He kept running his hands through his disheveled dark hair, his broad shoulders rising and falling in quick succession. Appearing as if he were trying to calm down, I relaxed a fraction.

Until he turned around.

And strode forward, every step toward me completely frightening.

Before I could step back, he reached forward and pulled me to him, his warm breath hitting my lips he was so damn close. When I dared to look up at him, his eyes held mine for a brief moment, something passing between us that neither of us understood.

Then he broke the connection.

"Did you fuck him, Sully?" he grated, his hold on my arms intensifying while he waited for my answer.

"No, we didn't do anything wrong. I swear it." I all but mumbled the last few words, the closeness we shared very confusing. I was scared of him, yet I hadn't realized I missed his hands on me until I'd felt them again. Even in his anger.

His silence threw me into another inner struggle. *Does he believe me? Is he going to punish me even if he realizes I'm telling him the truth?*

Without another word, he reached for my wrist and dragged me toward his bedroom. The only resistance I gave him was a slight tug of my arm, a gesture he completely ignored. Once inside his room, I glanced around the area where I'd laid my head since he'd left, suddenly missing the solace I'd been able to create for myself.

Releasing my arm, he looked around his room, incredulous eyes giving away what he was seeing. "Did you clean my room?" he barked, walking away to look in his closet, then in his bathroom. When he came back inside the bedroom, he shrugged off his cut and threw it over the back of the chair in the corner.

Why I would clean the area I spent the majority of my time in was surprising, I had no idea. But then again, he was a man, and in my short twenty years of life, I'd never known a man to clean up after himself.

"Yes," I answered, unsure if touching his things was going to push him over the edge or not. I stood near the door while he continued to look around, watching his every move and preparing myself for anything. While my body remained still, my eyes followed him everywhere, focusing on the stretch of his black T-shirt when he bent over to inspect underneath the bed. Although I wasn't quite sure why he was looking under there, I didn't ask; I remained silent, waiting to take my direction from him. His muscles strained against the fitted material, his multiple tattoos twirling around the thickness of his arms, beckoning me to . . . what? Feel them? Long for them to wrap around me and hold me close? The notion was ridiculous and I knew it, shaking my head to try and rid myself of the crazy thoughts.

"You didn't have to do that," he calmly said, advancing on me now that his curiosity was sated. I braced myself. When he saw the rigidness in my posture, he slowed, but never stopped. Standing incredibly close to me, he hooked his finger under my chin and raised my head to him.

"I didn't mean to scare you, Sully, but you have to understand you belong to me now. And if any other man puts his hands on you or looks at you like they want to fuck you, I will deal with them in the only way I know how."

"Violence?" I squeaked. I knew I was pushing my luck, but I had to make sure there was no misunderstanding him.

"Yes, violence. You know as well as I do that it's how things are done in our way of life. You can never show weakness or else you die." The intensity in his blue eyes frightened yet drew me in at the same time. Differing emotions pinged through me, and I had no idea which one to latch on to and ride out.

Maybe he'll make the decision for me.

"But Jagger and I were just watching a movie. Then we fell asleep. He didn't touch me," I promised.

"He may not have touched you, but he certainly wants you. There's no denying that." I opened my mouth to argue with him, but he wasn't having any of it. "I know what I saw when he looked at you, never mind that the little bastard tried to shield you from me, protecting you as if you were his."

"He's my friend," I whispered, our continued closeness making me shift from one foot to the other while he silently demanded my eyes remain on him.

He backed away before shouting, "He's not your fucking *friend*, Sully! The sooner you get that through your head, the better. I mistakenly sent him to babysit you, to keep you safe and out of harm's way until I got back. That's it. No more, no less. But he went and caught feelings for you. That much I'm sure." Redness stole over his face, and I knew he was becoming more enraged the longer he stood there ranting about Jagger. I chose to agree and let the topic die before he lost control and did something I feared.

"Okay," I mumbled, retreating a step to ensure there was a big enough space between us. Tears welled in my eyes and before I could stop them, they drifted down my cheeks and revealed my sadness.

"Goddammit!" he cursed, turning his back on me and walking into the bathroom. Slamming his fist against the countertop, he cursed some more before regaining some sort of calm.

Choking on my sobs, I tried to gather my wits and soothe myself before he reentered the bedroom, but he was too quick. I needed more time alone, but he stole those precious moments from me. Rushing toward me, he snatched me up and dragged me toward the bed, pushing me down on top of the mattress until I was completely vulnerable to him.

The long nightshirt I wore rode up my thighs the further I retreated. His gaze drifted to my exposed legs, and a sudden heat washed over me. Lust danced behind his beautiful blue eyes, but not in a way which scared me. I loved the way he watched me, even though I knew I should be on guard to any move he may decide to make.

Thankfully, I'd been wearing a bra, hoping and praying he couldn't see my body's reaction. My nipples pebbled and brushed against the soft material, their ache blossoming and making me fidget even more. My hopes were dashed that he hadn't noticed when his eyes landed on my breasts, his tongue snaking out and wetting his full bottom lip.

I wonder what his kiss tastes like.

What the hell was wrong with me? The man before me, my husband, could possibly decide to force himself on me, and I was enthralled with how his lips would taste against mine?

"You're so beautiful. You know that, right?" He reached for my legs and pulled me to the edge of the bed, prying my thighs apart with his large hands. "I didn't mean to make you cry, but what I told you was the truth. I don't want to talk about it again, though. Understand?" he asked, while continuing to open my legs to him.

What the hell is he doing?

I tried to move away again, but his hold was strong. "What are you doing?" I whimpered, not sure how I felt about being this defenseless.

"I never apologize," he affirmed, "but I want to make you feel better." Those were the only words he chose to speak before he ran his hands up the full length of my thighs, hooked his fingers in the band of my panties and removed the material from my body. His expression softened while he watched me, trying to calm me without words.

Was I ready to have sex with him?

Would he ultimately force me, taking the decision away from me?

Before another wayward thought barreled through me, I felt his warm breath between my legs.

THIRTY

Marek

THE SIGHT OF SULLY SPREAD bare before me was too much. I needed to taste her, make up for scaring her a few moments ago. I wasn't apologizing for anything I did, but I meant what I'd said. I wanted to make her feel better, to chase away all her fearful thoughts with the simple swipe of my tongue.

The entire ride home, I pictured exactly the position we found ourselves in, but I never really thought it would happen. I knew she was scared of me, even though it was obvious she also desired me. Then, when I'd walked in and saw her and Jagger on the couch, my rage bloomed to heights I'd never experienced before. I'd never been jealous over a woman, but I was quickly realizing things were much different with my new wife.

She was mine, and no other man was ever gonna have the opportunity to touch her.

But there was much I still had to learn about her. Like why she looked at me with lust in her eyes, her body reacting to the mere sight of me with hardened nipples and quick pants of breath, yet she denied herself my touch.

All other women would have readily thrown themselves at me, promising me the world if they could just get a taste. But the woman lying before me broke all those molds. She was different, and it intrigued the hell out of me. While there was no way I would ever force myself on her, I didn't think she realized that.

I guessed it was time for me to assure her.

Gently nipping at the insides of her creamy, toned thighs, her breath hitched as she waited for my next move. Her arousal was prevalent, her need for me wafting through the air and calling for me to act soon.

She rested on her elbows and waited, her eyes pleading with me to do something. Only problem was, I had no idea if she was too frightened to say anything or if she was waiting for me to dive right in.

Licking her inner thigh, dangerously close to her pussy, I uttered four words I'd never spoken before in my entire life.

"Can I taste you?" I asked, prepared for her to say no, but praying to God she'd say yes. I continued to lavish her with my tongue until she gave me the words I quickly became desperate to hear.

"I . . . I don't know. I've n-never had someone do th-that before," she stuttered. It wasn't a no, so I was halfway to tasting her on my tongue. The notion that no other man had eaten her pussy before was incredible, the best thing I thought I'd ever heard. Knowing my cock wouldn't be the first to enter her body was disappointing, but at least I could own this act.

I tried not to react to her statement, fueling the paranoia which was undoubtedly engulfing her right then. Instead, I chose to simply wait until she finally gave in. She watched me with careful eyes, silently pleading with me to do something, or stop altogether.

I chose to do something.

Lowering my head until the scent of her filled my nose, I opened my mouth and licked her slowly. One swipe of my tongue was all it took for her to moan out a throaty breath, collapsing back onto the bed in satisfaction. And reserve. She tried to close her legs again, unsure of what she was experiencing, but a simple growl from me told her to stop.

"Is that okay?" I asked, stunned I was even asking for permission. But I didn't wish to push her too hard, especially after frightening her with my outburst earlier. "Do you want me to stop?" I waited at least ten seconds and still she remained quiet. "Sully, do you want me to stop?"

"No," was her quick response, spreading her legs wider for me. I smiled big and tasted her again, this time with more urgency. I kissed and licked her as if I were eating my last meal, the scent and taste of her pushing me over the edge. Eating her out was different from fucking her, an act I wasn't sure she was quite ready for. But my cock didn't care, painfully pushing against the seam of my jeans, bouncing between pleasure and pain.

When my lips closed over the bud of her clit, she moaned loudly, fisting her hands in my hair and driving herself further into my mouth. "Marek. . . ." She writhed against me, trying to find a rhythm which would ensure her release.

"Cole," I corrected, continuing to push her toward the edge.

She stopped moving and pulled at my hair. "What?" she asked, breathless and needy for my next touch.

"My first name is Cole. That's the name I want you to scream when you come," I demanded.

She never responded, instead pushing my face back down so I could continue. I smiled wide. She was close to diving off the cliff, so it wouldn't take much to push her over. Thrusting two fingers inside her tight heat, I sucked on her clit until she almost shot off the bed.

"That's it," I encouraged. "Give me your pleasure. I want all of it," I commanded while driving her crazy. Crooking my fingers and hitting against the sensitive spot nestled deep inside her, she cried out my name and pumped faster against my face.

"Cole!" she screamed, her body locking up tight as her pussy clamped down on my fingers. Her panting drove me to milk every last bit of pleasure from her delectable body, my cock pushing even harder against its restraint, begging to take her and finally consummate our forced marriage.

No more words were needed from either of us as she rode out her high. As soon as she'd come back down, though, embarrassment stole over her, her entire body covered in a light pink tinge. I found it rather satisfying that she could let go completely during the act, yet be shy enough afterward for her body to betray her, revealing her true feelings to me without her consent.

When I crawled over her, I took notice of the scars I'd tried to ignore when my head was buried between her legs just seconds before. The mere sight of them fueled my simmering rage, this time for a different reason. The fact that someone had done such things to her was incomprehensible, but then again she'd belonged to one of the worst clubs I knew, which obviously meant nothing to those bastards.

Lightly tracing my fingertip over the harsh, jagged scar on her lower belly, she stiffened, trying to push away from me while not being too obvious about it. But I knew. I knew she was embarrassed or ashamed or whatever crazy emotion she was trying not to show me right then.

"You have yet to tell me who did this to you."

"Why does it matter?" she retorted, rising up on her elbows again so she could see my face. It was a brave move on her part, one I didn't expect at all. The fierceness in her chocolate eyes bore into mine, her black hair fanning around her like a cloak.

"It matters because I'll end whoever dared to mark your body."

"I know I'm disgusting to look at, but it's hardly a reason to go start a war on my club." Her eyes widened with the realization that she'd given something away. She struggled to pull her body free from underneath me, but she wasn't going anywhere. Not until I'd finally gotten some answers.

Pinning her to the bed beneath me, every part of me covered every part of her. Her mouth was close, so close I longed to see if her kiss was as sweet as her pussy. But I didn't move, instead choosing to focus on the effect I had on her. Resting on my forearms to try and keep some of my weight off, I stared down at her, keeping my eyes on her face even when she looked away. A single tear escaped and trickled down her cheek, hitting the bed below.

"Look at me," I commanded. When she finally did, I tried to ease her worry. Somewhat. "You're far from disgusting to look at, Sully. In fact, even with all your marks, you're rather stunning." I spoke the truth, and I hoped she believed me. Why it was so important she trusted what I was telling her was confusing, but I didn't have time to delve into it if I wanted her to tell me what I'd been asking since I'd taken her. "Who put those marks on you? Tell me now." My voice was calm but my body was tense, the slow tick of my jaw probably giving away everything.

She tried to turn away from me again, but I directed her face back to mine with a simple touch. Since she had no other choice, she finally gave me what I wanted, although hearing the words fall from her lips didn't prepare me for the onslaught of rage I was soon to feel.

"Vex and my father marked me." Just when I thought she was going to clam up again, she continued speaking, her tongue wetting her lips before her next words. I berated myself for wanting to kiss her again, all while she was exposing her soul to me, but I couldn't help myself. She was too enticing. Luckily, I was able to focus again before she caught the distracted look on my face.

"They are both responsible for the bruises—new and old. The burn marks on my lower back are from when my father thought I was providing information to the cops during a raid two years ago. They approached me and asked if I was okay. When I told them I was, pleading with them not to talk to me too long . . . Well, that piqued their curiosity. They took me into a back room and questioned me for a half hour, twenty-nine and a half minutes too long for my father not to automatically jump to conclusions. Immediately after they left, he dragged me into his office, ordered me to take off my shirt and bend over his desk. He then proceeded to burn me twice, my screams doing nothing but making him laugh." She spewed out word after word, as if she'd been dying inside by keeping the cause of her abuse secret. I saw a calmness drift behind her eyes when she finished the first part of her story, a weight lifted from her soul that she didn't even realize had bound her to agony.

There were so many things I wanted to say and ask her, but I knew if I did she would shut down again. So, with controlled breaths, I allowed her to continue without my barrage of thoughts on the subject.

"Vex claimed me from my father when I was fourteen. He was eighteen. My father had been raping me before Vex took me as his own, but stopped as soon as I belonged to another club member. He told Vex I was a lousy lay, but if he wanted to find out for himself, that was his choice. He's the one who stabbed me. Twice. Once when he thought I was flirting with one of the other members, and once just because he wanted to hear me scream. He was coked out of his mind and told me he needed some amusement." Another tear danced down her cheek. Mortification and shame stole her next breath, and I decided right then that I couldn't restrain my temper any longer.

Pushing myself off the bed, I paced in front of her, cursing before swiping everything off my dresser. The crash soothed me. A little. But it wasn't enough. I needed to hurt someone, and it would preferably be Vex and that fucker of an old man of hers. The president of the Savage Reapers. Hell would rain down on that club, the likes of which they'd never seen before.

All in due time.

Sully crawled up the bed, pulling her nightshirt down so she was completely covered. Her eyes glanced from me to the mess I'd made. I frowned at her sudden anxiousness, her switch in mood puzzling me. Looking for a distraction was probably her way of coping, but I still found it odd.

"What?" I questioned, keeping my eyes trained on her.

"I . . . I just feel out of sorts . . . when there's a mess. Especially in my bedroom." Her words weren't lost on me. She'd said 'my bedroom,' and like a giddy asshole it made me smile for some reason.

Feeling bad for her, especially after finally giving me answers, I tried my best to put her mind at ease. "I'll clean it up. Don't worry about it." I strode toward her, reached for her hand and pulled her to stand in front of me. Placing my hands on the sides of her beautiful face, I promised something I knew right then I would die to hold true.

"No one will ever hurt you again. Do you hear me?"

She nodded and relaxed in my hold, averting her eyes to the mess behind me. With a soft chuckle, I released her and began the task of cleaning up the scattered and broken items.

THIRTY-ONE

Sully

NEVER BEFORE HAD I IMAGINED what it would feel like to trust someone, to believe the words they told me and instinctually know they weren't a lie. I thought it was all fantasy. Those feelings of security only happened to other people. Not me.

Cole's promise to never allow anyone to hurt me again relieved a harrowing burden I hadn't realized I carried. Deep down, maybe I was waiting for my club to barge in and reclaim me, or maybe I thought Cole would change his mind, decide he made a mistake and return me himself. Either way, I was waiting to return to a life of pain and torment, thoughts of extinguishing my own existence a constant desire.

Every moment living in my new life brought me closer to allowing fate to right the wrong I'd lived so far. And although it was hard for me to have faith in anyone, I was beginning to open myself up and believe there were good people in the world.

Shoving aside that Cole had just brought me to the brink of bliss, pushed me over and brought me back all within mere seconds, I focused on what he was doing now. Cleaning up the mess he'd caused. He knew it was a source of anxiety for me, and it said a lot that he cared enough about my unease to want to help me.

While I watched him gather the broken pieces of clutter into his hands, I noticed how his hair kept falling into his face, the strands in much need of a simple cut.

Walking up behind his crouching form, I offered to help him out. "I can cut your hair if you'd like." Vex had always expected me to perform the simple act, never giving me a thank you or showing any kind of appreciation when I'd finished. One time, because he'd moved, I'd cut his hair crookedly, and even though I was able to fix it easily enough, I'd earned the wrath of his displeasure. My finger still throbbed when rain approached, even though the once broken appendage had been healed for years. I wasn't about to disclose any more war stories to Cole, though, fearing he would certainly go off the deep end and do something very dangerous. All in order to seek justice for me. While I found the thought comforting, I didn't wish to be the cause of something popping off and harming the club that was essentially protecting me.

When he managed to pick up the last piece of disarray, he rose to his feet and turned in my direction. "You don't like my hair?" he asked, tilting his head to the side, a gesture which caused more of his hair to fall over his eye. Blowing the intrusion off his forehead, he curved his lips up at my expression. I thought I'd insulted him and was instantly regretful, but his grin succeeded at putting me at ease.

"I like your hair just fine. It seems like the length is bothering you, though." I patiently waited to see if he was going to accept my offer or not.

"Sure, why not?" he said, ushering me toward the bathroom. Once inside, he took a seat on the edge of the bathtub, pointing toward the drawer of the vanity when I asked if he had a pair of scissors and hair clippers. I hadn't seen them when I was cleaning off the countertop in my urgency for order but sure enough, there they were hiding toward the back.

Pulling them free, I checked the quality and decided I could definitely work with what he had. Now all I had to do was keep my hand steady enough not to mess up his lovely thick hair. Stepping closer, I straddled his leg to gain better access. I worked quickly but efficiently, making sure not to cut it too short. He told me he liked a little bit of length on top. Running my fingers through the thickness of it, making sure to shake any loose strands free, excited me, for some reason. I'd had my hands tangled in his hair when he was pleasuring me, but the simple act of cutting it and checking my work almost made me feel normal for a brief moment.

A feeling I grasped onto and held tightly.

"How's it lookin'?"

"Good. Almost finished," I answered, twisting my body to check out the back. My foot slipped on the tile and I stumbled forward. Luckily for the both of us, the scissors were nowhere near his head.

His large hands steadied me, resting on my waist and gripping me firmly. "You okay?" His fingers continued to dig into my flesh, but he wasn't hurting me. In fact, his touch was exciting.

Cole Marek certainly had a way of disarming me, and since I knew I wasn't quite ready to take it there, I knew I had to keep my wits about me. What happened before was wonderful, but I wasn't prepared to have sex with him yet. Yes, he'd had his face buried between my legs and brought me untold pleasure, but joining with him was something else altogether. Maybe I was holding off because I wanted it to be special and not because I felt obligated. I had no idea because I had no frame of reference, every other time the act had been forced on me. All I knew was I wanted our first time to be different.

Plus, there was the small fact that I still battled with being kidnapped and forced to marry the president of our greatest enemy, even though I was coming around to the idea that fate had sent him to save me.

When I tried to back away, his grip held me in position, stable until he deemed it time to let me go. When he decided enough time had passed, he spread his legs and pulled me in front of him, leaning forward and resting his head on my belly. No words slipped from his lips as he found some sort of solace with being so close to me.

My heart thudded inside me, pushing against my ribs so hard I felt like it was going to explode. Every move he made was new, the gentleness of his touch foreign to me, although I was learning to expect such things from him.

Would he wait for me to decide when the time was right? Or would that be pushing things too far?

THIRTY-TWO

Marek

HER SMELL DROVE ME INSANE, a break with reality I most surely embraced. I had no idea why I chose to rest my head on her stomach. It simply felt right.

The woman standing before me was unraveling my carefully orchestrated existence. I was the leader of the Knights Corruption. I wasn't supposed to fall for a woman. A woman who was going to make me weak. A woman who was going to have the power to crush me if I let her.

A woman who was going to be my destruction.

I prided myself on my ability to detach myself from certain feelings, affections toward the opposite sex being number one. I used them just like they used me, for pleasure and nothing else. Then Sully came into my life—or I should say I barged into hers—and ever since then, I'd been questioning my choices.

Even though I'd basically just met her, I hated being away from her for the time it took Stone and me to deal with Yanez. I hated that I ended up leaving her alone with Jagger. I hated that I'd found out he'd developed feelings for her in their short time together, and that she seemed more comfortable around him than she was with me.

I hadn't spent much time with her since I'd brought her here, but all that was gonna change. If I wasn't involved in club business, then I would be with her, getting to know her. We *were* married, after all. Might as well get to know the old ball and chain.

Cringing at my callous thoughts, I focused back on Sully. I continued to lean my head against her body. When she didn't make a move to dislodge me, I took it as a sign to see how far I could take things. Running my hands up the backs of her thighs, over her plump ass and up her back toward her bra, I stopped only when I'd reached the clasp. Unhooking it before she said anything, I felt the breath leave her body in a rushed gasp. Slowly trailing my fingers along her soft skin, I stopped when I reached the bottom of her heavy tits, feeling the goose bumps which broke out all over her skin.

"Sully," I groaned, my cock thick and ready to come out and play. When she still hadn't made a move, I reached up and palmed her glorious mounds, pinching the already hardened nipples between my greedy fingers.

A moan fell from her lips as she took one step closer. Her hands wrapped around my wrists and held tightly. *I need more of her.* Raising her nightshirt over her head, and disposing of the thin material that had covered her breasts, I sat in front of her, admiring her glorious body. I'd seen her a few times before, but never like this. She allowed my hands to roam freely, and the experience was like none other I'd ever had before with any other female.

My tongue connected with her skin and she moaned once again. Taking a pert nipple into my mouth, I swirled my tongue around the aching bud while sucking it deep into my mouth.

She tasted like Heaven.

Everywhere.

"Cole . . ." she cried out. "Yes," she panted shamelessly. I switched to teasing her other one, groping her while sucking reverently. My free hand dropped to her pussy, gently stroking her while I tuned up her body as best I could. She'd never put her panties back on from before, and I'd never been so thankful to have such easy access.

"You're so wet. Do you want me to stop?"

Hesitation emanated off her. "Yes . . . No . . . I don't know," she mewled. Her confusion not only came from her mouth, but it was in her body language as well. She pushed her tits into my mouth but struggled when I tried to fuck her with my hand. She was at war with herself, and I had to do something about it.

Standing quickly, I picked her up by her waist and placed her on top of the vanity, nudging her thighs apart with my leg. Yanking down the zipper of my jeans, I pulled myself out and rubbed the tip of my cock through her swollen, wet folds. "Tell me to stop, Sully. Otherwise, I'm gonna take you so hard, you'll forget your own fuckin' name." I was ready to explode any second if she didn't give me an answer.

Placing her hands on my chest, she pushed me back, looking into my eyes before telling me something I didn't want to hear. "I don't think I can. Please don't be mad. I'm just . . . I'm not ready yet."

My control shattered. "But you were ready to have my face buried between your legs before?" I grabbed her chin when she tried to turn her face away from me. "What? Now that I want some relief, you're gonna deny me? Is that how this is goin' down right now?" I hadn't meant to say something so harsh, but it just came out. I berated myself for every single word, but for some reason I couldn't stop myself. The hurtful words flowed easily and it upset not only her, but me as well.

"I'm sorry," she whispered, her head jerking from my hold before she looked down at her own naked body.

"Yeah, I'm sure you are," I snarled, putting my cock away and zipping up my jeans. Backing away, I took one final look at her before retreating from the bathroom.

What I did was a prick move, but I didn't see it turning out any other way. I was pissed that she made me feel as if I was on guard around her, asking for permission to take what essentially belonged to me. I could have demanded she fulfilled her wifely duties and fuck me as many times as I saw fit, but I wasn't that much of a bastard. Although the way I reacted told a different story.

At least she seemed to crave my touch. Maybe, given a little more time, she'd come around and give me what I wanted.

But what to do until then, I had no idea. Not wanting to stick my dick inside the same old club whores, I was fucked and I knew it.

Soon, my club would know it too, my mood already cresting toward miserable.

———◆———

AFTER CALLING RYDER TO COME watch Sully while I made a trip to the clubhouse, threatening his life if he acted inappropriately with her, I hopped on my bike and rode to the one place I could escape from the woman twisting me up inside.

There was already a commotion as I stepped through the front door. A few of the brothers were gathered around, laughing and poking fun at whomever was in the middle of their crowd. Shoving my way through, I saw Hawke sitting in the center with a pissed-off look on his face. It took me all of a millisecond to figure out what he was so upset about.

His head was shaved.

And from the look on his face, and those of his brothers, he hadn't done that shit to himself. One guess who did it, however.

"What the hell happened to you?" I asked, coming to stand directly in front of him, slapping the back of his bare head before he could answer.

"That bitch happened," he groaned, rubbing his hand back and forth over his shaved head.

"I don't know why you keep her around, man," Breck said, shaking his head while continuing to laugh.

"'Cause I love the crazy cunt." He half-chuckled, his semi-laughter quieting as he continued to rub his dome.

Kicking his leg, I drew his attention back to me. "What. The. Fuck. Happened?"

He leaned back in his chair and prepared to tell me his story, one he'd obviously shared with the other guys, seeing as how they were already grinning.

"I must have gotten drunk last night, somehow made it home, and passed out in bed. When I got up this morning, Edana had shaved my fucking head."

There was certainly more to the story than that. "Why?" I asked, already losing interest in their crazy-ass relationship.

Actually looking embarrassed for once, he winced before revealing, "I guess I forgot to take the condom off before goin' to bed." Feeling the need to elaborate based on my confused expression, he blurted out, "We don't use condoms." Not something I ever wanted to know. "The one time she decides to wake me up with a blow job and that's when this shit happens," he grunts, rocking his chair back and forth until he'd had enough and jumped to his feet. Expletives flew from his mouth as he walked toward the bar, motioning for Trigger to hit him up with a drink.

Walking past him, I decided to hit him with a few words of condolence. "At least she didn't cut your dick off, Hawke. Be thankful for that shit." I smirked, slapping him hard on the back before walking toward the room I kept in the back of the clubhouse.

———— • ————

A LOUD NOISE WOKE ME from sleep, jolting me upright and ready to fuck someone up for disturbing me. A loud crash followed by men hootin' and hollerin', music playing way too loud and women's laughter emanated through the hallway.

Dropping my feet to the ground, I took a few seconds to tamp down my rage, but the extra time didn't help, not at all. I couldn't go back to my house, the shitty way I'd treated Sully still weighing heavily on my heart and mind, but it seemed as if I couldn't stay here either.

Jerking open my door, I thudded down the long hallway until I came to the common room, and the scene in front of me was astonishing. Well, maybe not astonishing, since I knew my men liked to throw a good ruckus, but I had no idea one was planned for tonight.

I glanced around the room, looking for my VP, but he was nowhere to be seen. *Who the hell's in charge here? Oh, yeah, that would be me.* Sleep still cocooned me in her cloak, the fogginess dissipating slower than I wanted, leaving me hazy and not too alert.

That was until I heard another loud crash and Hawke yelled, "Let's get fucked up!" at the top of his lungs, shattering any remnants of rest I had left. I moved toward the bar, my steps slow and steady until I found a seat in the corner. Luckily, Trigger was still there, passing out drinks to the willing and able.

"Hey, Prez, how ya feelin'?" he asked, sliding a beer my way. I guessed by the look of me, he wanted to start me off with something light and forgiving.

I chose to ignore his questions, instead asking one of my own. "What the hell is goin' on? Who planned a ruckus for tonight?" Swallowing a large gulp of the frosty beverage, my eyes connected with his once I'd placed the mug back down on the bar.

"Cutter suggested we should have one, you know, in honor of you and Stone making it back alive." Trigger laughed at his own joke, one I didn't find all too funny. "What's wrong with you, Marek? You always laugh at my jokes." His faux offensive stare almost had me smirking. Almost.

I felt a presence sneak up behind me. Before I turned around, someone threw their arm over my shoulder and leaned in to me. Fumes from too much bourbon hit my cheek and instantly made me tense up. *I'm in no mood for this shit tonight.* "He's just pissed his old lady isn't givin' it up yet," Tripp yelled into my ear. Swiveling around in my chair, I gripped him by his cut and slammed him against the bar.

How did he know she'd refused me?

Wincing in pain, then laughing it off simply because he was drunk, Tripp patted my hands which were still wrapped around his vest. What the hell was he even doing out of bed?

"Why would you say that?" I seethed, the look on my face sobering him up a little.

"Because you need to get laid, man. You're miserable, and everyone knows it." I released him, but luckily caught him before he toppled over, injuring himself so bad it would probably take him weeks to recover. Hell, he still wasn't anywhere near healed from being shot four times.

"What the hell are you even doing out here, Tripp? Adelaide would kill you if she knew you were out of bed, and drunk of all things."

"She's not the boss of me." He chuckled. "Although, I'd certainly let her boss me around in the bedroom, if ya know what I mean." I didn't know if he realized what he'd just said, but the way he was feelin' right about then I doubted he cared either way.

A quick turn of my head and I saw it coming, but I was powerless to stop it.

Trigger's fist flew through the air and connected with the side of Tripp's jaw, knocking him to the left. Again, I was able to react before he hit the ground, splitting open his many stitches.

"What the fuck, Trig! You can't go around punching him, even if he *did* say something about your niece. He's still recovering, or did you forget that?" I shouted, glaring at him and daring him to argue. Thankfully, he held up his hands in surrender, but not before leering at Tripp one last time. I knew he wasn't sorry, but at least he didn't continue his beat-down on our nomad brother. Pulling his graying messy hair back into a neat ponytail, Trigger went about his business as if nothing happened.

A little while later, while I was nursing my second drink, I saw Jagger approach from the side and my body instantly went into fight mode. My muscles tensed, preparing to beat the shit out of him if he said the wrong thing.

When he finally stood next to me, he opened his mouth and spoke. Quickly and quietly. "Prez, uh . . . Do you think I can talk to you?" he pleaded.

"No," I gritted, never turning my head to look at him. Thankfully, he got the hint. He walked away with his head down, brushing past a few of the wannabes who tried to talk to him.

I'd deal with him when I didn't have to fight the urge to kill him.

The rest of the night passed by without incident, the men having a great time, overindulging in pussy and alcohol. Even Hawke, with his newly shaved head, was back to his old antics, fuckin' around with some of the club whores. *He'll never learn.*

But then again, what fun would it be around here if he ever did?

THIRTY-THREE

Sully

"COME ON. JUST COME WITH me to the clubhouse and then we can go shopping," Adelaide pleaded with me. She told me she was in desperate need of some retail therapy, and I had to admit I thought it would be fun. Besides, it'd been three days since Cole had been home, no doubt still pissed because I wouldn't have sex with him. But at least he didn't force himself on me like I feared he might do. And even though he'd been cruel, he kept to his word and didn't hurt me. Well . . . not physically.

"I'm not sure if I'll get in trouble or not," I answered. Adelaide still didn't know the whole story surrounding me being there, but she never pried. The only thing she was aware of was that I always had someone watching over me, but she'd eventually admitted it was a normal occurrence with how protective some of the men could be.

Speaking of shadows, Ryder had been the newest chosen one since Jagger had been thrown out a few nights back. I didn't mind him hanging around, although, unless he was drinking, Ryder was a pretty quiet guy. His company was nothing like Jagger's, and I feared it was because Cole had threatened his life if he stepped out of line, which might be something as simple as engaging me in conversation.

"How are we going to convince Ryder? He won't let me out of his sight."

"Then we tell him he has to go with us." She smiled, and I knew exactly how she was going to 'convince' him to accompany us.

"Your uncle?"

"You know it." She laughed, tugging on my arm and pulling me toward the living room where Ryder was watching some show about Harleys.

A little while later, we were pulling into the compound, the heavy metal gates closing behind us while Adelaide found a parking space. My nerves took hold and shook me senseless. I had no idea if this one move would be the thing to send Cole over the edge. I'd believed him when he said no one would hurt me again, but was I pushing my luck by showing up unannounced? Did the man have his limits?

A single bead of sweat beaded on my brow. My hands became clammy and my breathing had stifled into short pants. I guess I was preparing myself for the worst, in case today proved to be the day I pushed the envelope one too many times.

A soft rapping made my head turn to the right. I hadn't realized Adelaide had left the car, but there she was, knocking on my window to get my attention.

"Come on, silly." She laughed. "You can't sit out here. You'll roast in the sun." The genuine smile on her face made me extremely happy I'd met her, but her warning didn't deter me from staying within the confines of her car.

"I'll roll down the window," I offered, fidgeting in my seat.

Opening the door, she reached for my hand and after a small amount of resistance, I allowed her to extract me. We walked through the courtyard of the compound, the sun blaring down on both of us and immediately heating us up to an uncomfortable level. Thankfully, we'd both been smart enough to wear light and airy sundresses. Adelaide's was a pretty pale blue color, hitting her just above the knee. It was strapless, and since she was smaller-chested than I was, it looked perfect on her. I, on the other hand, could never wear a dress without straps—too much up top to be comfortable. The dress I chose to wear was a beautiful multi-colored pattern, one Adelaide thought would look great. And, much like hers, my dress also hit just above the knee. A simple pair of flip-flops completed the outfit, although I probably should have worn more comfortable shoes after hearing about all the stores she wanted to visit. I'd chosen to wear my hair back in a stylish ponytail. It was practical and easy, plus it was off my neck, a smart decision given the sweltering heat.

When I gazed at my reflection in the mirror, I deemed it to be a lie. A stylish, vibrant young woman stared back at me, but I was anything but. Young, yes, but the other shit was a mirage.

My heartbeat picked up its pace the closer we came to entering the clubhouse, bikes lined up outside telling me there were a decent amount of members there today. We were walking too quickly for me to take the time to scan the area for Cole's bike, to determine if he was indeed inside those walls.

Opening the door, Adelaide reached for my hand once again and pulled me behind her, ensuring I wasn't going to take off running and abandon her. Although, something told me she would be just fine. All of the men in this club would protect her, or they'd have to answer to that uncle of hers. I wished I had someone in my life who had looked out for my well-being just a fraction of how he did for his niece.

Maybe in a different life.

The brightness of the shining sun was cut out once we entered inside. A few of the men milled around the open space and true to form, Trigger was behind the bar serving drinks to anyone who wanted them. It was only a little after two in the afternoon, but a few of the brothers were already well on their way to becoming drunk. I wondered if they were trying to mask a darkness in their own lives.

"Addy," her uncle called out, a genuine smile tipping the corners of his lips. "Tripp's in the back resting off last night." His expression faltered for a split second and I had no idea why. Until he squealed on himself. "Look, honey, Tripp's probably in a bad way." The look of confusion on his niece's face made him elaborate. "He was drinking with the rest of us last night, made some comment about you bossing him around . . . and. . . ."

"And what, Uncle Trig?" She leaned in closer. "Oh, my God! What did you do?" she exclaimed.

"Oh, calm down. I only punched him." When he saw she was starting to get upset, he tried to placate her. "I just punched him once. He's fine, but the amount of booze he shoved down his throat is enough to have him feelin' like shit today. You've been warned," he offered before talking to someone wanting a beer.

Adelaide turned her attention on me, asking if I wanted to wait out there or come with her to check on Tripp. I smartly chose to follow her toward the back of the building, not wanting to be a sitting duck in case Cole showed up.

Pushing open a small door toward the back, we both walked in on a naked man sprawled across a bed hardly big enough to fit the likes of his size. He looked to be at least a few inches over six feet, although lying down I couldn't exactly be sure.

I should have averted my eyes, but I couldn't help it; I stared at him like some kind of hussy, horny to get her next fix. The man's body, even with all the scars, was pretty impressive. Well-defined muscles, broad shoulders and thick thighs held my fascination, but they didn't elicit a need to touch him like when I gazed upon Cole's body.

Oddly, I could identify with Tripp in some small way because my body was also punctured and scarred. It was an odd connection but one I would accept.

Thankfully, Adelaide stalked forward and threw a sheet over his manhood, shoving at his shoulder with her small hand to try and wake him. "Tripp," she called out. "Get up." When he made no move to awaken, she tapped his cheek lightly, trying to rouse him that way. Still nothing. With one knee on the side of the bed, she leaned in closer to make sure he was breathing before tapping his cheek once more.

All of a sudden, strong hands gripped her shoulders and tossed her across him, landing on the other side of the mattress. At first, I thought he was having some sort of nightmare, like I had from time to time where I was lost between reality and a haze of fright. But when I heard his laughter, I knew he was playing with her, and the sight, although scary at first, had me smiling and wishing I had those types of relationships with people.

Adelaide was quickly becoming one of those people for me, which I would forever be grateful for.

Tripp's voice was deep and rough, no doubt the effects of high amounts of alcohol from the night before. "My guardian angel." He laughed, kissing her cheek before releasing her.

"You're incorrigible," she scolded, slapping his arm before rising from the bed. "By the way, we walked in on you naked, sprawled out for anyone to see." I thought she was trying to embarrass him, but the man had nothing to be ashamed of. Not in my opinion, at least.

"Did you like what you saw?" he asked, a cocky grin on his knowing face.

"I've seen better," she teased, making my own laughter erupt into the friendly atmosphere.

Gently shoving Adelaide to the side when she'd risen to stand next to him again, his piercing green eyes came to rest on me, noticing me for the first time since he'd woken up.

"Well, well, well. Who do we have here?" he asked, that same self-assured grin spread wide on his handsome face. Unlike many of his brothers, the only signs of facial hair were from a two-day-old growth. Scratching the side of his face, he managed to call my attention to his mouth when he licked his lips. Although I had no desire to kiss anyone but my husband, I could see how women would want to latch on to that full mouth of his.

Making sure to keep himself covered with the sheet Adelaide threw over him moments before, he leaned against the bed frame and watched me, waiting for introductions.

Taking a step forward, I said, "I'm Sully." I had no idea what else to add to that, but my friend did.

"She's Marek's wife," she added.

"Holy shit!" he shouted. "I heard about the infamous woman who'd trapped and tamed the president of the Knights Corruption." Arching a brow, he finished with, "You're even more beautiful than they say, sweetheart."

His compliment instantly made me uncomfortable, although I tried to hide it. I wasn't used to people telling me I was attractive, so I immediately thought they were only saying such things to make fun of me in some way. But just like when Cole had told me so, Tripp's assessment seemed genuine.

"Thank you," I whispered.

"You better behave yourself, Tripp," Adelaide warned, slapping his hand when he tried to reach for her. "You mess with Sully and Marek is going to bury you himself." I wasn't sure if she was teasing him or if she was serious.

Something told me it was the latter.

"Oh, I'm just having some fun. Keep your panties on . . . Or don't, it's up to you," he joked, looking at Adelaide with adoration. Turning his gaze back on me, he tried to comfort me, seeing the nervousness pouring off me in waves. "I'm harmless, sweetheart. Don't mind me. I love getting a reaction out of people." Glancing back to Adelaide, he confessed what happened the night before. "By the way, you need to tell your dear uncle to calm the hell down. Anytime anyone talks about you, he flips out." He instinctually rubbed his jaw. "He punched me last night when I made an innocent comment." Groaning when he touched a sore spot, he looked up at the woman at his side. "It hurts," he admitted, playing it up more than he needed to.

Stroking his face over the affected area, she lightly tapped him when he least expected it. "Ow!" he yelled. "What the hell, Adelaide?"

"Oh, I didn't hurt you. Stop being such a baby." She laughed then went about inspecting his numerous healing wounds. Tripp sat up straight so she could check his back as well. When she deemed everything looked good, she warned him about pushing himself too hard, like with the night before. "You shouldn't be drinking so much . . . and pissing my uncle off. You need to allow your body enough time to heal properly, Tripp. I mean it."

"Yes, ma'am." He saluted, reclining back on the bed. "Now, if you lovely ladies don't mind, I need some more beauty rest. Plus, my head's killing me." His groans sounded behind us as we left his room.

I liked Tripp. He had an aura about him which instantly relaxed me. He was funny, and humor was certainly something I needed more of in my life.

Stepping into the hallway, I continued to smile from the encounter when we ran into Jagger. His hands came up and landed on my arms, steadying me before I tripped over my own two feet.

"Sully, how are you?" he asked before retracting his hands. A black eye and split lip greeted me when I fully looked at him. His blond hair was disheveled, as if he'd just rolled out of bed, and his amber eyes were bloodshot. Honestly, he looked like hell.

"What happened to you?" I made a move to touch his face, but he backed up. "Did Cole do that to you?" I asked, suddenly furious with the man I hadn't seen in days.

Moving back another step, he looked reserved before answering. "No, it was from a fight I had two nights ago. A legit fight," he confirmed, his eyes roaming all over me in concern. "Are you all right? He didn't hurt you, did he?"

I knew exactly what he was talking about, and I put his mind at ease immediately. "No, he didn't hurt me." I tried to smile but I faltered. I watched him while he stood in front of me, shifting nervously from foot to foot. He wanted to talk to me, as I did to him, but the tension in the air prohibited us from continuing.

"Well, it was nice to see you. Take care," he said before walking past me down the hall and disappearing into a room a few doors down.

I didn't have feelings for Jagger other than as a friend, but the fact that we were forbidden to talk to each other really hurt me. Nothing inappropriate had gone on between us the entire time he watched over me, but Cole had freaked out just the same. My husband hardly spent any time with me, yet he didn't want anyone else to either. Of the male persuasion, at least.

Forgetting Adelaide was standing near me, her voice brought me back from my depressing thoughts. "What was that all about?" Her sincere concern for my situation was touching.

"Cole freaked out on Jagger because he thought we'd been doing something in his absence." Reaching to touch her shoulder, I confessed, "But we weren't, Adelaide. I swear." What the woman standing before me thought of me had suddenly become very important. Tears swam in my eyes as I tried to hold it together.

"I believe you, honey," she assured me, pulling me in for a quick hug. She knew I needed the comfort, and I was grateful she could read me so well. "I'm sure everything will blow over soon enough. Marek is a good man. Usually, he's pretty laid-back, but I think you might have him all twisted up inside. Let him get used to the idea of . . . well . . . you, and life will get back to normal." She smiled, linking her arm through mine and continuing down the length of the hallway.

THIRTY-FOUR

Marek

STANDING CLOSE BY, I HEARD a woman's voice say, "Now, let's go find Ryder so we can get our shopping on." Right then, I knew it was Adelaide and the hairs on the back of my neck bristled, but not because it was Trigger's niece. No, it was because I knew exactly who she was talking to.

Sully.

My wife.

But how could that be? Why was she here at the clubhouse when she should've been back at my house with Ryder? Quickly glancing around, I spotted Ryder in the corner, already locking his lips around a bottle of beer.

Both women entered the common room, instantly drawing the attention of all the men milling around. Most gave them a quick nod in acknowledgement, while one or two of the already-drunken bastards stared a little too long. Trigger was on alert as soon as his niece re-entered the room, and I was acutely aware of every movement Sully made . . . and of everyone who gazed at her longer than necessary.

It seemed Jagger wasn't the only one I had to worry about. Maybe I was being paranoid, but I would rather instill fear into them than let it go. "Zip!" I shouted over to one of our youngest members. "If you don't turn your fucking eyes away, I'm gonna pluck them outta your head. Feel me?"

"Sorry, Prez." He was halfway to passing out already and it was barely after two. But at least he had enough sense not to argue and did as he was instructed, gulping down the rest of his drink and turning his attention to whatever show was on TV.

My eyes found Sully's and like always, something passed between us. I was no longer upset with her for refusing me. Hell, I wasn't really angry with her for that reason to begin with. I battled between fighting the feelings she created inside me and giving in to them altogether. I'd lashed out and hurt her. Never mind that I hadn't been home in days because I was too much of a coward to face her.

Pushing all my errant internal ramblings aside, I approached them rather quickly. Blocking the pair from going any further, I reached out for Sully's hand. I had no idea what I was going to do or say but in that moment, I needed to touch her. As my fingers were about to skim hers, she pulled away, taking a half-step behind her new friend.

I wasn't gonna lie, it hurt. Was she still afraid of me? Or was she still upset that I'd yelled at her the way I had? Did she hate me now?

Part of me didn't blame her, not one bit, but another part, the Neanderthal part, didn't give a shit. She was mine, and there was no way I would allow her to embarrass me in front of my club. I felt everyone's eyes on the interaction, and I wasn't gonna be made a fool of.

"What are you two doing here?" I asked none too nicely.

Adelaide was the one who spoke, all while Sully kept her eyes on the ground. "I asked Sully to accompany me here to check on Tripp before we headed out to do some shopping." My eyes never landed on Trigger's niece, the whole time focused on my wife instead. Not until Adelaide mumbled something stupid, that was. "Well, I guess we'll be going now."

Two steps and I was standing directly next to my wife. Her body warred between leaning into me and pulling back. I saw it in her posture, and in her expression, even though her beautiful eyes were still avoiding me.

"No way are you two going anywhere without one of my men." A short and simple demand. Or so I thought.

"Look, Marek," Adelaide started, "I'm not involved with this club like that, so I can come and go as I see fit. No one will tell me what to do. Ever." Her voice raised an octave toward the end of her little speech. I had an idea that Stone had a little something to do with the unspoken reason for her 'I'm woman, hear me roar' rant.

"You're right, you're not. But she is," I said, pointing toward Sully. "She's my wife, and as such she's not allowed to go anywhere without me or one of my men." I didn't elaborate on my fear of her club coming to look for her, stealing her back right out from under my nose. No, Adelaide didn't need to know all that. Speaking of, I had yet to receive an updated report on their whereabouts. I found it odd that they hadn't tried to storm my club to reclaim her from us.

"Then *you* can come with us," she offered. What a ludicrous statement. I had better shit to do besides watching the two of them shop for clothes, or whatever the hell they were going out to buy. Although the thought of watching Sully try on different clothing was rather appealing. I wondered if they were going to one of those lingerie shops during their outing. What did that matter, though, when she wasn't ready to hop into bed with me? Then again, I *was* able to get her naked.

Yeah, that's where my head went, random thoughts bouncing back and forth inside my brain. I was beyond frustrated, and if I didn't sink inside her tight little body soon, I was gonna explode.

I noticed Sully had raised her head, turning her face toward me, waiting to see if I would agree to come with them or not. Would she be upset or relieved if I said yes? I figured I wouldn't know unless I answered.

After a few seconds of internal deliberation, I decided it was best for me not to go, so I declined her offer. However, I was pleased to see Sully's face fall, letting me know she was indeed upset that I'd refused. It gave me hope that she was on her way to forgiving me for acting like such an ass. Any normal man would apologize, and while the thought had crossed my mind, it wasn't how I operated. *Apologize for nothing, but make amends to right the wrong.* Although, the beauty in front of me was changing me in ways I didn't want to acknowledge.

A fierceness to protect her, even from myself at times, swirled powerfully through me, making me question everything. I'd already made the move to take my club legit, which was one less thing I had to worry about, even though I had to make sure it came to fruition. Anything which would put me in better light in her eyes was quickly proving to be a driving force for how I conducted my day.

Then stop yelling at her, Marek.

Suddenly wanting to be alone with her, I snatched her hand and pulled her behind me toward my room. "We'll be right back, Adelaide." The warmth of her palm had my cock stirring to life. Man, I was easy. All it took was her simple touch and I couldn't keep myself from picturing how she would look beneath me, driving her heels into the backs of my thighs as I drove myself inside her.

Closing and locking the door for added privacy, I spun her around until she was facing me. "Let me see your eyes," I demanded, a softness in my tone I meant for her to hear. Once I had her attention, I started in with my ramblings. "Listen, Sully," I said, my thoughts so twisted together it was hard for me to find the right thing to say. "I won't pressure you again to fuck me." *Yeah, that's the sentence my brain-to-mouth filter released. Real smooth.* "You just let me know when you're ready, okay?"

"Okay," she answered, her dark orbs focused on me. Before she looked away again, I needed to let her know she wouldn't be going on any shopping outing. Something which was surely going to upset her, but it was the best choice. I wasn't going to risk her safety because she wanted to flit about town with her new friend.

"I don't want you going anywhere with Adelaide without one of the guys. And since she's gonna give me a hard time about it, it looks like you two will have to do it another time."

Wrinkling her brow at something running through her head, she nodded and averted her gaze.

"What?" I asked, wondering what in the hell she was thinking.

"Can't Ryder go with us?"

"No." I decided to elaborate when I saw the desperate look on her face. "Ryder already started drinking. He won't be of any use if something happens."

"What's going to happen? We're going to be out in public with people all around us." The one thing I noticed about Sully was that she was becoming more comfortable when talking to me, which was a good thing, in most cases. In instances where I didn't want to hear another word about something I'd said, though, it was a pain in the ass. I was used to people taking my word as law, so to have someone push the envelope was quite the challenge.

"Your father and Vex haven't made a move to come and collect you. And, quite frankly, I find it odd, which tells me they're planning something. So, I'm not taking any risks." Turning my back on her to search for a clean shirt, I had a sneaking suspicion that the next thing out of her lovely lips was going to send me over the edge.

Call it a hunch, or intuition or whatever the hell.

Completely ignoring my statement about her family, she chose to bring up a topic she knew I would overreact to, yet she did it anyway.

"What about Jagger? He can come and watch out for us to make sure nothing happens."

Every muscle in my body locked up. My blood pressure rose and while I tried to convince myself to calm down, I couldn't help but grind my teeth together to snuff out the volcano erupting inside me.

Whipping around to face her, I moved closer. So close she backed up until she hit the wall, preventing her from escaping my temper. Before I started yelling, she placed her hand on my chest and pled her case. "I know you think there was something going on between us, but you have to believe me, there wasn't. He was a perfect gentleman with me. I swear. I don't have any feelings for him whatsoever. You can trust me." Her eyes stayed glued to mine, a gesture which helped to soothe me. Somewhat.

Gritting my teeth, I ground out my response. "You may not want to fuck Jagger, but trust me when I tell you this, Sully, he wants you. Badly. I saw it in his eyes, and I saw it in his body language when he thought he was protecting you from me. He won't admit it out loud, because he knows I'll snatch his life, but he does," I repeated.

Her hand continued to rest over my heart and I was doing my best not to explode right then, but it was becoming harder the more she pushed me about the prospect.

"But I don't want him, so what does it matter? He doesn't make me feel the way you do." She mumbled her last few words, but I heard them loud and clear. Taking another step closer, my chest brushing against hers, she inhaled a quick breath before leaning her head back against the same wall which held her prisoner to me.

"And how do I make you feel?" I couldn't help myself; she'd opened up the topic, and I was gonna explore it.

"Breathless. Scared. Excited." Her eyes glossed over as if she was going to break down, but I had no idea why. *Am I scaring her right now? Or is she excited?*

"You know I'd never hurt you, right? I may say things from time to time which will hurt your feelings, but I would never do anything to tear you apart." Lifting her chin higher so her lips rested a whisper away from mine, I inhaled her sweet breath. I wanted so badly to claim her mouth, but I hadn't been intimate with a woman like that in what seemed like forever. Although, before our encounter a few days back, I hadn't gone done on a woman in as much time, either.

Her full pink lips trembled, her tongue parting her mouth to wet the very same things I wanted to nibble and taste. Goddamn it! Every reserve I held tight started to weaken and crumble.

Her eyes suddenly closed, and it was then I decided to make my move. "Do you want me to kiss you?" I asked, hoping like hell she said yes. I'd never wanted to taste a woman as much as I did her right then. The suspense tore me apart and just before I was going to make the decision for her, she said the one word I was praying for.

"Yes."

Short and sweet and to the muthafuckin' point.

Without further delay, I crashed my lips to hers. The feeling was incredible, my increasing attraction toward her fueling the blaze of longing inside me. There wasn't an area on her luscious body I didn't wish to devour. And her mouth was the perfect place to start.

She obediently opened up for me, and the first time I felt her gentle tongue caress mine, I almost exploded in my pants I was so worked up. Her fingers grabbed at the fabric of my cut, desperately trying to pull me closer, but if I moved forward any more I was going to crush her to me. But maybe it was exactly what she was looking for, to be melded as one. Or maybe that was what I wanted, to be so lost to her that we became the same person.

"Sully," I groaned, breaking our kiss for the briefest of moments. "You taste unbelievable. Even better than your pussy," I added, with a tilt of my lips I knew she could feel when I kissed her again. Doing my best to dominate her with my kiss, she suddenly flipped the script and was the one who ended up controlling me. I forced my tongue inside her mouth but it was Sully who set the pace, sucking on my intrusion before playfully biting the tip. The woman was driving me mad, and I kicked myself for waiting so long to connect with her like this.

While I wasn't going to push her to let me inside her, I needed to relieve some of the pressure of my cock. Placing my hands under her ass, I lifted her up my body and wrapped her legs around my waist, the wall behind her an added anchor. I would tell her later on how much I preferred her in dresses. Easy access and all that happy shit.

Rubbing myself against her core only made me want her more, but I would stay true to my word and wait until she was ready.

THIRTY-FIVE

Sully

I WAS LOST.

Ripped away was everything I'd ever known, and in its place was a man who both conflicted and excited me.

He made me feel bad for my decision not to have sex with him in his bathroom, although I pretty much led him on by allowing him to go down on me, then again by exciting me with his lips wrapped around my breasts. But when he pulled himself free from his jeans, and started rubbing himself against my core, something told me to wait. I wasn't sure why because I'd wanted him then, but I knew enough to listen to my inner voice, something which had been missing for some time.

And yes, he yelled at me for denying him, but he'd never made a move to take what was rightfully his. By law I was his wife, so I had to give it up whenever my husband wanted it. Right?

Then he'd gone and backed me against the wall in his room at the club. Asking me if I wanted him to kiss me. Of course I did, and I voiced as much, because my inner self told me to go for it.

The hairs of his beard tickled my chin, but that wasn't what I focused on. It was his lips and the way they were making love to my mouth. It was his tongue and the passion he poured forth, letting me know how much he was enjoying me. That I could give him something which he craved was a heady feeling. It was the way his thickness pressed against my core, the slight sting of his rough zipper against my barely clothed body sublime, the slightest friction against my clit mind-numbingly erotic. And it was the way his fingers dug into my soft skin, possessing and claiming me as his.

"I want you so bad," he groaned against my lips. His kiss was amazing, making me feel truly wanted for the first time in my life. Whenever

Vex had kissed me, even in the beginning, it was rough and demanding.

Never gentle.

Never passionate.

Never like this.

It was true I didn't know much about Cole Marek, but I knew enough from the way he tried to protect me that he was a good man. I knew enough from his kiss that he desired me, and I knew enough from the way he talked to me to realize he was conflicted about his feelings for me.

But in a good way.

My instinct told me it was certainly in a good way.

A loud pounding on the door interrupted our little tryst, and it was me who complained by cursing into the air around us. We tried to continue devouring each other with a rawness I'd never experienced before, but whoever was in the hallway wasn't going away anytime soon. So it was best he address the intruder.

"What?" he yelled, before running his tongue along the side of my neck, only to stop to suck on my earlobe, tickling me with his breath when he whispered into my ear, "I wish we were back at my house right now."

"Me too," I confessed, telling him the truth, and in turn basically letting him know I would have given into whatever he wanted to do to me. He looked surprised by my admission, but the look quickly faded into growing agitation toward the person outside his door.

"Marek, open the fuckin' door, man!" Stone yelled through the thick wood. "Looks like I'll be taking these two shopping." He rapped on the door again. "Come on before I change my mind." I heard Adelaide say something to him but I couldn't really focus, not with Cole's mouth still so close to mine again.

"I'm gonna kill him. For real this time." He said the words, but I knew he didn't mean them. I saw the way he was with his VP, and it was like they were true brothers. They shared a special bond, a connection only death's grip could break. So, he could threaten him all he wanted, I knew they were just words said in sexual frustration. It actually made me smile.

"What are you smirking at, woman?" he asked, setting me down to rest on my feet before walking toward the door.

"Nothing," I lied. Watching him move would never get old for me. He possessed a certain swagger when he walked, a dominance which couldn't be taught.

Swinging open the door, he stared at Stone while waiting for him to say something else. A silent message passed between them, and it wasn't until Stone looked at me then back to Cole that I understood what they had communicated. He knew he'd interrupted something big, and his eyes were apologetic, as was his posture.

A couple tense seconds ticked by before anyone spoke. "I'll take them, Marek. You don't have to worry about a thing."

Looking back at me, Cole extended his hand and I readily accepted. He walked me out toward the front door, Adelaide and Stone following close by. Once outside and standing next to Adelaide's blue Honda, she gave up her keys, but not without a few choice words first.

"I'm fully capable of driving, Stone. Don't be so pig-headed." She huffed and puffed, but the look in her eyes while she verbally dueled with the man was very telling. I'd never told anyone what my new friend confessed to me about their 'relationship,' and I never would. Not that I had much choice, seeing as how I only talked to a few people, but I would still never betray her confidence.

"I'm not riding in the passenger seat like some kind of pussy, Addy. Now, stop giving me a hard time about this."

"Well, you could ride in the backseat if you want," she said, smiling because she knew how much her arguing bothered him.

"That's even worse." Opening the passenger door for her, he grumbled, "The man is supposed to drive. Always." As soon as she was completely seated inside the car, she tried to retort, but he closed the door right when she started talking. Chuckling to himself all the way around to the driver's side, he glanced up at us still standing there and said, "Come on, Marek. Say good-bye. I don't want to be gone all goddamn day."

"Fuck you," Cole answered, smiling as he opened the back door for me. Before I stepped a foot inside, he grabbed my waist and pulled me to him. "I'll bring something home for dinner. Then maybe we can watch a movie, if you're up for one." Such a simple plan for tonight, but it meant more to me than I could ever express. It seemed he was trying to turn over a new leaf, and the gesture went a long way in my book. When he placed a lingering kiss on my lips, all I wanted to do was wrap myself up in his arms again, but I knew it had to wait.

We were on the road for a full two minutes before Adelaide or Stone finally spoke. "What the hell was that back there, Sully?" Stone asked, staring at me through the rearview mirror. The confusion on his face was rather comical, and if he hadn't been so serious, I would have laughed.

"What do you mean?" I asked, fidgeting with the hem of my sundress.

"What do you mean, what do I mean? The goddamn kiss. Marek doesn't kiss anyone. Ever," he practically shouted.

"Calm down or you're gonna scare her," Adelaide scolded, hitting him on the arm for good measure. "Jeez, Stone. What the hell's gotten into you?"

"I'll tell you *who* I'd like to get into," he retorted, and had I not known about the two of them his reply would have completely gone over my head.

My friend huffed in the front seat, but when she turned around to check on me, she winked and smiled, masking her expression as soon as she faced front once again.

THIRTY-SIX

Sully

MY DAY WITH ADELAIDE WAS so much fun, more than I think I'd ever had. Her ease, confidence and humor soothed me, bringing out sides of my personality I hadn't even realized existed. Our banter back and forth wasn't forced but simply flowed, although Stone was the one who received the brunt of it when he started complaining we were taking too long.

I'd never had a girlfriend before, and while the dynamics of the relationship were new to me, Adelaide made it very easy.

My father chose to homeschool me my entire life, so I was never surrounded by girls my own age. Yes, our club had gatherings from time to time, and while there were other kids present, I often chose to keep to myself. Either the other kids made fun of me for how black my hair was, calling me a witch, or they'd call me a slut because my body decided to develop early.

When Stone and Adelaide dropped me off back at Cole's, it wasn't until I was standing on the front porch that it even dawned on me that I didn't have a key to his house. I was in mid freak-out, prepared to walk back toward the car to tell them I had no way inside, when the front door opened.

Cole stood on the threshold in nothing but a pair of black sweatpants, holding a white towel and running it back and forth over his wet hair. His bare torso was glorious, every muscle twitching with the exertion to dry himself. The beautiful artwork on his skin danced, and if it wasn't for the sharp burst of the horn behind me, I would have certainly lost time watching his every movement. Daring a glance below his waistline, I noticed the outline of his thickness through his sweats. And while I was utterly turned on, I was also a little wary that Adelaide had seen him as well. It was hard to miss, and I wondered how many other women had the pleasure of sneaking a peak at Cole Marek's goods.

A sudden feeling of jealousy wrapped its ugly arms around me and almost suffocated me. The emotion was foreign, and I had no idea where it had come from. *Is this how he feels when Jagger's around me? Is this why he almost killed him that night? Because if this is the same thing, I don't want any part of it.*

Realizing I was being irrational, I beamed a smile at him as he ushered me inside.

"Did you ladies have fun? I hope Stone behaved himself," he said, walking toward the kitchen to grab a bottled water. After taking a swig, he made a move to pass it to me, but then decided against it at the last minute. "I forgot you don't like to share my germs," he taunted, a smirk resting nicely on his lips.

I'd had the man's tongue in my mouth. What was so bad about sharing a drink with him?

"That's okay. I think I've changed my mind," I responded, reaching out to take the drink. After a satisfying gulp, I handed it back, waiting for his next move.

I wasn't gonna lie; the sight of him half-naked was doing wicked things to my body, and if there was any reservation before today about finally joining with my husband, all fears and concerns were washed clear away. First by his soul-crushing kiss earlier, and then by the feelings firing off inside me from the mere look of him.

"Did you just get out of the shower?"

"Yeah. I just had a quick workout and wanted to wash up before you got home." *Home.* What a weird concept. But he was right. His home was now my home as well, and the sooner I accepted it, the easier things would fall into place.

Leaning against the kitchen counter, Cole kept his eyes on me. His hair was sticking up in a few spots, but he'd never looked sexier. A few beads of water ran down his torso between his strong pecs, disappearing into the waistband of his pants. I watched the liquid vanish, and it wasn't until he coughed that I realized I was blatantly checking him out. Again. A light blush crept over my face, instantly giving away my embarrassment at being caught.

"Like I said before, it's your right to stare at me as much as you want." He grinned and turned around to grab a large white box. "I didn't know what you'd prefer, but everyone loves pizza. Right?"

"I know I do."

"Good." Gesturing toward the small table in the corner of the kitchen, we both sat down and he dished out a slice for me. We ate in silence, our gazes connecting every now and then. Neither one of us knew what to say, plus I was too famished to think about anything other than downing the yummy food in front of me.

Once I'd had my fill, I leaned back in my seat and reached for my drink. He'd finished off his initial water and ended up handing me a fresh one. This one I didn't share, drinking the majority of it after my meal.

"So," he said, startling me from the silence of the room. "What have you heard about my club?" With arms folded across his chest, his biceps popped even more. I itched to feel them wrapped around me again, but all in due time I supposed. He'd started a real conversation, and I would be an idiot not to snag the invitation.

Trying to hide my smile, because I now knew it was bullshit, I revealed the worst thing I'd heard about the Knights Corruption growing up. "Well, I heard that, twice a year, the members of your club were involved in a huge orgy, and at the end, one person was chosen to be sacrificed. The blood of the chosen a gift to ensure the club's prosperity, or some stuff like that." My lips curved up, but quickly fell when Cole leaned forward with a surprised look on his face. At first, I thought I'd said something which was in fact true, but seconds later he frowned before smacking the top of the table, laughter pouring from him in complete hysterics.

"Are you fuckin' shittin' me, woman? That's the kind of crap they told people we did?" His rumble of happiness was music to my ears, never mind that the sight of him smiling was mesmerizing. He was gorgeous. His ice-blue eyes lit up from the inside out, his lips provoking me to jump across the table and bite them, they were so alluring. I'd gotten so lost in the sight of him that I almost missed what he said next. "We only have the orgy once a year, and we sacrifice two people. Tell 'em to get their facts straight," he teased, winking at me while he continued to find amusement in what I'd told him.

A short time later, we found ourselves sitting on the couch. For as intimate as the space was, it was very homey. A single couch, recliner, and end table were the only furniture in the room. A big-screen TV was mounted over a huge fireplace, the beams of the log cabin becoming the second focal point of the home. There were no pictures hung, or any personal effects throughout his house, something I took notice of the first night I stayed there. The color scheme was brown and cream, the lighter color coming from a fleece blanket thrown over the back of the couch, as well as from the few pillows littering the sparse furniture.

"You really need some pictures or something in here," I offered, watching him move about in front of me while he decided which movie to pick.

"Okay. Why don't you pick something out then? Maybe on your next excursion with Adelaide, you can bring something home that you like." His back was turned toward me as he spoke, and while I wanted to look at his face, I wasn't too upset about having to look at the back of him either. He'd thrown on a white T-shirt after dinner, the fabric molding to his body in perfection. If I didn't watch myself, I would literally start drooling.

"How about a scary movie? What do ya think?" he asked, turning around to display a few of the horror movies Adelaide had initially dropped off.

I didn't want to disappoint him, but I knew from experience they weren't my cup of tea. I should have just said no, and asked for a comedy or action film. But instead, without thinking, I blurted out something I should have kept to myself.

"I tried to watch a scary movie with Jagger and I practically ended up in his lap, I was so scared." Initially, I chuckled at the recollection, but my choice of words hit a very tense nerve of his.

Gone was the laid-back look on his face, replaced with a controlled anger. The mere mention of the prospect had his jaw clenching and nostrils flaring, his large hands fisted so tight I thought he was going to lose all feeling in them. "Is that right?" he asked, the clench of his teeth, shouting at me how upset he was, even if he did try to hide it.

The only thing I could do was apologize, so that's exactly what I did. He may not say 'I'm sorry' for anything, but I grew up tasting those words every damn day.

"I'm sorry. I didn't mean anything by it. Honestly. I . . . I just don't like scary movies," I mumbled, hoping like hell he was going to let my slipup go. Turning his back to me once more, he rooted through the box and picked out a different movie, one he didn't show me before sliding it into the DVD player.

Just Friends was the title. One I'd seen with Jagger, but I sure as hell wasn't going to mention his name again.

A half hour into the film and my eyes started to drift close. It'd been a long day, one filled with warring emotions. I'd been scared, confused, aroused, happy, and conflicted, all within the span of twelve hours, and it seemed my body had had enough. Without even realizing, I cuddled closer to Cole's large frame, my hands tucked into my lap while I rested my head on his shoulder. I knew he watched me. I could feel his eyes on me, but I was too exhausted to read into it.

Wanting nothing more than to rest, I closed my eyes for good and gave into the dark slumber beckoning me.

THIRTY-SEVEN

Marek

I FIGURED OUT MY NEW favorite pastime was watching Sully, whether she was awake or off somewhere in dreamland. She'd fallen asleep barely past the beginning of the movie, and I knew it was because she'd had quite the day.

Carrying her sleeping form to our room, I removed her dress and bra and laid her on the bed. Since there was no place I'd rather be, I locked up the house and decided to join her, crawling under the covers and pulling her close to me.

She stirred slightly in her sleep, her lips parting in the softest moans I'd ever heard, but it wasn't clear if she was having a nightmare or dreaming of something naughty. I had my answer when she reached for me and whispered my name, the sound floating in the air above us, waiting to be snatched and held close.

"I'm here," I whispered, pulling her closer. My cock was at full attention, nestled against her plump ass, and it didn't help any when she started moving her hips and grinding her backside into me. Whatever restraint I still had control over was quickly fleeing. I didn't want to take advantage of her, but if she kept that shit up, I was gonna flip her over, spread her luscious thighs wide and take her once and for all.

"Cole . . . please," she cried out, that time louder than before. What was I doing in her dreams? Was I angry with her and she was pleading with me? Or was I teasing her and she wanted more? I couldn't wait to find out, so I shifted our bodies until she was lying flat on her back with me hovering over her, resting on my forearms so as not to crush her delicate form.

Leaning down, I ran my lips over the smooth expanse of her neck, licking, biting and kissing my way up toward her earlobe. "Tell me what you want me to do to you, Sully," I growled, low enough to not scare her, but firm enough to make her comply. When she didn't answer me, I nudged her legs further apart and settled myself in between, the rigidness of my cock brushing over her barely clothed pussy. I thought leaving her panties on would be a deterrent, a barrier to leave her alone while she slept, but everything changed when she called out my name.

Asleep or not, I had to act on that shit.

Softly kissing her jaw, making my way toward those delectable lips, I continued to demand she tell me what she wanted from me. Finally, once I laid my mouth over hers, our breaths melding together as one, she gave me something to work with.

"Cole," she cried out again. "Please take me, make me yours." Instinctually, she wrapped her legs around mine, digging her heels into the backs of my thighs just like I'd imagined she'd do. I could have easily freed myself and taken her, but I needed her to be fully awake for this, give me her permission before I finally claimed what was mine.

I wouldn't steal her passion like some thief in the night.

"Sully . . . Wake up." I kissed her lips once more, grinding myself into her to try and rouse her from sleep. "Sully," I said more harshly. "Wake up, baby."

Her eyelids fluttered open and it took her a few seconds to focus on me, to realize she wasn't still dreaming but was instead staring into the face of the man she'd just been fantasizing about. "Cole?" Confusion painted her lovely face. A beam of moonlight filtered into the otherwise dark room, illuminating her jet-black hair, which was fanned out over her pillow, the starkness of it against her creamy skin a fascinating contrast. Her dark chocolate eyes pinned me, and I was unable to move or speak. I wanted to drown in her gaze, and if she wanted we could stay like this for all eternity.

I was losing my reality with her, and I knew it.

Whatever hold she had over me grew, and I didn't foresee it ever stopping.

"What are you doing?" she asked, licking her lips while her eyes focused on my mouth.

"You were calling my name in your sleep, so I thought I'd wake you," I answered half-truthfully.

"By lying on top of me?" She smiled, the slight tilt of her pink lips entrancing me. Before I could answer, she tightened her legs and ground herself against me, my cock jerking from the pressure. I'd never wanted someone so badly before, and if she didn't give in to me this time, I thought I was literally going to go off the deep end. Dive over the cliff into insanity.

"Do you want me to kiss you again?" I wanted to start small then work my way toward my ultimate goal.

"Yes," she panted, raising her head to take the step before I could. Her soft tongue dueled with mine, the kiss even better than the first time. Although we were new to each other, our passion was an age-old dance, our rhythm falling into place rather quickly.

We teased and enticed.

We demanded and submitted.

We stole each other's hunger and returned it with a fervent desire, the likes of which I'd never felt before.

When I couldn't take it any longer, I dared to ask her the question I hoped she was ready for. "Do you want me to take you? To claim you as mine once and for all?"

An exhale of breath was all it took for her to respond.

No hesitation.

No waiting.

"Yes."

Changing positions so I was on my knees, I reached for the thin material around her hips and drew the fabric down over her legs, discarding them once they reached her ankles. Needing to savor the moment, I teased her skin with my mouth, working my way from her feet up to her knees, then finally resting just below the one place I wanted to bury myself. Raining light kisses all over her heated flesh, I brought my hand up to play with her, stretching her apart with two of my fingers, pumping in and out of her sweet pussy, my vision blurring with lust.

"Oh, God, Cole . . . Yes," she gasped, writhing under me and gripping the sheets in ecstasy.

Wanting to taste her desire for me once again, I licked her slowly, reveling in the way my touch made her feel. She cried out, calling my name over and over again until she finally clenched on my fingers and rode out her orgasm, my lips wrapped around her clit to draw out every last drop of pleasure.

Her satisfaction painted my face when I finally crawled up her body, pushed my sweats the rest of the way off, gripped myself and teased her opening with my thickness.

"Are you on any kind of birth control?" I inquired, praying she was so I could take her bare. I had condoms readily available, though, just in case.

A quick look of sadness infiltrated her eyes, putting me on guard instantly. "No, but I can't have kids anyway. So. . . ." She stopped talking, a sudden embarrassment stealing the rest of what she was going to say.

"How do you know that?"

"Trust me. I can't get pregnant." She turned her head so I couldn't see her beautiful browns. "Please don't make me talk about it right now," she pleaded.

I would get to the bottom of *that* statement, but I agreed with her, now wasn't the time. Instead, I chose to make sure this was what she wanted, asking her again for her consent.

She turned her head back to look at me and gave me a simple nod, a bite of her lip showing me she was ready and willing.

Pushing myself inside her, inch by agonizingly slow inch, was the best feeling in the world. Her tight walls gripped me like a fist, strangling the pleasure out of me before I even started. Making sure to take it slow so I didn't explode too soon, I stopped halfway in and leaned down to kiss her.

"I can't move right now or I'm gonna be done before I even start." I was in the middle of counting in my head when she thrust her hips up toward me, sheathing more of me than I was ready to give. "Fuck!" I yelled. It was another five controlled breaths before I was ready to stake my claim on her. Possess her with everything clamoring inside me.

"Goddamn it! You're too tight," I groaned, throwing her leg over my waist to open her up some more.

"Does it not feel good?" she worried, her fingers gripping my arms while I bucked into her.

"It feels *too* good. That's the problem."

"That doesn't sound like a problem at all," she said, her quiet laughter dying when I pulled out and pushed back inside her roughly. "Oooooo . . . Oh, my God . . . Do that again," she demanded.

Of course I gave her what she wanted.

Over and over, and over again.

Ten minutes and a lot of exertion later, I could tell she was close to detonating. Her moans had become more intense, her demands on my body more aggressive. I would have never pegged her for someone who would take such an active role during sex, her otherwise quiet demeanor indicating quite the contrary.

Pinning her hands above her head, I thrust deeper, letting go of the last strand of my control, punishing her body with my own, driving out every last cry and plea from her throat. Reveling in her pleasure, a cocky grin spread across my face as I nipped at her bottom lip, demanding entrance into her tempting mouth.

"Sully . . . I . . . I can't hold out any longer. Fuck! You're too much," I growled, pushing her further up the bed with my intensity.

"Make me come." She writhed beneath me, flexing her hands in my hold. Wrapping my free arm around her waist, I held her back off the bed and drove into her like some kind of wild animal, shouting out her name as soon as I felt her pussy clench around me, shivers of bliss firing off inside both of us. My vision actually went hazy, chasing after my own goddamn air just so I could breathe.

I buried my head in the crook of her neck, waiting while I came back down to reality. Licking at her salty skin, I realized right then that I would never get enough of her.

Her mouth.

Her skin.

Her pussy.

Just . . . her.

Everything about her called to me, and not strictly in the carnal way. Something inside her spoke to me. It was unknown what she was trying to tell me, but in due time I knew I would uncover the unspoken messages.

THIRTY-EIGHT

Sully

LYING FULLY SATED IN COLE'S arms was like a dream, the connection between us more than physical. Granted, we didn't really know each other that well—yet—but there was an undeniable attraction pulling us together. While he was the most beautiful man I'd ever laid eyes on, there was something within him which beckoned to me.

I felt it when he looked at me.

I felt it when he touched me.

I felt it when he called out my name.

The pain he tried to shield from me broke free when he thought I wasn't paying attention, his vulnerability where I was concerned teetering between awareness and obscurity.

My ears pricked to listen to his breathing, trying to determine whether or not he'd drifted off to sleep. He'd taken me twice more, once on top of the bathroom vanity and again in the shower. Each time was more exhilarating than the last, my fear of my new life abandoning me as I gazed into the promise of my future. Although my new husband had upset me with his words on occasion, I knew it was simply because he didn't know how to act.

Was I making excuses for his behavior? Yes.

Did I understand what it was like to have my world flipped on its ass, scrambling around to try and make sense of Fate's warped sense of humor?

Absolutely.

Although Cole Marek was the man who'd kidnapped me, he was the same man who'd essentially saved my life.

He'd forgotten to shut off the bedside light, its soft illumination dancing over his relaxed form. Propping my head on his chest, I stared up into his handsome face. His eyelids fluttered in his sleep, a half-smirk resting on his full and inviting lips. Breaths of soft, warm air hit my cheek, while his heart fell into a steady, easy rhythm. His body heat warmed me. The only thing we had draped over us was a thin sheet, the rest of the blankets were strewn over the bed in a crumpled mess, but I was nice and cozy lying half on top of him.

"If you don't stop admiring me, I'm going to be forced to take you yet again," he muttered, startling me from fantasizing about that very same thing.

"I thought you were sleeping." When I tried to move, he quickly changed positions until he had me pinned beneath him. As soon as I was on my back, I spread my legs wide so he could snuggle in between. The man was insatiable, but I quickly realized I was too.

"How can I sleep with you next to me? I'd be a fool to waste one precious second dreaming of you when I could have the real thing right now." He grinned, his self-assuredness quite the turn on.

To be desired, truly coveted, was the most intoxicating feeling in the world. I'd never had anyone look at me the way he did, even when he was upset with me, or confused about our new situation together. His blue eyes pierced me with the knowledge that he'd come to save me. Whether he was aware of it or not, I wasn't sure, but his soul spoke to mine.

His lips traced a line from my collarbone to my ear, a place he loved to tease with his tongue before making me break out in goose bumps, the contrast of wet skin against warm breath enough to make me squirm in delight.

"I wanna ask you something, and I pray you've come to trust me enough to tell me the truth," he prodded, his soft kisses on my skin a distraction to what was coming next.

Did I trust him?

I was beginning to.

Was I afraid of what he was going to ask me to reveal?

Unequivocally.

He withdrew his body from mine and sat back on the bed, pulling me up until I was in a seated position myself. *I can only imagine what he's going to ask me.*

"Earlier tonight, when I asked you if you were on the pill, you told me you couldn't have kids, to not worry about it. When I tried to ask you to elaborate, you shut down, a sadness filling your eyes I've unfortunately seen before."

I noticeably stiffened, preparing myself for the conversation he was going to force me to have.

I'd only told Cole a few things about what I'd experienced at the hands of Vex and my father, but he didn't know the half of it. Shit, he didn't even know a quarter of it, if I was being honest. He'd seen the scars covering my body, and I'd told him how some of them got there, but there was so much more to my story. A story I was ready to burn in the hottest fire, then watch as the embers of my tragic past floated away on the wind.

Instead of delving too far into the past, I decided to give him part of the truth. Steeling my nerves, my eyes flitted over his face but avoided his eyes. I knew if I looked directly at him, I would weaken and falter. I'd end up pushing myself back into the darkest parts of my mind, a place I never wanted to venture into again.

"Well," he prompted. "How do you know you can't have kids? You're a young woman, around twenty or so, right?" It was funny he wasn't sure, and I wasn't positive of his age either, yet there we were, sitting across from each other on the bed after a night of passion. Newly married and still discovering the little details about each other. "So what makes you think you can't pop out a few rugrats?" He grinned, his smile softening his callous choice of words.

Wrapping the sheet tighter around me so I wasn't so vulnerable, I fidgeted with my hands while I tried to find the right words. His stare burned through me and I knew he wouldn't wait long for me to respond, patience definitely not his strong suit.

I stared at my hands while I spoke, an action he didn't approve of; his finger moved to lift my chin so he could see my eyes. Taking the deepest breath, my anxiety expelling from me in waves, I mustered up enough strength to start.

"A few years ago, I was bl-bleeding pretty badly, so I was taken to the hospital. My father refused at first because he didn't want any outsiders in our business, but when he saw how bad I was, he reluctantly agreed." I tried to look away again, but his hold on my chin was strong. "The doctor told me there was too much damage, that the chances of me having kids were so minute, I would have more luck being struck by lightning. Twice." A lone tear escaped and trickled down my cheek. I hated that my past still terrified me, but I hadn't been in the company of the Knights Corruption very long. Even if they were basically keeping me safe and sound from my own club.

I hadn't allowed myself to give into the paranoia of what Cole had mentioned earlier, about being on guard and waiting for the Savage Reapers to come and collect what was rightfully theirs.

Me.

"But I don't understand. Why was there any damage to begin with?" His question was sincere, but his eyes told me he knew the worst part of the story was yet to come. By the look of expectancy on his face, he knew *who* was the cause of my dreadful tale.

I couldn't help it.

I broke.

"Cole . . . please," I begged. "Don't make me. . . ." I couldn't finish, my body shaking while tears streamed down my face. He'd finally released his hold on my chin, his body closing in on me and bringing me in for a hug.

"It's okay, Sully. No one will ever hurt you again," he promised, holding me so close he almost crushed me in his arms. "But I need to know. You have to tell me."

"Why?" I cried, pushing myself away from him. "Why do I have to tell you? Why do you want me to relive it? Why can't you just let it go?" I wanted to run, to barricade myself inside the bathroom for the rest of my life. I was ashamed and mortified that he was going to find out yet another awful thing that happened to me. Pity wasn't something I thought I could bear. Not from him.

He made a move toward me but I only backed up, desperately needing the added space if I was going to continue. Although I didn't think I would be able to.

"Because," he seethed, "when I finally put a bullet between their eyes, I wanna make sure they know *all* the reasons their lives are being snatched from them. Trust me, there's a long list as it stands, but to know their fate was sealed because of the damage they did to one of their own, will sink their souls into the deepest pits of Hell."

He said 'their eyes.' There was no mistaking he was talking about my father and the guy who'd tortured me for six long years. Vex.

Rising from the bed, I walked toward the window, moonlight slicing through and adding to the barest of light already encasing the room. I knew in my heart there was no escape from this.

Like a Band-Aid. Right off.

With my back toward him, I finished my story as quickly as I could.

"Vex had gone on a bender for a few days, shoving so much coke up his nose I'm surprised he was still alive. Never mind whatever else he'd ingested to help him fight off his demons. I was tucked away inside our bedroom, keeping to myself, but for some reason he thought I was messing around on him. His paranoia strangled him and no matter how much I pleaded, trying to make him see reason, he was convinced I'd been with someone else. Of course I wasn't, but there was no getting through to him.

"During one of his rants, he attacked me, smacking my head against the wall before shoving me onto the bed. My head was killing me, preventing me from trying to protect myself, but in the end I guess it didn't really matter. He always got what he wanted, no matter how much I fought in the beginning. Screaming at me that he was gonna make me pay for fucking around, he tied me to the bed, the rope so tight it cut into my skin whenever I tried to move." My shoulders trembled, but I steeled my reserve as best I could before continuing. "He raped me over and over. Violently. He left me tied up for two days, and when I'd made a mess because he refused to let me use the bathroom, he . . . he. . . ." I hiccupped, not thinking I could finish. Thankfully, Cole kept his distance, otherwise, I would have refused to continue. I needed the space. It was just easier that way. Well . . . 'easier' was probably the wrong choice of word.

"When his body was depleted, he raped me with anything he could find. His beer bottle. An old baseball bat he had in the closet. It went on for what seemed like forever, and no matter how much I begged and screamed, he never relented. I knew my father was aware something was going on because I heard them talking outside our bedroom, Vex telling him he was teaching me a lesson. I tried to call for help, but I was too beaten and broken." The horrific details rushed over me, prickling my flesh like the sharpest of blades.

Tears streamed down my face, my memories like a plague on my soul.

"He left me to bleed like an animal for a whole day, tied to the bed." Turning to face Cole, I needed to see his reaction. I knew he was going to be angry, infuriated even, but I had no idea how much rage one person could muster inside them.

His eyes turned dark, his skin heating like he was on fire from the inside. He stood before me a man ready to kill and right then, I knew he would never let anything bad ever happen to me again. Although he'd forced me to relive one of the worst things to ever happen to me, it made me realize I was no longer in danger, that the man before me would do whatever it took to keep me safe.

Closing the short distance between us, he took me in his arms and vowed to end the men who'd kept me a prisoner my entire life, beating and degrading me for their own amusement, suffocating whatever life burned inside me until they all but snuffed out my essence.

THIRTY-NINE

Marek

A MONTH HAD PASSED SINCE Sully told me what Vex had done to her. It had taken everything in me not to gather my men and hunt him down like the animal he was in that time.

Realizing I *was* gonna kill him one day—probably sooner than later—gave me solace. It wasn't much, but it was something I could cling to until the day arrived.

"Let's go!" I shouted from the living room. "We're gonna be late, goddamn it!" Not that I should care, but I was a stickler for punctuality, and the fact that the club cookout had started forty-five minutes ago and I was still waiting for Sully to finish getting ready was grating on me.

When I wasn't involved with the club, I spent every available second with my wife, ravaging her and making her scream out my name. She'd finally become comfortable with me, laughing when I playfully teased her, as well as dishing out her own form of medicine. I'd opened up a bit more about my past, as she did hers. I knew she still kept things from me, but I vowed not to push her anymore. Not until she was ready.

That the woman was still alive and going strong was a testament to how strong she was, having faced the Devil and spit in his face.

Every day that passed was one step closer to happiness. I hadn't realized when I snatched her from the pits of Hell that she would change me. It'd been a long time since I'd had a purpose in life, other than plotting the downfall of my enemy and taking my club legit. And while both things drove me each day, they were nothing compared to the woman I'd forced to marry me, thinking at the time it was just the perfect 'fuck you' to the Savage Reapers.

It was the first time in my life I felt whole, if that made any sense. My need to protect and watch over her was sometimes suffocating, probably because I'd never possessed such a need before. Yes, I strived to keep all my brothers alive, watching their backs as they did mine. But they didn't play on a loop in my head, wondering if they were happy, if someone was going to come and snatch them from my life. They were all adults, knew the risk involved, a risk which would hopefully diminish to nothing once we were out from underneath the cartel.

"Woman, if you don't show yourself in the next two seconds, I'm comin' in there and draggin' you out as you are. I don't care if your half-naked or not." I tried to be patient, but it just wasn't in me. I had a temper, and Sully had witnessed it on more than one occasion. Lately, she paid me no attention when I started spouting off at the mouth, our comfort level with each other rivaling those who'd been together for years. It was odd, thinking I'd only known her for a short time, yet I felt as if she'd always been with me.

Like I'd always been waiting for her.

"Don't get your panties in a bunch, Marek," she teased, appearing on the threshold of the living room, a sultry smile lighting up her face. She called me by the name she knew before she was aware of my given name during those times when she was either upset with me, or trying to ruffle my feathers. Like now.

"Oh, hell no!" I shouted, already crushing the distance between us and shoving her back toward our room. Her look of surprise was apparent, but I never gave her an opportunity to question me until she was planted in the middle of our bedroom.

"I thought you were yelling at me to hurry up. Well . . . I'm done." With her hands on her hips, she asked, "Why are you making us even more late?" She had to know there was no way I was letting her out of the house dressed in that skimpy-ass outfit.

She'd told me about how she was forced to dress when she was with Vex, always wearing baggy clothes for fear he would beat her for wearing something that actually fit. I never wanted to stifle her and make her feel as if she couldn't express herself, and the majority of the time, I didn't have much of a problem with the clothes she wore, dragging many a bag through the front door after a shopping trip with Adelaide. One of my men always accompanied them on their outings and while they complained, Sully knew I was protecting her, still not having heard a peep from the Savage Reapers. Every passing day only put me on guard that much more.

"Are you kidding me with what you have on right now?" I asked, feeling a mixture of incredulity and irritation. Her plain white tank top dipped in the front, showing off the cups of her bra, which were fucking purple. Every bastard's eyes would be ogling her tits, therefore forcing me to mess somebody up.

Her shorts were short, like *really* short, and because she'd thrown on sandals with a huge heel—I think she called them wedges or some shit like that—they made her legs look long . . . and her shorts minuscule.

I could only handle one thing at a time.

Taking a quick once-over of her reflection, spinning around to make sure she wasn't missing anything, she asked, "What's wrong with what I have on? It's hot outside, Cole. I'll probably still be dying in what I have on." It *was* rather hot outside, the California summer kicking it up with record highs. Her hair was pulled up into a messy bun resting on top of her head, no doubt preparing as much as she could for the stifling temperatures.

"I can't do it," I said, rifling through the closet to find her something else to put on. "You know I wouldn't normally tell you what to wear, but this is too tempting, Sully. The guys are gonna be drinking, and if any one of them looks at you too long, I'm gonna end up punching them the hell out."

"Oh, you're just overreacting," she admonished, moving to walk away from me. "Come on, let's go. Everything will be fine." When I didn't budge, she turned around and raised her brows at me, waiting for me to come to my senses and follow behind her.

"I'm not budging, woman," I gritted, reaching into one of her shopping bags and pulling out a thin strapped dress which still had the tags on it. While it was short, it was much better than what she was prancing around in. The dress was a cream color with a thick red stripe in the middle. It was nice. She'd obviously liked it if she bought it. Well, technically, I'd given her money to buy it, but who's fussing over logistics? "Here, put this on?"

The Sully who was forced into the Knights Corruption would have never said a word, taken the dress and changed immediately. But the longer she was with me, the more comfortable she was in expressing her thoughts and opinions, which was a good thing.

Most of the time.

But it was times like this when her newly formed strong will was a pain in my ass. And even though she tried my patience now and again, when it boiled down to it, I was her man, her husband, and as such had the final word. Most times I let her go, but when I felt strongly about something, whatever I deemed was law.

And this was one such time.

She stalked forward, stopping when she was a few feet away from me. "Are you serious?"

"Very."

We stared at each other, a battle of wills passing between us. But I wasn't relenting. After twenty tense seconds, she snatched the dress from my hand and stomped toward the bathroom, cursing under her breath the entire time.

"You can change out here, sweetheart," I teased. She slammed the door behind her before I could say anything else.

I thought it was the quickest she'd ever changed, emerging two minutes later. She was trying not to smile, but her sexy lips twitched while she watched for my reaction.

"Motherfucker!" I cursed. "That's almost as bad," I confessed, running my eyes up and down her seductive body. I had no idea the top of the dress was so form-fitting, and while the fabric flared out at her waist, it only came down to mid-thigh, those same damn sandals making her legs look like they went on for miles.

She looked beautiful. Too beautiful to be hanging around a bunch of horny bastards.

"I'm not changing again, Cole. There's nothing wrong with this dress and you know it."

Glancing at the clock, I mumbled under my breath as I took her arm and guided her out the door.

I'm gonna kill someone today. I just know it.

———◆———

"HOW LONG BEFORE YOU DECIDE it's time, Prez?" Zip drunkenly shouted, his body swaying into Hawke, who'd been standing next to him to hold him upright.

"Calm down, man. Not here. Save that shit for Chambers," Stone grated, his patience for the young member's hot temper waning. His cold stare shut Zip up just as he was about to spout off again. The boy was constantly itching to settle unpaid debts between the two clubs, only ever knowing about the destruction they'd caused in the past couple years against his brothers. He had no idea just how far back it went.

Motioning to Hawke, I tried to dispel any further rantings from Zip. It was a day for relaxation, a cookout in full swing as the sun dipped low in the horizon. "Go find him someone to occupy his time," I demanded, jerking my head toward the small group of females huddled together across the compound. "And make sure you don't offer yourself up as well, seeing as how Edana will be here any second." He laughed, but I gripped him by his collar. "I mean it, Hawke. I don't need her freakin' out. Can't handle that today."

"Don't worry. I'll be on my best behavior." He saluted, winking as he turned a staggering Zip toward the laughter of one of his future bedmates.

"I'll believe that when I see it," I muttered, taking a pull of my beer while I watched them walk away.

It was days like this that reminded me of who I was, what I was in charge of. Looking around the wide open space, the confines of the large metal gates keeping us safe, I watched as people enjoyed themselves, filling up their plates while they caught up with people they hadn't seen in some time.

Our cookouts were a time to chill and appreciate what was real in life, family and friends being the most important. Although, in our crew, friends *were* family. We had a few people who didn't always see eye to eye—Trigger and Stone being the two men who jumped to the forefront of my mind at the moment—but everyone here would take a bullet for the person standing next to them. Women included.

To be an old lady of one of the men, they had to love and embrace the club, and everything that went along with it. Good and bad. And that was a hard thing if someone didn't grow up in this life, which was why most outsiders weren't built for it. The only person I knew of who wasn't fully integrated, yet was around us from time to time, was Adelaide.

I knew something was brewing between her and my VP, and the best of luck to them for trying to figure it the hell out. There was many an obstacle in the way, her uncle only being one of them. But my boy deserved to be happy.

Speak of the devil and he shall appear. "Hey," Stone greeted, bumping my shoulder with his as he took a seat next to me. "Party's good. Weather's nice," he assessed. "And Sully sure looks hot as fuck."

It took me a quick second for his words to penetrate, and when they did I offered the only retort that would hit him right back.

"Adelaide sure looks tasty," I said, watching his expression fade from amusement to shock.

Then controlled anger.

The smirk I threw his way played with him until he cursed out loud and rose from his seat, making a quick beeline toward the woman I'd teased him about. He was becoming so predictable when it came to her, and if he wasn't careful, it was gonna bite him in the ass.

My eyes roved through the large crowd, men laughing and drinking, women gathering together to no doubt talk about the men, and children zig-zagging between the adults as their screams of happiness broke through the air.

A light tap on my shoulder made me turn my head to the right. Sully sat beside me before I fully realized it was her who'd called my attention. "Are you having fun, *Prez?*" She laughed, her beautiful eyes studying my face as if she were never gonna see me again and wanted to remember every line. When her gaze landed on my mouth, she bit her lip and fidgeted in her seat. The heat from her body warmed me, even though we were both already baking in the sun.

Her hands rested in her lap, her fingers clenched tightly to the hem of her short dress. Daring to sneak a peek at her exposed legs, my pants had suddenly become quite the hindrance. All I wanted to do was whisk her away and thrust inside her, making her scream my name, no matter if she was heard or not. But I'd not taken my hands off her for the past month, and it was as good a time as any to practice restraint.

"I'm good," I answered, finishing off the last of my beer. "Are you?"

"Yeah," she said, taking a quick look around. "I really am." She smiled wide and my heart flipped. Sully had been so reserved when she'd first come here, and rightfully so. I'd plucked her from her life and shoved her into a world she'd feared as long as she could remember. But my actions, as well as my club's, had proved she was safe with us, and every day since I'd seen her come alive. Breathing in the air as if it were truly a gift. I saw the world differently through her eyes. I appreciated the little things because, in a way, she was experiencing them for the first time herself. No matter if it was a walk along my property on a nice day, or running a mundane task such as grocery shopping, she treated each excursion as if it was the biggest deal. And for her, it was. She hadn't been allowed off her compound much at all, the world around her taunting and excluding her from a life she would never know.

Leaning in to give her a lingering kiss, her tongue captured mine and for a brief moment, our surroundings faded into obscurity. When we finally pulled back, I heard a round of gasps and someone whistled off in the distance. Turning toward the noise, I shook my head and huffed, the eyes of everyone attending glued to me and Sully.

"The hell you all lookin' at?" I yelled, a genuine smile on my face for the first time in what seemed like forever.

The woman to my right the sole reason for it.

FORTY

Sully

"COME ON, SULLY. WE'LL BE right back," Adelaide promised, snatching my hand in hers and pulling me toward her car. The sky had darkened, most of the KC members well on their way to not remembering the gathering. "It's just two little blocks down that way." She pointed to her right. "We'll be back before they even know we're gone." She smiled, and her expression was contagious.

"I don't know. If Cole finds out, he'll be pissed, not to mention it's still not safe." I bit my lip on the last word, watching my friend closely.

"Not safe from what?" she asked, tipping her head to the side.

Even though Adelaide and I were fast becoming close, I still held how I'd come to be there safeguarded. She would inundate me with questions, ones I couldn't even begin to know how to answer. Not wanting to taint her image of me, or put her in harm's way, I chose to keep my mouth shut.

"Just in general," I lied. "It's getting dark, and there are unsavory people lurking around every corner."

She shook her head in amusement and dragged me toward her car. "Come on. I have an unhealthy craving for nachos and cheese and they ran out a while ago. Plus, we could use a couple more bags of ice." Trying to convince me to go with her, she added, "Wait and see. They'll all be happy we had the foresight to think ahead, their beer warming as we speak."

"It's only two blocks away? And we'll be right back?" I prompted.

"Promise."

"Okay," I conceded.

She had to threaten the men guarding the gate, using her uncle as bait. I laughed every time she did it because the expression on the men's faces never failed to be priceless.

In my nervousness, I continually played with my wedding band, twisting it around and around, counting the seconds until we were back inside the KC compound. Uneasy about upsetting Cole was second only to the fear of my club kidnapping me right back from their sworn enemy. Then I could kiss everything good-bye.

Cole.

Adelaide.

My life.

Pulling into the parking lot, we both quickly exited the vehicle, my eyes searching our surroundings to make sure we were safe. We walked into the store and immediately noticed only two other people inside, and they were both women. "I'll grab the ice while you get what you need," I told her, making a beeline toward the freezer area. Opening the door, the cold waft of air hit me, instantly making me shiver. As I searched, I heard the ding of the bell over the front entrance. Tossing some damaged ice bags aside, I finally found what I was looking for.

Standing up, I allowed the freezer door to slowly close in front of me, gripping a bag in each hand and thinking about how much better I'd feel once we joined the party again.

Raising my head, I caught my reflection in the door, and in that split second I saw a man standing behind me. The image was quick, but there was no mistaking the one person who'd damaged me for years, torturing me for his own sick amusement and making me wish every day that fate would step in and take me from this cold world.

"Hello, *sweetheart*," he rasped, his voice pure evil. There was no time to defend myself, or to even scream for that matter. Painfully bruising my arm with his fingers, Vex leaned in closer and threatened me—not that his mere presence wasn't making me tremble already. A sharp pain erupted in my midsection, and it only took me a moment to realize he'd roughly shoved a gun into my ribs. "Make one sound and I'll kill that little bitch you came in here with. First, I'll make you watch me torture her, then I'll blow her fucking brains out."

I reacted quickly. "I don't know her. We just walked into the store together." Having no idea how long he'd been watching me, I tried to call his bluff.

"Nice try. But I've been watching you for quite some time. I know she's a friend of yours, just like I know it'll rip your heart out to watch her life slip from her . . . all because of you."

Shit! What was I going to do? The last thing I wanted was to put my friend's life in danger, but I knew if Vex walked me out of this store, I'd end up dead by his hands.

Or my father's.

The bags of ice dropped to my feet and hit the ground, barely making a noise. Adelaide was not where I could see her. I prayed she didn't show herself because, if she did, my situation would certainly become more precarious.

"Vex, please," I pleaded, which only earned me instant bruises on my arms from his grip as well as my side from the muzzle of his gun.

"Speak again, bitch, and I'll shoot you where you stand," he sneered. Tears instantly welled and my thoughts ran a million miles a second. More people suddenly filtered into the small store, and it was then he chose to make his move. "Don't come willingly and I'll make good on killing her. Test me."

The thing was I didn't need to test him. He was crazy enough to walk right up to her in front of witnesses and shoot her dead. Sanity had left Vex a long time ago; in its place was madness, worsening every day.

I had no idea why my father kept him around as long as he did. Actually, that was a lie. I *did* know why, but it still wasn't a good enough reason to excuse his recent behaviors.

Vex's father, Manny, had been my father's best friend, until he went and got himself killed, dealing on the side and hiding the profits away from the supplier. When my father tried to right the wrong and exact revenge for Manny's death, he put himself right into harm's way. It was Vex who'd rescued him, hence making him put up with his crazy shit for years. There were times I thought my father would say fuck it and put a bullet in Vex, but he never fatally punished him. It was during those times, where there didn't seem to be any consequences, that I used to think crazy needs crazy, and that my father would be lost in a way without Vex's instability.

Hell, Vex's unsettling nature probably made my father feel somewhat normal.

Yanked back into the horridness of the situation, I prayed for more time to come up with a plan of escape. But it wasn't to be. Vex found his chance to steal me when three young kids tripped into the store, drunk and causing a much-needed distraction. Ushering me quickly toward the front door, he shoved me through first, his gun still digging into my sensitive flesh. I never even tried to look for Adelaide, for fear she would see me and jump to my defense.

Once we'd made it outside, we walked toward the back of the building and straight toward a beat-up car. Throwing open the trunk, he shoved me inside before I could even think about protesting, even though I knew any resistance was futile.

I decided right then and there to save all of my strength.

I was going to need it if I hoped to die with any kind of dignity.

FORTY-ONE

Marek

"LET ME IN!" I HEARD a woman scream, her voice becoming shriller the more she was denied access into Chambers. Everyone knew women weren't allowed behind these closed doors, the only exception being when we made a back room into a makeshift operating area for Tripp, and Adelaide was the only one attending to him. Once he was well enough to reside in one of the regular bedrooms, he'd been moved.

"You know you're not allowed back there," one of my men called out, but the thickness of the doors muffled their voices enough that I couldn't tell who'd said it, nor who the female was who was trying so desperately to push past them.

I heard scuffling, then a fierce pounding on the door, followed by more shouting.

"What the hell?" I grumbled, catching Stone's focus while I rose from my seat. I'd pulled him behind closed doors a few minutes prior to discuss the phone call I'd received from Yanez. He told me they would be stopping by our club in the next week to finalize all details, something I thought we'd already done through him, but I guessed his boss wanted to speak to us face-to-face. I wasn't opposed to talking to Carrillo, finally being able to see his face while he promised me once again that my club could walk away from the cartel. It was just one more thing I had to oversee and handle to ensure the safety of my men.

But that was what I'd signed on for when I accepted the gavel, I supposed.

The handle turned with such vigor I was surprised it hadn't popped off altogether. Whoever was on the other side was adamant about getting in, and my curiosity as well as my anger rose with every heartbeat.

"Adelaide, calm down!" the man shouted, who I soon realized was none other than her uncle, Trigger. And for him to be restraining her from entering meant something serious was going on.

My mind instantly shot to Sully for some reason, if only because I knew how close the two women had become. Calming my thoughts, I settled on that she was probably trying so hard because Stone was with me. As soon as the thought breathed to life, I shoved it aside, realizing Adelaide wasn't like the women I'd had normal dealings with. She didn't seem to overreact to situations, instead being the calm one everyone gathered around to seek the same kind of serenity in times of panic. Tripp's situation being one such time.

As soon as her name drifted out of Trigger's mouth, Stone jumped to his feet and flew toward the locked door, twisting the handle and throwing it open. Adelaide looked frenzied, her wild eyes searching for someone. They landed on Stone first, passing him an unspoken message before shoving past him and toward me. My heart raced, the hairs on the back of my neck bristling with worried anticipation.

"Marek," she cried out, crushing the rest of the distance between us until she stood two feet from me. "Sh-she's g-gone," she hiccupped, tears breaking free and trembling down her reddened cheeks. "W-we were in the store . . . th-then she was gone." Her hysterics heightened my worry, but she was speaking so fast I could hardly make out what she was saying.

Grabbing her arms, I steeled her shuddering body and tried to calm her enough for her to make some goddamn sense. "Who's gone, Adelaide? What the hell are you talking about?" As far as I was aware, she hadn't gone off the compound, so talk of a store was ludicrous.

"It's all my fault," she offered, a hint of hysterics washing over her while she continued to plead with me. "You have to go find her, Marek. You have to go now," she urged, pulling from my grip and taking a step back. Stone was at her back. As soon as she sensed he was near, she turned around and wrapped her arms around his waist, finding comfort in his embrace. Trigger noticed and took a step forward, his fists clenched like he was ready for battle.

One look from me, however, and her uncle stopped all movement. He was smart enough to realize his temper wasn't welcome right then. Reservation smothered him as he kept his fury in check, forcing himself to focus on the bigger threat.

Turning Adelaide around in Stone's hold, I held her gaze while I asked for the last time, "Who are you talking about?" I knew, but I needed to hear her name fall from Adelaide's mouth to unfortunately confirm it.

"Sully." She tried to wipe away her tears but they kept falling. Finally, she gave up, her shoulders slumping forward in defeat. "I'd convinced her to run to the store with me and now . . . she's . . . she's gone. I couldn't find her anywhere." Her lips quivered. She was trying to be strong but she failed. Big time. "I'm so sorry, Marek," she confessed.

"Why did you go off the compound, Adelaide?" I yelled, all of my reserve suddenly gone. I could no longer control my rage, taking a single step toward the woman telling me the horrible news about my wife. Both Stone and Trigger stiffened, prepared for anything now that my stance threatened their woman, their family. "I specifically told you she wasn't allowed to go ANYWHERE without one of us. What the FUCK!" I'd never been so incensed and so frightened all at the same time.

"I'm sorry," she repeated. "The store was only two blocks away, and I really didn't think there would be any harm. We'd be back before anyone even knew we were gone."

"And now they have her!" I roared, my entire body set to explode. Stone stepped forward, shoving Adelaide behind him toward her uncle. Jerking his head in the older man's direction, Trigger ushered his niece out of Chambers, slamming the door behind him before I really lost it.

"Shit!" Stone rumbled, shoving his hand through his dark blond hair. His distress was enough to put me even more on edge, realizing the direness of the situation. I knew the Savage Reapers weren't gonna let this go. And now that they had her back in their grips, not only would they torture her, but they were most likely gonna kill her, especially after finding out I made her marry me.

It took me all of one minute to devise a plan, albeit a haphazard, careless one. But it was a plan nonetheless. We would storm into wherever she was being held and kill every fucker we came across. It was gonna be a bloodbath.

As soon as I shared my plan with Stone, he froze.

"Marek, we can't go in there guns blazin'. For one, we have no idea where they took her. Second of all, we can't risk the lives of every brother here just to get her back." The last word hadn't left his lips before I slammed him against the wall.

"She's my wife," I seethed, pushing my forearm further into his throat. Stone was a big guy, and although I didn't want to hurt my best friend, I needed for him to feel my rage.

"Yeah? So what?" he dared to retort. "She's your wife because you forced her to marry you. You're just pissed because those bastards bested you." Pulling back, I straightened myself until I was no longer leaning into him, but instead standing tall in front of him. Toe to toe. His eyes widened at my reaction. A swift tick of the clock passed before my right fist connected with his face. His head turned, but of course the force of my punch didn't hurt him. It was times like this when I hated that he couldn't feel any pain.

His shock, however, was satisfaction enough.

It had to be.

Pinning me with his glare, he said, "What the hell was that for?" There was no rubbing of his jaw to soothe the pain, but there was a trickle of blood which covered the corner of his lip. He felt the moisture, wiping it away before it dripped onto his white T-shirt.

"She's my wife," I repeated. "Therefore, she belongs to me." So many emotions battled together. Hurt, anger, confusion . . . but mostly fright. I was scared for Sully, and the longer we stood there arguing, the longer she was subjected to her club, mainly Vex and her father, Psych.

A pained expression washed over me. My eyes had become glassy, a reaction I had no control over. Fists clenched and nostrils flaring, I retreated until my back hit the wall. I hung my head so my VP couldn't see the expression on my face. Hell, I wasn't even sure what was happening to me. Clutching my chest, I tried to assuage the tightness, instinctually rubbing the area closest to my heart.

"Oh, no!" Stone called out, instantly garnering my attention. A knowing smirk appeared on his face. "You love her," he proclaimed, brushing his hair off his forehead. "Fuck, Marek. Why didn't you say something before?"

"Because I didn't realize it until right now," I affirmed, running my hands through my own hair in frustration.

"This changes everything," he said.

I quickly nodded.

"I'll gather the men. You start figuring out how we're gonna find her." He advanced toward the door, but before he disappeared from sight, I said something which stopped him right away.

"I had a tracker put in her wedding ring. If she still has it on, we'll find her."

I prayed whoever took her hadn't noticed the band, because they would have taken it from her. It was the biggest reminder that she was no longer a part of their club, the biggest 'fuck you' their enemy could shove down their throats.

FORTY-TWO

Sully

TWISTING THE RING AROUND MY finger over and over helped to soothe me. It was funny how things turned out. At first, the ring had been something that had shackled me to Cole, and his club. But now, I found solace in the gold metal band, as if in some way I was still connected to the man I'd ended up falling for.

I had to make sure Vex didn't see it, though. Otherwise, his rage toward me would be off the charts, and he'd probably kill me before returning me to the Savage Reapers.

Slipping the band from my finger, I quickly placed it into the cup of my bra, tucked securely under my left breast. No sooner had I pulled my hand from my clothing than the car came to an abrupt halt, jerking me forward in the trunk. Bracing for what I knew was coming, I prayed Cole would be able to find me. I had no idea how, but I prayed nonetheless.

A LIGHT HUMMING NOISE FILLED my ears, the only one of my senses on high alert. My eyelids were closed, too heavy to open even if I wanted to. My hands and legs were numb, and it wasn't until I tried to move them that I realized I was restrained. The shock of it wore off quickly, as soon as my memories flooded over me.

Vex had taken me. Shoved me in the back of a rundown car and driven for what felt like hours. It was the last thing I remembered before groggily waking up wherever I was now.

Was I back inside the Savage Reapers' compound? Or did Vex take me somewhere completely different? Instinctually, I knew if he'd taken me back to my father, I'd be dead before Vex could exact whatever revenge he felt he was entitled to.

Wriggling my hands behind my back, I heard movement behind me. "Good, you're awake," Vex said. "I thought maybe I gave you too much."

I opened my mouth to speak but no words came out. The only noise to escape was a low groan. My tongue felt like sandpaper, my lips cracking from the lack of moisture.

I had no idea what he'd drugged me with, but it obviously wasn't meant to kill me.

His finger lifted one eyelid, the light above my head infiltrating my pupils and causing me a great deal of pain. It was like tiny shards of glass poking at me, and it only stopped once he'd withdrawn his hand and my eye closed into darkness again.

"It'll take a few minutes for the drug to wear down enough for you to open your eyes. It's a bitch, isn't it?" he grated, happy with himself that he was able to impose pain on me yet again.

He rambled on for the next ten minutes about how much he was going to enjoy hurting me, that while I was away he had to resort to taking out his aggression on the countless club whores who were only too eager to jump all over him. That was, until he'd beaten most of them to within an inch of their lives. He'd even sliced up a few of them for added enjoyment.

Just when I thought I was going to throw up from the details of his rampage, my eyes flitted open. I tried to focus on something in front of me to calm my rising nausea, praying he wasn't the only focal point in the room. Thankfully, he was behind me. I'd chosen a spot on the wall in front of me, inhaling long, slow breaths. Silently blowing them out through my nose. Within seconds, my stomach calmed.

A shadow moved at my side then quickly in front of me as Vex crouched until he was at eye level. I tried to lower my head but he wasn't having any of it, his fingers roughly pinning my chin in place. He dug into my skin, instantly bruising the sensitive flesh.

I winced . . . and he laughed.

He had always enjoyed my pain.

His soulless green eyes pinned me, narrowing his gaze as if he was trying to read my mind. Funny thing was he was so far gone from reality that he probably thought he could. Whipping my head to the side before he stood, he cursed under his breath and walked away before uttering another word.

"Where are we?" I rasped, the vibrations in my throat instantly alarming me. I didn't sound like myself, and it scared the hell out of me.

"Somewhere nice and safe, *sweetheart*. Don't you worry about that." Clanking sounded behind me, and my heart raced the longer he stayed hidden from sight. "You see," I heard him say. "Your father wanted me to bring you back to him so he could do with you as he saw fit. But I couldn't do that." He tsked. "I needed to do my own thing first." More clanking. "He can have whatever's left of you when I'm finished. Or maybe I'll go back and tell him I couldn't get to you. Keep using that excuse day after day. Week after week. Hell, year after year." He slammed something down on a metal desk, whatever objects were on top crashing against each other and creating a loud noise. "I watched you for weeks, Sully. I only needed to find the right time to take back what rightfully belonged to me."

Following weeks spent with a man who let me speak my mind whenever I had something to say, I'd forgotten my place when it came to Vex. The words flew from my mouth before my brain could warn me against it.

"I don't belong to you. I never did."

There was no sound in the air around me before I felt his fingers around my throat. My body smarted at the aggression, my eyes bulging, my chest constricted the longer I was unable to take in oxygen. Just when black dots hazed my vision, he released his hand and backed away. Instantly, I went into a frenzied coughing fit, inhaling air as quickly as I could muster.

"You've always belonged to me. You were always mine. And nothing's changed," he sneered, his malevolent smile making my heart skip a rampant beat.

For someone to be so young yet so calculating—and dead inside—was something which had always baffled me about Vex. My father, I could see. He was much older, life having beaten him down. The only thing he had to cling to was his ruthlessness.

But nothing had happened to Vex to make him the way he was.

He was simply born bad.

FORTY-THREE

Marek

FORTY-FIVE MINUTES WE DROVE. EVEN though the odometer read a hundred miles an hour, it felt like we were driving at a snail's pace. My fingers curled around the steering wheel while my stomach twisted the further away from the club we ventured. I couldn't stop my mind from drifting to the image of Sully being hurt at the hands of that bastard, Vex. I tried my absolute best to keep her safe, always making sure either me or one of my men was watching over her, impressing upon her how important her safety was, yet she'd still made the decision to go off the compound without protection.

But I couldn't blame her alone. Adelaide was the other half of the equation, although she didn't know about the circumstances behind why Sully needed such protection. She probably just assumed I was being an over protective, possessive man, wanting his woman heavily safeguarded. While all that was in fact true, there was more to the story. Way more.

For as much as I wanted to point the finger at Sully and at Adelaide, I knew in my heart there was only one person responsible.

Me.

I should have paid more attention to her whereabouts during the party.

I should have drilled it into her how imperative it was that she not leave the compound without my permission.

I should have. . . .

Punching the dashboard, an immediate pain radiated through my hand, but I welcomed the quick distraction. It took my mind off the fact that if anything happened to Sully, I didn't know what I would do.

Wait . . . That was a lie.

Yes, I did.

I'd rip through the Savage Reapers with the vengeance of the Devil, and I'd snatch every last one of their lives. If I perished in the process, then so be it.

"We're gettin' closer," Stone confirmed. Sitting beside me, he studied the tracker to make sure we were headed in the right direction. I prayed her wedding ring was still on her hand, or at least somewhere on her body. I knew she was aware of the significance of the round piece of metal. Not only because it tied her to me, but if her club knew she'd married the president of their enemy, her life would be in even greater danger.

Hopefully, she'd had the foresight to hide the damn thing, all the while keeping it close.

Ryder and Hawke accompanied us, their silence in the back of the van a sign they knew how serious the situation was. I wanted to bring more men in case we ran into a few of the Reapers, instead of the single man who I believed had taken her, but I couldn't leave my club unprotected. While I believed Sully was in extreme peril, it could also have been a setup of sorts.

Either way, we were heavily armed, never mind that we had the element of surprise on our side. There was no doubt they knew we were coming, but I doubted they expected us to find her so soon.

"It's up ahead," Stone called out. "Turn here and shut off the lights," he demanded. I obeyed, not giving him shit for the first time in our lives.

He took our situation seriously, and I couldn't have been more thankful. The second he found out she was missing he was by my side, firing off question after question and gathering a couple of the men to come with us.

The creak of the sliding van door screamed into the silence of the night. Looking around quickly, we noticed a large plot of land surrounded by vast emptiness. There were no houses. There were no cars. Hell, there weren't even any people anywhere in sight. The further we walked, the closer we came to a small building set back in the middle of the wide open space, a tall chain-link fence barricading the structure into some sort of privacy.

The sun had long gone down, and in the absence of streetlights the only thing guiding us was the moon. We knew instantly we were in the perfect place to kill, or be killed, and no one would be any the wiser for days. Weeks even.

With the seemingly abandoned building a few hundred yards in front of us, we stealthily crept forward, the shadow of night cloaking us enough that we were able to sneak around without the fear of being caught.

I still had no idea what we'd walk into. Their entire club could be hidden inside, and although I had rage on my side, I was no match for the likes of an entire club. Or we could walk in on nothing, Vex having figured out we were tracking her, this stop-off point merely being a ghost hunt.

"Go left," I instructed Hawke and Ryder. "Stone and I will go around that way." I pointed to the right of the rundown building. Silence screamed all around me and the more the eeriness deafened me, the more alarmed I became. Pricking my ears, I listened for any signs of someone else there with us, but there was nothing.

Securing the perimeter, we'd all met up around the back and searched for a way inside. A busted-out window toward the middle was our best choice.

"I'll go first," Stone offered. When I tugged on his jacket, he wrenched his arm free. "I'm the obvious choice and you know it." He winked. "Besides, if anything happens, at least I won't feel a thing," he tried to joke. Under any other circumstance, I would have laughed, but the precariousness of what we could potentially walk into still had me on guard. No time for carelessness.

I moved to go first, but he shoved me back, a stern look in his eye only he could get away with flashing my way. "I mean it, Marek. Let me go first. I'll check things out and see if there's another way in. One where we aren't standing on each other's shoulders to get inside." His eyes gleamed as he tried to lessen my worrisome mood.

But again, nothing.

Just impatience . . . and fear.

Fear I would walk in and find Sully dead.

Fear I would walk in and not find her at all.

"Then go if you're goin'. Stop blabbering on and get in there." I cradled my hands together to make him a foothold. Raising him up, he took a quick look inside, as best he could with no apparent light, and lifted himself further until he was able to shove a foot into the corner of the window frame. Thankfully, the opening was wide enough for a man of his size, his broad shoulders skimming the sides.

We heard a thud, followed by a stream of cursing. At first, I thought he'd seen someone, but quickly found out a large piece of glass had cut his hand when he'd landed. The only reason he made any noise was because he had to rip a piece of his shirt to cover the wound.

He'd found a side door and beckoned us forth before we were caught like sitting ducks. Again, we had no idea if we were the only ones there, or if people were waiting to ambush us.

Twenty minutes it took the four of us to search around in the dark.

Twenty minutes of my heart in my throat.

Twenty minutes of agony while I searched for the woman who'd flipped me on my ass.

The vast space was cut into multiple sections, rooms disappearing into each other, plenty of hiding places to search. I wasn't even sure what kind of building we were running around in, what type of business it could have been used for. And I didn't give a shit either. All I cared about was finding Sully.

"Are you getting anything?" I asked Stone, pointing to the tracking monitor.

"Not really. Just a weak signal that keeps fading in and out, depending on where we are inside this shithole." The place smelled rank, a mustiness mixed with the scent of dead animals filling our nostrils.

We'd quickly discovered there were two levels to the place, the one we were currently searching and a lower one. Hawke found a door with steps which descended below. Was that were they were all waiting for us? Were we walking into a trap?

With the meager light of his phone, he opened the door and started his way down the steps, careful not to shout anything back to us. But he didn't have to because we were right behind him.

It was the last place we had to look and I prayed we found her or, at the very least, a clue as to where she could have gone. If she was even there at all.

Once we'd reached the bottom of the crumbling staircase, concrete falling away with every step we took, my eyes tried their hardest to adjust to the lack of light. It was even darker down there. Ryder flicked his lighter and as soon as the flame caught, we walked close to each other, huddled around that damn sparse source of light. My phone was well on its way to dying, as charging the device was the last thing on my mind before I rushed out to search for Sully. Hawke still had his cell out, but even with all three sources of illumination, the dank cellar was intimidating.

Fifteen minutes later, we concluded no one else was hiding away in the old abandoned building. As we headed toward the steps, I kicked something, sending the object rolling across the hardened floor. The metal *clang* instantly raised my hackles, and for some reason a feeling of dread settled down deep inside me.

Following the sound, I snatched Ryder's lighter from him and bent down to retrieve the item. Between my fingers was a ring. A thin yellow band.

Sully's ring.

She *was* here.

But where is she now?

Not having the concentration needed to drive, Stone took the wheel once we'd approached the van. We were on the road and headed back when Hawke's phone started buzzing.

"Yeah?" he sharply answered. "Hold on." Tapping me on the shoulder, he passed me his cell. "For you. It's Cutter."

"Yeah?" I answered, giving the same curt greeting.

"Prez, we think we have a lead on Sully," he rushed. "One of those fucks dared to show up at Flings, spouting off at the mouth to anyone who would listen about how the Reapers were going to own this town soon enough, so everyone better watch out. He was definitely high on something, which worked to our advantage because we grabbed him quickly and threw him in the back room. I have no idea where he ranks in his shithole of a club, but I figured it couldn't hurt to try and extract some information from him." Cutter was a man of few words, so his continued rambling was certainly telling.

"Fuck, Cutter, get to the point!" I shouted, losing any and all patience. "What do you know?"

"Sorry. After a little *convincing*, the punk sung like a canary." I rolled my eyes at his obvious enjoyment. Cutter wasn't shy when it came to making people talk. I wouldn't say he *enjoyed* what he needed to do from time to time, but I know that shit didn't bother him too much either. "He told us Vex might be holed up in some shitty motel somewhere on I5, maybe near Tulare. He's not sure where he's going, but he told us Vex was overheard telling a few people he was going to 'end the embarrassment once and for all.'" He took a short breath before continuing. "Are you guys anywhere near there?"

Catching a passing road sign, I concluded we were close to an hour from where Vex might be. "You don't happen to know what he's driving, do you?" I held my breath and prayed for the information to keep on flowin' my way.

"A red '75 Impala. Beat to shit but still good enough to keep runnin'."

"Thanks, man," I said, ending the call before shouting directions to Stone. I felt the van pick up speed, the engine whirling with the force of my VP's determination.

———◆———

IT SEEMED LIKE AN ETERNITY before we came upon the first shitty motel we could find, but after a quick scouring of the small parking lot, we deemed it wasn't the right place. For all we knew, the information given to Cutter had been utter bullshit.

So it went, crappy motel after crappy motel, until my hopes were dashed. At the rate we were going, there was no way I would ever find Sully. The only link I had was her wedding ring, and it either had been taken from her to be left behind at the abandoned building to taunt me, or she'd somehow dropped it.

My money was on Vex having figured out there was a tracker in it, leaving it behind on purpose. And who the hell knew how long they'd been there. I knew it couldn't have been too long, though, because as soon as Adelaide told us she was missing, we took off. But one *minute* was an eternity, knowing she was being subjected to God knew what.

The long stretch of highway had my mind all twisted up. Thoughts of Sully consumed me. She'd brought out parts of me I hadn't even known existed. The need to protect a woman so fiercely was beyond any scope of reality I'd ever lived in. She drew my attention, as well as those around her. If anyone's eyes lingered too long, I would become instantly engulfed in fury, threatening their very life until they looked away. And that just wasn't like me. I was a pretty laid-back guy. Normally. Before she'd come into my life, anyone who knew me would have attested to such a thing.

But I was possessive over Sully. I wanted all her time and focus. I hated when she was out of my sight, mainly because I didn't trust anyone to protect her the way I could, but also because I couldn't stand when other people made her laugh, or felt joy in a world where she belonged to me. I should've been the one putting those smiles on her face, enticing those intoxicating laughs from her lips.

And I did.

But others shared in that glory as well.

My bombardment of irrational thoughts was yet another one of her effects on me. They were unexplainable, and I wore myself out mentally trying to dissect my feelings.

Slowing the van, Stone jutted his arm out in front of me, startling me from my brief escape from reality. "Is that the car?" he asked, trying to lean over me to get a better look, all while doing his best not to veer off the road.

A small sign for a Motel Nine flashed in front of us and, sure enough, in the small dirt parking lot was an old, beat-up red Impala. "That has to be it," I affirmed, more to myself than anyone else. "Keep driving," I instructed, hitting the dash in anxiousness.

Stone read my mood quickly. "We'll get her, man," he said, tapping the wheel before proceeding further down the road, easing his foot off the accelerator so we didn't miss a good spot to hide.

We parked and slinked around the building. Hawke and Ryder walked toward the office to find out some more information. We had to make sure we had the right place; barging in on innocent people with guns blazing and murderous intent probably wouldn't be the best thing right now.

Grinning like a fool, and with bloody knuckles, Hawke came strolling out of the front of the building, Ryder quickly in tow. "He's in number three," he said, brushing past me toward the room.

All four of us rushed across the lot, guns drawn and prepared to kill if and when we deemed it necessary.

There was a good chance Vex had acted alone, stealing Sully like the true coward he was. Swooping in and kidnapping her only when he knew she was alone and defenseless. The only time he would ever be able to overpower her was when she was without protection. At least when I'd done it, we'd attacked their club like men, killing as many of those worthless bastards as we could.

"Vex is mine," I growled, gun cocked and aimed at the flimsy door ahead, prepared for anything. I prayed Sully was all right, but only time would tell what he'd actually been able to do to her. It only took a split second to end someone's life, and if that was the road he'd chosen to travel down, then he would be following her into the afterlife sooner than later. Although, before he stole his last breath, I'd make him beg me for death.

As soon as Ryder's big black boot made contact with the door, all four of us filtered into the room, no light inside except for a small table lamp in the far right corner. I'd never surveyed an area quicker than I did right then. Floral wallpaper from the seventies covered the walls, an old box-style

TV sitting on a metal stand, half of it bent from the weight buckling it. Two separate areas on the walls were faded, indicating a picture had once hung there. A queen-sized bed sat in the middle of the room with covers, which conveniently matched the wallpaper, crumpled into a ball. In the middle lay the woman I'd come to save.

There was a split second, the time between one breath and the next, when Vex looked stunned. Sitting hunched over the only chair in the room, he snorted a line of coke off the corner of the long dresser. His eyes were bloodshot and his nose was bleeding, but it didn't stop him from shoving that shit up his nostrils. A coked-out fucker was dangerous, and we all knew it.

They were unpredictable.

Jumpy.

Paranoid.

Hawke and Stone rushed forward, attempting to reach for Vex while I ran toward Sully. Her limp body was sprawled across the bed, her head lolled to the side so I couldn't see her entire face. At first glance, she looked dead. Her hair covered the only visible side of her face, so I was unable to assess any immediate damage. But the further down her body I scanned, I knew right away he'd injured her. But how badly was the question.

The cream dress she'd been wearing had turned one color.

Red.

Blood red.

Rushing forward, I said a silent prayer she was alive, that the illusion she cast was just that. "Fuck," I cursed loudly, jumping on the bed and cradling her head in my hands. Pushing back her hair, I gasped at what I saw. Both of her eyes were swollen, her right one on the way to being sealed shut because of all the damage. Her bottom lip was split and there was dark bruising around her entire throat. She'd been strangled.

My hands ran all over her body, searching for the cause of the crimson river. Before I could lift her dress to check, I heard a shuffle behind me, then a gunshot. Whipping my head around, I saw my VP on the ground, holding his side with one hand, his other propping up his upper body. Blood trickled over his fingers, hitting the faded, light green carpet.

"Goddamn it!" Stone roared. "Like I don't have enough fuckin' scars as it is." Yeah, that's what he was concerned about. I knew damn well he wasn't feeling any pain, instead worried about the vanity of it all. I would have laughed at him if our situation weren't so dire.

While I was on the bed with Sully, and Stone was holding his weeping wound, Hawke had tackled Vex and had him restrained on the ground, his knee pushing into the bastard's back to help keep him still. It worked in our favor that he was drugged out of his mind and although he got off a lucky shot, his reflexes were otherwise impaired.

Once I knew he was no longer a threat, I focused on Sully, the rampant beat inside my chest pushing fear into my heart.

"Ryder, come help me!" I shouted. He was next to me before I took my next breath. "Sully," I called out, reaching for her face and trying to wake her. Placing my hand on the side of her neck, I'd been able to find a pulse, but it was extremely faint. I knew it was only a matter of time before she drifted away from me for good, so I had to think fast.

With Ryder taking over and cradling her neck, I'd finally been able to push her dress up. Sections of the material stuck to her skin, which was not a good sign. After carefully separating the dress from her body, I discovered she'd been stabbed. A deep gash between her upper ribs. The warm stickiness of her life coated my hands, while I tried to find something to push down on her wound.

"We have to get her to a hospital. Now!" I felt myself starting to panic, something I never did.

"What about me?" Stone yelled. "I need a hospital too, man. Just because I don't feel it doesn't mean that damn bullet isn't ripping apart my insides." He slowly rose to his feet, wobbling a little before catching the edge of the dresser for support.

I scrambled off the bed, carrying Sully in my arms while I debated what to do. I knew she needed immediate medical attention, and lots of it, but so did my VP. Explaining a knife wound *and* a gunshot wound would surely bring in heat we didn't need.

We were close to a two-hour ride away from the club, and I wasn't sure if she would make it. But what choice did I have? I couldn't just drop her off at the hospital, all alone, but I couldn't very well carry her in there myself either. No, if I left her all by herself, the authorities could take her from me, or worse, her father could somehow find out and steal her right out from under their noses. Then I'd never get her back alive.

"What about the safe house, Prez? It's only an hour from here. Surely they'll both make an hour's ride," Ryder said hopefully.

I knew I brought him along for a reason.

Quickly glancing around the dreadful scene in front of me, I made the decision that the safe house was our only bet. It was a place we kept on the side in case of emergencies, and today it was going to serve a dual purpose.

To treat Sully and Stone . . . and to finally end Vex once and for all.

"Stone, are you okay to get to the van with Ryder?" He looked paler than he had a second ago, and I wasn't exactly sure how bad his damage was.

He stumbled again, but righted himself while he walked toward the busted door, fending off any help from Ryder. "Yeah, I'm good. We'll be right back."

"Hurry up," I yelled to their retreating backs. Stone was hurtin'. Maybe not physically, but his body was taking the brunt of his trauma.

I heard the screeching tires in no time, rushing out to place Sully in the back of the van. I'd swiped the comforter from the motel room to help make her as comfortable as possible, even though it was covered in blood. *Her* blood. But I didn't want to lay her down on the cold, bare floor of the vehicle. Rushing back inside, I grabbed my VP's gun, which had fallen out of his hand when Vex had shot him.

"Hawke, go out and get in the van," I demanded.

"What do you wanna do with him?" he asked, pushing his knee further into Vex's back. I'd insanely thought Vex was choosing to remain silent all this time. What I hadn't realized was that when Hawke had tackled him, he'd inadvertently knocked him out.

"He's gonna meet his maker tonight," I sneered. Hawke moved away from his body, allowing me to kick Vex then roll him over. I expected the unconscious bastard to wake up, throw some attitude my way, as if he were invincible, and then eventually plead for his life.

I wasn't particularly fond of torture, or at least being the one to do it, but I would thoroughly enjoy what I had planned for the man who'd made Sully's life a living nightmare. Day in and day out. I knew she chose to still protect me, or herself, by not divulging a lot of the things that went down when she was living with him, and because of that my imagination was my worst enemy.

Time quickly escaped me, and if I was gonna do something, now was the time. I had to make sure to get both Sully and Stone to the safe house as soon as possible.

A bullet to the head while he was unconscious seemed unfair. No, I needed for the bastard lying before me to suffer in ways I hadn't even thought of yet. Making the quick decision to bring him with us, although the thought of him breathing the same air as the rest of us tugged at the unraveling string of my sanity, I picked him up off the floor and threw him over my shoulder. Taking one last look around the disheveled room to make sure I wasn't missing anything, I closed the door and walked the few feet to the vehicle waiting for me.

Once we were on the road, I instructed Hawke to place a call to Trigger, asking him to bring Adelaide to the safe house right away.

Hopes were high that both of the people who meant the most to me would live to see another day.

FORTY-FOUR

Marek

HUNCHING OVER SULLY IN THE back of the van, I cradled her head in my lap, securing her to me while making sure she was as comfortable as she could be, given the circumstances. She was still out cold, her motionless body making my own tense in sorrow.

"She'll be okay," Stone assured, turning around in the passenger seat to look at me. Clutching his side, he tore his hand away to assess the damage, blood coating his entire side. It looked pretty bad, and I was extremely grateful my friend didn't feel an ounce of pain. His body's reaction to the intrusive bullet, however, was less than desired. All signs of life seemed to drain from his face, a pale shadow of disbelief coloring his features. His sitting form wavered, unable to fully control himself while Ryder drove like a maniac. I think it was the only time either one of them used their seatbelts.

"Are you okay, Stone?" I asked, not doing my best to hide the worry in my voice.

"All good, bro-brother," he stammered slightly. A deep breath later and his head lolled to the side. Ryder took a corner faster than he should have and Stone's body tipped over, his head hitting the passenger window with a thud.

"Goddamn it, Ryder!" I shouted. I wanted so much to berate him for driving so carelessly, but at the same time I wanted to urge him to go faster. He never said a word, all the apology I was looking for pouring forth from his reflection in the rearview mirror.

The rest of the trip was executed in silence. Stone had come to only to pass out once more before we arrived at our destination. Sully's body still lay across my lap, unmoving except for the shallow breaths of air she took into her lungs. And Vex form still laid in a crumpled mess across the back of the van, stuffed into the corner so Hawke could keep a closer eye on him. Primed to make a move in case he woke up and tried something.

So lost in my own head, I hadn't even realized we'd pulled into the garage at the safe house. The place was located in a normal residential area, hiding right out in the open.

Throwing open the side door, the first person to greet us was Adelaide. At first her composure calmed me, until she moved closer and was able to witness the destruction we hid inside the vehicle. Reaching forward, she touched Sully, her hands roaming all over her body to locate the source of the damage. When she skimmed her fingers over her friend's ribs, she jerked them back in horror.

"Oh, my God!" she cried. "Who stabbed her?" Her eyes were on me instantly, silently pleading for an answer, but there simply wasn't any time.

Jerking my head toward Ryder, who'd come around the back of the van, I indicated I needed his assistance. He carefully cradled Sully's body until I was capable of extracting her from the vehicle myself. With my wife in my arms, I shouted for whoever else was around to attend to Stone. I didn't need to tell Hawke to stay with Vex—he knew what he had to do until he was told otherwise.

Before I disappeared inside the house, I heard Adelaide's cries once she realized Stone was out cold inside the van, but I couldn't falter. I needed to ensure Sully was taken care of before I gave my attention over to my buddy. Being torn between two people was the worst feeling in the world, but I knew the woman lying lifelessly in my arms was my first priority.

If the roles were reversed, and it had been Stone carrying Adelaide and me bleeding out, he would make the same decision. I knew he cared for her as I did for my wife; I saw it in his eyes, and in the way he reacted to situations where Adelaide was concerned.

There was a flurry of activity inside the makeshift hospital room, aka the living room. Adelaide had set up rather quickly, calling in the assistance of her doctor friend, the one she'd relied on to help Tripp when we'd found him dumped outside the gate. They both worked diligently to repair the two broken people placed before them.

After what seemed like the longest five hours of my life, they were both on their way to recovering.

Luckily, most of Sully's wounds were only superficial, although her knife wound was certainly going to leave a nasty scar to match those already marring her beautiful skin. I viewed the newest addition as a testament to how strong she was, but I knew she would see it as yet another possibility for me to pull away from her, thinking such imperfections would make me change the way I saw her.

The way I felt about her.

Stone's wound was a bit more damaging, nicking his liver before it passed through his body. Thankfully, I'd been informed he wouldn't sustain any long-lasting effects because of it, the liver being one of the organs which rejuvenated itself rather quickly. The other plus to that was Stone didn't feel anything, other than Adelaide's anger when he'd tried to get up and move around too soon. We transported them both back to the clubhouse the next evening. I gave strict instructions not to allow either one of them to leave the confines of the compound, needing as many people around them for protection until they were both completely out of harm's way.

Plus, I needed time to deal with Vex before I followed them home.

———— ✦ ————

I NEEDED SOMEONE WITH ME who wouldn't think twice about what I had planned for Vex, so I placed a call to Cutter to meet me at the safe house. Any one of my men would have helped me out, but Cutter was fashioned from a different cloth. He didn't get off on torturing people—it wasn't an unearthed desire he had brimming below the surface. He was just able to switch something off and do whatever was necessary without a second thought.

Waiting in the hollows of the vast basement, I heard the garage door followed by the door to the kitchen creak open then close, the deadbolt locking in place soon after. Our safe house was a well-guarded secret, but just in case we'd been compromised, I cocked the gun resting in my hand, ready and able to take down any intruders who thought they could get one over on me.

I waited in anticipation while footsteps drummed down the wooden stairs, followed by unhurried walking down the short corridor. Not having to give direction to which room I'd be in, mainly because it was *the* room we used whenever we found ourselves in this predicament, the handle turned and very slowly, the door swung open.

Cutter loomed on the threshold, his short, graying hair perfectly styled in place. He'd come wearing all black, as was the necessary required uniform for someone about to torture another person.

A quick nod between us was all the greeting we gave each other before he moved further inside. Years ago, we'd transformed the room into a soundproof area. For obvious reasons. We didn't need to alarm any of the neighbors because otherwise, we'd have to find another location for our safe house. And, well . . . that was just a pain in the ass.

Vex had woken the previous night while Adelaide was tending to her two patients, but since he'd been confined to this room, which was directly below the living room, no one heard him when he started yelling obscenities to no one in particular. The only people who even knew he was there were me, Hawke, Ryder and Cutter. Maybe Stone knew, but he was so out of it for the majority of the night I doubted he'd paid any attention to what was going on around him. Other than Adelaide tending to him, of course.

Naked and bound to an old wooden table with coarse rope, Vex's crazy eyes followed me as I moved around him, making sure his restraints were still properly tied. I didn't need him busting out of them during what we had planned. A small piece of me wanted to free him, to best him with nothing but my brute strength, ending his life with my bare hands, but I didn't have time for it. I needed to save whatever reserve I had left for Sully.

She needed me whole.

Physically as well as emotionally.

The one thing I allowed Vex to have was his voice. I wanted to hear him beg for his life, all while I explained what was coming next. I wanted to hear his excuses, his reasoning for tormenting Sully for however long he had access to her. To hear why he chose to treat her like he had.

Did he have any regrets?

Was he sorry in the least for what he'd done to her?

Would he beg for forgiveness before pleading for his life?

We were about to find out.

Cutter stood off to the left while I remained close to the table, Vex continuing to follow me with his stare.

"So," I started. "Although I'm gonna snatch your life from you today, yours won't be a quick death." He closed his lids and exhaled a long breath, but remained silent. When his eyes connected with mine again, he looked . . . crazier? If that was even possible.

Whatever he'd told himself inside that fucked-up head of his was enough for him to hide his fear from the two men who would be the last to see him alive.

Going against my better judgment, I asked him a question. "Do you have anything to say before we get started?"

Glancing first to Cutter wielding one of his favorite knives, then to me standing directly beside him, he cracked his neck from side to side as if he were preparing to do battle himself.

"You stole my property. You barged into *my* club and stole what belonged to *me*. I saw you. I saw the way you looked at her, the way you tried to make sure she was safe when she wasn't with you. I've been watchin' for weeks. You have a soft spot for the whore, but know this. Even when I'm dead and gone, Psych won't rest until she's back inside our club. And how you found her at the motel will be nothing to what he's gonna do to her once he gets her back."

Though I tried not to react to whatever he said, he'd been able to rattle me. He'd been able to play on my fears. Vex was only *one* of the threats toward Sully, and we both knew it. Her father was diabolical, and if he ever got his hands on her, there was no way he wouldn't kill her soon after. Vex had only allowed her to live so long because I was sure he was gonna use her until he'd had his fill.

Deciding not to give the bastard any satisfaction, I steeled my posture and made sure my face was expressionless when I uttered one word.

"Cutter."

And just like that, his torture began. Neither one of us had a specific plan as to what we were gonna do to him. I simply knew it would be drawn out and painful.

Over the course of the next hour, my man went to work carving up Vex's chest, inch by inch. Some cuts were shallow, some were deep. Some were long, some were short. But each one was precise.

Stepping back after Cutter had finished, I could clearly make out the letters 'K C,' even with all the blood seeping from his open wounds. To have the initials of a rival club carved into the chest was one of the highest insults. The only thing equaling it was integrating one of their own, which I'd already done when I made Sully my wife.

While I thought Vex would beg and plead, scream and holler, cry and break down, he did none of those things. He grimaced every time the tip of the blade cut through his flesh, but not once did he say anything.

Which led me to believe one of two things.

Either he was strong-willed and brave.

Or he was certifiably insane.

I was leaning toward the latter.

Walking around the table until I stood next to his head, I leaned in close so he wouldn't mistake what I had to say. "We're just getting started, you fucker. Hope you like what we have planned next." His bloodshot eyes glared at me, his lips drawn so tight they'd lost all color. Although he chose not to utter a scream, the stress of keeping all his pain bottled up was wearing on him. His brown hair was matted to his forehead, his body's one indication he was indeed panicking on the inside.

He looked haggard.

He'd aged years in just minutes.

"Cutter, help me turn him over." Having no idea what I was thinking, he acted as instructed. No questions asked.

I debated on whether or not to knock Vex out before loosening his restraints, or to allow him to fight one last time.

What the hell. I enjoy a good challenge.

As soon as I loosened the ties around his feet, his body went into full fight mode, kicking and thrusting his legs every which way. His entire body twisted, his back arching off the table while he continued to thrash about.

Realizing he was gonna be quite the handful, I brought the butt of my gun down quickly on the side of his head, a lump swelling on his temple almost instantaneously. The blow was enough to stop him from freaking out, but not enough to halt him entirely. Which I welcomed.

What fun would it be if he complied completely?

Cutter held down his lower half while I freed his arms, flipping him over quickly so we could restrain him again. A low groan escaped his mouth as soon as his carved-up chest hit the surface of the table, blood steadily pouring from him and hitting the ground at our feet.

Widening his legs, I tightly fastened each ankle to the bottom of the table. He was most certainly going to resist his next and final punishment, so I had to ensure he was secure before making my next move.

Beckoning Cutter over, I leaned in close and whispered something into his ear, Vex's head turned to the side, his eyes roaming over the scene of his two assailants with vigor. There was no way he would know what was coming, and while I wanted nothing more than to surprise him directly before inflicting his much-deserved pain, I decided to give him a hint.

Let him sweat a bit beforehand.

Once Cutter had ascended the basement steps, I leisurely walked around the space, pacing and slapping my hand on various objects placed around the room. First it was a set of chains. Picking up the heavy objects, I tossed them into a tin tray, the noise startling even me, and I was prepared for it. Then I fingered the many knives lined up next to one another on the far side table. In view so he could see, but not so close he could make out the intricate carving details of each.

"Sully told me all about what you did to her." Choosing to remain silent while my words resonated, I waited to see if he would banter with me. A few moments passed . . . and nothing. So I continued. "She told me how you abused her for days before leaving her tied up to bleed out like some kind of animal." Footsteps sounded overhead. "And I'm gonna do to you what you did to her." Rounding the table so I could lean in close, I threatened, "Let's see how you like being fucked with a bat."

The last word left my lips and, as if on cue, Cutter strolled into the dank room holding an old, beat-up, wooden baseball bat. I kept my eyes on Vex the entire time, waiting for it to register just what was gonna happen to him. My satisfaction came when my fingers curled around the larger part of the bat. His eyes shut tightly before his body twitched on the table, his muscles locking up the closer I moved toward him with the weapon in hand.

"If you believe that lying whore then you're the idiot!" he yelled, breathing hard as he waited for my next move. "I never did any such thing to that bitch," he seethed.

"Maybe you just don't remember it," I countered. "Enough talk. Let's get down to it." I tapped the wood against his upper thighs, tormenting him before I even started. "Who knows, Vex, you might actually enjoy this." My laugh was sinister. I had no qualms about dancing with demons that night, every punishment I deemed appropriate as payback for all the years he'd tortured Sully. Not givin' a shit about her well-being, physically or emotionally. Tapping the bat against his ass that time, I finished with, "Or maybe not."

His howls were music to my ears; he'd finally broken. He was a soulless sadist who deserved every bit of pain I inflicted on him. After an hour, I blessed Cutter with the authority to finish him off however he deemed necessary. I gave him strict instructions to drop off Vex's rotting corpse somewhere his club would find him, and to leave the bat in place so they knew exactly what had happened to him—among other things.

FORTY-FIVE

Marek

TWO WEEKS HAD PASSED AND both patients were doing quite well. I'd taken Sully back home to my house—*our* house—and let her recoup under my watchful eye.

I'd forsaken the club to a point, vowing to care for my wife until she was completely healed. The area surrounding her wound remained red and puffy and she still experienced a bit of pain, but not nearly like she had. Every time she moved too quickly, or twisted the wrong way and winced, it sliced right through me. As soon as she witnessed the pain in my eyes, she was the one trying to comfort me.

Our affections for each other only grew stronger, and it was on a mundane Thursday evening when I decided I needed to finally tell her how I felt once and for all. Expressing myself wasn't necessarily my strong suit, unless, of course, I was angry about something. In those cases, I had absolutely no problem letting anyone know what was brewing inside me.

"Can I get you anything else?" Sully reclined on the couch, taking a small sip of water to wash down her pain meds. She was getting better with each passing day. Physically, anyway. Emotionally was a different story. Almost every night, she'd woken from nightmares, choosing each time to remain tight-lipped when I asked her what exactly plagued her. The only thing she would mumble was "Vex."

I saw the effects of what he'd done to her body, but I still had no idea about what had happened during the time she was with him, which had led to each and every bruise . . . and to the stabbing. My body clenched in rage every time I looked at the remnants of her abuse, but I always made sure to keep my fury in check so she didn't think it was directed at her in any way.

She'd asked me a few days after I'd rescued her if I'd killed Vex, the whimper in her voice almost indecipherable. I warred between thinking she was fearful he was still alive, and her expressing her sadness because she still felt something for him. Something akin to Stockholm syndrome, or some shit like that.

When I fessed up that he'd been taken care of, that he was no longer a threat, she breathed a sigh of relief. An action which immediately put all my fears to rest. I didn't go into detail over what we'd done to him, however. She didn't need to hear any of it.

She was relieved Vex no longer breathed the same air, and that was good enough for me.

Now, the only other person I had to worry about was her father.

I'd been in touch with Rafael, making sure our deal was continuing as promised. Soon enough, the Savage Reapers would be without a steady flow of income, and as soon as Psych and his men were vulnerable and desperate, my men and I would swoop in and end him and his filthy club once and for all.

"No, I'm fine," she answered. "Thank you." She turned her head and looked up at me as I approached. She smiled, her entrancing brown eyes beckoning to me. "You know you don't have to dote on me, don't you?" She licked her lips and waited for me to sit next to her. Once I was close, I reached for her hand and entwined my fingers with hers, the warmth of her touch calming my erratic nerves.

"I don't mind. Whatever I can do to help you, I will. Always." I meant to smile, but my face remained expressionless. There were so many things I wanted to say, so many questions I had, about everything, that curving my lips was the last thing I thought about.

And she noticed.

Turning slowly to face me, her hand covering her newest wound out of habit, she looked worried. "Is there something wrong, Cole? Why do you look so serious?" When the only response I gave her was silence, her eyes widened and she had a mini panic attack, as if I were about to ruin her with whatever was gonna come tumbling out of my mouth.

Clutching her hand tightly in mine, I leaned in and kissed her lips. It was gentle at first, then the more breath we shared, our entanglement became something else.

Raw.

Carnal.

Promising.

I love you. I think I fell for you the first time my world crashed into yours. There hasn't been a moment that's gone by when I haven't thought about you. About what you were doing. About how you were dealing with your new life. If you were attracted to me. If you thought about me as much as I thought about you. My life had very little meaning before I met you, and now . . . Shit! I have no idea what I would do without you. When you were stolen, my soul was crushed, the very thought of never seeing you again too much to bear. I exist because you exist. I hate when other men look at you, let alone dare to talk to you. I want to rip their eyes out of their heads, their tongues from their mouths. My heart hammers against my chest in anger when I'm not the only one who makes you laugh, who puts you at ease, for however long that might be. When I'm inside you, it's the best feeling in the entire world. Nothing else matters. The only sounds I want to hear for the rest of my life are the sexy-as-hell moans you make when you're coming. Whether it's from my mouth, fingers or cock. I could live with you, here, all alone, just the two of us, naked and satisfying each other for the rest of our lives.

I wanted to say all of that to her, but I didn't. Pulling back from her mouth, I said, "I'm fine. Just worried about how you're feeling."

Her face relaxed a little, short pants of air hitting my face while she tried to calm down from our kiss. "I'll be okay. Really. I've been through worse." She cringed at her own words, which in turn made me stiffen.

A few precious moments passed while be both studied each other. I knew what was rumbling around inside my head, but I had no idea what *she* was thinking. I knew she cared for me, deeply even, but she'd never really told me how she felt, only ever giving me whatever I craved, whenever I was craving it. Her. Always her. And she gave herself to me freely, each and every time since I'd officially claimed her as my own.

"Are you tired?" I asked, watching her face carefully.

"I think so. Yes." Her fingers danced over her shirt, mindlessly playing with the part of her that was bandaged. She'd needed twenty-five stitches to close the wound. While that was bad enough, it could have been worse, I supposed.

"Okay," I said, pulling her to her feet very gently. "Let me change your bandage and we'll go to bed."

"That's okay. I can do it. You've done so much for me already." For some reason, she looked down at her feet when she spoke.

"Look at me," I instructed, tilting her chin up with my finger so I could see her face. "I want to do everything for you. Please don't take that away from me." *I sound pussy whipped for sure.* But I wouldn't have it any other way.

She remained quiet.

"Okay?" I asked, my brow arched in question.

"Okay," she whispered, before leading me to our bedroom.

Once I helped her undress, a task which was painful for me because I hadn't been able to sink inside her in weeks, I crawled into bed next to her, careful not to push against her side. I was overly cautious around her recently and I knew it drove her nuts, but the last thing I wanted to do was cause her any kind of discomfort.

"I won't break, Cole," she mumbled when she saw the reservation on my face while I held myself back.

"I know. I just . . . I don't want to hurt you. Not after everything you've been through." I tried to smile but I failed. Again.

I was painfully hard as it was, and her writhing under the covers, even though it was simply to get better situated, was driving me insane. I couldn't help it. I felt like some kind of creeper the way my eyes roamed over her entire body, heat exploding in my veins at the very thought of how she felt underneath me. Over me. Next to me.

Thrusting inside her tightness, tasting her essence and exploding together had become my new favorite things in the world.

"If you keep looking at me like that, I'm gonna be forced to jump you. And since I can't put that kind of pressure on my body yet, it would be wise for you to stop." There was a playfulness to her tone, although I knew she was being serious.

Apparently, I was torturing her as well as myself.

"Sorry," I said, lying on my back and staring at the ceiling. The light next to her was still on, and it didn't take her long to ask me to lean over and shut it off. Carefully, I moved over her body and stretched for the lamp, my chest brushing against hers as I did so.

A soft groan fell from her lips. Shit! I hadn't meant to touch her afflicted area, but I was too big not to. "Sorry," I repeated, that time for a different reason. Before I pulled away, she put her hand on my upper arm and squeezed. While I remained frozen in place, she moved her legs apart, kicking one over mine so quick I was surprised she had the strength.

"What are you doing?"

"I said I can't jump you. That doesn't mean *you* can't jump *me*." A sexy smile appeared on her face, her tongue parting her mouth and licking her lips while what she'd just said registered.

"I don't want to hurt you, though."

"You won't," she assured me, spreading her legs wider. "Just be gentle," she urged, her night shirt riding up her body until I could see her pink lace panties.

Fuck! She was so beautiful. I should have declined. I should have lain back down and fallen asleep, allowing her more time to heal.

But I was greedy.

And I needed my fix.

Hovering until my body was completely covering hers, I grinned wickedly before taking her mouth, her sweet tongue unraveling the last of my restraint.

"The way I'm feeling right now, I can't be gentle. So I think it's best if we just go to sleep."

I thought I'd had my say, kissing her one last time and trying to remove my body from hers. But a firm grip on the back of my neck halted me. Her foot caressed the back of my thigh, digging in when she thought I was going to retreat.

"Then I challenge you to take me slow. And gentle. I want you to draw out my release. Make me lose my mind, Cole," she pleaded. To say I was stunned was an understatement. I was usually the one who talked during sex, telling her over and over how good she felt, her moans affirmation she loved the way I fucked her. But in all the times we'd had sex—and there were numerous occasions during the short time we'd known each other—she'd never openly expressed herself as much.

Never mind that she'd just challenged me. It'd been a long time since anyone had challenged me to do anything. How did she know I could never turn down such a thing?

"You dare me, do you?" I asked, amusement dripping from my tone.

"I do," she answered, both of her legs pinning me in place. Our lower bodies were still covered by thin material, hers by a flimsy scrap of pink lace, and mine by the fabric of my boxer briefs.

Reaching behind me to unlock her legs, I backed up until I could grab her panties, drawing them down her thighs and discarding them somewhere behind me. When I made a move to lie back on top of her, she stopped me with a confused look on her face.

"What?"

"Aren't you going to take yours off too?" she asked, pouting that I wasn't already completely naked.

"Don't worry about me, sweetheart. You'll feel me. Trust me." I moved to cover her once more but she stopped me. Again.

"Cole, I want you naked. I want to feel every part of your body on mine. I don't want a piece of clothing in the way." My woman sure was feisty, and I found I absolutely loved it.

Without another word, I quickly peeled off my boxer briefs before lying over her one more time. "Better?"

"Better," she responded, closing her legs tightly against my waist. "Much better."

Resting on my forearms, I captured her mouth, simultaneously running a finger through her swollen folds to make sure she was ready for me. It took me only seconds to find out she was indeed primed to go.

I lined myself up and gently pushed inside her, as slowly as I could manage. Her breath caught in her throat, the look on her face one of pure lust. While I wanted to quickly sheath myself, I made sure to adhere to her challenge. If she wanted it slow, I would give her what she craved.

Thrusting in a few more inches, I stopped to seize her hip, my fingers digging into her soft skin while I withdrew until only the tip of my cock remained inside. I felt her frustration when she ran her nails down my back, the slight sting of pain affirming I was driving her insane. Little did she know she was affecting me the same way. The softness and warmth of her body was pure torment. Pleasure spiraled through me when I pushed back inside, her tightness clenching around me until I thought I was gonna explode.

"You like that?" I rasped, barely able to hold onto the sliver of control still in my grasp. "How do I feel?" Sucking her bottom lip into my mouth, I swirled my tongue with hers before she could answer. I thrust in further, faster than I'd intended. "I could fuck you forever," I growled, dangerously close to throwing caution to the wind and taking her rough and hard. Thankfully, I didn't allow my baser instincts to take over because I would have surely hurt her. But gone was the need to prove a point, her dare flying right out the window as I forged ahead and rocked my body into hers.

My hand moved from her hip to her tit to roughly pinch her nipple, a satisfied moan falling from her gorgeous mouth as soon as my fingers released her. My lips closed around the puckered area, my teeth gently biting her before withdrawing. I knew what she liked, and it was my goal to make sure my wife was completely satisfied.

"Cole!" she cried out, her fingers gripping my hair tighter the more our bodies moved as one. Her eyes fixated on mine, her teeth capturing her bottom lip when she couldn't take it any longer. I knew she was close, could feel it in the way her muscles clamped down on me. We'd only known each other a short while, but I knew her body inside and out, and I knew when she was ready to lose herself into oblivion.

"Do you love how I fuck you?"

"Yes," she moaned.

"You like how my cock fills up that tight pussy?" I breathed hard.

"Yes."

"Fuuuccccckkkk! I'm not gonna last long. I need you to let go. I need you to come all over me, Sully," I demanded with ragged breaths. I swallowed her screams as she gave in, her body locking down tight underneath me. She threw her head back and broke our kiss, her moans filling the air around us. She was so incredibly sexy like this, lost to what her body needed.

I couldn't take any more torture. Wanting to draw out my pleasure simply wasn't a reality. Our harsh panting melded together, our bodies as one driving us both toward the edge of insanity. I captured her mouth, our kiss hard and unforgiving. When I felt her teeth pierce my lower lip in urgency, I simply lost it. I slammed into her over and over again until I felt the pull of bliss rock through me.

Grunting out my own pleasure, I filled her with my release, and it took everything in me not to collapse on top of her. I was spent, fully sated, but I remained mindful of her condition.

When I stopped twitching inside her, I withdrew from her body and fell onto my back, my arm quickly searching for her to pull her closer. Once her head rested over my heart, I breathed easily, counting my heartbeats because I knew every one of them belonged to her.

"I love you," I whispered. My resolve had snapped, but I wouldn't take back the words for anything. Busting inside with the overwhelming feelings, a first for me, I just had to let her know how I felt. I'd almost lost her once without her knowing. I wouldn't make that same mistake again.

No more holding back.

Instead of feeling her relax against me, she stiffened, rolling over on her back quicker than I could stop her. Did she not feel the same way?

Had I made a mistake by telling her? Instead of regret washing over me, waves of anger at her blatant denial forced me to say something I should have kept quiet.

I felt vulnerable right then, and when I felt out of my element, I lashed out.

"What's wrong with you?" I practically shouted. "Can you only love someone who beats the shit out of you?" Dick move, but what could I say? I hated feeling cast aside. I sat up in bed, throwing my legs over the side and giving her my back. I regretted the words as soon as they'd left my lips, which I knew would happen the second she moved away from me, but I couldn't help myself.

Silence tortured me, so many thoughts and regrets running through my brain. I screamed at her in my head to say something. Anything. Finish her rejection of my words if that's what it came down to, but make a fuckin' move.

She rose from the bed and walked toward the door, dragging the sheet to wrap around her. Jumping up to stop her, I gripped her arms and shook her. Not hard, but enough to garner her attention. There was no way I was letting her leave me right then, not without some kind of explanation.

"Answer me," I growled, my anger still simmering from her refusal. Instead of telling me I'd hit the nail on the head, she started shaking, lowering her head until I could no longer see her face. She kept sniffing, and I knew right then she was crying, trying to hide her emotions from me. Was my declaration so unwanted I'd upset her to the point of tears?

Just when I thought she would remain close-lipped, she spoke. "Why are you lying to me?" She kept her head down while her body continued to shake, her long hair shielding her from me.

My grip on her arms tightened, although I was far from hurting her. "Sully," I called, but still she didn't look up at me. I tried once more. "Sully, let me see your face. I won't ask you again." She shook her head, refusing me.

Quickly walking her backward, she hit the wall with enough force to snap her out of whatever she'd just lost herself to. Conscious of her bandaged area, I took care not to jostle her any more, just enough to pull her focus back to me.

"Why do you think I lied to you?" I asked, pure confusion muddling my overactive thoughts.

She drew a quick breath before answering. "Because no one has ever told me they loved me before. Not even my father." Imploring me with her eyes, she continued spewing garbage from her mouth. "I'm disgusting. I'm riddled with scars and marks. I know you're trying your best to be nice to me because you pity me, but you don't love me. So please don't torment me with such words."

My heart broke because I knew she truly believed everything she'd said, her self-image more damaged than I could have ever imagined. If there were any possible way for me to go back in time and snatch her from her club years ago, I would have done it. It was unreasonable, but I felt responsible for her, even before I knew her.

Yeah, how fucked-up was that line of thinking?

Holding her face so she had no choice but to continue to look at me, I poured out my feelings for her. Again. Only this time, I hoped she didn't reject me, instead choosing to believe me and accept my words as the truth.

"I *do* love you. That is the God's honest truth. You might not believe me now, but in time you will. I can't promise I won't say something that might hurt your feelings, or do something which would make you question my loyalty to you, but at the end of the day, you are the woman I want to spend my life with. I will never physically hurt you, but the heart is another matter altogether."

I knew I was about to touch on a subject I barely even gave thought to, much less voiced, simply because it was still too painful, but it was the perfect time to bring it up. "I'd seen the way my parents were toward each other and, while they loved each other deeply, jealousy ran rampant between the both of them. They would sometimes say things they would instantly regret, but their love was what got them through, the glue that held them together until. . . ." I stopped speaking, suddenly questioning whether or not I wished to delve into that part of my life. I thought I wanted to, but saying the words out loud was a completely different story.

With everything I'd just spoken, the part she chose to hang on to and question was the part about my parents. Maybe it was easier for her to digest than the feelings I harbored for her. In time, maybe she would come to believe me.

"What happened to your parents?" she asked. "Are they still alive?" She held her breath while she waited for me to speak again.

"They're both dead." The words cut me, even though I'd come to grips with their death. Reaching for her hand, I pulled her back to the bed and sat her on the edge, taking the seat right next to her. I wanted to get this over with, and then hopefully she'd allow me to lose myself in her for the rest of the day.

"Can you tell me what happened? Do you want to talk about it?" How the hell had our conversation started off with my telling her I loved her, to her rejecting my affections and calling me a liar, to talking about my deceased parents? Funny how life works, switching from one thing to the next in mere seconds. Sometimes without any warning whatsoever.

"My mom passed away in her sleep six years ago. The doctors said it was a brain aneurism." My eyes became glassy at the memory of her, but I pushed the thoughts aside. No time to dwell on that now.

"And your father? What happened to him?"

"Three years ago, my father and his VP, Stone's father, went on a run. Everything was going according to plan until the Savage Reapers interfered. Long story short, both my father and Stone's were killed during the battle. Hence one of the many reasons we're at war with those bastards."

It had always been difficult for me to discuss my father, mainly because I missed him immensely. Plus it was too much of a drain that evening, having other issues which required my attention.

Sully's body shook. "I'm so sorry," she cried. *Yeah, me too.*

After some time had passed, we were back in bed, lying next to one another in complete silence. I'd revealed a lot of things and it was best I let it sink in, giving her time to come to grips with the revelation of my feelings for her as well as the background as to why it was my ultimate goal to destroy the Savage Reapers.

"Cole," Sully whispered, breaking the silence of the room.

"Yeah," I answered, shifting over on my side so I faced her. Trailing a finger along her belly, I enjoyed the moment until she decided to continue.

"I told you I hated Vex, and I do. Well . . . I did, when he was alive. But there was a time when I told him I loved him. Once. I thought if he heard the words, he would have a change of heart and start treating me better. But the only thing my words got me was a black eye." Her body shook under my touch. "He told me I was trying to trick him, and if I ever told him that again he would kill me."

She turned on her side so we were staring at each other, her warm palm resting on my bearded cheek. "So you can see why I reacted the way I did when you told me you loved me. Rejection was all I'd ever known, but I see now with you it's different. While it might take me some time yet, for it to fully sink in, I do believe you love me." A lone tear trickled down her cheek, her eyes so full of acceptance, but there was a trace of fear still wedged beneath her stare. "As I love you."

My mouth was on hers before she could take her next breath. This whole sharing feelings and loving someone was a whole new world for me. Yes, it would take her some time, but I was willing to stick by her until she was completely mine.

Mind, body and soul.

EPILOGUE

Marek

"ARE YOU SURE YOU WANT me to come with you? I know how you get," she teased, walking toward me in a pair of jean shorts and a modest pink tank top. I say modest because her tits were concealed . . . well, as well as could be expected while still wearing a flimsy piece of material. My jealousies where she was concerned only seemed to worsen, not get better. I trusted her; it was everyone else I had a problem with.

Jagger knew to stay clear of Sully. I knew of a few occasions when I'd been in Chambers and she was helping some of the other women cook, or clean up around the clubhouse, and she and the prospect had run into each other. But from what I was told, their encounters were always kept short, and they never happened when I was present. I made sure of it, for all of our sakes. Sully had tried to plead her case every now and then that the two of them were just friends, but I shut her down every time, dismissing her rants as naivety. On one occasion, we'd gotten into such a heated debate over it I dropped her off at the house and stayed at the club for two days. It was my way of telling her to drop it, or else.

Was it mature?

No.

Did I get my way?

Abso-fuckin-lutely.

"Of course I want you to come. Stone and I have a quick meeting about club business, and then you and I are takin' off for a few days." Pulling her close, I pushed her long hair over her shoulder and nuzzled into her neck, inhaling her scent and dreaming of the exact second I could lose myself inside her again.

Kissing the sensitive spot below her ear, she laughed before flinching, but not before gracing me with one of her sexy moans. "Where are you taking me?"

"It's a surprise, so stop trying to ruin it." Giving her one more quick kiss, I turned toward the door and pulled her behind me.

We made it to the compound quickly, spotting Stone as soon as I parked. Having Sully on the back of my bike was amazing. The way she held on to me, clutching on for dear life sometimes, was extremely satisfying. She wasn't too familiar with riding, her father and that bastard hardly ever taking her off their property, let alone on the back of a motorcycle. A fact I relished more than I let on.

The more we rode together the more she relaxed, although she still had her moments, especially when I kicked it up a notch, traveling faster than was safe sometimes. But I couldn't help it; when I was on the open road with the woman I loved behind me, I let time and speed escape me.

She handed me her helmet as soon as she planted both feet on the ground, sidling up to me to give me a quick kiss before disappearing inside. "I'll be in the kitchen when you're done," she called over her shoulder. I was still staring after her when Stone punched me on the arm.

"Earth to Marek," he jested, a goofy smile on his face while he waited for my reaction. I didn't give him one, instead brushing past him to walk inside as well.

"What time will he be here?" I asked, rounding the table in Chambers and taking my seat at the head. We had a few other things to discuss before Yanez showed his ugly face. But it was necessary—vital, even. The encounter should be the last one we would need to have with the cartel before we were separated from them for good. I wanted to confirm everything else was in place, mainly the beginning of the inevitable demise of our biggest enemy.

"They," my VP corrected. Lifting my head, I tilted it to the side and questioned him with a furrowed brow. "Rafael is coming with Rico this time. They should be here within the hour." He smiled wide, knowing damn well I preferred talking to Carrillo than Yanez. It appeared my day was looking up.

"Good. Happy to hear it."

Leaning back in my chair, the soft leather of the seat conforming around me, I interlocked my fingers behind my head. Smiling wide, I couldn't help but feel as if my life was on the right path. My relationship with Sully was progressing in the right direction. The final piece of the puzzle of taking my club legit was falling nicely into place, and those around me seemed to be happier because of it.

Life was good.

Or so I thought.

STONE

This book is dedicated to the many wonderful friends I've met during this amazing journey. Love of books reaches worldwide, from here in the States to Europe to South Africa to Australia (you know who you are my sweets).

PROLOGUE

"YOU JUST MISSED HIM, SWEETHEART!" Barlow yelled from the other end of the bar while tending to his next customer. Any sane person who laid eyes on the man would have been intimidated. He was in his late thirties, built like a brick shithouse and covered in tattoos. Hell, even his bald head was inked. I knew he was a teddy bear at heart, but maybe I was the rare exception, someone who knew he was a big softie underneath all that scary brawn.

Barlow was the regular bartender at The Underground, a bar owned by the Knights Corruption MC. My uncle Trigger had been a member since before I was born. His club was his life, and even though I visited from time to time when called upon for my nursing skills, and briefly interacted with some of the members, he didn't want me to be a part of that life, a decision I readily went along with because it was quite dangerous.

Speaking of dangerous. . . .

"Hey, Addy," I heard a gravelly voice call from behind me. I knew exactly who it was even before I turned around, the deep rasp of his tone already sending a tremor of lust shooting right through me. My inner thigh muscles clenched tight, desperately trying to suppress the desire to have him buried inside me. I'd dreamed of that voice whispering naughty things in my ear when I was alone, my fingers caressing my skin while wishing they were his instead. But I knew the scenes which internally bombarded me could be nothing but pure fantasy, simply because I knew it wasn't in the cards for me to become involved with such a man. He was risky, in every sense of the word. A hothead who lost his temper at the drop of a hat. I'd seen it with my own two eyes on more than one occasion. Granted, the people who'd infuriated him had rightfully deserved his anger, but still . . . his reactions were never a good thing.

Slowly turning in my seat, I came face to face with none other than Stone Crosswell, the VP of the Knights Corruption. He stood so close I could smell his cologne—a subtle hint of the outdoors . . . and pure male. My eyes traveled over him from head to toe, taking him all in and committing him to memory. I would need it later when I was lying in bed, conjuring up his image in order to find my release.

When my eyes finally met his, he smiled wide, fully aware I was checking him out. A light blush crept over my skin at being caught, but I couldn't help it. He did it to me every time.

Dark eyes entranced me, promising me passion and a whole lot more before I finally turned away. Taking the seat next to me, he bumped my shoulder before situating himself. I knew he did it on purpose and I wasn't complaining, but he was only making things harder for me. He'd expressed his interest a few times, but I continued to turn him down. I had to give it to him, though—he was relentless.

"What are you doing here?" he asked, tapping on the bar to indicate he wanted Barlow to serve him a drink. If anyone was frightened by the bartender's appearance, they would be doubly hesitant to approach Stone. The man was the epitome of strength and masculinity, a high dose of testosterone emanating from every pore on his well-toned body. Standing at six-foot-two, he was a solid wall of muscle, tattoos inking the majority of his torso. Of course, I could only attest to what I'd seen, which was quite an eyeful when he'd walked down the hallway of his club in nothing but a towel wrapped around his hips, banging into me as I emerged from another member's room. My uncle had called me in to patch the guy up after he'd gotten into a fight, a knife wound sliced his skin open so badly he'd needed twenty-five stitches.

Stone's face was ruggedly handsome, his sharp nose and high cheekbones drawing my initial attraction. But it was his entrancing eyes which fascinated me. Eyes the color of mahogany. Eyes which held secrets only a lucky few would ever be privy to. His second most captivating feature was his full lips, which happened to be in direct contrast to the rest of him, promising a softness I wasn't quite sure was a part of his makeup. His mouth continually drew me in, countless minutes passing while I lost myself inside numerous daydreams.

"I was hoping to catch my uncle. I needed to ask him something." When Stone locked eyes with me again, I lost all train of thought. His dark blond hair was longer on top than it was on the sides, almost like a Mohawk, but not quite. His beard was longer than I remembered, but so help me God, he looked amazing. His leather cut made a rustling sound when he turned his body toward mine, and I couldn't help but take notice, yet again, of his muscled, tattoo-covered arms. His white T-shirt was the perfect contrast against his tanned skin, the detail of his artwork on the best canvas imaginable.

How I longed for him to wrap his arms around me and pull me in for the best kiss of my life. Of course, my fantasies remained locked inside my horny brain. There was no way I would give in to my desires; it wouldn't work out well for either of us. He would end up breaking my heart, and my uncle would end up breaking his neck.

It was a big no-no all around.

So why did I keep fantasizing about him? Was it because he was essentially forbidden?

"What did you need to ask him?" he questioned, licking his lips while he continued to pin me with his stare.

"What?" I whispered, all my focus on that delectable mouth of his. Full and plump, begging for me to bite it. *Good Lord, Adelaide. Get a freakin' grip.*

"What did you need to ask Trigger?" he repeated.

The mere mention of my uncle forced me out of my own delusional head. "Why so nosey, Stone?" I smiled, but it faltered when he moved closer.

"Because anything having to do with you is my business," he confessed, a stern look dancing across his face while he silently challenged me. What an odd statement. I would have liked to say it was the first of its kind he'd spewed at me, but it wasn't. Whenever I was in his presence, which wasn't very often, he'd made reference to me being his business, and that I was his, so to speak. I never read into those statements, simply thinking he was playing with me, albeit it was a weird way of flirting. But his words never alarmed me. In fact, they had the opposite effect. My lady bits tingled at the thought that he wanted to possess me in some way. I knew it was ridiculous and borderline insane, but I couldn't help how my body reacted.

"Is that right?" I indulged him.

He made a play for my hand, and before I could pull back, he threaded his fingers with mine and pulled me closer, his warm breath kissing my lips.

"That's right."

I was a puddle of hormones around the man, and no amount of reasoning made any difference. My heart kicked up a notch and I suddenly found the air around me stifling . . . quite difficult to breathe.

Wrenching my hand free before something happened, I stood from my stool and grabbed my purse. "I have to use the restroom," I blurted, hurrying toward the hallway before he could stop me. Every step I took away from the man invading my good senses was a step toward freedom. Freedom from my lust which held me captive whenever he was anywhere near me. I was growing weaker and weaker around him, and I knew it was just a matter of time before he caught me off guard and pounced.

Once I was finished talking to my reflection, warning myself that it was in my best interest to walk right past him and leave, I opened the bathroom door. I was two steps out when a strong arm wrapped around my waist and pulled me into a solid wall of muscle.

"I can't wait anymore," he growled. It was dark where we stood, but I could still see his eyes. His dark, beautiful, lust-filled, eyes. "I'm gonna kiss you now," Stone declared before leaning in to me.

Time froze.

I couldn't move.

I could hardly breathe.

My pulse intensified, the thrumming of anticipation pounding inside my chest, the beat thumping against my skin and making me hyperaware of the creature holding me prisoner. I parted my lips to say something—anything—but no sound poured forth. Instead, his mouth covered mine, his desire authoritative and demanding, but he never pushed me further than I wanted to go.

My heart skipped a beat at the promising contact, and it wasn't long before I was the one devouring him. Licking, biting and sucking at his mouth, hungry for his passion to envelop me.

To own me.

And so was the start of our dysfunctional story. He was arrogant and pushy, and I'd resisted as long as I could before inevitably giving in.

It was a constant battle between the two of us, but I wouldn't change a thing.

Well. . . .

ONE

Adelaide

"WHAT'S YOUR PROBLEM? WHY ARE you acting like this?" One frustrated breath after another tumbled forth the longer he cornered me in the empty waiting room. My workload had been fierce, and the last thing I needed was an unnecessary confrontation with the man who'd been driving me crazy as of late, both in a good and a bad way.

"I wanna know why you won't meet up with me later, that's all," Stone confessed, his rigid posture the exact opposite of his innocent question. He was poised for an argument, and no matter how many honest excuses I gave him, he saw them as just that—excuses.

"I told you I have to work a double tonight, and then I'm picking up an extra shift tomorrow for Carol. I can't get out of it now, I promised her." He'd backed me against the wall, and although he wasn't touching me, he was still holding me hostage in a sense, his arms braced on the wall behind me. He knew damn well I couldn't resist him when he was that close. And when my resolve slipped, he attacked, ghosting his lips over my own. I gasped from the sudden shock at his audacity, but I should have known he was going to play that card. When his tongue snuck out and stroked over my bottom lip, I was a goner. As I was about to give in, yet again, my name sounded over the intercom and knocked me out of my delirium.

Placing my hands on his chest, I tried to shove him back but he didn't budge, instead choosing to try and kiss me again.

"Stone, I have to go. I'm still working, and someone's looking for me." My tone was curt but had faltered slightly. I wanted to be consumed by the big, bad, biker crowding my personal space, but duty called. Thankfully. I was weakening around him more and more each time, and it was becoming quite dangerous.

To us both.

Stone Crosswell was fierce, in every way imaginable. I had no doubt he'd done things during his life he wasn't proud of, most of them probably illegal. I'd seen a few sides of him during the past year, our pseudo relationship—if you could even call it that—bringing out parts of him I was sure he didn't show the rest of the world.

He was possessive to a fault, even though we weren't technically together. We could never be, for various reasons. My uncle Trigger, for one. He would no doubt put a bullet in Stone if he ever found out the man was sleeping with his one and only niece, the apple of his eye. And although Stone had a condition where he didn't feel pain like the majority of humanity, a bullet could still kill him. And I wasn't going to endanger his life merely because he wanted to claim me publicly.

It was the thing we argued about the most. Sometimes he made me feel guilty for denying him, but other times he confessed he understood. He'd stated on many occasions how he didn't want me involved in *that* life. Except for helping the club out from time to time with some medical assistance, I wasn't akin to their lifestyle. My uncle wanted to keep it that way, as did Stone . . . depending on his mood.

Luckily, a lock of dark blond hair fell over his eye when he leaned in to kiss me again. When his hand swiped it back, I made my move. His large frame had been caging me in, but his small movement allowed me the room for escape I needed. Wiggling out from in front of him, I made it to the entrance of the room before he realized what had happened.

"I'm waitin' for you, Addy, so hurry up," he called after me as I ran down the hallway to find out why I'd been paged. I needed those minutes away to gather my senses, encouraging myself to stick to the plan I'd talked myself into earlier.

The plan to end things with the man I was falling for.

His club, although falling more on the legit side of the law as of late, was still dangerous. I'd seen some of the aftermath of their dealings with my own eyes. The most recent incident when I was called in to care for one of the nomad brothers, Tripp, after he'd been shot four times by a rival club. And then again when that same club kidnapped Sully, the president of the Knights Corruption's wife. My new friend.

Further delving into their world would surely put my life in danger more than it probably already was, and I'd worked so hard during my short twenty-six years to have everything ripped away. And for what? A man who rocked my world in the bedroom? I did my best to trivialize our relationship, demeaning it down to nothing more than sexual compatibility, but deep down I knew it was so much more. Stone was the man my heart belonged to. Too bad my head was going to win out this time.

I knew he wasn't going to take it well. I'd broached the subject a few times in the past, and he dismissed it altogether, telling me I was being ridiculous and that nothing bad would ever happen to me.

Although I believed he thought he was telling me the truth, I wasn't naïve. I knew as long as I was close to him I would always be in danger.

Walking toward Brenda, an older RN I'd become friendly with when I started at St. Joseph's Hospital two years prior, she handed me the phone, a big smile plastered on her adorable face. Believing she was at least in her early fifties, I viewed Brenda as cute. She was shorter than my five-six frame, had a head of dark curls, and the most adorable button nose. Her lips were thin, but her smile was contagious.

"Thanks," I said, putting the phone to my ear to find out who'd been looking for me. "Hello, this is Adelaide."

A brief silence greeted me before a male voice traveled down the line. "Adelaide. Hi, it's Dr. Weber. I had a cancelation and wanted to know if you could stop in for your annual, instead of waiting another two weeks. I know you said you were having some issues, so I thought you'd like to come in to put your mind at ease." His light tone comforted me, and it was a no-brainer. The sooner he could see me, the better.

Dr. Weber had been my gynecologist for the past four years, and the fact I now worked in the same hospital as him made things much easier whenever I needed to speak to him on the fly.

"Yeah, that would be great. What time?"

"Fifteen minutes? Does that work for you?" he asked.

"I'll make it work," I assured. "I have a break coming up soon. I'll just use it then."

"Great. See you soon." I hung up the phone and looked at Brenda for a brief moment. So many thoughts ran through my head. I was slightly worried about the unexplainable abdominal pains I'd been having. Ovarian cancer ran in my family, so I was at a much higher risk than normal. And although I was only twenty-six, I knew enough to realize I wasn't too young for cancer to take hold and rip my life apart. Better to be safe than sorry.

Keeping my worries to myself was weighing on me. I couldn't confide in Stone or my uncle, and my dad was the last person I wanted to burden. He'd lost his wife, my mother, to the awful disease five years back, and the last thing I wanted to do was cause him to worry over what could potentially be nothing at all.

I was lost in thought walking down the deserted hallway, completely forgetting there was a brooding man still waiting for me. A small scream tore from my mouth when big hands hauled me into the waiting room I'd escaped from five minutes prior.

Smacking him on the chest, I took a deep breath to calm myself. I hated being scared, the feeling instantly irritating me. His playful smirk did wonders for my mood, however.

"I'll come over when you're done with work," he declared, as if we didn't just have a semi-argument before I was paged. "I'll pick up some pizza since I know you're not gonna want to cook after being on your feet all day." Although the thought of some hot, cheesy goodness had my stomach instantly rumbling, I stuck with my former excuse.

"Stone . . . I can't." I took a few steps back. As soon as I made the move, he frowned, advancing on me before I could disappear from the room.

His warm breath hit my face, his lips so close all I wanted to do was taste them. *Get it together, woman.* "Why not? And don't give me that lame-ass excuse that you have to cover for what's her face."

"Carol," I corrected.

"Whoever," he grated, placing his hands on the sides of my face. "I wanna see you later. I *need* to see you later."

I had no other choice but to retreat once more. I held up my hand in front of me, letting him know not to crowd my personal space again. For some reason, he took the hint that time. "I have to go. I have an appointment to get to, and then I'm finishing off the rest of my shift. *Then* going home to bed," I finished, nodding with a small smile.

He didn't speak for a few seconds, and I foolishly thought he would let the subject go. But instead of continuing to be persistent about seeing me later that evening, he chose another topic altogether.

"What appointment?"

"What?" I asked, realizing exactly where our conversation was heading.

"What appointment do you have to get to?"

"Oh," I stalled. "Umm . . . My annual appointment."

"For that?" he asked, pointing toward my lower region.

"Yes, for *that*." I smirked, trying my best to lighten the increasingly tense mood before it got out of hand. "They called and told me they had a cancellation and asked if I wanted it. I told them I did, so they're expecting me in . . . ten minutes," I affirmed, glancing at the clock on the wall behind Stone. I purposely said 'they' instead of 'he.' For good reason.

"Is it with a man or a woman?" He had instantly changed the mood from slightly tense to borderline volatile. I could have lied, sure. But I wasn't a liar, besides the fact I sucked at it. No, lying would only make it worse, as if I was hiding something.

"Does it matter? It's with a *doctor*," I emphasized. I knew exactly what he was going to say and how he was going to react once he found out Dr. Weber was a man. He would go all Neanderthal. He might even start pounding his chest and pee on me to mark his territory, even though I wasn't technically his to claim. But try explaining that to someone as irrational as Stone.

My refusal to answer gave everything away. If jealousy had a look, Stone mastered it right away. His brows drew together in anger, his breathing accelerating while his fists clenched at his sides. A deep red color rose over his throat, spreading higher until his face was flushed with outrage. Moving toward me, he reached for my arms. Once he had a hold on me, he drew me closer. If I hadn't known him, I would have thought he was about to hurt me in some way. But the man I knew would never lay a finger on me in anger. He simply wanted to touch me, even though he was angry about the situation. He'd told me on numerous occasions I soothed him, now being one of those times, I assumed. Even though I was the direct cause of his fury.

Before he spoke, I knew I had to say something to calm him, bring his focus back around to what was really important. "Stone," I warned, my tone soft but firm. "You need to calm down. You're still healing from being shot, and even though you don't feel it, the stress you're exhibiting is surely causing all sorts of havoc, prohibiting you from making a quick recovery."

A few weeks prior, Marek's wife Sully, my new dear friend, was kidnapped by her crazy ex-boyfriend. Stone had gone with him to rescue her and in the midst of everything, he'd been shot. Thankfully, there was no permanent damage, but he wasn't one hundred percent healed, and stress of any kind always delayed the recovery process. I swore sometimes just because he couldn't feel anything, the man thought he was invincible.

He completely zoned out.

Not one word about his recovery registered; instead, he kept focusing on the fact I was going to see a male for my exam.

"You're gonna let another man look at your pussy?!" he grated through clenched teeth. Before I could answer his ridiculous question, he cut me off, all his insecurities pouring out of him like a siphoned hose. "Absolutely not. No way in fuckin' hell am I allowing another man, doctor or not, to look at what's mine." He raked his fingers through his hair in utter frustration. "No way," he repeated, shaking his head with such vigor I thought he was going to make himself dizzy. Pointing toward the door, he demanded, "Go cancel. Tell *him* you want a woman instead." A slight calm descended over him right then, probably because he thought I was going to obey. His posture became less rigid, but little did he know he was two seconds away from blowing a gasket.

To redirect his focus, I could have chosen to tell him about some of the issues I was experiencing. The pain I was having from time to time, the irregular test results I'd received a month before which caused me to make another appointment so soon, but I wanted to safeguard that information until I knew for certain if there was a problem or not.

Looking at the clock once more, I saw I had six minutes to get to Dr. Weber's office, a feat which was going to be tricky since he was on the other side of the large hospital. I knew he would be okay with me arriving a few minutes late, but I hated keeping him waiting, especially since he went out of his way to contact me after the last-minute cancellation.

Mustering all the strength I had left, I stepped forward and shoved my finger harshly into Stone's muscled chest. "Dr. Weber has been my gynecologist for the past four years, and I'm not switching to someone else simply because you're acting crazy. He is a professional, plain and simple. Now, stop acting like a complete ass and leave before we say something we're gonna regret." He didn't budge, instead becoming irate all over again when he realized his asinine ways weren't going to work. He might intimidate everyone else in his life, but not me.

Before our encounter escalated further, I was the one who chose to quickly make my exit, leaving a stunned maniac standing in the middle of a still-empty waiting room.

His little tirade wasn't the first and certainly wasn't going to be the last, not by any stretch of the imagination.

TWO

Stone

THE WOMAN WAS ABSOLUTELY INFURIATING. She'd warned me to calm down because I was still recovering from being shot, but I didn't care about that. She'd cautioned that, even though I couldn't feel the effects of the bullet's damage, stuff was still goin' on inside me, and my temper wasn't helping my recovery. It was times like this when I always threw caution to the wind, realizing I was pushing the limits of my own body, but I didn't care. Not when there were bigger issues staring me in the face.

It took all my reserve not to destroy the waiting room, knowing damn well security would have been called and I would have been banned from the premises. Not that I would have let that stop me.

While I tried to compose myself, because I'd had no other choice, she was flitting off to bare herself for some fuckin' guy, doctor or not. *New mission—find out everything I can about Dr. Weber.* If she wasn't gonna listen to me, then I would make *him* back off.

The open road helped to soothe my nerves, the ride back to the clubhouse allowing me the time I needed to try and focus on other things, although it was difficult.

When I'd finally arrived, I parked and took off my helmet, placing it on the back of my bike. There were a few people milling around outside, men and women alike. It was a warm day and I could have sworn we were having a cookout, but based on the lack of bodies, maybe plans were changed at the last minute.

"Yo, Jagger," I called out, striding toward one of the club's prospects, "we havin' a cookout or what?" Coming face to face with the young guy, I could see why a lot of the wannabees flocked toward him. He was a good-lookin' kid. He was also the ticketed fighter of our group, signing up and winning every single battle he'd been in. Mostly, they were underground fights, nothing professional. I'd even taught him a thing or two when he needed someone to go toe to toe with. My line of fighting was more for self-defense, even though I'd used many of my martial arts skills to take down our enemies, when it was called for.

"Hey, Stone," he greeted, walking up and slapping me on the back. "Yeah, just delayed by like an hour. We're still waiting on Hawke and Ryder to come back with the steaks."

The genuine smile on his face was contagious, my own lips kicking up in amusement. I liked the kid, but Marek didn't. I tried to warn Jagger to stay on the prez's good side, and he assured me he was trying. All it would take was one wrong move on the prospect's part, and he'd be tossed from the club without a second thought. Probably worse, depending on what got him ousted.

"Cool. All right, I'll go see what everyone else is up to," I said, leisurely striding past him.

"Hey," he called after me. "The ring is coming this week. Once we get it set up, you and me can start breakin' it in."

"You got it." He was excited we were finally gonna get in weekly workouts, honing his fighting skills enough to where he would be unstoppable. He was well on his way already, but a few improvements wouldn't hurt.

Now that Marek was taking the club completely legit, it was up to everyone to either be active in one of our legal endeavors or start up something for themselves, with the rule that a certain portion of whatever money they made came back into the club. The Knights Corruption was a main priority for all the men, so keeping it thriving was everyone's first duty, and we did so willingly.

Walking away, I heard a few of the girls who were hanging around giggle as Jagger approached them. With all the available pussy, I was surprised he never took advantage. He was always eager to hook up before, but something changed a couple months ago, and I wasn't quite sure what it was, although I certainly had my suspicions.

My phone rang, drawing me back from my speculations about Jagger. Pressing the button, I answered before identifying the caller. "Yeah?"

"It's Yanez. We're coming to see you tomorrow. Pass along the news to Marek." His choppy breaths came out strained, as if he'd run a marathon before he placed the call.

"Who's we?"

"Who do you think? Me and Rafael. See you around noon." He hung up before I could ask him anything else. Prick. I couldn't wait until we were free from the cartel altogether. I hated dealing with Rico Yanez, even though our interactions had been minimal. But any time spent indulging that worthless jackass was too much in my opinion. I knew Marek shared the same sentiment, although he had a different opinion about Rafael Carrillo. He'd saved the leader of the Los Zappas cartel's life, and because of it we were being rewarded with a few favors. One was that they were letting us walk away from our part in the drug smuggling business. And two, they were gonna cut off the Savage Reapers' supply as well, basically crippling them into oblivion, definitely a win-win for us.

I was inside the clubhouse for five minutes, chatting it up with Cutter and his son, Breck, when Ryder and Hawke strolled through the door, bags of food in each of their hands. I hadn't realized how hungry I was until right then. Food had been the last thing on my mind since my interaction with Adelaide. She frustrated me beyond belief, and it was a wonder I was able to interact with anyone else after she left me at the hospital.

She sure was a spitfire, and although it annoyed me most times—that day being a prime example—her feistiness often turned me the fuck on.

"It's about time you two bastards got back," Cutter joked, grabbing a few of the bags to inspect what they'd bought. "Where's the beer?"

"Right here, old man," Hawke interjected, shoving a case of alcohol at him. Before Cutter uttered another word, Hawke said, "Don't worry, there's more in the van."

Laughing, Cutter and Breck headed outside to grab the rest of the night's drink. While beer was high on the list, we also kept a stocked liquor bar. Every man had their poison, and while most of us could handle it, some could not—Ryder jumping to the top of that list. We made sure it was a rare occasion when he indulged, mainly because he became a mean drunk when he consumed the hard stuff. Beer flowed nicely through his system, but get some whiskey in the bastard and he was ready to take on every one of us.

That man had some demons lurking inside, a part of him he kept secret from the rest of us. The most anyone knew about his private life was that he had been married once, but she up and left him, taking their daughter with her. He never divulged the reason why, even when we tried to get it out of him while he was drunk, volatile or not. He was another brother who hardly took advantage of the available pussy.

Me, on the other hand, I dove right in, until I got mixed up with Adelaide a year back. Since her, I hadn't so much as touched another woman. She was all I needed.

But our relationship was complicated. Too many obstacles in the way of officially being together. Her uncle was number one. The club's lifestyle was number two.

The Knights were well on their way to becoming legit, the next day's final meeting with the cartel proving so. Now, all I had to do was make sure Trigger wouldn't shoot me, and then I could convince Adelaide to be with me once and for all.

THREE

Adelaide

AFTER THE DAY'S EVENTS, ALL I wanted to do was crawl into a hot bath and let the water soak away all my fears. Trying my best to calm myself until the results came back, my brain was suddenly consumed with one man.

Stone Crosswell.

I'd asked him one time how he'd got his road name and he told me that Marek had given it to him when they were kids. Said he was like a block of stone, never allowing anything to penetrate. No pain. Statuesque when any other normal human being would have crumbled under the agony of life's afflictions. Stone had what was referred to as congenital insensitivity to pain, and while he thought it was a blessing, it was really a curse. Pain was the body's alarm system, sounding off when something was wrong. Because of his condition, he was careless, flippant even when it came to keeping himself out of harm's way. Something which drove me absolutely insane.

His given name was Lincoln, but only a few people knew that. The only reason I knew his real name was because he let it slip one time when he was talking about his mother, and how she used to call him by his full name when she was upset with him. Lincoln DeLeon Crosswell. His revelation caught me so off guard I could do nothing but laugh. Only he could pull off a name like that, although Stone was quite fitting as well.

The only time he tolerated me calling him Lincoln was when I was extremely upset with him. And it was during those times he knew enough from my tone and choice of name to back off and give me my space. Come to think of it, he hadn't pissed me off quite to that level in some time.

I shouldn't jinx myself.

Driving home, I couldn't help but be grateful at the way some parts of my life turned out. I'd always done well in school. I wasn't a genius by any means, but I certainly was book-smart. Since I was a young child, I knew I wanted to be a nurse. Actually, I wanted to be a doctor but we didn't have the money for such an expensive education, so nursing was the next best option.

My mother had been in and out of hospitals since I was in grade school, battling one illness after the other, all the while her spirits shining bright. She was the strongest woman in the world, and I was devastated when she'd been taken from me at the tender age of forty-six. I was only twenty-one, and I wasn't ready to lose my best friend. Who was I going to talk to when I was having relationship issues? Who was going to help me plan my wedding, if such a thing ever happened for me one day? Who was going to teach me how to be a mother, if my life was ever graced with little ones?

My uncle Trigger was my mother's younger brother, and since her passing, he had become even more protective over me, especially during the times when I was at the club. I couldn't even count how many men he'd threatened when it came to me, or how many of them had met the end of his fist. Uncle Trig was just shy of fifty, much older than some of the men, but he had a mean right hook, so they knew enough not to piss him off. While I loved him dearly, sometimes my heart ached looking at him because of the resemblance he shared with my mother. It was quite uncanny. They had shared the same almond-shaped eyes and full cheeks, along with the same shade of brown hair, although his had been greying for quite some time.

Turning the key in the lock, I opened the door, but before I stepped inside, my next-door neighbor stuck his head out of his apartment and unintentionally scared me.

"Sorry, Adelaide. I didn't mean to startle you," Robby said, smiling quickly to relieve any fright he'd just caused me. Dropping the hand clutching my chest, I returned his smile.

When I moved here two years ago, Robby was one of the first people I'd encountered and I couldn't have been happier. He was six years younger than me, which put him right at the tender age of eighteen when I met him. For him to be living on his own was surprising, but when he explained he didn't have any family to speak of, I understood. He'd bounced around the foster care system his entire youth, and the second he could escape, he did. Graduating high school—which was a feat in itself, because he told me how much he struggled with his studies—he secured a job as well as his own place. He'd been living in the building ever since.

"That's okay, Robby. How are you?" I asked, stifling a yawn I knew was coming.

"Great," he replied, smiling wider since I was engaging him in conversation. I think he had a little crush on me, which was a nice ego boost, seeing as how he was quite the handsome little devil. Dark curls adorned the top of his head, defined cheekbones and full lips setting him apart from a lot of young men his age. He'd been much too thin when I first met him, but since then he'd filled out rather nicely. I tried not to notice because he was so much younger than me, but I was only human. Making sure never to encourage him, I treated him like I would my kid brother's friend, if I had a kid brother. "Hey, I tried out a new recipe. Wanna taste it?" His new thing was cooking, something I benefited from on numerous occasions.

"Not tonight. I'm exhausted. How about tomorrow?" I offered.

His face fell, but with the hopes he could indulge me the next day, his blue eyes lit up. I made a mental note to see if there were any available young women at the hospital I could set him up with. We were scheduled to have a new class of nursing students starting on Monday. I'd have to scope out the potential candidates.

"Okay. It's a plan." He smiled and waited until I closed my door.

There weren't too many apartments in the building—only four floors and I was on the top one, which I preferred. I didn't need to worry about hearing people above me, walking around at all hours of the night. Each floor housed four apartments. Robby and I took up two of those on our floor. One had recently been vacated, by a couple buying their first home, and the other had been empty for renovations.

My landlord was a nice older gentleman, who lived out of the area. Whenever I ran across a problem, he sent someone by right away to take care of it. Robby was forever telling me he could fix things for me, but I didn't want to rely on him too much, nor did I want him to get the wrong impression. I indulged him enough by trying out his new recipes from time to time because he didn't have anyone else to give him an honest opinion. Plus, they were always fantastic, so I kind of benefited.

A little while later, after my much-needed relaxing bath, I headed to bed earlier than planned. Checking my phone, I noticed Stone had left me five messages and two voicemails. Most of them were apologetic, but at the same time he was sticking to his justification for wanting me to make an appointment with a woman, instead of keeping Dr. Weber.

I never replied to his crazy rantings. Pulling the blankets up to cover me, I turned off the side light and gave in to the sleep waiting in the shadows to drag me under.

FOUR

Stone

"WHERE THE FUCK ARE THEY?" Marek asked, frustration written all over his face. Pacing back and forth in Chambers was only hyping him up, even more so than usual. Ever since we'd saved Sully, he'd been much more possessive over his time with her, despising some of the club's activities because it meant more time away from his wife. Okay, 'despised' was a bit harsh. But he definitely wasn't as integrated into the day-to-day dealings of the club as he had been. I was happy he'd finally found someone to share his life with, and even though they hadn't known each other long, he seemed to be over-the-moon happy. And his version of over-the-moon happy was the slight smile he displayed whenever he mentioned her name. It was a big deal for him, and I acknowledged it by taking over many of the duties which required special attention.

Our local businesses needed to be overseen, especially once we finally cut all ties with the cartel. I knew without Marek telling me, that we had to cultivate our new, and old, endeavors to make sure they were as profitable as possible. The Underground was the club's bar, the only patrons the club's members. Yes, occasionally strangers wandered inside until they realized who owned the establishment, then they quickly disappeared. No harm, no foul, most of the time. So that business wasn't necessarily profitable, more of a place away from the clubhouse where people could unwind and let loose.

Flings, the strip club we'd opened close to six months ago, was proving to be quite the moneymaker. Then again, pussy was a surefire way to secure a profitable income. Thankfully, there was no shortage of women willing to take off their clothes for some dough. A quick and easy way to earn money. The women were to follow the same rules as the rest of the Knights Corruption. No hard drugs. Plain and simple. We'd had an issue a few weeks back with one of the strippers snorting heroin before she went on stage. Not only was her performance shitty, but she had put us in jeopardy of getting raided if word ever got out there were drugs at the club. We possessed zero tolerance, and the bitch was fired as soon as Marek confronted her.

We didn't need any reason for that prick of a DEA Agent, Sam Koritz, to bust into one of our places and start tossing our stuff around like he'd done the last time he and his buddies made a surprise visit to our clubhouse.

Marek was planning to open two more pussy clubs in the next couple months, although now that his time was occupied every second he wasn't at the clubhouse, I doubted he would be overseeing anything when it came to location, liquor licenses, talent, etc. I'd probably have to step in and take over, and while the thought of interviewing potential talent was entertaining, I didn't think Adelaide would appreciate me gawking at naked chicks all day.

Fuck! I hated when thoughts of that nature even filtered through my mind. I shouldn't care what she thought. It was club business, and therefore none of *her* business. We weren't even technically together—not that she would have a say about it even if we were. But the thought of her finding out, then being pissed off and doing or saying God knew what, already had me wanting to pass the job off to someone else. Not that any of the other guys wouldn't jump at the opportunity.

I was so lost in thought I didn't even notice Marek standing at my side. He gave me a 'what the fuck' look before he resumed his annoying pacing. Before either of us spoke, I heard shouts coming from outside the Chambers door.

Our guests must have arrived. *About damn time.* Sneaking a quick peek at my watch, I noticed they were an hour late, their tardiness grating on my last nerve because they thought nothing of keeping us waiting. But as ballsy as we were most of the time, we weren't stupid enough to call and inquire as to their whereabouts. Even though Carrillo was repaying a debt to Marek of his own accord, we knew not to push the man.

Not waiting for direction, Marek and I exited Chambers and walked toward the common room. Standing by the front entrance were Rico Yanez and Rafael Carrillo, the two top men of Los Zappas cartel. While Carrillo looked put together and polished, his dark grey suit pressed to perfection, every strand of his dark hair in perfect place, Yanez looked anything but. He was wearing a pair of worn jeans and a T-shirt with two holes near the neckline. I was all for casual, but not for a man in his position. His greasy, graying hair was pulled back tight, making his face look even harsher than it already was. The man had beady eyes, which shouted he was not to be trusted. With anything. I was surprised a man as smart as Carrillo made him his second in command. There had to be a reason why, although I couldn't fathom what it could be.

Carrillo approached us while Yanez hung back, assessing every member inside the club as if he were prepared to pop off at any moment and start some kind of war.

"Marek," Carrillo greeted, gripping my friend's hand. His smile seemed genuine, which made me relax. That was until I laid eyes on his watchdog again. Then my hackles were up and ready for anything.

"Carrillo," I heard Marek return. "I hope your trip was uneventful." My prez kept a straight face, but his tone was airy. I knew he trusted the cartel leader, a feat I didn't possess myself. I was wary of most people, as was my friend. Normally. But I hadn't orchestrated the agreement the two men had made. I would back my leader up a thousand percent, but I still had my suspicions.

"Shall we?" Marek gestured toward an empty room at the back of the club, nothing inside except for a few chairs. No one stepped foot in Chambers except for the members. Women weren't even allowed back there. It was a hard and fast rule. The only exception was when Adelaide had to set up a quick operating room for Tripp when he'd been dropped off at the front gate riddled with bullet holes. And while I liked the guy just fine, even sharing a beer or two with him in the past, I hated the fact my woman was the one overseeing his recovery. She still checked in on him, which more than annoyed me.

Trying to focus on what was happening around me, I followed Marek and Carrillo into the room, Yanez walking closely behind me until we were all sheltered inside the small space.

Seeing as how it hadn't been our first meeting about dissolving the club's relationship, we wrapped up our little powwow in a half hour. Turned out Rafael Carrillo was indeed a man of his word. It took some time—a year and two months, to be exact—but we were finally at the turning point, and we welcomed it with open fucking arms. Not only would the Knights Corruption be on the way to legitimacy, but our enemy would fall to their knees, never to recover enough to be a threat to us ever again.

"If there's anything you need, just let me know," Carrillo offered, shaking Marek's hand while we all stood back at the threshold of the entrance to the club.

"And if you ever want a free lap dance, you let me know." Marek grinned, slapping Carrillo's shoulder in a good-natured gesture. We remained close-knit, saying our good-byes when I saw movement from the corner of my eye. For some reason, I knew to give whoever was standing there my full attention. I'd only been half engaged anyway, allowing Marek to take the lead, as he should have being the Knights' president.

Slowly turning my head, I lay witness to Sully crouching near the bar, and as if I were watching in slow motion, I saw the glass she was holding slip from her grasp and crash to the floor. There had been other noises floating through the air, mainly from some of the men laughing and ragging on each other, mixed with music pumping out of the surrounding speakers. For some reason, though, the glass breaking into tiny shards rang out loud, drawing a few other people's attention. Marek, Carrillo and Yanez not being a part of them.

Sully's eyes practically popped out of her beautiful head, her face stark white as if she'd seen a goddamn ghost. She suddenly started shaking, and the weird thing was that she was looking directly at us. Before I even made a move, she bent down and started cleaning up the mess she'd made, but there was something in her body language that put me on full alert.

Fear.

She was fucking riddled with it.

Striding across the open space then approaching her slowly so as not to startle her, I bent down and grabbed the last few pieces of broken glass. Reaching for her hand, I gently helped her to her feet and that's when I saw it. She'd been crying, her breaths short and choppy as she tried her best to control herself.

"What's wrong?" I asked, guiding her to sit on one of the empty bar stools. Standing in front of her, I turned around slightly and followed her gaze; when I realized who she was staring at, I frowned. Did she know Carrillo and Yanez?

Internally balking at my own stupid question, I realized she *had* to know them, simply because the Savage Reapers had an ongoing deal with them. *Well, until today, at least. No more.*

"That man," she whispered, averting her eyes to stare at her trembling hands resting in her lap.

"Which one?"

"I can't be here," she suddenly declared, trying to rise from the stool but stumbling, the metal legs of her seat screeching across the floor. The noise pierced the air and drew her husband's attention. Unfortunately, it also drew the attention of our *guests*.

As soon as Sully realized all three men were staring in our direction, she panicked. If I thought her complexion was white before, she looked like she was about to faint, all the blood draining from her face in rapid fashion.

Grabbing her shoulders, I tried to make her focus on me, but she was too lost to whatever was happening inside that head of hers. Shaking her did nothing but irritate my friend, who was briskly walking toward the both of us.

"What the hell is goin' on?" Marek asked sternly, reaching for his wife's hand and pulling her close. "What's wrong, Sully?" He physically had to turn her face so she would look at him; otherwise, her stare was latched on to the two men standing by the door.

"That man . . ." she repeated, her breath leaving her lungs in a desperate attempt to form a noise.

"Which one, sweetheart?" Marek cooed, starting to panic himself because of his wife's odd behavior. "Tell me what's wrong. You're freakin' me out." He placed his hands on her upper arms and pulled her in to him, whispering, "You can tell me. It'll be okay. I'm here. No one's gonna hurt you."

"Yanez," she cried, resting her head against her husband's chest for support. Or to hide. I couldn't distinguish which. Maybe it was both.

Something bad was about to be revealed, I knew it deep in my soul, but there was no preparation in the world that could have prepared me for what came flying out of Sully's mouth. "He . . . He—" she cut off, tears tumbling down her cheeks as she so desperately tried to continue, her entire body shaking in Marek's embrace.

"He what?" Marek seethed, gritting his teeth because he knew as well as I did that her disclosure was gonna be detrimental. She was visibly terrified, and we realized she wouldn't react in such a way unless something unspeakable had happened.

Finally connecting her eyes with her husband's, she whispered, "He raped me."

If ever I thought I'd seen my best friend enraged before, it was nothing compared to what he showed right then. Fire lit his eyes, his posture locking into place as his muscles coiled. The air around us thickened with deadly tension, the likes of which I'd never experienced before. I would go so far as to say I'd actually seen the pulse in his neck beating furiously, his body's reaction heightening it quickly. Too quickly. God knew what deadly thoughts were crashing into his brain right then.

Suddenly, Marek locked eyes with me, a desperation I'd never seen before putting me on edge. When I'd received his unspoken plea, I nodded and moved closer to his wife.

It was mere seconds before he was sprinting across the length of space separating us from the one man who was gonna feel the brunt of all his rage.

Reaching the bastard in no time at all, he cocked back his fist and let it fly, connecting with the side of Yanez's face before anyone saw the assault coming. The man's head whipped to the side and he instantly lost his balance and tumbled over, hitting the ground with a heavy thud. Marek was on top of him before the man could right himself, continually hitting him in the face. All the while, Marek never said a word, which was the eeriest part of the whole scene. Rage poured from him and onto the man lying beneath him. It was obvious Yanez had no idea why he was being attacked.

Or at least, that's what I thought.

Until he opened his fucking mouth and essentially sealed his fate.

"Her f-father gave her to m-me," he garbled, blood dripping from his nose and mouth as he tried to speak, his left eye well on its way to being swollen shut. "It was a fair exchange for doing business." Although I was clear across the room, I heard every vile thing the man spewed, sickened to my core at what Sully had endured at the hands of not only Yanez, but essentially her father as well. The one person who should have been wired to protect her. The same person who'd thrown her to the wolves. And I was sure it wasn't the first time.

Sully dropped her head, her hair falling forward and shielding her from the scene unfolding in front of everyone present. The cloak of black gave her some kind of solace, some detachment from reality she so desperately needed. Feeling helpless in all this, I wrapped my arm around her shoulders and pulled her to me, doing my best to show her we were all there to protect her. She'd come to trust us during her short time with the Knights Corruption, but right then she needed strength more than ever, and I was only too willing to offer it.

Marek managed to get in one final punch before he was hauled off the bastard by Hawke and Trigger. I wanted to be the one to stand next to him, but I knew he would have wanted me to watch over his wife. So I stayed put—for the time being, at least.

The entire time, Carrillo stood back, not saying a word or lifting a finger to try and help his right-hand man. A smug expression danced across his face, and I suspected the head of the cartel had little to no respect for Yanez, his allowing someone else to pummel him all the proof I needed.

Once both men were on their feet, Marek grabbed the gun hidden in his waistband, pulled it free, and pointed it directly at Yanez's head. There was no tremble in his arm, no hesitation in his stance, just a resoluteness which emanated from his entire body, as if shooting a man dead in the middle of the clubhouse was a normal occurrence. Which it certainly was not.

Sully leaned further into me. I supported her, silently promising her everything was gonna be okay, all while watching my friend threaten a member of the cartel. The very same cartel we'd just broken free from. How would Carrillo feel if Marek killed his second in command? Would he wage war on the Knights? Or would he be elated that we'd rid him of such a vile creature?

I guessed we were about to find out.

"You raped my wife!" Marek roared, stepping closer and pushing the gun hard against Yanez's temple. Almost immediately, a ragged sob tore free from Sully's lips, realizing everyone there had just found out what had happened to her. Mortification covered her skin, kissed her cheeks, and took hold of her body. Shaking and borderline hysterical, the only thing I could do was hold her tighter, kissing the top of her head and whispering, "Shhh . . . It's okay."

"I didn't know she was your wife," the man gritted, spitting blood on the floor after answering. There was no remorse in his tone, or fear on his face. He stood tall and glared at Marek the whole time he had a gun against his head. Yanez knew as well as I did that, if Marek shot him, his boss would be forced to retaliate.

Knowing I needed to step in before the situation escalated beyond control, my eyes darted around the room. "Jagger!" I hollered, seeing the prospect enter from the kitchen. "Get over here. Now." Once he was close, I carefully guided Sully toward him. "Get her out of here," I instructed. I knew Marek had a problem with the kid, but it wasn't the time to worry about such things. Jagger heard the urgency in my voice and didn't argue, ushering Sully into the kitchen where she would be hidden from whatever was gonna happen next.

Once they were both out of sight, I strode toward my friend, struggling to find the right words which would calm him enough not to do anything rash. But nothing came to mind. I put myself in his shoes. If Addy had told me some fucker had raped her, and that man was standing in front of me, I would have reacted the same way. Actually, the bastard would be dead by now, but that was the difference between me and Marek, which was why he was the president and I wasn't. He had more control than I did, even though he was teetering on the brink right then.

"Don't do anything stupid, man," I whispered in his ear. His rage was contagious, and it was hyping me up as well. Nothing good was gonna come of the situation if both of us wanted blood.

All of a sudden, Carrillo spoke up. "Marek," he warned. "If you take out my second in command, then you leave me no choice but to take out yours." The words were threatening, but the man's demeanor was anything but. The fucker was smiling at us, as if he were discussing the weather.

"He deserves to die," Marek argued. "He raped my *wife*."

Turning his head toward his man, Carrillo asked, "When did this happen, Yanez?"

"A few months ago," he replied, wiping his bloody mouth with the back of his hand.

Focusing back on Marek, the head of the cartel asked, "Was she your wife then?"

Silence was the initial answer, my friend trying to figure out what to say next. Truth was, the answer was no; it happened before we'd even snatched Sully. Which apparently had been the right move, because it hit home right then just how much the woman had been abused.

"Was she your wife at that time, Marek?" Carrillo asked again, taking a step closer to crowd my friend's personal space.

"No, she wasn't. But it doesn't matter. He has to die." His focus was rigid, and I feared he was gonna pull the trigger, putting us all in grave danger with such a rash, knee-jerk reaction. Like I said, the bastard would have been dead if Addy had been the one who'd been violated. But Marek was more levelheaded than I was, and right then I prayed for him to re-main somewhat calm and eventually back away without bringing the axe down on all our heads.

"No, he doesn't. While I don't condone what he did, you cannot exact revenge on him because he mistreated a woman you didn't even know at the time." Carrillo's words were calm but his tone was borderline deadly, realizing the possibility of a war erupting.

Placing my hand on Marek's shoulder, I leaned in and urged him to put the gun down. "Don't do this. Not right now. Sully needs you. Save it for another time." His breaths were still ragged from exertion, but he heard my words. What I'd said flipped some switch inside him enough to withdraw his weapon from the man's head.

"This isn't over, Yanez," Marek growled. "Now get the fuck out of my club."

Both men disappeared from the clubhouse, Carrillo glancing back at Marek with a look in his eyes which was something akin to an apology.

FIVE

Adelaide

"ARE YOU EVER GOING TO learn, Tripp?" I asked, laughing and gently hitting him on the arm. The man was something else, his prior wounds doing nothing to change his demeanor or attitude. If anything, he probably thought he was invincible. But I guessed being shot four times and surviving would make anyone think they were untouchable.

What had happened to him was horrible, yet it was another reminder why I chose to stay away from the club's lifestyle. Even though Stone promised me they were looking for ways to make sure their future was secure . . . and on the right side of the law.

Yeah, I would believe that when I saw it.

"Nope, not if I can help it, sweetheart," he jested, swallowing the last of his drink. He was not drunk by any means, but was well on his way to feeling nice and relaxed.

"You know you're not supposed to drink and take pain medication at the same time, don't you? Not such a smart move," I warned, my face suddenly becoming very serious. From what little I learned about Tripp during the time I watched over him after he'd been shot, I knew him to have a good heart. His laughter was rich, his jovial attitude standing out amongst the seriousness of his brothers. I was sure there was a dark side hidden underneath, but I couldn't determine whether or not what he showed to the world was a façade or the truth. Either way, I liked him.

He was forever flirting with me, but I knew he was harmless, although Stone would argue the exact opposite. When I'd asked Tripp if there was someone special in his life, a brief dark look clouded his piercing green eyes, but it disappeared too quick to read further into it. For any woman who was comfortable in this type of lifestyle, Tripp was quite the catch.

The man was gorgeous, a fact I made sure to keep to myself, just in case my admission fueled his flirtation into something more. Plus, I didn't need Stone to keep questioning me about him because I thought he was attractive. He did that enough already. He hated the attention I gave the nomad, but it was ridiculous. I'd overseen his recovery, no more, no less.

But Stone was a jealous, possessive ass sometimes. I knew this when I became involved with him, and it was another reason I was unwilling to become even more attached. Most times, I wanted to slap him for acting crazy. The other times, well . . . I just ignored him and went on about my business. Which drove him insane.

"I've been through the wringer and I'm still standing, ain't I?" Tripp asked, laughing and pulling me close. Swinging an arm over my shoulder, he leaned in and kissed my temple. "Don't know what I would have done without you, Adelaide," he confessed, kissing my cheek that time before letting me go.

But it wasn't quick enough because Stone and Trigger saw the whole thing.

"Shit," I muttered under my breath, putting a few extra feet between me and Tripp, who was oblivious to the death stares he was getting from both my uncle and the crazy man stalking our way.

"What the fuck?" Stone gritted, coming to a stop directly in front of us, his hands shoved deep in his pockets to keep from attacking his fellow brother, I was sure. Quickly glancing over at Trigger, he shouted, "What? You ain't gonna say shit to him about pawing at your niece? Why you always comin' down on me, but you clam up when *he* does it?" Stone's face was red with anger, and I found it both irritating and amusing. He worked himself up over nothing, and no matter how many times I told him I wasn't interested in Tripp, that I simply cared about him getting better, he didn't believe me.

Correction—he didn't necessarily believe I wanted Tripp. Instead, he was convinced the nomad wanted to get in my pants, although he used much more descriptive wording.

"I punched the fucker for making comments about my niece. He knows not to overstep again," my uncle proclaimed, although he still looked like he wanted to jump over the bar and clock Tripp once again.

These men are too much sometimes.

"Calm down, everyone," I huffed. "Tripp is not doing anything wrong. We're simply having a conversation, and he was thanking me for watching out for him. Making sure he's healing all right. That's it." Placing my hands on my hips, my lips parted to say more but Stone cut me off.

Glaring at Tripp, he asked, "When are you leavin', anyway?"

"Not enjoying my company?" he joked, smirking at Stone and egging him on.

"No," Stone answered, before turning his attention back to me. "If you're done fawning all over him, I need you to look at my bullet wound," he said, walking toward the bedroom he used when he stayed at the clubhouse.

I knew if I didn't indulge him he would blow up my phone or show up at my apartment or the hospital until I talked to him. I'd looked at his wound the other day and he was healing rather nicely, so I knew it was just an excuse to get me away from Tripp . . . and alone. Away from my uncle's watchful glare was another motivation.

"You don't have to do anything you don't want to, honey," my uncle said, his eyes questioning me more than his words ever could.

"I'll be fine. You know how much of a baby Stone is." I smiled to put him at ease.

"I heard that, woman," Stone called from down the hallway.

"Well, I said it loud enough for you to hear." I walked toward where he'd disappeared, laughing to myself that he was so easy to rile up.

Entering his room, I quickly came face to face with his bare chest. It wasn't like I'd never seen him shirtless before—hell, I'd run my hands all over his delectable body many times—but each time I saw him in all his glory, I was taken aback.

He was all man.

Powerful and virile.

A strand of blond hair fell over his right eye when he dropped his head. Even from that angle, though, his dark eyes connected with mine and a shiver coursed through me. I'd never been as attracted to another man as I was to Stone. Something innate called to me on a baser level. I didn't completely understand it, but it was there nonetheless. Pulsating under the surface, tempting me to let go and give in completely.

Was it lust?

Most definitely.

Was it something more?

Only time would tell, although I was leaning more toward yes the more time I spent with the infuriating man.

Walking the few feet to reach him, my hand connected with his wound, my fingers dancing over the area and inspecting it. His skin was still red and puffy, but the initial swelling had gone down. He was going to be left with a nasty scar, but it wasn't going to detract from his beauty. If anything, it only added to it.

His perfect chest was covered with tattoos, intricate designs swirling over his pecs, as well as the entire length of both arms. There was a fierce-looking hawk inked into his skin, the eyes of the bird ominous. The only other tat as entrancing was the club's emblem, a skull with flames shooting out from both sides, a large sword slicing through the middle of it.

"It looks even better than the other day." I was still staring at the affected area when I spoke, knowing as soon as I made eye contact he was going to flip the script and either give me a hard time about Tripp, or disarm me and make a move. He probably thought it would be fun to try and have sex with me right under my uncle's nose.

And I wasn't sure I was strong enough to resist him.

He hadn't been inside me in days, and the closeness we shared right then was weakening me with every passing second. But I knew if my uncle even *thought* there was something going on between the two of us, there would be a bigger issue. I had no doubt he would try and kill him, club brother or not.

Before I said another word, his fingers cupped my chin and raised my head until our eyes connected. I thought he was going to say something endearing, or sexy.

But what did he say instead?

"I swear to Christ, the next time that bastard touches you, I'm gonna fuck him up. You've been warned, Addy," he growled. "So if you don't want to see him all messed up again, then you better stay clear. He's healed up just fine. No need for you to fawn all over him anymore." Pulling back, he threw a shirt over his head and, for a microsecond, I hated that he was shielding his body from me.

Once I'd scolded myself for my weakness, his words really hit home.

He was being an ass. As usual.

Who did he think he was, talking to me like that? Essentially threatening one of his own club members. Nomad or not, Tripp was part of the Knights Corruption. But I guessed it wasn't anything my uncle hadn't proclaimed on occasion, not only against Tripp, but Stone and every other man who'd ever innocently flirted with me.

So many retorts fired off inside my brain, but I couldn't form the words for any of them. I was beyond pissed; I couldn't even think straight. So instead of engaging him in an argument, I chose to escape his presence altogether. When he turned around to search for something, I abruptly left the room, walking quickly down the hallway toward the common area. Waving good-bye to my uncle, I headed toward the exit. I was ten feet from my car when I heard Stone shouting after me.

There was no way I was turning around, because if I did and saw the irate look on his face as he stalked toward me, I would have engaged him in a verbal battle. And that would have certainly drawn the attention of everyone present, essentially making them question whether there really was something going on between the two of us. And I didn't need that getting back to my uncle. He already suspected enough as it was.

Peeling out of the lot, my tires kicking up gravel all around me, I sped off down the street, glancing in my rearview mirror to witness Stone pulling at his hair and no doubt cursing up a storm.

SIX

Stone

SHIT HAD GOTTEN WAY TOO intense earlier, what with Marek attacking then threatening Yanez. He could have unraveled all our hard work to break away from the cartel in one fatal moment. I didn't blame him for his rage, though. It was totally justified.

I asked him if there was anything he wanted me to do, fully onboard with whatever came out of his mouth. While I prayed it didn't put us in harm's way, the truth of it was that we were still in danger's path, and probably would be for quite some time to come. While Marek ushered Sully out the door, he told me we would devise a plan soon enough. He was taking her home, and I doubted anyone would lay eyes on them for a few days.

As if gracing me with a sense of calm after everything that'd happened, I'd never been so happy to see Addy's face than when I saw her across the clubhouse floor. Although, my feelings had switched from elated to enraged in a few short moments once I saw Tripp groping her. And she was laughing, as if it were totally acceptable to allow another man to touch her in such a familiar way.

I thought I'd won out when she followed me to one of the back bedrooms, luring her there with a false need to check my healing wound. But I couldn't hold my tongue, something I was famous for around here. My temper usually bested me, but no matter how I tried to control it, my anger won out every single time. It was useful during club battles, but not with Addy. I knew it, yet I failed to rein it in when she riled me up beyond the point of sanity.

When I turned around for a split second, she took off, peeling out of the lot before I could reach her.

Seems like she just invited me over for some more one-on-one time.

———— ♦ ————

ADDY LIVED THIRTY MINUTES FROM the club on a good day, but that day the California traffic was unreal. It took me close to an hour to reach her house, and I only prayed I hadn't wasted the trip. For all I knew, she could have ran errands or been called in to work. Blowing up her phone did nothing but irritate me, driving home how pissed she was when she didn't answer.

Not once.

Not even to tell me to go to hell.

Nothing.

Parking my bike in the lot attached to her building, I trudged up the four flights of stairs until I reached her apartment. I'd been inside quite a few times, and I prayed my impromptu visit wouldn't cause her to turn me away.

I knew I pushed her buttons, but she pushed mine right back.

Knocking three times, I breathed deeply, mentally going over what I was gonna say as soon as she opened the door. Looking down at my boots, I waited ten seconds before rapping on the door again. My fist was cocked back to knock a third time when the door finally opened, but instead of Addy answering, some young kid stood in front of me. He laughed and yelled something over his shoulder before his eyes connected with mine.

Who the fuck is this guy?

"Can I help you?" the little bastard greeted, a dimple showing on his ridiculously cherub-looking face. His innocence instantly pricked my nerves. Of course, I reacted without thinking, gripping the kid's collar and pulling him closer so I could intimidate him. His eyes widened and his mouth fell open in surprise. He was a few inches shorter than me, but he was no lanky fuck. Definitely built, his broad shoulders filling the doorway, he was still no match for me, something I needed to show him in case he had any ideas toward my woman.

"Who. The. Fuck. Are. You?" I enunciated clearly. "And what are you doing inside Addy's apartment?" Shoving him hard, he stumbled back inside, reaching out to grab something to steady himself, but he only found air. He fell backward and hit the ground with a heavy thud, his right arm going underneath him and twisting weirdly beneath his body. The grimace on his face told me he hurt himself when he fell, but I didn't care. All that was on my radar was finding out who this stranger was and getting rid of him quickly so I could finish my conversation with Addy.

Stepping forward and leaning over the kid, I reached for him one more time, but a shrill yell from across the room stopped me. I looked to my right and all I saw was a frenzied woman headed straight for me.

"Stone!" she screeched. "What is wrong with you?" Her voice cracked, her volume level increasing with each word she threw my way. It was her way of letting me know she was livid; her voice often rose an octave when she was extremely irate. Resting on her knees, she tended to the kid on the floor, checking him over to see if he was all right. He flinched when she touched his wrist, and for a split second I felt bad. But only for a brief moment. Until I remembered there was another male inside her personal space and I had no idea who he was.

Pointing, I asked, "Who the fuck is he, Addy?" My impatience was weighing heavily on me, and if I didn't get answers soon I was gonna flip out. And that wouldn't be good for anyone.

Helping him to his feet, she guided him to the dark leather sofa against the back wall. Closely inspecting his injury again, she rested it on the arm of the couch while she walked toward her small kitchen, grabbed a dishtowel and an ice pack before stepping in front of the kid again. I kept referring to him as a kid because I knew he was young, but he wasn't a teenager, which meant he was a threat to what was mine.

After she finished wrapping his wrist, she turned her fury-filled glare on me, walking toward me with such menace in her eyes, she instantly put me on alert. I'd definitely been on the receiving end of her anger before, more times than I could count, but this time was a little different. The kid sitting on her couch meant something to her, which put me in an even fouler mood.

The little spitfire stood her ground in front of me, her blonde hair falling in her eyes as she slapped my chest with her hands. Her sudden surprise attack made me jerk back a step, but only because I hadn't ex-pected her to react so fiercely.

"What is wrong with you?" she repeated. "Seriously, are you on drugs or something? Because that would sure explain why you're acting so damn crazy lately." She stood so close I could smell her perfume, and while I tried to maintain my stance, she disarmed me. Her scent wafted around me, making me think of pinning her on her back, and having her beg for my cock before ravaging her.

When I didn't answer, she slapped my chest again, this time grabbing my leather cut and trying to shove me back toward the front door. Even though she was beyond angered, there was no way she was able to physically move me. The first time I was caught off guard, but now I was resolute in my stance. I towered over her by at least half a foot and had her by a good hundred pounds.

I didn't answer her earlier question because I wasn't gonna dignify it with a response. She knew damn well I wasn't on anything. I guessed my behavior would have made sense if I was taking something, but it was all me. Ever since she'd come into my life up close and personal, I'd acted like a maniac. Moody and temperamental. More so than usual. Marek had called me on it, and now Addy was doing the same, although it wasn't the first time she'd made mention of it.

"Who is he?" I barked, my jaw clenched so tight I thought I was gonna shatter my teeth. "Answer me," I demanded when she remained close-lipped.

"No. I won't answer you. It's none of your damn business. We aren't together, and you have no right to come here and start assaulting my guests." She took a few deep breaths before continuing to tell me exactly what she thought. "You need to leave. Now," she said, pointing toward her front door.

"No." Short and simple. There was no way I was going anywhere, not until I found out who this guy was. As if sensing I was gonna erupt again, he rose from the couch and approached us, cradling his wrist in his hand, trying to keep the ice pack steady in order to do its required job.

"Addy, I can leave. I don't want to cause any problems." He looked pensive and a bit afraid of the scene unfolding in front of him.

Without turning in his direction, still locking her gaze on me, she said, "You're not going anywhere, Robby." Softening her tone, she urged him to take a seat. "Please sit back down. We're going to eat dinner as planned. That's not changing because my ass of a friend decided to bust in here and go all psycho."

Okay, a few things raised a red flag with me. First, she admitted she was having dinner with this *Robby* character, which made me angry since it'd been a while since she'd agreed to have dinner with me. Second, she referred to me as her *friend*, which instantly set me off. We were so much more than that. Hell, I wanted to claim her as my woman, but she was still giving me the runaround about the dangers of my lifestyle. I couldn't blame her for worrying, but I assured her the club was going legit, so the dangerous element which had followed us for as long as I'd been a member was diminished. I promised to protect her, assuring her I would never let anything bad happen to her, but still she had issues. I was sure I wasn't making the best case for myself with the way I was acting, but I had no impulse control. It was on my list of things to address, but right now wasn't the time.

Looking over Addy's head, I locked eyes with her guest. "We're much more than friends, *Robby*." Clenching my fists, I tried my hardest not to stalk over to him and snatch him up from the sofa. "We fuck! All the time!" I shouted, making sure he heard me loud and clear.

A quick gasp pulled my attention back to the petite blonde woman simmering in front of me. "Oh, my God!" she cried. "Are you *serious* right now?" When I only glared at her, she finally revealed exactly who Robby was, I assumed hoping to calm me down enough to leave. Little did she know, I wasn't going anywhere. "Robby is my neighbor, and my friend. That's it, so the fact that you're acting all crazy isn't justified. Not one single damn bit. You owe us both an apology before you leave."

"I'm not apologizing for anything," I said stubbornly. "No way."

"Then there is nothing more for us to say to each other." I didn't like her tone. It was different from our other fights. She gave off an air of indifference, as if she were dismissing me, not only right then but in the future as well. I was man enough to admit it scared me. I would never voice such a thing, of course, but it made me stop and collect myself.

Swallowing my anger, I blew out a frustrated breath and took a step back.

"Fine," I bit out. "I'm sorry I barged in here and reacted the way I did." My words tasted sour on my tongue, and if it weren't for the woman pushing me, I would have never admitted such a thing.

"That's it?" she asked, her tone starting to rise again.

Glancing over at Robby, I said, "Sorry you hurt your wrist." There, that was all I was gonna say. If that wasn't good enough, then oh well.

Robby rose from the couch and approached us, tentative at first until I silently gave off the vibe that I wouldn't attack him again. But when he put his hand on her shoulder, I felt myself tense up once more.

"Adelaide, I'm gonna go home. I'll talk to you tomorrow." He moved toward the door, but before he completely disappeared she spoke up.

"I'm sorry. I'll refrigerate your dinner."

"Don't worry about it. Why don't you two enjoy it. Sounds like you have a lot to hash out." Funny thing was, he wasn't being sarcastic, and for a quick second, I didn't wanna kill him.

He opened the door and walked into the hallway, and I watched to see which apartment he disappeared into. To my dismay, he lived right next to her. Shaking my head in disgust, I slammed the front door shut and turned my attention back to Addy, but she'd already walked across her place and busied herself wrapping up the food. I continued to stand near the entryway, and when she didn't say anything for the next minute, I took it upon myself to get comfortable. When I reached the couch, I leaned back, my eyes following her as she continued to distract herself in the kitchen. She was cleaning up, taking her time so she didn't have to deal with me. But that was fine, because I loved to watch her.

Her long hair flowed down her back, soft waves enthralling me, enticing me to run my fingers through the strands before gripping tight and anchoring her exactly where I wanted her. Even though there was a good chance she wouldn't give in to me tonight, I could still fantasize. Her dark jeans shaped every single curve, especially when she bent over to pick up something off the floor, her shirt riding up in the back to expose a bit of skin. Once she was upright again, she stretched her arms to reach the cabinet above the fridge, her ass pushing outward while she wrangled a container. I wasn't sure whether or not she was oblivious to the fact I was leering at her, but she never gave me any indication she was aware I was even in the same vicinity.

She was giving me the silent treatment, but again, I was okay with it.

Like I said, I was content with just watching her.

SEVEN

Adelaide

I KNEW HIS EYES WERE on me the entire time I busied myself with tidying up the kitchen. I'd lost my appetite the second he'd barreled into my apartment. Intuition should have told me he was going to show up at my place, and the fact I invited Robby over for dinner, the same dinner I'd declined the night before, was a stupid move.

But I shouldn't have had to worry about such things, fearing Stone's reaction if he happened to come by. I was beyond horrified for my neighbor. He was all of twenty years old and clearly not a match for the likes of the crazy VP of the KC MC.

"Are you almost done?" Stone asked, his tone portraying a calm which indicated he'd never even been upset in the first place. Out of everything, that was what irritated me the most. His voice gave everything away. How telling it was of the man himself. He felt justified, and once he'd exerted himself and the altercation was over, he went back to his *normal* self.

I swore running hot and cold, mostly hot, was in his genetic makeup.

I chose not to respond, my own anger still boiling close to the surface. Having no other way to show him his actions were downright unacceptable, I kept my mouth closed. Using my words did nothing but seem to irritate him further, making him spew his nonsense over and over again until he made me dizzy with aggravation.

Another minute passed and still I kept busy, scrubbing the counter for the third time. I was so lost in my own head I hadn't even noticed that he'd risen from the couch and walked the few feet to get to the kitchen. I startled when his arm wrapped around my waist, the scouring pad and spray bottle of cleaner I was using dropping to the floor. Before I could say anything he pulled me in to him, my back resting against the solid, well-defined muscles of his chest, his heat instantly enveloping me.

"You not talking to me now, sweetheart?" he whispered in my ear, the tiny hairs on the back of my neck springing to attention. He tightened his hold while continuing to tease me. Knowing damn well the effect he had when he touched me, he used it to his advantage, doing his best to throw me off guard, trying to make me forget about his little tirade moments prior. I berated myself for even contemplating giving in, but I couldn't help it; the call of his body to mine was overpowering sometimes.

Thinking hard about what to say to try and make him see the error of his ways was quite the challenge indeed. Stone wanted to be my man, exclusively. The thought of me with anyone else tore him up inside. He'd confessed as much. And the thought of him touching another woman drove me insane, but there was too much at stake not to address the issue of his temper.

I was happy with the occasional sex-fest—or so I tried to convince myself, at least—but he wanted more and kept pushing. Every time he saw me, which was more and more recently.

Sucking gently on my earlobe, his tongue flicked out and caressed the sensitive spot underneath, sending shooting tingles throughout my tensed body. He didn't play fair, and his faint chuckle proved so.

"No, you barbarian." I'd meant for it to be an insult, but he just laughed. Of course, he would find my name for him amusing, mainly because he probably prided himself on such things. To be compared to an uncivilized, savage type of being was a compliment to Stone. If I called him a caveman, he might drag me by my hair and show me just how caveman he could be.

"You don't have to talk to me. That's fine," he said before kissing my neck, his tongue sneaking out and adding to the teasing. "I just wanna hear you moan, then scream my name when I make you come," he growled, nipping the sensitive skin between his teeth before kissing it again to soothe the quick bite of pain.

I knew right then, that if I spread my legs for him, he would never learn. Never take me seriously. Never change his ways, and if we were to continue with whatever this was between us, I needed him to put a leash on that overactive temper of his, especially when it was directed toward people who didn't deserve it.

Aka any guy who talked to me.

Although my body screamed for me to forget everything my brain told me, I withdrew from his hold, which was hard to do because he was gripping on to me for dear life. Slapping at his hand, I finally wriggled away, putting some much-needed distance between us. He saw the look in my eyes, one of lust mixed with stubbornness, and for a brief moment, he grinned.

That was until the stubbornness overshadowed the lust. Then he knew he was in for it.

It was a rare occasion when I rejected Stone's advances, mainly because the man certainly knew what he was doing once he got his hands on me. And his tongue . . . His tongue was lethal. Along with other body parts, of course. But if I had any hope of the man tempering himself whenever he felt threatened, I needed to dismiss him and send him on his way.

Straightening my posture, I stood firm, although I was a quivering mess on the inside. Hopefully, he couldn't tell. I stared him in the eyes and rambled on. "If you think for one second I'm gonna sleep with you after you barged into my apartment with both guns blazing, attacked my innocent, defenseless kid of a neighbor, and then mockingly apologized for your actions, you need to have your head examined." I pursed my lips and shook my head for added effect. I had no idea why, but it seemed to amuse him more than me telling him I wasn't speaking to him.

Leaning his hip against the counter, he folded his arms over his chest, his muscles popping up and flexing underneath the long white shirt he wore which fit him like a glove. I'm not gonna lie—I looked. I loved every inch of Stone's physique. But I averted my eyes before he caught me ogling him. Or so I thought.

"Stop being so damn hard-headed. Fuck that kid," he spat when he saw my demeanor wasn't changing. Pointing his finger in my direction, he was the one who started babbling. "Don't tell me you don't know 'Robby,'" he said his name in air quotes, "wants to fuck you."

"Not sure why you're putting his name in quotes, dumbass. That's his name." I couldn't stop the sarcasm before it bubbled forth from my lips. He clenched his jaw and continued on his little tirade.

"He wants you. Anyone with eyes can see it." When I still hadn't responded, he continued on. "Trust me. As a guy, I know this shit."

"Oh, stop it. Robby's barely twenty. He's still a kid. And so what if he has a little crush on me? He doesn't act on it. I've told him, not in so many words, that I'm just interested in being friends. So it's no big deal." I huffed when I saw his eyes widen, trying desperately to figure out what

I'd said to warrant such a reaction. I replayed the words in my brain until it hit me.

I'd just admitted I knew he had a crush on me.

Stupid, Adelaide. Just stupid. Know your damn audience.

Pushing off the counter, he stalked toward me, and since I was in the corner of the small kitchen, I had nowhere to escape. Gripping my arms, he pulled me close, his warm breath cascading over my face. "You know he wants to fuck you? And you invite him over for dinner?" Shaking me gently to show me how serious he was, he added, "What's that about, Addy? Huh? Tell me. My big dick not enough for you? My tongue's no longer wanted on that pussy of yours? Huh?" I was in shock that he went there, but I shouldn't have been. This was typical Stone. I knew it was his insecurities coming to the forefront, but I didn't dare bring up such a thing while he was pissed off. Again.

When I remained close-lipped, he glared at me, biting his lower lip until he figured out his next move. I was at a loss for words, and nothing I said would've assuaged his ego or paranoia right then anyway, so I chose to say nothing.

After a few countless seconds, he gripped my hand in his, pulling me behind him toward the front of my apartment. Flinging open the door, we walked into the hallway, and before I could protest, his large fist pounded on Robby's door.

"What are you doing?" I asked, struggling to dislodge my hand from his, but his grip only intensified. "Let go, Stone!" I hollered, hoping to pull his attention away from whatever he was thinking of doing.

Before another word left my mouth, Robby opened his door. He had a peephole handy, so why the hell did he open up? Was he a glutton for punishment? His eyes fell on me before he looked at the infuriated man standing to my left, and I prayed his actions wouldn't be punished. There was nothing short of clubbing Stone over the head that would make him not do whatever he was about to.

"You wanna fuck my woman?" Stone yelled, moving closer to Robby.

The look on my young neighbor's face made my heart sink. I knew he held an innocent crush for me, and the fact Stone embarrassed him about it really rattled me. I would have cried from humiliation right then but I didn't want Robby to feel as if he had to defend me in some small way. Because if that happened, I had no doubt Stone would attack him.

"Well . . . do you?" Stone hollered again.

"N-no. We're j-just friends. I swear," Robby stammered, his eyes wide while short pants of breath left his mouth.

"If I so much as see you around Addy again, I'll make you disappear. You hear me?" he snarled. Robby made the mistake of looking at me, an innocence in his eyes which made me want to give him a big hug. Stone lost it. Poking his finger harshly into Robby's chest with his free hand, he shouted, "Don't fuckin' look at her." When my neighbor's eyes snapped back to meet Stone's, the crazy man standing next to me growled, "Do you hear me?"

"Yes." Robby said nothing else before quickly closing his door.

Running his hand through his hair, Stone turned toward me and dragged me back inside my apartment. He didn't fight me when I struggled to break free from his hold that time.

I was beyond livid, irate to the nth degree. My body was flush with rage, my chest quaking to take in breath after breath. I was so angry I didn't even know what to say.

"I know you're pissed. I can see it written all over your face. But it had to be done. I can't stand that he lives right next door to you," he confessed. "I don't like it one bit." He ran both hands over his face in aggravation before lowering his arms to his sides, staring at me and waiting for me to speak.

"GET OUT!" I roared. I stepped away when he drew near. "Don't you dare touch me, you ass!" I couldn't stop my voice from going nuclear. "How dare you embarrass me like that. Robby is no threat to you, yet you acted like a complete psychopath." Sucking in more air, I used it to help calm me. It barely worked. "You need to leave, Stone. I mean it. I don't even want to look at your face right now."

"Addy . . ." His voice dropped a level. "I'm just trying to protect you. You don't know the world like I do."

"Oh, yeah? And what danger is a twenty-year-old kid? Did it feel good to pick on someone seven years younger than you? You're nothing but a bully."

"Hey, watch it," he warned, his nostrils flaring in anger. "I'm not a bully, and you know it."

"Do I?" Feeling like we were getting off topic, I reiterated my need for him to leave. "You need to go. I don't want to see you anymore. I can't take your explosive temper. It's gonna ruin me." I had no idea I was even going to say such a thing until the words tumbled out, but there was no taking them back.

I thought he was going to explode again, but instead he looked completely shocked. His stunned expression told me that he really didn't think there was anything wrong with the way he'd acted. In his mind, he was simply protecting what he thought was his.

Me.

But he was too volatile. I could somewhat handle him threatening Tripp or any of the other club members when he thought they were getting handsy, or flirting with me. They were all equals and could handle their own, to a certain degree; Stone was a trained fighter, so there was only so much fairness to an altercation if he was engaged. But to threaten a twenty-year-old was so far past the line, the line was nonexistent.

"What the fuck do you mean you don't want to see me anymore?" he asked, his breath seizing in his throat while he waited for me to deliver the final blow. He was shocked and angry, but he was also afraid. I saw the emotion hiding behind his eyes. It disappeared before it battled to the forefront, but I'd seen it.

Calming myself even more because I didn't want him to think I was spouting off irrationally in the heat of the moment, I inhaled some much needed oxygen and backed up a few paces. "Look," I started, "we aren't even a couple. Yes we had fun, but it's time to end it. You need to find someone else who is better equipped to deal with you and your club life. I'm just not cut out for it. I'm sorry." Every single goddamn word cut me like a knife. Picturing him with someone else almost made me take it all back right then, but I knew I was making the right decision. I just had to convince my heart of the same thing.

I locked up my emotions so tight I was surprised I was even still able to speak. One tiny crack and I would crumble.

Realizing Stone was too proud a man to beg, I knew he wouldn't show that side of himself. If it even existed.

"Are you fuckin' serious, Addy? Just because I confronted him?" He had no clue, and his words only drove home how much he was in denial.

"It wasn't just that. It's everything. We can't ever be together for real, never mind the fact I can't handle your temper anymore." Averting my eyes, I declared, "This has to be good-bye. For real."

An explosion of expletives left his mouth before he stormed out of my apartment, slamming the door so hard behind him I thought he'd splintered the wood. A few minutes later, I heard the roar of his bike, but I couldn't bring myself to go to the window to watch him leave. It broke me to say good-bye, but deep inside, I knew Stone Crosswell wasn't good for me.

Any part of me, especially my heart.

EIGHT

Stone

"YOU'VE BEEN MOPING AROUND HERE for days, Stone. What's wrong with you?" Ryder asked, plopping down beside me on one of the couches in the common room, the beer in his hand almost empty. It didn't take much to notice he was already on his way to feeling good.

"Fuckin' nothing," I grated, my nerves shot to all hell since Addy kicked me to the curb almost a week prior. I blew up her phone for five days straight, even stopping by her place. But she wouldn't answer her cell or her door. She froze me out, and I couldn't say I blamed her. My temper was uncontrollable sometimes, but I would never hurt her. I thought she knew that. Was she afraid of me? Of what she thought I might do if I really lost control?

The thought alone made me chug down the rest of my drink, the whiskey burning my throat while it worked its magic of making me numb.

"Fine. Don't tell me. I'm perfectly content with sittin' here and gettin' drunk." Ryder chuckled and finished his drink, popping the top off another beer bottle and taking a few swigs.

We sat in silence, losing ourselves to the alcohol coursing through our systems. It wasn't until two days later that I peeled myself off the couch, showered, and tried to make some semblance of my life again.

I vowed to get Addy back, if it was the last thing I did. How? I had no idea.

———◆———

MAREK WAS STILL HOLED UP at his place, no doubt trying to repair whatever damage had been done to Sully's emotional state when she laid eyes on the man who'd raped her. I'd phoned him a few times, but the conversations were always short and to the point.

He's fine.

He's taking care of his wife.

He'll call me soon to discuss our next move.

Only there wasn't a next move to be had. We couldn't touch Yanez unless we wanted to bring down Carrillo's wrath on our club. Marek had fought hard to break us away from the cartel, and I wasn't gonna let him undo it all with a rash decision.

Again, he was a better man than me, but that was why he was leading the club. He *needed* to be the better man. For all of us.

"Stone!" Jagger shouted, jogging toward me with a big smile on his face. "Guess what arrived today?" The kid was like a pig in shit he was so happy. He bounced around on the balls of his feet in excitement, and for a brief second his mood was contagious. The corners of my lips turned up slightly, waiting for him to reveal the big surprise. When I cocked a brow, he said, "The cage."

"Is that right?"

"Yeah, do you have time to spar with me in a bit? Hawke's gonna help me set it up. He offered to go toe to toe with me, but you know as well as I do I'd knock him on his ass before he even knew what happened." Jagger laughed at his own joke, but the fact was, he was right. Hawke could hold his own in a fight, but not against the likes of Jagger. He would be too busy showboating, playing it up for anyone watching, and that's when the prospect would strike. He was young, and undefeated in the underground fighting world. Surprisingly, it hadn't gone to his head. Not yet, at least.

He may be a superstar in that world, but he knew not to overstep his bounds in the club. Remaining respectful toward the other brothers, he wanted nothing more than to be fully patched in, but for whatever reason, our prez wasn't a fan of the prospect.

And it was that very same day that I found out why.

An hour after the ring had been constructed, Jagger and I were both circling each other, adrenaline surging through my veins for the first time in days. I'd drowned myself in alcohol, trying to figure out what to do about Addy, but I had to admit it was nice to focus on something other than my battered ego. And heart, if I was completely honest with myself.

"Come on, old man," Jagger taunted, a wide smile on his face while he bounced around me. He was doing his best to make me dizzy with his fancy footwork, but he should have known I wouldn't be so easily distracted.

"Old man?" I'm half a decade older than your punk ass," I mumbled around my mouth guard, frowning at his audacity. Trying to annoy me was surely on the top of his list.

Both of our hands were taped, but we didn't wear any gloves. Or nut cups. There were rules, and we trusted each other not to break them.

No hitting below the waist, but everything else was game.

After countless minutes of Jagger pussy-footin' around me, I decided it was time to make my move. With a quick jab, I managed to graze the side of his jaw before his hands flew up to protect his face. I didn't blame him, though; he should protect that pretty face of his, unless he wanted to drive away all the free pussy that was endlessly thrown at him. Then again, women dug scars. So maybe I was just tryin' to do him a favor.

Chuckling at my inner thoughts, I reached forward and threw another punch. He was quicker that time, blocking it entirely, hitting back with a jab of his own and catching me in the ribs.

The guy was quick, I'd give him that.

But while he was talented, I had more experience. I faked another shot, drawing his attention to my left arm. Once I hooked him, I countered with a quick uppercut with my dominant hand.

"Fuck," he cursed, annoyed at his lack of attention. Come to think of it, he'd seemed a bit distracted when we started, but I thought it was just nerves from his upcoming fight later that night.

"Come on, bro. Keep your head in the game," I instructed, letting him get in a couple good shots to help fuel his drive.

We went at each other for the next twenty minutes, jab for jab, cross for cross, kick for kick, until we were both sweating and primed for more. I was just about to burn more energy when the roar of a bike drew our attention.

Kicking up loose gravel as he drove through the lot, Marek finally backed into his spot, extending his hand for Sully to find her footing as soon as he killed the engine. What were they doing here? I hadn't heard a word from him since the last time he'd rushed me off the phone, so to say I was surprised by their visit was an understatement.

Then again, a person can only hole up in their house away from everyone else for so long. Trust me, I knew.

I focused on Jagger once again, but he was still staring after Marek and Sully. Our prez had walked ahead a few feet and was chatting with

Ryder, Hawke and Trigger, their faces serious, while Sully hung back for a few minutes. I was about to yell at Jagger to get his head back into it when I followed his line of sight.

He was staring at Sully, a weird look of longing in his eyes as he watched her with an intensity that instantly unnerved me. The way he was looking at my best friend's wife was haunting. And it was right in that moment that I realized why Marek had a problem with the prospect.

There was no denying it. Anyone who paid enough attention would be able to pick up on it—the guy was horrible at subtlety.

Without warning, I approached Jagger from the side and pulled one of my infamous leg sweeps, taking him down before he even realized his feet had left the ground.

It was quick.

And effective.

Our underground fighting champ hit the mat with a heavy thud, a groan tearing from his mouth and drawing the looks from a few of the guys near the ring.

"What the hell, Stone?" Jagger shouted from the floor. His back twisted off the ground as he prepared to gain his footing. Standing over him, I leaned in close and gave him my best advice. Or warning. I couldn't decide which.

"You get caught looking at Sully like that again, and I'll beat the hell out of you myself." A swift kick to his ribs made my point. I was about to lay into the prospect again, just for good measure, when I saw Addy's blue Honda pull into the lot. I hadn't laid eyes on the woman in a week, and the mere sight of her pushed all the emotions I'd buried deep back to the surface with a vengeance.

Standing in place, I watched her get out of her car, take a few steps then wrap her arms around Sully in greeting. My eyes followed every movement my woman made, Yes, she was still *my* woman, even if she'd kicked me aside. It was a simple technicality.

Adelaide Reins would always belong to me.

My heart leapt in my chest when she turned her gaze to me, but before I could show any kind of reaction, my legs were in the air and I was falling to the mat below. My arms flew out to my sides, trying desperately to grab on to something, but only air surrounded me.

I looked over at Jagger, still lying on the mat, a shit-eatin' grin on his cocky-ass face.

Looks like he'd used one of my signature moves on me, knocking me on my ass while I was the one distracted.

Well played, fucker.

NINE

Adelaide

I KNEW COMING TO THE clubhouse was going to be a mistake, but I needed to be there for my friend. Marek called and asked if I could swing by and take Sully out for a few hours; he had some club business to attend to and didn't want to leave her alone.

I readily agreed, the utter concern in his voice sealing the deal for me. Of course, in good ol' Marek fashion, he appointed one of his men to join us. Tripp. Which I didn't mind at all because the man's charm had grown on me. Plus, I could make sure once and for all that he was fully healed. It was touch and go in the very beginning, but thankfully he'd pulled through with flying colors. Even though it pissed Stone off beyond reason, I was happy to check in on my favorite patient.

Standing a few yards away, I briefly saw Stone and Jagger going at each other in a boxing-type ring, which had to have been new because it wasn't there the last time I was. Berating myself for even being drawn to the infuriating man, I couldn't help but sneak a peek every now and then.

The man had an incredible body, and watching the way he moved while he sparred with Jagger was amazing. For some reason, they had both been on their backs when I'd first arrived, but for the past five minutes, they were really going hard at each other, throwing jabs and kicks faster than I thought humanly possible. The muscles in Stone's back flexed and constricted with every punch he threw, his thick thigh muscles holding him in place, waiting for Jagger's counterattack.

"You ready, ladies?" Tripp called from across the courtyard, striding closer and pulling my attention, distracting me from the rampant thoughts firing off inside my head. The nomad was pretty incredible-looking; add his charm and he was a lady-killer for sure. Too bad I wasn't interested in him that way. The only man who did it for me was the one fighting close by.

For some reason, I was curious to see what Stone's reaction would be to Tripp accompanying Sully and me on our little outing. He'd always reacted unfavorably when Tripp was around me before, I wondered if today would be any different. I was the one who told him it was over between us, and after a few days of him calling me nonstop and showing up at my apartment, he'd abruptly stopped.

Did he not care anymore?

Did I care?

Sadly, yes. More than I cared to admit, even to myself.

Throwing an arm over mine and Sully's shoulders, Tripp gifted us both with one of his signature smiles. I dared to glance over toward where Stone was and saw his entire body tense in anger. But he didn't say anything, merely glared at me before exiting the ring. I thought for sure he was going to come over and threaten Tripp, but instead he said something to Marek in passing and disappeared inside the clubhouse.

Marek strode our way and slapped the nomad on the back. "Don't fuck around. I'm trusting you with my wife's life." The two men exchanged a look, Tripp nodding when whatever message they'd passed to each other was finished.

I smiled and said, "Hey, what about me?"

"It goes without saying, Adelaide. You're as important to a certain someone as my wife is to me." His statement confused the man sent to babysit us, but I knew exactly who he was talking about. What had Stone told Marek about us? I guessed it didn't matter really, because there was no longer an *us*. "He'll watch over the both of you like his life depends on it."

"Fuck," Tripp mockingly grumbled. "I had no idea this was gonna be so stressful. I just thought I was hanging out with two hotties, shopping for clothes and shit." The twinkle in his eye put everyone at ease, even though Marek didn't want to show as much. He liked the guy, and apparently he trusted him.

When we approached my car, Tripp opened both of our doors before taking a seat in the back. Never in a million years would Stone allow a woman to drive while he was a passenger, insisting only pussies let their women cart them around. Then again, neither one of us belonged to Tripp, so it appeared he didn't have an issue with me driving my own damn car, or with Sully sitting in the passenger seat.

The day passed quickly. We were gone a little longer than expected.

Sully checked in with Marek a few times, nervous he was going to be upset she was taking so long, but her husband assured her it was all right, that he wanted her to have a good time.

I wasn't sure what was going on with my friend, but she looked distracted and down in the dumps, for lack of a better term. There was only so much we could talk about with Tripp close by, and I doubted she wanted to get into anything heavy with him listening. I promised I would stop by their house in the next few days so we could spend some quality girl time together. Marek would most likely be present but would busy himself in another room so we could really talk.

Sully knew all about me and Stone, just not about the part where I told him I no longer wanted to see him. I wasn't gonna lie; there were a few times when I had picked up my phone to return one of his many calls, but decided against it. Nothing would change and we would be right back to square one, going around and around until both of us were dizzy.

"So, Tripp," I started, licking my spoon clean of vanilla and peanut butter swirl ice cream before continuing. "Is there a special lady in your life?" I didn't know much about the nomad, but the fact he chose to stay at the clubhouse and not go back on the road after his recovery was intriguing indeed. I wondered if he had his eye on anyone local, which would explain his reasoning for sticking around longer than normal.

We were sitting in a local ice cream parlor, our shopping bags resting at our feet while we gorged ourselves on frozen treats. It was obvious Tripp was surprised by my personal question, and a fleeting look of regret crossed his features before he showcased his winning smile. After running his hand through his hair, he flicked his wrist and checked his watch.

"No one to speak of," he answered. As jovial as he appeared, my probing had certainly put him on edge.

"Come on," Sully prodded further. "No one at all? Not even someone casual you kind of like?"

Wrapping his lips around his spoon, he winked before pulling the utensil free. "Nope. There is too much pus—too many fine women to ever pick just one." Shrugging, he said, "It just wouldn't be fair to take myself off the market." His smile broadened when he heard us both laugh.

Before either of us could get all up in his business again, he announced it was time to go. The ride back to the clubhouse was quiet, but it was a comfortable silence, so I had no complaints. Pulling into the lot, I killed the engine when I saw my uncle up ahead. I hadn't seen him in days and wanted to say hello. He was engaged in conversation with Hawke, and God only knew what the two of them were talking about. Hawke was a crazy bastard. From what I heard from Stone, the man couldn't keep it in his pants. Therefore, his longtime girlfriend, Edana, was forever after him. Why she didn't just leave him was beyond my scope of reasoning. I would never tolerate Stone cheating on me, even if we hadn't officially been together.

That was an unwritten rule—no other women for him, and no other men for me.

But I guessed that had changed now. We were free to pursue whoever we wanted. Problem was I wasn't interested in anyone but him.

Could he say the same?

After promising Sully I would call her and set up a day and time for me to come by her house and hang out, and thanking Tripp for going with us, even though he'd pretty much been forced, I walked toward my uncle. As soon as he saw me approaching, he opened his arms wide and waited for me to nestle into him. I loved him dearly. His protectiveness over me was sometimes irritating, but deep down I didn't mind it so much. I would never tell him that, though, because he would only go further into the realm of crazy uncle protecting his only niece.

No, the current level of overprotectiveness he displayed toward me was good enough.

"How are you, sweetheart?" he asked, kissing the top of my head before releasing me.

"Good."

"How's work going?"

"Good," I answered again. Before he asked any more questions, I interjected and switched the subject. "Uncle Trig, Dad wants you to come over for dinner soon. You up for it?" My uncle and father got along just fine, often finding time to hang out before my mother died. But it seemed ever since her death, her brother and my father distanced themselves from each other. I wasn't sure if it was because the other reminded them too much of my mother, or if they had some sort of falling out. I had no idea. All I knew was that my uncle stopped coming around after the funeral. I found it odd but I never pressed, not wanting to step into something personal I had no business in.

"Tell him thanks for the offer, but I'm busy."

"You don't even know what day it is," I countered, looking at him in confusion.

"I'll be busy," he retorted, suddenly looking a bit uncomfortable.

"Okay." I sighed, deciding it was indeed best to change the subject.

We stood close to each other, but thankfully Mother Nature called before it became awkward. Excusing myself, I walked toward the entrance to the club, hoping and praying I wouldn't run into Stone.

Once I finished using the restroom, I opened the door and shut off the light. Taking a few steps down the hallway, I heard a noise coming from the bedroom Stone used. When I stepped closer, I realized it was a woman's voice.

"You like that, baby?" she said. "Come on, Stone," she urged. "What's wrong? Looking at my tits doesn't do it for you?"

Instant sickness flipped my stomach, and my heart felt like it had been ripped from my chest. Clutching at the walls to hold me up, my mind was quickly bombarded with images of Stone having sex with someone else, a faceless woman. A woman with a high-pitched, whiny voice.

He'd obviously moved on from me rather quickly, but could I really be upset? I was the one who told him good-bye, after all. It just would've been nice if he could have at least waited a few more days before jumping into bed with some club skank.

I heard him grumble something before his door flung open, and out walked a bleached-blonde, fake-titted bimbo. The dark circles under her eyes revealed she was beat, someone who would most likely spread her nasty legs for anyone willing.

In shock from witnessing what I did, I was still frozen in place when Stone appeared in the doorway, raking his eyes over my stunned face before he let a curse fly from his mouth.

"Goddamn it, Addy. What are you doing here?" He looked embarrassed and angry all wrapped in one.

"Don't mind me," I said sarcastically as I turned around. "I just dropped Sully and Tripp off and decided to say hi to my uncle. The only reason I came back here was to use the bathroom before I headed home." Having no idea why I felt the need to explain myself, I shut my mouth and started walking away. I didn't get very far before his fingers circled my wrist to halt me.

"Don't go, baby. Let's talk," he said, a softness to his voice I hadn't heard in quite some time. Outside of the bedroom, at least.

"I don't have anything to say to you, so why don't you *talk* to the skank who came out of your room," I seethed, anger pouring out of me before I could even think to suppress it.

Turning me around, he pulled me close. Lifting my chin so he could look in my eyes, he asked, "You pissed another woman was trying to get my attention? Because you're the one who threw me away."

He spoke the truth, but the words still killed me.

"You can do whatever you want. You're free to fuck as many lowlife, scum-sucking skanks you want. Just do me a favor and wrap it up, unless of course you don't care about your dick falling off." The venom in my voice wrapped around me like a warm blanket. I spewed the words so easily it was as if I'd been holding them back for some time.

His eyes widened at my choice of words . . . but then he smiled. Big. *Damnit!* He reveled in my irritation, and for someone who claimed they didn't care, I'd just proved the opposite.

"I don't want that whore. *She* came into my room and propositioned *me*. I told her to get lost. It was just unfortunate you were here to witness any of it." Leaning in closer, his mouth rested just above mine. "I only want you, Addy. Only you." His lips were so close I could taste him already.

Thankfully, we were interrupted before I gave in.

"Stone, there you are," Marek called out, walking straight toward us and completely ignoring the fact he'd almost caught us in a compromising embrace.

Staring at me for another few seconds, Stone finally broke our connection and stepped back. With a puff of his chest, he glided past me and followed Marek toward Chambers to no doubt talk about club business.

And I was left standing in an abandoned hallway, trying to figure out what just happened.

Stone

"I CAN'T TAKE IT ANYMORE, man. I have to kill that fucker or I'm gonna go insane." Marek paced back and forth, grabbing his hair in anger while he tried to figure out the best way to handle the issue with Yanez. We despised that the bastard still sucked air into his lecherous lungs. "Sully wakes up almost every night now, screaming and fighting, as if she's trying to push someone off her. Seeing Yanez again has brought back that night full force." He turned glassy eyes on me. "I feel so fuckin' helpless." It was rare to see such emotion on my best friend's face. It was a true testament to how he felt about his woman.

Not wanting to call him out on his brief moment of weakness, I chose to offer my undying support instead. "I'm ready for whatever you wanna do, but we have to be smart, Prez. We can't go on a killing rampage and expect nothing to happen. We'd be putting everyone we care about at risk. And for what?" The question left my mouth before I could take it back.

Fury blazed from my friend's eyes, stalking toward me with his fists drawn. "Sorry," I grumbled. "Wrong question." He composed himself before continuing to pace. Taking my seat to the left of his head chair, I leaned back and started spouting off scenarios that might work to our advantage.

"How about we mess with his truck and cut his brake lines? Or we could make it look like a robbery gone bad, kill him before anyone was the wiser?" So many thoughts rambled around inside my head I wasn't sure how they sounded when I said them out loud. Marek was still restless, so nothing had grabbed his attention yet. Flinging myself forward, I pounded my fists on the table and yelled, "I fuckin' got it, brother!" My lips curved up in a menacing smile. "We set him up."

"What do you mean?"

"Well, Carrillo seems like he's a man of his word. If he told you he was going to cut the Savage Reapers out of any further dealings with Los Zappas, only to find out Yanez is still doing some side dealings with them, then wouldn't that prove he isn't loyal to his boss, and that he's only looking out for himself? It questions allegiance and all that happy shit."

For the first time since we entered Chambers, Marek stilled and contemplated my suggestion. His eyes lit up, looking forward to something akin to a plan. I knew the man was itching to set things right, although no matter how many men he killed, it wouldn't take away the pain of knowing Sully had been abused, repeatedly. First by her father, then Vex . . . and now Yanez.

Were there more who needed to pay?

I could try to convince the man to eradicate all his guilty feelings at not having been there for the woman he loved when she was being violated. He hadn't even known her then. But I could imagine that I would feel the same exact way if the roles were reversed and we were talking about Addy. Even though the woman didn't want me anymore, I would still give my life to protect her, to avenge her against anyone who dared to wrong her.

"Yes," Marek said, drawing me back from my makeshift thoughts. "That could definitely work. And if I know anything about that piece of shit, we wouldn't really have to set him up. I have no doubt he would go behind Carrillo's back with some shady dealings. We just have to catch him in the act." Hope sprung to life in his expression, and I was only too happy to be the person who inspired the brief reprieve from his misery. "Then after Yanez seals his own fate, we'll deal with Psych once and for all."

With a plan set, all we had to do was decide who was gonna follow Yanez around while we put everything into place.

Adelaide

WARM BREATH STROKED MY BELLY, *firm yet soft lips trailing tantalizing kisses toward my center. The one area aching for his touch. His teasing made me squirm, and just when I thought I was going to break a hip trying to jerk closer to his mouth, a strong hand settled over my stomach, holding me in place.*

"Stop moving, baby, or I'm gonna tie you to the goddamn bed." Kissing my inner thigh, he asked, "Is that what you want? I think you enjoyed it last time." His voice lowered to a dangerous level, lust infused with impatience.

"I don't care what you do, just give me what I need," I demanded, a fire lighting up inside me so fierce I thought I was going to burn alive. Shivers bounced throughout my body, my pussy beyond drenched with desire just waiting to feel his tongue. A blast of cool air puffed against me and I jerked. "Stop teasing me, Stone." My tone became rather needy, even though I tried to will my voice to remain unfettered.

"Always so impatient," he teased before pushing my legs further apart. He used those talented hands of his to spread me open. At first, I thought he was going to continue to hold back, but when I felt his tongue swipe through me, I arched my back and pushed my ass into the bed. Even though I was waiting for his assault, it was already bordering too much. I was so revved up I almost came on the spot. My sensitivity level was high; a few more strokes like the first one and I would be sated before we really heated things up.

"I could eat you all day long," he rasped.

"And I would let youuuuuu," I agreed, the last word prolonged because he'd hit that one perfect spot.

"You're so hungry for me. I can taste it. Savor it on my tongue." His beard tickled my inner thighs while his tongue assaulted me. The feeling was out of this world. Mind-blowing. An ache bloomed deep inside, and that need coupled

with the spark of desire, courtesy of his talented tongue, was almost unbearable.

"Please . . ." I begged. One word, but it said so much.

"Okay, I'll give you what you want, but you have to promise me you won't see Stone anymore. I want you, Adelaide. Me. I can love you like he can't." Encased in the throes of ecstasy was a funny place to realize who you desired wasn't who was pleasuring you. Looking down, I saw the top of Robby's disheveled curly head of hair. Before I could speak, he pulled his mouth away and crawled up my body, licking his lips as he drew closer.

Movement in the far corner of my room caught my attention. Stone. He was sitting in the chair near the window, leaning forward and resting his forearms on his legs, shaking his head from side to side with a murderous look in his eyes. "I knew it. I knew you wanted him," he accused, pointing toward Robby, his voice barely above a whisper. "Well, I can't protect you now, sweetheart. You threw me away. I can't save you anymore." Stone lowered his head into his hands, his body shaking in what appeared to be grief and sorrow.

Turning my head back toward Robby, I saw a desperate look on his face and it baffled me. "All I wanted was for you to like me. But what did that get me?" he asked, pointing to his chest. At first, I thought he meant I broke his heart, but then I saw blood start to pour from an open wound. Leaning over me, his lips dangerously close to mine, he whispered, "Dead. That's what it got me."

Within seconds, I was covered in Robby's life source. I tried to scream but he put his hand over my mouth, silencing me before I could call for help. Finally wrenching free from his hold, I turned my head toward the corner of the room, my eyes desperately searching for Stone. But he wasn't there.

Instead, he was walking toward my bedroom door, mumbling, "I can't protect you anymore, Addy. You threw me away."

Then he disappeared into thin air.

My eyes flew open, my heart thrashing inside my chest so hard it actually hurt. Staring off into the darkness, I repeated, "It was just a dream," over and over again until my eyes finally adjusted to my surroundings. My ears prickled, on alert for the slightest noise which would tell me I was still locked up tight in the midst of my nightmare.

But nothing.

No noise.

No light.

No hope.

I kept hearing Stone tell me I threw him away, that he couldn't protect me anymore, and even though I'd been lost to my subconscious, his words—or better yet, his threats—certainly struck a chord. I did toss him aside, and in doing so I'd lost any sense of security I had where he was concerned.

No doubt about it, I did feel safe knowing Stone was only a call away if ever I needed him. Not only was he physically a force to be reckoned with, but his possessive need to protect me was comforting, until he'd crossed the line with his explosive temper. It was during those times when I could hardly handle being around him. He wasn't so bad in the beginning, simply grunting when he didn't like another man's attention directed toward me. It could have been a colleague of mine who stood a little too close, or a man taking a second glance if I walked past, or a club member joking around with me, or God forbid touching me in some small way.

The more time Stone and I spent together the worse he became, which could only predict what our future would hold if something didn't change.

I knew my refusing to take our 'relationship' public was the accelerant to the fire which surrounded us both. He'd said on more than one occasion, "How can I trust you when you won't even tell anyone we're together?" It all came down to some form of insecurity with him, and with me. Sometimes. I knew he was surrounded by overly willing tramps, but I had to trust he wouldn't engage them. There were a few times my jealousy burned hot and I flew off the handle about witnessing a blatant flirtation. The woman toward Stone, not the other way around. But never did I threaten anyone or act like a fucking psychopath. Well . . . not in public, anyway. Ask Stone and he may tell you a different story about my behavior behind closed doors.

We just fueled the bad parts in one another too often, getting worse with each passing day. No, my decision to end things once and for all was the right choice.

Too bad my heart was shredded to pieces because of it.

TWELVE

Adelaide

"DO YOU WANT ANOTHER DRINK, Adelaide?" Marek asked as Sully and I took a seat on the couch. Tucking my legs underneath me, I got nice and comfy before answering.

"No, thanks. I'm good." I smiled before turning my focus back on my friend. She looked better than I'd seen her in the past couple weeks, which was definitely a good sign. Something had happened a while back, and I was hoping she would finally open up and talk about it. I wouldn't pressure her, but I wanted to let her know I was there for her.

Marek was certainly good for Sully. She'd put on a few much-needed pounds since marrying the president of the Knights Corruption. Her personality blossomed as well. She wasn't the shy introvert she'd been when I first met her, even though it hadn't been all that long ago.

They complemented each other. Marek was fiercely protective toward her, but she seemed to appreciate it. Her husband, much like Stone, warned everyone not to get too close to her, but unlike my friend, I couldn't stand when Stone threatened someone just for looking at me.

But Sully and I were different people. Different pasts, different views on things. I knew she'd been abused when she lived with her old club. The Savage Reapers were every bit the bastards I'd heard they were. Even though I wasn't technically part of the 'club life,' I'd overheard my uncle and Stone talk about their enemies.

Kissing the top of his wife's head, Marek gave me a quick wink before saying, "I'll leave you two to talk about periods and sappy movies." He grinned before disappearing from the living room.

"Very funny," I called out after him, shaking my head and smirking.

Settling back against the plush couch, I directed my attention to Sully.

She looked like she wanted to say something but was a bit hesitant.

"What's up, woman?" I gestured, gently poking her in the side. She laughed and reached for my hand, suddenly becoming very serious.

"You know I value our friendship, right?"

"Of course." I nodded. "As do I."

Squeezing my hand, she added, "You were the first person to ever take a genuine interest in me. In who I was. In what I liked and didn't like. You were my first real friend. Still are." She looked bashful for a brief moment. "Cole is my friend too, but our relationship is on a different level, you know?"

"I do." I had learned bits and pieces about how Sully came to be part of the KC MC. Some from Stone, some from my uncle, and some from simply overhearing other members talk. I was happy Marek stormed the Savage Reapers and stole her from them. He'd essentially saved her, in my book.

Anyone with eyes could see they were gaga over each other, a side to Marek I'd never thought I'd see.

If only my life could play out so well. Except without all the abuse and kidnapping. Yeah . . . without all that, thank you very much.

I would have loved nothing more than to claim Stone as my man, but it didn't look like it was in the cards for us. No happy-ever-after like with my friend and her husband.

Sully looked hesitant, her mouth open to say something, but she decided against it at the last minute. Her eyes were downcast, her teeth raking over her bottom lip in concentration.

"What's wrong, honey? You can tell me anything," I comforted.

"It's just . . . I don't know." Leaning back to rest her head on the sofa, she blew out a soft breath before continuing. "I want so much to be able to tell Marek everything about my life and what I've been through, but it's so hard. He asks me all the time about what happened before he met me, and I share. Some things. But other things are too painful to dredge back up. I know he gets upset because he knows I'm holding things back, but I'm not ready to go there just yet. I already have nightmares about what happened right before he found me. I don't need any more."

She said 'right before he *found* me.' Funny how one's perception was altered when their life was changed for the better. I liked her version, though. Yes, Marek had certainly 'found' her all right.

Something she just said niggled at me. "Why are you having

nightmares? What happened?"

She'd dislodged her hand from mine a few minutes prior, resting them in her lap while she played with the hem of her shirt. Her long, black hair was pulled back in a messy bun, her face makeup-less. She was stunning, but her dark eyes were haunted. A whole different world resided behind her beautiful browns.

Because she looked like she needed to get something off her chest, I patted her leg and gave her a sympathetic smile.

A single tear escaped and slid down her cheek. After a minute of silence, she told me all about Yanez, what he'd done to her. What her own father had allowed to happen, as well as running into her rapist again in the common room of the clubhouse recently.

My own tears danced down my face listening to her tale. I wished I'd known her before. I wished I could have saved her from that life. So many things I wanted to say, but something told me no matter what I said, I would never even begin to touch the surface of understanding what it was like to live through something like that. So I simply listened, offering my support and friendship the best I could.

I'd delved into the story about me and Stone and how we were no more. I wanted to take her mind off her tragedy so I threw my own at her feet. Plus, it was nice to talk about it with someone. Roxanne, one of my oldest and dearest friends, had up and moved to Maine a few years back, and although we had the occasional phone call to catch up, it wasn't enough to dive right into the drama that was my life recently.

I had acquaintances at work, but no one I felt close enough to talk to about such things. Plus, they wouldn't understand, instantly judging Stone simply because he was part of the Knights Corruption. The club didn't have the best reputation around these parts. That was a lie—they had a horrible reputation. I saw the looks people threw my way when he visited me at the hospital, and that was enough for me to keep my mouth shut about anything pertaining to us.

An hour later, we decided to watch a movie. A comedy of course, seeing as how we both needed a pick-me-up. I moved to rise from the couch but was forced back down immediately, an immense pain shooting through my lower abdomen. My hand flew to my stomach, clutching at the area and trying to breathe through the discomfort. My face was telling, I was sure, because suddenly Sully was right next to me, leaning down to see what was wrong.

I couldn't speak. I couldn't tell her this wasn't uncommon for me. The only thing I could do was concentrate on how many heartbeats it would take until the pain faded.

"Cole!" Sully shouted at the top of her lungs, never once moving from my side in case I needed her. Her husband flanked me on my left side before I could utter a word of protest. The last thing I needed was for these two to be worrying about me. They had enough on their plates.

Not wanting to alarm either one of them, I tried my best to smile, but I failed.

Big time.

My voice squeaked when I finally spoke. "I'm fine. Really," I assured, straightening myself very slowly before making eye contact with either one of them. No one but my immediate relatives knew cancer ran in my family, that my mother had died from the disease, or that I was at a high risk of getting it as well. Stone didn't even know.

And I wanted to keep it that way. I was still waiting to hear back about my recent exam results. Actually, Dr. Weber had left me several messages asking me to call him back, but I'd procrastinated.

I didn't know what I would do if he told me something I didn't want to hear. Taking the stance of 'no news is good news' really didn't work in my situation, because he had news. I just didn't want to hear what it was.

Once I was resting comfortably back on the couch, and the pain had subsided, I drew in a deep breath in preparation for the questions which were going to come flying my way.

"What happened?" Sully asked, concern etched deep on her face while she gazed at me, her hand gripping mine in support.

"Are you sure you're okay?" Marek questioned next. "Do you want me to call Trigger?" He made a move to reach for his phone, but I stopped him.

"No, I'm fine now. I get spasms from time to time. It's nothing," I lied.

"That didn't look like nothin'," Marek argued. "That looked fuckin' painful." He reached for his cell once more.

"I'm good. I promise. Besides, I've already seen a doctor about it and he said I'm fine," I lied again. I couldn't help it; I didn't need him alerting my uncle to anything just yet, if at all. I could handle whatever was thrown my way—after I decided to call Dr. Weber, of course.

"Well, I don't like it," Marek said, running his hands over his beard in worry.

"You don't have to," I grated. Immediately calming my tone, I finished with, "Seriously, I appreciate your concern, but I'm okay." Turning my attention back toward the TV, I said, "Now, how about that movie?" I knew if I looked back at either one of them right then, I would crack and tell them everything.

Spew all my worries at their feet and try to find comfort in their concern.

———— ♦ ————

FORTY-FIVE MINUTES INTO THE FLICK, I heard the roar of a motorcycle pull up. The engine kicked off, heavy footsteps pounding up the steps then onto the porch, and the front door opened before I could even think to ask if they were expecting company.

Stone walked into the house, said something quick to his friend then spun his focus onto me. His posture was stoic, but the look of fear on his face told me everything he was feeling without him uttering a single word.

"Marek, I'm gonna kill you," I grumbled, knowing full well he'd called him right after my little 'episode.'

Marek looked unapologetic. "Sorry, but you wouldn't let me call Trigger, so you left me no choice."

I didn't even have to ask him why he chose to call Stone, because I knew deep down he knew there was something going on between the two of us, even if he wouldn't admit it. I was actually surprised more people hadn't said something to either one of us, but then again they were all probably scared to death of my uncle. Fearing if they voiced their suspicion, Trigger's retaliation would somehow reach them as well.

As Stone approached the sofa, Sully stood and walked toward her husband. "I'll leave you two alone," she said, looking back at me with a mix of concern and hopefulness.

"You don't have to go," I pleaded, praying Sully would stay and that Stone would realize he wasn't wanted. Or needed, for that matter. But she never said another word as she followed her husband from the room. Less than a minute later, I heard their bedroom door close.

Traitors.

Stone settled in next to me but didn't say a word. His presence was uncomfortable enough; I didn't need to hear his voice as well. The movie continued to play in the background, and I did my best to give it my full attention, but I couldn't. I knew he was watching me, waiting for me to address him, but I remained silent, having no idea where to even begin.

Should I tell him I might have made a mistake by ending things with him? Would I admit to such a thing, even when every other thought told me I'd made the right decision? Would confessing that I missed him terribly end the way I wanted it to? Funny thing was I had no idea how I truly felt about my decision to cut him loose. My brain told me one thing but my heart felt something completely different. Was I strong enough to go with the logical part of myself?

Countless moments passed before I bit the bullet and addressed the confrontation brewing between us. There was no other way around this. If I wanted him to leave, I had to engage him first.

So I did.

Finally.

"Why are you here?" I asked, never looking away from the TV.

Instead of answering my question, he threw one of his own at me. "What happened before? Are you having problems . . . down there?" he questioned, uncertainty and a bit of embarrassment laced in his words.

I couldn't help but smirk. *Men.* Anything to do with our lady parts and they all became queasy. Unless they had their mouths, hands, or cocks in that region, they didn't want to hear anything more about it.

I glanced over at him, the worry on his face disarming me. Even though I'd ended things, he still cared about me, as I did him.

Putting him out of his misery, I finally said, "I'm fine. Don't worry about me. Seriously, Stone." He didn't look convinced, however. He reached for my hand, but before his fingers touched mine I pulled away, scooting toward the far corner of the couch.

"Why?" he asked, his shoulders slumping forward in defeat. And heartbreak. He tried to put up a good front for those around him—hell, he even had me fooled sometimes—but I knew I hurt him. What I wasn't going to reveal was that I was just as upset, even more so because I thought I was falling in love with the temperamental ass.

It was one of the rare occasions I even allowed myself to think such a thing.

Not having to ask him what his question meant, I responded with, "You know why. I've already told you."

Sliding closer, he managed to capture my hand, threading his fingers with mine and squeezing. The pressure was light but enough to draw me out of my own head. I didn't know how else to explain my feelings, other than what I'd already revealed. The part about me falling in love with him was going to remain locked up tight. If he ever got wind of that, he would be relentless in his pursuit to start things up again.

"I call bullshit," he tempted. "Yeah, I have a temper and while I try to control it sometimes, it's like something inside me snaps and I'm power-less to stop it." Trying to wrench my hand free was futile. "But I would never hurt you, Addy," he promised, moving daringly close to me. "You believe me, don't you?"

His intoxicating scent floated around me and, for a brief moment, I envisioned myself wrapped up in his strong, secure hold. Closing my eyes, I allowed myself to feel the pull. To experience this weird connection between the two of us. But I couldn't remain in that world for too long. My heart could only take so much.

"I believe you would never hurt me physically, yes," I assured him. "But I'm not so sure about emotionally." I'd told him the truth. Now it was up to him to let it register in that thick head of his.

"What's the worst thing that's gonna happen? Huh? You tell me. That someone might get beat up because I don't like the way they're lookin' or talkin to you? That's not so bad," he retorted, trying his best to convince me.

My heart broke a little more because he just didn't get it. Foolishly, I was hoping for him to acknowledge he had a problem and at least offer to get help for his issue. Maybe go to anger management classes, a thought that made me laugh internally. I couldn't even imagine a big, tough, beard-ed, tattooed biker walking into such a meeting. Before I externalized my humor, I withdrew my hand from his.

"You need to leave," I urged, praying he would get up and walk out the front door. I feared weakening and giving in to him if he stayed too long, realizing I would be putty in his hands if he managed to touch me again.

"Not until we talk this through." He sat back and braced himself for a fight. I saw it in his body language, but I was tired of arguing. I didn't have the strength for it anymore, having had something else on my mind. And depending on the results, I would need to save all my energy for that fight instead.

"There's nothing more to say," I declared, rising to my feet and trying to walk from the room, but he halted me with a quick grab of my arm. Standing himself, he pressed his chest to my back. He quickly released me only to wrap his arm around my waist and tuck me further in to him, his power and essence wrapping around me like a security blanket.

My dream suddenly rushed over me, as well as his declaration. *I can't protect you anymore, Addy.* It was true I felt like I was flailing out there in the world without the reassurance of Stone having my back if I needed him at the drop of a hat. But it had been my decision to set him free, so I needed to deal with it.

"I can't let you walk away from me, baby," he promised, kissing the back of my neck. "I need you." His warm breath slid over my skin like velvet. "Don't you need *me?*" His whispers were driving me to the brink of sanity. He knew exactly what he was doing, using all the tricks in his arsenal to get me to cave.

And I almost did.

But then I remembered the look on poor Robby's face when Stone had threatened him, and I couldn't let it go. I grabbed the strong arm holding me captive and finally pried it loose, taking a step away before turning around to face him.

"I don't have anything else to say to you. You need to leave me alone." My voice trembled and I knew he'd heard it. *Damnit!* We stood there staring at each other for what seemed like forever.

Lost in the battle between reasoning and the overwhelming emotions of my heart, I was pulled back into the situation when a lock of his hair fell forward over his eye. A quick flick of his hand and he shoved the strands back in irritation. For some reason, I became lost in the sight of him, which was the last thing I wanted to do.

But there was no arguing that he was quite the specimen, and I allowed myself to take him all in and commit him to memory, because that was where he was going to reside.

His loose, dark-washed jeans hung off his narrow hips in the sexiest way, his muscular thighs hiding just underneath the material. He wore a black fitted, long-sleeved Harley T-shirt underneath his leather cut, his dark boots finishing off his casual yet intimidating outfit. Or maybe that was just him. *He* was intimidating.

"Then why are you lookin' at me like you wanna fuck my brains out?" he growled, taking a daring step closer.

"I'm not."

"Yes, you are."

"No, I'm not," I all but whispered. Our back and forth wasn't getting us anywhere, and I decided right then I needed to block him out. Darkness surrounded me for a few seconds, my eyes closed while I tried to gain my bearings. When I finally opened them, my gaze connected with his once more. "Leave."

Giving me a once-over, he huffed, squared his shoulders, and pronounced, "This isn't finished."

He disappeared out the front door before I even had a chance to respond.

THIRTEEN

Stone

FOR SOMEONE WHO BARELY VISITED the clubhouse, Addy was becoming quite the fixture lately. I didn't know if she was doing it to torment me, or if she consistently had a legitimate reason for hanging around.

Not being able to touch her was slowly driving me insane, and I only prayed she felt the same way, although the last time I saw her she made it perfectly clear she didn't want to have anything to do with me. Well, that was what she'd tried to portray with her words anyway, but the look in her eyes told a different story. Or was I just reading too much into the uncertainty I'd seen behind her beautiful blues?

Trigger was in his usual spot behind the bar, dispensing drinks to whoever was hanging out. The woman who had me all twisted up inside was sitting on one of the stools, leaning forward and engaging her uncle in conversation. Her laughter rang out and drifted through the air, a sweet melody which tortured me, simply because it'd been weeks since she'd laughed like that with me. Fearing I was never going to hear it again, I stalked toward her, hell-bent on making her end this stupid charade and give me another chance. I couldn't promise that I would be able to fully control my anger, but I would do my best. But only in those situations which didn't call for me to knock someone out.

Figuring out how to act nonchalant, I strode up next to her and straddled the empty seat to her right. As soon as she sensed I was near, her body instantly stiffened, and although it wasn't the reaction I wanted . . . it was something. If she didn't care at all, she would have blown me off completely, comfortable enough to either ignore me or breezily acknowledge my presence, much like with any other member. But the fact I could unnerve her in the slightest was indeed a good thing. It meant I still affected her.

I acknowledged Trigger with a quick nod before directing my attention to his niece. "Addy," I greeted. "How are ya?" I tapped the bar before allowing her to answer, desperately needing the smooth courage of liquor before she either ignored me further or actually chose to speak to me, for however long. Trigger gave me the stink eye before pouring me a shot of whiskey. It was early, barely two in the afternoon, but seeing her just two days after I'd rushed over to Marek's house pushed me toward the drink in order to rein in my . . . FUCK! I didn't even know what I was feeling right then.

Excited?

Pissed?

Confused?

Whatever it was, the burn of the alcohol helped to simmer it to a tolerable level.

"Fine," she curtly answered. "And you?" Her tone was as if she were talking to someone she barely knew and was merely trying to be polite. If her uncle wasn't standing five feet away, I would have dragged her back to my room and demanded she end this craziness.

But he was.

So I didn't have a choice but to remain calm.

"Why ya here?" I tapped the bar again, glancing at Trigger for another shot.

"I had to ask my uncle something."

"Yeah? What's that?"

All of a sudden, Trigger leaned forward and placed his hands on the bar, doing his best to intimidate me. What he didn't get was that, while these other guys might be scared of him, I wasn't. The only reason I didn't tell him I'd been sleeping with his niece was because I knew it would hurt Addy, and that was the last thing I wanted to do. Although, I guessed I'd failed in that regard anyway, seeing as how she ended things between us.

"That's our business," her uncle rumbled, irritation contorting his features. His displeasure for me grew daily, and even though Addy and I both denied any involvement with each other, the man wasn't stupid. He just didn't have any proof of our relationship. Not yet, at least. He'd certainly lose his mind if he knew I'd fucked his niece so good she hadn't been able to walk right the next day.

Suddenly bombarded with images of a naked Addy, I smirked to myself, probably looking like a cocky sonofabitch, but ask me if I cared.

Holding up my hands in surrender, I said, "Sorry, just tryin' to chit-chat."

"Don't you have to go scope out talent for the new club we got openin' next month?" he blurted, flinging a wet bar towel over his shoulder.

Addy's posture locked tightly in place, no doubt from what Trigger had just asked me. If she wasn't gonna give me what I wanted, which was her, then the only thing left to do at that point was to have a little fun. Gauge how much she still cared about me, about what I did.

"I was just on my way there when I saw your lovely niece and wanted to exchange pleasantries." I smiled, and he knew I was up to something.

"I'm not gonna warn you again, Stone. Proceed carefully or else."

One of these days, I'm gonna call his bluff for sure. But not today.

"You guys are opening up another one of *those* clubs?" she asked, a grimace plastered on her lovely face while she continued to look forward, ignoring me.

"Yup. Nothin' better than pussy on tap. Right, Trigger?" I laughed, but the man wasn't amused. Not in the least. I didn't know if it was because I was being so crass around Addy, or if he just couldn't stand me anymore. Shaking his head in annoyance, he walked toward the kitchen, thankfully leaving the two of us alone. I knew he was gonna be back soon, so if I wanted to provoke some kind of reaction from her, I had to do it quickly. I knew it was immature and childish, but she left me with no other choice. Asking her to talk to me, and being all nice about it, hadn't worked, so I was left with only one option.

"You should come by and check it out when it's up and runnin'. I think you'd like it." Taking a risk, I ran my finger up and down her arm, a gesture which made her flinch.

"I don't think so," she balked, jerking her arm away. "But hey, if used-up twats is now your thing, have at it." Shit! My game was backfiring, and fast. I wanted her to rant and rave, dare to forbid me from going there, but she only gave her snarled permission of sorts.

"Twats need lovin' too," I mocked.

"You're a pig," she sneered, pulling further away from me when I tried to touch her again.

Before I could respond, continue my banter with her, Hawke came up behind the two of us and threw his arms over each of our shoulders. "Whatcha talkin' about?" he shouted, the smell of alcohol on his breath rather potent.

Shrugging him off, I scowled until he backed up, but calmed my expression quickly enough because I was going to use him to my advantage. "I was just tellin' Addy she should come by the new club when it's open."

"Fuck yeah, you should. In fact, if you want a job, Adelaide, I'm sure we can find a spot for you." Funny thing was, Hawke was being serious, and it was right then I wanted to punch his teeth down his goddamn throat.

Whipping around on her stool, she lurched forward and angrily shoved her finger into his chest. "Are you callin' me a whore?" she shouted, drawing the attention of her uncle, who happened to be coming out of the kitchen right then. But he didn't need to come to his niece's defense. I was already all over it.

Quickly standing, I gripped him up by his cut and shoved him back. Hard. "Watch you're fuckin' mouth, *brother*," I warned. Rising to my full height, I braced myself to kick his ass if he said one more wrong thing.

"What?" he asked, completely confused by mine and Addy's outrage. "I just meant that she's hot and would bring in a lot of customers."

Clenching my teeth, I stepped closer, my fists ready to pay a visit to his face. He saw my angry expression and tried to better explain himself. "What I meant to say is that Adelaide is a classy-lookin' woman, that she would be the highlight of the night. Ya know? All the men would want to watch her. She'd be good for business. That's all I'm sayin'," he offered, backing up a few more paces when he eyed first me then Trigger, who'd incidentally come around the bar and was standing right next to me. The only time we would agree on anything was when it involved defending Addy.

"You better get the fuck outta here, Hawke, before I knock you into the middle of next week," Trigger cautioned, clenching his fists at his sides.

"What the fuck?" Hawke mumbled before walking away, shaking his head the entire time in utter confusion.

"Sorry about that," I apologized, sitting down next to her again.

"He's an ass," she chided. "Even though I don't think he meant it as badly as I took it."

"He still shouldn't have said it." A silent minute passed, the back and forth between us abruptly ending. Hawke's interruption only intensified the tension, giving us both time to gather our wits and decide what the next move was going to be.

Drumming my fingers on the bar, I desperately tried to think of something to say which would turn it around for us, but I came up empty. Finally, I decided it was time to go, even though it killed me I'd be leaving her.

"Trigger, if Marek is lookin' for me, let him know I'm at Flings." Standing back up, I was half turned away from her when her voice stopped me.

"You're really going to look at a bunch of naked women right now?" She had whispered her question but I'd heard her loud and clear.

There were so many ways I could play this, but for some reason I decided against it. I went with the truth.

"Yeah, club—"

"Business," she finished. "Yeah, I know." Irritated, she turned in her seat and looked up at me with sad eyes. Had we still been doing our thing, I would have passed off the job to a few of the other brothers, not wanting to witness the hurt on her face. But she'd ended things, so she had no right to make me feel any sort of way toward something I normally wouldn't think twice about.

I glanced around, making sure Trigger wasn't within hearing distance before leaning close and asking, "What do you want from me, Addy? Huh? Because you're confusing me right now. You don't want to be with me, but you're actin' all hurt because I gotta go deal with business."

Frustration poured off her in waves, a feeling I was quite familiar with as of late. Her mouth remained closed, her eyes pleading, but I was clueless as to what she wanted. She said one thing then did another. She'd tossed me aside, yet there she was, sitting inside my clubhouse, distressing me with her mere presence.

Just when I thought she was gonna let it go, her voice broke the silence. "I don't know, all right?" Flicking her hair over her shoulder, she steeled whatever reserve she had left and said, "Just go," before rising from her stool and adjusting her dress, her head down the entire time. "Do whatever you want." Defeat coated her words, and if I wasn't so hell-bent on teaching her a lesson, I would have grabbed her and demanded she take me back. But would I be content with continuing to keep us a secret? I knew I wanted her, more than anything, but I wanted us to be out in the open. And if I knew anything, I realized the stubborn woman standing in front of me wasn't there yet.

No more words were exchanged before she quickly walked away. And there I was, left to sit and wonder if she was ever gonna come back around.

Deciding I was tired of having my emotions jerked all over the damn place, I grabbed Hawke and Ryder, heading out to find the distraction I so desperately needed.

FOURTEEN

Stone

A HEAVY HAZE OF SMOKE blinded me as soon as I walked into Flings, the dim lighting making it nearly impossible to see the bar that ran the length of the wall to the left. Numerous tables and a few couches were scattered throughout, and circling the large stage in the middle of the room were single plush chairs where the men could sit up close and personal. Two smaller stages were placed to the left and right of the main one, and five private rooms existed toward the back for when the men wanted a little more privacy with one of the dancers.

We didn't put much thought into the décor of the place because . . . what the hell for? Men came to watch women take their clothes off. Plain and simple. They didn't care what color the walls were or about the texture of the couches and chairs. So, we threw up some red paint and the seating was entirely leather.

Simple and easy.

Just how the men liked their women.

I was a red-blooded male, through and through, someone who loved tits and ass as much as the next guy. But sitting through countless auditions of women stripping for a spot at the new club just didn't interest me. I couldn't be bothered. It was why I brought along two of my brothers. They'd be making the final decisions simply because my head wasn't in it.

The only naked woman I wanted to see right then was Addy, but that wasn't gonna be happening anytime soon.

Scantily clad females milled all throughout the wide-open space, waiting for their turn to bare everything for the three of us. In any other circumstance, I would have appreciated the variety of women who had come out today. There were blondes, brunettes and redheads. There was even one who'd dyed her hair pink. Some of them were shorter than others, but the one thing most of them had in common was that they were blessed with big tits. It didn't take a genius to see that the majority of the potential talent had been to see a doctor to enhance themselves, but that didn't make a difference to me. Tits equaled money.

The only rules we had were no hard drugs. Other than that, anything went, from lap dances to whatever else transpired between consenting adults. Everyone who walked through those doors knew not to step out of line, one wrong move by the customer and there would be some serious repercussions. While we didn't have a bouncer in the back rooms with the dancers and their clients, we had surveillance, and someone manning the booth at all times, in case someone got out of hand. Which rarely happened, because most people around here knew we owned the club and knew acting out of turn wouldn't be tolerated.

"Fuck!" Hawke shouted, coming up behind me. "I can't wait to see me some naked bitches bouncin' up and down on that pole." A wide grin lit up his face.

"You act like you ain't never seen a stripper before, man," Ryder grumbled, smacking him in the back of his still-bald head. "You better calm down before Edana gets all over your ass."

"How's she gonna know?" Hawke smiled at a few of the women standing around, waiting to be called up to the stage for their audition.

"Most likely by all the glitter you're gonna be wearin'," I said, shaking my head at the poor bastard. Sometimes he was so dense it was almost comical. He looked confused until I added, "Don't tell me you ain't gonna let some of them give you a private show."

He said nothing in response, only smiled and wiggled his eyebrows.

One after another, the women strutted across the stage, tearing off their clothes to the song of their choice. I tried to get into it and appreciate the moment for what it was, but Addy kept popping up in my head, those sad blue eyes of hers gutting me when she heard I was coming here. I berated myself for continuing to let her affect me the way she did, but I simply couldn't help it. Deep down, I knew she was gonna be mine again; it was just a matter of persuasion and time.

After the auditions were finally over, I leaned against the edge of the bar and allowed Ryder and Hawke to make their picks, giving the women the details on when and where to report. Tipping my head back and swallowing a shot of whiskey, the burn the perfect calm to my busy brain, I heard someone talking near me. It took me a second to realize the woman standing to my right was indeed trying to engage me in conversation.

Before Addy, I would have been all over her, taking her into one of the back rooms and giving her the ride of her life. But now . . . nothing. While she was attractive in the fake-tits, bleached-blonde hair, heavy-makeup kind of way, she didn't hold a candle to the woman who held my heart—and my nuts—in a vice. I felt like a pussy over the way I pined after Addy, an emotion which only served to piss me off the further I indulged it.

Once my eyes landed on the stranger, she took it as some sort of invitation, I guessed. "Hey, handsome," she enticed, pressing her implanted double Ds against my side. "In the mood for a lap dance? Maybe a little more?"

"No, thanks," I declined, briskly walking around her and toward Ryder who was sitting on one of the couches, sandwiched between two topless brunettes.

Once I stood two feet from him, I announced I was taking off. "I'm out. I'll see you guys later."

"Where you headin' to?" Hawke yelled, striding across the room, zipping up his pants with a mischievous look on his smug face.

"I got things to do."

"Like what?" Ryder pressed, his brows raised while waiting for me to respond to his nosy question.

His hand disappeared down the front of one of the brunette's thongs. Funny thing was, while he began to stroke her, he kept his attention on me, as if he wasn't doing anything at all. That's how used to this type of thing my brothers were, like it was second nature to finger-fuck some chick out in the open. Normally, I found it rather amusing, but my nerves were frayed and all I wanted to do was be alone until I could find Addy. Praying she would at least find it in her heart to talk to me, and maybe allow me the chance to explain myself one more time.

"Like none of your fuckin' business," I snapped. "How 'bout that?"

"Fuck you, Stone," Ryder bit back. "Your miserable ass needs to get laid." Shrugging, he continued on his little tirade. "Beats me why you won't take one of these broads in the back and let 'em suck your dick."

Before I could even respond, Hawke's loud mouth piped into the conversation. "Because the only chick's lips he wants wrapped around his cock are probably Addy's." He laughed. The bastard had the audacity to slap my back when he said it, too. An action which pushed me to see red. No one was allowed to talk about my woman like that, even if what he said was the absolute truth.

Snatching him up by his throat, I slammed him against the nearest wall, baring my teeth as if I was gonna rip his goddamn throat out. "If you ever talk about her like that again, I'll fuckin' kill you."

Hawke's shocked eyes were as wide as could be, until they weren't. "I knew it," he garbled. "You fuckin' love her, man." He tried to laugh, but there was only so much air I was allowing him, so his words came out more like a harsh whisper. Shocked by what I heard, I released him, backing up a step and preparing myself for whatever else he chose to point out.

Pointing toward Ryder, who was still seated on the couch, Hawke yelled, "I told you there was something goin' on between the two of them."

The stupid shit wasn't even fazed that I could crush him right then, too wrapped up in the fact he'd discovered some golden truth.

"You better shut the fuck up, Hawke, or I'll do it for you." My tone left no room for misunderstanding.

Throwing up his hands in a sign of surrender, he smirked and shook his head.

"All right, all right. Fine." Walking away, he mumbled, "I knew it. Ya'll don't think I pay attention, but I do."

"Hawke . . ." I warned, my temper on full blast at that point. While I was hot under the collar, I also started to wonder who else picked up on this thing between me and Addy. Trigger? Surely, he would have tried to shoot me by now if he seriously thought I was shaggin' his niece.

NEEDING TO CLEAR MY HEAD a bit, I decided to take the long way to Addy's apartment. The rumble of the bike between my legs caressed me into numbness. To a certain degree. So much stuff rattled around inside my head it distracted me from my main objective.

To get Addy back.

But then what?

Would she finally accept what we had and announce it to the world?

Would I be able to finally claim her for good?

Would she, in turn, claim me?

Fuck Trigger. Fuck anyone who objected. Fuck the nonsense spouting from Addy's beautiful mouth. And fuck my temper—which, by the way, was fully on its way to erupting the longer I even thought about all this.

The sun slowly dipped behind the horizon, colors of red, orange, and purple silhouetting the sky like some kind of artsy painting. Without sounding like a pansy, I could admit it was rather beautiful. And guess who I wanted to share that sentiment with?

Yup. Addy.

But she was freezin' me out. Punishing me for something I basically had no control over. She thought it was as easy as counting to ten and calming down. It was so much more than that, though.

What she didn't realize was, when I saw men looking at her the wrong way, touching her or making comments about her, I saw red. No matter how innocent any of it seemed to her, it meant war to me.

Addy didn't know what went on inside a man's head when he looked at her. He may be all nicey-nice up front, but all he'd be thinking about was fucking her, any and every which way he could. Some of it was as upfront as that; other times, sick fetishes fueled the imagination.

I'd met some pretty unsavory people in my life, bastards I wouldn't wish on my worst enemy, and that was sayin' a lot.

Well . . . never mind. I'd be okay with unleashing those sick degenerates on the Reapers.

I digressed.

Addy's innocence only saw one side, but I saw all the others. Not so much with my brothers because I knew them to be good men at heart. Even Tripp, although I wanted to punch him most times for the way he fawned all over my woman.

Anyone outside our circle, however, was a threat, and I would forever treat them as such. I just had to make Addy understand. Have her see it from my perspective, agree, and stop the bullshit about telling me she didn't want to see me anymore.

So lost in the goings-on of what was happening, and what was going to be, I didn't see it until it was too late. It would be easy to blame Addy for infiltrating my thoughts for the reason why I hadn't been paying attention to my surroundings, but the truth was, the guy came out of nowhere.

Barreling out from a side road, an older-model truck headed straight for me, the front left bumper crashing into the back right side of my bike, spinning me out of control. Screeching tires from the vehicle sounded as I was tossed through the air, the wind cutting my skin before the road rose up to meet me, asphalt kissing my body in the blink of an eye.

Everything after that was a blur, a flutter of activity surrounding me, but for the life of me I couldn't figure out why.

At some point, my helmet had either been removed or had flown off after I'd hit the pavement. I couldn't quite remember. When I'd gotten my senses back, I looked down at myself and realized I was lying on the opposite side of the road I'd been traveling on, sections of my jeans and shirt ripped open. Bright red blood covered my skin, but of course I couldn't feel any pain. Judging by the look on the people's faces, they were shocked.

At what, I wasn't sure, until an older woman spoke up. Squatting down next to me, I could see the concern etched on her face as she looked me over. Red hair pulled back into a severe bun sharpened her cheekbones, but it didn't take away from her sincerity. Her warm touch was comforting, and I relaxed a little while looking into her greyish eyes. I thought she was feeling for broken bones, but if she was looking for a reaction of pain, she would surely be disappointed.

"Are you okay, sweetheart?" she asked, leaning back on her haunches, continuing to eye me carefully.

Even though I couldn't feel if there was any damage, I did a quick assessment of my situation, moving my hands and feet and wiggling my toes. Nope. I wasn't paralyzed. Good sign.

I'd been lying on my back and when I went to sit up, the woman warned me otherwise. "I don't think you should move, sir. An ambulance is on its way. I think it's wise to wait for them." In the span of thirty seconds, this stranger referred to me as 'sweetheart' and 'sir.'

If she only knew.

"I'm fine. No need for help," I assured, slowly rising to my feet. I was a little light-headed, but otherwise intact.

"I don't think that's a good idea," a male voice said from behind me. Turning my head, I saw a young, dark-haired kid dressed in an oversized hoodie, ripped jeans, and shit-kickin' boots. He appeared to be in his late teens, but I couldn't tell for sure. His eyes raked over me and he looked . . . scared.

"Do I look that bad?" I tried to joke, but they didn't find it too funny. Looking past the woman and kid, I tried to locate my bike. Doing a quick visual search, I finally saw it lying down the road a bit, mangled to all hell. Fuck! I loved that bike. "Do you have a phone I can use?" I asked no one in particular.

"Yeah, man," the kid announced, shoving his huge cell into my hand.

The model we used were the old-fashioned flip phones. Basic. Easy to use. What he handed me was foreign. I made a face and he caught on to the reason pretty quick. Judging by the way I was dressed, and looked, it was safe to say he understood I probably wasn't into all that technical stuff.

Swiping his hand across the screen and tapping another button, a number pad screen popped up. "What number do you wanna call?" he asked, ready and waiting to help.

I gave him Marek's number. He didn't answer, as I assumed he wouldn't since it was a number he didn't recognize. But I left a message, telling him where I was and that I needed him to pick me up immediately. Never saying good-bye, I handed the phone back to the young kid and walked to the curb. Taking a seat, I prayed my friend was quick.

I could have assured his speedy arrival if I'd remembered to tell him I'd just got run the fuck over.

FIFTEEN

Adelaide

MY SHIFT WAS FLYING BY and I couldn't have been more pleased. Keeping busy was certainly the best thing because it allowed me to forget about certain painful aspects of my life. Stone in particular. I was a damn mess whenever he was around, confusing me and twisting me all up inside so much I could barely think straight.

"Bed four," Carol yelled to my back as I walked down the short hallway with a clipboard grasped in my hands, distracting me enough to push all thoughts of the infuriating man aside. For a brief moment, at least.

With my head down and my eyes gliding over the chicken scratch of one of the nurses, I came to an abrupt halt outside bed four. A rough rumbling voice pierced the air, stopping me in my tracks immediately. My heart fluttered uncontrollably, and then my stomach suddenly dropped. I stepped closer, tipping my head to the side as I strained to hear what was being said, but it was futile; his voice was too muffled, the words coming out in short grunts. The only thing I was sure of was that there was more than one person hidden behind the curtain, a thin green material which provided the illusion of privacy.

Closing my eyes and taking a deep breath, I gripped the side of the curtain. When the air finally escaped my lungs, I pulled it open.

Fast and harsh.

My eyes quickly scoured the scene in front of me. Screams would have bubbled up from my throat had I not been at work, trying to remain professional. Stone was sitting upright on the hospital bed . . . covered in blood. Marek lounged in a seat off to the left and acted as if it were a normal occurrence to be sitting in a hospital with his best friend all banged up. Then again, maybe it was. What the hell did I know? Stone never told me anything about club business, and if he'd gotten into a fight he'd never gone into details.

He'd had black eyes and cuts before. The man even had scars from being stabbed and shot, and still he remained close-lipped. But never before had he come to the hospital. Not that I was aware of, anyway. In recent times, I was the one who had taken care of the men whenever they required medical attention, and for all I knew he could have been under the impression that I wouldn't come to the clubhouse.

So he came to me.

Closing the drape for privacy, I stepped closer to better assess his situation. Red stains soaked his clothes, his jeans and shirt shredded, revealing gashes on his skin. His hair was pushed back, blood coating his hairline as well as his cheeks, but it looked like it was more from him running his hands over his face and through his hair rather than whatever had happened to his body.

"Addy," Stone finally spoke. "You okay?" he asked, worry laced in his voice for me. Which was so odd because he was the one who was hurt.

"What the hell happened?" I frantically questioned, rushing forward to inspect his damage up close. Flinging the clipboard on the counter next to me, my fingers grazed over his body before I even realized I was touching him. First his right thigh, then over his chest.

"He got into a fight with a truck. And the truck won." Marek chuckled from the corner of the room, leaning forward and watching his friend in amusement. Stone laughed at his buddy's comment, but when his eyes found mine again, that laughter quickly died.

"What. Happened?" I reiterated. They might think danger was funny, but I didn't, and if there were any confusion, my anger and worry was written all over my damn face.

"Some asshole crashed into my bike and I skidded across the road. Thank fuck my helmet stayed on or you'd be lookin' at a completely different person. My pretty face would have been all mangled." His smile returned full force. He reached for my hand to pull me close, but I dodged him, stepping aside to grab a hospital gown for him to change into.

"What happened to the driver?"

"He took off," he answered, as if it was no big deal that the person thought nothing of leaving another human being lying in the middle of the road, possibly dying. A shudder tore through me but I refused to give it life, my anxiety already kicking into overdrive picturing what could have happened to Stone had he not been so lucky.

"Here," I said, shoving the gown at him. "I can't do anything with your clothes on."

"Well, I like the sound of that," he teased. Hopping off the bed, he started to undress in front of me and Marek. No hesitation whatsoever.

"Let me know when you're done." I turned my back and stepped toward the front of the room, ready to leave and give him some privacy when his voice stopped me.

"It's not like you haven't seen me naked before, sweetheart." His tone was playful but also suggestive. I tried, I really did, but images of Stone in all his splendid nakedness infiltrated my brain.

Glancing over at Marek, my eyes practically bugged out of my head, shocked Stone had revealed something so private, a detail which was supposed to be secret.

"I knew about you two, even before this asshole said anything. It was so fuckin' obvious," Marek assured, rising from his seat and walking toward me.

"Where ya goin'?" Stone asked.

"I love ya, brother, but I'm not lookin' at your bare ass if I don't have to. I'll be in the waiting room if you need me." He disappeared without another word.

Once we were alone, I chose to keep my back to him, not sure if I should step out of the room or not. But, as usual, he made the choice for me.

"Addy," he called, the sensual rasp in his voice stroking my simmering lust.

"Yeah?"

"I need you to help me take my clothes off." I knew damn well he didn't need my assistance. He was simply trying to bring me close enough to work his magic.

I decided right then it was easier just to go along. That way, I could fix him up quickly and send him on his way. Yeah, I was doing this more for my benefit than his.

Keep telling yourself that.

"Fine." I gave in, turned to face him, and stepped forward. Marek had already removed Stone's cut because I saw it slung over the chair tucked in the corner of the room. "Let's get your shirt off first." I tried to keep enough distance between us so he couldn't touch me, but it was pointless because he wrapped his arm around my waist and pulled me closer, catching me when I stumbled forward.

"That's better," he said, a smirk lifting the corners of his full lips. Releasing his hold, he raised his arms in the air. I was careful when I gripped the hem of his tattered shirt and pulled it up his body. Instantly, I noticed he had two deep gashes on his right side. Blood continued to trickle down his chest with no hopes of stopping until I stitched him up. His array of intricate tattoos was blurred underneath his own life source, and it was extremely upsetting.

Tossing the blood-soaked material on the floor, I moved back so he had enough room to remove the rest of his clothes.

"Do you need my help taking off your pants?"

"You don't know how long I've waited to hear you say that, baby," he joked, although the look in his eyes told me he wasn't kidding around. Damn, the man could reduce me to a bumbling fool with a simple glance. Steeling my nerves, I arched a brow and not-so-patiently waited for him to be serious. Thankfully, it didn't take him long. "You're no fun," he grumbled.

"This isn't time for fun. You're injured—pretty badly, I might add. You're gonna need at least twenty stitches for each gash on your chest, and God only knows what you have going on underneath your jeans."

"You don't remember? Then maybe I need to give you a reminder." His eyes lit up with lust and I knew I was in for it. There was no quick patching him up then sending him away. He was well on his way to disarming me. My fear at seeing him so banged up played havoc with my anger toward our situation. Warring back and forth, I wanted him to wrap himself around me, to pull me close and take me with a passion only he could evoke from me. But at the same time, I wanted him to disappear.

To leave me alone to try and figure out my crazy emotions.

Something told me he wasn't going anywhere anytime soon, though.

Finally, his fingers quickly went to work on the button of his jeans. Pulling down the zipper, he kicked off his boots at the same time. Amazingly enough, his balance remained intact, but I wondered for how long. He might not be feeling any pain from his injuries but surely he was going to feel a touch of dizziness soon, especially with his body continuing to leak blood.

Once the fly of his jeans was completely open, he leaned back and rested his hands on the edge of the bed, thrusting himself forward and waiting for me to help him.

"What? You can't take them the rest of the way off?"

"I may not be a doctor, but in my condition I don't think you want me bending over. Do you?"

Smug bastard.

Without responding, I grabbed his jeans and slid them down his muscular thighs, lifting each foot to completely discard the tattered material. His legs weren't as bad as his chest, although there was quite the nasty road rash on his right thigh. I had no idea how hard he hit the pavement, or even how fast he'd been going when he was thrown from his bike, but the majority of the damage was on his right side. Which told me that was the side that hit the ground first . . . and hard.

Stone was left standing in front of me with nothing but underwear and socks. Normally, it would be a funny image, what with the socks, but nothing on this man was amusing. He was pure, raw sexual energy. Wanting to check every part of him, I reached down and discarded the fabric covering his feet.

I knew the next part was going to test both of us, and even though I would have preferred for him to remain somewhat clothed, I had to inspect his entire body to ensure I'd done my job thoroughly.

Or maybe that was just what I was trying to tell myself.

Hooking my fingers in the sides of his black boxer briefs, I drew the material down his legs, his ever-impressive cock rock-solid and springing back against his stomach once he'd been freed. I tried my hardest not to look, but I failed big time. What I hadn't realized was that I licked my lips, entranced with the sight of his naked body. I'd seen him bare countless times before, but I swore each time was like the first.

"Wanna taste it, Addy? 'Cause you keep lookin' at me like that and I'm gonna put you on your knees and make you suck my dick."

It took a few seconds for his words to register, and when they did I had the audacity to feign surprise over why he'd said such a thing. But I knew I *had* just been visually raping him. He had every right to say what he did.

"I don't know what you're talking about," I mumbled, moving toward the drawer to find what I was going to need to stitch him up. When I was ready, I held up a needle, preparing to tell him it was a local anesthetic to numb the area when I remembered he didn't need it. It was still very strange knowing a person who had his condition. He was lucky in a way, but unlucky in the fact he pushed himself beyond his limits most times, never knowing what damage he was causing inside his body.

Pain was the body's way of telling us there was something wrong, but in Stone's case he never knew if there was a problem. Other than seeing blood pour from him, as it was right then.

Focusing on the worst wound, I gestured for him to sit down so I could finally begin to work on him. He'd refused to put on the hospital gown I'd handed him earlier, and I simply didn't possess the mental energy to argue, realizing it would be utterly useless.

He never said a word while I worked, which I believed was more unnerving than him speaking. There were a few times when my hand brushed against his cock, and we both stilled for a brief moment before I continued.

It was pure torture.

Once he was all patched up, and I'd effectively wiped away the blood smearing his face, I stepped back to inspect my work. Everything looked good. I opened my mouth to speak but the air left my lungs when he pulled me hard against him, his rigid thickness pressing into my belly as he held me impossibly close.

"What are you doing?" I asked, afraid of the answer.

"I can't take this anymore," he growled. "And don't tell me it's easy for you either. I see the way you look at me. You still want me. I know you do."

I shouldn't have admitted it, but the words left my lips before I could stop them. "Of course I still want you. But that doesn't matter. You know that."

"No, I don't."

"You do," I confirmed, trying my hardest to break free from his hold. But he was much too strong.

"Kiss me," he demanded, licking his lips and leaning forward. His breath mixed with mine, a heady euphoria settling over me as I inhaled his air.

"No," I whispered breathlessly.

"Please," he begged. Stone never begged. He must have been desperate. Did he know I was just as anxious?

"I can't."

"You can. You know you want to. Don't deny me." His tongue teased my bottom lip. "Don't deny *yourself*."

Then, right there, in the middle of room number four, behind a thin green curtain, I gave in to a naked Stone. My hands gripped his shoulders while I attacked his mouth, nipping and tasting him with unbridled passion. I was like a woman unhinged. Every second since I'd ended things between us had been pure torment for me. I'd dreamed of his mouth on mine, his hands possessing every inch of my body while his cock filled and stretched me into pure bliss.

I missed his kisses.

I missed connecting with him, writhing around with each other for hours on end until we finally collapsed from sexual exhaustion.

I missed the security he offered me.

I missed his friendship.

I missed being able to tell him when I'd had a tough day at work.

I missed quoting our favorite movies together.

I missed laughing with him.

I just missed *him*.

Placing his hands on the sides of my face, he pinned me while he returned my hunger. His tongue danced with mine, sucking and gently biting the tip while he groaned in pleasure. The rumble from his throat excited me because I knew where such passion could lead. I allowed myself to give in, even if it was only for a kiss.

Breaking away, he panted as he looked deep into my eyes. "Come back to my house, baby. Let me love you," he enticed, kissing the corners of my mouth before devouring me whole again. Before I could muster up enough strength to answer, he pulled a bold move. Reaching for my hand, he circled my fingers around his cock. Talk about jumping the gun. But secretly, I loved it. "Feel what you do to me," he growled. "It's all for you. Every thick inch. All for you."

I realized if anyone walked in on us I would be out of a job, but right then I didn't care. All I cared about was the next few minutes, until I regained my senses enough to put an end to it. Gripping him tightly, I stroked him once from the tip to the base of his arousal before allowing him to fall from my hand.

Finally, when I knew I was surely testing fate, I withdrew completely and stepped away. "You need to get dressed before someone walks in."

Even though his face had fallen for a brief moment, the sad look in his eyes breaking my heart, for once he didn't argue, dressing quickly before settling back on the edge of the bed.

"So? Will you do it?" he asked, crossing his arms over his chest.

"Do what?"

"Come to my house. We need to talk and finally hash this out."

"There's nothing to hash out," I argued.

He jumped off the bed and stalked toward me. Running his thumb across my lip, bruised from his kiss, he cockily asked, "There isn't?"

No sooner had he dropped his hand when Dr. Weber pulled back the curtain. My heart fell into my stomach at the sight of him. I'd been ignoring him for what felt like forever, and seeing him standing in front of me made me feel really guilty.

"Adelaide, there you are," he said, glancing from me to Stone then back again. "Are you almost done with this patient?"

"Yes, I am," I answered quickly, giving him my full attention.

"Good. I want you to come to my office when you finish up."

"Okay," I conceded.

Out of the corner of my eye, I could see Stone tense up next to me, but thankfully he didn't say anything. I also counted myself lucky for the fact he had no idea who this man was. Not until Carol burst in, that was.

"Dr. Weber, you have a call on line two," she said, smiling at me before openly gawking at Stone. She caught herself and turned her eyes back to me before making a hasty exit.

"Thanks, Carol." Patting my shoulder, he said, "Duty calls. But I'll expect to see you shortly." Dr. Weber left before my next breath.

I was still turned to the side, so I couldn't fully see Stone's face, but I sensed he was putting two and two together and would be giving me the third degree very shortly.

"*That's* Dr. Weber," he said through clenched teeth. "Are you fucking kidding me?"

"What?" I tried to play ignorant, but I knew the reason he was about to blow his top. Working against Dr. Weber in Stone's eyes was that he was a man, first and foremost. The second thing was the man was movie star good-looking. Jet-black hair and bright green eyes were his finest attributes. Add to that his full lips and a Romanesque nose and he was quite enthralling.

But for as handsome as he was, I wasn't interested. Never mind he was married to a woman he happened to adore immensely.

"He's married, Stone. So don't get yourself all riled up."

"Since when does being married mean he'll keep his dick in his pants?"

"Stop overreacting. I mean it." I stared at him, preparing to have yet another fight over something which wasn't even worth discussing.

But surprisingly, he listened. His breathing turned heavy, but he didn't say another thing about Dr. Weber.

Pulling on his cut, he brushed past me, but before he disappeared from the room, he barked, "If you're not at my house later, I'm comin' to get you. I'm done with this shit." He narrowed his gaze. "Don't test me," he warned before walking out.

SIXTEEN

Adelaide

SITTING ACROSS THE DESK FROM Dr. Weber was extremely nerve-racking, to say the least. I'd been avoiding him like the plague, but I knew I couldn't stay away from the news any longer, whatever it might be.

Busily looking at something on his desk, he shuffled through the paperwork as if he were trying to buy more time. Maybe I was reading into something which wasn't there, or maybe I'd just hit the nail on the proverbial head.

"Adelaide," he started. "I'm not sure how to tell you this."

My heart instantly rammed hard against my chest.

I remained silent, petrified if I spoke my fate would be sealed even quicker, which was such an asinine thought to have. Whatever he was going to reveal would be the truth, whether or not I said anything. And that was one of the shittiest parts, that I had absolutely no control over what was going to pour from his lips. Bracing myself for the inevitable, I linked my fearful eyes with his hesitant ones and counted the seconds.

Instead of him remaining in his seat, he stood and walked around his desk, choosing to sit directly next to me. When he reached out and grabbed my hand, I couldn't hold back any longer. Tears dripped down my cheeks while I waited for the verbal blow.

"I'm so sorry, but your test results revealed you have stage two ovarian cancer. And while it's rare for a woman your age to be diagnosed, it does happen." He squeezed my hand for comfort, and for a moment I allowed his support to envelop me. When he'd conducted his exam a short time ago, he'd informed me there was a tumor on my right ovary, and he'd convinced me to let him do a biopsy, to make sure we covered all bases. Especially with my family's history. I readily agreed, even though my consent had instilled instant fear. Almost as if by saying yes I was agreeing to the diagnosis somehow.

I permitted his devastating words to swirl around inside my head, thinking of all the things I needed to do as well as who I needed to break the news to. Then a ludicrous statement came crashing over me. What if I kept the news a secret? What if I just dealt with it myself, sparing my family—and Stone—in the process?

Resigned to the idea I would brave the scary waters alone, I felt a little better. I knew I would do whatever Dr. Weber suggested; I trusted him and knew he wouldn't steer me wrong. I would see whatever specialists he had in mind, and follow a strict regimen if need be.

Stage two was a better diagnosis than stage three or four, the chances of survival increased. I knew because my mother didn't find out until she was at the last stage, and by that point there wasn't much the doctors could do for her but make her as comfortable as they could.

Because of what my mother had endured, I'd been very diligent in getting tested, and I'm glad I was. The sooner the cancer was detected the better, all things considered. Of course, I would rather have had Dr. Weber give me a clean bill of health, but it wasn't to be. So I had no other choice but to keep my chin up and forge ahead. There would be good days and bad days, I was sure, but hopefully the good outweighed the bad.

"There's one more thing, Adelaide." He shifted nervously in his seat next to me.

"What is it?" I asked fearfully, wrenching free from his hold and tucking my hands underneath my legs.

"As if the news isn't bad enough, I hate to add another thing in the mix. I can't believe I have to tell you this, but . . ." His words trailed off before he could finish, my fear spiking higher the more he remained quiet.

"Jesus, Dr. Weber. What is it?" I cried out.

He turned his body fully in my direction, his green eyes pinning me. Steeling his nerves, he blurted, "You're pregnant."

I zoned out for a brief moment, shutting down any reaction I should've had at him telling me I was going to have a baby. Would I have been happy if he hadn't told me the other news? Would there have been a smile on my face and hope in my heart otherwise? I simply didn't have an answer for such silly questions. The only thing I had to focus on was how a woman could carry to full term while having that poison inside her.

"That's impossible," I finally responded, a comforting numbness wrapping its cold arms around me, shielding me from feeling anything at all. Except surprise and denial, of course.

"Unfortunately, I'm afraid it's not."

Wanting to flee from his office and process the news in private, I urged him to finish. "So, what do we do now? Can I have treatment while I'm still pregnant? Will the chemo kill the fetus, or will it cause birth defects instead?" Being a nurse, I knew a lot about the human body, but this was definitely not my area of expertise, so I looked to him to guide me to the next step.

"Well," he said, shifting uncomfortably. It was then I realized it wasn't easy for him to have this talk with me, any more than it was for me to hear it. In that brief instant, I felt bad for Dr. Weber. "If you decide you want to keep the baby and try to carry to full term, we won't start treatment until the second trimester, to help prevent birth defects as much as possible. I believe you're around eight weeks pregnant, so that gives you a small window to make your decision. If you decide it's in your best interest not to have the baby, then we can perform a therapeutic abortion and start treatment almost immediately."

His words hung heavy in the air. I wanted so desperately for him to take them back but he couldn't.

Fate had decided my future, or possibly the lack thereof.

SEVENTEEN

Stone

I TRIED TO NOT FREAK out, to not rush back to the hospital and kidnap her. To force her to come to me. I wasn't a patient man by any stretch of the imagination, but I was smart enough to realize that, if I acted irrationally, I ran the risk of pushing Addy further away. Then I wouldn't have a shot in hell.

To help ease some of my frustration, I took a quick shower, rinsing away all the dirt and blood from earlier, being careful not to ruin Addy's handiwork. But the soothing water hadn't helped, so after throwing on some clothes I took to pacing in my living room. When that didn't work, I resorted to throwing back shots. But after four, I stopped. If . . . no, *when* she showed up, if I was drunk it would have the same effect as if I'd gone and stolen her from her job.

She wouldn't give me the time of day to try and work things out.

Plopping down, I rested my head on the back of the couch and tried my best to calm down. Anxiousness gripped me tight, and I knew if she made me wait much longer I was gonna crawl right out of my goddamn skin.

The clock ticked by slowly and painfully. It was nearing ten at night, and although I didn't like the thought of Addy traveling when it was dark out, I had no other choice if I wanted her to come over. Having forgotten to ask her what time she finished her shift, I reached for my phone and quickly dialed her number.

It rang only three times before her breathy voice caressed my eardrum. "Hello?"

"Where are you?" I asked, a sternness in my voice I hadn't even realized was present. It was extremely frustrating waiting for her and I took it out on her in the first two seconds of hearing her voice. Berating myself, I instantly corrected my tone. "Are you done with work yet?"

"Yes," she responded right away, but something seemed off. Her voice sounded raspy and raw.

"Were you crying, Addy?"

"I'll be there soon," she told me before disconnecting the call, completely ignoring my question. I redialed her number but it just rang and rang before going to voicemail. Trying two more times to reach her, I finally stopped and waited for her to show up.

Eighteen minutes later, I saw her headlights pierce the dark as she drove up my driveway. Striding toward the door, I thrust it open and jogged down the front steps, coming to stand by her driver's side door before she even shut off the engine. Impatience was certainly something I had to work on, but I knew something was wrong and the quicker I found out what, the quicker I could fix it.

I held the door open for her to exit the car, extending my hand to help her. As soon as the warmth of her palm hit my own, I led her toward the front entrance of my home before either of us said a word. Once inside, I ushered her toward the leather couch in the living room, images of the two of us suddenly springing to life. Her pinned beneath me as I thrust inside her over and over. Her on top of me and riding me until we both came undone. Bending her over the arm of the sofa, grabbing her blonde locks as I ruthlessly fucked her hard from behind, her moans so loud I was thrilled there wasn't a neighbor for miles.

"Do you want something to drink?" I asked, praying she'd accept so she could at least relax enough to have a real conversation about what was going on between us. If she remained as closed off and uptight as she had been, then I doubted the evening's visit was going to do anything, other than irritate me even more than I already was. "I think I still have some of that wine you like."

She nervously played with her hands, averting her beautiful blue eyes from me. "Just water, please."

"Are you sure? Looks like you could use something to take the edge off." I tried to joke, but it fell flat.

"I can't drink," she offered, a response I knew she hadn't meant to say simply because of her sudden reaction. She looked scared, fear crossing her face before she could hide it.

Forgetting all about trying to get her liquored up, I approached and sat down next to her, keeping a small distance between us. "Why would you say that?"

Completely ignoring the fact I'd just asked her for an explanation, she jumped off the couch and headed straight for the door. "I can't do this. I'm sorry." Before she disappeared outside, however, I caught up to her and stopped her. Wrapping my arm possessively around her waist, I hauled her back into the living room. No way was I allowing her to leave before we hashed out whatever this was between us.

"I don't think so, sweetheart. You're not going anywhere until you tell me what's going on." I was already anxious and she hadn't told me a damn thing. But maybe that was why I was all worked up, because she chose to remain tight-lipped.

"What do you want from me? Huh? You want me to lay all my issues at your feet? Ask you to save me? To be there for me when I'm not sure if I'll even make it?" Clutching strands of her hair, she pulled, as if the pressure was a relief for her somehow.

Something was really wrong, and I doubted it had anything to do with the original reason she gave me for not wanting to continue to be with me, mainly my explosive temper. No, whatever she was spouting off about was something much more dangerous, or sinister, or some shit I didn't even have a word for yet.

Grabbing her shoulders, I gently shook her, the dazed, far-off look on her face starting to scare me. "Addy, what are you talking about? Tell me now before I start to think the worst." Then something dawned on me. "Does this have anything to do with why that doctor wanted to see you?" I tried to keep my voice free from rage when I referred to *that* man, and hopefully I'd been successful. Realizing my anger was the last thing she needed to deal with drove me to calm my tone even more before speaking again. "Did he tell you something bad?"

Not one second passed between us before she answered. "Yes."

Moving closer, I cradled her to me, gifting her my support in the absence of words. At first, her arms remained at her sides, a stiffness holding her captive from accepting what I so freely offered. Then, before I knew it, light sobs tore from her throat while she clutched onto me as if her life depended on it. A fear, the likes of which I'd never known, ripped through me with such intensity it shook me to my core.

Pushing her back so I could see her face, I asked with trepidation, "What did he tell you?" My breathing kicked up a notch, adrenaline coursing through my veins in case I needed to react accordingly. Was she attacked and never told me? Was there something wrong with her I didn't know about? The questions were endless, but instead of torturing myself any longer, I asked my question again. "Baby," I soothed, "what is it? I need you to tell me."

Instead of speaking, she reached up on her tiptoes and crashed her mouth to mine, an action which completely caught me off guard. I knew what she was doing, though—she was deflecting my question by trying to lose herself in me. When I felt her tongue press against my lips I readily opened for her, tasting her sadness as well as her need for me. It was exactly how I'd hoped things would end up when I demanded she come to my house earlier—without the secret upsetting news, of course.

"Are you going to tell me what the issue is?" I asked, surprising myself by breaking free from her intoxicating kiss.

"After," she whispered, wrapping her hands in my hair and trying to pull me closer.

"After what?" My tone was cautious but hopeful.

Sinking back down to her natural height, she placed her hands on her hips and frowned, the initial fear in her posture gone for a brief moment. "After you fuck me." Biting the corner of her bottom lip, an action she knew drove me insane with lust, she smiled and leaned up to capture my mouth again. But before I gave in, I wanted to see if she would agree to something first.

"Do you promise to come back to me? To be mine? For good? For real?" I kept pushing, but I couldn't hold back. I needed us to claim each other, to declare it publicly. I knew there would be issues with her uncle, but I'd deal with Trigger when the time came, as well as anyone else who had anything to say about it.

"Stone . . ." she warned, releasing her hold and taking a step back. "I can't do that and you know it."

"Do I? Everything tells me the opposite. You want me. You *need* me, or else you wouldn't be looking for solace in my arms. Right?" I insisted she answer me or I wasn't gonna give in. God help me, no matter how hard I wanted to sink inside her, she wasn't getting anything from me until she finally agreed to give me what I wanted.

Once and for all.

When she finally spoke, her words floored me. More accurately, they amused me. "I can't protect you from my uncle." She was dead serious, which made me laugh out loud.

"I think I can handle your uncle," I promised, moving closer because I knew she'd just admitted she would be mine.

Before I could pull her toward me again, she placed her hand on my chest and looked deep into my eyes. "Stone, if we're going to do this for real, I need for you to make an honest effort to control your temper. With everything else going on, I don't think I'll be able to handle it." Her words weren't lost on me, and I'd push her to tell me everything, but only after I gave her what she wanted.

"I promise. Don't you realize the fact I couldn't claim you as mine only fueled my fury? Knowing whenever Tripp lounged all over you, or Hawke said that shit to you about the club, that I couldn't say a damn thing, couldn't warn them to back off because you were mine, killed me. You denying me made me react even more harshly than if you had allowed me to tell them you were my ol' lady."

"Your old lady?" she asked, the frown on her face telling me every-thing. Even though she didn't care for the terminology, it was exactly what she was.

My fucking ol' lady.

It meant something to her status in the club, which meant something to me, and hopefully to her once she became accustomed to it.

"Yes, my ol' lady. Better get used to it, sweetheart," I teased, placing a lingering kiss on her lips.

"Can't you just say I'm your girlfriend? Or your woman? Anything is better than ol' lady." Pursing her lips only made me want her more.

"I'll say those things as well, but 'ol' lady' is here to stay." A genuine smile splayed big and proud on my face as I realized what I'd been pushing for between us was finally coming to fruition.

"Fine," she pouted. "But I'm not ever referring to you as my ol' man. No way. Not gonna happen," she affirmed, a small twinkle in her eye.

"That's fine. Because soon enough, you'll just call me your husband." The words were out before I even realized what I was saying.

But I wouldn't take them back for anything in the world.

Because they were the absolute truth. And the sooner she got used to the idea, the better it would be for the both of us.

EIGHTEEN

Adelaide

I CHOSE TO IGNORE HIS last statement, simply not possessing enough mental energy to add to my list of things to ponder. Instead, I linked my fingers through his and guided him toward the bedroom. Needing to lose myself to Stone drove me to finally give in and agree to being with him again, officially this time. I had to admit, the thought thrilled me, and if I was excited, I was positive he was as well.

He'd been the one pushing for us to be a couple since the first time he kissed me, which was odd because usually it was the woman asking for the commitment. But I think the territorial part inside him wanted to possess me for all the world to see. And if his last statement were any indication where his head was at, I had no doubt he would try to make it legal sooner rather than later.

I would be lying if I said I hadn't constantly thought about it before. Because I had. But there were a few obstacles in the way.

My uncle.

The club life.

His temper.

I prayed that when he finally found out about the baby, and the cancer, that he would make an honest effort in trying to control his temper. He was smart enough to realize such continued stress on me would be even more detrimental given my current condition.

Although, revealing my secrets could have the opposite effect. He could become even more protective and controlling, giving me the excuse of looking out for his new family. I guessed I would have to see how it all played out when I finally took the plunge and told him.

Maybe what he said was true. Now that I'd agreed to be his, and he could assert his feelings for me in public, he wouldn't feel the need to blow up over other men paying me attention. Then again, Stone would always be Stone, but the fact other people would know I belonged to him would surely be a comfort to him nonetheless.

Dr. Weber's words changed my life forever. One thing alone was enough to deal with, but having both issues was staggering, and because of it I knew deep in my heart I needed Stone in my life. I needed his love and protection. His assurance that everything was going to be all right, with both the baby and the cancer. I would find strength in his arms, so I accepted everything he offered.

Plus an unwelcome thought plagued me, pushing me toward the man I truly wanted in my life.

I knew deep down when I ended things with him that I was going to eventually give him another chance. And seeing him all banged up in the hospital really hit home that I didn't want to have any regrets, especially if there was a chance I only had so much time left. Our mortality had been pushed to the forefront that evening, for each of us, so I chose to forge ahead with our relationship, hoping for the best and praying for many long years ahead together.

Once we entered his room, I flicked on the light and led him toward the bed. It was a strange turn of events indeed, because Stone was the one who always ran the show when it came to having sex. He was a downright control freak sometimes, tying me up just so I wouldn't get in the way of what he wanted to do to me. I smiled at the gesture he offered by allowing me to take charge this once.

Pushing him down so his back hit the mattress, I remained standing in front, still dressed in my uniform. Not wanting any reminder of my job, I quickly discarded my clothes, gazing at the lustful look on my man's face.

My man.

I loved the sound of that for sure.

Standing in nothing but my matching bra and panties, I'd never felt sexier. Whenever he was near, he was forever trying to touch me, consumed by connecting with me in any way he could. Whether it was through a kiss, a smack on my ass, or a full-on grope session, he claimed he could never get enough.

"Do you want me?" I asked, passion dancing over each word tumbling into the air around us.

"Fuck yeah, I do." He rose up on his elbows so he could see me better, his eyes raking over my entire form. First staring intently into my eyes as if he were communicating a secret message, then focusing on my mouth, licking his lips like he wanted to devour me whole. Afterward, his eyes fell over the rest of my body, burning me with a need I'd only ever felt with him. "Play with yourself while I watch," he suddenly demanded.

"I'm in charge here," I warned. "But since I was gonna do it anyway . . ." Slowly sliding my hand down my belly, stopping for a few seconds over the area which would soon grow swollen with his child, my fingers disappeared beneath the waistband of my white panties. Closing my eyes, I spread my legs wider and bucked forward when my fingers made contact with my clit. I was more than ready to go, likely to explode before we even started.

"Look at me while you touch yourself," he rasped. When my lids flew open, I was surprised to find he was sitting on the edge of the bed, his belt buckle undone and his zipper down. "Come here," he commanded, reaching to pull me close.

"I thought you were going to let me call the shots tonight," I argued.

"You know I can't wait to touch you, though. So how 'bout you can call all the shots as long as you always give me access to your body? How does that sound?"

"So I can't tie you up then?" I teased, taking the opportunity to ask him something unexpected.

"Ummm . . . no," he answered resolutely. I laughed because I knew there was no way he would ever allow me to restrain him, although the thought of him at my complete and utter mercy was an intoxicating turn-on.

I decided to give in, allowing him to touch me while I teased myself. Wanting him to see all of me, however, I gripped the sides of my panties and lowered them down my legs until they pooled at my feet. Taking another step forward, I unclasped the front of my bra, discarding the flimsy material as quickly as I could.

I stood before him in all my glory. I'd always been self-conscious of my smaller chest and plump rear end, but the way Stone worshipped my body made me accept myself more. He acted like he couldn't get enough, as if he were addicted to me. And to have a man like him desire me in such a raw, primal way was intoxicating.

"Goddamn it!" he growled. "I love your fuckin' body so much." His warm fingertips grazed over each nipple, pinching the hardened peaks before leaning forward and pulling me into his mouth. His tongue swirled and danced over my sensitive buds, his lips drawing the blood to the surface before releasing me with a seductive popping sound.

Desire pooled in my belly, working its way down to my core with such intensity that I would instantly detonate if he touched me there, which I was sure he wouldn't complain about. He prided himself on the fact he could make me come with his fingers, mouth, and cock. "A triple threat" he would sometimes joke.

He was holding me so close I couldn't move, and because I wanted to undress him, I shoved his shoulders back. After some reluctance, he finally gave in and leaned back. Shaking my head at the annoyed look on his face, I grabbed the hem of his shirt and pulled it over his head, quickly assessing my handiwork to make sure his stitches were holding.

"Are you sure you're okay to do this?" Worry pierced my brow for a brief moment, until he assured me he was all right.

"A few scrapes and bruises aren't gonna stop me. Plus, you know I can't feel that shit anyway," he assured. Normally, I would have denied him until I deemed him healed enough, but I was being selfish right then.

I needed him.

Desperately.

Crooking my finger, I gestured for him to stand. He did so willingly, and with a fat smile on his gorgeously chiseled face. Since his pants were already undone, they slid down his legs with ease. And the best surprise was that he was going commando underneath. His large cock sprang to life, twitching and aching for me to wrap whatever I could around the thickness of it. My mouth or hand, I was sure he wouldn't complain either way. No hesitation existed as I sank to my knees, the plushness of his dark carpet kissing my skin while I quickly situated myself.

His breath hitched when he gazed down at me. "Do you want me to suck your dick?" I asked, knowing damn well he was going to say yes. Stone was someone who loved to talk dirty during sex, so I was only doing my part, asking him direct questions I knew would only add fuel to his already out-of-control fire.

"You know I love when you talk like that," he groaned, tilting my chin up so he could see my face. Taking hold of himself, he pressed the tip to the seam of my lips, sliding it back and forth before commanding me to open. "Spread those pretty lips of yours, baby. Suck me in deep until I hit the back of your throat, then I want to feel your tongue lick me while I fuck your mouth."

How can I say no to that?

I did as I was told and pleasured him exactly the way I knew he liked, teasing him before sliding my tongue up and down his shaft. Gently cupping his balls in my hand, I sucked him deep, flicking my tongue every so often. Once I'd taken him in fully, I swallowed then hummed, an action which made him curse before grabbing the back of my head.

"Keep that up and I'm gonna shoot down the back of your throat in no time," he mumbled, so lost to the sensation he could barely speak. There was nothing sexier than hearing his excitement, knowing I was the one making him come apart at the seams.

Popping him free from the warmth of my mouth, I briefly looked up and asked, "What if that's what I want? To taste you on my tongue?" Before he answered, I decided to pleasure him a different way, a technique I'd done only a few times before. Heading further south, I focused on one of the most sensitive parts of his body, the area he identified as 'the boys.' Without warning, the left one disappeared into my mouth, giving him a gentle tug all the while carefully caressing him with my tongue as I applied a bit of pressure. His reaction was to tangle his fingers tighter in my hair and pull upward, the slight sting of pain urging me further. Releasing him from my mouth, I teased the other one, flicking my tongue over his sensitive skin while my hand stroked him, leisurely but firmly.

Stone thrust his hips forward a few times, a low growl rumbling in his throat before suddenly taking a step back. Confusion hit me at first, but when he hauled me to my feet and crashed his lips to mine I knew he was on the verge of losing control. He enjoyed what I was doing—maybe a little too much—and that realization made me grin.

"I want you on your back. Now!" he affirmed, an intensity in his voice I'd never heard before.

"You didn't like that?" I asked, knowing damn well he did.

"More than you know." Pointing to the bed, I did as instructed and lay on my back, spreading my legs because it was the position I thought he wanted me in.

"Not yet, sweetheart." He pushed my thighs together and climbed up my body. My confused look make him chuckle. When he was close enough, he placed a knee on either side of my head, grabbing himself and tapping my lips with his arousal. "Open up for me again. I'm not gonna be gentle, but I *will* be quick," he promised. Bracing himself by placing his left hand on the bed, he pushed past my lips and, true to his word, he fucked my mouth hard and quick. His growls reverberated through the air, driving me to finish him off even faster than I thought possible.

Wrapping my fingers around him, I stroked him, matching the intense force of my mouth. "Come for me," I urged, taking a quick break before sucking him back in.

"Fuck me!" he yelled. "Oh, shit, that feels too good. I can't . . . can't . . . Addy . . ." The muscles in his stomach tightened, the swell of his thickness pulsated, and before long he grunted, his salty essence coating my tongue before disappearing down the back of my throat. I milked every last drop before licking my lips clean.

After a few brief moments, Stone righted himself before moving down my body, resting over me on his forearms. There were no words spoken as our eyes locked. The look in his was one of passion, sure, but there was also a hint of reverence as well. He stared at me like I was the only other person in the world, as if his own existence would end if I wasn't near him. Lost in his gaze, I thought about what would happen to him if I didn't make it, how heartbroken he would be if he had to continue on without me. A lone tear escaped and trickled down my cheek, my determination to survive so strong I knew it was the only option.

"I love you," I confessed, cupping the side of his face with my palm, gingerly leaning up and softly brushing my lips against his. When my head rested on the bed once more, I thought I was going to be exposed, vulnerable after my admission, but instead I felt relieved. I'd meant to tell him how I truly felt a while back, but then I'd broken free from him and feared he would never know exactly what he meant to me. Maybe my recent diagnosis and unexpected pregnancy were all a gift. I knew it was a weird way to look at my situation, but maybe it was life's way of righting a mistake before it was too late.

It felt like hours had passed, but it was only mere seconds before his lips parted and he spoke. "I love you, too. Forever," he proclaimed, wiping away another one of my tears with his thumb before resting his mouth over mine. "Promise me you'll never leave me again," he demanded before firmly capturing my mouth, his tongue teasing me until I opened for him.

Our kiss was otherworldly, filled with passion and promises unspoken. I silently swore to fight for not only my life but the life of our unborn child, and I had a feeling he was trying to show me his intention to be a better man, in all aspects. The only issue I had with him was his temper, so if he could somehow get that under control he would be utterly perfect in my eyes.

Suddenly breaking our connection, he moved down my body and parted my legs, his warm breath hitting me right before his tongue snuck out and tasted my excitement. I was barely able to form a coherent thought his assault on me was overwhelming, my inner muscles already contracting and preparing for my climax, which was guaranteed to happen within minutes if he kept up that pace.

"I could eat you all day I'm so addicted to your sweetness," he mumbled, shoving his head back between my legs before I even registered what he'd said. Plunging two fingers inside, he closed his lips over my clit and sucked hard. The feeling was akin to a twinge of pain, the sensation immensely intense. He knew whenever he did that I came shortly afterward. And this time was no different. I tried to move back on the bed but he held me firm, fucking me with both his hand and mouth. Fierce and quick. Over and over. There was no stopping or prolonging it.

When I couldn't hold back any longer, I screamed out his name as I collapsed, my throat raw as my orgasm rocked through me before I even felt it building. Pulling his hair, I bucked against him, savoring the feeling until it was completely over.

After I'd come back down, he moved up my body until he hovered over me again, his lips so close he drove me crazy with desire. "Taste yourself on me," he urged, pressing his lips to mine, opening so I could do as he commanded. My arousal was sweet on his tongue, and I accepted him, teasing and tormenting him as much as he allowed.

When he'd had enough torture, he parted my thighs with his knee, reached down with his hand, and touched my clit. I jerked. "Too sensitive?" He laughed. All I could do was nod, ripe with anticipation knowing he was going to bury himself inside me in no time at all. Leaning close to my ear, his warm breath kissed my lobe before he spoke. "Are you ready for me to fuck you now? Wanna feel me deep inside you?" His whispers made me shiver in delight. So eager for the thrill of it, I couldn't answer. Instead, I thrust my hips upward, pleading with my body instead of with my words.

"Nope. Not good enough. I wanna hear you say it." His beard tickled my throat, but the sensation was quickly replaced when he sucked on my neck, teasing me with his sweet kisses and soft bites. "And don't leave anything out."

Trying to catch my breath, I finally spoke the words he asked for. "I want your big—" I latched onto his ass and pulled him closer "—thick cock so deep inside me it hurts. I want you to fuck me like you hate me." Apparently, it was the right thing to say because, before my next heartbeat, he pushed inside me in one quick, rough thrust.

"Put your hands above your head and don't lower them." Excited, I did as I was told. We'd experimented in bondage play before, but seeing as how neither one of us knew we were going to end up in bed tonight, he wasn't prepared. I guessed my compliance would have to do.

I loved when Stone ordered me around in the bedroom. Outside . . . not so much, but in there he could do practically anything he wanted to me and I would be ready, willing, and able. I trusted him wholeheartedly not to hurt me or push me too far. He could read my body better than I could, a feat which baffled me each and every time.

When my arms were firmly in place, he kissed me before lowering his head and drawing a nipple into his mouth. His teeth grazed over the tip and I stiffened, the bite of pain always catching me off guard, but when his tongue stroked the tight bud, all pleasure returned tenfold. He teased my other nipple the same way, bringing me to the brink right away.

"It's been forever since I've been inside you, so I'm gonna fuck you hard and fast. But rest assured, you'll be coming again before I finish." No more words were spoken before he stayed true to his declaration and quickly moved inside me. He withdrew until only his tip remained, then forced himself all the way back in, seating himself to the hilt.

He did this over and over, until he no longer pulled out, just fucked me like a man possessed. Hitching my right leg over the crook of his arm, he was in deeper than before, dragging himself along every sensitive nerve. I felt my body ramping up for its release, and no matter how much I tried to dismiss it, wanting our escapade to last as long as possible, there was no way to stop it. I climbed higher and higher, until I perched right on the very edge of the cliff. My cries and whimpers told him I was so close; he just needed to reach between our bodies and stroke me, sending me on a freefall to the desire swirling below.

As if reading my mind—or better yet, my body—his fingers connected with my over-sensitive clit, teasing me with the perfect amount of pressure until my pussy clamped down all around him.

"Lincoln!" I cried out in the heat of the moment, clutching the headboard to anchor myself. "I'm coming. Oh, God . . . I'm coming so hard,"

I sputtered, unable to inhale a full breath.

"I can feel you exploding, baby," he rasped, bringing his lips down to meet mine while he chased his own release. His kiss was demanding, so full of urgency it was overwhelming, but in the best way possible. His body finally bucked in release as his hot seed quickly filled me. Little did he know he'd already planted a part of himself inside me, forever linking us together.

When he finally rolled off me, he positioned himself on his back, pulling me with him so I was tucked safely into his side. Resting my head on his chest, I could feel the quick beats of his heart and, oddly enough, they matched mine exactly.

Two hearts beating as one.

"So," he said, startling me. "Lincoln, is it? I thought you only called me that when I pissed you off so badly you didn't know what to do?" He was clearly amused, and it made me smile.

"Well, I scream out your given name when you push me to the brink of sanity. So that could be in anger . . . or in pleasure." I smiled, and I knew he felt the curve of my lips against his chest.

"Sounds good to me," he replied sounding amused. We lay in each other's arms for a few minutes before he broke the silence again. "Addy?"

"Yeah?" I quickly answered.

"What news do you have to tell me?" His question was short and to the point.

"I'll tell you tomorrow," I promised. "I just want to take tonight and live in the moment. I don't wanna think about anything else but you and me." Snuggling in closer, I draped my arm over his waist and threw my leg over his muscular thigh.

"Addy?"

"Yeah?" I tensed, waiting to see if he was going to push me on the topic.

"Tell me you love me again."

I tilted my head and looked up at him, his gorgeous face beaming down at me. "I love you. With all my heart," I professed. I swore if I could combust with elation, I would have done so right then, the look on his face melting my heart. Stone was a gentle soul underneath his rough exterior, and I was so happy I was the woman he'd chosen to share his life with.

"Love you too," he said, before capturing my mouth once more.

After I'd rested my head back on his chest, he took a few breaths before choosing to speak yet again.

"Addy?"

"Yes?"

"You know I'm gonna fuck you a few more times before I let you sleep, right?"

I quickly relaxed back into him. "Yeah. I'm looking forward to it . . . Lincoln."

He laughed, the vibrations of his chest tickling my ear, a smile wide on my face as I waited for him to take me again.

NINETEEN

Stone

WAKING AS SOON AS THE light of dawn filtered through my bedroom window, I couldn't believe I finally had Addy back in my life, in my bed, and in my arms for me to hold and protect. And the biggest gift she could have given me . . . she did. Her heart, when she'd told me she loved me. Without sounding like a complete pussy, I was over-the-moon elated that she'd finally shared her deepest feelings with me. And I returned her affections wholeheartedly. I would have professed my love to her earlier but I didn't want to scare her off, not quite sure how she felt about me. I knew she wanted me, but I had no idea she truly loved me, as I did her.

She had no idea how much I'd missed her. I hadn't even allowed myself to realize the magnitude of what she'd done to me when she broke it off between us. From the first time I laid eyes on her, I knew she was gonna be mine. No matter how many times I was warned away from her, I persisted, defying all rational thought. I knew it was against the rules to be involved with family of another member, but try and tell that to my heart, mind and . . . hell, I can't believe I was even thinking this but . . . my fucking soul.

Sometime during the night, she'd rolled over, taking me with her because I wasn't about to let her go. Cradling her against my body, my dick pressed into the seam of her luscious ass. Small movements she made caused her body to back into mine, increasing the need for me to take her once again. She was probably a little sore from the previous night, but if she didn't quit tempting me, I'd throw all concern to the wayside and take her anyway.

Sure enough, she writhed against me once more, unraveling the last strand of restraint I'd so desperately held in my weakening grasp.

Leaning over her, I pulled her hair away from her face and gently kissed her neck. "Addy," I whispered, trying to rouse her from her slumber. She'd slept enough for one night, and I needed some more lovin'. "Baby," I called out, that time grinding my cock against her while bending her leg behind her and over my waist. Being sure not to make her uncomfortable, I spread her a bit more until I could see all of her. Stroking her with a soft touch, her body responded immediately, stretching around my fingers as soon as I entered her.

She groaned, pushing against me while I teased her, clutching the covers and rocking her body back to meet me. "Oooo . . . that feels amazing," she whimpered. Pleading with me not to stop, I fucked her with my hand until she came, her muscles clamping down on my fingers while she rode out her orgasm. Moaning out her satisfaction, she tried to turn to face me, but a strong hand on her side kept her immobile.

"I'm gonna take you like this," I told her, splaying her leg over the crook of my arm and completely opening her up for me. "Grab me and put me inside you. I'm gonna hold your leg in the air so I can fuck you deep." I barely finished instructing her before I was halfway sheathed. I stayed still while she worked me the rest of the way in, panting out pleas for me to take her hard. And rough.

As I started to move, building up momentum, my cell rang. "Don't even think about it," Addy warned, gripping my thigh and pushing herself against me over and over again. Since it was still early, I knew something was going down, but I was torn between pleasuring my woman and answering the phone. There was too much risky shit still up in the air with the club, so I decided it was best I took the call. I slipped from her tight little body and rolled onto my back. As I reached over the side of the bed to grab my jeans, my cell vibrating and ringing against the fabric it was hidden between, Addy hopped off the bed and walked away.

"Where the fuck you goin'?" I barked, flipping open the phone and resting it against my ear. Completely ignoring me, I watched her disappear from the room, instantly regretting my choice.

"Stone?" a voice called out over the other end of the small device. "You there, man?" It was Marek.

"Yeah, yeah. I'm here. What's up?"

"I need you at the clubhouse ASAP. We got some stuff we gotta deal with, that bastard Yanez being first and foremost, and we need all hands on deck." The urgency in his voice instantly put me on alert. Whatever we needed to do was time sensitive, and for as much as I didn't want to leave Addy right then, I had no other choice.

"Fuck!" I grumbled, throwing one leg over the side of the bed in a lazy-ass attempt to get up.

"You got somethin' better to do, brother?" he asked, annoyance strangling his tone. When it came to Yanez, Marek was jumpy, wanting desperately to avenge Sully in the worst way. He'd become somewhat obsessed with disposing of the man who'd raped his wife. If the roles were reversed, I would go to the ends of the earth to exact my revenge and wrath on the prick who'd done that to Addy.

"Nope. Just tired is all," I answered, hoping my pitiful excuse would fly.

"Then wake the fuck up and get here." He hung up before saying anything else, which was probably for the best because Addy came strolling back into my bedroom, naked and sexy as hell.

"I have to go," I said, sitting on the edge of the bed, running my hands through my hair in frustration. "But I'd like to finish what we started." I grabbed her waist and pulled her in to me, spreading my legs so she could move in closer. My hands snaked around her back and gripped her ass, burying my face in her chest and trying to convince her to give in.

"We need to talk," she whispered, trying to push me away. I'd meant to make her tell me her news before we fell asleep, but we'd both been so exhausted we passed out before I could push her to open up. And now I had to go handle club business.

"I know. But it's gonna have to wait until I'm finished." When she pushed my chest again, I had no choice but to let her go. Rising to my full height, I hooked my fingers under her chin and raised her head. The fire in her eyes confused me. I wasn't sure if she was upset at me or at the situation. While there wasn't a damn thing I could do right then, I still felt horrible for leaving her before she'd been able to unload whatever was bothering her.

I wanted to be there for her in every way I could, but there were gonna be times, like this, when I had to put the club first. If we weren't directly in the middle of a shit storm, I would have told Marek to carry on without me.

But we were.

And I couldn't.

"Will you wait here for me?"

"No," she answered quickly. Too quickly.

Something was off, and I pressed even though I knew damn well I didn't have time to pursue her sudden temper.

"Why not?" I took a step forward, crowding her personal space. Right then it didn't make a bit of difference that both of us were still naked. We were pushing each other. A battle of wills, so to speak. I loved her sass and spunk, but sometimes I wished she was more submissive, doing as I asked instead of always asserting herself. I knew I probably sounded like a bastard, but I really didn't care.

"Because I have stuff to do. I can't wait around for you all day."

"Do you have to go to work?"

"No."

"Then what's the problem?" I prompted, feeling my blood pressure rise because I knew she wasn't gonna make this easy for me. All I wanted her to do was wait for me until I was done with whatever I needed to do at the club. Then we could talk, discuss whatever was bothering her, maybe have some dinner, and then lose ourselves in hours of pleasure.

Looking more than annoyed, her blue eyes lit up with anger, a hint of sadness splayed underneath, which confused me. "Just because I finally agreed to be with you for real doesn't mean I'm gonna be waitin' on your ass whenever you want me to. I have a life, Stone. My own life, with my own friends and a job, which demands a lot of my time. I'm not gonna give all that up because life decided to throw a whopper of a curveball at me, punching me in the face before I even knew it was happening."

If anyone could have seen the look on my face they probably would've laughed their asses off. "What the fuck does all that mean?" I asked, a deep frown of confusion painting my expression. I knew before she answered that it wasn't gonna be good. She was too worked up for her outburst to be solely about me making a simple request for her to stay back at my house until I returned. Something prickled at me, but I had absolutely no time to delve into it and we both knew it.

Looking a little sheepish, she realized she'd gone overboard in her response. "Nothing," she lied.

Because I had no time to do anything else, I quickly dressed before pulling her into my embrace. Her body was still, but as I continued to hold her, praying whatever was weighing on her mind would ease up some, she molded herself into me. Wrapping her arms around my waist, she placed her head on my chest and exhaled a strangled breath. I kissed the top of her head before releasing her.

"I'll call you when I'm done, and if you have time I would love for you to meet me back here." Every word I spoke was controlled, and as much as I wanted to demand she wait for me, I knew she would tell me to go to hell and storm out of my house. And even *I* realized it wasn't the smartest thing to do right after she'd agreed to take me back.

Stone

"WHAT'S GOIN' ON?" I ASKED, flinging myself into my appointed chair, glancing around the room at all my brothers. It seemed Marek had called everyone in, but for what I wasn't sure yet. My friend sat at the head of the table, looking quite volatile while he waited for the room to silence. Tripp and Hawke were holding their own sidebar while Ryder and Trigger boisterously laughed about something Jagger had said. Cutter, Breck, and Zip leaned back in their chairs, their eyes half open considering how early in the day it still was.

Another round of laughter erupted, but instead of having my eyes on the brothers scattered around the large oblong table, they were focused on Marek. I saw his jaw tick and his eyes narrow. I didn't even have to follow his gaze to see who he was intently staring at—Jagger. I'd figured out why he seemed to not like the guy, and under other circumstances Jagger would have been kicked out of the club. But the money he brought in was a nice sum, helping us get away from all the illegal shit which constantly threatened our very lives.

That, plus the kid knew, if he truly stepped out of line, Marek would end him. Prez wasn't normally an aggressive guy. Some had even said he was rather laid-back, but ever since Sully had come into his life, his temper was short, his protectiveness over the woman off the charts. He rivaled me with the temper and possessiveness traits, and I was only too happy to have the company.

Marek leaned forward, quickly assessing everyone with a simple glance. Running his hands over his face, his expression changed from mere annoyance to self-satisfied, mixed with a hint of rage. His blue eyes blazed, his posture rigid; he just looked pissed-off.

As soon as he began to talk, everyone shut up and paid attention, as if the man were speaking some sort of gospel. "I tasked Zip with keeping tabs on Yanez, which is why this is his first time back with us in a few days. The day that vile fucker and Carrillo walked out of here, I'd been given assurances we were free and clear from the cartel, as well as the fact Carrillo was going to immediately cut the Reapers out of whatever deal they'd had with them. No more supply, which means no more money funneling into that cesspool of a club."

There was only a small group of men in the club at the time when Yanez and Carrillo visited, so not too many were aware of the chaos that ensued as soon as Marek had learned what Yanez had done to Sully. But word traveled fast, and I had no doubt every member sitting around the table found out what had happened.

"Yanez has to die. Plain and simple," Marek said, rage blossoming behind his eyes again. If Carrillo's right-hand man didn't cease to exist soon, I feared my best friend was gonna go off the deep end.

"You know if we just up and kill him, there will be a shit storm raining down on us faster than we can prepare for it," Cutter yelled out, slapping his hand against the table.

"Yeah," a few of the other men grumbled. While they would have the prez's back, no questions asked, they were looking forward to the days ahead. Days of not having to worry about the DEA knocking down our door. Or our biggest enemy trying to pick us off one by one. Everyone realized breaking free from the cartel, and having them cut the Reapers off, was the best thing to happen to us in a very long time.

Marek had a vision for how he wanted to lead the club, and while some griped about not being able to earn as much without running the cartel's drugs, they quickly came to realize we would be just fine. Yes, we would have to scale back a bit, but there was no reason we couldn't indulge now and again. Our businesses would make us enough money to keep us afloat . . . and then some.

Flings was quite prosperous, and the new titty bar would be too. The Underground was sort of a wash, but at least we weren't losing money there. Marek had talked about getting into other businesses as well. Maybe a few more bars scattered around the local area. Booze and pussy would certainly be our biggest moneymakers.

"I know," our leader agreed. "That's why we have to catch him going behind Carrillo's back. There's no way that greedy fuck isn't gonna make some shady-ass deal with the Reapers, and when he does, we'll be there to catch him. Then I'll take it to his boss." Swiping his palms against each other, he said, "And that will be that. The cartel can't afford to have such disloyal people in their midst. When they find one, they get rid of him. I just have to convince Carrillo to let me have Yanez, with the promise to dispose of him." Leaning back in his chair, he huffed out a breath before slamming his fist on the table. "But only *after* I make him pay for what he did."

There was a lot of nodding, everyone in agreement of what was laid out before us.

Turning my attention toward Zip, I asked, "Did you see anything when you were watching Yanez?" I knew if it were anything substantial, we would've already been on our way to see Carrillo, but at that point any information we could gather on the bastard would be better than nothing.

"Not too much so far. He's gone to meet with his boss a few times, as well as some guy I didn't recognize, but other than that he's been keeping a rather low profile," Zip answered. I could tell by the look on the kid's face, and the way he carried himself, he'd been honored that Marek had appointed him to follow the guy. Zip always went above and beyond to prove his loyalty to the club because his father had turned out to be a rat, and he didn't want to be known as the same. So tailing someone who was so important to Marek was of the highest honor in Zip's eyes. His green eyes gleamed proudly, his chest puffing out like a proud peacock. But I couldn't blame him. Not one bit.

At the same time I asked what the other guy looked like, Zip pulled his phone from his cut and flipped it open. Not long afterward, he shoved his phone toward Marek, showing him a picture of the mystery man.

"Motherfucker!" he shouted. Passing me the phone, I saw immediately who he was referring to.

The man looking pleased as all hell shaking hands with Rico Yanez was none other than Sam Koritz, the DEA agent who'd raided our club a few months back. We knew he was dirty, so I wasn't sure why we were surprised he was in bed with the cartel. While we could certainly find a way to use this information to our advantage, the real connection we had to make was between Yanez and Psych, the leader of the Reapers. Sully's father. Only then could we convince Carrillo to hand over his man.

"Fuckin' Koritz!" Trigger shouted, passing the phone from one person to the next. Every one of the men was onboard with getting rid of the DEA agent for good. He'd caused too much heartache for our club. It was one thing for a man of the law to come after us because we lived on the other side of said law, but for a crooked bastard to do the same was inexcusable.

A few minutes later, Marek wrapped his hand around the gavel and ended the meeting with, "Be ready at a moment's notice if we find what we're looking for. Hopefully it'll be anytime now, but just in case, keep your eyes and ears peeled for anything strange. Other than the impending issue with Koritz, I'm sure the Reapers were made aware of the fact they're no longer doing business with the cartel, and I imagine they'll be looking to find out why. As soon as they do, I have no doubt they'll be gunning for us."

With nothing left to say, he slammed down the gavel and rose from his chair. Clapping me on the back, he gave me a nod before exiting the room, everyone else filing out right behind him.

I knew this was coming, but that didn't stop me from wishing like hell we didn't have to deal with it. All I wanted was for our club to be totally legit, put the cartel and the Savage Reapers far behind us, and move on with enjoying life.

I prayed for the day when the biggest issue I had to worry about was whether or not I'd pissed off Addy.

Adelaide

"ARE YOU SURE YOU'RE OKAY, sweetheart?" my dad asked, placing the back of his hand on my forehead. "You feel a bit warm." The concern in his eyes was mild. What would they look like when I finally worked up enough nerve to tell him not only that was I pregnant with his first grandchild, but I was sick on top of it? More than anything, I wished I didn't have to put my father through any of this. He'd seen enough horror years before when he sat by my mother's side, every single day, doing his best to tend to her and lift her spirits, all the while completely forgetting about himself.

And he'd stayed lost. Not one time in the five years since the death of my mother, his loving wife, had he ventured out on a date with anyone. Brian Reins was a very attractive man. "Fit and fifty," I would tease him. His dark hair was greying at the temple, making him look even more distinguished, his deep brown eyes shining bright whenever he saw me. Too bad they didn't light up for anyone else. I often prayed for him to meet someone, grab life by the balls and at least try to be happy, but my prayers never came true.

My dad worked as an accountant and, contrary to popular stereotypes, he wasn't boring. Or at least he hadn't been. He had an adventurous soul, always looking for the next big thrill. I couldn't even begin to count how many times he'd convinced my mother and me to step outside our comfort zone and experience life. Swimming with the sharks in Hawaii, or jumping out of a plane were just some of the thrills he wanted all of us to experience. When he started talking about cave climbing, my mother and I had to put a stop to it. A small smile found its way on my face remembering all the fun we had as a family.

But after my mother died, everything stopped.

The thrills.

The laughter.

Life as we knew it.

I'd trudged through, focusing on school and finishing my degree. I was lucky enough to find a great nursing job at Mercy Medical Center. My hours were long sometimes, but I really enjoyed being in a position where I could make a difference for someone. I supposed the fact I couldn't help my own mother drove me to want to dedicate my career to helping others.

And now here I am, the one who's sick and will be in need of someone . . . well, like me.

"I'm fine, Dad," I assured him. Sucking down any courage I thought I had walking through his front door, I gave him a faint smile before twitching in my chair.

"If you say so."

"I say so," I joked. Since I wasn't going to wait around for Stone back at his house, I decided to wing it and see if my dad was free for lunch. Thankfully, he was. We hadn't spent much time together lately because of my crazy schedule at work, and his hours were picking up because tax time was fast approaching. Even though he set his own office hours, seeing as how he owned the accounting firm, he was still very diligent with attending to his customers. A great work ethic was one of the many things he'd passed along to me.

"So, where do you want to go for lunch," he asked, scrolling through his e-mail while he waited for me to decide.

"How about the new Thai restaurant near the ice cream parlor we used to always go to?"

Never taking his eyes from his phone, he nodded.

"Are you sure you have time, Dad? It seems like you're distracted." I placed my hand on his forearm to get his attention. It worked.

"What? Oh . . . Sorry, honey." A little hesitant, he gave me a half smile before changing our lunch plans. "Do you mind if I just make us something here? It's just that I have to go into the office earlier than I thought, and it would make it easier for me to fix us something instead of traveling back and forth to a restaurant." Looking hopeful, he asked, "What do you think?"

There was no hesitation; as long as I was able to spend time with my dad I was happy. I needed his love and support now more than ever, even if he had no idea what was going on with me.

"Of course."

"Good," he said, clapping his hands together in excitement. "What shall I make us?" He contemplated his future dish, tapping his finger on his handsome chin. "I know!" he exclaimed. "I'll make my famous chili." Scouring the kitchen for the necessary ingredients, he looked lighter than he had in past visits. I wondered if I was missing something, or had it been that long since we'd spent any time together.

Deciding to ask a question which had fallen from my lips many times before, one he seemed to not like, I forged ahead and inquired anyway.

"So, are you seeing anyone? You know, I hear some of those dating sites aren't half bad. Just stay away from Tinder," I teased, drumming my fingers on the countertop, watching him start to prepare our lunch.

Without making eye contact, he said, "No one special."

No one special.

Did that mean he'd at least gone on a date recently? And recently could have covered the past year.

I couldn't help myself; I just had to pry. "Does that mean you're getting out there? Are you finally dating again?" I knew without a doubt no one my father would meet would ever come close to filling his heart the way my mother had, but there had to be someone out there he could connect with, and hopefully fall in love with again.

But what the hell did I know? I was in love with a pompous, overbearing, ill-tempered, possessive ass. But that wasn't all he was. Even though Stone was all those things, he'd also shown me a different side to him, a side I doubted many had the pleasure of seeing, if any. He was kind, thoughtful, loving, affectionate, protective, funny and sexy as all hell. Okay, the last one wasn't a personality trait, but it definitely worked in his favor.

"Don't worry about me, honey. I'll meet someone when I'm ready," he assured.

"But it's been five years. I just want you to be happy again."

Slamming down the spatula he was using to brown the meat, he turned toward me and scowled.

"I'll do it when I'm ready. Don't push me." His aggravation was mild but still very much present. Slouching, he immediately apologized. "I'm sorry, sweetheart. I'm just a little stressed right now, and the last thing I want to think about is committing to someone."

Who said anything about committing to anyone? I was simply asking if he'd met someone. Was there something going on I didn't know about? My father and I were really close, but I was sure there were some things he kept hidden from his only daughter.

As there were things I kept hidden from him.

Placing my hand on his shoulder, I leaned in and kissed his cheek. "I just want you to be happy. You deserve it." Moving back, I walked toward the quaint kitchen table and pulled the chair out, sitting before he even had the chance to turn around.

Silence ensued, but it was exactly what we both needed. So many things rattled around inside my head, and although they were very different from what was probably bombarding my dad, I knew we were both experiencing our own stressors. Although I was positive that cancer and pregnancy, at the same time, could be classified as more than a mere stressor.

I was fully aware of my precarious predicament but it almost seemed like it wasn't real, as if Dr. Weber had told me the news but my mind refused to accept it, therefore making it null and void. Telling my father the news would be heart-wrenching. Well . . . part of it, at least. Hoping the other part would thrill him placed a small smile on my face.

But how would he feel about Stone, his future grandchild's father?

For that matter, how would Stone feel about becoming a father? He could go either way, really. We'd never even discussed the possibility of having children, too busy sneaking around and having our fun. The thought never crossed my mind, and I wasn't sure whether or not it was even on his radar.

The clink of ice cubes pulled me out of my own head. "Do you want some iced tea, Addy?" my dad asked, reaching into the refrigerator and pulling out a large pitcher of my favorite nonalcoholic drink.

Before the news, I would have readily accepted, gulping down the refreshing drink and asking for more. But since Dr. Weber had told me I was pregnant, the thought occurred that maybe I shouldn't be drinking caffeine. I was probably going a little overboard, but so many things could happen during a pregnancy, and considering I already had to go through some future treatment, I wanted to ensure I wasn't eating or drinking anything I shouldn't.

"I'll just have water, please," I responded, hoping like hell he wasn't going to delve into why. Throwing me a funny look, he simply shook his head and poured me a glass from the water cooler.

"Here you go," he offered, placing the glass on the table. "We should be eating in about a half hour. You know how I love to slow cook as much as possible." He winked before returning to stirring the chili. Before long, my stomach rumbled, loud enough to pull my father's attention.

"Damn, was that your belly?"

"I guess I'm just excited to eat your food. It's been a while," I confessed.

"I'd say so." Coming to sit next to me, he placed his hand over mine, tapping it lightly before smiling. "So, are you seeing anyone special? You can tell your old man."

Old man.

I couldn't help but think of the conversation I'd had with Stone about me being his ol' lady and how I'd protested calling him my ol' man. Only one person held that title, and it wasn't a gorgeous tattooed biker.

"Funny you should ask." I hadn't planned on telling him any of my news for a little while yet, but the opportunity presented itself and I plunged in headfirst. Plus, it wasn't as if my dad was going to run and tell my uncle; otherwise, I would have kept my mouth shut, fearing his reaction and what he would do to Stone. I knew my man could definitely hold his own, but the fact I was—or rather *we* were—going to draw a wedge between the two of them, I would be lucky if Trigger didn't try to put a bullet in the club's VP like he'd often threatened.

"Oh?" he said, straightening in his chair, his hands clasping together to hear my news. All of a sudden, I'd become quite warm, my belly protesting in hunger while my heart picked up pace in anticipation of what my dad's reaction would be. I knew damn well he would flip his lid when he found out I was dating someone in the club, and while I knew I could do nothing to mitigate his fears of being involved in that lifestyle—something I myself was worried about—I would have to do my best to convince him I was safe and well taken care of.

The words bubbled up in my throat, but before I released them in a huff of air I decided to leave out certain details about Stone. Him being part of the Knights Corruption for one. Later on, I would tell him, but not now.

"I'm seeing someone. Actually, I've been dating him for just over a year now." I hadn't lied; technically Stone and I had been seeing each other for the length of time I'd specified, it had just been our little secret. Plus, the coated lie would be a softer blow when my dad found out I was pregnant. At least the man who'd knocked me up wasn't a one-night stand or a meaningless fling. He was someone I loved. "I've known him for years, however." That part wasn't a lie either. I met Stone right after I'd received my nursing degree. Although my uncle didn't want to involve me, he didn't have a choice. One of their men had been injured, and there was no way they would take him to the hospital; stab wounds often brought about many questions . . . and the cops. So he'd called me in, swarming around me the entire time, shielding me from any communication with the men who were present.

Stone had walked in on us while I was patching up one of their nomad brothers, who'd come for a visit and gotten into a fight when he'd stopped by some bar beforehand. As soon as Stone entered the room, I knew my life was never going to be the same again. The way he looked at me, having no idea who I was at first, was as if he were staking his claim. Silently, of course, because he never uttered a word, simply looking in my direction, making eye contact, then disappearing without so much as a hello.

From that point on, any time I was called to the club he'd watch me, his eyes following every movement I made. Although I'd caught him a few times, he was rather slick about it; there was always someone next to me, and as soon as I saw him looking, he would direct his attention to whoever was standing nearby. My uncle had warned every man in the club that, if anyone messed with me, he would snatch their life. And I had no doubt he meant it.

Eventually, Stone started talking to me. At first, it was simple greetings, then his interactions with me escalated each time he would see me, engaging me further and further. Fortunately—or unfortunately, depending on how I looked at it—I was called to the clubhouse quite a few times. And while I was happy to help my uncle out, putting my nursing skills to use outside of a regimented hospital environment, I was still on edge every time I pulled into their lot.

Danger surrounded them all the time, so danger licked at my heels whenever I was present as well.

One fateful evening when I'd gone to The Underground to search for my uncle, for a reason I couldn't recall for the life of me now, Stone finally made his move. Cornering me in the hallway of the bar, he called my desire for him to the forefront, brazenly kissing me before I even had a chance to defend myself.

But I loved it.

And he knew it.

And from then on, he'd been a permanent fixture in my life. The only difference now was the fact I'd agreed to officially be a couple and stop sneaking around.

My dad's brows knit into a tight frown. "What do you mean you've been with him for a year? Why am I only hearing about him now?" I wasn't sure whether he looked offended or angry.

Taking a slow sip of my water to buy me some time, I averted my eyes and stared at the family portrait on the wall behind his head. It was the last picture taken of the three of us, six months before my mother passed. She looked healthy, not like a woman who was going to leave us forever in less than a year's time.

"Well?" Dad prompted, pulling me back from my haunted memories.

Taking the plunge, I started explaining. Sort of. "It wasn't anything serious until recently." His lips parted to grill me some more when my phone rang. Quickly searching my purse, I pulled it out and glanced at the screen.

Speak of the devil.

"Do you have to take that?" he asked, reaching for my glass to refill it.

"I'll call him back. Now, how about some of your infamous chili?" No sooner had the words left my mouth than my stomach growled, threatening to eat itself if I didn't provide some sort of nourishment.

It was the perfect question to distract my dad from probing further into my relationship with Stone.

TWENTY-TWO

Stone

I HATED WHEN SHE DIDN'T answer her phone. It drove me fuckin' nuts, and I'd be sure to let her know as soon as she answered the damn thing. I was controlling to a fault and I didn't see any reprieve in sight, although I knew I had to curb it enough to not drive her completely away from me again, even though she'd promised not to run away going forward. I knew she loved me almost as much as I loved her, and I prayed those feelings were enough to convince her to stay when I overstepped my bounds. Because, let's be honest, although I would do my best to calm my temper, I knew there would be times I would cross the line. I wasn't delusional enough to think I'd be able to completely change who I was.

Trying her phone an hour later, she finally answered.

"Hey," she casually greeted.

"Hey, yourself. Where are you?" Nothing like cutting right to the point. Finished at the club, I wanted nothing more than to have Addy back in my arms again, begging for me to fill her until she collapsed underneath me. I couldn't help it; it was where my head went whenever I heard her sexy voice.

"I'm at home now."

"Now? Where were you?" I tried to keep the curt tone out of my voice, but I failed big time.

Huffing into the phone as if my question had just annoyed the hell out of her, she grumbled something incoherent. If I had to guess, she did it on purpose, riling me up even more than I already was. Stress of the club and aggravation over not being able to lose myself completely in Addy were driving me to the brink.

"What?"

"I was with my dad," she bit out. "We had lunch at his house. Wanna know how long it took me to get home and every move I've made since then?" Obviously, she was being sarcastic, but her anger wasn't lost on me. I knew I was a lot to handle, and I knew I drove her nuts, but I couldn't help myself.

"Knock it off," I warned. "I just wanted to see you, that's all."

"That's not all and you know it." She was borderline explosive, and it rattled me.

I had no idea what had crawled up her ass, but it wasn't like her to get so defensive with me so quickly. Usually, it took a buildup over a few days of putting up with me and my demands before she blew up and told me to go straight to Hell.

Curiosity wrapped its risky arms around me, and before I could stop myself, I engaged her in an argument.

"What the hell is your problem? I asked you to wait for me until I was done at the club and you refused. I let you leave and when I finally called you, you didn't answer. Numerous times. What am I supposed to think? Huh? You tell me." The anger poured out of me like lava, each word packing a harder punch than the last.

"You *let* me leave?" she hollered. "You don't *own* me, Stone! I can do whatever I want, whenever I want to. If you think for one second that just because we're official I'm gonna let you dictate any part of my life, you're sorely mistaken." Short pants of anger hit my ear, and I knew right then if I didn't bring it down a notch she would hang up on me and deny me any kind of access to her for the next few days. It was her go-to thing when she'd had enough of me. For most men, the silent treatment was a godsend, but for me it was utter torture.

"All right, calm down," I soothed, my voice instantly becoming quieter, pushing all anger aside in an effort to make sure she didn't go nuclear. "I was just concerned is all. You know I worry when you don't answer your phone." A full fifteen seconds of silence followed my sort of apology. I actually thought she'd hung up on me.

I was the first to break. "I would love to see you. Can I come and pick you up?" I hated asking for any kind of permission, but I knew if I came off as arrogant as I wanted to, she would dismiss me altogether.

"Fine," she mumbled.

"Okay, I'll be there within the hour."

"Fine," she said again, hanging up before I could say anything else.

Oh, boy! This was going to be something. I could just feel it in my bones.

TWENTY-THREE

Adelaide

BY THE TIME STONE ARRIVED, I'd managed to calm myself enough that I wasn't upset with him anymore. I knew exactly the type of man I had agreed to be with, and short of slapping him upside his head, I knew it was going to take some time for him to lose some of his arrogant and possessive ways. Otherwise, I would freeze him out until he complied, which had worked in the past. Sort of.

I was praying he would calm down once we'd told people we were an item, an occurrence I both looked forward to and feared. For many different reasons.

A loud knock rapped against my door.

Because he'd arrived quicker than I'd expected, I jumped at the loud noise before reaching for the handle and pulling the door open. Every single time I laid eyes on the man crowding the entryway, I crumbled. I tried to put on a good front, but there was no way he didn't notice the effect he had on me. My eyes devoured the very sight of him. Never mind the fact my body reacted accordingly—nipples pebbling into tight buds, thighs clenching together to ease the building ache, the feeling of pure desire wrapping around my entire body.

The first thing I noticed was the ravenous look behind his beautiful dark eyes. The way he stared at me made me forget I had been even remotely upset with him. As if that weren't enough, licking his full lips drew my lust to the surface, blood rushing to the one place I wanted to be consumed by him. My eyes finished devouring the rest of him, from his black T-shirt which fit his chest and arms like a glove, to his dark jeans which hung low on his narrow hips, enticing me to find the prize he hid lower still.

"Keep starin' at me like that and you'll be on your back before you can take your next breath." He entered my apartment, closing the door behind him before stalking toward me. Not once did his eyes waver from mine, other than to quickly take in my state of undress.

Tiny jersey shorts and a tight cami were the only clothes I wore, and the way I was feeling right then, mixed with the way Stone was looking at me, I'd come to the conclusion that I was indeed overdressed. I'd taken a quick rinse when I came home from my father's house, needing the warmth of the shower to help chase away the twinge of nausea as well as the worries which racked my nerves.

"Where are we going?" I asked, backing up a few paces the closer he came. We wouldn't be leaving my apartment if he had his way, and while I was good to go with what was probably running through his head, I needed a distraction from the issues I tried my hardest to run from, even though I knew I had to face them, and soon. But I needed more time, even if it was only a day.

"What?" he asked, reaching for me. I smiled and continued to back away, the backs of my legs eventually coming to rest against the edge of the couch.

"You said you wanted to pick me up," I answered, resting the flat of my palms on his chiseled chest. "Where are you taking me? Out on our first official date?" I teased, knowing full well Stone wasn't the type of man to *date*.

He stopped suddenly, cocking his head and narrowing his gaze. "You wanna go out on a date?"

See? I hit the nail on the head.

Deciding it was the best opportunity I would have to take it all the way, I indulged myself. "Yeah, sure I do. I think you should dress up in a nice suit and pick me up for a proper date, complete with flowers and a nice, fancy restaurant." I couldn't help myself, a small smile giving everything away.

Never in a million years could I imagine Stone dressed in anything other than his normal day-to-day attire. He was rugged and sexy, not refined and polished. If I'd wanted a man like that I would have dated any one of the doctors at the hospital who'd asked me out.

No, Stone was exactly the type of man who revved my engine. Even though he drove me insane sometimes, he also drove me out of my mind with lust. One look from him and I was a total goner for sure.

Something he was totally taking advantage of right then.

Pulling me in to him, my breath escaped on a strangled hiss, our bodies pressed so close I had to tilt my head back in order to see his face. Lowering his mouth, he kissed me. Sweetly. His lips skimmed over mine, but he never took it further. A slight flick of his tongue was the only action that told me he would delve deeper if I gave him access. But I was too enthralled with whatever game he was playing to completely give in. And rest assured, he was up to something—I was sure of it. Any other time Stone was able to get his hands on me was a rushed effort to bring us both pleasure.

This was something different. Did he feel bad about berating me over the phone? Was he trying to calm his reactions when it came to his daunting ways of handling things? Was he trying to apologize for his craziness earlier?

I had no idea, but I was about to find out.

Pulling back, he gazed deep into my eyes. The look was overwhelming, allowing me to see a part of his soul. The connection between us had always been undeniable, but it was times like these which told me he was it for me. Better or worse, Stone Crosswell was the man I was meant to end up with. Despite everything.

A pang of hurt crushed me. Would I be able to give him all of me in return? Would we grow old together? Would we share the joy of the child growing in my belly?

Would we be happy?

Dismissing my fears, I focused back on the gorgeous creature staring at me.

"Did you trim your beard? It doesn't look as long as usual." Yeah, that was where I chose to focus. Everything else pinging back and forth inside my head was too much.

"Yeah, I did. It was getting a bit too much. You like?"

"I approve." I smiled and playfully yanked on his trimmed facial hair.

He'd gone quiet for a few seconds, something obviously on his mind enough to not talk right away. When his lips finally parted, he said something I never would've imagined.

"If you're serious about me wearing a monkey suit and taking you to a fancy restaurant, I will. I would do that for you because you deserve it, Addy." He kissed me gently again. "You deserve everything."

I was floored.

I was completely playing with him, but I guessed it backfired on me.

Well, not backfired, per se, but it was definitely unexpected. That was for sure.

"While the idea is tempting, how about I hold onto that one, calling it in whenever I want?"

"Deal."

"Deal," I repeated. "So, where are we going?"

"I thought we could grab some takeout and head back to my place," he said, linking his fingers through mine and pulling me toward my bedroom.

"Where are you going?" I asked, thinking he wanted to ravage me before we left. And to be quite honest, I wasn't about to object.

"You have to get changed. You're not goin' outside dressed like that." He waved his hand over my body, drawing my attention back to the fact I was barely clothed.

TWENTY-FOUR

Adelaide

STRAPPED TO THE BACK OF his impressive ride, my arms wrapped tightly around his strong body. I relaxed and allowed myself to revel in the moment. There was a certain freedom which came from being on the back of a motorcycle. Allowing the open road to possess me. The wind whipping all around, making me aware I was part of something bigger.

It was intoxicating.

I understood why the men chose to take their bikes when they had to go on long runs. There was nothing like it, and although I was sure they were tired after the long distance, it must have been well worth it, an escape which was sometimes definitely needed.

I'd closed my eyes as soon as we hit the stretch of highway away from my house, but I'd immediately become alert when I noticed we were traveling toward the club. I knew the distance and turns like the back of my hand.

The roar of the engine was too loud for him to hear me, never mind we were both wearing helmets. I decided not to freak out, though; I was sure there was a good explanation why he needed to stop there. But that didn't stop me from tensing up the closer we approached, hoping and praying my uncle wasn't anywhere near the place.

When we finally arrived, Stone backed his bike into his appointed spot like he'd probably done thousands of times before. Swinging my leg over, I came to stand beside him, pulling off my helmet before he even shut off his engine.

"What are we doing here?" I asked, my lip quivering in uneasiness the longer he remained silent. Tearing off his own helmet, his strong thighs continued to straddle his ride. He didn't answer me, instead reaching for my hand to pull me close.

"Addy . . ." he started, giving me a look of apology as well as intent.

"No, no, no." I shook my head and pulled my hand from his grip. "We can't do this now," I pleaded. "I'm not ready."

Dismounting, he stalked me as I backed up with each step. "Yes, you are," he affirmed, a thread of steel to his voice I was all too familiar with. "There's no time like the present. We have to get this over with if we're gonna move forward. And if that means dealing with Trigger, then so be it."

He seemed so sure of himself, standing before me like a mountain of strength. My uncle was going to flip out, and there wasn't a damn thing I could do about it. I hated that I was going to upset him, but I was even more distressed at the potential harm he would inflict on Stone. And while Stone wouldn't technically feel the physical effects of my uncle's wrath, it could most definitely be life-changing.

My uncle was *that* crazy protective when it came to me, and I had no doubt he would threaten Stone's very existence, no matter what pleas fell from my lips.

After some more back and forth between the two of us, I gave in. I tried to walk in front of him to scope out the club and see who was present, but he pulled me back, grabbing hold of my hand and forcefully gripping it in his. He wanted there to be no doubt we were together, and if seeing our hands entwined was the first start, then so be it.

I continued to struggle, but that only earned me a tightened grasp as well as an annoyed look.

"Stop trying to get away from me," he warned. "It's happenin', so the sooner you get onboard the better."

If he wasn't afraid of what was going to happen, then why was I? While I tried to relax and let everything play out as it will, I couldn't escape the fear inside me. This was the last thing I needed to deal with right now. I still hadn't told Stone anything about being pregnant or sick, and there he was, adding another thing to my plate I just didn't need to deal with.

As we walked across the expansive lot, I noticed a few members milling around. First, Hawke came into view. His head was down, looking at something displayed on his phone. When he heard us approaching, he picked his head up, staring at our combined hands before a knowing look appeared on his face.

"'Bout fuckin' time, brother," he acknowledged, addressing Stone before looking my way. "Hi, Addy," he gleamed, his smile telling me everything. How the hell did he know we were together? Had Stone announced our business to people before I'd even agreed to be his?

Before I could ask, Stone answered my silent question. "He guessed."

That's it?

Hawke wasn't the sharpest tool in the shed, but I had noticed he liked to people-watch. Was that how he'd picked up on whatever was between us? Were we that obvious? How many other people had taken notice?

The next people I saw were Ryder and Tripp, huddled around the fighting ring toward the back of the lot. Jagger and Zip were sparring, Jagger's skill outweighing his opponent at every turn. All four men were too engaged with what was going on to pay us any mind. That was until they heard their president's voice.

"Are you fuckin' kiddin' me right now, Stone? This is the last goddamn thing we need, messing things up inside the club." Marek briskly walked toward us, fists clenched at his sides and an incredulous look painted across his face.

"I'm not hidin' it anymore, Prez. She's mine, and I want everyone to know it." Stone stood tall next to me, challenging his friend—and leader—with a simple look.

"Fuck!" Marek shouted, coming to stop directly in front of us. Looking back and forth between us, he finally focused on me, realizing his friend was too far gone with determination. "Addy, is this something you want to divulge right now? Your uncle's inside, but he'll be out here any second."

I never got the chance to speak before Stone spouted off at the mouth. "What the hell, Marek? I told you it's what's happenin'. Of course Addy's scared of Trigger's reaction, but she wants this as much as I do." Stone tightened his hold on my hand on the last word.

"Is that true?" Marek asked me again, completely ignoring his VP.

It *was* what I wanted. I just didn't want to do it right then. Thinking we had some more time before anything about us being together came to light, I'd pushed the notion from my mind until I was ready to do it. I never thought he was going to force me into it so early after I'd accepted to be with him.

But it looked like I had to make a decision and quick. Or rather, give my response—my decision had already been made for me, the man holding my hand hostage unwavering in his resolve.

"Yes," I whispered, averting my eyes from Marek's intense stare and quickly glancing around, looking for any signs of my uncle. Thinking maybe it would be easier for him to hear the news without us touching, I continued to struggle out of Stone's hold, but he was relentless.

"Stop it. I mean it," Stone grumbled, yanking on my arm. "It's either you continue to hold my hand, or I'll shove my tongue down your throat as soon as I catch sight of Trigger." He continued to stare straight ahead. "Your choice."

I had no doubt he would do exactly as threatened, so I stopped fidgeting. And no sooner had I stilled when I saw my uncle walking toward us. Marek was blocking the middle of us, where our hands were joined.

Breathing in and out deeply did nothing to calm me. Shit was about to go down, and I was hastily trying to think of ways to calm the situation as soon as it erupted. I could beg and plead with him to be rational, or I could stand strong. Remind him I was grown and could make my own decisions, including who I was going to share my bed with.

Okay, maybe I shouldn't say anything referring to us having sex.

Everything happened so fast. First, my uncle was smiling at me then he was staring at our hands, the look on his face switching in a split second. Confusion danced over his features before fury took hold.

Coming to stand next to Marek, he glanced from Stone to me to our hands again. His entire body tensed and, rising to his full height, he became quite an intimidating force. Disappointment and anger dueled behind his eyes, and I felt awful that I was partly the cause of his anguish.

"What. The fuck. Is this?" he seethed, pointing toward us with a sharp gesture. His focus wasn't on me, however, but on Stone. He was impatiently waiting for an answer when I began to speak.

"Uncle Trigger, please let me explain before you start yelling," I pleaded, trying to step closer to comfort him in some small way. But I couldn't move because Stone was still tightly holding onto me.

My uncle's gaze never wavered. It was as if he never even heard me speak.

"Why are you touching my niece?" he bit out, advancing closer, menace pouring off him in waves. When Stone didn't answer, my uncle shoved him. Hard. Finally breaking our hands apart. "Answer me, you bastard! Why the fuck are you touching my niece?" he repeated, stepping dangerously close to him again. All the men surrounding the ring heard the commotion and came rushing over. A firm hand grabbed my wrist and pulled me back. I tilted my head to the side and saw it was Tripp. Pulling me further away, he said, "You might not want to see this, Adelaide."

"This is happening because of me," I assured him, not taking my eyes off the two men preparing for battle.

"No, this is all on Stone, sweetheart. He knew better. He knew he shouldn't have gone after you, but he did. And now he has to deal with the consequences." Tripp's tone was unaffected. The words he spoke were so matter-of-fact, it was scary.

Sidestepping the nomad, I shrugged off his hold and moved back out front to witness what came next.

"I warned you what would happen if you so much as touched Addy!" my uncle shouted, his hands running over the top of his head in anger, strands of hair loosening from his ponytail. Without saying another word, Trigger reached behind him and pulled a gun from his waistband, aiming it directly at Stone. My eyes bugged out of my head at the horror which was about to unfold. Surely, he wouldn't make good on his threat and kill the VP of his club. Marek wouldn't allow it.

Or was Stone's decision to 'go after' me that detrimental?

Hands tried to pull me back again, but I fought against them; I assumed it was Tripp but I couldn't be sure. I rushed forward until I stood next to the president of the Knights Corruption.

"Do something, Marek!" I cried out. "You can't let this happen." I tugged on his arm. "You have to stop this." He never even looked at me, instead jerking his head toward the two men about to go to war.

"Trig, just don't kill him. Okay?" Marek bristled with some kind of emotion, but I couldn't pinpoint what it was. I was sure he was pissed two of his men were at odds with each other, but it was more than that. He acted like he was powerless to stop what was about to unfold, but didn't he realize he held all the authority necessary? He was the president, after all. His word was law. Even I knew that much.

Realizing their leader wasn't going to intervene, I raced forward to shield Stone. Or I tried to, at least. As soon as I was close enough, both my uncle and Stone shouted for someone to remove me.

At least they were on the same side when it came to keeping me safe. But I didn't care. I knew Stone would never harm Trigger, but it looked as if my uncle was hell-bent on teaching Stone a lesson.

"Uncle Trig, please put the gun down," I begged. "Please don't do this." Tears clouded my vision, but I couldn't afford not to see every single movement either one of them made. They danced around each other,

Stone keeping his eye on his opponent's weapon.

"He knew what would happen, Addy. I told them all."

"Don't be crazy," I pleaded. "Can't we just go inside and talk this out?" Even as the words left my mouth, I knew they were ridiculous.

"Addy!" Stone shouted. "Let it happen. Then we can move on."

"You'll never move on with my niece. After I shoot you, you won't so much as be able to whip it out ever again."

"Trigger . . ." Marek warned. "Be careful what you do. I mean it. You can graze him, but if you disable my VP in any way, you and me are gonna have an issue."

Oh, God! Had they all lost their minds?

They weren't going to back down. My uncle had Marek's approval to shoot Stone, and Stone was simply standing there, waiting for his punishment. Did he know all along he was really going to be shot?

Was he crazier than I thought? Did he want to be with me so badly that he was willing to take a bullet because of it?

I couldn't move.

I couldn't breathe.

I was paralyzed with fear.

Suddenly, my brain formed a thought, and before I could properly filter the words, they fell from my lips before I could stop them.

"I'm pregnant!" I shouted, stepping forward to make sure they heard me. For some reason, it didn't dawn on me to worry about Stone's reaction over the news. All I wanted to do was distract my uncle enough to refocus his attention.

But it did the exact opposite.

"You knocked up my niece?" my uncle roared, steadying the weapon in his hand and resting his finger over the delicate trigger.

Before I could say another word, he fired.

TWENTY-FIVE

Stone

I'D BEEN TOO SHOCKED BY what came flying out of Addy's mouth that I took my focus off her uncle. And it was in those few precious seconds that he made good on his threat and fuckin' shot me.

The ol' bastard really did it.

While I didn't think his threats were idle, I hadn't really put any stock in them either. Worst-case, I thought he was gonna come at me and throw a few punches, which I would have let him seeing as how I *did* go against one of the codes. 'Never mess with anyone in another member's family.' But I couldn't help myself; Addy and I were meant to be together, and nothing—and no one—was gonna get in the way.

The force of the bullet pushed me back, throwing me on my ass before I even realized I'd been shot. Of course, there was no pain, but pressure exploded toward the top of my thigh. When I looked down, I saw a hole in my jeans, blood pouring from the wound and dribbling to the concrete below, causing quite the mess.

"You're fuckin' crazy, Trigger!" I yelled, throwing off my cut before taking off my T-shirt. Placing the material over the wound, I knew I had to stop the bleeding before my body decided to revolt against me. I didn't know how badly I'd been injured, but I was sure Addy would tell me any second.

"I warned ya," he said cockily before turning around to walk toward his niece. "You need to come with me, Addy. Now." He reached for her hand in anger and, family or not, that shit pissed me off.

"I'm not going anywhere with you. You just shot a man and walked away. One of your own brothers," she cried. "How could you do that?"

"How?" he shouted. "Because he knew what the punishment was

for messing with you. That's how. Now, come with me so we can talk."

"No. I love you, but I'm beyond livid with you right now. You need to leave me alone until I calm down," she insisted, pulling her hand from his and retreating until he took the hint. A defeated look held him in place before he turned toward the clubhouse, no doubt going to pour himself a stiff drink. Something I could have used right about then.

I rose to my feet before Addy reached me, terror laced behind her beautiful blue eyes. "I'm okay," I said, standing up straight after tying my shirt around my leg. "Let's get inside so you can patch me up before it gets worse."

I tried to focus on anything but the words she'd shouted for everyone to hear. 'I'm pregnant.' Upset she chose to openly reveal something which should have been done in private, I shrugged away from her when she reached for me. I should have been the first person she told, not my whole goddamn club.

Refusing to have our conversation in front of everyone present, I walked ahead and disappeared inside the building. True to what I thought, Trigger was already behind the bar pouring himself a drink.

I glanced in his direction briefly before heading down the hallway to my room. I had just stepped inside when Addy appeared right behind me, closing and locking the door for added privacy.

She rushed forward and reached for my leg, but before she could attend to me, I grabbed her arms and pulled her close. So many things fired off inside my brain I had no idea which topic to tackle first.

The fact she chose to hide the pregnancy from me.

The fact she chose to shout out the life-altering news in front of everyone, making me look like an idiot that I found out right along with my brothers.

The fact she obviously didn't trust me enough to come to me the minute she found out she was carrying my baby.

The fact she finally agreed to be my woman, but chose to hide the first thing that cemented us in each other's lives like a horrible secret.

Maybe I was being irrational, overthinking and playing into the paranoia flooding me, but what else could I do?

I wanted to hear her out, I really did, but betrayal built quickly in my veins. "Why the hell didn't you tell me you were pregnant? You ashamed that's my baby or somethin'?" She tried to step back but I held her close, refusing to allow her to escape before she answered me.

Her face fell, looking as if she was insulted I would ask such a thing. Swallowing the words bubbling up her throat, she shook her head and silently pleaded with me. For what, I had no idea.

"Answer me!" My temper took hold and battled inside me. I knew I had an issue, but if shit like this didn't happen then the beast would never rear his ugly head.

Was it too much to ask for people to not piss me the fuck off?

Finally pushing her away, I sat on the edge of the bed, not caring that the blanket was soaking up the river of red seeping from the hole in my leg.

"Of course not. How could you ask me that?" Her eyes misted with unshed tears. Normally, I would have comforted her, but I was too upset—not necessarily at the news, but at the way everything had played out. I could deal with the ramifications of choosing to be with Addy, with being shot like some kind of dog in front of everyone because I'd chosen to disobey Trigger's warning. But what I was having a hard time dealing with was the fact she was growing my kid inside her and chose to keep that information from me.

"How long have you known?" I asked, playing with the button of my jeans, knowing full well I had to dispose of the material soon. Addy's eyes kept flitting toward my thigh, hoping I would let her tend to me before I managed to lose more blood.

"I just found out."

"When?" Had she harbored the news for weeks? Months? I'd just seen her naked and hadn't noticed anything different about her body, so I assumed she wasn't too far along, but what the hell did I know?

"Yesterday," she finally confessed. "After you left the hospital, Dr. Weber called me to his office and delivered the news." Her head was down, locks of her blonde hair falling forward and framing her face.

Tensing at the mere mention of the doctor, I knew I needed to focus on something else or I would explode. So I stood up, popping open the button of my jeans, and dragging my zipper through its metal teeth. As soon as she realized I was trying to undress, she rushed forward, untied the T-shirt I'd wrapped around my leg, and gently tugged my jeans down until they were a tangled mess around my feet.

Realizing she hadn't known long helped to simmer the heat swirling around inside me. After countless seconds of silence, I concluded that shock had played its hand in the delay of her coming to me and filling me in that our lives had been forever altered.

A few breaths and I was well on my way to calming down.

"I thought you were on the pill," I said, kicking the jeans away so there was no restriction for when she inspected the damage her uncle had caused.

Kneeling in front of me, her delicate hands brushed over my skin, inspecting the wound to determine her next move. "I am . . . I was. But it's not a hundred percent reliable. Things happen."

"Things happen?" I repeated incredulously, running a hand through my hair in disbelief.

Completely choosing to ignore me, she focused on fixing me. "I still can't believe he shot you," she uttered, the sudden frown on her face expected. I loved that she worried about me, but it seemed there were bigger issues which required her attention.

Our baby, for one.

Stilling her hands, I tilted her chin upward and forced her to look at me. Children had never been on my radar, even while I was pursuing her. But the thought of her swollen with my child somehow suddenly pleased me, a feeling I never thought I would have.

"Are you happy about it?"

"It?" She half smiled. "Do you mean our son or daughter?" While she made an attempt at lightheartedness, there was worry etched deep into her expression. No matter how hard she tried to hide it, her apprehension shone bright for me to see.

"Yeah, that's what I meant."

She averted her eyes and rose to her feet. Placing her hand over my heart before looking at my face again, she confessed, "It's complicated, Stone. There's other factors at play. I'm not sure what I'm going to do, or even what's gonna happen for that matter."

Forgetting all about the fact I was standing in the middle of my room at the club in nothing but my underwear, blood continuing to trickle down my leg, and reeling with the news I was gonna be a father, I blanked with a response to her off-the-wall statement.

"What the hell does that mean?" Moving closer until she backed against the door, I pinned her not only with my body but with my stare. "You thinkin' 'bout not having my kid?" The thought she would want to exterminate a piece of us was beyond any scope of reality I was unexpectedly thrust into.

Instead of answering me, she ducked under my arm, but wasn't quick enough. "I can't do this right now," she cried. "Please . . . just let me go."

"Not a chance in hell. Not until you tell me whatever else it is you're hidin' from me." Dragging her toward the bed, I forced her to sit, taking a seat next to her, demanding she clue me in to the craziness inside her head.

"What do you want from me?" she asked. My silence forced her to continue, albeit hesitantly. "I'm shocked at the news of the baby, among other things." She mumbled the last part of her sentence, but I'd heard it. I had excellent hearing, something she hated whenever we argued and she tried to slyly get in the last word. It never worked because I always heard her grumblings, therefore officially having the final say.

Panic stole over her, and I would have bet if I placed my hand over her heart it would be racing. "What's wrong? You need to tell me now before I think the worst. I can't begin to fathom why you're this upset over finding out you're pregnant. I mean, yeah, it's a shock, something we didn't plan for, but it happened all the same. Did you think I would be angry or somethin'? Did you think I would demand you get rid of it? Because I would never do that. *Ever.* That kid," I said, pointing to her belly, "is half you and half me, therefore perfect." I smiled, but my expression did nothing to calm her.

Instead, she started to cry.

Tucking her under my arm, I rained kisses down on top of her head, whispering soothing words in her ear to let her know I was there for her, in whatever way she needed me to be. My initial thought that she wanted to abort my child quickly disappeared. I saw the look in her eyes, and it was one of acceptance of our newest addition. But something was clouding her happiness. Something dire, I was sure, even if she refused to speak the words.

Clearly, she wasn't gonna fully open up about whatever else was weighing heavy on her, so instead of continuing to force her confession, I redirected the focus onto me.

"Wanna patch me up now?" When she lifted her head, my eyes stayed glued to hers, waiting for the smallest sign she was gonna crack and break down again. But she didn't, instead turning her attention to my leg.

Trigger had managed to remove a chunk of flesh, the bullet piercing and exiting my limb. Thankfully. It would have been one hell of a pain in the ass to cut out a lodged bullet, and with Addy in her current state, I didn't think she would have the strength to tackle the repair right then. And even though I didn't care about the wound, I knew it wasn't smart to leave a foreign object inside my body.

Like I said . . . thankfully, it was a clean shot.

Since Addy had been called upon more and more in the past few months, she left a few basics at the clubhouse. Instructing me to put pressure on my wound, she disappeared from the room, returning moments later with her hands full of supplies. After cleaning the wound and deeming the bullet hadn't hit any major arteries, she went to work stitching me up. It was really more of a superficial wound, but based on the worry plastered across her beautiful face, anyone would have thought Trigger had shot me in the heart.

When she finally finished, she retook her seat on the bed next to me, staring at me with a blank expression. I could see she was tired, the events of the day quickly catching up to her.

"Wanna go home?" I asked, linking my fingers with hers.

"Yes, that would be great. It's been a long, strange day, and I want nothing more than to relax in my tub."

"Well, you can do that at my place." I rose and pulled her up with me. When I tried to walk forward, my right arm was tugged behind me, the look in her eyes turning from confusion to instant disbelief.

"Stone," she said calmly. "I'm going home. To *my* place. Not yours." Her body didn't move, her feet glued to the floor.

"No."

"No?" she asked, her voice rising in surprise.

Turning toward her so there was no misunderstanding, I yanked her closer and gave her my final words, already dismissing the argumentative words forming in her brain.

"You're gonna have my kid. There's no more 'your place' or 'my place.' There's only *our* place, and the sooner you get on board with that, the better it will be for the both of us. So we'll swing by your apartment so you can grab some things for the next few days, but hear me now, woman," I demanded. "You're moving in with me, and I don't want to hear another thing about it."

I had no idea I was even gonna suggest such a thing so soon, but it fit. It just seemed right. Ever since Addy finally agreed to be mine, I would be lying if I said I didn't think about the day when she would finally live under the same roof as me.

Looks like fate made it happen sooner rather than later.

TWENTY-SIX

Adelaide

THE MAN CONTINUED TO EXASPERATE me to no end. While I was annoyed he tried to push his weight around, there was a small part of me which was relieved. Living with Stone was certainly going to be a challenge, but I was happy to spend more time with him. I grew more accustomed to the thought of having a baby with each passing day, and even though the cancer still festered inside me, and terrified me greatly, I knew he would be there for me.

No matter what.

One hundred percent.

I just had to learn to live with his overbearing ways.

Or learn how to ignore him better when he aggravated me.

Not a week later and he had rounded up a few of the men to help move my stuff into his house. I should have known he wasn't going to waste any time at all. We'd decided to give the majority of my furniture to charity since his was newer and nicer, although I insisted I keep a chest of drawers that had belonged to my mother. As soon as he knew how important the piece was to me, he readily agreed.

His home was quaint, and I liked it much better than my small apartment, but I couldn't help feeling as if I were on his turf. I was careful with cleaning up after myself, as well as making sure to straighten up as much as I could. I acted like I was a guest, and it annoyed him. He told me it was as much my house as it was his, but it was going to take me some time to not only believe him but also feel genuinely comfortable there.

My safety had become Stone's utmost concern, so it worked out well that his house was equipped with the best security system there was. Actually, I'd come to learn all the men in the club had a top-of-the-line system. One of the hazards of being part of the lifestyle, even though Stone continued to assure me they were now legit. "Toeing the legal line," as he would put it. It took him a half hour to teach me how to use the damn thing, changing the code to the date we'd become official, which I thought was sweet.

Stone was tough. He was arrogant and a royal pain in the ass most times. His temper was explosive given the right—or wrong—circumstance. But he was also sweet and caring, the security code just one of the many examples. It was small but it meant a lot to me, showcasing a part of his sentimental side not many people bore witness to.

———◆———

"WE'RE GONNA BE LATE, WOMAN. Let's go!" Stone yelled from the kitchen, his deep voice drifting through the air. I rounded the bottom of the stairwell when he appeared around the corner, almost knocking me over in his haste to rush me along.

"Calm down. You don't have to freak out. We'll be there on time," I assured. Grabbing my purse, I flung it over my shoulder and walked past him toward the front door. He mumbled something incoherently as he followed behind me. The only word I caught was "fuck," which he said a lot.

Since the sky had decided to open up, we were forced to take his truck, something I wasn't complaining about. Even though I was still early into my pregnancy, I had already started to feel a little uncomfortable, my body quick to become tired and achy. The thought of being strapped on the back of his bike for the next twenty minutes or so was not appealing at all.

Reaching across the console, he interlocked his fingers with mine and pulled my hand to rest on his thigh, the gesture relaxing me for some reason. Nerves coiled tight, my upcoming ultrasound was a source of stress for me. I still hadn't told Stone about the cancer, and the further along I became, the quicker the time approached when I would have to start treatment.

"I'm gonna get the green light for sex today, so prepare yourself, baby." He laughed, although he was dead serious. He hadn't touched me since he found out, afraid and unsure of what sexual activity would do to the baby. I tried to assure him it was okay to engage in our favorite pastime, but he wouldn't budge. It was worse for me as the days ticked by, and even though I didn't feel the best on most days, I was horny as hell. The mere sight of a clothed Stone was enough to send me over the edge, never mind when he was stark naked, just a touch away. Teasing me, torturing me with his ruggedly handsome face, and his sculpted, intricately inked, gorgeous body.

He insisted we shower together as much as possible, but since he refused to ravage me, I made up excuse after excuse why I couldn't join him under the hot spray of the shower. Morning sickness or being plain dog-tired worked every time.

"I've told you we can have sex, but if you need to hear it from Dr. Weber, then so be it." As soon as I finished speaking, his hand tightened around mine, his grip borderline painful, which I was sure wasn't intentional. I knew what garnered the reaction—the good doctor's name.

"Do we have to see him?" he asked, an angered expression stealing over his face while he continued to look straight ahead.

"We've been over this before. You need to let it go already. You're being irrational, and I think even *you* know it." His hold relaxed a bit, enabling me to wiggle my fingers for good measure.

Dr. Weber had been a godsend, pulling some strings for me at the hospital to allow me to take a couple weeks off work at the last minute. I had plenty of built-up vacation time, so I took advantage, but that ended today. I was set to go back to work tomorrow, so I was going to relax and enjoy the rest of the day. No matter what developed.

Stone remained silent for the rest of the drive, speaking only when he asked where we were going once we entered the hospital.

As soon as I signed in, we were ushered into the nearest office. While I took a seat on the edge of the exam table, Stone paced back and forth, pieces of his blond hair falling forward while his impatience ate at him.

In order to take my mind off the upcoming exam, the uncertainty of what might be revealed unintentionally, I chose to focus on the man in front of me. His signature dark, loose-fitted jeans and black T-shirt covered his body, but did nothing to hide the impressive physique underneath. Or maybe that was just because I knew exactly what was under those threads. Either way, my hormones kicked into overdrive. The rustle of his leather jacket echoed through the silent room, his deep voice rumbling as he talked to himself, finally coming to lean against the nearest wall. His chiseled features and full lips entranced me, had me envisioning us writhing around for hours on end. With any luck, after he received the go-ahead he was so eager to hear, he would take me straight home and fuck me well into the evening.

Leaning back on the table, I etched the sight of him deep into the recesses of my brain—not that he didn't already reside there. I wanted to commit this moment to memory, however, our small piece in time before the rest of our lives.

Piercing dark eyes pinned me to the spot, turning a lust-hazed glare in my direction. "Why are you looking at me like that?" he asked, pushing off the wall and inching closer until he stood in front of me, spreading my legs so he could fit comfortably between. The warmth of his skin hit mine when he rested his hands on the top of my thighs.

"Am I making you nervous?" I joked, reaching forward and clutching the lapels of his cut in my hands. Our mouths were close, his breath fanning over my face as our eyes remained locked.

Without uttering a single word, he ghosted his lips over mine, tormenting me in the sweetest way. Placing a soft kiss on the corner of my mouth, he backed up just as Dr. Weber quickly knocked on the door before entering.

"Hi, Adelaide," he greeted, placing his hand on my shoulder in an innocent sign of affection. After returning his welcoming, my eyes searched for Stone. I knew what I was going to see, and as predictable as his temper was, I witnessed him stand tall and fall into rigidness. He was too busy watching the doctor to notice me silently pleading with him not to do or say anything out of line. Finally, when Dr. Weber took a seat on the stool, Stone looked my way.

Subtly shaking my head at the infuriating man, making sure he caught my unspoken message, I attempted to make the introductions.

"Dr. Weber, this is Stone. He's the baby's father—" I didn't even get a chance to finish what I was going to say before Stone cut me off.

"And her man," he affirmed, glaring at me before adding, "We live together."

Dr. Weber turned his full attention to the man standing behind him, rising from his stool and extending his hand. "Nice to meet you, Stone. Congratulations." His hand hung in midair for a second too long, but thankfully Stone returned his greeting, pumping his hand and no doubt exerting his strength in his handshake. If Dr. Weber was in any way intimidated by the rough-looking, tattooed, leather-clad biker, he didn't show it.

Once they broke away, Stone opened his mouth to speak, and what came out embarrassed the hell out of me. But I should have expected nothing less, realizing he was going to have an issue with my doctor.

"So," he started, wrapping his arm around my shoulder in one of his signature possessive moves. "You a pervert or somethin'?"

"Stone!" I scolded, heat instantly flooding my face. I tried to shrug away from his arm but he held me tightly; instead, I placed my head in my hands. But before I shielded myself in mortification, I caught the amused look on Dr. Weber's face.

"It's okay, Adelaide," he comforted, patting my knee before continuing. I heard Stone growl next to me at his gesture. Yes, he actually *growled*, like some kind of animal. "Are you asking me why I became a gynecologist, Stone?"

"Yeah, I guess I am."

He wasted no time in explaining something I didn't even know. "Well, my mother and sister both passed away from cervical cancer when I was younger, so I made it my vow to dedicate my education to learning all about the female body and helping any way I could so other families didn't have to experience the heartbreak and tragedy my father and I endured."

I'd uncovered my face halfway through his explanation, mortified Stone's stupid question made him feel as if he needed to explain his chosen path of medicine. And I wasn't sure if it was wrong or not, but I felt a little better knowing he'd experienced the same thing my father and I had with my mother's cancer . . . and her death.

Stone was actually at a loss for words, but instead of manning up and apologizing, he simply nodded and turned his attention back to me. Dr. Weber accepted his nod and wheeled his stool closer to the table. There must have been some coded language which passed between the two men suddenly crowding me, and as much as I wanted to read into it and figure it out, I let it go. I knew my attempt would only leave me even more confused.

A few breaths later and we all focused on the reason for my visit, which was to find out how far along I was and to hopefully hear the baby's heartbeat.

"So, how have you been feeling?" Dr. Weber asked before instructing me to lie back on the table.

"Okay, I guess," I answered, squirming on top of the exam paper underneath me.

"Hmph," Stone grumbled, quickly pulling my focus.

"What does that mean?" I asked, daring him to speak up. Dr. Weber lifted the hem of my shirt, uncovering my belly to apply the gel needed for the ultrasound.

"It means you've been sick most of the time and exhausted as all hell. And let's not forget moody." His tone was serious, but the twinkle in his eye told me he was also playing with me.

Turning my head back to the doctor, I agreed. "Yeah, everything he said."

"Well, that's to be expected. A lot of women experience morning sickness and exhaustion throughout their entire pregnancy." Placing the wand over the gel and moving the instrument back and forth, he finished with, "Hopefully that's not you, though."

A foreign sound suddenly erupted in the room. A fast-paced drumbeat of sorts. I knew exactly what the noise was, but Stone had no idea. The confused look on his face was comical. Dr. Weber noticed it as well.

"That's your baby's heartbeat, Dad," he said, smiling big when he met Stone's gaze. Most people would have either been intimidated by the biker, or at the very least offended with the question he'd asked earlier. But not Dr. Weber. The man was beyond professional, and super friendly. It was why I liked him so much.

Squeezing Stone's hand, I looked adoringly into his eyes, smiling at his reaction. All of a sudden, the biggest grin appeared on his face, and it was in that moment I knew he was going to be the best father to our child. If I could pinpoint the moment he fell in love with the baby, it would have been right then.

"That's his heartbeat?" he asked incredulously.

"Yes, it is," Dr. Weber answered. "Confident the baby's a boy?" he joked.

"Damn right, it's gonna be a boy. I can't handle a girl . . . yet." He laughed, but I knew he was completely serious, his eyes still locked on mine while we both experienced a true gift. A miracle.

Focusing back on me, Dr. Weber had more news. "Well, it looks like you're right around twelve weeks, which means we can start discussing the treatment options," he said, withdrawing the wand and wiping off the excess gel from my stomach.

Stone didn't miss a beat. "Treatment for what?"

Both Dr. Weber and I looked like a deer caught in headlights. I had no idea what to say, no clue how to break the news that the woman he loved was battling for her life. And poor Dr. Weber suddenly looked beside himself, quickly making up some excuse about being late for his next appointment before disappearing from the room.

Sitting up on the table, I adjusted my shirt to cover the rest of me and hopped down, praying he would forget all about what he'd just heard. But it wasn't to be. Typical Stone; he just wouldn't let it go. I'd wanted to tell him, to be able to confide in and lean on him when I needed it, but I simply hadn't come up with either the right time or the right words.

Reaching for my purse, I tried to push past him toward the door, completely ignoring his question, but he stopped me with a firm grip on my wrist. Pulling me back to him, he imprisoned me near the wall and tipped my head up so I had no other choice but to look him in the eye.

"What the hell was he talking about, Addy?"

Figuring this wasn't the appropriate place to reveal what I'd been hiding, I lied. "Just pregnancy stuff." Normal people would probably be able to pull off the falsehood, but not me. I sucked at lying, and Stone knew it as well as I did.

"Stop fucking lyin' to me," he demanded, his voice displaying his rising anger. "Tell me right now what he meant by 'treatments.' And if you lie to me again, so help me God, I'll drag that doctor back in here and *make* him tell me."

"He won't tell you anything. Doctor/patient confidentiality and all." My tiny rant pretty much gave everything away. I'd basically confessed I was indeed hiding something. Stone didn't have a medical background, but he wasn't stupid. He knew the word 'treatment' had nothing at all to do with the baby, and I was only making him more upset the longer I denied him the information he wanted.

"I won't ask you again," he warned, crowding my personal space until I was completely uncomfortable. Emotionally, not physically.

Our eyes remained connected—mine pleading for him to let it go, his demanding answers. A small bead of perspiration broke out on my forehead, my hands suddenly becoming clammy. My intake of air was choppy at best, my heart racing with a sudden surge of adrenaline. Or was that fear?

"I think you need to sit down," I suggested, gently trying to push him away so I could think. Thankfully, he backed up a few paces, giving me room to collect my thoughts.

And breathe.

"I'm waiting," he said impatiently, his fists clenching into tight balls the longer he waited for me to speak.

"I don't know what to say."

"How about the truth. Start there."

It was extremely awkward between us, physically standing so close but emotionally miles apart. The deafening silence only made it worse, and the only way it was going to end was by me telling him I had cancer.

I wasn't sure which torture I preferred, though.

The silence . . . or the truth.

TWENTY-SEVEN

Stone

I'D BEEN ONLY TOO THRILLED to come to this appointment today, sharing in the joy of our unborn child, as well as getting the go-ahead to ravage my woman. But our trip turned into something else altogether.

Addy was definitely hiding something. I'd sensed it ever since the night she agreed to be mine. At first, I thought it was the pregnancy, a revelation which blew my mind, but after seeing her and Dr. Weber's reaction after he'd spoken of treatments, I knew it was something bigger than my child growing inside her.

But what it was, I had no idea, and the possibilities were endless. I didn't allow my mind to wander too far because I'd drive myself insane. Instead, I demanded answers, and I wasn't leaving the room without them.

I remained standing a few feet away, giving her the room she asked for, but if she didn't open her mouth soon and start talking I was gonna pin her against the wall again. My heart raced inside my chest, a slow burn of paranoia drifting through my veins.

Suddenly becoming very warm, my vision hazed with the passing of time. I stood my ground, showing her I wasn't backing down until she gave me what I wanted. Her shoulders slumped, her posture one of defeat. Blonde strands fell loose around the edges of her face, her blue eyes pleading with me to let it go, to allow her to leave without speaking a single word.

But I didn't give in.

"Addy, tell me now."

She took a small step back, her body inches from the wall. Was she looking for an anchor, something to hold her up when she finally spilled the words she'd kept hidden?

"Stone . . . I . . . I don't know how to tell you this." I remained quiet, the slight tick of my jaw the only real indication she was testing my patience. Her nervous stare pleaded with me, but I held firm.

Finally steeling her reserve, she blurted out, "I have cancer."

Within seconds, all the air had been sucked out of the room, leaving me silently gasping for breath. The world as I'd known it spun around me, tilting on its axis and threatening to toss me into the oblivion of the unknown.

I heard her words.

I saw her fear.

I felt her terror.

But did she feel mine?

She hid the truth from me, choosing to deal with not only the baby but with the awful disease killing her slowly all by herself. I knew her mother had died from ovarian cancer, a fact she had only shared with me one time. She never wanted to talk about it, and I never pushed because I didn't blame her for not wanting to discuss something so awful.

"What kind of cancer is it?"

"Ovarian." As soon as the word left her lips, I deflated. Whatever air I'd managed to suck into my lungs was suddenly forced out in a heavy whoosh, my head falling forward while my body quaked. Before I drowned in the firing emotions, I allowed the cold arms of denial to wrap tightly around me.

She stepped closer, reaching out to try and touch me. But instead of accepting her gesture and being the one to comfort her, I backed away. Shaking my head, I spilled forth everything bubbling up inside me, powerless to stop the barrage of fear her words had created.

"No. That's not true."

"It is. I'm sorry, but it's the truth."

Why the hell is she apologizing to me?

"You need to get another opinion. They gave you the wrong results. It's not true," I repeated, barely more than whispering. I retreated until my back hit the wall, pulling at my hair so tightly a twinge of pain shot through my head, the follicles on fire from the brutality of my grip.

"Stone, look at me," she pleaded, the heat from her body enveloping me the closer she stepped. "Baby . . . please. Look at me." Pure torment laced each word, and it took everything in me not to collapse to the floor. Slowly lifting my head, taking my precious time before looking into her eyes, I swallowed each breath and prayed I possessed the strength needed to finally offer her the solace she needed.

As soon as our gazes connected, I saw the tears well up behind her eyes, breaking free once she saw the panic written all over my face. "I'll be okay," she cried, her uncertainty a direct contradiction to the words she spoke.

More tears.

More lies.

"Don't lie to me. I can't take it if you lie to me." My chest expanded as if I'd just run a mile, and before I could stop myself my arm shot out and connected with a tray of instruments. The loud clank of metal objects hitting the floor jolted her back, surprise and understanding in her nod.

She'd had time to digest the news. But not me. I'd only had minutes, so my reaction was warranted. In my head, at least. Needing to purge myself further, I reached for the stool Dr. Weber had sat on and flung it across the room, instantly putting a dent in the wall. Anguish tore from my throat, and all the while I kept thinking how unfair life was. I'd finally managed to convince Addy to be with me, to tell the world she was mine, only to have it cut short. I had no idea what our future held, or even how long it was for that matter, but it didn't stop me from reacting the only way I knew how.

My temper controlled me, and since it was a familiar feeling I gave in, relinquishing all rationality and diving head first into the depths of rage.

I tore the doctor's office apart, whipping whatever wasn't nailed down against the walls and reveling in the noises they made, hoping to drown out my own disbelief.

After a few minutes of me losing myself, I finally calmed enough to lean against the wall, shoving my hands deep in my pockets for fear I would explode and start destroying the room again.

Addy had stood in the corner of the room watching me, tears coating her cheeks the entire time. Her body shook in sadness, but she allowed me the time I needed to succumb to my feelings. I loved her more than I had before she told me the news, and I knew right then I would stand beside her and fight for her life just as strongly as she would.

Without delay, I crushed the small distance between us and drew her into my embrace, promising her my strength while she continued to cry.

"I'm sorry if I scared you, but I had to do something. And since I can't eradicate the sickness inside you, I had to, well . . . destroy something."

"I know. That's why I let you go. But now that it's over, I need to know if you're okay with what's going to happen going forward." Pulling back so she could look at me, she trailed her hand down the side of my cheek, looking at me as if it was the last time. "I completely understand if you can't do this. It's a lot to ask someone, and I don't blame you if you walk away. If I'm able to carry our baby to full term and deliver, I would never cut you out of his life, but that doesn't mean you have to stay with me. You can move on and find someone healthy."

Her rant only served to infuriate me. She was willing to let me go, but what she didn't realize was that I would die without her. No matter what, I was in this for the long haul, and nothing she could say would change my mind.

"Are you serious? Why are you saying this to me?"

"Because we've only been together for a short time, and it's too heavy to put on you. So I'll understand if you can't deal with it. Really, I will." She continued to cry as she gave me an out, her puffy eyes and trembling lips cutting through me like a knife.

Not another second ticked by before I demanded she stop spewing her garbage. "Addy, shut the hell up. Right now. I'm not goin' anywhere. I love you and no matter what happens, I'm right here for you. *With* you. So if you say another word about me leaving, I'm gonna be really pissed off." She remained silent. "Understand?" I couldn't stifle the anger in my tone.

"Yes," she whispered, wrapping her arms around me and holding on for dear life. While she tried to portray strength by telling me she was releasing me, her hold told me she'd hoped I would stay.

"Now let's get the hell out of here before they make me pay for the damage I've caused." That prompted a soft chuckle from her. Kissing the top of her head, I led her toward the door, already wondering what our next move would be.

Yes . . . *our* next move.

Not just hers.

We were in this together from here on out.

Life or death.

TWENTY-EIGHT

Adelaide

"I CAN'T JUST UP AND quit my job!" I yelled, aggravated he chose to wage this battle with me over and over again. "I've worked too hard to get where I am. Do you have any idea how lucky I am to have a job at St. Joseph's? No, I'm not giving that up." I stood strong, bracing myself for yet another argument about me continuing to work.

My hands rested firmly on my waist, prepared to defend my stance all night long. The fact we both stood naked in the middle of our bedroom was hardly distracting. To him or to me. My sixth-month-swollen belly protruded more with each passing day, one of the reasons he consistently brought up the subject of me quitting.

"Yes, you can!" he shouted right back, his muscles rigid in anger. "You can barely get through the day now, how the hell are you gonna be in another month? In another week?" Stone paced in front of me, his frustration intensifying the longer I remained stubborn. "I have more than enough money, so you don't *need* to work."

He'd mentioned his financial status on more than a few occasions. Not bragging, simply informing me he was more than capable. Thing was, I didn't need or want him to take care of me. I was fully able to do that for myself.

"But I *want* to work," I protested. While I fought against his pighead-edness, secretly I wanted to take a break from my job. The long hours on top of the pregnancy and chemotherapy were killing me. More figuratively than literally, thank God.

At thirteen weeks, I'd begun my first round of treatment, Stone accompanying me each and every time. The regiment Dr. Altosh, the oncologist Dr. Weber had recommended, suggested included six cycles of therapy, each one given every three weeks. My condition was closely monitored, simply because it wasn't only my life at stake, but that of my unborn child as well.

The side effects I experienced were mild compared to some I'd heard about. Fortunately, I didn't lose my hair, but I experienced extreme nausea, although I wasn't sure if it was because of the baby or the chemo. Maybe it was both. Either way, it was difficult to keep any food in my system for a full week after the treatment. Then the feeling would lessen, while still being present, until the next round of dosage.

"Well, I'm only givin' you another week and then you're givin' your notice. I'm not having you run yourself ragged, battling cancer and going through this pregnancy *and* working crazy-ass hours. Just because you *want* to. No, you need to slow down and take care of yourself . . . and our son." Stone had been right all along—we'd found out we were having a baby boy soon after the appointment where I revealed what I'd been hiding from him. Stepping closer, he imprisoned me with his angry glare. "Don't test me, woman, because you know what I'll do if you don't follow orders."

Choosing to ignore his thinly veiled threat, which I was sure had everything to do with confronting anyone he could at the hospital, I focused on the one word which threw me into a world of surprise. Although it shouldn't have; I should learn to expect these types of things to come flying out of his mouth.

Baffled at his audacity, I balked. "Orders? Are you kidding me?"

"Nope." A cocky smirk found its way onto his infuriatingly handsome face. No matter how upset I was with him, I couldn't help but admire his looks. Maybe it was the constant surge of hormones, or the fact the man standing before me was the most gorgeous specimen I'd ever seen. Either way, I berated myself for the way my body reacted to him.

Even in anger.

His and mine.

"Well," I huffed, "I don't know who you think you're talking to, but I'm not gonna stand by and let you dictate the way my life is gonna go. So you can forget—"

"Oh, shut the hell up, Addy," he grated, his eyes flicking over my body with heated appreciation. It was so easy for him to switch from arguing to fucking. And although I hated to admit it, he made it easy for me as well. Striding toward me, he reached for my waist and pulled me close, his arousal thick as it pressed against my belly. "I don't want to talk about it anymore tonight." He pressed his lips to mine quickly before breaking away. "All I want is for you to ride my face until you drip in cum, then I want to bury myself inside you until the sun comes up."

While my anger toward him, and the whole working situation, remained on a low simmer, my need for him was greater than I cared to admit.

And just like that, I'd gone from angry and stubborn to horny and willing.

TWENTY-NINE

Stone

THE DAY ADDY WOULD GIVE her notice to the hospital had quickly approached, and even though she fought me tooth and nail, she'd finally agreed to quit. I knew how much her job meant to her, and if it wasn't for her being pregnant and having cancer, I wouldn't have said anything. One of those things alone was cause enough to take a break, but both together and she was lucky I'd held out as long as I did.

Being financially sound was something I'd always been grateful for, now more than ever. The fact I could provide for all of us for the rest of our lives was more than comforting. The majority of my money had initially been from illegal activities, but what I'd done with that money was certainly legal.

Investments.

Lots of them.

The majority of the club's members had followed suit, investing in up-and-coming businesses as well as dabbling in the stock market from time to time, securing their futures as best they could.

"Where are you going?" I asked, watching her walk past me toward the front door. Quickly chewing the remainder of my ham and cheese sandwich, and washing it down with a quick gulp of water, I rose from the couch and approached her before she turned the handle.

"You know where I'm going," she sulked. I remained silent, knitting my brows as an indication I was lost. With a huff, she threw her purse over her shoulder and gave me a sassy glare. "I'm going to the hospital to give them my two weeks' notice."

Two weeks? Oh, hell no. I'd told her today was the day she quit. For good.

"I'm sorry, what?" I asked, drawing closer while wiping the remnants of food from my mouth. "Two weeks? No, that's not what we agreed on. You're supposed to tell them you quit. End of. Meaning you're no longer going to work there. Like starting immediately."

"First of all," she started.

Great . . . here we go. I swore if I didn't love her as much as I did, I'd be beyond annoyed with her mouth. Truth be told, she kept me on my toes, constantly pushing back, my stubbornness and temper just a few traits she battled against. But she wasn't innocent either. Her attitude mixed with her mouth were enough to drive any man crazy, and while I was pushed to the brink most times, she turned me on when she acted like that.

It meant she was feistier in bed.

And I had no complaints there.

None whatsoever.

I cut her off before she riled herself up. "Listen, you're not gonna win here. I'll drive you in, you'll tell them you're quitting, and then we'll come back here and enjoy each other." I smiled, a devious twinkle in my eyes as I challenged her. The look on her face was priceless. She was flabbergasted, feigning as if she wasn't interested in what I'd proposed, and for some reason she felt like she had to fight me on it, just like she did with everything else. The woman wasn't the easiest to get along with, but she was mine and I cherished her more than she would ever know.

Pulling her close, her big belly bouncing against my stomach, I leaned down and captured her lips before she could argue. Again. Teasing her mouth, I begged for her to open up and let me taste her warmth. It was only a few seconds before she complied, her lips parting and meeting my tongue with her own. Passion danced around us, swirling our need for each other so intricately I never wanted to part from her.

My hand snaked around the back of her neck, holding her firmly in place while I promised her everything with the sweep of my tongue and the press of my lips.

"How about you just call in and tell them?" I panted, breaking away briefly to make my plea. "Then we don't have to leave at all, and we can continue this in the bedroom."

She backed away, keeping her hands on my chest while she looked into my eyes. Before she spoke, I took the opportunity to admire her newly acquired body. I loved Addy's figure before the pregnancy, but it was nothing compared to the way she looked while carrying my son. Her hips had filled out, her womanly curves calling for my touch every time

I saw her. Normally, her chest was on the smaller side, something I never minded; in fact, I loved that she fit into the palms of my large hands. But I had to admit I was just as turned on at the sight of her plump tits, sitting high and full, begging for my lips to wrap around her pink nipples.

She'd complained she could no longer fit into her jeans. When I suggested she purchase actual maternity clothing, she'd dismissed me with a roll of her eyes, holding on to the idea that she could still wear what she wanted, which was why she'd switched to loose-fitted dresses. I didn't care. Whatever she wanted to wear was fine with me, as long as she was comfortable and it made her happy. Plus, the clothing she wore only meant easier access for me. No buttons and zippers to contend with, just a simple lift of the material and I was well on my way to fucking my woman.

"You know you look amazing right now, don't you? It should piss me off that your tits are on full display and you were gonna show them to every man at that damn hospital, but I can't help but want to tear that dress off you and take them into my mouth until you're begging for me to ruin you." I'd completely switched it up, ignoring the fact she was arguing with me a few seconds before, now trying to entice her to let me have my way with her.

"Oh, stop it," she said, playfully slapping my chest before trying to take a step back. When I kept my hold tight, she challenged me, her eyebrow arching impatiently and waiting for my release. Finally, I gave it. She parted her lips to speak but quickly closed them, throwing her hand over her mouth at the same time her beautiful blue eyes widened.

She was gonna be sick.

She was too far from the bathroom so I hauled over the empty garbage can, her gratitude speaking volumes while I held her loose blonde curls behind her head. Expelling the small breakfast she'd had earlier, her complexion paled after she'd finished. It was right then that she stopped fighting me about quitting, about feeling the need to travel to the hospital simply to tell them the news.

Helping her lie on the couch, I placed her favorite throw over her after removing her sandals. "I'll be right back," I promised, moving away only after she nodded. Quickly cleaning out the can, I brought it to rest beside her in case she felt the need to be sick again. I also brought her a small glass of ginger ale. Because of the chemo treatments, she hated taking any additional medication for nausea, so the soft drink was her only slight reprieve. I made sure to stock up on it as soon as she told me it helped.

"Here," I said, handing her the phone. "When you feel better, make the call and tell them." It wasn't a suggestion and she knew it, too tired and sick to even try and argue. She knew I was right, even though she would never admit it.

The rest of the day passed easily enough. She'd only been sick one other time, quickly recovering enough to hold down a small dinner of chicken and carrots. She loved pizza and pasta, but her body rejected the overly starchy meals more often than not. Actually, I was surprised she was able to gain weight with the amount of times she threw up, but she and the baby received a healthy diagnosis along the way, so I forced myself to not worry as much.

Most days, it worked.

THIRTY

Adelaide

THE NEXT FEW DAYS PASSED better than the previous ones. I'd been able to hold down my meals, as well as eating a little extra to make up for what my body lacked. At least it was the way I justified it, gobbling down bowls of ice cream and indulging in some weird cravings—Oreos and pickles, to be exact. I guessed it was the combo of sweet and salty.

I'd followed Stone's advice—rather, his *demands*—and quit my job. For the time being. I would beat this rotting disease inside me, give birth to a beautiful baby boy, and then decide how I wanted to proceed. Helping people had been my calling and I didn't want to give it up altogether, but I did agree that I had to focus on both my health and my child for the next few months or so.

Not being able to financially contribute to the household drove me nuts, even though Stone refused my money while I was still bringing in a paycheck. I had a small amount in savings, but I didn't like that my cushion wasn't growing each month. Instead, I had to rely on Stone to provide for everything—food, utilities, baby items, even my clothes. He promised he had more than enough to take care of us for the rest of our lives, but I didn't want to take advantage.

He rebuked my arguments each time the conversation came up, until one day he laid it all on the line for me, confessing he had millions saved, the interest on that money more than enough for us to live on.

Admittedly, I felt a little better after hearing a figure, but I still couldn't stand being hindered in some way.

As far as my cancer went, I hadn't told anyone but Stone. Worrying my father and uncle was the last thing I wanted to do, and I chose to wait until after the treatments were finished to decide what to do next.

Hopefully, the therapy would work and there would be nothing to tell, but until I received the results, I was keeping my mouth shut.

———◆———

"HOW YA FEELING TODAY?" STONE asked, tracing my arm with his fingertips. We were still lazing about in bed, the early morning sun dancing through the window, trying to entice us to rise and enjoy the gift of the day.

"Why? You have something in mind?" On my last word, I backed my ass into his groin, eliciting a soft groan from his throat.

"Keep doin' that and I'll be inside you before your next heartbeat." Gingerly continuing to stroke my arm, his warm breath cascaded over my neck, shivers shooting through me with deliciousness.

"What if I want you inside me?" I prompted. "I've missed you . . . so much," I moaned, rocking against him again. It'd been days since we last had sex. Between me not feeling well and the time he had to spend at the club, we hadn't had much quality time together, and when we did, I was exhausted. Stone had been very patient, but I knew it was driving him insane that he couldn't touch me the way he wanted to.

Hell, it was driving *me* insane.

"Don't tease me, woman. I don't think I can handle it." Seizing my hip, he pushed his thickness against me, rubbing himself in sweet antici-pation. Craning my neck, I locked eyes with him, and with a simple look I gave him the go-ahead. Licking his lips, he grabbed my jaw and turned me toward him so he could capture my mouth.

Teasing and promising.

Torturing and relieving.

"Stone," I moaned, my sudden need for him almost too much, weigh-ing down on me so heavy the only relief would be when he filled me and destroyed the ache cresting inside me.

"It's Stone? Not Lincoln?" he teased, nipping my bottom lip before kissing me again.

"We'll see what happens in a few minutes." I smiled, but it disappeared as soon as his fingers found my nipples. My breasts had become super sensitive since becoming pregnant. A couple months before, he'd been able to make me come just from playing with them, sucking and knead-ing the pliant flesh until I rocked into bliss. It was a first, but it certainly wasn't the last. Once he realized how responsive I'd been, he teased me unmercifully whenever we were alone, no matter what we were doing. Watching a movie, cleaning up after dinner, simply passing by each other after a shower—any time he could get his hands on them, he was game.

I knew he'd loved my body before I'd become swollen with his child, but his appreciation for my new curves certainly made me feel like the sexiest woman alive.

"You like that?" he asked, gently twisting the erect buds between his fingers.

"You know I do," I whispered, barely able to get the words out before my body bucked under his touch. Gripping his strong thigh, I dug my nails into his skin, unable to hold back the orgasm slowly cresting to life. "I can't . . . Oh, my . . . Yessss."

"Do you love my hands?" He tweaked my nipples with a bit more pressure. "Do you love my mouth?" He kissed my neck. "Do you love my tongue?" He teased my lower lip with the softest sweep of his tongue. "Do you love my cock?" He pressed his body against me, grinding hard until all the air was forced from my lungs in a harsh moan.

"Yes . . . Yes to all of it. Please stop teasing me."

"What do you want me to do to you?" He rolled me on my back, moving down my body until he neared my waist. Sitting on his haunches, his large hands gently spread my thighs. "Tell me. I'll do anything you want." Need licked at my core. Arching my back, I widened my legs for him. Or was that for me? The desire in his eyes was one of the most erotic sights, looking like he wanted to devour me whole, and the sooner the better.

He placed his hands on my belly for a brief moment before lowering his head between my legs, and it was right then that something happened. Something he'd never experienced before.

"What was that?" he asked, jerking his hands away from my tummy and looking frightened.

I'd felt our son kick quite a few times before, and each time he did, Stone was either not present or the baby stopped before his father could feel him.

"Are you okay?" he asked, worry distorting his expression as he moved to sit up.

I grinned, so excited he'd finally been able to feel his son. "That's your boy."

"Oh," he said, still confused by what he felt. "Does it hurt?" Placing his hands back on my belly, he waited for our baby to make another move.

Thankfully, he didn't have to wait long. Another flutter erupted inside me, Stone's eyes flashing wide before a huge smile tilted his lips.

"It doesn't hurt, just feels . . . weird."

Looking at me with such adoration, he leaned in close and captured my mouth. "Thank you, Addy."

"For what?"

"For giving me a son. I never even realized how much I wanted to be a father until fate made the decision for me." His entrancing brown eyes glassed over, the moment very emotional. While he held back, I bawled like a baby. Or like a pregnant woman whose hormones were all over the place. One minute I was fine and the next . . . well, it was like this.

"Don't cry," he soothed, kissing my lips over and over, wiping away my tears until finally I'd calmed down enough to actually speak.

"I'm sorry, it's just sometimes you're too sweet."

With a slight shrug, he said, "I know," kissing me once more before attempting to hop off the bed.

"Wait," I cried out. "Where are you going?"

"I'm gonna grab a drink. Why?"

"I thought we were gonna have sex," I pouted, rising on my elbows to see him better. He took a few steps back, pulling on his T-shirt while still engaging me.

"Not after I felt him. No way are we having sex now that I know I'll probably hurt him." Stone's fears were irrational, although many men shared the same thought. I'd done a stint in obstetrics when I first became a nurse, and I remembered having many a conversation with the parents about this very same topic.

"Stone," I pleaded. "For as large and in charge as you are—" I chuckled "—there is no way you're gonna hurt, or even reach, the baby. Trust me, he's pretty far up there." Thinking he would take me at my word, I relaxed on the bed, waiting for him to come back to me, but he only moved further away. Walking across the room, he shook his head, showing he didn't believe me. A few seconds later he disappeared and left me lying there in utter disbelief.

It wasn't until our next doctor's visit, after Dr. Weber thoroughly explained the ins and outs of where the baby resided in the womb, and how far into the vagina the penis went—even for someone as well-endowed as Stone—that he finally believed I was safe enough to have sex.

Although it was the last thing I wanted to talk about with my doctor, it was necessary to calm Stone's nerves and frantic irrational thoughts.

When it was all said and done, though, we had some of the best sex of our lives.

So thank you, Dr. Weber.

Stone

THE ENTIRE RIDE TO MAREK'S house was bittersweet. I hadn't been able to spend much time with my buddy these past few months, only meeting to discuss club business—Yanez, in particular—so I was looking forward to catching up. But on the other hand, all I wanted to do was laze about with Addy, soaking in as much of her as I could while we still had time alone together. While my love for my son grew every single day, I knew once he came into the world our lives were gonna change forever.

"Are you sure you're feeling okay?" I asked, reaching across and placing my hand on Addy's knee. As much as I wanted to spend time with Marek, I knew she was itching for some girl time with Sully as well. The mere mention of going to their house for dinner had Addy smiling big, and as much as I wanted to keep her all to myself, I realized that was selfish. She needed her friend, just like I needed mine.

"Yes, I'm fine. Plus, this will be my last good meal until I go for my next round of treatment tomorrow. Then you know what happens." She tried to smile, but the knowledge that she was gonna be sick for at least a week after treatment would instill an uneasiness in anyone.

Adelaide Reins was the strongest woman I knew. She battled cancer like a trooper, while carrying our baby. There were times she cried when she was sick or when she was tired—hell, there were times when she was sick *and* tired—but she never complained. She never questioned why this had happened to her, at least not out loud. Taking the cards life dealt her, she made the best of an extremely difficult situation, all the while putting up with my mood swings.

I tried to stifle my outrages, mostly my jealous rants, and I believed I was successful, but there were a few times I couldn't help it. Like when

Hawke commented on how sexy Addy was with her new tits. Yeah, the fucker actually made that comment. Or when Tripp embraced my woman, kissing her cheek before placing his hands on her growing belly.

That earned him a punch in the face, the brazen bastard.

He laughed.

Addy . . . not so much.

I still didn't like the relationship she had with the nomad, but I guessed I had to deal with it because Addy considered him a friend. And if I forbade her to talk to him, all that would get me would be a few days of the silent treatment, and I couldn't deal with that. Plus, I didn't want to add any extra stress in her life.

So I sucked up their interactions, reacting when I felt he pushed the envelope too far.

When we finally arrived, I cut the engine and exited the truck to make my way to Addy's door. I may be part of a notorious biker club, albeit legit now, be tattooed and look a bit rough to some people, but I opened the door for my woman. I waited on her hand and foot whenever I could, and showed her a side of me no one else was privy to.

"Well, it's about time, brother," Marek greeted from his front porch, leaning in the doorway as he acknowledged his dinner guests. Addy insisted on bringing a salad, and when she was close enough she shoved it into Marek's hands, walking past him through the front door.

"Where's Sully?"

"She's finishing up getting ready. You can go back in the bedroom to hurry her along if you want," he offered.

"Okay, be right back," she called over her shoulder, leaving the two of us alone to talk.

"Want a beer?" He walked into his home, me following directly behind him.

"Sure thing." I accepted the drink and sat at the kitchen table while Marek took the seat next to me.

He and I were best friends, had been since we were young. We knew everything about each other, our best attributes as well as our weaknesses. Experiencing the death of our fathers together made our bond even stronger, the pain we felt sealing our place in the world as brothers. We didn't share the same blood, but it made no difference to him or me.

Recently, though, we'd fallen out of sync. He was busy with cementing his relationship with his wife, and making sure the club stayed on the right path. All the while waiting for the opportunity when he could catch Rico Yanez doing some shady dealings behind the cartel's back. Only when he was able to take Yanez's life would he be able to rest easy.

And me. Where did I even begin with what I'd been dealing with? Addy made me swear not to tell anyone in the club about her cancer, fearing even if I told Marek in confidence he might somehow innocently let it slip to Trigger. Therefore defeating the purpose of trying to protect her uncle, and eventually her father. I didn't agree with her decision. I felt her family had a right to know, to offer her their love and help, but when it came right down to it, it wasn't my call.

Then there was the baby. Only a few of the men in the club had kids, but no one I was close enough with to seek out any kind of advice. Ryder had a daughter he hardly saw because she lived across the country and only visited once a year. I found out recently Cutter had a daughter as well, but he didn't want anything to do with her. Something about keeping her and her mother safe all these years, but I wondered if all that would change now that we were eliminating threats toward our club.

Our lives had certainly changed in the past year, but it was for the better. We both had a woman to love, something I would have never envisioned for myself before Addy, and certainly not for Marek.

"So," my friend started, pulling me back from my thoughts. "How's it goin'?" A short and simple question, but it spoke volumes. He was asking me about my relationship with Addy as well as impending fatherhood all rolled into those three little words.

Nodding, I took a large swig of my beer. Only after the cool liquid had cleared the back of my throat did I form the words to answer. "Everything's good. Addy's still sick most days, but she's trudging on through."

"Well, I guess she doesn't have a choice, now does she?" he joked.

"Nope, she doesn't. But she sure is a trooper, man."

"Especially since she's gotta deal with your unpredictable ass on top of being pregnant." He laughed, a little more that time because it was the truth.

"There's that," I responded, tipping the nose of my bottle at him before drinking. Turning my head to the side to make sure we were still alone, I asked him what I'd meant to for the past few days. "Any new developments with Yanez?"

He shifted in his chair, his expression quickly turning to frustration. "No," he grated. "I still have Zip watchin' him, and while we've been able to gather a bit more info on his interactions with Koritz, it's not enough to bring to Carrillo yet."

"Well, at least we'll be able to take that fucker out as well when the time comes. I'm still pissed about him raiding our club." Sam Koritz was a shady DEA agent and his time would come. Payback was certainly a bitch. Switching the subject, simply because I was curious, I asked, "Does Sully know you're biding your time until you can kill him? Have you told her anything of your plans?"

"Fuck no. I don't need her worrying about that shit. I'll tell her when it's done; otherwise, there'll be no mention of it whatsoever." He looked at me like I was slow. "Got it?"

"Really? You even have to ask me that?" My jaw muscles ticked while my face scrunched up in disbelief. I was insulted and he knew it.

"Sorry, I know you'd never say anything, Stone. I just . . . Sully . . . Sometimes I wish I could purge *for* her. You know?"

Sadly . . . I did.

I savored the next few minutes before bringing up a topic I knew was touchy. He hadn't said as much in so many words to me, but I was quite observant. "Hey, man, listen. I think we should start sending a guy or two with Jagger when he's fighting."

Marek bristled with unspoken aggravation, calming himself before meeting my stare. "Why?" he deadpanned.

"From what I understand, the purse is getting kinda large, and I think he could use some extra support in case anyone gets any ideas." Taking another pull off my beer, I leaned back in my chair. "He's gettin' to be a pretty big deal in that world."

"Well, if he's so big then can't he take care of himself, seeing as he's the one winnin' all the fucking fights anyway?" Reclining in his chair and mirroring my stance, he threw one arm over the back of his seat and rested the other on the table, drumming his fingers across the top. He was contemplating my suggestion, even though the prospect was probably one of the last people he wished to discuss right then.

"What's up with the two of you?"

"What do you mean?" he asked, rising from his seat and grabbing another beer from the fridge. Tipping the bottle at me to ask if I wanted another, I simply shook my head. One drink was good enough since I was driving. No way in hell I was makin' my pregnant woman cart my drunk ass home.

"Why don't you like Jagger?"

"Who said I didn't like him?"

"Your expression and body language any time you're around him," I replied quickly. Rocking back and forth in my chair, I waited patiently for him to answer, amusing myself until the women joined us.

"If you must know, he's got a thing for Sully." He leaned against the kitchen counter, his hands clenched into tight fists as he freed the words from his mouth.

"Yeah, I know," I admitted, smirking I'd finally been able to make him admit it to me. While I was amused, it was actually no laughing matter. I hated the way Tripp acted toward Addy, but at least I knew he didn't have a thing for her. There would be no telling how I would react toward the nomad if I thought otherwise.

Marek looked like he was ready to read me the riot act, but thought better of it. "If he's goin' around tellin' people, I'm gonna kill him. Quite literally."

Deciding it was best to put my dear friend out of his misery, I confessed how I knew the prospect had feelings for Sully. "Look, the boy's not stupid. This club means everything to him. He's not about to fuck that up, plus risk you snatchin' his life, all for a little crush."

"Little crush?" he shouted, lowering his voice once he realized how loud he sounded. "It's not a little crush. I think he's in love with her."

I shook my head at his theory. "I really don't think so. I don't think it's anything more than a simple crush. Sully is beautiful, after all. I'm surprised more men aren't following her around." Ribbing him was probably not the smartest idea, so before he freaked out, I continued telling him what I really thought. "In all seriousness, his infatuation will pass . . . in time. All we have to do is hook him up with as much pussy as possible."

"Well, I'll leave that up to you," he grated, pushing off the counter and walking around the table. "Where the hell are those two?"

Needing to know where he stood about what I'd proposed a few minutes back, I repeated my question. "So, what's your take on sending a couple guys with Jagger to his next fight? I think it's in two days."

"Fight?" Sully asked, rounding the corner with Addy close on her heels. "Are you guys talking about Jagger's upcoming fight?" She closed the small distance between her and her husband, pecking his lips before turning around to face me. "Hi, Stone," she greeted.

"Hi, Sully. How are ya?"

"Good." She leaned in to Marek, seeking his comfort, but he pushed her away so he could look at her.

"What do you know about his fights?" he asked, his question surely poised for an argument. All of a sudden, the air bristled with tension, both women confused by the change in my friend's voice.

"I overheard Tripp and Ryder talking about it the last time I was there." She looked down for a brief moment, giving everything away. She was lying, or omitting something, and the both of us knew it. Before things turned unbearable, she chose to confess, not even realizing she was being scrutinized during those few seconds of silence. "Plus, he told me when I ran into him." She talked quicker, hoping to dispel any anger her husband felt at the fact she'd conversed with the prospect. "I was waiting for you to finish up talking to Trigger when I ran into Jagger in the kitchen. We were just chitchatting, Cole," she offered, realizing he was about to blow.

"Did he invite you to his fight?" he seethed.

"No." I could tell she answered truthfully that time.

"Hey, I have a great idea. How about we all go to his next bout?" Addy asked, completely oblivious that there was an all-out war about to erupt in the kitchen.

"Hell no!" Marek and I both shouted at the same time, cementing the answer, just in case there was any doubt.

"Why not? It might be fun," she pressed, lowering herself to sit on my lap.

"For one, you're six fuckin' months pregnant, never mind I would never allow you in that kind of environment. It's too dangerous."

"But you guys would be with us. Therefore, we'd be safe." Addy smiled as if she had just solved it.

"Give it up, Adelaide," Sully said, nestling closer to Marek. "Even if Stone let you go, my dear husband wouldn't follow suit. He thinks Jagger likes me, so there's no way he'll let me go. Even though I've told him he doesn't."

"Wait . . . what? Am I missing something? Why do you think Jagger likes Sully?" she asked Marek, evoking the anger he'd been able to dispel to the back burner.

"'Cause he does," he answered brusquely.

Before his wife could interject with her rebuttal, I spoke up. "He does, Sully. But I think it's a harmless crush."

Addy nodded, indicating she agreed with me. "He's young. I'm sure that's all it is."

I couldn't hold my tongue, even though this wasn't our argument. "Just like your neighbor, 'Robby'?" I said, crooking the first two fingers on each hand as I finished speaking.

"Again, that's his *actual* name. Not sure why you're using air quotes. Besides, he's not my neighbor anymore." The subject was still a little sensitive for the both of us, so I wasn't sure exactly why I'd brought it up. She tried to stand, but I held her close with a firm grip on her waist.

"Let's forget I brought it up," I offered, realizing full well it was the last thing either one of us wanted to talk about. It was in the past, and there it would remain, until I deemed it necessary to bring to light again.

The rest of the evening was calmer, thank God. We shared many laughs, making fun of some of the club members. Namely Hawke. He was a good guy, but dense as hell sometimes.

We enjoyed Sully's homemade chicken pot pie, a recipe she wanted to try out on us to see if it was any good. Marek had told me she'd really taken to cooking, as well as baking. Of course, I couldn't let a comment like that slide by without a retort, patting his belly and joking that I could tell she was feeding him well. Truth be told, Marek was in the best shape of his life, much like me. Although, I might be okay with putting on a few pounds if Addy took to the kitchen the way Sully had.

But I liked my balls too much to make the suggestion.

THIRTY-TWO

Adelaide

"I'M NERVOUS. IT JUST SEEMS the further along I get in this pregnancy, the more I want to protect our son from the poison they inject into me." I turned my head to the side, trying my best to hide my building paranoia from Stone. "Maybe I should stop until after I give birth."

He moved closer, his knee brushing my thigh when he reached for my hand. "Addy, look at me." I obliged the first time he asked. "If you want to stop treatment until after he's born, then I support you. But remember that Dr. Weber said the baby looks perfectly healthy, and the last time you brought up postponing chemo, he advised against it."

The decision to forgo treatment until after the delivery had been weighing heavy on me, but instead of focusing on that, I chose to direct my attention to the fact that Stone had said Dr. Weber's name without reservation. I smiled.

"What?" he asked, clueless as to why I was grinning from ear to ear.

"I think you're growing." He glanced down at himself, confused as all hell.

"What are you talkin' about, woman?"

"You said Dr. Weber's name without following it up with a threat of some sort."

"Oh. Yeah, I guess I did." He mirrored my enjoyment, a smile curving up the corners of his beautiful mouth. "I guess he's not so bad," he offered, which I knew was a big deal for him to say. "Plus, he's going above and beyond, working with Dr. Altosh to make sure your treatments are the best option for you. To save your life." The seriousness of his last state-ment stole both of our smiles. While both doctors were fully invested in my case, they weren't God. And if my maker wanted to call me home sooner than I wanted to leave, then there was nothing anyone could do about that decision. It was beyond all of our reaches.

After a long pause in our conversation, Stone broke the silence by speaking again. "So . . . does that mean you do or don't want to go for your dose today?" His fingers remained entwined with mine, his love and support pouring from him the entire time I internally dueled with what to do. This time of my life was the hardest so far, and while I prayed to make it through with both my life and the life of our son growing inside me, I wasn't naïve. But not wanting to travel down the road of self-doubt right then, I squeezed his hand and nodded.

"I only have one more treatment after today, so I may as well get it over with." I wasn't one hundred percent sure, but ninety percent was good enough, right?

"Okay then. I'll grab your jacket." Even though the temperature outside would reach the high eighties today, I often got the chills directly after the drugs were introduced into my system. All things considered, the side effects I had to endure weren't terrible. Thankfully. Other than the nausea which quickly followed and stuck around for almost a week, and the tiredness my body succumbed to, the only other side effect was that my skin was drier. Almost as if the drugs sucked the moisture right out of me. Something Stone said he didn't mind so much, because he loved rubbing me down from head to toe with lotion twice a day.

Any reason for him to have his hands all over my body and the man was in Heaven. Hey, I wasn't complaining either.

My cancer and pregnancy brought out the protective side of Stone in spades. He never allowed me to lift a thing, whether it was cleaning up after we'd had dinner, or carrying a load of laundry. Dealing with all the household tasks was his way of making sure I was taken care of. When he couldn't be home because of the club, he'd send one of the other men over to help me out, even though he would be home later that evening. He never wanted me to go without, and he hated the fact I spent time alone without him. Worrying about me all day long had taken over the majority of his life, and while I felt bad that I caused him to fret over me so much, it was nice to have someone there when I needed him.

Carrying my jacket in one hand, he guided me toward the front door with the other. The warmth of his palm calmed my rising nerves, giving me strength to tackle another day. I wasn't gonna lie; many days were a test for me. I tried my hardest not to let him see me crumble, but whenever I had a few hours to myself, I allowed my fears to come to the surface, my tears doing their job of ridding my body of such overwhelming emotion. If Stone had noticed my red and puffy eyes, I placated his worries by telling him my tears were because of my overactive hormones. He believed me. At least, I thought he did.

I'd decided to go ahead and finish the regimented treatment sessions. After this one, there was only one left. One more and then I would find out whether or not they had worked.

Waiting for that day was going to be nerve-racking for sure. Either way, I knew I had the love of a good man, and the will to fight another day.

THIRTY-THREE

Stone

"I'M NOT SO SURE THIS is such a great idea, Addy." I tried to reason with her but for some reason she chose to ignore me, flitting about our bedroom and searching for her other sandal.

"You'll be fine," she soothed, excited when she'd finally located the missing shoe. Strapping it into place, she stalked toward me with purpose. Standing on her tiptoes, she linked her fingers around the back of my neck and pressed her mouth to mine. Her tongue drifted across my bottom lip, the sensations of lust and need spiraling through me in mere seconds. All it took was a simple touch and I was prepared to throw her down on the bed and fuck her like I hadn't seen her in weeks.

"Stop trying to distract me," I growled, capturing her mouth for a quick kiss before pushing her back. "Besides, I need my wits about me if I'm gonna meet your father. I have no doubt that once he finds out I'm part of the club he'll be pissed. I would be if I were him."

"What does that mean?" Her confused look would have been funny if she hadn't been so serious. Tugging on the hem of her blue jersey dress, the color making her eyes pop, she backed away from me, her gaze pinned to mine.

"You know damn well what it means." She remained silent, forcing me to explain further. "He's gonna look at me as nothing more than a criminal, stealing his daughter's future before it even starts. And sometimes I think he'd be right to think such things." I couldn't believe I'd voiced my insecurities, thoughts which sometimes buried me in self-doubt. But it was the truth. I regretted my choice of words as soon as I saw a single tear dance down her cheek. Reaching out to calm her before she became more distressed, I tried to grab her hand but she quickly retreated.

"Don't say those things," she whispered, breaking eye contact and looking down at her swollen belly. "It makes me think you'll leave me. If you think you'll ruin me . . . you'll disappear, and I don't know how I would live if you ever did that to me." The desperation in her voice struck a severe chord with me. I wasn't used to her appearing vulnerable, sickness and pregnancy alike. She was always strong, pigheaded even. Never exposed.

When I tried to make contact again, she withdrew further, but before she fled the room, my fingers latched around her arm to halt her. Pulling her to me, I kissed the top of her head and poured my heart out. I needed to make sure she knew I wasn't going anywhere before she worried herself to death. She had enough on her plate; she didn't need to add *me* to the list, or the future of our relationship. In reality, if anyone left it would be her, when she was finally fed up with me. Another thing I would never seriously let happen.

Addy was mine forever, and no one would get in the way of that.

Including either one of us.

I directed her face upward until I could see her eyes. Placing a lingering kiss on her lips, I spewed out everything I was thinking. My thoughts were all over the place so what came out of my mouth was jumbled, but it made sense to me.

"I'll never leave you. Ever. I don't care what your father thinks or even what I think from time to time. Are you too good for me? Absolutely. But does the selfish part of me care? I should . . . but I don't. You're mine. End of story. I'll piss you off countless times over the course of our life together, but I'll apologize and hopefully you won't get sick of hearing the words." More tears leaked from her eyes, my own becoming glassy at seeing her so upset. "I love you. Now and forever. Nothing will change that, I promise. If anything, I'll probably have to live with Marek from time to time because you'll get sick of me and kick me out." While I tried to lighten the conversation with a joke, I was being completely serious at the same time. I could clearly envision Addy demanding a few days alone to allow her anger toward me to lessen, for whatever reason.

Her arms wrapped tightly around my waist while her head pressed against my chest. "He'll make you stay at the clubhouse instead." There was no laughter in her voice, even though what she said was a comical retort.

"Yup. You're probably right. And every night away from you and our son will be torture. So I'll do my best not to let that happen."

I hugged her back with a fierceness that showed her I was serious about everything I'd said, all while not crushing her belly.

"If we don't get goin', your father is surely gonna blame me."

"Fine, fine," she mumbled, snatching a short-sleeved sweater from the chair to go over her dress. The weather outside was beautiful, but the sun was going to dip below the horizon soon enough, and although I would still find it warm out, Addy would get the chills. One of the many side effects from her treatment.

Over an hour later, we pulled up in front of her father's house, arriving later than I'd wanted because I needed to take a detour toward the clubhouse in order to check in on some business. What I thought was going to be a quick stop turned out to be an ordeal. Trigger and I had words . . . again. As soon as he laid eyes on his niece and the ever-growing proof I went against his steadfast rule, he had no qualms about telling me what he thought of me. His anger toward me didn't affect me in the least—what was done was done. Addy was mine now, and there was nothing he could do about it. He'd exacted the punishment he thought was fitting by shooting me, and if he didn't move on soon . . . I'd force him to do so.

How? I had no idea, but I was sure with the help of my friend, and president, we'd come up with something. Plus, every time he said something to me in front of Addy he managed to upset her. And that was unacceptable.

Coming around to her side of the truck, I opened her door and extended my hand. Once I felt the warmth of her skin on mine, I relaxed. Sort of. As tough as I tried to appear, there was nothing that would calm my nerves about meeting her father. Someone who was gonna judge me before he even heard me speak. Someone who was instantly gonna think I was unworthy of his daughter, strictly because I wasn't him. Fathers always wanted to be the only men in their daughter's lives, solely because no one else could ever measure up.

Plus, I was the man who'd knocked up his little girl.

Yeah, this is what I'm up against.

Clasping her hand in mine, she walked beside me as we approached the front door. I wouldn't give in to the erratic thumping of my heart, or the heavy quick breaths which bombarded me with each step forward. I refused to let Addy or her father see me sweat. If I deserved her, and I did, I had to man up and get through the dinner unscathed.

"I hope you're hungry," she said, raising her fist to knock on the door. Her nervousness was apparent in the back-and-forth shuffle of her feet while she waited for her father to answer.

"Well, considering the only thing I had to eat today was pussy, I could certainly go for some food."

The door flung open before Addy could respond, her eyes wide and staring right at me with a mixture of surprise and humor.

"Addy, honey. You know you don't have to knock," her father told her, stepping forward and bringing her in for a hug. We were still holding hands, but were separated in order to allow her to return her father's embrace. I continued to stand on the threshold of his home while he greeted his daughter, his gaze never once resting on me. Not until Addy made the official introductions.

"Dad, this is Stone . . . I mean Lincoln Crosswell." Turning her head toward me, she said, "This is my father. Brian Reins."

We assessed each other in mere seconds. He sized me up and while I returned the favor, I patiently waited for him to welcome me. Extending my hand in greeting first, a few palpable seconds passed before he took it. The next breath to leave my lips was one of relief.

While it was ungodly warm outside, I chose to wear a long-sleeved white shirt, mainly to hide the fact my arms were completely covered with ink. I also thought it would be smart if I left my KC cut at home, not wanting to shove the fact I was involved in a club he would surely have an issue with.

First impressions and all.

"How are you feeling, sweetheart?" he asked, his hand instinctually finding her swollen belly. "While your mother constantly complained she felt like a beached whale, she never looked more beautiful than when she was carrying you." A quick look of love and sadness erupted behind his eyes. "You have that same look," he confessed.

"Of a beached whale?" she teased.

"Oh, stop it. You know damn well you look beautiful." He leaned down and kissed her temple before ushering her toward a seat in the kitchen.

His focus was mainly kept on his daughter, but after a little while, he knew he had to pay me some kind of attention. My first impression of Brian Reins wasn't of rudeness or aloofness, but one of a man portraying the alpha male. He was letting me know I meant nothing to him, that he was in control and I was now on his territory.

Trust me, I understood. More than I wanted to. But it didn't erase the fact that, although he thought he had the upper hand, he didn't. Not anymore. I'd already claimed my woman, my child growing inside her as proof. For as much as I wanted to pound my chest and declare being top dog, I knew it was Neanderthal-like. And downright immature. I was more secure in myself than that, although I had questioned my worth a few times before we'd arrived.

He turned his attention to me after holding the chair out for his very pregnant daughter. And it was then he chose to engage me in conversation. Finally.

"Why in God's name are you wearing a long-sleeved shirt?" he asked, pinning his eyes to mine and crossing his arms over his chest. His question may have sounded innocent enough, but every word spoken was calculated. From the moment he opened his mouth, he was judging me. And honestly . . . I didn't blame him. *If Addy and I have a daughter someday, I'll probably be worse, never allowing any male to come near her.*

Addy spoke up before I could say anything. "Dad, he's trying to be respectful."

"What does that mean?" her father asked, frowning at his daughter's answer. I was sure all sorts of things went through his head, and before he lost himself to the catacombs of possibilities, I parted my lips and answered.

"I'm covered in tats, and since Addy told me you don't have any of your own, I didn't want to offend you by making you stare at mine the entire time."

Leaning back against the kitchen counter, his eyes roamed over me. Head to toe. I was sure I was quite the sight. My hair was shaved on the sides, my blond strands longer on top and fashioned back in a Mohawk kind of style. My beard, although shorter than I normally wore it, was long. And mix in that I was covered in ink . . . well, I wasn't the ideal choice for the likes of his daughter. So I wore long sleeves to hide at least one of those things.

"Nonsense. I don't have any because I could never find something I wanted permanently marked on my body. But that doesn't mean I don't appreciate a piece of art when I see it." His body relaxed, his arms drifting down and coming to rest at his sides. Nodding, he gave me a lazy grin before turning around to check on whatever food he'd put in the oven.

His noncommittal acceptance was gonna be short-lived, however.

THIRTY-FOUR

Adelaide

AT FIRST, I THOUGHT MY father was going to deny Stone entry into his house. He'd told me on previous visits that he wasn't looking forward to meeting the man who got me pregnant. The man who didn't have the decency to come to him, like he ought to, and ask for my hand in marriage. To do the right thing.

My father, although only fifty, was extremely old-fashioned. He believed that men and women shouldn't live together before marriage, and should definitely not have children unless they were legally committed to each other. And if such a thing happened, as in my case, the man should make an honest woman out of his future child's mother.

We'd argued on a few occasions when I told him I didn't want to rush things, and that I wasn't going to get married just because he thought it was the right thing to do. In the beginning, Stone had agreed with me, but as my belly grew, he'd mentioned getting married more and more. I was also convinced that because I was sick, it fueled his urge to make me his wife.

What if I didn't make it?

What if my life was cut short before he was ready to let me go?

Before I was ready to leave?

Pushing those depressing thoughts aside, I tried my hardest to focus on the two strong men in the kitchen with me. My father busied himself preparing the dinner he insisted on making—chicken Marsala, one of my mother's favorite dishes. And as such, it was one of mine as well. Over the years since she passed, my father had taken up cooking. He didn't have much of a choice; if he didn't want to survive on fast food alone, he had to learn to cook for himself—more than his infamous chili, that was.

"Lincoln, can you set the table? I don't want Addy lifting a finger," my father insisted, staring at Stone until he rose from the table and walked toward the cupboards. Instructing him on where he kept the plates and silverware, my father turned toward me and smiled. He loved that Stone did what he was asked without reservation, and although I knew he wanted to impress my father, Stone's own insecurities about the meeting eating away at him, he wasn't a man who took orders very easily. Other than from Marek, and only when it was about club business.

Once all three place settings were arranged, my father took the chicken from the oven and placed it in the center of the table. A bowl of mixed veggies along with some fresh rye bread and butter completed the dinner. It'd been some time since I ate this particular meal, and the nostalgia of it all had suddenly become overwhelming. Pushing back the building tears, I reached across the table and grasped my father's hand.

"Dinner looks wonderful, Dad. Thanks for having us."

"Anything for you," he said, patting my hand before cutting into his chicken. Moments of silence passed as all of us consumed the delicious dinner, eyes glancing from one person to the next without uttering a single word. The only sounds to fall from my lips were those of satisfaction at how tasty the food was.

"The chicken is wonderful," I exclaimed, shoveling in piece after piece until I'd eaten the entire thing. Finishing off my spoonful of vegetables, I buttered some rye then leaned back in the chair to get more comfortable. I took a small sip of water before placing the warm bread between my lips.

"Damn, girl!" Stone exclaimed, "You sure ate your meal quick." He chuckled, reaching under the table to pat my leg before continuing to finish off his chicken.

"What can I say? Our son's hungry." With laughter falling from my lips, my gaze locked onto my father. His face was void of expression, which was odd since he was such an animated guy. I couldn't tell right then if he was angry or sad. Was the mention of our son pushing him to his limits? It wasn't like he wasn't reminded that I was pregnant as soon as he saw me.

Breaking his connection with me, my father focused on Stone. "So, Lincoln. Tell me about your parents . . . your family. Do they live around here?"

I instantly tensed, realizing the topic of his parents was surely a touchy one. Since I hadn't told my father much about him, always putting off the topic because of the way I knew he would react once he found out he was part of the Knights Corruption, I definitely never mentioned his parents. I probably should have just so we could have avoided the uncomfortableness.

Turning my head toward Stone, I implored him to silently pass me a message with his eyes. Let me know if he was going to be all right with discussing a topic he barely talked about with me. I would interfere on his behalf. All he had to do was blink a few seconds too long, or hold his breath a few more heartbeats . . . or grimace. Something. Anything.

But the man was as cool as a cucumber, even though I knew he was probably agitated on the inside.

Giving my father his full attention, he spoke quickly, hopefully making it clear he didn't wish to expand on the topic.

"Both of my parents are dead." I knew talking about his family was very difficult for him. The one time I'd asked him about them, he gave me short answers, telling me his father was killed a few years back along with Marek's, and that his mother had died from a drug overdose when he was only twelve years old. Other than the one-time bout of information, he refused to discuss them further. I tried on one other occasion, only to be shut down with a grunt and a shake of his head. I knew enough not to push him, and I feared my father was going to try just that.

"I'm sorry to hear that," my father sincerely offered, and thankfully he read his body language well enough to not ask him anymore questions. Although I think I would have preferred the tension of talking about his deceased parents over what he asked him next.

"How did you two meet? Addy never told me." His eyes pinned his dinner guest, refusing to look at me as if I would dismiss the question altogether. And I guessed he was right to think so. Our visit had been going well up until that point. I hated to ruin it, so the only thing I could think of to do was be deceptive.

Beat him to it and lie about where we'd met.

"We met at work. He came in after he'd been in an accident and I was the nurse who stitched him up." Stone visibly flinched from my response, but I'd deal with his mood later, after we were far away from my father's interrogative stare.

"Is that right?" my father asked, taking a pull from his bottled beer. Stone had refused the drink, thinking it best not to partake in alcohol since this was their first meeting and he needed all his wits about him. I wouldn't go as far as to say that he was nervous, per se, just cautious not to make the wrong move, or say the wrong thing.

Well, all that came to an end when he decided to speak up and answer the next question.

"What do you do for a living?" My father finished off his drink and set it on top of the table, reclining in his chair while folding his arms over his chest again. I knew that move. That was the 'I suspect something isn't right, and you better tell me the truth' move.

"Actually, I work with Addy's uncle Trigger." My breath caught in my throat and my body locked up tight. Panic engulfed me before I could convince myself to calm down. My father knew damn well his brother-in-law was knee-deep in the club. Had been before he even met him, which was quite a long time ago. My father had often told me he was extremely happy I was never integrated into that life. Both he and my mother made sure of it. The good thing was that my uncle agreed wholeheartedly with them, protecting me every chance he had.

When I started going by the club at my uncle's request to help out, we decided it best to keep that piece of information from my father. It would only upset him, and he had enough to deal with since my mother passed; he didn't need to worry about my well-being. It was why my uncle was so damn adamant about everyone leaving me alone when I visited. It was why he threatened every member to stay away from me, and it was the reason he felt it was his just duty to shoot the father of my unborn child when he'd learned Stone hadn't adhered to his threats.

Clanking silverware drew my attention back to my father. He leaned in close and gritted his teeth when he spoke again. "What do you mean you work with Trigger?"

I had to interfere and do it quickly. "He means he's worked with Uncle Trigger in the past." I opened my mouth to say something else, not quite sure what, when Stone interjected, placing his hand over mine and giving me a light squeeze. He was assuring me it was best to get this out in the open. To deal with it and move on. Just like he did when my uncle shot him. Thankfully, my father didn't own a gun; otherwise, our visit might have turned out completely different.

"I'm a member of the Knights Corruption, right along with Trigger. We've been involved with starting up a few different types of businesses to ensure the livelihood of the club going forward." I wasn't sure whether he was going to continue speaking, but it didn't matter because as soon as he took another breath, my father rose from his seat and started shouting, deflating any hope I had at a peaceful evening.

"What the hell are you saying? What are you telling me right now? That you're part of that cesspool of a club? They're nothing but criminals, preying on the weak and dealing in drugs and God only knows what else. No!" he hollered. "I won't have my daughter involved with anyone from that place." Suddenly turning his eyes to me, he asked, "Does Trigger know you're with him? Because he assured me he would protect you at all costs. To make sure you never fell prey to the likes of anyone involved there."

"He knows," Stone interrupted, rising from the table himself, pulling me right along with him until I stood next to him. His arm wrapped around my waist, and the gesture wasn't lost on my father. He was claiming me, and it was the worst possible time for his possessive side to come out to play. My father slammed his hands on the table and kicked his chair behind him, the shrill sound of metal legs against tiled floor unnerving. "The bastard even shot me because of it." There was no amusement or fear in his voice when he confessed this to my father. There was just matter-of-fact resignation.

"Good. At least he kept his word to me. Sort of. Although you snuck past him, I won't allow you to take this relationship any further. I forbid you to see my daughter any longer!" my father shouted. "I won't keep you from your child, but as far as you and Addy are concerned, you're done. So help me God, if you don't listen to me, you'll regret it." Heavy footsteps sounded as my father rounded the table and came to stand directly in front of Stone, his fists clenched at his sides, prepared to do battle if that's what it came to.

While I knew he wouldn't be okay with me being involved with someone in the club, I seriously didn't think he would take it this far. Threatening Stone if he didn't leave me alone. Ready to pound on the father of his unborn grandchild. He'd gone too far, pushed so far past the line it was nothing but a flimsy blur.

"Dad!" I shouted, reaching out to grab his hand. But he pulled away, denying my touch before it registered. His reaction hurt, but I had more important things to worry about right then.

Like making sure both of them didn't somehow come to blows. They were both fiercely protective of me, and the last thing I wanted or needed was for them to be at war with one another, simply because they were each trying to assert their role in my life.

I pressed on and tried to diffuse the escalating tension between the two men who meant the world to me.

"Dad!" I tried again. "While I know you're concerned for my well-being, I'm grown. You can't dictate who I involve myself with." Looking toward an increasingly agitated Stone, I confessed, "Stone would never let anything bad happen to me. Fate has done that already," I mumbled, more to myself, thankful neither one of them heard my grumbling.

"Addy, you don't know what they're capable of. They're nothing but a bunch of murdering, drug-dealing, lowlife scumbags."

Just when I thought things couldn't get worse, Stone erupted, gripping the edge of the table for leverage. Otherwise, I feared he would have attacked my father.

"I tried to be respectful. I tried to bite my tongue, praying the night wouldn't end like this, but I can't do it any longer. You weren't gonna give me the time of day regardless; I saw the way you judged me as soon as you laid eyes on me. But know this. I'm in love with your daughter, she's having my baby, and very soon we'll be married. And there isn't a damn thing you can do about it. As far as my club goes, my brothers are nothing short of extraordinary men. Sure, we've done some things in the past which resided on the other side of the law. I'm not gonna lie about that. But things are different now. We're done with anything that will endanger our lives as well as the lives of those we love. I would give my own life to make sure Addy and my son are safe, and if you don't believe or trust me then that's your problem. Not mine." Stone's face had become red, his chest expanding quickly while his jaw ticked uncontrollably. Turning my head toward my father, I saw he mirrored Stone's reactions.

The only thing I could do to alleviate the thick tension was to leave, allow my father time to calm down, and hopefully let what Stone had said sink in.

"I think it's best we go," I said, reaching over and touching my father's arm. That time, he didn't pull back, instead looking at me with fear in his eyes. I knew I meant the world to him, and the fact I was upsetting him tore me to shreds. But I loved Stone. I was carrying his child. I needed him, more than I could ever explain to my father. "I promise I'll call you in a couple days. Trust me to know that what I'm doing is right for me," I pleaded.

Taking a step back, I reached for Stone's hand and pulled him toward the door.

Thankfully, he followed me without hesitation.

THIRTY-FIVE

Stone

THE MAJORITY OF THE RIDE home was done in silence. The explosive encounter with Addy's father continued to attack the protective side of me. To hear him challenge me, to insinuate I wasn't man enough to care for and protect his daughter, really hit a nerve, mainly because it was an insecurity of mine. I'd hoped for the best that evening, but I was a fool to think he would welcome me with open arms.

Addy sat beside me, her hand resting on the top of my thigh. She never spoke but her support, and apology, shone through her simple touch. We were a few miles from home when she finally spoke.

"I'm so sorry about the way my father behaved. I really think he'll calm down in a few days, realize he was out of line." Her head was turned toward me and I knew she was staring at the side of my face, willing me to look her way. But I kept my stare straight ahead.

"But that's the thing. He wasn't out of line. And that's what's messing with me." My grip on the steering wheel tightened as I tried to rein in my fleeting temper. I was upset. More than upset, if I was being honest. But confusion riddled me, making me feel helpless. My brain was on overdrive, thoughts of attacking her father for making me feel worthless mixed with admiration for the man that he'd stood up to me and tried to protect his daughter. Because I knew I would do the same damn thing, if ever the situation arose.

"Please don't believe anything he said. He's just hurt, and scared for me. He doesn't know you, or the guys at the club for that matter. He knows what a good man my uncle is, and in time he'll see you in that light as well."

"Don't hold your breath," I shot back at her. Calming my tone, realizing she didn't deserve any of it, I took a few deep breaths and continued to stare ahead, focusing on the road instead of the distraught woman sitting next to me.

When we finally arrived home, Addy exited the truck quicker than I could get to her, walking briskly toward the front of the house without a second thought of waiting for me. She had the door unlocked and had disappeared inside before I stepped foot in front of my truck. The last thing I wanted to do was upset her, but that was exactly what happened tonight. Although I wasn't really to blame, I was the one who had to calm her, to assure her everything would be all right. I knew how close she was with her father, and although I knew I wasn't gonna be seeing him anytime soon, I knew I had to convince her to talk to him sooner rather than later. She had enough stress in her life; she didn't need to be worrying about the status of their relationship on top of everything else going on.

Finally following her inside, I threw my keys on the side entry table and kicked off my boots before walking toward the kitchen. I needed a beer like no one's business, and since I was home I felt it was safe to indulge. I needed something to soothe the rising fire inside me. The more I repeated his words over and over in my head, the more conflicted I became. *'They're nothing but a bunch of murdering, drug-dealing, lowlife scumbags.'* I knew it wasn't all true. Well . . . the low-life-scumbag part anyway.

Swallowing half my beer in a few long gulps, I wiped my mouth with the back of my hand before setting the bottle on the countertop. I didn't want to get too carried away, and if I finished my drink too quickly, I would just reach for another. Then another. And another.

I knew eventually Addy would need to talk about what happened, and how would it look if I was sloshed off my ass, and not there for her to discuss the new stress weighing her down?

Having time alone before I searched for her, I found I was able to calm myself a little more. Rational thought drove me to wash away most of my insecurities, and while I wasn't completely convinced I was good enough for Addy, and never would be, I felt better about my role in her life. Her father spoke from a place of love, I realized that, but his attack on me and my club still cut deep. But I couldn't focus on that any longer. I had to stop worrying about myself and how I felt, and start worrying about the woman who was dealing with the brunt of the situation. She was caught dead center in the middle of this new war between me and the man she loved more than anything. Pushing out a harsh breath, I steeled my nerves and vowed to be the bigger person. I had no idea how, since I'd never had to take on such a role before, but with her help I would figure it out.

I was gonna be the last person she would need to worry about. If only her father knew about her cancer, I bet he'd change his entire tune. It wasn't my place, however, no matter how much I wanted to inform him of his daughter's precarious condition.

Finally having enough solitude, I strode down the short hallway toward our bedroom. I figured she'd disappeared inside to get away to collect herself, much like I'd done in the kitchen. The door was open, a small light on in the corner of the room. My eyes searched the space quickly, but I couldn't find her. Stepping inside, I walked toward the closet, thinking she was changing, but she wasn't in there either. There was only one other place she could be. Slowly pushing open the bathroom door, I spotted her sitting on the edge of the tub, her head hung low and resting in her hands. Her long locks covered her face, but I didn't need to look into her eyes to know how upset she was. I saw it in the shake of her shoulders, in the way her fingers threaded through her hair, and I could hear it in her voice when she spoke.

"I can't talk about it," she cried. "I just can't deal with it right now, so please don't ask me to." Reaching out to caress the top of her head, she leaned in to my touch and it was right then I knew I would do everything in my power to keep her safe and unharmed. I would make it my life's mission to make her the happiest woman in the world, even when life got in the way.

"You don't have to talk about anything you don't want to. Just know I'm here for you. Always," I promised. I continued to stroke her hair, moving closer in case she needed more of my strength.

Her breathing was short and choppy, but she soon regained some of her composure. Lifting her head, her eyes pinned me and what I saw surprised me. I thought for sure she was gonna lose herself in sorrow, but like always, her will to move past things, if only for a while, told me of the type of woman she was. Addy never wanted to wallow in the heartache of the moment; she took time to process, felt the emotions rushing through her, and then pushed forward.

This time was no different.

Reaching for my fingers still running through her hair, she held onto me for support, rising from her seat so she stood in front of me.

Her beautiful blues spoke volumes without her having to utter a single word. My woman needed something desperately. And I had a good idea what that was.

Wrapping her arms around my waist, she leaned up on her tiptoes and softly pressed her mouth to mine, her tongue drifting over my bottom lip in the quickest of teases. "Will you make love to me?" she asked, as if she even needed to pose the question. "But not soft and gentle. I need a distraction right now, and I need to feel you take me with a need like never before."

I was stunned to say the least. Not that she wanted to have sex, but that she was asking me to unleash a bit of the beast inside me. Glancing down at her belly, then back to her face, I bit my lip in reservation. And lust. Right then, I wasn't sure which emotion was gonna win out, but they were splayed all over my face and she read me like an open book.

"You're not going to hurt him," she promised. "I'm not asking you to have crazy rough sex with me. I'm just askin' you to not treat me like I'm gonna break. That's all." Her hands shot to my belt buckle before I could respond, tugging it open and pulling it free from the loops in one swift motion. The clank of the metal hitting the floor startled me. I was entirely focused on the look of lust spreading not only over her face, but throughout her body, her nipples pebbling behind the soft material of her bra, her dress unable to disguise her reaction.

"Are you sure?" I asked, licking my lips as she grasped the button of my jeans, popping it free and sliding the zipper through its many teeth. "I guess so." I laughed, seeing as there was no stopping her now. Not that I was complaining. Once she pushed my jeans down my thighs, I stepped free and kicked them behind me, tugging off my socks just as quickly. When I reached for the hem of my shirt, she stopped me, replacing my hands with hers and slowly drawing the white fabric up my torso. The tickle of her fingertips made my skin come alive, every nerve ending on high alert the more of my skin she exposed. When my shirt cleared my head, she tossed it behind me, raking her nails down the length of my chest until she came to the waistband of my boxer briefs. She told me with a quick flick of her eyes to remain still until she'd completely undressed me.

Normally, I was the one who was in charge of undressing the both of us, but I had to admit I loved letting her take the lead. Her desire for me fueled mine to heights I'd never known before. I was forever learning new things about Addy, pleased when she slowly showed me another side to her, making sure to keep me on my toes. Keeping the mystery alive,

I supposed.

Slightly caressing me with her fingers, she ran her hands behind me, tugging the material of my underwear away from my body so she could slip underneath. While she teasingly lowered it, she grasped my ass, pulling me to her while she placed random kisses all over my chest. Flicking her tongue over my nipple, I choked on a ragged inhale, my mouth suddenly popping open while my eyes stared straight into the depths of hers. Tucking an errant strand of hair behind her ear, I lifted her chin and took her mouth. I wasn't gentle, but I wasn't as harsh as my body wanted me to be. I couldn't fully unleash myself on her until after she had my son. Only then would my reservations go away.

For as idiotic as it may seem to others, I held back when claiming my woman, fear always threatening that I could do some kind of damage, especially if I really gave in to the animal inside clawing to get out.

When our mouths parted, she took the opportunity to tell me something she thought I should hear. "I love you. You're a wonderful, albeit infuriating, man, but I couldn't ask for a better partner or father for our son." What she didn't say was, 'Don't let my father's words fester inside you, making you second-guess the type of man you are.'

Pushing the last piece of fabric covering my body down my thighs, her hand quickly wrapped around my cock, tightening her hold while I tried my hardest to regain my composure. The heat from her hand undid me, and if she decided to stroke me a few times I couldn't be held accountable for my body's reaction.

Threading my fingers through her hair, I yanked her head back until her throat was exposed, the pulse of her desire thumping so strongly I saw it through her creamy white skin. She continued to grip me, her other hand on the hard planes of my chest. I needed to connect with her in the worst way, so before I knew what I was doing my mouth found the soft expanse of her neck, nipping and biting her the more she drove me out of my goddamn mind.

"I want you so bad," I groaned, my hand falling from her hair to cup her plump breast. I swore every day her tits seemed to get bigger, and while I loved every change our son caused, I hated when other men noticed as well. Choosing not to mentally go down that path right then, I focused back on Addy, ravaging her mouth, nipping her lip and swirling my tongue with hers, until she exhaled and the sexiest moan fell from her mouth. I was gonna explode in two seconds if I didn't bury myself inside her soon.

Breaking our connection, both of us pleading for air, I abruptly turned her around and told her to place her hands on the edge of the vanity. Nudging her legs apart with my thigh, I nestled in between and flipped her dress up, exposing her delectable ass. I wasn't slow with any of my movements, ripping her panties from her body before she even realized what I was doing. She gasped in surprise, but I saw the satisfied smile plastered across her face in the reflection in the mirror.

Smirking, I yanked down the top of her dress, exposing the rest of her without pulling the material all the way off. Addy was overly sensitive about her body, and while she was proud of her belly, she was still self-conscious of it at the same time. As if that made a lick of sense. I loved every inch of her, but right then I didn't want to have to deal with any of her insecurities. So I let the remainder of her dress cover her stomach, all the while gazing intently at her tits in the mirror and running my hands greedily over the plump globes of her backside.

"Couldn't wait until we made it to the bed?" She laughed, backing herself into me as I pressed forward. All amusement died when she felt my rigid length teasing her swollen folds, her wetness coating me. "Oh . . ." she moaned, her head falling forward while her arms locked in position.

"No." I teased her clit with the tip of my cock. "Look at me, Addy. Look at what you do to me," I demanded, continuing to torment her body until she started to shake.

Raising her head so I could see her eyes in the mirror, I licked my lips before covering her with my body, placing my free hand on her waist and pulling her back to meet me. It was a tug of war.

Pull back.

Press forward.

Lining myself up at her entrance, I thrust inside her in one swift motion, holding her steady until I was completely sheathed. Her body shook, her knees buckling while her arms dropped from the edge of the sink. I pulled her back until she righted herself, standing tall while I slowly started to move inside her. "You okay," I asked, fearful I was hurting her in some way.

"Yes, never better," she said, turning her head to the side so she could see me. She smiled, but the curve of her lips disappeared when I hit that perfect spot inside her. "Oh, my God. Yes . . . yes . . . right there," she moaned, the sounds wafting in the air around me, pushing me to make her come as soon as possible.

Bending my knees slightly, I withdrew almost completely, and it wasn't until I heard her groan in frustration that I pushed back inside, repeating the move until I thought she was gonna kill me. "Sorry, baby, but you feel way too good, and if I fuck you like I want to, this is gonna be over before we know it." Trapping her lovely face, I bent down and smashed my mouth against hers, biting her lip in utter recklessness. A faint smell of copper filled my nose and I knew I'd made her bleed, but she didn't seem to care, licking at my mouth while she searched for my tongue, doing her best to devour me.

She tugged on the strands of my hair, eliciting a slight sting of pain, something which only spurred me further. While one arm held her close, my free one roamed over her body, kneading her tits and pinching her puckered nipples between my fingers.

I was trying to hold out, tease the both of us to make this last as long as possible, but the all too familiar pull in my balls warned me I was close to exploding. "Lean over. Place your hands back on the sink and don't move." She did as she was told and once I knew she was braced for my attack, I gripped her waist with both hands and rutted inside her like I was never gonna have her again. I knew she was close, her gasps coming quicker than before, her full lips parted while she anxiously waited to detonate.

Stroking her body with my own, I needed to tip her over the edge before my orgasm claimed me, so I ran my finger over her most sensitive area, applying a bit of pressure while I swirled my movements.

Faster and faster.

Until her body locked up tight.

Her muscles milked me to come deep inside her. As soon as her cries hit my ears, I slammed into her a few more times before falling over the edge right along with her. The jet of my release filled her so completely it dripped down her thighs, and there was nothing more fulfilling than seeing my seed painted on her skin.

Locking eyes in the reflection of the mirror, we both smiled in satisfaction. Our bodies had found a release, sure, but I reveled in the comfort that I'd been able to make her forget the unfortunate turn of events that evening for the briefest of moments.

THIRTY-SIX

Adelaide

"OF COURSE. I'LL BE RIGHT there. Okay . . . I know. Yeah, that's fine." Slowly opening my tired eyes, I managed to catch the end of Stone's phone conversation, which wasn't hard to do since he was pacing around the room. And while his voice woke me up, I was never so happy because I was gifted with the sight of his naked body, his muscles bunching in frustration the longer he engaged whoever was on the other end of the phone.

His club kept him extremely busy these days, and while I missed him when he was gone, I enjoyed and made the most of my time alone, catching up on movies I'd wanted to see or books I'd been meaning to read. Whenever we were together, we couldn't keep our hands to ourselves, so most times we ended up enjoying each other for hours on end, then lazing about until it was time for bed. And while I wasn't complaining one bit, sometimes I simply needed some solitude.

He flicked his cell closed and glanced in my direction, smiling when he saw I was awake. "Sorry, babe. Did I wake you?" he asked, rounding the bed to come and stand next to me. Reaching down, he played with the strands of my hair, tucking them behind my ear before tracing a line down the side of my cheek, his thumb running over the seam of my lips before suddenly pulling back.

"Why did you stop?" A puff of frustration barreled forth from my mouth before I could stop it. "I was kinda hoping we could . . . ya know . . . before you have to leave."

His frown was comical, mainly because Stone was so damn rugged-looking any confused expression on his face always amused me for some odd reason.

"You said some nasty stuff last night. Now all of a sudden this morning you can't just say you want to have sex?" He laughed before sitting on the edge of the mattress, the pads of his fingers tracing the length of my arm. After our tryst in the bathroom, he'd managed to take me twice more, both times colorful phrases pouring from my lips as if I'd turned off my brain-to-mouth filter. But what I'd chosen to say turned both of us on, the freedom to tell him exactly what I wanted to do to him, or what I wanted him to do to me, quite exhilarating.

"I'm still half asleep, so stop makin' fun," I pouted. "Besides, it's too early for such talk."

Leaning over me, his mouth claimed mine before he spoke again. A quick flick of his tongue enticed me, shoving away whatever sleepy cobwebs still remained. Stretching my arms above my head, the sheet inched down and exposed my breasts, my nipples already pebbled from my body's reaction.

A quick gasp from Stone had my eyes studying his face, trying my hardest to determine if he was going to stay and take me once again, or tell me he had to leave me for a bit. Before I could open my mouth to ask, however, he stood and walked toward the closet.

"While I would love to stay and . . . you know," he said, turning his head and smirking, "there's something I have to tend to at the club."

I couldn't help it, my curiosity getting the better of me. "What do you have to do?" I asked, sitting up in bed but not covering myself. Normally, I never ask him about what goes on inside his club, but for some reason I decided to. He'd assured me they were well on their way to becoming a clean, legit club. The only thing he'd ever shared with me was that they had to tie up some loose ends before everything turned around for them. And while I hated the sound of his cryptic message, I had no say whatsoever, so I held my tongue and prayed for the best.

"Nothing to worry yourself about, Addy. You know that." His tone had instantly changed from playful to serious. I knew he hated that he couldn't share certain aspects of his life with me, but I also knew he did it to ensure my safety. The only good thing was that those days were numbered. Once the Knights were riding on the right side of the law, there would no longer be a need for him to hide things from me, something I was sure would be a huge relief for both of us.

Tossing the covers aside, I placed my feet on the ground and very slowly stood up. My belly was growing more and more each day, making me extremely happy but also very uncomfortable. My poor bladder took the brunt of it, threatening to explode every half hour. Okay, maybe not that often, but it sure felt like it.

Before I disappeared inside the bathroom, he halted my steps with a firm grasp on my waist, his body pressed against my back. "I wish I could stay in this room with you forever," he whispered, his warm breath fanning across the side of my face before he leaned down and kissed my shoulder. "But I have to go."

"I know," I breathlessly replied, my body pressed tightly against his. It was the sweetest torture. I loved the feel of him, his skin warming my own, but I knew our shared moment was fleeting. This time, at least. I had nothing planned for the day, so as soon as he returned home he was all mine, and I was sure I could convince him to retreat to this very room until the sun rose the next day.

Kissing my temple, he stepped back and retreated into his closet to find some clothes. Once he was fully dressed, he headed toward the bathroom to brush his teeth. I was already inside, relieving my bladder. Shortly later I joined him at the sink, washing my hands and reaching for my toothbrush, We both smiled and went about our mundane task, and all the while I couldn't help but to think that I was the luckiest woman in the world.

I couldn't explain my contentment, other than to say it was times like this that a serene mood wrapped around me and held me tightly. Standing close to each other, the only sound coming from the bristles cleaning our teeth, was peaceful. If that made any sense. Outside our house, the world was frenzied—my own body was chaotic at times—but here, tucked inside our spacious bathroom, I found peace. If only for a few short moments.

———— ◆ ————

MY LAST ROUND OF TREATMENT was completed three weeks prior, and today was the day I found out if all I'd gone through had worked . . . or not. I'd chosen to keep my upcoming appointment a secret from Stone because I didn't know what I would do if I had to handle my own emotions on top of his if Dr. Weber delivered news I didn't want to hear.

I warred back and forth with needing Stone's strength if the news was bad and shielding him from the devastation if my body was still riddled with the destructive disease. Realizing he would be upset with me for not including him, whether the news was good or bad, I decided I would deal with one thing at a time.

Our growing child was my number one concern. I would make him refocus on our son, instead of being upset with me for trying to protect him from the deliverance of the diagnosis.

I had a few hours before I had to meet with Dr. Weber, so I took full advantage of the time to do some shopping for the nursery. Thankfully, our home had three bedrooms, one of which we turned into the baby's room. Stone had already constructed the crib, working tirelessly until the wee hours of the morning to make sure he'd finished it on time. His time. I reminded him we still had a couple weeks, but he insisted on completing it as soon as possible. At one point, he got so frustrated with the damn thing he called in Marek to help him. Two tough, grown men cursing and pounding away on defenseless pieces of wood was quite the amusing sight.

Sully had accompanied her husband, and while our men took out their frustrations on the crib they were trying to assemble, we lounged in front of the television, catching up on each other's lives while partly paying attention to the cheesy reality show that was on.

Throwing a light jacket over my tank top, I grabbed my keys from the side table and walked outside, inhaling the fresh air and allowing myself to take those few precious moments to really appreciate the gift of another day.

Once inside my car, I called Stone to let him know I was running a few errands but would be back at the house before he returned. There was a back and forth between us I knew was going to happen, mainly because he wanted to send one of the men over to go with me, to keep me safe, but I reminded him I was okay by myself. Long bouts of silence passed between us before he finally relented, but only after I'd agreed to call him to check in every hour. It was a small compromise, so I agreed.

The drive to town was relaxing. I enjoyed the hustle and bustle of the people going about their daily routines, running their own errands, laughing and enjoying the beautiful summer day.

California was ungodly hot sometimes, but today was perfect. A slight breeze carried the promise of better days, the sun shining on all of us trudging through yet another day of life. Thankfully.

Once I'd completed all my errands, I drove the short distance to the hospital, preparing to meet with Dr. Weber about my diagnosis. My heart was in my throat waiting for him to walk through his office door. A slight panic rushed through me when I saw the handle turn, sweat breaking out along my hairline when he stepped into the room.

If his tight smile was any indication, I knew I should prepare myself for the worst.

THIRTY-SEVEN

Stone

IT'D BEEN MY DUMBASS IDEA to bring up the topic of having a couple men accompany Jagger to his next fight, and apparently it had blown back in my face. Marek had told me the prospect's next bout was fast approaching and he wanted me and Tripp to attend, reporting back anything we deemed unusual or of concern.

I tried to talk my way out of it, but it was part of club business so Marek wanted me to take an active role in our other source of income. Jagger brought in a pretty penny for us, winning every fight, no matter the size of his opponent. None of these fights were legal, which meant there were no rules. No consequences in case someone was seriously injured. But all the fighters knew the potential risks they faced as soon as they stepped into the ring.

Thankfully, Jagger was truly gifted, his speed and agility enhanced under my guidance and tutelage. Our sparring sessions, although fewer in the past couple months, were very beneficial for him. He was quick. I had a lot on my mind as of late, and the prospect took full advantage, striking when he knew I wasn't giving our sessions my full attention. But it was all good. He was learning how to hone in on his opponent's weaknesses, whether it be physical or mental.

"Stone, you with us?" Marek shouted, pounding the table to garner my attention. I'd been so lost inside my own head I missed the rest of what he'd said.

"Sorry. What?" I asked, leaning back in my chair while running my hands over my face in irritation.

"We keepin' your ass from somethin'?" Trigger inquired, glaring at me from across the table, his arms folded tightly across his chest. The man was probably my biggest enemy these days, although he reduced the amount of times he gave me shit for messing with his niece. Every day he seemed to further accept the idea of Addy and me, our child the solidification needed for him to know I wasn't going anywhere. But it was times like this when he chose to take advantage of his dislike for me. I didn't care, though, because all I had to do was say something, which in turn pissed him off more.

"Yeah . . . your niece," I fired back, leering back at him with equal intensity.

Sucking air through his teeth, he told me to go fuck myself before turning his attention back to the leader of our group. I grinned over my brief moment of victory.

Trigger and I loved to push each other's buttons, but I just wasn't in the mood for his antics right then.

Turning to face Marek, I nodded to indicate I was focused on the conversation once more.

"As I was sayin, Zip finally has some info on Yanez. Something I think we can use against him." Motioning toward the young member, he waved his hand to give him the floor.

"Last night, I finally caught a meeting between Yanez and Psych. I have no idea what they were talking about, but I managed to snap off a few incriminating pictures," he said, tossing a few of the aforementioned photos on the table for us to see. "There's even one in there where they're exchanging a black duffel bag for an envelope of what I can only assume is money."

When the pictures finally made their way into Marek's hands, he smirked, realizing he finally had the evidence he needed to meet with Rafael Carrillo about the fate of the cartel's right-hand man. Marek knew Carrillo would kill Yanez after finding out the scumbag went behind his boss's back and continued to deal with the Reapers.

It would come down to convincing Carrillo to allow Marek to have the privilege of snatching the man's life, an argument I think my friend would win considering Carrillo knew what had happened to Sully.

A pregnant pause shrouded the room, all the men looking back and forth at one another, waiting for someone to speak and break the growing tension.

Frustrated with the lack of communication, something which was dragging out our meeting and therefore keeping me from getting home to my woman, I blew out a breath and leaned forward in my chair. "So, what's the next move, Marek?"

Locking eyes with me, he said, "You and I set up a meet with Carrillo. On the side. Away from Yanez. It's gonna be difficult, but I think we can arrange something soon."

Damn it! Something else I didn't want to do, but I knew I had to help my friend seek the revenge he needed.

Tapping my finger on one of the many pictures of Psych and Yanez, I asked a question I knew grated on Marek's mind every single day. "You heard anything from Psych . . . or his club? I think it's weird they haven't tried to . . . you know." My words drifted off, not really wanting to complete the sentence.

All the muscles in his body locked up tight, his fear and rage pouring out of him for all of us to witness. "I know." He nodded. "And no. We've been watchin', but nothing. I was shocked when Zip was able to capture these pics of Psych because the man has been virtually missing for the past few months." Running his hands through his dark hair, he straightened himself before finishing his thoughts on the subject. "I've been waiting for him to come for her, but he stays locked away in the shadows. I know damn well he's planning to attack, I just don't know when."

"Then why don't we just attack them again and take him out?" Ryder offered, slapping his hand against the solid wood of our meeting table.

"Because we've been watchin' their club and Psych is rarely there. I don't care about the rest of them. All I need to do is take out the head of that fucking club, then all will be quiet."

"Yeah, but what about Rabid? Psych's VP?" Ryder kept on pushing the topic and I saw what it was doing to Marek, his face scrunching in irritation, although everything Ryder was asking was legit.

"What about him?!" Marek yelled. "The man's not gonna do anything once his prez is dead. He doesn't have the balls to come after us. That much I know for sure."

He was right. Rabid was definitely a follower, not someone we had to worry about seeking vengeance for the death of his leader. If you could even call Psych that.

Holding his hands up in surrender, Ryder cocked a brow and tilted his head, letting Marek know he meant no harm with his questions. A simple nod from his prez let him know everything was good between them.

"Anything else we need to talk about?" Marek asked the group, looking from one man to the next. The table was full, everyone in attendance and eagerly waiting to hear what business had to be dealt with next. Fortunately, we were all on the same page when it came to the club, all of us realizing what had to be done in order to solidify our futures.

Just when I thought our meeting was over, Tripp spoke up, breaking the silence dancing around the room.

"I wanted to let you guys know that I'll be heading out in a few days. I'm fully recovered now, and well . . . there's no more need to be shacked up here any longer." His eyes danced with appreciation toward every one of his brothers, including myself. Even though I hated the relationship between him and Addy, I knew he would never overstep his bounds where she was concerned. He viewed her like a sister, only goading me for a reaction when he was in need of some amusement.

Marek was the first to speak, beating us all to the punch. "Actually, Tripp, I'm gonna need you to stick around a bit longer. If you don't mind." Although it appeared as if our leader was asking, he wasn't. He needed the nomad to stay put, for a reason he was about to divulge. "With everything else we need to take care of, I need someone to oversee Flings as well as the new club we have opening in a couple weeks. Pussy on tap, brother. Nuthin' better, right?"

I knew what my friend was doing. He was enticing Tripp to stay with the mere mention of naked broads. Little did he know the nomad needed no such allure. He would stay simply because his president needed him to—nothing more, nothing less. I saw the far-off look in Tripp's gaze when he thought no one was watching. He wanted to stay with us, but didn't want to wear out his welcome. I was sure being a nomad was lonely, and his time with us had to bring out his need for brotherhood more than usual.

Tripp's head jerked upward. "Whatever you need, Prez," was his simple answer.

THIRTY-EIGHT

Adelaide

I FELT LIKE I WAS experiencing déjà vu, sitting across from Dr. Weber in his office. His attention was focused on whatever he was reading on his computer, glancing in my direction every few seconds. Why? I had no idea, but I had an awful feeling he was going to tell me something I didn't want to hear.

Standing, he rounded his desk and came to sit next to me, much like he'd done when he'd initially delivered the bad news. My stomach dropped, fear coursing through me and preparing me for the next few minutes of my life.

It was funny how quickly regrets flashed in front of me, realizing I was about to be told something awful. Again. I wished right then that I hadn't fought so hard against being with Stone, that I'd spent more time with my father, that I'd developed more friendships with the people I worked with, that I'd traveled more.

The list could go on and on if I let it.

Grasping my hand in his, Dr. Weber pulled my full attention before he parted his lips to speak. "Addy, your CA-125 bloodwork test came back a little higher than I would have liked to see after your rounds of treatment. While your levels are lower than before, I don't think you're out of the woods yet."

His words became muffled the more he spoke, as I had no idea what CA-125 meant, and honestly I didn't really have enough energy to care. I knew right then I'd made the wrong decision by not telling Stone about the appointment, needing his support more than ever. The air surrounding me suddenly became too thick, my heart threatening to burst out of my chest the more Dr. Weber continued to talk. Orbs of light clouded my vision, and if I hadn't known any better, I feared I was about to pass out. Pulling my hand away from Dr. Weber, I gripped the arms of my chair, steadying myself while I tried my best to calm down. Taking slow and steady breaths until everything eventually came back into focus.

"... and that's why we'll wait until you have the baby before taking the biopsies."

His words shoved me back into the reality of our conversation, even though I'd missed the majority of what he'd just said.

"I'm sorry, what?" Leaning closer, I furrowed my brow, urging him to repeat himself.

"I know this is a lot for you to process, Adelaide, but you need to start thinking about what you want to do once your son is born." Staring at the still-confused look on my face, he took a breath before continuing. "We are going to schedule an appointment after the birth, where I will take a biopsy of both of your ovaries, just to be sure. If you still have the cancer, like I suspect you do, we'll discuss future treatment options. We can be more aggressive after you give birth, so at least we won't have to worry about your baby's health on top of yours. The only thing is that you won't be able to breastfeed. Well, it's not highly recommended, at least, not while you're undergoing treatment." Patting my hand, he finished with, "The good news is that your levels are lower than before, meaning you are not any worse off than you were before you started receiving chemo." A small smile tipped his lips, trying his best to be positive during a meeting which was anything but.

Tears streamed down my face before I even knew what was happening, our conversation suddenly becoming too much to handle on my own. Dr. Weber passed me a box of tissues before patting my hand once more and walking around his desk to sit in his chair.

"Is there someone I can call for you? Stone, perhaps?" His question hit a nerve with me, only because I'd foolishly hidden this appointment from him. Now, not only did I have to process everything the good doctor told me, but I had to relive it again once I told Stone everything.

"No, I'm okay. It's just . . . I didn't expect to get this kind of news, you know? I was hoping to leave here with a weight lifted off my shoulders."

"While it's not the news either of us was expecting, it's not the worst either. Please focus on that fact while we forge ahead with what we're going to do in the upcoming future." His kind eyes tried to calm me, but he wasn't the one with cancer destroying him from the inside.

Nodding, I withdrew another tissue from the box before placing it back on his desk. Taking another minute to compose myself, I finally stood and exhaled a lungful of air. "Thank you, Dr. Weber. I'll be in touch in a few days to discuss more of this in detail. I just need some time."

"I understand." Rising, he walked me to the door, his hand resting on my back and offering me his silent support. "Please call me anytime, day or night, if you need to talk. I'm always here for you, Adelaide." His kind words made me cry again, wiping away the tears as I exited his office.

My head hung low while I walked down the hallway toward the elevators. The last thing I wanted to do was make eye contact with anyone, prompting people to ask me if I was okay. The truth was . . . I wasn't.

Rounding a small corner to reach the bank of elevators, my head still down, I bumped into a large frame, my hands coming up to instantly brace myself.

"Addy," a deep voice called out. It was mere seconds before I realized who it was.

My father.

"Dad? What are you doing here?" He ignored my question, instead focusing on my red, puffy eyes and the tears still dancing down my cheeks.

"What's wrong, honey? Is the baby okay?" His worried tone forced me to answer.

"No, nothing is wrong with your grandson," I promised, trying my best to smile, but the gesture was moot. My lips simply wouldn't turn up, my sadness forcing them into more of a frown than anything.

Grabbing my hand, he pulled me toward the elevator, pushing the button before I could protest. Neither of us spoke another word as my father led me from the hospital and toward the parking garage.

"You're coming with me, so don't argue. I know something's wrong and if you won't tell me here, you will tell me when we get to my house." I remained silent, realizing I desperately needed to speak with him. Not only about the blowup that happened between him and Stone when we went to visit, but about the cancer as well.

I'd spoken to my father a few times since the huge argument, but all our conversations were short and curt. Our love for each other was strong, and I knew we would resolve our issues in time. I guessed my unfortunate turn of events was going to be the deciding factor to ending the uneasiness between us once and for all. Once I told him I was sick, he was going to forget about everything else, realizing it simply wasn't important. The last thing I wanted to do was worry him, however, so the entire ride to his house I kept quiet while deciding the best way to break the news.

His devastation was going to push the reality of my situation to the forefront, and there would be no chance of escape after the words fell from my lips.

———◆———

TWO HOURS AND MANY TEARS later, my father and I had finally finished discussing my cancer, his fears, and my hopes for what the future held. He wasn't an overly emotional man, but when it came to his family he didn't care who saw the cracks in his demeanor. Whether he was freaking out and threatening the father of my unborn child, or sobbing like a baby at the thought of losing his daughter to the very same disease which claimed his wife, he laid everything out on the table.

Brian Reins was a man I would forever look up to, seek his approval and look to for guidance while I threaded through this journey I called life.

Since my car was still in the parking garage at the hospital, my father gave me a ride to pick it up. I had to admit, being forced to finally let him in on the one thing I'd kept him shielded from was a huge weight lifted. The secrecy had been killing me, even though I was doing what I thought was best. Turned out, telling him helped me more than I could have ever imagined.

Once we'd arrived, he walked me to the driver's side, pulled me close, and gave me an extra-long hug, his love wrapping around me to keep me safe.

After he left, I sat in my car for a bit before I turned the engine over, finally checking my phone only to see that I had eight missed calls from Stone. Slapping my hand to my forehead, I'd totally blanked on calling him over the last few hours. He was probably worried sick something had happened to me.

He answered on the second ring, shouting into the phone so quick I hardly made out anything he'd said.

"Addy! What the hell is wrong with you? Are you okay? Where are you?" He fired question after question at me, never once taking a breath to allow me to answer. His ramblings went on for another twenty seconds, and even though he would have normally irritated me with his over-protectiveness, for some reason I found his paranoia comforting.

I needed to be reminded that I had someone who cared for me. Someone who loved me so much he was worried all the time whenever he wasn't with me. Had I not been sick or pregnant, I would have never tolerated such behavior, but I completely understood it right then.

Finally, after he finished his interrogation of sorts, a brief moment of silence fell between us, the only time I was going to get to speak.

"I'm sorry I haven't called you, but I had a quick meeting with Dr. Weber then I ran into my father, which is where I've been for the past couple hours."

Not wasting one more precious second he asked, "Where are you now? Are you heading home?"

"Yes."

"I'll meet you there. And Addy?"

"Yeah?"

"Go straight home. We need to talk."

Oh, God. Now I know why men never liked to hear those four words. That particular phrase had my mind running wild, all sorts of scenarios running through my already muddled mind. It wasn't until I pulled up in front of our house and saw him standing on the porch that I began to calm down. Seeing his intensity when I walked closer pricked my awareness that whatever he wanted to talk to me about was serious.

And I had a feeling it had nothing at all to do with what I'd been hiding from him all day.

THIRTY-NINE

Stone

FINALLY SEEING THE ONE PERSON I wanted to lay eyes on all day long made me both furious and relieved. How many times had I asked her to check in with me when she was out of my sight? I knew I should have never let her flit about town by herself. Well, lesson learned. It was never gonna happen again.

I knew my reaction was because I'd been scared, even more so after Marek declared a lockdown at the club. Something popped off with the Reapers and until we figured out just what that was, we were to bring everyone to the clubhouse where they would all be safe.

Only thing was I hadn't been able to get in touch with Addy.

Walking down to meet her in the driveway, I latched on to her arm and helped her up the steps, guiding her through the door and toward the stairs so she could pack a few things.

"What are you doing?" she asked as I hurriedly ushered her up the staircase and toward our bedroom. "Stone, stop pushing me and tell me what's going on." She suddenly stopped walking, turned to face me, and wouldn't budge unless I told her what she wanted to hear.

No use beating around the bush.

"There's a lockdown. I need you to grab some things, because you'll be staying at the clubhouse for a couple days." Turning her back around, I made sure she walked the rest of the way down the hallway, gently shoving her inside our room and toward the closet.

"I don't understand," she said, all while she did as she was told and packed some clothes from both our dressers. Stopping off in the bathroom, she swiped a few necessities into her toiletry bag, coming to stand in front of me when she was finally finished.

Surprisingly, the whole event only took her ten minutes.

"I can't explain everything. All you need to know is that we need to leave. Now," I urged, taking the bag from her and leading her from the bedroom.

Our entire ride to the compound was in silence. I detected from her body language there was something amiss between the two of us. She was hiding something from me, but then again, so was I. Although my secret had to do with the club and was essentially none of her concern. I didn't need her worrying about me any more than I was sure she already did.

She rarely asked me about any of the goings-on inside my club, but I saw the curiosity in her eyes whenever I gave her a blanket statement of having business to attend to. Hopefully soon, though, I would be able to give her all the information she wanted. Once we were done with the Reapers altogether.

Which meant after we wiped out Psych and anyone else we felt was a threat. Initially, we were going to allow the severing between the cartel and the Reapers take its toll and wait until our rival club disintegrated amongst themselves. But now with the news that Yanez was going behind Carrillo's back, we knew that option was no longer viable.

We had to obtain the go-ahead to take out Yanez, a permission Marek was desperately waiting for, then take out Psych, disposing of him once and for all. There was no concern whatsoever of Rabid, Psych's VP, taking over simply because the man wasn't that smart. Always been a follower. Never a leader.

After the iron gates opened for us, I drove forward and found my parking space. The lot was practically full, men milling around with weapons in their hands, and on their hips. It was the last image I wanted Addy to have, but there was nothing I could do.

Walking around to her side of the truck, I opened her door before she had the opportunity to do so and escorted her from the vehicle, grabbing her bags from the backseat before guiding her toward the entrance to the clubhouse.

"Are you hungry? You want me to grab you something from the kitchen before you get settled in?"

Shaking her head, she walked ahead of me toward the room which was reserved specifically for me. Most of the men, minus the prospects, had a designated room inside the clubhouse, which made times like this a bit more comfortable. Each family could set up camp in their own area;

even though it might be a tight fit, it was hopefully only going to be for a few days.

Sitting on the edge of my bed, Addy stared up at me, watching every move I made before parting her lips to speak. "Stone, why can't you tell me what's going on?"

"Because it's not your concern."

"Not my concern?" Her voice rose in octave. "Are you kidding me? You whisk me away from our house as soon as I get home and tell me I have to stay here for a few days. But you won't tell me why?" She rose from the bed and started unpacking our things, mumbling to herself as she did so.

I should have been concerned with finding out if Marek knew anything more about the threat to our club, but all I could do was watch every movement Addy made. I couldn't help it; I was mesmerized by the woman. Her long hair fell toward her face when she bent over, so she tucked the errant strands behind her ear so she could finish what she was doing. She was wearing one of her stretchy jersey dresses, her tits practically spilling over the top they were so plump. When she bent over again, I caught a peek of her white cotton panties. Gone were the thongs she used to wear, explaining they were much too uncomfortable the bigger she got, but I had no complaints. While she grumbled about her underwear hardly fitting over her ass, I loved the sight of her cheeks protruding beyond the confines of the soft material.

Her annoyances became my pleasure.

Striding up behind her, I pushed her hair to the side and whispered in her ear. "Don't you dare bend over in front of anyone else, because I can see your panties." The rasp in my voice made her breath hitch. Or was it because my cock was hard and pressed against the seam of her ass?

"Stop trying to distract me," she mumbled, a slight trace of humor in her voice when she responded. Once she finished unpacking our clothes and toiletries, she sat back on the edge of the bed, reaching for my hand to come and sit beside her. There was no hesitation on my part, parking my ass on the bed next to her right away.

Staring into her eyes for the briefest of moments, I knew she wanted to divulge something but was holding back. "What are you not telling me?" I prompted, hoping she wasn't gonna procrastinate before telling me whatever was on her mind.

She fidgeted next to me, her uneasiness blanketing her and giving everything away. Well, almost everything.

"I . . . I went to see Dr. Weber today."

"Did you have an appointment?"

"Yes." She bit her bottom lip in nervousness before breaking eye contact.

"Look at me," I demanded, turning her head when she refused. "Why didn't you tell me about this appointment? What were you meeting with him for?"

Silence.

We stared at each other for what felt like forever, but in reality it was only seconds. Five very long seconds, to be precise.

Just when I thought she wasn't gonna say anything, she clutched the hem of her grey dress and bunched the material in her hands. "I met with him so he could give me the results. You know, to see if the treatments worked or not."

A lone tear slipped from her eye and slid down her cheek. My heart practically burst out of my chest waiting for her to speak the words I knew I never wanted to hear.

My tone belied what I was feeling inside. "And?"

"He said the cancer is still there, although it's not as prevalent as before. But he won't know more until he takes a biopsy.

"And when is he doing this?"

"After I have the baby." Her answers were short and to the point, something which unnerved me for some reason. Maybe it was because she'd had time to process everything, whereas I was just hearing all of this for the very first time—a trend with her which I hated immensely.

Rising from the bed, I paced in front of her for a few minutes, digesting everything she'd told me. I tried to find the right words to comfort her, but I failed, instead allowing my worry to cloak me like some kind of shield. A mask of paranoia I'd become defenseless against.

Halting my steps, I faced her when I asked, "You said you ran into your father, right?" She quickly nodded. "Did you finally tell him? About the cancer?" She nodded again, and for some reason I found comfort in her answer. At least someone else knew and could share my fear, even if that same person despised me.

I went back to pacing but was interrupted when Addy rose to her feet and walked toward me, pushing herself against me until my arms wrapped around her. She was trying to ease my trepidation with her body . . . and it worked. For the most part.

"I'll be okay," she whispered, cradling herself into the crux of my arms. "I promise."

I knew she couldn't promise me any such thing, but I chose to believe her.

What other choice did I have?

FORTY

Adelaide

TENSION WAS HIGH BETWEEN EVERYONE inside the clubhouse. The women did their part in trying to keep everyone calm, cooking and serving the men and children as best they could. To do their part, the men tried their best to keep all talk of business contained behind Chambers, but the frustrations of the members spilled over into the common area, their offhanded comments heard by not only myself but some of the other women as well.

There was talk of retaliation against the KC, Ryder drunkenly spilling some of the secrets the more he drank. I wanted so desperately to know what was going on, but based on the bits of information I'd already heard, I decided I wanted to remain in the dark when it came to the threat against us.

I had too many things to worry about as it was; I certainly didn't need to add any more to my list.

Eyeing Tripp standing in the corner near the kitchen, I walked toward him with purpose, reaching him before he even saw me coming. My abrupt presence startled him but he quickly recovered, leaning forward and placing a quick kiss on my cheek.

"Adelaide, so nice to see you again. How are you feeling?" he asked, glancing down at my protruding belly.

"As good as can be expected," I answered, giving him a genuine smile.

"How are *you* feeling?" I asked in return, moving out of the way of racing children so I didn't get run over.

"I'm back to normal, I suppose. In fact, I was gonna take off in a few days, but Marek asked me to stay on and oversee the two clubs." A remote look drifted over his face for a brief moment. Before I could even think to question it, though, it was gone.

"Well, I'm glad to hear you'll be sticking around. I think I'd miss you," I teased, reaching out to touch his shoulder. There was something about Tripp which drew me to him, my protective side emerging whenever he was near. Maybe it was simply the caregiver part of me recognizing something was amiss in his life, offering my support even when he hadn't asked for it.

"I won't miss this," an all too familiar voice rumbled from behind me, grabbing my waist and pulling me into him so my back rested against his chest. "You need to find a woman of your own, Tripp, and stop hittin' on mine."

The only part of Stone I could reach from my position was his leg, so I smacked his thigh in annoyance. "Knock it off. He's not hitting on me. Not at all. Actually, I'm the one who approached him, if you must know."

Stone's grip on me tightened slightly, his irritation prominent in the way he held onto me.

"Yeah? And why's that?"

"I came over to tell him that someone better put Ryder to bed, because he keeps mumbling things I'm positive shouldn't be heard by anyone other than the men. Things I'm sure were said in private."

Both Stone and Tripp cursed at the same time, walking away from me to wrangle up Ryder and lock him away inside his room before he stirred up more shit.

Fortunately, the rest of the evening was quite uneventful. Everyone had retired to their respective rooms, the common area becoming deserted well before midnight. There were only a few men milling about, walking in and out of Chambers, whispering their business away from the rest of us.

The whole scene was quite surreal. I'd never been around when there was a lockdown, only ever hearing bits and pieces from my uncle when I'd overheard him talking to one of the other members. I knew enough not to inquire, however, because it had never had anything to do with me before. But everything was different now, ever since I'd become officially involved with Stone.

While I couldn't be happier that I was finally with the man I was meant for, my reservations barreled forth. Times like this were exactly why I'd denied him for so long. There was no going back, though, so I kept my chin up and followed his instructions, something which was hard for me to do without complaint.

I was just about to hop in the shower for a quick rinse before bed when Stone walked into the room, his disheveled hair quite telling of the day he'd had so far. First, he'd been consumed with the goings-on here, with his club, and then I broke the news that I still had cancer. Even after all the treatments I'd endured. And now, he was still dealing with a possible threat toward everyone he cared about.

I wanted to do something for him, not wanting to wallow in self-pity about my situation, instead focusing that energy onto him. If he felt better, I would feel better.

"Wanna take a shower with me?" I coaxed, lifting the hem of my dress up my body and over my head, standing before him in my white cotton bra and panties.

Briskly walking toward me, he guided me toward the bathroom before his response left his lips. "Yes." Kicking off his shoes and socks, he unbuckled his belt and unzipped his jeans, pushing them down his muscular thighs and taking his boxer briefs right along with them. The last thing to go was his shirt, tossed on the floor at his feet with the rest of his discarded clothes.

A naked Stone was the most beautiful, erotic sight I'd ever been gifted with. The toned, rippled muscles of his torso called for my touch. The need to run my fingertips over his sculpted chest bombarded me each time I was given the opportunity. I stood there staring at him as if it were the first time I'd ever seen him naked.

"Are we jumping in this shower, or do you want to stare at me a little while longer?" He laughed, licking his lips as he leaned his hip against the sink. Crossing his arms over his chest only spurred my incessant desire to visually devour him that much more.

"Give me a minute." I chuckled, moving forward and running my hands down his chest, pulling at his arms until they fell at his sides. I'd touched him hundreds of times before, but for some reason this time was different. Having no idea if the bad news I'd received earlier had any bearing, I pushed all thoughts of my sickness aside and committed every line and plane of his body to memory, needing to focus on him instead of the persistent cancer inside me.

My fingers trailed down the rest of his body, settling on his defined abdominal muscles, sinking lower still until his thickness filled my hand. When he inhaled quickly, I knew he was enthralled with my fascination, jerking his hips forward until I grasped him tighter.

"Addy . . ." he moaned, threading his fingers through my long hair, caressing my scalp with a lazy massage.

"Do you like that?" I asked, knowing damn well what his answer would be. Releasing him, I traced the rest of his warm skin with the tips of my fingers, unintentionally tickling him as I skated around the back of his body. Looking deep into his dark, expressive eyes, I pulled him closer, leaning up and capturing his mouth before he could react.

His tongue pressed into my mouth, drawing out my lust until he'd essentially held me captive with his kiss. Nipping at my bottom lip, he broke our connection for the briefest of moments, pulling back so he could peer into my eyes. "I would have never guessed you'd be in the mood for this," he said, gesturing back and forth between us. "What's gotten into you?"

"Well . . . I'm kinda hoping you'll be the one 'getting into me.'"

His gravelly laugh made me smile.

"As you wish, but let's get in the shower first. That way, I can clean you right after I dirty you all up." The gleam in his eyes sealed the deal.

A half hour later, we snuggled under the covers and tried our best to get some much needed sleep.

Even though we were essentially trapped inside the clubhouse, a very real threat to the livelihood of all the members and their families, there was no place on Earth I would rather be than wrapped in Stone's arms.

EPILOGUE

Stone

ANOTHER MONTH PASSED.

Another month of silence on the part of our greatest enemy.

Psych still had not made a move to come and collect his daughter, Marek's wife. He was either planning some kind of elaborate attack or he had more sense than any of us gave him credit for, realizing we would kill him on sight. If I was gonna go with either scenario, though, it would be the first one. Unfortunately.

Psych Brooks was one crazy motherfucker, and I had no doubt he'd been lying low the entire time because he was biding his time until he found what he believed to be his prime opportunity. But he'd better hurry if he wanted a chance for retaliation; otherwise, we were gonna snuff him out of existence as soon as we seized the chance.

The president of the Savage Reapers had to die, and the sooner Marek was able to accomplish it, the better. He was completely focused on disposing of Rico Yanez because of what he'd done to Sully, however. Although, if my opinion counted for anything, I believed her father to be a more satisfying prize to eliminate, solely based on the few things my friend had revealed to me. I was aware that Psych had raped his own daughter. Repeatedly. As well as beating her whenever he saw fit. The man had also handed his only child over to the likes of that despicable bastard Vex, which in and of itself was more than enough to snatch his life.

But Marek viewed the situation differently. He wanted to kill Yanez. Then, and only then, could he redirect the rest of his rage on Psych Brooks, extinguishing his very existence so he no longer breathed the same air as the rest of us.

Marek had successfully set up a meeting with Carrillo a while back, taking me along for both physical and emotional support, although he would deny it if asked. While Carrillo was visibly angry with the evidence we showed him of his right-hand man clearly still engaged with the Reapers, it wasn't enough in his eyes to sign his death warrant. Instead, the head of the cartel assured us he would do his own investigating, promising to hand over what was left of him after he exacted his own punishment, assuring Marek that Yanez would still be breathing when he got his hands on him. It was the best deal we could get, so we agreed. Honestly, we really didn't have much of a say in what happened to Yanez, so the fact Carrillo offered any part of the soulless fucker to us was a win.

Addy's belly continued to grow, and since she was two weeks past her due date, she was beyond frustrated that our son decided to stay nestled inside her, refusing to come out and greet the world. I did as much for her as I could, including rubbing her feet and back when I saw the slightest look of discomfort slide across her lovely face. I knew her so well I could read her like an open book, something for which she was both grateful for and annoyed by. It meant she couldn't hide anything from me anymore, as I paid extra-close attention to her, even when she wasn't aware.

We'd gone over some names, but we still hadn't decided which one to go with. She said she wanted to wait and see him first, that once she held him in her arms she would know the perfect name for him.

Addy had set up an appointment with Dr. Weber, one I was included in because I had some questions about what was going to happen with her treatment going forward. The good doctor described the tests he'd performed, and that Addy's condition was better than it had been. However, he believed the cancer was still present, and he was going to take a biopsy of her ovaries after the birth of our son. Just as Addy had told me earlier. But it was different, more affirming, hearing it directly from the horse's mouth, so to speak.

All things considered, life was good. Her dad still didn't want anything to do with me, but I could only hope in time, once I'd proved I could take care of his daughter and grandson without issue, he would come around and at least acknowledge me as a permanent fixture in their lives.

———•———

MY CELL VIBRATED ON TOP of the table, interrupting Marek as he spoke about our latest issues. Normally, we weren't allowed to bring our phones into Chambers, as they were simply a distraction. However, since

Addy's due date had come and gone, I needed for her to be able to reach me at any time.

Glancing at my screen, I saw it was indeed my woman and, for some reason, I looked across the table and caught Trigger's attention with the widening of my eyes. I'd called Addy before we came into the room, telling her to only call me if it was an emergency; otherwise, I would call her whenever our meeting ended. I knew she wouldn't take that lightly, so the fact her beautiful face was lighting up my phone, I knew something had happened.

Flicking the phone open, I answered quickly. "Hello? Is it time?" An ear-splitting grin appeared on my face at her confirmation.

Marek slapped my forearm and said, "Well, men, looks like we're gonna postpone business." I heard him speak, but I was so focused on the strain in Addy's voice I never responded, instead rising from the table and hurrying outside toward my bike. I swore I broke every traffic rule there was trying to get to her as fast as possible.

Once I arrived, I rushed toward the reception area of the hospital, hurriedly asking the woman for Addy's room number. I raced toward the bank of elevators down the nearby hallway, praying the entire time for her safety as well as for our son's. I pounded continuously on the floor button, cursing out loud because it took so damn long for the doors to close. Thankfully, I was alone, or I would have probably scared someone. So many thoughts invaded my brain. Would my son be healthy? Would Addy be okay during the delivery, and after? I flip-flopped from smiling wide to chewing on my lip in nervousness. Fear and elation battled within me. Too bad the warring emotions would stay with me until I knew for sure that both mother and baby would be fine.

Practically tripping into her room, I saw Addy lying in the hospital bed, already hooked up to a monitor. Sully was at her side, holding her hand and talking her through the pain. The two women had been doing some last minute baby shopping when I got the call. I had quickly learned her contractions were only five minutes apart, a fact I found unbelievable since Addy had just called me not twenty minutes prior. Apparently, she'd been experiencing them for a few hours, but failed to mention anything.

Approaching her bed, I reached for her other hand and leaned down to kiss her. "Why didn't you call me when you first started getting them?"

"Because I wasn't sure if they were real or Braxton Hicks contractions." She pushed a breath of air from her mouth. "I didn't want to bother you if it was nothing," she confessed.

"Bother me?" I asked incredulously. Shaking my head, I gave her a stern look before leaning over to kiss her again. "I should be upset with you, but all I want is to help you through this."

Sully took that as her cue to give us some privacy, rising from her seat and leaning down to give her friend a quick hug. "I'm gonna wait for Cole in the waiting room. No doubt he's on his way with the other guys." She smiled at me before walking around the bed and heading toward the door.

I'd thought we would get some time alone, but it wasn't to be. If Dr. Weber wasn't paying Addy a visit, we were talking to nurses, several who had come and gone for the day, changing shifts. Addy had been in labor for hours on end with no relief in sight, until finally Dr. Weber said she was close to ten centimeters dilated and it was gonna be time for her to start pushing soon.

For some odd reason, she decided not to have an epidural, a decision she was definitely regretting. She'd tried to convince Dr. Weber to give her one, but he'd informed her that her window of opportunity had closed. If I could have given her my condition, I would have. In a heartbeat. To witness someone I love writhe around in pain, to realize there wasn't a damn thing I could do about it, tore at me. It destroyed me. But I couldn't focus on myself, I had to give her my strength, offer her something else to focus on beside the agony tearing through her.

"I don't think I can take much more of this," Addy complained, her face scrunching in a grimace when the next contraction hit. Clasping my hand tightly, she held her breath and shook her head back and forth.

"You have to breathe." I stroked the top of her hand. "Breathe through the pain," I said, thinking I was helping to remind her of what she needed to do. Once the pain had passed, she loosened her grip, turned her head to look at me, and told me just what she thought of my suggestion.

"Easy for you to say. You've never felt pain a day in your life. What the hell do you know about this?" Tears of frustration slipped from her eyes, pulling her hand from mine in anger. "I'm in so much pain here, and all you can do is tell me to breathe. Really?" she asked, glaring at me as if she wished the floor would open up and swallow me whole.

Before I could come back with some sort of retort, Dr. Weber strolled into the room, looking the part of the calm, comforting doctor. As soon as Addy laid eyes on him, she changed her demeanor right away, smiling at him as if he held the golden ticket. At first, I was pissed, but then I realized the only reason she was floating on cloud nine in front of the doctor was because he was there to help move the delivery along, essentially ending her pain.

"How we doing?" he asked, smiling as he wheeled the stool closer to the edge of the hospital bed. I wasn't gonna lie; the fact he was looking at Addy underneath her hospital gown, up close and personal, angered me, but for the sake of everyone involved, including Dr. Weber, I held my temper in check. Addy took notice, however, reaching to touch my arm to bring my attention back to her. Giving me a slight smile, she turned her head back to Dr. Weber.

"I'm ready," she confessed. "My God . . . I'm ready."

"Yes, please," I answered as well. "Can't we move this along? I'm fearing for my life over here," I half-joked.

Dr. Weber smirked, shaking his head at my ludicrous statement. I may be a tough bastard, but my woman could destroy me with a single look.

Fiddling underneath the sheet, Dr. Weber mumbled something to himself before wheeling his stool back. "Addy, the baby is not in the right position. You're fully dilated, but I can't have you start pushing yet." More tears coursed down her face. "The baby is in what we call a transverse position." The confused look on our faces forced him to explain further. "The baby's head is sideways. I'm going to try and move him so he is facing down. Now, I have to warn you, this is probably going to be a little uncomfortable. Okay?"

She simply nodded, clutching my hand in anticipation for what was to come. I wasn't stupid; I knew damn well he had to reach inside her to try and turn the baby. The thought infuriated me, and I tried not to focus on the fact he was going to cause my woman intentional pain, even though he needed to do it in order for Addy to start pushing. Regardless, it didn't soothe my need to cause him bodily harm.

As soon as she shut her eyes and bit her lip, I knew she was in pain. Thankfully, Dr. Weber was successful in moving the baby, and did so relatively quickly.

When he wheeled back and rose from his seat, he patted Addy's knee before excusing himself, telling us he would be right back.

My instinct was to protect her, but there wasn't a damn thing I could do for her right then, other than sit by her side until our son was born. She was exhausted and in tremendous pain. From where we sat, it seemed like there was no end in sight, more so for her than for me.

I was man enough to realize her yelling at me before was the anguish talking, but it still struck a nerve. I was also smart enough to realize I shouldn't mention it—not until after the baby was born, at least. Or maybe never. Yeah, never talking about it was probably my best bet. Especially if I ever wanted to get her pregnant again.

Jesus! I'm already thinking about more babies with her.

"What are you smiling at?" Addy shouted, gripping my hand again to help her through another contraction.

Dr. Weber chuckled, catching Addy's words to me as he walked back into the room. "Game face, Stone. Don't mess around over there." He winked when I looked at him, and I had to admit I actually liked the guy, even if he did piss me off from time to time by touching Addy or looking directly at the one area no other set of eyes should ever see.

Wheeling himself in front of her again, he placed her feet in the stirrups and gently pushed her legs apart. Two nurses had come in behind him, waiting to assist in the delivery.

"Well, it looks like we're ready to go," Dr. Weber said, raising his head briefly to smile at her. She returned his gesture, grateful she was going to welcome the newest member of our family very soon. "The next time your body signals for you to push, I want you to bear down, okay?"

She nodded, glancing over at me with fear and happiness all tangled together.

I leaned over and we quickly shared a kiss before all the action began.

Two short minutes later, Addy began pushing, my ears ringing from the sounds of her effort. Every scream tore at my heart. Every tear sliced through me so deep all I wanted to do was hold and comfort her. But she was strong, in every way possible. The woman put me to shame with her bravery and will, her desire to persevere even when life threw her the biggest curve ball.

"That's it, Addy, keep pushing. You got it," Dr. Weber encouraged, cheering her on the entire time. "I can see the head. Okay, okay, hold on. Don't push." I had no idea what he was doing down there and when he spoke again, this time directly at me, I startled. "Stone, do you want to see your baby being born?" He smiled, and it was certainly contagious.

I gave him a quick nod before taking the couple steps toward the bottom of the bed. One of the nurses immediately fell into place, taking my position on Addy's left side.

Let's be truthful for a second. Childbirth, while truly being a miracle, is disgusting. There's just a lot of *stuff* going on, but that being said, I don't regret for one moment witnessing my child coming into the world.

"Okay, when you're ready . . . bear down," Dr. Weber instructed. A scream tore from Addy's lips. Her back rose off the bed, and when she pushed down with all her might our baby's head popped out. "Stop pushing now, Addy. I have to clean out the nose and mouth. Bear with me."

"Oh . . . my . . . Please, Dr. Weber. I have to push. I have to push," she repeated, lying back on the bed in utter exhaustion. Both nurses whispered encouragements, brushing her hair off her forehead and looking at her in awe, as if she were the only woman who had ever given birth.

"Go ahead, Addy. Time to meet your baby." She gave one final push and the baby was fully out, a patch of light colored hair adorning the top of his head. Dr. Weber's eyes instantly found mine. "Do you want to cut the cord?" At first, I shook my head, afraid I was going to harm the baby in some way. But once he told me he would walk me through it, that I would do great, I took the instrument from his hands and clipped exactly where he showed me.

My attention ricocheted back and forth between the baby and Addy, concern instantly stealing my breath because I wasn't sure who to focus on first. I was now responsible for this brand new life, and while I welcomed the joy he would bring to my world . . . I was terrified. Dr. Weber had said something, but I was so caught up in my thoughts it took a few seconds for his words to register.

"Stone? Earth to Stone," he teased. When my eyes finally met his, he glanced down at the tiny being in his hands. "Would you like to hold your daughter?" he asked, pushing the towel-wrapped infant toward me.

I heard his words that time, but they didn't seem real. It was as if he were asking me a question which couldn't possibly be true. Why was he mixing up the sex of my baby? Why was he saying daughter when he should have been saying son? Staring unbelievably at everyone in the room, their faces full of happiness and joy, I'd realized that Dr. Weber spoke the truth, that he wasn't playing a joke on me.

And it was right then when my entire world slammed to a stop.

"It's a girl?"

He placed the baby in my arms before answering.

"Looks like we're all a bit surprised, now aren't we?" He laughed before continuing to take care of Addy.

Staring down into the face of the most beautiful creature I'd ever seen, my eyes became glassy, a lone tear slipping from the corner before I could stop it. Clearing my throat, I steeled my reserve before turning to look at the woman who'd given me the greatest gift.

"It's a girl," I said, shaking my head because I was still trying to come to grips with my new reality. "I'm not gonna do well with this," I confessed, instant panic engulfing me. All sorts of thoughts ran through me. If Addy thought I was possessive before, she was in for a rude awakening. No boy was ever going to get close to our baby girl. I would threaten and kill anyone who tried—once they were of age, of course. I wasn't about to go around threatening little boys on the playground, not unless they hurt my daughter in some way.

Oh, God! I'm gonna go to jail someday in the future. I just know it. My anxiety heightened with each random thought, and I had no idea how to relinquish it all and just enjoy the gift that was my daughter.

It was also during my mini breakdown that something hit me with such force, my eyes widened in shock.

Oh, God! Now I get it! I totally understand why Addy's father hates me.

I saw Addy grinning out of the corner of my eye, no doubt knowing what was going through my head. Holding out her hands for our baby, I kissed the top of my child's tiny head before giving her to her doting mother.

"Is it wrong I already feel bad for the torment you're going to put her through as she gets older?" she asked, laughing before I even responded. She must have found my expression comical, but I was far from amused. My brows furrowed, a strong feeling of protectiveness engulfing me so tightly I felt as if I couldn't breathe. Addy reached for my hand and linked her fingers with mine.

"It'll be okay. Just breathe," she whispered.

———•———

Adelaide

Two months later

"CAN YOU SEE WHO'S AT the door, babe?" I shouted from the nursery. I'd just finished changing our daughter, Riley, and didn't feel like rushing downstairs to see who'd come to visit. All the men from the club had stopped by at one time or another. They were all very sweet, bringing by stuffed toys and diapers by the boxes. It was funny to watch the transformation from tough bikers to baby-talking softies as soon as Riley was placed in their arms.

At first, Tripp and Ryder were hesitant to hold her, afraid they were going to drop her, but after I positioned her just so, they felt better about the interaction with the tiny human.

Stone found comfort in that he had all the men on his side when it came to protecting his little girl. Both Trigger and my father had come to accept Stone as the man in my life, mainly because they figured it was life's ultimate payback that he now had a daughter of his own. They teased him that he got what he deserved, and although all their ribbing was in jest, they adored the newest member of their family to pieces.

"Marek and Sully are here!" Stone shouted from the bottom of the stairwell. "Is Riley sleeping?"

Rounding the corner to come and stop at the top of the stairs, I responded, "Well, she wouldn't be now with all that yelling." Shaking my head, I descended the steps, locking eyes with the man who'd become my entire world.

Meeting him at the bottom, he leaned down and gave me a quick but passionate kiss, his tongue swiftly tracing my bottom lip before pulling back.

"Stop teasing me," I whispered, moving past him to greet our guests, but he stopped me before I took another step.

"Can I take her?" The love in his eyes for Riley poured forth in droves, almost making me jealous. Almost. I couldn't be happier that our daughter had Stone for a father, knowing he would love and protect her to a fault. I envisioned many an argument between the two of them as she grew older, turning to me to talk some sense into him. But what she would come to realize was that she not only had to worry about her father, but her grandad, her uncle, and every other man in the Knights Corruption brotherhood.

Poor little thing was doomed and she didn't even know it.

But it would all come from a place of love.

Handing Riley over, I walked toward the kitchen to grab a bottle so he could feed her. He loved the bonding experience with her . . . as did I. I chose not to breastfeed because I was nervous about having any residual chemo drugs in my system, although I was assured I was all clear. And by all clear, I meant the cancer was no longer detectable. I underwent a needle biopsy soon after Riley was born, the results coming back positive, which I'd expected. But since I no longer had to worry about possibly impeding the health of my child, I underwent a heavier, more extensive bout of treatment, essentially doing the trick and giving me a clean bill of health.

Entering the living room where everyone was gathered, I saw the look of pride on Stone's face as he showed off his daughter to our closest friends. No one was aware that I'd come into the room yet, so I continued to take it all in. All three of them were fussing over the tiny girl wrapped in Stone's arms, and when I saw a brief look of sadness pass between Marek and Sully, I knew I had to make my presence known before Stone inadvertently said something he shouldn't. But I was too late. The words fell from his lips before I could say anything.

"So, when are you two gonna have one?" he asked, glancing first at Marek then at Sully, an unknowing smile plastered on his face while he continued to fuss over his daughter.

The pained look on Sully's face broke my heart, only second to the regretful one on Marek's. It was during a conversation Sully and I had once when shopping for baby clothes that I asked her the same thing. At first, she simply told me she was unable to have children. I asked her why and she changed the subject, only later telling me the actual reason.

I broke the rising tension by barreling into the room, causing such a commotion Stone had forgotten he'd even posed the question. "Here you go," I said, pushing the bottle toward him so he could feed her.

"Thanks, babe."

"Wow!" Marek exclaimed, quickly washing away whatever thoughts had just held him hostage. "I never thought I'd see the day when you'd be excited about feeding a baby." His best friend teased him, but I knew he was beyond happy for Stone.

"Yeah, well, things change, man." There was no way he was going to let the ribbing from his dear friend deter him from coddling Riley, making funny faces at her while she suckled on the end of the bottle.

"They sure do," Marek attested. "Hey, speaking of change . . . I got the call." A coded look passed between the two men, one which instantly put me on edge for some reason. And I wasn't the only one. Glancing over at Sully, who was sitting directly across from me, she shared the same worried expression.

"*The* call?" Stone asked, shifting his daughter from one arm to the other.

"Yup. Time to put this to bed, brother," Marek affirmed, nodding in earnest before reaching for his wife's hand. Interlocking his fingers with hers, he leaned over and kissed her temple, pure love pouring forth in one simple gesture.

I knew the answer I was going to get when I asked the question, but I had to ask regardless. Maybe since they'd actually spoken in front of us about something which was obviously top secret, they would let something slip.

"What call are you talking about?" I asked them both simultaneously, glancing back and forth between the two men.

"It's club—"

"Business," both Sully and I answered at the same time. "Yeah, we know," I joked, realizing that, although they chose to speak in code in front of us, there was no way they were ever going to elaborate on the dealings of the KC.

The rest of the day passed in a blur, the four of us talking well into the evening, sharing funny stories as well as our vision for the future. Marek and Stone assured Sully and me that their time being eaten up by the club was coming to an end sooner rather than later. I knew there would be some sort of threat to the club for a while yet, mainly because they'd dealt on the wrong side of the law for far too long. And even though they were doing what they had to in order to end that part of their lives, diminishing the risk going forward, it would still take some time for them to be in the clear.

Instead of focusing on such things, however, I glanced around the room and realized just how lucky I was. Dealing with a life-threatening sickness made me take stock in what was truly important—the love of a good man, a healthy, beautiful baby girl, and wonderful friends, just to name a few.

I was truly blessed.

JAGGER

Jen, without our little brainstorming session I probably never would have stumbled across the idea which ended up being one of the most unique parts of this story. Thanks schmoopie! ☺

PROLOGUE

"WORTHLESS PIECE OF SHIT!"

I swore those were my father's favorite words. His preferred insult. Normally, he spewed the offense alone, but then there were times, like now, when he followed them with his fists. The contact with the side of my face jolted me back, the sting of pain forcing me to feel something. Anything. Otherwise, I remained in a constant state of numbness, my own kind of self-preservation.

Hitting the wall behind me, my head thumped off the plaster and created a small dent, but I didn't dare move; if he saw what I'd done, he'd become even more irate. If that were at all possible.

I'd come to expect his outbursts, especially when he drank. Which happened to be most of the time. Growing up with an alcoholic parent was tough, and that was putting it lightly. He'd hated me my entire life, his abuse escalating the older I became. He blamed me for everything that went wrong in his life, from the death of his wife, my mother, to gambling debts he'd incurred, to losing his job. I couldn't win, no matter what I said or tried to do to help.

I'd gotten a paper route at the tender age of eleven, handing over all my wages, but all that earned me was a swift backhand. He thought I was being disrespectful, essentially telling him he couldn't take care of us. Which was the absolute truth, but I never uttered those words. We'd lost our house soon after and had been moving from place to place ever since. My father couldn't hold down a job because of his excessive drinking, and no matter how much I tried to stay out of the way, he'd always find fault with something I did, punishing me so badly sometimes I didn't dare go out in public for fear people would see the damage he'd caused.

For as horrible as my father treated me, he was the devil I knew. The thought of being yanked from the only life I'd known and placed with strangers was enough to cause me to silently endure all of his beatings.

Both verbal and physical.

He'd told me my entire life that I would never amount to anything. That I'd probably drop out of school and end up being a bum for the rest of my life.

But I'd proved him wrong.

Holding my cap and gown, I'd thought my graduation day would have finally made him proud of me, but instead my accomplishment only made him rant his insults harder and faster.

"You think just because you skated by and passed by the skin of your teeth that means you're somethin' special?" he roared, his spittle hitting my cheek he was standing so close. His version of "skating by" was me graduating with second honors, and while most kids would be proud of that achievement, I had to hide it from him. Otherwise, he'd think I was boasting, rubbing it in his face that I was smart.

I stood in front of him with my head hung low, knowing better than to answer. He'd already struck me once, and although his fists didn't hurt as much as when I was younger, I still didn't want to have to deal with any more. I'd never retaliated against my father. Never raised my own fists in return. No, I took his rage because a part of me thought I deserved it.

Guilt ate at me from the inside that I was the reason my mother had died. I'd killed her simply by being born, and my father never let me forget it. Unfortunately, his lack of love for me fueled my anger toward others. It was why I'd been expelled from more than a few schools, constantly getting into fights with kids who'd picked on me because of the shoddy clothes my father forced me to wear. He simply refused to spend money on his growing son.

But something good came from my rage. I'd perfected my fighting skills, often sparring against other kids for money. Some were my age and some were years older, but no matter what, I'd win every time.

Every opponent was my father.

Every knockout was my father hitting the floor.

Every win was my way of telling my father to go fuck himself.

My father staggered backward in his drunken state, bumping into the kitchen table before stabilizing himself. Running his pale hand over his balding head, he looked like he was going to explode. Gritting his teeth, he stepped closer. "I hope you don't think you're gonna live under my roof now that you're grown," he seethed, his bloodshot eyes looking like they belonged to some sort of demon. "Well? Answer me, boy," he demanded, stepping even closer. He reeked like alcohol, the smell making me instantly nauseous.

"No," I answered, keeping my head down so I didn't have to look at the loathing in his eyes, his hatred making me feel the way he truly saw me.

Worthless.

Dreadful silence danced around the both of us, the drumming of my heart the only sensation I allowed myself. I'd shut down, but in the next few minutes I'd be free forever from the evil bastard standing in front of me.

Spitting at my feet, he shoved past me, but not before driving the emotional knife in deeper, slicing me apart from the inside. "Get your fuckin' shit and get out." A ragged breath passed. *Here it comes.* "It should have been you who died that day," he said, venom cutting each word perfectly. I wished I could have said he'd never spoken those words before, but then I would have been lying.

He said them often.

Only that time would be the last I'd have to hear them.

ONE

Jagger

"KILL HIM!" THE WORDS ECHOED in my ears, the air swirling around me suddenly thicker than it was seconds before. I dismissed the lump forming in my throat and focused all of my attention on pummeling my opponent, my fists flying so fast his blood coated the ground beneath us in no time. Taking a quick reprieve, I allowed him a few precious seconds to regain his footing; otherwise, our bout would be over too fast. And where would be the fun in that?

So many people united in the thrill of the fight. They'd paid good money to witness bloodshed, to be part of something they were too terrified to do themselves.

Fight.

For sport.

But not me. I lived for the surge of adrenaline that slithered through my veins. To know my skills outmatched anyone who had stepped in the ring with me. Plus the prize money wasn't anything to sneeze at.

I'd been involved in the underground world of MMA fighting for a few years, and I was undefeated. Confidence and cockiness were often separated by a thin line, but I wasn't in it for the recognition, or the women, or the power trip it gave most fighters. To me, the ring was the one place I could release all my pent-up rage. A place I could lose myself to the chants of the crowds and the smell of blood and sweat.

A place where I wasn't . . . worthless.

A sharp pain in my side shoved me back into the heat of the fight. The kid in front of me was two years younger and certainly not as skilled, even though he'd just managed to catch me off guard. But it wouldn't happen again. I knew his weaknesses—his left knee, for one. He'd hurt it badly a year back and unfortunately for him, I was gonna make him relive that excruciating pain. The other obstacle working against him was that he was a known drug addict, fighting strictly for money to fuel his demons. While he possessed some talent, he wasn't focused or disciplined. Two things working in my favor right then.

Locking eyes with the guy who would give me my next win, I faked an uppercut, drawing his attention to my hand while my foot shot out and connected with his previously injured knee. As soon as his leg bent in the wrong direction, I knew the fight was over, but just to lock in the victory I finished him off with my infamous right hook.

He never saw it coming.

And I never expected for my hit to be the final blow.

The final action which stripped his soul from this life.

An unnerving sound reverberated in the air around me. No one else heard it, but the crackling noise boomed inside my ears, pounding so fiercely inside my head I thought for sure everyone knew what I'd just done.

I hadn't meant to.

All I'd wanted to do was make sure I remained at the top of my game. There was no saving him, though. I jumped back and watched his body free fall in slow motion. His head hung from his shoulders while his body twisted in an awkward position, his legs bending while the pull of gravity embraced him.

So many people cheered, the applause and shouts making me feel as if my ears were bleeding. My heart pounded inside my chest so fiercely I feared I was gonna join him in the afterlife if I didn't get a fucking grip on my new reality.

Blood poured from his nose and mouth, but there was no other sign of life emanating from him.

He'd broken his neck. Or rather, *I'd* broken his neck.

His body lay limp on the ground.

Not a twitch.

Not a breath.

No hope whatsoever that it was all a bad dream.

Death.

He was dead.

I'd killed him.

I'd only intended to put him out of commission from fighting, not from life itself. My wrapped hands pulled at the sweaty strands of my hair, blowing out a disbelieving gush of air as I tried to wrap my head around what just happened. I'd never killed anyone before. Well, let me clarify—I'd never killed anyone *in the ring* before.

Outside the solace of the ropes, I'd snatched a few lives alongside my brothers of the Knights Corruption.

A strong grip ripped me backward toward the ropes, making me stumble and fall onto the stool in my corner of the ring. I heard someone speaking but the sound was muffled, as if their hands were covering their mouth while they yelled incoherently.

My body shook under the solid hold of someone, and it wasn't until I finally raised my head that I saw who it was. Stone, the VP of our club, stood over me with an intense worried look in his eyes. His lips were moving but I couldn't make out what he was saying. Then, without warning, all the muffled noise came into focus and it suddenly became too much to bear. My hands hastily covered my ears, drowning out the sound of the chaos of what I'd done.

The shock of killing my opponent twisted me in ways it shouldn't have. As I said, I'd killed before, but it was always justified; battle of the clubs warranted fatalities now and again. But when I was in the ring, my ultimate goal was to win. To be the victor and to show everyone I excelled at something. To prove to those around me that I had amounted to something because my entire life my father had drilled the exact opposite into me, telling me I was a mistake and would either end up in jail or dead. He told me once he hoped it was the latter. I was only ten when I first heard those words, and while I'd tried not to let him see me upset, tears spilled forth at the very notion that my own father hated me.

It was his face I saw most often when I beat the hell out of someone, wishing my fists pulverized the man who'd given me life.

"Jagger!" Stone shouted. "We have to go. Now!" He held the ropes open for me and once my feet hit the ground, two men flanked me, one on each side. Ryder and Tripp. I hadn't even known they were there that evening, my focus solely on my fight and nothing else.

"Let's grab your winnings," Tripp yelled in my ear, "then we can get the hell outta here." As soon as I came out of the office with my prize money, we hastily headed toward the back of the warehouse, the red blinking exit sign my sole focus. But our escape was interrupted by someone blocking our path.

Hyped from my fight, with disgust and a twinge of guilt shooting through me, I hardened my restraint when I realized the man standing in front of us was none other than Snake, the brother of the guy I'd just killed. And as luck would have it, Snake just so happened to be part of our most hated enemy.

The Savage Reapers.

Normally, members of the two clubs would never be in the same vicinity, not unless we were warring. But the unspoken rules were bent under these types of circumstances. The underground fighting world brought out all sorts of characters, and unfortunately for us, it meant the scum of the Reapers often visited the fights. I tried to keep that part of my life separate from the club, although the two worlds were blending more and more recently. Plus I knew if our president, Marek, found out he might've put a stop to me participating in the bouts. He already didn't like me, suspecting I held certain feelings toward his wife. Feelings he'd misread. Regardless, I didn't want to give him any reason to take away one of the few things in life I thoroughly enjoyed.

But now that secret was out in the open. Stone, Ryder and Tripp circled me, a protective gesture which wasn't needed, but was definitely appreciated.

"What the fuck are you doing here?" Stone seethed, clenching his fists at his sides as he glared at Snake. "Do you have a death wish?" Tripp and Ryder stayed close, prepared to jump in if anything popped off. Even though the Reaper was surrounded by the enemy, it didn't seem to faze him. In fact, he looked like he was enjoying himself, knowing his presence was pissing us off even more.

Completely ignoring Stone's question, Snake turned his stare to me, puffing up his chest and stepping toward me. "You killed my little brother," he gritted, strands of his long dark hair falling loose from the tie that held it away from his face.

I wanted to tell him it wasn't on purpose, that it was an accident, but I didn't dare open my mouth to explain. It would be portrayed as weakness, so I kept my lips sealed.

I meant to keep my eyes on Snake, but I was curious to see what my brothers' reactions were to his statement. Now that they knew the man I'd killed was a sibling to a Reaper, they had to have guessed I knew our enemy had visited the fights. Would they rat me out to our leader? And if so, would I be kicked out of the club? Surely my omission would be the proverbial nail in the coffin. The final straw that would allow Marek to get rid of me.

I'd heard stories of other clubs never allowing their members to leave in anything other than a body bag. But I knew Marek didn't rule like that. Brothers who no longer wanted to be part of the life simply left, no bad feelings or ill wishes. The club wasn't for everyone and Marek knew it. Although I could've counted the number of men who'd left on one hand, and none since I'd been accepted as a prospect two years ago.

A quick hit to the chest pushed me back a step, and I was thrust out of the ramblings inside my own head and back into the situation. He'd dared to put his hands on me, and because I was distracted he'd been able to do so. Before anyone else could react, I shoved past the bastard and walked toward the exit. Some might have construed my actions—or lack thereof—as a pussy move, but I needed air. I needed to clear my head, and the last thing I needed was to take out all my frustrations and shock on the brother of the man I'd just killed.

Thankfully, Stone, Ryder and Tripp followed me without so much as a word, lining up alongside me as we escaped the confinements of the old, abandoned warehouse.

"The next time I lay eyes on you, you're fucking dead," Snake shouted after me. He continued to spout off at the mouth, but the harsh click of the metal door closing behind us cut him off.

Hunching forward in the backseat of Stone's truck, I rested my head in my hands and prayed that some potent alcohol would help me lose myself. Even if just for an evening.

I'd deal with life, and the consequences, when the sun came up.

TWO

Jagger

THE MORNING LIGHT INFILTRATED THE common room, my hungover ass burrowing further into the couch and shielding my eyes just so I didn't have to witness the dawn of another day. Because I wasn't a full-fledged member, I didn't have my own room at the club, so taking the couch was my only option.

After my fight the prior evening, the guys had brought me back to the clubhouse instead of dropping me off at my dismal apartment all by myself. They knew I'd have a problem with what I'd done, even though it hadn't been intentional. Still, to kill by accident was much worse than when it was done on purpose.

Tripp and Ryder had joined me while I'd drowned myself in alcohol. Stone on the other hand had to get back home to Adelaide and their new baby, Riley. I viewed the VP of my new family like a brother, even more so than the other men. We had a special bond. Maybe it was because we were both skilled fighters, or maybe it was because Stone had taken me under his wing when I'd first become part of the club, looking out for me when things went a little off the rails.

The cushion near my feet dipped, the weight of someone who I'd yet to identify taking up some of my personal space. Shoving at my legs, a rough voice vibrated through the air, and even though my eyes were still shielded, I knew exactly who it was.

My fellow drinking buddy. Ryder.

Thankfully, he'd stuck to beer; otherwise last night would have had a much more dire outcome. Ryder didn't do well with hard alcohol and we all knew it.

"You gettin' up anytime soon, prospect? It's just after two. You've slept the majority of your day away," he chided. Kicking at him only made him laugh, punching my leg before slouching back on the couch.

So much for losing myself to slumber for the rest of the day.

Before long, other voices filled the room, rousing me from my half sleep once and for all. Sitting upright, my hands instantly cradled my head, the intense pounding threatening to stay with me for hours.

"Wow, buddy, you look like shit."

When I spread my fingers to look and see who'd given the compliment, I saw it was Hawke. The wide grin he sported soon disappeared when his crazy woman, Edana, walked up behind him. She mumbled under her breath before shoving past him, heading toward his room at the back of the club, her wild auburn hair flowing behind her while she strode off with purpose. The pissed-off look on her face was telling. Those two had such an explosive relationship; I had no idea why he kept her around. "Great pussy" was something I'd heard him say before, but ain't no pussy worth putting up with that much shit on a daily basis. The fact that Hawke never kept his dick in his pants just added fuel to that out-of-control fire. But to each their own.

Hawke's eyes darkened before he dropped his head and followed Edana, probably gearing up for another all-out brawl from the look on his face.

Slowly rising from the couch, I walked toward the kitchen in search of food. I needed something to settle my stomach, and I'd found that greasy food always did the trick. Although I doubted I'd come across something already made and waiting for me to snatch up.

My head was buried in the refrigerator when I heard someone enter. Paying no attention to who it was, I continued to scour the shelves, hoping there was something edible for me to digest. Rooting through the choices, I decided to grab one of the small cardboard containers from the bottom shelf—leftover Chinese food of some sort. I opened the lid and gave it a whiff before deciding it was still good enough to eat. Someone was gonna be pissed I ate the rest of their chicken and broccoli, but I was too hungover to care.

Closing the fridge door, I turned around to find a fork when I came face-to-face with Sully. Her sweet smile calmed me some, my headache becoming a dull annoyance more than anything. For some inexplicable reason, any anxiety I'd carried around on a daily basis was lessened whenever she was near. I didn't understand it, and I stopped trying to months ago. It started when Marek summoned me to watch over her while he was away on club business with Stone after she had first come to stay with us. I'd thoroughly enjoyed our time together, loving that I'd been able to bring her out of her shell a bit by making her laugh. Normally, I was pretty reserved, but every now and again I could shoot the breeze with the best of them, coming up with witty banter just like everyone else.

Our budding friendship had been cut short, however, when Marek got it into his head that I had feelings for his new wife.

Was he right?

Sort of.

To myself, I would admit I found Sully very attractive, and while she was thinner than what I normally went for, she had a great body. Come on, I'm a young, red-blooded male after all. I noticed. What can I say? I won't apologize for it, although I would never make my appreciation known out loud for fear of retaliation from my president. I valued the club—and my life—way too much to do something so stupid.

But it was more than Sully's physicality that drew me in. It was something inside her which spoke to me, an inexplicable pull. Maybe it was the way I truly let my guard down in the presence of a female for once, not second-guessing whether she wanted to get into my pants or simply use me as a stepping stone to gain some kind of status within the club.

Maybe it was the short role of protector I was forced into while I watched over her for those few days. I'd seen how broken she was when she'd come to be with us, and even though she seemed much stronger and happier with each passing day, I'd discovered some of the things she'd had to endure at the hands of her club. Mainly her father and Vex. Thankfully, Vex was dead; if Marek hadn't already disposed of him, I probably would have.

I'd also been at the club the day the leader of the Los Zappas cartel visited, along with his right-hand man, Rico Yanez. Apparently, Yanez had raped Sully before Marek had stolen her, a situation which played heavily on our leader's mind day in and day out—anyone with eyes could see it. He'd changed over the time she'd come into his life. There were times he seemed lighter, but as soon as he'd found out what had happened to her, finding himself face-to-face with one of the men who'd violated her, something inside him had turned off—or on, depending on how you looked at it.

The need for vengeance and blood was strong with him, and I couldn't say I blamed him. I just hoped when the time came he would allow me to assist in the demise of that worthless piece of shit.

"Hi, Jagger," Sully's soft voice greeted me, looking toward the door to see if anyone else was going to enter. For the time being, we were alone, which probably wasn't the safest thing. If Marek walked in and saw us together, he'd flip out. And although his demeanor around me wasn't as aggressive as it had been initially when all the shit went down about my new friendship with his wife, the tension between us still bristled whenever we were near each other. I just didn't want to do or say anything which would shove me back into "I'm gonna fuck you up" status.

"Hey." I gave her a tight smile before moving past her, continuing to look for a fork. "How are you?" I asked, keeping my eyes diverted just in case someone did interrupt us. At least they couldn't say we were engaged in anything inappropriate.

"I'm good." She hesitated before speaking again, and I had a good idea why. It was obvious she knew what had happened at the fight, and was deciding whether or not she should ask me about it. Leaning against the counter, I shoved food into my mouth while I waited for her to say something, daring to finally look at her.

Worry laced the faint lines of her expression and I wanted nothing more than to comfort her. To tell her I was okay . . . or at least I would be. I was a survivor. If my bastard of a father had taught me anything, it was how to throw up walls to protect myself from the harshness of the world. Most of the time it worked, but there were instances—like with my interactions with Sully—where the walls started to crack.

"I heard about last night," she confessed, taking a few steps closer until she reached out and placed her hand on my shoulder—an action which was definitely appreciated, but not necessary. I didn't want anyone's pity, most of all hers.

Shrugging away from her touch, I gave her another tight smile before nodding. Continuing to eat was the distraction I needed, and thankfully Sully picked up on the vibe I'd thrown out. She probably thought I was scared to talk to her, but that was only partly true. While I could hold my own with Marek—and when I say hold my own, I mean letting him treat me any way he saw fit without retaliation—the last thing I wanted to do was cause Sully more heartache by creating an argument between them. She had enough to deal with, and I didn't want to add to it.

"No big deal," I lied. "Part of the risk we all take when we step into the ring."

Her lips parted to respond when someone barreled through the kitchen door, locking eyes on me as soon as I came into view.

"Yo," Breck interrupted. "Prez wants to see ya." He glanced quickly to Sully, then back to me before exiting the room.

"Fuck," I cursed, slamming the container of food on the nearby counter. Marek either wanted to see me because I was alone with his wife, or for the previous night. And seeing as how no one knew we were alone in the kitchen, my bets were on the latter.

"I'll go talk to Cole before he sees you," Sully offered, turning toward the door before she allowed me to respond.

Quickly walking past her, I reached for her arm to stop her. "No," I gritted. "I'll deal with it. Besides, I doubt it has anything to do with you."

Choosing not to utter another word, I pushed the door open and walked into the common room. I was halfway toward Chambers when I heard Marek shout, "Where the fuck is he?"

Great! Nothing like walking into the lion's den, and apparently he was hungry.

Blowing out a frustrated exhale, I breached the threshold of the room where we held all our meetings.

This should be fuckin' good.

THREE

Jagger

AS SOON AS I STEPPED inside Chambers, I noticed that almost everyone was present, with the exception of Cutter and Trigger. I hadn't even seen the majority of the members milling around the club, but then again, I was too busy trying to function with a raging hangover.

To say Marek was beside himself was quite the understatement. He looked ready to rip someone apart. Sections of his dark hair stuck up, his hands gripping his head in frustration as he paced in front of everyone present.

His blue eyes darkened as soon as he saw me, halting his anxious stride before making a beeline in my direction. I didn't flinch, even though the furious look on his face unnerved me. An unkempt beard covered his face, his eyes red and haggard-looking. He wasn't getting any fucking sleep and his body paid the price. I knew he was biding his time until he could make Yanez pay for what he did to his wife once and for all. And if I'd overheard Stone correctly, his wish was gonna come true any day now.

Grabbing my cut, he drew me close. Ominous silence stretched between us while he prepared the words he wished to spew at me. His brow furrowed and the muscle in his jaw ticked, but still I showed no fear. To show weakness was detrimental, not only in the club but in life in general. That much I knew.

I could have shrugged Marek off me but I didn't dare, and the reason boiled down to one thing and one thing only.

Respect.

"Why the hell didn't you tell us the Reapers were hangin' around your fights?" He shoved me before giving me a chance to explain, and I was oddly thankful for the space he'd offered. Straightening my vest, I steeled my resolve and stood up straight, looking him in the eyes the entire time.

Words zipped through my brain at warp speed, and while I tried to nail down enough of them to form a coherent sentence, Marek shouted, "Answer me, goddamnit!"

His spike in temper forced me to speak right away.

"I didn't know any of those bastards were there until last night. I swear. I never pay attention to anyone other than who I'm fighting. Never get distracted by the noise," I said, turning to the VP of the Knights for affirmation. "Right, Stone?" I asked, hopeful he would back me up right then.

Stone gave me a simple nod, followed by a quick smirk.

Slamming his hand down on the table, Marek shot daggers toward all of us before speaking. "You need to be on guard every fucking second of the day. You need to make sure you know who is around you at all times. Do I need to remind any of you what's at stake?" Silence followed his outburst. "Do I?!" he roared, the vein in his temple threatening to burst if he didn't calm the hell down.

"No," everyone collectively answered, including me.

"Those bastards still haven't made a move for my wife, and every day that passes puts me even more on edge, just waiting for what they're gonna try to force me into. Force *all* of us into," he corrected. Plopping down in his chair, he expelled a breath and leaned forward, his fisted hands resting on top of the oblong table. "Get your heads right, fucking pay attention and be ready for anything."

No one broke the intensified silence, instead nodding and waiting for direction. And Marek gave it with a slam of the gavel, the boom ringing out and dismissing all in attendance.

As we headed toward the door, Marek's harsh tone stopped a few of us. "Stone, Jagger and Tripp, stay behind."

Once everyone else had left, the three of us turned all our focus toward the man who commanded our attention.

"I want you guys at every one of his fights," he said, pointing at me. "If there are Reapers showing up, we need to make our presence known. Stay in the background, though. Watch. Listen. We need as much information as we can get to make sure we're prepared for whatever they're planning. And trust me, they're planning something. Psych Brooks won't leave his daughter alone much longer." Gripping his chest, he affirmed, "I can feel it."

We each nodded our understanding before he dismissed us.

"You got off lucky," Tripp mused, slapping my back hard before shoving past me toward the common room. The nomad was quickly becoming a friend, even though he gave me shit all the time. Whenever he saw me sparring in the ring we'd constructed in the corner of the lot of the clubhouse, he teased that he could take me down, telling me I hit like a little girl. Yet he hadn't made good on his threat, still hadn't stepped up to show me what he was made of. Don't get me wrong; the guy was huge, standing at six-four and easily weighing in at two-twenty. But although he was a great match for me, he didn't intimidate me. I may have been a bit smaller, but I was quicker, a trait I used to my advantage every time an opportunity arose.

Taking a right, I walked toward the exit, needing some air to help soothe everything tumbling around inside my head. I was still unnerved about what had happened the night before. I'd tried to forget by losing myself to the bottle, but all that did was give me a wicked headache. No, I needed to do something else, but I wasn't sure what that was right then.

This fuckin' sucks.

"Yo, Jagger," Stone shouted from behind me. "Wait up."

Turning on my heel, I watched him slowly jog toward me, a pensive look on his face the closer he came.

"Sup?" I mumbled, just wanting to leave. I needed to take a ride, but where I was gonna go I had no idea.

"You okay? You don't look so great," he acknowledged.

"I'll be fine. It's just. . . ." I cut myself off because I didn't want to verbalize what was bothering me. I was sure Stone knew what the problem was, so there was no need for me to elaborate.

"I get it, man," he consoled, grabbing my shoulder for a quick show of support. Stone's friendship rattled me sometimes, but in a good way. I wasn't completely used to having someone show a genuine interest in my well-being.

"Did you want to talk to me about something?" I asked, gripping the back of my neck to help assuage the knotted muscles.

"When's your next fight?" Without even saying it, I knew having to accompany me to each of my upcoming bouts was the last thing Stone wanted to do, even though he enjoyed a good show. He had a new family waiting for him at home, a situation I very much wanted for myself. Well, maybe not the baby part, but definitely a woman. I was lonely, plain and simple. Sure, I had chicks throwing themselves at me all the time, but I was tired of pump-and-dumping every woman who spread her legs for me. I was looking for something more—which I was sure sounded odd coming from a twenty-two-year-old guy, but there it was. I knew enough not to verbalize that to anyone, however. If I did, I'd never hear the end of what a pussy I was, or whatever other clever names they'd come up with.

No, I'll keep my thoughts to myself.

"Two days."

"That's kind of soon, isn't it?" he asked, a confused look distorting his expression.

"It is, but ever since . . . well, what went down, I'm apparently a hot ticket. The purse has nearly tripled, and while I don't want to fight again so soon, I just can't pass up the opportunity at that kind of money." Looking sheepish for a second, I added, "I don't have the financial security you guys do. Just trying to make my way and all."

Stone nodded. "I get it." He swung his arm around my shoulder and pulled me close. "I do, but don't do it for the money. Not if you're not right in here," he said, tapping the side of my head with his finger.

"Easy for you to say," I grumbled. "You don't have to worry about money." I shoved him away, the annoyance with my situation propelling my anger further. "I don't want to keep living like this, Stone."

"Like what?"

"I live in a shithole. My president can't stand me. Hell, I'm surprised he hasn't kicked me out of the club by now. I ain't got no woman," I exclaimed, throwing my hands out to the sides. "I fight 'cause it's my escape, but if I kill again, in the ring, I won't even have that anymore." Clutching my chest, a sharp pain shot through me. I knew it was just nerves, though. Anxiety. "And if I can't fight, I don't know what I'll do."

Baring my soul to someone was new to me, and had it been in front of anyone else, I would've kept my mouth shut. But I knew Stone wouldn't give me shit like the others would.

Sympathy washed over him while he stared at me, trying to think of a retort to my mini outburst. "First, if you don't like your place, fucking move. Second, Marek doesn't *hate* you." I cocked my head to the side in disbelief. "Well, you're not his favorite person, but he acts better toward you than he did. He knows you're loyal to the club, that you would do anything for your brothers. Plus, you bring in a nice chunk of change." Stone grinned, but his smirk was fast replaced with a solemn look.

"Then why haven't I been fully patched in yet?"

"Time, brother. Give it time. You know Marek doesn't just patch someone in because they think they're due. But I promise it'll happen." I knew Stone couldn't guarantee such things, but I appreciated his faith in me, and in our leader. "Now," he said, "as far as a woman goes, you have your pick. What's wrong? I see the way all these chicks throw themselves at you, panting for your dick." He laughed, but I didn't find it funny.

I know, I know—poor young, good-looking guy. Pussy all around, wantin' to fuck me. I get it.

I just . . . I just want something more.

"It's not what I'm interested in anymore. I want what you guys have." Right then, Sully and Marek came strolling outside, his arm wrapped protectively around her waist as they approached. I couldn't help it; my eyes instantly latched on to hers, and while she gave me a quick smile, she looked away just as fast. And thankfully, so did I. Focusing back on Stone was my safest bet.

I thought Marek was gonna say something to us, but all he did was nod at Stone and give me a quick scowl before leading his wife toward his bike. They were gone before I registered that Stone had started talking again.

" . . . so you just have to wait until the time is right." I completely missed what he'd said, the lost look on my face telling him everything. "You didn't hear a word of that, did you?"

"Sorry, man. My mind is firing off in all different directions."

"I said"—he took a deep breath—"you'll find someone to settle down with when the time's right." He slapped me on the back. "Besides, aren't you a bit young to be thinking about getting married and having kids?"

The look on my face was comical, I was sure. "What the fuck? I'm not looking to get married and start breeding," I practically shouted, then lowered my voice. "I just want to have some kind of connection with someone, in addition to sexual." A cocky grin spread wide on my face. "I wanna be interested in fucking her *and* hearing what she has to say about stuff, you know?"

"Yeah, I know."

Taking a few more steps, Stone gave me a quick look before straddling his bike. I walked toward my own ride, grabbing my helmet when my friend's voice broke the silence. "About the fights," he started. "Don't worry about what *could* happen, Jagger. Just give it your all and everything else will fall into place."

FOUR

Jagger

NORMALLY, THE ENTIRE WORLD DWINDLED away when I prepared for a fight. An unusual peace rained down over me, as if all my troubles had faded into obscurity, my only focus defeating my opponent.

It fueled me.

I craved it.

The adrenaline was my drug of choice, my shield against the world.

Sitting in one of the empty back rooms of the warehouse, however, all I could concentrate on was whether or not this fight would end up with another fatality. My internal warring weighed heavily on me, and right then I desperately prayed for a distraction. But the close confines of the tiny room offered nothing.

Thankfully, before I went out of my mind waiting to be summoned, Stone and Tripp strolled into the room, closing the door behind them so we could have some privacy before the bout.

"How ya feelin'?" Tripp asked, leaning against the wall while Stone sidled up next to me.

"Good."

"You sure?" Stone asked, grabbing the wraps from the table and raising my fists. Normally I took care of wrapping my own hands, had been doing it since I started fighting, but that night I let Stone do it. I had a lot on my mind and could use his help with the simple, yet important task.

"Yeah," I muttered. Not really having much else to say, I remained quiet, my pulse quickening with each tick of the clock. Each pass of the second hand was like a boom inside my head. Breathing deeply, I closed my eyes and tried to will my pounding heart to calm the fuck down.

Tightly grasping my shoulder, Stone leaned in close and calmly said,

"You'll be fine, brother. Stop freakin' out." While my demeanor was calm, my face expressionless, he knew exactly what was going on inside me without me saying so. He could read me better than I'd expected, but for some reason that didn't shock me. Stone was very perceptive, although he tried to hide it most times—not wanting to get mixed up in other people's drama, I was sure.

The click of the door startled me, my gaze flying toward whoever had entered the room. It was Marty, one of the organizers for the fight. He was in his late forties, a sorry excuse for a comb over covering the top of his head. He reminded me of someone who lived alone, eating a ton of microwavable dinners while watching *Jeopardy!* Ask me why I pictured him in that scenario and I'd tell you I had no idea. It just fit.

"Five minutes," he announced, leaving the door open after he exited.

Before long I heard the announcer say my name. The floor beneath my feet vibrated, the excitement from the crowd undeniable. Their hype only served to unnerve me more than I already was, but I had to push past my apprehension if I was going to keep my undefeated status.

I was fighting Marcus Hill, an underground up-and-comer who had only lost one out of his last fifteen fights. Having done my own research, I'd been able to easily identify his weakness—his right shoulder, which was injured six months back. Since then, it popped out of its socket if twisted the wrong way. Or right way, depending on who was inflicting the damage.

Jumping up, I cracked my neck from side to side before throwing out a few shadow punches. Pushing out the breath I'd held hostage in my lungs, I locked eyes with Stone and Tripp before walking toward the door.

Here goes nuthin'.

Barreling my way through the crowd, my brothers tight on my heels, I focused on the guy already dancing around inside the ring. *Never get distracted by the noise.* It was a mantra I'd adopted from Stone. He'd yelled it at me a few times when we started sparring together, and it just stuck. It made total sense, and it always kept my attention on what was right in front of me, whether it was in the ring or handling club business.

Marcus hyped up the crowd, trying his hand at some fancy footwork and entertaining the audience until I approached. Once I was close enough, he stopped jumping around and turned fully toward me. Raising his arm, he pointed at me and shouted, "You're dead." I was surprised I heard him over the sound of everyone screaming. And the fact that he would use those exact words had me instantly furious. The fucker was going down hard—in and out, quick defeat. Then I'd escape and drown myself in a bottle of whatever would do the trick that evening.

Tripp grabbed the ropes and parted them enough for me to pass through, planting my feet directly in the corner while waiting for the fight to begin. Since I was involved in the underground fighting aspect of MMA, there weren't many rules. Actually, there weren't any rules to speak of, but I was sure it was frowned upon to kill someone during a fight.

Even in the absence of guidelines, the people who set up the bouts tried to pair the fighters as best they could, putting them in similar classes. Ours was the middleweight category, putting us both around a hundred and eighty-five pounds. Marcus and I were similar in stature, him only standing an inch shorter than my six-foot frame. While we were both lean, I was cut everywhere it counted. Marcus was in decent shape, although he carried a few extra pounds around his belly. It was in that added weight I would find more weakness.

I barely heard the ring announcer finish his speech, spouting off our names and fight histories, before it was time to put this guy on his ass and claim my prize money. Slowly approaching, we sidestepped each other, our gazes locked and ready for any unexpected moves. He was quick . . . but I was quicker. I kicked out and slammed the top of my foot into his ribs, making him stumble backward, a grimace instantly lighting up his face. Not taking a few seconds to compose himself before coming at me was his mistake. He should have thought about his next strategic move, but he was eager to show everyone what he could do.

Too eager.

And it was his downfall in the end.

Rushing toward me, he managed to land a blow to my side, but when he attempted to strike again, he missed as I danced away. While he staggered forward, I surprised him with a few rapid blows to the kidneys, knocking the breath from his body before he even realized he'd been hit.

While I normally reveled in the thrill of the fight, stretching out my time in the ring as long as possible because it was the only place I'd actually felt at home, that time was different. The fear of accidentally killing someone else drove me to distraction.

All I wanted to do was end the bout, lose myself to a few stiff drinks and possibly give in to one of the wannabes who'd been shamelessly throwing themselves at me. I could use a warm body for an hour or two.

Deciding enough was enough, I struck like a coiled snake. With a sudden right hook, I knocked Marcus flat on his back, dazed and confused. While he tried to right himself, I dropped to the mat, wrapped my legs around his body and captured his right arm, rotating it harshly in the wrong direction. As soon as I heard his shoulder pop out of place, I knew the fight was over.

With his free hand, he tapped the mat, signaling his submission.

I jumped to my feet and strode to my corner of the ring, waiting for my name to be announced as the winner. Stone and Tripp were there, huge smiles of pride on both their faces as they slapped my shoulder and shouted out congratulations, making me grin for a brief moment.

I turned toward the center of the ring to see what was going on. As soon as my eyes connected with Marcus's, I sort of felt bad, but only for a brief moment. Anyone looking at him could tell he was in agony, one of his buddies trying to pop his shoulder back into place. Contrary to popular belief, I didn't get off on going around hurting people. Yes, injuries—and apparently death—were all on the table as soon as we stepped into this ring, but that didn't mean the smell of blood made me high. No, I honed my skill to the point that I was undefeated in this world, and all I wanted was to go against a worthy opponent. So far, I hadn't had many.

Jerking my head toward Stone and Tripp after I'd been declared the winner, I silently communicated for them to follow me. All winnings were picked up in the back office, and while the door was guarded by two large buffoons, I wasn't scared in the least. Knowing I could take them both out in five seconds flat hitched a swagger to my gait.

"Tripp, can you do me a favor and grab my bag from the room?" I asked before disappearing inside to grab my prize money.

"You got it," he replied. "Be right back." He disappeared while Stone stood outside, waiting for me to re-emerge. No one was allowed to accompany the fighters inside the office. They'd been robbed in the past, hence the two roided-out guys standing watch.

The purse that night amounted to fifteen thousand dollars, the most I'd won to date. I wasn't stupid; I knew the result from my last fight upped the ante. At least something good had come out of it. Morbid way to look at the situation, but it was all I had.

Tripp walked toward us, my duffel bag slung over his shoulder. He threw it to me and I stuffed the envelope full of cash inside, zipped it back up and headed toward the exit. There were a few more fights scheduled for that evening, but I wasn't stickin' around. All I wanted to do was go back to the clubhouse to hopefully get drunk and get laid, in no particular order.

"At least we didn't see any of those fuckin' Reapers here tonight."

"Yeah, one less thing we have to worry about right now, at least." I had no idea who was saying what, Stone's and Tripp's voices melding together at some point. All I could focus on was getting out of there, the smell of piss, smoke and body odor more potent the longer I remained inside the confines of the old, dilapidated building.

Just as we were about to walk through the door and escape, a flurry of movement to my left caught my attention. Then I heard a panicked female voice saying something I couldn't quite make out, but I knew enough to recognize that she was in some sort of trouble. There were throngs of people milling around all over the place, so I wasn't quite sure why the hairs on the back of my neck bristled. Something warned me to stop and take notice, though. And the closer I stepped, pushing past some of the people blocking my view, the more amped up I became.

"Why won't she look at me?" a gruff voice shouted. Shuffling closer, my brothers close on my heels, I could finally see what was happening. Initially, they'd been confused as to why I'd turned around, but as soon as they'd heard what I had, they'd followed me, ready to jump into action if necessary.

"Because she doesn't want to have anything to do with you," one of the women yelled back. "She hasn't responded to any of your texts, so take the hint." A spitfire with shoulder-length blonde hair stood toe to toe with none other than Marcus Hill, challenging him as best she could. Physically she was no match, but that didn't stop her.

I caught bits and pieces of their argument, realizing she wasn't fighting for herself, but for another person. But who? And where were they? Stepping so close I was standing directly behind the shouting female, my eyes wandered all over the place, trying to see everyone who was in close proximity.

"Well, I'm not goin' anywhere until she at least lets me explain what happened," Marcus threatened, his left hand gripping his right shoulder, pressing his fingertips into the swollen flesh. He still hadn't seen me, too focused on arguing with the blonde.

Peering over the feisty woman's shoulder, I finally saw another woman crouching in the corner, her head down and tilted to the side. All I could see of her was her long dark hair, strands that shielded her face from everyone there. Protecting her. Assessing her body language, I could tell she was frightened. The slight tremble of her shoulders infuriated me, bringing out a fierceness I'd only possessed while enthralled in one of my fights.

"If you don't leave her alone right now, I'm calling the cops," the blonde woman threatened, fisting her hands at her sides in an attempt to gain some semblance of control. Without knowing her, I instantly liked her. Anyone willing to stick up for someone else was okay in my book.

Marcus looked around at the numerous sets of eyes watching the situation unfold, angry he wasn't getting what he wanted. When his gaze landed on me, the tick in his jaw told me my presence was about to make things worse. Not only had he been denied from talking to the dark-haired woman, but the victor of his fight was watching intently, ready to pounce if given the opportunity. I knew his shoulder was still throbbing and there was no way he wanted to tussle with me again, so he smartly decided to let it go.

"Fine," he bit out. "She's a *freak* anyway," he emphasized, taking a step back. The dark-haired woman snapped her head up at his comment, and it was then I was able to finally see her. A shiver shot straight through me, an audible gasp forced from my mouth. An angelic face with the most entrancing caramel-colored eyes glared at Marcus before quickly connecting with the woman to her left, her features and expression in direct contrast to one another. Glancing back and forth between the both of them, I could tell there was some sort of relation. Sisters, maybe?

Stone and Tripp walked up beside me, watching with as much interest as I was. Marcus backed up another step after he'd seen all three of us standing side by side. He could act as tough as he wanted in front of two helpless females, but he knew I'd pound him into the middle of next week if he made a wrong move.

Before I could open my mouth to tell him to fuck off, the dark-haired female tugged on the other woman's arm, raised her hands in the air and signed something to her. The blonde woman responded, signing back at a rapid pace. I had no clue what they were saying to each other, but I was fascinated by the scene unfolding in front of me.

Idiotically, I thought that I'd be able to identify a deaf person simply by looking at them, but I now knew how stupid that assumption was. Caught up in watching the two of them communicate with one another, it took my brain a few extra seconds to register what Marcus had just said about the deaf woman.

I stepped forward and grabbed him by his throat, pushing him against the nearest wall. "Don't you ever say that about her again," I seethed. "You got it, Hill?" I said his name with disgust, shoving at his injured shoulder when he refused to answer me. Instead of words, a howl flew from his mouth, his body crumpling against the wall behind him.

When I deemed him no longer a threat, I released him and turned around, striding toward the two women. My gaze was fierce enough to deter anyone else from getting involved. The crowd who had initially been surrounding us dispersed, leaving only myself, Stone, Tripp and the two females remaining.

"Are you all right?" I asked both of them, not quite sure who to direct my question to. I knew she couldn't hear me, but that didn't stop me from flitting my attention to her as well.

"Yes, thank you," the blonde woman replied, throwing her arm over the other woman's shoulder and pulling her close.

"Do you want us to escort you and your friend outside? Just to make sure Marcus doesn't try anything else?" I waited patiently for her to let me know what my next move was gonna be.

"My sister."

"What?" I asked.

"She's my sister. Kena. And my name is Braylen."

Pointing to myself and then my buddies, I said, "Jagger, Stone and Tripp." I was talking to both of them but I'd kept my eyes on Kena, watching her every reaction. Locking eyes with me, a small smile graced her full lips, and it was right then that I knew I was done for.

Changed forever.

FIVE

Kena

THE THREE MEN WHO HAD thankfully come to our aid wore their appearance of intimidation well. But I guessed at a gentleness underneath, a trait I was sure not many people bore witness to. I saw it in the way they'd tried to protect my sister and me, in the softness in their eyes when they reassured us that Marcus wouldn't be a problem any longer.

I'd mistakenly gone on a date with Marcus Hill a few weeks back. He'd come into my family's restaurant a few times and had always seemed nice, never giving me any reason not to trust him. I know it sounded weird since I didn't know him, but I naively thought I could spot an asshole right out of the gate. As it turns out, some jerks conceal their assholishness during the initial encounters, sucking their victim in and revealing their true selves only when they deem it necessary. Such as when they'd had too much to drink. As was in my case.

He knew about my handicap, although if I referred to myself as impaired around my family they lovingly scolded me. Despite realizing I was different, he'd asked me out anyway, and after some persistence on his part, I'd agreed. But on one condition—that Braylen tagged along. I wanted her with me for two reasons. One, because I hadn't been on a date since my senior year of high school, and two, so she could help communicate for me.

My sister and I met him at a bar he'd chosen, which was the first mistake, because all he did that evening was throw back shot after shot. When he'd become quite intoxicated, we told him we were leaving, which was when he became a little too handsy with me, completely ignoring the horrified look on my face. He ended up shoving my sister to the side when she grabbed his arm to let me go. When I turned hysterical with fear, I must have hit a nerve because he backed away and allowed us to walk out without further incident. I had no idea if it had dawned on him just how aggressive he'd become, or if he simply thought I wasn't worth the effort after I refused his advances.

When Braylen had begged me to come out to the fight that evening, I had no idea Marcus was going to be there. He'd briefly mentioned being involved with fighting, but it was such a fleeting statement I never paid much attention to it. So imagine my surprise when I saw him saunter down the narrow walkway toward the ring. Because of where our seats had been, he hadn't seen me. Until later. As soon as I saw him, I'd wanted to leave, but the other guy who had entered the ring after him kept me glued to my rickety chair.

An undeniable fierceness shrouded him, a potency which drew me in right away. A sensation I couldn't comprehend, but I knew I had to stay until the end. Luckily, Marcus had lost, making the mystery fighter the victor. Or at least he was a mystery to me. To the fans shouting his name, he was obviously well-known.

Standing outside and finally breathing in some fresh air, I'd managed to calm down some, thankful these three men had come to our rescue. I had no idea how far Marcus would have taken it if we were left to deal with him all by ourselves. Not that I didn't have faith that Braylen would have jumped on his back like an angry spider monkey if he refused to leave me alone, of course. She was fiercely protective of me. And I loved her all the more for it.

Jagger tentatively approached me, a curious look on his face while he attempted to converse with me. He'd seen my sister and I signing to each other so he knew there was something different about me, but I bet he had no idea what it really was.

"Is she all right?" he asked Braylen, turning his head toward her at the last minute. "She's not hurt, is she?" He looked worried about me and I found it rather sweet. I didn't know him, yet there was a strange pull between us. I felt it, and I noticed he did as well. His expression was one of a child looking at something wondrous for the first time, the innocent curiosity which came from being exposed to something unknown and . . . different.

Braylen smiled at Jagger then turned her attention toward me. Raising her hands, she signed, *He's quite the hottie, isn't he? Look at those arms of his, and that butt. Wow! Did you see his butt, Kena? And what about his two buddies.*

Holy shit, woman. We couldn't have been saved by hotter men.

I smiled, responding with, *Jagger is hot, for sure. I hope none of them know what we're saying.* I glanced at Jagger and saw him intently watching the exchange between Braylen and me, waiting for my sister to confirm that I was indeed all right. *Tell him I'm fine.*

Do you want me to give him your number? she asked. I looked at her like she'd lost her mind. *What? You can text, can't you?*

What I strangely felt toward Jagger was nothing I'd ever experienced before. Maybe it was simply hormones. Or maybe it was the knight in shining armor syndrome. Whatever the cause, I couldn't deny I felt something toward the mysterious fighter. So I allowed myself a moment to consider Braylen's question. But in the end I declined, not being in the right frame of mind to put myself out there.

Tapping my index and middle finger against my thumb, I signed, *No.* I saw the disappointment on her face right away, and I knew she wasn't going to let me dismiss him that easily. I would have thought she'd be onboard with my refusal because of what had transpired with Marcus, but she still pushed me.

Why not? she asked. *I really don't think he's anything like that asshat. Plus, you need to get out more. Stop hiding behind this bullshit,* she signed, pointing to my throat. *Live a little, and what better way to do that than with this fuckable man?*

My eyes widened and she laughed. I dared to glance at the guy in question, and thank goodness he still had no idea what we were saying to each other.

After Braylen gave me a subtle glare, she turned toward Jagger and said, "Kena is fine. She was a little rattled, but she's okay now. She also wants me to thank you and your friends"—she looked over at his buddies quick before locking eyes with Jagger again—"for helping us out. Kena is forever in your debt. And because of that, she wants me to give you her phone number." I grabbed her arm to try and turn her toward me, but she wouldn't budge. Instead she was smiling, extending her hand for his phone.

"How are we gonna talk on the phone?" Jagger asked slowly, as if my sister hadn't realized this.

"You can text, can't you?" Braylen retorted, smiling even wider.

The whole time they were conversing, I couldn't stop the embarrass-ment from creeping up and stealing over my skin, my face no doubt bright red. Continuing to try and get my sister's attention was futile; she was dead set on fixing me up with Jagger. After she'd finally put my number in his phone, he raised his head and pinned me with his entrancing amber-colored eyes. Biting down on his lower lip, he seemed to be struggling with something. Maybe he only took my number to be polite. Or maybe he wanted to speak to me. I had no idea, but I wasn't complaining about having to look at him for a few more minutes.

"I don't know if I can do this," he suddenly blurted. My heart fell, rejected before he even got to know me. I should have felt nothing, since I was the one who had initially refused my sister's persistence, but his dismissal hurt all the same. "I think she's absolutely beautiful, and I would love to get to know her, but how the hell am I gonna talk to her?"

I wasn't quite sure who exactly Jagger was talking to, because his eyes roamed from Braylen to his friends, only resting on me for a few seconds before looking at the ground. He seemed put out all of a sudden, as if it were a burden to be mixed up with someone like me.

It made me feel less than.

Inadequate.

Without thinking, I grabbed Braylen's arm, and that time she gave me her attention. I signed furiously. *You tell him not to bother with me then. Don't call me. I'm not someone to be tolerated. To hell with him if he doesn't want to get to know me.*

Braylen looked at me strangely. "I'm sure that's not what he meant, Kena." She didn't sign to me that time.

"What did she say?" Jagger asked, suddenly looking interested again.

"Nothing. Don't pay attention to her. She's just flustered. It's been a long day." I tried to turn Braylen toward me once more so I could tell her something else, but she refused. "I'm not looking at you, little sis, so stop trying." Stomping my foot like an errant child did nothing but make her laugh. "Not gonna work, so stop it," she chided. Folding my arms over my chest, I blew a strand of hair out of my face before turning and walking away. If she wasn't going to listen to me, I was done. My feelings had been hurt, and all I wanted to do was go home. Maybe soak in a hot bath before turning in for the night. The thing was . . . I knew Jagger would run on a constant loop in my head until I finally succumbed to sleep. Even while still being upset with him, as well as with my sister.

Maybe I'd taken what he'd said the wrong way. Or maybe I hadn't. Either way, I was used to people ignoring me, never giving me the time of day because I was different.

I briskly walked away from the small group, but didn't get very far before a firm yet gentle hand wrapped around my upper arm, stopping me.

When I turned my head, I saw Jagger staring at me like I was a piece of lost treasure. His eyes roamed my face, focusing a little too long on my lips before connecting with my eyes.

Everyone else stood back while we had our own private moment. "I'm sorry if I offended you, Kena. That wasn't my intention at all. It's just . . . I'm not sure how to talk to you. Look at me now. You can't hear anything I'm saying and I have no idea how to tell you . . . well . . . anything. You're so fucking beautiful that I'm losing all my sensibilities just being near you." He stepped closer, his scent wafting around me and making me dizzy. In a good way. "I guess there's no harm in telling you that I'd love nothing more than to kiss you, to feel the warmth of your mouth against mine. I have no idea why I'm saying this, except for that I guess I'm safe to do so because you can't hear me. Which sucks, by the way." The more he spoke, the more uncomfortable he appeared. "Listen to me ramble on. Sorry, I have no idea why I keep talking except that I have this overwhelming need to tell you that you do something to me. You make me feel . . . relevant. If that makes any sense at all, which it probably doesn't." His tongue snuck out and ran over his bottom lip, immediately drawing my attention to his delectable mouth.

As if a lightbulb had switched on inside his head, he suddenly asked, "Can you read lips?" Turning around to look for my sister, he yelled, "Can she read lips?"

"No, she never bothered to learn." Jagger instantly relaxed, but it was short-lived. "But she can hear everything you're saying." Braylen strolled up behind Jagger, put her hand on his shoulder and leaned in close. "You see, Kena's not deaf. She just can't speak. Whatever you just told her is now ingrained in that brain of hers, so it better have been good." My sister chuckled as she grabbed my hand and pulled me away. "Time to go now, boys. Thanks again for your assistance." She looked back at Jagger. "You better text her. You'd be a fool not to."

Daring to take a look back at the guy who just threw my world into chaos, I saw the wheels turning, watching him come to the realization that I'd heard him tell me he wanted to kiss me. That I made him feel relevant.

I had no doubt he would have never told me those things if he thought I could hear, but I loved that he'd bared a piece of himself. Even though he thought his words fell on deaf ears.

Every pun intended.

Before we slipped inside Braylen's car I heard one of his friends say, "Looks like you'll be learnin' some sign language, my man."

SIX

Kena

WHY DID YOU GIVE HIM my number? I asked Braylen while she flitted around her room trying to get ready for work. It'd been two days since I'd met Jagger and still he hadn't reached out. I tried to convince myself that I didn't care, that it was for the best, but I was disappointed. He'd been attracted to me; he'd said so. He told me he wanted to kiss me, so why the silence?

My sister ignored me, mumbling words every now and again. She drove me nuts refusing to answer. Before she became even more distracted, I grabbed her arm and spun her toward me, letting her know I wasn't going to let up until she answered my question.

Sighing overdramatically, she tucked her hair behind her ear and stared at me for countless seconds before opening her mouth. "Because you need to get out, Kena. You need to stop shying away from people and put yourself out there more. Hiding at work and then back at home is not doing you any good." Braylen only signed to me when we were in the company of others, and when she wanted to talk about them. Otherwise, she spoke to me like any other normal person, something I thoroughly appreciated.

I'm not hiding.

"You are. I love you, but you're in denial, sis." Throwing a pair of jeans on her bed, she brushed past me toward her closet to search for a shirt.

When she emerged, I signed more emphatically. *I would have thought you wanted me to stay clear of all fighters, especially after what happened with Marcus.* Shifting from one foot to the other, I patiently waited for the line of crap she was going to lay on me.

"You can't group all of them together. Plus, I don't know . . . ," she stalled. "There's something about Jagger I found calming. Weird choice of word for his type, but there it is. Plus, the way he was watching you when you weren't paying attention was endearing."

Endearing or stalker-ish? I smirked before she tossed a pillow at my head. *Either way, I'm not getting mixed up with him. You say there's something calming about him, but I detect there's a very dangerous element surrounding him.* What I'd really been referring to was him being hazardous to my heart.

"It's up to you either way. I think you should give him a shot if he texts you, though. Take it slow. Give it time and get to know him. If you're not interested, let it go. But if I'm right about him, and I really think I am, he could be good for you." After Braylen finally decided on an outfit, skinny jeans and a red tank top, she threw on her sneakers and grabbed her smock. She was running late and would have to leave right away if she was going to make it to work on time. Thankfully, her best friend owned the hair salon, Transform, where she worked.

Sensing there was nothing left to say, I followed her toward the front door, walking past her while she locked up. Happy to head into work, I started my trusty Nissan and decided I would welcome the distraction of my job; otherwise, I'd overthink the entire situation involving Jagger.

Braylen and I hadn't ventured far from the nest, renting a house ten minutes from my parents, eight minutes from the restaurant and five minutes from the salon.

I never had any big dreams of traveling around the world, or going away to school far from home. I was a homebody, attending a nearby college and earning my accounting degree, which enabled me to take care of the finances for my parents' lucrative restaurant. They were doing so well there were plans to branch out a few towns over. They paid me a nice salary, so I couldn't complain. Sure, I could have gotten a job at a large accounting firm, but because of my "challenge" I was simply more comfortable around my family.

In most cases, I coped rather well in life, but there were moments, like with the altercation with Marcus, where I found myself shutting down. I hated that I couldn't scream at him to leave me alone, leaving my older sister to fight my battles for me yet again. She'd been the first one to stick up for me, defending me against the bullies at school. Little did she know, sometimes she did more harm than good. When she called out those little bastards, they teased me relentlessly whenever she wasn't around. I never told her because I didn't want to make her feel bad.

My parents wanted me to have as normal a childhood as possible, which was why they had enrolled me in public school. Sure I couldn't talk, but I could hear just fine. I'd write down any questions I had for the teachers, and everything worked out fine until fifth grade, when the bullying just got worse. The kids called me a mute, which I was, but the way they said it made me feel like a freak, as if I had a choice in what had happened to me.

When I was an infant, I'd contracted a viral infection which had damaged the nerves in my larynx. A freak thing. There was optimism that the damage wouldn't be permanent, but as the years passed and I still wasn't able to form a sound, the doctors said there was no more hope. Because of that, I'd never spoken a day in my life. In the past, I often wondered what my voice would have sounded like, fantasizing about all the things I would've loved to say to my family, and to the few friends I'd made growing up. To tell someone I loved them, for them to hear me say the words, was what I had dreamed about the most. But it would never happen, so I let those fantasies die long ago. No use dwelling on the impossible.

The bullying had gotten so bad that one day during sixth grade my parents found me bawling my eyes out, tucked into the far corner of my closet. After some prodding, I finally spilled the beans, signing so fast I was surprised they understood me at all. Finally deciding enough was enough, they'd moved me to a school for the deaf. At least there I'd be around kids who had to communicate the same way I did.

Signing was my main way of communicating, but for my family, since I could hear what they were saying, they'd simply spoken. Occasionally, there were times when they would talk, stop to sign, and then go back to talking.

Almost like speaking Spanglish, but for sign language.

SEVEN

Kena

PULLING INTO THE PARKING LOT of the restaurant, I noticed we were rather busy. Crowds sometimes gave me anxiety, so I was thankful there was a back entrance, something I used quite a bit. Walking down the short hallway toward my office, I heard my phone ding, alerting me to a text message. Rooting through my purse, I found the device buried at the bottom. I hurriedly swiped the screen, thinking it was Braylen switching plans for later, but to my astonishment the message was from an unknown number. All it said was *Hello*.

My heart thumped against my chest, my breathing suddenly coming in short spurts. *Is this him?*

Closing the door behind me, I walked across the room and sat behind the desk. My office was small but it did the trick, locking me away from everyone else. The walls were painted a neutral tan color, which I found oddly soothing. My desk was big enough to house a computer, phone and lamp. I often listened to music while I worked, so I had a docking station as well, which charged my phone while Pandora played.

Five minutes had passed and I still hadn't responded to the text. There was a chance it could be a wrong number, but deep inside I knew it wasn't. Still . . . I hesitated.

Did I want to start talking to Jagger?

Open myself up only to be disappointed in the end?

Being guarded was a natural defense, but after warring back and forth with myself for another ten minutes, I finally gave in and typed a response.

Kena: Who is this?

Three little dots appeared on the screen.

Unknown: Jagger.

Unknown: How are you?

My breath caught in my throat, small beads of perspiration forming by my hairline. I had a sneaking suspicion it was him, so why was I so nervous? What about him had me suddenly flustered? Closing my eyes, I brought forth the memories of when I'd met him two nights prior. Fast-forwarding past the unfortunate encounter with Marcus, I focused on when my eyes first met his. I'd been so infuriated after hearing that ass call me a freak that I hadn't seen anything but red. Still in the throes of anger, I soon calmed when I'd realized that someone had come to our rescue.

A stranger.

A gorgeous, tattooed, tough and intimidating-looking fighter.

The first thing I noticed about Jagger was his eyes. I knew it sounded all dreamy and lovely and cliché, but it was the truth. His eyes captivated me as soon as our gazes met, the amber color almost mesmerizing. The shade was beautiful, but it was the intensity behind them which drew me in and held me prisoner.

To what, I had no idea.

Not yet, at least.

I'd only had seconds to rake in his entire being before I came across as some sort of visual stalker, so I'd made it count. My eyes darted from his dark golden hair, to his strong jaw, to his full and inviting lips. Then my gaze went lower, noticing his muscular arms which were covered in ink before dropping to the cut physique hidden underneath his clothing. I'd seen him earlier in all his glory while he was in the ring, only wearing a pair of black shorts, his chest bare and on display for all to see. Based on the shouts of the women, they were enthralled with him as well—not that he paid any attention. And not that I'd noticed.

Kena: I'm fine.

Shaking my head, I'd instantly wanted to delete my response, but it was too late. I was sure he'd already seen it, seen what a doofus I was. Not having used that word since I was a kid, it seemed to fit perfectly. My lack of flirting, even over text, proved how out of practice I'd been. Not that I'd ever had much experience, of course.

Throwing my phone in my desk drawer, I busied myself with numbers. Work needed to be done, plus I needed a very real distraction. My impatience to hear Jagger's response annoyed me, though, and it was simply one more thing to add to the growing list of reasons why I'd chosen to keep myself hidden from the world as much as possible. My family didn't understand it—Braylen, mainly—but they didn't have a handicap they had to endure. Sorry, not handicap . . . challenge. No, to hell with that. It was a handicap, no matter how they tried to spin it. Don't get me wrong, I wasn't a "poor me" type of girl, but I hid behind it when it suited me. Which was quite often.

My cell vibrated inside the drawer, drawing me back from my internal deliberations. Closing my eyes, I willed my inner strength to barrel forth, to deter me from glancing at his response, but it was futile. Curiosity won out and I pulled the drawer open to retrieve my phone, swiping the screen so I could see his reply.

Jagger: I'll text you later. Have to take care of something.

The door to my office came crashing open, my surprise at the intrusion swallowing the disappointment I felt reading Jagger's last text.

Mom, you scared me, I signed before relaxing in my chair.

"Sorry, sweetie, the door flung open too easily," she said, smiling widely as she approached. My mom, Caroline, was a beautiful woman. While she was short in stature, matching my five-foot-three frame, she made up for it with her feistiness, a trait my father often told us he loved. Although there were a few times I was sure he wasn't a big fan, mainly when they argued. Thankfully, those occasions were few and far between.

Did you need me? I asked, waiting to find out why she'd burst in.

Rounding the desk, she came to sit on the corner, tucking an unruly strand of hair behind my ear. She hesitated before speaking, which told me she was going to say something I didn't want to hear.

"Kevin is going to be an hour late for his shift," she said, turning her eyes away from mine for a brief moment. "He said he has personal business to attend to that he can't get out of." Fidgeting, she finally looked at me again before asking, "Do you think you can help out in the kitchen until he gets here?"

I knew my mom wouldn't ask me to help out unless she absolutely had to, so as it turned out I really didn't have a choice at all. Well, I did, but I'd do anything to eliminate the look of worry in her eyes right then. My dad wasn't feeling well so he hadn't come in, and my sister was already at her other job. So it was either I help out or my mother would have to run back and forth between the kitchen and helping wait tables, since we were down a waitress at the moment. Given the option, I would much rather help cook than take people's orders, seeing as how I couldn't answer any of their questions and all.

Our regulars knew I couldn't speak, but whenever newbies came in . . . Let's just say I was thankful for my office hidden in the back of the restaurant.

Who's going to be helping me out until Kevin gets here?

"Eddie. It's a little busy right now, but it's starting to calm down. The two of you will be fine. Then when Kevin gets in, you can come back here and finish up."

I liked Eddie a lot. He'd always managed to make me laugh, entertaining me with one of his crazy, adrenaline-infused stories. Plus, he wasn't too bad to look at. With shoulder-length black hair—which he always had tied back when working—and brown eyes, he was certainly a cutie. Not my type, but good-looking nonetheless.

Okay, just give me two minutes and I'll be right there.

She leaned over and kissed my cheek. "Thanks, sweetheart. I really appreciate it." Giving my mom a faint smile, I waited until she left my office before taking a few deep breaths to steel my nerves.

I wasn't a recluse or someone who shied away from all social interactions, but I did become slightly unnerved when thrown into a situation I wasn't completely comfortable with. I'd get over it, though. I always did.

Tying my hair back, I ventured out toward the front of the restaurant. Ten minutes later and I was in full swing, helping cook some of the lunch specials for the day. The time flew by. Between orders, Eddie regaled me with stories of his latest thrill-seeking adventure. A month back he went base jumping with a few buddies of his, said the feeling was unlike anything he'd ever experienced. I listened attentively, nodding and smiling so he knew I was paying attention.

Although Eddie was only twenty-four, three years older than me, he seemed much older—not necessarily looks-wise, but in experience. I guessed it had to do with him living his life to the fullest. I was sure he had fears, everyone did, but he never exposed them or let them hold him back.

Glancing at the clock, I noticed two hours had passed. As I was about to search for my mother, Kevin barreled into the kitchen, furiously tying his apron around his back so he could take over. Leaning in, he kissed my temple and gave me a thousand-watt smile.

"I'm so sorry I'm late, Kena. Please forgive me," he pleaded, holding his hand over his heart while he gave me the puppy dog eyes. And boy, what eyes they were. Pools of dark blue which promised wicked nights of fun, with full, lickable lips to match. Kevin was quite the sight, standing before me awaiting my faux absolution. Little did he know I could pardon him almost anything, his dimpled cheeks persuading me rather quickly.

He remained motionless until I smirked and signed, *You're lucky I like you.*

Kevin had learned sign language when he was a kid. His aunt Louise had been born deaf, so communicating with her that way had simply become second nature for him and his entire immediate family.

Love you, pumpkin, he hastily signed before taking the spatula from my hand. I laughed at his ridiculous nickname for me, shaking my head and walking back toward my office.

Braylen had often asked me why I never gave him a chance, seeing as how he'd asked me out a few times in the past. Repeatedly I'd explained that while he was rather attractive, much more so than Eddie—not that I was comparing them to each other—I simply wasn't interested. To clarify, I *had* been interested in accepting one of his invitations for dinner and a movie, but after I saw the way women threw themselves at him after one of his shows, I decided not to put myself into a situation which would only serve to hurt me in some way.

Kevin was the lead guitarist for a local rock band called Breakers, and they had quite the following. Braylen and I had gone to a few of their gigs, and had really enjoyed ourselves. The last time he asked me out, which was two months ago, I'd finally told him the reason why I wouldn't accept. Instead of trying to convince me otherwise, he simply nodded and kissed my cheek, telling me if I ever changed my mind, he would be the happiest man alive.

After another couple hours, I'd finally finished my work, so I texted Braylen and told her to meet me at home when her shift ended. Checking my phone one more time, I saw Jagger hadn't texted again, and it was with vast disappointment that I drove home. I vowed right then not to allow myself to get all worked up over some guy I didn't even know.

EIGHT

Jagger

ANNOYED I HAD BEEN PULLED away from texting with Kena, I tossed my cell on the table outside Chambers before entering. No one was allowed to bring their phones inside when we were discussing club business except on rare occasions, which always had to be approved by our president.

Walking around the large oblong meeting table, I settled into my assigned seat and impatiently waited to find out why we'd all been gathered last-minute.

The men filed in one after another, taking their seats and conversing amongst themselves. Marek and Stone were the last to arrive, their expressions hiding the direness of what was about to unfold.

Once our leader pulled his chair closer to the table, he rested his folded hands on top of the etched wood. A frown decorated his face, his dark hair disheveled and sticking up in several places. There were a few more lines around his eyes than from months prior, telling the amount of stress he'd been under. Steering the club away from the Los Zappas cartel was taxing, and even more so on Marek and Stone, since they worked so closely together. I knew our prez was still waiting for the green light to snatch Rico Yanez's life, and then he would focus his attention on ridding the world of Psych Brooks, Sully's father. If anyone could even call him that. The man made the Devil look like a pussycat.

"I have news," Marek announced, silencing those who were holding their own sidebar conversations. Everyone turned toward the head of the table, eagerly awaiting the next words to fall from his mouth. Brief silence danced around the room, each member taking comfort in the unknown, for as brief as it was. "I got the call I've been waiting for." After briefly locking eyes with his second in command, he leaned forward and pinned the rest of us with his intensity. "Rafael Carrillo called me to tell me we could have Yanez." Everyone remained silent, fearing they'd miss something if they uttered a word or moved a muscle. "He instructed a few of his men to follow Yanez, gathering his own intel to support our claim that his right-hand man was continuing to deal with the Reapers after he'd cut off all dealings with them. Apparently he found what he was looking for."

Marek turned his head toward Zip. "Good work." Two words and the youngest member beamed with pride.

Zip had been tasked with following Yanez a while back, trying to obtain any kind of evidence he could to give to Marek, who in turn would bring it to Carrillo to show him just how disloyal the shady bastard had been to the cartel. He'd snapped pictures of Yanez with Sam Koritz, a corrupt DEA agent who'd raided our club, as well as photos with Psych Brooks. It was those pics with the president of the Savage Reapers which had apparently spurred the cartel to take action.

Looking from one man to another, I wasn't quite sure where to rest my attention. The room had remained silent, Marek's words festering for all of us. He was finally going to get justice for his wife, and while the thought pleased me, I wasn't afraid to admit to myself that I was a bit unnerved at what it could mean for our club. With an integral part of the cartel now being extinguished, would they look to make up for the loss?

I knew Marek and Carrillo had some sort of agreement, the head of the cartel releasing us from their grip because of it, but I still didn't trust the guy. Who was to say he wouldn't go back on his word in the future, forcing us back under their wing whenever he deemed necessary? I hadn't been privy to any of the meetings that had taken place, so I only had my suspicions to go on, but I prayed with everything inside me that my concerns would remain unjustified.

"Don't make any plans," Stone said, directing his instruction to the entire room. "We're gonna need you all ready to go when the time comes. Some will come with us to the safe house, others will stand guard at various locations. If anything pops off, we need to be ready." Stone nodded at Marek before leaning back in his chair.

The club kept a safe house an hour away, a place that was used in cases of emergency. It was situated in the middle of a residential area, hidden in plain sight. With a soundproof basement, it was perfect for dealing with unsavory people. The last time I knew of anyone making use of it was when Marek and Cutter had tortured and killed Vex, the guy who'd tormented Sully while she lived with her club.

The boom of the gavel sounded, signaling the meeting was officially over. Rising from my seat, I walked toward the exit, my mind on what was going to happen in the next few days. I was eager to assist Marek in resolving the issue of Yanez, even though I was positive he would never ask for my help, content with leaving me in the background when it came to club business.

As soon as I walked from the room, I grabbed my cell from the table where I'd left it and glided my fingers over the keyboard to text Kena. Just as I was about to hit Send, the phone was suddenly ripped out of my hands. Snapping my head up, I saw Tripp grinning, rifling through my privacy.

"Is this the chick we met at your fight? The deaf one?" he asked, continuing to smile at my unease. Why I was nervous I couldn't say. I just was.

"She's not deaf," I snapped. "She just can't speak."

"So, you gonna fuck her or what?"

"Gimme back my phone," I demanded, my anger rising the longer he held my cell captive. The bastard towered over me, but if he didn't watch it I'd knock him on his ass. Or at least imagine such a thing. While I was quite lethal in the ring, Tripp could certainly give me a run for my money if we ever got into a serious altercation.

"Answer my question first."

"None of your business," I quipped. A need to defend Kena abruptly took over, even if Tripp had just been messing with me.

Looking at my phone, he chuckled before tossing it back to me. "If you need help with sexting, just let me know." He walked away before I could respond, his cocky gait making me want to throw something at the back of his head.

Sending Kena a quick text, I hoped she was near her phone so she could respond. Walking toward the bar, I nodded toward Trigger to pour me a drink. I liked the resident member of the club, his no-nonsense attitude quite amusing most of the time. Thankfully, I'd never been in his line of sight before. Stone took the prize for that one. Ever since he got with Adelaide, Trigger's niece, there's been an all-out battle between the two of them, Trigger going as far as shooting the VP when he found out. Although, since the birth of Stone and Addy's daughter, the tension has seemed to lessen between the two men, only erupting when Stone wanted to get a rise out of Trigger, and vice versa. Using Adelaide as leverage, of course.

Jagger: Did you officially add my number to your phone so you don't think some random creep is texting you? LOL

LOL? I'm not an LOL kind of guy.

Throwing back a shot, I nodded for Trigger to hit me again.

"You know it's still early, right?" he asked, flinging a white dishtowel over his shoulder. He could ask me all the questions he wanted, as long as he poured me a drink.

"So?"

"Don't you have to train or something for your upcoming fight?"

"That's not for another two weeks," I retorted, growing agitated that I had to explain why I wanted another shot. I knew I was just the prospect of the club, but although the guys treated me well, it was times like this that I felt as if they undermined me. Or was that just concern? I had no idea and didn't have enough energy to deem it one way or the other right then.

Sliding the drink toward me, I tossed it back then slammed the glass on the bar before leaving my seat and walking toward the couch. Plopping down, I gripped my phone, willing Kena to respond so I had something to occupy my time. I didn't have anything planned for that evening. No fights, and it appeared as if my services weren't needed with the club yet. Having no desire to sit in my small apartment by myself, I lounged on the sofa and waited.

Thankfully, I didn't have to wait too long.

Kena: Who is this?

Did she have that many guys texting her that she honestly didn't know who it was? That we hadn't just been communicating before? And why did that thought irritate me?

Jagger: It's Jagger. Did you really forget about me that fast? Or do you have a slew of men begging for your attention?

No way was I gonna come across as insecure. Chicks hated that shit, right?

Kena: I know who it is. I'm just playing with you. Plead the fifth on the last question.

Before I could read too much into her last text, another one came through.

Kena: And yes, I added you to my phone. Hopefully, you won't make me delete you.

She certainly had some spunk, a trait I hadn't expected. I liked it.

Jagger: I'll try not to.

"Ask her to send you a pic of the twins," Tripp shouted as he walked past me on the way to the bar.

"What are you, fifteen?" I yelled back.

"No, I just haven't seen a nice pair of tits in a while, and from what I remember, she looked like she had some nice ones." I knew Tripp was just bustin' my balls, but his comments made me want to punch him in the face.

"Don't pay the nomad any attention," Stone instructed, sitting down next to me. "He likes to get under my skin with Addy, and he's just doin' the same shit with you. You texting that girl from the other night?"

"Yeah."

"You like her?"

"Yeah," I repeated, counting the seconds until she responded.

Oh God, I can feel myself growing a vagina.

"Then why don't you ask her to do something?" he asked, slinging his arm over the back of the couch and settling in.

"Because I can't talk to her in person. I know she can hear, but what about when she tries to say something to me? I-I mean . . . communicate with me, I know she can't speak," I explained, frustration tripping up my words. "I won't be able to understand her and I'll look like an idiot." Leaning my head back against the cushion, I let out a breath and tried to figure out what to do. I really wanted to get to know Kena, but would it ever go further than just texting?

"Do you like her?" Stone asked a second time, arching his brow in waiting.

"I already told you I did," I snapped.

"Then get off your ass and figure it out," he chided, rising to his feet and towering over me. Confident he'd given me the best advice known to man, he walked toward the exit of the clubhouse.

As I parted my lips to shout after him, my phone chimed.

Kena: Do you have any plans tonight?

Jagger: Why do you ask? Way to play it cool.

Kena: Friend's band is playing. Wanna go?

Jagger: I'm not into chick music, but I'll go if you want me to.

I frowned after re-reading my response, realizing I'd probably come off like a douche.

Kena: Ouch! I think you just shit all over my gender's music. BTW, my friend isn't a girl.

Jagger: Sorry, that didn't come out right. What's the name of the band?

Kena: I don't know if I should tell you now.

Is she seriously pissed off?

Radio silence for what seemed like forever. Just when I thought I'd blown my chances of seeing her that evening, an occurrence I hadn't even thought possible until her suggestion, she responded.

Kena: Breakers.

Jagger: I know them. Who's your friend?

How did she know any of the members? Did she go to school with them? Did she date one of them? More than one? Were they friends with her sister instead? So many questions rattled me.

Kena: Kevin. He works at my family's restaurant.

Jagger: Which restaurant?

Kena: Nope. Not gonna tell. You could be a crazy person. Don't need any sexy fighters showing up and stalking me.

There was no way to identify a tone through text, but I knew she was only messing with me. I wouldn't push for the information, however, in case she was being slightly serious. Plus, I didn't blame her. At least she was being safe, even though it was directed toward me.

Jagger: Smart move. You think I'm sexy?

Kena: :)

Allowing her compliment to boost my ego, I wanted to go out on a high note, ending our messaging tryst with one final request.

Jagger: Text me the name of the bar and the time to meet you. If I can get away, I'll see you later.

Appearing aloof had always worked in the past in garnering female attention, and I prayed my indifference worked with Kena. With each stroke of the keys I knew I was putting myself out there more than I'd initially intended, but I couldn't help myself. My heart pounded at the very thought of seeing her again, her communication with me crystalizing the possibility as a very real one.

Tucking my phone into my back pocket, I leaned forward and rested my forearms on my thighs. Bowing my head, I threaded my fingers through the strands of my hair in distraction. It wasn't a smart move to appear too eager, and although I looked forward to seeing her again, I tried to convince myself that she was just another girl.

A vibration thrummed against my lower back, but I ignored it.

Let's see how well restraint works in my favor.

NINE

Kena

OH MY GOD! GIVE ME back my phone. My hands were going a million miles a minute, my aggravation prevalent in the way my fingers danced through the air and created words. Sentences. Threats to my sister for stealing my phone and texting Jagger.

Only Braylen would be so carefree, flirting with him via messaging. She knew damn well I would've kept my responses short and sweet. And although I probably would've sounded like a dork, it was me and I wasn't going to change for anyone. A stubborn trait which irritated my older sister to no end.

But she didn't understand.

She didn't have anything holding her back from being "normal." While I longed to join the rest of society, I was forced into the shadows, watching everyone else live the life I wish I could. Warped or not, it was my view of the world.

Braylen danced around me, dizzying me into submission, if only until I regained my senses. "Oh, come on, lil' sis. You know damn well you would've let him slip through your fingers with your nonchalant responses and ill-conceived notions of what you think flirting is." She laughed harder with my pathetic attempts to tackle her and retrieve my cell.

Huffing, my face turning a light shade of red, I finally stood still and glared at my infuriating sibling. You would think being three years my elder would've made her more mature, but nope. I'd give her credit, though; with every birthday that passed, she refused to shed her childlike enthusiasm for unexpected situations. I guessed she viewed my predicament as such.

With my hands on my hips, I refused to plead again, instead choosing the effective stance of patience. Although it wasn't my strong suit. Eventually, she'd tire and pass me my phone. Moments prior, I'd caught a few of her responses to Jagger, but she'd been too quick, hopping off the bed before I could snatch the phone away from her.

Finally, after she deemed enough was enough, she crossed the small space between us and gave me a hug. Kissing my cheek, she said, "I did it for your own good. You'll thank me one day," she promised, returning my property.

Sauntering toward my closet, she disappeared inside and rooted around, the slight clang of the hangers drawing my attention. Re-entering the room, she shoved a dark purple tank top at me, flirty ruffles embellishing the front. "Wear those skinny jeans that make your booty pop. And those black heels you never wear."

Which ones? I loved how she could switch my mood from irritation to curiosity.

"The ones that make your legs look like they go on for miles, with the studded spikes on the back."

I'll break my neck. There's a reason I only wore them once. I cringed, remembering the time we'd gone out for drinks and I'd tripped walking back from the ladies' room, almost falling on my face.

"Stop being a baby and just get them. We have a few hours before we have to leave, so make sure you sex it up."

Taking my time, I indulged in a long shower. Thoughts of the upcoming evening took hold as the foam from my vanilla-scented shower gel coated my skin, lost in hopes that something good would finally happen. Not that I'd had a bad life, because I certainly had not. But most days, it seemed like I was simply existing, trudging from one day to the next with snippets of joy laced between.

I wanted to experience all life had to offer.

Passion.

Drama.

Love.

Okay, maybe not the drama piece so much, but the other two would be wonderful.

An hour later, I curled the last strand of my dark hair, flinging it behind my shoulder and integrating it with the rest, using my fingers to soften the look. I slipped on my heels, smoothed down my shirt and checked out my butt. Hey, I had to make sure the jeans still did their job. Deeming myself presentable, I snatched my wristlet from my dresser, flicked off my bedroom light and strode down the short hallway to my sister's room.

Pushing open her door, Braylen gave me an enormous smile when her eyes landed on me.

An impervious whistle cut through the air. "Now that's what I'm talking about," she exclaimed. "Wait until he gets a load of you. He's gonna bust a nut for sure." She teasingly smacked my ass on her way toward the front door. "Let's go, chica. There is some fun to be had."

———— ◦ ————

NERVES SHOOK ME THE FURTHER we walked toward the entrance to Rustic, the trendy bar where Kevin's band was set to play that evening. I'd wanted nothing more than to lay eyes on Jagger again, but with every swift tick of the clock, reservation suffocated my hope. In its place, anxiety and fear riddled me, threatening to shut down my evening before it even started.

"Calm down," she soothed. "I see you're getting nervous. Don't get lost inside that head of yours tonight," she said, tapping my temple to help shock me out of my own inner paranoia. "If he shows, great. If he doesn't, we're gonna drink and be merry. Even flirt a little with whoever catches our fancy." She laughed, seizing my hand and dragging me through the entry, steering me directly toward the bar ahead. "Let's get started, shall we?"

There were a few different levels to Rustic, making it a popular hangout for the locals. The first floor housed the main bar and the stage where the bands played, numerous high-back booths as well as tables and chairs scattered throughout providing plenty of seating for the patrons. If people wanted to experience more of a club feel, they ventured down to the basement where another bar stole the entire back wall, a large dance floor stretching across the majority of the open space. The seating on the lower level was selective, only a few couches spread out around the room.

Two cosmopolitans in and I felt nice. Relaxed. Ready to allow the night to unfold and thrust me into unforeseen possibilities—of the good kind, of course. Listening to Braylen chatter on about some of her salon clients, my nerves lessened, having something other than my anxiousness to focus on. Plus, the alcohol licked my veins, pulling me into a nice fog. In the middle of my sister telling me about some hot guy who'd walked into her work, a strong hand clutched my waist, pulling me back into a strong chest. Stumbling backward a step, the mystery guy helped to steady me before making his identity known. My sister was all smiles.

Turning my head to the side, I saw Kevin grinning at my shocked reaction. Leaning in, he kissed my temple before releasing me.

"I'm so happy you two made it," he said, leaning his hip against the bar so he was facing both of us. "You haven't been to a show in a few months." Quirking his brow, he looked lost in thought for a moment. "Yeah, it's been at least six months," he affirmed, a beaming smile lighting up his face once more.

As I brought my hands up in front of me, preparing to sign, an eager-looking redhead sauntered past, eyeing Kevin like she wanted to eat him up. "Hi, Kevin," she cooed, pushing her tits out to make herself more tempting. She was attractive enough, if you found desperation appealing.

"Hi, sweetheart," he answered, winking at her before turning his focus back on us. "Fans," he chuckled. "Comes with the territory."

You certainly don't mind, I signed, smirking at the way he tried to look affronted.

"I'd give it all up in a heartbeat if you'd agree to be mine, pumpkin," he teased, encircling my waist with his arm and pulling me close, kissing the top of my head. "Just say the word." I knew Kevin was attracted to me, but I also realized he was only playing, enjoying getting a rise out of me whenever he could.

You'd never be able to live without all the fans fawning at your feet night after night, I jested, resting my hand on his upper arm in a comfortable touch of friendliness.

Contemplating a retort, he wiggled his brows and bit his bottom lip. "Yeah, you're right." I enjoyed the easiness between us, thankful Braylen had convinced me to come out. Plus, Kevin took my mind off Jagger, which was a good thing.

After five minutes of easy banter between the three of us, Kevin spotted his buddies, announcing he had to do some last-minute sound checks before the show. Once we readily agreed to stay until their set was over, he embraced the both of us before sauntering across the room and hopping on stage with his bandmates.

"You having fun?" Braylen asked, bumping my shoulder with hers, a hopeful look in her eye that her baby sister was letting loose and enjoying herself.

I really am. I smiled, harboring a deep appreciation toward her for constantly looking out for me. *I can't believe I'm saying this, but thanks for forcing me out tonight.*

"You're welcome, sweetie. I just wanna see you live a little, ya know?"

Nodding, I turned my attention toward the drink she pushed my way, sliding it across the dark polish of the bar. The alcohol promised an eventful night, dark liquid fingers dragging me into a soft oblivion if I wasn't careful.

Last one. I don't want to get drunk, I signed.

"Why not? It's not like you have to go into work tomorrow if you don't want to." Chewing on her straw, she took quick sips before placing the drink back on the bar. "What's the harm in totally losing yourself tonight?"

Well, for one, I don't want to be throwing up all night. And two . . . , I stalled, *there's no two. I just don't want to be sick and then feel like crap all day tomorrow. Plus, you know what a lightweight I am when it comes to drinking.* Bringing my hands down to rest on the edge of the bar, I reached for my third and final drink of the evening, circling my fingers around the cool glass and gingerly bringing it to my lips.

"Well, you might change your mind," she prompted, her eyes suddenly fixated on someone across the room. Grinning from ear to ear, she looked back at me before broadcasting, "Someone decided to show up after all. And he looks fine as hell."

Slowly turning my head, my eyes locked on Jagger propped against the wall behind him, hands in his pockets and looking quite magnificent. Even from across the room, I knew his gaze rested on me, his beautiful eyes so intense it made me shudder. An undeniable pull existed between us, and all I wanted to do was go to him.

Or run and hide.

I couldn't decide yet.

TEN

Jagger

I WASN'T GONNA LIE. FOR as tough as I appeared, I was a nervous wreck on the inside. Self-doubt propelled itself forward, casting me in the unrelenting shadows of unworthiness. What if she became frustrated because I couldn't communicate with her? Would she deem me undeserving and move on? Even over the distance separating us, I witnessed the comfortability that existed between her and Kevin. His attraction to Kena was obvious, but was she to him? It sure looked like it.

The aloofness I played while texting her came back to kick me in my stubborn ass. Maybe I shouldn't have ignored her last message. Maybe I should have let her be the one to end the back and forth between us. Either way, it was too late now; what was done was done. If she had certain feelings about it, or me, I was sure she'd let me know as soon as I approached.

I hid in the dimness of the bar until Kevin left. Only then did I reveal myself, still while hanging back and watching her. Parts of me felt like a creeper, but when it came to Kena, all bets were off.

Hopefully she's still interested; otherwise, I fear stalking charges in the near future.

Dispelling all unsure thoughts, I shoved off the wall once I knew Kena and her sister had seen me. While I took my time reaching them, I calmly repeated, *Don't fuck this up. Don't fuck this up. This one is special.* My little mantra had the opposite effect, though. My sudden nerves ricocheted inside me, my heart thumping hard against my chest and threatening to stop altogether the closer I advanced.

Expelling a quick breath, I dodged the ever-growing crowd and finally came to rest a few paces from Kena. Braylen's stare was intense, but the lilt of her smile helped to ease some of my trepidation. I realized Kena would consider her sister's advice when it came to interacting with me, so I knew I had to impress both of them.

"Hi," I greeted, standing so close to Kena our shoulders brushed. Her body trembled from the touch and I prayed it was from excitement, not regret of having invited me that evening. Not wanting to come across as lustful as I felt being near her, I kept my eyes on her face, drinking in her image as best I could before moving on to her sister. Giving them both a genuine, yet apprehensive smile, I eased a little when I saw they both appeared happy to see me.

"Thank God you came," Braylen gushed. "I was beginning to lose all faith in your intentions toward my sister." She laughed, throwing her arm over Kena's shoulder and pulling her close—a protective stance of sorts. Right away, I liked Braylen. A fire lit behind her eyes in warning, although hope danced alongside. The warring emotions both confused and elated me. She loved Kena more than anything, and while she wanted her to be happy, she would slay anyone who hurt her.

"I wouldn't miss seeing you again," I admitted, meeting Kena's eyes briefly before looking away again. Not wanting to reveal too much, I changed the subject. "What are you both drinking?" I asked, signaling for the bartender who was chatting it up with some chick.

Kena raised her hands and signed something to her sister, a look of hesitancy holding her captive.

Braylen responded before turning her attention to me. "She's fussing because she doesn't think she should drink anymore, but I told her to relax and live a little. You never know what can happen," she goaded.

Kena gave Braylen a death stare of sorts before shyly looking over at me, the uncertainty in her beautiful caramel-colored eyes undoing me. The need to assure her that everything would be fine overwhelmed me, a strong urge of protectiveness wrapping its warmth around me. I couldn't explain it, and I didn't think I wanted to; if I unraveled those feelings too much, they might float away and leave me in a place where I no longer wished to exist.

Before my brain could filter my words, I opened my mouth and said, "I won't let anything bad happen to you." I hadn't meant to be so forward, but every syllable was the absolute truth. She smiled at me before looking back to Braylen.

It was clear Kena was nervous, but did she realize I was as well?

Hiding my emotions had been ingrained in me since I was a kid, my father's constant hurtful words toughening me up faster than was deemed healthy. The only time I'd let my guard slip was when I'd met Sully. Like Kena, she'd elicited my protective side, and just like this situation, I couldn't explain it.

"Kinda heavy for a first date," Braylen chuckled. "But I like it." Kena hurriedly signed something again, embarrassment stealing over her skin like a cloak. If I had to guess why, I would have said it was because her sister referred to this as a date, something I wasn't completely opposed to. Ignoring Kena, Braylen looked at me when she said, "I'm going to go check out when the band's gonna start. Be back soon." On her last word, she smiled at her sister before walking toward Kevin and his bandmates.

I'd known Kevin for a few years, as we went to the same high school. He was slightly older than me, and while we weren't technically friends, we'd been to a lot of the same functions—football games and parties, to be specific. I had no issues with him, and I wasn't aware of any negativity he harbored toward me.

I'd chosen not to wear my Knights Corruption cut to the bar that evening, not wanting to draw any unnecessary attention to myself. Don't get me wrong, the pride I felt toward my club would never waver, even though I still only held the title of prospect. Something I hoped changed in the near future. But we didn't have the best reputation around the area, and I didn't want to scare Kena off before she had the chance to get to know me.

The silence between us was palpable, and a tad uncomfortable. I could speak to her, but she couldn't reply—not in a way I understood, at least.

Not yet.

I vowed to rectify that soon, though.

Hoping to rely on body language and common sense, I took a chance and started speaking. "You look beautiful, Kena," I said, figuring it best to start off with an honest compliment.

She blushed before bringing the pads of her fingers of her right hand to her chin, touching briefly before pulling them away. After the gesture, she looked surprised she'd done it, probably because she knew I didn't know what it meant. But I could have guessed, given what I'd just said to her.

"Does that mean 'thank you?'" I asked, smiling when she emphatically nodded. "There's hope for me yet, isn't there?" I saw the quake of her chest, and her lips kicking up in a smile, realizing she was laughing, although not a single vibration of noise escaped. For the first time since I'd met her, her eyes lit up with a subtle hint of joy. Granted, this was only the second time I'd been in her presence, but she wore her emotions on her sleeve—which I found perfect since it made reading her moods much easier. And the more I got to know her, the easier it would become. I was sure of it.

Because I wanted to find out more information about her relationship with Kevin, I decided to cut to the chase and simply ask her, a yes or no the only response necessary.

"So, you and Kevin . . . Are you strictly friends?"

She swiftly nodded.

The bartender finally broke away from the chick he was fawning over and approached. I placed my order for a beer and for him to refill whatever it was Kena was drinking, before returning my full attention back to her.

"Did you ever date him?"

She shook her head.

"Did he ever ask you out?"

She briefly averted her gaze before looking me in the eyes again.

She nodded.

The air thickened around us as I prepared to ask my next intruding question, but I couldn't help myself; I needed to know. Curiosity as well as ego propelled me forth.

"Did you *want* to date him?" I intended to be casual but the more I engaged her, the more I wanted to know about the nature of their relationship.

Looking hesitant, she finally nodded, just as my fingers brushed over hers on top of the bar. An electric jolt passed between us—literally. I shocked her and she pulled her hand back before giving me an innocent smile.

Damnit! She had wanted to be with Kevin at some point. Did she still? I had to find out before I pursued this thing between us.

"Why didn't you, then? Be with him, I mean?" It wasn't until she frowned that I realized she couldn't answer me; I'd strayed off the path of simple yes and no questions. Reverting back, I changed my inquiry. "Do you still want to date him?"

No time passed before she shook her head, placing her hand on my wrist before pulling back once she realized she'd touched me. She looked confused, like she didn't understand her own reaction.

Her response soothed me, and from the intensity in her eyes, I knew she was being truthful. For some reason, she'd wanted to take things beyond friendship with Kevin, but had chosen not to.

Assuming, I pressed, "Was the reason why you chose not to be with him have anything to do with him being in Breakers?" *Depending on her response, I might be in the same boat, once she finds out about my club.*

Another nod.

Choosing not to rush things, and needing to save the information of my being involved with the Knights Corruption for another time, I offered a nod of my own before taking another pull of my beer. I dissuaded myself from interrogating her more about Kevin, not wanting to come off like an untrusting asshole.

Moments passed before Braylen returned. While I wanted to spend more time alone with Kena, there were only so many questions I could ask before our encounter would turn even more awkward.

"What are you two talkin' about?" she asked, taking a healthy sip from her drink, eyeing me first before looking at her sister. Kena signed something, and Braylen glanced at me skeptically before speaking. "Jagger, let me ask you something." *This should be good.* "My sister tells me you were asking her about her relationship with Kevin. Do you believe her when she tells you they're just friends?" Placing her hand on her hip, she leaned in to her sister while waiting for my lips to part and answer.

"Yeah." I wanted to add "For now," but thought wisely against it.

"Good. Because the last thing Kena needs is some possessive ass trying to stake some kind of claim on her. Understand?"

Kena shifted her feet, not sure who to look at.

"Completely."

"Are you possessive and territorial?" she threw at me, taking me by complete surprise.

"Not typically, no."

"What does that mean?" Kena's hands worked feverishly, but Braylen wasn't paying attention, her focus on me and me alone.

"I haven't met someone I've wanted to protect before. That's what I meant." I knew I'd stretched the truth a little when I'd answered. Sully popped into my mind, but I wasn't about to bring her up, because I didn't want the both of them getting the wrong idea. Besides, the way I felt toward Sully was completely different from the way I felt about Kena.

Worlds apart.

"I vouched for you, so don't mess this up," the feisty blonde said, taking a step back and finally turning toward Kena. Braylen shook her head and signed back to her sister. Whatever they were saying, they wanted to keep secret.

Note to self: learn sign language as soon as possible.

ELEVEN

Kena

FINDING A BOOTH CLOSE TO the stage with a perfect view of Kevin and his band, I sat next to Jagger, Braylen sitting across from us. I'd become flustered when Jagger started asking about Kevin, but I didn't want to lie. Yes, I'd been attracted enough to want to date the guitarist, but I decided against it because I didn't want to have to deal with all the drama that came with his fans. Namely the brazen women fawning all over him. So instead, we'd remained friends, and it was the furthest our relationship would ever develop.

I found nothing wrong with his questions on the subject, but apparently Braylen did. She liked Jagger, had encouraged me to give him a chance, but as soon as she found out he was asking about my feelings toward Kevin, the protective side of her busted through. And while she hadn't been aggressive with Jagger, her tone indicated her seriousness. It both comforted and irritated me.

I'd pleaded with her to let it go, and we had a mini argument of sorts. Thankfully it was quickly resolved, with me promising not to take things further with the fighter if I felt he was turning into a jealous freak.

An hour later, the band was in full swing. While I tried to lose myself to their music, all my attention was geared toward the devilishly handsome guy to my left. Jagger wore a dark green, button-down shirt with the sleeves rolled up, exposing the ink on his skin. And every time he moved his hand, I saw the muscles in his forearm twitch.

Playing with the stem of my glass, I tried not to pay too much attention to him, but it was impossible. Every so often, he'd nudge my arm or brush my shoulder, asking if I was enjoying myself. My only response was a curt nod. I knew he gazed at me, and each time I turned my head to check, he would simply smile and occasionally lick his lips, which then made me think naughty thoughts.

My imagination ran wild, picturing his naked body. Images of how he'd look hovering over me while he spread my legs, impaling me onto him until he filled me completely. I fantasized what his kiss would taste like. Was he aggressive or gentle, or a little bit of both? The thoughts shocked me, mainly because I'd never felt the touch of a man before. Yes, I'd kissed a few boys when I was younger, but because I shielded myself from normal dating situations, I'd never found myself in the position where I was thoroughly tempted to go all the way. Not that I didn't think about it. Often. Because I did. Being a twenty-one-year-old virgin was a status I wanted to rid myself of, but not with just anyone. While I wanted to shed my innocence, I wanted it to mean as much to the person I'd chosen to give it to as it did me.

Brushing my hand with his, Jagger called my focus when he leaned in close and asked, "Do you want another drink?" His warm breath danced over the side of my face and made me shiver. Finding the perfect opportunity to gaze at him openly, I turned toward him and we locked eyes. Gently shaking my head, I waited for him to speak again, to say anything that would keep me engaged so I didn't have to look away.

His hand lingered near mine and I didn't pull away. I loved the contact more than I let on because I didn't wish for him to view me as clingy. I had no idea what he thought of me, other than I believed he found me attractive.

"Do you want some water instead?" Realizing I definitely should have some, I nodded. Since I blocked his exit, I shuffled to the edge of the booth and stood when I cleared the table. "Braylen, do you need another drink?" he politely asked, scooting the rest of the way out of the booth until he stood directly beside me, his hand resting on my lower back. The warmth from his touch instantly ignited my desire, and it was difficult to keep such a thing in check.

But I managed.

Barely.

"Thanks, but this should be my last," she responded, holding up her drink for him to see. "But I'll take a water as well, if you don't mind."

"Not at all." He smiled at me before walking toward the bar.

A second after I sat back down, my eyes following every move Jagger made, my sister burst in on my visual stalking.

"Wow!" she exclaimed, hitting the top of the table with her hand. "You really like this one, don't you?"

Shrugging, I tried my best to play nonchalant, but she saw straight through me.

"Don't play coy with me, missy. I see the way you keep trying to sneak a peek at him. Even now, you can't keep your eyes off him, probably staring at his ass. But hey, I don't blame ya. He's gorgeous. Plain and simple."

He's certainly attractive, but I'm not gaga over him if that's what you're implying. So what if I'd told her a little white lie. I thought I was trying to convince myself more than her.

"Uh-huh," she mumbled, following my line of sight to Jagger, which only confirmed she knew I'd just fibbed. "Either way, it's nice to see you having a good time for once." Bringing the glass to her lips, she tipped it back and swallowed the rest of her drink.

I have fun, I argued, my hands taking on the frustration my voice wouldn't allow.

"When?"

When we go shopping or watch a movie. When we're just hanging out.

"That's not the same thing, Kena, and you know it. All I'm saying is that it's nice to see you interested in getting out there, putting your heart on the line, no matter the risk."

Whoa, slow down. Let's not get crazy. I smiled at her assumption that I was diving headfirst into the thought of me with Jagger. It was only the second time I'd seen him, and although I wanted there to be more occasions of the same, I wasn't naïve enough to think he'd break down all my walls with a few encounters.

Before Braylen and I could continue our conversation, Jagger sauntered back over with our waters in hand. He'd also gotten himself another beer. He didn't appear inebriated in the least, even though I'd witnessed him put away at least four of them. It should have alarmed me, but his actions and words hadn't been anything shy of respectful, so I pushed the thoughts from my mind as soon as they appeared.

I slid into the booth, allowing him to take the seat near the edge. Bringing the cool liquid to my lips, I swallowed a few sips before placing it on the table. *Thank you*, I signed, hoping he remembered what it meant.

He smiled. "How do you sign "you're welcome?"" he asked, never taking his eyes off me.

I brought the pads of my fingers to my chin, like before, and then pulled them away.

"I thought that was "thank you"," he said, rather confused, glancing back and forth between me and Braylen.

"It is. You can use the same simple gesture to reply after someone signs "thank you,"" Braylen explained. "It's similar to when people say "aloha" for hello and goodbye."

Jagger thought Braylen's clarification was amusing, the corners of his full lips kicking up into a breathtaking smile.

"I guess that's easy enough," he chuckled, bringing his fingers to his chin and forming the gesture. "Did I do it right?" he asked, uncertainty scouring his face as he looked at me afterward. A simple nod from me and he relaxed, reaching for my hand and giving it a small squeeze.

His touch warmed me. I liked him, but I didn't really know him. I wanted more than anything to see him again, but I also didn't want to appear desperate. My battling feelings drove me crazy.

When he withdrew his hand, I had to resist appearing distraught. To distract myself I ran my fingers up and down my glass of water, the condensation making the pads of my fingers slippery.

"So," Jagger blurted suddenly, "are you two going anywhere afterward?"

I shook my head, all the while silently pleading with my sister to back me up. While I thoroughly enjoyed my time with Jagger, it was emotionally draining. I needed the rest of the night to decompress, maybe talk it out with my sister back at home.

"It's been a long day, so we're just gonna head on home in a few minutes," Braylen affirmed, tapping her fingers against the wood of the table. Every once in a while she'd turn her attention to the band, trying to give Jagger and me some privacy, even though we were all sitting together.

Ten minutes later, we rose from the booth and started walking toward the exit. I glanced back over my shoulder to make eye contact with Kevin, trying to let him know that we were leaving. Initially we'd told him we'd stay until the end, but Braylen was right; it'd been a long day and while I wanted to spend more time with Jagger, I was tired. Kevin acknowledged our good-bye with a jerk of his head, but when his eyes fell on the guy walking behind us—my "date," of sorts—a frown painted his expression. I wasn't sure why, though. Maybe he thought we'd picked up some random guy, or maybe he thought we were leaving because he'd been bothering us. I wasn't sure, and right then I didn't have enough energy to care.

Even though the warmth of the night air was soothing, a shiver shot through me at the close proximity of Jagger's body to mine. There was certainly a connection between us, but would it move past that evening? I figured only time would tell.

"Well, I had a great time," he stated, reaching for my hand once more. Holding it tight, he gave me a sultry smile. "Thanks for inviting me." I hadn't revealed that it was in fact Braylen who had invited him, but I guessed none of that mattered now.

A fleeting moment passed when I thought he was going to lean in and kiss me. My heart leapt in anticipation, but that was quickly squelched when Jagger's eyes darted past my sister and me and locked on someone behind us.

"Fuck," I heard him grumble. I tugged on my hand, still clasped tightly in his, but he ignored me. Instead, he shoved me behind him in one quick move, my sister standing close by me. Jagger shielded the both of us, and I had no idea why.

Until a man stood two feet from him and shouted, "This is payback for killing my brother." As his words nestled deep in my brain, the man pulled a gun from his waistband and pointed it at Jagger's head.

TWELVE

Jagger

EVERYTHING HAPPENED IN A SPLIT second. I went from thanking Kena for inviting me out to shielding her and Braylen from Snake, his gun pointed right in my goddamn face.

There was no getting out of this without someone hitting the ground. And that someone wasn't gonna be me.

Threat aside, I understood the man's hatred toward me, but that didn't give him the right to pull up on me right out in the open. If he wanted to exact his revenge against me, he needed to step inside the ring in an attempt to right the so-called wrong I'd done him.

"Are you out of your fucking mind?" I yelled, releasing Kena's hand and throwing my body toward him, catching him off guard, and in the process knocking the gun from his hand. There was no reasoning with the guy and I knew it, making a snap decision in order to spare not only my life but everyone else present. Mainly the two women behind me.

Snake was part of the Savage Reapers. Even if he didn't have a beef with me for accidentally killing his brother, his hatred toward our club would be enough of a reason to pull the trigger, possibly killing anyone else who got in the way.

I heard a few screams behind me, and I was sure one of them came from Braylen. Not having enough time to turn around and explain, I followed Snake to the ground, landing on top of him to break my fall. My fist connected with his face before he had time to react, blood spurting from his nose and mouth and covering my shirt. But I didn't care. Not only had I probably blown any shot I had of seeing Kena again, I was enraged this bastard had the balls to pull a gun on me. He knew the dangers of the ring as well as I did; he couldn't possibly have thought I killed his brother on purpose. Either way, I showed him I wasn't gonna tolerate being threatened. Add in the fact he was part of our most hated enemy and my aggression poured from me with ease, beating the man unconscious. He never had a chance, which was why he'd brought his weapon with him in the first place.

Two bouncers rushed outside in the midst of the commotion, and luckily for Snake they pulled me away before I killed him. It would have been another accident, so to speak, although I wouldn't have let his death eat at me like his brother's did.

Staggering to my feet, I ran my bloodied hand through my disheveled hair, trying my best to catch my breath. Once security realized I'd calmed down, they approached the limp body lying on the sidewalk, grabbing the fallen weapon before tucking their hands under his arms and dragging him around the corner, away from any spectators.

Turning around, I assumed I'd be met with the absence of Kena and her sister, but they were still there, staring at me with matching looks of horror. Braylen more so than Kena.

Taking a tentative step forward, I threw my hands up in surrender, showing them no more threat was present. "Are you okay?" I asked to no one in particular, although my question should have been poised directly to Kena. She looked down at the ground as soon as I took another step closer, her shoulders trembling in fear.

Regret shrouded me that she had to witness what just happened, but I didn't have another choice, unless she wanted to see my brains strewn all over the sidewalk. Call me crazy, but I thought that would have been more disturbing.

Braylen stepped in front of her sister, shielding her entirely from me as I approached. "Don't take another step," she warned. When I stopped, she came at me, albeit verbally. "What the hell was that, Jagger? What are you into? Did you really kill someone? Are you part of a gang?" She peppered me with question after question, her ranting making me mentally dizzy. Never allowing me a chance to respond or explain, she seized Kena's arm and dragged her away. "Don't contact her again or else," she threatened, both of them disappearing around the corner before I could even think to stop them.

I reached for my phone to text her when all of a sudden it rang, the shrill sound slicing through the air and distracting me enough to answer it.

"Yeah," I shouted, clutching the cell to my ear so tight my lobe started throbbing. I'd welcomed the pain.

"Hey, man," Stone chastised. "What the hell's up your ass?" I opened my mouth to answer when he cut me off. "Doesn't matter. Get to the clubhouse. Now. We're making a plan tonight." Silence greeted me on the other end as he hung up.

———◆———

ARRIVING AT THE COMPOUND, I parked my bike and rushed inside to find out what the hell was goin' on. I had a feeling, but I wanted to hear it from our leader's mouth. Throwing my cell on the table outside Chambers, I rounded the table and took my seat. Hawke, Ryder and Zip strode in behind me, Trigger and Cutter following after them. Marek, Stone, Breck and Tripp were already seated. Once everyone was prepared to start, Marek uttered four words which would change the course of our night completely.

"We're pickin' him up." Resting against the worn leather of his seat, he thrummed his fingers on the tabletop, the rhythm he created hypnotic. A calm descended over our prez, and I knew why. Finally, after what seemed to be forever, he was gonna seek the justice he needed to avenge what had happened to his wife. Hopefully after the deed was done, they could both start to heal and move on.

The need to desecrate the man who'd violated Sully ran deep in my veins. Adrenaline coursed through me in waves and I prayed Marek would allow me to be part of Yanez's death in some way, although I'd never request such a detail. He tolerated me, his harsh demeanor toward me lessening each time we interacted, but I didn't want to do anything to jeopardize our "progress."

"Where?" Stone asked, worry etching deep into the lines of his face. He had more to lose than most of us, Addy and his daughter waiting for him at home. I couldn't even imagine how he felt, realizing he was walking into an unpredictable situation. But I was sure Marek wouldn't send us into enemy territory. Not intentionally, at least.

"Reynosa," he answered, expelling a deep breath.

"Fuckin' Mexico!" Trigger shouted, lowering his voice once he saw the glare on Marek's face.

"Yeah, fuckin' Mexico," he yelled back. "Carrillo is doin' me a favor by handing Yanez over so we can finish him off. He's been holding him for the past four days, delivering his own brand of justice for going against the cartel." He took a moment to compose himself. "He said if we want him, we have to come and collect him. Obviously, I agreed."

Leaning forward and resting his arms on the table, he laid out the carefully orchestrated plan. "Stone, Tripp, Ryder and I are takin' the cage." Pointing at Cutter, he said, "You take Trigger and Breck to the safe house and get set up." Turning his head toward Zip and Hawke, who were sitting side by side, he instructed, "You two are gonna stay behind and man the compound. No one knows about the trip, so you shouldn't have an issue with any surprise attacks. But just in case, I put a call in to our Laredo chapter. Salzar is bringing ten of his best guys with him. They'll be here tomorrow night."

A solemn air fell all around us, thoughts of the assigned duties driving home the severity of the upcoming event. And by event, I meant the torture and death of Rico Yanez.

Marek had stopped talking to the group at large, instead having his own sidebar with his VP. It appeared everyone had their orders—everyone but me, that was. Chancing an argument, or the silent treatment, I interrupted Marek and Stone.

"Prez," I called out, counting my heartbeats until he looked my way. "What do you want me to do?" I held my breath in anticipation. He could dismiss me altogether, or acknowledge me and treat me as a rightful part of this club, even though I wasn't fully patched in.

Stone nudged his friend with his arm, leaning in and whispering into his ear. Marek nodded before turning his attention back on me.

"You'll go to the safe house. We need someone to clean up, after all." A cocky grin tilted his lips, and I realized he was giving me a shit job. But I'd take it. When I disposed of Yanez, I'd gain my own sense of closure over what had happened to Sully, burying the bastard where no one would ever find his body—or what was left of it.

"When do we leave?" Trigger asked, smoothing his straying hairs back into place.

"We leave first thing tomorrow. You guys will head to the house later on. So get as much rest as you can because we have a long couple days ahead of us." Striking the gavel against the wood signified our meeting had come to an abrupt end. The sound boomed, slicing through hesitation and tension. Everyone knew what they had to do, and because we were loyal to our leader, we all did as asked without a second thought.

With everything else going on, I barely had enough mental energy to deal with the issue with Kena. Thinking I'd completely blown my shot with her, I threw all caution to the wind and decided I didn't have anything to lose. It'd been a couple hours since the incident at Rustic, and there was a good chance she'd turned in for the evening, but I decided to contact her anyway.

Jagger: Are you awake?

I ventured home after our big meeting, but instead of passing out for the evening, I stayed awake in the hopes I'd get the opportunity to explain myself to Kena. All different excuses ran through my mind, but none of them were any good. Some were the truth, some elaborations on fact, but all were clearly not sufficient enough to warrant her ever giving me another chance.

An hour passed.

Then another.

And another.

As I sprawled across my bed, phone clutched tightly in hand, my eyes drifted close. The faint light in my bedroom slowly becoming dimmer, until there was nothing left except blackness. A few more minutes and I would've been out cold, but the alert from an incoming message jolted me back awake. I swung my hand up so fast to check that the cell slipped from my fingers and plonked me right in the face. Curses flew from my lips while I clutched the bridge of my nose, massaging away the quick bite of pain. When I finally swiped the screen, I saw a response from Kena. Wasting no time, I checked her message.

Kena: I don't want you to contact me anymore.

Jagger: You don't? Or Braylen doesn't?

Kena: Both.

I had to convince her to let me fully explain myself, but I sure as hell didn't want to do it over text. I wanted to do it in person, but that wouldn't be for another few days at least, depending on how long Marek was gonna keep me at the safe house.

Jagger: I have to go away for a few days, but when I get back can we please meet up? I need to explain what happened. And if you don't want to see me ever again after that, then I won't bother you. But please just give me a chance to tell you my side.

Breathing had quickly become difficult. My palms started to sweat the longer I waited for her to respond. Having no clue why it meant so much to me to have Kena hear my excuses threw me into instant aggravation.

I hated feeling defensive, like I had to justify my life to someone, but I also knew she was different. I couldn't explain it, though; I just . . . felt it. Deep inside.

A text popped up, and with it hope that she'd give me an opportunity to right what she thought was a wrong.

Kena: Kevin said you're part of an illegal biker gang. Is that true?

Fuckin' Kevin.

Jagger: Yes and no. Yes, I'm part of a biker club. Not gang. And no, it is not illegal.

May as well disclose everything.

Jagger: Not anymore.

The detail about finishing off Yanez I'd keep to myself. Residual tactics had to be dealt with, but the Knights were more legit than not.

Twenty excruciating minutes passed before my cell dinged again. I really should have put the issue on the back burner until I was able to give her my full and undivided attention, but the need to explain weighed heavy on me.

Kena: I don't know.

Jagger: You don't know what?

Kena: If I should see you again.

I hated that I couldn't talk to her, that she couldn't hear the sincerity in my voice when I explained I would never hurt her. That I didn't want to scare her. I just wanted one more chance. My fingers slid over the keys when a thought popped to life.

Jagger: Can I call you?

Kena: Did you forget I can't speak?

Jagger: No, but I have an idea.

THIRTEEN

Kena

UNEASE SETTLED AROUND ME WHILE I curled up in the corner of the couch. Phone clasped in hand, I stared at the screen, re-reading Jagger's texts. There wasn't a lot of information in them, but for some reason the strange need to allow him to explain possessed me. Plus curiosity pushed me to hear his side of the events.

Danger had never been a friend of mine. Nor was drama. I stayed tucked away in my own little bubble, never venturing too far outside my comfort zone. Then one day I allowed Braylen to convince me to go to an abandoned warehouse where men would pummel each other for money. And it was at that match that Jagger had come to my rescue. Fighting whatever feelings he'd evoked within me, I'd never retracted my sister's invite for him to meet us at Rustic.

Even now, I still had this pull toward him. My head told me to run far, far away from the sexy, dangerous fighter, but my heart told me to take a chance and hear him out.

Damn emotions.

He wanted to call me. I had no idea what he thought he'd achieve by doing so, but again, I was intrigued as to what would happen. The one thing I was positive about was that his voice would surely undo me, destroying any uncertainties I had toward giving him another chance. The rasp in his tone did strange things to me, and I knew if I heard him on the other end of the line that I'd cave and give in to whatever he asked of me.

Before I typed my reply, my mind wandered to Braylen and how upset she'd seemed on the ride home. She'd ranted all the way back to our house about how I'd better never see "that lunatic" again. She confessed her initial judgment of him had been misconceived, and I lost count how many times she apologized for pushing me toward going out with him. Seeing someone pull a gun so close to where we were standing shocked and terrified her, as it did to me. But whereas she closed the door on Jagger altogether, I left it open just a crack. I wasn't ready to shut him out completely. Not just yet. Not until I'd at least heard what he wanted to tell me.

Making sure my door was shut, I walked back to my bed, crawled on top and rested against the headboard, my phone staring at me like it held the answer to some great riddle.

Blowing errant strands of hair away from my face, I chose two letters which just might change my world as I knew it.

Kena: Ok.

A few seconds passed before my phone rang. I had no idea how to lower the volume, seeing as how no one had ever called me. For obvious reasons. But no mind; I swiped the Answer button and held the device to my ear.

Then waited.

"Kena, thank you so much for taking my call," he said breathlessly. Even if my voice had worked, I wouldn't have been able to speak right then, nerves strangling my thoughts, let alone any words I would have been able to form in my throat. "I know you can't answer me in the traditional way, so I thought if I asked you a yes or no question, you could tap one of the buttons as your response. One tap for yes and two for no. Can you do that? Does that make sense?"

I waited a heartbeat before hitting a key one time. I swore I heard the smile in his voice when he spoke again.

"Good. That's good," he affirmed, his deep breaths helping to soothe my wayward nerves. He had no idea what he did to me. Even now, he had no clue that my heart raced inside my chest, that my breathing had become erratic at hearing the growl in his tone. My mind raced with images of him, picturing him sitting next to me at the bar, the way his touch jolted me when he brushed his fingers over mine, or when he clasped my hand in his. How warm I'd felt from the contact.

"I wanted to tell you how sorry I am that you had to see that. I'm sure you were scared, and I hate that I put you in that position." He sounded sincere, and I couldn't help but feel as if I should've been the one comforting him in some way. "Anyway, I wanted to know if I could see you again when I get back in town. Shouldn't be any more than a week, at most. Please let me apologize in person, Kena. Then, if you never want to see me again, I won't bother you. I promise."

Silence made the hairs on the back of my neck stand at attention. Contemplating his request, I mentally weighed the pros and cons, the cons vastly outweighing the pros. Something dangerous surrounded Jagger, and the night's events only proved my suspicions. He belonged to a biker gang—sorry, "club." Although I had no idea what the difference was. Kevin told me they were into some illegal shit, but wouldn't explain any further. Maybe he didn't know, or maybe he'd tried to spare me the gory details. Either way, he had warned me away from the likes of Jagger, promising nothing good would come from seeing him again. Kevin told me they'd gone to the same high school, and while he wasn't friends with him, per se, he told me Jagger was always getting into fights, trouble following him all the time. Then there was the little fact that a scary-looking man had tried to shoot him, out in the open, without a care in the world, screaming that Jagger had killed his brother.

Red flags littered my internal struggle, shrouding me in waves of uneasy doubt. And even though I shouldn't have ever granted his request to call me, I had. For some inexplicable reason. And because confusion over my lack of sense baffled me, I decided to give in to him once again, agreeing to see him so he could apologize in person.

Only then would I know how I wanted to proceed.

My forefinger hovered over a key, prepared to answer his question. It was a simple response but one which eluded me. His voice cut through the line again, startling me before I'd made my decision.

"Please," he begged. "Can I see you again? To explain?" The voice drifting through my ear was poignant. Gentle. Convincing.

Without hesitation, I pushed a random number key.

One time.

Yes.

A quick exhale of relief barreled down the line. "You won't regret it. I promise. I'll text you in a few days and you can decide where you want to meet. Good night, Kena," he said before disconnecting the call. He hurried off, but I couldn't say I blamed him, probably afraid I would change my mind if given more time to think about it. And while I appreciated he didn't keep me on the phone, I hated the absence of his voice.

Lying in bed, I stared off into the darkness and prayed I'd just made the right choice. Although I was sure Braylen would tell me otherwise.

FOURTEEN

Jagger

RAMPANT THOUGHTS KEPT ME AWAKE the rest of the evening, sleep continuing to evade me. Taunting me with promises of submersion, only to be thrown back into consciousness. Even lying in the pitch black, my shallow breaths the only sound cutting through the air around me, I couldn't let go and give in. My mind raced, first to thoughts of Kena and how she felt about everything she'd seen, then to how she truly felt about me.

Was she as intrigued with me as I was with her?

Did she feel the same pull toward the unknown like I did?

Did she rationalize against it?

When I wasn't thinking about Kena, my brain switched to thoughts of Sully. I couldn't even imagine what she was going through. I would've loved nothing more than to be her true friend, out in the open, but her husband wouldn't allow it. Maybe once he saw I was interested in someone, he'd rid himself of the silly notion that I was in love with his wife.

Knowing the men didn't divulge club business to their women or families, I wondered if Marek had hinted at the reason for his departure. Maybe she'd want to know that the man who'd attacked her would be disposed of, never to walk the earth or breathe the same air as the rest of us again. It would give her solace. Some, at least.

Before long, the soft burn of the sunrise sliced across the horizon. An orange glow lit up the sky, the white haze of light filtering through my bedroom like fog billowing across the moors. Stretching, I yawned and allowed my body to flex and constrict before finally mustering enough energy to rise from the bed. Planting my feet firmly on the ground, I massaged the back of my neck. Tight muscles had always been my dead giveaway of the stress I'd harbored inside, whether from an upcoming fight, tension whenever Marek and I were in close proximity to each other or impending club business.

Specifically revenge.

Padding across my bedroom, the worn carpet cushioning the soles of my feet, I walked into the hallway, lost in thought of the upcoming hours . . . days. Not only did I have to do my part in the death and disposal of Yanez, but I had to convince Kena of my regret at her having witnessed something which most likely terrified her. If I weren't in the lifestyle I was, I would've been unnerved, and that's putting it lightly. Though I knew the threat against the club was dwindling, after what transpired with Snake, how did I convince her she'd be safe with me? That I could protect her? Because honestly, I had my doubts at times.

My life was my own. I took care of myself the best I could, but I hadn't thought about what it would mean to bring someone else into my world. For as bad as I wanted her, for as desperate as I was to have her in my life, I could admit the thought of something happening to her frightened me.

Don't get ahead of yourself. She just agreed to hear you out. Nothing more.

How people outside my club perceived me had never mattered before. I was proud of being involved with the Knights Corruption, even at the prospect level, and being an undefeated fighter in the underground world always spoke volumes to the type of man I wanted to become. One who had the loyalty of his brothers, and someone who was feared in the ring.

Turning on the water, I busied myself with brushing my teeth until the temperature warmed. Finally stepping inside the shower, I exhaled a satisfying groan, the spray helping to ease the stiffness from my limbs. I stood still and let the water cascade over my body, my head hung low while the heat drenched my hair. If I could've stayed in there until it was time to travel to the safe house, I would have.

My hands skated over my chest, then my arms, around to my back, then finally down my legs. I washed away not only the prior evening, but the early morning residual sleep as well.

Fully awake, my thoughts returned to Kena. Her beauty stunned me. Her body turned me on, but she was more than her physical appearance. A quiet desperation lived behind her eyes, a plea to be more like everyone else—to be "normal," without a handicap. But in reality, everyone had their own challenge to overcome; some were physical, while others were mental or emotional. She didn't strike me as someone who felt sorry for herself, but I had a funny feeling she hid from the rest of the world, only showing a close few her true self.

I want to be included in her inner circle.

New goal: penetrate Kena's world.

Oddly enough, or expectedly enough, my brain instantly flooded with images of her naked, fantasizing what she would look like silently pleading with me to possess her. Before I realized, my fingers circled my arousal and I pumped it from root to tip. My grip tightened the more I pictured her underneath me, writhing in pleasure as she clawed at my back, hooking her legs around my waist and anchoring herself to me. With every jerk of my hips, I imagined thrusting inside her, the warmth of her flooding over me and ruining me for all others. I wanted to draw out my pleasure, but my orgasm threatened to rock through me at any moment. My spine tingled while my balls drew tight. My stomach muscles clenched, an ache I hadn't realized was present until it was too late. Kena's delectable mouth was the final image I saw before my release rushed forth, my moans infiltrating the enclosed space, echoing against the easy thump of the water hitting the tiles.

Damn, I needed that.

As soon as my breathing slowed, I shut off the water and stepped from the shower, doing a quick pat down before tying the white towel around my waist. Shuffling down the hall, I entered my room and rooted through my closet, grabbing the first pair of jeans I could find. Opening the drawer of the only dresser housed inside my small bedroom, I grabbed a pair of socks, boxer briefs and a plain white T-shirt, quickly dressing before shoving my feet inside a worn pair of brown boots.

I lounged around for the remainder of the day, ordering takeout to ensure I had something in my belly before I got the call. Who knew when I'd eat again? Or would want to, for that matter. Having no idea what type of actions I'd be expected to perform, I wanted to at least have the vigor to contemplate the severity of them. Nervous energy surrounded me while I watched the sun disappear, its soft glow illuminating the night, promises of calm and tranquility a lie.

Passing out on my worn fabric couch, I awoke to the piercing sound of my cell. Rubbing the sleep from my eyes, I turned the phone over and saw Cutter's name flash across my screen. The man rarely called me, but since he was assigned to the safe house, along with his son, Breck, and Trigger, it wasn't a complete shock that he'd called me.

With a flick of my finger, the call connected. Before I could say hello, however, his raspy voice paraded down the other end of the line.

"Get a move on, prospect. We're headin' to the safe house in an hour. Meet you there," he said before hanging up. I'd quickly learned Cutter was a man of few words. I'd heard he had a daughter he never saw, but other than that personal tidbit of information, the man was a mystery to me.

Rising from the sofa, I took a quick look around and counted my blessings, as meager as they may be. While my apartment was humble, at least it provided me with a roof over my head. I preferred to spend my time at the clubhouse as much as I could, though, simply because I was around other people. When I was home, I was alone. And if the solidarity wasn't enough to deter me from staying there a lot, the lack of décor amped up my loneliness. Finally having some money in the bank, courtesy of the fights, I thought it was time I seriously considered buying a few things to spruce up the space. But who would help me? I didn't know the first thing about tackling such a feat.

The couch I'd crashed on earlier was a dark green sofa. Or at least it had been, the color fading over the years since I'd bought it. Even then, it was secondhand. A barely held-together TV stand and an end table were the only other items in the living room. My bedroom consisted of a simple queen-sized mattress, sans frame and box spring, a small dresser and nightstand.

I didn't require much, but some new things would certainly put me in better spirits when I stepped foot inside my home.

Snatching my keys, I twirled them around my finger while I walked toward the front door, locking up before I headed outside.

While I straddled my bike, I prayed everything would go according to plan and that I could put the upcoming days behind me as soon as possible.

FIFTEEN

Jagger

WE'D BEEN AT THE SAFE house for almost two days, impatiently awaiting Marek's return. Which wouldn't be for quite some time yet. He wanted everyone ready to go, and while Trigger, Cutter and Breck occupied themselves with games of poker, I vegged out in front of the television, watching hours of mindless shows. But at least we'd kept up with the cable; otherwise, I would've been sitting around twiddling my goddamn thumbs.

The safe house had timers for everything, from the sprinkler system, to the lights, to the television. It always appeared as if someone lived here, or the neighbors would be a bit more suspicious than I was sure they already were.

As the many hours ticked by, the building eagerness rattled me. While I wasn't a newbie when it came to killing, torture was a whole new ball game. And if I knew anything about Marek and what he'd been through, Yanez would beg for death more often than not. I knew where our leader's head was at; he wanted justice for Sully. While I was completely onboard, the unknown distressed me, something I kept secret for fear the other guys would think me to be soft.

And how would it look like if the fighter of the group showed an ounce of indecision? Bad. It would look bad. No, I'd buck up and help orchestrate Yanez's demise when the time came, if Marek wanted my help at all. He might just need me to clean up like he'd mentioned during our last meeting.

"Yo, prospect," Breck shouted from the kitchen. "Grab me a beer." The only reason I didn't tell him to get fucked was because I knew my place in the pecking order. Still trying to prove myself, I had to take orders, no matter how small, like this one. What Marek would require of me later would be considered a big one.

Night and day, but I was obligated to do both.

Normally, I liked Breck, but during times like this I wanted to show him how much damage I could do to him with a quick shot to the jaw. Slowly rising off the couch, I walked the short distance to the kitchen where he was playing cards with his father and Trigger. Even though the fridge sat directly behind them, I still proceeded without a single complaint uttered. Internally, I told him right where to go. Roughly pulling open the door, I reached inside and grabbed a beer, flicking off the top before slamming it down on the table in front of him.

No 'Thanks."

No ''Bout time."

Just a cocky smirk before he tipped the bottle to his lips and swallowed half of the alcohol in a few short gulps. Wiping his mouth with the back of his hand, he focused back on the game, his face scrunching up in con-centration as he tried to win the pot of money in the center of the table.

Twisting an empty chair around, I straddled the seat and rested my arms over the back. "Who's winning?" I asked, looking first over Trigger's shoulder and then Breck's.

"I am," Cutter divulged. "These two bastards been losin' their money to me all evening." After fifteen minutes of watching them bluff and curse each other, I'd had enough.

"Do you guys need me for anything? If not, I'm gonna catch some shut-eye until they get here." As I hopped up from the chair, Trigger's phone rang. He glanced at the screen, then quickly at all three of us, a warning look in his eyes he couldn't hide even if he wanted to.

"Yeah?" he answered, nodding while intently listening to whoever had called. A few more intense seconds of waiting and Trigger finally ended the conversation.

"They're a few hours away." He jerked his chin in my direction. "Brew some coffee, prospect. It's gonna be a long fuckin' night."

———◆———

HEADLIGHTS LIT UP THE DARKNESS, and everything became real when the heavy garage door started to open. Then the screech of the van's engine sounded as it lurched inside. We all scrambled to our feet, wired and ready to jump into action. Flinging open the door which separated the house from the garage, we rushed forward, coming to a dead stop when we saw Marek and Stone heave a limp body from the side of the vehicle.

Yanez.

His head was down, and at first it appeared as if he were unconscious. But when they jostled him, soft, pained moans escaped his mouth. Dropping him, Yanez hit the ground with a heavy thud, more groans cutting the otherwise silent air. Seizing his arms, Tripp and Ryder pulled him behind them as they walked up the three steps into the house. Yanez's body awkwardly slid over every bump and rigid surface as he was dragged through the kitchen and eventually down into the soundproof basement below. As I walked behind them, careful to keep my distance and not get in their way, I heard Yanez's head hit off every single step, the sharp thud jolting me each and every time. Don't get me wrong, the despicable piece of shit deserved whatever Marek had planned, but that didn't stop my body from reacting. My heart hammered double time, my palms starting to sweat in expectancy.

"Put him on the table," our leader shouted, switching the light on and walking across the small room. Shrugging off his cut, he laid it across the chair in the corner, cracking his neck briefly before fiddling with what sounded to be knives of some sort. His back faced me, and while Tripp and Ryder heaved the barely alive man onto the table, Stone walked up behind Marek, talking so low I couldn't make out a single word.

Cutter walked past me, his shoulder brushing against mine when he entered the dank room. The light above slightly illuminated the space, shadows dancing next to us and creating the perfect atmosphere.

For death.

"What you gonna do to him, Prez?" Cutter asked, rounding the table and glaring down at Yanez, although the barely breathing man hadn't taken notice. Instead, he turned his head to the side, the loud clanking sounds Marek made drawing his attention. I moved closer while still being mindful to stay in the background until instructed otherwise. Not sure whether or not I wanted to witness Yanez's ultimate demise, I pushed all doubt to the side and just watched the scene unfolding in front of me.

Turning around, Marek stepped toward the table, a pair of pliers in his hand. He spun them around and around before lightly tapping them against his temple. In the soft light, the leader of the Knights Corruption resembled a deranged lunatic, the lost look in his blue eyes hazed over with a sort of delirium. Fear ripped through me right then, and I had no doubt his victim felt it as well. In that moment I couldn't help but envision hearing Rob Zombie, the unease of his music a perfect fitting to the horror-type scene unfolding.

Shaking my head to rid myself of the odd thoughts, I glanced toward the men milling about the room. All of them were there because of their loyalty to Marek, as was I. Even though I knew he didn't like me, I would do what was asked of me without second-guessing him.

Locking eyes with Cutter, Marek's voice finally rang out, hatred and desperation mixing together to form an odd sound. "Remember what we did to Vex?" Cutter nodded right away. "Worse than that," Marek declared.

"Fuck," I heard Tripp and Ryder mutter. Everyone, including myself, heard about what Marek and Cutter had done to Vex. After carving the letters 'KC' into his chest, they finished him off by using a bat. And not by beating him with it.

Marek stood next to the table, Yanez's beady eyes intently trying to watch him as best he could given the damage to his face. Carrillo's ex right-hand man was beaten to a pulp, both of his eyes so swollen I was surprised he could see anything at all. He was littered with cuts and burn marks, on his face as well as his neck and what I could see of his chest, his tattered shirt torn to reveal parts of his damaged skin. Normally, I would have hated to see someone treated like this, but he certainly deserved it for what he'd done to Sully. And if I had to wager a bet, she wasn't the first woman he'd brutalized.

Rico Yanez lived in darkness, his soul blackened with what I was sure he'd done during his wretched life.

Raising Yanez's hand, Marek inspected it briefly before letting it drop back to the table. "Looks like Carrillo beat me to it," he mumbled, walking around the table to look at the man's other limb. I moved closer, wanting to see what he meant, but before I opened my mouth to ask Stone, who stood in front of me, I saw it.

Yanez's fingers were missing.

All ten of them.

Whoever had cut them off had also cauterized the wounds. My guess was so he didn't bleed out, ending his torturing sessions too early.

"Oh well," Marek said dismissively, waving his hand through the air like it was no big deal. "Looks like we'll just have to get right to it, then." A glaze washed over our leader's face, and right before my very eyes I saw him shut down, going into whatever headspace would allow him to deliver justice for his wife. Briefly turning around, he fiddled with a few things before donning a pair of latex gloves. Then he reached for a dull scalpel-type knife as well as a vice grip before walking back toward Yanez's limp body. "Prospect," he addressed, turning his gaze to me. "Grab some gloves, then yank down his pants."

My mind was a flurry of thoughts, but I had no time to indulge any of them. Hurrying across the room, I threw on a pair of the same gloves, a bead of perspiration trickling down the side of my face. Hesitation held me prisoner until I heard Stone clear his throat behind me.

"You good?" he asked, concern slithering around those two words. I quickly turned around and saw him quirking his brow in wait.

"Yeah," I muttered before taking the few steps necessary to put me right next to the table. I had an idea what Marek had planned, and while the thought sickened me, I knew it was the only way for him to purge. My fingers fumbled with Yanez's belt buckle, and once it was undone, I popped open the button of his jeans and tore the zipper down. After dragging the material down his legs, I stepped back, my eyes locked on my president.

"The underwear too," he instructed, a sick sort of smile tilting up the corners of his lips. Marek looked haggard, deep stress lines marring his face. His eyes were bloodshot and his hair stuck up around the edges of his head. Again, he looked a bit deranged, but plotting revenge and then finally seeing it through had to take some sort of toll on the mind and body. Hell, probably even the soul.

Yanking down the man's briefs made him come to life—well, whatever was left of him, at least. He tried to struggle, but his strength eluded him. Instead his eyes bulged as best they could and he tried to speak, his garbled voice incoherent to the rest of us. I thought he said, "Please, don't," but I couldn't be sure. Either way, it didn't matter; his fate had been decided, and no amount of begging would change it. If anything, his whimpers would do more harm than good, although I couldn't fathom what "more harm" would entail at that point.

Marek stretched his arm across the table and passed me the vice grip. "Put his dick in this, then grab his balls tight."

Those were the ten most menacing words I'd ever heard.

Yanez knew what was coming, and although he tried to fight again, it was useless. His death was imminent, but how long would it be before the reaper came to steal him from this life?

With every slice Marek made, separating two of the three body parts which made Yanez a man, he whimpered uncontrollably, thrashing as much as he could while in our grasp. There was an unwritten rule among men: Never go for the nuts. That being said, what Marek was doing to Yanez was justified. In our eyes, at least.

My arm jerked back when Marek had finished, my eyes instantly going to the area between Yanez's legs. Blood poured forth in spurts. It would only be a matter of minutes before he bled out completely, I was sure of it.

With his free hand, our president wrenched a piece of duct tape he'd pre-cut from the edge of a utility cart. "Tripp," he called, "open his mouth." The nomad jumped into action, prying Yanez's jaw wide and holding steady while Marek shoved the man's balls past his stretched lips. As soon as Tripp released his grip, our leader slapped the piece of duct tape over his mouth, pressing down to make sure it was securely in place.

Stepping back, Marek gazed at his handiwork, a look of satisfaction covering his face as his eyes roamed the full length of his victim. Nodding hastily, as if he'd agreed with a silent conversation he'd been having with himself, he jerked his chin toward Stone and Ryder.

"Bring him to the corner so we can string him up," Marek instructed. The two men shot into action, dragging the ex-cartel member from the table and across the room. Standing him upright, they placed his wrists in the shackles built into the wall, letting him dangle once they'd released him. The position would allow him to bleed out quicker than lying on the table. And if blood loss wouldn't cause his demise, then suffocation would.

We all stood there watching Yanez struggle during the last minutes of his life. Silence comforted us while we witnessed the warranted punishment.

Five minutes turned into ten, which turned to twenty.

He still breathed.

Another five minutes passed.

Finally deciding enough was enough, Marek walked toward the strung-up man and raised his hand to Yanez's nose, pinching his nostrils to hurry his death along.

A slight twitch was the only form of life still left inside him.

Two minutes later, he was dead.

Finally.

SIXTEEN

Kena

"WHAT?" BRAYLEN SHOUTED. "ABSOLUTELY NOT. Don't you even think about it, Kena," she continued, pacing in front of me while she tried to control her sudden outburst. "There is no way in hell I'm going to allow you to meet him. No," she said, suddenly stopping to look me in the eye. "He's not the guy I thought he was. You have to see it too." She resumed pacing. "You just have to." Pushing loose blonde strands away from her eyes, she pinned me with a concerned look. "I made a mistake when I encouraged you to give him a chance, a mistake I regret with every fiber of my being. Putting you in harm's way is the last thing I ever wanted. And now you're telling me you want to hear him out? No," she repeated, shaking her head in earnest.

Because my sister's back was to me, I couldn't respond. Breaching the few steps between us, I reached for her shoulder. Turning her around, I narrowed my brows and cocked my head slightly to the side.

I know you're concerned for me, but I'm a big girl. I can make my own decisions, so stop treating me like a child. My hands fell to my sides in exasperation. I parted my lips, expelling the air from my throat, but no matter how much I willed the words to take flight, it was utterly useless. Most days I accepted and even reveled in being mute, but then there were instances where the silence kept me chained to a frustrating existence.

Stilling her movements, Braylen unexpectedly pulled me into a hug, wrapping her arms tightly around me as if she thought I would disappear. After countless seconds she pulled back, her warm breath fanning the side of my face. "It's my job as your big sister to look out for and take care of you." I tried to distance myself to respond, but her hold on me intensified. "I know you're not a kid anymore. I do," she said dejectedly, as if she wished the opposite were true, "but that doesn't mean I won't stop trying to protect you. I don't care if you're fifty. I'll always look out for you." A small smile tipped her lips upward, the love she held for me shining brightly in her brown eyes. "And as such, I'm warning you to stay away from Jagger. For your own good." She finally took a step back, allowing me the distance I craved in order to respond to her ludicrous threat.

Every muscle in my body locked up, anger dancing on the edge of every gesture I made. *And if I don't? What will you do?*

At first I thought my sister had been bluffing, mere worry for me pushing her toward an argument. But it wasn't until her next statement that I completely understood how far she'd go to make me comply.

"I'll tell Mom and Dad."

My mouth dropped open, and it was a good thing for her right then that I couldn't speak because I'd be cursing her every which way to Sunday. So instead, as usual, my hands were a flurry of activity, gesturing so fast I was sure she missed most of what I told her.

I can't believe you would stoop so low as to tattle on me like some five-year-old brat. You know damn well Mom and Dad would worry themselves sick if you filled their heads with lies. She started to speak but I cut her off with a fierce scowl. *While I realize what happened was bad, the last thing they need to do is worry about me. You telling them would only make things worse. Please.*

I started off angry, but by the end I pleaded with her not to interfere. I couldn't explain my incessant need to see Jagger again, not even to myself, but the one thing I did know was that I'd never felt this way toward anyone. Even with my lack of experience with the opposite sex, I felt the pull, the undeniable connection between us, and I wanted to see him again to make sure I hadn't made it up in my mind, that I wasn't crazy.

Braylen just stood there, hands planted firmly on her hips, waiting. For what I wasn't sure, but at least in silence I could hope she relented. I should've known better, though.

"I swear I'll bring our parents into this if you agree to see him, Kena," she warned. A standoff ensued between us, her unwavering and me staring at her in utter disbelief. When I realized she wasn't going to give in, I offered what I thought was a fair compromise. At least I hoped she would see it as such.

How about if you come with me when I meet him? That way, you'll know I'm safe. Plus you'll hear what he wants to tell me and find out for yourself that he's not someone I should be afraid of.

"I don't think *Jagger* is the person you should fear, but the types of people he surrounds himself with. But then again, what the hell do I know? I thought he was a safe bet. His coming to our rescue that night fooled me. I let my guard down because I saw the way he looked at you, and I wanted so badly for you to open up to someone. To really start living, experiencing life, instead of hiding away in the back of the restaurant all the time."

If I looked up "stubborn" in the dictionary, there would be a picture of Braylen, smiling and flipping off the reader. I knew whatever reply I gave wouldn't deter my sister, but I tried anyway. *Don't judge him on one incident.*

"That was a pretty big fucking incident," she yelled, anger wrapping around her like a blanket. Waving my hand in her direction in frustration, dismissing our entire conversation, I walked past her, my shoulder bumping into hers as I headed out of her bedroom. She saw the look on my face, I was sure, anger mixed with sadness. "Kena!" she shouted. "Wait."

I ignored her, snatched my keys from the table near the door and rushed out of the house. Clicking the key fob to my car, I got in and turned over the engine, sitting in silence for a few minutes. Maybe I'd hoped Braylen would chase me outside and plead with me to forgive her. What did I get instead? A lousy text message telling me she wouldn't budge, no matter how angry I was with her. She was only looking out for me, blah, blah, blah. I didn't need her love and protection, though. Even though I didn't have much experience when it came to guys, I really thought I could handle myself. Being mute didn't thwart my knee from connecting with Jagger's balls if I felt I needed to fight back for some reason. Although, the last thing I wanted to do was hurt his family jewels. No, I could think of many other things I wished to do with that region of his body.

Simply thinking of him caused a warmness to float through me, shivers of delight shooting to my own nether region. Lost in dirty thoughts of writhing around with the fighter, the sudden knock on my window made me jolt. My hand flew to my chest in surprise and I inhaled a quick breath of air. Glancing to my left, I saw Braylen watching me, probably wondering what the hell I was doing just sitting in the car. Thank God she wasn't a mind reader; otherwise she'd be giving me the riot act about my daydreams.

Her fist pounded again, that time with a bit more urgency. Finally lowering the window, I expected to hear an apology, but no such words came out of her mouth. She did say something that made me happy, however.

"Okay. Fine," she relented. "I'll go with you to meet him. But it has to be out in the open with lots of people around, and it has to be in broad daylight. Preferably Neelan Park."

I could certainly accommodate her request, especially if it meant I could see Jagger again without worry she'd find out and make good on her threat to bring my parents into the situation.

Braylen never waited for my response, instead turning on her heel and walking back inside the house. But that was okay; I'd gotten the answer I'd wanted.

Now all I had to do was wait for Jagger to contact me again. He'd told me he'd be away for a few days, but if he didn't text me soon, my sister would surely tell me "I told you so," and the last thing I wanted was for her to be right about him.

I wanted to prove her wrong in the worst way.

SEVENTEEN

Jagger

EVERYONE HAD LEFT THE SAFE house except for Cutter and me. It was up to us to dispose of Yanez's body. Well, to be more factual, it was my job to get rid of him, but Cutter volunteered to help. I had no idea why, but I welcomed his assistance nonetheless.

Silence teased us while we busied ourselves in unchaining Yanez from the wall, laying him on top of the thick green tarp we'd readied, rolling him up and carrying him out to the garage. The guys who'd gone to pick up the ex-cartel member caught rides back with Breck, who'd thought ahead and brought his truck, leaving the van for us to use. Stuffing the dead man in the back of the vehicle was the easy part. When Cutter sat his ass down in front of the television, I knew I was on my own with cleaning up the mess in the bowels of the house.

Oddly enough, while I hosed the blood off the concrete ground, the red-tinged water sliding across the surface and disappearing down the drain set in the floor, Kena popped into my head. At first, it disturbed me that I thought of her while cleaning up after a kill, but it was exactly why the images of her bombarded me.

The world I'd immersed myself in was dangerous, no doubt about it. I realized selfishness drove me to pursue her, even though I knew she didn't belong anywhere near me. Yes, the Knights were going legit, but we still had shit to clean up, and until everything was put to bed, the threat against all of us was grave.

Yanez had finally been dealt with, which meant there was only one remaining loose end to tie up.

Psych Brooks.

Sully's bastard of a father.

When and where that man would cease to exist still baffled me, as I was sure it did Marek and the rest of the guys. Everyone itched to finish the war between us and the Savage Reapers, and we all realized more blood would be shed before it was over.

But how much, and whose, were the real questions.

Throwing the rags I'd used to clean off the table into a nearby garbage bag, I glanced around the room one last time to make sure I hadn't missed anything. Shutting off the light, I ascended the stairs and announced I'd finished. Clicking the remote, Cutter rose from the sofa and led the way back out to the garage.

The club's safe house wasn't used for disposal of bodies, and from what I'd heard, there had been quite a few. You don't shit where you eat, so to speak, so we drove for an hour before turning down a partially hidden dirt pathway. The secluded area was perfect, far away from both of the areas the club used.

Tossing me a shovel from the back, Cutter and I made quick work of finding the perfect spot to bury Yanez. Flashlights resting on the ground illuminated the darkness while we worked, flinging sodden dirt behind us while we unearthed his new home. It'd rained hours prior, which made the soil heavy, requiring a bit more muscle, but neither of us complained.

A few times I'd opened my mouth to make chitchat, but every time I ended up thinking better of it. What were we gonna talk about, the weather? No, the situation called for concentration and quiet. The quicker we finished the better.

After a grueling two hours, we'd managed to dig deep enough to conceal the body without worry, cover him back up and start the drive back to the clubhouse. I would've ridden my bike but I'd asked Stone to take it back for me, realizing I'd be in no condition to be out on the open road with a tiredness which would undoubtedly get me killed.

Resting my head against the passenger side window, I closed my eyes and wondered when my life would start to fall into place. Question after question arose.

When would Marek decide me worthy enough to patch me in as a full member, solidifying my loyalty for good?

Would Snake decide to come after me again? Would he end up getting lucky and kill me?

As slumber beckoned me, Kena's beautiful face popped into my head. In my mind she spoke, telling me how much she wanted to be with me.

Fantasy, I knew, but it was the peace I needed to drift off during the last stretch of our ride. I only hoped she wouldn't go back on her promise to meet me.

———◆———

WITH A JOLT, THE VAN came to a stop. "Fuck," I groaned, rubbing the side of my head while Cutter grunted out some garbled noise. Clutching the door handle, I pulled the lever toward me and flung the door open, practically falling out of the vehicle I was so uncoordinated.

The last couple days had drained me, especially that evening. I was physically and mentally exhausted, and all I wanted to do was crash for the night. Didn't matter where; the couch inside the club would do just fine.

Lazily strolling across the lot, my eyes stayed on the entrance to the building with one goal in mind: forget everything that had happened in the past twelve hours.

The waiting.

The uncertainty of my role in the revenge against Yanez.

The torture.

The dismemberment.

The blood.

The burial.

The end of Yanez, once and for all.

The last part comforted me while the rest of it sickened me. I played the tough, unaffected guy, but deep down I was unsure of a lot of things in life. My sense of self had been warped since I could remember. In some small way, my father still held power over me, making me question my worth every now and again. It was why the Knights were so important to me, and why I would do whatever was asked without question.

Loyalty.

I'd never had it before I'd become a part of them. Even though I was the low man on the totem pole, tasked with the worst jobs from time to time, I knew every one of those members would have my back if and when I needed them.

It was why I held my tongue when Marek gave me a verbal lashing whenever he felt he needed to. It was why I never retaliated with my fists when he punished me for getting too close with his wife when he'd asked me to watch over her.

And it was why I respected his dislike for me, staying clear of Sully when I saw her, even though all I wanted to do was make sure she was okay. The innate need to protect her battled within, though I wasn't quite sure why. Maybe because of the way she'd looked so lost when she first came to stay with us. Or maybe it was because I saw a woman trying to make sense of her new life, silently pleading for someone to help her.

Maybe I read into things which weren't there.

Maybe I didn't.

All I did know was that as time passed, and wrongs against her were righted, she would start to heal.

"Prospect! Come here," Marek demanded, standing in the entryway to Chambers, looking beat down and tired as hell. With my shoulders squared, I huffed and silently counted to ten as I approached, dodging the throngs of men who were partying it up like we hadn't just tortured someone. Almost a dozen members from the Laredo chapter had arrived a day or so before, setting up camp to make sure nothing popped off while we were gone. And now that the ordeal was finished, it was time for them to party, to engage in a ruckus, although I wanted no part of it this time.

Standing a foot away from Marek, something in his bloodshot eyes softened when he looked at me, but it was gone before I could read further into it. Moving to the side, he allowed me to pass and enter the room where we met about all things club-related. The good and the bad.

The click of the door closing jostled me. I'd flinched, but Marek had been facing away from me so he hadn't noticed. He strode toward his seat at the head of the table, never uttering a single word while he situated himself. Still locked into place, I remained quiet until the silence tore at me, threatening to undo my sanity if he didn't speak soon. Pressing my luck where he was concerned, I opened my mouth and forced five words past my unsure lips. "Did I do something wrong?" I asked, fisting my hands and slowly unfurling them, over and over.

"Sit." He gestured toward a chair closer to him than my assigned seat at the far end of the oblong table.

Hesitation briefly gripped me, but I dismissed my reluctance before it got the better of me and sat a few seats away from him. Drumming my fingers against the wood of the table did nothing but increase my jumpiness, never mind that the noise also served to irritate Marek. A quick pull of his brow and I'd stopped the incessant tapping. Laying my palm flat, I waited for him to speak, to finally find out why he'd called me in there by myself. It'd been a long time since Marek and I had been alone together.

Not since he'd saved me from getting my ass jumped by four members of the Savage Reapers. But to be fair, I'd been the one to initially jump in and help him and Stone out when they were ambushed by a handful of our enemy's club, not realizing who they were before I stuck my nose into their business.

It seemed like forever ago, but it had only been two years since Marek had accepted me, bringing me into the club as a prospect with promises of money, loyalty and girls. And hey, what twenty-year-old guy would turn down such a proposition? I'd been undeniably grateful, humbled by his acceptance of me when all I'd received my whole life was rejection from the one person who should have been wired to love me unconditionally.

My shitbag father.

I'd learned the rules of the club quickly, thankful to have fallen upon the opportunity to finally belong somewhere. To be accepted by a group of men who emanated nothing but confidence, strength and smarts. Sure, they gave me shit from time to time, but that was all part of the ritual of belonging.

While Marek had been the one to essentially save me from myself, giving my life a purpose, it was Stone I eventually gravitated toward. Something about the VP seemed familiar to me, and while I couldn't pinpoint exactly what that had been, I welcomed his friendship with open fuckin' arms. He became more like a big brother than anything, helping me with my fighting techniques and offering his advice, even when I hadn't asked for it.

Clearing his throat, Marek brought me out of my own head and back to our impromptu meeting. Jerking his head toward me, his gaze locked on me the entire time, he asked, "You good?"

Inquiring if I was okay was his subtle way of finding out how I'd felt about everything that went down with Yanez earlier. Marek's concern was masked with aloofness, although I'd been smart enough to read between the lines. Or between those two simple words.

Was this his proverbial olive branch?

If so, I'd take it, grab on with both hands if it meant slowly creeping my way out of the dog house.

Many different words jumbled together inside my head, but for some reason none of them would leave my mouth. So instead, I simply nodded.

Leaning forward, his elbows resting against the etched wood of the table, he scrutinized me for a few seconds before continuing to speak.

"What I asked you to do was a bit more than I'd ever required from you before. More . . . gruesome than what you're probably used to." Roughly running his hands through his messy dark hair, he blew out a pained breath. "Hell, maybe not. I've no idea what you've seen before you came to be part of us. Either way, it's a lot to deal with. I realize that. Just wanted to make sure you're okay with everything."

This was the most he'd spoken to me without gritting his teeth, or looking at me like he'd wanted to kill me, in a long fucking time. Stunned stupid at first, I shook off the surprise and answered with the first thing that came to mind.

"I'm fine. Nothing I can't deal with." What I didn't divulge was that I'd probably have a nightmare or two over holding Yanez's balls in my hands while Marek stole them from him.

A few more seconds passed before he rose from his chair. "Okay then." Walking toward the door, he shouted over his shoulder, "If you wanna sleep in Stone's room, go right ahead. He went home already."

Another offering I'd gladly take, seeing as how I doubted I'd make it home in one piece if I dared to ride my bike with fatigue nipping at my heels.

I'd meant to text Kena before I fell asleep, but as soon as my back hit the mattress I passed out cold, hoping the nightmares weren't waiting for me in the shadows of darkness.

EIGHTEEN

Kena

IT'D BEEN FOUR DAYS SINCE I'd last heard from Jagger, and I started to believe that he didn't want to meet up after all. Maybe after some consideration, he thought I wasn't worth the trouble. Why should he feel as if he had to explain anything to me? Sure, our attraction was strong—at least it was on my part—but maybe he viewed me as just another person who came across as demanding, eluding his advances until he justified himself. Perhaps he only wanted to get me into bed, and after thinking of all the work he'd have to put in, apologizing and trying to make me see things from his point of view, it was too much effort. He'd just move on to the next one; surely there wasn't a shortage of women lining up to sleep with him.

As the thought permeated my brain, I cringed. I hardly knew the guy, yet the thought of him having sex with someone tore at my heart in a big way.

Braylen stopped asking me if I'd heard from him, the disappointed look on my face enough to tell her I'd been upset at his lack of communication.

The day had passed by like the previous ones. I'd woken up, showered, gotten dressed and gone to the restaurant to work for the day, filling in for Kevin when he'd been late. Again. Thankfully, he hadn't brought up the incident with Jagger. He'd done his friendly duty in warning me against him, but he didn't bombard me with questions about the situation every time he saw me.

When I dragged myself back home, I plopped my tired ass on the sofa, leaned my head back against the soft material and closed my eyes. Thoughts of Jagger infiltrated, but I shoved them aside because I refused to keep thinking about him when I clearly wasn't on his mind. A weightlessness grabbed hold and started to pull me under. Wanting to take a quick nap, I gave in, but was quickly jostled back to reality when I heard my phone chime, indicating I'd received a text. Doing my best not to get my hopes up, thinking it was most likely Braylen messaging me, I reached over to the table near the couch where I'd thrown my purse. Rummaging through it, I pulled out my cell and stared at the screen.

The message was from Jagger.

Breath eluded me.

My mind went blank.

The heightened beat of my heart thrummed against my chest the more I stood there staring at the tiny device.

After what seemed like hours, I swiped my phone open and read his message. For a full minute, my eyes stayed focused on the first word he'd written, fearing if I read the entire text I'd be disappointed in some way. Finally, I read it all, my heart leaping in my chest as I finished.

Jagger: I hope you still want to meet up with me. You're all I've thought about for the past few days.

His blatant admission surprised me, although it thrilled me just the same.

Kena: Yes. It's only right to hear you out, give you the opportunity to explain yourself in person. I hope you don't mind, but the only way Braylen would let me see you again is if I agreed to let her come with me.

He texted back right away.

Jagger: That's absolutely fine with me. Although I'm confused as to why Braylen has any say over what you do. You're grown.

How did I explain my sister to him in a way that wouldn't make him run for the hills? Braylen had always been there for me, sticking up for me and defending me growing up—and even as an adult, the awful encounter with Marcus the most recent. She'd attack anyone without a second thought if she thought they posed a threat toward me. I loved her for it, although it was times like with Jagger when I wished she'd take a step back and let me handle my own business.

Kena: She's only concerned for me, that's all.

I decided to downplay her protectiveness; no need to scare him off too soon.

Jagger: You're lucky to have her watching out for you, then.

An exhale of relief escaped that he understood and hadn't tried to persuade me to come to meet him alone.

Jagger: Where did you want to meet? Totally up to you. You tell me the time and place and I'll be there.

Well, he's sure accommodating.

Kena: Do you know where Neelan Park is?

Jagger: Yes.

I knew Braylen didn't have work the next day, so the timing was perfect.

Kena: Meet us tomorrow at noon by the picnic tables.

Jagger: I'll be there. Can't wait to see you.

Now all I had to do was make sure Braylen hadn't changed her mind. I fired off a quick text letting her know that Jagger had contacted me and we were going to meet him tomorrow. I gave her the time and place, although she'd insisted on the park initially. Either way, happiness danced in my heart I'd see Jagger again.

Would it be for the last time?

———— ◆ ————

A SINGLE BEAD OF SWEAT trickled down my back under the blaring sun. Thank heavens I chose to wear a tank top and shorts, or I probably would've passed out by now. The temperature had already reached the mid-eighties and it was barely noon.

Braylen and I patiently waited by the designated area for Jagger to show up. We'd decided to arrive a few minutes early; somehow my sister had convinced me we'd have the upper hand if we were there first. Because I hadn't felt like arguing, I just agreed with her.

Glancing at my watch, I saw that it was exactly noon. While we'd been waiting for the past fifteen minutes, Jagger wasn't technically late. Not yet, at least. Huffing beside me, Braylen rolled her eyes when I turned my head toward her.

Hey, you're the one who insisted on coming with me. My own frustration escaped, and if I had to sit in this heat for much longer, I feared my mood would switch from tolerable to volatile. I didn't do well with the hot weather, becoming ornery rather quickly.

"You know damn well I wasn't gonna let you come alone, so just let it go," she argued, taking a swig from her icy bottle of water. Just as I raised my hands to respond, I caught a glimpse of two men walking briskly toward us. Even though a vast amount of space separated us from them, I knew one of them was Jagger.

The closer they moved, the more anxious I became. Excited to lay eyes on him was second to the nerves gripping me from the inside. I believed Braylen's presence, along with whomever he'd brought with him, made for a very tense meeting. Flustered at what would happen in the next few moments, I closed my eyes and willed my erratic heart to stop its furious pounding. But all the will I could muster didn't matter.

My sister had finally noticed our visitors, hopping up from the picnic bench before I could beg her not to embarrass me. I followed behind, walking up to meet Jagger and his friend. Both guys looked quite menacing from afar, but up close I could see the vulnerability in Jagger's expression. His friend, on the other hand, looked like he would rather be anyplace but there with us. Both wore a leather vest with patches all over. I assumed it had something to do with their club, and because Jagger had worn it to meet me, he was essentially introducing me to that part of his life. While I appreciated the small gesture, I was sure my sister did not.

Finally standing before us, Jagger reached for my hand and pulled me close, kissing my cheek before stepping back.

"Nice to see you again, Kena," he greeted, his amber eyes glistening with appreciation. Turning toward my sister, his smile faltered slightly when he said, "Hi, Braylen. Thanks for letting Kena come and see me today."

"Uh-huh," she responded, tilting her head to the side while her hands found their way to her hips. She could be quite intimidating when she wanted to be, to men and women alike. "Who's this?" she asked, pointing toward Jagger's buddy.

"Oh, sorry. This is Ryder. He's one of my brothers."

"Didn't know you had a brother. Then again, we didn't know a lot about you, Jagger," she gritted, his name sounding like acid on her tongue. "Like you killing someone, or belonging to a gang."

Oh Lord. If I didn't shut her down she'd haul me away before he ever had the chance to explain.

"First off, *sweetheart,*" Ryder chastised, stepping closer until he towered over my sister, "you don't know anything about him. Or me, for that matter. So I'd suggest you keep your mouth shut and let these two talk."

For once in my life, someone had rendered my sister speechless. Her cheeks flushed, her eyes popping wide in astonishment that someone had the balls to talk to her like that. I would've laughed if I hadn't feared the whole situation was on the verge of blowing up in my face.

Before Braylen could respond, Jagger opened his mouth and apologized for his friend's behavior. "Braylen, you'll have to forgive my friend here. You see, he's just sticking up for me, like you are for your sister." The words sounded sincere, but the smirk on Jagger's face told me they were anything but.

Reaching out, I grabbed hold of my sister's arm, jerking her to the side before she made our encounter any more awkward. Turning her fully toward me, I let my hands do the talking.

Please don't embarrass me. I'm begging you. Just ignore his friend and let Jagger and me have a few minutes alone. She stared at me with her mouth agape, probably still stunned into silence from what Ryder had just said. *Please,* I begged.

"If you think for one second I'm gonna hang back with that ass Jagger calls a friend while you two traipse off, letting him fill your head with God knows what, you're outta your mind."

"Well, nobody wants to be alone with you either," Ryder snickered, crossing his arms over his chest in a defensive stance. For some reason, his willingness to engage my sister—or better yet, *enrage* my sister—amused me. He had every right to defend his friend, even if he came off as aggressive doing it. Looking the man up and down, I decided that I kind of liked him. Short dark hair neatly adorned his head, while a shadow of a beard painted his face. He was tall; if I had to guess he was just over six feet. Well-built and handsome made him a catch for any woman. Well, anyone except my sister. She apparently didn't like his mouth, although those lips of his could certainly entice any woman out of her panties.

Oh my God! What is wrong with me, I thought, thankful no one could read my mind.

Clearing his throat, Jagger brought me back to our uncomfortable little standoff, his eyes silently apologizing for his friend's retort. He moved a step closer, and when Braylen made a move to step in front of me, I pulled her backward with more force than I thought I had in me. Seizing her arm, I dragged her away until we had some privacy.

I love you, but if you don't let me talk to Jagger alone for a few minutes, I swear I'll make you regret it. I don't know how, but I'll think of something. I mean it, Braylen. You have to back off and let me handle this.

For the second time that day, my sister was at a loss for words. I'd never been so forceful with her before, but right then I didn't have a choice. I couldn't allow her to run my life, making my decisions for me, even if she only did it out of love. Concerned or not, she had to let me live my own life without always interfering.

"Fine, but don't come crawling to me when he breaks your heart. Or worse, gets you killed because of whatever he's mixed up in."

Well, if I'm dead I won't really be complaining much, I signed quickly, more to get her goat than anything, showing her how ridiculous she sounded.

"Not funny," she replied, walking back toward the two guys waiting on us. Brushing past the both of them, she planted herself on the picnic bench, crossing her arms over her chest and mirroring Ryder. When I glanced over at him, I saw a hint of a smile lift the corners of his lips. Clearly my sister amused him, even if he gave off the impression she annoyed him. The wheels of my mind started spinning, thinking that if I could somehow hook the two of them up, maybe she would leave Jagger and me alone.

I knew I'd gotten ahead of myself, but a girl could dream, couldn't she?

NINETEEN

Kena

WARM BREATH FANNED ACROSS MY ear and sent a shiver of delight pulsing through me. "They'd make one helluva couple, don't ya think?" His raspy voice unraveled the last thread of restraint I held close. If I turned my face an inch to the left, Jagger's lips would brush over mine, and although I wanted that more than anything, it wasn't going to be in front of the two brooding people standing close by.

Feeling brazen after threatening my sister to cool it, I grasped Jagger's hand and led him toward a secluded area of the park not far from where we stood. Needing to be away from prying eyes, he readily followed, tightening his hold in mine the further we walked. When two enormous oak trees finally shaded us, I removed my hand from his and took a reluctant step back. My boldness slipped when I found myself alone with him, a sudden shyness wrapping around me and strangling me. I wished I could be more like other girls my age, throwing caution to the wind and just going for it, whatever the situation may be. But sadly, I didn't fall into that category.

Staring down at my shuffling feet, I startled when Jagger's fingers lifted my chin, his eyes boring into mine in the most intimate of ways. Tucking a piece of my hair behind my ear, his hand lingered near my face, almost as if he wanted to stroke my cheek. But he didn't, instead choosing to break the connection right away.

"Thanks again for agreeing to hear me out. I'd hate for you to think of me as someone I'm not," he said, biting his bottom lip in sudden nervousness. I found his uneasiness slightly endearing, rendering him the opposite of his big-bad-biker persona. There was much more than met the eye with Jagger, and I only hoped I'd have the opportunity to find out what.

For a split second I'd wanted Braylen next to me to translate, but I knew I had to do this on my own. While it had been difficult to fully communicate with him, I appreciated the attempts he'd made so far. Sure, he'd only asked me yes or no questions, but at least he'd tried.

"Well, I guess I'll get right to it so we can get it out of the way." His lips kicked up in a sexy grin, and I just about pounced on him. The way his eyes roamed over my entire body, then fixated on my face, studying every feature as if he'd never see me again, both worried and titillated me. I *wanted* to be studied by him, and I hoped this wouldn't be the last time we'd be in each other's presence.

Leaning back against one of the oak trees blocking out the blaring sun, I bent my right leg and rested my foot on its trunk, entwining my hands in front of me while I waited for him to continue.

"What you saw, what you had to witness . . . I'm so sorry that happened. Had I known he would be there, I would've made sure you were nowhere in sight. Of course, I couldn't have known he'd come after me, although I should've expected it after what happened, but still," he rambled on, then stopped himself. "I'm getting off topic. Sorry. That guy came after me because I'd accidentally killed his brother in the ring. I swear it wasn't intentional, and it's been bothering me ever since." He took a deep breath before continuing. "What else?" he asked, more to himself than to me. "I'm part of the Knights Corruption MC, and although we've been involved in some illegal shit in the past, we no longer are."

Something in the way he averted his eyes every now and again told me he omitted certain important details from his explanation, but I couldn't very well ask him about it since he would have no idea what I was trying to get at. Better left for another time, I supposed.

"I'm an underground fighter, as you well know, and currently I'm undefeated." A proud smile appeared when he spoke about being unbeatable. "My club brothers mean the world to me and I would do anything to protect them, as they would for me." He went back to biting his bottom lip, rocking back and forth on the balls of his feet while trying to figure out what to tell me next. His slight anxiety in turn made me nervous, so I stepped forward and reached for his hand. When our palms touched and our fingers intertwined, I felt an overwhelming sense of safety. As if Jagger would go to the ends of the earth to protect me from harm, much like he'd explained he'd do for the members of his club.

I smiled at him when he faltered for his next words, trying to gift him my calmness to continue. Normally, I'm a Nervous Nellie around the opposite sex, never mind someone as gorgeous as Jagger, but there was something about him which spoke to me on a level even I didn't completely understand.

His hold on my hand tightened, pulling me closer until our faces remained just inches apart. "I really like you, Kena. And I would love it if you would give me the chance to get to know you better." His subtle scent of cologne, mixed with a muskiness that was all him, invaded my nose, the smell so heady I wanted to bottle it up and inhale it whenever I thought of him. "Can you give me that chance?" he asked, his beautiful smile returning in full force.

I just couldn't say no.

I nodded, displaying my own happiness with my expression.

"Good." When he leaned in closer I swore I could taste his lips, but we were interrupted before anything happened, Braylen power-walking toward us with intent.

"Are you guys done? Because I can't take any more of that guy," she shouted, pointing over her shoulder toward Ryder. Her face scrunched in anger, and I found it funny that she'd allowed someone to rile her up so much. It had to mean something, or maybe I just hoped for something that wasn't there.

Breaking apart, our intimate moment ruined, I smiled at Jagger before turning toward the feisty blonde I called a sister.

We're finished now, thank you very much.

Glaring at the guy standing next to me, Braylen passed him some sort of silent warning before turning her attention back to me. "Are you ready to go? I have more important things to do than stand around here all day," she huffed, tapping her foot in restlessness.

"Actually, I thought I could give Kena a ride home," Jagger interrupted, stepping closer and reaching for my hand again. Braylen saw the interaction and scoffed, raising her eyes from our entwined hands to stare at me in astonishment.

"Don't tell me you let him sweet talk you?"

I tried to respond, but Jagger held on to me. It wasn't until I tugged again that he let go. "Sorry," he said, "forgot you needed that." His apologetic smile undid me, and all I wanted to do was wrap myself in his arms. But instead, I had to deal with my overprotective sister.

I didn't let anyone sweet talk me. He's nice, and I like him. That's all there is to it. So let it be.

Standing firm, I placed my hands on my hips and waited for her to give in. Thankfully, I didn't have to wait long.

"Whatever," she mumbled, as she walked away. "It's your life. You're the one who's gonna have to deal with the repercussions."

Shaking my head, I turned back toward Jagger and grinned. I hadn't felt like this . . . ever, now that I thought about it. Sure, I'd had crushes on people before, but never had I been so consumed with thoughts of someone. Especially someone I hardly knew.

Heading back to the picnic table, I saw Braylen saunter past Ryder, waving him off when he tried to touch her arm. *What the hell happened while we were gone?*

"Nice to meet you, sweetheart," Ryder yelled after her, laughing as he watched her fling open her car door.

"Can't say the same," she shouted back before starting the engine and taking off.

Lightly smacking my upper arm, Ryder continued to laugh when he said, "Wow! Your sister is a piece of work. Is she always that intense?"

I wanted to shake my head but that would have been a lie, so I settled between nodding *and* shaking my head from side to side. Indecisive, but they both understood what I meant.

"I like it," Ryder said, before clasping Jagger on the back. "Well, if you kids don't need me anymore, I'm out." Without another word, he strode across the lot and swung his leg over his motorcycle, the engine coming to life with the turn of a key. It was then I realized the bike next to Ryder was most likely Jagger's. He said he wanted to give me a ride home, but I'd never ridden on the back of something so dangerous before. They looked so unsafe, no protection from anything.

"Text me your address." I quickly pulled out my phone and messaged him the information. After he glanced at the screen, he put his phone back inside his vest. "Shall we?" he asked, placing his hand at the base of my spine and guiding me toward his ride. Reaching for his helmet, he passed it to me before swinging his leg over the impressive piece of machinery. Scooting up some, he started it up, the fierce sound of the bike startling me. Glimpsing back, he seemed confused as to why I hadn't already straddled the seat, but one glance at the reluctance on my face told him everything. "Let me guess. You've never ridden before."

I shook my head.

"Well, you're in for a treat, then. It's the best feeling in the world. Well, the second best feeling in the world," he teased, winking while a slight tinge of pink stole over my cheeks. He did his best to put me at ease, but I truly didn't think I'd be able to go through with it. *Maybe I should text my sister and ask her to come back for me,* I thought. "I won't let anything happen. I promise." He reached out, the flat of his palm facing upward, waiting for me to accept his invitation.

I trusted him to keep me safe, so I placed my hand in his and allowed him to help me onto the bike, scooting up behind him until my front pressed against his back. Having no idea what to do, I placed my hands on my thighs, waiting for further instruction.

"Wrap your arms around my waist," he said. When I'd done as he'd instructed, he pulled them snugger. "There, just like that. Hold on tight, and lean into any turns I make." My fingers grazed over his abdomen, and even though I was petrified, I quickly took the opportunity to explore the hard planes of his stomach over his shirt. I remembered exactly what his torso looked like, and a warmth spread through me the more my hands snaked around his body. He patted my hands in reassurance. "Don't worry. You'll be fine. Trust me." As the last word fell from his lips, he took off slowly, allowing me time to adjust before increasing his speed. Once he turned onto the highway, he let loose, thrusting forward with a quickness I knew had to be dangerous.

I held on for dear life, probably ensuring he would never want to have me on the back of his bike ever again. After a few minutes, however, I breathed deep and celebrated the feel of the air whipping around my body, and the freeness of the open road. The leather encasing him was warm to the touch, and I wondered what his bare skin would feel like against mine. Being so close to him toyed with my imagination, but before I could lose myself to any more of my thoughts, he turned left off the highway. We were only a few minutes from my house, and never before had I been so disappointed.

When he finally killed the engine, he unlocked my arms and helped me find my footing. After I stood without wobbling, I removed the helmet and placed it on the seat I'd just vacated. A second passed before Jagger swung his leg over and joined me on solid ground.

"So, did you enjoy your first bike ride?" He seemed hopeful, and I didn't want to disappoint him, so I nodded. "Are you lying?" he teased, reading me better than I thought possible. While I'd been terrified in the beginning, I relaxed after a few minutes and really did enjoy myself. So when I nodded again, I truly meant it. "Good, I'm glad. It's the first of many."

Shrugging, at a loss for what to do next, I pointed toward my house, signaling he had the right place.

"I'll walk you to your door," he offered.

Flashing him a genuine smile, I turned my back and started walking the few yards toward the porch. Once we stood on the bottom step, I nervously played with the flap of my cross-body purse, finally delving inside to retrieve my keys. My eyes kept flicking from his face to my hands and back again.

"Do you think I could use your bathroom quick before I head back?" Because I wanted more time with him I readily agreed, nodding before turning around to put the key in the lock. Glancing around the street, I realized Braylen wasn't home, which worked out just fine in my book.

Opening the door, I moved aside so he could enter. Our ranch home wasn't anything fancy, but it was nice. Cozy. And apparently Jagger thought so as well.

"I like your house," he said, glancing from the living room, to the kitchen and then toward the small hallway to the left. "Bathroom?"

I signed, *Second door on the left,* briefly forgetting he had no idea what I'd just told him. But instead of showing him where it was, I held up my forefinger and middle finger in a V shape, then tapped my other hand against the wood of the front door, then pointed down the hall. I wanted to see if he caught on to what I tried to tell him, although it appeared as if I'd been playing charades more than anything else.

A frown appeared, but a few seconds later he grinned. "Second door down the hall?" I nodded. I did a lot of that with him, but I had no other choice. "On the left or the right?" I pointed to the left. He walked away, and I headed straight for the kitchen. I needed a drink like nobody's business, and while I could've definitely used a glass of wine, I opted for a bottled water instead. I'd just finished half of my drink when Jagger reappeared, striding straight for me, his lips curved up in the most enticing grin. He appeared happy. Even his eyes shone brightly. Was it because of me? Or was he normally a happy-go-lucky kind of guy? I hoped for the first option. Well, and the second, but more the first.

We stared at each other for a short while, neither of us knowing what to do. Until he broke the silence, his voice wrapping around me and threatening to never let go. "Well, I guess I better get going. Have some stuff to take care of."

Again, more nodding on my part.

Looking like he battled between leaving and wanting to hang out for a little while longer, I couldn't help but share his silent indecision. Desperately wanting more time with him, my brain fired off warnings that if he didn't leave soon, I might be tempted to throw caution to the wind and do something I may regret.

Once we neared the front door, he turned around and stepped toward me, his lips so close all I could do was stare at his mouth. Without touching me or saying a single word, he'd somehow managed to drive me insane with want. His warm breath tickled my lips, and when I'd finally dragged my eyes up to his, they bored into mine and tried to communicate a silent message of sorts.

The impending anticipation before the first kiss drove me crazy, although I'd never wanted anything more. After what seemed like forever, the both of us frozen in time for countless seconds, he placed his right hand on my waist, digging his fingers into my skin. Not hard, just the right amount of pressure to tell me he needed to touch me, to connect with me in some way before he left.

"Can I kiss you?" he asked, looking tentative, preparing himself for rejection. But it was a denial which never came. I nodded and leaned in, waiting for him to crush the remaining space. Greedily accepting my invitation, he brushed his lips against mine, the softness of them teasing me in just the right way. At first, I assumed he'd hold back, offering nothing more than a simple peck, but the longer we remained fused together, the clearer it became our first kiss would surely be electrifying.

His right hand traveled up from my waist until it rested at the nape of my neck, gripping me softly and pulling me further toward him. His lips pressed harder. When his tongue slipped from his mouth and teased my lips, I instantly opened for him. Allowing myself to lose some of my inhibitions where he was concerned was the most freeing thing that'd happened to me in a very long time. His warmth enveloped me, and we spent the next few minutes exploring one another's tastes, enjoying the other while we could. My fingers dug into his shoulders as he devoured me, his desire for me fueling my own to even greater heights. His kiss was dominant yet permissive, firm yet tender. The two wavering contradictions certainly kept me intrigued.

Jagger's free hand explored my body, yet he remained respectful. Dipping his fingers under the fabric of my shirt, he skated across my skin, eliciting goose bumps. Freeing my neck from his hold, both of his hands glided behind my back, holding tightly and pulling me impossibly close, as if he wished to meld his body with mine—and judging from the hard length poking me in the stomach, it was exactly what he wanted to do. But he never pushed me further than I was willing to go. He didn't grab my ass or grope my breasts, and while I appreciated him remaining a gentleman, there was a small part of me that wished he'd cross the line and show me just how much he wanted me.

Breaking apart, his short pants of breath hit the side of my face as his lips moved toward my ear. "I can't stop kissing you," he whispered, nipping my lobe before kissing the tender flesh just below it. Pulling back so he could see my flushed face, he asked, "Do I affect you the same way?" There was no mistaking the wanton look on my face, but just in case, I gave him a simple nod. "Good, at least it's not just me who feels like I'm going crazy," he mumbled, hitting the proverbial nail on the head. I shared in his delirium, yet I'd never been so happy.

Gifting me with one last kiss, he stepped back and adjusted himself, sheepishly grinning when he'd been caught. "Sorry, but I couldn't help it." All I could do was rest my head against the door and smile. I wished for time to stand still, to never move from the spot where I stood. But like all good things—spectacular things, even—our connection had to come to an end at some point. "Well, I guess I should go now." Disappointment snared my vision, but I quickly reeled it in. I knew he liked me, as I did him, immensely, but I also didn't want to come across as needy. Treading carefully for fear I'd offer him too much of myself, I continued to lounge against the door, doing my best to plaster a nonchalant look on my face. I wasn't sure if I pulled it off, though.

My body felt like jelly, so to ensure I wouldn't sink to my knees, I took a few extra seconds and gazed at Jagger. Truly looked at him. Studied him, really. I needed to commit every image I could to memory. The way his dark golden hair had flecks of sun-kissed blond spattered all around his head. The way a small dimple appeared in his left cheek when he grinned. The tiny chip in his front tooth that was unnoticeable to most, but because I'd been scrutinizing every facet of him, I'd noticed. Oddly, it added to his ruggedness. I glanced down and peered at his forearms, the ink and corded muscles flexing with every gesture he made. Right then his hands fisted and unclenched, over and over again, and I thought maybe it was a nervous tick.

Finally moving away from the door, I twisted the handle and opened it, waiting to hear if he'd say anything before leaving. Luckily, he didn't disappoint. "I'll text you later and we'll set up a day to do something. Sound good?" He fiddled with his own keys that time, glancing from his hands to my face, back and forth until I cupped his cheek. Smiling, I leaned forward and captured his mouth with my own, getting my fill until the next time we'd see each other. I not only found Jagger quite intriguing, but I liked the person I became when I was around him; I remained shy, but my wall of reserves faltered when in his presence. I couldn't explain it, nor did I wish to.

As my lips broke away from his, saddened at the loss, I took a tentative step backward. I wanted nothing more than to taste him again, but I realized that if I didn't allow him to leave something bigger might happen. And while I could certainly picture myself pinned beneath him, offering him my most precious gift, there was no way I wanted to rush things between us.

Not yet.

Not until we knew each other better.

Pushing a heavy sigh from his mouth, Jagger looked dazed. A fleeting look skipped across his face, one so quick it disappeared before I could dissect it. "We'll talk soon," he said, squinting his eyes shut when he realized what he'd just said. "Sorry," he apologized. "Y-you know what I mean." I simply smiled, doing my best to communicate that I didn't find offense with what he'd said. Actually, I found his screwups quite endearing.

He soon disappeared from my house, and as I watched him walk away, I couldn't help but regret my decision to let him leave.

TWENTY

Jagger

WITHOUT SOUNDING TOO MUCH LIKE a pussy, I felt as if I were floating on cloud nine. I spent the entire ride back to my apartment picturing her mouth against mine. The way our tongues melded together, teasing and tasting. The way her skin warmed from my touch. The look of longing on her face when she'd given in and demanded as much from me as I did from her.

The wind swathed me as I rode, the rumble of my bike's engine eradicating some of my frustrations. Of the sexual kind, of course. Wanting desperately to take Kena to bed, the image of the two of us entwined, writhing around in blissful pleasure, bombarded me while I drove. I wouldn't rush her; however, there was too much at stake, for both my head and my . . . heart?

I'd never allowed a female to consume my thoughts before, choosing only to use them for sexual gratification and nothing more. I'd also never pictured myself in a relationship before, electing to stay as detached as possible when it came to the opposite sex. Not that Kena and I were in a relationship. Well, not yet, at least. But hopefully in time, she would deem me worthy of being her man.

Although I wanted nothing more than to be with her, I knew danger lurked around every corner. Psych still hadn't made a move to come and collect Sully, something which unnerved Marek, as well as the rest of the club. Plus, Snake would surely come after me again, and where would I be the next time? At one of my fights? Out with some of the guys? Or maybe out with Kena?

While I despised the thought of putting her in that situation again, I couldn't help but be selfish.

I wanted her.

And I knew there was no way my head was going to win against my incessant need to possess her.

Before long, not remembering a single mile of the travel home, I veered up the incline of my street, whizzing past the parked cars and imagining what it would be like to live in a house filled with a family. Because my mother died giving birth to me, the only family I knew was my father. Obviously, I used the word "family" extremely loosely when referring to that man.

But then I'd stumbled upon Marek and Stone, jumping in without regard for my own safety in order to help them out. My assistance was rewarded when Marek insisted I stop by their clubhouse the following day.

As they say, the rest was history.

Or at least history in the making.

As I dismounted, clutching the black helmet in my hand, I strolled toward the front entrance, a tilted smile encroaching. For once, after a very long time, hope swirled inside me, and it happened because of one person.

The one woman who challenged me to be a better man without even realizing it.

Once inside, I pulled my T-shirt over my head, catching the faint smell of vanilla. Inhaling the only remnants of her, I took my fill before tossing the shirt to the floor in the corner of the bathroom. I imagined my sloppiness grating on her nerves, triggering many an argument, and while the subject should've served to irritate me, I could only grin. Wanting nothing more than to share my life with someone, daily struggles and all, I'd embrace each and every moment she gifted me.

To be thinking of her as if she were the one didn't scare me, although it probably should have. I was only twenty-two, too young to even think about settling down, but I knew deep inside that she differed from every other woman out there.

Felt it deep inside my broken soul.

Continued images of her lifted my spirits as I washed the day off me, my fingers circling my arousal in an attempt to tamper the need surging through me to claim her, if only in thought. Desiring someone so desperately both unnerved and exhilarated me.

Two contradictory emotions, neither of which I gave in to completely.

I had no idea what the future held for me until it smacked me in the face. Drifting off to sleep, the only thing I kept praying for was to get what I'd wanted. I figured fate would deliver soon enough.

Or not.

———◆———

"WHATCHA LOOKIN' AT?" ADELAIDE ASKED over my shoulder, snatching my phone from me before passing me her daughter. She smirked before taking a few steps back, completely out of my reach from my lounging position on her couch. I cradled Riley in my arms, the baby's presence dispelling any frustrations I'd had at Adelaide's prank. I ignored her, concentrating on trying to make the four-month-old baby smile. Normally I wasn't a kid person, but Stone and Adelaide's child was surely someone special. She had the entire protection of our club behind her, and she didn't have a clue how much shit we were gonna give any boy who came near her as she got older. Poor thing.

Riley's tiny fingers clutched my thumb, gurgling and staring at me like I was some kind of large toy. Her bright green eyes marveled at the sight of me, and I returned the favor.

"Why are you looking up books on sign language?" Glancing over my shoulder, I saw Adelaide's curiosity written all over her face, her brows knitted together while she continued to stare first at my phone's screen, then at me.

"There's this girl I met," I answered, repositioning Riley so I could turn around without fearing I was gonna squish her. I'd planned on leaving it at that, not going into too much detail, when Stone ambled into the living room, running a towel over his head to help dry his hair. Bare-chested, drops of water running down his torso, it was obvious he'd just hopped out of the shower. Thank fuck he had enough sense to put on a pair of shorts before strolling out.

"You talking about the girl from the fight?" He leaned in to give his woman a kiss before walking toward me and reaching for his daughter. If life ever granted me children, I could only hope to be half the father Stone turned out to be. He loved his daughter with a fierceness I'd never seen before, coddling and fussing over her constantly. Or at least that's the way he was whenever I was around.

"Oooo, what girl?" Adelaide teased, biting her lower lip and wriggling her brows. She passed Stone a bottle of formula, all while keeping her stare glued to me. Obviously she wasn't gonna let up until I gave her a bit of information.

"Just some girl," I replied, the words erroneously riddled with non-chalance to throw her off the trail. As soon as Stone opened his mouth again, I knew more details would be demanded, so I crossed my ankle over my knee and settled in for the interrogation.

"Just some girl, my ass," Stone mumbled, tipping the bottle higher so Riley could eat. "He's gaga over this chick. Don't let him fool ya." He sat down beside me, hitting my shoulder with his as he looked down at his daughter. If Stone wasn't such a good friend, I would've up and left the house, refusing to allow anyone to rib on me just because they felt they could. But in truth, I'd come to their house because I'd secretly hoped to talk to him about her. The other guys at the club would razz me, blowing off whatever I felt toward her as nothing more than needing to get laid.

"All right," I confessed. "So she's more than just some girl." Throwing my arm over the back of the sofa, I said, "I really like her, but. . . ."

"But what?" Adelaide asked, handing back the phone she'd grabbed from me moments earlier.

"She can't talk, so I need to learn sign language in order to understand what she's trying to tell me."

"Wait, I'm confused," Adelaide said. "Is she deaf?"

"No, she just can't speak. So while she can hear me, if I ask her any-thing other than a yes or no question, she has to sign. And as of right now, I only know "thank you."" Puffing out my cheeks in frustration, the stress of not being able to communicate properly with Kena already weighing on me, I threw my head back and closed my eyes.

"Sully knows sign language. Maybe she can teach you." The last word barely left Adelaide's mouth before I had already jumped to my feet. The knowledge that someone I knew could help thrilled me, but then reali-zation hit. No way would Marek allow us time together. As quickly as I became excited, defeat rained down all over me. Slumping my shoulders, I walked toward their kitchen and pulled open the refrigerator. Grabbing a beer, I popped the top and took a big swig.

"Help yourself," Stone grunted, turning his brief attention away from me and back to his daughter.

"What's the problem, Jagger?" Adelaide asked, sitting next to her family.

"Marek will never go for it." She opened her mouth to speak but I cut her off. "Trust me, he won't, which sucks because I need to learn this shit like yesterday."

"We'll talk to him," Stone offered, passing Riley to her mother to finish the feeding. Rising, he walked past me and grabbed his own bottle of beer.

"Yeah? How long's that gonna take?"

"No time at all," he answered. "He and Sully are on their way here now."

TWENTY-ONE

Jagger

I WOULD'VE BEEN LYING IF I'd said being in such close proximity to Sully and Marek together didn't play on my nerves. The only thing settling me was that he seemed to have softened toward me somewhat over the previous couple weeks. Okay, maybe softened was the wrong choice of word. His borderline hatred of me had lessened, tolerating my presence more and more as the days passed. Hey, any little bit helped.

Taking a seat in the lone recliner, facing the sofa where everyone else perched themselves, allowed me to follow along with their conversation while keeping to myself. Laughing right along with Stone and Adelaide while they regaled us with some of their stories of Riley tempered some of the tension swirling in the air. Or was that just around me?

"But when she looks at me like I'm her whole world, it just does somethin' to me, man." Stone smiled, glancing over at his best friend. Adelaide grazed the back of his head with her hand, and when he turned to look at her, she kissed him. A simple gesture of affection, but it made me long to be with Kena. I wanted so much to be wrapped up in her, just like Stone was with Adelaide. Hell, even the way Marek was with Sully.

I'd coyly snuck peeks at my prez's wife, watched her glancing at her husband every now and again, and I desperately prayed Kena would gift me with the same adoration someday. Minus the sorrow laced behind her eyes, an emotion which confused me because I had no idea where it had come from. I would like to have said Sully and I were friends, and I thought we were . . . to a point. But we'd never been able to explore and strengthen our relationship because of her husband.

Marek's stubbornness aggravated many people, but that trait had also helped the club in immeasurable ways. His quest to never give up on getting his hands on Yanez, for one. Something which had paid off, because the world was now free of such an evil, despicable human being. If I could even call him that.

Moments of fussing over Riley filled the ensuing silence, all of us fascinated with the tiny human. When the baby was placed in Sully's arms, a heart-wrenching look passed over her face, one that was gone too quickly to discern exactly what it had meant.

"So," Adelaide started, reaching over and stroking Riley's head while Sully held her close, "Stone and I wanted to know if you and Marek would be Riley's godparents." For a brief moment, I'd almost felt like I was intruding on a sacred moment between close friends, but it quickly passed when I saw the smiles light up all their expressions, especially Sully's. She was elated, and it pleased me to see her so happy.

To see all of them so happy.

"We don't go to church," Marek blurted, "but we'd do it if you could find a way around that little issue." He kissed Sully's temple before placing his hand over Riley's tiny chest. "We'd be honored, is probably the response you wanted," he chuckled.

"Well, yeah, I guess it is," Stone agreed, reaching over and smacking his friend on the back. "I don't go to church either, and while Addy is a practicing Catholic, she kind of fell off attending as well. But she has a great relationship with her church's priest, and he said he would officiate Riley's baptism, no problem."

"We were thinking of having it at the clubhouse, if that's okay with you," Adelaide said, glancing from Stone to Marek and back again.

"I'm pretty sure that question was to you, buddy," Stone said, jerking his head toward Marek.

"Of course. Yeah. Whatever you two need, we'll do it." They all continued to smile, and their joy seeped into me and calmed me further.

And then Adelaide opened her mouth and started talking to Sully.

About something which involved me. A topic which would surely get under Marek's skin and squash all the happy vibes floating around the room.

"Sully, you know how to sign, right?" Adelaide asked, continuing to stroke the top of her daughter's head, calming her as soon as Riley started to cry.

"Yeah, why?" she answered, her gaze never wavering from the child in her arms, not until Stone had cleared his throat. Even he knew what was coming, preparing himself to deal with whatever blowback would possibly occur.

"How do you know it?" I blurted out, not even realizing I'd asked the question until after the words had left my mouth. Marek picked his head up and looked at me, but thankfully his expression was void of anger. Irritation may have been at the forefront, but not anger.

"I didn't have much going on when I lived. . . ." She trailed off before taking a breath and continuing. "I had to be inventive, fill my days with something, so I watched videos and convinced my father to allow me to buy a book on the subject. I would sit in my room for hours on end and have conversations with myself just so I could practice." She smiled, but the curve of her lips waned. Handing Riley back to Adelaide, she tucked a strand of her black hair behind her ear before resting her hands in her lap.

"Why the sudden curiosity?" Marek inquired, looking at everyone, including me.

"Jagger's interested in someone, and she can't speak. So he needs to learn sign language in order to understand her," Adelaide offered. If Stone had been the one to talk, he probably would've been a bit crasser about my situation, no doubt throwing in that I wanted to get Kena into bed and needed a way to tell her so, or some shit like that.

"Is she deaf?" Sully asked, quickly glancing toward Marek to see how he was faring with her talking to me. Luckily, he didn't seem to have minded, but maybe that was because his wife and I were not alone together.

"No, she just can't speak," I responded, scratching the side of my head as a distraction.

"So she can hear, just doesn't wanna talk? Is that what it is?" Marek asked, confused by the turn of conversation.

"No," I said, a little more intensely than I'd intended. "She physically can't talk. I haven't worked up the nerve yet to ask her what happened. It might be a touchy subject." *Breathe deep.* "And yes, she can hear. But for right now, I can only ask her yes and no questions, because otherwise . . . I just can't understand her when she tries to communicate with me." Annoyance trickled through my veins because they'd forced me to talk about Kena's condition, and although the conversation was one derived from simply curiosity, I felt as if I were betraying her in some way.

"Oh, how awful for her," Sully said, a frown suddenly appearing. "I'd love to help you, but I'm not sure I can." Without realizing, she caught her husband's eye before turning back toward me. She silently asked permission with the quick look they'd shared. The last thing I wanted to do was turn the joyous nature of the day's visit into one filled with bristling tension, but I had no other choice.

With every moment that ticked by where I couldn't properly communicate with Kena, I feared she'd deem me not worthy and move on to someone who could understand her. Someone like Kevin. Someone who fully comprehended her situation and could give her something I couldn't.

So I decided to risk Marek's anger and pushed Sully on the topic.

"Anything you could teach me would be awesome. I really like her. It'd mean a lot to me." I leaned back in my seat and patiently waited to see what would happen. Thankfully, Stone's woman interjected her two cents.

"It's the perfect solution. Isn't it, Sully?" Adelaide asked, first locking eyes with her friend, then with Marek, silently challenging him to disagree. Adelaide wasn't afraid of anyone, and I truly admired that about her. She'd put Stone's volatile ass in check on quite a few occasions, and while the leader of the Knights Corruption unnerved me at times, he had no such effect on Adelaide.

Tense, uncertain seconds passed without a single word spoken from anyone. I swore they heard my heart thrumming inside my chest, felt the uneasiness wrapping around me, but still the silence continued.

Deciding to end it, I finally spoke up. "It's okay. I'll figure something else out. No biggie." Slumping back in my chair in defeat, I ran my hand through my hair in uncertainty.

"Nonsense," Adelaide pushed, handing Riley to Marek to hold. A distraction tactic at best, and I think it worked; everyone loved the little girl, Marek being no exception. "Jagger, Sully will help teach you what you need to know. It's not every day someone special falls into your lap."

"That's a whole other topic, sweetheart," Stone teased, grabbing his woman by the waist and pulling her impossibly close.

Shoving his shoulder in mock annoyance, she turned back toward me, an amused look on her face. "I'm serious. We need to help him out. And if anyone here has a problem with that, they'll have to deal with me." A smile still danced on her lips, but everyone present knew she was dead serious. Even Marek.

All heads turned toward the dark-haired leader of the club, breathlessly waiting for him to speak. Would he assert his dominance over the entire group? Or would Adelaide's not-so-subtle demands win out?

Marek's chest rose and fell, an unsettling sigh his only response until he finally opened his mouth. "At the clubhouse. Be there tomorrow at noon." Leaning forward, he pointed a dangerous finger in my direction. "If I so much as see anything inappropriate, you'll regret it, prospect."

"Oh, stop playing the big bad biker, Marek," Adelaide teased. "Save all that testosterone for when Riley starts dating." She laughed at her own joke, but her words only served to rile up her man.

"Hell no!" Stone shouted. "No dating for my baby girl. Nope. Not gonna happen."

We all laughed, even though I knew Stone stood firm behind his outburst.

Poor Riley was gonna have a hell of a time dealing with not only her father, but every other man in the club as she got older. Their protection over her already something fierce, it would only intensify as she became interested in the opposite sex.

TWENTY-TWO

Kena

"I CAN'T BELIEVE THAT GUY," Braylen grated. "I mean, who the hell does he think he is?" For the past two days, my sister had been going off about both Jagger and his friend Ryder, flip-flopping between the both of them so often it was hard to keep straight who she'd been pissed at.

Who are you talking about? And why are you so upset? I'd never seen my big sister so riled up over any guy. Yeah, her concern about me getting involved with Jagger was understandable, but when it came down to it, I could make my own decisions. But for her to still be this upset over some guy she'd just met was rather telling. What had happened between them when Jagger and I left them in search of some privacy at the park? We weren't gone that long.

"I'm talking about his friend. Ryder," she blurted, running her hands through her hair in annoyance. I had no idea how we'd gotten on the topic of either one of the men, but there we were, and since she needed to get something off her chest, there was nothing I could do but sit back and hear her out. Plus, it amused me to see her so irked over Jagger's friend and club brother.

What happened between you two? I wriggled my brows in jest, but it only served to irritate her more.

"Absolutely nothing," she replied too quickly, a slight pink tinge stealing over her cheeks.

Come on, Braylen. You're not telling me everything. I rested my hands at my sides and squinted at her, doing my best to read her body language. Other than the embarrassment which covered her skin, I had no idea what else she'd been leaving out of our conversation.

"He's a pig," she'd finally disclosed. "When you guys walked away, he told me that I needed a good fuck to calm me down. He even offered to be the one to "fuck me senseless,"" she said, switching her tone to a deeper voice, no doubt imitating Ryder.

I couldn't help it.

I smiled. Big.

My sister was certainly intense, especially toward those she had an issue with, justified or not. And because Ryder had called her on her shit, he was all right in my book. Maybe my sister did need to get laid, although she'd never had any issues in that department before. If she had someone else to focus on, maybe she wouldn't be so overbearing when it came to Jagger, and my decision to keep seeing him. A decision she didn't know about yet. I hadn't even told her about the kiss. Needing to keep something to myself, I decided to tell her when I deemed necessary, or when she'd moved past her dislike for him.

I guess I shouldn't hold my breath on that one.

"It's not funny," she pouted, although the slightest hint of a smile graced her mouth.

It kind of is, I signed back. *Plus, Ryder's kind of hot.*

I half expected her to make some kind of grossed-out face, as if the mere mention of Ryder's looks would send her into a tailspin of sorts. Spouting off how much she couldn't stand the sight of him, and if she ever saw him again it would be too soon. That kind of stuff. But instead, she gave me a half smirk before turning around and walking toward the kitchen. When she returned with a bottle of unopened wine and two glasses, plopping down on the couch next to me, I couldn't help but shake my head and smile again.

Raising my hands, I signed, *You like him.* It wasn't a question, instead an observation.

"What?" she practically screeched. "You're out of your mind." Leaning closer, she scrutinized me. "Are you already drunk, Kena? Because that's the only way you could be serious right now." When I just sat there staring, she continued with her mini outburst. "Are you for real, or are you messing with me? Because if you honestly think that I would ever like that man, no matter how good-looking and mysterious he may be, I might need to have you committed." Popping off the cork, she took a big swig straight from the bottle. Scrunching up my face, I tore the wine from her fingers and poured myself a glass before she finished off the contents.

So you do think he's good-looking?

"Duh." She rolled her eyes. "Anyone can see he's fucking gorgeous. Too bad he's crass and arrogant." Pouring herself a glass, she took a few slow sips, the look plastered across her face telling me she was contemplating an issue, an internal dialogue I was sure she wouldn't allow me to be a party to.

Settling back into the comfortable couch, I pressed the remote and flicked on the television. We'd planned on watching a movie, but something told me we'd be discussing some of the members of the Knights Corruption instead.

Placing the wine glass between my legs, I asked, *Why don't you give him another chance? If he still acts the same, then you'll know he's not right for you.*

Only my sister could chug wine and not make it look uncouth. "Give him another chance? Now I *know* you're drunk." Plunking back against the leather sofa, she folded her legs underneath her. "I don't want to be anywhere near that man. Besides, when or why would I even be in the same room with him again?" Her question lingered in the air, more of a serious inquisition than a rhetorical one.

I'm going to see Jagger again soon. I could ask him to bring Ryder along if you want. Maybe we could all grab something to eat. For a split second I believe Braylen considered it, but then her stubbornness kicked in and she tossed aside the mere notion of ever laying eyes on Jagger's friend again.

"No, thank you," she emphatically said, pouring another glass of wine. "Can we please not talk about either one of them anymore, and just watch this damn movie?"

Okay, okay. Don't get testy, I signed before pushing Play. For the next hour and a half, we lost ourselves in the comedic world of Kevin Hart.

Later that evening, as I snuggled under my thick comforter, my air conditioner on full blast, a message came through on my phone. My heart skipped a beat from the mere thought that it could be Jagger texting me. Unhooking my cell from its charger, I swiped the screen and saw it was indeed him.

Jagger: Would you like to grab a bite to eat next Friday? Say around seven? I'd make it sooner but I have a lot of stuff I have to deal with. Plus I have a fight coming up in a couple days I need to train for.

When he'd left my apartment days ago, I'd expected him to contact me right away. But he hadn't, and while I'd been disappointed, I understood our situation wasn't the norm for him. Or for me either, as a matter of fact. I'd accepted my limitations, but I was smart enough to realize it might take him some more time. My condition certainly wasn't an easy thing to handle, so I silently berated myself for not being patient.

While excitement raced through me at seeing him again, my nerves also took over. There were only so many yes and no questions he could ask me in person.

Kena: Next Friday sounds good. See you then.

Jagger: Great. I'll text you tomorrow. Good night.

I fell asleep that evening thinking of Jagger, much like I had since the day I'd first laid eyes on him. Thoughts of him infiltrated my brain more often these days. I found it hard to concentrate at work, or while I hung out with my sister or just doing mundane everyday tasks. Consumed with when I'd see him again became my not-so-favorite pastime.

Picturing his face and remembering what his kiss tasted like lulled me to sleep, dreams sneaking out from the recesses of my subconscious and pulling me under into a blissful slumber.

TWENTY-THREE

Jagger

"STOP MESSIN' AROUND AND BE serious for a minute," Sully demanded, her tone belying the words she'd spoken. Trying to appear the serious teacher, her face lit up at the interaction between us. Sitting next to her on the couch in the clubhouse common room had been our daily meeting place for the past five days, and she'd taught me a lot. We'd also managed to have a bit of fun along the way as well.

"I *am* serious," I said, smirking at the disbelieving expression on her face. "I just keep forgetting some of the letters. This shit isn't easy."

"No one said it was gonna be, so stop pouting and get with it. Besides, aren't you taking her out in two days? Because that's not a lot of time to practice. I think we're gonna have to extend our sessions a bit. What do you think?" Sully glanced at the book in her lap, the one she'd been teaching me from since we started the lessons. She knew a lot without even glancing at it but because she wasn't fluent, she had to refer back to the book every now and again. But she was a much better teacher than YouTube.

"What about your husband? What's he gonna say about that?" Marek had handled our little sessions a lot better than I thought he ever would. At first he hung around, often sitting at the bar to keep an eye on us, but after the third day, he'd disappeared into Chambers, most times with Stone and Tripp, to discuss routine club business. All the important topics required all of our attendance, but thankfully that didn't happen all that often lately.

"I've discussed it with Cole already and he's fine with it. As soon as I told him how much Kena means to you, he kind of gave up the notion that you're in love with me." Sully swallowed nervously and brushed her hair from her face, glancing at me quickly. "I told him he was crazy, that you never felt that way about me, but he dismissed my ramblings. Anyway," she muttered, "he's fine with all of it."

Sully and I had talked about how Marek had treated me after the day he attacked me in his living room when he'd returned home early from his trip. Seeing his wife sleeping against my shoulder had set him off, and I caught the brunt of his anger that night. Then for the months that followed, he barely tolerated my presence. It wasn't until recently that his behavior toward me started to thaw, the turning point happening after killing Yanez.

The next two hours passed by ridiculously fast, the both of us giving it our all, communicating with nothing but our hands. We weren't allowed to speak to the other, and while I'd messed up a few times, I'd certainly made progress. An accomplishment I treasured, as did Sully, beaming brightly with her own teaching achievement.

Rising to my feet, I raised my hands above my head and allowed my muscles to stretch. Craning my neck from side to side helped to wake me, which I'd needed because I had to prepare for that evening's fight.

"Hey, Ryder!" I shouted over my shoulder as he walked by. "You seen Stone?" Figuring it was probably a good idea if I engaged in some last-minute training, I squeezed Sully's hand in thanks and went in search of my sparring buddy.

"Yeah, he's in Chambers with Marek."

Nodding my thanks, I strolled across the room, and knocked on the door before entering. Peeking my head through the small allowance, I locked eyes with Stone before turning to Marek.

"You need something, prospect?" the club leader asked, a look of irritation strangling his features. Was that for me? Or for another reason? With no time to waste, I answered right away, hoping to get in at least an hour in the ring before I had to leave. I'd wanted to shower and contact Kena for a little bit before heading to that night's fight location.

"Yeah, sorry for interrupting. Sully and I are done for today, and I wanted to know if you," I said, switching my attention to Stone, "could go a few rounds in the ring with me."

Stone looked a bit unnerved, as if whatever he and Marek had been discussing had been heavy. But it was obvious it wasn't weighty enough to require all of us to be involved, so I dismissed it as none of my business.

"Sure. I'll be out in five," the VP acknowledged, waving toward the door, essentially dismissing me. I took the hint and closed the door, striding toward the bathroom so I could change into a pair of shorts. I planned on working up a sweat, and jeans just wouldn't be the proper attire for me to whoop on Stone.

———◆———

"WHO'S COMING TONIGHT?" I ASKED, wiping the sweat from my brow after Stone and I finished dancing around the ring, both of us energized after our little bout. My friend had a red mark forming on his side where I'd kicked him, but the bastard never even flinched, his ability to never feel pain pissing me off. Not that I wanted to harm him, but for ego sake, it would have been nice if Stone had at least made some kind of pained expression.

Normally, I wouldn't train the same night I had a fight scheduled, but I'd needed to release some of my aggression. Saving all my energy for my opponent that evening might have proved to be detrimental, and there was no way I wanted a repeat of what happened before, ending someone's life unintentionally.

"I can't make it, but Ryder and Tripp will be there with you." Stone ran a towel over his dampened hair, tossing it at me with a devious smirk on his face. "That's for good luck."

"Gross, man." Tossing his sweat rag to the floor, I threw him the middle finger before lifting the top rope of the ring so I could exit. "I'll text them the address." Jumping to the ground below, I snatched my shirt from my duffle bag and threw it on, heading toward my bike so I could make it home in time to relax before I had to leave again.

An hour later and I'd washed off the remnants of my training, my mind focused on one person and one person only. Although, given I had a fight later that evening, my mind should've been on my upcoming opponent and not on the one woman who'd captured my undivided interest.

I'd tried texting her as soon as I arrived home but she never responded. Assuming she was busy, I didn't think anything of it until my phone suddenly chimed with her reply.

Kena: Sorry, I meant to text you back earlier but I was with Kevin.

What. The. Fuck? What was she doing with Kevin? She'd told me there was nothing going on between the two of them, even though he'd asked her out and she'd been interested at some point. Had she changed her mind? About him? About me?

My fingers glided over the keys without a second thought. Normally I wasn't a jealous person, but all of that changed right then. She belonged to me, and the thought that she spent time with another guy more than irritated me.

Jagger: Why were you with Kevin? I thought you weren't interested in him.

I had a few other choice words on reserve but thought better of expressing them, especially so new into our budding relationship. Not wanting to scare her off before we'd spent more time together, I kept my temper in check. From our messages. At home alone, I brewed in my anger, cursing out loud as I paced back and forth waiting for her to respond.

Kena: I'm not. His band wrote a new song and he wanted to know if I could listen and give my honest opinion. That's all.

Jagger: Are you sure that's all it is? Because I have a right to know.

I need to calm down before I type something that'll be out there forever.

Kena: Yes. Why are you acting like this?

Why am I acting like this? Maybe because you're spending time with another guy, someone who's expressed interest in you. Wants to date and no doubt fuck you. My inner ramblings never made it into text, thank God, because if they had she might never respond. Deciding to completely ignore her question, I switched the subject and invited her to my fight. Normally I would've thought it best to keep her far away from that part of my life because of obvious danger, but I wanted to see her. To look into her eyes and see if she still felt about me the way I did about her. I had to make sure the torture that kept me awake most nights was shared. I'd meant to save my surprise for when I saw her on Friday, but because of the revelation with Kevin, someone who could readily communicate with her, I needed to show her I was on the same level.

Someone worthy of sticking with.

Jagger: Why don't you and Braylen come to my fight tonight? Tripp and Ryder are going. I'll make sure they watch over you two, just in case Marcus is lurking around.

No response for ten minutes. *Maybe she's asking her sister. Hopefully that's the only reason for delay.* Finally, a message flashed across my screen, but unfortunately it wasn't from Kena.

Tripp: We'll meet you there a few minutes beforehand.

I never texted him back, instead impatiently waiting for Kena to get back to me. Countless minutes passed, driving me insane with edginess. Had I fucked up calling her out like I had? I could've said so much more, but I did my best to keep it in check. My heart raced at the thought that she'd changed her mind about me, and even though there wasn't a damn thing I could do about it right then, I still berated myself for becoming so entranced with her. Nothing good was gonna come out of it, so why did I insist on pursuing her?

Because you feel something for her you can't explain.

Over the next twenty minutes, I drove myself crazy. Finally deciding I had to pull my focus back from her and onto my upcoming bout, I tossed my cell on the table near the door and walked down the hall toward my bedroom. Gripping the sides of my hair, I pulled tightly, eliciting a sting of pain which helped to soothe the rampant fire burning inside. Lost to the ramblings inside my head, I almost missed my phone ringing. Realizing it had to be someone from the club, I lazily strolled back toward the living room, grabbing my cell and turning it over so I could see who was calling.

To my surprise, Kena's name appeared on the screen, which was quite odd seeing as how she couldn't talk.

"Hello," I tentatively answered, holding my breath in confusion.

"Listen, we'll go, but you better tell that ass of a friend of yours to stay away from me because if he says the wrong thing, I'm gonna deck him. You got it?" Braylen spewed her words faster than I could understand. It took my brain a few extra seconds to comprehend what she'd said, but apparently it was too long because she started in on me again. "Jagger," she shouted. "Did you hear me?"

"Yeah, I heard ya. I'll warn Ryder that he's gonna get junk-punched if he steps over the line." He'd told me why she left the park so pissed off that day. His telling her she needed to get fucked probably hadn't sat so well with her, and while I found it funny, I cautioned him to cut the shit because he could potentially ruin things between Kena and me. Her familial loyalty to her sister no doubt surpassed anything she felt toward me.

Chuckling to myself so as not to piss her off, I complied with her amusing demands and wasn't even offended when she hung up on me. Seconds later, a text message came through.

Kena: Sorry about that but she refused to go unless she talked to you first.

Jagger: No problem. I won't be there until nine thirty, so I'll see you then.

A tentative smile lifted the corner of my mouth, and while I'd been thrilled Kena had decided to come that evening, I couldn't help but feel like something bad was gonna happen.

TWENTY-FOUR

Kena

THE ROAR OF THE CROWD should've excited me like it seemed to do for everyone else, but instead it frightened me. I hated watching grown men fight, and while I came to see and support Jagger, I couldn't wait until we could leave.

As soon as we entered the basement of the abandoned warehouse, two men in leather cuts flanked us on either side. I recognized Ryder from the park, and I believed the other guy's name was Tripp, briefly remembering him from the night I'd first met Jagger. I raised my hand to both of them in greeting and they returned the welcome with a simple nod.

I saw Ryder lean down and whisper something to my sister, the slight flush of her cheeks warning me she was set to explode. Grabbing her hand, I hurried down the narrow walkway and toward two empty seats in the middle of the growing crowd. Once seated, I raised my hands and asked, *What did he say to you?*

Biting her bottom lip, she tilted her head to the left where Ryder stood, then looked back to me before saying, "That his offer still stands in case I'm interested."

I instantly smirked, a reaction which made my sister scoff and slap my arm in irritation. Her admonishment only made me smile bigger.

While I'd thought Ryder and Tripp would sit next to us, they chose to stand on either side of the aisle instead. Our lookouts, or bodyguards I supposed. It should've been a warning of things to come, but as soon as the lights dimmed and the announcer started speaking, all I could think about was Jagger. And sure enough, as if my mind willed the sight of him, I spotted him moments later coming down the walkway, fans patting him on the back as he took his time advancing toward the ring. Women shouted obscene things, vying for even just a second of his attention. Right away, I was thrust back to the reason why I'd denied Kevin a date.

Fighters were no different than band members.

Although, what I'd felt toward Kevin didn't even compare to what I felt about Jagger. Not even in the same ballpark. So I dismissed my insecurity and tried my best to focus on him as he approached. When he turned his head to the right, we'd locked eyes and everyone else ceased to exist. I found it hard to breathe, let alone make any kind of movement while I continued to stare at him.

Jagger wore a pair of black shorts which hit just above his knees, and as my eyes traveled the length of him I noticed he was not only bare-chested but also barefoot. As naughty images of the two of us penetrated my mind, he winked before continuing toward his destination. Spreading the ropes, he stepped inside the ring and walked to the far left-hand corner, his opponent already boring holes through him like he wanted to rip him to shreds.

Both men were cut, but Jagger looked more powerful. Maybe it was the way he carried himself, confident the other guy never stood a chance. Jagger *was* undefeated, after all. I'd heard it from his mouth as well as from his buddies muttering the same before Braylen and I took our seats.

My mind raced to the explanation he'd given me about why that scary guy had pulled a gun on him, and I wondered if every time Jagger stepped foot in the ring he was worried about ending another man's life.

The sound of the bell rang out and I couldn't help but become fascinated with the dance both fighters performed. But it quickly changed as soon as Jagger's head shifted to the side after his opponent landed a punch. From that moment on, I looked away often, dreading what I'd see when I lifted my eyes to the gruesome scene in front of me. Braylen, on the other hand, cheered right along with everyone else, often standing on her seat so she could have a better view of the action. A sentiment I definitely didn't share.

While my head hung low, someone sidled up next to me. At first I had an uneasy feeling, but when I raised my head, I saw Tripp casually standing there, his hands in his pockets while he watched the fight with appreciation. When he finally turned toward me, he started to speak but because of the noise, he had to lean down quite a bit so I could hear him properly.

"Don't worry about him. He's just messin' around with the other guy. Workin' him up some for the sake of the crowd. It makes him more valuable." Leaning back, Tripp gave me a megawatt smile.

A simple nod from me and I looked to the ring in enough time to watch Jagger land a hard punch to the side of the man's face, tossing him to the ground like he weighed nothing at all.

The fans went crazy.

Jagger had just knocked out his rival.

He jumped out of the ring and walked directly toward me, not participating in any of the showboating that went along with winning. Leaning over Tripp, Jagger extended his hand to me and I readily accepted. Pulling me forward, I glanced back at Braylen to let her know we were leaving when I saw Ryder say something to her. But instead of looking pissed as usual whenever he was near, a shadow of a smile ghosted her lips. I left them to attend to whatever it was they were doing, allowing Jagger to lead me to the back of the crowded space.

"I just have to rinse off, change and grab my money. Then we're out," he said to both me and Tripp, before disappearing inside a back room. He'd emerged five minutes later fully dressed in a white T-shirt, dark jeans and worn brown boots, his hair still damp from the shower.

Damn, he was fine both in and out of clothes.

Leaving me alone again with Tripp, Jagger disappeared inside a small office. I'd fidgeted with the hem of my blue shirt, shuffling my feet anxiously waiting for him to come back.

"Want out of here that bad, do you?" Tripp asked, leaning against the wall behind him. His piercing green eyes swallowed me whole, but not in an inappropriate way. More like he'd taken over the role of protector in Jagger's absence.

Balling my fist, I placed my thumb over the rest of my bent fingers and bent my hand forward. His brows knit together in confusion. I'd realized I'd just signed *yes*, but of course he had no idea what I was trying to tell him.

Jagger reappeared quickly and translated for me, which was completely unexpected.

"She said yes," Jagger announced, grabbing my hand firmly in his before leaning in to capture my mouth. The sudden gesture surprised me, although I would have been lying if I said the kiss didn't thrill me. Even in front of hundreds of strangers. Not having enough time to even contemplate what other words he'd learned in sign language, he pulled me toward the exit, Tripp following closely. Once outside, I peered around the both of them and tried to locate my sister.

Sneaking his arm around my waist, Jagger pulled me close, planting a kiss on my temple before smiling down at me, the gesture indeed intimate. My heart sang, but my head told me to remain alert.

Ryder and Braylen suddenly appeared out of nowhere, rounding the corner of the building and heading straight for us. My sister's face was expressionless, while Ryder's was the exact opposite. In fact, he looked to be quite animated, a cocky smirk playing on his features and softening his hard-around-the-edges look.

When all three men circled around us, I couldn't help but notice the strength they emanated. Jagger was the only one not wearing his leather vest, but he looked just as intimidating as the other two. All of them were at least six-foot, Tripp being the tallest and towering over his friends by a few inches.

Jagger took a few steps forward, releasing my waist only to latch on to my hand. Intertwining his fingers with mine, he pulled me behind him, telling his buddies he'd see them the next morning. I turned my head to look back at Braylen, and it was then I saw the look she gave Ryder when she thought no one was paying any attention.

Especially him.

She liked him.

For as much as she tried to convince everyone of the opposite, the man clearly intrigued her. Catching my eye, she shrugged. It made me smile. Braylen was a tough woman, didn't take shit from anyone, so it was nice to see her express interest in someone. Someone who challenged her, albeit in a way I'd never thought she'd go for. Ryder came across as the silent type, brooding even, but when he was around my sister, something switched inside him. I didn't know him well at all, but I knew enough to see he liked her. And that was good enough for me.

If he was half the man Jagger was, he was okay in my book.

Jagger's warm breath hit my ear before I'd even realized he'd leaned in to me. "Ryder's gonna walk her to her car and follow her home. You wanna say good-bye?" he asked, taking a step back to look at my face.

I tugged my hand from his and strode back toward Braylen, Ryder stepping aside so I could talk with my sister before we parted ways.

Are you all right with this? I gestured, glancing over at Ryder and the other two who were all now huddled together and talking about something so low neither of us could hear.

"Yeah, I'm good. He's just going to walk me to my car and make sure I get home safe." When she looked down at her feet, then back up at me, she laughed and blurted, "He's not that bad, I guess."

Shaking my head in amusement, I gave her a hug before heading back toward Jagger. As our small group dispersed, a blur of commotion caught my attention, but before I could see what happened, Jagger stepped in front of me, essentially blocking my view of everyone.

"Let's go," he urged, doing his best to keep his tone casual. But a slight tremor escaped. Before I could read into it, he placed his hands on my shoulders and turned me around. Once I faced away from the crowd, he threw his arm over Braylen's shoulders and steered her away as well, the three of us walking down the sidewalk as if it had been the plan all along.

My sister tried to break free, confusion riddling her expression at the about-face, but Jagger's hold never wavered. "I'm gonna follow both of you home." He offered no other explanation. Even though I knew something happened, I didn't quite know what, and something inside my curious brain told me not to ask.

Otherwise, I feared whatever relationship I had with Jagger would go up in smoke.

TWENTY-FIVE

Jagger

MY SELFISHNESS TO BE NEAR her, to show her I was the man for her, put her in danger yet again. Only this time, I'd been able to shield her from what I feared could've been fatal.

Either for me or, God forbid, Kena.

Constantly questioning her safety had become the new norm for me, and while I knew deep in my soul that she'd be better off without me in her life, I just couldn't break away. No one else had managed to make me feel the way she did.

"Why did you drag us away so fast?" Braylen asked, continuing to try and glance over her shoulder every few steps. She'd clearly made some sort of plan with Ryder that evening, and because her night had switched to something else entirely, Kena's sister was not too happy.

"Ryder and Tripp forgot they had to head back to the club. Had to sort out some business." I hurried them down the remainder of the block, their car parked smartly underneath a bright street lamp. "I'm sure you'll hear from him," I tried to reassure her, but her pissed-off attitude told me she wasn't taking his abandonment lightly.

She mumbled incoherently before rounding the car to jump in the driver's seat. Reaching for the passenger handle, I waited until her sister clicked the locks before opening the door for Kena. But she didn't get in right away. Instead, she stood there looking up at me, confusion mixed with a sprinkling of fear behind her eyes. The frustrating thing was that she couldn't just come out and say what she wanted, ask me the many questions mulling around inside her head. It wasn't the time or place, anyway. I'd answer as much as I could later on, but not now. Not here.

Needing them to leave, I gestured toward the inside of the car with a jerk of my head, hoping she understood so I didn't have to push further. Averting her eyes from mine, she turned slightly to the left and took her seat inside the car.

"I'll follow you to make sure you get home safely. I'm parked down there a bit," I said, pointing back toward the warehouse. "But don't wait for me. I'll catch up." The words lingered in the air, but the swift slam of the door sliced them to pieces before another breath escaped my lungs.

The ride to their house filled me with trepidation, a feeling I was all too familiar with these days. Before Kena, I only worried about myself and my club, which was more than enough, trust me. But ever since she'd come into my life, fear riddled me. Always worrying whether or not being mixed up with me would endanger her triggered many a sleepless night.

I portrayed someone filled with confidence, a guy who took life's punches as they came—literally and figuratively—before quickly moving on.

I joked.

I laughed.

I had my brothers' backs. Always.

I got drunk occasionally.

I used to partake in the endless flow of pussy.

I tried to do right by others, shielding them the best I could, when I could.

No one ever bore witness to my insecurities. I feared I'd never be good enough for the Knights Corruption family. I feared Kena would eventually tire of me and move on, leaving me in the dust to fumble my way back toward my warped sense of reality.

There was no doubt I was a work in progress, but then again, weren't we all?

Winding down the curvy road, I finally came to stop behind Braylen's car, the small white Toyota's engine shutting off just as the driver and passenger doors sprung open.

Braylen looked back at me before turning toward the front of their house, walking briskly toward the door and disappearing inside before I'd even come to stand next to Kena. The last thing I wanted to do was explain why I'd rushed them home so fast, so I was happy Braylen left so abruptly; out of the two, she'd obviously be the one to shower me with endless questions.

One minute Kena and I were walking along, minding our own

business, and the next I'd been shot a warning look from Tripp, a silent order to escort the women out of there right away. Out of the corner of my eye, I saw Snake approach our group like a man on a mission, one of his friends accompanying him this time. Before an ambush erupted, Tripp and Ryder formed a wall, essentially separating the threat from me, Kena and her sister.

Stupidly thinking the Reaper wouldn't dare show his face at one of my fights so soon after our last encounter proved to be an almost lethal mistake on my part. I had no doubt he'd come to finish what he'd started, snatching my life for killing his brother. In his head, I had to perish, and now I knew he wouldn't stop until he'd accomplished his mission.

So wrapped up in my head, Kena's warm palm on my cheek threw me back into the here and now, and I leaned in to her touch like it would give me solace. But sadly, it didn't; if anything, her concern rattled me. Looking deep into her eyes, I tried my best to smile, and for the most part I'd succeeded, even though I knew she realized something was off.

"It's getting kind of chilly out. You better head on inside," I urged, removing her hand from my face, kissing her palm before lowering it to her side. Too many contradictions flew at me, and right then I didn't have time to indulge any of them. I had to head back to the club and find out what the hell ended up happening after I'd left.

A frown knit her brow, but before she read further into my dismissive words, I leaned in and grazed my lips over hers. For a brief moment, I thought about staying right there with her, wrapping her in my arms and never letting her go. But I knew it was only a fantasy, one which had to end in mere moments.

Kena's hands snaked around my neck, her fingers threading through my hair, the strands long enough for her to tug them in excitement. Her tongue pressed against mine, the dance intoxicating and breathless. If I hadn't known better, I would've thought she was trying to convince me to stay. But was she that brazen? What would happen if I followed her inside? Would she give herself to me?

For as much as I wanted to find out, I knew I had to head back to the clubhouse so I could do my part in the situation I'd created.

Breaking free from her embrace, I silently cursed myself before looking at her beautiful face. "I'd love to stay, Kena. You have to believe me. But I have to go. I can't explain everything right now, but just know that I'd rather stay here with you." I could see she wasn't sure if I was telling the truth or not, so I pressed my entire body against hers, pinning her to the side of the car. My arousal was quite evident when pressed against her stomach. Her caramel eyes undid me, pleading for me to stay and make good on what my body promised. Or did I read her expression wrong?

No matter. I had to go. Now.

Capturing her mouth once again, I traced her luscious lips with my tongue, my hands resting on either side of her face to pin her in place. When I broke free once more, I finally took a few steps back, my hands falling to my sides in disappointment.

"I'll text you later. I promise." The only movement she made was to nod, a fallen look taking over her expression. I hated that she thought I didn't want to spend more time with her, but I couldn't get into why I had to leave. She continued to remain motionless while I watched her, and it became evident that she wasn't venturing inside anytime soon. Not without some encouragement. "Kena, I need you to go inside," I pressed. "I'll wait here until you do." Reaching behind me, I snagged my helmet and waited for her feet to carry her forward.

She remained unmoving.

And while I found her stubbornness amusing, I didn't have time to play games. Tilting my head to the side, I gave her my sternest look, but still . . . nothing.

Instead of compliance, her body straightened. Pushing back her shoulders, she held her head high and challenged me. I smirked but quickly thinned my lips to show her I'd meet her challenge head-on, eventually winning the little battle of wills she'd started.

"Kena . . . ," I warned, taking a step forward.

She signed something, her frustration pushing her to communicate even though she thought I didn't understand. But I did. I'd wanted to let her in on my surprise earlier, but then everything happened and I wanted to savor my secret until our next encounter.

However, now was as good a time as any to let her know I understood her, returning my slight annoyance with her jerky movements.

"I know you just signed my name."

Her eyes widened fractionally before switching up and squinting at me. She'd tried to hide her surprise, but I'd seen it.

Her hands were a flutter of activity after that, and while I tried to remain as serious as possible I couldn't help the laugh which erupted. No doubt she'd thought I'd learned a few simple things, like "yes" and my name. Although, she'd soon learn the opposite was true.

Taking another step toward her, I smirked before saying, "You just asked me if I wanted to kiss you again. And the answer is a definite yes." A slight blush kissed her cheeks, the tinge of color arousing me even more than I already was.

Again her hands rose and hit together, making a few sweeping motions before settling at her sides. She threw me a lopsided grin, figuring what she'd signed was too complicated for me to understand.

Without hesitation, I answered back.

"There's no way I can understand you? Is that what you just signed? Or did you ask me how it is that I can understand you? I'm still new to this, so you have to be patient." I waited for her response.

I asked you how it is that you can understand me.

I decided to test out my signing skills in response. *My friend Sully has been teaching me. How am I doing?*

Very well.

Her smile lit up the world around us, and all I wanted to do was attack her mouth again in reciprocation, but I knew if I moved toward her, I wouldn't be able to break free. Not again.

A brief moment of awareness encapsulated us, one where we realized we'd just crossed a barrier. She could communicate with me now, other than nodding in response to a yes or no question, eliminating the boundaries that had trapped us since the day I'd first met her. It was a freedom both of us felt right then, perpetuating our connection even deeper than before.

"Well," I spoke up, breaking the silence, "I do have to get going, but I promise I'll text you later. If it's not too late, message me back." Thankfully, she'd turned around after throwing me one last smile and walked toward her front door. After she'd disappeared inside, I grinned, a real weight lifted from my shoulders.

But it would soon be replaced with another as soon as I pulled into the clubhouse lot.

TWENTY-SIX

Jagger

I SWUNG MY LEG OVER the seat of my bike, planting both feet firmly on the ground. While walking toward the clubhouse, my phone vibrated against the inside of my pocket, startling me into the seriousness of the new situation. I had no doubt Tripp and Ryder had *detained* the two Reapers, our biggest enemy not getting the hint to go into hiding, never to resurface.

Marek had seen to it that their drug supply had been cut off from the cartel, a stipulation—or promise, depending on how we looked at it—for our prez saving Rafael Carrillo's life once upon a time. The mere inconvenience that the Reapers kept coming after us screamed how stupid they really were.

The mistake they'd made, however, was showing up to one of my fights. Yet again. Only this time, the brazen fucker had thought ahead and brought one of his pathetic brothers with him, realizing he'd get knocked the fuck out again if he came alone. But in the end it didn't matter.

Marek wouldn't allow them to go back home.

They had to die.

And I knew I was gonna have to take part in their demise, eliminating one more threat to me and my club.

Then the only danger remaining would be the guy who led the Savage Reapers.

A club that stood for nothing other than greed and bloodshed.

Psych Brooks.

"Yeah," I finally answered, gripping the handle to the clubhouse's door.

"Get to The Underground. Now. Back room." Seven words . . . then silence. At first, it sounded like Cutter, but once I'd allowed my brain to register his voice, I realized it was Ryder who'd called. Then hung up on me. The inflection in his tone left no room for argument. Besides, I knew better than to piss him off. Although he'd come across as sullen most times, joking with some of the brothers from time to time, I knew a darkness nestled deep within him. From what, I had no idea, but surely time would reveal some of his secrets.

Time, or some hard-ass liquor. A substance he definitely didn't handle well. All the brothers were aware. It was why Ryder was closely watched whenever alcohol was served, beer not only his preference to remain on the sane side, but all of ours as well.

I'd only witnessed the club's resident mechanic volatile from consumption one time, and believe me, it had been eye-opening.

Snatching my hand away from the door as if I'd been burned, I turned on my heel and walked back toward my bike, all sorts of thoughts of the long evening ahead invading my brain.

Because of the late evening hour, traffic hadn't been an issue, and I'd arrived at the establishment our club owned in no time. Striding through the door, I saw a few of the members lounging in different areas. Breck and Zip hung at the bar, talking with Barlow, The Underground's bartender, breaking the conversation between them every few seconds to laugh about something one of them had said.

Hawke slunk off his barstool and stumbled toward the hallway, no doubt headed toward the bathroom to either piss or puke. He looked like shit, no doubt drowning himself in alcohol over his woman, Edana. The two of them had made me think twice about becoming involved with someone, their crazy relationship a deterrent to most young guys. But when I looked at Marek and Sully, or Stone and Adelaide, my faith in the possibility of attaching myself to a woman had become renewed.

And then I met Kena.

Don't think about her right now. Not when you have to do something you're gonna take issue with.

No one noticed me as I slinked past toward the darkened hallway. The last room on the left called to me. Inhaling a deep breath, I grasped the handle and turned.

"Get in here and close the door," Tripp grated, circling the two guys slumped against the worn leather sofa situated in the corner of the room. As my gaze danced over them, I realized they were in pretty rough shape, although not nearly as bad off as I would've thought. The nomad, while more of a laid-back member, had a temper when prompted. And members of the Savage Reapers coming after me provoked that shielded part of his personality.

"What are we doin'?" I asked, leaning against the wall and shoving my hands in my pockets. Bending my right leg, I rested the sole of my boot behind me, locking me into place because I had no idea what else to do with myself.

"What do you think we're doin'?" Ryder spoke up that time, taking a swig from his bottle of beer before slamming it down on top of the desk. "We gotta get rid of 'em." The look on his face told me two things. One, Ryder didn't want to be there anymore than Tripp or I did. And two, he wasn't as settled with disposing of our enemies as he would've liked to portray. I honestly didn't think any member of the KC MC *liked* to kill, even if their victim was our most hated enemy. As far as I knew, no one craved bloodshed. No, if it had to be done, it had been out of necessity.

Retribution for attacking one of our own.

Revenge for Sully.

Payback for constantly threatening us, and essentially threatening our families.

Pushing off the wall, I strode toward the couch with determination. I wanted to snuff out their existence once and for all, send a message back to the Savage Reapers that every time one of them came after one of us, it would end in death. For them. But the other part of me wanted to spare their lives, give them the option to cease fire here and now. So with a tentative glare, I opened my mouth and made an offer I was sure wouldn't be accepted readily, by them or by my brothers, and essentially Marek, who I was sure knew about our little hostage situation.

"I have an offer for you, Snake. You and me. Right now. We fight, and if I win you walk away and never come after me again." Rocking on the balls of my feet, I clarified my statement. "Me or anyone in my club."

He didn't speak, but then again he didn't have the opportunity to do so because both Tripp and Ryder started shouting over each other.

"No fuckin' way, Jagger," Tripp yelled.

"Ain't gonna happen, brother," Ryder chimed in. My eyes pinged back and forth between the two of them, the muscles in my neck tensing from the added stress.

"The only way either one of them is leavin' is in a body bag." Gripping the shortened strands of his hair, Tripp blew short, rough bursts of air through his nose. Looking to the left, I saw Ryder mirroring his frustrations.

"He wants to destroy *me!*" I roared back. "Me. So give him his shot. But he'll do it with his fists and not a fucking gun like a coward." All I wanted to do was punch something, but I knew I had to save all my energy for the possibility of a fight. I feared my brothers weren't gonna give in, but eventually they accepted the offer I'd thrown out.

"Fine," Ryder gritted. "But you better fuckin' win. Or so help you." His threat left no room for argument. I knew he'd look out for me, as I would him, but right then much more was at stake than just me winning for myself.

I had to win for the good of the club.

"So, what do ya say?" I kicked Snake's boot, pulling his attention away from his friend. "Want a chance to try and take me down? Finish what your brother couldn't?"

Snake lifted his head, rage blossoming behind his eyes as he glared at me. Most times a pissed-off opponent fought sloppily. What I'd said demeaned him, in more ways than one, but I'd pulled it from my arsenal of tricks in hopes he'd make the fight an easy one. There was no doubt he'd be a poor match for me, lacking the necessary skills to fight someone of my caliber, but I knew enough not to underestimate the effect of rage. A slight possibility existed that he'd be able to best me; hatred and the need for revenge could give him the push he'd need to defeat me.

Slowly rising to his feet, Snake walked toward me, a slight limp emerging the closer he advanced. Blood crusted the corner of his lip, his left eye cut, and well on its way to becoming swollen. His shirt was torn, exposing multiple darkening bruises on his torso. But for as fucked up as he appeared, it wasn't enough to hamper him from fighting.

Standing two inches shorter than me, he almost matched my physical prowess. Almost. The Reaper was no lanky fuck, and the upcoming battle between us would most certainly make me break a sweat. Pushing strands of his long dark hair away from his face, he gave me his best scowl, and had I not been a fighter, confident in my skills, I might have been unnerved.

"Where we doin' this?"

His question had me turning toward Tripp, who happened to be standing off to my right.

"Outside," the nomad grunted.

Not five minutes later, we stood under the dark shield of night, the dim light above the back door our only illumination. Enough to see each other. Snake's buddy remained inside, Ryder keeping a close watch over him in case he tried to escape.

Foolishly I thought we'd speak before beginning, but Snake charged me, catching me completely off guard. Fuck! Stumbling backward, he'd managed to knock me off balance, but because of my training, I quickly recovered, sidestepping his next move. He tumbled forward but swung around quickly, bringing his right arm with him.

His knuckles grazed the side of my jaw, but it wasn't enough to do any damage. He hadn't even managed to stun me. Instead, all his fist did was piss me the hell off. I knew going into our fight that it wasn't gonna be pretty, and that most likely my adversary wouldn't make it out of there alive, but I kept a tiny shard of hope that I'd defeat him and he would return to his club the loser, never to come after me again.

Twisted fantasy, I knew.

"I'm gonna kill you!" Snake roared, lunging at me before he'd fully restored his balance. His technique was sloppy at best. No way in hell he would manage to take me down.

Enough shittin' around. I need to end this and do it soon. Bracing myself for his next move, I deflected his punch with a block of my arm and returned a powerful right hook, directly to the side of his face. His head snapped to the side and we wobbled but didn't fall over. The stunned look in his eyes told me I'd definitely fazed him, but unfortunately for me it wasn't enough to knock him out.

For the next ten minutes, he tried his best to hurt me, but he failed every single time. Punch for punch, I warred with him, two men battling for victory. Only I had skill on my side; he had rage, and nothing more.

Faltered steps showed me he was tired, and it was then I took full advantage. Pummeling him with my fists, his head snapped from side to side. Blood matted hair stuck to his face, hiding most of the damage from sight. But I kept at him.

A harsh gut shot.

A kick directly to his knee, bending his leg back awkwardly. The move sent him on a free fall, and on his way down I hit him with a swift, hard upper cut.

Down to the ground he went, but oddly enough he remained alert, spitting blood and attempting to rise from the dirt. "When I'm done with you, I'm goin' after that fuckin' freak you like," he growled. Spitting more red saliva on the ground, he spoke again, sealing his fate once and for all. "I'll take her back to my club and pass her around to every single member of the Reapers, but not until after I've broken her in." He smiled, one of his front teeth now missing, and thought he'd won. Stupidly thinking if he angered me in return, I'd lose all control and somehow he'd best me.

What he didn't realize was that after the last despicable word left his filthy mouth, he'd essentially chosen to give up his life. Without even realizing it, he'd played on one of my biggest fears—Kena coming to harm all because of me. Terror gripped my insides and squeezed. I saw red and before I could stop myself, I pounced on top of him, pounding him with my fists so fast I was surprised I kept my balance.

All my anger poured forth, driving directly into his jaw. His cheekbones. His nose. His temples. I would never allow anyone to touch Kena, especially this piece of Reaper shit. As the seconds passed, disorientation set in, shrouding my reality.

I heard someone yell my name, but I never stopped. The only thing I could focus on was the man lying beneath me. I had to make it so that he was no longer a threat to Kena, and if that meant beating him into unconsciousness then so be it. Doing whatever I could to protect her, I continued to desecrate his bloodied form.

"Jagger!" I heard once more, only that time strong arms wrapped around my shoulders and heaved me backward. My ass hit the dirt, my arms still swinging in front of me. Lost in a daze, it took some time before my delirium subsided. "Come on, brother. You're done."

Recognizing Tripp's voice, I blinked a few times and did my best to catch my rapid breaths. Lines of sweat dripped down the sides of my face, the ache in my hands making me wince.

"I'll kill him," I seethed, trying to rise to my feet so I could go at him again. With a stern look, warning me to stay put, Tripp leaned over Snake and placed his fingers on his neck.

"Looks like you got your wish," he stated matter-of-factly. It hadn't even dawned on me that I might actually kill him. Well . . . no, I lied. It had occurred to me that it might be the end result, but I hadn't gone into the fight planning for such a thing to happen. I truly did want him to crawl out of there afterward, return to his cesspit of a club and finally understand that he couldn't beat me. He couldn't harm me. He couldn't end me.

But he had, in a way. Threatening Kena had sliced through me, splintering me in two. And when both halves came back together, I'd become a different man.

Someone who sat on top of another and literally beat him to death with nothing but my fists.

Would I kill for Kena?

It appeared I just had.

Adrenaline coursed through me, and I hadn't even noticed that Ryder had dragged the other Reaper outside, shoving him to the ground right next to Snake. Pulling a gun from his waistband, Ryder aimed it at the guy's bald head, but before he fired, the guy sputtered something so fast I almost missed what he'd said.

"Prez is comin' for ya. He's gonna get that bitch and kill off your entire club." He spit at Ryder's feet, grinning as if his words would somehow free him from his ultimate demise.

"Well, you ain't gonna be with him when he tries," Ryder taunted, pulling the trigger before the man could reply. The blast cut through the dismal night's thickness, shards of truth falling to the earth all around me.

We'd just killed two men—albeit our enemy, but still. We'd snatched two lives, and although I'd beat myself up over the death of Snake's brother, I felt justified over these kills.

Numb even.

Without a single word spoken, I ran from the scene, hopped on my bike and raced toward Kena's house, hoping and praying she'd make me feel something again.

TWENTY-SEVEN

Kena

SLEEP EVADED ME. MY EYES fluttered closed but my mind raced, thoughts of Jagger flooding in. My inner voice warned me of danger, but my soul soared whenever we were together. I found it hard to explain, even to myself, so all my inner ramblings were pushed to the wayside by my feelings for him.

Because I couldn't fall into the blissful arms of slumber, I'd decided a hot shower might calm me enough to try again. Running my hands over my soapy skin, I imagined they were Jagger's instead. My brain immediately went back to the kiss earlier that evening. The way his taste invaded my senses proved even more powerful than the last time our mouths had collided. Nipping and suckling, tasting and devouring. On top of it all, the revelation that he'd learned sign language just about undid me. My heart burst at the seams, splintering apart before becoming whole again, only this time I was more vulnerable than before. Realizing he cared for me more than I thought scared me, but only because I feared him tearing me to pieces with a simple denial. Of what magnitude I didn't dare think.

Finishing up, I finally turned the handle and shut off the water, wrapping a towel around my body before running another over my wet hair. Steam kissed my exposed skin as I stepped from the stall into the middle of the bathroom. Music drifted from my phone's speakers but when the song ended, I heard a noise coming from the living room.

Leaning my ear against the door, I heard Braylen shouting at someone. Who the hell would be here at this hour? Had Ryder found out where we lived and showed up to apologize for blowing her off? Curiosity pushed me to crack open the door, allowing the chill of the air to barrel in.

"I need to see her, Braylen. It's important. Please let me in." Jagger's gruff voice traveled down the hallway, my fear escalating as to why he'd shown up on our doorstep at nearly two in the morning. Needing to find out the reason, I threw my towel to the ground before wrapping my short black robe around me, cinching the belt at the waist before rushing toward the front of the house. In my haste, I'd almost tripped over my feet, but luckily managed to remain upright.

As soon as I entered the living room, I saw Jagger standing near the front door. Apparently his plea had convinced my sister to let him in, although her body blocked him from going any further.

What happened to you? I signed, hastening my advance toward him in desperate concern. His wet hair told me he'd recently showered, but the water didn't wash away the damage littering his body. His left eye was cut near his brow, the skin surrounding it puffy and red, well on its way to becoming a nasty black contusion. The flesh on his cheekbone and jaw was colored a dark red, the edges already turning a tinge of purple. When I glanced down at his fists, I noticed his knuckles appeared raw, as if he'd run them over a cheese grater.

When he'd left me earlier, he never mentioned having to fight that night, so I could only assume something bad had taken place. Something frightful enough to push him to come to my house afterward.

Taking a step toward me, he pulled me close and wrapped his arms around me tightly. His warm breath fanned my wet air, triggering a chill to break out all over my body. Pulling back briefly, he asked, "Can we go to your room?"

Nodding, I gave my sister a half smile before reaching for Jagger's hand, threading my fingers with his and pulling him behind me back down the shortened hallway. Once inside my bedroom, I closed the door before removing my hand from his. I walked toward the bed and sat on the edge, waiting for him to tell me why he was there. Watching him pace in front of me should've unnerved me, but the opposite was true. His anxiety calmed mine, taking my mind off my own unease and pushing the focus onto him.

When he stopped, he turned toward me and locked me in his stare. He opened his mouth to speak but no words tumbled forth, an action which happened to me more times than I could count. But I had a reason. He didn't, other than struggling with what to tell me and what to keep hidden. The more he remained still, the heavier his breathing became. I swore I saw the pulse in his neck throbbed.

What happened? I asked him again, resting my hands back in my lap after signing.

"I can't talk about it," he answered, looking regretful right away.

Why?

"Because I can't."

Then why are you here? I expected silence but instead he moved toward me, hovering so close I had no choice but to lean back on the bed, my arms behind me for support.

"Because I need you, Kena. I need you to calm me." His thumb gently stroked my bottom lip. The look in his eyes made me hyper-aware that my robe barely hid my nakedness. An ache only Jagger could elicit began, the throbbing between my legs almost unbearable. Could he sense it? Did he have any idea how he made me feel?

No more words were spoken as he kicked off his shoes, and climbed on the bed until his body hovered over mine. I'd pushed myself further back on the mattress, coming to rest when I settled in the middle. Holding himself up on his forearms, his face was mere inches from my own, his warm breath dancing over my lips.

Tempting me.

Tormenting me.

"I need you," he repeated, before crushing his lips to mine. Our kiss turned frenzy, the heat of our mouths fusing us as one. I lost myself to his taste, just like I had the other times he'd completely consumed me. My hands wrapped around his upper arms while he kissed me with such passion I'd become drunk on it.

Jagger's one arm roamed the length of my body, stopping at the hem of my robe before dipping underneath. As he explored my skin, his fingers skating higher and higher, I suddenly became nervous. I pulled my mouth from his and pressed further into the bed, gripping his bicep in slight warning.

His hand stilled on my hipbone, but his finger brushed back and forth over my heated skin. I didn't think he even realized he was doing it, so I didn't stop him.

"What's wrong?" he asked, dipping down to give me a quick kiss. A reassuring kiss, of sorts.

I didn't know how to respond so I simply shook my head. His eyes penetrated my own for a brief moment before he pushed himself off me. Standing at the side of the bed, he reached for my hand and pulled me to my feet, directly in front of him.

Clutching my robe tightly around me, I made sure my belt hadn't come undone before releasing my hands.

"What's wrong? You can tell me. Do you not want to be with me? Am I going too fast?" The look of concern on his face relaxed me. I knew I'd made a big deal of him touching me, but my inexperience made me stiffen. I wanted nothing more than to give Jagger my virginity, but I knew I should probably tell him the reason for my hesitation.

I raised my hands in front of me, his eyes lowering to watch me tell him something. *I've never done it before.* Embarrassment stole my next response, so I patiently waited for him to say something in return.

Cocking his head, his eyebrows knit together, causing him to wince from the deep cut set above it. Gently touching his wound, he gave me a lazy smile before speaking.

"Does that mean what I think it means?"

My shy expression gave him the answer.

Pulling me into his arms, he kissed the top of my head, his lips lingering for added affection. "We don't have to do anything you don't want to, baby. I would never rush you." Taking a step back while still holding my arms, he continued to comfort me. "Besides, I wouldn't want our first time together to be in the same vicinity as your sister." He laughed. "I think she'd try and cut my dick off." He chuckled some more, making me break out in the biggest smile.

Bringing his arms around me again, he gave me a lingering hug before releasing me once more. "Do you mind if I stay over, though? I just want to be near you. I swear I won't try anything," he promised. "I just wanna hold you."

I pulled him toward my bed and threw back the covers, releasing his hand as I climbed in. Once he'd disrobed, leaving on his white boxer briefs, he snuggled in next to me. Turning on our sides, he drank in my essence, tracing his fingertips up and down my arm. My eyes started to close after a while, but quickly opened when the pad of his thumb came to rest on my throat.

"What happened, Kena? Why can't you talk?"

Swallowing against his touch, I knew I owed him an explanation. I just didn't like talking about it, fearing it made me appear weak, even though I knew the mere thought was ludicrous. I inched back a little so I could put some space between us.

When I was a baby, I contracted a viral infection. It damaged the nerves in my larynx.

"So you've never spoken? Not a day in your life?"

No. Not one word.

"Oh, man. That sucks." He closed his eyes in regret the instant he'd said it. "Sorry."

Don't worry about it. You're right. It does suck.

In order to abate the awkwardness that followed, I decided to ask him a question I'd been wondering for quite some time. Since we were sharing and all.

Is Jagger your real name?

"No."

Care to tell me what it is?

"No." His lips kicked up in the cockiest of grins. "Just kidding, although I don't like it, so please don't ever use it."

Oh this should be good. Wait, don't tell me. Let me guess. Tapping my forefinger against my lips, I appeared to be contemplating his name. *Is it Milton?*

Laughing, he quickly said, "No, but nice try."

Okay, okay, hold on. I got it. Is it Arlo?

"Arlo? What the hell kind of name is that?" He shook his head, laughing.

No more kidding around. I know your real name. I licked my lips, drawing his attention to my mouth as a distraction. *It's Beauford.*

With a faux shocked expression, he attacked me, tickling my side and throwing me into a fit of hysterics. Although he couldn't hear my laughter, he could see me smiling, writhing around uncontrollably. Finally coming to rest on top of me, he pinned my hands above my head, essentially rendering me "speechless."

"You sure do have an active imagination, woman. No, my first name is not Beauford. If you must know," he stalled, averting his eyes briefly, "it's Harold."

I wriggled my wrists in his hold, trying to let him know I wanted to respond. Releasing his grasp, I made a few quick movements with my hands. *Harold's not that bad. Why don't you want me to use it?*

A dark look stole over his face. "Because it's my father's name."

And you don't get along with your dad?

"No." His curt answer warned me not to push, but I did it anyway.

Why not?

"He hates me . . . and the feeling is mutual. Look, I don't wanna talk about him, okay?" He pushed off me, flipped over and came to rest on his back, folding his arms over his chest in unease. Upsetting him was the last thing I wanted so I nestled close, hinting that I wanted to comfort him.

Without a second thought, he unfolded his arms and pulled me to him, allowing me to rest my head on his chest. The rhythmic thumping of his heart calmed me, and a short time later, I drifted off to sleep, cushioned in the safety of Jagger's embrace.

TWENTY-EIGHT

Jagger

"CAN I BORROW ADELAIDE FOR a few hours?" As soon as the question left my mouth, I knew perhaps I should've rephrased it. Yeah, no doubt the way I blurted out such an odd request would surely piss off Stone.

Stalking toward me, he balled his fists at his sides while he glared at me.

"What the fuck does that mean?" he growled, advancing on me quicker than I thought possible.

I held up my hands in surrender, realizing Stone's protectiveness over his woman rivaled Marek's for Sully.

"Sorry, I didn't mean to ask like that." I smirked, although taking his anger lightly could surely prove dangerous.

"You better wipe that grin off your face, Jagger, before I wipe it off for you." Stone took another step, but halted as soon as Adelaide entered their kitchen. We both watched as she rounded the table and approached me, gently cupping the side of my face.

"You need to protect yourself more when you're fighting," she instructed, slightly shaking her head before kissing my cheek. A concerned smile graced her features when she pulled back, an expression I both appreciated and detested. I hated the thought that she might find out exactly why I'd received the cuts and abrasions, not wanting her image of me to be tainted. Irrational, I realized, but the thoughts flitted through my head nonetheless.

I'd always liked Adelaide, even more so since she'd brought such happiness into my friend's life. Although, glancing at his hardened expression, he appeared anything but right then.

"What brings you by today?" she asked, busying herself preparing a bottle to feed Riley.

"Funny you should ask," I replied, moving closer to her and further away from her man. "I need help furnishing my place and I thought that, since you did such a great job with your house," I complimented, gesturing with a wide sweep of my arm, "you could help me."

My eyes quickly surveyed the adjacent rooms, pops of color set amongst a neutral backdrop. No doubt Stone had chosen the tan wall paint, as well as the dark, brown leather furniture, but it was his woman's eye for detail which set the room apart from most. A multi-colored, intricately woven area rug sat underneath their chest-type coffee table, pulling the non-descript wall color into its design as well as the red and yellow throw pillows. Colorful artwork adorned their walls, as well as antique-looking knickknacks placed on shelves Stone had installed after Adelaide moved in. I'd seen the transformation during my visits to their house, so I knew she would be the perfect person to ask for this task.

Adelaide smiled. "Flattery will get you everywhere." I thought I heard Stone grunt, but tried not to pay him any mind. "Of course. Can you go today?"

"Yeah. Today would be perfect, in fact."

I'd wanted to invite Kena over, but no way would I expose her to the current state of my place. She deserved better. Besides, I'd meant to spruce up the place for a while now; Kena just happened to give me the push to forge ahead.

Thinking of her, I hated that I'd left her house so abruptly a few days before, but I needed time by myself to process everything that had happened. Leaving her sleeping form had been extremely difficult, but I knew if I'd stuck around, she'd somehow try to force me to explain why I'd shown up at her house in the middle of the night. And no way was I ready to divulge that sort of information. Not now. Maybe not ever.

So I decided to leave her a note, apologizing for leaving before she woke but that I'd text her later that day. And I did, but unfortunately, all we'd been doing was texting. Realizing I hadn't been in the right state of mind, I came up with excuse after excuse as to why I couldn't see her, but I knew she'd become frustrated with my absence. Her texts proved as much, her replies short and to the point.

"Hello," Stone called out, snapping his fingers in front of my face. "What the hell are you thinkin' about?"

"What?" I startled, leaning against the counter to brace myself. "No one," I uttered.

Realizing my mistake did nothing to stop the barrage of questions Adelaide hurled my way. "No one?" she asked, smiling while she glanced back and forth between me and Stone. "This is for that girl you learned sign language for, isn't it?? Oh, this is getting serious." Clasping her hands together, she let out an endearing, albeit frustrating, yelp of glee. "It is, isn't it?"

"Stone . . . a little help here," I pleaded.

"Nope," he mumbled, opening the cabinet to hand Adelaide the top to the bottle she was making for their daughter. "You wanted her, so there you go. Take her." He grinned, earning him a slap on the arm from the mother of his child.

Tightening the lid of the bottle, she handed it over to Stone, which he readily accepted. I'd never seen a man so enthralled with the day-to-day dealings with his child as much as I'd seen with Stone. A tiny shard splintered a piece of my heart at the thought that I'd never received even an iota of compassion and love from my own father. And while I'd missed out on one of the fundamentals in life, protection and encouragement from a parent, I was thrilled Riley would receive it in spades her entire life. Not only from Adelaide and Stone but from all of us. The poor thing would be smothered in love, so much so I was sure she'd find an issue with it at some point.

"Let me get changed and we can go," Adelaide announced, gifting Stone with a quick kiss before disappearing around the corner.

As soon as she was out of sight, I leaned in close, choosing to lower my voice for what I had to say. "I'm assuming you heard about what happened a few days ago." I'd said it more as a statement than a question, garnering a raised brow from Stone.

"Of course I did," he replied, leaning against the same counter and mirroring my body language—arms crossed over the chest, muscles tensed in a touch of anxiety. Me more so than him. "You good?"

What a simple yet loaded question. How did I feel about everything that had happened in the span of less than a week? I supposed I hadn't allowed myself to fully digest what I'd done, choosing to focus on eradicating the threat to Kena more than anything else. Stone and I were locked in the same headspace when it came to destroying the risk to those we cared about, so I knew he'd understand why I'd flown into a rage and ended up killing Snake. Besides, that piece of shit belonged to our enemy. I could've walked up to him on the street and shot him dead and Stone wouldn't have looked at me twice in question. Well . . . okay, maybe not in that situation, but pretty similar.

"To be honest, I've tried to block it out. I don't have the mental energy to deal with the consequences of what I've done. All I thought about while I beat him was that I needed to eliminate any threat possible toward Kena." His confused expression spurred me to explain. "He told me he was gonna snatch her and pass her around his club, but only after he'd had his fill." I ran my hands over my face, careful not to further aggravate my cuts and bruises. "I lost it, man. My vision tunneled into near black and I let my fists take over. The only reason I stopped was because Tripp pulled me off him."

Stone slapped my shoulder, a sign of support. "You did what you had to. Don't ever doubt that. I know it, and Marek will too as soon as you explain what happened."

Shit! I'd completely forgotten about Marek and what his reaction would be to us killing two of our enemy. He held great contempt for them as well, but that wouldn't justify taking two of them out without a good reason.

But I had one. Didn't I?

I could only hope he saw the situation like I had.

Protection.

Pulling out a chair, Stone plopped himself into it and thrummed his fingers on the tabletop, the hammering noise rather annoying. Smirking, he gestured toward the chair to his right. Taking the invitation, I leaned back against the seat and folded my arms over my chest again.

"So, what happened to the two fucks afterwards?" he asked, taking a drink of water after asking me a question I didn't have the answer to. Well, not exactly. I only knew what Ryder had told me; I never followed up with him afterward to find out if he had any issues.

"Ryder said he was gonna drop them off at their club. And I'm gonna be honest. While I loved the idea, I wasn't sure it was the smartest move. Shoving the kill in their faces like that." Unfolding my arms, I rested my hands on top of the rounded table. "Especially after what his buddy told us right before Ryder put a bullet in his head."

"About coming for Sully?" When I looked confused, he added, "Ryder told me."

I looked down at my hands briefly before making eye contact with him again. "Yeah. That."

"Doesn't matter, brother. We already know Psych is planning something. We just don't know what or when. But rest assured, we'll be ready. No doubt."

I opened my mouth to ask him if he had ever thought about breaking away from Adelaide, before she got pregnant with Riley. Before his feelings for her had intensified and grown stronger. I wanted to know if he'd ever thought about sacrificing his happiness in order to keep her safe from our way of life, but the woman in question strolled into the kitchen with Riley on her hip and her purse slung over her shoulder.

After she passed their daughter to Stone, she kissed them both, whispered something in my buddy's ear and walked toward the front door. "Shall we?" she called over her shoulder, not waiting for me to catch up before disappearing outside.

TWENTY-NINE

Kena

FIVE DAYS HAD PASSED SINCE I'd laid eyes on Jagger. Boy, the guy ran hot and cold, his lack of presence certainly speaking volumes. I tried my hardest not to read too far into things, but what choice did I have? The only thing I had to go on was what he told me, which was zilch thus far. Lame excuses about having to work for the club, or handle business for the club. However he'd put it didn't make any sense to me whatsoever. In my head, if he truly liked me, he would make the time to see me, not confuse the hell out of me, day in and day out.

It seemed every day—no, every *hour*—I fluttered back and forth between deciding to give him his space and demanding answers to why he avoided being with me again. Sometimes my patience won out, and sometimes my aggravation shook the sense right out of me.

I was the furthest from a pushy person. In fact, I preferred to stay in the background, observing those around me instead of being up front and center. It was why I kept to myself, shielding myself from fully living. Until I'd met Jagger. Something about his soul spoke to mine, begging me to open up and give him a chance. So I'd stepped outside my comfort zone to meet him halfway. But his current behavior had me rethinking my decision to delve headfirst into what I'd hoped had been a budding relationship between us.

The way he looked at me whenever we were together was unlike anything I'd ever experienced before. His silent promises made my heart soar, but would whatever he held secret end up destroying us before we even got started? Did I think him worth it enough to take that chance? To risk my heart?

I didn't have to think about it too long.

Of course he was.

Any guy who would study sign language just to communicate with me, especially when he hadn't known me very long, ranked high on my list of keepers.

After he'd showed up at my house at two in the morning, kissed me silly, then cuddled with me for the rest of the night, I'd mistakenly thought we'd moved forward with whatever was happening between us. But I'd been wrong. When I woke, I saw he'd left a note. And sure, he stayed true to his word and texted me later that day, but that was all we'd been doing.

Texting.

I wanted nothing more than to see his face. Hear his voice. Feel his arms around me. Savor his kiss. But something bothered him and I had no idea what it could be. Maybe his fights weighed heavier on him than he cared to let on, but I wanted to let him know I would be there for him if he needed to unload and talk about . . . whatever.

Deciding enough was enough, my fingers glided over the letters as I typed out a text which cut straight to the point.

Kena: Why are you avoiding me?

Sitting on the couch, a glass of wine on the end table waiting to be consumed, I impatiently counted the minutes until he answered. *I could be here all night, or he could decide to put me out of my misery and respond right away.*

Five minutes.

Ten.

Twenty minutes later, my phone finally dinged.

Jagger: I'm not avoiding you at all. Is that what you think?

I should've made him sweat a little, but I didn't want to drag this out any longer than necessary, so I responded immediately.

Kena: You confuse me. You show up at my house late at night, looking like you've just been in a terrible fight, kiss me until I can't think straight, and then end up holding me until we fell asleep. Never once did you tell me what happened to you, and to make things worse you left before I woke up.

Jagger: I left you a note.

Grinding my teeth in frustration, I threw the phone on the cushion next to me and grabbed my glass of wine. Not having the patience to savor the red liquid, I swallowed a few large gulps, allowing the alcohol to permeate my aggravated mood.

Finally, I reached for my cell and typed out my retort to his pitiful excuse. *Men.*

Kena: Just because you left me a note doesn't excuse your rude behavior. If you don't want to see me anymore, just tell me. Be a man about it.

Before I could stop them, tears flowed down my cheeks, frustrating me even more than before I'd contacted him. Sorrow washed through me that whatever I thought was happening between Jagger and me would die before it even took flight. The chance I could have found "the one" quickly disappeared, evaporating into thin air before I could even hold the possibility close. I knew my emotions ruled me, as they always had. I just never had anyone on the receiving end before. Harmless crushes, sure, but nothing like this.

Jagger: I'm calling you.

Kena: I'm not answering.

Jagger: Yes, you are.

Kena: No, just tell me.

My breath caught in my throat, threatening to suffocate me if he made me wait much longer. The chime from my phone pushed the air through my nose in relief. Or was that delayed frustration?

Jagger: Please answer your phone when I call.

Realizing I desperately wanted to hear his voice, I gave in and agreed to hear whatever it was he wanted to tell me.

Kena: Fine.

Instead of another message, my phone vibrated in my hand, my generic ringtone slicing the air around me and managing to startle me, even though I'd been expecting his call.

Swiping the Answer option, I placed the device next to my ear. I'd learned to accept my challenge a long time ago, but during times such as this, all I wanted to do was speak my confusion. Unload all my uncertainties in a way which would make sense to him. But instead, all I could do was to either text with him or allow him to speak his mind.

"Kena, listen," he started, breathing heavily as if he'd just run a mile. "I'm so sorry for making you think I don't want to see you anymore, because that's simply not true. In fact, I want to be with you more than ever. The other night. . . ." He stalled, and if I had to guess he was probably pacing back and forth, his words temporarily failing him. Thankfully, the silence didn't last long. "There are things I'm trying to work out. Take care of. And until they're finished, I can't really talk about it. I hope you'll give me the time I need and not give up on me. I care about you. A lot," he confessed, the deep timbre of his voice unraveling any doubt I'd held about his feelings toward me. "Can I see you? Tonight?"

I hadn't expected for him to ask me such a thing, and right then I regretted my sort-of ultimatum. It hadn't been blatant, but he'd surely read between the lines. Not wanting him to feel as if he *had* to see me, I let the silence exist between us, perpetuating uncertainty on both our ends.

"I *want* to see you," he stressed. "It's not because you gave me some sort of half-ass ultimatum, either." I heard the lightheartedness in his tone, his amazing ability to read me without being anywhere near me.

I wouldn't know the true depth of his feelings until I could look into those penetrating amber-colored eyes of his, so I gave him what he wanted.

What *I* wanted.

I pressed a number on the keypad one time, the sound booming in my ears, releasing the tension I'd carried since I'd first texted him that evening.

"Great. You won't regret it, Kena. I promise. Can I pick you up in an hour?"

I pressed the key again. One time.

Yes.

"See you soon," he promised, hanging up the phone and in turn erasing some of the reservation I'd allowed to rattle my emotions.

THIRTY

Kena

TRUE TO HIS WORD, JAGGER showed up on my doorstep an hour later, looking as fantastic as ever. The cuts and bruises I'd seen days earlier had turned different shades, but he appeared to be healing nicely. My eyes lingered on his mouth; I couldn't help it. Every time I saw the guy, I wanted to throw myself at him, wrap myself in his embrace and latch on to those delicious lips of his.

I knew what he held within his kiss, and I'd wanted to feel the promise of something more right then. But I held back. How would I look to him if I attacked him, when only a short while ago I'd come off as upset? Never mind what kind of precedent that would set for us going forward. If there even was an "us" after that evening. He'd know that all he'd have to do was be near me and he'd get his way. And let's face it; he'd mess up a lot.

He *was* a guy, after all.

Stepping to the side, I allowed him to enter my house, his arm brushing mine as he walked past. A tiny shiver coursed through me at the slight contact, and I berated myself for being so weak.

The thick rustle of his leather vest tore me from my inner ramblings. The way he moved throughout the small space had me gasping for my next breath. He reminded me of a predator, assessing his surroundings before pouncing. Even though he tried to give me space by keeping his distance, the pull between us encapsulated my entire being.

I couldn't think.

I couldn't breathe.

I couldn't wait to be consumed by him once again.

My eyes wouldn't stop devouring the very sight of him. Dark, loose jeans hung low on his hips. His grey T-shirt clung to his torso as if it had been made specifically for him. All I wanted to do was run my hands over him, head to toe, but I remained unmoving. I wanted him to make the first move. Explain why he'd been avoiding me, even though he'd said he hadn't been.

I fidgeted with the hem of my tank top, hoping and praying he would end the silence soon. Although I could spend all day just staring at him, the uneasiness of the quietness drove me insane.

Jagger's eyes lit up the closer he stepped, his gaze lingering on my mouth, as I had done to him moments earlier, and I couldn't help but to wonder if the thoughts running through his head mirrored my own.

Without notice, he brought his hands up in front of him, and at first I couldn't focus on anything other than the scrapes and bruises desecrating his knuckles still. Wanting so desperately to reach out and touch him, I held back. Whatever he wanted to say to me had to happen in order for us to move forward.

Placing his fist against his chest, he rubbed it in a circular motion. *I'm sorry*, he signed, the apologetic look on his face replicating his message.

Although I appreciated the sentiment and effort, I couldn't help but wonder how many times I would see that specific gesture.

Why? My one-word question was all I could think of to ask in response.

Reaching out, he captured my hand and led me to the couch, jerking his head for me to take a seat. Once I settled in, he joined me, continuing to hold my hand as he turned his body toward me. "I know we don't know each other that well yet, but I hope you'll give me the chance to stick around. I really like you, and I think we could be really good together." I tried to tug my hand from his but he only tightened his grasp. "I need to get this off my chest before you start asking me more questions."

More questions? I'd only asked him one, although it *had* been an all-encompassing one.

He licked his lips and exhaled a heavy breath. "There are some things I can't divulge right now. Things that have to be secured, taken care of so there's no more threat to me or my club." I knit my brows at his unexpected statement. "I'm just trying to be honest. Well . . . as honest as I can be right now." Shifting closer, his knee bumped mine, the slight touch distracting me. "I'm just asking that you be patient and not get angry when I can't explain certain things. Can you do that? Can you give me the time I need to straighten some things out?"

His thumb danced back and forth over the top of my hand, his gentle touch a complete contradiction to the guy sitting next to me. His intimidating appearance warned the world not to get too close, his club's emblem etched on the back of his leather cut enough to scare most people. But from what I could tell, Jagger—and his friends I'd had the pleasure of meeting—seemed to be good men, even though a secrecy shrouded them, clinging to them so closely it was hard to see them for the people they truly were.

I realized my impression of them could've been misguided, but my gut told me they were good people.

I gave him a simple nod before brushing my lips against his. I hadn't meant to fold so easily, but Jagger's words, combined with his pleading look, assured me he was telling me the truth. As much as he could, anyway.

Surprised, he leaned back and searched my face for an explanation to my complete one-eighty. But he didn't find one, because I couldn't explain it myself, except to say I trusted him.

Explicitly.

For the next twenty minutes, we made out like a couple of teenagers, although we weren't too far removed from that age group. He'd repositioned me so I straddled him, his apparent arousal pressing against the most sensitive part of me.

Hands explored.

Kisses promised the world.

My heart beat so fast I feared it would burst from my chest the longer Jagger continued to tease me. A warmth flooded my insides as an ache I'd come to recognize well blossomed deep within, pulsing and demanding release. My body reacted to his, no doubt threatening to detonate if I continued to refuse what should have come naturally.

Although inexperience held me captive, I knew Jagger would be the one I'd give myself to.

Utterly and completely.

He'd already captured my mind and soul.

The only thing left to offer was my body.

With trembling hands, I gripped the hem of my top, inching the material higher until air flowed across my belly. Jagger's fingers had been entangled in my hair, but when I attempted to remove my shirt, he pulled back, resting his hands on my thighs and gently kneading my skin.

"What are you doing?" he asked, a reserved smile tentatively lifting the corners of his lips.

Letting go of the material, I answered. *Removing my shirt.*

"Why?"

A sudden flush doused my skin, but irritation quickly replaced the abrupt embarrassment I'd felt. *Why do you think?*

"I'm not ready for that," he said, chuckling once he realized what he'd said. "Let me clarify. I'm not ready for *you* to be ready for that. Does that make sense?"

No.

"Kena," he huffed, "I don't wanna rush you into something I don't think you're ready for."

But I am ready, I pouted, the incessant ache intensifying between my legs.

Removing me from his lap, he rose from the couch before reaching out and waiting for me to place my hand in his. Once I did, he led me toward the front door, completely disregarding that we were just talking about possibly having sex. Tugging my hand from his, I took a step back.

"What are you doing?" he asked, turning around to face me.

Where are you taking me?

"To eat. I'm hungry. Aren't you?"

Yes . . . but not for food.

Clenching his jaw, Jagger decimated the space separating us and tugged my arms behind my back, pinning my wrists with one of his hands. Spinning me around, he trapped my back against the wall and leaned close to my ear.

"Trust me, I want nothing more than to sink inside you, but not here. Not now." Nipping my earlobe, his warm breath prickled my skin, a shiver my sole reaction to his teasing. The smooth skin of his cheek rubbed against mine, the closeness undoing the last strand of my restraint. But I kept myself in check because the last thing I wanted was for Jagger to keep refusing me, landing blow after blow to my suddenly fragile ego. "Understand?"

A nod from me and he released my wrists, pulling me behind him out the front door.

We spent the next few hours enjoying a meal at a small Italian restaurant we both loved, talking about everything under the sun, from my job at the restaurant, to our favorite movies, to places we dreamed of visiting someday. Surprisingly, we both wanted to travel to Europe, taking in as many countries as could be afforded.

That evening, the connection we'd shared snared deeper than before. We'd learned a lot about each other, and when he dropped me off at home, walking me inside and giving me another heart-melting kiss, I knew he was it for me.

The one.

The person I wanted to spend all my time with.

But for now, I'd keep those feelings tucked safely away, patiently waiting for a time when I could express them. When I knew he felt the same.

THIRTY-ONE

Jagger

THE NEXT COUPLE WEEKS FLEW by in a blur. Our club hadn't heard a peep from the Reapers, much to our amazement. I'd talked in length to Marek about what had happened that night, and he assured me he would've done the same thing.

His icy demeanor toward me had certainly started to melt, accepting me more and conversing with me at length many times. Sully had visited the club often, and whenever I saw her we talked without the fear of her husband retaliating. Oftentimes, Sully and I communicated strictly using sign language. Her assistance helped me to hone my silent skills until I'd become completely comfortable, only messing up a few times when talking with Kena.

Kena: Can't wait to see you later.

Her message made me smile. Amongst everything else going on in my life, the club, the fights, she'd become my constant. My rock. Someone to turn to when things weighed heavy on my mind. Granted, I could only reveal so much, choosing to keep a lot of my life hidden until the time I deemed necessary to fill her in, but her support gifted me with a calm I hadn't even realized I'd needed until she came into my life.

I loved Kena's sense of humor, poking fun when I'd sign the wrong thing, innocently teasing me until I'd break out in laughter, being sure not to take myself so seriously.

I never thought I would feel joy, the concept of such an emotion foreign to me my entire life . . . until I met the woman I was put on this earth for. The first time I'd laid eyes on Kena, I knew my life would change; I just hadn't realized to what extent.

Jagger: I'll be there soon. You're staying over tonight, right?

The first time she'd spent the night was a little over a week ago, and I'd been thrilled to share my bed with her, although we didn't have sex. She'd wanted to, at least I thought she did with the way she kept rubbing herself against me while we made out on the couch. Then again, I returned the favor, seeking comfort for my constant hard-on. I was sure if I'd made the suggestion she would've been onboard, but something told me to hold back. To allow her more time to be sure.

Tonight, however, I was gonna broach the topic, and if I didn't see any hesitation in her response, I'd give in to what we both wanted. On every other occasion, there had been a tremble in her hands, or she would avert her eyes when she'd let me know she was open to having sex. All signs pointed to her being slightly unsure.

I didn't want her uncertainty.

I wanted her to *want* it to happen. Without a doubt.

A half hour later, I pulled up in front of her house. I'd brought my truck, the chill of the night air a bit too much for a ride on my bike. Hopping out of the driver's side, the front door swung open and Kena rushed outside, slamming the door behind her in haste.

Rushing forward, I asked, "Is everything okay?" Her face flushed, her lips turning up into an awkward grimace.

I think Braylen's having phone sex with Ryder.

Not able to contain it, I burst out laughing, having no doubt the man was talking all sorts of dirty to Kena's sister. What surprised me was that Braylen had given him the time of day. I thought she couldn't stand him. However, I had witnessed a few tiny cracks in her façade whenever he was around, or was mentioned.

"That's awesome," I chuckled.

Ewww. It is not. She acted as if the thought of it repulsed her, but secretly I thought she enjoyed the idea of the two of them together.

Drawing her close, I nuzzled my lips against the underneath of her ear, kissing her slowly and teasing both of us. She squirmed, often telling me I gave her the chills when I did that, but no way would I release her without gettin' my fill.

She lovingly slapped my chest and I finally pulled back, giving her a quick kiss on the lips before walking her toward the passenger side of my truck. As I opened the door for her, she turned and gave me a sexy smile, earning her a smack on the ass before she climbed into the vehicle.

I can't wait to get my hands all over her later. Adjusting my raging arousal, I circled the truck, taking an extra second to compose myself before I ended up attacking her, lifting her dress and taking her right on the front seat.

Grabbing some takeout, we headed back to my place for the evening. I'd actually been proud to show off my apartment, all the new furnishings having been delivered a few days before Kena had come over for the first time. I'd forever be in Adelaide's debt for helping me pick out some things which helped spruce up the drab space. The furniture was a mix of modern and contemporary, sleek lines and beautiful craftsmanship going into every detail of each piece. I ended up being drawn to the darker wood, although the coffee table was a mix of glass and metal, only adding to the overall layout and design of the living room. I'd painted the walls a cool beige color, adding colorful pictures and pillows as accents, extending the same concept into the bedroom.

The small fortune it had cost to decorate had been the best money I'd ever spent. Now when I opened the front door, it felt like a home.

The hours ticked by way too fast for my taste, but it did mean one thing: time to see if Kena was ready to fully give herself to me. As the final credits rolled on the comedy we'd just watched, I reached over and seized her wrist, tugging her toward me. Patting my lap at the same time, she took the hint and straddled me, her thighs pinning me on either side.

Gazing deep into her beautiful browns, I knew she was it for me, and tonight would only solidify that she belonged to me. The final step in her becoming mine. As my mouth captured hers, my kiss asking permission to forge ahead, my hands drifted under the hem of her blue sundress. Running my fingers up and down her back at first, she seemed relaxed, complacent even. Until I gripped her backside and pushed her against my thickness; then she broke the kiss and stared at me with her mouth wide open. Surprise and expectation laced together in one simple response.

"You ready for this, sweetheart? Because if you're not, we can wait a little while longer." While I prayed for her to say yes, I knew I cared about her enough to wait as long as it took.

Placing her hands on my chest, she pushed herself back until she found her footing and stood in front of me. Reaching out, she wiggled her fingers, letting me know she wanted me to take her hand.

An offering of herself to me.

And I readily accepted.

I led her down the hall to my bedroom, kicking the door closed behind me once we were inside. I'd left the bedside lamp on, so there was plenty of light without being overpowering for such an intimate moment. I wanted to see her, every part of her, but since this was all new to her, the bright overhead would make her that much more self-conscious.

I let go of her hand and allowed her the time she needed to direct the scene. For her to run the show. While I couldn't wait to be inside her, I wanted her to take all the time she needed.

Giving me her back, she swept her long dark hair over her shoulder, turning her face slightly toward me. It took me a couple seconds, but when I realized she wanted me to help her out of her dress, I stepped forward and took hold of the zipper. Each inch of exposed skin aroused me further, her silky skin begging for my kiss. Taking my time, I drew the metal fastener through its teeth, my racing heartbeat drumming in my ears.

When I placed my lips on the side of her neck, I felt her pulse strumming underneath, and I couldn't help but smile. No hesitation; I knew she was finally ready to give her body over to me.

Would her heart follow?

Once her dress hit the floor, she kicked it aside, turned around and stood before me in nothing but a white see-through lace bra and matching panties.

Gorgeous.

The only word fitting to describe her right then.

Taking my fill, I raised her chin to meet my eyes. "We'll go slowly. You stop me anytime you feel it's too much, okay?"

A simple nod from her was all I needed.

I'd never taken my time with anyone before. I'd never relished the feeling of just being with a woman, always in a rush to fuck and get it over with so I could move on.

But with Kena, I didn't want any of our moments to end. I wanted to savor every second with her. Sitting on the edge of my bed, I drew her close, spreading my legs so she could move in further. Her perfect breasts were directly in my line of sight, but her bra still shielded her from me. Without allowing another second to pass, I reached around her back and unhooked the clasp, pushing the straps off her shoulders and tossing the material to the floor to join her discarded dress.

My eyes were alight with pleasure at the mere sight of her exposed skin. So appreciative she'd picked me to give her virginity to, I treated her with gentleness until the rapture of the moment became too much. Threading my fingers through her long strands, I brought her mouth to mine and nibbled at her lips, begging to enter her warmth.

I needed to taste her.

To breathe her in.

After I'd bruised her mouth with my kiss, I trailed my lips down her throat, the moisture from my tongue eliciting goose bumps across her skin. I reached her collarbone, my teeth coming out to play for a brief moment, something I found she liked. Next I moved toward her pert breasts, begging to be tasted.

Sucked.

Pinched.

So I gave her what her body demanded.

Taking a pebbled nipple into my mouth, I swirled my tongue around the heated flesh, gently biting and teasing her until all she could do was throw her head back in pleasure. She pushed herself further into me, and I ravenously accepted. Once I was done, I switched to the other, giving it as much attention as she deserved. I went back and forth, mouth over sensitive skin, fingers pinching the erect buds until I felt a rumble in her chest, telling me she enjoyed the torture I offered her.

I claimed her lips once more, spinning her around and pinning her to the bed beneath me while our tongues danced together. Spreading her legs, I broke from her delectable mouth and moved down her body, taking my time to experience every bit of her she'd laid bare to me. Hooking my thumbs in the waistband of her flimsy panties, I drew them down her toned thighs, stopping by her calves, too entranced with seeing her bare pussy to go any further.

Daring to glance up at her, realizing the look on her face would spur me to hurry, I held my breath and controlled my movements. With a sexy smile, she bit her lip as she writhed on the bed, widening her thighs to display more of herself. Her modesty fled, pleasure and want taking over and driving the course of the evening.

"Should we get rid of these?" I teased, tugging the lacey material the rest of the way down until they finally fell from around her feet.

Kena was the most beautiful woman I'd ever laid eyes on. She was shy yet eager. Reserved yet willing. She bit her nail while she looked down at me, my head nestled between her opened legs. I'd thought for sure she would've been more reluctant when we'd finally ventured to this point, but instead I saw desire driving her to expose her vulnerability.

"I've wanted to taste your pussy for so long," I groaned, running my fingers up the inside of her leg, quickly following the touch with my mouth.

When my warm breath caressed her core, her muscles tightened, and I knew what she'd offered was a true gift.

THIRTY-TWO

Kena

AS SOON AS HIS TONGUE swiped through my innocence, I knew I'd never be the same. Every touch he laid on me I treasured. It'd seemed as if I'd waited forever to be with Jagger, and I couldn't believe it was finally happening.

I thought I would've been more reserved, but the way he loved my body, the adoration in his eyes when he looked at me, all of me, was nothing short of glorious. How could I want to hide any part of myself when his gorgeous stare undid me? Before I realized, my hands snaked down my body and found his hair, tugging his strands tighter each time his tongue flicked over me. When the tip of his finger entered me, I tensed, but his words worked to soothe me.

"I'll take it slow. I promise. The last thing I want to do is hurt you." I trusted him, so I relaxed and reveled in the pleasure he brought me. Just when I thought his skill couldn't get any better than his mouth and finger working me simultaneously, he buried his tongue inside my heat. My back arched off the bed, and in turn I shoved his head further into my pussy. He laughed, pulling back to ask, "You like that, huh?" My only answer was thrusting my hips back toward his face. "So greedy," he mumbled, before continuing to devour me as if he'd never have another taste.

I'd brought myself to orgasm many times before, but the buildup Jagger offered became so much more. My breaths came quick and short, my heart ramming against my chest in expectation for what my body prepared to do. Throwing my head back, I clutched the bedsheets with my free hand and ground my pussy closer to Jagger's mouth, silently begging for him to push me over the edge. To make me come so hard I wouldn't know which way was up.

His ministrations increased, his mouth promising the sweetest release. Fingers teased my opening, dipping inside every few seconds to add to the sweet torment.

"I know you wanna come," he spurred, driving his finger further into me while his lips wrapped around my clit. I would have shot off the bed had it not been for his hand splayed across my belly and holding me as still as possible. Pulling back, he blew his breath across my wetness, the chill he created making me jerk back in surprise. Nothing sexier existed than witnessing Jagger positioned between my thighs, licking me and bringing me to the brink of explosion. The sight alone almost undid me.

"Come on my tongue, Kena. Please," he begged, sucking on my clit once more, his hand working to make his plea come to fruition.

A harsh buzz deafened me. The light from the corner lamp became dimmer the closer I flew to heaven. At one point I thought I forgot to breathe altogether.

"I can feel you holding on. Let go," he urged. "Let go and come for me, baby." The deep rumble of his voice added to the pleasure, the vibrations from his throat tickling my clit, splintering my last shred of restraint.

My body locked up.

My muscles contracted and released, spasms throwing me into paradise.

Lights danced behind my eyelids the more intensely my orgasm racked through me. I gave in fully to the bliss, my thoughts so scattered I couldn't even think straight. All I could do was feel, ride the wave of ecstasy for as long as it lasted.

Finally my release subsided, allowing me to slow my erratic breathing. My limbs felt like jelly. I couldn't move. I couldn't even bring my hands up in front of me to answer Jagger when he asked, "How was that?"

All I could do was smile, locking my gaze with his in hopes he understood.

And he did, the wicked grin on his face proof enough for me.

When I'd finally regained some mobility, I raised up on my knees.

"What are you doing?" he asked as I moved toward him, my intent obvious. Or at least, I thought it was.

I want to taste you.

"No."

No? Oh, you don't like that?

"I'm a guy. Of course I like that. I love it. But tonight, I just want it to be about you."

Can you at least take off your clothes, then? I don't think I like being the only naked one here.

"That I can do," he replied, kicking off his shoes and socks while he removed his shirt. His intricate tattoos only added to his sexiness, dark lines mixed with colorful swirls painting his skin so beautifully. I'd been staring so long at his chest and arms that I hadn't even noticed he'd removed his jeans . . . and his boxer briefs.

Standing in front of me in all his glory, his sweet smile did nothing to detract me from the huge erection he sported, his cock jutting out as if it had a mind of its own. Maybe I should have reconsidered. I thought I was ready. I mean, I wanted to be with Jagger more than anything, but I hadn't truly considered what would happen.

Don't get me wrong. I knew exactly what he and I would be engaged in, and I hoped I would love it, but looking at his thickness, realizing that part of him was going to be deep inside me, made me hesitate for a few seconds.

I berated myself for acting so childish, but for someone who'd never had sex before this moment was a huge deal. For me, at least.

"Are you okay?" He moved toward the bed, his fingers circling his excitement. As if second nature, he lazily ran his hand up and down his shaft, keeping his eyes on me the entire time. Averting my gaze from that part of him, I watched the way his muscular thighs carried him closer. The way his stomach muscles clenched with every pump of his hand.

Jagger crawled up the bed and moved his body over mine until my back hit the mattress, all before I could answer. "I know you're nervous. I can see it in your eyes. In the way your breaths skip. But please realize we'll only do what you want. What you can handle."

My heart melted. Placing my hands on the sides of his face, I pulled him to me and crashed my lips against his. I didn't want to wait one moment longer to connect with him.

"Fuck," he groaned. "You have no idea what you're doing to me." He continued to nip at my mouth, lavishing me with kisses, stopping briefly when he jumped up to snag a condom from his back pocket. Sheathing himself, he lowered on top of me again, bracing his weight with his forearms. "Are you ready?"

I nodded. I wanted more than anything to appear sexy and confident, but the truth was my nerves fired off every which way.

"Open your legs. Wider." His lips brushed over mine again, distracting me when the tip of his cock pressed slowly inside me. "Don't tense up," he cautioned. "You'll only make it worse."

Worse? I thought. Right then I couldn't help but give in to my unease, knitting my brow and digging my nails into his biceps. I swore if I bit my lower lip any harder I'd taste blood.

Pulling back a little, I saw his concern. "Okay, we're gonna stop. Maybe it's not the right time yet." When he tried to move away, I clutched on to him for dear life. The last thing I wanted to do was come across . . . well, as I had been. It was time for me to woman up and do what I'd wanted to do for quite some time now. There wasn't another man alive who I wanted to be my first, so before Jagger leapt off the bed, I wrapped my legs over the backs of his and tightened my hold. Reaching down, I grabbed his delectable ass and ground myself against him, his cock sliding through my folds with ease.

He didn't ask me if I was ready, or if I still wanted to do this. Instead, with as much gentleness as he possessed, he pushed himself inside my tightness, stopping every few seconds to allow me to adjust.

The way he swirled his tongue with mine when he ravished my mouth helped take my mind off the sting of pain once he'd fully sunk inside me. Eventually, we melded together, the friction of our bodies coming together, eliciting a pleasure I'd never even thought possible.

"Goddamnit!" he growled. "I'm not gonna last much longer." Slowing his thrusts, he breathed deeply before pulling back to rest on his haunches, taking me with him so our bodies remained connected. Seizing my waist, he pulled me roughly toward him, slamming into me with a controlled frenzy, withdrawing slowly before repeating. "Is that okay? Am I hurting you?"

No.

The last thing I wanted to explain was that while my body ached with delicious pleasure, I didn't want him to stop. I needed him to take me the way he wanted, trusting him to not go overboard and fuck me with wild abandon. I craved his lust, his unabashed desire for me. So yeah, *no* would be my only response.

Jagger's mouth parted and his head fell back, his grip on my waist tightening all while he tried not to speed up. "I can't . . . I can't hold back."

Just when the familiar tingles began, sprinkling their tease throughout my insides, he withdrew completely. Moving quickly up the bed, he turned me on my side until his body cradled mine from behind.

"I wanna be close to you," he whispered, kissing the shell of my ear. "Plus, I'll have better access to this," he said, trailing his hand down my belly until he rested the pad of his finger over my clit.

I reached behind me and threaded my fingers through his hair, opening my legs when he nudged them apart with his thigh. Pushing into me from behind, his fingers continued to play with my sensitive bundle of nerves, heightening the thrill until I thought I'd shatter into a million pieces. I rocked back into him, finding my rhythm rather easily. Restrained panting hit the side of my face, Jagger's tongue lavishing the skin of my neck, nipping and sucking while his body claimed mine.

The pressure built.

My muscles locked up tight. Again.

Like the sweetest of roller coasters, dragging out the ascent to the top, the anticipation of the strongest climax teased me.

"I can feel you start to clench around me," he grunted. "And it's the best fucking feeling in the world, baby."

Lowering my hand from his hair, I gripped his thigh, my nails digging into his skin and anchoring me in place. I tried to hold out as long as I could, never wanting his sweet assault to stop, but my body had other plans.

"Are you gonna come?" he asked, adding more pressure to my clit. All I could do in response was nod, one hand clutching the covers while the other held his leg. "Then fall with me, Kena. Let go and crash," he grunted, his speed increasing until he'd shouted out his blissful release.

The sounds he made thrilled me, ramping my own orgasm even higher. Our bodies continued to rock together until both of us had come back down from our sexual high, tangled in each other for the next five minutes. Eventually, he rolled onto his back, taking me with him so my head rested on his chest.

The wild thud of his heart slowed with the tick of the clock, and it wasn't long before I'd drifted off to sleep. Thoughts of Jagger infiltrated every facet of my mind as I gave in to some much needed rest.

THIRTY-THREE

Jagger

IN THE PAST, EVEN THOUGH I hated to even think about it now that Kena was in my life, the girls I'd fucked had no problem letting me know when they were about to get off. Their moans and pleas for me to fuck them harder because they were right on the edge were a constant.

But with Kena it was completely different. I had to rely on her body to tell me how she was feeling. Watching her eyes glaze over in the sexiest of ways, or the way her nipples became erect, or the way her pussy drenched my cock in her excitement. She'd pushed me to the brink faster than ever before, her tightness fisting me until I had no other choice but to give in to the speeding train of pleasure barreling down on me.

I'd managed to make her come twice, and that was only the beginning. While I had to take it easy until she became accustomed to me, I looked forward to having quite a bit of fun with her, teasing her endlessly for hours . . . or minutes, depending on how hyped we both were. Images of all sorts of positions enticed me, and I couldn't wait.

Slowly rolling Kena to her side, I managed to sneak off into the bathroom without waking her, tossing the condom in the trash before returning. The mattress dipped from my weight and still she didn't stir, too wrecked from earlier. I sported a huge grin as I nestled in behind her, pulling her close so I could fall asleep as well.

I'd only known Kena a short time, had only slept in the same bed with her as many times as I could count on my fingers, yet it was as if she'd always been in my world. I knew I was falling for her, in a big way, and although the thought terrified me, for various reasons, I knew in the end she was the woman I wanted by my side.

I'd go to the ends of the earth to protect her, to shield her from harm any way I could. The fear of the unknown rattled me, but I couldn't focus on the "what ifs." I had to take each day as it came, hold on tight and enjoy the motherfuckin' ride.

Lost in a dream, it took me a minute to realize the shrill sound cutting through the darkness of the room was my cell. Fumbling through my jeans to find it, I quickly pulled it free from the pocket and squinted at the bright light on the screen.

"What?" I whisper-barked, pissed that whoever called had no concept of time.

Hurried breaths flew down the line, instantly putting me on alert. Swinging my legs over the side of the bed, I grabbed my clothes and walked into the hallway. I knew I'd have to leave. I just didn't know why yet.

"Get to the clubhouse now, Jagger!" Stone yelled, hanging up before he'd even allowed me to ask questions. Once I finished dressing, I scribbled out a quick note to Kena, reached for my keys and quietly closed and locked the door behind me.

I shouldn't have, but I sped all the way to the club, ignoring all the traffic lights. Lucky for me, there weren't many people out on the roads, seeing as how it was still very early.

There was an urgency to my step as I pulled open the door, entering the common room and absorbing the electric somberness drifting through the air.

Stone stood in the corner talking to Marek. Zip, Cutter and Breck lounged on the couches, drinks in hand and looking a little worse for wear, while Trigger busied himself serving alcohol to whomever requested it.

"What the fuck is goin' on?" Ryder shouted, entering the clubhouse looking like he'd been hit by a truck, hair all disheveled with red-rimmed eyes.

No one answered, serving to annoy him as he took a seat at the bar. Finding my own words, they caught in my throat when I heard shouting, followed by a barrage of curses coming from the hallway. Whoever was back there was angered beyond all rational thought.

Then I heard a door slam.

The eruption of noise floated toward us all, the expectancy for something explosive to follow. First I saw Tripp, his downcast eyes a telltale sign something bad happened. Then I saw Adelaide, and it was then I realized shit had hit the fan. In a big way, grand enough to warrant her presence. No doubt she'd been called in to help patch someone up; otherwise, there was no way Stone would have his woman here so late.

Still I kept my questions buried, watching and waiting for everything to unravel.

"How is she?" I heard Marek ask, moving closer until he'd reached Adelaide, a stolen look of concern and anger in his expression.

"She's pretty awful," she answered. "They did quite the number on her, so bad it's going to take her quite a while to recover. She really should go to the hospital, but I get why you don't want that, so I did the best I could." Sidestepping our prez, she saddled up next to Stone, turning her head into the crook of his arm and curling into his protective embrace for support.

For what, I still had no idea.

Until I saw Hawke slowly walking down the same hall Tripp had just emerged from, someone frail huddled next to him. At first, I wasn't sure who he shielded but the closer he stepped, the more I realized he was holding Edana. His woman. Only she didn't look like herself. She wore a baggy T-shirt and grey sweatpants, no doubt Hawke's clothes. But why? I'd never seen her in anything but skintight jeans and shirts which left little to the imagination. Her auburn hair was pushed back off her face, wet and tangled from a fresh shower.

When they both stood only a few feet from me, I saw the damage that had put everyone on edge. Nasty welts and bruises covered her face, her right eye swollen shut and her upper lip split open. The haggard way in which she walked indicated there was more damage to her body; she winced every few steps when Hawke unknowingly picked up his pace.

"Sorry, baby," I heard him mumble as they passed by. Up close, Edana looked worse, the red and purple bruises distinct and grotesque. Hawke dwarfed her small frame even more than normal, the fragility of her presence screaming out to all of us.

What the hell happened?

"I'll fuckin' kill every last one of 'em, Prez," he roared, walking toward Marek, coming to a brief stop while still sheltering his woman. "They raped her. I don't . . . I can't. . . ." Hawke stopped speaking. Anyone close enough to hear the pain in his voice knew that if he'd continued talking, he would've broken down right then.

"We'll get them for this," Marek promised. "For fucking everything." A quick glance between them, a silent plan of action already formulating in their heads, I was sure, and Hawke led Edana toward the exit.

Once they were gone, I walked toward Stone, pulling him to the side once the conversation ended between him and Marek, our president turning his attention to Tripp who'd been firing off questions as soon as an opportunity presented itself.

Adelaide stuck to Stone's side, but I didn't care. I wanted to talk to both of them actually.

"What the hell happened to Edana? And who does Hawke want to punish for it?" A niggling sense of who'd attacked her whispered in the back corners of my brain, but I needed to hear it out loud.

"Those goddamn Savages jumped her outside Indulge. They beat her with their fists, forced themselves on her and taunted her, telling her the only reason they were gonna let her live was so she could pass along a message."

Indulge was the club's newest titty bar, and normally security was pretty tight, so I was surprised to find out some of the Reapers were able to not only sneak near our establishment, but attack Edana.

One of our brothers' old ladies.

Without me pushing, Stone continued. "She went there looking for Hawke, no doubt to chew his ass out, boundless guilt he's no doubt dealing with. Anyway, they told her they were comin' for everyone we loved, and they wouldn't stop until Sully was back in their club." Marek had heard Stone's words, no doubt not for the first time, and threw a punch at the wall behind him, pushing his fist through the crumbling drywall.

We all knew our enemy wouldn't stop until they had Marek's wife back with them, her father orchestrating the ambush. We'd been waiting for quite some time now for him to make his move, and it looked like the wait was over.

But who would be next?

I hesitated leaving the club, needing to stick around in case I was needed, but I wanted to head back to my place. Kena was no doubt still locked in sleep, but she was there alone.

All of a sudden, my heart skidded to a stop, loathsome fear fueling my choppy gasps.

Her image filtered in, her innocent smile slicing me apart because I knew what I had to do.

THIRTY-FOUR

Kena

ROLLING OVER, I THRUST MY arm outward and expected to feel Jagger sleeping next to me. But his side was empty. And cold, indicating he'd left the bed quite some time ago. I'd glanced to the alarm clock next to the bed and saw the bright red numbers, reading 6:08 a.m.

Stretching to chase away any residual sleep, I threw off the covers and planted my feet firmly on the ground, shuffling from the room and toward the living area, expecting to find him there.

But again . . . nothing.

He was nowhere to be found. His place was small, and unless he was holed up in the bathroom, he'd left me alone in his apartment. Trudging toward the kitchen to find some coffee, it was then I saw a small note lying on the counter. Barely legible handwriting told me he had gone to the clubhouse. He didn't say why, but I knew enough about him to realize it had to have been important for him to leave me.

Thoughts of the previous night rushed over me and I smiled. I'd never felt like this about anyone before, and the notion that he cared for me as I did him made me the happiest woman in the world.

The way Jagger looked at me, touched me, whispered concerns in my ear as he worked inside my body thrilled me. His gentleness soothed my worries about my first time, and it couldn't have been more perfect. I wouldn't have traded that moment for anything in the world.

Bringing the brewed tastiness to my lips, my hand shook in surprise when I heard the jostle of keys in the lock. The front door flew open and in walked Jagger, looking like he'd been put through the wringer. What had happened during the time he'd been gone? Walking across the threshold, he closed the door behind him and headed toward me, his eyes on me the entire time.

Once he was close, he circled his arm around my waist and pulled me in to him, burying his face in the crook of my neck, inhaling me before placing a lingering kiss on my skin. His tensed shoulders and reserved demeanor instantly put me on alert.

Stepping back, he held my hands in his and looked at me, saying nothing. He just stared, as if his goal was to memorize my every feature.

Finally, after a few intense moments, he dropped my hands and walked toward his bedroom. "I better take you home now, Kena," he called out over his shoulder as he disappeared down the hallway.

I was left standing in the kitchen in nothing but his T-shirt and a dumbfounded look on my face.

Following him back into his room, I searched for my clothes, locating them half kicked under the bed. Gathering them in my hands, I walked toward the bathroom, closing the door behind me. I felt vulnerable right then, and the last thing I wanted to do was expose myself to Jagger— physically or emotionally.

Re-entering his space, I saw him sitting on his bed, his hands cradling his head. It wasn't until I knocked on the wood of the nearby dresser that he looked up. Slowly rising to his feet, he crossed the room and brushed past me without a word.

When he opened the front door I stopped him, grabbing his hand and tugging him back toward me. Once I had his attention, I asked, *What's wrong? Why are you taking me home so early? Did I do something wrong?*

The look on his face told me something serious was about to come flying out of his mouth, and as his lips parted, I held my breath, not wanting to hear any of what he was going to tell me.

Bracing my hands against my sides, I counted the seconds, but no sound ever left him. Instead, he looked like he was going to break down, so before that happened, he turned back around and walked out into the hallway, expecting me to follow.

Which I did.

Confused.

Angry.

Scared.

The entire ride back to my house was in silence. Had I misread his feelings for me?

Had he tricked me into bed, telling me whatever I wanted to hear in order to steal my innocence?

Did he view me as a challenge, nothing more?

If he would only talk to me I'd be able to find out what was wrong, but he remained tight-lipped, only asking if I was cold when he saw me shudder. The temperature had nothing to do with my shivers, just the obstinate guy sitting next to me.

He pulled down my street, the time ticking by too fast, bringing me closer to a situation I knew would upset me. Shutting off the engine, he gripped the wheel tightly, dipping his head for a brief moment before reaching for the door handle. Stepping out, he came around to my side, but I'd already exited the vehicle, standing next to his truck with my arms clutching my purse.

Part of me wanted to walk ahead and disappear inside, never giving him the opportunity to tell me whatever it was that weighed so heavy on him. But the other part of me wanted to demand he tell me why he wanted to get rid of me so fast.

I struggled between the two, but in the end I remained standing exactly where I was, leaning against the passenger side door, fiddling with my keys.

"I'll walk you inside," he finally said, speaking quickly before ushering me forward. The heat from his palm on my lower back warmed and chilled me at the same time.

He remained silent while I jabbed the key into the lock, pushing the door open and walking inside. I took a few steps to the side and watched as he hovered in the doorway, uncertain if he should come inside or turn around and leave.

Not being able to stand whatever this was between us any longer, I raised my hands in front of me and let loose, a bit of anger jerking my motions to let him know he'd upset me.

Why the silent treatment? Tell me what I did. I deserve to know.

I advanced toward him but he retreated, his back hitting the door, a conflicted look crossing over his face.

Listen, Kena, what happened last night was a mistake. It should have never happened. I found it odd he chose to sign to me instead of speak, but I had no time to wonder before I saw his expression change, appearing resolute and void of any feeling. As if I'd just been another notch on his bedpost, which I knew in my heart wasn't the case. Although he was making a strong case to prove otherwise.

Why would you say that?

He didn't answer, instead shoving his hands in his pockets, averting his eyes from mine every few seconds.

When I signed again, he stared at my hands, avoiding my face at all costs. Until he couldn't.

Stop being a coward, Jagger, and tell me what's going on. Tensed moments pinged between us, my heart beating so fast I feared it'd burst from my chest.

Did you use me? Did you just want to get me into bed? Was that your main goal? I lowered my arms to my sides and fisted my hands. My nails bit into my palms and I welcomed the sting of pain.

Would you hate me if I said yes?

Inhaling a ragged breath, I took a step back, my backside bumping into the chair behind me. My lips parted, as if I'd wanted to speak, but I knew that was just stupid. I didn't want to show him how hurt I was but I couldn't help my body's reaction, my heart breaking in two at the thought that the guy standing in front of me was nothing like I'd thought. I didn't know *this* Jagger. I hated this version of him, making me ache inside so badly I wanted to crumble to the floor and weep uncontrollably.

Instead, I held back the tears and answered. *Yes. I would.* For as much as I tried to convince myself that my answer had been truthful, I knew it was a lie. I wanted to hate him, to despise him for hurting me, but I knew I loved him. Even though we'd only known each other a short time, my feelings would seem silly to anyone else, but they were real to me.

And I told him my secret before I could stop myself.

But I love you, I signed, finally allowing the first of many tears to escape. I detested my vulnerability, but I couldn't shield it any longer.

His sharp intake of air told me I'd managed to shock him. Then again, if he'd only chased me because he wanted to get me into bed, I was sure telling him I loved him was the last thing he expected from me.

But didn't he know?

Couldn't he feel it in my kisses?

Couldn't he see it written all over my face when I looked at him?

Didn't he feel it last night when I gave myself to him?

Apparently not.

I'd been the biggest fool.

You don't love me, he replied, running his hands through his hair, his eyes appearing glassy . . . until they didn't. *I'm not the guy for you, and I'm sorry if I led you to believe that I was. We had fun, but I don't wanna see you anymore. I'm sorry,* he said, dropping his hands.

I don't believe you. Tell me, I demanded. *I want to hear you speak those words out loud.*

Shaking his head, he turned his back to me before reaching for the door handle.

I couldn't shout at him to turn around and look at me.

I couldn't yell at him, demand he take back his soul-wrenching words.

The only thing I could do was watch him disappear as the front door closed behind him.

THIRTY-FIVE

Jagger

CONSUMING A LOT OF ALCOHOL was the only way I could stop the pain, my heart feeling as if it had literally splintered in half. Two weeks had passed since I'd lied to Kena, and each day it only got worse.

She'd called me out, saw the weakness splayed all over my body when I told her I didn't want to see her anymore. She knew damn well I wouldn't be able to speak those wretched words out loud, so I had chosen to sign them instead.

The ache in my chest blossomed rapidly, making it difficult to breathe, the slow burn of whiskey dulling it only moderately. Hunching over the bar at The Underground, I embraced the liquor, not paying much attention to anyone around me. Until I had no choice.

A strong hand gripped my neck, and because I'd invited the drink to soothe me, my reaction was nothing less than . . . well, immobile. Trying to raise my head, the weight of my world too heavy to accommodate such a simple action, it fell forward before I could stop it, the hard wood of the ledge catching it instead of my hands.

"Fuuuuuck," I moaned, rubbing the affected area with fingers that felt like lead. Even the slow rise of my arm should have screamed I'd had enough to drink, but since I could still somewhat form a thought, I knew I wasn't done yet.

"You're a fuckin' mess, brother," Ryder growled from behind me, releasing my neck before settling in the seat next to me. He didn't say anything for a moment, or maybe he had and I hadn't heard him, too lost to the numbness finally encasing the tortured parts that remained.

"I got . . . got this," I mumbled, bringing the shot glass to my lips and tipping my head back, the motion throwing my entire body backward.

Thank God Ryder had been there to catch me; otherwise, I'd have been lying on my back, hopefully knocked the fuck out.

Barlow approached, giving me a once-over before shaking his head. "How did you get that, Jagger?" Before allowing me to answer, he turned his attention to Ryder. "I cut him off two drinks ago, but apparently the slick little fucker still managed to snag some more." A harsh crack of his cleanup towel hit my neck, the sting just what I needed to push myself back into reality, albeit slowly.

"Ow! What the fuck, Barlow?"

"That's for not listening to me," he yelled over his shoulder, already walking toward the other end of the bar.

"I think you've had enough," Ryder confirmed, "but before I drop your ass off at home, I wanna know why you cut her loose." From my peripheral I saw him lean forward and rest his forearms on the bar. Although he hadn't been looking at me, it didn't mean he didn't expect me to answer.

I played dumb, however.

"Who?"

"You know damn well who. Braylen's been calling me, screaming at me as if that shit was my fuckin' fault."

Wincing, I could only imagine what Kena's sister had said to him. She was one ballsy, speak-her-mind kind of chick. But her desire to protect Kena made me smile. Well, not smile, but glad she had someone willing to call the likes of Ryder and bitch him out for something he had no hand in. No doubt she'd left me some nasty voice mails as well. Only I'd been too consistently wasted to even bother to check.

Barlow walked back in our direction, placing a tall glass of water in front of me. "Drink it," he demanded, stepping away before I could argue.

"Hey, gimme a shot," Ryder yelled. "You know what I want."

"Fuck no," Barlow shouted back, flipping that damn towel over his shoulder before busying himself with pouring a beer. Ryder opened his mouth to protest, but the bartender cut him off. "There's no way I'm serving you hard liquor, Ryder. I actually like you."

Thankful I had something else to pull my focus, I glanced back and forth between them, curious who'd win out. The two men were pretty much even in height, weight and muscle. The only difference being that Barlow had a shaved head covered in tattoos, his appearance giving him slightly more of a menacing edge.

"What the hell does that mean?" Ryder adjusted himself, one foot planted firmly on the ground while the other rested on the rung of the barstool.

"I don't want to have to call in reinforcements to beat the shit outta ya once you get out of hand." Advancing toward us again, he slid the beer toward Ryder, smirking before turning his back.

"Fuck you."

"You're welcome," Barlow responded, completely ignoring us for the next fifteen minutes.

I expected Ryder to press me for answers, but instead he let me wallow in my self-pity. Because Barlow wouldn't serve me anymore and I had my own personal watchdog hovering over me, I couldn't even lean over the bar when the bartender wasn't looking and snag a bottle, the one I'd taken earlier resting at my feet. Empty.

But the silence was short-lived, Ryder bumping my arm with his before he began his interrogation. "So, why did ya do it? I thought you really liked this one," he goaded, forcing me to talk, although he wouldn't like my response.

"Mind your business. I'm not sittin' here spillin' like some sort of bitch," I slurred, my head lolling from side to side, the room spinning so fast I had to close my eyes to make it stop. Only my lack of sight made it worse.

"It became my business when you dragged me into it, fucker." The bass in his voice dropped threateningly low.

"I don't wanna be with her," I lied, tapping the bar to get Barlow's attention, even though I knew he was simply gonna ignore me.

"Why?"

"Let it go," I shouted, pounding my fist against the wood that time.

"No, I won't. Not until you give me a good reason, one I can tell Braylen when she no doubt shows up at my fuckin' place. Again."

Snagging the opportunity to switch the subject, I dove right in. "She been to your place? So, what . . . You datin' her?" I grinned, my smile no doubt lopsided as all hell. Taking a few gulps of water, some of it dripping down my chin, I patiently waited to see if he'd take the bait.

Sadly, he didn't.

"We're not talkin' about me. Now, if you don't give me a reason why you're not seeing Kena anymore, I'm gonna drag your ass back to her house, drunk or not, and leave you there."

My heart sped up, fear he'd actually do that making me sit up as straight as I could manage. "I'm not good enough," I finally revealed. "She's in too much danger bein' with me." Gripping my hair, I said, "You saw what happened to Edana, man. I'd die if they ever got their hands on Kena." It was the absolute truth. If something bad ever happened to her because of me, I had no idea how I'd go on afterward.

"You can't stop livin' because you think somethin' bad might happen. If that was the case, no one would ever get with anyone." Pushing out a breath, he continued. "You think Marek doesn't worry about Sully every minute of the day, especially knowing Psych's plannin' on coming for her? Or that Stone isn't sick with worry every time Adelaide and Riley are out of his sight?"

"What about Braylen?"

"What about her?"

"Don't you worry she'll get hurt?"

"Nope." Swallowing half his beer in a few gulps, the glass clanked against the bar when he put it down. "Besides, we're just fuckin'. And ain't no bastards gonna stop me from gettin' my dick wet." He spewed his nonchalant words my way, but I saw the hesitation on his face. Braylen meant more to him than just someone to stick his dick in. But I decided not to call him out on it, although I should have because then it would've diverted the conversation. I was too drunk to mentally play games with him, though, his sobriety no doubt giving him the advantage.

So I settled on a dismissive approach. "Whatever."

Finishing off the rest of his beer, he stood and reached for my upper arm, pulling me to my feet. "Let's go."

I tried to shrug him off but it was futile. "Where we goin'?"

"You're gonna fix this. If not for yourself, then for me, 'cause I'm tired of hearing Braylen's shit." Effortlessly pulling me toward the exit, he added, "I can think of better things to occupy her mouth." He laughed at his own joke, continuing to force me outside and into his vehicle.

Realizing fighting him was useless, I tried to convince him I was too far gone, using my inebriation as the perfect excuse. "I'm too goddamn drunk to see her."

"That you are," he agreed, kicking over the engine and throwing it into gear. "I'm gonna get you some coffee. And Jagger?" I turned toward him. "If you puke in my truck, I'm gonna kill ya."

"Then stop drivin' like an asshole."

"I'm only goin' five miles an hour," he retorted, shaking his head. A few miles down the road he stopped at a drive-thru, ordering two large coffees. Black. Handing me the first one, he jerked his head at me. "Drink it."

Knowing I'd see Kena sooner rather than later, I didn't argue, bringing the hot liquid to my mouth, burning my tongue at first contact. But I soldiered on, needing to be somewhat sober when I finally laid eyes on her.

Ten minutes passed without either of us speaking, the tension between us faltering some. "How do you know she's even home?"

"I already checked with Braylen." That's all he said, keeping his focus on the road ahead.

Settling further into my seat, my alcohol-induced haze lessening with each fleeting mile, my brain formed many questions.

Did she know I was on my way?

Did she even want to see me?

Would I give in and beg her for another chance?

Would she forgive me?

I guess I'll have answers soon enough.

THIRTY-SIX

Kena

BRAYLEN HAD BEEN ACTING EXTREMELY weird for the past couple hours, looking out the window every once in a while. When I asked her why, she'd waved her hand at me and shrugged, not giving me a definitive answer.

Every day over the past two weeks crawled by, each passing second consumed with thoughts of Jagger. I knew I should have never been involved with him, fearing my sister's warning would eventually come true. That he'd break my heart.

And it was exactly what he'd done.

Although, I felt much worse than I ever thought I would. With Jagger, I pictured us making it for the long haul, envisioning us moving in together someday and forging a future.

I was old enough to know that not everything would be perfect, but I wanted to explore the next chapter of my life with him. Unfortunately, the first time I laid my heart on the line it'd been sliced from my chest and crushed under the weight of his rejection.

I'd chosen Jagger to give myself to, and he'd taken advantage of my vulnerability.

The thought that he'd only chosen me because I presented as a challenge enraged me. Did he laugh at me with his buddies? Brag about getting into the mute girl's pants? Anger washed over the hurt when I'd allow myself to fully contemplate what had happened between us, coming to grips with the fact Jagger was a bastard, feeding on my innocence any way he saw fit.

Braylen backed away from the window, mumbled something to herself and walked toward the front door. Glancing at the clock on the wall above the television, I saw it was closing in on eleven, the later hour nudging me to let out a full yawn.

When she looked in my direction, I signed, *I'm going to bed. I'm tired.*

A knock rapped on the door, drawing my attention right away. "Don't be mad at me, but for as much as I want to punch Jagger in the face right now for hurting you, I know he truly cares about you." I rose from the couch and took a step toward the hallway. She held her hands up in front of her as a sign of surrender. "I know. I know. I can't believe I'm even asking you to give him a chance to explain why he did what he did, but trust me. There's something more he's not telling you. Ryder texted me before and told me he's been miserable for the past two weeks, drinking himself silly just to get through it."

I didn't want to hear any more of what she had to say. Taking another tentative step away from her, the pounding on the door broke the building tension between my older sister and me. *How dare she do this? How dare she make me face the one person who crushed my entire world?* At first I thought I was being a bit overdramatic, but try telling that to my heart, to the sadness embedded in my brain every time I thought about him.

But although I hated that he'd destroyed me, I couldn't just stop loving him.

Is that him? I knew the answer before she responded.

"Yes. Ryder's out there with him. He had to sober Jagger up before he got here."

So it wasn't even Jagger's idea to come over, then? It was yours and Ryder's? That's even more humiliating.

Never mind that I felt like shit, I looked like it too. My hair was pulled back into a messy up-do, not having washed it in five days. I wore a yellow cami and wrinkled pajama bottoms, not caring that they hadn't been cleaned in as much time either.

Braylen moved toward the front door, her fingers circling around the handle, ready to welcome the two of them into our house.

Don't you dare, I warned.

"I hate seeing you like this, and if there is anything I can do to help . . . I'm gonna do it." On her last word, she flung open the door, stepping to the side as Ryder entered first. Jagger followed behind, making sure to stay near the entryway. *Smart move,* I thought.

I could have strangled Braylen right then. She'd been all over the place when it came to Jagger and me. First she liked him. Then she couldn't stand him. Then she liked him again. *Come on, woman, make up your mind already.*

"We're gonna give you some privacy," Ryder announced, seizing my sister's hand and pulling her from the house, her astonishment heard all the way to his truck, complaining she wasn't even dressed. But somehow I thought he wouldn't have a problem with the lack of clothing she wore, an oversized T-shirt the only thing covering her decency.

A rumble of the engine and a slight squeal of tires told me they'd really left me alone with Jagger. And while I was infuriated, my eyes couldn't stop drinking him in. I thought I looked bad, but it was nothing compared to him. His hair was a mess, and a faint shadow of a beard prickled his jawline. He looked tired, haggard even. Faint lines were etched into his face, accentuating his hollowed appearance. While he looked a little worse for wear, he was still the most handsome guy I'd ever seen.

But I couldn't think like that. No way would I allow him to affect me like he had before he broke my heart. I couldn't take it if he said something endearing or begged for my forgiveness. Because I just might crumble and give in, opening myself up for a bigger disaster down the road.

He continued to stand near the door, his eyes following my every movement. Knowing he wouldn't leave until I broached the topic of him being there, I took a step closer. I held steady, glaring at him to try and mask my true feelings.

Devastation.

What are you doing here?

"I had to see you," he answered, licking his lips in nervousness.

You had to see me, or you were forced here to see me?

"Both," he replied, surprisingly admitting that Ryder had dragged him to my house. "Kena," he started, advancing on me until I held my hand up for him to stop. "I'm so sorry for the way things ended between us. I didn't mean to hurt you. I hope we can still be friends."

So . . . you're not here to get me back?

"No."

I'm not gonna lie and say there wasn't a part of me that was distraught from his admission. While I'd vowed not to give him another chance, I at least thought he'd come to his senses and realized he had feelings for me. Feelings that hadn't disappeared just because he had.

Now I was beyond irate with Braylen, and whatever part Ryder had played in this whole charade. Why compound the hurt I'd felt? Just to see if there was a chance he'd come back around and want to be with me again? Had they even asked him if he *wanted* to see me? Talk to me? Try and get me back?

It was obvious they hadn't.

So then, what are you doing here? I asked again, fisting my hands at my sides so I didn't rush forward and slap the shit out of him for turning me into a pathetic person, drowning in hurt all because he'd bested me. Lied to me. Made me believe he'd cared.

"I wanted to apologize for my behavior and tell you that I didn't just go after you to get you into bed. That wasn't my intention at all. I genuinely cared about you. Fuck," he grumbled, running his palms down his face in frustration. "I still do. I just . . . I can't be with you."

I refused to beg him to explain further. He stood before me, telling me again that he didn't want me. And no matter how much I wanted to throw myself into his arms and plead for him to change his mind, I stood strong. I valued myself too much to act like such a fool.

Then there's nothing left for you to say. You can leave now. Besides. . . . I dropped my hands before I finished, realizing I'd only be inviting drama into my life, when all I wanted to do was forget everything and crawl into bed. Sleep until my sister forced me out of bed days later.

But it was too late.

I'd piqued his interest, his brow furrowing while he continued to stare at me. "Besides what?"

I just shook my head, refusing to fulfill his curiosity.

"Besides what, Kena?" he asked, a hint of anger lacing his voice when he'd said my name. "Are you trying to tell me you're seeing someone else? Is that it?" His entire body tensed, the flare of disbelief lighting up his eyes. "Tell me," he demanded, taking a step toward me, his carefully orchestrated reserve slowly crumbling.

He deserved to feel hurt, or betrayed, or jealous, or whatever emotion sliced through him right then.

"Is it Kevin?" His question shocked me, but it shouldn't have. He'd obviously had an issue with our friendship, although he'd never given me shit about it before.

I never answered, biting my lower lip in nervousness, a tick I'd seen him do before. But it was enough to appear as if I'd answered yes. A barrage of expletives flew from his mouth before his eyes turned dark and he snarled at me in fury.

My initial intention was to make him jealous. Of course it would've been with a lie, but I hadn't followed through. Although, it seemed I didn't have to; his imagination ran wild, and I did nothing to stop it.

The wildfire of his emotions cut through the air, engulfing us both in its tight grip.

"Let me tell you something right now. If I ever see his hands on you, I'm gonna rip them from his body and beat him with them. Don't test me, Kena. I mean it," he threatened, stepping closer until he stood only a couple feet away from me. The growl in his voice kicked me back into the reality of the situation. He had no right at all to threaten Kevin, even if he was my fictional boyfriend. Something he'd come up with all by himself. All right, I knew I hadn't dissuaded him otherwise, but still . . . He was the one who tossed me to the side, and in a cruel way I might add.

You have no right to say that to me. You broke up with me, so why do you care who I date? Again, I fed into the lie but I couldn't stop myself, part of me smug that he was jealous.

"So I broke up with you, and already you're spreading your legs for someone else? Is that it? Now that you're no longer a virgin, you'll jump on any cock ready and willing?"

I gasped at his audacity, but of course he could only see my reaction, not hear it. His words mixed with his hateful tone triggered me to do something I never thought I would.

Especially to him.

I slapped him so hard I'd jolted his head to the side. From the shocked look on his face, he clearly hadn't expected it either. Clenching his jaw, trying to keep his temper in check, he turned around and strode toward the front door, whipping it open before slamming it hard behind him when he left.

Tears coursed down my cheeks that I'd been reduced to someone who would strike another person.

And Jagger, of all people.

But he'd deserved it. Hadn't he?

THIRTY-SEVEN

Jagger

"WHAT THE FUCK DID YOU do?" Ryder roared, knocking me off the barstool before I'd even realized he was near me. Lucky for him, I was drunk. Again. Otherwise I would've knocked him the fuck out for coming at me like that.

Lolling my head to the side, rubbing my jaw from the impact of his fist, I slowly climbed to my feet, clutching the ledge of the bar and using it as an anchor until I found my footing.

"What the hell?" I muttered, continuing to rub my face. The man packed one hell of a punch, and like I said, he was lucky I was incapacitated.

"What did you say to her?"

"Who?"

"Kena."

"None of your damn business," I said, righting myself on the stool and tapping the bar to get Trigger's attention. The clubhouse was practically empty, except for a few men milling around. Marek and Stone had been holed up in Chambers a lot recently, only breaking away to ensure their families' safety. Hawke appeared every now and then, wanting to hear details of retaliation, but so far there hadn't been any.

Marek knew what had to be done, even though some of them disagreed. Patience, although not our strong suit, had to be practiced. But I had a feeling he had something else up his sleeve, even if he denied it. I could've been wrong, however. I didn't even know how to run my own life, let alone how to run an entire club, or at the very least, offer any suggestions.

"Like I told ya before, it's my business when Braylen won't give it up because she fears I'm just like your dumb ass."

Finding some liquid courage, I asked, "Thought you guys were just fuckin', so what do you care? Can't you find another slut to stick your dick in?" Yeah, liquid courage wasn't always the smart way to go.

No one would have ever believed I was a trained, undefeated fighter right then. Not with the way Ryder managed to grip me up and pin me against the side of the bar. "If you don't fix whatever you said to Kena, I'm gonna make you regret it." His fists clenched tighter, the rustle of my cut echoing in my ears.

"Fine," I agreed. I made him believe his threat scared me, but in reality I knew I had to apologize for what I'd said to her. I was out of line, even if the thought of her with Kevin enraged me all over again.

Releasing me, he strode across the empty space and disappeared outside, leaving me alone with my thoughts. Trigger had taken off somewhere as soon as Ryder started in on me, and the other guys lounging around were now outside, probably tinkering with their bikes.

Straddling my seat once more, I pulled my phone from my back pocket and brought up the keypad. I doubted she would respond, but I had to send her a message regardless.

Jagger: I'm sorry.

Right away, my phone chimed.

Kena: GO TO HELL!!

Jagger: I'm already there. Trust me.

A half hour passed before she finally responded again, although my last text probably confused the hell out of her. It did me. I couldn't differentiate my emotions. At first, my heart broke that I had to set her free, realizing the danger she would be in if anyone knew she was attached to me. Then I was enraged at the thought she was seeing Kevin so soon after we'd broke up, but it wasn't her fault. I was the one who ended things, so why was I upset?

Because you love her.

And I did, although I could never tell her that because I knew we couldn't be together. Telling her those three words would kill us both, offering a hope that neither one of us could grab on to.

Kena: I'm not seeing Kevin. Never was. I just let you think that because you deserved it.

I had to re-read her text five times before it fully sank in. My lips kicked up in a smug grin, happy what I'd thought wasn't even true. The palm of my hand smacked my forehead, remembering what I'd accused her of, the reality of the situation hitting me like a freight train.

So I broke up with you, and already you're spreading your legs for someone else? I can't believe those words actually came out of my mouth. And just because I'd still been partially drunk didn't excuse my behavior. Not at all. That wasn't me, but my anger had gotten the best of me.

Jagger: I'm so sorry. Can you forgive me? Can we still be friends?

Kena: I don't want to be your friend.

Ouch! But I totally deserved it.

Jagger: I understand. Just know that I'm really sorry.

Kena: I can accept that you don't want to be with me anymore, although it hurts because you know how I feel about you. I'll forgive you someday, just not right now.

I had no idea what to respond, so I didn't, dropping my phone on top of the bar. Once Trigger had returned, coming out of the kitchen with a big fat sandwich in hand, I asked for another shot.

"Don't you think you've had enough?" he asked, chewing while talking.

"Not nearly," I admitted, drumming my fingers on the wood and irritating the both of us.

Sliding my order toward me, he moved closer, a genuine look of concern on his face. I'd always liked Trigger, although the guy was quite intense on occasion. Mainly when it had to do with Adelaide. Protecting his niece was crucial to him, and when Stone had overstepped those boundaries, I thought he was gonna kill our VP. For Christ's sake, he'd shot him! But in his eyes, Stone deserved it. Thankfully, they'd moved on—but only barely, Trigger still giving him shit every now and again.

My phone dinged but I ignored it, choosing numbness instead.

Kena

OVER THE COURSE OF THE next few weeks, Jagger had texted me numerous times, asking how my day was, apologizing over and over for the things he'd said and telling me he still wanted to be friends. But again, I'd told him I wasn't interested in only being his friend. Although my face lit up every time my phone did, it didn't mean I'd forgiven him for hurting me.

I had a decision to make, and every time I thought I had it figured out, I'd change my mind. Wasn't it my right as a woman? Braylen went back and forth just like I did, some days being Team Jagger, telling me I should give him another shot. Although what she wasn't understanding was that he didn't want another chance, he only wanted to be my freaking buddy.

Then other days, she cursed the day he'd come to our rescue, insisting he'd put some kind of voodoo hex on me. Her moods depended on whether or not Ryder had been giving her a hard time about something, pissing her off so badly she'd needed a glass of wine as soon as she stepped foot inside the house.

I figured only time would tell what would transpire between Jagger and me, but I did know one thing. I'd force him to tell me the real reason he broke it off.

So help me God . . . I had a right to know.

———— ♦ ————

SNATCHING MY PHONE OFF OF my dresser, I decided tonight was the night I'd agree to meet up with Jagger. He'd asked me a few times to come over and have dinner, or for him to come to my place. I didn't think he was suddenly embarrassed to be seen with me in public, but not once did he suggest actually going out to a restaurant. Yeah, the only options were his place or mine.

Either way, he had no idea I planned on ambushing him with my need-to-know question. If he'd told me the truth, maybe I would've been more understanding. Less hurt. Although I didn't see how the last part would ever have been true.

I still hurt.

A lot.

And I continued to suffer because there wasn't a clean break between us. Yet, I continued torturing myself for some reason. Case in point, the message I'd sent to him.

Kena: Are you free tonight?

I wondered if he'd been waiting for me to message him, his response coming through right away.

Jagger: Of course.

Kena: Wanna cook me that dinner?

Jagger: Absolutely.

Kena: 7?

Jagger: Works for me. I'll pick you up then.

Kena: I'll just drive over.

I wanted to be the one able to leave at the drop of a hat, in case anything happened and I needed to make a hasty exit.

Jagger: No, I'll pick you up.

Kena: Then I'm not coming.

Jagger: Kena . . .

Kena: Jagger . . .

His response took a few minutes to come through, no doubt hating that he had to concede and give in. He couldn't control the situation and I knew it irked him.

Jagger: Fine. This time.

This time? Did he think there was going to be another time? The only reason I'd set up these dinner plans was because I wanted—no, I *needed*—answers.

Kena: See you at 7.

Jagger: Can't wait.

I took extra time preparing for the upcoming evening, choosing the perfect outfit, a pair of dark skinny jeans paired with a billowy cream-colored top. A pair of heels complemented the ensemble, making me appear sexy yet not over the top. I wanted him to take one look at me and instantly regret tossing me aside. I desperately needed it for my ego.

I chose to wear my hair down in loose waves, while going light on the makeup. I wanted to look good, but I didn't want to appear as if I'd been trying too hard.

Heading toward my car, I stopped abruptly when I saw that I had a flat tire. Stomping my foot, I made no qualms about cursing—inside my head, of course. Pulling my cell from my purse, I texted Braylen and asked when she'd be home. Her response was immediate, telling me not until late.

I had two choices to make. Either I could cancel on Jagger or I could convince him to just come to my house instead. No point in him coming to pick me up just to drive all the way back over to his place. Tapping my foot against the pavement for a solid minute while I thought things through, I finally decided to ask Jagger to come over.

Once back inside, I threw my purse on the couch, my phone still in hand.

Kena: I have a flat. Can you just come over here for dinner?

Braylen would be gone for hours, so there was no chance she'd run into him, probably giving me shit about letting him come over. Depending on her mood, of course.

Jagger: I made lasagna, so let me pack it up and I'll be there soon.

As soon as I read his message my stomach rumbled.

I had a decision to make. Either I wanted to forge ahead and accept him as my friend, or cut him from my life altogether. Looking at my pathetic self in the mirror, running my fingers through my hair and checking my lip gloss, I knew I wasn't strong enough to cut him out completely. Not yet.

Thirty minutes later, three knocks sounded. Checking my reflection one last time, I blew out a nervous breath and opened the front door. And the sight before me was worth every internal debate, every mixed emotion and every self-doubt I'd possessed over the past few weeks.

Jagger stood on my stoop, holding a tray of lasagna. He was the dish I wanted to devour instead of the carby goodness he held in his hands. As soon as he looked at me, I knew the night would become complicated. For me, at least. The intensity in his eyes gave away his secret, one he'd probably deny if I'd asked. He still desired me, but would he act on it? Go back on his ridiculous notion of us not being . . . well, *us*?

Widening the door, I stepped aside until he'd entered. Without instruction, he walked toward the kitchen and placed the pan on the counter.

"We're probably gonna have to nuke it for a few seconds before we eat. It's still warm, but it'll taste better piping hot. Don't you think?" he asked.

Sure.

Reaching into the upper cabinets, I took down two plates, grabbed a couple of forks from the drawer and removed the lid from the tray.

"I'll get that," he offered, suddenly appearing behind me, his warm breath hitting the back of my neck. His closeness rattled me. I didn't want to feel vulnerable around him, but I couldn't stop my heart from speeding up, or tamp down the need to turn around and press my lips to his.

Placing his hands on my waist, he gently moved me aside, busying himself with dishing out a piece of lasagna for us both, popping them in the microwave for ninety seconds to ensure the temperature was just right.

The clattering of dishes called my attention back to the table. I'd been staring at the back of him, watching the way his muscles flexed every time he moved. His jeans fit him perfectly, teasing me with the image of what I knew lay just underneath. He'd worn a white button-up shirt, the sleeves rolled up to his elbows, exposing muscular, inked forearms. And so help me, I swore it was arm porn.

Clearing his throat brought my attention back to his face. Blushing lightly because I knew he'd just caught me staring, I moved to the seat next to where he stood, sitting down and focusing on the plate of food he'd set in front of me.

Don't look at him. Don't look at him. I kept repeating this over and over, not wanting to give him any indication that he'd been affecting me since he'd walked through that damn door.

"Kena." I kept my eyes on the table. "Kena," he called a bit louder. "Look at me."

Slowly raising my head, I raked my eyes over every button on his shirt, the skin of his throat, his chin, his lips, his nose . . . and finally his eyes.

He didn't say anything at first, instead taking his time studying me in turn. His scrutiny put me on alert, and I swore if he didn't say something in the next few seconds, I was going to jump over the table and attack that perfect mouth of his.

"Ready to eat?"

Yeah, not what I'd expected him to say, even though the food he'd cooked sat directly in front of us.

Nodding, I picked up my fork and cut into the steaming dish. Funny thing was I'd suddenly lost my appetite, my nerves making me semi-nauseous. But I didn't want him to realize how uncomfortable I'd suddenly become so I started eating, appreciating how tasty the meal was.

I smiled between mouthfuls.

"I hope you like it. It's the best thing I can make." He laughed, the tiny dimple in his left cheek appearing.

I gave a simple nod.

Jagger looked like someone people should be afraid of, his tough exterior the first thing everyone saw. But when he smiled, I saw the guy underneath. When he'd made love to me, I'd felt his gentleness. When he looked at me like I was the only person in the world, I saw his vulnerability.

Too bad I couldn't claim him as mine anymore.

Just a friend.

But I'd take what I could for the time being, until it became too much and I became tired of torturing myself.

After dinner we retired to the sofa. I kicked off my shoes and tucked my legs underneath me, sitting far enough away from him that we wouldn't accidentally touch. I needed the distance, craved it for my sanity to remain intact.

Awkward moments passed until I couldn't take it anymore. *So what now?* I signed. *How does this friend thing work?* I smiled but I was anything but happy. Nervous was more like it, sitting but a couple feet away from Jagger, trying to appear unaffected, but I was anything but.

Shrugging, he replied, "Not sure. I've never been friends before."

Never?

"Nope."

Leaning back, I untucked my legs and brought them up toward my chest, resting my hands on my knees. *We'll figure it out together, then.*

"Okay." He smiled and reached out to touch me, his fingers briefly running up and down my arm. Pulling back, he settled into his seat again, his eyes drifting over my face before focusing on the television. I'd flicked it on before we'd sat down.

"Hey, my club's having a cookout this Saturday. Do you wanna go? And before you say no, I think Ryder invited Braylen, so at least you'll know a few people." He grinned, lifting his glass of water to his mouth. I watched him swallow the cold liquid, and I wanted more than anything to lick the droplets of water off his lips. "Kena? Did you hear me?"

Startled, I looked away, but not before I heard him chuckle.

I don't know, I answered, still avoiding his face while literally twiddling my thumbs.

The cushion next to me dipped, and when I looked up, Jagger had moved closer, our thighs brushing against one another's.

What are you doing?

He moved closer, cupping the side of my face, and even though I fought it, I leaned in to his touch.

"I don't know," he confessed, his lips only inches from mine, his warm breath tickling my mouth. So badly I wanted him to kiss me, and I think he wanted that as well, but we were toying with very dangerous territory.

With my hands pressed against his chest, my fingers playing with the fabric of his shirt for a brief moment, I pushed him back. I needed the distance. I could barely breathe, his closeness suffocating me in some strange way.

Don't.

"I'm sorry. I shouldn't have done that."

I hadn't meant to ask him, but I couldn't help myself. *Why did you break up with me? Why throw away what we had only to settle for this?* I asked, waving my hand back and forth between us.

Irritation lit up his face as he rose to his feet. "Do you think I wanted to let you go? Do you think I like feeling like my heart is missing from my chest? I had no choice," he mumbled, gripping the back of his neck and squeezing. "It's not safe for you to be with me right now, Kena. There are things happening in my life that I can't get into. Just know I would be with you if I could. Maybe in the future, after everything gets sorted out . . . but not until then."

Rising to stand in front of him, I let my anger take hold and dictate which words my hands would form. *So, what? You're gonna string me along, keep me in the shadows until you deem it time for us to be together again?*

"It's not like that."

I think it is.

"Kena, please," he begged, stepping closer, but I backed up, knowing if he touched me I'd break. "I swear I wish it were different. I really do. We're trying to deal with the threat, and then we'll be good."

He spoke in code, not making any sense at all. *I don't know if I can hang on until then,* I confessed.

Completely disregarding my last statement, a pretty important one, he proceeded to ask me the question he'd asked minutes earlier.

"Will you go to the cookout with me on Saturday?"

You just said I wasn't safe with you, I countered.

"There's no safer place than the clubhouse. All of us will be there." He didn't elaborate or even fully explain what the hell he'd been rambling about seconds prior. His back and forth made me dizzy, and before I said something I would forever regret, I gave him an inch.

No doubt he'd find a way to take a mile, though.

I'll think about it.

For once, he was the one nodding, words escaping him for a response. Soon after, we called it a night, him kissing my cheek before finally leaving.

As I lay in bed, tucked comfortably under the covers, I couldn't help but wonder where I stood in Jagger's world. Would fate allow us to be together again soon, or would her sometimes cruel hands tear us apart for good?

THIRTY-NINE

Jagger

IT TOOK EVERYTHING IN ME not to pin her on her back and attack that luscious mouth of hers, but I knew if I had, I would have hurt her more than she already was. But there were times, like when I was sitting right next to her, inhaling her sweet scent, entranced with the way she stared at me, that I wanted to throw caution to the wind and go for it. Fuck the consequences.

Fortunately, the next day, after some much-needed prodding, Kena agreed to go to the cookout. I tried to pretend I was the sole reason she'd agreed, but I knew Braylen had a hand in it.

After our mini argument, I knew I had to back off a bit and give her the space she needed. It was just as hard for me as it was for her, dealing with our relationship, whatever status we were in.

Jagger: What are you wearing?

Kena: Are you trying to get cute with me?

Her slight flirtation shocked me, but I loved it. It meant she was on the slow road back to forgiving me.

Jagger: Damnit! You caught me.

Kena: Nice try, but I'm not telling you. You'll just have to see for yourself.

Jagger: Seriously, asking because I need to know whether I should bring my bike or truck.

Kena: Oh . . . Truck.

Jagger: See you soon.

THE PARTY WAS IN FULL swing by the time we arrived, men and their women socializing as if we weren't on the cusp of a war. But I understood.

Sometimes, we needed to take a step away from it all and enjoy what's important in life—friends and family. The carefree day only shielded the stress we'd been experiencing, however. And by stress, I mean the daunting horror that any one of us, or someone we cared immensely about, could be snatched away in a heartbeat.

Willing myself to focus on the happiness playing out right in front of me, I reached for Kena's hand, surprised she'd given it, and strolled across the lot. A small clearing came into view the further we walked, a couple large tents pitched with picnic tables underneath.

The smell of steak and burgers made my stomach rumble, reminding me I hadn't eaten very much. "Do you want me to fix you a plate?" I asked, still gripping tightly to her hand. My eyes drifted over her face, down her body to her feet, and then back up until our eyes connected. I hadn't meant to do it, but I couldn't help the way she made me just want to stare at her. Her hair was pulled back in a ponytail, her face makeup-less but for a sheer sheen on her lips. It was under the bright sun that I noticed a splattering of freckles across her nose, making her appear younger than her twenty-one years.

The way her body looked in the outfit she'd chosen made me want to hide her from every brother's sight. The red tank top she wore fit her like a glove, a hint of cleavage popping out and making me want to strip her naked just so I could caress her skin with my tongue. And don't get me started on her shorts. Yes, they were modest, not hot pants or coochie cutters or shit like that, but the cut of them hugged her ass and made her toned legs look longer than they actually were. A pair of flip-flops adorned her feet. Her required casualness for the cookout was a win, although she looked sexy as hell to boot.

Tugging on my hand, I turned to look at her, wondering why she wanted to escape. She did it again. "You don't want to hold my hand?" I asked innocently, though a slight tremor of hurt mixed in with the words.

Again she tried to pull away, the annoyance on her face quite telling. As soon as I let go, I found out why she'd been trying to dislodge her hand from mine.

How easily you forget I need my hands to answer.

Quirking up the side of my mouth, I apologized. "Sorry."

She smiled and my heart leapt inside my chest. *You just wanna show all the other guys that I'm off-limits.* As soon as she lowered her hands she looked away, instantly regretting her response.

Hooking my fingers under her chin, I lifted her head so she would look at me. "Yes, that's partly the reason, but more than that, I love touching you."

Gone were any traces of playfulness. *You can't say things like that to me. I'm really trying to give this friendship thing a chance, but when you look at me like that, and tell me you love touching me, and admit that you're warning other guys to essentially stay away from me, it confuses me. And quite frankly, it hurts.*

I reached for her arm but she quickly walked ahead, spotting her sister and Ryder sitting under one of the tents. Tentatively walking up behind her, I placed my hand on her shoulder and leaned in to whisper in her ear, Braylen glaring at me the entire time.

"I'm sorry. I didn't mean to hurt you. Again." Inhaling her vanilla scented skin, I kissed her temple and rose back up to my full height. "I'm gonna grab some food. I'll surprise you." Trying to make light of a tense situation, I headed over to where Cutter was manning the grill.

Call me the master of mixed signals, but I simply couldn't help it. *I was conflicted, so I had no doubt Kena's warring emotions matched my own.*

"Who the hotties sittin' with Ryder? And what the fuck do they see in that grumpy bastard?" Cutter asked, flipping a couple of the steaks before tending to the dogs and burgers.

Cutter was a strange sort of guy. And by strange, I meant I could never get a good read on him. He mostly kept to himself, often called upon for his skills with disposing of people. I'd heard about it with Vex, and I'd seen it firsthand with Yanez. I wouldn't go as far as calling him creepy, per se, because he only did what was necessary, but I sure as shit wouldn't want to be on the receiving end of his "attention."

His son, Breck, on the other hand, was the complete opposite. They barely shared the same features, let alone a similar personality. I liked Breck just fine, most times. Other times, he was lucky I hadn't knocked him out, his cockiness getting the better of him. Especially when he was three sheets to the wind. Besides, I was a prospect; I couldn't touch a full patched member unless I was defending myself, which thankfully had never been the issue with him. Or any of the other brothers.

Slapping some cheese on two of the burgers, I stood back when Cutter gave me an annoyed look. "The blonde, Braylen, is sort of dating Ryder, and the gorgeous creature next to her is mine." I hadn't meant to claim her so possessively, but I had no doubt a few of these guys would make a play for her if they thought she was single.

Technically she is single, dumbass.

Shaking the absurd yet poignant thought from my head, I reached for one of the hotdogs and got my hand slapped with the spatula. "Fuck, that hurt," I groaned, giving him a death glare, one he returned ten-fold.

"Don't touch the food while I'm cooking, prospect." Raising his bottle of beer, he took a few gulps before placing it down on the side of the grill, its own perfect little holder grooved into the cut of the steel appliance. "I didn't know ya had a woman," he grunted, never once turning to look at me.

"Yeah, although . . . Yeah, it's complicated."

"Complicated? You postin' some fucked-up status on Facebook or somethin'?"

"What the hell do you know about social media, old man?" I laughed, still keeping watch over Kena out of the corner of my eye.

"I know enough. And if I were you, I'd un-complicate that shit. Otherwise, my son is gonna have her on her back before you know it." His words cut right to the heart of me. Sure enough, when I turned fully around to face the three of them—or should I say four of them—I saw Breck sitting across from Kena, laughing at something Ryder said but keeping his eye on my woman. Where the hell had he come from?

"How the hell did you see him? Your nose is in the goddamn grill."

"I don't miss shit," he said, tossing some food on a plate and shoving it toward me. "Here. Now go away."

Swiftly walking toward the table, my adrenaline fueling the anger coursing through me, I stopped right next to Kena and set the plate in front of her. I'd meant to grab some sides and drinks, but no way would I allow Breck any more time in her presence without realizing she wasn't available.

Single or fucking not, Kena was taken.

She was mine.

Placing my hand on her shoulder, I glared at the guy brazen enough to try and grab her attention, staking my claim like some sort of animal. "Here you go, babe," I said, talking to her but keeping my eye on Cutter's son.

"What's up, prospect? Can we help you?" Breck laughed, the lilt of his tone indicating he was well on his way to feelin' good. No doubt he'd started drinking hours before.

"Yeah, you can stop hittin' on my woman," I said with a controlled tone. All I wanted to do was reach across the table and knock him on his ass, but I refrained. Sliding into the seat next to Kena, I threw my arm over her shoulder and pulled her close, scowling at Breck the entire time. I knew my behavior was less than stellar, but I was powerless against the surge of testosterone rapidly flowing through my veins.

"No way this fine piece is yours," he countered, pissing me off even more. Before I could respond, Kena elbowed me in the side, dislodging my arm from around her. Turning toward me, her face scrunched in annoyance. Bringing up her hands, she signed so fast I almost missed a few of the words.

Your woman? Why are you all of a sudden being so possessive? Are you trying to show off or something, because I don't like it.

Trying to figure out an apology, I was caught off guard when Breck opened his mouth.

"Holy fuck! You got you a woman who can't talk?" Slapping the table, he continued his drunken rambling. "You lucky sonofabitch. How awesome is that? You don't have to hear her yapping all the time, naggin' you and shit."

I hopped to my feet and reached over the table, but Ryder had already beat me to him, grabbing Breck in a choke hold and lifting him from his seat so quickly he stumbled backward. He slurred his words while trying to figure out why Ryder had attacked him. And while a few of the other guys turned their attention toward us, none of them approached, realizing that Breck had probably deserved whatever was coming his way.

And he did. Without a doubt. The rule about a prospect not putting his hands on a full patched member unless it was in self-defense? That went right out the fuckin' window as soon as he said what he did about Kena. Surely Marek would have pardoned my actions, had I been the one to teach Breck a lesson.

I'd been so amped up with attacking him I'd failed to see how Kena had been faring from his heartless comments. When I sat back down, I turned my body toward hers but she moved away. It was only by an inch or so, but I hated any distance between us.

I'm so sorry about what he said. I'd decided to sign, hoping it would somehow alleviate whatever embarrassment or anger she'd been feeling right then. She shrugged as if she hadn't been affected, but when a tear danced down her flushed cheek, I knew she was upset. And I didn't blame her. Not one fucking bit. Hastily wiping away a few more tears, she rose from her seat and started walking away from the table.

"Where are you going?" I jogged up next to her and tried to take her hand but she pulled it back, continuing to walk ahead of me. "Kena!" I shouted. "Where are you going?"

She turned around, signed, *To the bathroom*, and continued on her way. I kept my distance but there was no way in hell I was gonna leave her alone, especially when she had no idea where she was going.

FORTY

Kena

EMBARRASSMENT COURSED DOWN MY FACE the further I walked away from the whole scene. I heard Jagger's steps behind me, but I knew if I turned around I'd start sobbing uncontrollably, seeking comfort in the arms of someone who may or may not want me.

Coming across the first building I saw, I turned the handle and entered, the wide open space shocking me with its sheer size. A few couches littered the area, with single leather seating spread throughout. A large bar occupied the entire back wall, an area I was sure got a lot of use. There were a few closed doors, so I walked to the nearest one. My fingers curled around the knob, but before I could turn it, Jagger's hand covered mine.

"Oh no, sweetheart, you can't go in there," he warned, a softness to his voice abating his command not to enter.

Withdrawing from his touch, I asked, *Why? What's in there?*

He opened his mouth to respond, but someone beat him to it. "Chambers. No women or nonmembers allowed inside their sacred meeting room," a beautiful woman mocked, smiling big while her eyes raked over me. She seemed rather friendly, so why did a twinge of jealousy grapple with my good senses?

Placing her hand on Jagger's shoulder, she shoved him out of her way, bringing her hands up in front of her and signing, *Hi. I'm Sully.*

My smile widened because there was someone besides my family—and Jagger, of course—who I could communicate with. She obviously wasn't deaf, or mute, so I wondered how or why she knew sign language. Was she a teacher for the hearing impaired? Or was it because of someone in her family?

I'm Kena. Nice to meet you.

You as well. Jagger has told me a lot about you.

"Yeah, and you're not supposed to use any of it against me," Jagger cautioned, smiling as soon as his eyes connected back with mine.

Continuing to smile at Sully, I hoped she hadn't seen my unease bridled underneath my façade. The day had been trying enough, and it was still early. Whatever was going on between Jagger and me—or *wasn't* going on between us—bothered me. Add that asshole with his comments, and I was ready to go home.

"Sully! Where are you, woman?" a man hollered, striding across the room until he came to stand behind the black-haired female. His tone indicated he'd been frustrated, but as soon as he touched her, he seemed to calm. The man was very attractive, his blue eyes quite entrancing. Unnervingly so. Circling his arms around Sully's waist, he pulled her close and kissed her neck, taking a few extra seconds before he raised his head in our direction. "Who's this?" Apparently he was a right-to-the-point kind of person.

"Kena. Jagger's girlfriend," Sully answered, instantly making me even more uncomfortable. Not so much because I didn't like the title, but I knew for sure Jagger would rebuff the statement, hammering home our odd situation for everyone.

But he never made the correction. Instead, he put his arm over my shoulder, the heat from his hand resting on my skin burning me up. I squirmed, my body suddenly engulfed with a blush I couldn't control, no matter how hard I tried. Ever since I'd met Jagger I'd started to slowly come out of my shell. His attentions for me brought out some of my hidden confidence, but being surrounded by people I didn't know, I started to revert back to my old shy self.

And it only got worse when more people filtered in.

"What do we have here?" Stone shouted as he approached, carrying a baby girl, the sight so precious . . . yet odd. It was strange to see someone like Stone, a tough-looking guy whose skin was covered in more ink than Jagger's, cradling a baby to his chest, making funny faces and noises every few seconds. I assumed the baby was his, but maybe not. Maybe he loved kids so much he snatched one up right from under an unsuspecting woman's nose. "Hi, Kena," he said, before handing the baby to Sully. I watched the interaction, Sully's expression tugging at my heartstrings, even though I didn't know her at all. But it was hard to miss the look of longing clinging to the gaze she fixated on the child.

Another female's voice cut through my thoughts, bringing my attention to someone strolling up to our newly formed group.

"Hey, babe," Stone greeted. "I think Riley needs her diaper changed." He smirked, kissing the blonde woman on the mouth quickly, but passionately.

"So you handed her to Sully?" she admonished, slapping his arm in mock annoyance. "Why didn't you just do it?"

"Because I did the last two. It's your turn."

"I'd be happy to do it," Sully interrupted, shifting the attention back to her. Watching everyone's interaction helped reduce my pang of anxiety—until they turned their attention back on me, of course.

"So . . . this must be Kena," the blonde said, stepping forward and pulling me in for a hug. She'd surprised me, but I appreciated her kindness. "I'm Adelaide. Sorry, I'm a hugger," she chuckled.

"As long as your hugs are directed only toward females, we're all good," Stone griped, the look on his handsome face showing he was riling her up.

"Don't even start," Adelaide grumbled, flipping her hair over her shoulder. Turning her focus solely on me, she asked, "So, Kena, tell me. Why is it that Jagger has kept you hidden until now?" She flicked her eyes toward the guy in question before looking back at me.

I had no idea what Jagger had told his friends and what he'd decided to keep secret, so I shrugged, not knowing how else to respond. Honestly, I'd thought Adelaide had asked a damn good question, one I was curious about myself, even if he'd given me some lame-ass reason.

"Well, she's here now," Sully shouted over her shoulder, walking down a hallway with the baby. My eyes followed her because I wasn't quite sure where else to look.

"Yes, and we're going to take full advantage," Adelaide said, smacking Jagger's arm off my shoulder only to replace it with her own. "Any woman who can get Jagger to settle down is a keeper in my book." Again I blushed, hating how much everyone kept referring to me as his girlfriend. But I wasn't about to correct all of them right then, causing more of an uncomfortable scene than necessary. I'd talk to Jagger later, begging him to tell these people we're just friends, even though the thought killed me. I wanted to be so much more, but apparently he didn't. Or did. What he'd told me conflicted with the way he'd been acting ever since we arrived earlier.

"Don't scare her, Addy," Stone said, coming to my defense and stealing his woman from my side.

"Oh shush," she muttered. "Kena, are you free tomorrow? I have to pick up something I ordered for Jagger's place, and it finally came in. I'd love to hear what you think, seeing as how you probably spend a lot of time there." Her smile was infectious, and for a few moments I allowed myself to live in a world where Jagger and I were together, and this was just one of many conversations I'd had with people who obviously cared for him.

So that's why your apartment looks so nice? She helped you decorate?

"Yes, she's the reason my place looks so good," Jagger confessed, grinning at Adelaide before turning his heart-stopping smile in my direction. All I wanted to do was throw my arms around his neck, pull him close and kiss him silly. But of course I couldn't—or wouldn't, to be more accurate.

"So are you? Free, that is?" Adelaide repeated.

What could it hurt? I nodded.

"Great, I'll get your number from Jagger and I'll text you tomorrow."

Sully re-entered the room right then, heading straight for our little circle.

"All done," she stated, passing the baby to her mother. "Well, I'm starving, so I'm going back out to grab some food." Turning toward me, Sully affectionately touched my upper arm. *It was great to meet you, Kena, and hopefully I'll see more of you. Maybe we can hang out sometime.*

Adelaide and Sully had been so nice; it was a shame I'd probably never get the chance to forge any kind of friendship with them. I feared my visits to the club were not going to be too often, today being a special occasion because of the cookout. But I told her what she wanted to hear.

I'd love that.

Once everyone had disappeared outside, I found the perfect opportunity to tell Jagger I wanted to leave. I'd loved meeting more of his friends—well, most of them—but I was tired, still reeling from all the emotions pinging back and forth inside me.

Can you take me home now?

He looked shocked. "Why? Is it because of what Breck said before? Don't pay any attention to him."

It wasn't just what he'd said. It was everything. My uncertainty about what was going on between Jagger and me, being overwhelmed with the sudden intrusion of his friends, although they were lovely, the heat, my hunger, my sudden headache. The list could go on and on, and all I wanted to do was go home and lie down. Maybe dissect Jagger's behavior toward me today.

I raised my hands to respond when a group of men entered, their laughter and shouting ensuring Jagger and I wouldn't be having any sort of conversation in front of them.

My gaze was still locked on the strangers who'd entered our space when Jagger intertwined his fingers with mine and led me down the same hallway I'd seen Sully walk down before.

He ushered me into a bedroom, closing the door and locking it behind him, the click forcing my heart into my throat. When I dared to look at him, knowing full well something was about to happen, I did my best to stay strong. The pull he had over me was palpable, desire wrapping its arms around me and urging me to fall into his embrace. To allow his mouth to claim me.

"Kena." He said my name on a groan, as if I'd been torturing him simply by being in the vicinity. Moments passed in silence, me standing in the center of the room while he remained by the door. All but a few feet separated us, yet it felt like miles. The way he looked at me confused me. His eyes devoured the very sight of me, promising me endless hours of pleasure, but his body language remained on reserve, fighting the urge to walk to me and do God only knew what. His conflictions were contagious, and I knew right then I needed to leave.

I didn't think my heart would be able to handle another letdown.

FORTY-ONE

I WANT TO GO HOME, I repeated. He took a step forward, forcing me to retreat.

"Why are you putting distance between us?"

Because you're being cruel. You're confusing me, saying one thing yet doing another. You've told me we can't be together because it's not safe, yet you take me to meet your entire club.

"I told you it's—"

I cut him off before he continued spewing his pathetic excuse.

Then you get all possessive when your buddy says something to me, although I thank you for putting that ass in his place. But still, you act like I'm yours, when in fact the opposite is true. Either be with me or don't. I can't take the back and forth, the stolen moments between us before you act like we're nothing more than friends again. We both know we're more than that, but I fear it'll be too late when you realize you let me slip through your fingers.

I witnessed his inner struggle. The frown now apparent on his face, the quick breaths to gain some sort of semblance of control, the way his hands fisted and relaxed over and over again. Finally, when I figured he'd made some sort of decision, he stalked toward me and drew me into his arms, slamming his mouth over mine before I could even think to react. To prepare myself for some sort of sexual onslaught.

Our kiss became frantic, holding on to each other as if we'd simply slip away otherwise. There were so many things I wished to say, but there was no way I wanted to pull my hands from his body. Winding my fingers into the strands of his hair, I tugged harshly, my excitement getting the better of me. He moaned, apparently more than a little turned on. The evidence of his excitement pressed against my belly, no mistaking what else he wanted to do with me.

Jagger took a step forward, forcing me back. Much like before . . . minus the space between us. He kept advancing, making me retreat until the edge of the bed stopped me. The gentle yet firm caress of his tongue made all my thoughts jumbled, halting all rationale.

I was lying on my back before I could protest, Jagger's body covering mine completely, his mouth stirring up all sorts of sordid desires. We'd only had sex once, but it was enough to know how amazing he'd felt deep inside me, throwing me into wave after wave of immense pleasure.

I certainly had my reservations, but the way he nipped my lips and swept his tongue through my mouth to taste me excited me. The way his breath mixed with mine as if we were one thrilled me.

Nothing less than exhilarating.

"I need you so much," he growled, trailing his hands down my body, slowly lifting the bottom of my shirt and ghosting his fingers over my heated skin. I squirmed beneath him, trying to dispel the effect he had on me, but it was useless.

I thought he would've moved his hands toward my breasts, giving me more time to consider the idea of stopping him, but instead he popped the button of my shorts, pulled down my zipper and tugged at the waistband of my panties. His fingers disappeared inside, running through my swollen folds all while he continued to ravage my mouth with his dominance. Slipping a finger inside me, I inhaled a sweet breath before biting his lower lip at the shock of the sudden, yet welcome, intrusion.

"Fuck!" he groaned. "You're drenched." Taking his time, he pleasured me, crooking his finger inside me and hitting that perfect spot. Widening my legs, I'd accidentally trapped him, making it so he couldn't move his hand. He chuckled before withdrawing his finger. Switching positions, he knelt at the foot of the bed, gripping my shorts and trying to drag them down my legs. But I stopped him, my hands on his persistent.

"What's the matter?"

I had to let go of him in order to respond, so I only hoped he'd allow me to answer before continuing to try and undress me.

I don't think we should do this.

"Why?"

Because I don't think it's a good idea. Given the circumstances.

"That we're at the clubhouse?" He truly looked confused.

No, not that. Well . . . yes, that. But more because of the fact that we aren't together.

"Yes we are," he stated matter-of-factly, looking at me as if I'd gone crazy.

Maybe I *was* crazy. His back and forth certainly confused the hell out of me so badly I couldn't even think straight. Had I missed something? Had we gotten back together and he hadn't told me? When he hadn't corrected the girlfriend comment from his friends, was that when it happened?

Instead of giving in, I disputed the entire concept, even though it was the last thing I wanted to do. I wanted the words he'd spoken to be the truth, but the little voice inside my head told me to stop hoping for such things.

Jagger, we're not together. You broke it off with me, remember? Then you wanted to be friends. Only friends. Until you deem it safe to bring me back into your world and out in the open. But technically, I'm not yours and you're not mine. Not in the way that counts.

Placing one hand on his chest and the other on mine, directly over our hearts, he said, "This is where it counts."

While the sentiment made me well up with a whole new batch of emotions, I knew he'd never see our situation from my point of view.

I'd planned on some elaborate speech, but all I could come up with was, *It's not enough.*

His face fell and all I wanted to do was comfort him, when in reality I was the one who had been the most affected by his decisions. It seemed that way to me, at least. While I'd witnessed his affection for me every time he looked at me, touched me, kissed me, it was *my* heart breaking every time he averted his eyes. Or withdrew his hands from me. Or broke the intoxicating connection between us by removing his lips from mine.

I'd meant to remain strong, but when Jagger rose from the bed and held his hand out to help me up, a lone tear escaped the corner of my eye. I tried to quickly wipe my sadness away before he saw. But it was too late.

"I'm so sorry, baby," he soothed, pulling me close and wrapping his strong arms around my trembling body. And it was then I allowed Jagger to witness my frailty, sobbing until I was sure I'd released every last tortured heartache. He never said another word the entire time he comforted me, simply stroking my hair and kissing the top of my head every now and again.

After what felt like forever, I managed to calm down. Pulling away from his embrace, I fastened my shorts and flattened my slightly twisted shirt.

Reaching for my hand, he said, "Come on, I'll take you home."

We re-entered the large common area when I saw Braylen and Ryder come in from outside. As soon as she saw me she rushed forward, frowning at what I was sure was my disheveled state.

"Are you okay?" She didn't even give me a chance to respond before she seized my free hand and ripped me away from Jagger, dragging me clear across the room. "What happened? Why were you crying?"

I'm fine. Really. It's just a little too much all at once. Being here with all these people. Dealing with Jagger and our feelings for each other. Not being together but being together. I don't know. I lowered my hands because I knew I wasn't making any damn sense, her drawn features proving as much.

"Men!" she exclaimed, sneaking a peek at Ryder when he wasn't looking. I'd thought for sure she would've pummeled me for information, but luckily she didn't press. "Do you wanna leave? We can veg out at home if you want." While I appreciated the offer, I knew damn well my sister didn't want to leave Ryder yet, so I let her off the hook.

Jagger is taking me home. We were actually on our way out to find you to say good-bye when you came in.

"Are you sure? Because if you don't want to go with him, I'll take you. Just say the word."

Thanks, but I'll be fine.

A swirl of activity erupted, giving Jagger and me the perfect opportunity to escape without too many questions. More so for him than me.

As I lay in bed later that evening, I dreamed of a life where Jagger and I could be together without issue. Praying someday that we'd get back together, forging ahead into what I knew would be a great life together.

Little did I know we'd have to travel through hell first.

Kena

MY PHONE DINGED, SHOVING ME away from the remaining shadows of sleep. Turning my head, I noticed my alarm clock read 10:08 a.m. Stretching my limbs before sitting up in bed, I couldn't believe I'd slept so late. Normally, I was quite the early riser. Although, ever since becoming involved with Jagger, I'd noticed all my old habits flew right out the window. The very thought of our predicament drained me, no doubt pushing my mind, as well as my body, into total exhaustion.

Hence the late hour. Or rather, it was late for me. Braylen, on the other hand, could sleep until noon if I'd let her. Swiping the screen, I saw I had a text message from an unknown number. Curiosity took hold, so I opened it and started reading.

Unknown: Did you still want to get together today?

Poised to type a response and ask who it was, my phone pinged with another message.

Unknown: BTW, this is Adelaide.

Duh! It was then I remembered she'd invited me to go shopping. But was I up for traipsing around town with a woman I'd only just met? Besides, she didn't know how to communicate with me like Sully did, so would our day be spent in silence, nodding and quick smiles filling up the uncomfortable pauses?

As if reading my mind, she'd sent another text.

Adelaide: I've sat in on the occasional lesson with Jagger, so I know a small amount of SL. Although I'm sure I'll mess something up, so please be patient with me.

Some of my nerves melted away. The people Jagger surrounded himself with seemed wonderful. Their support of him shone through, and anyone could see they genuinely cared for him.

I seriously contemplated backing out of the day's trip, but something inside nudged me to forge ahead. To get out of my comfortable little bubble and make new friends. I had a good feeling about Adelaide and knew she and I would get along well, despite the communication barrier.

Kena: I'd love to. Just tell me where to meet you.

Adelaide: Nonsense. Zip will be joining us. Only to keep an eye out, per Stone's crazy request. I hope you don't mind.

Assuming Zip was one of the members of Jagger's club, I should have listened to my instincts when she'd said he'd be joining us, wondering why he'd been asked to tag along. But I didn't.

Adelaide: I promise you won't even know he's there. Besides, if he becomes a pain, I'll just threaten him with my uncle. Fill you in on that little trick of mine when I see you. ☺

Adelaide's ease for the situation soothed me, so I typed my response right away.

Kena: Looking forward to it.

I added her name and number to my contacts and texted her my address, informing her I'd be ready in an hour.

———— ◆ ————

SLIPPING INTO THE BACK OF a red muscle car, Adelaide turned in her seat and smiled at me, the excitement on her face brightening my mood. Any hesitation I'd held slowly evaporated into thin air. The driver, however, stared at me through the rearview mirror, never cracking a grin or saying anything to either of us before pulling out onto the street.

"Don't mind him, Kena. Zip's just grumpy because he was tasked with escorting us." The guy in the driver's seat grumbled incoherently before tightening his grip on the wheel. "Besides, he knows if he doesn't lighten up, I'll tell my uncle he misbehaved." She laughed, but Zip didn't find what she'd said funny.

"You better not sic that ol' man on me," he warned, being sure to keep his tone toward her respectful.

"Ol' man? Wait until I tell him that."

"Shit!" he grunted. "Adelaide, have mercy on me. Please." He looked unsure as to whether he should take her seriously or not.

Ten minutes later, Zip pulled the car into a parking lot, shutting off the engine before turning toward his passenger. "You know the drill. Please don't get me in trouble by ditching me. You know damn well Stone will hand me my ass if you do. Never mind what Trigger will do to me." His expression was serious.

"Fine. But don't hover over us. Deal?" Adelaide reached for her door handle, staring back at Zip and waiting for him to tell her what she wanted to hear.

"Deal," he conceded.

I watched him exit the car, my reaction kept in check when I noticed the gun tucked in the waistband of his pants. The dark black weapon screamed that maybe this wasn't such a good idea. Adelaide caught me staring and assured me, "Don't even give it a second thought, Kena. All the men carry."

All the men? Did Jagger?

As if sensing my inner turmoil, she continued with, "It's just a precaution. Nothing more." Somehow I feared she wasn't being completely honest, but not knowing much about the two of them or their club, I only had her word to go on.

I was still a nervous wreck, but I tried to overshadow my thoughts by listening to Adelaide talk about how excited she was that Jagger asked for her help in decorating his place.

"You should have seen his apartment before I got my hands on it," she cringed. "There was a ratty couch and crappy TV in the living room. That's it. Can you believe it? And his bedroom was even worse, just a mattress on the floor and a single, broken-down dresser. I think the door fronts were falling off too."

I frowned thinking of Jagger living in such a place, but at least that was no longer the case. Thank God.

I'm sure he was stubborn at first, I signed.

"Did you say he was stubborn?"

I nodded, a little surprised she'd understood me.

"I know the sign for that word," she laughed. "Sully used it a lot when she was teaching him." Leading me toward a small, trendy-looking furniture store, Zip jumped ahead of us and held the door open. At least he was a gentleman, although I was sure most of the public didn't view him as such.

When he relaxed, he looked to be a little younger than me. He wasn't overly tall, probably just shy of six feet. His leather cut and baggy jeans did well to hide his thin build, but I was sure he was lethal with that gun of his. Otherwise, I doubted Stone would have asked him to watch over his woman.

Zip's dark hair was slicked back, his green eyes watching every move Adelaide and I made, while remaining at a distance which allowed us to float around the store with ease.

"Don't worry about him," she said when I glanced back at him a few more times.

Are you scared?

I had no idea why I'd asked her such a question, but my hands were gesturing before I could stop them.

"I'm not sure what you just asked me." She looked embarrassed, and I hated we couldn't talk freely. But I was aware this would happen, so I spelled out the last word, hoping she knew the alphabet.

Thankfully, she did.

"Scared? Am I scared? Is that what you're asking me?"

I nodded.

"No," she answered without hesitation. "Zip's temper is enough to scare off anyone if they rile him up. Besides, he's a good shot." She chuckled, but quickly stopped when she saw the uneasy look on my face.

Linking her arm through mine, she led me toward one of the sales associates. "You're safe, Kena. And I know there's something amiss with you and Jagger. No doubt his stubbornness," she said, bumping my shoulder with hers, "is getting in the way. But he'll come around. I've never seen him this over the moon about someone before. It'll work out. Have faith."

Have faith. Easy-enough concept. Or was it?

After Adelaide spoke with the associate, we headed back toward Zip, his nose buried in his phone as we approached.

"You almost done?" he asked.

"Yeah. They'll bring out the lamp, and then we can go." Turning her attention toward me, she asked, "Are you hungry?"

Yes.

My stomach rumbled from the mere mention of food. I hadn't eaten anything before I'd left my house, too nervous.

"I can run through a drive-thru but that's it." Zip's nose was still buried in his phone.

"No," she countered. "I want to go to the diner next door and sit down."

"Can't do it," he pushed back. "Prez wants me back as soon as possible."

"Why?"

"You know I can't tell you that." Zip and Adelaide squared off, staring at each other while I stood off to the side, not knowing what to do with myself.

After a few more tense seconds, she huffed and gave in. "Fine."

"Here you go, miss," a man said, handing Adelaide the most beautiful lamp I'd ever seen. I knew it was only a lighting fixture, but it was gorgeous. The top part was a sphere, etched lines of colors swirling around its entirety. A curved spine connected with the base, dark, thick wood making up the rest of the piece. Jagger made the right move in asking his friend to help decorate his place. She certainly had an eye for design.

We decided to skip the drive-thru, Adelaide offering to whip us up something back at the clubhouse before taking me home. I wasn't sure who would give me a ride, however, seeing as how Zip had been the one driving. But I knew they wouldn't leave me stranded, so I didn't give it another thought.

Adelaide had chosen to sit in the back with me, chatting away about various topics, her daughter most of all. I smiled, nodded and listened intently, thoroughly enjoying our day together.

"I'm going to have Sully teach me sign language just like she did Jagger. I have a feeling you're going to be sticking around for quite a while." Her enthusiasm for my place in Jagger's life tugged at my heart. I had no clue if what she spoke was the truth or not, but I loved the idea.

I continued smiling at her when all of a sudden we were both thrust back into our seats, Zip having picked up considerable speed.

"What the hell?" Adelaide grumbled, clutching the door for support. "Slow the hell down!" she shouted.

"Fuck!" he yelled in response. He grabbed his phone before shouting, "Put your seat belts on. Now!"

Reaching for my restraint, I buckled it into place while having no idea what was going on. Adelaide had done the same, Zip speaking again right after the click of her belt sounded.

"Someone's followin' us. Hold on while I try to lose 'em."

I never had time to look and see who was behind us.

To ask Adelaide a question.

To contemplate whether or not my life was in danger.

To wonder if I'd see Jagger again.

To think anything at all.

Another vehicle slammed into us from behind, sending us careening into the opposite lane. Closing my eyes and holding my breath, all I heard were screeching tires at first. Then it was as if we'd been thrown into the air, the car tumbling down the highway, rolling over and over until we'd finally halted, skidding to a stop with the roof of the car beneath us.

Everything had happened so fast, I barely had the opportunity to dissect our predicament when I heard heavy, booted footsteps running toward us. Mumbled voices shouted to each other.

Had someone come to help?

My head throbbed as soon as I pried my eyes open, my vision blurry when I looked around the inside of the car. Broken glass was everywhere, so I was careful where I placed my hands when trying to support my weight upside down. Turning my head to my left, I saw that Adelaide was awake, taking in the scene just as I was, but the look on her face was more alert than mine. I couldn't see Zip, but I heard him groaning, no doubt hurt from the accident.

It was an accident, wasn't it?

Or did someone purposely run us off the road?

Before I could allow my brain to contemplate whether or not that was true, I heard people just outside the car. Then I heard the driver's side door open, the metal screaming with every pull. At first I thought the men who'd approached were there to help, but the thought was quickly doused when I heard someone say, "Kill him then grab those two."

My heart skidded to a stop when I saw two arms reach inside the car and drag Zip from his seat, flinging him into the road with no regard as to whether or not he'd been hurt. Then I remembered what had just been said.

From my position in the back of the car, I saw Zip roll onto his side and reach behind him. He was going for his gun, but before he pulled it free, a deafening, soul-piercing shot rang out.

His arm fell awkwardly behind him, his lifeless body kicked onto its back, pinning his limb beneath him. A river of blood seeped from his head and coated the concrete. I would've screamed right then if I'd had a voice. Instead I started to cry, my fear of being shot like an animal in the street so overwhelming I could do nothing but release my terror in the form of tears.

"Oh my God! Oh my God!" was all I heard Adelaide cry. She was just as terrified, but neither of us had time to comfort the other with false promises before both of our doors were ripped open, the same ear-piercing sounds of metal being jarred away from the frame of the car.

Two men clad in leather and smelling like alcohol and smoke leaned inside and freed us from our seat belts. Grabbing us underneath our arms, they roughly yanked us from the car. With whatever strength I had, I started to flail about, figuring there had to be other people surrounding our accident.

Someone besides these cold-blooded killers.

But I never had the chance to see before I was struck on the head, darkness stealing my hazy sight.

FORTY-THREE

Jagger

SO MUCH COMMOTION STOLE MY focus. Various screams and shouts blocked my chance to concentrate on any one man or the enraged words they spewed amongst each other.

Having no idea what had happened, I braced myself for the worst, but nothing could have prepared me for what happened next. I had no idea my world was about to be flipped on its goddamn ass. That my heart would be ripped from my chest and sliced into such tiny pieces there was no possible way it'd ever be whole again.

Gathered around the table in Chambers, every man stopped their rantings when a phone rang. I looked around the room, trying to decipher where the noise had originated from. When I glanced toward Marek, I saw the small device in his hand.

A look of rage mixed with fear shadowed his hardened features.

After pressing the Answer button, silence ensued.

Until a harsh voice destroyed the quiet, tearing our world apart.

Our leader had put the cell on speaker, allowing all of us to hear the caller. Which should have been the first thing to alarm me, but I was too focused on trying to figure out why every brother beside me looked like they wanted to kill.

"After all this time, did you really think I'd just let it go? Let you take my daughter without retribution?"

Oh shit! Psych!

I leaned as close as I could, making sure I didn't miss a single word. At least now I had one piece to the puzzle, but I was still confused as to what was going on.

"What do you want?" Marek asked in a slow and dangerous voice. The muscles in his neck strained, and I knew as soon as this call ended he'd let loose and explode for all of us to see. Focusing on Stone next, I saw that he'd mirrored his friend's body language. He was also enraged, but there was something about his expression that unnerved me to my very core. The fear that bound him frightened me, a shiver racing through me at what was going to be revealed in the next few seconds.

"I want Sully. You give her to me and I'll give you back the two bitches we rescued on the highway." He said the word "rescued'" slowly, telling us with the inflection of his tone that he'd done the opposite. Whoever he'd "rescued," he'd kidnapped. No doubt about that.

"And what about Zip?" Marek growled.

What the fuck happened to Zip, and who are the two "bitches" he's referring to? With everything going on, I hadn't even noticed Zip was missing from the room.

"He's dead. My men left him in the middle of the road." Psych spoke so matter-of-fact it was as if he'd been talking about a car that'd broken down on the side of the highway.

Marek slammed his hand down on the table, the thunderous sound vibrating throughout the room. Dread pulsed through my veins, and it was all I could do not to rush from the room to retrieve our fallen brother.

"Mark my words, you soulless fuck. My face will be the last you'll see before I rip your fucking heart from your chest," our leader threatened, pounding the table a few more times for emphasis. Stone leaned back in his chair and ran his hands over his face, terror seizing his expression while waiting for Psych to speak again.

"Mark *my* words, *Marek*," Psych taunted, "I'll fuck your VP's woman until she bleeds. Until she begs for death. Then I'll move on to her little friend. Although I don't think that one can speak, so that'll be a whole lotta fun."

Stone kicked his seat behind him when he suddenly jumped to his feet. "Don't you fucking touch her!" he yelled, whirling around and punching his fist through the wall. The sound jerked me out of my daze. It'd taken my brain a few seconds to catch up to what was going on, my denial surely trying to protect me.

But when Stone's eyes latched onto mine, when he watched as Psych's words slowly registered, I knew this shit was for real. I froze in place, unable to move. The breath in my lungs stilled as I fought back the vomit creeping up my throat.

"GIMME BACK MY DAUGHTER!" Psych roared through the phone, gutting everyone in the room. The hair on the back of my neck stood up, and I knew right then there was a very real possibility I'd never see Kena alive again.

Would Marek give up his wife in exchange for Adelaide and Kena?

Did he even have a choice?

If he didn't comply, he'd ensure their deaths for sure. And while he might not lose too much sleep over Kena's, I was sure he would torture himself over Adelaide's demise.

His best friend's woman.

Trigger's niece.

Before Marek could deny the demand, Stone stole the phone from the table and answered. "When and where?" Three simple words, but when put together, they meant a shift in everything we'd ever known.

Marek jumped from his chair the same time I had. In fact, all of the men were on their feet, realizing something was about to go down right here inside Chambers. Volatile looks and controlled fury threatened to annihilate anyone daring to move the wrong way, or say the wrong thing. And it wasn't just from Marek or Stone. It was from Tripp. And Ryder. And Hawke. And Trigger. And Cutter. And Breck.

And me.

Before one of us went nuclear, a noise erupted from the other end of the line, silencing the rage we'd all felt by replacing the emotion with stifling dread.

Screams.

Haunted screams.

A woman's screams.

Adelaide's screams.

"Don't you fuckin' touch her!" Stone thundered again, punching the wall behind him once more in his haste to expel some of his fury.

"She sure is a looker, Crosswell. I bet her pussy's real nice." Psych's eerie laughter made us all cringe, the idea that he'd violate his captives a very real possibility. If he hadn't done so already.

Thoughts of Kena rushed over me. I tried to keep it together, do my part in whatever needed to happen before allowing myself to feel the mixed bag of emotions threatening my sanity. But the flood of rage, despair and heartache took hold and I feared I'd never be the same again.

"I'll call back with the information. Oh, and boys, don't even think about pulling a fast one. If I get a whiff you're up to something, I'll gut them both like the whores they are."

Psych ended the call, and as soon as the silence creeped in, the entire room exploded into chaos.

FORTY-FOUR

Kena

HUDDLED IN THE CORNER OF a dank, musty room, I clutched my knees to my chest for solace. I had no idea where I was or who had taken us, too terrified of the possibilities of what could happen to properly think straight.

Clutching my hands to my head, I tried to soothe the thunderous pounding between my temples, but nothing I did helped. I'd cried enough over the past few hours to last me a lifetime, so I'd eventually stopped. Whether that was because I'd willed myself to do so or because my body had finally depleted the emotion, I couldn't say.

The door creaked open and someone stepped inside. But I couldn't look. If I saw who it was, then this was all too real. I buried my head deeper into my hands, my elbows coming together while my fingers touched at the base of my spine. But no matter how much I shielded my sight, my ears continued to prick at every noise.

"Get up," the rough voice demanded, stepping closer when I didn't budge. A strong grip wrapped around my wrist, hauling me to my feet. He started to walk toward the door, and something told me to fight. I had no idea where he intended to take me but I knew it wasn't somewhere safe. All I had was my struggle, so I allowed it to pour from me in waves.

I jerked my arm back the best I could, but it was ineffectual. The large man standing in front of me looked pissed off. And scary. His face was shadowed with a heavy beard, his dark hair cropped close to his head. If I hadn't known any better, I would've thought he had been in the military at some point in his life, the haircut very similar to those of Marines. But I knew from one look into his dark eyes that he had done no such thing. There was nothing honorable about him.

He yanked me forward. "No use resisting. Prez wants a test drive." No remorse. No concern or amusement in his tone. Dead. He was empty inside, alarming me even more than I had been before. "Says the other one is too much trouble."

My thoughts flew to Adelaide. I hadn't seen her since the accident— or rather, the intentional car crash. When I came to, she was gone. I'd thought I'd heard her screams, but tried to convince myself I'd been hallucinating. My denial served as self-preservation, but right now this man was shattering it to pieces.

Again I tried to resist, but that time it only served to anger him, delivering a backhand so harsh my head whipped to the side and I stumbled backward. I hadn't fallen, though, his hold on my arm too fierce to allow a slap to break the connection.

I whimpered.

I cried.

But of course he heard none of it.

"Tough little cunt, aren't ya?" he laughed, pulling me out of the room and down a narrow hallway. "Maybe when Psych's done wit' ya, he'll let me go a round. I like a bitch who resists."

I may have been inexperienced before Jagger, but I was smart enough to know exactly what he'd been referring to. I steeled my reserve the best I could, covering my cheek with my free hand to help stop the blossoming ache. I'd never been struck before, the radiating pain becoming worse and worse with each step I was forced to take. Licking my lip, I tasted blood. But at least the pain served as a distraction, blocking me from thinking about what was going to happen next.

We stopped outside a steel door. I tried to free myself from his grasp again, but to no avail. He knocked three times before the door swung open, an intimidating man appearing on the other side. As soon as he looked past my captor, he grinned, raking his eyes over me from head to toe. I cursed my earlier decision to wear a dress that day, wishing I'd thrown on some jeans instead. But how was I to know the car I'd be in would be run off the road, the driver would be killed and I'd be one of two people kidnapped?

Oh my God! Guilt tore at me that I hadn't thought of him before now.

Zip.

I can't believe they killed him.

Right in front of us.

I didn't know the guy, that was true enough, but he seemed to be friendly with Adelaide. Plus, he was a member of the Knights Corruption, and therefore someone of importance to Jagger, as well as the other men of the club.

Jagger. Oh my God! Did he even know we'd been taken?

Had our kidnappers made contact?

Was it even about the club?

Or were we going to be sold into slavery? I'd seen my share of documentaries before. Sexual slavery happened all over the world, even in America. The thought I'd be sold to strangers for nothing more than pleasure heightened my terror.

"Bring her in," a gruff voice called out. Passing by the man who'd answered the door, I was thrust toward another standing in the middle of the room. The guy in charge, I assumed. He was older, probably somewhere in his late forties. Maybe even early fifties. Haggard lines had stolen the remnants of whatever youth he'd had, the signs of a hard life certainly lived. His dark, shoulder-length hair greyed at the temples, the strands shaggy and unkempt. He licked his thin lips while assessing my body, inhaling the air around me as he advanced closer.

"You smell nice," he said, his compliment certainly a lecherous one. I averted my eyes, quickly taking in the room. I noticed a worn, stained mattress in the corner, an unconscious Adelaide lying across it. Her hair was matted with blood, either from the accident or from whatever she'd endured at the hands of these men. Only one side of her face was visible. And from what I could see, they'd beaten her. But had they done something worse? The man who'd brought me here indicated they hadn't, but I didn't know if that was the truth or not. I prayed it was.

"Can you hear me?" he asked, reaching out to touch my breast like he had every right to violate me. I shouldn't have done it, but I couldn't stop my body's reaction, slapping him across the face the second his hand fell away.

The man behind me grabbed my hair and yanked me back, slamming me into his hard chest. "You're gonna pay for that," he seethed, shoving me toward the man I'd just assaulted.

The older man tilted his head, running his fingers over his cheek, a redness starting to appear from where I'd struck him. He grinned, as if he'd found what I'd done amusing. "Now, let's try this again," he sneered. "My men tell me you haven't uttered a sound since they found you."

My eyes must have bulged out of my head. Found me? What a warped sense of reality he possessed. "Can you hear me?" he repeated through clenched teeth.

I nodded.

"Good. Then you'll understand when I tell you that you and that bitch over there are being traded for my daughter. But that doesn't mean I can't have some fun with you until then."

Vigorously shaking my head, I raised my hands in front of me even though I knew he'd never understand me.

Jagger will kill you if you touch me.

"Put your hands down," he growled. "I don't understand retard, so save it." His insult shouldn't have hurt, not in the least considering what type of man he was, but it did. Turning his attention to the man behind me, and the other standing near the door, he waved them off with a flick of his wrist. "You can leave us now. Make sure to keep an eye out. Just in case the Knights try some slick shit. For all I know, these two have trackers on them."

"You got it, Prez." The clank of the closing door made me jump, my fright amusing this horrid man I was now alone with. Well, technically Adelaide was also there, but the poor woman was still unconscious. I pushed the thought away that she could be dead. He'd just said we were being traded for his daughter, so would he be stupid enough to kill one of us? And who was his daughter?

"Do you have a tracker on you?" I shook my head, but he stalked toward me anyway. "I don't think I believe you," he taunted. "Looks like I'm gonna have to check for myself." A few more steps and he'd backed me against the wall. Trapped. Nowhere to go. I was at his mercy and we both knew it.

I tried to make a run for the door, but he caught me mid-stride, wrapping his hand around my throat and squeezing. I clawed at his hold but it was useless. "Nice try, but you're not goin' anywhere until I say so. But I can let you in on a little secret." He licked the side of my face, his rancid breath making me instantly sick. "No one is gettin' out of here alive except me and my men. When your precious little boyfriend comes for you, along with his buddies, we're gonna slaughter them all."

Surprised he was able to read my mind so well, or rather the look on my face, he spoke again, his rough voice no doubt the product of too many years of smoking. "Yeah, I know who you are, sweetheart. You're the fighter's woman. Since I couldn't snatch back my daughter, I grabbed the next best thing. Stone's woman. You just happened to be with her. Two cunts for the price of one," he laughed, the evil sound strangling the hope out of me.

Snaking his free hand down my body, he hoisted the hem of my dress, trailing his fingers up my inner leg until he reached the apex of my thighs. I tried to squirm away from his touch, but he only tightened his grip on my throat. Moving my panties to the side, he shoved a finger inside me. I winced, the burn of his intrusion rocketing through me. I closed my eyes to block him from sight, needing the shield of darkness to help my brain flit off to somewhere else. But it was useless.

"Nope, no tracker up there. How about your sweet little ass?" My eyes flew open when his hand trailed toward my backside. Before he could enter me there, his attention was drawn to the other side of the room.

"Leave her a . . . lone, you bas . . . tard," Adelaide croaked out, her voice raw and throaty.

"Well, well. Look who decided to join the party." He released his hand from around my throat and propelled me toward Adelaide. "Go join your friend while we wait."

I thought for sure he was going to do something to one or the both of us while we waited for the men to show up, but he didn't. He walked from the room and left us to ponder our future.

Or lack thereof.

FORTY-FIVE

Jagger

"THERE'S NO WAY IN HELL I'm letting Sully go!" Marek shouted, pacing back and forth like a caged animal. His head whipped up every few seconds to look at his VP. His best friend.

"So you're gonna let Addy and Kena die? Is that it?" Stone yelled back, doing a bit of his own pacing.

I was torn. I wanted to shout at Marek to listen to Stone and allow Sully to be traded for the lives of our women, but then I didn't want Sully to come to any harm either. I could only imagine the torture he grappled with; I had no idea what I'd do if I were in his shoes. My initial answer would be the same, but would I eventually come around and devise a plan that would enable me to save my woman, along with the other two?

My thoughts turned to Kena, my heart breaking at the thought they were touching her. Hurting her. I knew I should have never brought her into my life, but I'd been a selfish prick, wanting her up close and personal. Then shit went down with Edana, and it was enough to wake me up. But it'd been too late. I wondered if I hadn't allowed her to go with Adelaide, if she would be at home safe and sound right now.

But she never would've allowed me to get away with forbidding her from accompanying Adelaide, nor would Stone's woman tolerate such pigheadedness from me.

I should've left Kena alone after coming to her rescue the first night I met her. My decisions would forever haunt me, but now was not the time to focus on such things. I had to do my part in the planning of what we were going to do next.

"I don't know what to do, Stone, but I sure as fuck am not handing my wife over to her father. He'll kill her and you know it."

"Well, he'll kill Addy and Kena if you don't," Stone countered, his face red with bridled rage.

"Fuck!" Marek roared, throwing his chair against the wall, his predicament weighing on all of us. The rest of the men sat in silence, waiting for orders. We were all ready and willing to act at a moment's notice.

A soft knock rapped against the large wooden door, our heads whirling toward the sound. Since I was closest, I rose from my seat and turned the handle. Sully stood in the doorway, her eyes red and puffy, indicating she'd been crying. I hadn't even realized she was there. When I'd been called in, I knew it was an emergency but I had no idea what had happened. I'd later come to find out Zip had managed to call Hawke, allowing him to hear everything that had transpired after he'd been dragged from his car. Marek must have brought his wife to the only place he knew was safe. The gates were locked and armed, so there was no fear of someone sneaking in while we were held up in Chambers.

Marek attempted to block Sully from entering but she shoved past him. No women were allowed in here, but no one said a damn word, realizing the circumstances warranted a bit of leeway.

"Baby," Marek soothed, "what do you need?"

"You need to take me to him, Cole," she said, preparing herself for one hell of an argument.

He looked shocked that she not only knew what we'd been discussing, but that she'd offer to go back to her father. The man who'd raped and beaten her throughout her life. The man who'd passed her off to Vex and who'd so freely given her to Yanez.

"Never," he growled. "I'll never let him get his hands on you ever again." When he saw the look on his wife's face, he pleaded with her instead. "Don't ask me to do that, Sully. I can't. Please," he practically begged, a trait none of us were used to.

"He won't kill me." For her to even speak those words about her own kin made my blood run cold. It spoke to the true evil of her father. Shit, he was worse than my old man, which was saying a lot.

"He will and you know it. Maybe not right away, but he'll end your life as surely as you stand before me." He shook his head. "No, forget it. It's not happening."

"Then I'll leave you," she warned, standing tall with her head held high. She never took her eyes from her husband, challenging him to comply before things got out of hand.

"What?" he asked, astonished she'd threatened such a thing. Grabbing her before she could retreat, he pulled her close, his face mere inches from hers. "What the fuck did you just say?"

Sully never flinched. "I'll leave you if you don't let me go. I'm the key to saving both of them, and I can't sit by and do nothing. If my father wants me, then make the trade. He won't do anything. I promise. He'd rather keep me alive and torment me than end my life. Besides, I can endure him again until you come for me, because I now know what love is." She placed her hands on either side of his face and kissed him gently. "You've saved me, in every way possible, and it's you I'll think of when things get tough. But I'll survive. I promise. Just come for me soon, okay?" She smiled, but it quickly faded.

"I can't do it," he repeated, resting his forehead against hers. At some point, Stone had approached his friend from behind. He placed his hand on Marek's shoulder, but his touch was quickly dislodged. "Don't fuckin' touch me," he barked, never breaking away from his wife.

"Don't be mad at him, Cole. Wouldn't you ask the same of him if the roles were reversed?" Marek never responded, but we all knew his answer would've been yes.

"So either way I lose you."

"But if you trade me, you'll get me back. The time frame just depends on you."

"Fine," he conceded before releasing her. "But you're coming back with us right along with Adelaide and Kena." Grasping his wife's hands, he pulled her toward his seat at the head of the table. "Now we wait for him to call back with instructions."

AN HOUR LATER WE TRAVELED north toward Modesto. The place we were to make the exchange was an old abandoned warehouse, a building so dilapidated I was shocked it hadn't been torn down yet. What Psych hadn't realized was that I knew the place well. I'd fought there quite a few times, finding hidden back entryways into the building for the sole purpose of avoiding all the hoopla that went along with the fights. All I wanted to do when I battled was get in, win, collect my money and get the hell out.

No doubt Psych would have half his fucking club waiting to ambush us, but we had a plan of our own. Stone and I sat in the front of his truck,

Marek and Sully huddled in the back, capturing their last fleeting moments before she was handed over.

Marek had placed a call to Salzar, the head of our Laredo chapter, as soon as he'd heard about the kidnapping. And again when Psych had given him the directions to the warehouse. So we had men hiding out everywhere, waiting for orders to attack. Some were hidden around the warehouse we were headed, some were back manning our compound, and others had been dispatched to hide out near the Reapers' compound and wait for instructions.

Stone turned down an unpaved path, the warehouse about half a mile down the road. My heart sped up, fear and adrenaline fueling the erratic thumping. What if something went wrong and Psych killed Adelaide and Kena anyway? Were they even still alive? Stone had asked to speak to his woman when the Reapers' president called back a second time, to which he heard Adelaide screaming, but that was a while ago. A lot could have transpired since then.

As we approached the building, the garage started to open, two men standing guard just inside and guiding us through. Both Reapers were armed, their weaponry strapped across their chest, probably not the only ones they had on their bodies. Coming to a stop a few feet after entering, our doors were yanked open and three additional men appeared, extracting us from the vehicle and shoving us forward, but only after patting us down and stealing our weapons. The entire way, Marek had his arms wrapped tightly around Sully, protecting her as best he could with Psych's men crowding them.

We were ushered through a narrow hallway, down two flights of steps and around a few corners. It would've been easy to get lost, which was probably why Psych chose that place in particular. It was enormous, and anyone inside was like a rat in a maze. Unless you knew your way around, of course. Which I did.

Eventually, we came to a stop, one of the men knocking three times on a large steel door. It opened right away and none other than the president of the Savage Reapers stood before us, grinning like he was privy to the biggest fucking secret.

Little did he know *we* were the ones who held the secret.

"Come in," he said, stepping back and allowing us to enter. The room was huge, but my eyes instantly found Kena. She was crouching in the far corner, hovering over Adelaide's body, when she saw us. The look on her face gutted me, and I'd never forgive myself for putting her in danger. Stone had seen them at the same time I had. Both of us moved to rush forward but we were shoved back, guns pointed directly at our heads. "Don't fucking move until I tell you to," Psych warned.

"Adelaide!" Stone shouted. "Is she okay?" His voice became frenzied when he couldn't get to her. Sully buried herself in Marek's embrace the entire time, clutching on to him knowing she would have to stand next to her father soon enough.

She's unconscious, Kena signed.

"What did she say?"

"She said she's unconscious," I translated.

Turning his fury toward Psych, Stone shouted, "What the fuck did you do to her?"

"Your woman has a mouth on her." That's all he said, but we were smart enough to fill in the blanks. The gun pointed at Stone's head wouldn't have stopped him from attacking Psych, but the fear Adelaide would be killed in the struggle somehow was the only thing that stopped him from crushing the Reapers' leader. I knew because it was the only reason I hadn't rushed him either.

Leering at his daughter, Psych motioned her closer. "Come here, Sully." She withdrew from Marek and stood straight. After a single step, her husband stopped her.

"Not until you release them."

"Well," Psych huffed, then turned to Stone. "Seeing as how your bitch is out cold, how do you think that's gonna happen?"

"Then let Kena come over," I interjected, desperately needing to touch her. Protect her.

I'm not leaving her, Jagger.

"This isn't up for debate," I responded, pissed she was putting herself in more danger by not listening to me.

She shook her head, refusing to budge.

"Kena!" I shouted, taking a single step forward only to be shoved back once more, the same gun now pressing into my forehead. Kena's hands flew to her mouth, but she finally listened and rose to her feet. When she tucked her hair behind her ear in nervousness, I saw the side of her face was swollen, her lip cut and bleeding.

"Come now," Psych demanded, his patience nonexistent the longer his daughter kept him waiting. Marek leaned in close and whispered in

Sully's ear before reluctantly releasing her. Both women walked at the same speed, Kena coming to stand next to me as Sully reached her father.

While I welcomed Kena into my arms, careful not to explode and kill every motherfucker present because someone had hurt her, Psych's reaction to his daughter was the exact opposite.

"You know you'll be punished for consorting with them, don't you? You married the president, for fuck's sake," he said, his anger on a slow simmer. "You disgust me."

Sully never said a word, waiting to see what he would do next.

We all were.

Then it happened so fast, none of us saw it coming. Psych clenched his fist, raised his hand and punched his daughter, the slam to the side of her face sending her crashing to the floor. Her hand flew to her cheek to hide the damage as she crawled toward the wall. Unfortunately, I knew some of the abuses Sully had suffered at the hands of her father, and this wasn't the first time he'd struck her. She knew what she was agreeing to when she'd insisted Marek trade her for the lives of the two other women. Observing her abuse firsthand, however, was entirely different than hearing about it, and if I ever got the opportunity to repay him for what he'd just made me witness, I would. And I'd take every bit of pleasure I could squeeze from it.

"You're gonna pay for that!" Marek roared, quite possibly shedding the last of his sanity right before our eyes.

"Don't," Sully squeaked, raising her hand to warn Marek not to retaliate.

"Yeah, don't," Psych mocked, the evil smirk on his face making me wish I could kill him where he stood. But all in due time. "You know I never intended to let you leave, right? Any of you. Our clubs' war will end tonight, retribution for everything you've done to us, mainly cutting off our supply with Los Zappas. That one really hurt," he said, scratching the top of his head as a deranged look took hold.

His men flanked us, promises of our ultimate demise drifting in the air. Before anyone made good on any threats, though, gunfire was heard faintly in the distance, pulling us all back into the severity of the situation. Not that we hadn't resided there to begin with. Swinging his eyes toward Marek, our prez shocked the fucker when he announced, "And you know you're not walking out of here either, right?"

Psych laughed.

He actually laughed, making me believe he'd truly earned his road name. He was definitely psychotic, teetering on the line between reality and madness.

"I knew you'd bring all your men with you," Psych said. "That's why I sent my men to your compound. So even if you made it outta here alive, you'll have nothing to go back to." The leader of the Reapers grinned, thinking he'd bested us. Yet again. When would he ever learn?

"Seems as if we anticipated each other's moves."

Psych's brows knit tightly together.

"What does that mean?" he asked, glaring at Marek with intent to do him harm very soon.

"It means your compound is already in ruins. So, if by the grace of God, *you* somehow get outta here alive, you'll have to run and hide because you'll have nothing to return to. No shelter."

Both men locked eyes, their fierce intentions battling the other for dominance. Little did Psych know we would be the victorious ones. We'd always win when it came to them. They may have bested us here and there, attacking our brothers and now our women, but in the end it would be their club that would perish into dust. Not ours.

From the look on Psych's face, the time for talking was over. The gunfire we'd heard in the distance had breached the warehouse's walls. There were men yelling, their words still muffled enough we couldn't make out what they were saying, but we all heard the urgency in their tones.

Someone pounded repeatedly on the other side of the door. I wasn't sure if they wanted to get inside, or wanted someone on our side to come out. It could've been one of our men, or one of Psych's. Either way, we weren't to open that door until the situation had been handled.

By handled, I meant the men holding us hostage no longer had breath in their lungs, and Psych was shackled, ready to be transported back with us.

The plan was to keep him alive long enough for Marek to make him pay for everything he'd ever done to us, but more importantly everything he'd ever done to Sully. The latter taking precedence.

My eyes stayed glued to Psych. All it would take would be a nod, or a wink, or a flick of his wrist to tell his men to pull their triggers.

All of us remained stock still.

We had a plan.

All we had to do was wait to make our move.

FORTY-SIX

Kena

MY EYES FLITTED FROM ADELAIDE'S unconscious form, to Jagger, who continued to stand close to me, to the man who'd orchestrated our kidnapping. I briefly glanced at Stone, Marek and Sully as well, struggling with the belief that she was related to that madman.

It wasn't until I was taken that I fully realized Jagger's hesitation to be with me. I had no idea. How could I? My world before him had been all butterflies and roses compared to the way he lived. While I believed the men of his club to be good people, they'd obviously been involved in things which put their lives and their families' lives in jeopardy. I felt horrible for giving him such a hard time about us, never in a million years seeing things from his perspective. But again, I didn't know any of this danger existed, another facet he'd tried to protect me from.

Jagger's hand brushed against mine, pulling me back from my drifting thoughts. My eyes connected with his and I saw his warning. It was quick and subtle, but because I'd grown up honing my ability to read people's body language, I instantly knew he was telling me to get down with a simple flick of his eyes toward the ground.

One moment there was an unsettling silence inside the room, all of us waiting to see what would transpire in the seconds ahead.

And the next there was complete anarchy.

"Now, Sully!" Marek shouted. At the same time his voice rang out, Jagger shoved me toward the corner before swiftly ducking away from the gun pointed at his head. He swept his leg out and the man standing closest to him lost his footing, his arms flailing, dropping his gun in the process. The weapon skidded across the floor and stopped in front of me, but instead of picking it up, I kicked it back toward Jagger. Thankfully he'd been able to retrieve it before one of the other men saw the exchange. Marek and Stone had been able to disarm their men as well, their opponents no match against their fighting skills.

When I looked toward the opposite side of the room, I saw Psych on the ground, clutching his upper thigh. From my position, I couldn't see anything other than he was still alive and looked to be in tremendous pain.

My eyes darted back toward Jagger, watching him stand over the man he'd disarmed. Without looking at me, he said, "Kena, look away. Now!" The urgency in his tone was enough to make me shut my eyes and bury my head in my hands.

A gunshot rang out, the thunderous sound making me jump. Two more shots sounded, and I knew all three previously armed men were dead.

"Are you okay?" Jagger asked, crouching next to me and pulling my hands from my face. "Look at me, baby. It's okay." When I finally pried my eyes open, I saw blood spattered on his face, hands and clothes, the result of shooting someone at close range. But fear didn't shake me; gratitude that he'd survived did. Tears poured from my eyes as I swung my arms around his neck and pulled him impossibly close.

Jagger helped me find my footing, kissing me as he removed my hands from around him. "I'll be right back." I nodded my understanding before he walked toward Marek and Sully.

Stone had run to Adelaide as soon as the threat had been eradicated, bending down to gather her in his arms. Stopping next to his brothers, he'd demanded they leave immediately because he was worried about her still-unconscious state.

Marek turned toward Jagger. "Can you get them outta here?"

"Yes," he simply answered.

"I'm not going anywhere without you," Sully cried, throwing herself into her husband's arms. "I can't . . . I won't survive if something happens to you."

"Nothin' will happen to me," he reassured, lifting her chin so he could look into her eyes. The love between them was palpable, and I felt like an intruder watching their interaction, but I couldn't look away. With everything that had just happened, I clung to the love they shared, allowing it to fuel my strength to survive. To get out of here alive and forge ahead with Jagger once more. If he'd have me. What happened may have solidified his need to stay away from me, but I simply wouldn't know until after we got ourselves away from this place.

Clasping my hand, a gun in his other, Jagger pulled me toward everyone else. "Follow close behind me. I'll take you the back way." Looking toward Marek, he said, "Once I get them out of here, I'll call Salzar. He should be close by." No one said another word as Jagger cautiously opened the door, peering into the hallway to see if it was safe for us to leave.

We followed him down multiple winding passages, stopping every hundred feet or so and waiting for the threat of armed men to pass. Luckily the lighting inside the building was dim, some areas left in complete darkness. After hiding out in one of the numerous rooms, Jagger deemed it safe to continue on. Finally, after walking up two flights of stairs and down a few more narrow hallways, Jagger led us into an area which looked like a dead end.

"Are you sure you know where you're going?" Stone whisper-shouted from behind me.

"Yeah. The back exit is just up ahead."

Sure enough, after a few more feet we came upon an old run-down-looking exit. Jagger withdrew his hand from mine and passed me the gun while he pried the weather-beaten door open, the squeak of the metal hinges sounding much louder in the quiet space.

"Hurry up, man," Stone grunted, shifting Adelaide's weight in his arms.

Flinging the door the rest of the way open, Jagger walked ahead of us. "Hold on a sec. I wanna make sure no one is waiting to ambush us outside." He disappeared and my heart leapt inside my chest. Fear of the unknown fueled the tremor of my hands. I could barely catch my breath when Jagger popped his head back in, giving me a half smile before reaching for my hand once again. "Come on. All clear."

Sully walked close behind me, followed by Stone carrying Adelaide. We trudged through an open field for what felt like miles, but it probably only seemed so long because I was utterly exhausted. Mentally as well as physically.

Jagger shoved his gun into his waistband, reached around me and held out his free hand to Sully. She clasped on to him without hesitation. I suspected she and Jagger were close, and I couldn't have been happier he was looking out for her. Witnessing the brief encounter between her and her father told me she'd endured horrible abuse at his hands. I saw the fear in her eyes when she'd stood next to him, the complacent acceptance when he'd hit her, as if she were not only expecting his backlash, but was used to it.

We eventually came across a clearing, jogging the rest of the way, conscious of Stone having to carry Adelaide. Otherwise we would've run as fast as we could just to put that much more distance between us and the place where we could've spent our last moments.

My ears pricked when I heard a whistle off in the distance. I squeezed Jagger's hand. "Don't worry. That's for us." And sure enough, just a few more yards ahead, there was a large SUV waiting, men jumping out and surrounding us. I didn't recognize anyone besides the guy who'd insulted me at the cookout, and Ryder.

Filing into the vehicle, Sully and I huddled close together while Stone continued to cradle Adelaide in his arms, the worried look on his face increasing the longer it took her to wake. She'd flitted in and out of awareness the entire time she and I were held captive in that room. My only guess was that they must have hit her in the head at some point.

"Gimme a phone," Jagger demanded, holding his hand out to Ryder. Walking in front of the truck, he blocked out some of the illumination from the headlights. Returning moments later, he came around my side and leaned in, clasping my hand. "Kena," he started, the tense flick of his jaw preparing me for what he had to say. "Wait for me back at the clubhouse. You'll be safe there."

Instantly I tried to snatch back my hand. I vigorously shook my head, trying yet again to tug my hand from his. But he wouldn't let go.

"Go. I promise I'll meet you there. I have to help Marek." He released me. Bringing his fist to his chest, he rubbed it in a circle. *I'm sorry.* Then he did something completely unexpected. Unclenching his fisted hand, he held up his thumb, index finger and pinky, the two remaining fingers bent forward.

I love you.

I sobbed, clutching the area over my heart to help ease my despair. It didn't work. Sully comforted me the entire way back, offering as much support as she could. Her husband had also chosen to remain behind, and I couldn't help but wonder if either of us would see the men we loved alive again.

EPILOGUE

Jagger

LEANING BACK IN MY CHAIR, my hands folded on top of the table, I wanted to be engaged in the conversation but I was too distracted. Looking around Chambers, my eyes stilled on the vacant seat diagonal from me.

Zip's chair.

He was a good guy. Occasionally a little hot under the collar, but his anger was often fueled by his need to make the Reapers pay whenever they'd crossed us. Zip was loyal to the club one hundred percent. And he would be missed.

Hawke and Tripp had gone to the site of the accident, but they never found Zip's body. After calling every hospital in a fifty-mile radius, we learned he'd been picked up by paramedics who'd arrived at the scene shortly after Psych's men had snatched the women.

Marek had been the one to claim his body, seeing as we were his only family. And since he spent most of his time at the clubhouse, it was only fitting he be buried behind it. The Knights owned close to ten acres surrounding our compound, so we designated the perfect spot for his grave, a shady area under an old, strong oak tree. We gathered to pay homage and said our good-byes four days after his death, drinking to the lost soldier of our group well into the early morning hours.

Before we'd walked into that warehouse, we had devised the plan that Sully would smuggle in a knife. We knew she'd be checked for weapons, just like the rest of us, but we'd prayed they'd overlook the one hidden in her boot. They had. Luckily. She knew to wait for the signal before striking, to plunge the blade deep in his leg and twist so the wound refused to close. We didn't want her to kill him, just temporarily put him out of commission. Thankfully, she'd succeeded.

For as evil and corrupt as Psych was, he wasn't very smart; he'd only had a few men in the room to protect him. The absence of his own weapon continued to baffle me. The only thing I could chalk it up to was arrogance. Which had been his downfall. Sure, he probably figured since his men had disarmed us, he had the upper hand, but he should've known better.

After calling Salzar and giving him detailed directions as to where he could find us inside, I headed back toward the room we'd escaped from. I wasn't shocked to find Marek standing over Psych's bloodied body, his knuckles raw from beatin' the hell out of Sully's father. Seeing the look of gratitude on Marek's face when he saw me return was all the thanks I needed.

"Stone will let you know whose shift is up next," Marek said, smirking at his VP. The tension between the two men had finally dissolved. They threw themselves back into the daily running of the club, focusing more on their immediate plans for Psych, who just so happened to be shackled in the basement of the safe house. For the past two weeks.

Our prisoner of war, I supposed.

The men took turns checking in on him to make sure he was as destitute as possible. We fed him the bare minimum, only giving him the amount of water needed for survival until Marek decided to finally end his wretched life. I knew he was cooking up something good, and Psych's death was definitely something I wanted a hand in. Not only had he hurt Sully her entire life and injured Adelaide, who thankfully was recovering nicely, but he'd had the audacity to touch Kena as well.

She'd told me what he'd done to her. He'd violated her, and for that alone he needed to pay dearly.

Every day Kena's face looked better and better, the bruises fading to a light yellowish color. She wore her hair down a lot, trying to shield the damage from me because she knew how angry I became seeing evidence of what I'd essentially allowed to happen. Even though she argued, telling me it wasn't my fault.

I didn't believe her, though. Most times I would concede because I wanted to move on and not focus on the guilt that ate at me on a daily basis. I'd talked in length with Stone about what I'd been going through, and he asked me one simple question: Did I love her? I told him the truth. I did. I had no idea how I'd lived on this earth without her by my side all these years, but I thanked fate for bringing us together.

I vowed to never leave her side again. Something she seemed more than pleased about, except of course when I'd become overprotective about her going places alone. But because of what had happened, she hadn't argued too much, realizing her safety was my number one priority.

We spent a lot of time joined at the hip, the guys in the club referring to me as pussy-whipped, but I didn't care. I welcomed their jabs because it meant Kena was really mine. Hell, we'd already started talking about moving in together someday in the near future.

Lost to thoughts of my woman, I missed most of what the men had been discussing. Until Marek shouted my name. "Prospect! Are you fuckin' listenin'?" he yelled, glaring at me.

I knew he'd been under a tremendous amount of stress dealing with Psych. Then add to that he worried about Rabid, the Reapers' VP. Our prez wanted to make sure the man stayed hidden. He'd never been an issue before, seeing as how the man had no backbone, but things sometimes changed when a leader was dethroned, so to speak. People sometimes rose up and wanted to assume power, even though the Savage Reapers had no sustainable source of income to speak of. Once the cartel cut them off, they'd been slowly drowning, selling subpar product they'd either stolen or bought off one of the local gangs, the drugs utter shit. And their customers knew it.

"Prospect!" Marek yelled again. Shit, I was two for two. I really needed to pay attention.

"Sorry," I said, waiting for him to speak again.

"Come here," he demanded. When I finally stopped in front of him, I glanced around the room, but none of the other men gave me a clue as to what was going on, their faces expressionless. "Gimme your cut," Marek said, grabbing my vest as soon as it slid past my shoulders. "Ever since you came to this club, you've done as asked, no matter how degrading or dangerous the request." Stone handed Marek a knife. I glanced down at my cut lying on top of the table, the prospect patch being pried away from the leather. Every stitch being ripped apart.

"Over these past few months, you've really proven your loyalty. First with helping to dispose of Yanez, then with being the reason we all made it out of that warehouse alive. So I think it's time," he said, pulling something from the inside pocket of his vest, "that you become a permanent member." On his last word, he handed me back my cut along with a full member patch.

Two words sewn onto a thick piece of material.

Knights Corruption.

No more prospecting.

"If your woman can't stitch it on, I'll have Sully do it," he offered. I stared at the patch for what felt like forever, my eyes becoming glassy, but I knew they'd never let me live it down if I allowed my emotions to escape. So I tipped my head back, allowing the water building in my eyes to recede.

When I finally looked at Marek, he was smiling.

Full-blown.

At me.

The gesture alone almost made me gasp in shock. But I returned the sentiment, beyond thrilled that I'd finally been accepted as an equal to all the brothers in the club.

Kena

WAITING OUTSIDE THEIR MEETING ROOM killed me, but I was so excited for Jagger. Braylen had grabbed me as soon as I came out of the bathroom, shouting for me to get dressed, that we had to get to the clubhouse as soon as possible. At first, I thought something was wrong, but she quickly explained it was a good thing.

Today was the day Jagger was being fully patched into the club.

Ryder had told my sister it would be real nice if I was there when he came out of Chambers. His exact words.

In past conversations with Jagger I knew most of the hierarchy of his club, some of it confusing me so he'd go over it again. To which I'd give him a blank stare. But the one thing I did know for sure was that it was a huge deal to become a fully patched member. He loved that club, almost as much as he loved me. At least that's what he'd told me. I wasn't fully convinced it was true—not yet, at least—but he was making promising strides to prove it to me.

I heard shouts and laughter behind the large wooden doors, hyping my excitement to the next level. A few moments later, the handle turned, the large room coming into full view.

And there he was, standing tall and proud, a smile so big I would've thought he'd won the lottery. Then again, in his eyes, I was sure that's how he felt.

Jagger was a good man. He deserved life's every happiness, and I was thrilled he'd chosen me to join him in this next chapter of his life.

"Hey, babe!" he shouted, breaking away from the others and heading straight for me. The prospect patch on his cut missing, nothing in its place.

Why is there nothing in place of the patch?

"It's right here," he answered, holding up his hand. "Do you know how to stitch?" His smile was infectious, my breath catching in my throat looking at the pure joy on his face.

I do.

Drawing me into his arms, he pressed his eager lips to mine, his tongue teasing me in the most delicious way. Just like that, I wanted to be alone with him. To celebrate privately.

Breaking the kiss, his mouth found my ear, whispering, "I think I like those two words. I might just make you say them again real soon." His warm breath tickled the side of my neck. Leaning back, I stared at him, waiting for him to tell me he was joking, but he never did. Instead, he winked before kissing me once more.

"How about we go back to my place and celebrate?"

I loved it when he read my mind.

TRIPP

If there is ever a time you feel like you just want to give up, dig deep to find your strength and continue to forge ahead. The results will be that much more rewarding.

PROLOGUE

"*STOP*! IT'S NOT WHAT YOU think," she cried, clutching the back of my cut and trying to pull me off the man I found in our bedroom. In *our* fucking bed. "Tripp, please. . . ."

I wrenched my body to the side. It took only seconds before she got the hint and her hands fell to her sides.

"If you don't back the fuck up, Rachel, you're gonna regret it," I warned. The blood pumping in my veins was thick, my heart threatening to explode the more enraged I became. I'd never put my hands on a woman in anger before, but this bitch was pushing my limits for sure. Bad things happened when I lost control, and although I'd be justified to flip the fuck out right then, I still tried to keep it together. As best I could.

My thoughts pored over the past couple months, trying like hell to shove the haze of red from my vision. The mysterious incoming texts late at night. The sudden trips out with friends she hadn't spoken to in months, if not years. The out-of-town trips she suddenly had to take to visit a sick relative, someone I'd never heard her mention before. All of her excuses should have screamed she was fuckin' around, but I'd been so busy with all the shit goin' on at the club I simply took her at her word.

What a big fuckin' mistake.

"You think you can fuck my woman and get away with it!" I roared, slamming the stranger against the wall, the thud of his head hitting the plaster echoing around the room. "I hope she was worth it 'cause now I'm gonna kill ya."

The guy sucked in a strangled breath, his eyes popping wide as I tightened my grip around his throat. He clawed at my hands, but it was useless. I knew I wasn't gonna snatch his life, but I sure as hell wasn't gonna tell either one of them that.

What the fuck did she see in this guy, anyway? His long hair was unkempt, his beard scraggly at best. I towered over the guy, and while I realized I was larger than most, my size didn't detract from the puniness of the man she'd chosen to fuck around with behind my back.

In retrospect, I'd stupidly decided to be faithful to Rachel. I'd had plenty of opportunities to fuck around, but I'd made a commitment. I thought we both had. I was a one-woman type of man, which was quite the conundrum in the lifestyle I'd chosen. Pussy flowed easily for everyone involved in the Knights Corruption. Shit, for all the clubs I'd known. And while most chose to partake, there were a select few who chose one woman and one woman only.

Foolishly, I'd been one of them.

As I glanced at Rachel, my heart splintered a little more with each passing second. She was still trying to convince me to let go of the guy, fear in her eyes at what she thought I was gonna do. She had feelings for this fucker, which meant whatever she'd felt toward me had waned. We had our issues but I thought we were good . . . all things considered.

"Please," she continued to beg. "Let him go, Tripp. I promise it won't happen again." She grabbed my arm and tried to yank me back, but her feeble attempts only served to irritate me further. I needed to get outta there, but not until I'd finished teaching them both a lesson. Squeezing tighter still, I only released my grip when the guy's eyes closed, his lungs ceasing to struggle for air. I hadn't killed him, although I wanted to; I'd merely choked him out. As soon as I backed away, releasing my hand from around his throat, his limp body slumped to the floor. I waited to see if Rachel would rush toward him but she didn't, although her eyes kept flicking from mine to his and then back again.

Turning fully toward her, I shook my head when I saw the look of fright on her face. She had no idea what I had planned for her, probably thinking I'd killed her lover and that she was next. Apparently, she didn't know me at all. Or did she? I'd killed before, sure. Numerous times, in fact, but always in retaliation or defense. Never because of infidelity. Although, I'd never been put in this type of situation before.

Stalking toward her, I assessed her body language.

Fear.

Regret?

Didn't matter. I was done with her, but that didn't stop me from retaliating. Her back slammed against the wall, her hands coming up in front of her to protect our bodies from colliding. I came to a halt inches from where she stood pinned, my jaw clenched and nostrils flaring. I was so enraged I had no idea what to say. I wanted to wrap my hands around her throat just like I'd done with that fucker, but instead I kept them at my sides. My nails dug into my palms, drawing some of my attention away from thoughts of hurting her.

When moments passed and still I hadn't moved, she reached out and cupped my face. "I'm so sorry, baby. It'll never happen again. I swear." She flicked her eyes to the unconscious man and then back to me. It was then I noticed her pupils were dilated. She was on something, but since her choice of drug varied, I had no idea what it was. "I've just . . . been so lonely. You're always gone, and when you're here, you're not really with me."

I gasped as if she'd sucker punched me in the gut. "Are you fuckin' kiddin' me? You're trying to blame me for you bein' a whore?" Fury boiled my blood. I jerked my head away from her hand, her fingers falling from my face. I stepped closer, my chest brushing against hers. She stood before me completely naked. Having caught them in bed together, she'd never had the chance to throw on clothes. And while the thought of fucking her senseless normally arrested me whenever I saw her big tits and round ass, her standing before me with not a stitch of clothing on right then only served to disgust me.

Another man had been inside her. Tasted her. Promised her God only knew what, and from the looks she kept sneaking at him, she professed her own hopes and dreams to that bastard as well.

She reached for my hands, but I shrugged her off. "I'm not blaming you. But you can't blame me either. I know you've fucked around on me, and although I didn't cheat to get back at you, I'm not gonna stand here and let you intimidate me anymore."

"What the fuck are you talkin' about?" I yelled. "I haven't fucked anyone else for the past two years. Ever since we agreed to be together." As for the other bullshit she spewed, I couldn't help it. At six four and two hundred thirty pounds, I couldn't help but intimidate most people, even her. I admitted that I used my size to get what I wanted most of the time, and if I were being honest, I loved that she felt inferior right then.

Her eyes darkened, her posture becoming rigid all in the blink of an eye. Rachel could be a bitch when she wanted and right then was a prime example, trying to turn the tables on me to excuse her abhorrent behavior.

"You can say whatever you want, Tripp. I know you've fucked around, but I'm not gonna stand here and try to convince you to come clean." Pointing toward the man on the floor, she said, "I fucked him. Plenty of times. And now it's over, so the sooner you forgive me the sooner we can get back to us." Rachel had done a complete one-eighty in the span of minutes. At first, she played off her actions with remorse, apologizing with a look of guilt plastered on her face and riddled in her voice. And then she tried to blame me for fuckin' around, acting as if her cheating was merely a bump in the road of our relationship. As if that shit was normal and should be forgiven with no questions asked.

I wasn't gonna lie. She hurt me. But I wasn't gonna sit there and cry about it either. I refused to embarrass myself by givin' her the time of day any longer. No, she fucked up . . . and good.

I need alcohol.

Slamming my hands on the wall, one on each side of her head, I shouted, "Fuck you!" A quick thought of head-butting her flitted through my brain, and while the image satisfied me, I would never do such a thing. Retreating a step, I said, "We're fuckin' done. Get your shit and get out." Turning my back on her, I strode toward the hallway, shouting over my shoulder. "When I get back, you better not be here."

I heard her yelling but ignored her as I slammed the front door behind me. Two minutes later I was on the open road, embracing the wind and the feel of my bike between my legs. The rumble and vibrations calmed me. My grip on the handlebars loosened the farther I rode, putting as much distance as I could between me and the woman who fucked me over.

Had I known how my night would turn out, I might have stayed at home and watched her leave instead.

ONE

Tripp

LYING IN BED I TOOK a deep breath, willing the ache from my body, but it was useless. The evidence of the life I'd lived riddled my skin. I'd been shot more times than I'd like to recount, though thankfully nothing had happened to me in the past year. It was a nice change of events.

Absently tracing the scar near my heart, I thought about what I had to take care of later that day. Sighing, all I wanted to do was close my eyes and go back to sleep, but Marek wanted me to check out how shit was goin' at the new titty bar, Indulge. I had a hand in hiring the last round of talent, and four out of the five were still employed. We'd fired one of them for doing drugs; that shit just wasn't tolerated.

I believed someone had been hired to replace the chick we got rid of, but I wasn't sure. I'd been out of the mix for the past couple weeks, helping my prez deal with the final obstacle we faced.

Psych Brooks.

Leader of our most hated enemy, the Savage fuckin' Reapers.

All the brothers had taken turns standing guard to make sure that bastard got exactly what he deserved. Strung up like an animal in the basement of our club's safe house, he'd been deprived of adequate food and water, only being provided with the minimal amount to keep the breath in his lungs.

Daily beatings occurred, mostly at the hands of Marek, then Stone and Jagger. And that was because Psych had fucked with all three of their women. Sully had received the brunt of his abuse her entire life, seeing as how she was the daughter of the evil bastard. Her father never protected her, not once in all the years she lived with him. Shit, I hated even calling him her *father*, because he certainly was not.

When I broached the subject of Psych's demise, asking Marek when he was gonna end the fucker's existence, a sadistic grin lifted the corners of his mouth. Normally the image would have been out of character for the leader of the Knights, but whenever the subject of his wife's father was mentioned, the look was expected. "I'm not done with him yet," Marek would always respond. I understood, and while I agreed that he should drag out the man's torture as long as possible, I also wanted to be done with him. We needed to move on, and put the last link to our old life to rest once and for all.

But all in due time, I supposed.

Swinging my legs over the edge of the bed, I quickly stood and stretched my arms above my head, chasing away the last traces of sleep. Padding toward the bathroom, my mind was a flurry of thoughts, none of them bringing me an ounce of comfort. I was up next in the rotation at the safe house, and while I didn't mind gettin' a little bloody in the name of payback, I'd much rather chill out at home.

After a hasty shower, I grabbed some clothes from my closet, dressed, and snatched my keys. An hour later I pulled up to the safe house, shutting off my bike's engine and glancing around the garage to see who else would be joining me, if anyone. Looked like I was the first to arrive. Never paying much attention to who was scheduled to show up when, I strolled inside the house with thoughts of gettin' this shit over with so I could hit up The Underground on the way back. My home away from the clubhouse. The club's bar didn't bring in much of a profit, but it was my go-to when I didn't want to be surrounded by everyone.

We were on strict orders to keep shit as quiet as possible, so no more than three men were allowed at the house at any given time. Marek feared if people came and went at all hours, we'd draw too much attention and the neighbors would get suspicious. My thought, however, was that anyone who lived close would keep to themselves, fearing what would happen if they butted their noses into our business. The few times we did see our neighbors they averted their eyes and hustled inside their homes, slamming their doors before we even had the chance to nod hello. Not that we were out to make friends, but a welcoming acknowledgment here and there couldn't hurt. At least, that was my take on it.

Strolling through the kitchen, I snagged a beer from the fridge before venturing into the basement. The creak of the wooden steps echoed through the enclosed space, the ominous sound perking my ears with each thump of my foot. The scene I walked into was straight out of some horror movie.

A man shackled to a wall, head hung low and beaten so badly he was barely recognizable. But it wasn't some low-budget film; it was fuckin' real life, and the strung-up man was evil personified. Psych Brooks deserved every bit of pain he'd endured, plus whatever was left in our arsenal to deliver. So far, most of his teeth had been knocked out and his jaw was broken, which made eating impossible. The leader of the Reapers was on borrowed time since he could no longer take in food, so we made good with the time he had left. All the fingers on his right hand had been broken, along with his left femur. He'd howled when Stone had taken a sledgehammer to his leg, his wails the sweetest sound to our club's VP.

I was more of a subtle torture kind of guy—rubbing salt into tiny slits in the skin, shoving sharp objects under the fingernails, that sort of shit.

Once I'd hit the last step, I covered my nose with my hand. "Holy fuck, it reeks down here!" For a split second I thought I saw Psych lift his head and grin, but it could have been my eyes playing tricks on me. The man was more than beaten down, holding on to the last remaining threads of his life.

Marek had told us all that with each of our visits we were to inflict some sort of pain on Psych, making sure to save the big shit for him. Broken bones, stretching his limbs by tugging on the chains—all that sort of shit was permissible, but no one was to slice him open or cut off anything. That was to be left for our prez.

Ever since Sully had come into Marek's life, I'd witnessed the changes in him. Before her, he was a serious guy, but pretty laid-back. Not too much rattled him. He took things as they came, reacting when necessary and taking appropriate action.

These days, Marek barely cracked a smile, except when his wife was around. He'd aged a few years in the short span of time since her arrival. His expression was a constant grimace, and his eyes had taken on a darkness only a few of us could relate to. But it was all understandable. Knowing what Psych had done to his daughter her entire life, what he allowed others to do to her, gutted Marek. He didn't have to voice it in order for it to be known to all of us. I only prayed that after he finally had the chance to purge, after he was able to rid the world of Psych, he'd go back to the man I once knew.

Revenge had a funny way of flipping you on your ass, however. For so long, thoughts of getting even fueled the desire for justification. But when it was all said and done, sometimes all you had left was a shell of your former self.

As I reached for the chains, knowing my form of torture that day was gonna be to stretch Psych's arms so far above his head he'd have to step on his tippy-toes or else risk popping out his shoulders, I heard footsteps above me.

"Grab me another beer," I shouted toward the stairs, not givin' a damn who was there as long as they brought me a replacement. I was gonna be there for a while and wanted extra suds to help deal with what was to come. I'd never say I was a fan of inflicting pain, but the shit didn't faze me either.

"A please would be nice, brother," Hawke responded, pounding down the steps so hard I swore I heard one of them crack. He tossed me the bottle before plopping down on a metal stool in the corner, rubbing his hand over his head. His hair was finally growing back after having been balded when his woman had found out he'd cheated on her. Their relationship had taken a turn after the incident which still gutted my little brother.

"You actually left Edana's side?" I asked in surprise. Ever since his woman had been beaten and raped by some of Psych's men, Hawke never left her alone, bringing her to the club every single time his presence was required. Marek had given him a short reprieve from dealing with some of the club's business, the trips to the titty bars on hiatus until he knew Hawke could handle it without being distracted. I'd talked at length with him over what happened with Edana, but in the end he was the one who needed to come to grips with it and decide what needed to be done.

"Yeah," he answered, taking a slow pull on his bottle. "I figured it was time for me to step up and start doin' my part again."

I'd always been protective over my younger brother, going to bat for him and sometimes helping him clean up his messes. An incident happened a few years back, a scuffle with some random guy who went after him after finding out Hawke had fucked his wife. And because I was tired of jumping to his defense because he couldn't keep his dick in his pants, I'd stepped back and let the guy get in a few good punches, my arms crossed over my chest, just watching the two of them battle it out. I knew Hawke could handle his own, even with traces of alcohol flowing through his blood, so it was merely seconds before my sibling had the man on his back, turning the tables and beatin' the shit out of him. I'd finally intervened when I saw that Hawke was doing some damage, dragging him off the half-conscious man. I'd also warned him that the next time he messed with a married chick and the husband found out, I'd jump in with the stranger and help teach Hawke a lesson.

One glance at the Reapers' leader and Hawke's eyes darkened with anger. "So what are we doin' to him today?"

"I think he's in need of a bit of a stretch, don'tcha think?" I grinned, glancing at Psych to see if he was even aware he had company. The slight shuffle of his feet indicated he was, and I had no doubt he knew he was in for one helluva day.

Nothing but pain.

"TWO MINUTES," CARLA ANNOUNCED AS she walked up behind me, looking at me through the mirror in front of my station. "Then you're up, hon." Even after a month of working at Indulge, nerves still managed to rattle me before each performance, something I feared would never go away. Then again, the moment I became comfortable with this job should be the exact moment I quit.

Carla disappeared to attend to the other girls, mending some of the outfits for the night's performances. The club's manager used to be a stripper, but all that ended the day she met her husband, Brian. She'd stopped taking off her clothes for money but stayed in the business to help the younger girls starting out, offering advice and keeping them out of trouble.

In the short time since I'd known Carla, she'd helped me tremendously, teaching me how to deescalate any situation, learning to read the men's body language and how to protect myself if they ever got a bit rough. I'd never had anyone look out for me before, and Carla would forever have my gratitude for seeing me as a person and not just an object. A commodity to own and possess.

Adjusting my auburn wig, I finished my makeup with another coat of mascara before standing and assessing the costume I'd chosen for my routine—a naughty schoolgirl outfit. Cliché but it worked, arousing the customers to ensure tips would be plentiful. With one final glance in the mirror I headed for the door, my heart thrumming fast.

"Good luck, sweetheart," Carla shouted behind me. I turned halfway around, enough to flash her an appreciative smile before focusing on what came next.

The whole stripping scene was new to me, but it provided me with an income, something I was never allowed to have before. Refusing to even think about my past, I focused on the remaining beats of the current song, blew out a long breath, and strode toward the back of the stage. I was up next.

I lost myself to the rhythm of my routine, allowing the spotlight to block the prying eyes watching my every move. The club was almost at capacity, which was both good and bad. I would surely go home with enough money to cover my room and put some food in the mini fridge that was supplied at the motel, but because of the number of patrons, I would surely be putting Carla's advice to good use. Most of the men were well on their way to Drunkville, their eyes surely not the only thing trying to get their fill of me that evening.

With each piece of clothing I removed my mind hid, drifting off to the only time I'd felt safe, loved—my childhood. Memories of vacations with my parents filtered in. Playing Army with my older brother because where we lived there were no other children. Escaping to my room after I'd been punished for misbehaving, only to have my mom come and comfort me. She'd explain why I'd been in trouble but always made sure to tell me she loved me to the moon and back, kissing my forehead before giving me her stern look telling me that I was still grounded. My dad calling me his little princess as he twirled me around in his arms, blowing raspberries on my cheeks until I laughed so hard I could barely breathe.

As the song increased in tempo, unwanted scenes barreled forth. Tears pricked behind my eyes but I refused to allow them to fall. My whole world imploded the night two police officers knocked on our door.

An accident.

Icy roads.

One driver, two passengers.

No survivors.

Thrusting myself back into the present, I focused on the numerous strangers watching me while I danced to the music, counting the seconds until I could disappear backstage once more.

THREE

Tripp

"I NEED YOU TO TAKE my place at Jagger's fight tonight," Stone said, straddling the barstool next to me. "Addy's goin' to her dad's for dinner." He tapped the bar and signaled for Trigger to grab him a beer. The resident bartender scowled and disappeared in the back, completely ignoring Stone's request altogether. Those two didn't have the best history, not since Stone went against club rule and got involved with Trigger's niece, Adelaide. Now the mother of his kid.

Hell, he and I didn't have the best relationship either. He forever gave me shit about hittin' on his woman, but he'd got it all wrong. Adelaide cared for me after I'd been dropped off at the gates of the club, shot four fuckin' times, bleeding out and left for dead. It was Adelaide who had nursed me back to health, and because of the bond we shared, our friendship had blossomed. Which was quite odd for me, seeing as how she was the only true female friend I had. I innocently flirted with her, sure, but who wouldn't—the woman was gorgeous. But she was more like a sister to me, and as time passed Stone had come around to the fact that I would never fuck someone I viewed as family.

Don't get me wrong, Stone and I battled. Quite a few times. Shit, he even punched me in the face for puttin' my hands on her belly when she was pregnant with Riley. But I let it slide because, as a man, I understood his possessiveness. Didn't stop me from fuckin' with him, though.

Every once in a while I could still rile him enough to throw me daggers.

"If she's goin' to her dad's, then why do I have to take your place at the fight?" I lifted my beer and drained the remaining liquid.

"'Cause Riley is sick and I need to stay home with her. Addy hasn't seen her dad in quite a while and doesn't want to cancel." Leaning over the bar, he grabbed a mug and poured himself a drink before sitting back down. "That good enough of an excuse for you?"

"What's your problem?" Certainly used to Stone's aggravated tone, I knew when something was amiss.

"Nothin', man. Just . . . I don't know. Shit, I don't wanna talk about it right now." Tipping his head back, he swallowed half his drink in two gulps. "Besides, I sure as hell ain't talking about Addy with you." Gone was his usual tone of contempt, replaced with a slight wave of familiarity, as if he didn't completely hate me.

Slapping his back, I gave him something to contemplate. "Well, if you ever wanna talk. . . ." I left it at that, not about to get all sentimental with Stone's ornery ass. He knew where to find me if he needed to get somethin' off his chest. Although I imagined he'd seek out Marek before anyone else, seeing how close the two of them were.

The club's VP opened his mouth but quickly snapped it shut when his phone rang. Pulling it from the inside of his cut, he glanced at the screen before answering. "Hey," he said before vacating his stool and walking toward the room he used when at the clubhouse. I had no doubt his wife was on the other end of that call.

The rest of the day passed quickly. Nothin' much goin' on at the club besides making sure everyone took their turns visiting Psych.

———— ✦ ————

I ACCOMPANIED RYDER TO JAGGER'S fight, standing guard outside the dismal office inside the ratty old warehouse until the prize money was secure. Ever since Jagger had killed a guy in the ring, the younger brother of a Reaper, he'd become the hot ticket of the underground fighting world. The prize money quadrupled and because Jagger was still undefeated, the pot grew with each bout.

"All good?" I asked, moving to the side as soon as the office door opened.

"Yup," Jagger answered, his black duffel bag swung over his shoulder as he walked past me. He instantly sought out his woman, having no patience for anyone else. Kena was huddled in the corner with her sister, Braylen, and of course Ryder was close by. The guy wouldn't admit it but he had it bad for her. He tried to play it off as nothing more than sex, but I noticed the way he watched Braylen when he thought no one was paying attention.

Kena's hands were going a million miles a minute and after Jagger responded, she grabbed his hands and smiled. When Kena was an infant, she'd contracted a virus, which had damaged the nerves in her larynx, prohibiting her from ever uttering a single word. Jagger had learned sign language in order to communicate with her, but there were times when he messed up, like right then.

"What did you tell her this time?"

"Shut up, man. You try and learn this shit and not mess up." Jagger's frustrations quickly disappeared when his woman signed something before kissing him.

I grinned as I turned my attention to Ryder. "You almost ready?"

"Fuck yeah I am." He looked pissed, which wasn't out of the ordinary where he was concerned, especially when Braylen was around. I swore those two were always arguing about something. "Remind me I can't strangle her," he mumbled as he brushed past me, completely ignoring the blonde-haired woman walking briskly behind him.

"I heard that," she shouted, smacking his arm when she'd finally caught up to him.

Shaking my head, I turned back to Jagger. "You're set to go there now, right?" He was up next in the rotation at the safe house.

"Yeah, Kena and Braylen drove so I'm right behind you. Just let me say good-bye first." Taking her hand, he led Kena past me and out of the dank building where he'd won yet another fight.

The newly patched-in member took joy in dishing out pain on the bastard shackled in the basement. Psych dared to orchestrate the kidnapping of Kena and Adelaide. And to make matters even more serious, he'd been brazen enough to put his hands on Jagger's woman.

I'd only been paired with Jagger a few times since we'd taken Psych, and every time I inwardly cringed, witnessing the former prospect's rage toward the leader of the Savage Reapers. Or I should say ex-leader, seeing as how his life was gonna be snatched soon enough. Although, if it were up to Marek, Psych would live the next ten years rotting away in that basement.

Once outside, Jagger and Ryder walked the women to their car. Kena was all smiles while Braylen's scowl was enough to make *me* flinch. A couple of minutes later, the two men strolled back to where we'd parked and straddled their rides. We all kicked over the engines at the same time, the rumble of the three bikes sounding like fifty, echoing around us in the empty streets.

A sense of calm descended over me as I gripped the throttle, picked my legs off the pavement and drove off down the street. Jagger and I hooked a right toward the safe house while Ryder turned left, no doubt headed back toward the clubhouse. Something had been bothering Ryder lately, and I knew it was more than the arguments with Braylen, but damn if he clammed up every time I asked why he had a stick up his ass. Instead of answering, he would grunt and reach for a beer. If and when he got his hands on hard alcohol, then and only then would I be truly concerned.

The hard shit and Ryder just didn't mix. I'd witnessed it a couple times and never wished to again. That man had some demons lurking inside him, and for some reason his whole personality completely changed with the consumption of whiskey.

Pushing thoughts of Ryder aside, I focused back on what I had to take care of in the upcoming week. After that night, I had a few days to myself, my only obligation making sure everything was running smoothly at Indulge.

Little did I know a simple check-in at our newest titty bar would change everything.

FOUR

Reece

TAKING A DEEP BREATH, I shoved all nervousness aside as I stepped on stage. The music I'd selected began to play, the beat of the tune vibrating from the speakers and wrapping around me like some sort of blanket—which was an odd sentiment, seeing as how I was about to take off my clothes in front of a bunch of horny men. Losing myself to the music was the only way I managed to continue stripping. I closed my eyes and allowed the thrum of the song to live within me, swaying to the idea that my life was exactly where I wanted it to be.

Which was false, of course.

No little girl dreamed of dancing naked, straddling a pole while lusty men looked on. I certainly hadn't. But I didn't have a choice. When I mustered up enough courage to leave my life in the shadows, I had fifty dollars to my name. Taking my clothes off was the quickest way to make the money I needed to survive.

Shield myself from my past as best I could and hope for a better life.

A calm life.

A safe life.

Swinging my legs around the pole, I hoisted myself until I neared the top, slowly positioning my body until I was turned upside down. My strong thighs stabilized me while my hands gripped the pole so I didn't fall if I accidentally slipped. Which had happened before, but thankfully only when I'd been practicing my routine, not live on stage.

I unlocked my legs and spread them into a wide V, strategically placing my arms so I had a better hold. I slowly lowered my body until I reached the floor, going into a split before bouncing my ass up and down on the stage to the climax of the song. I soon let go of the pole, seductively crawling toward the edge of the stage and the men who were waving their money in the air.

The outfit I'd chosen that evening was a men's white dress shirt, buttons opened to my navel. The sleeves were rolled up twice and a dark gray tie hung loosely from my neck, dipping between my abundant cleavage. A hint of teasing without showing everything. Not until I decided to. Of course, what was underneath the shirt left very little to the imagination, the white lace thong barely covering me. I always wore wigs while working, a helpful tip from Carla. That night I wore a short blonde hairstyle, quite the contrast to my long chestnut-colored hair.

I only had a few minutes left on stage, choosing a longer rendition of "Gone" by The Weekend. His voice was sultry and seductive, perfect for dancing and enticing men out of their hard-earned money. At my core, I was innocent and naïve, but whenever I stepped on stage I took on a different persona. A woman out to get as much from a man as I could. Ensnare them. Make them think they're the only guy in the room. Make them *want* to keep watching me long enough to get paid.

Pushing myself on my knees I slowly unbuttoned the rest of my shirt, pulling the material apart once the last button slipped through its hole. Running my hands over my breasts, I shielded them from view until I'd received a few more bills tucked securely in the garter around my left thigh.

"Let's see those tits, sweetheart," an older, balding man yelled, swaying from side to side from obvious intoxication.

"Yeah," his buddy agreed from behind him.

Giving them both a sexy grin, I pointed to my garter. For as drunk as the bald guy was, he stuffed his money under the lace wrapped around my leg with ease.

Gripping both sides of my shirt, I slowly pulled the material away from my body. This was the part I hated, losing what little clothing covered me. But it was part of the job, so I mentally flitted away from the scene in front of me. I never allowed myself to see the men once my shield had been stripped away.

Their images all blurred together.

Faceless people in the crowd.

I knew it was my choice to strip, but it didn't make it any easier. And since there was a strict no-drugs policy at the club I couldn't even contemplate taking something to help numb me. I had to endure until I came up with a better way to support myself.

If that ever happened.

Shrugging the shirt off my shoulders, I tossed the material to the side of the stage. I knew what they expected and I gave it to them. Kneading my breasts, I pinched my erect nipples a few times before running my hands down my body. Knowing my song was coming to a close soon, I rose to my feet and sauntered toward the pole. Twirling a few times, I came to rest in front of it, sliding down slowly until my ass was a few inches from the ground. I played with the flimsy strands of my thong, teasing the men surrounding the stage with small glimpses of my bare pussy.

Indulge was a fully nude club, and even though I was required to rid myself of all clothing, I chose to always do so when I didn't have much time left on stage. Other dancers spread their legs wide when they bared themselves, but I never did.

I couldn't.

Standing and swiveling around so my back was to the crowd, I bent over and hooked my thumbs under the lace of my thong, slowly dragging my panties down my toned thighs. As soon as the scrap of material pooled around my ankles, I stepped free of them and kicked them toward the back of the stage.

The last few chords of the song drew near. I turned back around to face the crowd and caressed the pole as if it were a lover, running my hands up and down the metal, the coolness of it distracting me from the countless pairs of eyes staring at me. I trailed my hands down my body, shielding my pussy quickly before baring everything.

Thankfully the last note of the music sounded, signaling that my time was up. Bills were thrown toward me once they knew my show had ended. Gathering the money tightly in my hands, I continued to plaster a smile on my face, winking at a few of the men before finally disappearing off stage.

Each of us had a secure locker in the back of the club. Stuffing the wad of cash in mine, I pulled out my next outfit for the evening, complete with my favorite red wig. I sipped on my watered-down vodka on the rocks to help take the edge off.

If I'd known how my evening would turn out, I would've ordered a few more drinks.

FIVE

Tripp

IT'D BEEN THREE DAYS SINCE I last visited the safe house. My next rotation was in a day or so, depending on when Marek decided to pull the trigger—either literally or figuratively—and fuckin' snatch Psych's life once and for all.

Striding through the back door of Indulge, I passed by a few of the staff, nodding in acknowledgment as I headed toward the front. I spotted Hawke near the bar, throwing back shots as I approached.

"Bout fuckin' time, brother," Hawke shouted over the music, slapping me on the back. "What took you so long?" His brows rose but his attention wavered once one of the strippers walked by, throwing him a smile before heading toward a table of men.

"Thought you were all done with that." I signaled the bartender for a drink, turning back toward Hawke after ordering.

"I am," he said, "but I can still look. As long as I don't touch." His smile faltered, and I knew he still struggled with what happened to Edana. She'd gone looking for Hawke and had been viciously attacked by a few Reapers right outside this place, only allowing her to live so she could deliver a message that they were comin' for everyone we loved. Retribution for Marek stealing Sully away from her father.

I knew Hawke still harbored guilt for putting his woman in that situation, even though it hadn't been his fault. Yes, he'd had a hard time keeping his dick in his pants, but all that changed after Edana's attack. He confessed he hadn't touched another chick since, and I believed him. I saw the look of pure terror and pain in his eyes when he held Edana, doing his best to comfort her and assure her that he would rain all hell down on the Reapers for daring to touch her. As volatile as Hawke and Edana's relationship was, they loved each other, although at times it seemed only logical to question.

"How is she?" I didn't have to say her name for him to know who I was talking about.

"She's healing physically, more each day, but she's still fucked-up in the head." Hawke finished the rest of his beer, slamming down the bottle in frustration. "She's been having fuckin' nightmares, and when I try to hold her she lashes out and hits me. She doesn't even know it's me until she's fully awake." Running his hands through his hair, he dropped his head and groaned. I'd heard his anguish because I stood so close, but to everyone else, it just appeared as if he was drunk. "I don't know what to do for her. I feel so goddamn helpless, man," he confessed.

I had no idea what he was going through, but my heart bled for him just the same. Shit like this was one of the main reasons I chose not to get attached to a woman. Bad things happened all the time in our world, and the less people I brought into it, the better. Besides, the last chick I'd shacked up with betrayed me, and who the hell wants to deal with that fucked-up situation again?

"It'll get better in time. Just be patient."

"Easier said than done," Hawke grumbled. As he was about to say something else, Arianna, one of the dancers, shimmied next to me and wrapped her arms around my neck, pushing her fake tits against my chest. Rising up on her toes, still significantly shorter than me even in heels, she pressed her mouth to mine.

"Hey, baby," she cooed, licking her glossy lips before trying to kiss me again. But I was prepared that time. Unlocking her hands, I gently pushed her away. Yeah, I'd fucked her a few times when I was drunk and horny, but settling between Arianna's legs again wasn't something I was interested in any longer. To be honest, it shocked me that she'd been able to convince me to fuck her more than once. But like I said, I was drunk for all three occasions.

"Not tonight," I warned, keeping my voice as casual as possible. She reeked of cheap cologne, no doubt from giving a few guys some up close and personal time. Disappointment shrouded her face, but the emotion quickly disappeared when Hawke leaned over me and gave her his winning smile.

"I can take you both on if that's what you want. It doesn't have to be just the two of us." She batted her heavily coated eyelashes at me before turning her attention to my younger brother.

I'd been around the block and was no stranger to threesomes, but never with another guy. And sharing this chick with my brother was the last thing that was goin' down tonight. No fucking way was I crossing swords with him.

"No," I said more firmly, pushing her back another step to clear her from my personal space. "Not gonna happen, so stop tryin'."

She gave me a fake pout before winking at Hawke. Fortunately, a few guys seated close to the stage caught her attention and she strutted toward them without glancing back at us.

Well, that was easy enough.

"You hittin' that?"

"Not anymore. I should've never started shit with her to begin with," I confessed, taking a healthy swig from my beer.

"Why? She cray?" Hawke asked, grinning because he knew I hated when he talked like some teeny-bopper.

"Cray? Really?" He laughed before hitting my shoulder with his. "To answer your question, Arianna's probably in the vicinity of crazy, yes, but I never paid much attention to say for a hundred percent." Finishing off my drink, I gestured for another.

"Same thing, sweetheart?" Carla asked, wiping down the bar in front of us.

Before answering her question, I asked, "Why are you serving drinks tonight? I thought we just hired someone to do that." Swiping the bottle she'd passed me, I gulped half of it down before she responded.

"She called off. Said her kid was sick or something." Waving to someone at the far end of the bar, she smiled before leaving to tend to a customer.

I liked Carla. She was an ex-stripper turned manager. Anyone who spent five minutes with her knew she had a good head on her shoulders. Smart. Savvy. Compassionate. She kept the patrons in check with her stern, no-nonsense tone, all while helping the dancers, whether it be with costumes, dance routines, or talking them through a bout of stage fright.

Carla was a powerhouse of a woman. Not in stature, standing at just five foot five, but in personality. She was attractive, although not my type. If I had to guess her age, which I would never do out loud, I'd put her in her early to mid-forties. Her shoulder-length, honey blonde hair was styled into a flattering bob-type hairdo. Thin yet curvy, she definitely caught the attention of many of the men who frequented the club, a fact her husband, Brian, didn't appreciate. He'd almost knocked out one of the men ogling Carla when the drunken patron decided to get a bit handsy. Luckily, our security stepped in and threw the guy out on his ass before Brian attacked him.

Flinging the bar rag over her shoulder, she slid a shot glass toward Hawke and gave him a wink. He responded with an appreciative nod before throwing back the amber liquid, slamming the glass on the bar when he finished. Carla had a nurturing way about her, and when she'd found out what had happened to Edana, she tried to comfort Hawke in the only way she knew how—by giving him a drink right before he knew he even needed one.

"Hey, I meant to ask you this earlier. How's the new dancer working out? Any issues?" Finally sitting on the barstool, I rested my right foot on the rung, my left on the ground. Strumming my fingers on the bar top, I patiently waited for her to respond, my eyes taking in the action around the club.

"She's quite somethin'." Carla chuckled, the teasing tone to her voice enough to draw my attention back to her. Smiling big, she jerked her chin toward the stage. "In fact, you can see for yourself. She's up next."

SIX

Tripp

THE TONE OF CARLA'S STATEMENT had me on edge for a reason I couldn't explain, except that I knew something was about to change for me very soon.

Apprehension stole the air from my lungs.

Swiveling around, my eyes darted toward the area of the stage I knew the girls emerged from, my posture becoming more rigid with every breath I took. Before I could berate myself for being ridiculous, Craig's voice, our announcer, crooned through the speakers.

"Call your wives and tell 'em you'll be late tonight, fellas, because our next dancer is gonna grace us with one more performance. She's sexy. She's alluring. She's temptation incarnate."

A thunderous roar erupted before he'd even finished speaking, the spotlight hitting the stage and the music pumping from the sound system in time to the appearance of the next dancer.

It was a sensual song, one I never expected to hear in a place like this, but I guess that's what made her performance unlike any other.

A thin blanket of smoke rolled across the stage, quickly dissipating when the mystery woman appeared. Seduction drifted off her in waves as she walked toward the pole. Every step she took was predatory, the sway of her hips and the confidence in her body language instantly grabbing my attention. Hell, she entranced every fucker in the club. I saw the evidence as I quickly scanned the room.

Hopping off my barstool, my heart pounded faster as I approached the stage. Hawke shouted something behind me, but I couldn't hear him. My only focus was on her. I had to find out what the invisible pull was drawing me toward her. My breathing accelerated as I moved closer, and I realized right then that I was powerless to stop whatever was happening to me.

When I stopped a few feet from the stage, I finally saw what all the fuss was about. Everyone around me faded into nothingness, the once-deafening shouts from the men muffled. The thrum of the music lessened as my eyes latched onto the woman rocking my world.

She was the most beautiful creature I'd ever laid eyes on, and I'd seen plenty of gorgeous women in my thirty-two years. I had no idea what her name was, however, because Craig's announcement had been shrouded by the shouts of excited men.

She wore a tiny, white sheer top tied just underneath her full breasts, accompanied by a skirt so short it barely covered her ass. But I guess that was the sole purpose.

Her long red hair fell to the middle of her back, the curls bouncing and moving with every step she took. Her stomach was flat and toned, her legs long and lean. When she turned away from me and bent over I thought I was gonna come in my pants. Her heart-shaped ass was a work of art, and the only thoughts I had were of me sinking my teeth into her soft, pliable flesh.

Before I knew it, I'd advanced closer, surely blocking the view for some of the other patrons. But ask me if I cared. Besides, even if they had a problem with me obstructing their view, they weren't stupid. If they didn't know me personally, they could easily see from the cut I wore that I belonged to the club who owned this place. And if that weren't enough of a deterrent, my sheer size would have them thinking twice about opening their drunken mouths.

Our newest dancer slowly moved around the middle of the stage. Her delicate fingers popped the buttons of her shirt, purposely taking her time for the much-needed buildup, working up every man in the place. Her actions fueled something inside me, an unfamiliar rage simmering deep within. I wanted her performance to be for me and me alone. But the thought was stupid.

She's a fucking stripper.

Of course her little dance was directed at whoever would throw her money. Another fact which stirred my fury from a simmer to a slight boil.

What the hell is wrong with me?

The song picked up tempo and her lithe body contorted around that damn pole with expertise. Her shirt was wide open, exposing her full, natural breasts for everyone to see. She took a spin around the pole, jumping and hooking her legs above her head before slowly sinking down toward the floor.

She was magnificent.

I was knocked back from my fantasies when I saw her approach, her eyes locking with mine as she came closer.

I found it difficult to breathe, as if all the air had been sucked out of the room. I was stuck in place, entranced by the woman in front of me, and the gleam in her eyes proved she was aware of my new predicament.

A small smile tilted up her full, luscious lips as she watched my re-action. Reaching up, she grabbed her shirt and slowly let it slip off her shoulders, then off completely. Keeping her gaze pinned on me, she grabbed her breasts and pinched her nipples, twisting her hips to the beat of the music.

I couldn't look away.

What I really wanted to do was jump onto the stage and whisk her away, but not before covering her up. I couldn't stand that there were at least a hundred pairs of eyes raking all over her exposed flesh. It was driving me insane, but there wasn't anything I could do about it.

Was there?

Before I could entertain my odd thought, she sank to her knees and crawled toward me, engulfing me further in her web. It wasn't until she was a few feet away from me that I noticed something different about her. From afar, she appeared every bit the stereotypical stripper, playing her part to make her money, but up close, her bluish-gray eyes told a different story. They held an innocence, an inexperience which just didn't seem plausible. It was the oddest contradiction.

They say the eyes are the windows to the soul. If that were true, then I could see that all of her hopes and dreams had been dashed, yet she forged ahead, seeking a light that might be just within her reach.

Hope and desperation battled for dominance behind her beautiful pupils, the dueling emotions rather intriguing. I tried, but I couldn't look away. I thought I heard Hawke's voice yell for her to take it off, but I ignored him, even though I wanted nothing more than to punch him in the face for watching my woman get naked.

My woman?

So entranced with my new feelings, I hadn't realized she was so close. Her soft palm caressed the side of my face, her touch pushing all of my other thoughts to the side, and causing my lungs to seize up. I knew right then that if she continued her silent assault on my senses, I was gonna cause quite the scene. Picking up on my body language, the tick of my jaw and clench of my fists quite obvious and telling, she removed her hand and moved back, eventually lying on her back and spreading her legs wide in front of me. In front of everyone.

I'd never wanted to fuck a woman more than in that moment. I kept picturing burying my cock inside her, feeling her clench around me as I made her come over and over again. Absently, I reached down and palmed my dick, trying to calm my arousal so I didn't embarrass myself in front of her and every other fucker present. Even though I tried to will my dick to soften, it only became harder, painfully straining against the fabric of my jeans.

I almost lost it when her fingers hitched inside the waistband of her tiny skirt, shimmying the material down her long, shapely legs until she was wearing nothing but a thong. After thirty seconds of pure torture, she rose to her feet and stepped back toward the center of the stage, her fingers dancing over her skin, continuing to tease and torment me.

She continuously honed in on me as if I were the only man in the room, something I quite liked, although I knew it wasn't true. The final beats of the song faded before she'd had the chance to remove her last piece of clothing. Indulge was a fully nude club, but right then I'd never been so happy to see one of our dancers break the rules.

She disappeared from the stage, taking with her our brief yet binding connection.

SEVEN

Reece

CATCHING MY BREATH BACKSTAGE HAD nothing to do with the exertion I'd endured during my performance. Instead, it had everything to do with the man who'd thrown me into another world. Dammit! I'd been so distracted with him that I'd never removed my thong. Rules of the club were to get completely naked, and I broke that rule. I sure as hell hoped I didn't get fired because of it.

Pushing aside my building paranoia at the thought of losing my job, I reverted back to thinking about the man who'd distracted me. It was weird to acknowledge, even to myself, but the painfully handsome stranger made me feel things I hadn't felt in years . . . if ever. He seemed different than every other man present, locking eyes with me like he wanted to expose his innermost secrets. A strange thread of connection quickly formed between us, still lingering in the air even without being in his presence.

Shaking my head, knowing my thoughts were utterly ridiculous, I tried like hell to forget about Mr. Tough and Sexy as I prepared for the rest of my evening, which thankfully was close to being over.

After quickly freshening up, I ventured back into the lounge area to search for someone who was receptive to a private dance. I'd become rather popular during my short employ at Indulge, so I never encountered any problems earning my keep. The entire time I searched for my next customer, my eyes flitted around the spacious room in search of the gorgeous stranger who'd made my heart leap in my chest just moments earlier. But I didn't see him. Maybe he'd done both of us a favor and left.

Berating myself for acting like some kind of lovesick puppy, I squared my shoulders, raised my head high and plastered on the most seductive smile I could muster. Striding across the room and looking for my next customer, I eyed a table full of businessmen. They seemed harmless enough, as harmless as men could be with naked women surrounding them and alcohol flowing freely.

Circling the table, I stopped next to a good-looking, dark-haired, younger guy, touching him on the shoulder to garner his attention—not that his eyes weren't already on me the entire time. "Hey, handsome. Do you want a private dance?" There was no way he would turn me down, not with the lust-induced haze he battled while leering at me. I shut down my inner voice, deciding I needed to right the wrong of not shedding all my clothes earlier. Besides, there had been many times when I'd had to grind up on a fat, ugly man, so when I encountered the chance to entertain someone pleasing to the eye, I jumped all over it. Figuratively as well as literally.

Grabbing my hand tightly, he said, "You don't have to ask me twice, sweetheart." He rose from his chair, practically knocking it over in his haste. "Let's go." His friends egged him on as I led him across the club, the smell of alcohol around him evident but not quite at an alarming level.

As we headed toward the private rooms located in the back of the club, my eye caught sight of someone off to the right, sitting in one of the more secluded sections of the establishment.

Him.

The one who drew me in with nothing but his mesmerizing green eyes.

The one who spoke to my soul.

I guess he didn't leave after all.

Desperate to distract myself from wishing I were with the mystery stranger instead, I practically ran toward the room I needed.

Closing the door to the private space, I guided him toward the single chair in the center. Once he sat, I stepped back, being sure to give him my sexiest smile before turning around to hit the button for the music. All of the selections in the private rooms were seductive beats, nothing fast-paced. The idea was to drag out the dance as long as possible, hoping the customers would engage in another. Most times, it worked.

After my stage performance, I'd changed into a simple, short black dress which buttoned up all the way. It fell just below my plump ass cheeks and dipped very low in the front, practically exposing my very erect nipples. The cold blast of the air conditioning was always kept on high, ensuring our *arousal.*

Shutting my eyes, I allowed the steady strum of the song to guide the flow of my body, swaying my hips while my hands danced over my skin. In my head, I was somewhere else. Alone. Not about to take off my clothes for some man I'd never met before. Just when I'd found my happy place, *he* popped into my head. The way his eyes bore into mine while I was on stage. The way his breaths increased and the slight thumping of his pulse intensified the closer I stalked toward him. The way his jaw muscles clenched when I saw him glance at the other men surrounding the stage. He didn't like that their eyes were glued to me, much like his were. It was slight, and quick, but I didn't miss his possessive demeanor toward me. And I should have been frightened, but I wasn't. I wanted his attention. Hell, I think I even wanted his hands on me while I danced, although that was definitely against the rules.

I circled the guy's body, all while lightly touching him. First it was on the shoulder, letting my fingers trail over the fabric of his jacket. Then I ran my hand down the front of his chest, slowly unbuttoning his shirt halfway. Pleased when I felt defined muscles underneath, the guy was a nice change of pace from some of the men I had to deal with. So why couldn't I stop picturing *my* gorgeous stranger?

Straddling my customer's lap, my thighs pinning him to the chair, I ran my hands through his thick hair. Gripping his curly tresses, I yanked his head back so he was looking straight up at the ceiling. I heard a rumble erupt from his throat, knowing he was completely turned on—as if the evidence of his arousal straining against his pants wasn't already a sign.

But then he tried to touch me, and that was a big no-no. A violation of the rules. Well, *my* rules. I knew for a fact there were girls here who had sex with some of the men who came in, but I wasn't into that. The show I gave them was just that, a show. Dancing. That was all I'd ever do with these customers.

Apparently, this guy had other intentions.

"Nuh-uh-uh, big boy. No touching allowed," I gently advised as I pried his hands off my ass and put them back on the arms of the chair.

"Ah, come on. All I want is to touch you. I won't bite, I swear. Well, not unless you want me to." He winked as if the gesture would make me change my mind. The lights were dimmed low but I could still make out his every feature, as I'm sure he could mine. I knew he noticed the warning look on my face, and when he made a move to grab me once more, I quickly removed myself from his lap and backed up.

I needed the money, so instead of calling security in to remove him, I tried my best to dispel the intensified moment. And fast. Needing him to focus on me and not my unwillingness to let him grope me, I grabbed the top of my dress and slowly pried it apart, the buttons making a delicious sound as each one popped open.

And we have success.

He licked his lips while his eyes devoured the very sight of me, his anticipation heavy for my next move. The skin of his hands turned pale, his grip on the chair certainly intense. Until it all became too much for him. Slipping his hand down his pants, he started to stroke himself, and I knew my situation had gone from tricky to unnerving. The way his eyes darkened frightened me, but I tried like hell not to show it.

My hands stilled on the last two buttons of my dress and I stopped dancing. Taking one step back, I told him, "There's no touching allowed in here, honey." A fake smile plastered on my face, my tone left no room for argument. I prayed he'd see I was serious and simply comply so I could finish, but something told me that scenario wasn't going to play out for me.

"But I'm not touching you," he responded, looking confused.

I pointed at his crotch. "No touching at all, not even yourself."

Instant irritation contorted his expression, his eyes suddenly becoming darker than before. I knew he'd been drinking, but as the situation unfolded I realized there was something else wrong, something more dangerous. If I had to guess, I'd say he was high. On what, I had no idea, and I didn't want to stick around to find out.

"That's a fucking stupid rule if you ask me," he shouted, rising from the chair and taking a single step in my direction. "I'm paying good money, and if I can't touch you then I sure as hell should be able to stroke my cock if I want." There was fire in his eyes, and I knew I'd lost control of the situation. I frantically tried to figure out how I was going to move past the irate man and escape.

While I contemplated my next move, I put as much distance between us as possible. "Well, those are the rules and you have to abide by them if you want me to finish my dance." I didn't want to finish, not at all, but I'd say anything I needed to. "Can you please sit down so I can finish for you?" I asked as I popped another button, plastering on another fake smile to trick him into thinking he wasn't frightening the hell out of me. The plan I'd come up with was to make him sit back down before I ran toward the door. Toward safety.

But he had other ideas.

Still standing, he barked, "How about you get fuckin' naked and do what I'm paying you to do." He crushed the space between us in two long strides, grabbing my arms before I could retreat. Standing at five foot eight, decently tall for a woman, I appeared much smaller with him towering over me. I'd been in these circumstances before, unfortunately—a hazard of the job—but usually the men were weak and drunk, easily persuaded to comply with my rules. This guy, however, was different. He scared me, and if I didn't escape soon I feared he was going to attack me, uncaring if he hurt me or not. For all I knew, he *wanted* to hurt me.

"Please let go," I pleaded, trying to shrug out of his bruising hold. When his grip intensified, I started to tremble. "You're hurting me." Still nothing. "Let go of me," I screamed. "Now." I tried to appear strong and fearless, but my tone betrayed me.

"You're not going anywhere until I get what I paid for, you little slut." With his final word, he shoved me so hard I fell on my ass, instant pain shooting up my back and breaking out at my shoulders. Shock knocked me dizzy, allowing him to start to disrobe. He loosened his tie and ripped his shirt open in a flash, the muscles I thought were so appealing minutes before terrifying me now. His fingers popped the button of his pants before quickly working on his zipper as he approached my crumpled form.

Thankfully, the daze I'd been in dissipated and I shot to my feet, making a run for it. He caught my wrist as I rushed past, however, whipping me around and slamming me against the nearest wall. I tried to fight him off but I was simply no match. "Get off me, you bastard!" I cried, fear setting in that no one was going to hear me. Not over that damn music, both inside our room and out. My only saving grace would be if someone happened to be walking by at that exact moment.

"Now," he said, as he gripped the sides of my dress, "we're gonna have some fun." Popping the remaining button of my dress, he ripped the material from my body and tossed it to the floor beside me. I tried to cover myself, but he grabbed my hands with one of his and held them above my head. Trying to kick him did nothing but earn me a punishing grip to my slender waist. "Keep on fighting me, sweetheart. I love a good struggle."

There was nothing I could do. I was utterly helpless. My arms were restrained and his hips were pinning my own to the wall, adhering my fears to his excitement. His lips roamed over my neck, biting and licking me as if he wasn't forcing me into this position.

I continued to struggle, but the only thing I accomplished was wearing myself out. When my attempt at escape became futile, I started to cry. Honestly, I'd been surprised it'd taken me that long for the tears to start flowing. While I was lost to my breakdown, his free hand moved from my waist and down my body, traveling over the skimpy material covering my sex.

He rubbed his fingers over my core, trying to gain entrance by sliding the lace to the side. "You'll like this. I promise," he mumbled, his ministrations becoming more persistent. I wriggled in his hold, finding a spurt of energy, and as he took a small step back I finally found my opportunity to attack.

His face was mere inches from my own when I struck his nose with my head. A chilling sound erupted from his mouth before he released me and stumbled back, his hands instantly flying up to cover his face. Blood coated his fingers, but I didn't hear bone crunching so I doubted I broke his nose. *Pity.*

Before I could skate around his enraged form, he leapt at me and tackled me to the ground. "You fucking bitch!" His knees made good work of pinning down my arms, so the only thing I could do was shake my head from side to side. As if that was going to help me. I closed my eyes, willing my mind to float off to a safer place, but I was stuck inside that darkened room with a man who was hell-bent on taking what he thought he was owed.

Drops of his blood hit my cheek, forcing me to open my eyes and face the reality of what was going to happen. I decided to plead with him once more. "Please don't do this. Please just let me go." I begged him over and over, but it was no use. And my silly attempts to buck him off barely registered. He was simply too strong.

His hands wrapped around my throat before another word left my lips. Dots flashed behind my eyes. I started to fall under an all-too-familiar darkness, and although I did everything in my power to stop it, I feared all of my efforts were in vain. If I fell unconscious, he'd surely have his way with me. Not that I could do much while I was awake, but at least if I were lucid, I'd still have a shot.

The darkness would still my struggle.

The light would give me a fighting chance.

EIGHT

Tripp

I RESTED MY HEAD AGAINST the top of the booth, taking in all the activity of the club, but nothing I saw distracted me from *her*. The mysterious woman who not ten minutes prior had burrowed into the deepest parts of my brain.

"I thought you were leaving," Hawke yelled, slapping my shoulder before taking a healthy swig of his drink.

After *her* performance I knew there was no way in hell I was leaving any time soon. My inner voice had convinced me to stay, so I slinked into the nearest booth and attempted to cool my overactive thoughts with some hard alcohol.

"Nah," I responded nonchalantly. "I'm gonna hang out a bit longer." I never made eye contact with my brother for fear he'd pick up on something I wasn't completely sure of myself. Hawke may play a dumbass most times but the guy was super observant.

"Uh-huh," he mumbled, throwing back a shot before his head twisted to the side. Slapping the table, well on his way to becoming drunk, he shouted, "'Bout time you fuckers got here." Turning my head, I saw Ryder and Breck approach, both of them looking like someone killed their dog, if they'd had one.

Neither one of them said a word as they nestled into the booth next to Hawke and me, spreading out enough so we weren't crammed together, which would just be weird. Ryder reached for my scotch but I slapped his hand away before he'd grabbed the glass.

"What the fuck, nomad?" he yelled, quickly retracting his hand.

"You know damn well you ain't gettin' any of this shit."

"Who died and made you my keeper?" His scowl would have scared most people, but not me. Besides, I knew Ryder enough to know that he wouldn't make good on any threats while he was sober. And by sober I meant no hard alcohol flowing through his veins. Otherwise, all bets were off.

"Beer," I said, taking a healthy swallow of my drink.

"What?"

"Beer, you bastard. That's all you're gettin'."

"We'll see about that," he growled, shoving Breck from the booth so he could get out. Luckily, I caught Carla's attention and shook my head while pointing at Ryder who was fast approaching the bar. But my warning was unnecessary; everyone who worked the bar knew not to serve Ryder anything but beer.

Turning my attention back on Breck, I asked, "Why the face?"

No hesitation before he spilled. "Marek's ridin' our asses about the rotation with Psych. He's coming unhinged and it's scaring the shit out of me."

"*Coming* unhinged?"

"Well . . . more than usual." He shook his head as if he disagreed with some sort of inner dialogue, locking eyes with me before he frowned.

Ryder striding back to our table pulled all of our attention.

"You fucker. That chick wouldn't serve me what I wanted," he griped before pushing Breck farther into the booth so he could sit back down.

"Why you want that shit anyway?" Hawke shouted over the music, tapping the top of the table in beat with the song.

"I could just use a shot of something to help take the edge off."

"Why?" Hawke repeated. "Braylen getting on your nerves?" My brother laughed, and seeing the look on Ryder's face only made him laugh harder. "Shit!" he exclaimed. "Never thought I'd see the day when the big bad Ryder was all twisted up from some fuckin' broad."

"Fuck you. I don't even know what Edana sees in your dumb ass," Ryder goaded, knowing damn well Hawke was gonna retaliate. Which he did, seconds after Ryder shut his mouth. Hawke jumped up from his seat and lunged over the table, reaching out to grab Ryder's cut, the volatile look on his face warning everyone around him he was set to explode.

Pulling him back, I shoved Hawke back in his seat, throwing my arm across his chest to try and keep him contained. Which was quite challenging because he kept trying to go after Ryder, who sat across from us with a fuckin' smirk on his face.

"Calm the hell down!" I shouted to my brother, putting more pressure on him to stay still. Finally he did, reaching for his drink and draining the rest of it before tossing the empty beer bottle at Ryder. Thankfully our Sergeant-at-Arms ducked at the last minute.

"Isn't it your duty to make sure there's no chaos in the club?" I asked, glaring at Ryder. He knew damn well any mention of Edana was a sore subject, the guilt that consumed my brother on a daily basis over every-thing that had happened to her borderline debilitating.

"What? Like keeping the peace and shit?" He laughed, shaking his head in disbelief at the idea.

"Yeah, you ass."

"Like that'll ever happen." Ryder slumped back in the booth, baiting Hawke with the narrowing of his eyes. It was as if he wanted to fight with him.

Deciding to change the topic, I coaxed Breck into telling me more about his outburst. "So, is someone not doing their part babysitting our prisoner?"

"No. Everyone is doin' their part."

"So what the hell is the problem?"

Tapping the table as a distraction, Breck glanced to Ryder before speak-ing. "Marek feels we're not inflicting enough pain on Psych." From the tone of his voice I knew the subject bothered him. Breck had no problem inflicting pain on someone when necessary, especially to the likes of that fucker, but I knew he didn't get off on that shit either. None of us did. Well, apparently Marek did, but could I blame him? The man had every right to inflict as much agony on Psych Brooks as possible, but at some point he had to let go and move on.

"He's draggin' this shit out. It's not good. Not for him or any of us."
Bingo.

Leaning forward, I gave Breck my best advice. "Look, this whole situ-ation with Psych will be done whenever Marek deems it so. He's working through some shit, not only for himself, but for Sully." Resting back against my seat, I finished with, "We're just gonna have to be patient. He can't prolong it forever. Have you seen Psych's condition? If I were a betting man, I'd give him a few more days at best."

Swallowing the rest of my drink, I shoved it toward Ryder. "You can suck on my ice cubes if you want. I'm sure there's some scotch left on them." The corner of my lip twitched in amusement watching his reaction.

"Fuck you," he grated, grabbing two of the cubes from the glass and throwing them at me. I dodged them, but Hawke hadn't been so lucky.

"What the fuck?" he yelled, tossing them right back at Ryder. A hint of a grin appeared on my brother's face, but it was gone before anyone else saw it. At least they weren't tackling each other to the ground.

The thing with men that many women didn't understand was that we could argue, and even go to blows, but a few minutes later it was done with. We were all brothers and, as such, we had each other's backs. Sure, we got on each other's nerves, and sometimes a battle ensued, but we didn't hold grudges. When it was done, it was done.

With the exception of Trigger and Stone. Trigger still harbored some ill feelings toward Stone for going against code and gettin' with his niece. Their relationship wasn't as bad as it once was, especially after Riley was born, but anger still reared up every now and again when Trigger spoke to the club's VP.

The antics at our table took my mind off *her*. Slightly. Peering around the club, I still didn't catch a glimpse of her. I wondered if she left for the evening. All of a sudden, thoughts of where she lived, how she got there, and if she was being careful bombarded me. Why I cared about the safety of a woman I'd never met baffled me, but the questions and concerns were present nonetheless. After ten minutes, I decided to put my crazy thoughts to rest.

Straddling a stool at the bar, I waved Carla over. "Did the new girl leave already?" I tried to appear as disinterested as possible, but her smile told me she knew I was anything but. I averted my eyes but her silence pulled my attention back to her. "What?"

"I told you she was quite somethin', didn't I?" She smiled bigger at my intrigue. I didn't answer. Instead, I raised a brow in irritation. Carla laughed. "No, she didn't leave yet. I believe she's in the back room giving a private dance."

My hands instantly clenched the edge of the bar, the look on my face surely telling Carla that I was less than pleased with the news. Although I couldn't explain why, not to her and certainly not to myself.

Rising from my seat, I walked across the open area and headed toward the private rooms. Only one was in use at the moment, the green sign above the door reading 'Occupied.' Every step closer had me on edge, my heart racing so fast I swore it was gonna beat right out of my goddamn chest if I didn't get a fuckin' grip.

I was ten feet away when I heard a man shouting. Then I heard a woman's screams, pleading with him to get off her. And I knew I only had seconds before something horrific happened to her, if it hadn't already. Not stopping to check if the door was unlocked, my shoulder hit the thick wood and splintered the frame.

Berating myself for ever taking my eyes off her in the first place, a mistake I would never make again, I rushed into the room and threw myself at the man pinning her to the ground. My sheer size, mixed with my surprise attack, was enough to knock the guy to the ground in no time, wailing on him with my fists while he did his best to defend himself. He tried to throw a punch, but all that got him was a broken wrist. My rage poured from me in droves, the adrenaline coursing through my veins hyping my need to end the fucker. My fists were still flying at him when hands grabbed at me from behind, tugging me backward to get me to stop.

"Tripp!" Ryder shouted. "Come on." I tried to shrug him off, but he wasn't the only one pulling at me; my brother was helping to diffuse the situation as well.

"Bro, he's right. Come on. You did what you needed to. It's over." Hawke had no idea what was going on, but he knew I would never attack someone without a damn good reason. It took me a few extra seconds to calm down enough to hop to my feet, leaving the other guy on the floor still breathing. Unfortunately.

Gripping my hair, I turned around and found the woman I'd rescued cowering in the corner, her knees pulled tightly to her chest as she buried her head from view. I could see her body trembling from clear across the room and I wanted nothing more than to protect her, to soothe her worries and comfort her. A stranger. A woman I'd seen for the first time on stage, dancing for a crowd of men. A woman who willingly came into this room with a stranger because she wanted to make extra money. A woman who would put herself into this very same situation again in the future.

Not if I have anything to say about it.

Disregarding my crazy thought, I moved toward her with my hands held in front of me to show her I meant no harm. The commotion caught the attention of not only my men but Carla and the guy we had working security that evening.

"Oh my God!" Carla cried. "What happened?" She took a step toward the woman, but I stopped her.

"Don't. I got her," I said, crouching and resting my hands on her shoulders. "Look at me." She ignored me and kept her head down. "Look at me," I said more forcefully, while still keeping a hint of compassion in my voice. Finally, she complied, lifting her head slowly until her eyes connected with mine. "What's your name?"

"Reece," she whispered. Tortured blue-grays shredded me, the hurt and fear lingering in her gaze pumping my anger to new heights all over again. It was then I noticed she'd been choked, the bastard's fingerprints bruising her delicate neck, the reddened area already starting to darken.

Barely controlling myself, I reached for her hands and guided her to her feet, pulling her into me to shield her nakedness from everyone present. Without turning around, I shouted to Hawke, "Get him the fuck out of here and make sure he understands that if he ever comes near this place, or her, again that we'll snatch his life from him."

As Hawke and Ryder dragged the bastard past us and from the room, she began to tremble more, wrapping her arms around my waist and trying like hell to disappear. If she could've climbed inside my body, I swore she would have. After what felt like forever, I dislodged her hands from around me and took a small step back. I shrugged off my cut and wrapped it around her. The sight of how it swallowed her up was almost comical, but at least she was covered.

"Thank you," she said, her voice small and frail. I nodded before turning my attention to Carla, who was still standing close by. "Can you stay with her for a second?"

"Absolutely." Carla drew Reece into her embrace, whispering something in her ear in an effort to comfort her.

Stalking toward the security guy, I grabbed his collar and shoved him against the wall. "Where the fuck were you? Why weren't you watching the cameras?" I roared, slamming him against the wall once more. "You could have prevented what happened to her." Stunned, the guy went mute on me, eyes widening in fear for his life. "Where were you?" I repeated.

"I'm sorry. I . . . I was . . . busy," he stumbled over his words.

"Busy doin' what? Gettin' your dick sucked?" The surprised look on his face told me I'd hit the nail on the head, and it took everything in me not to snatch him by his throat and squeeze the life out of him. "Well, I hope it was worth it because you're fired. Get your shit and get the fuck out of this club before I make it so you can't walk outta here," I threatened.

Spinning around, I headed back toward the two women. "Carla," I said, pulling Reece from her arms and back into mine, "I need you to tell all the girls they aren't to mess with the men when they're on duty. Ever. And give the guys the same message. Because if this shit happens again, I'll rain holy hell down on whoever fucks up."

"I'll take care of it," she assured, glancing quickly at the younger woman and then back to me before giving me what looked like a thankful smile.

Once it was just the two of us standing in the middle of the room, I stepped back to put some distance between us. With my fingers under her chin, I slowly lifted her head. "How's your neck? Because it looks pretty fuckin' bad."

"Nothing I can't handle," she confessed.

"Fuck!" I shouted, calming my tone once I saw her flinch. "Sorry. You don't have to be afraid of me. I won't hurt you. I promise."

"I know."

Looking into her beautiful, soul-captivating eyes, I knew she meant what she'd said. Those two simple words of acknowledgement were all I needed to forge ahead with my plan.

NINE

Reece

WHAT I FELT WHEN IN this man's presence was unlike any other emotion I'd ever experienced. His concern wrapped around me like the warmest of blankets, his desire to protect me settling my wayward nerves. My nakedness shielded by his large leather vest, I clutched it tighter and walked next to him as we headed toward the exit. I had no idea where he was taking me, and for the briefest of moments I didn't care. All I wished to do was live in the existence that a stranger rescued me. A stranger who captivated my attention and never let go. I didn't understand the pull I felt toward him, but after the night I'd had, all I wanted to do was forget about what happened and try and salvage an ounce of dignity before I broke down in front of the large man walking beside me.

"You're not working here anymore," he blurted, making me stop dead in my tracks while he continued on ahead. He hadn't realized I stopped following him until he happened to turn his head to the side, expecting to see me beside him. The look of anger mixed with fear on my face propelled him to walk back toward me. "What's the matter?" he asked, as if he hadn't just stolen my livelihood right out from under me.

Cinching his vest tighter around me, I narrowed my eyes before speaking, trying to choose my words wisely. But as soon as my lips parted, I rambled like some sort of fool. "How . . . how is it my fault? I didn't provoke him. I swear. I was only trying to give him a lap dance, and then he stroked himself and when I told him to stop he got angry, and when I tried to escape he got angrier and came after me and . . . and . . . I'm sorry." After all that, I ended up apologizing for being the cause of the eruption at the club that evening.

The stranger's head cocked to the side and studied me for a moment before asking, "Why are you . . . ? What's the matter?" Truly looking confused, he rested his hands on my trembling shoulders.

"I need this job," I pleaded, lowering my head in nervousness. "Please don't fire me. I swear it won't happen again." How I could promise such a thing was beyond me, but I did. I'd say anything I needed to, no matter how ridiculous, to ensure I kept my job. I wasn't above begging and groveling, having been doing it for years. Raising my chin I stared at his broad chest, covered by a thin white T-shirt. Imagining what his naked torso looked like distracted my overactive brain, if only for a few seconds. Lifting my chin higher, I had no choice but to finally look at him, the frown marring his handsome face quite puzzling.

"I'm not firing you for what happened. But I won't lie and tell you that you're gonna continue to work here. It's not happenin'." His fingers trailed over the tops of my arms, and even through the thick leather covering me, the contact heated my skin to scorching levels.

I needed space.

"I said I was sorry. It'll never happen again." *There I go again with my half-assed promises.*

"You're goddamn right it won't happen again. I'll make sure of it." The muscles in his jaw jumped, his fingers digging into my arms in what appeared to be anger.

I couldn't figure out why he blamed me entirely for that bastard attacking me.

Shrugging out of his grasp, my own anger took hold, but experience told me to watch my tone. Although, all reasoning aside, there was something about the man brooding in front of me that told me he wouldn't physically lash out at me.

"What makes you think you have the authority to fire me?" I grasped at straws, but hopefully throwing a legit question at him would make him take his attitude down a notch.

Apparently, I was about to be schooled.

"First off, I told you I'm not firing you. Well, not exactly. And second, who *I* am is your boss. See the patch on that vest coverin' ya? It says 'Knights Corruption.' The very same club that owns this place." Cocking an arrogant brow, he leaned down and said, "So I hold all the authority, sweetheart."

Captured in a good old-fashioned stare-off, it wasn't until Carla placed her hand on my shoulder that I turned my attention away from the man in front of me and on to her.

"You okay, hon?" she asked, concern for my well-being written all over her pretty face.

"Yeah, but . . . I just got fired." I tried to remain strong, but the hitch in my voice gave me away.

"What do you mean?" Stealing my space, she stood in front of me. "Tripp, what is she talkin' about?" Pinning her hands on her hips, she asked, "Did you really just fire her?"

Tripp?

"She's not workin' here anymore." The look on his face left no room for argument, but that didn't stop Carla.

"She didn't do anything wrong and you know it."

"I know that," he argued.

"Then why?" Carla pressed, reaching behind her and grasping my hand, funneling her support through her touch.

"I'm not justifying my choice to you or anyone. It's done. Let it go." He stood taller and crossed his arms over his broad chest, his muscles stretching the fabric of his shirt.

His size should have intimidated me, but it did the exact opposite—I felt safe next to him, protected, like nothing in the world could harm me. And even though he'd just fired me, I couldn't help but commit every facet of this incredible man to memory. Carla's next words shoved me out of my assessment and back into the increasingly tense situation.

"Stone left it up to me to find Heather's replacement, and I did. So you can't stroll in here and undermine me. That's not how any of this works." Tripp remained still, only the repeated arch of his brow a giveaway that he was even listening. Carla huffed and stepped closer, releasing my hand in the process. Shoving a finger into his thick chest, she said, "You don't scare me, Tripp, so stop trying."

His response was sudden. He reached around the club manager and snagged my wrist, gently pulling me behind him as he strode quickly toward the door. "It's done, Carla, so find another girl."

When I ventured a glance behind me, I saw Carla shaking her head, her lips moving so rapidly I was sure she was having quite the conversation with herself.

"Where are you taking me?"

"Home," he answered, never bothering to look at me.

"I don't need you to take me anywhere." I tried to pull free from his grip but he only tightened his hold. "I'm fine by myself. You've had your say. You've fired me, so stop confusing me with pretending you care what happens to me. I can make my own way home."

He continued on, walking so fast I tripped over my feet in my haste to try and keep up. When I smacked into his back on my lurch forward, he stopped and spun around, his hands instantly steadying me. "Sorry," he apologized. "I walk fast when I have a purpose." Then he did something which completely threw me off-kilter—he smiled . . . and I swore I thought I was gonna faint. In an instant, all the anger and frustration I'd felt toward him melted away.

The way his green eyes lit up captivated my soul. Odd sentiment, I know, but so very true. The breath in my lungs stung after endless seconds, but I wanted to remain frozen in the moment, relishing the odd peace catapulting me into a different place in time.

"Are you okay?" he asked, his fingers dancing over the tops of my arms once more. Closing in on my personal space, he stood so close I had to crane my neck just to see his face. His warmth enclosed me, his intoxicating scent flicking on a switch inside me that had been off for a very long time.

I wanted nothing more than to wrap my arms around his waist and nuzzle myself into him, to rest my head against his chest and feel the thrum of his heartbeat, but of course I held back. He'd think me some kind of fruitcake if I did such a thing. Instead I stood tall and allowed myself to escape inside those entrancing orbs of his.

"You okay?" he repeated, cocking his head to the side while waiting for an answer.

"Y-yeah. I'm fine," I finally responded, my hold on his vest unrelenting as I used it to keep myself covered. "But I'd like to get dressed before we leave." Knowing he wasn't going to make the first move and back up, I retreated a few steps, his hands falling to his sides.

Music vibrated from the speakers. Men shouted at the naked performer on stage, their hoots and hollers blending into one another's. A glass shattered in the distance, followed by a few choice words from Carla. A woman's laughter rang out into the sexually charged air, but none of it registered completely. It was as if I existed in a daze, everything around me a mirage. As if it weren't really happening. But dead center in the mix of the cloudy vision of the club stood two people, everyone else fading into obscurity with each second ticking by.

Tripp and me.

Our eyes devoured the other, the air between us shared.

Our worlds were colliding, exploding and threatening everything we thought and knew. I saw the shared experience in the twinkle of his eyes and in the way his full lips kicked up in the corners, smiling because he saw the same recognition in me.

Finally, after what felt like an eternity, Tripp nodded before pushing a strained puff of air through his lips. "Go. Put some clothes on and grab your things. I'll be waiting right here." His tone told me everything, and I knew I'd better hurry before he lost his patience and dragged me out of the club. Naked or not.

TEN

Reece

"ARE YOU FUCKIN' HIM?"

I knew exactly who'd asked the abrupt question, my locker door thankfully blocking the woman from sight. But I couldn't hide behind the metal barrier forever. Once the latch clicked closed, I turned my head and gave her a fake smile.

"Can I do something for you, Arianna?" I asked, wishing she'd just leave me alone. Ever since I started working at the club she'd given me a hard time, throwing me nasty glares, hiding my costumes and makeup, and making snide comments. I got it—she didn't like me, although I couldn't fathom why. I'd never done anything to her, but I gave up caring, especially when Carla told me she was only acting like that toward me because she was jealous of all the attention I was getting from the customers. The same customers who used to fawn all over her.

"You hard of hearin'? I asked if you're fuckin' him," she repeated, haughtily crossing her arms over her chest and pushing her fake tits up higher.

"Who are you talking about?"

"Tripp."

"You know him?"

"Oh, honey." She laughed. "I know him *real* well." She winked and licked her thin lips, dropping her arms to her sides before stepping closer. "I fucked him so many times I've ruined him for any other bitch."

If Arianna weren't such a nasty person she'd actually be attractive. Close to my five foot eight, she had a nice build, although she'd gone a little overboard with her implants. Only my opinion, of course. She also caked on the makeup, something I thought was a waste of time because the men weren't too concerned with our faces. She wore wigs like the rest of us, but the first time I saw her natural reddish hair, all thick and wavy, I'd been jealous. That was until she opened her mouth and snapped at me, asking why I was leering at her. Ever since then I'd tried my best to stay clear of her whenever we worked the same shift, but she always seemed to seek me out for her own amusement.

"Well?" she pressed when I remained silent.

"I just met him." I had no idea why I gave that answer, but I couldn't think of anything but the truth.

"Well, he won't want your simple ass anyway, so don't even bother."

I chose not to engage, pushing past her and grabbing my purse and bag from the bench, along with Tripp's vest.

As soon as Arianna's eyes latched onto his leather, she gave me the nastiest look. "You just met him? Then why do you have his cut?"

"His what?"

"His cut," she sneered, pointing at the vest in my hand.

"He gave it to me until I got changed." I hadn't wanted to continue the conversation, but I found myself babbling on nonetheless.

"Well, since I'm going home with him tonight, I'll give it back to him." She reached out and tried to snatch it from my hands but I moved back, clutching his property tightly. A possessiveness I'd never encountered before took over. I couldn't explain it and I didn't have time to, not before Arianna stepped closer and tried to grab the vest once more. Thankfully, Carla interrupted us; otherwise, I had no idea what would have happened. I'd already endured enough that evening, and another fight was the last thing I needed.

"Arianna, you're not done with your shift. Let's go," Carla demanded, pointing toward the door for her to leave.

"Fine," she scoffed, "but remember who he'll be fuckin' later, sweetheart." She narrowed her eyes, trying her best to intimidate me before knocking into me on her way out the door.

"What the hell was that all about?" Carla's compassion for me was comforting, but I was tired and the only thing I wanted to do was leave. End this night and lose myself to sleep until the dawn promised a new day.

"I have no idea," I lied, not wanting to explain because I didn't completely understand myself.

Following Carla, I walked across the main room until I stood behind Tripp. He didn't know I was there, as was apparent by his conversation with whoever was on the other end of the phone.

"That's fine. Yeah, I don't care. Whatever you need." He sighed. "I said I don't care." Those were his final words before he hung up. Tucking his cell away, he turned around and practically bowled me over since I'd been standing so close. He looked confused for a moment, grabbing a strand of my hair and twirling it around his fingers. I'd removed my wig, my long chestnut color clearly a surprise to him.

"I was beginning to think I'd have to come and collect you." No smile traced his lips that time, which led me to believe he was completely serious. Did he not trust that I'd leave the club on my own accord? That he'd have to personally escort me out? And why was he insistent on driving me home? Why not just put me out and be done with me? I'd just met this man, yet already he confused the hell out of me with not only the way he looked at me but the way he made me feel. I should've been infuriated with him for firing me, but I wasn't. Well . . . I was, but I also wanted to spend more time with him, defying all reason and logic.

Placing his hand on the small of my back, he guided me toward the exit. Before we made it, though, Arianna came out of nowhere and grabbed Tripp's arm. "I'll see you later, baby," she fussed, glaring at me quickly before looking back at Tripp. Before he could answer, she pressed her nasty lips to his and strolled away.

A twinge of jealousy roared through me as I put one foot in front of the other rather quickly and walked farther away from Tripp. I should have known he wasn't going to let me get too far ahead of him, the feel of his hand on my waist annoying yet comforting.

"I don't know what she's talking about," he said, pushing the door open for me.

Without looking back, I responded. "None of my business. Just like it's none of your business who I go home with." Being snarky wasn't a trait of mine, but I found it came in quite handy just then.

I half expected him to come back with a retort but he remained silent. I knew my comment bothered him, though; I could just feel it.

The darkness of the evening was a perfect shield, so I kept my eyes straight ahead while we walked side by side across the large parking lot. I had no idea where I was going, but I kept on anyway. Eventually, I'd figure it out. The motel I was staying at was only a mile down the road. Worst-case, I'd walk the entire way, although the heels I had on would kill my feet before I made it there.

"I'm parked over here," Tripp announced, grabbing my hand and hauling me toward a motorcycle. Once we neared his ride, I shook my head and retreated. "What's the matter?"

"I'm not gettin' on that," I refused, pointing toward the hunk of steel. "I'll find my own way back."

"I won't let anything happen to you. I promise." Reaching out his hand, he waited for me to come closer, but I never did.

"I don't want to." No way was I going to straddle that machine. There was absolutely no protection between me and the pavement if something went wrong. Helmets only helped to protect the head from being crushed. What about the rest of my body? I just couldn't trust my safety to a complete stranger, even though said stranger was most likely an excellent rider. Fate had lashed out at me enough during my life, I wasn't about to tempt the fickle bitch and simply hope for the best.

While I was caught up inside my own head, he pulled his phone out and dialed a number. "Get out here. In the parking lot. I need your keys. Because I said so." He hung up, not once taking his eyes from me. Moments later, the door swung open and a man walked straight for us. He was good-looking, his dark hair the same shade as Tripp's, and the closer he came the more I could see a resemblance between the two.

"How am I getting home?" the man asked, throwing me a smile before tossing his keys at Tripp, staggering to the side before righting himself.

"I'll have someone come get you."

"Why don't you just let me take your bike?" His jumbled words gave away that he was a little more than tipsy.

"Because, brother or not, I'd have to kill ya if you put a scratch on my bike. Seeing as how your ass is drunk and all."

"I'm not drunk. Just feelin' nice," he blabbered, winking at me before turning his attention back to Tripp.

"Shut the fuck up and get back inside." Tripp stepped closer and whispered something in his brother's ear before ushering him back toward the club. Turning around, he strolled toward me, grasped my hand and led me toward a dark-colored truck. "I would've introduced you, but he's not in any shape not to be crass, or even remember he met you for that matter. It'd just be a waste of time."

Opening the passenger door, he waited until I'd slid inside and buckled up before rounding the vehicle to his side. Turning over the engine, he drove across the lot and came to a dead stop at the edge, glancing over at me for directions.

"Take a right. My motel is a mile down the road." I settled into my seat and waited for him to propel the truck forward, but we remained immobile. "What?" I asked, admiring his profile during the ensuing silence, losing myself to the image of his chiseled jaw and slight stubble.

"The Buckshot Motel? That's where you're staying?" he asked incredulously, turning on the interior light and shaking his head before peppering me with more questions. "How long have you been there? And why . . . why in God's name would you choose that place? Do you know what a cesspool it is? Of course you do, but what I can't figure out is why you're staying there." He rambled on until he wasn't even directing his words at me any longer. His demeanor was borderline snobby, which was quite comical coming from someone who looked like him. He was the furthest thing from uppity, yet he took it upon himself to condemn the only place I could afford, essentially making me feel worse about my predicament.

"Well?" he asked, raising his voice as if I hadn't been paying attention the entire time.

"Yes, I'm staying there, and it's because I can't afford anywhere else. I've just moved here and I had a whopping fifty bucks to my name. I was lucky to find a job right away, so at least I wasn't out on the streets." Turning my body toward him so he didn't miss the angry look on my face, I continued, "But now you've gone and fired me—for something that wasn't my fault, I might add—so now it's a great possibility that I'll be homeless in a few weeks if I don't find another place to work. So thanks for that." The more I spoke, the angrier I became, although I tried to rein in my temper because my feet were killing me and the thought of walking a mile in the dark in these damn heels was too much. If I watched my tone maybe he'd follow through and give me a ride back to the 'cesspool.'

We stared at each other, the slight tick of his jaw and squint of his eyes telling me something was going on inside that gorgeous head of his. He bit his lower lip, and I wanted nothing more than to dislodge it from his straight white teeth and suck on it. *Oh my God! What is wrong with me?*

Moving my body to face the front once again, I said, "Please just take me home."

"Home?" he scoffed, flicking off the light before pressing on the gas and turning left.

"Where are you going? I said to take a right."

"You're not going there."

"But my stuff is there."

"We'll get it tomorrow," he said matter-of-factly.

"Where are you taking me?"

"To my place. You can stay there until you find something better. No way am I dropping you off at that shithole, and since I don't trust that you'd be safe there, I'd be forced to stay with you . . . and no way that's happenin'."

There he goes rambling again.

ELEVEN

Tripp

I CAN'T BELIEVE SHE EXPECTED me to drop her off at the Buckshot Motel. The place was well known for druggies and whores. They even rented the rooms by the hour, for Christ's sake.

"How did you get back and forth to work? I know you don't have a car if the only thing you could afford was that fuckin' place." My hands tightened on the wheel, my impatience for the entire evening coming to a halting close.

She remained silent for a few moments before answering, most likely pissed at me for putting down her choice of living arrangements. But I didn't give a shit. Someone had to tell her, and that someone may as well be me. "I'd walk," she answered, angering me more than I already was, "or I'd hitch a ride with Carla or one of the other girls who live close by." The entire time she spoke she avoided lifting her head. Why did her refusal to look at me bother me so much?

I couldn't believe I hadn't thought about this before, but I wondered if she had someone waiting for her back at the motel. "You got a man?" I blurted, holding my breath until she uttered a response.

"No."

"Good."

"Why good?"

"'Cause if you told me you did, it wouldn't stop me from bringing you to my place." I had no idea why I was saying what I was, but the words tumbled out before my fuckin' brain could filter them. I only prayed I wasn't freaking her out.

Miles passed before she spoke again. "Tripp?"

"Yeah."

"Is that your real name?" she asked, resting her elbow on the frame of the door.

"Is that what you were really gonna ask me?"

"Yes." She answered so quickly I knew her response was forced.

"I don't know you well enough to tell you my real name, sweetheart," I countered, smirking at the sudden back and forth between us, the topic thankfully lighter than before.

"But you're willing to take me back to your place. Which, by the way, I don't think is a good idea."

"Oh yeah, and why's that?"

"Because you're a stranger. And I don't make it a habit of going back to strangers' homes." Her arm fell from the doorframe and both hands rested in her lap, picking at the edge of my cut.

"If that's bothering you"—I gestured toward my vest—"you can throw it in the back. I'll grab it when I get out."

"No, it's fine. The heaviness of it is actually keeping me warm. California nights sometimes get a bit chilly."

"The way you said that I'm assuming you're not from here."

"No, I'm not." She wasn't gonna give me anything more unless I pressed.

"Where are you from, then?"

"Maine."

"Why did you move here? You chasin' a modelin' career or somethin'?"

"Yeah, I was hoping to get my big break twirling around the pole." She chuckled. "It obviously didn't work." A lightness drifted off her and whatever tension had been strangling the air between us lessened.

"So why California, then?" I asked once more.

"I'd rather not talk about it." Short and to the point, the tenseness creeping back into her posture warning me to let it go. So I did, for the time being.

She didn't speak again until twenty minutes later when we turned down a narrow, darkened gravel road. I'd been renting a cabin ever since Marek had asked me to stay on and oversee the progress and daily running of Indulge.

Clearing her throat, she blurted, "You're not planning on killing me, are you?" A nervous laugh escaped, irritating me more than I let on.

"Do you think I'd save you from that asshole only to turn around and kill you?"

"I hope not." Another uneasy laugh. "Thank you for that, by the way. I really appreciate it, even though I got blamed for it."

"Why do you keep saying I blame you for him attacking you? Because it ain't true. The only one to blame is that fucker. Him and him alone, so please stop sayin' otherwise."

She twitched in her seat, her nerves getting the better of her. I could tell she wanted to confront me, yell at me, tell me right where to go, but for some reason she held back.

"What?" I asked, finally pulling to a stop in front of my place.

"If . . . if you don't blame me, then why did you fire me?" When I opened my door the interior light came on, illuminating her beautiful face and her confused expression.

"Because I don't want you to ever put yourself in that situation again. It isn't safe." I climbed out of the truck and shut the door before she could come back with a retort. When I arrived at her door, I opened it up and extended my hand. Hawke's truck was high and I didn't want her to lose her footing while climbing down.

As soon as her palm touched mine, I closed my eyes and reveled in the warmth of her touch. It was brief, yet calming. I took her belongings, including my cut, from her hands and led her toward the porch.

"You have a beautiful home," she said in awe, her voice like the softest silk, weaving its hold around every fiber of my being and entrancing me.

"Thank you, but it's not mine. I'm just rentin' it for now. But if I stay on, I have the option to purchase." A large front porch ran the entire length of the cabin. Sometimes I'd sit in the lone rocking chair with a beer in hand and watch the sun disappear behind the horizon, often wondering what the future held for me and my club. There were plenty of nights I'd wished to share the scenery with someone, but until I met Reece, I hadn't realized how lonely I'd been.

She walked quietly beside me, the only sound coming from the rocks of the pathway kicking up beneath our feet.

Once inside, I tossed everything I'd been carrying on the nearest chair and walked to the kitchen. "Do you want something to drink?"

"Water will be fine."

After I handed her a bottled water, I intently watched her twist off the cap, raise it to her mouth and take a healthy gulp before licking water droplets from her plump lips. When she finished, she placed it on the table closest to her and stood in front of me, playing with her hands in nervousness.

When the silent awkwardness became too stifling, I spoke up. "I have some clothes you can change into."

"Are you married?" she asked, stepping back and bracing herself on the chair behind her. Her bluish-gray eyes widened, and although I didn't understand her appall, all I wanted to do was put her out of her misery.

"No, I'm not married."

"Oh," she said, rushing out a breath of air. "I thought when you said you had some clothes for me that you had access to women's clothing."

"No, I meant I have some shorts and a T-shirt you could wear. Or not. If you prefer to sleep in the nude, please don't let me stop ya." I chuckled to help relieve some of the tension, but it did nothing to stop her body from reacting. Averting her eyes, her cheeks flamed the sexiest shade of pink. How someone could take their clothes off for a living yet look so embarrassed by the mention of sleeping nude was quite the conundrum. She certainly wasn't what I expected at all.

Dismissing her slight discomfort, she switched the subject, although what she chose to say irritated me. "I don't want to be in the way when Arianna gets here, so if you'll show me where I'll be sleeping, I'll get out of your hair."

"What the hell are you talkin' about? Why would Arianna be coming over?" My entire body tensed. I hated that Reece thought there was anything going on between me and that bitch. Yeah, Arianna was a bitch. I saw the way she talked to everyone at the club; I just chose to ignore it when I buried myself between her legs because I was obviously out of my mind.

"Because she told me she was."

"When?"

"When I was getting changed at the club. She cornered me and asked me. . . ." She trailed off before finishing, becoming quite flustered again. Her blush intensified.

Oh this is gonna be good.

"What did she ask you?"

"I don't remember," she lied, lowering her head to avoid further eye contact.

"Reece. . . ." She kept her head down. "Look. At. Me," I demanded, the gruffness to my tone leaving no room for argument. After several seconds, she finally raised her head. "What did she ask you?"

Her teeth played with her bottom lip in nervousness. All sorts of images of what I'd love to do with those lips ran through my head, but before I lost myself to them, she answered. "She asked me if I was fu-fucking you." Surprisingly, she kept her eyes on me after speaking, probably counting the seconds until I broke the suddenly charged connection.

"What did you say?"

Her mouth fell open. "What do you think I said? I just met you earlier tonight." Her mouth opened and closed a few more times, but no words escaped.

"So . . . you don't wanna sleep with me?"

"I didn't say that. I mean, that's not what she asked me." Her hands twisted errant strands of her hair. "Wait, what are you asking me?"

Rattling her was quickly becoming my new favorite thing.

Having too much fun to let it go, I pressed her further, crowding her personal space for the full effect. "It's simple. Do you want to sleep with me?"

"I don't know you."

"So what? It's a simple yes or no. Do you want me between those sexy thighs of yours or not?" She looked like a deer in headlights. "Okay, we'll table that question for another time." I should've been more sensitive to what she'd been through earlier, but I couldn't help but goad her. Besides, I took comfort knowing I'd never let anything bad happen to her again. From here on out she should consider herself safe. "And just so you know, Arianna won't be stopping over."

"Is she your girlfriend?"

"Hell no!" I shouted, lowering my voice back to a normal level after I saw her flinch. "Sorry. No, that chick is certainly not my girlfriend. Since you seem to want to pry into my business," I said, giving her a faux look of irritation, "I'm not involved with anyone."

"Oh," she simply responded, twirling a strand of hair around her finger again. A nervous tick?

"So you know what that means, don't ya?"

"No." Her voice was meek and unsure, a contradiction to the woman I believed her to truly be.

"That means you're free to hit on me as much as your little heart desires."

She blushed again, but at least that time her flush was accompanied by a smile.

Walking away was hard, but I turned my back to her and headed toward the kitchen once more. "You hungry?" I asked over my shoulder, rummaging through the fridge for something to make in case she said yes. I didn't have to face her to know her eyes were glued to me. As much as I wanted to turn around and catch her ogling me, I remained in position, acting as if I weren't completely distracted by her standing twenty feet away.

"No. I don't have much of an appetite," she admitted.

Closing the fridge, a rush of strangled breath passed my lips before I finally turned to face her and saw I was right. Her eyes were glued to me, but when her tongue peeked out and licked her lips I had to hold back from rushing toward her and crashing my mouth to hers.

Fuck! What was I thinking bringing her to my house?

Before I could delve into my confusion, my cell rang, 'Prez' flashing across the screen and pulling all of my focus.

"Yeah," I answered, my voice rushed, trying to tamp down my irritation.

"You're up."

"I thought that wasn't until tomorrow."

"Change of plans. Let's go," Marek demanded, hanging up on me before giving me the chance to ask if someone could take my place. Cursing under my breath, I glanced at Reece, hating that I had to leave her. But at least at my place she'd be safe. It was a small comfort.

If I'd had a choice, I would've stay holed up in the cabin for days—weeks, even. Who was I kidding? I'd stay locked away from everyone else for months if that's what it took to drive away my new obsession with this woman.

TWELVE

Reece

WHAT THE HELL WAS I thinking coming here?

My actions were completely out of character. Never mind that Tripp was a stranger; even though he'd rescued me, the way my body bristled when I was near him should've been a warning in and of itself. He was dangerous. The way his eyes devoured me. The way his body called to mine on the basest of levels.

All my thoughts became muddled whenever he crowded my personal space. Hell, even with the space currently between us I found it hard to think of anything other than being wrapped in his warm embrace.

Maybe it was nothing more than knight-in-shining-armor syndrome. Was that even a thing? I'd never had someone come to my rescue before, so maybe his saving me from that bastard earlier was the sole reason for my confusing feelings toward him. Even as my brain tried to convince me this was the real reason, my heart and soul knew differently.

"Come on," he instructed, striding from the room after speaking and leaving me no choice but to follow. Correction—I had a choice. I could have stayed glued to the spot, but my brain spurred me to follow him. Or was that curiosity? Or tangible attraction?

He disappeared around the corner and I had to jog to keep up, which resulted in crashing into the back of him, bouncing back and almost losing my balance. Luckily my hand shot out and I braced myself against the wall.

"You okay?" he asked, spinning around and grabbing my arms.

"Yeah, I'm fine," I said, quite embarrassed. "Your long-ass legs are to blame, you know." I tried to make light of my clumsiness, and from the smile on his face, it'd worked.

"My long-ass legs?"

"Yeah. I had to run just to keep up with you. What are ya, seven feet tall?" He stood taller and smiled bigger, his rugged beauty almost knocking me on my ass for real that time.

"Six four."

"You're the biggest man I've ever seen," I blabbered, continuing to crane my neck just to see his face. My confession rattled me even though it was an innocent statement.

"You ain't seen nothin' yet, sweetheart." He chuckled, licking his lips before turning away from me and strolling into what I assumed was his bedroom.

Standing in the doorway, I watched him dart about the room, disappearing into a closet before reentering the space. Grasped in his hands was a plain red T-shirt. "Will this do?"

"For what?"

"For bed. Or like I said, you could sleep in the nude. But if you go with that option, you better lock this door or I'll be payin' you a visit." He wriggled his brows and I found him even sexier than before. A playful Tripp, albeit inappropriate, tugged at something inside me, but I didn't want to dissect any of what I was feeling right then.

"What about the shorts?"

"What shorts?"

"You said you had a T-shirt and shorts I could change into. So, where are the shorts?" I shuffled my feet but beyond all reason kept my eyes pinned to his. I found our banter soothing, although the sexual attraction toward him ran rampant inside me, threatening to erupt at any moment if he didn't walk away.

With a few simple steps, he towered over me, holding his shirt in front of me. "I think this will be plenty. It'll hide . . . everything." Why did he look disappointed after he spoke? Standing so close tested my restraint. I feared if he didn't move back, and do it soon, I'd throw myself at him and beg him to have his way with me. Which, much like going home with a stranger, was completely out of character for me.

Pulling me back from my fantasies, he pointed toward the bathroom and said, "You can change in there."

———— ◆ ————

"WHAT SMELLS SO HEAVENLY?" I rounded the corner as my stomach threatened to eat itself.

"I thought you said you didn't have much of an appetite," he responded, wiping his hands on a nearby dishtowel.

"Well, it's back in full force now." Walking up behind him, I moved to his right to try and peer around him but he shifted at the last second, blocking my view of whatever he was dishing out on the plate. Because I couldn't see the food he'd prepared, I did the next best thing. Taking a deep breath, I inhaled the delicious aroma, closing my eyes and allowing the savory smell of bacon, eggs, and pancakes to waft through my nose.

"Did you just smell me?"

I was still lost to the aroma of a home-cooked breakfast when Tripp surprised me with his question. My eyes popped open and my lips parted in surprise. I took a step back and fervently shook my head. Words escaped me, and in my silence I allowed myself to quickly take in the man in front of me. The smirk on his face was most definitely arrogant, but for some reason it worked for him. Made him sexier, if that were at all possible. His shirt stretched across his broad chest and the image of what lay just underneath was anything but hidden. He wore dark-washed jeans, the fabric fitted in all the right places. When I looked lower I saw he was barefoot. I'd never been so happy to see a man's feet before.

"Well . . . did you?" he asked again.

"Uh . . . what?" I shook my head and tried a different response, something that didn't have me sounding like a complete idiot. "No, of course I wasn't smelling you. I was smelling the food."

"Are you sure? Because I've been told I smell incredible."

"I'm sure you have, and by plenty of women at that."

"Not anyone who counted," he offered. A fleeting look passed over his features but was gone before I could read into it. Retreating a step, he glanced at me from head to toe, similar to what I'd just done to him. His quirked brow made me self-conscious all of a sudden, even though I was fully clothed. "I like you in my shirt."

Finally peeling my eyes from him, I looked down at the oversized shirt covering my body. With my gaze still averted, I responded. "Yeah, it does the trick."

Tripp cleared his throat, but it wasn't until he did it again that I raised my head. The way he stared at me was as if he wanted to eat me alive, and given the sexual tension between us I could only imagine exactly where he'd like to start on my body. Clenching my thighs together, I tried to squelch the sudden throbbing, but it was useless; the only thing that was gonna help me right then was a cold shower. I tried to think of something to say but the only thing my lust-induced brain could come up with was "You have a stain on your shirt."

"Where?" He pulled the material away from his body and I caught a peek of his lower abdomen. *Look away.* But I couldn't. "I don't see it," he huffed, pulling his shirt higher up his body so that I had a full view of his stomach. Can men have eight-packs? Because he sure as hell did.

"It's right there," I answered, tearing my eyes away from his naked skin and stepping closer until my hand covered his, moving the shirt until I touched the stain. "Here."

He smiled, looking at where our hands touched. "Hazard of cooking, I suppose." Swallowing my sudden brazenness, I stepped back and pulled my bottom lip between my teeth. I was nervous, sure, but it was more than that. Desire. Want. Lust—you name it.

"Looks like I better take this off before I stain it again."

Before I processed his words completely, he lifted his shirt, revealing first his defined abdominals and then his pecs. Furrowing my brow at the sight of the many scars littering his torso, I didn't ask what had happened, figuring it was too personal for him to reveal such a thing to a stranger, even though he'd insisted said stranger stay with him that evening.

When his shirt had finally cleared his head, he tossed it on the seat closest to him, his eyes pinned to mine. Watching, waiting for some kind of reaction.

"Better?" he asked, leaning against the counter so I could take him all in. My mouth suddenly went dry. My heart hammered inside my tightly coiled chest, and an ache I was becoming familiar with bloomed between my thighs. "Reece? Are you okay?"

"Huh?" I continued to visually devour him, committing every facet of his incredible body to memory. I was completely shameless.

Tripp pushed himself off the counter, his muscles flexing and taunting me. *Yeah, completely shameless.* "I asked if you were okay." The deep gravel of his voice ricocheted through me and made my lustful state even worse. *Get a grip, woman.*

"Oh yeah, I'm fine. Sorry, I didn't mean to stare. You just caught me off guard when you stripped in front of me." My nervous laughter told him everything.

"I hardly call that stripping. Now, if I took off my jeans. . . ." The corners of his full lips kicked up in amusement again.

I knew if I didn't change the subject I would completely embarrass myself in front of him. No doubt he was used to women throwing themselves at him, and the last thing I needed, or wanted, was to be included in that group. No, Tripp was a stranger, someone I'd just met earlier that night. Even though I essentially owed him my life for his protection, it didn't change the fact that I didn't know him. Sure, I was attracted to him, but that's all it was—physical attraction. Nothing more.

He must have realized I'd become uncomfortable, although I doubted he knew the extent of why, because he turned around and finished dishing out the food he'd cooked. "Sit down," he ordered, his tone demanding yet gentle.

As soon as I situated myself, he placed the plate in front of me. "It's the only food here. I hope you don't mind breakfast." He stood beside me stock-still until I made a move, so I dug in to keep from focusing on him any longer. Only then did he walk out of the kitchen, returning several minutes later fully clothed. And although I was thankful that he'd covered himself, I couldn't help but feel a pang of disappointment.

THIRTEEN

Tripp

I TOYED WITH FIRE. BRINGING her back to my place wasn't the smartest move I'd ever made, yet I couldn't seem to help myself. From the first time I laid eyes on her I knew I never wanted to look away.

I just about lost my shit when she entered the kitchen wearing nothing but my shirt. Yeah, it covered her completely, but her full tits pressed against the material, drawing my attention right away. I'd seen her naked earlier when she danced for me . . . and every other man at the club. And it was knowing what my shirt hid that tortured me.

Regretfully I had to leave her to take care of club business. I was already late, and I knew Marek would lay into me even worse if I didn't hurry my ass up and get to the safe house.

"I have to go." Eyeing her plate, I saw she'd eaten every last morsel.

"Where? Will you be gone long? You're going to leave me here all by myself?" She showered me with questions, her nervousness wafting off her in waves.

"I have to tend to some business at the club. I probably won't be back until tomorrow. Late morning. But feel free to make yourself at home. If you wanna take a shower, there're plenty of towels and anything else you'll probably need. Not so much chick stuff, but shit to get the job done." All at once, I felt heat rush through my body. Not only was I picturing her naked in my shower, with her hands running all over her toned and supple body, but I rambled on like some kind of idiot. Taking a much-needed breath, I finished with "You'll be fine until I get back."

Grabbing my keys off the table, I walked toward the door, telling myself not to turn around for fear I'd never leave. But her voice stopped me, the innocence of her tone undoing me.

"Tripp?"

With my back still facing her, I answered. "Yeah."

"I'm scared." The lilt of her voice tugged at my insides, urging me to swing around and pull her close. But I understood myself enough to know that if I drew her into my embrace I wasn't gonna let her go.

"Why?"

"Because of everything that happened earlier."

Shit! There was no way I couldn't face her, the fright she felt lacing each word. Letting go of the handle, I spun around and walked toward her. Her fingers toyed with the hem of her shirt. *My* shirt. Her breath quickened the closer I stepped, and the fear I heard in her voice was mirrored by her expression.

"He won't hurt you again. I promise."

"I know."

"Then why are you scared?"

"I don't know. When you told me you were leaving, I just got nervous. I can't explain it, other than to say that I feel safe when you're near. I know I don't know you, and you could very well still be a killer," she nervously joked, "but it's how I feel." Looking around the wide-open space, she added, "And now you're gonna leave me here all alone."

Reaching for her hand, I intertwined my fingers with hers. "You'll be fine. This place has a state-of-the-art security system and you're out in the middle of nowhere." Grimacing, I realized that probably wasn't the best thing to say. Nothing like making her feel even more secluded. "What I mean is that the chances of anyone approaching this place are nil to none. You'll be safe until I get back. But if it would make you feel better, I'll give you my number in case you need me. I mean, need to call me." *There I go again with the awkward fuckin' rambling.*

"Okay," she agreed, pulling her hand from mine to root through her purse. Finding her cell, she handed it to me and I input my name and number before giving it back. "I feel better knowing I can reach you."

She looked like she wanted to say something else, possibly apologize for being so scared, but she remained silent.

"Call me if you need to. Okay?"

"Yeah."

Uncertainty weighed me down as I walked out of the cabin, and while I had no idea why, I knew the woman standing on the other side of the door had just changed my life forever.

FOURTEEN

Tripp

THE SMELL OF BURNING FLESH assaulted me as soon as I stood at the top of the basement stairs. Pulling my shirt up to cover my nose, I tentatively walked down the steps, curious as to what the hell was goin' on down there.

"How does that feel, you motherfucker?" I heard Marek shout, the roughness of his voice quite unsettling. I knew Psych's demise was being carefully cultivated by our leader, but it wasn't healthy anymore. Not that any type of torture was *healthy*, but his revenge against Sully's father was taking a toll on him none of us could have predicted. He was coming apart piece by piece, so quickly I feared there'd be nothing left to the man I followed without question and admired immensely. He was transforming into someone else, and there wasn't a damn thing anyone could do about it. We just had to wait and see what hell he'd eventually succumb to when this shit was all over.

Stepping into the shrouded darkness of the basement, a single dull overhead light doing its best to illuminate the dank space, I saw Psych still shackled to the wall, hanging limply from the iron restraints above his head. The man was a shell of his former shelf, his dark, shoulder-length hair greasy and limp. He looked like death. Fuck, he even smelled like it.

Marek stood in front of him, a blowtorch in his right hand. The flames lit up the darkened corner of the room, and when the torch touched Psych's chest, his garbled groans filled the air. I hated the leader of the Savage Reapers as much as anyone else, but what Marek had been doing to him since he'd taken him had become too much. I wanted to slit the guy's throat and end it already, but I would never steal Psych's last breath. That was for Marek to do. His final 'fuck you' to the man who'd been his biggest enemy. The man whose club had killed his father during a routine run. And the man who'd abused Sully her entire life.

The Knights and the Reapers had been at war for as long as I could remember, going back decades; that alone was justification for killing Psych. But add in all the evildoings that he horrifically subjected his own daughter to, and it was a recipe for . . . exactly what had been going on ever since they'd stolen him from the warehouse where he held Adelaide and Kena hostage.

"Prez." I walked up behind Marek and placed my hand on his shoulder. He flinched but never turned around. Removing the torch from Psych, he lowered his arm, the flame still on and bright.

"'Bout fuckin' time you got here, Tripp. What the fuck took you so long?"

"Sorry," I said, continuing to talk to his back. "Had some stuff I had to take care of."

"Does that stuff include the new stripper from Indulge?"

What the hell? How does he know about Reece?

I didn't respond, instead trying to remove the torch from Marek's hand, a gesture he didn't appreciate. "I'm not done yet. Step back," he ordered, raising his arm and bringing the torch so close to Psych's leg the flame licked the hair before burning through the flesh of his thigh. Psych's head shot up and at first I thought he'd tried to plead with me, but the sounds coming out of his mouth were nothing more than hallowed moans. Sounds of torment so unnerving I had to turn my back and block out the image in front of me.

After several minutes, Marek finally laid the torch on the metal rolling cart, the clanking sound grabbing my attention. I thought maybe he was done for the evening, that he'd grab his cut he'd laid over the chair in the corner and walk from the room without another word.

How wrong I was.

What happened next flipped my leader's world upside down, ripping his guts from him, taunting and clouding everything he'd ever known.

Psych's lips parted and incoherent sounds poured forth. He was trying to say something, but we couldn't make out what exactly until he cleared his throat, wincing in obvious pain before attempting to speak again.

"What did you say?" Marek shouted, stepping close to the shackled man.

"Family." One word, mangled or not, we both understood.

"You don't know the first thing about that fuckin' word," Marek spit at him, his fists clenching uncontrollably. The vein in his neck throbbed and I feared for my leader's life if he didn't get ahold of himself.

"Maybe you should just ignore him, Prez," I encouraged. "Nothin' this piece of shit says is worth listening to."

"I know." Even though Marek acknowledged what I'd just said, it didn't stop him from probing Psych to continue.

"Fuc . . . kin' fam . . . ily," Psych spoke again, the two words not making much sense to us.

Gripping the strands of his hair, Marek balled his fist and punched Psych in the face, snapping his head to the side from the jolt. "What are you tryin' to say? Spit it out already."

Psych inhaled a shallow breath before opening his mouth once more. "I said—" He coughed, garnering whatever strength he had left before continuing, "Fuckin' family." Another short breath. "How does . . . does it feel . . . to fuck . . . your family?" Each word was strained, each syllable rattling the unbearable tension in the air. Psych didn't make any sense, but he pressed on nonetheless. The evil glint in his eyes proved he knew he'd gotten his captor's attention. Even in his current state, barely hanging on to life, he reveled in fucking with Marek's head.

"What the fuck are you talkin' about? You're not makin' any sense," Marek growled, his frustration rubbing off on me.

"Yeah, what the hell are you trying to say, Reaper." His club's name tasted like poison on my tongue, but I refused to say his name. Something tangible bristled in the air surrounding all of us, and had I known what it was I would have killed Psych before he parted his lips once more.

Shifting his feet, the clank of the chains binding him to the wall filling the air, Psych lifted his head the best he could and glared at Marek. "Why do you . . . think . . . this war started, boy? Huh?" He dropped his head for a brief moment, doing his best to gain momentum for what was coming next. With a broken jaw, it was hard for him to speak so when he did, he did so slowly, mumbling most of his words.

"Because your fuckin' club couldn't stick to your territory and got greedy. The Reapers intercepted a shipment meant for the Knights, and shit popped off. A few of our men, my father's men, paid the ultimate price. All because of you."

The lines on Marek's face deepened, the redness of his eyes intensifying with the stress barreling around inside him.

The prickling unease in the room heightened, drawing us all into its clutches. I moved closer to Marek. It was intentional. My gut told me he was gonna need my support in the next few minutes.

"That's not why," Psych said, coughing up blood before spitting it out, the string of saliva hanging from his lips while he spoke again. "It's because I fuc . . . ked your. . . ." His words trailed off while he succumbed to another coughing fit. Strangled breaths of air tempted his life, but he pressed on. "Mother," he finally finished.

Marek's eyes widened as he took a step back. I read his body language; all he wanted to do was decimate whatever was left of Psych's body, but he restrained himself. Barely. Marek glanced toward me, a silent plea in his gaze before he turned his attention back on the Reaper.

I was now certain that the Knights Corruption leader would be lost in a haze of rage . . . and perpetual agony.

"You're lyin'!" I shouted in Marek's defense.

Completely ignoring me, he continued to focus on the man unraveling in front of us. "I'd say ask your ol' man, but . . . he's rottin' in the ground." Psych could barely breathe, yet he somehow mustered up enough strength for a sinister laugh. The man was evil incarnate; I was convinced of it now more than ever before.

"You're just sayin' this shit to fuck with me because you know I'm gonna snatch your life from you soon, and there ain't a damn thing you can do about it." Marek began pacing, mumbling to himself the entire time.

"I'm not. It's . . . the truth." Psych's chest constricted, more blood spurting from his mouth and hitting the concrete under his feet. "Forcing that bitch wasn't what fucked with your ol' man," he spit out. "It was when she . . . she got kno. . . ." He took a breath. "Knocked up . . . that did it."

Marek halted all movement and whipped his head toward Psych. I tried to interfere but I was too late. He rushed toward the wall and pressed his forearm across his enemy's throat, screaming and shouting at him the entire time. I saw the look in Psych's eyes. He knew he'd gotten to him. He'd managed to pluck at the raveling thread holding Marek together and completely destroy it.

"You worthless piece of shit! You'll say anything just to goad me. Why? Do you want me to end your pathetic existence? To relieve you of this torture? Because that ain't gonna happen. So spew all the garbage you want because I know it's a lie." Marek took a quick breath. "My mother was only pregnant one time. With me."

Psych pushed back against Marek's arm, getting as close to his face as he could. "I know."

All of a sudden I found it difficult to breathe, my lungs seizing in astonishment. And if I'd felt that way, what the hell was Marek goin' through?

"You know . . . what . . . that means? Do ya . . . *son?*" I swore I heard the last piece of Marek's sanity splinter apart. "I'll ask ya . . . again." Psych's chest convulsed in a short coughing fit, blood dripping off his chin, making him look like a madman. "Do you like . . . fucking family?"

Vehemently shaking his head, Marek released his hold on Psych and backed up, knocking into the rolling cart. "You're fuckin' lyin'!" he roared. "You'll say anything at this point."

"'fraid it's true. Son."

"Stop saying that!" Marek cried out, unraveling further with every second. "No," he whisper-shouted. "No, it's not true. You would've said something before today. You would've tortured my ol' man with that shit." Marek's eyes darkened the longer he engaged Psych.

"You th . . . think I'd ever claim yo . . . you? You're the fuckin' enemy. The sh . . . shit under my shoe," he sputtered, more blood escaping his mouth.

"Shut the hell up, Reaper!" I shouted, stepping closer with a knife gripped tightly in my hand. His eyes flew to the weapon and when I took another step toward him, he grinned. He wanted me to stab him, probably prayed for it, but I wouldn't give him the satisfaction of killing him. For as much as I wanted Marek to end him right then, I knew he'd do it when he saw fit.

"Tell me . . . somethin' . . . son," Psych goaded, "how does it . . . feel knowin' you were . . . fuckin'—"

"Shut the fuck up!" I yelled, hoping my shouts would drown out his garbled words. But they didn't. Nothing would stop Psych from having the final word, pushing the president of the Knights into madness.

"Your sister?" Psych finished, grinning like the biggest fool before his head fell in utter exhaustion.

FIFTEEN

Tripp

EVERYTHING HAPPENED SO FAST I didn't have time to intervene, which was probably for the best, all things considered. I didn't want to be the one to step in and try to calm Marek down enough to reason with him. Otherwise, *I'd* probably be the one sucking in my last breath.

In the blink of an eye, Marek grabbed a knife from the cart and barreled toward Psych, the old man's eyes widening a fraction before the corners of his thin, cracked lips curved into an ominous grin.

"Marek!" I shouted, not quite sure what else I was gonna say after calling out his name. Whatever he did to Psych was justified, but I feared if he killed him now he would never get the answers he needed. But maybe he didn't care about that. Hell, he didn't appear as if he cared about anything but snatching Psych's life and sending him straight to hell. Exactly where he belonged.

His arms were a blur of movements, blood spurting forth from Psych's body so fast his life source coated the floor in mere seconds, expanding and covering ground so quickly I had to take a step back or the crimson river would have surrounded my boots.

Marek had finally lost it, his hand plunging the knife into the Reaper over and over again, ripping open the thinly veiled skin covering his organs. At one point, soon after he first attacked, Psych's bowels started to spill from his body. But that didn't stop Marek. It seemed to only fuel his rage, pushing him beyond the scope of sanity. Surprisingly, Psych was still alive, his short breaths few and far between, his lungs amazingly still functioning. That was until Marek plunged the knife through Psych's chest, directly into his heart. Twisting the blade ensured our enemy would leave this world in the next few seconds.

When he finally exhaled his last connection to this life, Psych's entire body went slack, pulling on the chains and testing their hold. Dropping the knife to the floor, Marek finally retreated until his back hit the wall, his eyes on Psych the entire time, as if he weren't completely convinced he'd died. My eyes followed my prez's steps. When he finally slid down the wall and hung his head in his hands, his mind, body and soul completely defeated, only then did I glance over at the state of our enemy.

The sight was something out of a fuckin' horror movie. It looked like Jason Voorhees had destroyed Psych with a machete. His stab wounds were so extensive I couldn't tell where one ended and the next started. Most of the skin was completely shredded, half of the damage coming from being burned off, the rest from Marek's uncontrollable rage. Some of Psych's organs were exposed and hanging from his still form, the image regrettably burned into my memory forever.

"It can't be true," Marek whispered. The room was eerily silent, allowing me to hear every disbelieving word he uttered. "He was lyin'," he continued, speaking to himself more than to me. But I needed to answer and try to bring him back to reality, whatever that might look like now.

"Fuck, Prez," I comforted, squatting down so we were closer to eye level. "He could have definitely been lying." What I failed to say was, *"And he could have been telling the truth. Sully could really be your sister."*

Dropping onto my ass, I braced myself against the wall and mirrored the leader of the Knights. And that's how we stayed for at least an hour, both of us trying to come to grips with what Psych had said. Whether or not Marek wanted to admit it or not, the Reaper could have very well been telling the truth, saving his final blow of retaliation for the end.

———— ◆ ————

"IT AIN'T GOOD, BROTHER," I exhaled into the phone. I'd called Stone when I didn't know what else to do. "He's completely lost it. You need to grab a couple of the men and get over here." A few choice words from the VP of our club and he fell silent. "Oh, and make sure to bring the cage 'cause Prez is in no shape to ride back on his own." Finishing the conversation, I hung up and paced in the kitchen, looking inside the fridge a few times, hoping that some alcohol would magically appear each time the light went on.

I tried to persuade Marek to come upstairs, but he refused to budge from the spot he'd glued himself to on the floor. Every now and then he'd glance over at Psych, vehemently curse, and then drop his head again, mumbling incoherently and sounding like a certified crazy person. Maybe he was. Maybe he'd gone off the deep end and split from reality. Looking at him, anyone would agree. Parts of his hair stuck up, his hands gripping the strands in delirium. His eyes were bloodshot. His month-old beard was unkempt, and blood covered his hands and clothes.

He looked like a deranged killer.

Well . . . truth wrapped its ugly hands around that new reality.

I jumped to my feet two hours later when I saw headlights pull up the driveway, the squeak of the garage door solidifying that reinforcements were there. Rushing to meet them, I rounded the van to the driver's side. "Stone, thank God!" I wasn't normally one for such exclamations, but the situation I was in surely called for one.

"Where is he?" Ryder patted me on the shoulder as he passed, Trigger and Jagger hot on his heels. Their only priority was getting to their president, but I needed to fill them in on just what they would walk into once they breached the basement door.

"Hold up," I shouted, following them through the kitchen. Trigger grabbed the handle and just as he tried to yank the door open, I slammed my palm on the wood to make sure I had my say before they went down there. "I've seen some nasty shit in my life. I've *done* some nasty shit, but what's down there is somethin' else." The seriousness of my tone left no room for doubt. Only when I had all of their attention did I continue. "Marek lost his shit. For real, and Psych paid the price."

"Good," Jagger sneered, his jaw clenching while he waited for something more to come out of my mouth.

"I'm not sayin' he didn't deserve every bit of our leader's fury, but something was said down there that pushed Marek over the edge. And I'm not sure if he can come back from it, especially if it's fuckin' true." I mumbled the end of my statement but I knew damn well every man standing in front of me heard me.

"What the fuck are you talking about?" Stone rushed forward, grabbing the handle and trying to pull the door open. But I kept it closed, even when our VP gave me a stern, disapproving look.

"I think I should let Marek tell you." Yeah, I wasn't about to tell them that our president may have married his own half-sister.

"Then back the hell up and let us down there, nomad," Trigger gritted out, mirroring everyone else's look of anger.

"Just be warned that it's quite the sight," I cautioned before removing my hand from the door. Trigger pulled it open and one by one they hurried down the steps. I debated whether or not I should go back down into the basement, and after several minutes of contemplating, I finally gave in and joined my brothers.

SIXTEEN

AGAIN I ASKED MYSELF WHAT the hell I was thinking going home with a complete stranger. The same stranger who left me all alone in his house, who took off in the middle of the night, explaining that he'd be back sometime the next day. And to add to the already odd scenario, he never told me the code for the alarm system, essentially locking me inside until he returned.

Having no idea what else to do, I grabbed my phone and dialed the number for Indulge, hoping and praying that Carla was still working. I desperately needed someone to talk to, and I feared if she'd already gone home that I'd sit and stew all night. I cursed Tripp, angry with him for firing me, or whatever he called it, all while still remaining thankful he'd come to my aid earlier. The situation was complicated to say the very least.

The phone rang three times before someone finally answered. "Indulge" was the only greeting that came through the line.

"Hi. Is Carla still working?"

"Who's this?" I knew without asking it was Arianna, and if she knew it was me she'd probably hang up. I couldn't risk it so I lied.

"Her sister." I tried to change the tone of my voice when I answered, still fearful she'd end the call.

"Hang on," she responded, shouting over her shoulder and away from the phone. Breathing a sigh of relief, I counted the seconds until Carla came on the line.

"Heather? Is everything okay?" she asked in a small panic. "Why are you calling so late?"

"Carla, it's me. Reece. Sorry about that, but if I told Arianna it was me I think she probably would've hung up on me."

"Yeah, you're right." She chuckled. "That one is a bit touched in the head, if you know what I mean. Why couldn't it have been her who Tripp kicked out tonight?" A brief silence ensued. "Sorry, honey. I didn't mean it like that."

"Well, that's why I'm calling. Sort of." Slouching back against the couch, I tried to get as comfortable as I could.

"Hold on a sec. Let me take this in the office. Too noisy out here." I waited until I heard the background noise of the club diminish, taking that extra time to figure out why exactly I'd called Carla in the first place. "Okay, all good." I didn't have to be standing next to her to know she was smiling, that she was exuding her support through the phone. "What's up?"

"I don't know. I. . . ." My words drifted off, but it wasn't long before Carla picked up on exactly what my worry was.

"Where are you, Reece? Are you safe?"

"Yeah. I think so."

"What do you mean you think so? Where did Tripp take you?"

I hesitated for a moment, knowing my answer would certainly raise some flags with her. "Back to his place."

Carla gasped. "Why? Why wouldn't he take you to your motel room? Well, I guess I understand why he didn't take you there. I've told you that place is dangerous, that you'd be much better off staying someplace else, but what the hell do I know, right? I've only lived around here my entire life." She rambled on for another minute before finally taking a breather.

"Are you done?" I kept my tone non-defensive because I knew Carla had my best interests at heart, and she was only worried about me.

"I think so."

"Good. Now can I continue?"

"Go ahead." Her smile had returned. I just knew it.

I wavered before letting her in on what Tripp said on the drive home. "He felt the same way . . . about me staying there, and since it was late, and I had nowhere else to go, he just took me back to his place."

"Where is he now?"

"I don't know," I answered truthfully. "He said he had some stuff he had to do for his club, and that he'd be back sometime tomorrow. That's all I know. But until then, I can't leave because he set the alarm and never told me what the code was. So I'm essentially trapped here." Closing my eyes, I tried to picture Carla's reaction, but the only image I could muster was of Tripp. The concern in his eyes when he'd crouched down in the private room at the club to make sure I was okay. The annoyance on his face when I'd told him where I'd been staying. The way his full lips kicked up in a smirk when he told me I was free to hit on him anytime.

"Tell me where you are. I'll have someone close up for me and I'll come get you," she offered.

"I don't really know where I am exactly. He lives out in the middle of nowhere." Then I suddenly remembered that his brother was at the club. Or at least he was when we left. "Is his brother still there?" I asked, hoping she'd say yes.

"Hawke? No, he left already. One of his buddies came to get him about a half hour ago."

"Oh, okay," I dejectedly responded. "I guess it's just as well, seeing as there's still the small issue of his alarm."

"Oh, I don't give a shit about that. I'll bust you out of there and he can deal with whatever happens."

"You'll bust me out of here?" I laughed.

"You know I will." Carla's amusement faded, quickly replaced by a serious tone. One which kind of freaked me out.

"Do you think I'm in danger here? You can tell me the truth." My heart rammed against my chest in anticipation of her answer. She obviously knew Tripp more than I did because of the way she spoke to him when he was in the midst of dragging me out of the club earlier.

"With Tripp? No. Not from what I know of him. He can be quite intense sometimes. Other times . . . he's laid-back, joking around to stifle a tense situation. He's a good guy. I don't agree with him taking you to his place, however. Although. . . ."

"Although what?"

"I'm sure I read it wrong."

"Carla," I said as sternly as I could. "What the hell are you talking about?"

"It's just . . . the way he kept looking at you. I don't know. It was off." What she told me momentarily freaked me out, until she finally explained herself. "Sorry, what I mean is . . . I've known Tripp for some time now and I've never seen him look at anyone the way he was looking at you tonight. Yeah, I've seen him interested in women before, but not like he was with you. He seemed bothered by the fact that you were even there, all while being intrigued at the same time. Again, I could be reading too much into it, so. . . ."

Out of everything she'd just said, it bothered me when she mentioned him being interested in other women. A small pang of jealousy surfed through me, even though I realized it was ridiculous for me to even feel such an emotion.

"Reece? You still there?"

"Yeah, sorry." I expelled a deep sigh. "I'm just thinking about what I'm gonna do for a job now." Then a thought suddenly came to me. "Carla, do you think you can talk to Tripp? Make him reconsider and let me come back to work?"

"Do you think that's such a good idea? Especially after what happened?"

"I don't have another choice. Not until I'm able to find something else. I need this," I pleaded. "I need this job. Please."

"Of course. I'll talk to him."

"Thank you." After several minutes we finally ended the call, Carla promising she'd do her best to try and convince Tripp to let me stay on at Indulge until I found another job.

I should've been pissed. I should've been scared. But I was neither. Carla's reassurance helped to ease some of the anger and panic I'd felt. I had no idea what I would have done without her. Even though I'd only known her a short time, I considered her a true friend.

Deciding not to delve too far inside my various thoughts, I deemed it best to try and distract myself by exploring Tripp's home. If he was gonna leave me all by myself, then he should expect I'd go snooping through his things. Curiosity won out as I opened the drawer of the end table in the living room, finding nothing inside except a few motorcycle magazines and a remote for the television. Everything stacked neatly. Looking around the small living space, it was then I noticed that not one single thing was out of place. A few pillows were strategically arranged on the couch, a comfy-looking blanket thrown over the back. Not a single item littered the coffee table, or floor for that matter. Everything seemed to have its place, and the thought that Tripp was some kind of neat freak made me smile.

Wait . . . aren't serial killers anally neat? I lost my smile for a brief moment before I laughed out loud. "Get a grip, Reece," I mumbled to myself before heading toward the kitchen to grab some water.

Walking through the cozy cabin, I took it all in, immersing myself in Tripp's world. A small glimpse inside the man who'd saved me. The place was small, the only rooms in the front the kitchen and living room. A large stone fireplace took up the majority of the wall, and with the way the evening had dipped into the lower digits, I imagined relaxing on the brown leather sofa while a fire warmed me.

Toward the back was a short hallway which led to two bedrooms and a bathroom. Peeking my head inside Tripp's sanctuary, I glanced around the room and smiled. Again. What was with my lips kicking up whenever I thought about the gorgeous man who'd forced his way into my life? Taking a tentative step inside, looking behind me as if he was gonna show up out of thin air and catch me snooping, I marveled at the state of his room—neat, just like every other inch of this place. An overly large bed took up a lot of space, but seeing how big Tripp was, it made absolute sense. An end table and a five-drawer dresser were the only other pieces of furniture, a small walk-in closet tucked into the corner housing the rest of his belongings.

Glancing at the alarm clock, I saw it was late, reminding me that I was most certainly beyond tired. Raising my arms above my head, I stretched as best I could and bellowed out the loudest yawn before turning and exiting the room. Walking only a few feet I came upon the bathroom. The thought of losing myself to a hot shower suddenly seemed like the best remedy to the horrible night I'd had.

As soon as the water beat down on my body, the steam enveloping and soothing me, I relaxed and pushed all thoughts of what had happened to the back of my mind. It was what I was best at—denial, oblivion. Over the years, I'd gotten very good at shoving life way deep down. It was the only way I could survive. Old habits were certainly hard to break, and because I didn't know any other way to cope I chose denial once more.

After my shower, I pulled Tripp's T-shirt back over my head, inhaling his lingering scent before pulling it down to cover my body. Images of the sexy biker rushed forward, and it was all I could do not to fantasize what he would look like completely naked. Normally such thoughts never entertained me, not even when I encountered a good-looking man while working. I always tried to keep that life separate from my real one, never mixing the two worlds for fear of the uncertainty. And even though I'd only been stripping for a short while, my promise to never mingle the two worlds had proved beneficial. *Until tonight.*

Tripp made me feel things without even trying. I'd never come across such a man before, someone who made me question my logic and instincts. I'd drive myself insane if I gave in to the need to try and understand why

I'd suddenly become obsessed with him. Why he'd done what he had for me. Why I shoved aside my inner voice and got into his truck, allowing him to take me to his place. Why I'd thought about him almost every second since he'd left.

Deciding to forgo making myself crazy, I trudged back toward his room and crawled onto his bed, laying my head gently on the pillow. I would have curled up in the guest bedroom had there been a bed, but it appeared as if it was being utilized strictly for storage, the numerous boxes stacked perfectly. Not a shocker.

As I lay there, I took a deep breath and recapped everything that'd played out that evening. I refused to focus on anything that happened before Tripp had come to my rescue. No point in frightening myself over something I couldn't change. I strangely thought my body would refuse to succumb to sleep, that I'd unfortunately be awake for the rest of the night. But as soon as Tripp's face appeared in my mind, I smiled and slipped into the darkness of a comforting slumber.

SEVENTEEN

Tripp

"WHAT THE FUCK?" STONE ASKED, pacing back and forth in front of Psych before moving toward his best friend and leader. "Marek. What the hell happened, brother?" was all he could ask.

But Marek never answered. Instead, he remained on the floor where I'd left him, his head still in his hands as he mumbled the same thing over and over again.

"It can't be true. It can't be true."

He was slowly losing his mind, and so far I was the only one who knew why. The smell of the room had intensified over the past hour, and because no one had made a move to clean anything up, we were completely exposed to Psych's lifeless body and all the horrible smells his dead flesh emitted.

"Why does he keep saying that?" Jagger asked after pulling me to the corner of the room. My answer didn't come as easily as I thought it would've. There was a part of me that wanted to protect Marek as long as possible. Maybe if I told the others the reason he kept repeating "It can't be true," it would become all too real. So I stalled, trying to think of what to say. "I know you know something, Tripp. You were the only one here with him. Other than that fucker over there." Jagger pointed toward Psych, his eyes lingering on the dead Reaper for only a few seconds before his attention was back on me. "What can't be true?"

I waited, for what I had no idea. My lips remained sealed while my heart picked up its pace. Marek stepping back into reality and shouting for me to remain silent would have been extremely welcome at that point. But there was only silence. Even Ryder, Stone, and Trigger were quiet, whispering to each other every few minutes. All of us were contemplating the next move, but shock about the situation kept us locked into ambiguity.

Before Jagger could press me again for an answer, Stone closed in on us, his presence leaving no room for anything but the truth. "What the hell happened down here?" He looked back and forth between Jagger and me, but obviously I was the only one who could answer.

"What does it look like happened?" I whisper-shouted, doing my best to deflect from giving him—giving them all—the answers they truly wanted. "He fuckin' lost his mind and took it out on Psych."

Stepping closer, Stone gripped my shoulder. "Why did he all of a sudden lose his mind?" The VP of the Knights stood a couple inches shorter than me, but his domineering presence was larger than life. The stern look in his eyes told me he wasn't gonna let up until I told him something.

Quickly contemplating what I should say, my eyes veered over to glance at Marek, hoping he'd look at me and give me some kind of signal on how to proceed. But he did nothing, continuing to mumble to himself while he shook his head back and forth.

Tightening his grip, Stone demanded I let him in on what exactly happened. Why his president was on the fuckin' floor and actin' like some kind of mental patient. "Tripp, I swear to fuck if you don't tell me what happened. . . ." He didn't need to finish his sentence because it didn't matter what he threatened me with. I'd never let it get that far. We were dealing with enough shit as it was; there was no need to add to it.

Stepping back to give us as much privacy as possible, I blew out a breath and started talking. "When I came down here, Marek was torching him and shit. Fuck. I thought I was gonna lose my lunch from the smell. Anyway, out of the blue, Psych started talkin' about family and why the war really started between us and them in the first place."

"Greed and territory," Stone interrupted. "That's how it started."

"Not according to Psych."

Stone frowned, leaning against the wall while waiting for me to clear up the confusion. Jagger continued to listen, keeping his mouth shut so he could take it all in. Ryder and Trigger were across the room, crowded around Marek and trying to talk to him, to get him to snap out of whatever delirium held him captive.

"He lied. Whatever that fucker said . . . he lied." Stone's temper rose, but he kept it under control. "What did he say?" he pressed while clenching his fists.

"He said that the war started because he raped Marek's mother. That the Reapers and the Knights went to war because he raped her . . . and knocked her up."

"Fuck!" Jagger and Stone yelled at the same time, looking over at Marek to see if he heard what I'd just told them. But he didn't, still lost in his own world, which was probably for the best right then. At least until we got the hell out of there.

"That's not the worst part," I continued, running my hands through my hair as a stall tactic.

He hit my shoulder in frustration. "Out with it, nomad." Stone and I didn't have the best relationship, but it had been getting better over the past year. And if I didn't want to go back to him constantly giving me shit every time he saw me, and meaning it, then I better just spill the rest of what happened so we could all move on and deal with it. No matter the consequences.

"Psych indicated that he was Marek's father and asked Marek how he liked fucking his sister." I let the words linger in the air between us, allowing them the time to process what I'd just said. It didn't take long at all, their reactions mirroring what I'd gone through when it was being said for the first time.

"Is it true?" Jagger asked, staggering back a step before bracing himself.

"I don't think so," I answered.

"But it could be. Holy shit," Stone said, lowering his voice. "It could be."

"How do we find out if he was lyin'?" My question swirled around all three of us, waiting for someone to come up with a plan to either put Marek out of his misery or drive him further into it.

"Fuck if I know," Jagger muttered. His dark blond hair, which was normally strategically styled, was all over the place, looking more like Marek than I cared to admit. After telling them the reason for their leader's meltdown, Jagger tugged at his strands, practically ripping out chunks because he didn't know what else to do with his hands. He couldn't punch the wall; he needed them for his fights, his way of earning for the club.

Stone's eyes widened for a brief moment before he walked across the room and pulled open a drawer. Slamming it closed he looked inside another, then another before he found what he was looking for. With a baggie in hand, he grabbed a cloth from the rolling cart and closed in on Psych. Running the fabric down the dead man's chest, Stone tossed it in the baggie. Then he ripped out a chunk of hair from Psych's head, throwing that into the same baggie.

Heading back our way, he showed me the bag and said, "I'll have Addy contact someone and rush the DNA sample. Now all I have to do is convince Marek. He might fight me on it because of his fear that it could be true."

"Can you blame the guy?" I asked.

"Nope." That was all he said before we all dispersed.

EIGHTEEEN

Reece

GROGGILY WIPING THE SLEEP FROM my eyes, I swung my legs over the side of the bed. Tripp's bed. Resting my feet on the cool floor, I inhaled the moment and tried my best to take in my new predicament. Not only the room where I'd spent the night, but that I was now jobless. Jobless and essentially held captive. Okay, held captive might've been a bit strong of a sentiment, but it was kind of on point. Sort of.

While I sat on the edge of the bed, I recalled my phone call with Carla the night before, choosing to focus on certain parts of our conversation more than others. For instance, when she'd told me, "I've known Tripp for some time now and I've never seen him look at anyone the way he was looking at you tonight." Why did the recollection of her telling me that cause a flutter in my belly? Being careless in the past had led to some of the worst decisions I'd ever made, essentially endangering my life, and it was precisely why I needed to keep my head straight. No matter how attracted I was to Tripp.

Deciding I needed a shower to wake me up, I shuffled across the room with my head hung low and swung open the bedroom door, running right into a naked, muscular chest. Quick hands reached out and grabbed me as I stumbled backward, righting me before I ended up on the floor.

"Jesus Christ, woman!" Tripp exclaimed, his fingers still wrapped tightly around my upper arms. The heat from his touch instantly warmed me. No, scratch that—his touch enflamed me, torched me from the inside. So hot I thought for sure he'd snatch his hands back from the burn. My belly fluttered like it had once before while my heart beat furiously inside my chest. Licking my lips, I broke free from him and retreated, which was a mistake because I could see more of him. But distance was most definitely needed; otherwise, I feared I'd allow my hormones to take over and literally throw myself at him. Try and climb his massive, sculpted form.

"Sorry," I mumbled, trying like hell to avert my eyes from the practically naked man standing in front of me.

"No, I'm sorry if I scared you. I saw the door was closed and didn't wanna wake you. Although, come to think of it, it's almost noon." He smiled and crossed his arms over his chest. "Do you normally sleep in this late?"

I heard him speak but his words jumbled together. As if in some kind of trance, my eyes trailed over his body, devouring the sight of his rigid, cut muscles, the V of his abdomen disappearing behind the white towel wrapped around his waist.

When my gaze moved upward, trailing over his arms still crossed and muscles popping, I saw him lick his full lips. His smile intensified, and it wasn't until I finally looked him in the eye that I saw the glint of amusement. His short dark hair was wet, a few water droplets dripping off the tips and running down his neck.

"Like I said before, you can hit on me anytime." Dropping his arms to his sides, he brushed past me and walked toward his closet. I tried but I couldn't seem to peel my eyes away from him. The way he walked was mesmerizing, his gait confident and authoritative. Before I could even think to apologize for leering at him, his towel fell to the floor without warning. And there before me was the sight of his naked ass. His glorious, tight, round and muscular ass. I knew if I didn't turn around in the next second he was gonna ruin me for all other men going forward.

"You still there?" His voice rumbled through the air and startled me, but it was exactly what I needed to regain some of the composure I'd lost when he'd dropped his towel.

I flipped around to give him some privacy. "Um . . . yeah. Sorry. I was . . . just shocked." I could hear the rustle of his jeans as he pulled them over his thighs, followed by the zipper and finally the clank of his belt buckle as he finished dressing.

"You can turn around now, sweetheart. I'm decent." He chuckled, the deep timber of his laugh making me clench my thighs together. It was obvious he loved getting a rise out of me. Was I that easy to rile up? Apparently so.

"Sorry," I repeated, sheepishly grinning to try and hide my

embarrassment. I hated how he could fluster me so easily.

"Am I that awful to look at?" he teased, stepping closer until he was only a few feet from me. His eyes stayed pinned to mine, and the lazy way the corners of his mouth curved up was probably the sexiest thing I'd ever seen.

"You know you're not."

"You're quite the contradiction, you know that?" Intrigued by his odd statement, I took the bait.

"I don't understand. What does that mean exactly?"

"Well, for starters, you're a stripper. Or rather, you *were* a stripper." I couldn't help the slight irritation that flowed through me at the mention of my job loss. "You took your clothes off and danced for countless strangers, put yourself in a sexual environment all the time, yet you blushed when you saw me naked."

"How do you know I blushed? You were turned around."

"Because your cheeks are still red." He reached out and ghosted his fingers down the side of my face. I hadn't expected him to touch me, and when he did I couldn't stop my body from reacting. Again. My breath came out in short spurts as if my lungs had stolen my air, yet I welcomed the strange feeling. Before I did something stupid like lean in to him, I retreated.

"I have to go," I whispered, watching him closely for any sudden change in expression. Would he be angry that I wasn't fawning all over him? Especially when it was obvious he was attracted to me? Would he find me challenging and pursue me, try to convince me to stay to see if he could get what he wanted from me—even though I had no idea what that was? Well . . . I could take a guess, but would he be so brazen? Of course he would. I didn't see him as the type of guy to beat around the bush when it came to things he wanted.

But did he want me?

Oh my God! My brain was firing off in all different directions, most of my thoughts confusing the hell out of me.

"What's goin' on in that head of yours?"

"Just thinking that I overstayed my welcome," I lied, fiddling with the bottom of his shirt which still covered me. His eyes drifted to where my fingers gripped the material.

"I think that's my new favorite shirt," he confessed, veering the conversation—what little of it there was—in yet another direction. Holy shit, we were all over the place.

"Well, it's yours, so that would make sense." I had no idea what else to say, other than to make idle, meaningless chitchat. After several heartbeats, I chose to get back to the main point. *What was that again? Oh yeah. . . .*"I have to go."

"Where?"

"Back to the motel."

"I told you that you're not going back there," he snapped, reining in his sudden temper once he realized his outburst. He crossed his arms over his chest and stared at me, as if trying to will me into submission. I was sure most people followed Tripp's orders, but I wasn't gonna be one of them. Not when what he was saying was completely asinine.

"Where else am I gonna go?" Wanting to mirror his resoluteness, I put my hands on my hips and challenged him back. I was sure I was quite the sight, standing there in nothing but his T-shirt, hair tousled and looking a mess.

"You can stay here."

"With you?"

"What's wrong with that?"

Was he offended?

"Um . . . let's see. I don't know you, for starters. Besides, you fired me, remember? What makes you think I'm still not pissed off at you?" My arms stayed glued to my waist.

It was then he decided to make a move, reaching me in only a few long strides. He stood so close I had to tilt my head back to see his face. "Are you?" His warm breath fanned my face and I couldn't help but wonder what his kiss would taste like.

"Am I what?" I asked dreamily, so lost to the image of his lips pressed against mine that I'd lost all rationale.

"Pissed at me?" He reached out and tucked an errant strand of hair behind my ear, the pads of his fingers trailing over the sensitive area just below my earlobe.

"Huh?" My eyes were half closed at that point, and my mouth had suddenly become quite dry.

Chuckling, he leaned down until his mouth was but a whisper away from mine. "Are you still pissed at me? For letting you go from the club? Or are you imagining yourself kissing me? Is that where that beautiful head of yours is at?"

I couldn't do anything other than stare at his mouth, the questions he'd just asked not even registering before I rose up on my tippy toes and pressed my lips to his, completely oblivious to how inappropriate my actions were.

"Aw . . . fuck it," he muttered before giving in and kissing me back.

NINETEEN

Tripp

WITH REECE'S LIPS PRESSED AGAINST mine, it didn't take long before I lost all control and demanded everything from her. I hadn't thought of anything else since the first time I saw her, which had been less than twenty-four hours before.

Our situation hadn't started off ideal, but that didn't seem to matter. Life threw me a surprise that flipped me on my goddamn ass, and I had no choice but to roll with it and see what happened. I wasn't a deep thinker. I wasn't a man who questioned "what does it all mean" or even considered something as unrealistic as fate, but I couldn't deny the attraction and pull I felt toward Reece. An odd feeling, one I'd never experienced before, not once during my thirty-two years. There was something different and special about her. About us together. I knew she was attracted to me, could see it every time she looked at me, but did she feel that same undeniable force?

Our mouths collided while our tongues dueled, both of us desperately trying to savor the taste of the other. When she nipped my bottom lip I swore my dick became so hard I thought I was gonna explode right then and there. With the way we were goin' at each other, it sure as hell wasn't gonna take much anyway.

"Let's get this off you," I growled, breaking away from her mouth and raising the hem of her shirt—my shirt, to be exact—until it cleared her belly. Several seconds passed. I waited, impatiently I might add, but she didn't protest, so I lifted the material over her head and tossed it somewhere behind me. My eyes traveled the full length of her, first stopping to take in the magnificent view of her round and perky tits, then moving lower to glance at the tiny pair of panties she wore which barely covered her. I stepped back to better take her in, and that's when I saw her skin blush the sexiest color of pink. When I remained silent, she became self-conscious.

"What?" she asked, swallowing nervously while I continued to devour the sight of her.

"You're perfect. Absolutely fuckin' perfect." I wanted my mouth to cover every single inch of her, starting with those full, kiss-bruised lips. Pulling her into me, I crashed my mouth to hers again, demanding she open up for me once more with the thrust of my tongue. I pulled back long enough to remove my own shirt, and then I was back to tasting her for what felt like forever.

She moaned, digging her fingernails into my shoulders as I walked her backward toward my bed. Reaching under her ass, I pulled her up my body and she instinctively wrapped her legs around my waist. The warmth of her chest pressed against mine felt like heaven. I could only imagine what it would feel like to slide inside her, the heat of her pussy surely enough to send me over the edge.

Once we reached the bed, I crawled on top and gently laid her beneath me, careful not to crush her delicate frame. The prickling awareness that she was gonna allow me to fuck her soon excited me all while making me nervous. To be more exact, I was nervous for her, not me.

I'd been with many women over the years and it never failed. Every time they discovered what I was packing down below, their eyes widened. Some of them had even looked a bit worried.

I was a large man. Everywhere.

My hands trailed along her sides, goose bumps covering the surface of her skin the more I explored. Gently biting the tip of her tongue, I pulled back and stared at her, loving the fact that she looked like she did because of me. Her skin was still tinged pink, her plump lips battered from my demanding kiss. Her eyes were half closed, desire pooling underneath so heady I could only imagine what I'd find if I ran my fingers between her legs. No doubt she was soaked.

"Tripp." She whisper-moaned my name when my fingers played with the top of her panties. Shifting positions, I sat back and tugged the material down her thighs until her bare pussy was no longer covered.

"I can't wait to taste you," I said hastily, ripping her panties the rest of the way off before spreading her legs and burying my head in between. But before I could savor her sweetness, she uttered three words which stopped me dead in my tracks.

"Make me forget."

She spoke the words quietly, but I'd heard them loud and clear. I clenched my jaw, knowing damn well I couldn't continue on without making sure she was ready to fuck me because she wanted to, and not to escape from what happened the previous night.

After the attack she appeared okay, only a slightly frightened reaction moments after I busted into that back room. I stupidly thought she was completely fine, even thinking she was over it. But I should have known better. Of course, she'd suppress her feelings. I didn't know of a single woman who wouldn't be shaken after something like that, which was all the more reason I'd never allow her to put herself in that kind of situation again.

You hardly know her. How can you protect her?

Choosing to ignore my inner voice of reason, I pushed off the bed and stood at the edge, contemplating my next move. Fuck, this was hard. There she lay, naked and ready for me, and my dumb ass refused to fuck her unless she was doin' it for the right reason. Goddamn, I hated having a conscience.

"What's the matter?" she asked, closing her legs and leaning up on her elbows. I wanted to wipe away her look of self-doubt and confusion, but I couldn't. Not until I made her tell me why she'd said, "Make me forget."

"Reece . . . ," I started, running my hands through my hair, tugging at the strands in sexual frustration. My cock pressed against the seam of my zipper, throbbing for a release I had a feeling wasn't gonna happen any time soon. My hesitation made her even more aware something was wrong, so she pulled the covers over her to hide her nakedness.

"Why did you stop?" she gasped, remaining silent for a moment before saying accusingly, "You really are married, aren't you?" She shuffled back on the bed.

"I'm not fuckin' married. I told you that before."

"Then why? Why did you stop?"

"Why do you want to fuck me?" I asked crassly, wincing at the harshness of not only my words but my tone.

"Because . . . I like you. And I thought you liked me too."

"Is that it?" I arched a brow and set my expression to skeptical. She remained silent, not quite sure how else to respond. "Do you want me to make you forget what happened, to take your mind off being attacked?"

It was she who winced that time. "Yes," she replied honestly.

Shaking my head, I reached for her hand and waited for her to give in. Once the heat of her palm connected with mine, I helped her from the bed, the blanket still wrapped loosely around her body.

"I can't do this." She opened her mouth to speak but I continued on, not allowing her to say anything. "I'm not fucking you until I'm the only thought in that head of yours."

"I don't understand," she responded. "I'm not thinking about anyone but you." She tried to tug her hand from mine but I only tightened my hold. In fact, I pulled her closer.

"You need me in order to help you forget. You said so yourself." Taking a breath, I continued, "You've been through a lot, and that's on me for thinking you were okay with it. I should have known better, but I got caught up in you. In the thought of us together." To relieve her of some of her mounting anxiety, I kissed her, my lips lingering over hers for several seconds. "I don't want our first time together to be tainted by your need to escape from something else."

My eyes widened in shock when she started to cry. At first it was a single tear, but then many more quickly followed. Her shoulders shook as she finally released what had been pent up since the attack. Without hesitation, I wrapped my arms around her as she expelled her anguish. I normally didn't do well with a crying woman, but with Reece it was different. All I wanted to do was comfort her, to promise her that everything would be okay, even if I didn't truly believe every word myself.

A tightness gripped my chest, the anger I felt about what happened to her rising to new heights. Such vulnerability and confusion on her part had me wanting to erase the memory of the night before. But I couldn't. I didn't know how to help her, and that alone killed me.

TWENTY

Reece

I COULDN'T BELIEVE ALL THAT had happened in the course of twenty minutes. First, Tripp undressed in front of me, comfortable as could be with that unbelievable body of his. Then I fell under some sort of spell when he neared me, imagining all sorts of dirty things I'd love to do to him, and him to me. Then, as brazen as could be, I was the one who made the first move. With all of Tripp's flirtation, I was the one to kiss him. I was the one who encouraged what happened next without question. I allowed him to take over, to take off my clothes and lay me on the bed beneath him. I was the one who allowed him to put his head between my legs, and I was the one who essentially stopped it with my admission that I needed him to help me forget all that had happened in the past twenty-four hours.

As soon as Tripp rescued me I had something else to focus on entirely, whether it was the anger from being fired or my lusty attraction to the stranger who swooped in on one of my darker moments. What I wasn't doing was dealing with the near rape that had occurred. A part of me was used to violence, but I thought once I moved to California I'd be able to leave all of that behind me. The incident at the club proved otherwise, and instead of dealing with all of those raw emotions, I chose to deflect. To shove everything so deep down it was as if nothing happened.

But it had, and now I had to deal with it. Breaking down in Tripp's arms was apparently the first step.

After I'd dried all of my tears, I dressed in a pair of sweatpants and a fresh shirt he'd given me. Of course I looked ridiculous in the overly large clothing, but Tripp grinned when he saw me enter the kitchen, taking me in from head to toe. A flirty smile I was becoming all too familiar with played on his lips as I sat down to a bagel and glass of orange juice.

"Sorry, it's all I have right now."

"It's more than enough," I said before taking a bite.

I ate in silence, my breakdown before quite embarrassing. Looking up every now and again, I saw that Tripp was watching me. He would go from frowning, to biting his lower lip, which was extremely sexy, to cocking a brow. An internal debate no doubt wreaking havoc on his thoughts.

Eventually one of us had to speak. It just so happened that we decided that very same thing at the same time.

"So," both of us said, amusement in our tone at the coincidence.

"You go first," he insisted, taking a sip of his coffee. I watched the muscles of his throat swallow the hot liquid, then stared at his mouth as he licked his lips. "Reece?"

"Sorry. Um . . . well . . . I guess I should be going. Can you give me a ride back to the motel?" I'd hoped he wasn't going to give me a hard time about going back there. In reality, I had no place else to go.

"No." His answer was final. He placed his mug on the counter and crossed his arms, looking like he was preparing himself for an argument. Well, he was right. I hardly knew him; I wasn't going to let him dictate anything for me.

"No?" I asked incredulously, my tone raising an octave in disbelief, although his answer shouldn't have shocked me. I pushed my empty plate away and stood from the table, bracing myself behind my chair for support.

"No. I already told you you're not stayin' there. You can stay here. With me."

"I can't do that."

"Why?"

"Because I don't know you. Plus, it's . . . inappropriate."

He laughed, uncrossing his arms and stepping forward, mirroring the way I rested my hands on the back of the chair. "Why is it inappropriate? Unusual. Quick. Those are the words I'd use before saying it would be inappropriate." Clearly he found me amusing, a sentiment which irritated me.

My brain couldn't function when he stood so close, so I couldn't come up with a defense as to why I'd chosen that word. Instead, I blurted out something else which came to mind. "I just can't stay. Please. If you won't take me back to the motel, then I'll find my own ride."

"You *can't* stay? Or you don't *want* to stay?"

He just wouldn't give up.

Looking away, I said, "I don't wanna stay." I lied, of course, but I figured he'd relent if he knew I didn't want to be there with him. Thankfully, it worked. But when I glanced back at him, I saw a look of disappointment and hurt cross his face. It was brief, but I caught it.

"Fine. But you're not goin' back to the motel. I'll find you a place you can crash at until you get back on your feet." I opened my mouth to object, but he cut me off. "No argument, Reece." His hardened expression softened. "Let me do this for you. At least I'll know you'll be safe."

I eventually nodded, giving him the go-ahead to make the arrangements.

TWENTY-ONE

Tripp

I LEFT REECE IN THE kitchen while I stepped out on the porch, closing the door behind me for added privacy. Since I couldn't force her to stay with me, I had an idea where she could stay. I just needed approval first.

"What?" Marek practically shouted into the phone, no doubt losing all his patience for . . . everything.

"Sorry to bother you, Prez, but I was wondering if I could set someone up at Zip's place. I need somewhere safe, and close to the clubhouse."

"For *her?*" His tone was curt, his question irritating me right away. But since I detected a slight slur to his words, I let it go.

"Yeah."

"Is this rash move on your part gonna come back on the club in any way?"

Confused, I answered as honestly as I could. "No."

"Then I don't give a fuck." He hung up before I could thank him.

Zip's place was the perfect solution, but as I smiled at the compromise, I couldn't help thinking about our fallen brother.

Zip was a good kid. Always trying to prove his loyalty to the club, even though there was never a need. Marek had entrusted him to follow Rico Yanez, Rafael Carrillo's right-hand man. And when the leader of Los Zappas Cartel found out Yanez went behind his back and continued to deal with the Savage Reapers, our most hated enemy, it was enough to seal his fate. The proverbial nail in the coffin. When they'd finished with Yanez, they passed him on to us on Marek's request, where he was tortured and finally disposed of once and for all. Revenge for what he'd done to Sully.

When Psych found an opportunity to exact his own kind of revenge against our club, he'd managed to kidnap Adelaide and Kena, Stone and

Jagger's women. Zip had been the one assigned to accompany them on their shopping trip, and devastatingly enough, he'd been killed when the Reapers ran him off the road. This club was everything to Zip, and we paid him homage by burying him on the compound. He spent most of his time at the clubhouse, so we found it only fitting.

Walking back inside, I saw Reece pacing in the kitchen. Her head was down, sections of her dark hair shielding her face from me. As soon as she heard the creak of the door behind me, however, she looked up and directly into my eyes. I swore a jolt of something indescribable ricocheted through me.

"So, I found a place for you to stay." Shaking off the odd sensation that'd just racked through me, I leaned my hip against the counter. Her fingers had been playing with an area on the bridge of her nose, and when she caught me looking, she dropped her hand. It was then I noticed a small scar, a dent in her skin indicating she'd broken her nose at some point.

Jerking my chin at her, I asked, "What happened?"

Her response was immediate and deflective. "What do you mean?"

"How did you break your nose?"

"How . . . ?" She gently touched the scar again. "An accident. I'd had too much to drink one night and tripped over the curb. Clumsy, really." Her nervous laughter screamed she was lyin', but I didn't know her well enough to demand the truth. So I let it go.

Deciding to focus on something else, I raked my eyes over her, her appearance making me smile. The woman was drowning in the clothes I'd given her, but she'd never looked more beautiful. No makeup, her long hair piled loosely on top of her head. Something innocent about Reece tugged at my soul, and I'd be damned if I wasn't gonna find out what it was exactly that made me feel the way I did whenever I was around her.

Staring into her eyes calmed me, all the while heightening my need to protect her. I could spend hours, days even, trying to dissect my newfound feelings, but I wanted to live in the moment with her.

"I can't let you do that." She broke into my thoughts by responding to my original comment about Zip's place.

"Well, it's done." I tried to come off as cool and casual, but my clipped words gave me away. More than anything I wanted her to allow me to do this without an argument, but with the small amount I knew about her, it shouldn't have come as a surprise when she pushed back.

"Tripp, I really appreciate everything you've done for me. Besides firing me, of course. But I can take care of myself."

The next words to leave my mouth were certainly a surprise. I didn't want her anywhere near Indulge, but I also knew I shouldn't stand in the way of her making a living either. Maybe if I relented then so would she, taking me up on my offer to put her up at Zip's place.

"If I agree to let you go back to work at the club, in a different position, will you stay where I want you to? Where I know you'll be safe?" Zip had installed top-of-the-line security, as we all had, and his place was close to the clubhouse, which turned out to be rather convenient.

After his parents had died years prior, Zip had assumed all responsibility for the place, even thinking ahead and leaving it to Marek in case anything happened to him. He was young, and whereas most guys his age weren't even thinking about wills and what would happen to their shit when they died, most didn't have danger creeping around every corner, threatening to snatch their lives in the blink of an eye.

"What position?" she asked skeptically.

"You can assist Carla with bartending. She's been on us to hire someone to help her out, so I doubt she'll have any complaints about the new arrangement."

There was but a minute of contemplation on her part before she answered.

"Okay," she said enthusiastically. "Yes, I'll stay where you want me to, but only until I save up enough money for my own place."

I could have offered her the money she needed, but I selfishly wanted her close by so I could check on her anytime I wanted. With her permission, of course.

"All right then, let's grab your things from the motel and I'll take you to your new place." I gestured for her to walk ahead of me, resting my hand on the small of her back. She flinched from my touch, but I saw from the flush of her cheeks that she liked it.

———◆———

"I STILL CAN'T BELIEVE YOU stayed here," I growled, walking around the small room and tossing her stuff into a bag she had opened on the bed. The place was fuckin' filthy, the walls a dingy white and the seventies shag carpet a horrible shade of worn green. And the smell—holy fuck, it smelled like stale smoke, vomit, and piss. A white-hot surge of anger strangled me at the idea that she thought so low of herself she chose to stay in this dump. "What the hell were you thinkin', Reece?" I stopped in front of her and lifted her chin so she had no choice but to look at me.

Embarrassment stole over her skin and she tried to move her head, but I tightened my hold, all without hurting her.

"What were you thinkin' stayin' in this shithole?" I repeated.

"Stop it," she whispered, placing her hands on my chest and shoving me away from her. I stepped back only because I saw the sad look in her eyes and I didn't want to add to her already distressed state. "I told you I didn't have any money. This was the only place I could afford."

I couldn't help but press her for more information. More personal information. "Why didn't you ask your family for money, then? I'm sure they'd help you out."

With her back turned toward me, busying herself with gathering the rest of her things, she said, "I don't have any family. My parents and brother died in a car accident." She took a deep breath. "And I left my house so quickly I didn't have time to think about what I'd do once I got wherever it was I was going."

"What does that mean?" I tried to turn her around but she shrugged away from me, zipping her bag before quickly walking toward the door. Once outside, I decided to let the conversation die—for now.

I still had Hawke's truck from the night before, and thank God because it had started to rain on the way to the clubhouse.

"When can I start back to work?" Reece asked, tapping her fingers on the door rest.

"Tomorrow, if you want." My hands tightened on the wheel, a reaction she most definitely noticed.

"What's wrong?"

"What makes you think something is wrong?" My knuckles were turning white.

"Because of that," she said, pointing to my hands.

"I hate the thought of you around all those fuckin' men," I grunted.

"Are those men the same ones who keep making your club money?" She smirked, toying with a strand of her hair while giving me the coyest smile. While I didn't like the topic of conversation, I had to admit that I liked the relaxed mood she appeared to have switched into, especially since she seemed so upset moments earlier.

"Yeah. Doesn't mean I like you being in their line of sight, though." Blowing out a frustrated breath, I loosened my grip on the wheel. "Just stay behind the bar during open hours and we'll be fine."

"You mean *you'll* be fine," she teased.

"Yeah." I knew it was a lie as soon as the word left my mouth.

TWENTY-TWO

Tripp

TWENTY MINUTES LATER I PULLED into the clubhouse lot. "I'll be right back. Just have to grab the keys." I jumped out of the truck and was about to close my door when Reece's voice cut through the air.

"Can I use the restroom?" she asked, clenching her thighs together. "I really have to go and I don't think I can hold it." Her face scrunched up while she squirmed in her seat.

"Yeah, okay. Come on."

Leading her inside, I directed her to the bathroom while I headed toward the bar, having spotted Marek hunched over talking to Trigger. Slapping him on the back, I took the stool next to him. "How ya doin'?" I asked tentatively. His only response was a grunt, followed by a slew of drunken words.

Looking to Trigger, I frowned, to which he simply shook his head. He mouthed, "Not good," before serving Marek another shot. The only guys who knew about what was goin' on with our prez were the men who were at the safe house. We agreed not to tell anyone else until we found out whether or not Psych had been telling the truth. Once the DNA results came back, then we'd let Marek decide what to do next. Until then, we swore to keep our mouths shut.

Marek's cell vibrated on the top of the bar, Sully's face flashing across the screen before he reached over and rejected the call. "I can't," he mumbled before shouting to Trigger to pour him another drink.

"Are you sure, Prez?" Trigger asked, slinging his bar towel over his shoulder. "I think you've had more than enough. Don't you want to sleep it off? Or better yet, do ya want me to take you home? I'm sure Sully's worried about you. She keeps calling." Trigger looked to me for assistance, which I readily gave.

"Yeah." I tugged on his arm. "Come on. One of us will give you a lift home. I'm sure your wife is worried sick." I looked back to Trigger. "He hasn't been home yet, has he?"

"Nope. Been planted on that fuckin' stool the entire time. I'm surprised his drunk ass hasn't fallen off yet."

"I ca . . . can hear ya," he muttered, finally staggering to his feet and walking toward Chambers. "Bring me a bottle," he shouted before slamming the door to the club's meeting place.

He left his phone on the bar, and when it rang again, I answered. I probably shouldn't have, but I knew Sully would be worried. No doubt she'd already spoken to Adelaide and knew Stone had returned home.

"Hey, Sully."

"Oh. Hi." A brief silence ensued before she spoke again. "Who is this?"

"Sorry, it's Tripp." Trigger stared at me, disbelieving that I'd actually answer Marek's phone. He shook his head and walked into the kitchen, most likely not wanting to be part of me going behind our prez's back.

"Is Cole there? Why do you have his phone? Is he okay?" she asked, her words coming out faster and faster the more she spoke. "Did something happen to him?" Short pants of air hit my ear and I knew I had to calm her before she really freaked out.

"Marek is fine. He's just. . . ." I trailed off, not quite sure what to say to her.

"He's what?"

"Drunk." Short and to the point.

"Drunk? Why? What happened?" Before I could answer I heard someone in the background—Adelaide. Then I heard Stone's voice.

"Sully, give the phone to Stone. I need to speak to him." I thought for sure she'd give me a hard time, insisting I tell her about Marek, but she didn't.

"It's Tripp," I heard her say before Stone came on the line.

"Everything okay?" he asked.

"Not really. Marek's at the club, drunk and mumbling all sorts of craziness."

"Can you blame him?" he whispered. I heard the women's voices fading into the background and knew Stone had walked away from them for more privacy.

"Not at all. But you need to calm Sully down before she freaks out and makes things worse. Whatever you do, keep her away from here."

"Yeah, I got it."

"Good. Hey, did you give Adelaide that shit to get tested? Did you tell her whose it was?"

"I'm not an idiot, Tripp."

"Well, that's debatable."

"Fuck you. And no, I didn't tell her anything except that I needed her to put a rush on it. She knew enough not to question me about it."

"And by that you mean she asked and you had to promise her some kind of sexual favor to let it go." I laughed because I'd witnessed the dynamic between the two of them, Adelaide certainly giving our VP a run for his money.

"Fuck you," he repeated before hanging up on me.

I'd been distracted from the call and didn't notice Reece walk up behind me. She gently touched my arm to let me know she was finished and ready to go.

"Hey, babe," I greeted. *Babe? Where the hell did that come from?*

She looked as shocked as I felt, but smiled nonetheless while stepping back when I stood up. Guiding her toward Chambers, I asked her to wait for me while I disappeared inside. Once I'd retrieved the keys from Marek, who was slumped over the table while simultaneously yelling at me because I didn't have a bottle of booze with me, I took hold of Reece's hand and led her back outside.

"What the hell, Tripp?" someone yelled across the courtyard. When I turned, I saw Hawke jogging toward me. "You still got my truck," he accused.

"I know. You were too damn drunk last night to drive so I did you a favor."

Glancing behind me, he jerked his chin at Reece before looking back at me.

"Who ya got here?"

Now that my brother was sober, I guessed it was time for official introductions. *So help me if he tries any slick shit, I'll put him on his ass.* Although he'd told me he was done with steppin' out on Edana, he still had a long way to go before I actually believed it.

"Hawke, this is Reece. Reece, meet my younger, uglier brother, Hawke."

"Don't you wish?" Hawke glared at me before nodding toward Reece, who was still standing behind me. "Nice to meet you," he finally said. "But I think you might have something wrong with you, you know . . . up here," he said, pointing to his temple. "Anyone willing to hang out with my brother just can't be right in the head." He laughed but soon grimaced when I punched him in the chest.

"Shut the hell up," I grated, a half smirk on my face when I finally turned away from him and walked back toward the truck, Reece quickly following. "I'm takin' your truck again. Be back later."

———◦———

ZIP'S HOUSE WAS A FIVE-MINUTE ride from the clubhouse, which put me at ease knowing I could easily check in on her. In case she needed me, not for my own selfish need to see her.

Yeah, keep tellin' yourself that.

We entered the modest home and I gave her the condensed tour, although there wasn't that much to see. The living room was first, followed by a dining room and finally the kitchen toward the back of the house. Upstairs, there were two bedrooms and a small bathroom. The entire place was void of any fancy décor, but it was clean and was a million times better than that fuckin' shithole of a motel.

Watching Reece take it all in, I knew I'd made the right decision bringing her here. Going over the security system left Reece in a panic, so I wrote down the instructions on how to arm and disarm it, explaining everything in more detail as I jotted it down.

Rooting through Zip's hallway closet, I came across a fresh set of sheets and a new blanket. After making up the bed in his room, knowing that's where she'd be sleeping, I said good night and instructed her to set the alarm as soon as I left.

As I walked back toward the truck I was struck by an odd sense of anxiety about leaving her all alone.

TWENTY-THREE

Tripp

BAG OF GROCERIES IN HAND, I unlocked the front door. As I approached the keypad to disarm the alarm, I noticed Reece had never set it. Annoyance and a hint of fear coursed through me that she was left unprotected all evening. Looked like we'd be having quite the conversation as soon as I saw her.

Placing the bag on the kitchen counter, I filled the coffee pot before checking out the contents of the fridge—empty except for some condiments. Like I said, Zip spent the majority of his time at the clubhouse, so it didn't shock me that he didn't have any food.

While I waited for the coffee to brew, I went in search of Reece, taking the steps two at a time and quickly reaching the top. I tried to tell myself not to appear too eager, or enthusiastic, or whatever would make me seem as if I'd been counting the minutes until I laid eyes on her again. Dispelling my impatience, I told myself the reason I was quickly walking toward her bedroom was because I needed to have a talk with her about safety. The sooner that issue was resolved the better.

Looking down at my watch before entering her room, I saw that it was just after eight. By most standards, including mine, it was still kind of early, so I assumed she was still in bed.

As soon as my eyes landed on her sleeping form, I relaxed, breathing a sigh of relief that she was safe. To be this worried about a woman I barely knew was uncharacteristic of me, but there was just something different about Reece. I felt it the first time I saw her dancing on stage, and again when I rescued her from that asshole. Every time we interacted, or touched, or laughed, I knew my world was changing.

Reece had thrown the covers off her at some point, the nightshirt she wore riding up enough that if she moved even an inch I'd be able to see her panties, if she was even wearing any.

I can dream.

Her hair fanned out on the pillow. Her arms were raised high above her head, and the first image that popped into my brain was her splayed out underneath me, instantly making me as hard as stone. My imagination took hold and I envisioned her in every position possible, all in the span of a minute. Before I even realized what I was doing, I'd reached out to touch her, but she moved before I could do so.

Then she moved again, mumbling something in her sleep as her chest began to quickly rise and fall. Tossing her head to the side, she opened her mouth as if to say something but no sound came out. Lowering her arms, she clenched the bedsheet and groaned. At first I thought she was having some sort of erotic dream, but that notion quickly flew out the fuckin' window when the word "no" left her lips. Over and over again. Then she began pleading with someone not to hurt her, that she wouldn't do it again. Was the guy who attacked her coming back to torment her in her dreams?

I knew I had to wake her from her nightmare. I tried to be as gentle as possible, knowing that I could frighten her even more if I tried to shake her awake, but the more she writhed around, I knew I had to pull her out of her dreams quickly.

"Reece," I called out, gripping her by the shoulders. "Reece, wake up. It's only a dream." I grew frustrated the longer she remained asleep, and it wasn't until I practically shouted at her that her eyes popped open. It took her a few seconds to realize where she was, and that whatever she'd been dreaming about was no longer a threat. Before that realization took hold, however, she scooted back on the bed and threw her hands up in front of her, as if to protect herself from me.

I knew it was instinctual on her part, but it didn't hurt me any less. I would never do anything to harm her, and I kept telling her that with the look of concern in my eyes. Eventually, the fright she felt faded, and it was only when the relief set in that she lunged at me. At first I thought she was gonna try and attack me, which I would've let her do to help her purge whatever haunted her, but I quickly understood that she needed me to comfort her.

"Tripp," she cried, flinging herself into my arms and snuggling into my chest. While I hated that her reaction stemmed from her nightmare,

I couldn't help but love the feel of her against me.

"Was it that bastard who attacked you?" I asked tentatively, not really wanting her to answer but knowing she needed to in order to start moving past what happened to her. She remained quiet, hanging on to me for dear life. After several intense moments, I unlocked her fingers from around me and pulled back enough for me to look into her eyes. "Was that who you were dreamin' about?" She started to shake her head but then quickly nodded, looking down when she saw the frown on my face. "Reece. . . ."

"I don't remember." I knew she wasn't telling me the truth simply from the way she kept avoiding my eyes.

"Well, you're safe now," I soothed, running my hands up and down her arms in a show of comfort. I decided not to grill her about her dream. She relaxed, and so did I. "Come on. I brought you some food."

"Did you make coffee?" she asked, swinging her long legs over the side of the bed.

"Sure did." Those were my last words before I walked from the room, leaving her behind me to do whatever she needed to before she came downstairs.

———— ◆ ————

"I HAVE SOMETHING TO TALK to you about," I said, waiting until she'd taken a seat at the table, a forkful of scrambled eggs poised at her lips, ready to be devoured.

"Okay," she responded, looking rather worried.

"The alarm," I started. "You have to make sure you arm it. Every time. I don't care if the door is locked. You can't mess up on this." She remained quiet. "It's very important. Do you understand?"

She nodded.

"No, I need you to tell me you get it. That you hear what I'm telling you," I pressed.

"Yes, I understand. Sorry."

"Okay. If I come here again and find out you didn't set it, I'll be forced to spank you." I meant to lighten the mood with a joke, but as soon as the words left my mouth, I knew I shouldn't have said them. That was until I saw her skin turn pink, the blush rising from her neck up to her cheeks. Her teeth captured her bottom lip and she briefly closed her eyes before looking at me again.

Because of her reaction, I never apologized, instead letting my sexual threat linger in that beautiful head of hers. Her eyes widened when I stepped closer, her breath hitching when I reached toward her to snatch her mug for a refill. A rush of air left her lungs when I turned around, and I couldn't help but adjust myself. I was so fuckin' hard that if she made a move on me I'd carry her back upstairs and fuck her so many times she wouldn't walk right for a week.

Needing another topic of conversation to focus on, even one I didn't particularly care for, I chose work. Reece now stood in front of the sink, washing out her cup and rinsing off her plate. My eyes were glued to her backside the entire time, until she turned around and caught me leering at her like some kind of creep. Or horny man. Yeah, I was goin' with sexually frustrated, horny man.

"Listen," I said, clearing my throat, trying like hell to get back on track and force all of the sordid images from my brain, "I have to head to the clubhouse to take care of some business, but I'll be back to pick you up at five for work."

"Why?"

"Why am I gonna pick you up?"

"Yeah. I can find my own way there. I don't want to put you out. You've done enough for me already." She shuffled her feet in nervousness.

"I don't mind," I insisted, my body language giving everything away, I was sure. My go-to intimidating stance was crossing my arms over my chest and spreading my feet, and while the last thing I wanted to do was bully her, I played on the only tool I had right then. I needed her to give in and do as I demanded; otherwise, I feared I'd go out of my mind with worry. And if I was constantly focused on Reece's safety, I'd be hampered from doing whatever I needed to for the Knights. Then I'd have bigger issues.

"I really don't—"

I cut her off, my aggravation increasing by the second.

"This conversation is over, Reece. I'll pick you up at five. Be ready to go." I gave her a fleeting smile before walking out of the house, a preemptive strike to any argument she may have come up with.

TWENTY-FOUR

Reece

MY FIRST TIME BEHIND THE bar didn't go exactly as I'd hoped, but with each passing hour I'd mastered some of the skills needed not to break every damn bottle stacked on the shelves.

Tripp stayed true to his word and picked me up at five on the dot, hanging out at the club until Carla insisted his presence was only adding to my nervousness. He left reluctantly, but only after telling me what he thought of the outfit I'd chosen to wear—a short black skirt paired with a low-cut Indulge tank top. Carla had passed out the shirts to every woman who worked there, telling us to wear them to promote the club. Good for business and all that. They were designed to leave little to the imagination, but that was the point, to draw in men who would spend their hard-earned money on the girls.

"I hate the thought of all these men leering at you," he'd whispered in my ear while I poured one of the customers a beer.

"At least I have clothes on," was the only thing I could think of to say. He left soon afterward, peering around the club one last time before he disappeared outside. I had no doubt he'd have eyes on me in his absence, and I was proved right when his brother strolled through the front door not an hour later.

———◆———

"I'M GONNA CHANGE REAL QUICK. I spilled beer all down the front of me," I yelled over the music. Carla smiled and nodded, tending to the multiple men waiting to be served.

"There should be extra shirts in the back. If you can't find any, check my locker. It should be open." She turned back toward one of the customers who wasn't taking waiting too well. Luckily, Carla knew exactly how to handle those types of guys. Besides, new security had been hired on to assist, just in case.

Once I'd reached the back room, I spotted a pile of the club's tank tops neatly stacked on top of one of the dressing tables. My bra had been soaked as well but there wasn't anything I could do about that, so I tossed my beer-soaked shirt on the floor and quickly pulled a fresh one over my head. I'd been too distracted with trying to hurry that I never heard her come into the room.

"Well, who do we have here?" Arianna sneered, the disgust she held for me certainly not hidden. I kept my back to her and didn't respond, engaging with her the last thing I wanted to do. My plan was to ignore her and head back out to the bar, but that never happened.

As I moved toward the door, Arianna stepped in front to block me.

"I thought they fired you," she cackled. Yes, *cackled*. It was the only word to properly describe the sound she made, the noise like nails on a chalkboard.

"Just from taking my clothes off. Apparently Tripp doesn't want any other man to look at or touch what's his." The words left my lips before my brain could filter them. I hadn't meant to goad her, but I had to admit that it certainly felt good. Really good. Arianna was nothing if not a bully, and if what I said was enough to leave her speechless, if only for a brief moment, then I considered that a success. No matter how short-lived.

When the shock finally wore off, she attacked. "You're lying. There's no way Tripp would ever hook up with the likes of you. You're . . . beneath me." She blew a strand of her over-processed hair out of her face. "He'd never bother with you after he had a taste of me."

The image of Tripp and Arianna together bothered me, although it shouldn't have. I had no claim on the man. I barely knew him. And even though it was apparent we were attracted to each other, that's all it was. But I didn't need to let this bitch know that.

As I was about to say something else to rile her up, my cell rang. And as luck would have it, Tripp's name flashed across the screen. What were the odds?

Turning my phone toward her so she could see who was calling, I smiled big and said, "Well, would ya look at that. Right on time." Arianna gave me the nastiest look as I swiped to answer the call. "Hi, sweetheart," I cooed enthusiastically, probably a little overboard but I couldn't help myself.

Arianna stood there in utter disbelief before she finally stomped out of the room, shouting at whomever was in her way before slamming the door behind her, leaving me extremely satisfied.

"Sweetheart? Well, that's unexpected, although I can't say I don't like it." The sound of Tripp's laughter soothed me, while the roughness of his tone anchored me into calmness.

"Sorry. Arianna was givin' me shit about you, so I decided to mess with her a bit."

"Don't pay her any mind, Reece. Seriously, she's not worth it." His words were clipped, which only spurred my next question.

"Do you still hook up with her?"

"What? Who told you that?" Tripp sounded flustered, which was odd coming from him. He seemed as if nothing would faze him.

"She did." Silence. "So, do you?"

"No, I don't."

"It's true, then? You did sleep with her?" I had no idea why I pried into his business, other than curiosity. And jealousy. Let's not forget about jealousy.

Letting out a ragged sigh, he answered, "Yeah, in the past. A few times. But no more. It was a mistake. One that'll never happen again."

"Which one was a mistake?" I pried further.

"What?"

"Which time you slept with her was a mistake?"

"Every time." A frustrated pant of air hit my ear. "Look, I don't wanna talk about her, so can we please drop it?"

Since Arianna was the last person I wished to discuss, I did as Tripp asked and let it go. He proceeded to change the subject, asking when my shift ended. I told him around three, and that he didn't have to worry because Carla would give me a ride home, to which he insisted on coming to pick me up. He was so adamant that I relented.

Besides, I really wanted to see him.

As soon as I ended the call, my phone instantly rang. I never bothered looking at the screen, simply figuring it was Tripp calling me right back.

"I know. I won't go anywhere until you get here." My tone was light with laughter, but when there was only silence, I pulled the phone from my ear and looked at the screen. Unknown. It wasn't Tripp who'd called me back.

"Hello?" Still no answer. "Hello?" I asked again. That time I heard someone breathing and my stomach flipped over in nervousness. "Hello?" I asked more timidly, praying the person on the other end would hang up without saying a word.

I got my wish when the call disconnected.

TWENTY-FIVE

Tripp

EVERY SINGLE DAY FOR THE past week, I'd seen Reece. I'd picked her up for work, hung out for an hour or so, and then returned later on to drive her home. She'd become more comfortable with her new role at the club, and although there were a few times when some of the drunk customers got a bit handsy with her, she seemed to handle them with no problem. That didn't mean I trusted anyone around her. Quite the opposite, in fact. If I wasn't there, I had one of the guys posted until I could return. We'd also hired additional security, not only for Reece but for all of the women at the club. Had to protect the club's investment, right?

On Reece's day off, we went grocery shopping. Something so mundane yet I enjoyed every second. Watching her flit from aisle to aisle brought a smile to my face. Even though the way we met wasn't ideal, it didn't deter me from delving into who she really was underneath.

During our many late-night talks, I'd convinced her to open up more about her family. She'd tell me stories from her childhood but then would quickly shut down as soon as she broached the subject of their accident. It was obviously still too painful for her to talk about. I'd switch the topic to that of past boyfriends, for my own torture, and she'd give me vague answers, her finger subconsciously rubbing the scar on the bridge of her nose. The desperate look in her eyes told me let it go, and I did. For the time being.

Something about Reece brought out my overprotective side, which I knew drove her crazy sometimes. She'd roll her eyes when I'd become a little more than animated trying to stress the importance of being aware of her surroundings. So in order to try and teach her a lesson, I went as far as to hide around the corner of Indulge, grabbing her when she'd come outside for some fresh air. She didn't particularly care so much for that little stunt of mine, shrieking out in fright before pummeling me with her tiny fists.

————◆————

"I DON'T UNDERSTAND WHY THE hell you won't tell me," I yelled, trying like hell to control my temper. But I failed. Big time. Only when Reece shrank back farther into the couch did I release a heavy breath and silently counted to ten. Tentatively approaching her, I stopped by the side of the sofa so as not to crowd her. "Sorry. I just want to get to know you, that's all. The good and the bad." I attempted to lighten the mood with a smile but couldn't. My body wouldn't allow the simple expression to form while my blood ran hot inside my veins.

"There's nothing to tell," she lied, pulling her knees to her chest in a protective stance. "Besides, I don't know anything about *you*," she threw back at me. "You won't even tell me your real name. Or anything about your family. Or how you came to be part of your club. I hear the other men call you 'nomad' every now and again. I've done some research. Nomad means you don't belong to any one place."

"Charter?"

"What?" She looked confused by my correction.

"They're called charters." The sofa dipped with my weight. I needed to sit for this, knowing damn well she was gonna take advantage and ask me all sorts of questions.

Rolling her eyes, something she'd been doing quite often, she asked, "Why did you decide to stay here?"

I knew what she was doing, deflecting to take the focus off her. I'd asked her about her previous relationship, again for my own torment, but she refused to give me any details.

The anger I'd felt just moments before slowly started to fade, although traces of it continued to pump through my veins. "Okay, fine. You wanna know some shit about me, I'll tell ya." I took a deep breath, giving off the impression I was annoyed. It wasn't totally off base. "You already know that Hawke is my younger brother, and although he can be quite the pain in the ass most times, we're close. I'd do anything to protect him, even if it's from himself. What else . . . ," I said, tapping my finger against my chin. "I've been with the Knights since my early twenties. Although he was never part of the club, my father had been friends with Marek's ol' man, as well as Stone's. I knew the guys growing up, so it just made sense to join. My father often worried about the goings-on within the Knights and didn't want me or Hawke involved, but he also knew enough about us that we wouldn't be deterred so easily."

"What does he think about it now?"

"He passed away last year. Cancer." I couldn't help the sadness that crept over me. Both Hawke and I were close with the old man, and it was a dark day when he died.

"I'm sorry," she said, reaching over to stroke my hand, her touch most definitely welcome.

"Thanks. Anyway, we were young and thrived on danger." I smirked but quickly stopped when I saw her reaction.

"Wait, what do you mean danger?" A worried look drifted over her face.

"Not anymore. Nothing for you to worry about where the club is concerned." I refused to elaborate. "Anyhow, I've always been sort of a loner, hence being a nomad." Judging by her expectant look, I continued on, revealing something I hadn't told anyone—the real reason I'd been in town the night some of the Reapers had attacked me, leaving me for dead in front of the Knights' clubhouse, four bullet wound scars a constant reminder of my carelessness.

"One night, I came home to find the woman I'd been living with fucking some guy. In our bed. Needless to say, I wasn't too happy. I almost killed him. I wanted to, trust me, but I didn't. After telling her it was over, I left and hopped on my bike. Before I knew it I'd arrived at The Underground, our club's bar. Because of what'd happened, I got drunk. Really drunk. And when I stumbled outside, there were a few Reapers waitin' for me. Still to this day I have no idea how no one saw them creepin' around outside." I took a deep breath. "They shot me, then dropped me off outside the clubhouse."

I paused to allow her to digest it all, her eyes wide with fright and concern. "I almost died. If it weren't for Adelaide, Stone's woman, I probably would've. She patched me up and looked after me while I recovered." I smiled at the recollection of how pissed Stone had been when Adelaide watched over me. I liked to think I was the reason he got his head out of his ass and finally pursued making them a legit couple.

"Who are the Reapers? Are they still after you?"

Hmm . . . how to answer that question.

"The Savage Reapers are a rival club. Real scum of the earth. And no, they're not still after me." Deciding to be as truthful as I could, I added, "Well, because of the hatred our clubs have toward each other, there's always the chance we could run into them. You know, not on accident." The worried look never left her face. "But now that their president is dead, I don't see them being a problem."

"He's dead? Did you . . . kill him?" she asked meekly, her bottom lip disappearing between her teeth in anxiousness.

"No, I didn't kill him." It was mostly the truth. While I'd assisted in his demise, Marek was the one who ended his wretched life.

Wanting to change the subject from something so grim, I allowed her to ask me a few more questions, hoping that by me opening up she would do the same.

"What else do you wanna know?" I prompted.

"Do you have any other siblings?"

"No."

"Is your mother still alive?"

"Don't know."

"Why wouldn't you know that?"

I tried not to appear as angry as I felt. "Because she took off with another guy and left us when Hawke and me were still young."

"And you never saw her again?"

"No. Next question," I barked. Reining it back in again, I said, "Sorry, I just don't wanna talk about her."

There she goes again biting that damn lip. All I wanted to do was reach over, pluck it from between her teeth and suck on it.

"That's okay. I know how that feels. Some things are better left in the past."

And there it was. She'd essentially just let me know that she wasn't open to discussing anything from her past. Eventually she'd have no choice, but we weren't there yet.

"Okay, I have one more question for you." She smiled so I relaxed.

"Shoot."

"What's your real name?"

"Cavanaugh."

"That's your first name?"

"Last name." While she was still processing my answer, albeit not the one she wanted, I asked for hers in return. "What's your last name?"

I thought for sure she would've refused, but surprisingly she answered. "Kendrick. Now tell me your first name," she insisted.

Shaking my head, I moved closer and ghosted my fingers down her arm, doing my best to distract her. I refused to give her the answer she wanted, but it wasn't because it was anything horrible. I simply loved playin' with her, knowing my refusal annoyed her.

"Nope.

"Are you running from the law or somethin'?"

"I told you my last name. Besides, if I were hiding from the police, do you honestly think I'd be involved with a well-known biker club?"

"Maybe. If you think about it, it's the perfect cover. Hiding in plain sight." She laughed, the sexual tension between us increasing. She continued to look at me expectantly.

"Not gonna happen, sweetheart. I don't know ya well enough yet to tell ya."

"Still?" she huffed, moving to tuck her legs underneath her. Turning toward me, she rested her arm on the back of the couch. "You've found a place for me to live, have picked me up and taken me home every night I had to work, seen me naked, and kissed me so passionately you made my toes curl."

"I made your toes curl, huh?" I winked, the corners of my mouth curving up in a wicked grin.

"You're so arrogant," she teased, slapping my arm in jest and allowing her fingers to grip my bicep a few seconds too long. Before she could pull away, however, I grabbed her hand and pulled her close, positioning her until she straddled my lap.

"What are you doing?" she asked breathlessly, short pants of warm air hitting my face her mouth was so close to mine. She moved on top of me to better adjust herself, and the second she rubbed herself over my cock I almost lost all gentleness and tore her clothes off right then and there.

Reece was still fragile. She tried to pretend otherwise, but I saw the pain hidden behind her beautiful eyes. An incident that would merely startle someone else sent her into a panic, if only for a few seconds. Glass shattering from one of the mugs behind the bar. Shouts from the customers when they got excited, which was quite often given the club they were in. No matter what it was, though, she always collected herself quickly, and if I hadn't been paying so much attention to her, I probably never would've noticed.

"What do you want me to do?" I asked. Placing my hands on her hips, I ground myself against her, licking my lips and drawing her attention from my eyes to my mouth.

"I don't know what you mean." She still tried to play coy, and admittedly I kinda liked it. Lifting the bottom of her tank top, my fingers grazed over her skin, her breath hitching from the heat of my touch. "That feels nice," she whispered.

"You know what else would feel nice? Great, in fact?" I continued to raise her shirt until I'd finally removed it altogether. She never protested. Never answered my question. She didn't do anything except wait for me to make my next move.

TWENTY-SIX

I'D BE LYING IF I didn't say that most of my thoughts were consumed by Tripp. The way he'd looked when he dropped his towel in front of me, baring his naked self and acting like it was no big deal. The way he'd watch me when he thought I wasn't paying attention. The way his kiss tasted when I'd been the one to shamelessly throw myself at him the day after I'd met him.

The way he made me feel safe.

The way he made inappropriate sexual jokes, like telling me he'd spank me if I forgot to arm the alarm system.

The way my body reacted to that statement.

The way he noticed.

So to be sitting on his lap, straddling him, our most intimate areas touching even though we were still clothed, left no room for imagination any longer. I knew exactly what he wanted to do.

And I wanted to do it too.

I wanted Tripp to strip me naked and have his way with me. As many times as he wanted. I needed to feel his lips against mine, to feel the warmth of his breath covering my skin as he positioned himself between my legs. I wanted to taste him on my tongue, to drive him so crazy with lust that he was barely able to control himself.

As soon as he unhooked my bra and tossed it aside, I finally gave in, knowing what was to come would be climactic, every pun intended. The chemistry that existed between us was palpable.

Undeniable.

Electric.

"Yes," I moaned, writhing on top of him and pushing my breasts closer to his face. Needing him to take me in his mouth, I brazenly taunted him until whatever resolve he had left shattered into pieces.

"Fuck," he groaned, latching on to my breast while toying with the other. The sensation was too much. Every flick of his tongue over my sensitive nipple. Every gentle tug of his teeth, his tongue soothing the bite so the line between pleasure and pain blurred together. "These are mine, baby. Do you hear me?" he asked, switching from one breast to the other, pinching the erect buds until I could barely stand it.

Tripp rose from the couch while holding me exactly in the same position. I wrapped my legs around his waist to ensure I wouldn't fall. Hell, I never wanted to separate from the man ever again. Our mouths found one another's as he climbed the steps and hurried toward my bedroom, our tongues dueling for dominance. But it was no contest; he took control like he always did, and I'd never been so happy to submit.

Once inside my room, he wasted no time before laying me on my back and ripping my skirt from me, quickly followed by my panties.

"I can't wait to fuck you," he groaned, kicking off his boots before removing the rest of his clothing, standing before me in all his glory. As my eyes trailed down the length of him, starting with his gorgeous face, to his sculpted chest and abs, then down to his . . . *oh my God!*

With furrowed brows, I leaned up on my elbows and stared right at his package. His overly large, extremely rigid, previously well-hidden surprise. I knew he was gifted down below when I'd felt it against my thigh earlier, but I never would have imagined just how big he was.

"What's the matter?" he asked, glancing down at himself before finally nodding. "Uh . . . never mind. I know what that look's for."

TWENTY-SEVEN

Tripp

SCRAMBLING UNTIL SHE WAS ON her knees, a position I'd envisioned her in too many times to count, she shook her head and looked at me with a twinge of fear in her eyes. "You don't honestly think that'll fit inside me, do you?"

If I weren't so fuckin' hard right then, the situation probably would have made me laugh. Reece pointed at my dick in disbelief, and while I found the whole scene flattering, I knew there was a chance I'd hurt her. And that was the last thing I ever wanted to do.

Before I could respond with some sort of reassurance, Reece crawled toward me, her tits heavy and begging for my mouth again. I wanted nothing more than to flip her on her back and plunge inside her, but I knew I could never do that. Not the way I wanted. Not until she became comfortable with my size.

Inching closer still, she glanced up at me before wrapping her hand around me, my cock twitching in her tight hold. "Fuck me," I growled. "Don't tease me too much or I'll be done before I even start."

"It's just so big," she whispered, stroking me from base to tip. Slowly. Tentatively. In awe at the sheer size of it. When a drop of precum coated the tip, she swirled it around with her thumb, stroking me quicker than before.

"Reece . . . ," I warned, the look of failing restraint plastered all over my face. "You can't keep doin' that. Not unless you want me to come." My eyes were pinned to hers the entire time, and when I saw a small smile tilt her lips, I knew she was up to no good.

"I just wanted to touch it."

"Well, don't stop there, sweetheart." A wolfish grin spread across my face. "You can taste it if you want." On reflex, my cock jerked in her hand, emphasizing my offer for her to wrap her lips around me.

"I might just take you up on that," she said, licking her lips as if already preparing to swallow me whole. Well, not whole because I'd never fit.

The heated look in her eyes, mixed with the heaviness of my balls, told me that if she took me in her mouth I'd never last.

"Never mind. I don't want you to do it."

"No?" She drew closer until her lips hovered over me, the sight of her about to suck me into her mouth pushing me toward the edge.

"Reece," I warned again. "I'm serious. Don't. Not yet. I don't wanna come down your throat." No matter what I said, it didn't deter her from doing what she wanted. Sure, I could have stopped her, but there was a part of me that wanted to see what she'd do. She was clearly fascinated with me. Who was I to stop her from exploring my dick?

"I'll just do it for a second," she promised, opening her perfect mouth and wrapping her lips around me. Her tongue swirled around the tip, her cheeks hollowing as she sucked me in as far as she could, which wasn't much. But it was enough, all the same.

It took every ounce of control I had not to thrust inside her wet, hot mouth. So, to steady myself, I grabbed her hair and positioned her where I wanted her. She tried to take more of me but I pulled back, only allowing the tip to remain inside. I felt the ache in my balls building, threatening to explode soon if I didn't pull out all the way. But it felt too good—amazing, even.

"Goddammit!" I roared, restricting her movements every time she pushed to take more of me. Knowing it would all be over too soon, I pushed her back and I finally fell from her mouth. I swore it felt as if I'd run a fuckin' marathon. The air pushed from my lungs in heavy spurts, my chest rising and falling simply from lust alone. "You're gonna be the death of me," I told her, watching her smile widen. Her saliva made it easier for me to stroke myself while she watched, the desire in her eyes taking over in the form of sheer fascination. "Do you like watching me do this?"

She nodded, biting the corner of her bottom lip in excitement.

"Lie back," I demanded, kneeling once her back hit the bed. "Spread your legs."

"Tripp, I'm nervous," she admitted, worry etching faint lines around her eyes.

I'd better put her mind at ease, or she's gonna chew the hell out of that poor, abused lip.

"I'm not gonna fuck you yet. Not with my cock, anyway." Widening her legs, I lowered my head until my breath spread over her glistening pussy. "I can see you're ready for me, but just to make sure. . . ." I slid my tongue between her folds, the taste of her driving me insane.

There was no slow buildup before her back arched off the bed, her fingers pulling at my hair and thrusting her pussy against me. My tongue slid inside her, followed by two fingers, stroking that sweet spot until her toes literally curled.

"Oh . . . oh my God . . . yes," she panted, over and over again. With my free hand, I played with her tits, pinching her nipples and adding to the sensation racking her body. "Tripp. . . ." My name was like a prayer on her lips. A promise. An ode to something bigger.

I knew as soon as I wrapped my lips around her clit that she'd fall. While I wanted nothing more than for her to come on my tongue, I was also being quite selfish. The wetter she became, the easier it would be for me to push inside her.

"Does that feel good? Do you wanna come?" I asked, continuing to tease her until she answered.

"Please," she panted, her fingers gripping my hair to the point of pain. But I didn't mind. Not at all. It meant she was close to the edge. All I had to do was finish her off.

With one final stroke of my tongue, I sucked on her clit and pumped two fingers inside her simultaneously. Reece cried out, her moans the best sound I'd ever heard. The sight of her undid me, my own need to claim her intensifying the longer she rode out her orgasm.

When she'd finally come back down, she started to laugh. "Oh my God!" she exclaimed. "That was amazing."

"Then why are you laughing?" A smile toyed with my lips until I was full-on grinning. Her expression was infectious.

"Because I can't believe I've missed out on that all these years." While what she'd said was a compliment, I didn't ask her to elaborate because the thought of her with another man would torture me.

"Glad I could be of service." I moved up the bed and covered her still-quaking body with mine. "Do you know how many times I've pictured you like this, legs spread and ready for me?"

"Probably not as many as I have," she answered, a sly smirk staring back at me.

"Oh really?" I laughed at the casualness of her statement. The same woman who blushed when she'd seen me naked for the first time.

"Yeah, really," she teasingly taunted. She tried to move up the bed but my weight kept her pinned right where she was.

"Am I crushing you?"

"No, but I'm starting to freak out about . . . you know."

"My dick?"

A raised brow from me had her smiling again.

"Yeah."

"Don't worry. We'll take it slow." The last thing I wanted was for her to be so tense she didn't enjoy herself. But the reality was that my size was sometimes more of a hindrance than a blessing. I know, poor me, but that was the truth of it.

"Okay," she said, her muscles already tensing.

"Try to relax," I coaxed, kissing her sweetly to let her know everything would be great. We were meant to fit together; it just might take a bit more work on my end to ensure she felt nothing but pleasure.

Rising up on my forearm to balance myself, I reached for the condom I'd pulled out earlier and quickly sheathed myself. Lining myself up at her entrance, I teased her with my finger one last time to make sure she was completely ready.

"Tripp?"

Looking down into her trusting eyes, I knew I was never gonna be the same man ever again. "Yeah?"

"What's your real name?"

Without hesitation that time, I said, "James."

TWENTY-EIGHT

Reece

FINALLY. HE'D TOLD ME HIS real name. Then again, he couldn't use the excuse that he didn't know me well enough, seeing as he was poised to have sex with me.

Every time I thought about the size of his cock, what it would feel like stretching me open, I tensed. I tried to listen to him and relax, but he wasn't the one who was gonna get a huge dick shoved inside him. Most women would be ecstatic to find out the guy they were gonna sleep with was well-endowed, but this was going overboard just a bit.

"Are you ready?" he asked, concern mixed with lust dancing behind his beautiful green eyes.

"I think so."

He lowered his mouth to mine, his tongue sliding over my bottom lip and deliciously teasing me. The thrust of his tongue soon mirrored the thrust of his body. Gentle and patient. If his restraint teetered on the edge, he didn't show it. Placing his hand under my knee, he widened my legs, pushing my thigh up toward me to open me up a little more.

"You're beyond tight, baby," he groaned, nipping my lip before kissing along my jaw, eventually burying his head in the crook of my neck and panting heavily. "Are you okay? How do you feel?"

"It hurts a little, but it feels good at the same time." And it did hurt, even with how wet he'd made me. But it wasn't as painful as I thought it would be.

"I have an idea," he said before pulling out of me. "Come here." He grabbed my hips and pulled me down the bed. He rested back on his haunches and spread my legs as far apart as possible. His hands braced underneath my knees, pressing my thighs back toward me like he'd just done with my leg moments earlier. "Wrap your hand around me and put me inside you." When I looked hesitant, he said, "Trust me. Do it."

With my hand fully wrapped around his cock, I lined him up at my entrance. He swiveled his hips before pushing back inside me, that time going in with much more ease, although he still took his time. An ache that'd bloomed inside me intensified, my body hungry for every inch of him. After slowly working himself in, we were fully sheathed. I felt so incredibly full. Tripp remained still until he took a few deep breaths and pulled back an inch.

"I'm gonna start to move now." His expression looked pained and I wondered if I was somehow inadvertently hurting him.

"Are you okay?"

He clenched his jaw. "I'm more than okay. I'm just tryin' to hold back so I don't hurt you. But it's so hard." The sexiest moan flowed from his incredible lips, seducing me even more than he already had.

"Yes it is," I said, laughing after I realized how cheesy my reply was. He chuckled, and whatever tension had existed between us instantly evaporated.

Every corded muscle of his chest constricted as he rocked in and out of me, the vision in front of me purely animalistic. His lips parted, his eyes hooded as he lost himself to the feel of my body. The sight of Tripp lost in his own bliss was intoxicating, and if I were a woman who could come from an image alone, it would have happened right then.

Several minutes later Tripp found a steady rhythm, thrusting inside me, gently at first and then a bit more aggressive the more my body opened for him. All traces of pain disappeared. Every time he swiveled his hips, he hit my sweet spot, the strangled "yes" which flew from my lips affirmation enough.

"Right there?" he asked, hitting the sensitive place inside me over and over. He knew damn well that was the spot.

"Yes. Oh . . . yes. Right there." I tried to move with him, but the position he had me in made it near impossible to do so. "Tripp, let go of my legs. I want to feel you against me. Please," I begged. It didn't take but a second for him to comply.

Resting on top of me, some of his body weight held up by his forearms, his mouth found mine again as he fucked me senseless. "I can't believe you're takin' all of me, baby. So fuckin' good," he panted. "You feel incredible. So warm. Tight. Do you love my cock?" The only response I could muster was a moan. "Tell me you love my big cock," he demanded, plunging his tongue into my mouth. I should have known Tripp would talk dirty, his past sexual innuendoes surely laying the groundwork.

As we continued to taste each other, I felt my body crest on the wave of pleasure, climbing higher and higher until the sensation was so overwhelming there was nothing to do except count the seconds until my body detonated into the abyss of my impending orgasm.

I couldn't believe the words that were about to come out of my mouth, but before I could stop myself, I shouted, "Fuck me harder. I'm right there. Oh my God. Yes . . . I'm right there." My fingers clenched his tight ass as he picked up his pace, reaching underneath me to pull me closer while he pounded into me, although I suspected he still restrained himself. A twinge of pain erupted but was quickly absorbed by my orgasm. Every nerve inside me fired into the heavens, the feeling so strong and powerful I almost lost my breath. Tripp latched on to my mouth and swallowed my screams, his own moans mixing with mine as he lost himself to his own high.

When we'd finally come back down, our breath regulated and reality came back into focus. Tripp remained on top of me, his weight starting to crush me the longer he laid there. I tapped his ass. When he still didn't budge, I slapped his rear.

"Ow," he grumbled.

"You . . . have to . . . move." My strangled words were enough for him to roll off me.

"Sorry." He laughed. "I forget my size sometimes."

"You could've killed me," I teased, turning on my side to face him.

"It'd be a hell of a way to go out, though, don't ya think?"

I never answered, the curve of my lips enough to tell him I agreed. To look at him right then was the best sight I'd ever laid eyes on. A thin sheen of sweat covered his large, muscled body, the tips of his hair sticking to his forehead from all of his exertion. I never thought a sweaty man could be alluring, but Tripp had proved me wrong. His semi-erect arousal lay across his belly, the condom he'd worn disposed of in a nearby wastebasket.

Lost to the image of the man lying next to me, he startled me when he reached out to pull me close. He smiled and kissed my temple, wrapping his arm around me as I snuggled into his side. Without thinking, the pads of my fingers danced over his skin. When I came to a scar, I stopped, but only briefly before continuing on.

"Does it still hurt?"

"Sometimes when it rains, but other than that, not really."

I decided to continue to be inquisitive, hoping in his contented state that he wouldn't hold anything back. "I thought all big bad biker boys were inked up. So where's yours?" I continued to trace his skin, the circling rhythm comforting me enough I felt my eyelids grow heavy.

"First off," he said, grabbing my hand and placing it over his manhood, "I ain't no boy." He thrust his hips for effect and laughed when I playfully pulled back and smacked his arm. "Second, people usually get inked to tell a story. My wounds are my story." His words were poetic yet haunting. I couldn't even imagine what he'd experienced, the horrific ordeal he had to live through. But live he did, which proved Tripp was a fighter. If I hadn't realized it before, I did in that moment.

To lighten the mood, I decided on a lighter topic. "Where did you get your nickname from?"

"Well, if you must know," he says, licking his lips, "girls were always tripping over themselves to get my attention. Hence the name Tripp." He stopped talking and just stared at me, and it wasn't until he grinned that I realized he was just messing with me. Although I had no doubt that women did trip over themselves to gain his interest.

"Nice one." I laughed.

"Seriously, though, I was quite the clumsy fucker when I was younger. I was always trippin' over my own damn feet. Always fallin' and breakin' somethin'. My dad was the one who gave me the nickname." His eyes darkened for a brief moment, no doubt at the recollection of his father. Before I could inquire, however, his mood switched back to one of light-heartedness.

"Ready for round two?" He turned his head toward me and captured my lips. I was sore but definitely up for some more of what he was offering.

"I guess so," I answered, rolling my eyes on purpose as if his request was an inconvenience. He flipped me on my stomach and slapped my ass, but as soon as his hands parted my legs, his cell rang.

"Dammit!"

"Do you have to get it?"

"Yeah. Shit's not good right now, and it could be important."

Hopping off the bed, he snatched his phone from the end table and strode toward the hall, returning a minute later. He looked pissed while he quickly dressed, sitting on the edge of the bed to pull on his boots.

"Look, I have to get goin', but I promise I'll be back as soon as possible."

"Can I ask what it is you have to do?"

"You can, but that doesn't mean I can tell you."

I shrank back on the bed, annoyed by his statement. I'd dealt with secretiveness before and it only led to bad things.

Seeing the look on my face, Tripp laced his fingers with mine and tried to make me feel better. "Listen, Reece, when it comes to the club I won't be able to tell you about a lot of stuff that goes on. I hope you can understand."

"I do," I lied. What else was I gonna say? Demand he tell me everything? We'd only slept together one time, and while I wanted nothing more than to claim Tripp as my man, the truth was we still didn't know each other all that well.

"You okay?" he asked, leaning over to give me a parting kiss.

"Yeah."

"You sure?" His questioning gaze comforted me.

I nodded that time, pressing my lips to his before he rose from the bed.

"I'll set the alarm before I go."

"Hurry back." I pouted, disappointed he had to leave so soon after we'd been together. He shot me his sexy grin and winked before disappearing from the room, the close of the front door signifying when he'd left the house.

Lying back against the headboard, I couldn't stop my heart from racing to keep up with the adrenaline and giddiness I felt. I knew we'd only just met, but whatever was happening between us was exciting. The sexual chemistry was off the charts, but more than my attraction toward him, I felt safe, which was something completely new for me.

For the next twenty minutes I lost myself to thoughts of the man who'd just left my bed, and what'd we'd be doing as soon as he returned. Then a sudden noise from downstairs drew my attention. At first I thought I heard something hit against the front door, but then I couldn't be sure. Sitting up in bed, I strained to listen for any signs that Tripp had returned. When all was silent, I laid back on the bed only to jump to my feet when the alarm shrieked through the air. Wrapping the sheet around me, I raced toward the top of the steps, the front door wide open below.

I didn't hear anything over the piercing sound. I should've locked myself in the bedroom, but instead I slowly descended the stairs and cautiously peered around the room. After shutting the door, I punched in the code and the alarm finally silenced. I checked out all of the rooms. No one else was in the house, but that realization didn't stop my heart from pounding against my chest so rapidly I feared having a heart attack right where I stood.

TWENTY-NINE

Tripp

WHEN I'D WALKED INTO THE clubhouse, Trigger, Ryder and Jagger were crowded around the door to Chambers, talking quietly while they glanced over at Marek every now and again, who was subsequently slumped over the bar. I knew exactly what'd they'd been discussing. The possible relation between Marek and Sully seemed like the only topic we talked about when together.

When Stone ripped out a chunk of Psych's hair and swiped his blood on a piece of cloth, he did so when Marek was in the middle of his break with reality. It wasn't until the next day that he revealed to his best friend and leader just what he had planned. At first Marek refused, but after a little coaxing he relented, realizing it was better to know either way than to continue to torture himself. He'd given Stone some of his hair as the final step.

"What the hell are we gonna do with him?" Jagger asked, pacing in front of us like he was the only one put out by the new state of our president. "He can't go on like this."

"We know," Ryder barked, glaring at the rest of us as if we were the cause of the new shit storm.

"Calm down. We don't need to deal with your pissy mood on top of everything else." Trigger gave Ryder a look before turning his attention to me. "Where are we with the results for that fuckin' test?"

"I don't know. Stone gave the stuff to Adelaide and asked her to put a rush on it. That was a week ago."

The tension brewing between the four of us was enough to push any one of us over the edge with anxiety, as if the energy we shared was tangible, feeding on our state of mind.

"What the fu . . . fuck are ya yellin' 'bout?" Marek slurred, slapping the top of the bar for emphasis, although with the way he wobbled on top of his seat, I was surprised he had enough energy to even raise his hand. I'd seen Marek fucked up before—actually quite a bit over the years—but never like this, and not for this long. While I completely understood his turmoil, I also knew it was in his and his wife's best interest to do something about it, and quick. Otherwise, I feared shit was gonna hit the fan, and irreversible damage was gonna be the result.

No one answered his outburst. In fact, we tried to give him his space, although what he'd been doing with that space had been destructive. From what Stone had told me, Marek and Sully had been fighting—or to be more accurate, Marek had been blowing up at his wife for no reason. None that Sully could understand, at least. He'd barely spent time at his house, only stopping in for a few minutes at a clip before coming back to the clubhouse, where he proceeded to get shit-faced.

"Trigger!" Marek yelled over his shoulder, almost falling on his ass from the simple movement. Once he righted himself, he shouted, "I need another fuckin' drink."

"Goddammit," Trigger growled. "I can't take much more of this." He continued to grumble to himself as he walked across the room and then behind the bar.

"And don't water it down," our prez ordered.

"I *should* water that shit down. Maybe then you'd sober up and take your ass home." Bold move on Trigger's part, but someone had to say something.

"Fuck you!" Marek shouted in response, rising off his stool and stumbling toward the back, no doubt heading to the bathroom to either piss or vomit.

As soon as he disappeared, the door opened and in strolled Stone. At first I was happy to see the guy. Then Adelaide and Sully appeared right behind him.

"What the hell?" Ryder quickly walked over to him and pulled him aside. They huddled in the corner, our VP glancing over at his woman and Sully every few seconds. I knew their presence wasn't gonna go over well as soon as Marek came back from the bathroom, and I only prayed he'd passed out back there.

Approaching the two women, I gave them both a tight smile. "What are you doing here?" I knew Stone never told Adelaide exactly whose

DNA was being tested, but she wasn't stupid. And while I believed she'd never guess what was really going on, she had to know something was off. Stone's moody ass had only intensified.

In truth, all of us had been on edge since that fateful day when Psych spewed his final admission. Or lie. The truth was yet to be determined.

Jerking her head to the side, Adelaide had me follow her until we stood away from Sully. Once her friend was out of earshot, Adelaide started talking. "Sully called me this morning crying because she's worried about Marek. He won't talk to her, snaps at her for the smallest things, and he hasn't spent the night at home in a week." She looked at me expectantly, as if I was gonna tell her something her own man wouldn't. "I don't know what the hell is going on, Tripp, but this is bullshit. She's been through enough. She doesn't deserve this, and if you know what's goin' on you need to tell her."

"You know I can't do that." My shoulders slumped forward. I wished I could put their minds at ease, but it simply wasn't my place. Marek had to handle this on his own, and although I didn't agree with the course he'd taken, it was essentially his call.

"Why?" Her voice rose. "Is it some kind of man code? Is he cheating on her?" she finally asked, lowering her voice to ensure Sully didn't hear. The whole time we'd been standing off to the side talking, Jagger had been keeping Sully occupied, giving her a quick hug when she started to cry.

"No, it's nothin' like that. That much I can tell you," I told her honestly.

"Then what is it?"

I opened my mouth to tell her she wasn't gonna get anything out of me when I heard a crash come from down the hallway. The noise grabbed everyone's attention, and I held my breath for what was to come. I knew damn well Marek wouldn't be happy when he saw Sully, which was awful. If anything he should've been seeking comfort in her arms, but he turned the other way, hurting her in the process.

The whole situation was beyond fucked-up, and the longer he had to wait to find out if his wife was actually his fuckin' sister, the more he unraveled.

The second Marek appeared all conversations ceased. Everyone turned toward him and waited to see his reaction. At first he didn't see his wife; it was apparent in the way he ambled back toward the bar, stumbling over his feet and almost falling on his face. Twice. He was a sad sight and when I glanced over at Sully, the tears flowed more freely than before.

Adelaide had left my side to console her friend, and it was when a sob erupted from Sully that Marek finally turned around, noticing her for the first time. A mix of anger and torture distorted his expression at the very sight of her. As if his heart was being ripped out all over again. I walked the few feet and stood next to the women and Jagger, Ryder, and Stone approaching our group as soon as they saw Marek's reaction.

None of us knew what he was capable of at that point. Would he ignore his wife or rant and rave until he forced her to leave? He'd never lay his hands on her, that much we knew, but what words would come out of his drunken mouth was anyone's guess.

It seemed as if time stood still as Marek and Sully locked eyes with one another, the tension in the air building until Marek finally spoke.

THIRTY

Tripp

"WHAT THE FU . . . fuck is sh . . . she doin' here?" he slurred, walking as swiftly toward us as he could in his inebriated state. His eyes were bloodshot and his hair disheveled. He reeked of alcohol and his clothes were a little worse for wear. All in all, he looked like shit.

The closer he came the more we huddled around Sully, preparing to deter him from whatever he planned on doing.

When he stood a few feet from his wife, he wobbled and tried to reach for her, but Jagger stepped directly in front of her. His move of protectiveness only served to infuriate Marek, the look of astonishment on his face quickly giving way to boiling anger.

"Move!" Marek shouted, continuing to sway on his feet.

"Not gonna happen, Prez," Jagger said, crossing his arms over his chest but looking a little apprehensive. "Why don't you go sleep it off?"

Stone stepped in and stood directly in front of his friend. "Yeah," he agreed. "Why don't you go sleep it off? You can talk to her later."

"I don't wanna talk to her," he growled, clenching his fists until his knuckles turned white.

"Why?" Sully suddenly shouted, shoving past Jagger so she could look at her husband. "What did I do? Why won't you tell me?" Her voice trembled, tears cascading down her cheeks while she waited for him to answer. "I love you, Cole. Why are you treating me like this?" She stepped closer—too close, in my opinion. Emotions ran high and I feared the worst.

Before anyone could stop him, Marek grabbed Sully's arms and drew her in, their noses almost touching they were so close. "I. Don't. Want you here," he enunciated. "Go home." He shoved her back, but not hard enough to cause her to stumble. He took a step back, glaring at her the entire time.

I understood why Marek didn't want to fill Sully in on exactly what was goin' on, not until he absolutely had to, but there was no reason for him to be treating her like this. It was uncalled for, and certainly unnecessary. Then again, he wasn't in his right mind. Hadn't been for a while now.

As if shit weren't already spinning out of control, Adelaide stalked toward Marek, Stone trying to pull her back before she reached him. "I don't know what's going on, but you're a real shit for treating your wife like this. A real shit," she repeated, hitting his chest for emphasis. "You better get your act together, and soon, before you lose the only good thing that's ever happened to you." They stood toe-to-toe, Adelaide throwing Marek icy daggers and Marek swaying from side to side, trying to keep his balance.

"Stone, get your fuckin' woman outta my face or else," Marek threatened, continuing to clench his hands at his sides. The sight disturbed me. The guy I knew would never raise a hand to a woman, yet there he was essentially threatening Adelaide. Would he really do something? I had no idea, and that realization rattled me.

The icy expression that crossed Stone's face alarmed everyone present. "Don't you fuckin' talk to her like that. You hear me?" he asked, stepping in his best friend's face. His drunken, out-of-his-mind, heartbroken, and confused best friend. I would've bet Marek's mental state, drunk or not, was the only reason Stone didn't physically attack him.

As the two men squared off, we all backed up to give them some room to sort out their issue, if that was at all possible right then. After an intense stare-down, Marek still wobbly on his feet, Stone leaned in and whispered something in his ear. Resting his hand on Marek's shoulder, Stone continued to speak, but only on a level our prez could hear. A minute later I saw some of the tension evaporate from Marek, although he still appeared to teeter on the edge. Shaking his head, he stumbled back before turning around and heading toward the hallway to no doubt escape everything and everyone.

Sully continued to cry, resting her head against Jagger's chest while she expelled everything she'd been feeling.

"Stay with her," Stone told Jagger, grabbing Adelaide's hand and tugging her behind him into Chambers. He motioned for the rest of us to follow with a jerk of his head. Normally, women weren't allowed inside Chambers but this was one of the rare exceptions, the last time being when Sully had forced her way inside to demand that Marek trade her for Adelaide and Kena after her father had orchestrated their kidnapping.

I had an idea what Stone wanted to ask his woman, and the seclusion of the room would certainly provide the privacy we needed. The tension coming off the VP built and built until he looked like he was gonna explode. Pacing in front of all of us, he ran his hand through his hair before clenching his fists at his sides, much like Marek had done moments before.

"Why haven't we heard anything back about those results?" he asked to no one in particular, although there was only one person present who could give an honest answer.

Ryder and Trigger mirrored Stone, pacing and glancing over at Adelaide every few seconds. I'd chosen to lean against the wall, content to just listen to whatever was about to unfold. Someone had to be the semi-calm one.

"Like I told you yesterday when I called them, the lab is backed up. There's nothing I can do about that," she said. "Why is that DNA so important, anyway?" There was a small part of me that thought maybe Stone had told Adelaide everything, but thankfully I'd just been proven wrong.

Stone ignored her question, instead edging closer until he towered over her. "You didn't call today?"

"Not yet, no."

"Are you fuckin' kiddin' me right now, Addy? I told you how important those results are. That I needed them back right away," he bellowed, the veins in his neck bulging the more he continued to speak. Or rather yell. Stone started pacing again, mumbling incoherently to himself.

"What the hell is wrong with you?" She looked to each of us standing in the room, her nervousness displayed on her face. "Whose DNA is it?"

"None of your business," Stone yelled over his shoulder. I'd seen those two shout at each other before but this was on another level, and Adelaide knew it. Before she could respond, however, Stone gripped the back of his neck in frustration and headed toward his woman again, backing her against the door before she could react. He loomed over her once more, intimidating her with his size and aggression. "Get your fuckin' ass on that phone and get the goddamn results, Addy. Now!" He slapped the doorframe above her head for added effect.

My eyes popped wide as I looked around at everyone in the room. To say we were surprised Stone had yelled at his woman like that was an understatement. Sure, our VP was hotheaded and went overboard sometimes, but I'd never heard him speak to Adelaide in such a way.

Sure enough, in true Adelaide fashion, she didn't let him get away with it. I saw what was gonna happen before Stone did, her hand cracking across his face before he took his next breath. The sound shook the room and everyone gasped, me included—an odd reaction coming from three grown men, but it was the truth. We'd all been through the mental wringer for what seemed like forever with no end in sight, and right then was the culmination to the ever-growing tension.

Stone backed away, the look on his face softening as if she had indeed just slapped some sense back into him. "Baby, I'm sorry," he apologized, reaching out to touch her, but she shrugged away from him.

"Don't even think about touching me," she fumed. Stone had a condition where he was immune to physical pain, but right then I could see that he was hurtin'. Not from the slap, of course, but because he knew he'd crossed the line, and it'd take quite a while for him to grovel enough for Adelaide to forgive him. She never put up with his shit, pushing back as often as Stone tested her.

Shoving him, the adrenaline pulsing through her surely enough for her to move him, or he allowed her to do so, she continued to speak. "There's obviously something detrimental going on here to have Marek treating Sully like shit, and for you to have lost your damn mind and yelled at me like that." Adelaide was the one to advance on Stone that time, looking up at him and throwing him a stern glare. "You better get your head out of your ass, Stone, and until that happens you can stay here. I don't want you at home."

Again Stone tried to draw her into him but she dodged his touch. Looking every bit the apologetic man, he raised his hands in submission. "I'm sorry. I was outta line. It's just . . . there's so much goin' on and—"

"I don't care what's goin' on here. That's no excuse for you to talk to me like that." Anger and hurt shrouded her expression.

"I know. I'm sorry, baby," he repeated.

Adelaide continued to glare at him, even when he attempted to grab her hand, which he failed at yet again.

"Don't," was all she said before she threw the door open and hurried from the room, Stone hot on her heels. I could hear him apologizing over and over, but it was no use. Adelaide was as stubborn as Stone, and I knew—we all did—that his sullen ass would be staying here at the clubhouse for at least the next few days.

As if whatever had just transpired in the past hour hadn't been enough, I noticed two missed calls from the alarm company when I pulled my phone from my pocket.

Tripp

RUSHING INSIDE THE HOUSE, I shoved past the officer standing in front of Reece and pulled her close. "Are you okay? What happened?" I looked between the both of them, impatiently waiting for one of them to answer me.

"I'm fine." She tried to pull away but I wouldn't let her.

"Do you live here?" the officer asked, flashing me a stern look before glancing back toward Reece. The guy was young, a rookie maybe?

"Yeah," I lied, deeming him unworthy of a full explanation. "What happened?" I repeated.

"Apparently the front door was opened, setting off the alarm." Nothing further from him before he jotted something down in a notepad.

"How the hell did that happen?" I finally let go of Reece and neared the doorframe, searching for any sign of foul play but not readily finding any. "Did you check the house?" I wasn't sure who I directed that specific question to.

"Yes," they both answered, Reece dipping her head for a moment before looking back at me. I had a suspicion she was hiding something from me.

"And?"

Reece spoke first that time. "I checked the house after the alarm went off, and thankfully didn't find anyone. Officer Bauer did another check when he arrived. Just in case." She gave the cop a thankful smile, and I didn't like it. I saw the way he kept checking her out, right in fuckin' front of me. Brazen little shit.

Needing him to leave, I threw my arm around her shoulder and leaned down to kiss her. "Well, it looks like maybe a faulty door. I'll have it checked out. No need for you to stay here." My tone left no room for misunderstanding. Or argument.

He gave me a final once-over before smiling at Reece. "Miss." He nodded before leaving, still writing something down on that damn notebook of his.

After I'd shut the door, I asked, "Are you sure you're okay?"

"Yeah. Just a bit frightened. But that alarm probably scared me more than anything." Putting her finger in her ear and wriggling, she said, "It's really loud."

"That's the point. A deterrent." I took some time before blurting out my next statement, figuring it was as good a time as any to let her in on my plans. Plans that had formed on my way over. "You're gonna stay with me at my place."

I expected some sort of argument, some sort of refusal, but she had none. A simple nod from her and I'd been put right back on edge when I should have been relieved.

She was definitely hiding something from me.

THIRTY-TWO

Reece

DESPITE THE FRIGHT I'D ENDURED two days back, I never imagined my life could turn out normal. Well, as normal as it was working in a strip club and being involved with a biker. I was smart enough not to put too many hopes and dreams on a new relationship, if that was even what this was, but I couldn't help but picture myself with Tripp for the long haul.

His incessant need to make sure I was safe was sweet. Something I certainly wasn't used to. He'd increased security even more at the club after the mysterious issue with the front door. Not sure why, seeing as how it had happened at the house and not at Indulge, but I couldn't help but feel a sense of relief either way.

What I failed to tell Trip was that I'd been a little more than freaked out, and while I tried not to show my vast relief at his suggestion to stay with him at his house, a calm had descended over me when he uttered the words.

"You wanna go dancing after work?" Carla asked, giving me a quick smile while she poured a beer for a customer. "I know a place that's open late."

She busied herself wiping off the counter and taking orders while I contemplated her offer. After the hang-up I'd been worried. Then when the door at the house had been mysteriously opened, thankfully setting off the alarm, I'd been rattled to my core. For as much as I wanted to relieve some of my anxiety about both incidents, I knew I shouldn't go anywhere Tripp wasn't able to accompany me, and I highly doubted he was the dancing kind.

"I don't think I should," I finally answered.

"Oh come on," she prodded.

I gave her my most apologetic smile. "Maybe another time."

"Does this have anything to do with Tripp? Is he keeping you under lock and key?" Her question wasn't meant to be a serious one, but when she saw the fleeting widening of my eyes, she changed her tune. "Are you serious, Reece? Did he tell you that you can't go anywhere without him? I've noticed how the two of you have been attached at the hip recently. The man is relentless, and while I think Tripp is a good guy, don't let him push you around. You do what you want, when you want. Do you hear me?" Her hands found their way to her hips, her brow arched in wait.

"It's not like that." She looked at me skeptically. "Honestly. He just wants to keep me safe." Carla had no idea what I'd been through in the past. If she did then she'd fully understand my need to relent to Tripp's slightly overbearing tendencies.

"Fine, but if I think he's being too possessive over you, I'm gonna say something to him."

I had no doubt she would. Carla had come to be a good friend over the short time I'd known her, so I didn't take any offense to her threatening to stick her nose further into my business. Besides, I thought it just might be worth watching that interaction between the two of them. For amusement purposes.

The next few hours passed relatively quickly. The crowd grew in size, and thankfully everyone seemed to be on their best behavior. Surely the overly large bouncers spread throughout the club didn't have anything to do with it. Coming back from the ladies' room, Carla caught me before I walked back behind the bar.

"Hey, there's a guy over there asking for you."

Craning my neck around her and the few men blocking the view to the other end of the bar, I didn't see anyone I knew.

"Is he a customer?"

"I don't think so."

Again I tried to see anyone who might look familiar, my heart racing inside my chest all of a sudden. "What does he look like?"

"Cute. Tall. Slim build. Blond hair. Oh, and he has a small scar on his chin." Carla nodded toward one of the dancers needing her assistance before leaving me to stand there all alone, my fear taking hold and wrapping its horrid arms around me so tightly I suddenly found it hard to breathe. My eyes bounced all over the club and still I didn't see him.

Not until one of the drunken patrons hopped off his stool and staggered toward the stage.

A terror I was unfortunately all too familiar with ripped me apart from the inside, threatening to destroy my very existence. My sudden panic stole my remaining breath as soon as my eyes connected with his. A wry, lecherous smile spread across his face before he shoved away from the bar. Each step he took toward me warned me to run, but I couldn't. My body froze, locking me in place. My heart rammed against my ribs as fearful tears stung my eyes.

A cold sweat broke out over my skin when he'd finally reached me, his fingers curling around my small wrist and tightening. He saw fear in my eyes, a reaction he'd come to love from me.

"What's wrong, sweetheart?" I didn't answer. I couldn't. My brain fired off a plethora of words, but my lips refused to give them sound. "You didn't honestly think I'd let you leave me? That I wouldn't find you?" He sucked on his teeth while he shook his head, an indication that harm was about to find me. But surely he wouldn't do anything in public. Right?

Breaking eye contact, I glanced around the club in a panic, desperate to find one of the security men Tripp had hired. I saw a couple of them, but they were busy keeping the customers in line. I screamed in my head for one of them to look over at me but it was useless. They obviously couldn't hear me as they weren't mind readers. Next I searched for Carla, but she was busy serving drinks.

When my eyes found his again I flinched. His cold stare froze me. The way he looked me up and down, wearing a disgusted expression as he did so, told me his rage was building.

"What the fuck are you doin' here, anyway? And dressed like some kind of street whore?" His hold on my wrist intensified, making me wince from the pain.

"Please let me go," I pleaded. "Please."

All of a sudden we were nose to nose. "Don't you think you deserve to be punished for running away?" My only reaction was to shake my head. He disagreed with my silent response. "I think you do." His eyes darkened as his other hand seized my upper arm, turning me around and shoving me in front of him toward the hallway. I tried to look over my shoulder to see if anyone had noticed the man gripping me up, but the club was packed. As he pushed his way through the crowd, I knew there was no hope of being rescued.

THIRTY-THREE

Reece

DREAD FILLED MY VEINS AS he shoved me into one of the empty private rooms. In that moment I would have preferred that bastard who'd attacked me the night Tripp saved me over the soulless man standing in front of me right then.

The way his cold stare devoured me made me feel weak and pathetic. Gone was any ounce of strength I'd gained since fleeing from him all those weeks prior, only to be reduced to the sniveling, pleading shell of a woman pushing short pants of air from my lungs.

"Rick . . . please don't do this," I begged, raising my hands in front of me as if my feeble attempt to ward him off wasn't laughable.

"Don't do what?" He cocked his head. "Make you see the error of your ways for taking off? For forcing me to hire someone to track you clear across the fucking country?"

I'd been so careful, disposing of the single credit card I had and only paying with cash. I thought I'd fled far enough, leaving him back in Maine, but his daunting presence just reiterated how much of a fool I'd been to think I could ever escape him.

With each word he spoke his voice became louder, raising the hairs at the nape of my neck. I knew what would happen once he ran out of rhetorical questions.

Threats.

Pain.

Bruises.

"Fuckin' answer me," he roared, spittle hitting my face as he backed me against the wall. "Did you really think I'd let you go?" Running his fingertip down my arm, he sneered at me before puncturing my skin with his nails. Blood trickled down my arm and I flinched in pain, praying this was the worst he'd subject me to. But I should have known better. "I swear to Christ if you don't answer me, you're gonna regret it." The lower half of his body pinned me to the wall behind me.

"No," I meekly whispered.

Placing his fingers at his ear he said, "Sorry. What was that?"

"No," I repeated, choking on my fear.

"Then why did you leave?" His voice was low and deep. Menacing. I wasn't sure which I preferred, him shouting or the calm tone he chose to use right then. Both warned me of what was to come.

He slammed his palm against the wall by the side of my head, his breaths coming out harsh and quick. "Why do you make me do this, baby? Why do you keep testin' me? You know once I'm angry I can't control myself." I saw the devil in his eyes when his fingers wrapped around my throat. Images of Tripp flashed before me, and my heart ached at the thought that I'd never see him again. That pain was worse than anything Rick could ever inflict on me.

The tighter he squeezed the closer the darkness crept, bursts of light behind my lids warning me I was going to dive into unconsciousness very shortly. Just as my vision tunneled, someone banged on the door.

We hadn't been in the room but for five minutes, although it felt like a lifetime. More banging, followed by a man yelling. "Reece," he shouted. "Open the door." More pounding against the locked door. Surprisingly Rick released me, and as soon as I drew in air I started coughing, rubbing at the tender affected area around my throat. Rick reached for the handle, flipping the lock before swinging open the door. I was too busy trying to breathe to bother to see who had thankfully interrupted us.

"What the fuck do you want?" Rick growled, shrouding the doorway so I couldn't see who it was. Not until Mike, one of the bouncers I'd tried to signal earlier with my silent plea, shoved past him and approached me.

"Reece, are you okay?" He reached out to touch me but I shrank toward the wall, confused as to what was happening. My wits hadn't fully returned yet, my body still in preservation mode, trying to take in as much air as my lungs would allow.

"She's fine. Now get the fuck outta here," Rick yelled, stepping in front of Mike, his back facing me.

Before Mike could forcefully remove Rick, Tripp appeared in the doorway, his eyes instantly finding me. He seemed frozen in place, taking in the entire scene in front of him, but it only lasted for a few seconds before he rushed inside and shoved both Rick and Mike away from me.

"What the hell is goin' on here?" he asked, never taking his eyes off me. The vein in his neck bulged and I knew he was doing his best to control himself, his gaze pleading with me to fill him in on why I was in one of the private rooms with a man he didn't know and one of the club's security men.

Tripp's eyes trailed over my face before falling to my throat. I hadn't even realized my fingers were still rubbing at the area. When he gently removed my hand I swore I saw his eyes turn red with rage. "Who did this to you?"

"Don't touch her!" Rick shouted, sidestepping Mike and shoving at Tripp's shoulder. Rick was a tall guy, lean but certainly strong, although he was no match for the likes of Tripp—and he was about to find that out very soon.

Spinning around, Tripp lunged toward Rick and pounced on him, both men falling to the ground with a heavy thud. "You dare put your hands on her?" Tripp roared, his fist connecting with the side of Rick's face. I didn't feel sorry for the beating Rick was about to endure, but the last thing I wanted was for Tripp to be dragged into my mess.

"Tripp!" I shouted. "Stop. Please." I took a step forward, but Mike moved in front of me.

"Not a good idea," he warned, flicking his eyes back to the two men on the ground. Tripp was on top of Rick, expelling his rage onto the man who'd terrorized me for years.

A garbled sound erupted from the bastard's mouth but was quickly silenced by another hit from Tripp. In a blur of movement to my left, Hawke and Ryder rushed into the room and ran toward Tripp, attempting to pull him off Rick. After the third try they were finally successful.

Tripp stumbled backward until he righted himself, but as soon as Rick tried to speak Tripp attempted to go after him again.

"What the fuck?" his brother shouted.

Leaving the scuffle, Ryder asked me, "Are you okay?"

"Yeah, I'm fine," I lied. I was anything but fine, but the last thing Tripp needed to see was just how scared and upset I was. It would only add to his fury.

Once Rick had finally risen to his feet, he stupidly tried to approach me. His eye was already starting to swell, his nose and mouth all bloody, but that didn't stop him from boldly trying to shove past the man who'd just beaten him and try to get at me. It showed how crazy he was when it came to me.

"Don't you fuckin' touch her," Tripp growled, his voice dipping low with unbridled rage.

"Don't *you* fuckin' touch her," Rick retorted, wiping the blood from his face and then running his palms down the front of his jeans.

"Are you insane?"

Little did Tripp know the answer to that question was a resounding yes.

With a crazy look in his eyes, Rick stood rigid, glared at Tripp, and then uttered the words I'd feared as soon as I saw Tripp enter the room. "Get away from my wife."

THIRTY-FOUR

Tripp

I MUST HAVE HEARD HIM wrong.

Did he just say that Reece was his wife?

She's married?

Whipping my head in her direction, my feet quickly followed until I loomed over her. Her head was lowered, her eyes either closed or staring at the goddamn ground. I couldn't tell, but either way she was gonna look at me and tell me what the hell was goin' on. No way she was married, and to that fuckwit to boot. My brain refused to believe it. Plain and simple.

"Reece," I bit out, anger, adrenaline and confusion battling for first place. "Tell me what's goin' on," I demanded, the bite in my tone obvious. Still no movement from her, except for the shudder of her shoulders. Trying a softer approach, I lifted her chin with my finger until she finally looked me in the eyes. Hers were filled with unshed tears, but as soon as she saw the look on my face, an expression I wasn't sure was clear as I battled with pinging emotions, they fell down her cheeks.

"I'm so sorry," she said, grabbing my arm.

"Tell me it's not true," I pleaded, brushing off her hold before finally backing up. She cried harder before looking toward the ground again. "Tell me, Reece. Tell me right now that it's not true," I repeated. "Tell me you're not really married."

"She is," the bastard behind me yelled.

Desperately needing privacy, I instructed Hawke and Ryder to take him to another room and wait for me. I refused to acknowledge that he was her husband, even though I knew in my heart it was true. And even though I was sure she had a good explanation, it didn't change the sting of betrayal that sliced me in half.

Reece and I didn't know each other that well, this was true, but the connection I'd found with her was unlike any other I'd ever experienced. I knew the feeling was reciprocated. I saw it in her eyes when she looked at me, felt it in her kiss when she demanded more from me. But to think that she was hiding such a huge secret made me question everything I'd been feeling for her.

Once we were alone, I paced in front of her, silence compounding the tension which now existed between us. Finally, after what felt like forever, a soft sound drifted through the air and caught my attention.

"Tripp, I'm so sorry," she whispered, the lilt of her voice softening my anger toward her and the entire situation. "I wanted to tell you . . . but I didn't know how. I just wanted to forget."

"Forget you were married?" I crushed the small distance between us and crowded her personal space once more, giving her no other option than to look me in the eye while she tried to explain. Trust me, the last thing I wanted to do right then was deal with this shit, but I knew it would only fester and drive me insane, making me even angrier if we didn't have the damn discussion.

"Yes." Because of her anguish, her eyes took on a deeper hue of blue than gray. "I've left Rick a few times, but he always finds me." I hated the sound of his name on her lips, but I did my best to rein in my simmering fury. She slowly raised her hand and traced the scar on the bridge of her nose. "He threatened to kill me if I ever left him again. He probably would've had Mike not interrupted him.

"Was he the one who broke your nose?" I already knew the answer, but I needed to hear it from her.

"Yes." She blew out a pent-up breath before quickly revealing what'd happened. "He'd come home drunk, like he often did, and accused me of cheating on him. Even though I wasn't, and never had. It was the first time he'd punched me." A few tears escaped and trailed down her cheeks. "Before, he would only grab me and slam me against the wall, or slap me across the face. But he never balled up his fist, not until that time."

The silence was deafening as I continued to try and process everything Reece had just told me. My emotions had me feeling like I was on a damn roller coaster, jolting me back and forth between sadness, anger, betrayal and, oddly enough, possessiveness.

"I knew I should've never let you leave my house," I mumbled more to myself than her. But she'd heard me loud and clear.

"There's no way you could've known. I didn't lie to you, per se, but I did omit certain things about my life."

"Which is the same as lyin', by the way. Just so you know." I couldn't help the anger in my tone, pushing to the forefront of my tangled emotions. "You definitely should have told me before we fucked."

My crassness startled her, and the look of regret on her face tore at me. A deep sadness shrouded her eyes. It'd been there the first time I saw her, but I'd dismissed it to the lifestyle she'd chosen. Apparently it hadn't been from her choice of profession but from years of being beaten down so much she never thought she was worth anything. While I was still very upset with her for not confiding in me, I knew I had to protect her from her husband.

Fuck! I hated even thinking that word, but there it was.

Reece was married.

But that wouldn't stop me from claiming her.

THIRTY-FIVE

Tripp

AS IF I DIDN'T HAVE enough shit to deal with, now I had to take care of the issue with the shitbag who'd made Reece's life a living hell. Even though she'd only divulged a small amount of their life together, I knew there was much more to that damn story.

The last thing I wanted to do was leave her alone, so I instructed Mike to stay with Reece until I returned, knowing damn well she was still scared after what happened.

Striding toward the room where Rick was being held, I took a deep breath before turning the handle, knowing I had to control myself so as not to kill him right then and there. Don't get me wrong; I had no problem snatching his life, but taking such a rash step wasn't smart. If it came down to whether or not he had to die, I wanted to make sure everything was set in place before he drew his last miserable breath. Killing was never something I aspired to do, but I knew it was necessary sometimes.

Rick was slumped over on the small couch set against the far wall. Drawing my brows close together, I stared at Ryder with a questioning look, since he was the one closest to him.

"What?" Ryder asked, shrugging. "I saw Reece's neck. Just thought I'd make him see the error of his ways." The slow smirk on his face would have been comical had I not been so torn up inside over the whole situation.

Nodding, I approached. I slapped the side of Rick's head, a groan escaping him before lifting his head up. His eyes rose to mine briefly before closing. He was coherent enough to hear what I had to say. "You are never to come near Reece again. Do you hear me?" No response from him except an incoherent grunt. "I know you understand what I'm telling you, but let me break it down for you, just in case. If I so much as see you anywhere in the same vicinity as her, I'll kill you. Slowly. If you don't believe me then just test me, although it'll be the last thing you ever do." I stood to my full height. "Reece is mine now. Forget you ever knew her."

Jerking my head toward Ryder and Hawke, I instructed, "Break his legs."

"Both?" Ryder asked.

"I said *legs*, didn't I?"

"Okay, just making sure." I would have done it myself but I needed to get back to Reece. Ryder grinned while stepping toward Rick. My brother closed in on his other side and the two of them dragged the no-good piece of shit from the room and out the back door of the club.

Even if he tried to come after Reece again, it wouldn't be for quite some time.

THIRTY-SIX

Reece

I COULDN'T EXPLAIN MY EMOTIONAL roller coaster where Tripp was concerned. I'd been through the entire gamut since I'd met him, starting with fascination when I first saw him standing at the edge of the stage during one of my routines, to undying thankfulness when he'd rescued me from that bastard in the back room, to anger when he'd fired me, to sexual unease—of the good kind—when he looked at me like he wanted to devour me, to guilt for not telling him I was married. Then back to untold gratitude when he saved me yet again.

I'd never felt so alive before, yet I feared whatever was developing between us would fizzle out and die. Nothing good ever lasted in my life, and while I'd come to accept that, I could honestly say I was teetering on the edge, waiting for the other shoe to drop, so to speak. And it almost did when Tripp found out I was married. I really thought my betrayal would have driven him away, but he'd proven again that he was a good man.

We talked for hours and, justifiably, he went back and forth. One second he understood my need to withhold the truth about Rick, and the next he'd tell me it was wrong of me not to share that kind of information. We eventually agreed to move on and put the incident behind us. Easier said than done, of course, but at least we both made the attempt.

Before I could dismiss the topic of Rick altogether, though, I needed to know what had happened to him. Tripp didn't want to tell me at first, but thankfully he realized I had a right to know. Initially, all he would reveal was that Rick had been taken care of, and my heart skipped a beat. At first I assumed he meant that Rick had been killed, a thought which made me both uneasy yet relieved. I pressed further, practically begging him to tell me exactly what happened. I'd held my breath in case he told me that my first assumption had been correct. It turned out that Tripp had spared Rick's life, although he'd had him incapacitated by breaking both his legs. He also told me that he warned Rick that if he ever came near me again he'd kill him. I believed that he'd actually follow through if given another opportunity.

While there were so many things I had yet to learn about Tripp, what I did know told me he was a good man, present debacle included. Not the 'put your best foot forward until you finally show your true colors' type of man, but a genuinely good-hearted, 'do right by you' type of man.

While I hated that my brain conjured up images of Tripp and Rick together, I couldn't help but compare the two. Tripp had a good heart while Rick did not. Of course, Rick had been nice in the beginning, and me being so young I simply didn't have the experience to spot a wolf in sheep's clothing.

He'd come into the restaurant I worked at after school and sat at the counter, making small talk for two hours. I thought he was handsome with his shoulder-length sandy blond hair and green eyes, eyes which were deceptively perilous, although I didn't know it at the time. A handsome stranger paid attention to me, and I ate it up.

Rick showed up every time I worked, and once when I joked that he'd been stalking me, he simply shrugged and gave me a mischievous yet what I thought was an endearing smile. Looking back I should have seen the signs, but like I said, I was young and inexperienced.

When Rick found his opportunity he pounced. And I say pounced because he was most certainly a predator. We soon began dating and when the accident happened, the only person I had to turn to was Rick. He had become my only family, readily taking me in and letting me live with him. He dug his clutches in deeper after we'd been together about six months. I'd finally decided I was ready to have sex, and soon afterward the sides he'd kept hidden started to emerge. Becoming enraged when I talked to another guy, even when they were customers at the restaurant, he'd accuse me of cheating. I'd vehemently deny it, of course, because it wasn't true.

After I graduated from high school we were married. I'd convinced myself that once I became his wife he'd no longer have a need to be jealous. How wrong I'd been.

I had big plans of going to college, but Rick only became more suffocating, refusing to allow me to go anywhere without him. I had to quit my job, solely relying on him for everything. About a year into the marriage, he started drinking more, and that's when the real abuse started. At first he shook me when he yelled at me. Then he graduated to slapping me across the face until he eventually elevated to punching and kicking me. Since I didn't have a job, or go to school, or socialize with friends, and had no family to speak of, I had plenty of time to heal after one of his beatings. No one to witness the abuse.

The first time I tried to leave him was when one of his beatings had caused me to miscarry our child. I was twelve weeks along and although I was only twenty, I desperately wanted the baby. In some warped way I thought if we had a child that he would change, but in fact my pregnancy only heightened his paranoia and abuse, claiming he wasn't the father and that I'd been messing around on him. Looking back, having miscarried my child had been a blessing in disguise. I had no right bringing another person into that kind of world.

Over the course of our relationship, I left him a total of four times, this last time being the fourth. He'd made good on his promises and had found me each and every time. Only this time, I hoped and prayed Rick would heed Tripp's warnings and stay away from me for good.

Against Tripp's advice, I returned to work the following night, reminding him that there was no way Rick would be bothering me anytime soon—his words. I repeated them to him to drive home that I was safe. True, there was a part of me that believed Rick would saunter right back inside Indulge and hurt me, even kill me, but then I remembered that he couldn't walk.

———◆———

"MOVE," ARIANNA DEMANDED, SHOVING PAST me without giving me the opportunity to shuffle to the side to allow her to pass. Her mood toward me had shifted from mere annoyance to downright hatred, or something very close to it. I knew the reason why, but I never played into her sourness by engaging her.

Coming back from the restroom she bumped into me again, that time pushing me against the wall. "What the hell is wrong with you?!" I shouted, pissed off that she wouldn't give me a break. Whatever her issue was with me was all on her. I did nothing wrong and I wasn't going to let her give me shit any longer. I had enough on my plate at the moment as it was.

She stopped and spun around, advancing on me until she stood so close I could smell cheap men's cologne all over her. "My problem," she sneered, "is that you waltz in here and think you're the best thing that's ever graced that stage."

"I don't work the stage anymore, or did you forget?" Not working the pole any longer was just one of the things she hated about me, Tripp's interest in me being the main reason, of course. At every available opportunity Arianna would sneak up next to him and press her fake tits against him, pawing at him and offering herself. She wasn't subtle about it, making sure to remind me that they'd been together every chance she had. He assured me that he wasn't interested in her, and that the times they did hook up he was drunk, and that he never wished to repeat that mistake ever again. Even with his admissions, though, I couldn't help the jealousy that captured me whenever she touched him.

"You're stupid if you think he'll keep you around for much longer. Tripp loves variety, always coming back to me in between his new interests." She'd completely switched topics, focusing on the one that was the real reason why she'd decided to harass me that evening.

"What does that say about you, then?" I asked, scoffing when she looked confused. "If that was true, which it's not and we both know it, he'd just be using you until he found someone better. You're the idiot for waiting around for whatever scraps he'll throw your way."

If looks could kill I would have been dead already. I could tell by her expression that she didn't know what to say, but she was trying to think of something anyway. Several awkward seconds passed with us simply glaring at each other, until finally she mumbled, "Fuck you," and walked back toward the front of the club.

Rolling my eyes, I took a moment to compose myself before returning to the bar. Even though I tried not to let Arianna see me flustered, my insides were twisting and turning from the implication that Tripp would eventually go back to her.

As soon as I stepped behind the bar I saw Tripp, and low and behold Arianna was standing next to him, jabbering on about nonsense, I was sure. A fire lit my temper and, with barely controlled fury, I stalked to where they stood. He saw me approach, his eyes never leaving mine as I wrapped my arms around his neck and pulled him down for a sensual kiss. As soon as my tongue found his, he growled into my mouth and pulled me close, shoving Arianna away from him at the same time. I heard her gasp but I wasn't about to break our kiss to look at her. After I regrettably pulled back, Tripp had the biggest grin on his face.

"I think I know what that was for, but I don't care. You can stake your claim on me anytime your little heart desires." He gave me a quick peck on the lips before taking a seat.

"Since you've given me permission, you should be prepared for me to stake my claim over and over again." I'd meant to keep the tone light but I couldn't help it, even though I'd silently warned myself earlier not to go there. "You need to stop letting her hang all over you like that."

"I will. I promise." *Well, that was easy enough.* "You're the only woman I want hangin' on me. Pinned underneath me. Sittin' on top of me." He cocked his head to the side and appeared as if he were deep in thought. "What else?" he asked, tapping his chin with his index finger.

"Bending over in front of you," I offered, letting out a startled shriek when he grabbed me and pulled me on his lap.

"That's my girl." He laughed, nuzzling my neck before sucking on my earlobe.

I heard Carla laugh, not even realizing she was paying attention to us. I should have known better, though, as she had become protective over me, warning Tripp that if he ever hurt me he'd have to deal with her.

I'd decided to tell her everything pertaining to Rick, from my history with him up until what had just happened at the club. She was my one true friend, even though there were times when she was more like a mother figure.

THIRTY-SEVEN

Tripp

LOST TO MY OWN THOUGHTS about Reece and everything that'd just happened with that shitbag husband of hers, I nearly ran right into Stone when I walked into the common room at the clubhouse.

"We finally got 'em," he hurriedly announced, completely disregarding the fact that I'd almost knocked him over.

"The results?"

He nodded.

The last thing I wanted to deal with was this shit, but I knew it was of the utmost importance, the future of our club, and our president, basically hanging in the balance.

"Where's Marek?" I glanced around the room, trying to locate our downtrodden leader.

"He just went to piss."

"Is he drunk?"

"What do you think?"

Ryder waltzed out of the kitchen with a half-eaten sandwich in hand, stopping and looking at us standing together. "What?" he mumbled as he shoved the rest of the food in his mouth. Once he swallowed, he asked, "What's goin' on?"

"We got the results back," Stone offered, glancing down at his watch.

"Fuck," Ryder grumbled, looking between the two of us. "Wait, is that good news or bad?"

"Let's wait for everyone to get here first, and then we'll tell him together."

As soon as Stone stopped talking he looked uncomfortable, which immediately made me uneasy. I'd known Marek for years, and without sounding too much like a pussy, the first time I'd seen him really come alive was when he met Sully. Well, more like 'took.' Or 'saved' was more the honest truth. Over the time they'd been together, married for all of it because he'd initially forced her into it, I'd seen his eyes light up with life. Again, not wanting to sound all pussified and shit, but he'd changed.

While he'd become more on edge where his wife was concerned, constantly fretting about her safety knowing her father had still been out there, he smiled more. Okay, so I wouldn't go so far as to say he smiled, per se, but the corners of his mouth curved up more than ever before. And the way he looked at Sully, watched her when she wasn't looking, told me he'd fallen head over heels in love with her. Their beginning had certainly been the furthest from ideal, but they were meant to be together.

For all the happiness Sully brought into our president's life, she also brought him a ton of worry. Waiting for the other shoe to drop where her father was concerned, the constant fear she'd be taken from him, it all weighed heavy on him, showing in the deepened lines around his eyes. Then when he found out about what Rico Yanez had done to her, which unfortunately was the same thing Vex, her ex-man of sorts, and her father had done, he started to slowly unravel.

We'd all witnessed his slow descent into hell, his main focus not on club business but instead on making Vex, Yanez and Psych pay for what they'd made Sully endure, even though all that shit happened before Marek had even met her. It didn't matter, though, and I now understood his need for justice where she was concerned. I knew without a doubt that I'd snatch Rick's life if he ever came near Reece again.

To add something like this to the mix after everything Marek had been through, I feared he'd dive off the cliff of sanity and never resurface. I only prayed the results would be the ones he needed. The ones we all needed them to be if we wished to keep our president. Our leader. Our friend.

Ten minutes later the rumble of bikes sliced through the growing tension, my unease heightening with the thought that we were about to possibly deliver the worst news of Marek's life.

The door to the clubhouse swung open and in walked Trigger and Jagger. Thankfully no one else was with them. Marek had made us swear not to tell anyone else what was going on until he figured out what to do, which he never did. Instead, he chose to shut out his wife and drink himself half to death. The other guys had questioned the change in Marek, and we all chalked it up to his dealings with Psych. And by dealings, I meant Psych's torture and death. Cutter wasn't buying it, though, insisting Marek would have taken great pleasure in exacting revenge on the Savage Reapers' leader and not shut down afterward. Even though he was suspicious, he stopped trying to get any of us to talk after the third time we didn't give him anything.

"Hey," Jagger called out, coming to stand by my side, looking as reserved as the rest of us. Trigger mirrored our expression but remained silent, feeding off the palpable strain surrounding all of us.

We chatted amongst ourselves about the upcoming meeting when the man of the hour stumbled down the hallway and into the common room.

"What the fuck?" he growled, heading straight for us, albeit slowly so as not to fall on his face. "Is this a fu . . . fucking irrevention?" He looked haggard, but that was nothing new.

"No," Stone answered, striding the few feet until he stood directly in front of his best friend. "This ain't no intervention. We got the results." It took but a few seconds before understanding crossed Marek's face, and just when I thought he'd be relieved to finally find out whether or not Sully was actually his half-sister, he almost crumbled. Holding on to Stone's shoulder for support, Marek's eyes became glassy, unshed anguish pooling behind his blue orbs.

"I don't think I can do this," he garbled.

"You can, and you will," our VP gritted out. "Enough is enough. This shit's gotta stop. Today." Placing his hand on Marek's shoulder in return, he leaned in and whispered something in his ear, our president's face falling even more before he reluctantly nodded.

"Let's do this in Chambers," Trigger suggested. "Just in case some of the other guys show up."

All of us agreeing, we entered our sacred meeting place, shut the door and took our seats.

THIRTY-EIGHT

Tripp

"I SWEAR TO CHRIST, IF someone doesn't say somethin' soon I'm gonna lose it," Jagger blurted, pounding the table in frustration.

"Calm down," Trigger berated him, quickly glaring at him before turning his attention back to Marek, who was leaning back in his chair with his head tilted and looking up at the ceiling.

All concern was focused toward our leader, preparing for the results to be bad but hoping for the best. The envelope in Stone's hand was still sealed, indicating he himself didn't even know yet. We were all in limbo.

The tearing of the envelope made me shudder, but my reaction was nothing compared to Marek's. Forcing himself to his feet, he kicked his chair behind him with as much force as he could muster.

"I c-can't fuckin' do th-this," he stammered, the reality of his predicament sobering him slightly. "I can't," he mumbled before heading toward the door. Stone jumped up from the table and rushed forward, stopping Marek before he turned the handle.

Flinging the results toward me, our VP shouted, "Just open it."

My fingers trembled slightly as I pulled out the folded piece of paper. I scanned the document but had no idea what the hell I was looking at. There were multiple columns with a bunch of numbers.

"Well?" Stone shouted over his shoulder, pinning Marek against the wall to ensure he finally faced what he'd been running from ever since Psych fucked with his head.

Stone had given Adelaide Psych's DNA as well as Marek's, both in their own baggie. He feared if he labeled one 'Father' and the other 'Child,' she might've been a bit more suspicious, and that would've opened up a whole other can of worms. Instead, he just asked that they be tested to see if the two samples were related.

"I don't know what the hell I'm lookin' at," I grumbled, trying to read over the piece of paper once more. "Give me a sec." Starting from the top, I searched for anything that made a lick of sense to me. It wasn't until I reached the bottom, after all the bullshit columns, letters and numbers that I came to the fields I needed.

Probability of relation . . . 0%

I read it again just to be sure. Releasing a breath, one I hadn't even realized I held trapped in my lungs, I looked over to Stone and slowly shook my head, making sure to accompany the gesture with a grin.

"Oh, thank God," I heard Ryder say under his breath, understanding quickly spreading to Jagger and Trigger as well.

The rustle of Stone's cut bristled in the silence. I saw his grip on Marek's shoulders tighten. "She's not your sister, man." Marek raised his head. "Psych wasn't your ol' man, which means Sully is not related to you."

I thought Marek would've been elated, but instead he crumpled to the floor and the eeriest sob escaped. "Motherfucker. I can't . . . can't believe I push . . . pushed her away," he cried out, knocking his head against the wall a couple times. Stone sank to the floor beside him and threw his arm around his shoulder before looking to us and jerking his head toward the door. We understood right away, all of us disappearing from the room so they could have some privacy.

If anyone had any chance of consoling Marek, it was his best friend.

THIRTY-NINE

Reece

THE NEXT SEVERAL WEEKS PASSED way too quickly for my taste, but at least Tripp had remained in my life. Even after everything with Rick happened he stayed true to his word and stuck around, insisting I stay at his place with him.

"I want to talk to you about something," I said, tugging on the hem of my nightshirt as I walked toward the bed.

He swung his legs over the side and reached for his phone. Quickly checking a text, an annoyed expression passed over his face before he placed the device on the nightstand. "If this is about you paying for shit, I told you I don't want your money." He leaned back on his elbows, his nakedness completely distracting me. The way his muscles flexed with any simple movement entranced me. The man had the most amazing body, and I knew he was using it to sidetrack me. "My eyes are up here," he joked when he saw I'd been staring at . . . well, all of him.

"Very funny, but I'm serious."

"Then if you're so serious stop gawking at me like I'm a piece of meat." With one sudden movement, he hopped off the bed and picked me up off my feet, hooking my legs around his waist before I even realized what he was doing. "Or maybe some meat is exactly what you need right now."

"I told you we can't do that. Not for the next couple days." A mischievous grin appeared on his gorgeous face. "What?"

"There's always the back door." I gave him a blank stare. "You know . . . anal," he clarified, just in case I'd been confused on what 'back door' had meant, which I wasn't.

"Are you serious?"

His only response was to wriggle his brows.

I gripped the back of his hair and tugged. "If you think for one second I'm gonna let you stick that anaconda in my ass, you're crazy."

"Anaconda?" He laughed at my word choice, but that was exactly what his dick was.

No way. Not gonna happen.

"Fine. For now. We'll work up to it."

I attempted to object but he silenced me with his mouth, his tongue teasing my bottom lip before deepening the kiss. One hand gripped my backside, anchoring me to him, while the other held the back of my head, his fingers seizing my hair and positioning me exactly how he wanted. Tripp took control every time we'd been intimate, and this time was no different.

"Wanna wash up?" Already en route to the bathroom, his strong legs carried us toward the shower. Placing me on top of the vanity, he spun around and turned on the faucet, testing the water until it heated to the temperature he wanted.

While his back was to me, I removed my nightshirt. The only piece of clothing remaining was my black panties. When Tripp caught sight of me topless he groaned, reaching for his cock which already seemed painfully hard.

"What are you doing to me, woman?"

"What? We're gonna take a shower, aren't we? Well, I have to get naked before I get in, don't I?"

"Yeah, I guess." His eyes roamed my entire body, and when I hopped down from the counter and lowered my panties, he growled—literally growled, like some kind of hedonistic animal. It was extremely hot.

"Give me a minute and maybe I'll think about giving you some. As long as we're in the shower," I made sure to add. I acted like I was doing him some kind of favor, but in reality it was me who was going crazy over not being able to have sex with him. Tripp had become like some sort of drug. The way his touch ignited my skin. The way he looked at me, which made my body hum. The way his kiss made me wet. The way he moved his body when deep inside me like the most blissful, erotic escapade.

"Hurry up." He disappeared, but not before giving me one of his famous smirks.

I called for him to come back inside once I'd finished taking care of necessary business, stepping under the water while I waited for him to appear. A gust of air cooled my skin when Tripp opened the shower door. I soaked in the sight of him, taking my time raking my gaze over every inch of his body. When my eyes landed on his, he smiled. No smirk, no mischievous grin, just an honest-to-goodness happy, peaceful, enthralled smile.

Clicking the door shut, he backed me against the far wall, slowly reached for my hands and pulled them above my head. "Tell me you want me," he instructed, dipping his head and kissing my neck, licking and sucking until his lips nipped my earlobe. "Tell me how much you want me to fuck you." His warm breath triggered goose bumps across my skin.

"Yes," I panted, licking my lips and praying he'd kiss me again soon.

"Nope. Not what I wanna hear." His teeth snagged my lower lip, the quick shot of pain exciting me more than I thought possible. "I want you to tell me how badly you want my cock. Don't be shy either." His hold on my arms tightened while his lower half held me in place, the cool tiles warring with the heat of the spray.

I wasn't particularly skilled in the art of dirty talk, but if Tripp wanted to hear some filthy things then I'd try. But first I was gonna have some fun.

"I love your big penis," I moaned, holding back the smile threatening to give me away.

He pulled back, and the faux irritated look on his face was already making the corners of my lips twitch. "What the hell, Reece? 'Penis' is such an unsexy word. In fact, I can feel my *penis* deflating as we speak." He was lying, of course; his arousal was hard and thick, pressing against my belly. "Try again," he urged.

I kissed him quickly before pursing my lips as if in deep thought about what I should say. "I'd love for your cock. . . ." I paused for effect, to which his eyes lit up. " . . . to fill my vagina—" Tripp cut me off before I could continue with my 'sexy talk.'

"No *vagina* either."

I couldn't help it, the laugh I'd been holding bursting forth.

"I knew you were fuckin' with me." He chuckled, reaching down and lifting me up the wall. "Stop messin' around and tell me what I wanna hear or else."

I wrapped my legs around his waist and anchored myself to him. "Or else what?"

"Or else I'll spank that plump ass of yours," he threatened, the tilt of his mouth telling me he might just like to do that.

"You keep threatening to spank me. What if I want you to?" I teased, biting my lip while waiting for his reaction, which was immediate.

"Then I'd say that in a couple days when we can really play, I'll redden your ass, all while making you beg for me to fuck you hard."

I swore my temperature rose ten degrees, and it had nothing to do with the hot water raining down on me. "Well, until then. . . ." I took a deep breath, and leaned in to lick the shell of his earlobe before spouting, "I want your big, thick cock deep inside me." His muscles tensed. "I want you to fuck me like you've always wanted. Don't hold back."

"Fuck me," he growled before releasing my hands and unhooking my legs from around his waist. He didn't say another word, instead surprising me by spinning me around as soon as my feet hit the floor of the shower and pushing between my shoulder blades to bend me over.

"What are you doing?" I stupidly asked, knowing damn well what he had planned.

"I'm gonna take you from behind," he answered, his authoritative tone screaming for me to obey without reserve. "Brace yourself against the wall."

As my hands connected with the tile, he palmed my breasts, teasing one and then the other until my nipples were painfully erect. "Spread your legs for me, baby. Good." The sounds of the water and our heady breathing were quite intoxicating. Anticipation licked at my insides, warmth flooding me with eagerness and hunger. As I opened my mouth to plead with him to give me what I needed, he aligned himself at my entrance and slowly pushed inside.

"Yes," was all I could manage to say as he worked himself in inch by inch. At that angle I took him deeper, his thickness hitting against the sensitive spot inside me. He grabbed my hips and dug his fingers into my skin, pushing in and then pulling back, his cock electrifying all my nerve endings as he thrust in and out of me.

"You feel amazing," he panted, his grip bordering on painful. "I can't get enough. I don't ever wanna stop," he confessed, driving me higher and higher toward a place I'd quickly become addicted to. His touch had awoken me, promising me a life I'd never dreamed possible before I'd met him.

I moaned his name over and over as the first wave of my orgasm crested, pushing back against him every time he drove himself deep. Tripp was still holding back. I could feel it in the way his fingers bruised me, his muscles tensing when he thought he pushed too hard.

"Let go, Tripp. Take me how you want," I begged, my muscles beginning to clench in pleasure.

"I'll hurt you," he said, continuing to drive me insane with his body. "I . . . I can't," he mumbled, the spray of the shower muffling his refusal.

"Oh God!" I cried out. "I'm gonna come." My lungs seized my breaths as I rushed toward ecstasy at top speed. "Oh . . . Tripp . . . please. Please let go and fuck me." I steadied myself when a string of expletives flew from his mouth. Within seconds his grip punished me while his body destroyed mine. His harsh thrusts swirled pain and pleasure into the most beautiful, mind-numbing feeling.

"Goddammit!" he roared, pulling me back until I was flush against his chest. He rocked into my body over and over until he pushed me over the edge, free-falling so deliciously I couldn't think straight.

Euphoria.

It was the only word I could think of to describe the way he made me feel. He fell right after me, the warmth of his seed filling me, making me even slicker.

Our bodies continued to glide together, slowing with the passing moments. Still pressed against one another, he turned my face toward his, his lips drifting over mine before he demanded more from me. The man certainly knew how to kiss, that was for damn sure. Our tongues battled, his taste slowly imprinting on me for life.

All too soon, he slipped from my body and turned me to face him. "Did I hurt you?" He genuinely seemed concerned, and it was sweet.

"Nothing that won't pass in a few minutes," I assured. I knew my answer was sort of cryptic but I didn't want to tell him that he had hurt me a little, especially after I begged him to let go and fuck me with wild abandon. Truth was Tripp was overly large, so sex with him so far had been slightly painful, but the pleasure he evoked definitely outweighed the twinge of discomfort.

Tripp frowned at my response but when I rose up on my tippy toes and linked my fingers behind his neck, he relaxed. Pressing my lips to his, all of the worry quickly evaporated. His posture relaxed and we melded together.

"I'm clean," he blurted.

"Oh, you wanna get out of the shower now?" I asked, confused by his sudden statement.

"No. What I meant was that I'm clean. You know, no rashes or shit down below," he joked, chuckling when I realized what he'd meant.

"Oh. Good. Yeah, I guess we should have discussed that before going bareback, huh?"

How could I have been so careless? I seemed to lose all reason as soon as Tripp looked at me, let alone touched me. "I got tested at my annual exam, and since Rick and I hadn't had sex for a few months prior. . . ."

I stopped talking when Tripp's jaw muscles clenched and his nose flared in anger. He pushed away from me and flexed his hands at his sides.

"The last fucking thing I wanna picture is you with that prick." I'd seen Tripp angry before, usually when he was defending me, but his re-action right then was different. It was like he was upset with me, a feeling I certainly didn't like.

I lowered my head and apologized. "Sorry, I just wanted to let you know that you're safe." I stared at his feet, fearing that if I looked back up at him I'd start to ramble and reveal something else he didn't want to hear.

"Shit," he mumbled. Hooking his finger under my chin, he raised my head until our eyes met. "Listen, Reece. I'm sorry. I didn't mean to snap at you like that. I just don't ever want to hear that bastard's name. I can't fathom the thought of him touching you. And what he did to you . . . I should have done more than had his legs broken."

"No, you shouldn't have. I don't want you any more involved than you already are." It was the truth. While Rick deserved worse than having his legs broken, I didn't want his evilness to infect Tripp, making him feel as if he had to deal with Rick on my behalf. Silence wrapped around us both, and before things became tense between us, I decided to change the topic.

"Are you ever going to invite me to your club?" I would've been lying if I'd said I wasn't curious about where Tripp spent a lot of his time. I didn't even know if women were allowed there, but it couldn't hurt to ask.

"Funny you should ask," he answered.

FORTY

Tripp

"I'M NERVOUS," SHE WHISPERED, FIDGETING in the passenger seat of my new truck. Reece continued to be adamant about not riding on the back of my bike, something which I was definitely gonna remedy someday soon, so I went out and purchased something she felt safe riding in for the time being.

"Don't be. They're gonna love you." Reece had been a bundle of nerves ever since I asked her to come with me to Riley's baptism. She smiled but I knew she was on edge, and no matter how much I tried to calm her, my efforts were useless.

Stone and Addy had finally set a date to have Riley's ceremony at the clubhouse, and the day had arrived. That precious little girl was the apple of not only her parents' eyes but the rest of us as well. I tried not to fawn all over her whenever they brought her around, but she stole my heart. So innocent. When she looked up at me, I saw the trust in her eyes. Her tiny smile always made me happy, even when I'd had the shittiest day. It wasn't until I met Reece that I had even entertained the idea of having one of my own, although it was way too soon in our relationship to even discuss something like that. But nonetheless, the thoughts were forming.

"Do I look okay?" she asked, fiddling with the hem of her light blue dress.

"You're gorgeous," I confirmed. When she'd strolled into the living room earlier that day and twirled around, I caught sight of the back of her dress. The majority of her skin was exposed. She'd worried it wasn't appropriate, but with the hemline hitting just above her knee and the dress covering everything in front, it was more than suitable. Before we left the house, however, I showed her just how sexy I thought she looked, my desire for her uncontrollable as I backed her against the nearest wall, lifted her dress, moved her flimsy panties to the side and devoured her. Her taste was still on my tongue.

Pulling off the main highway, I drove another half mile until I reached the compound. The gate was open and manned by a few of the newest prospects. If these guys turned out to be half the man Jagger was, our club would be stronger than ever.

Once inside I easily found a space, most of the lot still empty. Once I'd killed the engine I glanced over at Reece, the anxious flush of her cheeks making my dick twitch. She reached for the door handle but I stopped her. "Here, let me get that for you. One second." I jumped out and hurriedly walked around the back, coming to stand by her side in a few seconds flat. I extended my hand as soon as I opened the door, the heat from her palm promising the warmth her body would provide mine once this shindig was over.

Leaning down I placed a chaste kiss on her mouth, knowing she was anxious and doing my best to try and calm her. "You'll be fine. Trust me. After about ten minutes, it'll be like you've known them forever. The women are super cool, so you'll have no problem there. The guys are as well, although if I notice any of them being *too* nice, don't get freaked out if I let them know about it." I winked, but she knew from the tone of my voice that I was deadly serious on that last point.

"Oh stop," she chided, slapping my arm in mock annoyance, doing anything she could to help ease her worries.

I walked beside her, my hand resting on the middle of her back. My fingers brushed back and forth over her bare skin. "I hate that you're showing so much skin," I rumbled.

She stopped walking and turned toward me. "You don't like my dress? Why didn't you say something back at the house? I know my back is exposed, but I thought you said it was appropriate for today. Besides, I'm not showing any cleavage or anything." She would have continued to ramble had I not interrupted her.

"Calm down, baby. I just meant that I hate that you're showing *any* skin. Not because the dress isn't nice, because it is, but every fucker here is gonna notice." I tried to smile but my expression was strained. "You look gorgeous. Stop freakin' out." I snatched her hand and led her the rest of the way through the large open lot.

Stone and Adelaide had picked a perfect day. The sun was shining and the light breeze helped to soothe the midday heat. A large tent with numerous tables and chairs littered the grounds, providing shade and seating for everyone attending.

"Nomad!" Breck shouted as he walked toward us, beer in hand and already half empty. I liked Breck just fine, until he consumed a few drinks; then he became sort of obnoxious. Usually, I'd just shout for Cutter, his father, to reel him back in or I'd be forced to deal with him. Most times, Cutter would intervene if he was there. If not, and I had to take care of business myself . . . let's just say that Breck had been knocked out once or twice. He wasn't my favorite, but I didn't dislike him either. He was loyal as fuck to the club, and that went a long way in my book.

"Get ready for this one," I warned Reece, the flare of her eyes almost making me laugh.

"Breck," I greeted, tightening my hold on Reece's hand unknowingly.

"Ow," she whined. "My hand."

"Sorry." Turning my full attention back to Breck, who was now staring at my woman, I took a step closer and crowded his personal space. "Don't even think about it, man. She's mine." The gravel in my voice was unmistakable.

"What?" He played dumb. "I didn't say anything." He grinned.

"You didn't have to. I know you." We stepped around him to join the others, but not before I warned him. "And don't get shit-faced, Breck. We're not at a fuckin' ruckus."

He mumbled something before walking in the opposite direction.

"What's a ruckus?" Reece asked, walking quickly just to keep up with my long strides. I slowed down when I noticed.

"It's a party the club throws every so often when we're celebratin' something or need to blow off some steam. But there's no wives or girlfriends allowed, just wannabes and the guys." I had no idea all of that shit was gonna come flyin' out of my mouth until it was too late.

Why the hell did I just tell her all that? Damnit!

She stopped walking and yanked her hand from mine. I closed my eyes in regret and tried to think of something to say that would undo some of the damage I'd undoubtedly just caused.

"What's a wannabe?"

"Women looking to attach themselves to one of the members. But it never happens. They're pretty much there to entertain the guys."

Oh my God! Seriously . . . shut up, Tripp.

"What?" Her question was accompanied by an indiscernible look on her face. Was that confusion? Jealousy? Anger?

"I have no idea why I just told you all that, Reece."

"Does your club throw these types of parties all the time?" She'd ignored my last statement.

"They used to. But not so much anymore." I was being honest, so I prayed it would gain me some brownie points. "We actually haven't had one in quite some time."

"If another came up, would you go?" She crossed her arms in front of her and kept her gaze on me the entire time. The heat of her stare fueled me. She was tryin' to lay claim on me and I found it exciting. I wanted to test her, to see how far she'd go, either with her words, her expression or her body language.

"Yeah, I'd go." I ran my hand through my hair, gripping the back of my neck as if I weren't giving much thought to her line of questions about my club. I'd told her the truth. I would attend the next ruckus the club had. I just wouldn't participate in the free pussy that was offered.

"Why?" Reece attempted to mask her anger.

"Because it's a club party. Why not?"

"Would you sleep with one of the women who came?"

"Do you care if I sleep with one of them?" I knew how irritating it was to answer a question with one, but I wanted to see what she'd say.

"Yes, I would care. A lot."

It was all I needed to affirm that she felt something deeper for me than just the byproduct of our rushed circumstances. I'd come to develop strong feelings for Reece, no matter how annoying I felt they were. After all, feelings equated to possible hurt and agony in the future.

"Then you have my word that I won't sleep with anyone else. But you have to promise the same. I meant what I told Breck. You're mine."

A look of what I could only describe as happiness fluttered across her gorgeous face when I verbally staked my claim on her. "So does that mean that we're . . . ?" Her eyes darted from me to the ground then back again.

"Together?" She nodded. "Yes. That's what it means."

She smiled, which made me smile, the thud of my heart relaxing into a steady rhythm, a calm spreading through me I'd never experienced before. In truth, it terrified me.

We stood there staring at each other, allowing the brief silence stretching between us to comfort us. There were so many things I wanted to say, but if I rambled on right then I'd come across as some crazy man. And after everything she'd been through, not only with Rick but since I'd met her, the last thing I needed to add to her list was an all-consuming man who wanted to possess her. My emotions were a lot for me to handle, and I could only imagine how she'd feel if I tried to express them.

FORTY-ONE

Reece

"RELAX," TRIPP SOOTHED, KISSING MY temple in an attempt to calm me. His touch soothed me, but not enough to stop the fluttering anxiousness in my belly as we approached some of the people already gathered.

"I'm trying," I answered, grasping his hand tighter. There were a group of women huddled together at one of the tables, laughing and having a great time together. It was then that I longed for someone, other than Carla, who I could let loose with and confide in. Don't get me wrong; I was beyond grateful that Carla was in my life, but sometimes I wish I just had a couple more girlfriends. Rick had kept me so secluded that the few friends I had back home had eventually stopped trying to reach out to me.

"You'll have fun. I promise," Tripp said, raising his free hand to someone who'd acknowledged his arrival. Our arrival.

"Well, look who decided to show up," a dark-haired man called out, quickly walking toward Tripp to greet him. He was handsome. Very handsome, in fact.

"Prez. How are ya?" They shook hands and did that half-hug thingy guys do. Since I had nowhere else to look, I studied both men, hoping to God I wasn't being obvious. The interaction between them was intriguing. They passed a silent message back and forth with the flick of their eyes and a subtle nod. Their body language was even heightened, elongating their coded communication.

"I'm good. Better."

"How's Sully?" Tripp's question caused his friend to tense, but only for a second. Had I not been paying such close attention I would've missed it for sure.

"She's good. We're gettin' there." Finally looking away from Tripp, the handsome stranger looked in my direction. "Who did ya bring with you?"

"This is Reece." Tripp looked at me for the other part of his introduction. "Reece, this is Marek, our club's president." It was then that my eye caught the 'President' patch on the front of his leather vest.

"Nice to meet you," I greeted, flashing a small smile before looking toward the ground. Bad habit after years of being with Rick. If I looked at another man for two seconds too long he became angry.

"Glad you could come today. Someone's gotta keep this guy in line."

I looked back up at the both of them and found two pairs of eyes on me. Marek's comment was one made in jest, but his expression remained stoic. Something told me the guy was more on the serious side, which I guess made sense seeing as how he was in charge of the entire club. But there was something hidden beneath the blue of his eyes that indicated there was more to him than what he revealed to others. Mainly strangers.

Tripp leaned away from me and spoke in a low voice, Marek acknowledging what he'd said with a jerk of his chin and a slight twitch of his lips. After they parted, Marek stood straight, glancing back at me one more time before turning around and walking toward a building to the left of where we were standing.

We continued to walk forward, and it was only then, as I scoured the expansive area, that I came to realize there was no baby present. I wasn't Catholic, but I knew enough that the child was usually clothed in a white gown of sorts for the ceremony, which would have made her easily detectable. Then again, maybe these people did their own thing, had their own traditions.

"I wonder where Stone and Adelaide are," he mused, as if he'd read my mind.

"I was just thinking the same thing."

He opened his mouth to speak but quickly snapped it shut, his recent smile morphing into a vicious scowl. The faltering of his steps put me on alert. Tripp cursed under his breath, and as I perused the crowd I knew exactly why.

"What the hell is *she* doing here?" I asked.

"I have no goddamn idea, but I'm about to find out." We stalked toward the person in question—or I should say that Tripp stalked forward, dragging me behind me. His steps were rushed and I had to break out into a slight jog just to keep up with him.

"Arianna," Tripp barked, startling not only her but the couple people standing close by. Lowering his voice so as not to call anyone else's attention, he said, "What are you doing here?"

I'd told Tripp about the way Arianna had treated me at work, telling me that I wasn't gonna hold his interest and that he would eventually choose her over me. I'd also revealed how she taunted me with their past escapades. I'd tried to play off her antics as juvenile and those of a jealous woman, but she'd managed to affect me. Tripp and I were still so new it was only logical I'd have my doubts.

Tripp shut down every insecurity I had where she was concerned, assuring me that he'd never touch her again, even if I weren't in the picture.

"I was invited, of course," she said sweetly, false bravado spewing forth as she put on airs she couldn't quite pull off. Her outfit was inappropriate for such an event. If I'd thought my dress was borderline questionable because of the open back, my reservations halted at the sight of her short, red, skintight excuse for a dress. Sure, some of the others' dresses were form-fitting, but they weren't slutty. There was a time and a place for such clothing, and a baby's baptism celebration wasn't one. Her face was overdone with way too much makeup, and her hair was high and ratty. Tame everything down and she'd pass for attractive, but not like this.

"By who?" he asked. Her eyes flicked to mine, narrowing slightly before focusing back on the man standing next to me.

"Breck."

"Of course," Tripp mumbled before shouting for Breck, who was fast approaching with a beer in hand. He stopped next to Arianna and snaked his arm around her waist.

"What?"

"Why did you invite her here?"

"Because I could. What's it to you?" Breck's eyes shot to mine before a lascivious grin flashed across his face. "Oh I get it. You fucked her so now you don't want anyone else to have her. Well, too bad." Breck pulled Arianna close and she laughed, but her eyes never left Tripp.

"I don't give a shit who you fuck." I believed he was speaking to the both of them, but couldn't be sure. "Just make sure you stay away from us, or else." Tripp stopped speaking, turned around and guided me back toward the parking lot. I heard Breck and Arianna mumble something behind me, but again we were walking so fast I couldn't make out any of it.

"Tripp, please slow down. I'm gonna break my neck in these heels." I yanked on his arm for emphasis.

"Sorry." He slowed but not by much. Once we were far enough away, he dropped my hand and leaned against the building Marek had entered not ten minutes prior. "I'm sorry you had to hear that, Reece. If I could change parts of my past I would."

"Ditto," I responded, leaning in to him so I could feel the heat of his body. Was I upset at the reminder that Tripp had been with Arianna? Of course. Did I believe he wanted nothing more to do with her? Whole-heartedly.

Tripp's arms encased me, drawing me in so I could rest my head against his chest. The hasty thrum of his heartbeat told me he was upset. Over the next several minutes we remained silent, existing in the comfort the other provided. His fingers danced over my exposed skin, heat blossoming between my legs at his subtle touch.

"Reece," he whispered, his fingers pressing harder on my back before lowering to cup my ass cheeks. Pulling back to look into his face, I saw a plethora of emotions cross his features. His green eyes darkened with remorse and apology, but a deepening lust existed just under the surface, overpowering his regret at the situation that had just occurred. "Can we escape inside so I can show you how sorry I am that you had to endure that?"

I knew it wasn't his fault. He had no idea she was gonna be there, and I wanted more than anything to give him a reprieve from his guilt, if that was even the correct word to describe what he'd probably been feeling since the encounter. However, I knew it wasn't the right time or place. The last thing I wanted was to be caught by his friends, especially since they didn't know me. It was important these people viewed me as someone other than just the stripper Tripp hooked up with from the club.

Rising up on my toes, I pressed my lips to his. When he groaned into my mouth, I thought for sure I would've thrown all caution to the wind and taken him up on his delicious offer, but I restrained myself. Barely.

"This isn't the place. But I promise that as soon as we get home I'll let you apologize over and over again."

He ignored me, instead pressing his lower half into mine. "Please. Don't make me beg, baby," he pleaded. "I'm so fuckin' hard right now." His warm breath fanned my face before his mouth descended over mine, the flick of his tongue enough to tempt me once again.

The roar of motorcycles interrupted our heated moment. Three bikes followed by an SUV soon entered the lot, gravel kicking up around their tires before they backed into the available parking spaces.

The engines kicked off and the men rested their feet on the ground on either side of their impressive machines as they removed their helmets.

"Yo," one of the men yelled, laughing at something one of the others had said while approaching us. "I thought for sure you'd be the last to arrive." He stopped a couple feet away, his smile wide and inviting. He appeared younger than the rest of them, probably somewhere in his early twenties. The way the sunlight hit his dark golden hair, it appeared as if he had natural highlights—an attribute any woman would kill for, me included. His amber eyes flicked from me to Tripp a few times before any introduction was made.

"I'm not the one who's always late. That's Ryder."

"Stop callin' me out," a dark-haired man yelled from across the lot, continuing to talk to the others as if he hadn't just had an outburst.

"You're a close second," the guy jested, his hand extended to me in the absence of introduction. "I'm Jagger," he said, snagging my hand as soon as I raised my arm. He seemed pleasant.

"Reece. Nice to meet you," I replied, relaxing in the acceptance of his friend.

"Why are your women already here?" Tripp asked his friend. "Some business I should know about?"

"Nope. Nothing that exciting. They didn't wanna ride with us 'cause they didn't wanna ruin their outfits." He shook his head as if the women were being ridiculous, but I completely sided with them. "Hey, before I forget. Can you come to my next bout? Ryder was supposed to but he said he's got somethin' going on."

"Yeah. No problem." Tripp had told me that they had an undefeated, underground MMA fighter in the club. I guessed this was him.

"Great. Okay, I better go find Kena before Breck makes another attempt."

"Fuckin' Breck," Tripp grumbled. "He brought Arianna with him."

Jagger's eyes flicked to mine. "Asshole."

"Yeah."

And that was it for their exchange. Jagger rushed across the lot, and I found his eagerness sweet. Or maybe it was to protect his woman from the likes of Breck. Either way, I liked him.

The next to approach was Hawke. Him I knew, having talked to him on occasion at Indulge when Tripp had sent him in to watch over me. He'd told me he was just there to make sure there were no issues, but I knew his presence had been geared toward me. I couldn't say I minded, though; after everything that'd happened, I welcomed the extra sense of security.

"Hey, Reece. How are ya?" Surprisingly, he leaned in to kiss my cheek, a gesture which earned him a growl from his older brother.

"All right," Tripp admonished. "That's enough."

"What? I'm just sayin' hello." Hawke chuckled, seeming to love riling up his brother.

"Uh-huh." Tripp looked around the lot before asking, "Where's Edana? I didn't see her with the others."

Hawke's expression darkened. "She didn't feel good," was the only explanation he gave. Tripp had told me that his brother had had a rough go of it lately due to his girlfriend being attacked. But he said he was getting better each day, although still much more reserved than he used to be.

"Maybe next time," Tripp said, gripping his brother's shoulder in a show of support.

"Yeah. Maybe." Hawke flashed us a tight smile before disappearing.

Before anyone else could advance our way, the driver's door to the black SUV opened and out stepped a tall, blond man in a dark blue suit. His hair was shorter on the sides than on top, pulled back in some sort of faux Mohawk. He looked nervous.

The other men standing around hooted and hollered at the sight of him, and I guessed he was another member of the club, although I wasn't sure because he didn't match their attire of leather vests and jeans.

"What the fuck?" Tripp whispered next to me.

"Who is that?"

"Stone. He's the VP. And Riley's dad." We watched him open the back door and fiddle around for few seconds before exiting with a little girl in a long white dressing gown. I guessed they were sticking to tradition after all. The sight of him holding who I naturally assumed to be Riley was beautiful. In that short amount of time, I could tell how much he loved his daughter. The way he ignored his friends and focused on the little girl, as if he was lost in her, instantly told me he was a good man.

He walked around the vehicle and opened the passenger door, and soon a woman came into view.

"Is that Adelaide?" The woman was stunning. Her dress was sleeveless and the most beautiful shade of pale yellow I'd ever seen. The material hit just below her knee, and even though it flared out at the cinched waist, there was no hiding her gorgeous form. Her beautiful blonde hair was pulled back in a stylish half updo.

"Yup. Sure is." Tripp smiled wide at the sight of her, and as soon as she caught his attention she returned the expression, striding over to us within seconds. Once she was near, she wrapped her arms around his neck and gave him a big hug.

"Not today, Addy," Stone shouted across the lot. The look on his face was part serious, part joking. The little I did know about the woman was that she had tended to Tripp after he'd been left for dead just outside the club's gates. She nursed him back to health and still checked in on him from time to time.

"Oh shush," she shouted over her shoulder, turning her attention to me when she looked back. "And you must be Reece," she said, pulling me in for an impromptu hug. She was certainly friendly, I'd give her that.

"Yes, I am." I smiled, and for once it hadn't been forced. My nerves had loosened their hold and I reveled in the feeling. "So nice to meet you. Tripp has told me a lot about you."

"Well, this guy," she laughed, gripping his upper arm, "and I have a special bond. I hope you don't mind that, because I know Stone certainly does."

"No issues whatsoever." I'd spoken the truth. My newfound jealousies didn't extend to Adelaide. "I'll be forever thankful that you saved him."

"Okay, okay. All this mushy talk is gettin' to me." Tripp leaned in and kissed Adelaide's cheek before walking away. He'd snatched Riley from Stone's hands, turning his back on his friend so he could fuss over the precious little one.

"He loves that little girl. They all do," Adelaide revealed. "I just hope she doesn't mind so much as she gets older."

FORTY-TWO

Tripp

"I NEVER THOUGHT I'D SEE the day." I held Riley close while her father fixed his tie.

"What are you talkin' about?"

"I'm talkin' about you in a monkey suit. What the hell's gotten into you?" Riley grabbed my finger and tried to suck on it, but I pulled it away at the last second. "Where's her sucky thing?"

"Her binky?"

"I don't know what the hell it's called."

"It's in the truck." He opened the back door and rooted around for what felt like forever.

"If you don't hurry up, I'm gonna let her suck on my finger, and you probably know where that's been." I laughed at the words that came out of his mouth. I would've never done such a thing, but the fact that Stone thought I would, and how distressed he became, made me laugh harder.

Gently placing the binky in Riley's mouth, he said, "I know where those hands have been. Keep them away from my daughter."

"Oh relax." Looking closely at him, I saw he was nervous. "What's wrong with you? Seriously? Why so uptight?"

"No reason." He shifted his attention away from me and onto his woman, who was chatting with Reece. "How's that goin'?" He jerked his head toward the women. "Heard you had some issue with her husband. Not cool fuckin' around with a married woman, by the way." His dark eyes chastised me. He obviously didn't know the full story.

"I'm not fuckin' around with a married chick. Well, she's technically married, but she doesn't wanna be." Stone stood there staring at me, waiting for the rest of the story. I didn't want to bring it up, but I didn't want him thinking badly of Reece either. "He beat and terrorized her for years. She finally got away, but he tracked her across the country. He found her at the club, and thank God we got to him before he dragged her out of there. He probably would've killed her this time." I hadn't realized how much the entire situation had affected me until I clutched my chest after speaking. The thought that Reece could've been ripped from my life gutted me.

"Fuck," Stone replied. "Sorry, man. I didn't know that." He looked back toward Reece and Adelaide. "Is she okay now? And where is her hus . . . that bastard?"

"Ryder and Hawke broke his legs in warning never to come near her again. I would've done it, but I probably wouldn't have been able to stop at just his legs."

"Speak of the devil," Stone interrupted as Ryder drew closer.

"I'm the devil? I think someone sold their soul for an Armani suit." Ryder chuckled. "Why you all dressed up?"

"Will everyone get off my back already," Stone sneered, shoving his hands in his pockets in another bout of nervousness. It was extremely odd to see our VP acting in such a way. It almost made me think something else was up with him. But he wouldn't tell me even if I asked, so I let it go.

Cutter and Trigger joined us, coming out of the clubhouse and smelling like booze. Nothing too crazy, though.

A black sedan pulled up in front of the gates, the prospects inspecting the vehicle before allowing it to pass. As soon as the car came to stop, a priest stepped out and smiled at Stone. Adelaide appeared suddenly, stealing her daughter from my arms.

"Time to get things started," I heard Stone shout as we all walked toward the back of the compound.

———— ◆ ————

THE CEREMONY WAS QUICK. MAREK and Sully had been chosen as Riley's godparents, and I had to admit that Stone and Addy had definitely chosen wisely. I saw the longing in Sully's eyes when she held the little girl, and I only hoped they could have one of their own someday. Marek stood rigid beside her, although he relaxed some when she reached for his hand. I could sense they were still dealing with the strain of what'd happened, but there was a light back in Marek's eyes that had been missing over more time than I cared to acknowledge.

We were an hour into the party when Stone stood, clearing his throat to gain everyone's attention. Once all eyes were on him, including Adelaide's, he finally spoke.

"Addy and I want to thank everyone for coming today to help us celebrate. And if Riley could talk, she'd say thank you too." Everyone smiled, glancing at the baby girl before turning their gazes back to Stone. "You're all aware of the difficulty Addy and I went through while she was pregnant with Riley, and it was by the grace of God that she was able to give me a healthy child. Now I'm not a religious guy at all." He looked over at the priest. "Sorry, Father Houston, but it's true." The collared man simply nodded. "But I'd never prayed as much as I did during those months."

A solemn look briefly passed over everyone present. We'd all been praying for not only Adelaide's life but for the life of their daughter. She'd been dealt a tough hand, having been told she had ovarian cancer *and* that she was pregnant. Thankfully everything turned out great, and Adelaide was in remission.

"After everything we've been through, baby, I don't want another day to go by without the world knowing how much I love you." Stone moved toward Adelaide, gently taking Riley from her arms and passing their daughter to Sully. Then he helped his woman to her feet and did something I never thought I'd see—he lowered himself to one knee and took her hand in his. Wide-eyed and astonished, Adelaide's lower lip started to tremble. "I even asked your dad for permission, so that tells you how serious I am." She laughed and looked across the table at an older man sitting next to Trigger. He looked back at her with such love there was no mistaking that he was her father.

"Baby . . . ever since I met you I've become a better man. I'll admit there've been hurdles along the way, and I'm not sayin' I won't trip and fall on my face from time to time, but knowing you're there to help me up and make me see the error of my ways means more to me than I can ever say." We all laughed because we knew Stone had a temper which landed him in hot water with Adelaide sometimes. But he always came around, and my God did he love that woman.

He licked his lips and blew out a nervous breath. It was then that I understood his previous anxiety and the reason why he'd decided to don a suit. He wanted to put forth the effort Adelaide deserved. "Adelaide Reins . . . will you marry me?"

"Of course I will," Adelaide proclaimed, tears streaming down her beautiful cheeks. She pulled him to his feet and threw her arms around his neck. Everyone clapped in celebration. Stone kept it clean, even though I knew damn well all he wanted to do was make a spectacle and kiss the hell out of her. But her father was present, and I knew even though his relationship with him had been rocky, he respected him enough not to openly defile the man's daughter in front of him.

FORTY-THREE

Tripp

I STAYED AS CLOSE TO Reece as I could, with the exception of when I had to piss or grab another drink. I knew she was still a bit nervous, although she'd relaxed some over the past couple hours. Adelaide and Sully had engaged her in conversation, doing their best to make her feel welcome. Kena and Braylen had even sat down next to her in an attempt to get to know her.

While Arianna made sure to stay away from Reece, I saw her staring at me from time to time. I never acknowledged her presence, which I knew irritated the fuck out of her, but I didn't give a shit. Reece had caught one of Arianna's glances and stiffened beside me. I relieved her tension with a soul-scorching kiss, almost forgetting we weren't in private. It wasn't until Hawke yelled for me to let her breathe that I pulled away from her delectable lips.

"Wanna join us?" Sully asked Reece, shuffling past us in a hurry.

"Where you goin'?" I asked before Reece could.

"Bathroom. If that's okay with you," Adelaide snickered, half sloshed herself, no doubt celebrating her engagement. Good thing Stone was driving them home.

"Want me to join you?" I asked my woman, laughing at her reaction.

"You can't go in the bathroom with us."

"Who says?"

"We say," Adelaide and Sully replied in unison. They pulled Reece away from me, and I hated to admit that I already missed her.

Fuck! I have it bad.

I couldn't draw my eyes away from her, staring after her like a lovesick puppy. Thoughts of her beneath me consumed me, and I counted the seconds until I could make the images in my head a reality.

I knew someone had sat down next to me, but I took a sip of my drink and ignored whoever it was, having a feeling I knew exactly who dared to approach me.

"You know she can't satisfy you the way I can."

Anger instantly boiled in my veins at the sound of her voice. I didn't respond, not until she shifted closer and put her hand on my thigh, too close to my dick. I seized her wrist and tossed her hand away as if she'd burned me.

"Don't fuckin' touch me, Arianna. I mean it. Do it again and I'll have you thrown out of here." I was doing my best not to cause a scene, but she tested my patience for sure. "Where's Breck?"

"I don't know. I think he's passed out somewhere. Besides, he can't keep up with me. He's not like you, baby," she slurred, daring to touch me again. I jumped up from the table and backed away, glaring at her before turning toward the clubhouse. No way was that bitch staying here without Breck present. I strolled inside and walked across the common room, finding the guy in question passed out cold on the couch.

"Goddammit!" I swore, punching the back of the couch. He didn't even move. As luck would have it, one of the prospects came out of the kitchen carrying two trays of food. "Hey, prospect. Call a cab."

"For who?" He was young and new. Too new to realize he didn't ask the questions, only did what we told him to.

"Just. Do. It." I turned on my heel but not before Arianna stumbled into the common room, no doubt having followed me inside. This was all I needed. Reece would be walking through there any second and I didn't want her to have to deal with my past mistake yet again.

"There you are," Arianna cooed, batting her heavily coated, fake lashes at me. "Wanna take me in one of the back rooms? Or we can do it right here if you want." She didn't bother waiting for my refusal before she hiked up her skirt and leaned against the bar. She wasn't wearing anything underneath.

"Pull your skirt down," I barked. "No one wants to see that shit." I was pissed, even more so when Arianna pushed off the bar and stalked toward me, her skirt still hiked up to her waist and exposing herself.

"You still want me. You know you do. Stop wasting your time with that skank." I found it funny that she referred to Reece as a skank when it was she who fucked anyone willing, often for money. Thank God the few times I'd been with her I'd been smart enough to use a condom.

I'd been so enraged that she'd put me into this position, I hadn't noticed Reece had walked into the room, halting her steps once she saw the scene in front of her.

Arianna hanging on my arm with her skirt around her waist.

FORTY-FOUR

Reece

TO SAY I WAS LIVID would have been an understatement. The sight of that bitch hanging all over Tripp, and with her skirt bunched up showing everyone her goodies, made my blood boil. Heat shot through me and my skin flushed red. My fists clenched at my sides and while tears formed, they were from anger. Not sadness or hurt. Okay, part of me was hurt, but mostly it was from anger.

Although rage best described what I felt right then.

I didn't misconstrue the scene in front of me. I knew damn well Tripp didn't want to have anything to do with Arianna. I saw it in his rigid posture, in the way his eyes flared with his own fury that she dared to come near him after he'd warned her earlier. It was then I saw Breck passed out on the couch, explaining why that bitch made her bold move on my man.

I'd finally found my sliver of happiness and there was no way in hell I was gonna let some low-class whore snatch that away from me. I was done brushing off her attacks, done second-guessing my relationship, done giving in to the small bouts of paranoia that maybe what Arianna spewed was true. That Tripp would eventually tire of me and go back to her.

It was time I stepped up and claimed what was mine. Oh yeah, my possessive side came bursting out, and I embraced the hell out of it.

Slowly walking toward the two of them, Tripp shoved her aside as I approached. "Get the hell away from him," I seethed, trying to convince myself not to tackle her and beat the hell out of her once and for all. For as much as I wanted to teach her drunk ass a lesson, this wasn't the time or place. I didn't want to make a scene, nor did I want the women behind me to think badly of me.

"Or what?" She tried to put her hands back on Tripp, even though he took a few more steps away from her. Before I could answer or even reach her, a blur of blonde hair pushed past me and headed straight for Arianna. Grabbing her by the back of her hair, Adelaide pulled her toward the door, Arianna stumbling behind her the entire way, trying to catch her footing.

"Get off me, you crazy bitch!" she yelled, trying to dislodge herself from Adelaide's hold. But it was useless; she was simply no match.

Adelaide was stronger than she looked. I laughed out loud as she finally tossed Arianna out on her ass, screaming, "Don't ever show your ugly face around here again or you'll regret it!" before she slammed the door on her. Turning toward us, she threw up her hands and said, "Anyone else need disposing of?"

We all burst out laughing at what she'd done. She saw the look on my face and decided to step in on my behalf, and I'd be forever grateful to her for doing so. She winked at me and said, "I got your back, sweetheart."

When Tripp drew me into his side, he kissed me before saying, "I told you they were cool chicks."

"They certainly are," I agreed.

All of a sudden a serious look shrouded his face. "Do you want me to fire her? I know you said you didn't want to see anyone lose their job, but I think she's only gonna get worse. Especially after tonight."

That time I didn't have to think too long before answering. "I think it's time. After the shit she pulled tonight, she's gone too far."

"Okay, consider it done. Now how about we get outta here so I can ravage you properly." The seductive tremor in his voice instantly made me wet, the ache that had been present the entire day kicking into overdrive.

"How can I say no to that?"

"You can't." He reached for my hand and pulled me toward the exit. Once outside, we walked right into another commotion. At first I thought Arianna still hadn't left, causing one last scene before she was finally booted off the property.

But as we approached, I saw a few of the men crowding the gates, a car on the other side with a woman blaring on the horn. It was obvious she wanted to come inside, but for who I had no idea.

Not until she laid eyes on Tripp.

I would have liked to say that the rest of the evening passed without incident, but I would've been lying.

FORTY-FIVE

Tripp

MINDLESSLY WALKING TOWARD THE GATES, I tried to dispel the image in front of me, but no amount of blinking or wishing would make her disappear.

"Tripp," Rachel shouted. "Tripp, tell them to let me in."

My only response was to shake my head, releasing Reece's hand as I prepared myself for one helluva scene. I had to make sure she was real. That she was really there. Only then would I summon up the anger necessary to tell her to go to hell.

"How the fuck did you find me?" Out of all the questions rattling around inside my confused brain, that was the one that chose to escape. Peering at her through the bars, gripping the metal tightly while I pushed angered breaths from my mouth, I shouted again, "How did you find me?"

"I . . . I remember you telling me about this place." Even in the dim light of the lot I could see her pupils were dilated. She had an issue with drugs back when we were together, but I always chose to look the other way because it hadn't affected me. Well, not until I found her fucking some guy, her lapse in judgement surely a side effect of the drugs. Or maybe it was simply because she'd been a selfish bitch. *Yeah, let's go with that second one.*

Other than her eyes, she appeared okay, even though I knew she wasn't. "What are you doin' here?"

"I need to talk to you."

Looking at Rachel now, I realized I'd never loved her. She was simply someone I'd fucked and had a good laugh with on occasion.

"What could you possibly have to talk to me about? I haven't seen you in over a year. What could be so damn important that you just show up here out of the blue?" I backed up and turned away from her, fully intending on hightailing it back inside the security of the clubhouse to bark orders at someone to make sure she left without further incident. But I didn't make it that far. The next words out of her mouth froze me to my spot, disabling any thoughts from forming, let alone allowing my body to flee as I'd initially intended.

"Your son."

I whipped around so fast I was surprised I didn't fall over. The weight of her words crushed me. No way. It wasn't true. She wasn't pregnant when I left her. Or was she? I had no idea, but then again why would I have even bothered to ask? She'd cheated, and the guy I'd found her with probably wasn't the first. If she'd popped out a kid, what were the chances that he was mine? Slim. The chances just had to be slim. Otherwise, I had no idea what I was gonna do.

Instead of confronting Rachel with her ridiculous allegation, I sought out Reece. I didn't have to look too far, seeing as how she was standing next to Sully, the look on her face utter disbelief. We'd just started our relationship; how would she handle me having a son all of a sudden? That was a lot to ask of someone. I clearly had deep feelings for her if I was more concerned about what she thought than what I was goin' through.

Striding toward the woman who'd taken over my entire world, I reached for her but she simply shook her head and stepped back. I could hear Rachel shouting something behind me, but all of my focus was on Reece. The look in her eyes told me she was confused and . . . was that embarrassment?

"Reece." Her name was the only word I could form. I had no idea what to say, but I knew damn well I needed her to talk to me, to tell me what was goin' through that head of hers. I could only imagine, but I refused to give in to my own paranoia. Maybe it wasn't that bad . . . or maybe it was worse.

As I opened my mouth to say God knew what, she turned on her heel and fled toward the clubhouse, rushing inside and disappearing as my world fell down around me. For the first time in my life I was happy, genuinely happy. It figured my contentment with life wouldn't fuckin' last.

All because that bitch at the gate decided she wanted to swoop in and ruin everything. Anger tore through me as I finally lost my temper and hauled ass toward Rachel.

"Open the fuckin' gates!" I roared, shoving past whoever stood in my way. "Now!" The creak of the steel fueled my rage, the match to ignite the inferno swirling around inside me. Once I stepped foot on the other side I came face-to-face with her.

"Tripp!" I heard Stone shout, but my name was muffled. My only focus right then was ripping the truth from her filthy, lying mouth if it was the last thing I did.

"You better tell me right now that you're lying," I seethed as I towered over her. Rachel was selfish, proving it when she fucked around on me. She didn't care about me then and she sure as hell didn't care about me now. Rachel was only there because she didn't have anywhere else to go, no one else she could think of who'd help her. If the kid turned out to be mine then I'd have no choice but to step up, but if I found out this was just a ploy of hers to wriggle back into my life, she was gonna regret it for sure.

Her shoulders shook. Her body trembled. Her eyes filled with tears, though I highly doubted they were genuine. Rachel had always been good at playing upset to get my attention. I'd fallen for it in the past, but not anymore.

"I'm not lyin'," she muttered. "He's your son."

My eyes scoured the length of her. She didn't look like she'd had a baby, but then again she had always been conscious of everything that passed her lips—with the exception of dick, of course. My fury heightened and it wasn't from the memory of her fuckin' someone else. I didn't care about that. I didn't care about her. I cared that she was messin' with my relationship with Reece by just being there.

"Where is he?"

She remained silent and pointed toward the back door. The muscles of my jaw ached from clenching so hard, but my expression was enough to make her move out of my way as I reached for the handle.

As soon as I ripped the door open, I saw a tiny baby sitting in a car seat, his eyes wide and staring right back at me. His lower lip quivered, so before he started wailing, I looked behind me to search for someone I could trust to help. I didn't want to touch the little guy for fear my anger would transfer to him and scare him more than I was sure he already was. But I needed to see him up close, and I sure as shit didn't want Rachel handing him to me.

I caught Sully's attention and motioned for her to come over with a simple jerk of my head. Marek released her hand but he didn't look happy about it. Rachel never objected as Sully brushed past her. She knew I'd shut her down or make her leave before I'd even seen my so-called son.

Sully silently reached inside the car and pulled the baby from his seat. The infant wasn't even strapped in, nor was the car seat securely in place. *Careless bitch.*

Cradling the baby in her arms, Sully held him out to me. Still Rachel said nothing. All she could do was fidget next to me.

"I can't." I just wanted to look at him up close, but under the illumination of the security light I couldn't determine if he truly belonged to me or not. All goddamn babies looked the same at that age.

Speaking of which, I asked, "How old is he?"

"Three months."

"Three months? How in the world can you possibly say he's mine? You got knocked up months after I left you." I took a step to the side and stood so close I pinned her against the car. "Did you think I couldn't add? That I was so fuckin' stupid I'd think this kid was mine when there is no humanly way possible he could be? Unless you saved my cum and had someone inject it inside you months after I took off. Is that what you did?" Before she opened her mouth to lie, I yelled over to Adelaide, interrupting her conversation with Stone. "Addy, how long is cum good for?"

"What?" she shouted back, confusion written all over her face. She started toward me, Stone hot on her heels.

When she was near, I repeated, "How long is cum good for?"

"If you're asking how long semen is viable, the answer depends on what's being done with it."

"Stop it," Rachel shouted, slapping my chest with both her hands. I didn't move. She'd always hated when I intimidated her by standing so close, but I'd only acted that way whenever we really went at it. I'd never laid my hands on her, my presence enough to shatter whatever shit she'd tried to lay at my feet. Whether it was coming home drunk dressed like some kind of whore, smelling like men's cologne, or high as a kite, stumbling into our place in a daze I thought she'd never come down from. I excused her behavior and I think deep down I knew not to trust her. When I caught her cheating, it was more of a shot to my ego than anything else, but I took the opportunity for what it was and finally walked away. And what happened afterward set the direction of my future. I couldn't blame Rachel solely for me getting piss drunk, jumped by the Reapers, and shot to all hell, but I held her partly responsible.

"Stop what?" I shouted right back.

"I have nowhere to go," she cried, a few dramatic tears escaping and falling down her cheeks. "I can't take care of him by myself. It's too much."

"It's only too much because you're still addicted to that shit." It was an open-ended statement. 'That shit' could be anything. She'd tried it all, her dilated pupils and sunken skin proving she'd engaged the devil just hours prior. Cocaine was her favorite, though. No doubt if I searched her purse there'd be a vial in there.

"I'm tryin'," she lied.

"You're not," I countered. "And now I want you to take your kid and get the hell out of here." Lowering my face to hers, I said, "And if you ever come back, you *will* regret it."

"Please," she begged. "Please just take him." Whatever light had been hidden somewhere inside her had been completely blown out. Her blank stare worried me, not so much for her safety but that of her kid.

"I'm not takin' care of your son, and I sure as hell ain't raisin' some other fucker's kid." I turned my back on her, the sight of her sniveling pissing me off. She had no right to just show up out of the blue, claim the kid was mine, when he clearly wasn't, disrupt my night, let alone my relationship with Reece, and then beg me to take her baby off her hands.

What the hell is wrong with her?

Selfishness.

Drugs.

That's what's wrong with her.

The baby started crying, all of the commotion happening around him finally tipping him over the edge. Sully held him close, whispering something to him while rocking him back and forth. He seemed to have calmed in her arms, and while I didn't want to take him from her, he had to go back to his mother. I used that term loosely because I could already predict what kind of life this poor kid would have—a mother chasing whatever high she craved, caring only for herself and putting her kid second.

When I turned around to reach for the baby, Rachel made her move. She jumped back into her car and kicked over the engine.

"Don't you fuckin' dare," I shouted, racing toward the car as she hauled ass in reverse. "Rachel!" I yelled. "Get back here!" The bald tires squealed as she whipped the car around and took off, kicking up rocks and dust in her haste to escape.

What the fuck just happened?

FORTY-SIX

Reece

STARING INTO THE MIRROR, I tried to get a handle on everything that'd just happened outside. Some woman showing up claiming Tripp was the father of her baby. What the hell? I knew the other shoe was gonna drop, so why was I surprised? Because for once in my dreaded life I thought I'd finally get my happily ever after.

Did he know she was pregnant when he left her? He told me briefly about their relationship and how she'd cheated on him. Tripp never seemed torn up about it, though, telling me he never really loved her, although he may have thought so at the time.

What if the baby if his? What will I do? Continue our relationship, or allow him to try and work it out with her in an effort to give his sudden family a chance? I guess I won't find out until I leave the bathroom I've been holed up in for the past ten minutes.

Slowly turning the handle, I reentered the common space inside the club. Kena and Braylen, who I'd met earlier that day, were standing close together in the far corner. Kena's hands were going a mile a minute, her sister trying her best to interrupt her at every turn. Tripp had told me about Kena's condition soon after I'd met her, explaining that she wasn't deaf but that she simply couldn't speak.

I needed to see Tripp, to talk to him and try to figure out where we stood. Before I reached the door, it flung open and a crowd of people barreled inside. As soon as Tripp saw me he rushed forward and pulled me into a hug. His embrace was strong, borderline suffocating, but I relished the feel of his arms around me.

"I'm so sorry, Reece. I had no idea. I never expected to see her ever again." He stroked my back in reassurance, but all I wanted was answers.

I pulled away from him so I could look into his eyes when I asked my question.

"Is it true, then?" I held my breath until he answered, which thankfully didn't take but a millisecond.

"No. The kid is too young to be mine. I have no idea what the hell she was thinking." He vigorously shook his head. "That's a lie. Yes I do. She's so far gone she actually thought I'd buy into her bullshit. Hell, she was high when she came here."

Looking around the room I saw the baby, but no Rachel. "Where is she?"

"She took off." He raked his fingers through his dark hair. "She fuckin' took off and left her kid here. And now I gotta deal with it."

I parted my lips to tell him I would help him when he squeezed my hand before walking toward Sully, who'd been coddling the infant.

I walked behind him and stood next to Adelaide, who was on the other side of Sully. I felt so out of place, but I didn't want to add to Tripp's stress by letting him know as much.

"He's adorable," I said, reaching over to touch his tiny hand. He had the bluest eyes I'd ever seen on a baby, although to be honest I hadn't seen many infants up close.

"He sure is," Sully whispered, nuzzling him close when he started to fuss.

"What the hell am I gonna do with a baby?" Tripp asked no one in particular. I gave him his space, continuing to stand next to Adelaide and Sully while he tried to work it out. I searched the rest of the room and saw Kena next to Jagger. They looked content, although she still looked frustrated, something definitely weighing heavy on her mind. She smiled at her man, but worry halted the expression from reaching her eyes. Next I saw Braylen standing next to Ryder, his arm slung over her shoulder while she rested her head on his chest. They were silent, watching everything unfold in front of them.

"Can you take him? Until I find Rachel?"

"Who the hell are you talkin' to?" Stone asked, looking over his shoulder as if there were someone standing behind him Tripp had been speaking to.

"Come on, brother. You already have one. How hard is it to take care of another one?"

"Are you kiddin' me right now? You have no idea how hard it is to raise a kid. I love my daughter more than life itself, but she requires constant attention. We hardly get any sleep, and forget about sex. No, we can't do it. You're gonna have to take him until you find that bitch. We just can't take care of two kids," Stone argued.

"Well, you better get used to it, sweetheart," Adelaide yelled over her shoulder, turning her attention back to Sully and the infant. "And that bullshit about no sex is a lie. How else did I get pregnant again?" She smiled, waiting for realization to dawn on her soon-to-be husband.

FORTY-SEVEN

Tripp

"COME ON, ADDY. I DON'T wanna hear that shit," Trigger yelled from across the room. He was behind the bar serving some of the guys a drink. That was gonna be my next stop for sure. I could definitely use a stiff one.

Stone mumbled something before crushing the small distance between him and his woman, reaching her in only a few strides. "What did you say?" The look on his face was priceless, and I had to stop myself from busting out laughing at his astonishment.

"You heard me." Adelaide kissed him before placing his hand on her belly. "Riley is gonna be a big sister." The light in her eyes filled me with warmth. I knew how much shit she'd gone through not that long ago, and to be able to have another kid was definitely a blessing for them both. Stone nodded before finally smiling. He pulled her close and kissed her, all the while remaining silent. He was obviously shocked. Shit, we all were.

"We can take him," Sully blurted, diverting the conversation and suddenly looking desperate to keep the baby in her arms. "I can watch over him while you try and find her." She looked over at her husband who was sitting at the bar, the pleading look in her eyes pulling at my heartstrings.

"I don't think that's a good idea, baby," Marek answered, sorrow laced deep in the lines of his face. He tipped his shot glass and swallowed the contents before rising to his feet.

"Please. I know it's not permanent. I promise I won't get attached to him." Sully looked down into the infant's face and smiled, the baby's tiny hand wrapping around her finger.

"You're already attached," Marek said, coming to stand next to her.

Deciding to add in my two cents, I said, "Come on, Prez. I promise I'll find her as soon as possible. I could really use your help." I rested my hand on his shoulder for emphasis.

Several tense seconds passed, keeping us all on edge as to what he would decide. Finally he huffed out a frustrated breath and relented.

"Fine. But you better find that bitch soon, Tripp. I mean it," he admonished. Even though he appeared put out by the request, his eyes filled with something akin to pride when he gazed at his wife holding the little one.

"I will. First thing tomorrow, I'm on it." Giving him a quick nod, I turned my attention to Reece. "Any time you wanna leave, just say the word. I know it's been one helluva day, and I don't blame you at all if you just wanna get outta here."

Whatever tension she'd been holding onto dissipated as soon as I wrapped my arms around her.

"I'm okay to stay a little while longer."

"Are you sure?"

"Yeah." Pulling back, she rested her hands on my chest and looked up at me, the thrum of my heart picking up speed from her simple touch. "Go talk to your friends. I'll be on the couch with my new favorite badass." Looking over her shoulder, I saw Sully and Adelaide had moved to the sofa, huddled together and fawning over the baby.

"I think I can take her," I teased, winking at Adelaide when she briefly looked over at me.

"I don't think so." Reece laughed. "You're no match for that woman."

"You might be right about that." Leaning down, I pressed my mouth to hers, the softness of her lips conjuring up all sorts of sordid images. Before I became a slave to what my body wanted, however, I ended our kiss. "I won't be long." I lightly smacked her ass before sauntering toward the bar to join some of the men. Marek occupied the corner seat, nursing his drink, while Stone was surprisingly engaged in conversation with Trigger. As I neared I could hear them discussing the VP's future child. Words such as 'karma' and 'hope you have another daughter' flew from Trigger's mouth, a smirk lifting the corners of his lips as Stone's face turned ashen.

Slapping Marek on the back, I swung my leg over the stool and sat down next to him. "How ya doin'?" It was meant to be a rhetorical question at first, but after the words left my mouth I really wanted to know how he'd been faring, especially after everything he'd been through. Him and Sully both. I'd asked him a similar question earlier and he gave me a coded look accompanied by a generic sort of answer, which was to be expected seeing as how Reece had been present.

I was the guy who witnessed the first slice into Marek's soul when Psych spewed the lies about the two of them being related. I saw all hope fade from his eyes, only to be replaced by fear and uncertainty. I saw it only fitting that I was the one who delivered the good news by reading the DNA results, almost coming full circle from desperation to elation.

"I'm good," he answered, continuing to nurse the amber liquid in his glass, the ice cubes clinking together and drawing out the staleness of his response as he lowered his drink. Marek glanced over at me when I simply bumped his shoulder. "What?"

"You know damn well that answer ain't gonna fly. Not now. Not after everything we've been through." Sure, Marek had been the one to bear the brunt of Psych's lies, but I'd been affected by his reaction to the entire situation.

"What do you want me to tell ya? That I withdrew so far into my own pain and misery that I practically pushed Sully away, treating her like shit and not givin' a fuck about how she was feelin'? That I thought about eatin' a bullet if it turned out that she was indeed my half-sister because my heart would've been shredded and there wouldn't've been any reason to live in a fuckin' world where she wasn't mine?" He ran a hand through his hair, the blue hue of his irises darkening with his still-present pain. "It took everything in me not to grab her and hold her close, fearing the outcome every second of every goddamn day. But Sully didn't deserve to be put through that shit, to drive herself crazy waiting for the final results."

"And you did?"

"It was my cross to bear," he answered quickly, and I truly believed he thought he spoke the truth. "Anyway, we got through it."

"Barely," I uttered, flashing him a smirk when he turned to look at me once more.

"Yeah. Barely."

The chatter in the clubhouse swirled together, all bodies present involved in their own conversations, allowing me time to delve deeper into what happened when he finally told his wife the reason he'd withdrawn from her.

"How did Sully take the news? You know, when you eventually fessed up as to why you were actin' like such a prick?"

A gruff laugh escaped my fearless leader.

"She was beyond livid." Marek leaned over the bar and grabbed a bottle of whatever he could reach. Normally Trigger would be on point in serving the drinks, but he was still too busy razzing Stone. "Actually, I'd never seen her so furious. She called me every name in the book. Not that I didn't deserve it."

"I can only imagine."

"No, you can't. I'm tellin' ya, I saw a side to my wife I never even knew existed. She was pissed that I chose to hide what her father said from her, sure, but she was more hurt than anything. She thought I didn't love her anymore and that eventually I'd leave her altogether. She told me she kept thinkin' she'd done something to deserve the way I treated her, that she was just waiting for the emptiness to creep back into her life when I finally decided to walk out the door for good." Marek hung his head, breathing quickly to regain his fleeting composure. "All of her hurt and fear manifested into rage. She almost scared me, and I'm man enough to admit that."

A slow smile spread across his face as if he was proud of his wife's reaction, that she was able to let go and not bottle everything up inside. Then again, it proved what I'd always thought about Sully, that she was a fierce woman underneath all the calm. His smile disappeared as quickly as it had appeared, however. "I'll always regret putting her through what I did, treating her as if it was her fault that I couldn't even bear to look at her, let alone touch her."

Clasping his shoulder, I said, "You two will get through this. I can already see that she's forgiven you. No one can mistake the way that woman feels about you, man."

"Forgiven, maybe, but it'll be a long time before I can prove that I'll never hurt her like that again."

I didn't know what else to say in support so I chose to remain silent. That was until he started his own sort of interrogation on me.

"What the fuck happened with that crazy bitch showin' up here like that?" He abruptly changed the topic and I couldn't say that I blamed him. Marek wasn't a touchy-feely kind of guy, and the fact that he told me as much as he had was a rarity in and of itself.

"I have no goddamn idea. I'm still tryin' to wrap my head around it. I haven't thought about Rachel since the night I left her, and for her to show up out of the blue, and claiming she has my son of all things, is mind-blowing. Then she fuckin' takes off and leaves her kid behind." A heavy exhale passed my lips. "Everything happened so fast. One minute she was here and the next she was gone."

"Crazy shit," Marek mumbled before pouring himself another drink.

"You can say that again."

A half hour later, we were all still trying to relax and find our footing after the evening's events. Riley and the baby boy, whose name we didn't know, were resting in one of the back bedrooms. It seemed like the night was gonna end on sort of a good note when all of a sudden one of the prospects—I believed his name was Cod—rushed inside.

"You guys better get out here," he shouted, the panic on his face unmistakable.

FORTY-EIGHT

Tripp

"FUCK!" MAREK YELLED. "WHAT THE hell is goin' on now?" All the members hurried outside, the women following close behind. But as soon as we saw who was waiting for us, I turned toward the females and shouted for them to go back.

"I got 'em," Trigger offered, thankfully following the confused women back inside the clubhouse.

As we approached the gates, badges were flashed and a few more SUVs appeared.

"Open the gates, Marek," Sam Koritz shouted. The crooked DEA agent who'd raided our club, and who was still in bed with the Savage Reapers, I was sure, had the audacity to show up out of the blue, without cause, and put the cherry on top of one of the shittiest days I'd had in a long time. Granted, I hadn't been there when he and his goons had stormed in, but I heard all about it.

The man was around ten years older than me, yet he looked at least twice that. A huge potbelly hung over the top of his cheap khaki pants, a laughable comb-over doing shit to hide his receding hairline.

"Why?" Marek's stance was unyielding. He didn't want to deal with Koritz any more than the rest of us did, but being in our position it was part of the deal, I supposed.

"Do it or we're gonna ram 'em."

"Why don't you go set up someone else?" Hawke shouted from behind me. I twisted around and shot him a warning look. We didn't need any reason for Koritz to put a target on our backs again. Granted, the club was legit now, no longer dealing with Los Zappas Cartel, but we did have a few decomposing bodies under our belt. Recent ones, at that.

Koritz signaled for the men still occupying two of the SUVs to back up, no doubt waiting for his go-ahead to lurch forward and slam into our gates.

Before they could make another move, Marek threw up his hand and rotated his finger in the air, signaling for the prospects to open the gates. The defiant part of me wanted to stand in front of the gates and tell them to fuck right off. In order to get rid of them, however, we had to comply.

The groan of the metal infuriated me. None of us understood the reason for Koritz's visit, but I was sure he was gonna fill us in real soon.

All five SUVs entered the compound, our men stopping them from going much farther than the entrance. No way in hell they were gonna make themselves at home and traipse all over our lot. My heart picked up pace the longer we stood in silence, waiting and wondering just what the hell brought them all out that evening.

Koritz finally stepped closer, a few of his men behind him with their hands on their weapons. None of us were armed. Well, let me clarify. As soon as Cod ran into the clubhouse shouting for us to come outside, all of us strapped up, the cold of the metal tucked safely in our waistbands. But Koritz didn't know that, and we sure as hell weren't gonna let him in on our little secret. For all he knew we were unarmed. Element of surprise and all that shit, in case it all went south.

"What the hell are you doin' here?" Marek spit out, taking a single step closer to the bastard stupid enough to think he could just show up out of the blue and there wouldn't be any consequences.

"We're looking for Psych Brooks," he cockily responded, arching a brow as if that reaction alone was enough to make us think he knew what we'd done to the Savage Reapers' president.

"What makes you think we know where that piece of shit is?" I took my place by my prez, offering a united front of sorts, denying any involvement in Psych's disappearance. A lie, but they'd never know that little tidbit of information. Henry 'Psych' Brooks was exactly where he should be—rotting in the ground. Marek had done the world a service when he'd extinguished that bastard's existence. Granted, his demise had been more brutal than what we were used to, but the ends justified the means.

"I have it on good authority that you were the last ones to see him alive."

"Oh yeah? Who told ya that?" Marek questioned. I personally couldn't wait for the day when we could teach Koritz a lesson, snatching his life once and for all.

Did I mention that the Knights were riding the legal side of the fence these days? Because that theory gets tested every once in a while.

A man who was a couple inches taller than Koritz sidestepped one of the DEA men and came into full view. It was dark and I couldn't make out much except that he was bald and stalky. When he moved under one of the lamps, however, I saw he wore a cut, but I couldn't make out the patch.

"You know where he is, and if you don't tell me I swear to Christ I'll rain holy hell down on your club." It was then I recognized his voice, had heard it a few times before. Unfortunately.

All of a sudden, an eruption the likes of which I'd never experienced before exploded around me, men screaming and barreling toward the intruder.

Rabid.

VP of the Savage Reapers.

Psych's right-hand man.

He dared to set foot on Knights soil?

Inside our compound?

The closest any fuckin' Reaper got to our clubhouse was outside the gates when they'd left me for dead, shot to all hell.

Koritz, along with his men, drew their weapons, and it was then we decided to show our cards as well. The smirk on the DEA agent's face would have been alarming if I'd thought enough to give a fuck.

"Well, it looks like you boys are in a bit of trouble." He puffed out his chest as best he could given his girth. "I'm sure those guns aren't registered." He made a move but stopped when Marek started shouting.

"Take one more step and I'll blow your head off, Koritz. Agent or not." The malice in Marek's voice left no room to wonder if he'd actually follow through or not. A glint of reservation flashed in Koritz's eyes, his men looking to one another for guidance. But they wouldn't find it. They dared to disrupt us, to show up on our doorstep asking about a worthless piece of shit. Adding to their stupidity, they brought Rabid with them. We should've killed them all just for that shit, but we didn't just have ourselves to worry about right then. The women in our lives took precedent over our need to show those fuckers who was boss. That didn't stop Hawke, Jagger, Stone, Ryder, and Cutter from spouting off at the mouth, though.

"Just get rid of 'em," someone shouted behind me, everyone's voices blending together and making it difficult to distinguish who was saying what.

"Fuck them for bringing that Savage piece of shit here," another yelled. If Marek didn't do something soon, all hell was gonna break loose, that much I knew for sure. Thankfully, Trigger had been able to keep the women away from this shit; otherwise, I had no doubt we'd be engaged in a whole other kind of standoff. And fuck Breck for passing out earlier. We needed all hands on deck in case shit went down, and based on all the hardware pointed at everyone's heads anything could happen.

Tense moments passed and still we all stood there, threatening the others in complete silence. Until our prez finally spoke up. I released the breath that was stuck in my lungs. I had no idea what Marek was gonna say, but at least it was somethin'.

"We don't know where Psych is, and we don't care. We're done with the war, have been for some time now," Marek spewed, his conviction a practiced one. If I hadn't known better I would've believed he spoke the truth. "Now unless you have a warrant, get the fuck outta here."

I got the feeling Marek wanted to say something else, but he surprisingly held his tongue. Probably for the best. We didn't need to invite any more trouble into our lives than was already present, although I was sure Koritz wasn't gonna stop until he'd buried us somehow. Literally or figuratively. Either way would be bad.

And Rabid . . . fuck! I thought for sure we were done with the Reapers, what with extinguishing their leader and all. But it looked like he was itchin' to start up a whole new war with our club.

Koritz eventually lowered his weapon, his men following suit. "I'll be in touch. You can count on that." The only thing we could do was watch in silence as they filed back into their vehicles and slowly backed out of our lot.

There was no resolution that evening, and there wouldn't be one for a very long time. I was sure of it.

Rabid knew our club was the last to see Psych alive, Marek, Stone and Jagger agreeing to meet him at the warehouse to exchange Sully for Adelaide and Kena. The rest of the men who'd accompanied Psych that day had all been extinguished, and looking back we should have chased down Rabid and taken him out as well, tied up all loose ends. But the VP of the Reapers had always been a follower, and we honestly thought once his prez was no longer in the picture, along with their supply being cut off from the cartel, that their club would've imploded from the inside.

Our arrogance had just come back to bite us in the ass.

EPILOGUE

Tripp

THE PAST TWO MONTHS HAD flown by in a blur. No matter how hard I tried, I couldn't find Rachel. It was as if she'd disappeared off the face of the earth, abandoning her kid like she didn't give a shit about the little boy. Then again, actions spoke louder than words, and while I'd initially been outraged at what she'd done, I came to believe that she knew she wasn't a fit mother, her selfishness for drugs clouding any maternal instinct she could have possibly had toward her own baby.

Even though only a short time had passed, the infant was growing quickly. Whenever Sully brought him by the clubhouse, there was a look of love and adoration in her eyes for the baby she cradled in her arms. I saw a peace come over not only her but Marek as well. The tension between husband and wife seemed to have evaporated, replaced by exhaustion, mostly due to late nights with the little boy would be my guess. If I asked my prez I was sure he'd tell me he'd prefer sleepless nights caused by a baby over all the other shit that had kept him up until the early morning hours.

All had been quiet where Reece's ex-husband had been concerned. She'd filed for divorce but her lawyer couldn't locate Rick, which wasn't a surprise to me, although I never let Reece in on that little tidbit of information. Not until now. I couldn't hide my secret any longer. Sure, I'd been a vault in the past, most of the club's dealings requiring the utmost discretion, and even though that would always remain, the situation with Reece was different. Outside the scope of what I was used to dealing with, so to speak.

"Reece?" I whispered. "Are you awake, baby?" She groaned, snuggling closer and slinging her arm over my chest, her head buried in the crook of my neck. The heat from her naked body made my dick twitch, as if I hadn't just exhausted him over the past couple hours.

"Reece?" I repeated, trying my best not to move because the feel of her next to me was too good.

"Uh-huh," she grunted, sleep still struggling to steal her from me.

"It's about Rick," I confessed. I hated bringing up his name while lying in bed with Reece but I had to tell her what happened. What I'd done. I knew I was risking her, risking *us*, but I didn't want that kind of secret between us.

Her eyes fluttered on my chest, her lashes causing an odd tickling sensation. The strands of her long hair cascaded over my arm as I continued to hold her tightly.

"I don't wanna talk about him." She was more awake than before but still groggy. "He's dead to me."

"Well, speaking of. . . ." I waited for the dawn of recognition to blossom in her brain. It didn't take long. She pushed herself up and bent her legs behind her, waiting for me to elaborate.

"What?" she prompted, rubbing her eyes with her palms to drive away the sleep once and for all. "Why did you say it like that?"

Not sure how to start off this particular conversation, I reached for her hand, wound my fingers with hers, opened my mouth and let the words flow. "He tried to come after you again." She gasped and I shook my head to stop her from responding. "Hawke was the one who actually spotted him. That guy was brazen."

I couldn't stop her from interrupting that time. "Was?" She tried to pull her hand from mine but I only held on tighter. "What are you telling me?" Her voice shook and her eyes widened. I feared she wouldn't understand what I'd done, even though she'd lived with the fear he'd find her and most likely would've ended up killing her.

"When Hawke saw him waiting in his car across the street from Indulge, he called me right away. My blood boiled at the thought that he was never gonna leave you alone. Never," I reiterated, trying like hell to drive home that she would've been in constant danger as long as he still breathed air into his lungs. "When we approached him, he tried to leave, but I ripped open his door and flung him onto the pavement before he could. Hawke did a quick search of his car and found a loaded gun in the console, along with a half empty bottle of whiskey."

"What did you do?" she whimpered, finally withdrawing her hand from mine. She moved back on the bed, the small distance between us like a knife to the chest.

"I had to, Reece. I had to get rid of him. Right before I shot him, he drunkenly confessed that he was gonna punish you for leaving him. That he was gonna kill you and then kill himself."

"He said he was gonna kill me?"

I wasn't sure why she was shocked by that.

"Yes."

"So you shot him?"

"Yes." My expression was blank. I wanted to smile, knowing Rick would no longer ever be a threat to Reece, but I knew it wasn't appropriate.

"Dead?" She looked to be in a state of shock.

"Yes." I kept repeating the same one-word answer, but it said every-thing. The truth. I'd snatched lives in the past, but this one felt more justified than most.

Because I loved her.

"Oh my God." Her eyes never left my face. Her expression mirrored my own, which was not good. It meant I couldn't get a read on what she was thinking or feeling.

So what did I do? I revealed feelings I'd been harboring for a little while now, blurting them out at the most inopportune time.

I reached across the bed and drew her close. Thankfully she didn't struggle, her surprise at what I'd told her incapacitating her refusal. Placing my hand on the back of her head, I pulled her so close the tips of our noses touched.

"I love you."

Her warm breath hit my lips, the need to kiss her more powerful than ever before. Her mouth parted but she didn't speak, not for an ex-cruciatingly long minute.

"You do?"

Not the response I was hoping for, but at least she didn't pull away in revulsion.

"Yes." Again with the one-word answer.

She continued to speak, glossing over the fact that I'd just told her that I loved her. Maybe she was in shock. Maybe she didn't feel the same. It didn't matter. I wasn't gonna lie; I would've loved to hear her say those three words back to me, but as long as she didn't run from me after hearing what I'd done, everything would be fine.

"I can't believe I made you kill him. I'm so sorry, Tripp. I never meant to drag you into my mess."

Wait . . .

What?

I pulled back so I could see her whole face. I needed her to really hear me, to understand that she wasn't responsible for any of what I'd chosen to do.

"You didn't make me do anything. I made that decision. More so for me than for you." Her frown showcased her confusion. "When I realized he'd never leave you in peace, it gutted me. To know that you could be snatched away from me at any given moment terrified me. And the only way to extinguish that worry was to snuff out the threat. So when I got the call from my brother, I seized the opportunity and ended it. Ended him."

Silence stretched between us, the slightly uncomfortable kind that was mixed with realization of our new reality.

I'd killed someone who had meant something to her at some point in her life, even though he turned out to be her worst mistake—her words, not mine.

When I couldn't take the quiet any longer, I asked, "What are you thinking?"

Reece moved the few feet toward the edge of the bed and swung her legs over, sitting upright next to me. She hung her head, her hair covering the side of her face. Gripping the edge of the mattress, she crossed her legs at the ankles. Her nakedness distracted me for a split second, memories of burying myself inside her enough to make my dick start to harden. Then she finally spoke, pulling all my attention back to the topic at hand.

"I'm not sure," she confessed. "On one hand I'm relieved that Rick will no longer come after me." She raised her head and looked at me. "I'll never be able to repay you for making me feel safe, Tripp. For the first time in my life . . . I feel free."

"But. . . ." I knew there was a 'but' in there somewhere.

Tears pooled behind her eyes. "But you killed him."

"Yeah, I did." A pain rippled through my chest, my breathing strangled and debilitating me while she continued to lock me in her gaze. I silently pleaded with her not to leave me because of a decision I felt I needed to execute—every fuckin' pun intended.

"I'm glad he's dead," she whispered, averting her eyes while lowering her head. "Does that make me a bad person?"

I gripped her thigh, my desire to touch her mixed with the need to gain her approval for what I'd done. "Does it make me a bad person that I killed him?"

"Yes." My heart sank. "No." A faint tremor of hope appeared. "I . . . I don't know."

This shit was all new to her, but unfortunately for me, it wasn't. Reece wrapped the sheet around her and stood, walking across the room and only coming to a stop when she'd reached the bedroom door. "I need some time to think," she said, clutching the sheet tighter before walking away from me.

———◆———

Reece

FOR AN ENTIRE WEEK, I'D successfully avoided Tripp. He'd given me the time and space I wanted without complaint. He refused to budge when I'd suggested staying somewhere else. Instead, he said he'd stay at the clubhouse until I decided to talk to him again. He understood why I needed to think about what'd happened, but the truth was that him killing Rick was only part of the reason why I needed to be alone.

The other reason was so I could wrap my head around the fact that his child was growing inside me, and I had no idea how he'd feel about that. His reaction to Rachel showing up and claiming he was the father of his child had set him off. Understandably, he was upset because he knew she was lying. Add in the mix that she'd cheated on him and it was a recipe for disaster when they saw each other again. But how much of his anger was because he thought for a brief moment that the baby was actually his? Did he even want kids? Would he react in a similar manner when I told him my news?

I could move past him killing Rick. I really could, even though it scared me that he'd taken a life. And while such a thing should terrify me, I hadn't been completely shocked. I may have been somewhat sheltered, all due to Rick's overbearing and suffocating ways, but I wasn't stupid.

Tripp was part of the Knights Corruption. They hadn't always been choir boys. Okay . . . 'choir boys' was a bit of a stretch, but my point was made. The men were intense, Tripp being no exception, but their love for their families overshadowed any wrongdoings that had been committed.

Naïve? Maybe, but I'd had the opportunity to really get to know Tripp, and what I knew was that . . .

I loved him.

Unequivocally.

Even before he'd expressed his feelings for me, I knew I'd fallen for him. The way he'd treated me, the way he'd made it his mission to keep me safe, the way he'd smile at me, touch me, kiss me—it all proved he loved me well before he'd uttered the words.

After another restless night's sleep, I'd finally decided to talk to Tripp and tell him everything.

———— ◆ ————

I PACED AROUND THE KITCHEN, glancing up at the clock for the millionth time that evening. How was I gonna broach the topic? Would I just blurt out, "I'm pregnant?" or would I beat around the bush, never quite finding the right words? What would happen if he didn't want the baby? If he no longer wanted me? I tried to put myself in his shoes, but I couldn't see past my own fears and paranoia. Our relationship was still new, and although we were learning more about each other every day, to introduce a baby now could destroy what we'd been trying to nurture.

My hand rested on my belly. I wasn't showing yet. I'd suspected I was pregnant the night Tripp told me everything, but I needed to see a doctor to confirm what the three store-bought tests revealed. The doctor said I was around eight weeks, and when I'd done my calculations, I figured it had happened when we had sex in the shower, the only time we hadn't used protection. We'd had discussions about birth control, both of us wanting to stop using condoms, but my body had always had a negative reaction to the pill. Funny thing was I'd made an appointment with a gynecologist to discuss other options. That appointment was set for the following week. I guessed there was no need to keep it anymore.

The roar of a motorcycle cut through my thoughts, increasing my anxiety over how our conversation would go. If Tripp decided that he wanted no part of the baby, or me going forward, then I'd walk away and raise him or her on my own. I knew it would be hard, and my heart would be broken, but my love for my unborn child was already growing deeper with each day that passed.

Taking a few deep breaths, I turned the handle of the front door, opening it up as Tripp walked up the front steps. I stepped back to allow him to enter, and as soon as he walked past me I knew I'd be more than heartbroken if he decided he didn't want to be a father. I'd be devastated. Seeing him again only drove home how much I loved him.

He headed toward the living room, choosing to stand near the couch instead of taking a seat. "Why did you want to see me?" His question was straightforward, a small bout of hesitation wafting off him. He was nervous. *Join the club.*

My eyes raked over him as he stood in front of me. His dark hair was disheveled, and three-day-old stubble prickled his jawline. He looked tired, but he had also never looked more beautiful. Odd word to describe a man like Tripp, but it was the God's honest truth. He was beautiful, inside and out. The rustle of his leather cut was a most welcome sound, and I had to remind myself to stop ogling him and get straight to it.

"Maybe you better sit," I instructed, pointing toward the sofa directly behind him. Without a word, he plopped down on the cushions, glancing up at me and waiting for me to tell him the reason I'd asked to see him.

"Okay, you're startin' to freak me out," he said, trying to grin but his expression fell flat. "Why don't you come sit next to me?"

"I need the space."

"Don't you think I've given you enough space? I mean, I know it's only been a week but I haven't called you, or shown up at the club to bother you. For fuck's sake, Reece, I told you I loved you and all you said was that you needed some time to think. I know you're unsure of me because of what I did, but don't tell me that you don't sleep better at night knowing that sick fucker can no longer hurt you." He took a deep breath, and I knew he would have continued had I not blurted out the real reason why I'd asked him to come over.

"I'm pregnant." My eyes widened at my bluntness. I'd planned on a different delivery, but I wanted him to stop rambling and saying things that only made me feel badly about the way I'd chosen to handle things between us.

He rose to his feet, his presence overwhelming me more than normal. He took a single step closer. "What did you say?"

Was he angry? Disappointed? Happy? I couldn't tell. His face was void of any expression.

"I'm . . . I'm pregnant."

He reached for me but I retreated. I had no idea why. Was I preparing myself for the hurt I'd start to feel as soon as he uttered the words I feared?

Was I still in a state of shock myself over the news that I was gonna be a mother? That my life was forever changed?

"Reece." My name flowed from his lips, his tone soft yet commandeering. "Come here." He reached out his hand and left it in midair, waiting for me to accept. He didn't have to wait long. As soon as our palms touched, I felt his love. His acceptance. He drew me closer, the small quirk of his lips telling me everything. He wasn't upset at all. The longer we looked at each other, the more apparent it became that Tripp was happy about my news.

"So you're not upset?" His delicious smell intoxicated me, almost to the point that I'd forgotten what we were talkin' about. Almost.

"Why would I be upset? Sure, it's a shocker, one I'm not quite sure how to process right now seeing as how we always used a condom, but I could never be upset about you telling me you're gonna have my kid."

"It happened when we had sex that one time in the shower . . . when I had my period," I blurted.

"That can happen?"

"Apparently," I responded.

"Good to know for next time." He chuckled, his attitude and demeanor toward the news making me love him that much more.

"There's something else I have to tell you." I snaked my hands around his neck and pulled him down so I could kiss him. He was so damn tall that sometimes I forgot how much shorter I was than him.

His breath tickled my lips. "If you tell me it's twins, I think I'm gonna have to sit back down for a minute." Although he was joking, I saw the flash of nervousness in his eyes.

"If I were having twins, I'd be joining you on that couch."

"So what is it?" His arms held me close, his fingers interlocking behind my back.

"I love you." No use in waiting a second longer to tell him how I felt. I should have said it the night he told me.

"That's the hormones talkin'." He tried to joke, but I knew he wanted to hear me say it again, possibly believing I hadn't meant those three precious words.

"No it's not." I smiled before pressing my lips to his once more. I needed to taste him, to breathe his air into my lungs and steal a small piece of his soul for my own. "I love you. More than I ever thought I could love someone. Ever since the first day we met you made me feel safe and protected. You gave me back a piece of myself that'd been missing for as long as I could remember." Tears welled up in my eyes, and although I told myself not to cry they came rushing forth anyway. "I can never repay you for that."

"You just did," he said, smiling before resting his hand on my belly.

RYDER

Elmarie—I dedicate the final ride of this series to you, someone I'm honored to call a friend. I adore your enthusiasm for my stories and truly appreciate all of your wonderful feedback.

PROLOGUE

MY HAND COVERED MY INJURED cheek while my lips moved in silence, praying to be saved from the monster who'd attacked me. Again. I wished for his death, and sadly, even at the tender age of seven, there were moments I wished for my own.

Still whispering my pleas, I finally opened my eyes. That was when I saw him standing in the doorway to my bedroom, huffing and puffing as if he'd run a hundred miles just to get to me.

Words formed in my throat, but when I opened my mouth to plead for him to leave me alone, only silence sounded. His black eyes stared me down, the intensity enough to make me cower on my bed. With my hands clutching the superhero blanket beneath me, I closed my eyes once more and tried to escape what was going to happen next. Unfortunately I knew all too well the pain I was about to endure in the next few minutes, although it would certainly feel like hours.

"Look at me, you little shit!" he thundered, pounding the doorframe for emphasis. When I refused, I heard him shuffle his heavy feet across the wooden planks of my bedroom floor. "What did I tell you about interrupting me and your mother?"

I'd woken to the sound of my mom begging him to stop. I knew what was happening and, although I was terrified, I had to help her. After racing from my room, I'd flown down the steps and found her crumpled on the living room floor, clutching her belly with one hand while the other was raised in the air to try to stop his next attack, blood dripping from her nose. As I ran toward her to try and protect her, I was hit so hard I flew across the room and crashed into the far wall. I was a small kid, weighing nothing at all, especially compared to the man terrorizing us. She tried to crawl toward me, but he stepped on her back, pinning her to the ground. With defeat in her voice, she told me to go back to my room, promising that she'd be all right. I didn't believe her but I didn't want her to watch him hit me again, so I scrambled to my feet and ran back to my room.

I heard him getting closer so I squeezed my eyes tighter, but my loss of sight didn't stop my mouth from opening.

"You're hurting my mom," I cried out.

"That's none of your business," he spat.

I tried my hardest not to appear scared, but I was. When I pried open my eyes, I saw him standing directly next to my bed, his hand on his belt buckle.

"I'll teach you not to interfere," he slurred, his stinky breath making me sick to my stomach. He'd been drinking that brown liquid again. He took another step closer, the belt loosening and sliding through the loops of his pants. Instead of holding on to it, however, he tossed it on the foot of my bed. "You'll learn your place in this house," he threatened as he unzipped his pants, a stranger than normal look in his eyes as he snagged my ankle and yanked me down the bed. Without much effort, he flipped me on my belly and knelt across my lower legs to keep me from getting away. "Don't fight me or you'll hurt yourself." I didn't understand what was about to happen.

Why wasn't he hitting me?

Why was I on my stomach?

Why was he taking his pants off?

Before I formed another silent question, I heard my mom screaming at him to get away from me. When the pressure on my legs lessened, I turned around and I saw that he had ahold of her hair, her arms swinging wildly, trying to hit him. "Don't you touch him, you bastard," she gasped, her breath coming in short spurts as she winced with every movement. She didn't care that she was bleeding, that bruises were forming on her face and arms, that some of her ribs were probably bruised or broken. Her only concern was for me.

He shoved my mother to the ground, grabbed the belt that had been tossed on my bed, knelt down next to her and wrapped it around her neck. Everything happened in slow motion and yet at a frenzied pace all at the same time. Her green eyes bulged wide, while her fingers scratched at the rough leather robbing the breath from her lungs.

"Noooo," I screamed as loud as I could, watching the life slowly start to drain from her face. Finding my last bit of strength, I launched off the bed and flew toward her, trying to loosen the belt, but it was useless. He was too strong.

When all of the fight had left my mom, he let go of the belt and stumbled backward, mumbling something only he could understand before disappearing from my room.

Burying my face in her neck, I cried harder than I ever had before, praying she would start breathing again. Hoping this was all a nightmare and I'd wake up any minute.

But it wasn't a nightmare.

My mom had just been murdered, a tragedy that shaped the person I would eventually become.

ONE

Ryder

THE MUSCLES IN MY HAND burned, the ache intensifying with no sign of relief. My knee was wedged into his back, holding him steady against the gravel beneath me. Rage bubbled inside me, overtaking any sense of rationality I had left, which was but a frazzled thread. Words tried to escape, but nothing passed my lips except my harsh breaths, panting like some kind of rabid animal.

Fury.

Revenge.

I felt it in spades but I couldn't move from the spot I was frozen in. I tried so hard to exact my kind of justice, but my mind was spiraling out of control, ensnaring me deep in its tight grasp.

"Ryder." I heard my name as if it'd been whispered. I'd been staring into the face of the man who'd changed my world forever, but his lips never moved. "Ryder," I heard again, that time a little louder. Before I could shout out and ask who said my name, the man I'd been pinning down vanished, as if he'd never even been there.

All of a sudden a sharp pain radiated through my leg. "Ryder!" A female voice captured the letters of my name, shouting out in fear and anger, both emotions mixed together to form a jolt that thrust me from whatever world had dragged me under, trapped in the deepest recesses of my mind. My eyes were already open, but as my vision tunneled and then expanded, I realized that Braylen was lying on her back . . . and I was pinning her to the mattress. Her legs were spread wide and flailing, my knee wedged between them to keep them apart. I'd captured both of her arms with my large hands, trapping her so she was utterly defenseless. That was until another wave of pain shot through my calf again.

"Fuck!" I yelled, staring down into the face of the woman who'd been sharing my bed for the past five months. Her wild blonde hair was fanned out on the pillow, the look in her eyes telling me she was gonna lay into me as soon as I fully came back into the moment.

"Get off me," she cried out. "You're hurting me." She bucked beneath me and, although she didn't possess the physical ability to budge me, her show of strength was enough to tell me she meant business. Before I could move, however, she kicked me again, that time the heel of her foot grinding into the tensed muscle of my calf.

"Goddamnit, Bray, stop fuckin' kickin' me."

Of course, she didn't listen, as was evident when another surge of pain hit. Knowing she wouldn't stop until she was released, I rolled off her and hit the mattress on my side of the bed. For as much as I wanted to massage my leg, I remained still, doing my best to catch my breath, trying to understand why I was on top of her in the first place.

"What the hell is wrong with you?" She sat up straight, scooting down the bed to put some distance between us. "I can't deal with this much longer. Your nightmares are getting worse, this time affecting *me*." It wasn't until I saw her clutching her forearms that I tried to move closer. I glanced from her arms to her face, cursing silently when I saw the first tear fall. I reached for her, but she moved back. "Don't touch me," she rasped, more tears falling down her reddened cheeks.

"I'm sorry." It was the only thing I could think of to say, although I knew those two words weren't enough to tell her how much I hated myself for hurting her, even though I had no idea I'd been doing it. I'd been trapped in another nightmare, helpless because I had no control when the past came to claim me.

Several minutes passed, allowing both of us to regain some sense of calm. When she finally cast her gaze toward me again, I saw her red and puffy eyes. Her breaths were still short and choppy, but not as erratic as when I'd first released her. I hated that I'd marked her, bruised her tender flesh while in the throes of my darkness.

"I'm sorry," I repeated, hoping she could see from my expression that I meant it. I was used to being guarded, keeping my past from everyone around me, including all of my brothers at the club. I figured if I told anyone it would make it real. I knew how ridiculous it sounded, my reasoning beyond irrational and fucked up, but it was how I chose to deal with my mother's death—keep it close and private. It was the only way to protect the last piece of myself.

"Why won't you ever tell me about your nightmares? Maybe I can help you," she whispered, already preparing herself for the anger she knew was coming, even though I knew damn well she didn't deserve any of it. Not that time, at least. Braylen certainly knew how to press my buttons, challenging me every single time she found an opportunity, but right then she was simply concerned.

An attribute I both appreciated and loathed.

Inhaling deeply, I clenched my jaw before shouting, "I told you I don't remember my fuckin' nightmares, so how the hell are you gonna help me?" I hopped off the bed and strode toward the bathroom, slamming the door before she could even respond. I knew she knew I was lyin', but I didn't want to give her a chance to call me on my bullshit.

After a hurried shower, I walked back into my bedroom only to be greeted with an empty space. Braylen left. I wasn't surprised, though. Not in the least. I'd been a real ass, first by bruising her, then yelling at her as if she was at fault for my fucked-upness.

I should've chased after her.

I should've called and attempted some sort of half-assed apology.

I should've told her what haunted my dreams.

But I couldn't do any of it. Instead, I collapsed on top of my bed, hoping she wouldn't curse me out too bad when I finally did contact her.

TWO

Ryder

SLAMMING BACK MY THIRD BEER, the alcohol did nothing to soothe my nerves. It'd been two days of silence from Braylen. Normally, I'd give her the time she needed, especially since I was usually the cause of her anger. Although for some reason, this time was bothering me more than normal. Was it because what I felt toward the woman had been intensifying over the past month?

But safety lived in silence and denial. It was how I'd survived this long, and I refused to change because of a woman.

Trying to push aside all thoughts of Braylen Prescott, I focused on gettin' piss drunk and passing out. And since Trigger refused to serve me hard liquor, knowing damn well what happened when that stuff coursed through my veins, I had to drink what he offered—beer. But as long as it did the trick, I wouldn't complain. Not too much, anyway.

"You're unusually ornery tonight," Trigger acknowledged. "What's up your ass?" Slinging a towel over his shoulder, he went about cleaning up behind the bar. Trigger was the club's resident bartender, lending an ear to those who needed it and givin' shit to those who deserved it. Apparently I was the latter. Tucking strands of his graying hair that had come loose from his ponytail behind his ear, he locked eyes with me and waited for me to engage.

"Ornery? Since when did you start breakin' out the big words?" I swallowed the rest of my drink, tapping the bar to indicate another. "Did you get one of those 'word a day' calendars? Deciding to test out your fake smarts on the likes of us?" My laugh was humorless. Giving someone else a hard time helped to take the attention off myself.

"Just because your dumb ass has a limited vocabulary doesn't mean we all do," he retorted, sliding a fresh glass my way.

I never let on that I was a smarty in school. High honors and all that good stuff. School came easily to me, numbers and theories the easiest. It was how I was able to help invest a lot of the club's earnings years back, setting us all up for life with the returns.

"Whatever." Focusing on losing myself to the suds in front of me, I zoned out and thought of nothing except becoming sloshed enough to barely keep my head up. But I should've known it wouldn't be that easy, not planting my ass on a barstool at the club. When I'd arrived earlier, only Trigger was present, the rest of the guys out taking care of what they needed to before gathering back together.

Most days I loved the company, even though I was more on the quiet side, sittin' back and takin' it all in. But right then, I wanted nothing more than to be left alone.f Those hopes were dashed as I heard Breck, Cutter, Jagger and Tripp stride through the entrance.

"Holy shit!" Tripp shouted. "What brings you here, stranger?" The nomad of the club strolled toward me, clasping me on the shoulder once he closed in on me. "Where the hell you been?"

"I was just here the other day," I gritted, keeping my simmering temper in check.

"Last week," Cutter said as he walked toward the kitchen. If I thought I was a quiet one, Cutter had me beat, usually only speaking when he wanted to call people out on their bullshit.

"He's too busy wrapped up in Braylen's pussy," Breck taunted, taking the seat next to me. *Does he have some sort of death wish?* "Tell us, Ryder, does she have a magic cunt?" He laughed, but it was cut short when I jumped up and hauled him off his chair by the scruff of his neck. There was a quick flash of fear in his eyes, but it was gone seconds after glancing at my drink of choice. Had I been drinking hard liquor, he probably would've pissed himself because he knew what I was capable of when it passed my lips. They all did. They'd seen it. Hell, they'd had to beat and restrain me to get me to calm the fuck down. Or pass out. Whichever came first.

"What?" Breck laughed. He was the complete opposite of his father. His unkempt shoulder-length brown hair and beard were way past due for a trimming. The biggest difference, however, was his ability to spout off at the mouth and irritate the fuck out of most of us because he never knew when to shut up. "It's an honest question. We all wanna know." He brought his drink to his lips even as I held him tightly in my grasp, spilling the contents down his front when I shoved him away from me. "Fuck," he mumbled, wiping the dots of beer off his cut.

After chugging down the rest of my beer, I attempted to leave but Tripp stopped me, stepping in front of me and arching a brow. "You good?" Two simple words. Too bad he had no idea how complicated his question really was.

"Yup."

"Good, 'cause you're up tonight."

"For what?" I racked my brain to try and figure out what he was talkin' about, but I came up short.

"Jagger's fight. It's you and me, brother." A slight smile curved up the corners of Tripp's mouth, trying his best to lighten my darkened mood. The nomad knew I had secrets, a mistakenly shared word here and there during our convos, but he had no idea what I'd been through before becoming a part of the club. None of them did, and that was how I wanted to keep it. I didn't need anyone's sympathy or pity. That would only make it worse.

"Fine," I agreed, sidestepping his large frame. "Send me the time and location," I shouted over my shoulder as I approached the door to leave.

Straddling my bike and kicking over the engine, I couldn't help but be annoyed at the fact that I had to attend Jagger's fight that evening, simply because I wasn't in the mood. But before I let the thought rattle me too much, I remembered there was a good chance Braylen would be there, seeing as her sister, Kena, was Jagger's woman. And far be it from Braylen to let her little sister out of her sight for too long.

THREE

Braylen

THE LAST THING I WANTED to do was attend Jagger's fight with Kena, but I hated leaving her alone, even though I knew at least two of the other guys from the club would be there, protecting Jagger and his winnings, even though Jagger could take out anyone who challenged him. There was more to their show of support, and while I didn't know the full story, I knew it was serious. Something coded spoken once about the Savage Reapers.

Ryder and Jagger sheltered my sister and me as much as they could, which sometimes seemed a bit too much. I fought Ryder when he made ridiculous demands, but somehow he always won. It was quite infuriating, to say the least.

Usually I was the last person who would shrink away from confrontation, but I'd been deliberately avoiding him. Well, his phone calls, to be more precise. Surprisingly he hadn't shown up at the salon where I worked, giving me time and space instead. And while I had no idea whether or not he'd be at the fight that evening, chances were good that he would be.

Why don't you wear this? Kena signed, a tentative smile on her beautiful face while she waited to see if I'd give her any sort of resistance.

My younger sister had developed a viral infection when she was an infant, damaging the nerves in her larynx which prohibited her from ever speaking a single word. My family had learned sign language, even though many times we chose to speak since she could hear us.

"I'm really not up to going. I'm tired," I lied, walking past her to grab my cell from the charging dock. Checking to see if I had any messages, even though I wouldn't respond even if Ryder had contacted me, I busied myself unlocking the device. I kept my head down since that was a surefire way of avoiding my sister.

Strands of my blonde hair flew around me as fabric suddenly covered my vision. Swiping at the material, I realized it was the top Kena had just presented to me. The bitch had thrown it at me. Normally my sister was docile, but apparently not then.

"What the hell?"

Stop avoiding him. Besides, don't you want to make sure nothing happens to me? The smirk on her face told me she knew damn well what she was doing—drawing on my need to perpetually keep her safe. Normally, Kena hated my overbearing ways, but right then she played on my fears that something would happen to her if I wasn't around to protect her. My fears weren't all that irrational, however. It wasn't long ago that she'd been kidnapped right along with Adelaide, the VP's woman. They'd been taken by the Reapers but thankfully had been retrieved unharmed, except for some physical bruising. The mental aspect of the incident, however, was something my sister chose to keep to herself, even with all of my incessant prodding.

"I'm not avoiding him. I've just been busy." I saw from the quirk of her manicured brow that she didn't believe one word of my careless untruth. "I'm not," I repeatedly lied.

I'd told her about what happened with Ryder, how he'd held me down while trapped inside some crazy nightmare, essentially scaring me half to death in the process. While she'd been concerned about me, she'd also been worried about Ryder. Kena had become fond of the brooding man, explaining that any guy who could periodically render me speechless had to be someone special indeed.

You and I both know you're hiding from him, but if you really don't wanna go tonight, then don't. I'm sure I'll be fine. She pouted, telling me she didn't want to go by herself, for whatever reason.

After several very long seconds, I relented. "Fine, I'll go, but I'm not gonna enjoy myself."

We'll see about that.

"I guess we will," I mumbled, more to myself than anything.

After I finally finished dressing, I glanced at my reflection in the mirror, making sure I looked appropriate enough for public view. I wasn't vain by any means, but I did care about how I looked when I stepped outside. My highlighted tresses fell just below my shoulder blades in soft waves. As far as my makeup went, I chose to keep it simple with two coats of mascara and a lightly tinted lip gloss.

You look great. Dressing up for anyone in particular? Kena teased, plopping down on the edge of my bed.

"What are you talking about? I'm not wearing anything special." Looking down, I was confused as to why she thought I'd put any extra effort into the clothes I'd chosen. A simple black tank top that scooped low in front to show a bit of cleavage, paired with my favorite dark skinny jeans and my go-to red heels were oceans away from being special. While I believed I looked good, my outfit wasn't anything out of the ordinary.

My sister smiled wide. She loved to get me going, probably paying me back for all the times I aggravated her. Ours was a special sisterly relationship, both of us caring for the other deeply. But there were times, like right then, when one of us couldn't help but razz the other. It was all done in good fun, so I smiled back and released most of the tension pent-up inside me.

"You look nice too," I said, playfully shoving her shoulder as we walked toward the front door. Holding my phone tightly, I chanced a look at the screen once more before the night air hit me.

Ryder

THE SMELL OF BODY ODOR, piss, and cheap cologne drifted to my nose as I positioned myself against the farthest wall, waiting for Jagger to emerge from the back room. His impending bout started in five minutes, the screams and shouts from numerous groupies making my ears ring they were so damn excited.

Surprisingly Kena and Braylen hadn't arrived yet, an odd fact since Jagger told me they were coming. I hadn't asked him—he'd volunteered the information, mumbling something about some goddamn look on my face, how it was sad and pathetic. I'd ignored him, choosing to focus on what would happen once I saw Braylen. Would she continue to ignore me? Would I ignore her in turn?

Shaking my head to rid my brain of the back and forth, I lifted my chin toward Tripp when I saw him enter. A few strides and he'd sidled up next to me.

"What the fuck is that smell?" he asked, grimacing as he pulled the top of his shirt over his nose. "It smells horrible in here. Jagger really needs to find other places to fight."

"Who cares what the place smells like? As long as he wins and gets paid, nothing else matters."

"Still. . . ."

Dropping the material shrouding his nostrils, Tripp opened his mouth to say something else when Jagger came bursting out of the back room, searching the area before settling his eyes on us. Stomping forward, he reached us in record time, looking worried and frazzled.

At first glance, the guy looked in control. Fierce even. His dark blond hair was shaved on the sides, the top strands longer than the rest. Slicked back and in place, the style was enough to ensure he could see his opponent without obtrusion. It also enhanced his etched features, which were pinned with worry for some reason.

"Where is she?" he asked, looking past us into the adrenaline-filled crowd.

"Who?"

"Kena. She's supposed to be here. She said she'd be waiting for me before my fight. It's not like her to be late." His fists clenched at his sides, the sign that he was subject to blow in a few seconds if he didn't find what was keeping his woman.

Kena was punctual, though her sister was always late. If they were coming together, it could explain her absence.

I couldn't deny that Braylen had somehow burrowed inside me, alighting on my nerves in both aggravation and intrigue. Passion and annoyance. The woman was something else, a firework in the darkest of nights.

I would've loved to say there was a quiet innocence and grace about her, but anyone who knew Braylen knew that wasn't entirely accurate. An embellishment of the highest degree, to be more exact. Every time she entered the room, she lit it up with her presence, her fierceness and undeniable sex appeal. Although the last trait was for me and me alone. She'd shoot off at the mouth at the drop of a hat, misinterpreting situations quite often. She ranted and raved first, then asked questions, but only after she'd calmed down enough to allow me to speak. And by speak, I mean kiss the hell out of her until she had no other choice but to calm down.

"Here they come," Tripp announced, pulling his phone from his pocket and taking a step toward the aisle. "You got this?" He cocked his head toward the two women fast approaching.

"Yeah."

"Be right back." No doubt he was checking in with Reece, his woman, who was pregnant with his kid. It seemed everywhere I looked lately the guys were knockin' up their ol' ladies. First Stone and Adelaide, and now Tripp had fallen down that rabbit hole. I didn't have anything against kids—I had one of my own—but I sure as hell didn't want to start all over again at thirty-four.

Jagger pulled Kena toward him, wrapping his arms around her and giving everyone quite the show. Damn, the guy was smitten, but I couldn't blame him. Kena was pretty damn cool, never seeming to give my friend much of a problem. Not like her sister with me.

Speaking of . . .

Braylen shot me a warning glance before trying to shuffle down a nearby aisle, squeezing past a few guys who seemingly didn't want to keep their hands to themselves. As I pushed off the wall, intent on wiping the floor with the asshole who dared grab her ass, my steps faltered when I saw her whip around and slap the guy across the face. Even over the roar of the frenzied crowd, I heard the impact.

Thankfully, for her and for me, the fucker seemed embarrassed enough to mouth something before looking down at the ground. Was it because he feared another smack from the feisty blonde, or could it have been the death daggers I shot his way when he looked around to see who'd witnessed the assault? While I was proud of Braylen for sticking up for herself, she had no idea how much danger she'd just put herself in for slapping that bastard. Had I not been present, would he have snatched her up and hurt her? I knew how the world worked, about all of the evil contained within, but Braylen was clueless. For as ballsy as that chick was, she lived in a bubble. Something we fought about on occasion.

I was always right, and she hated when I pointed it out.

Peering over at me, she looked away as soon as our eyes connected. She wanted to appear unaffected by my presence, but I saw the way her body reacted when she knew I was looking—no, staring. Her taut muscles locked up tight and the heave of her chest increased; it was slight but noticeable. Her tits looked amazing in that fuckin' black top, her ass round and delectable in her painted-on jeans. If I wasn't so intent on playing aloof, I would've approached, snatched her up and taken her back to my place right then and there. But because I wasn't entirely sure she wouldn't sting my cheek with a smack, I stayed planted against the wall. Not that I didn't encourage a bit of feistiness in the bedroom, but it wasn't the time or the place.

I knew Braylen well enough to know that if I pushed her too far, she'd continue to give me the cold shoulder. And while her silence gave me the room to try and come to grips with the shit I'd been dealing with—or pushing back down for my subconscious to bury again—I needed to be with her. To feel her against me. To taste her.

I could toss it up to simply being horny, but even though I knew it was more than hormones, I refused to acknowledge the fact that I was becoming more and more attached to her. My survival was key, emotional as well as anything else.

Entirely consumed with my own thoughts, I hadn't even seen Tripp approach, grumbling to himself as he came to stand next to me once again.

"Fuckin' women," he muttered, shoving his hands in his pockets while looking off into the distance.

He'd just given me the opportunity to focus on someone other than myself for a moment. "Reece okay?"

"Yeah, she's great. Just ask her." Sarcasm dripped off him. Tripp looked a little more than put out, and even though he'd be the first to poke fun at me, he'd also be willing to lend an ear.

"What's the problem? She not givin' you any now that you knocked her up?"

Cocking his head, he narrowed his eyes before flashing an arrogant smirk.

"No problem there. In fact, she's all over me." Bending his leg, he braced himself on the wall behind us, his smirk fading as quickly as it had appeared. "She told me she wasn't feeling well before I left, so I convinced her to call off from work. But when we just spoke, she told me she decided to go in after all." He stopped talking, looking at me as if I had a fuckin' clue as to what the problem was.

"So?"

"What do you mean 'so'? She's fuckin' pregnant. Every time she goes to work she puts herself and my kid in danger. I've told her I want her to quit, and she agreed, but she keeps pushing back the date. First it was gonna be last month, but then she told me that Carla needed to keep her on until she found her replacement. I spoke to Carla. Reece lied to me. Problem is I have no idea why." Becoming more upset the longer he spoke, he released a barrage of curses before slamming the sole of his boot against the concrete wall.

"Maybe she's pissed you're makin' her quit," I blurted, not entirely believing what I was saying. I couldn't even imagine how much my ears would be ringing if I ever tried to convince Braylen to quit her job. Granted, the salon where she worked was worlds different than Indulge, one of the club's strip joints, but Braylen still had male clients. Customers who wanted in her pants. I was positive of it.

"*She* agreed with me. So why would she be pissed?"

"That's like asking me why the sky's blue, my brother. I'm as clueless as you are when it comes to understanding how chicks think." Tearing my eyes away from Braylen—who continued to ignore me, even though

I saw her look in my direction every now and again—I gave Tripp my full attention. "From what you've told me, your woman's been through some shit. Maybe her job is some kind of security or somethin'. And now that she has to give it up, it's messin' with her." I sought out Braylen again. "My guess, anyway."

Before we could continue our conversation, Jagger stepped into the cage, cracking his neck from side to side and bouncing on his feet. He'd never been the showboater the other fighters were, but he seemed to steal the audience's attention each and every time.

The next fifteen minutes passed with the both of us just watching everyone else, on guard in case any unwanted guests showed up. Ever since Koritz, the crooked DEA agent, showed up at our club—and with Rabid, the Savage Reapers' VP, no less—an unsettling awareness shrouded everyone involved with the Knights Corruption.

The men were uneasy, just waitin' for shit to pop off, and the women were affected by our moods, even though they had no clue what was really going on.

We thought we'd put the war to bed between our two clubs when we took out Psych, only to find out that his club was hell-bent on finding out where he was and what had happened to him.

Too bad they'll never know . . . or find his rotting corpse.

As Jagger was declared the winner, he strode from the cage and barreled toward Kena, snagging her hand and pulling her toward the back of the room. Lifting his chin toward me before kissing his woman, he pointed toward the office on the second floor. It was code for "Watch my woman while I get my money."

Tripp flanked me on my left side while the women stood on my right. Braylen had still made no move to talk to me, and after another five tense minutes, I deemed enough was enough.

FIVE

Ryder

"WATCH HER," I INSTRUCTED TRIPP, referring to Kena, and seized Braylen's wrist, pulling her behind me toward the Exit sign. At first she didn't fight because I'd caught her off guard, but as we entered the night air, she tried to pull her hand from mine.

"Let go," she shouted, yanking her arm back a few times before I finally released her. "What is wrong with you? You can't just manhandle me whenever you want to."

Ignoring her question, I fired off one of my own. "Why didn't you respond to any of my texts or take any of my damn calls? You can't still be that pissed at me for the other night." As soon as I asked the question, I knew my fuckup. What I referred to was when I balked at her before disappearing into the bathroom, not the memory of pinning her to the bed beneath me.

"Are you kidding me?" she yelled, taking a step backward. I reached for her but she shook her head. "I wake up to you lying on top of me, bruising my arms because you were holding me down while you were dreaming. You had no idea I was even there until I shouted your name."

"And kicked me," I reminded her. A half smirk found its way onto my lips.

Not the right time.

"It's not funny, Ryder. You could've choked me to death."

"My hands weren't near your neck," I rebuked.

"But they could've been. What happens next time when you decide to wrap your hands around my throat?"

"I wouldn't do that."

"You had no idea what you were doing the other night, so how can you be so sure?"

"Because I would never hurt you." Scratching at the hairs covering my jawline, I did my best to convince her I believed the ridiculous words spewing from my mouth.

"Not intentionally," she whispered, the breeze stealing her words and swirling them around me like a tornado. Braylen put another foot of space between us.

"Stop moving away from me like you're scared of me, Bray. I don't like that shit." My head ached, all muscles in my body suddenly becoming too sensitive to the anxiety coursing through me. I hated the look of doubt shadowing her eyes, as if she wanted to come to me yet refused to move because she wasn't sure she should.

Hell, I didn't know if she should either.

I'd battled with the fear that I could've hurt her that night. I could've snuffed out her life, all the while having no fuckin' clue I'd even done it. Not until I woke up. Then what would I have done? How would I ever explain something like that to the club? To her family?

Dangerous.

The only word to describe what I was when it came to Braylen sleeping next to me, innocent and unknowing.

Silence drifted between us because neither of us knew what to say at that point. I hated the physical space separating us but I understood it, although I'd never let on.

Don't show any vulnerability. It was my motto since I was a kid, and in that moment it was being put to the motherfuckin' test.

As her lips parted to finally speak, a rousing burst of noise erupted behind us. A large crowd of people emerged, halting any thoughts that I'd get any further with Braylen right then.

"Come back to my place," I said, clenching my hands at my sides in preparation for her refusal.

"No." Blunt and to the point.

"Why?"

"Because there's something going on with you, and until you can tell me what it is, I can't help you." She bit her lower lip, averting her eyes to behind me every few seconds, no doubt waiting for her sister to join us.

"It was one night. One incident. Let it go," I rasped, pissed that I had to defend my fucked-up dream once again. I didn't want to delve back into my past, and that was exactly what would happen if I entertained telling her.

"It wasn't just one night." Her voice rose over the shouts of the people milling around us. "You've been acting weird for at least two months."

Dammit! That was about how long it'd been since the nightmares had returned.

Again, I refused to acknowledge what she said as anything but crazy talk. Before my brain could formulate a response, however, the back door to the building flung open. Tripp, Jagger, and Kena appeared, laughing and looking like everything was peachy fuckin' keen.

Well it wasn't.

Not for me, and apparently not for Braylen either.

One look from her sister and Kena rushed to her side, pulling her farther away from me and signing frantically, glancing back at me a couple times. Realizing I'd lost the battle, I gave up trying to convince Braylen to come home with me and joined my buddies.

"What's up with those two?" Tripp asked, slapping me on the back before removing his phone from his cut. Putting the device to his ear, he gave me a sideways glance while waiting for whoever he'd called to answer.

"Who the fuck knows," I grumbled. I had no desire to talk about it right there in the middle of the goddamn street. Jagger walked toward the women, watching the back and forth between the two of them before turning his head to look at me. He smirked, no doubt lovin' that I was the one in hot water. I hated that he could understand everything they were signing while I stood there like a dumbass, completely ignorant.

Finally, Jagger walked back toward me, grinning and shaking his head.

"Fuck off."

"Hey, I'm not the one givin' you shit." Jagger chuckled, slinging his black bag over his shoulder.

"What was she sayin'?" I didn't want to ask, but the need to know gnawed at my insides like some kind of insect.

"That she really wishes you would open up and let her in. That she's really concerned about your emotional sanity and wants to be there for you, to help you through whatever drama has you trapped in such a state that you shut down and lash out whenever something happens."

At first, I thought Jagger was telling me the truth, that she'd really said all that stuff, until he burst out laughing.

"What the fuck?" I growled, flashing him my most menacing look, but apparently I was losing my touch, or Jagger knew me well enough to not be afraid of me.

"Sorry, I couldn't resist, man."

"What. Did. She. Fuckin'. Say?"

"She said you're actin' like an ass, and that if you don't start talkin' soon, you can forget about her . . . or somethin' like that." Jagger walked away before I could ask him to repeat what he'd said, laughing at my misfortune of having to deal with Braylen's stubborn ass.

I knew Jagger was heading back to their place, so I straddled my bike, turned over the engine and took off down the street, not once looking at Braylen as I passed. I couldn't. Otherwise, I'd toss her over my ride and kidnap her, kicking and screaming.

And something told me that wouldn't go over too well.

SIX

Braylen

ALL I COULD THINK ABOUT while lying in bed that evening was Ryder and how clueless he was to just how detrimental his actions toward me had been. And how he refused to tell me exactly what was going on with him. He played it off as no big deal, as if it was normal to attack someone while in the throes of a nightmare. But it sure as hell wasn't.

Ryder had been acting funny for a couple months, although I couldn't pinpoint exactly how. It was a gut feeling, a warning that something explosive would erupt soon enough, and I wasn't entirely sure I wanted to be around to help pick up the pieces.

While I cared for him—more than I wanted to, honestly—I feared that he'd destroy me if he continued to keep me in the dark.

If secrets festered long enough, they would devour a person's soul, leaving them black and dying on the inside, blocking the smallest glimpse of healing light.

———— ◆ ————

"WORK YOUR MAGIC, SWEETHEART." TAKING a surprised breath, I lowered my arm to my side, the lightweight shears almost slipping from my fingers. I'd been lost in thought yet again and had completely ignored the client sitting in my chair. Taking a step back, I tried to gather myself, but it was too late. He'd seen my loss of focus. "Are you okay?"

"Um . . . yeah. Sure. Sorry about that. Now where were we?" I plastered on a big fake smile and turned his chair to the side so I could better assess the length of his hair, which hadn't grown too much since I'd seen him two weeks prior.

George had become a regular client of mine, his incessant need to make sure his hair was trimmed every couple weeks kind of amusing. But hey, I wasn't complaining. Besides, he was a great tipper.

I had the good fortune to work at my best friend's salon, Transform. Sia offered me a job as soon as I graduated cosmetology school, promising me a lucrative career with her clientele. I not only worked with all things hair, of course, but I was also certified in nails, waxing, etc. Name it, and I did it, which put me a leg up from most of the other women who worked there.

After only a year, Sia offered me the manager position, telling me she was desperate for someone with my organizational and people skills. And while the offer, complete with generous salary, was indeed tempting, all I wanted to do was come in, handle my shifts, chat with my clients and perform the magic on them they'd come to expect from me.

Sia was disappointed but understood. She ended up hiring a string of interim managers, none of them having what it took to help run an upscale salon. Because I felt bad and wanted to help her out until she found someone more permanent, I agreed to assist with some of the duties if she handled the rest—mainly dealing with the staff. I took care of inventory and bookkeeping while she dealt with scheduling, the stylists and whatever else popped up that required her attention.

"Just the usual today." He smiled at me as I turned his chair back toward the mirror.

"You know, I might start to think you have a crush on me," I teased, snapping the black cape closed that I had draped over him to protect from hair shavings.

"Who says I don't," he replied, winking at my reflection before flashing me his pearly whites. "Why do you think I come in so often?"

"I thought you had an agenda." I returned his smile as I ran my fingers through his short tresses. There wasn't much for me to do except clean his edges and polish him up. After ten minutes, I'd done all I could, turning him from side to side to make sure everything looked even.

I walked around his chair to stand in front of him, bending down to check out the front of his hair. My eyes were glued to his blond strands while his were glued to my breasts. My V-shaped top certainly showed a bit of cleavage, nothing obscene, although apparently the display was enough. Clearing my throat, his green eyes popped up to mine, a wolfish grin on his face at the knowledge that he'd been caught, although he didn't appear embarrassed by it. Not entirely, at least.

I figured there could be worse things in life than having the attentions of a handsome man. George appeared to be close to my age of twenty-four, although he could've been a couple years older. He looked young but distinguished. During one of our conversations, he'd told me he was a corporate lawyer of some sort. He stopped talking about his job when he saw my eyes glaze over. I'd apologized, telling him I didn't understand anything he'd tried to explain. He didn't seem put out by my lack of interest, thank God, as was apparent with the fifty-dollar tip he left me, and when he returned time and time again to sit in my chair.

On top of being successful before the age of thirty, he was stereotypically handsome. A full head of thick hair, light green eyes, and a sculpted jawline. His face was clean-shaven, giving him that younger appeal. The only thing not symmetrical on him was a tiny bump on the bridge of his nose, but it did nothing to detract from his good looks. But for as handsome as he was, he just wasn't my type.

Apparently my type was a dark-haired, rugged-looking, stubborn biker who was a pain in my ass as of late. Oh hell, who was I kidding? Ryder had been a pain in my ass since the first day I met him. Since he'd so eloquently told me that I needed a good fuck to calm me down.

"So, tell me, Braylen. Do you have a man?" George's words drew me back into the present. He was staring up at me, waiting for me to say something, but when I opened my mouth to answer, a rough voice cut me off, shutting down any reply I had. Stealing my choice to tell him I was indeed involved with someone, although we were kind of going through some stuff at the moment. Of course, I would've censored my response.

"Yeah, she does." Whipping around, I saw Ryder standing ten feet behind me, glaring at George's reflection in the mirror, looking all intimidating and . . . sexy.

Oh for the love of God, stop lusting after him while he's embarrassing the hell out of you.

"What are you doing here?"

"Apparently interrupting something." His mood was sour. His tall, broad frame was drawn tight, the muscles of his bare forearms dancing under the weight of his obvious displeasure. Ryder stood there in all his stubborn, infuriating glory, dressed in dark-washed jeans, a white T-shirt, and his Knights Corruption leather vest—or cut, as he often referred to it. He'd just witnessed another man openly flirting with me; I knew it was only a matter of seconds before he snapped. I had to do something and fast before the situation escalated out of control.

"I'll be right back, George," I offered, giving him an apologetic smile before removing his cape.

"Sure thing. I'll wait right here." What he said was innocent enough, but Ryder jumped all over him anyway.

"I think it's best you get outta here before I toss you out on your ass." Ryder took a step forward, but I stepped in front of him, blocking his advance toward my client. Pushing on his chest, I tried my best to move him back, but he continued to shoot daggers at the guy. I thought I heard George snicker, but I couldn't be sure. Either way, I had to remove Ryder from the salon before he really caused a scene. As it was, a few of the other employees and their clients were casting wary glances toward us.

"Go outside," I rasped, unable to contain my anger any longer because of the embarrassment he'd caused me. "Now!" I whisper-shouted as I shoved at him once more. The man was like a goddamn marble statue, unyielding except for the flicker in his eyes telling me he'd comply.

Reaching for my hand, he clasped it tightly and practically dragged me from the salon, walking briskly down the sidewalk until we were out of sight from any onlookers inside Transform. Thankfully there weren't too many people milling around outside, everyone locked up inside the shops and spending their money.

"What the fuck, Braylen?"

"What is wrong with you?" I asked, choosing to ignore his question. "What are you even doing here?" My back faced the concrete wall between a high-end boutique and a fancy shoe store. I kept my eyes pinned to his, and for several seconds we entered some sort of deranged staring contest, both of us trying to mentally overpower the other.

Ryder eventually broke. "What are *you* doing?"

"Working. What does it look like?"

"It looked like that guy was hitting on you and you were lovin' it," he snarled, the veins in his neck protruding with every spoken word. *I walked right into that one.* "Tell me I'm wrong. I dare you." His dark eyes turned black in his self-induced delirium.

I couldn't believe he thought I was interested in George, or any other man for that matter. He had to know that, even though I was upset with him and needed some time, I only had my sights set on him.

"Yes and no," I answered, huffing out a breath when his nostrils started to flare. "You need to calm down, Ryder. That's not what I meant."

"What the fuck did you mean, then?" He took one step closer, the warmth from his body igniting my own. He looked savage, and although I chastised myself for even feeling this way . . . I was undoubtedly turned on.

"George is harmless."

"*George* is not harmless. That guys wants to fuck you."

Our conversation wasn't going as planned. Not at all.

"Maybe he does." Ryder flinched, his hands curling into fists at his sides. *Wrong thing to say.* "But does that mean he gets to? No, of course not. I'm not interested in him. I only engage him because he's a great tipper."

Without hesitation, he growled, "Well I got a fuckin' *tip* for ya: stop flirtin' or you'll never see him again. Got it?" His fists uncurled, and his flattened hands ran the length of his jeans as if he was somehow self-soothing, doing his best to calm down. He took another step toward me like some sort of feral predator. Anger danced behind his eyes, along with jealousy, but I knew he wouldn't physically hurt me. Not while he was awake, at least.

As I opened my mouth to reply to his outlandishness, Sia approached us, her hands on her hips as she took in the scene. "You okay, Bray?" My friend and employer was all of five feet two with short pink hair. She looked whimsical and fierce all wrapped into one. She could be your best friend, as she was mine, or your worst enemy.

While I loved her concern, she was the last person I wanted to deal with. I had enough on my plate.

"She's fine," Ryder answered for me, not once turning to look in her direction.

"Well, I'm not asking you. I'm asking my friend," she shot back, taking a few steps closer. "Do you want me to call the cops?"

That question had Ryder whipping his head toward Sia, glaring at her as if he wanted her to crumble into pieces in front of him.

"No, of course not. It's all just a misunderstanding," I lied. "Ryder was just leaving." I held eye contact with her, silently pleading with her to return to the salon so I could convince Ryder to leave without further incident.

Tapping her foot, she narrowed her eyes before turning around and walking back toward her livelihood.

As far as I knew, Sia had no issue with Ryder. She'd met him on a few different occasions, and the main thing she'd uttered was that he was hot. But then he went and messed with her business, potentially scaring off one of her clients, which she undoubtedly took personally. And I couldn't say that I blamed her.

"You have to go." My back was pressed against the cool wall, my hands coming up in front of me to ward off Ryder's attempt to pull me close.

He ignored my nonverbal communication and advanced, regardless of the hesitant look he saw on my face. Or at least I hoped that was the look I portrayed. Because there was another one—lust. For as maddening as the man standing before me was, he was everything I'd ever dreamed of in a partner.

Well, mostly. I'd prefer him without the secrets and the potential danger following him everywhere. While he swore his club was no longer involved with anything illegal, that they'd gone legit a while back, it didn't assuage my feelings that something bad could happen where he and the rest of the Knights Corruption were concerned.

Refusing to give life to all the random thoughts firing around inside my brain, I tried my best to focus on one thing at a time—specifically Ryder and his incessant need to drive me crazy, of both the good and bad persuasion. The silent battle of wills wore on me, to the point that I was the one who caved that time around.

"You need a haircut." I had no idea why I said what I did, but it seemed to relax him, all while doing the opposite to me. The last thing I wanted was to be in such close proximity, touching him, staring at him to make sure my work was impeccable. Ryder naturally kept his hair short, but as of late the strands were a little longer than normal, hitting his collar. I thought he looked sexy no matter what style he chose, so I suppose my offer was my way of extending an olive branch. Of letting go of the need to keep the distance between us, even though I was uneasy and on guard with the way he continued to exclude me from certain aspects of his life. I understood the need for privacy with his club, but what I couldn't wrap my head around was why he wouldn't share anything about his past with me.

He never spoke of his family. I asked him once, and he shut me down right away. I figured I should consider myself lucky he'd told me his real name, Roman, although he asked me not to use it. When I asked him why, he shook his head and never answered. From his demeanor I knew not to pry again, or at least for a very long time. Maybe as the months passed, he would become more comfortable with me and want to open up, but as of yet, the topics were off the table.

"Why don't you come back to my place and give me one, then?" His fingers danced over my side before pulling me close so our chests were touching. I could feel his muscles, even beneath the thin white fabric, hard and chorded, twitching and warm.

"Why not just come in the salon and we can do it right now?" I countered, focusing on his full lips while waiting for him to answer me.

"Because if I see that guy, I'm gonna put him flat on his back. Besides, I don't think your friend would appreciate it."

He was right. Sia would definitely disapprove if Ryder waltzed back into the salon.

"Fine."

"Fine?"

"Yeah, fine. I'll come over when I'm done here."

"How about I pick you up?"

"How about you don't push your luck?"

He gave me a tight smile before releasing me and retreating, shoving his hands in his pockets as he waited for me to make a move. Only after I'd turned and started walking back toward Transform did I hear the roar of his bike before he raced off down the road.

SEVEN

Ryder

AS I WATCHED BRAYLEN ROLL out her little black bag across my kitchen counter, I couldn't help but stare at her ass. I mean, come on, it was right in my direct line of view. The way her jeans cupped her cheeks was enough to make me want to tear them from her body. Her legs looked killer, even though they were covered by dark fabric. They seemed to go on for miles, even when only wearing her sneaks.

"Are you staring at my ass again?" she asked, looking over her shoulder just in time to catch me in the act.

"You know damn well I am, woman. Your ass is one of the things I love about you." I hadn't meant to say *love*; it popped out of my mouth before I could stop it. Braylen noticed as well, judging by the stiffening of her shoulders as she turned back around.

We weren't there yet, expressing our feelings and shit. Yeah, I cared about her and wanted to be around her more often than not, but I sure as hell wasn't in love with her. Hell, I'd never been in love with anyone before. I wasn't quite sure I even knew what it felt like.

I'd been involved in a long-term relationship many years back, but thinking about it now, I was never in love with Rose. She'd gotten pregnant a month in and I did the right thing by sticking with her. In the end it just didn't work out, the danger surrounding the club too much for her, which I completely understood. I wanted her to take my daughter and move far away, outside any reach our enemies would've had.

Which brought me to another point—Braylen didn't know I had a daughter. I'd meant to tell her a few weeks after we started hanging out, but it just never seemed to be the right time. And now . . . fuck, too much time had passed for her *not* to know. Or so I'd been told by Jagger, Tripp, and Stone, Jagger being the one person I feared revealing my business before I could. After all, his woman was Braylen's little sister. But he assured me it was my news to tell, so he promised not to say a word to Kena.

"Okay, let's do this." She walked toward me with a pair of scissors in one hand and clippers in the other. She looked like a woman on a mission, pointing toward the chair she'd set in the middle of the kitchen, silently instructing me to take a seat.

Braylen shocked me from time to time, either with her sass and stubbornness or her ability to hold a grudge and give me the cold shoulder. During the time we'd been together, I could safely say she kept me on my toes. Life certainly wasn't boring where she was concerned. I just hoped her intentions were on point that evening.

"You're not gonna shave my head because you're pissed at me, are you?" My thoughts immediately flew to when Hawke's woman, Edana, shaved his head when she'd found out he'd been cheating on her. She did the deed while he was sleeping, cutting off his long hair like Delilah did to Samson.

Hawke was no damn biblical figure, though. He was a guy who couldn't keep his dick in his pants, until his woman had unfortunately been attacked—raped and beaten, to be exact—by some of the Savage Reapers a while back. Since then, he'd been towing the straight and narrow, watching over Edana like never before, glued to her hip whenever she left the house. It was a side none of us ever thought we'd see, but unfortunately it took a devastating incident to wake him the hell up.

"No, not unless you give me reason to," she teased, spraying my hair with a water bottle. "Now keep still or you're gonna end up with a funky do." She smiled, and it was the best sight in the world—next to her lying beneath me, of course.

Braylen was the most beautiful woman I'd ever seen. And sexy as fuck. She knew I lusted after her, and if she didn't know just how much I'd be sure to remind her very shortly.

We'd started off a bit rocky, me running my crass mouth and her telling me exactly what she thought of me. "Arrogant" and "cocky" were the two descriptive words she used the most, but after being around her a few times, I'd managed to wear her down enough to convince her to give me her number. A few phone sex sessions later—me always initiating because I couldn't stop myself from picturing her naked—and she'd agreed to come over to my place. To be alone. Just the two of us.

I happened to be a pretty good cook, so the first time she came over, I made her spaghetti and meatballs. I knew it didn't sound like anything too fancy but it was tasty, and she agreed.

She'd gotten a splash of sauce on her chin, and when I leaned over to wipe it away with a napkin, I couldn't help myself. I'd used my tongue instead. Remembering the first time I'd kissed those pouty lips of hers was enough to make my dick hard, a happenstance that occurred on the regular whenever she was near me.

"Almost finished," Braylen whispered, the warmth of her breath tickling my earlobe, a strand of her hair gently brushing my neck. She was inspecting her work, leaning in so close I could smell her shampoo, some kind of mango scent. Closing my eyes, I sucked in a breath while she clipped away here and there, the buzz of the clippers jolting my gaze from the darkness and back to her.

"Be careful with those damn things," I warned, nervous she was gonna exact some kind of revenge because I'd embarrassed her earlier.

"Stop being a damn baby. I'm just trying to clean up your sideburns." Her tongue snuck out from between her delectable lips, wetting the bottom one and teasing the fuck outta me. When she was done with the sides, she circled me until she was standing directly in front, moving closer until she full-on straddled my lap.

"What are you doing?" Surprise and excitement filled my veins, thickening other parts of my body as the realization hit that she was sitting on me.

"I need to get close so I can inspect the front of your hair."

"You better not sit like this with your clients. So help me Christ, Braylen." I couldn't help it, the words tumbling outta my mouth before I could even think to stop them as my imagination ran wild. My heart picked up pace, ramming against my ribs like it wanted to break free from my chest altogether.

"Oh stop it. You know damn well I don't."

"Do I?" I couldn't stop.

"Do you want me to have an accident with the clippers? Because that can certainly be arranged."

A stare off ensued, both of us vying for dominance with raised chins and narrowed eyes. Eventually, she continued her work, turning my head from side to side multiple times. Finally, she blew out a satisfied breath and placed the clippers and scissors behind her on the table, all while still sitting on my lap. "There. All done." Our eyes locked again and although only a few seconds passed, it felt like a lifetime.

I lived in the brief silence. I existed there, reveled in it.

Looking deep into her eyes made me nervous. Not from what I saw, which was something deeper than lust, but because I knew my feelings for Braylen were stronger than I let on. To her and to myself. It was my place in the club to try and keep the peace, to make sure everything went off without a hitch. Granted, I'd done a shitty job as of late, but I continued to try. Whatever was happening with Braylen and me, however, was making me second-guess myself, questioning how I saw the world and the people around me.

Maybe I was losing my mind. Or maybe I was just desperate to get Braylen naked and fuck her until neither one of us could move.

When she finally did make a move to stand, I grabbed her waist and pulled her back, thrusting upward as she came down. The friction of our bodies connecting, albeit still covered in clothing, elicited a shiver of maddening desire. Far be it for me not to explore the possibility that she'd feel the same and give in to what I had planned. She had to know this was where we'd end up as soon as she stepped foot in my house. Especially when she straddled my lap, feigning it was part of her hair cutting process. *I call bullshit.* She knew exactly what she was doing, taunting and teasing me with her body, the way her thighs clamped on the sides of mine, the way her eyes drank me in when she thought I hadn't been paying attention. The way her tits pressed against my chest as she ran her fingers through my hair.

Yeah, she knew what she was doing all along. Probably had this whole scenario planned out on the drive over.

"Don't do that, Ryder." Placing her hands on my shoulders to hoist herself back up, she struggled against my hold. I refused to let her go until I knew she was completely over being upset with me. Not only for earlier but for the other night when she'd left in a huff.

"I'm not letting go until you kiss me."

"Not gonna happen, so you may as well let me up." She tried to remove herself again, but again I stopped her. "Ryder," she said threateningly, "let me go." She was so cute when she tried to be authoritative.

"Nope. Not until you plant your lips right here," I said, tapping my mouth with my index finger.

"One kiss? Then you'll let me up?" She looked skeptical. I didn't blame her.

"Uh-huh." A smirk found its way onto my face. I tried to hide it, but I failed big-time, causing her to cautiously study me.

"Fine."

"You like that word, don't you?"

"Do you want me to kiss you or not?" I nodded. "Then zip it," she said, a twinkle of mischief lighting up her brown eyes. The corners of her lips tilted upward, a secret only she was privy to, right before she leaned in and pecked me on the mouth.

Quick.

Chaste.

No emotion.

She drew back and tried to stand once more.

"What the fuck? That's not a kiss," I growled. Wrapping the thick strands of her hair around my hand, I tightened my grip and pulled her close. "This is." Crashing my lips to hers, I teased her mouth with my tongue, begging for entrance into her warmth as my free hand disappeared down the back of her jeans, pressing her closer to create the contact I needed.

It wasn't long before she opened for me, tangling her tongue with mine as a deep groan escaped from the deepest part of her. It was matched only by one of my own.

I bit her bottom lip.

She sucked on my tongue.

I cupped her ass.

She stroked my cock through my jeans.

Fuck! This was more than a kiss, and we both knew it. Rising from the chair, I kicked it behind me and walked toward the kitchen table, planting her on top of it before breaking away from her mouth. "God-damnit, woman! You drive me crazy. Do you know that?" I tugged at her shirt, pulling it over her head with ease when she offered no resistance.

"You're just horny," she whispered breathlessly, fumbling with my belt buckle and pulling me toward her as she tried to unhook the leather strap. When she finally freed it, she unbuttoned my jeans and hastily unzipped them, pushing the material, along with my white boxer briefs, over my hips until my cock sprang free. I was painfully hard, and I feared if Braylen was just messing with me I'd lose my shit. If it was all a joke, her sick way of getting back at me for making her angry earlier, I'd beg to fuck her if that was what it took.

I grappled with whether or not to restrain her, tease her until she pleaded for me to fill her. Thankfully I didn't have to do anything, losing myself and all of my reason when her delicate fingers circled my thickness, stroking me from base to tip over and over again.

"You better stop or I'm gonna come before we even get started."

She rolled her eyes and shrugged, as if what I'd warned couldn't possibly happen. Granted, my stamina was pretty impressive, if I did say so myself, but we hadn't had sex in a few days, and I was more than amped up to blow.

Cupping the back of her head, I brought her mouth to mine again, kissing her so deeply I felt it in my goddamn toes. She tasted so sweet, her lips, tongue, and teeth enticing me to strip her bare and claim her until she begged me to stop.

"Let's get these off you." I reached for her jeans, practically ripping off the top button and tearing them down the front. As soon as the fabric parted, I pushed her onto her back, hooked my fingers into the waistband and shimmied her jeans over her hips, much like she'd done with mine. Only I took them all the way off her, tossing them over my shoulder before tearing off her white lace panties.

Pulling her back into a sitting position, I reached behind her back and unhooked her matching bra, flinging that somewhere behind me as well. All the while, Braylen continued to stroke me, softer than before because she didn't want me to come yet any more than I wanted to.

"I'm still upset with you," she said, smearing a drop of precum over the crown.

"I can live with that," I rasped, mentally counting to ten to calm myself. "Just as long as I get to bury myself inside that sweet pussy of yours." She loved when I used that word—pussy. It turned her on beyond all reason.

"Say it again," she whimpered, moving toward the edge of the table and spreading her legs. Her arousal glistened between her thighs, the sight enough to almost make me lose it right then and there.

Leaning closer, I nipped her earlobe. "Pussy."

She shuddered, her fingers tightening around my cock.

"Careful, sweetheart." Braylen flashed me a wicked grin before lining me up at her entrance. "Do you want me to fuck you now?" She nodded, lowering her fingers to cup my tightly drawn balls. I groaned into her mouth as I seized her lips once more, thrusting inside her in one quick motion, joining our bodies before either of us could take our next breath.

We'd stopped using condoms a month prior; we were both clean and she was on the pill. Taking her bare was the best feeling in the entire world. No barrier, just skin on skin. Heightened pleasure for us both.

She gasped, her own moans swallowed by our kiss. "Ryder!" she screamed, bracing herself on the table as I withdrew before roughly plunging back inside. There was nothing sweet and calm about how I took her. Braylen loved it rough and so did I. We both needed the aggressive sex more than ever, anger still simmering inside both of us for various reasons.

The legs of the table screeched against the tiled floor, the back-and-forth rhythm matching the erratic beat of my heart. I wanted so badly to fuck her with wild abandon, but I toed the invisible line between having rough sex and eviscerating her.

As soon as I hit her sweet spot, she threw her head back and arched her tits in my face. Without a second thought, my teeth grazed one of her nipples, my fingers pinching the other hardened bud. "Oh my God!" she cried out. "Yeah . . . right there. Yeah . . . yeah." She pumped her hips toward me as I drove into her, neither of us giving in to the other. We were both chasing our high, the sweet bliss of release that was inevitable.

"I love fucking you, baby," I roared, moving to bite down on the tender flesh of her throat, running my tongue over the affected area to soothe away the bite of pain.

I marked her.

I claimed her.

I fucked her until her pussy started to clench.

"That's it. Come for me." I pushed her body to the limits, forcing her to look at me while she came all over me. Her body squeezed my cock, shooting tiny spasms down my shaft until I was barely holding on.

Braylen shouted my name as she came, her fingers diving into my hair and yanking while she rode out her wave of pleasure. Tinges of pain erupted at the roots of my hair follicles, but it only drove me to fuck her faster, stretching her orgasm out as long as possible.

When she was finally sated, I chased my own climax, my bruising grip on her waist crushing her to me. "Oh fuck!" I shouted over and over until my balls drew tighter, the all-too-familiar pull starting at the base of my spine.

I wanted to last longer but her body demanded so much from mine. I gave her greedy pussy everything, spilling every last drop inside her as my orgasm threatened to pull me under and never let go.

EIGHT

Braylen

STILL SITTING ON THE TABLE, Ryder's face buried in my neck and his cock still jerking inside me, I realized there was no other place I'd rather be. Call it hormones, or the high from my orgasm, but something pulled me toward this man time and time again. I couldn't pinpoint exactly what the connection was, and after trying to dissect it for weeks—months even—I came to the conclusion that it was inexplicable.

All I wanted to do was melt into the man pinning me in place, but I couldn't release all of myself. Not completely, without reservation. Especially since there were so many things up in the air between us. We were like oil and water, and other than a few rare moments sprinkled in between, the only times we meshed as one were when we were having sex. Or leading up to the utterly delicious act.

As the pace of my heart steadily slowed, my eyes roamed around the space of Ryder's home. His place exuded masculinity, rustic décor everywhere, yet I found it cozy. A hearty fireplace took up the center wall of his living room, a few pieces of camel-colored leather furniture surrounding the focal point. His kitchen was small yet updated, all the latest stainless steel appliances glimmering in the condensed space. One of my favorite areas of his house, however—beside his bedroom, of course—was his en suite bathroom. The antique claw-foot tub called to me each and every time I spent the night. Although I wasn't sure I'd be sleeping over again anytime soon, not with the threat of him possibly maiming me in my sleep.

Hell, possibly worse.

From what I understood, most of the men in the club lived close to the compound, yet on their own parcel of land, with top-of-the-line security installed to deter any unwanted guests. Ryder's house was no different.

Sitting on three acres of land, he was housed in solitude yet close enough that he didn't live in the middle of bum fuck Egypt.

"Let's get you cleaned up," he mumbled before lifting his head to look at me. Several seconds passed of looking into each other's eyes before he placed a chaste kiss on my lips. It was almost as if he wanted to tell me something but thought better of it. Ryder fell from my body, pulled up his boxer briefs and jeans and tucked himself back into place. He reached for a box of tissues sitting on the counter.

"What?" He pushed my legs apart to wipe himself from my inner thighs.

"Nothing. I just like when you take care of me after sex. It's nice."

"Nice?

"Yeah."

He mirrored my expression, his smile melting my heart. Ryder was a tough guy, his appearance matching his personality. It was only during these tender moments that I glimpsed another side to him. A more intimate side I cherished because I knew it would disappear soon enough. I realized that sounded odd, seeing as how the act of sex was intimate, but sometimes sex was just sex. Primal urges between two people. It was the aftermath that could sometimes be more rewarding.

After he finished, he hoisted me off the table and helped to steady me until I found my footing. Grinning widely, he turned and moved to retrieve my clothes. Normally, I'd be self-conscious standing naked in front of a man. I had a little more junk in the trunk than I'd like, and my belly wasn't as flat as it used to be—I was a sucker for sweets—but the way Ryder stared at me made me feel like the most perfectly shaped woman in the world. I felt sexy and confident whenever his eyes raked over me, clothed or otherwise.

Walking back toward me, he held my clothes but made no attempt to hand them over.

"Can I get dressed now?" I asked, extending my hand so he could pass me my bra, panties, and outfit.

"What's the rush?"

"*You're* dressed."

"I kinda like you naked, though. You know, you can stay that way all night if you want. No complaints here."

"Nice try," I replied, snapping my fingers. With a loud sigh, he passed them to me, and within a minute I was fully clothed.

When I came to his house to cut his hair, I hadn't planned on having sex with him. Not really. I knew it was always a possibility, but I thought my smoldering anger would've blocked my lust.

I guess that didn't work out too well.

Ushering past him, I took a seat on his couch, crossed my legs and leaned back against the cushion. "We need to talk." I tried like hell to appear as if fighting was the last thing on my mind, but the reality was we would most likely end up there.

"The four magic words every man loves to hear," he griped sarcastically. Fiddling with the television remote, he clicked on a sports station before giving me his full attention. "What's up?"

His question was guarded, and I couldn't say that I blamed him. We still had a lot of unfinished business to discuss, and no doubt our conversation was going to turn heated. We were both stubborn, neither of us ever wanting to give in. When our fuses were lit, there was no stopping the explosion.

I wasn't a submissive person—not outside of the bedroom, at least. And Ryder sure as hell was domineering. He'd said on multiple occasions how he wished I'd just do as he asked without issue, but he'd been with me long enough to realize that was not how I was wired.

Crossing my arms over my chest, I braced for impact, ripping off the Band-Aid and blurting out, "I want to know what caused you to do what you did the other night."

His chest expanded as he inhaled a deep breath. Then his lips parted, expelling the air in the form of a shout.

"Jesus Christ! Are we goin' over that again?" Pacing in front of me, he ran his hand through his newly cut hair. "I told you I don't wanna talk about it. Look, I'm sorry for holding you down while I was dreamin', but it won't happen again." The vein in the middle of his forehead bulged, his breathing increasing the more aggravated he became.

"You can't say that."

"Yes I can," he gritted, tossing the remote on the couch next to me.

"If you talk about what's bothering you, you'll feel better."

"Nothing is fuckin' bothering me. Let it go, Bray." The rasp of his demand should've halted any further discussion on the matter, but of course, I just had to push.

"You need to let me in if we're gonna continue doing whatever it is we're doing."

"Fuckin'?" A look crossed his features so quickly I didn't have time to dissect it. Was it disgust? Uncertainty? I just couldn't be sure.

His choice of words hurt. Ryder was guarded, and I feared he always would be. If I was a sane woman, I'd just walk away, wish him well and move on. But I never claimed to be in my right mind when it came to the infuriating man.

"That's what we're doing? Nothing more than fucking each other?"

"Yeah. No." He planted his ass on the arm of the sofa at the far end. "I don't know. What I *do* know is that I'm not delvin' into my deep-seated feelings about what may or may not be bothering me. And if you can't deal with it, you can leave," he said, pointing toward his front door.

My lungs seized, taking in air seeming too difficult a task. He kept spouting off at the mouth, hurting me more and more with every syllable. The muscles in my chin started to quiver, so before he bore witness to the tears that would surely follow, I rose from the couch, grabbed my keys and bag from the kitchen counter and hustled toward the door.

But not before tossing "Fuck you" over my shoulder, then disappearing outside and slamming the door behind me.

NINE

Ryder

"SHE JUST HAD TO FUCKIN' push, didn't she? Couldn't leave well enough alone," I mumbled, whipping my beer bottle into the hearth of the fireplace, the shattering glass doing a less than stellar job of releasing any of my pent-up fury. "Fuck!" I roared, adrenaline coursing through me with no end in sight.

My cell rang, vibrating on top of the end table and cutting through the expletives I continued to yell into the silence around me.

"Hello," I shouted into the receiver.

"Hey, it's Stone. No time to ask what's up your ass, man." No break between words before he asked, "Do you know if anyone visited Braylen at work? Or approached her on the street? Anything weird?" His words were clipped and quick.

"What are you talkin' about?"

"Are you with her right now?"

"No, she just stormed outta here a few seconds ago. What the hell is goin' on?" I'd begun pacing again once I answered the call but I halted, fear of the unknown freezing me in place.

"Addy and Sully were approached on the street by some guy, telling them that they would get what was coming to them soon enough. The whole club would. Same fuckin' thing happened to Reece and a few of the strippers at Indulge and Flings."

"Who was it?"

"Don't know. He wasn't wearin' a Reapers cut, although that doesn't mean anything."

"I'll call you right back." I hung up on Stone while he was still talking, ran out the front door and raced down the steps toward Braylen's car.

Thankfully she hadn't left yet; she was sitting in the driver seat texting someone.

Whipping open her door, I grabbed for her hand to pull her out of the car. Startled, she dropped her phone, but when she realized it was me, she shot me daggers before leaning farther into the vehicle.

"I don't have anything to say to you," she yelled, bending over to retrieve the fallen device. Her blonde hair looked disheveled, as if she'd been tugging at it, and her eyes were red, almost like she'd been about to cry. No time to feel bad about upsetting her, though. There were more pressing things to deal with right then.

"Did anyone strange approach you recently?" My forearm hung over the top of her door, refusing to budge in case she tried to slam it shut.

"What?"

"Just answer the question, Bray. Did a man approach you recently? Spouting off at the mouth about getting what's coming to you?"

"No." Worry etched deep around her eyes. The last thing I wanted to do was freak her out, but I needed to make sure she was safe.

"Listen, put everything else aside. I need you to trust me. Don't go anywhere alone. I mean it. Not to work, not back home. Nowhere."

"You can't seriously think you're gonna tell me what to do, especially after what you just said to me in there," she spouted, angrily pointing to my house. "Because I'm not listening to anything you have to say."

"You can be as stubborn as you want, woman, but I'm fucking serious. There's a possible threat out there and I'll do what I have to in order to keep you safe. Even if that means being your goddamn shadow."

Unlocking her phone, she frantically started typing a message, biting her lip in concentration while waiting for a response. "Where's Jagger?" she asked. "Is he with Kena? Is *she* safe?"

"I'm sure he's with her. He won't let anything happen to her."

"I need to go. I need to find out where she is. She's not texting me back now." She said something under her breath before turning the key in the ignition. Grabbing the door handle, she tried to close it, but I still had it braced open.

"I'm following you home," I instructed, my tone deadly serious.

"Fine. Hurry up."

As I removed my arm from the door, she slammed it shut, threw her four-door sedan in Drive and peeled out of my driveway.

That woman was gonna be the death of me yet.

TEN

Braylen

FIVE DAYS HAD PASSED SINCE Ryder freaked me out with his sudden and random interrogation. I'd asked him later that night, when he insisted on following me home and then walking me inside, if I was in any real danger. He said no, but I couldn't help but feel that he was lying to me.

Against my wishes, he'd continued to show up at my house to follow me to work, then at Transform to follow me home, making me promise to call him right away if anyone strange tried to talk to me. I'd wanted to ask him to define "anyone strange," but I had a gut feeling he wouldn't be too happy with my lack of concern about the situation, one I was still left fumbling around in the dark about.

Ryder and I weren't any better off than when I'd rushed out of his house the previous week. He refused to open up and I refused to keep quiet about his lack of sharing. Maybe because there wasn't anything in my past worth shielding, I didn't fully understand the ramifications of guarding secrets. And I would've been okay with allowing him to open up when he was good and ready, but then he basically attacked me in his sleep. He could've killed me. If he ever wanted me to share his bed in the foreseeable future, he'd better start talking.

Then again, maybe I didn't mean anything more to him than someone to *fuck*, as he so eloquently put it. The thought alone had my chest tightening, but if that was how he felt, there wasn't a damn thing I could do about it.

So why try and protect me?

And men say women are confusing.

"ARE YOU SURE YOU DON'T mind me hangin' out with you two to-night? It's been a long day and I could use the company." Tucking my leg underneath me, I plopped down on the couch, wineglass in one hand and a bowl of popcorn in the other.

"It's your place," Jagger said, smiling at me before wrapping his arm around Kena's shoulder and pulling her closer. "Besides, I need a witness to prove that your little sister does indeed fall asleep during movies." Jagger laughed, but not before Kena slapped his thigh for making fun of her.

It was in fact true; I couldn't recall a movie I'd watched with her where she'd made it all the way through to the end. That wasn't the case for me, however. I was always up for a good flick. If it held my interest, I was in for the long haul—or the typical hour and forty minutes, give or take.

"What did you put in?" I asked, throwing some air-popped goodness in my mouth while watching the opening credits. The lights were dimmed low, and we were all sitting comfortably on the couch, Kena between Jagger and me. No doubt, my sister would be lightly snoring in T minus thirty minutes.

Far from the Madding Crowd, Kena signed, flashing me a smile before resting her head on Jagger's shoulder. He groaned, earning him another playful tap on the leg. Maybe it'd be more like T minus fifteen minutes before she passed out.

The way Kena and Jagger snuggled on the couch made me think about Ryder. I tried to stop it and focus on the film, but his image kept popping up in my head.

He'd obviously made his decision not to integrate me further into his life, and while it hurt because I'd grown fond of the broody, arrogant man, I took the opportunity to gain some space as well. Though that didn't stop Ryder from continuing to follow me to and from work or calling me multiple times throughout the day and night.

The man was infuriatingly confusing.

After two hours the movie finally came to an end. Exhaling a breath of satisfaction at seeing what I deemed a wonderful film, I stretched my arms over my head and groaned out a hearty yawn.

"My damn leg's asleep," I bellyached, untucking it from underneath my body and straightening the appendage, pins and needles in full force.

"And so is your sister," Jagger teased.

"How long did she make it this time?" I was so engrossed with the movie right from the beginning, I hadn't taken notice of exactly when

Kena fell asleep.

"She made it forty minutes," he replied, shifting slightly so as not to wake her. "I'm impressed."

"Me too." Rising from the couch, I stretched once more, tugging down the hem of my yellow cami before striding toward the kitchen. "Do you want something else to drink? Another beer?"

"Nah, I'm good. I should be going."

"Oh. You're not staying over?" Even though Jagger slept in Kena's room with her when he stayed the night, I felt safe knowing he was under the same roof.

Scratching the light dusting of hair on his jaw, he cracked his neck from side to side. "Wish I could but I can't. Have to deal with something at the club." Gently picking Kena up from the couch, he rose and tucked her back into him before walking out of the room.

A few minutes later he returned, yawning and doing a bit of stretching himself. Jagger's hair was sticking up in the back and a little bit on the sides, but he somehow still pulled off the tough guy look. I'd come to enjoy his company, even though I hadn't been his biggest fan in the beginning. Scratch that. I was, then I wasn't, and then I was once more.

Pulling on his club's vest, he snagged his keys from the coffee table. "Make sure you lock the door behind me," he warned. "And use the new deadbolt too."

Before he opened the door, I seized his arm.

"You'd tell me if we were in some real danger, wouldn't you? You wouldn't hide something like that from me? From Kena?" Worry bubbled forth on every word. I'd meant to simply ask if he thought whatever threat they were concerned about was viable, not appear shaken and nervous, riddled with stress over the whole situation. If only I knew exactly what was going on; then maybe I could relax. But nothing was simple and upfront with these guys.

Codes.

Underlying messages.

Secrecy.

"We're just being cautious, Braylen. That's it."

"You promise?"

Jagger had the decency to look away for a brief moment, inadvertently telling me everything I didn't want to know. "Ryder will be here in the morning. He'll meet you outside as usual."

"If he's just being cautious, then I don't need him to continue to follow me to and from work. I think it's overkill, don't you?"

He knew what I was doing, trying to trick him into revealing that they weren't simply being vigilant. There was some sort of real danger and it could possibly involve Kena and me.

"Don't."

"Don't what?" We were both standing near the door, a battle of wills ensuing the more hush-hush he remained.

"Just let him do this for you. It puts his mind at ease. Mine too, and no doubt your sister's."

"Had to play the sister card, didn't you?"

"I do what I have to." He winked, a small smile tilting his lips. His phone rang, killing anything else he would have said. "I gotta go. Call us if you need us."

For a brief moment, I'd thought about texting Ryder and telling him I didn't need him to babysit me any longer, but I had a feeling he'd either call to argue or show up on my doorstep to convince me otherwise. The energy required for such a confrontation was my sole deterrent.

ELEVEN

Ryder

"SETTLE DOWN," MAREK DEMANDED, LOOKING a little worse for wear. Although the stress of the Reapers most likely being responsible for threatening some of the women, and knowing our enemy was certainly planning some kind of retaliation for the absence of their president, Psych, the Knights Corruption leader looked to be in control. For the first time in what seemed like a very long time.

After everything he and his wife, Sully, had battled, there wasn't anything he couldn't push through, knowing damn well he had a great woman waiting for him at home. And although Sully had technically been kidnapped and forced to marry the man sitting at the head of the table, their love was one for the ages.

Not that I was all sappy or anything, but everyone knew those two were meant to be together.

Placing the gavel to his right, Marek leaned back in his chair and not so patiently waited for the chatter to cease. All of the men's words soon faded as we focused on our leader.

"I'd bet my life it's a fuckin' Reaper who's rattling our women, and for that alone he'll pay with his life."

We all nodded. Even though our club had gone legit, cutting off all ties with Los Zappas Cartel and the drug trade, we still dealt with whomever we deemed a threat. There wasn't anything we wouldn't do to protect our family, both at the club and at home.

"Has anyone been able to describe the guy?" Trigger asked, fidgeting in his chair like he was uncomfortable with the topic. He had every right to be twitchy; not only was he concerned about his brothers, but his niece, Adelaide, was involved with Stone. They even had a kid together, with another on the way.

"All they could tell us was that he was about six foot, had short dark hair and tats runnin' up both arms," Tripp offered, the nomad becoming quite the permanent fixture at the oblong wooden table. He'd come to stay with our club, giving up the open road for the time being. When Indulge first opened, Marek had asked him to stick around and see that everything fell into place. It just so happened that he met his woman, Reece, there, pulling out all stops to keep her safe, which unfortunately included dealing with her crazy ex-husband. And by dealing with . . . well, I supposed it was self-explanatory.

"That could be any of 'em," Cutter replied, shaking his head in obvious disgust. Breck was sitting to the right of his ol' man, pissed off right along with him. Hell, we all had the same anger bubbling up inside, threatening to explode given the right time and opportunity.

"Yeah it could be," Stone said. "We'll just have to take out every one of those fuckers. That'll solve the problem," he grunted, leaning forward and resting his forearms on the hard surface of the table.

"No one is gonna do a damn thing until I give the go-ahead," Marek warned, looking to Stone first, then the rest of us. "Just like with everything else in the past, I know you all want revenge, and to put this threat to bed once and for all, but we have to be smart about this. More now than ever before. That sonofabitch Koritz is gonna be watchin', waiting for us to fuck up. And now we have to also deal with that bastard Rabid."

"Who knew *that* guy would be a threat?" Jagger asked, scratching his jaw with one hand while drumming the fingers of his other on the edge of the table.

Marek leaned closer, his blue eyes darkening in seriousness and anger. "I underestimated him. It won't happen again." The rasp of his tone indicated he held the majority of his temper at bay.

A bout of silence ensued, all of us processing what could potentially take place in the upcoming days, weeks and even months. We simply had no idea what to expect, except the unexpected. If history was any sort of indication.

"Do we have eyes on Rabid?" I asked, looking around the room before finally resting my attention on Marek.

"Hawke."

Without thinking, I blurted, "Is that the smartest choice?" I took a breath to continue to speak but Hawke cut me off by slamming his fist down and shooting me the dirtiest look. Hawke and I had our issues, mainly itching to always get a rise out of the other, but there was no bad blood between us.

I may've just changed that.

"What the fuck does that mean?" he shouted, rising halfway from his chair as if he was set to lunge over the table at me. His eyes were wild with ferocity and I feared if he didn't get a grip soon, we'd be goin' toe-to-toe in the next several seconds.

Tripp sat next to his younger brother. The nomad shot me a disbelieving look before placing his hand on Hawke's shoulder, doing his best to try and calm him down before things escalated out of control.

"Settle down, man. I just meant that you might be a little too close to this, more so than the rest of us." Confusion shrouded his expression. "After everything that happened with Edana, can you seriously tell us you won't do something drastic if given the opportunity?" I had my doubts he'd be able to restrain himself. Not that I'd blame him, but when it came to being strategic, we had to hold off until Marek gave the orders. Any other move and a shitstorm could blow back our way and devastate the entire club forever.

Slowly lowering himself back into his seat, he replied, "I'm not gonna fuck it up." He closed his mouth and turned toward Marek, no longer wanting to engage me in any further conversation.

"I didn't say you would."

"Yes you fuckin' did. When you questioned me." He was still facing Marek when he responded.

"All right. Calm down. Both of you," Marek shouted, then sighed. "I'm too young for this," he mumbled, pushing his chair back from the lip of the table.

"What about that fucker who's making threats to our women?" Stone threw out that question, locking eyes solely on his best friend for the answer.

"Keep watch over them." Stone's mouth dropped open. "Hey, he came up to Adelaide *and* Sully. Don't forget that. My wife is just as upset as your woman."

"I know. I know," Stone said, shaking his head in aggravation. "I just hate the thought that anyone has the balls to approach Addy and freak her out with some lame-ass threat. I'm stressed out the way it is, constantly worrying about her and Riley. And now that Addy's pregnant. . . ." Stone stopped speaking, emotion rising in his voice and threatening to crumble the man right in front of all of us.

I feared for Braylen's safety every day. I could only imagine how I'd feel if she was my fiancée, or wife, or had my kid. It would only amplify the issue until I was giving myself a daily heart attack.

"We'll get 'em. He can't hide forever. Until then, keep your eyes and ears open. If you have to deal with family stuff and need someone to replace you in the rotation at Jagger's fights, or checking in on things at Indulge and Flings, just let me know. We're all in the same boat." Grabbing the gavel, he said, "Is there anything else?"

Everyone just shook their heads.

Braylen

LOUD VOICES OUTSIDE WOKE ME from sleep, rousing me only hours after I'd drifted off to dreamland. I couldn't make out what they were saying, but the longer I laid there, the more evident it became that the voices were familiar.

One was from the man who continued to confuse the hell out of me, twisting me all around until I didn't know which end was up, and the other was from the man who was completely head over heels for my sister.

I threw off the covers and groggily shuffled toward my window, tossing it open and leaning my head outside.

"What are you two doing?" I yelled, the night's breeze blowing strands of my blonde hair back in my face. I was sure I looked the sight, but ask me if I cared. Not a minute later, I heard my bedroom door open but didn't bother to look behind me, knowing it was Kena who had come to see what all of the commotion was about.

"He insisted I bring him here," Jagger finally answered, supporting Ryder under his left arm to help hold him upright. Ryder wasn't drunk off his ass but he was definitely feeling no pain.

"Oh yeah? Why's that?"

"'Cause I need ta see ya," Ryder slurred, shoving Jagger away from him. "Ya need ta stahhhh . . . stop ignorin' me, toots."

Kena tapped my shoulder. *Toots?* She rubbed at her eyes, smiling at me and then down at the sight on the street.

"Sorry for waking you, baby," Jagger shouted, louder than he needed to. He'd been drinking as well, but not nearly as much as his buddy next to him.

"Go home," I said, leaning back into my room. As my hands came up to pull down the window, Ryder started shouting.

"Woman! If you don't let me inside I'm gonna bust down your front door."

"No he won't," Jagger jumped in, having the decency to look somewhat embarrassed.

"I will. I'll da . . . do it."

"Why?"

"'Cause you won't get outta here," Ryder confessed, pointing to his head before taking several steps toward our front door. Within seconds the pounding started. Jagger was still under the streetlight, shaking his head and shrugging when Ryder just wouldn't let up.

"Fine, but stop banging. We do have neighbors, you know."

"I don't shit."

"I'm sure you do," Jagger razzed, laughing full-on when Ryder tried to swing at him, almost falling on his ass.

"You kn . . . know what I meant," he garbled.

Kena and I walked through the house until we reached the front door. As my fingers circled the handle, my sister tapped my arm once more.

Are you sure you want to let him in? If you really don't want to see him, I'll tell Jagger to take him away. Your choice. She stood back to give me space, gifting me with a sympathetic look. She knew I was torn up over Ryder because I'd confided as much after a few glasses of wine the other day.

"May as well get this over with." My sister nodded. I pulled open the door and was almost hit in the face. Ryder had his fist raised, ready to pound the wood when I'd suddenly appeared.

"'Bout time," he grumbled before entering our house, not a care in the world that I'd told him to go home moments prior. "You got anythin' to drink?"

"You've had enough," Jagger and I said simultaneously. Grinning, Jagger kicked the door closed behind him before grabbing Kena's hand, leading her back to her room and leaving Ryder and me alone, standing in the middle of the entryway just staring at each other.

After neither of us spoke, I flipped the deadbolt and turned around, heading toward the couch. I doubt he'd be able to make it much farther, so the sofa seemed like the best idea.

Planting myself down, I folded my arms over my chest, much like I'd done at his place right before we started arguing about him not opening up.

"What do you want? What couldn't wait until a decent hour?" My eyes raked over him as he leaned against the wall, no doubt needing the structure's support to hold him up. His dark eyes were glazed over and droopy but he was still coherent. He looked scrumptious, even while inebriated. His dark hair was sticking up on top, the result of him tugging at it I was sure. His teeth captured his bottom lip while he contemplated his answer. "Well?" I prompted.

"I wanna see ya."

"Why? You made it perfectly clear you don't wanna let me in. That we're nothin' more than just fuck buddies, so why the scene? Why all the dramatics?"

He pushed off the wall and slowly put one foot in front of the other. The look in his eyes was definitely predatory. Drunk or not, Ryder had a way of making me feel all hot and bothered with a simple glance.

Damn him, and damn my overactive hormones.

"Stop right there," I warned. "We're not doin' anything. You can sleep on the couch, but then you have to leave in the morning. I'm not staying out here with you, and you sure as hell aren't coming to my bedroom." I made a move to stand, but he was on me before I could get my feet underneath me.

His hands wrapped around my waist and as he crashed down on the couch, he spun me around and hoisted me on top of him. It happened so fast I had no time to fight him. The only thing I could do was plant my hands on his hard chest to ensure I didn't fall over. I straddled his lap, and he wasted no time leaning in and trying to kiss me, but I dodged his advances before his mouth could connect with mine. While I wanted nothing more than to give myself to him, he'd only hurt me. One way or another.

"Stop it, Ryder. I mean it. You can't just wake me up in the middle of the night, barge into my house and have sex with me. It doesn't work that way." I struggled to get off him, but his hold was fierce. Not painful but definitely strong.

"I can't."

"You can't what?" He didn't answer me right away, so I tilted my head and repeated, "You can't what?"

"I can't get you out of my head." He leaned forward, his warm breath lapping over my collarbone. The smell of beer would've been overpowering had his other scents not filled my nose as well. One of leather, the outdoors and his natural male scent.

"So you said."

"I'm not foolin' 'round here, baby." He raised his head and his mouth was millimeters from mine, his tongue wetting his bottom lip and turning me on like he normally did. I hated my body's reaction, and the last thing I wanted to do was give in to this type of behavior, but I feared my heart and hormones were going to win the battle against my brain.

"Really? 'Cause I thought that's all we were doing." I arched my brow, leaning back so our faces weren't so close.

"I didn't mean it," he confessed. "You just got me all twisted up inside." He threw his head back against the top of the couch, his hold on my waist still ironclad. "I can't stop thinkin' about you. All I do is worry."

"What do you mean 'worry'?" I knew the answer as soon as I asked, but thankfully he didn't remind me of the supposed threat.

Again I tried to move and again he held me to him, my thighs on the outside of his muscular ones. If I sat in the same position for too long, I'd start to cramp up, and then he'd have to let me up. Unfortunately I was probably close to ten minutes from that situation.

And a lot could happen in ten minutes.

Bodies could become one in ten minutes. Then again, hearts could be crushed in ten minutes as well.

"Can't you forgive me?" he asked, that time looking directly into my eyes. I studied every facet of his face, like I'd done many times before, only this time there was a sadness and vulnerability laced behind his stunning browns that I hadn't seen before. Maybe he really was all twisted up inside like he'd said.

"You never apologized," I reminded him. "Not once did you say you were sorry."

His hands moved from my waist and traveled up my body, finding their place on my cheeks. He pulled me close, his mouth practically touching mine when he said, "I'm sorry, baby. Please forgive me."

My answer was to seal my lips to his, my tongue searching for his warmth as he writhed beneath me. His hardened excitement elicited a primal need inside me, one I was powerless to control, let alone stop. The heat from him fueled my own, the need to crawl inside him such an odd feeling, yet it made perfect sense to me. As he dominated me with his kiss and while his hands cupped and squeezed my breasts, pinching my nipples through my thin camisole, I couldn't help but think that if we had sex right then, nothing would change.

Ryder would continue to keep me at bay, throwing me tiny scraps of affection and wilted promises whenever the mood, or alcohol, struck him. If I had any hope of recovering from the already brutal attack he'd had on my heart, then I needed to stop giving in to him.

One more second.

Okay, two more seconds. Then I'll pull away.

Oh hell, I had to slowly count to twenty before I ended the kiss, pushing off his large frame and stumbling to my feet. He reached for me, the frown painting his face enticing me to jump right back into his arms.

This man is dangerous.

"I need to go back to bed now." I backed up a few steps, keeping a close eye on him for any sudden movements.

"I'll come with you," he offered, trying to push off the couch, a feat which failed miserably as he simply couldn't find his footing. Our sofa was worn in and super comfy, the cushions molding to the body like a second skin. Add in a large, muscular man, whose reflexes were compromised from drinking, and there was no way he was getting off the couch without some help. And I knew if I approached him, he'd just yank me back down on top of him.

Ryder quickly gave up, his eyes starting to close as his body leaned to the side. Eventually he ended up lying on his back, his right foot resting on the floor while his left one was stretched out in front of him. Reaching behind me, I grabbed a blanket from the recliner and draped it over him. Pulling off his boots, I tossed them to the side and tucked the edges of the blanket underneath him. I watched as his breathing evened out, a peace drifting over him as if nothing in the world bothered him. Too bad I knew it was only a façade. Ryder was plagued by things he deemed too dark to ever confess.

When I turned and quietly walked across the room, about to turn the corner, I heard him say, "I saw him kill my mom. How do I ever get over something like that?"

I stopped dead in my tracks, every muscle on lockdown while I waited for another confession, but no other words filled the air.

THIRTEEN

Ryder

THE BLARE OF A CAR alarm jolted me awake, my hands instantly clutching my head to try and stop the pounding. Normally, I didn't suffer from hangovers; I must've drank an awful lot of shitty beer last night.

I hadn't been so out of it that I didn't remember what happened, however. I knew damn well I'd threatened Jagger to drive me to Braylen's house, the need to see her greater than I'd ever felt before in my life. With minimal reluctance, he'd finally agreed, not so much to help me out but because I was sure he wanted to spend time with Kena. Either way, mission accomplished.

I remembered pulling Braylen on top of me as I fell onto the couch, then apologizing and spewing something about not being able to get her out of my head. Then kissing her sweet lips. Then trying to get off the couch but failing, my body finally giving in to exhaustion, the alcohol flowing through my veins thickening and rendering me useless.

As I struggled to sit up, I suddenly remembered the worst thing of all. My hands came up to cradle my face, a groan of disbelief barreling from my mouth as I tried like hell to wish it away. I'd said out loud that I saw my mother killed in front of me.

Did she hear me? Had she left the room by the time the words escaped? If she did hear me, will she ask me about it? So many questions, none of which I would find the answer to unless I brought it up.

Reaching inside my jeans, I pulled my phone out to check the time—5:00 a.m. A sudden feeling of nerves took hold, so I scrambled off the couch, almost fell the fuck over, righted myself and went in search of Jagger. I needed the keys to his truck. I had to get out of there before Braylen woke up, before she decided to *shrink* me into telling her all about my sordid past.

———— ◆ ————

AFTER BRIEFLY RETURNING HOME, I showered, changed and headed toward the club, remnants of my drunken haze still lingering. Being alone with my thoughts was the last thing I wanted to do. I needed a distraction, and who better to gift me with such a thing than my brothers. While it was still relatively early—six thirty, to be exact—I was sure someone would be there. And if not, then I'd set up at the bar and start *forgetting* right away.

Forgetting I'd made a fool of myself by showing up at Braylen's house, drunk and insistent she see me.

Forgetting I'd basically passed out on her couch after having a taste of her sweetness.

Forgetting I'd mentioned my mother.

Forgetting Jagger was gonna be pissed that I'd taken his truck without his knowledge.

Forgetting I even cared.

I was close to ten minutes away from my destination when a vehicle unexpectedly cut in front of me, crossing lanes without any sort of warning. Besides being pissed, something screamed at me to pay attention, more so than I normally would have. An Oldsmobile Cutlass with faded and peeling blue paint, along with a bumper that was held on by duct tape, careened into the opposing lane before righting the wheel, slowing down and then speeding up. I kept my distance when normally I would have sped up and passed him off. At first glance it appeared as if a drunk driver was behind the wheel, but I quickly realized that wasn't the case.

The Cutlass pulled closer to the side of the road but never stopped completely. I let up on the gas, slowing the truck even more. The next thing I knew something was tossed from the passenger side window, and as soon as the object cleared the car's interior, the driver gunned it and took off like a shot. I was honestly shocked the ol' girl had so much gumption left in her.

Several moments later, I pulled over to where the Cutlass had slowed, my tires kicking up gravel until I eventually came to a stop. I had no idea what had been discarded, but I knew I couldn't leave without checking what it was. It could've been a bag of trash, the bastard too lazy to dispose of it properly, although my gut was telling me otherwise.

Throwing the truck in Park, I exited and walked around the back until I came to the side of the road closest to the small embankment. And that was when I saw a white garbage bag with black handles. Upon closer inspection, I saw the bag was moving ever so slightly. When I was a few feet away, I finally heard a noise, a whimpering sound trapped inside the confinement.

What the fuck? I proceeded with caution. For all I knew the guy could've tossed out a raccoon he'd caught, or a skunk, or any other kind of rodent. The closer I got the more I knew the animal inside wasn't any of those things. Crouching down, I cautiously untied the knotted black plastic handles, pulling apart the ends of the garbage bag until I could peer inside.

Looking back up at me were a tiny pair of pale blue eyes, a face so bewildered it tugged at my heart. It was a puppy. I'd always been an animal lover, even had a dog I loved with all my heart when I was young, so when I saw what that bastard threw out of his window, fury pounded through me. My skin was hot, my heart thumping wildly inside my chest.

I had a choice. I could hop back in my truck and take off after him, or I could tend to the defenseless puppy. Without much deliberation at all, I chose the puppy.

Tearing the rest of the bag away, I inspected the tiny creature. It didn't take long to discover that the puppy only had three legs—two front ones and the back right. From what I could tell, it looked like the missing limb was a birth defect and not the result of some sort of accident or mistreatment. Checking underneath, I saw the puppy was male, his tiny tail tucked under when I scooped him up.

He looked to only be around six weeks old, yet there was an old soul to this dog as I stared into his eyes. It was the oddest moment, but I swore to Christ I bonded with the little bastard, right there on the side of the road. While I wasn't sure exactly what breed of dog he was, his coloring was quite unique: gray and white fur covered his body, with a black patch circling his left eye.

Walking back to the truck, the little guy tucked close to me, I grabbed a blanket Jagger had in the back and threw it over the passenger seat before climbing back behind the wheel. Turning over the ignition, I gently placed the puppy on the blanket.

He started to shiver, so I put my hand over him. Surprisingly he stopped, licking his little lips before closing his eyes, as if he knew I wouldn't harm him.

I drove the rest of the way to the club with a discarded, three-legged animal next to me and an odd feeling of affection in my heart.

FOURTEEN

Ryder

STRIDING THROUGH THE DOORS OF the club, I hid the puppy underneath my cut. The morning air was crisp and the poor guy had been through enough; the least I could do was try and keep him warm.

No one was out in the common room, and the door to Chambers was wide open. There was a strong possibility some of the guys were sleeping in one of the rooms in the back. There were plenty of designated spaces for us to crash if we needed to. A night of overindulgence or a fight with an ol' lady—whatever the reason, all the men had a place to stay if the occasion called for it.

Disappearing into the kitchen, I rooted around for something edible I could feed the pup. What the hell did I even give him? We certainly didn't have any puppy chow on hand. Opening the refrigerator, I saw some leftover fried chicken, so still holding tightly to the dog, I wrangled the plate from the shelf, kicked the door closed and set up on the counter.

A whimper escaped the little creature when I removed the saran wrap from the dish, my own stomach rumbling from the smell. It was then I realized I hadn't eaten since early the day before, choosing to drown myself in alcohol instead of food.

"I know, little buddy. Just give me a minute." Deeming I needed the use of both hands, I found a dishtowel near the sink, folded it to create a little cushion and placed the puppy on top, far enough back on the counter that he wouldn't fall if he decided to become a bit lively.

"Talkin' to your dick again, are ya?" a gravelly voice sounded behind me, shuffling feet approaching before I had a chance to recognize the voice. Hawke.

He sidled up next to me and peered over my shoulder. "Well if I was, what's your excuse for trying to sneak a peek?"

"You wish." He took a step back and leaned his hip against the counter. Wearing an old KISS T-shirt and boxer shorts, Hawke looked a little worse for wear, his dark hair sticking out all over the place and a pillow line running down the entire length of his cheek.

"Rough night?" I teased, my hands busy tearing the chicken from the bone and putting aside small pieces for the pup.

"You could say that?" he gruffed, narrowing his eyes at me while he watched me destroy the food. "What are you doing? Isn't it a little early for leftovers?" Running his hand through his hair and making it worse, he pushed off the counter and grabbed some orange juice from the fridge. Chugging back a few gulps straight from the carton, he wiped his mouth afterward before putting the drink back in the fridge.

Hawke still hadn't seen the surprise visitor sitting patiently on the counter next to me. Not until he heard him whimper.

"What was that?" His confusion was comical. Looking all around the room first, he glanced up at the ceiling as if something was gonna drop down on top of us.

The puppy whimpered again. Before Hawke started shouting for me to tell him what was making the noise, scaring the dog in the process, I moved out of the way so he could see the little guy.

"Some asshole threw him out of his car while driving in front of me." I didn't have to say any more before Hawke approached the puppy with his hand out so the dog could smell him, a goofy smile appearing as he gently pet the puppy's head.

"I can't believe someone would do that. That's seriously fucked up."

"You're tellin' me."

"What are you gonna do with it?" he asked, picking him up so he could get a better look. It was then he noticed the puppy was missing one of his back legs. "What the hell?" he shouted, startling the little guy. "Did they cut it off?" He turned the creature from side to side, lifting him up to the light to see him better.

"I think he was born that way," I offered, finishing my hack job on the chicken. "Here, gimme him."

Hawke passed him to me, continuing to pet him as I fed him small pieces of chicken. He was hungry enough, biting my fingers in his eagerness to eat, his little teeth like razors. That bastard probably starved him as well, although he didn't look too gangly from what I could see.

"Are ya gonna keep him?"

"What am I gonna do with a puppy?" The thought had briefly crossed my mind on the way to the clubhouse, but then I decided against it. Puppies were a lot of work, let alone one with a disability. No, it was better if I did what I could, then passed him off to one of the no-kill shelters in the area so they could find him a permanent home with people who had the time to care for him.

"You need somethin' to go home to, man."

Ignoring his observant comment, I asked, "Speaking of, why didn't you go home last night?" I knew things had been rough between him and Edana. Ever since she'd been attacked, she'd been having some nasty nightmares, pulling away from Hawke which in turn strained their already tumultuous relationship.

"I can't help her. She doesn't wanna talk about it, and every time I even try to touch her she freaks out and starts cryin'." He ran his hands over his face. "I don't know what to do. She wants to go stay with her sister in Florida."

"Maybe it's the best thing right now," I suggested. Even as the words left my lips I knew I would've never followed my own advice if I were in his shoes. I'd be fighting to keep my woman close.

"Well, apparently I don't get a say. She's already packed a fuckin' bag." He plopped down in a nearby chair and hung his head. "I just don't know what to do," he mumbled.

I'd never seen Hawke so despondent. Normally, he was taunting the guys, crossing lines to where they'd retaliate and put him in his place. Or at least try to if Tripp wasn't there to interject.

After a few minutes of him wallowing and me feeding the rest of the scraps to the puppy, we both acknowledged our conversation was over with a simple nod, then proceeded to walk out into the common room.

Sitting on the sofa with a beer in hand and the puppy next to me, I welcomed the sweet arms of numbness. I needed one last ride to oblivion before I had to man up and deal with my shit with Braylen. I had to decide if I wanted to let her all the way in or let her go. It wasn't fair to string her along and I knew it. We'd both be worse in the end if I didn't make a decision once and for all.

FIFTEEN

Braylen

I SAW HIM KILL MY mom. How do I ever get over something like that? Those words kept me awake for an hour after I'd left Ryder on the couch. Who did he see? How did his mother die? What happened to the man who did it? How old was he?

I wanted so desperately to push him to tell me more, but I knew in his state he'd either refuse or ignore me completely. Much like he'd do if he was sober. The only difference between him being intoxicated or lucid, however, was that in his oblivion, he'd let something personal slip through. I wasn't even sure if he knew he'd said anything out loud.

His statement explained a lot, like the nightmares. Hell, even when he'd unknowingly attacked me in his sleep. In his dreams, was he trying to protect his mother? Had he tried when it happened for real? I was riddled with questions, but I knew enough about Ryder that no amount of persuasion would make him open up. Irritatingly, he had to come to that step all on his own; the more I pushed him, the more he'd shut down and distance himself.

———— ◆ ————

RYDER WAS GONE WHEN I woke up. I tried his cell to make sure he was okay but it went straight to voice mail. Apparently, he'd stolen Jagger's keys while he was sleeping and took off at God knew what hour of the morning. I prayed he had at least sobered up before he left.

Kena was off from work, so I gave Jagger a ride home before heading to work. He asked me to wait until one of the guys could pick him up so they could follow me to the salon, but I insisted I was fine. It was the middle of the day; what could possibly happen? He tried Ryder on his cell, and he also got his voice mail. After some reluctance, Jagger agreed to let me leave.

How gracious.

It was noon when I finally arrived, and since my first client of the day was waiting for me, I wasted no time diving right in. I could certainly use the much-needed distraction from all things Ryder.

———— ◆ ————

"I'M SORRY IF I CAUSED any kind of tension between you and your boyfriend," George said, flashing me an apologetic smile while I worked on his hair later that afternoon.

"He's not my boyfriend," I blurted, slamming my mouth closed as soon as I'd spoken. It was the truth, but George didn't need to know anything more about my personal business.

"Oh, I thought—"

"It's complicated." I kept my eyes down, pretending I was focusing on what I was doing, but the truth was I didn't want to talk about Ryder with him. Or anyone for that matter. The topic only served to upset me.

"If you ever want to uncomplicate things, just let me know. I'll be the first in line to take you out." He chuckled, trying his best to lighten the mood. Too bad for him mine was already soured.

Five minutes later I was done. He came in so often it didn't take long to shape up his hair. "All finished," I announced, unsnapping the cape from behind his neck. "Did you want to make an appointment for next time or just call?"

"Just book me in two weeks."

I should've known.

"Sure thing." After he paid and left me a large tip as usual, Sia strolled out from the office, looking exhausted and a little unwell.

"Are you feeling okay?" She'd changed her hair from pink to light purple, and I swore she was one of the few women who could pull off the look.

"My stomach's a little upset. I think I may be coming down with something. Do you mind closing up for me?"

"Not at all. Tammy and Michelle left already, and I don't have any more clients. Do you mind if I finish what I'm doing, then close up early?" *Please say yes.* The last thing I wanted to do was wait around for another hour just in case someone decided to pop in.

"Of course," Sia agreed. She slung her purse over her shoulder, gave me a weakened smile and walked out to her car.

Music was what I needed in order to make the mundane task of sweeping not so bad, so I flicked the switch for the sound system and got to work. Both Tammy and Michelle were great stylists, but when they were done for the day, they were done. Which meant that sometimes they didn't sweep up their stations or put their used towels in the back room to be washed. And since I told my friend I would close up, I wanted to ensure the salon looked its best when opened the following day.

Ten minutes into my task, I heard the bell over the door ring, alerting me that someone had walked in. "I'm sorry but we're closing early for the evening," I called out over my shoulder.

No answer.

Silence.

And the door's bell didn't ring again, indicating the person had left.

Maybe they didn't hear me over the music, although I'd kept it a reasonable level. Resting the broom against one of the stations, I slowly turned around, goose bumps prickling my skin with the oddest sensation of unease. I wasn't even fully facing the person before his hands were around my throat, my eyes popping wide in fear as he backed me against the nearest wall.

Looking into the face of a complete stranger, one who was intent on doing me harm, was the scariest thing I'd ever encountered.

Terror raced through every cell.

My lungs seized.

My heart raced.

My vision tunneled.

My body went on lockdown, all of my senses heightened in fear.

I had no idea who the man was or what he wanted. Well, I could guess what he wanted, but I hoped he was just there to rob the place. Maybe he was a drug addict looking for his next fix. Or maybe he was looking to do something a bit more sinister.

He was tall and lanky, but there was no doubt he was strong, his grip on my throat rendering me powerless. My fingers scratched at his hands but it only served to anger him more than he already was, so I dropped them to my sides, hoping and praying he'd let me go soon.

Looking at him was painful, and would no doubt give me nightmares for years to come, but I wanted to be able to describe him in case I made it out of there alive. Eyes the color of coal peered back at me while I struggled to breathe. His shoulder-length hair was light brown, but there were streaks of gray running through it. Scars riddled his face, one in particular standing out amongst the others—a long-since healed, jagged mutilation ran from the corner of his mouth all the way up to his hairline.

"You sure are a pretty one, aren't ya?" he asked, leaning closer and inhaling the air around me. His breath smelled like garlic and smoke, one whiff of it enough to make me wanna pass out. "I think maybe I'll take ya for a test drive as well." I wanted to shout, 'As well as what?' but obviously I couldn't.

Cocking his head ever so slightly, a menacing grin spread across his mouth, warning me something bad was about to happen. When his free hand shot out and seized my breast, I found my strength to struggle once more. If he was going to rape me, then I'd give him the fight of his life. Tightening his grip around my neck, he kicked my legs apart before lowering his hand to cup me between my thighs.

"You're gonna like what I do to you, bitch. So much you're gonna go runnin' back to your boyfriend to tell him what a real man feels like inside your cunt." Spittle hit my cheek as he tried to unbutton my jeans. I rocked my hips from side to side to try and escape his touch, but he was just too strong. "After I've had my fill of you, I'm gonna sample your little sister. Don't think that fighter is gonna stop me," he blurted, laughing when he saw the pure horror light up my face.

All of a sudden I didn't care what he did to me, as long as he didn't touch Kena. How did he even know about her, or me for that matter?

As he unzipped my jeans, the bell over the door sounded once more. It was then I mentally berated myself for not calling Ryder to see if he was going to meet me there to follow me home. I'd been so stubborn about him being my shadow that I'd inadvertently put myself in danger.

"We have to go," another stranger shouted. I couldn't see who it was because the man throttling me blocked my view of the front door.

"We have time," my attacker said, pulling the waistband away from my jeans, his fingers fumbling with the material of my panties. I closed my eyes and tried to imagine I was somewhere else, but it didn't work. I felt every callus on his fingers, smelled his breath as it hit my face and heard his breathing increase as he scraped his rough hand over my shivered skin.

"No we don't," the other guy warned, a touch of panic in his voice as he stood guard, openly allowing his friend to assault me. "We gotta get outta here before he shows up. You know he's coming."

Is he talking about Ryder?

Pulling his hand free from my jeans, thankfully not touching my most private of areas, he smirked before releasing me. My hands instantly shielded my neck, flinching at the already forming bruises.

Taking a step back, he spat, "Fuckin' Knights. They took out our prez, and now we'll stop at nothing until we wipe out every last one of 'em."

Without another word, the evil bastard spun around and walked out of the salon as calm as could be. His partner in crime had already disappeared before I could get a good look at him, but I figured none of it mattered. All that was important was making sure that Kena was safe.

After my initial shock finally wore off, I grabbed my phone from the counter and texted my sister. No response. I sent her another message. Then another, and another. Still nothing. Before leaving the salon, I made sure the coast was clear, locking up before racing toward my car. I dialed Jagger's number, but it only went to voice mail after a few rings. Leaving him a rushed message to call me back right away, I hung up and tried to call Ryder, but he wasn't answering either.

What the hell?

Why isn't anyone answering their phones?

Thankfully we lived close, but that didn't stop me from speeding home so fast I swore I broke every traffic law. I barely put the car in Park and shut off the engine before I was racing toward the front of our house, keys in hand and fumbling with the lock before practically kicking open the door.

"Kena!" I shouted, running from room to room searching for her. But she wasn't home. I tried texting her again, but again she didn't respond. I called Jagger but still nothing.

Frustration fueled my emotions, switching from shock and fear for what I'd been through to an unbearable need to protect my sister from the man who'd attacked me.

Barreling out of the house, I jumped back in my car and took off toward Ryder's, trying him again as well. When my calls continued to go unanswered, I tossed my cell on the passenger seat and concentrated on getting to Ryder's as fast as possible.

As it turned out, he wasn't home either. Slumping down on his front porch steps, I cradled my head in my hands and finally allowed myself to release what I'd been feeling as soon as that bastard had left the salon. Tears rushed down my cheeks, the adrenaline of trying to find Kena finally wearing off. My body trembled until I expelled every last bit of anxiety swirling inside me. Minutes later, I gathered myself, wiped away the rest of my tears and headed back toward my car.

There was only one other place I could check. I just hoped I remembered how to get there.

SIXTEEN

Ryder

STONE AND HIS WOMAN STOPPED by to talk to Marek before heading out to shop for more baby stuff. Adelaide was just over four months pregnant, and the bigger she got, the more Stone had a permanent look of worry imprinted on his face. The last time she found out she was pregnant, she also found out she had ovarian cancer, and while she was now in remission, the fear was there that the disease could always return.

The club's VP cradled his daughter, Riley, close to his chest when they'd approached and saw that there was a ball of fur on my lap, resting peacefully from a very trying and dramatic day. I'd told them both all about what had happened, and that was when Adelaide recommended Dr. Rubin. Of course, she fussed over the little guy, petting him and then stealing him from me, showing him to Riley before finally handing him back a few minutes later.

Luckily, the vet's office was able to take me on short notice, especially after I gave them a rundown of what had happened. The doctor confirmed the puppy was in good health, and a purebred to boot. A border collie. He also placed him at around six weeks, exactly what I'd guessed.

I had just been coming back from the bathroom, Hawke watching over the dog in my absence, when I heard a commotion outside. Before any of us could find out what it was, the door burst open and in ran Braylen, her blonde hair wild and matching the look in her eyes.

Terror.

Rushing forward, I reached her in no time, my eyes landing on her neck, the skin discolored from forming bruises.

"What happened?" I yelled, gently touching her throat. She flinched, which only served to infuriate me. Not at her but at whoever dared to put their hands on her. Every passing second restricted my breathing, a fierceness racing through my veins the likes of which I hadn't felt in a very long time. "Who did this?"

"I don't know," she confessed. Braylen looked around the room before giving me her attention. "Where's Kena?"

"I have no idea. She's probably with Jagger."

"Where is he?" She was frantic.

I shook my head, looking to Stone before turning toward Marek, who'd been hanging out in the doorway of Chambers.

"Anyone know where the hell Jagger's at?" I asked.

"I'll call him," Marek offered, reaching for his phone and dialing Jagger's number right away. After the third try, he'd finally gotten through. "Where you at?" Seconds of silence. "Is Kena with you? Then get to the clubhouse ASAP." Another second of silence. "Now, and make sure to keep an eye out on the way here." Our prez tossed his phone on the table next to him and said, "They're on their way."

I saw Braylen relax a little, but she was still freaked out, and I couldn't blame her. "Tell me exactly what happened," I coaxed, guiding her to the couch to take a seat. I kicked Hawke's leg for him to move and he got up, walking over to the bar without complaint. Crouching in front of her, I hooked my fingers under her chin and raised her head. She flinched but then steadied herself as soon as she looked at me.

"Sorry," she whispered, a lone tear coating her cheek. Wiping it away, she began telling me, and everyone standing around us, what happened to her. "I was closing up early at the salon when a guy came in. I didn't see him at first because my back was to him, and by the time I turned around, it was too late."

I couldn't help it. My anger bubbled forth before I could halt it. "Why were you there by yourself, and why didn't you lock the door?"

"Ryder," Adelaide warned, frowning at my brief snap of interrogation. "Stop." Her voice was softer on her last command.

Taking a breath, I nodded at Braylen, silently asking her to continue.

"He wrapped his hands around my throat and pushed me against the wall. And then when he tried to take off my jeans . . . I really thought. . . ." Her gaze drifted away as if lost to the horrific ordeal all over again.

"Fuck," I growled, my hands instantly curling into tight fists. My outburst threw her back into the moment. She fiddled with the bottom of her shirt, not quite knowing what to do with herself. When another tear appeared, I placed my hands over hers and tried to soothe her, letting her know I was there and no one was gonna hurt her.

"What did he look like?" Stone asked, approaching from the side. "Did he say anything specific?"

"Back up," I warned, throwing him a threatening look before hoisting myself off my haunches and taking the seat directly next to Braylen.

"We need to know, Ryder," Stone rasped, taking a step back when he saw I was about to lose my shit. Adelaide placed her hand on Stone's arm and gently shook her head as if to tell him to wait.

Braylen started speaking, answering Stone's questions before I could ask her anything of my own. "He was tall and skinny, shoulder-length gray-brown hair with facial scars. One long nasty one from here to here," she said, running her finger from her mouth to her forehead. She took a moment before continuing, glancing from each person present to the next before opening her mouth again. "He said something about you taking out their president, so now they're gonna wipe out every last one of you."

Shivers racked her body, but when I slung my arm over her, offering her comfort and protection, she leaned into me. I was wrought with guilt from not protecting her from that asshole, but I sure as hell wouldn't make that mistake again. "Oh, and there was another guy with him, standing by the door." Turning to face me, she uttered, "They know all about me and you . . . and Kena. How do they about my sister?" Her voice became panicked, and streams of tears began to fall again.

I pulled her close and kissed her temple over and over. "It's okay. No one is gonna hurt you or your sister. I promise." I heard some of the guys mumbling something to each other, but I wasn't about to leave Braylen's side to find out what. Not right then.

Ten minutes later, Jagger and Kena finally arrived at the club, rushing through the door because they knew Marek had meant business when he called.

"What's going on," Jagger asked, looking all around and waiting for someone to fill him in.

"Braylen was attacked," Adelaide blurted, looking at Kena specifically when she said it.

Right away, Kena raced forward and sat on the other side of her sister. *Are you okay? What happened?* She didn't even wait for Braylen to answer before she was hugging her so tightly I thought they'd never separate. But they finally did.

"I'm fine now. I'm just worried about you," she confessed, pulling Kena in for another hug. When they finally broke apart for the second time, Braylen looked up at Jagger. "Please make sure you don't let anything happen to her. Stay glued to her side if you have to. Please, Jagger," she begged, more tears welling in her eyes as she pleaded with him to keep her little sister safe.

"You have my word. Nothing will ever happen to her."

In reality, none of us could keep our women safe, not 100 percent, no matter how much we wanted. Not unless we had a . . .

"We need to go on lockdown, Prez," I yelled, standing and walking toward him with purpose. "Enough is enough. We need to find out who the fuck keeps threatening us."

"We know who keeps doing it," Hawke said, walking right up to us. "And the bastard Braylen described sounds exactly like one of the guys who attacked Edana." His posture went rigid, the look in his eyes one of determination. "Do you know how lucky your woman is, Ryder?"

I did, but I wanted to be sure Braylen wasn't leaving anything out, no matter how difficult it was to tell me. Spinning around, I was back next to her in three long strides. "Did anything else happen? Did he . . . ?" She knew what I meant and shook her head. "You can tell me." Even as I said the words, I had no idea what I'd do if I found out she'd suffered the same fate as Edana.

"No, nothing like that."

I thought someone was gonna put up a fight about my demand for a lockdown, but all of my brothers simply nodded.

"Okay," Marek agreed. "We go on lockdown till we can find 'em."

I should've been relieved. I should've been happy that Braylen would be at the clubhouse safe and sound, but I wasn't. Not entirely. Yes, she would be safe under our constant watch, but because we had to go in search of the bastards threatening our club, and our families, we were sure to get bloody.

SEVENTEEN

Braylen

RYDER EXPLAINED WHAT A LOCKDOWN meant, and while my initial reaction would've been to reject such a thing, I was only too happy to stay at the club until they sorted everything out. "Eliminated the threat," as Jagger so casually stated. I wasn't sure what that meant exactly, and I didn't think I wanted to.

The guys had taken Kena and me back to our place to pack a bag, enough for a week's stay. They said it shouldn't take any longer than that. Once back at the club, Ryder showed me to his room, placing my bag on the chair and pulling me in for a hug. I knew he was upset about what happened to me, but the one good thing that came out of it was that he seemed to be showing more of an affectionate side. A more tender side, to be more precise. Maybe it took an incident so drastic to finally make him realize that his feelings toward me might be more than what he wanted to let on.

No matter how tired I was, I just couldn't fall asleep. Ryder told me that he had to leave for a bit but would be back as soon as he could. He wouldn't tell me where he was going, other than that it was club business, but he assured me he wouldn't be in any danger. I wasn't so sure I believed him.

After another half hour of restlessness, I gave up, pushed off the covers and left his room, walking toward the front part of the club where a few of the members were still gathered, straddling the barstools and throwing back shot after shot.

It was close to eleven at night, and I had a feeling these guys were just starting their evening. Kena and Jagger weren't present, so I assumed they were in his room. My anxiety had started to come back, thinking about my sister being in danger, when Sully came striding out from the kitchen. I hadn't seen her in some time, and she was certainly welcome company.

"Hey, Braylen," she greeted. "How are you holding up?" Ryder had told me a few things about Sully's past, and I thought she was the bravest woman I knew. Surely the club's lockdown was nothing compared to what she'd been through.

"I'm all right, I suppose. Just worried, ya know?"

She gestured toward the couch, and I followed, sitting next to her and smiling at her genuine kindness.

"Try not to fret too much. The men will handle it." She sounded so sure. "They'll die before they let anything happen to us."

"That's what I'm afraid of," I whispered.

"Sorry, I probably shouldn't have put it like that." Sully shot me an apologetic smile, patting my hand before leaning back against the sofa. Her dark eyes roamed over the space of the common area, smiling while watching the mundane task of men drinking and talking. Looking back toward me, she said, "You probably think I'm crazy for smiling, but I'm still getting used to this life."

"But I thought you've been with them for quite some time now."

"I have, and while it was a little bumpy in the beginning between Cole and me, the entire club has always treated me well. I constantly waited for the other shoe to drop, but it never did. Not with them." Her smile was infectious, and I soon find myself mirroring her expression. "So tell me, how are things with you and Ryder?"

"Bumpy." We both chuckled at my word choice, but it fit perfectly. I caught glimpses of another side of Ryder, but just when I thought he'd show me more, he'd throw those walls back up. It was frustrating, to say the least.

"Give him time. He cares about you. A lot. He tries to hide it but I see it, and so does everyone else." Her words gave me comfort, something I very much needed after the day I'd had. Twisting her black hair up into a messy bun on top of her head, she threw her arms over her head and stretched, a yawn coming out of nowhere. "Oh my God, I'm so sorry. It's not you, I promise." She chuckled. "It's just that I haven't been getting much sleep lately.

"Because of everything with the club?"

"No. Sadly I'm used to that. It's because of Kaden."

"Who?" I didn't remember Ryder mentioning anyone named Kaden.

"The little boy Cole and I have been caring for. Tripp's ex dropped him off out of the blue, claiming he was his when in fact he wasn't. When she didn't get what she wanted from Tripp—although who knows what that even was—she took off and left her baby here. He hasn't been able to locate her as of yet." A mixed look of hope and sorrow took over Sully's expression, and I couldn't help but feel bad for her.

"So he's been keeping you up late?" I wanted to take her mind off whatever plagued her, and the mere mention of the baby had her smiling once again.

"Yes, but I'm not complaining. I've always wanted children. I know he's not really mine, but I can't help feeling an attachment to him. It's one of the reasons Cole was hesitant to take him while Tripp searched for his ex. He knew how hard it would be for me to give him back when he finds her." She let out a hefty sigh. "But I can't think of that right now, can I?" Her question was rhetorical. A brief moment of silence lingered between us before she asked, "Do you want kids someday?"

"Do I want kids?" I repeated. "Well, it's not like I've never thought about it, but I guess I just never settled on an answer. I guess . . . I don't know. With the right guy, I suppose I'd be open to the idea."

She bumped my shoulder with hers. "Could that be Ryder?" She wiggled her brows and I laughed.

"I'm not sure." *Better to be neutral, right?*

"I wonder if he wants any more. Then again, I doubted Cole would come around to the idea of Kaden, but when I see him with the little boy now, my heart swells. He's fallen in love with him as much as I have."

I stopped listening after she uttered the first sentence.

"Wait. Go back. What did you mean by 'any *more*'? Does Ryder have kids?" My voice rose higher than intended, drawing the attention of Hawke, who was busy drinking at the bar.

Sully's eyes widened before she mumbled, "Shit." Turning fully toward me, she continued with, "Sorry, Braylen. I thought you knew. He has a daughter. I think she's around ten."

Tears of anger flooded my vision, but I refused to cry. Pulling in a deep breath, I exhaled before speaking again. "No. I didn't know. I guess he didn't want to share that with me." What did that say about his feelings toward me, that he wouldn't tell me he had a child? Just when I thought he might be coming around to the idea of us being more than a casual thing—in his eyes, at least—he abolished all of those crazy notions with his secret. One of many, apparently.

"I'm so sorry. Truly. Maybe he just wanted to make sure you were it for him before he told you?" I knew Sully was only trying to help, but she was inadvertently making it worse.

I rose from the couch while trying to keep my composure, and it was at that exact moment that Ryder walked through the door, amused at something Stone had said.

His eyes instantly found mine. He muttered something to the club's VP before advancing toward me, but when he saw the irate and hurt look on my face, he stopped midstride.

"Braylen?"

"Don't come near me," I shouted. I hadn't meant to cause a scene, but my temper escaped before I could rein it in. I clamped my mouth shut before hurrying off toward the back of the club, heading straight for his room. I prayed there was a lock on the door; otherwise, I couldn't be held accountable for my actions if he came after me.

I heard Sully apologizing to him as I slammed the bedroom door with such ferocity I swore it shook the entire clubhouse.

EIGHTEEN

Ryder

"GODDAMNIT, SULLY. WHAT WERE YOU thinking?" I paced back and forth. "This is why I keep my shit private," I gritted, flashing everyone a pissed-off look even though I knew none of them deserved it. This was all on me.

"You better watch how you're talkin' to my wife," Marek growled, appearing out of nowhere. "It's not her fault you didn't tell Braylen about your kid."

Not acknowledging him or his truthful spewing, I hauled off toward the back of the club, knowing damn well I was the last person Braylen wanted to see. I had to deal with the issue before it escalated. Part of me wanted to leave it alone and get drunk, but the other part, the one that had developed feelings for the feisty woman, wanted to apologize and see if I could make things right between us. We'd been at odds for weeks, and I wanted the stress to stop. I had enough on my mind with the threat against the club; I needed to check her forgiveness off the ever-growing list.

Without knocking, I flung open the door to my assigned room and found her. She was sitting on the edge of the bed, the bag she'd packed resting on her lap.

"Where do you think you're going?" I hadn't meant to sound so gruff, but there was no way in hell she was leaving. Not until we'd eliminated the threat, which could take days.

"I'm not staying here."

"You're not leaving."

She raised her head and glared at me. Clutching her bag tightly, she said, "You can't keep me here against my will. That's called kidnapping, Ryder. Look it up."

"Well, then I'll kidnap you if I have to. You're not going anywhere." She parted her lips to respond, but I took a step closer and cut her off. "I know you're aware of the threat against us, and unfortunately that threat extends to you and your sister." Underhanded move, but I had to use it. Her breath hitched. "So until we can take care of it, no one is allowed to leave."

"You can leave." It wasn't a question.

"I have to help keep us safe, so yeah, I do get to leave."

"That's not fair," she mumbled, fidgeting with her bag again before standing and walking across the room, farther away from me. I didn't know if she thought by releasing the bag she was surrendering to her fate for the next few days, but she refused to let it go. "I want to be alone. You need to leave."

"No." I braced myself for impact. She'd been through a lot; surely all of her fear, anger, and uncertainty was gonna come bursting from her in the next few seconds.

"No?" she yelled, her mouth agape in astonishment. I wasn't goin' anywhere, not until I convinced her she was safe with us at the club. Not until I gained her forgiveness for not telling her about my daughter. Not until . . . fuck! I didn't know what else I wanted from Braylen, but it sure as hell wasn't for her to be standing so far away from me, looking at me like she didn't know who the fuck I was. Admittedly, I had a lot of demons, personal and shared with the other men of the Knights, but I was just me. A man fumbling through life trying to find some goddamn meaning.

Braylen was the sliver of light in an otherwise dark and lonely world. I'd always had an inferno burning inside me my entire life, and the woman standing in front of me was the first person to ever calm me. I couldn't explain it—I just knew she was it for me. I just had to convince her that I wanted her once and for all.

No more mixed signals.

No more thoughtless words.

No more secrets.

"Braylen," I said softly, relaxing my tensed muscles before erasing some of the distance between us. "I need you to listen to me."

"Listen to you? Why? Because you wanna lie some more?" Before I saw it coming, she launched her bag at me, hitting me in the chest and knocking me back a step. "Oh, sorry," she spat sarcastically. "Not lie. Just omit everything!" Her voice rose a few octaves. If I didn't calm her down, and fast, I knew our business was gonna be made public for the entire club to hear.

"Calm down."

"No, I won't calm down. You won't share any of yourself with me. You refused to tell me why you attacked me in your sleep, and then you kept something as huge as having a child from me." She backed up a step. "Do you know how that makes me feel? I know I may appear strong and brave, but I'm hurt." Her bottom lip quivered, and it almost gutted me. "You hurt me," she said softly. "You've basically told me that I mean nothing to you. That I'm just someone to pass the time with when you're bored. Someone to have sex with when you're horny." A lone tear fell and she wiped it away with an irritated swipe of her finger.

"You know that's not true."

"No, I don't."

"Yes, you do." I took a tentative step closer.

"Don't" was all she said before lowering her head, breaking eye contact with me and essentially giving up.

"Braylen."

Nothing. Not a single muscle moved in her body. I swore she held her breath as well.

"Braylen," I said with more authority, hoping she'd hear something in my tone that would make her look at me.

Still nothing.

"Goddamnit, Braylen! Fuckin' look at me." Apparently when I shouted it worked.

She finally picked her head up, her stare cutting into me like a thousand knives. More tears streaked her cheeks, and I couldn't stop myself. I rushed forward and pulled her into me before she could stop me, wrapping my arms around her so tightly I feared I'd bruise her ribs.

"Just let me go," she cried, feebly trying to push me away, but I refused.

"I can't." She trembled in my arms. "I'll tell you anything you want to know," I promised, kissing the top of her head, continuing to crush her distraught body to mine. "No more secrets."

It was in that moment that I fully let go, relieved I could finally share myself completely with someone. A ton of bricks dropped from me as I felt her nod against my chest.

Here goes nothin'.

NINETEEN

Braylen

I SAT ON THE EDGE of the bed while Ryder pulled up a chair so he could sit in front of me. Hesitancy stroked the air around him but he pushed on, taking a deep breath before he started to talk.

"You heard what I said back at your place, didn't you?" His brown eyes bored into mine, searching for something I was unclear of in that moment. "Before you left me on the couch?"

I wanted him to be truthful with me, so I made sure to return the favor. "Yes." Short and simple, yet it was anything but. Even though I had an idea he knew what my answer would be, he still looked a little shocked. He quickly regained his composure, wasting no more time before he told me what happened to his mother.

"Richard came into our lives when I was just five. From what I could remember he seemed okay, bringing me a toy whenever he visited, but it wasn't long after they met that he moved in with us. And that's when things changed. Most of my memories of him after that point are of him being drunk, and when he'd been drinking, he'd whale on my mother. When I tried to help her, I got it too."

I reached forward and captured his hands, offering him support while he worked up to the worst part. Even though I was still hurt, and angry with him, I knew I had to put all of my emotions aside and allow Ryder to tell me his story.

Breathless moments passed where the both of us remained silent, him working up the courage to tell me the reason he seemed so closed off and secretive, and me silently contemplating if I had the energy to forge ahead with a relationship with the very intense and complicated man sitting in front of me.

He loosened his hands from mine and pulled back, running them down his thighs in uncertainty. "One night it got really bad. I woke up to her screaming, and when I ran downstairs, I saw her on the ground, bleeding and clutching her stomach. I tried to save her, but I couldn't. She begged me to go back to my room and I did." He rose from the chair so fast it skidded behind him. "Fuck!" His fingers gripped his hair and I watched him slowly losing it. "If only I hadn't gone down there that night, maybe she'd still be alive."

"What do you mean? You just said he was beating her."

"He was, but when I tried to help her, he came after me. Came up to my room and tried to—" He suddenly stopped talking, and I knew reliving his past tore him up inside. So I waited, giving him the time he needed before finishing. "Looking back, I think he was gonna rape me, and when my mother saw his pants unzipped, pinning me facedown, she screamed for him to leave me alone. That's when he wrapped his belt around her neck and strangled her to death."

A shocked gasp escaped me. I couldn't stop it. Ryder muttering "I saw him kill my mom" when he was drunk did nothing to prepare me for the full story. I couldn't even imagine what he went through, watching his mother's life extinguished right in front of him.

"You were only trying to protect her. It's not your fault. The only one to blame is him. Only him," I repeated, hoping my words would break his irrational thought. I stood and tentatively approached him, his back to me as I walked up behind him. Resting my hand on the middle of his back, he flinched but then quickly relaxed.

Turning to face me, he looked emotionally beaten down. I knew it had been difficult, but I was thankful he'd finally told me, even after everything that'd happened between us.

"I wasn't sure I wanted you in my life," he announced. "Not permanently. After my mother's death, I closed myself off from everyone, only giving people the bare minimum. I think that's why I kept putting off telling you about my daughter."

His confession hurt, but at least now I understood him a little more. "And now?"

He seized my hands and placed them on his chest. "Now I can't imagine my life without you. I can't explain the pull you have over me, but I know I don't want to lose you. Ever." He circled his arm around my waist and drew me forward. "Please forgive me for not telling you sooner."

I looked deep into his eyes, drew his undivided attention because I needed him to really hear me. "I need some time to think about . . . us."

His arm fell to his side and he took a step back, my hand sliding off his chest. Ryder looked distraught, but for as much as I wanted to wipe away his sadness, I needed to make sure forging ahead with him was what I truly wanted.

I completely understood what he meant by the pull that existed between us because I felt it as well. Attraction, chemistry and raw passion certainly weren't an issue either. But could I trust him? Not only to continue to share himself with me, but with my heart?

I was in love with Ryder, but was it enough?

"Okay. Fair enough." He strode toward the door, but I didn't want him to leave just yet. So I decided to change the subject.

"Was there a puppy out there?" My question told him I was open to talking about something other than us, that I wanted to engage him while still taking the time I needed to process everything.

"Yeah," he answered over his shoulder, his hand gripping the door handle. "Come on, let's go see him."

———◆———

"WHAT ARE YOU GONNA NAME him?" I asked, accepting all of the puppy's kisses and trying not to smother him because he was so damn cute. Ryder told me how he found him, and while my heart broke for the little guy, I wanted to find the asshole who discarded him so carelessly and beat the hell out of him myself.

"I'm not."

"Why?"

"'Cause I'm not keepin' him." I looked at him like he was nuts, to which he said, "Bray, I can't have a puppy. You know how much work they are?"

"And? What's your point?" I passed the dog to Ryder, and without an ounce of hesitation, he took him, clutching him close to his chest. "You've already formed a bond with him. Don't give him away."

He didn't answer because he knew what I said was true.

"I'll take him," Hawke yelled from across the room. "He's a cute little fucker." He laughed when Ryder turned around and gave him a threatening glance.

"See. You don't wanna give him to anyone."

"No, I just don't want to give him to that jackass."

"I heard that," Hawke shouted before finishing off his drink.

"Good," Ryder replied, a small smirk appearing on his gorgeous face. Looking back at me, he shrugged. "You're right. Even though it's only been a day, I'm already attached to him, but I don't think I'm up for the commitment."

"What if I help you?" I offered, surprised the words came out so freely. *So much for needing time to think about us.*

"I thought you said you needed time to think about whether or not you wanted to be with me." His voice lowered as he spoke, and I knew it was because he wanted to keep our conversation as private as possible.

"We still have a lot to work through. Namely you telling me all about your daughter—the full story—but I'm not going anywhere, Ryder." I smiled and snatched the puppy from him, kissing his furry little head before walking toward the exit to take him outside. Ryder jogged until he caught up with me, smacking me on the ass as he ushered me forward.

TWENTY

Ryder

SIX DAYS THE LOCKDOWN LASTED.

Six days of knowing Braylen was safe.

Six days of not knowing if or when we'd ever catch the break we needed to finally move forward and put a plan in place to end the war between us and the Reapers once and for all.

"We got a hit," Marek shouted as soon as he walked into the clubhouse. "Chambers. Now." He strode into our meeting room and everyone present followed after him. The only ones missing were Stone and Breck. I knew our VP was in his room with Adelaide, and while I didn't have to guess what they were doing, it was gonna have to be cut short because we had an impromptu meeting.

After making sure Braylen was still asleep in my room, I rapped on Stone's door.

"Go away," he barked, grunting incoherently while I continued to bang on the door. I really didn't need to hear them goin' at it, but I had no other choice. His presence was needed, and I wouldn't walk away until he answered.

"Stone. Let's go."

"What the fuck?" I heard his heavy footsteps right before he yanked open the door, looking at me like he wanted to kill me. I could see Adelaide in the background, lying on the bed with tousled hair and the bedsheet pulled up to her neck. She was laughing, which only served to make me smile. "You better have a good reason, brother."

"Marek wants everyone in Chambers. Now. Then you can go back to trying to satisfy your woman." I moved back as he swung at me, practically tripping because he was using the door to shield his dick from view.

"Let's go, lover boy," I shouted over my shoulder as I disappeared down the hallway.

Walking into Chambers, I could feel the tension and worry pouring off every member. We probably all had the same question popping around inside our heads: *When the hell will all this end?* Unfortunately, there was gonna be more bloodshed before it was all said and done.

Once Stone joined us, throwing me another annoyed look to which I just smiled, Marek grabbed everyone's attention when he started to speak.

"I just got a call that a guy fitting the description of the one who attacked Braylen was spotted going into the Overbrook. He's not alone, though. Two other guys are with him." The Overbrook was a low-class stripper joint close to forty minutes away, a place we knew most of the Savage Reapers visited.

"Who called you?" Jagger asked, looking around the room and seeing everyone present except one man. "Breck?"

"Yeah," Marek affirmed.

"So what now?" Cutter asked, his stare darkening and looking none too pleased that his son was close to the enemy without any backup. "Are we goin' to get 'em? Just give me five minutes and they'll spill their guts, literally and figuratively."

Cutter wasn't shy about torturing when the situation called for it, but I'd have to intercede on this one, for at least one of the Reapers. The fucker who dared to put his hands on Braylen was gonna die a slow and painful death, whether or not he gave us pertinent information on his club. His fate would be sealed as soon as we captured him.

"I know our club has been through a lot over the past year or so, and normally I'd tell ya to be patient. That the time to react should be planned out." Marek slapped the table. "But fuck that!"

A few of the guys shouted, "Yeah!" while the rest of us just nodded. Of course, we'd follow whatever our prez said, but we couldn't hide our excitement that we'd be able to do something about our predicament sooner rather than later.

Marek doled out instructions like he always did, forever the leader. "Jagger, Tripp, and Cutter, you're goin' to meet Breck. Call him to find out exactly where he is. You know enough to stay in the background, showing yourselves only when necessary." He withdrew a plastic baggie from inside his cut, tossing the package on the table and sliding it toward where they sat. Trackers. "Put these on any of their bikes you see." The devices were small, would be virtually undetectable by the human eye, but for as high tech as they would undoubtedly be, they would only last two weeks. Three, tops.

The Reapers thought they were safe visiting the Overbrook, no doubt meeting whoever for deals as well as harassing the strippers. We'd never stepped foot there before, but we were always aware of their comings and goings throughout the years. We were just waiting for the perfect opportunity.

Looks like it's here.

"I want in on this one, Prez," I said, leaning forward and placing my hands on the table.

"And you will be. At the safe house, when they bring those bastards there. Take Hawke with you."

"What do you want me to do?" Trigger asked, intent on receiving his orders.

"You're gonna stay back with Stone and me."

Trigger gave a curt nod, the relief on his face that he'd be able to stay behind to watch over his pregnant niece more comforting to him than retaliating against our enemy. I couldn't say I blamed him. If I weren't so focused on making the scarred Reaper pay for what he did to Braylen, I'd be completely okay with staying back at the clubhouse with her.

"Anything else?" Marek looked to each man, giving us the opportunity to say whatever was on our minds. We only shared in the taste for revenge, so there was nothing but silence and anticipation swirling all around us, thick and heavy.

The gavel struck the wood with a thunderous sound, vibrating through the air and amping us up for what was gonna happen soon enough.

TWENTY-ONE

Braylen

I WOKE TO THE MATTRESS dipping beside me. Brief panic enveloped me until I realized it was Ryder. I felt safe whenever he was close, which was quite the conundrum since it was because of him that I'd been attacked and was now involved in his club's lockdown, essentially trapping me inside their clubhouse until they deemed otherwise.

"Sorry, babe. Didn't mean to scare you." I loved when he used terms of endearment. I knew it was corny, but they made me feel like he was truly mine.

"It's okay. Are you coming to bed?" I turned to face him, conscious of the puppy lying close to me, one eye open to see what all the noise was about.

"Not yet. I have to leave, but I'll be back. I promise." Even though he tried to mask it, I heard the worry in his voice. Ryder was a tough-looking man, had the personality to match, but there were times, like right then, when he was simply a human being. A flawed, unsure, slightly nervous person. It was his flaws that kept me interested in knowing the whole man. If that made any sense, because it sure as hell didn't to me most days.

"Where are you going? I thought the club was on lockdown." I was confused, and from the look on his face, I soon became alarmed. More for him than myself.

"Marek, Stone, and Trigger will be here to watch over you all. The rest of us are leaving. We have business to take care of. When it's done, we'll be back."

"But I don't want you to go." Sitting up, I moved the puppy to the other side of the bed so I could be closer to Ryder, wrapping my arms around his neck and pulling him to me. "Please don't go," I pleaded, having a bad feeling something was going to go terribly wrong. Having no idea where they were even headed off to, I still knew in my gut it wasn't a good thing.

"If I could stay here with you, I would, but I can't." Tension laced his words, but rather than argue with him, which was what I would have done before, I gave him what he needed—my acceptance of the situation. Besides, there wasn't anything I could do to change his mind. I knew when it came to his club, he would do what he needed to, come hell or high water.

He gave me a quick kiss, unhooked my hands clasped behind his neck and stood up. "Make sure to take care of Brutus."

"Who?"

"Brutus," he repeated, pointing toward the bundle of fur drifting in and out of sleep next to me.

"I thought you weren't gonna name him. Does this mean you're definitely keeping him?" With everything going on, I still couldn't hide my smile. I considered it a small win.

"Yeah, so make sure you watch over him." Ryder grabbed a few things from the dresser and tucked something into the waistband of his jeans before stopping by the door. Without looking at me, he said, "We'll talk more when I get back."

⸺ ♦ ⸺

THE MINUTES TURNED TO HOURS and still I heard nothing from Ryder, and neither had anyone else. At least I didn't think so. I doubted Marek or Stone were going to give me a play-by-play regarding their club's business.

Adelaide and Reece carefully sat down next to me, Adelaide rubbing her belly and grimacing. "I swore I wasn't gonna let that man come near me again after I gave birth to Riley." She smiled big when Stone's eyes caught hers. "But I just can't resist his charms."

"I don't think it's his charms that got you pregnant," Reece countered. I laughed, but it felt empty.

Seeing the worry on my face, Adelaide soothed, "It's better you know this now rather than years in. The club does stuff that won't make you happy. Ryder won't be able to tell you things, and it's frustrating, but he'll do it for your own good. For your safety." She continued to rub her stomach. "Stone's always telling me that there's an end in sight, that the danger toward the Knights won't always exist, but then shit like this happens."

"What exactly *is* going on?"

"Hell if I know. Just because I'm engaged to the VP doesn't mean I'm privy to information."

"How do you deal with not knowing, always wondering if he'll come back unharmed? Or at all?" I squirmed in my seat while looking at both of them, hesitant to hear the answer.

"When he goes away and can't tell me why, I remind him why he has to come back to me. That we have a family, and that if he stupidly puts himself in danger, I'll marry Tripp."

Reece chuckled at that one, her blue-gray eyes lighting up at the mention of her man. She was aware of the special bond Adelaide and Tripp shared, and she apparently had no issue with it.

"In all seriousness, there's nothing I *can* do but wait and pray he stays safe."

"That's it?"

"I'm afraid so." She gave me a grin before getting to her feet, Stone watching her and rushing right over. I thought it was adorable how much he fussed over her.

"Damnit, woman, you need to go lie down."

"Wanna come with me? Finish where we left off before?" Marek overheard their conversation and lifted his chin toward his VP. "We have your friend's approval. Now help me back to your room."

Stone just shook his head as he picked up his fiancée, carrying her down the hallway instead of allowing her to walk.

After briefly chatting about her own pregnancy, Reece and I soon followed suit and went back to our respective rooms.

The more I slept, the sooner Ryder would come back to me.

TWENTY-TWO

Ryder

MY MIND RACED WITH EVERYTHING I still wanted to tell Braylen, but I knew I had to focus on what was going to happen as soon as Breck, Jagger, Tripp and Cutter arrived. I had no doubt they'd snag the Reapers and bring them to us to be dealt with.

Hawke and I were in the basement of our club's safe house, which was only an hour away from our compound. It was located in an average-looking residential area—hiding in plain sight, so to speak.

The room was soundproof, which made it perfect to do what we needed to and remain inconspicuous with our neighbors. I was sure they often wondered about who lived there, but they never saw any of us long enough to inquire. We visited mostly at night, pulling directly into the garage and sealing out the rest of the world until our job was finished.

That night would be no different.

"I can't take this much longer," Hawke complained, pacing while driving the both of us crazy.

"If you don't stay still, I'm gonna put you on your ass, brother," I threatened, his anxiety increasing my own.

"Fuck you."

"No, thanks. I got a woman for that."

"Yeah, a woman those fuckers attacked."

He just had to go and throw that back at me, didn't he? I advanced on him, shoving him against the nearest wall, my hands clutching his cut and barely keeping him still.

"I know exactly what they did to her, one bastard in particular. Don't forget that shit." I drew my hands back but stayed planted in his personal space. "I know you want revenge for what they did to your woman. I only have a sliver of an idea of the rage flowing through your veins, but you need to rein it in. And do it before they get here. Otherwise you could do something that'll blow back on all of us."

Hawke's expression was blank, his eyes glazing over before becoming glassy. If I didn't know any better, I would've thought he was about to cry, and I knew it would have nothing to do with him being scared or sad or any of that crap. I knew it was because the fury ricocheting through him was almost too much, and his body needed some sort of release.

After several minutes of the both of us standing toe-to-toe, the silence both our friend and enemy, he gathered himself and nodded, the glassiness of his eyes disappearing as if it never existed.

My phone dinged a half hour later with a text message. Looking to Hawke, I said, "They're coming down the street now."

————◆————

I SHOULD'VE BEEN USED TO blood-curdling screams from these bastards, but I wasn't. It took me a few minutes after Cutter started in on one of the two Reapers they'd ambushed at the Overbrook to regain my steel composure. The smell of blood, piss, and vomit filled my nostrils and turned my stomach.

Breck had been keeping watch in the dark across the street from the strip joint when a man fitting the description of the one who attacked Braylen pulled up on his bike, two more of his buddies flanking him on his right side. More of them had arrived after his initial call to Marek. I was sure if anyone saw Breck, they would've thought he was some sort of creeper, hiding in the cage—aka van—with a large pair of binoculars attached to his face.

Once backup had arrived in the form of his father, Jagger and Tripp hid in the back until Breck told them their opportunity had arrived. Two stumbling Reapers appeared outside and briefly argued, their scene enough of a distraction to allow our men to swoop in and snatch them. Jagger had explained it had been easy—a few punches and both of the enemy's men had been rendered unconscious.

Now they were both strapped to chairs, their hands and feet bound so they had no chance of escape. They'd die in this basement, their bodies never to be discovered. Their disappearance from the Overbook would be speculated over, but no one would be able to prove what happened to them. Much like their president, Psych. They all figured we had something to do with him vanishing, but they had no proof.

And they never would.

The guys had put trackers on all of the Reapers' bikes sitting outside the joint. We knew their club would recover their rides and take them back to their relocated compound. The night Psych had Zip killed, kidnapping Adelaide and Kena, we'd called in reinforcements from our Laredo chapter, wiping out the Reapers' clubhouse, killing as many as we could during the battle and setting their compound ablaze.

Circling the two men, reveling in their distress, I cracked my neck from side to side, thinking about exactly what I wanted to do to them. The one with the jagged scar more than the other fucker.

"I'll tell you whatever you want to know," one of them cried. "Please just stop." Cutter had detached a few of his fingers and was preparing to take off his right thumb when he pleaded with us to cease the torture.

"Man the fuck up," Breck yelled. "You knew what you were getting into when you joined that cesspool of a club." He landed a harrowing punch straight to the guy's nose and blood spurted everywhere. "We don't need to hear anything you wanna tell us."

"The time for talkin' is over," Hawke mumbled loud enough for the two men to hear.

The crunch of bone had the man screaming once again, the look on Cutter's face stoic . . . and a bit unnerving. Once his thumb had been severed, the man passed out. It was the only time Cutter smirked.

Knowing he was up next, the man who'd attacked Braylen smiled, although there was a fleeting look of fear that passed over him as his eyes flitted to each of us. He completely ignored his buddy, instead choosing to try and intimidate us with his lack of fear. Little did he know that Hawke and I had something special planned for him.

I'd snapped pics of both of them and sent them to Marek, asking him to show them to Braylen, Adelaide, and Sully. I was still waiting for a response when Jagger spoke up.

"Listen, as much as I'd love to hang out and see these two take their last breath, I wanna get back. Do you need me for anything?"

"I think we're good," I said. "Take my bike. We're definitely gonna need the cage to get rid of 'em."

"I'm gonna go too," Tripp announced. "I need to make sure this whole thing isn't stressing Reece out too much. Don't want anything to happen to her or the baby."

"You can take my bike," Hawke said to his brother. "But if you do anything to it, I'm gonna kick your ass."

"You'd like to think you can," the nomad responded, snatching Hawke's keys midair before giving him the finger. Jagger and Tripp ascended the basement steps, leaving Cutter, Breck, Hawke and me to take care of the two Reapers. The guy who'd passed out was slowly coming to, and as soon as his eyes finally focused, his body started trembling.

"Oh for fuck's sake," Breck barked. "I can't take this guy anymore." Before any of us could stop him, he pulled his gun from his waistband, pointed it at the guy's chest and pulled the trigger. Perfect aim. Right to his heart. The man slumped over as blood coated his shirt, his cut hanging open so we could all see the fatal damage Breck had caused.

My hands flew to my ears. "Goddamnit! You could've warned us," I roared. "My fuckin' ears are ringin'" To say I was pissed was an understatement, but it wasn't me who shoved Breck. It was his father.

"What were you thinkin'?" Cutter asked.

"What's the big deal? The room is soundproof."

"Yeah, but it's not idiot-proof," Hawke retorted, wiggling his finger in his ear while throwing Breck a nasty look.

"I don't wanna be here all night," Breck continued. "We snatched these two, now let's just kill 'em. Get it over with." Tossing his gun on the metal tray in the corner, he stared at his father, then looked to Hawke and me. "What?" He threw his hands up in frustration.

"Cutter, maybe you and Breck should go. We'll take care of these two," I said, knowing damn well it was gonna come down to Hawke and me finally ending the lone Reaper's life.

A hesitant look flashed across Cutter's face.

"Are you sure?" He reached for a rag and wiped some of the blood from his hands.

"Yeah, we got it," I replied, glancing to Hawke before turning back to father and son.

"Okay. We'll see ya back at the clubhouse."

Cutter had driven his truck to meet Breck at the Overbrook, so that was what they took back with them. As soon as we heard the squeak of the garage door, Hawke and I stood in front of the Reaper, feet spread wide and our hands resting in front of us.

"Then there was one," Hawke uttered, rolling his shoulders and fisting his hands. "You know we're gonna fuck you up, don't ya?" Hawke asked, landing a punch to the Reaper's ribs, knocking the breath from him before taking a step back.

It was then my phone dinged, and I hoped and feared it was the answer I'd been waiting for. Opening the screen, I saw the reply from Marek. He said that while Adelaide and Sully didn't recognize him, Braylen did. Closing my eyes and desperately trying to gain some sort of control, I took a deep breath, but it was useless.

No words were spoken as I landed a few quick jabs to his face before turning to face Hawke. "It's him," I confirmed. "Braylen identified him from the pic I sent Marek." I knew in my gut he was also the one who'd raped Edana, the description on point from what Hawke had told me.

The next few minutes were a blur of Hawke and me going at him, one after the other, until he was covered in blood and air barely filled his lungs. Only when we took a quick reprieve did he attempt to goad us.

"B . . . big tough guys," he gasped. "Un . . . untie me. Then we . . . we'll see." The enemy bargained for freedom but he wasn't gonna get it. It wasn't about beating on a man who was tied up, his hands and feet restrained so he couldn't fight back. Under other circumstances, we would've gladly released him, given him the chance to defend himself. But he lost that privilege when he raped Edana and attacked Braylen. They were defenseless. Helpless. But that didn't stop *him*.

"If we released you, it'd be over too soon," I taunted. "And we wanna have our fun."

Blood spilled from his mouth when he coughed, the grimace on his face indicating we'd broken some of his ribs. However, his injuries didn't stop him from further sealing his fate.

"The kind of fun I had with your wo . . . woman?" His head lolled but he kept eye contact with me briefly before glaring at Hawke. "But I gotta say . . . I prefer the sweet taste of redheads." The evil smirk that appeared on his ugly-ass face sparked the simmering rage rattling around inside Hawke.

He lost it.

His eyes darkened.

His movements became meticulous.

Swift.

Deadly.

Before I could stop him, Hawke snatched the hatchet from the metal rolling tray beside him and buried it in the top of the Reaper's skull.

TWENTY-THREE

Ryder

IT WAS CLOSE TO NOON when we finally pulled into the clubhouse lot. Tired, dirty and sore, I flung open the driver door and stumbled from the cage, catching my footing before I fell on my face. Hawke didn't say a word as he exited the other side of the vehicle, trudging across the open space until he disappeared inside the main building.

After he'd abruptly snatched the life of our enemy, we drove an hour out to the secluded area we'd used to get rid of countless other bastards, disposing of the Reapers without so much as another thought.

We never knew their names. Didn't matter. The only thing that was important was that we were able to exact revenge on the man who'd attacked Edana and Braylen, and rid the world of two more of their kind.

I didn't make it ten feet from the truck before Braylen came sprinting out of the clubhouse, Brutus doing his best to keep up with her, his missing leg not much of an obstacle. She ran straight for me, throwing her arms around my neck and jumping on me. She wrapped her legs around my waist and pressed her lips to mine as I held on to her for dear life.

Never in a million years would I have pictured that exact scene unfolding in front of me. Braylen was stubborn and mouthy, with a fiery temper to match. To see her fear and elation mixed together—for me, of all people—kicked me in the ass while making my heart thump a little faster.

"Miss me?" I chuckled, welcoming the breath of fresh air that was this woman. Especially after everything I'd just dealt with.

She hugged me tighter, essentially answering my question. But for as hurriedly as she welcomed me, she held no punches either. Unhooking her legs from around my waist, she lowered to the ground and steadied herself before smacking my chest. Hard.

"You're an ass," she chided, stepping back and planting her hands on her hips, her expression angry.

There she is.

"Man, you go from one extreme to the next. You on the rag?" I knew my mistake as soon as I said it. Never, ever say that to a woman. It only intensified her mood, as I soon witnessed.

"Shut up. No, I don't have my period." She narrowed her eyes and silently cursed me. "I was worried about you. You couldn't call? Text? Nothing?"

"Bray—"

"No, you don't get to give me some stupid excuse that you can't contact me when you're dealing with 'club business.'" She used air quotes when she said it, like that was not what I was really doing. "Not after everything you've already put me through. Understand?"

Her brown eyes darkened, the fire behind them turning me on like never before. Here was this petite, feisty woman, throwing orders at me as if she held the reins in our relationship. Like she was in charge. For as much as it annoyed me, it made me want to hike up her skirt and fuck her right there in the open. Her pouty mouth and adorable scowl only added fuel to my overactive horniness.

Bending over and picking up Brutus, who was busy sniffing my boots, I cradled him under one arm and snatched Braylen's hand with my free one. I dragged her behind me and made it to the clubhouse door in no time. Luckily, Reece was on her way out, Tripp following swiftly behind her, so I was able to snag the door with my foot since my hands were full. For the quick glance I'd given them, it looked like they'd been involved in some sort of heated conversation. I didn't have the time or energy to ask if he was okay, and the annoyed look he'd shot me was enough of a warning to keep my questions and comments to myself. Besides, I had someone of my own I had to deal with, and I couldn't waste any more time.

"Slow down," Braylen shouted, tugging on my hand to free hers, but her attempts were laughable.

As soon as I entered the space, I saw Adelaide standing near the kitchen talking to Kena and Sully. Walking toward them, I untucked Brutus from under my arm and passed him to Braylen.

I finally released her hand. "You stay here. Talk to them," I said, gesturing toward the other women. "I'm gonna take a quick shower." She took a step closer, as if she wanted to come with me. "No." I walked off before she could argue, hurrying toward my room to wash off the remnants of the past two days.

After the quickest shower of my life, I strode out into the common room, a towel slung around my waist and water droplets running down my chest. Braylen was still in the same place I'd left her, engaged in conversation, when I walked up behind her. Without warning, I swung her around and she let out a surprised shriek. I tossed her over my shoulder before she realized what was happening and practically ran back to my room. I heard everyone's laughter follow us but I didn't care.

As soon as we entered my room, I slammed the door behind me and locked it.

"Let me down, you Neanderthal," she shouted, pounding on my back as if she could convince me to do so with her tiny fists. "What is wrong with you?" Walking toward the bed, I flung her down onto the mattress, straddling her before she could attempt to get up. "Seriously, what's wrong with y—"

I cut her off by crashing my mouth to hers, nipping her bottom lip before thrusting my tongue inside.

Braylen moaned, the vibration and sound making my dick harder than I ever thought possible. When the shock of what I'd done finally wore off, she gave herself over to me completely, sucking on my tongue and even biting me back. "I can't stand you sometimes, you know that."

"You love me," I goaded, realizing what I'd said right after the words left my mouth. I thought for sure she would deny it, but she said nothing, just stared at me before pressing her lips to mine once more.

Swinging my leg over so I was kneeling next to her, I whipped off my towel before hastily taking off her clothes.

"No foreplay?" she asked, smiling as she asked the question.

"Not today. Now spread your legs for me. Let me see you."

She inhaled a ragged breath, desire filling her eyes as she did as she was told. Her arousal was staring me in the face, and I thought she'd never looked so damn delicious. I restrained myself, albeit briefly.

I raked my eyes over her, from her gorgeous face to her toned legs. The woman was perfection, and yet she had no idea. When I couldn't take one more second of not being inside her, I moved closer and positioned her legs so they draped over my shoulders. And for the next hour, I made her scream my name, over and over again, until her voice finally fell silent.

———◆———

LOUNGING FLAT ON MY BACK with my arms tucked behind my head, I turned my head toward her, the hesitancy on her face telling me that she wanted to talk about something. So I did something I would've never done before—I encouraged her. "Go ahead. Ask me what you want to."

She didn't refute or deny, instead parting her lips and saying, "Tell me about your daughter." Without thinking, I groaned. I hadn't meant to, really I didn't. It was just a reflex. "Ryder, you have to tell me eventually."

"I know, and I'm fine answering anything you want. Old habits, ya know?" I flashed her a smile before starting. "Zoe is gonna be eleven in a few months."

"Zoe? That's a pretty name."

"It fits her. I didn't pick it, though. Her mother did."

"What's the story there? With the two of you?" Braylen flipped onto her side, and I did the same, running my fingers up and down her arm, then resting my hand on her side, pulling her closer so I could kiss her.

What the hell is happening to me?

"Rose and I met in high school, believe it or not. We weren't high school sweethearts or anything like that, but we did date on and off. Well, when I say date, I mean. . . ."

"Yeah, I get it." She shook her head and smiled, placing her hand on my chest and drawing circles. I didn't even think she knew she was doing it, but the motion soothed me. And I certainly needed it after what I'd recently dealt with.

"Anyway, we hooked up again a few years later and decided to give it a go. Thing was, she got pregnant a month into the relationship, and even though I didn't see it working out in the long run, I stuck with her. You know, for Zoe. But it crumbled, just like I thought it would. She left and moved to Illinois. She had family there still."

Braylen rose up on her forearm. "She took Zoe with her? Didn't you have a problem with that?"

"Yes and no. While I missed my daughter, I knew it was for the best. Our club wasn't the safest then, so I was okay with them both being away from me. After they moved, I went to see Zoe twice a year or so, calling her often."

"I can't wait to meet her." There was a brief silence before she spoke again. "Do you get along with Rose?"

"Yeah, for the most part." I rolled her on her back and pinned her to the mattress. "Are you done with your questions?"

"For now." She laughed, wriggling beneath me to try and escape, but the only thing she was doing was sealing her fate.

For the next half hour, at least.

TWENTY-FOUR

Ryder

BRAYLEN LOOKED SO PEACEFUL WHILE she slept, her hair fanned out on the pillow, lips slightly parted. She'd been staying at my place, taking the bed while I slept on the couch. We'd argued about the separation, but I couldn't take the risk of attacking her again while I slept.

Sure, I'd let her in, more than I ever had for anyone else, but I still had walls thrown up. And for them to start to crumble, I had to put the final piece of my past to rest before I could move forward.

Clutching a piece of paper in my hand, I quietly exited my bedroom, gently closing the door behind me so as not to wake her. I'd left her a note telling her I had club business to take care of and that I wouldn't be back until the following day. I'd also told her that Hawke would be stopping by to follow her to and from work, and for her to not try and ditch him because I'd be royally pissed off. I could picture her rolling her eyes and mumbling to herself after she'd read it, and the image made me smile.

I knew damn well if I'd told Braylen in person that I had to leave, she would've seen the look of indecision on my face and known I was lying. She would've questioned me until I'd either revealed the truth, something I wanted to shield her from, or we would've started to argue. And that was the last thing I needed to deal with, especially since we were in a pretty good place. We'd finally turned a corner.

It'd taken me a while to get there, of course. I'd been a dick and had made her believe that she meant nothing more to me than someone to just hang out with, a chick I hooked up with when the mood struck me. She had every right to pull away, and at the time I even welcomed the distance; it meant she was less likely to be pulled into my club's shit. But then I'd been proved wrong.

When that fuckin' bastard paid her a visit, I knew the only way she would be safe would be if she was by my side. Once and for all. But in order for her to forgive me, I knew I needed to finally let her in. Tell her things about my past I'd kept secret from even my brothers. It was difficult but necessary. In my gut, I knew Braylen was the woman for me; I just had to get out of my own goddamn way and see her for the blessing she was.

Straddling my bike, I kicked over the engine and took off down the long and narrow dirt road, heading toward the highway. I welcomed the solace of the early California breeze, allowing my thoughts to drift from the woman I'd left sleeping in my bed, to the threat against my club, to what I was about to do. My mind fired off in all three directions, flitting back and forth and driving me crazy.

Being on the open road was normally therapeutic. The freedom it provided usually helped to sooth my anxiousness—put everything back into perspective. But this trip wasn't like any other.

For more reasons than not, it paid to know people in law enforcement. The Knights had certainly taken advantage of the information we'd obtained, giving us the edge we needed, whether it was locations for drops or addresses for people we needed to pay a visit to. Granted, we didn't bother with such leads anymore, not since the club cut ties with the cartel, getting out of the drug trade a while back. But I'd called in a favor, and it was because of that favor that I was on my way to Roseburg, Oregon.

I'd had the information for two months but only now decided to act on it. The first night I received the news, I had my first nightmare. How convenient, right?

The mind was a strange thing. No matter how much I tried to suppress the memories, they still bled out, finding a way to terrorize me all over again as soon as I closed my eyes.

———— • ————

CLOSE TO EIGHT HOURS LATER, I was finally creeping up to my destination, the address scribbled on the piece of paper held in the palm of my hand as I pulled off to the side of the road. The house in question was two blocks away, and since I needed the element of surprise, I made sure to hide my bike between two large SUVs.

I wasted no time advancing with purpose, darkness settling in, the low dim of the streetlights barely illuminating the sidewalks. The area was residential, and while the homes had seen better days, it certainly wasn't the worst place I'd seen.

The building in question had faded green siding with dingy white shutters. A few cracked steps led to a small porch. Normally I was heavy-footed, especially with the shit-kickin' boots I had on, but I tried to tread lightly. The creaky floorboards weren't so forgiving, however.

I heard the click of a recliner's footrest going back into place. I waited several seconds while the footsteps trudged across the floor. Blowing out a rushed breath, I widened my stance and opened the screen door.

"Is someone there?" I heard a man croak out, walking the final steps until the large wooden door slowly opened. "Can I help you?" He opened the door wider, leaning forward so he could see me better.

Standing on his doorstep with the intention of finally ridding myself of the guilt and fear that had stolen my peace my entire life, I was surprised when a pair of dark brown eyes looked back at me. This wasn't the man I remembered. Not at all. The man standing before me was old, possibly in his early seventies. Feeble. Gone was his intimidating presence, the power he had wielded over me years before. His hair was closely cropped to his head and stark white. Deep lines etched his face, the evidence of a hard life of abuses.

The years had certainly not been a friend to him, weakening his muscles and aging his body faster than I thought possible. But then again, it had been decades—although for me it felt like months, days even.

It was him, though. There was no doubt about that.

I wasn't sure how I was gonna feel as soon as I saw him again. In truth, fear was a strong assumption, but then I had to remind myself that I wasn't scared or weak any longer.

Instead, anger and hatred mixed together to form the perfect cocktail as soon as my eyes landed on my mark.

"What do you want?" The longer I stood there in silence, the more uncomfortable he seemed to become. I couldn't blame him, though. He wasn't blind. He knew I meant him harm, as was evident when he took a quick step back and tried to slam the door in my face.

"I don't think so," I finally said, pushing until he stumbled back and almost fell over. Entering his house, I kicked the door shut behind me, making sure to lock it so we wouldn't be interrupted.

"I don't have any money." He held his hands up in front of him as if he was surrendering. Little did he know he'd be doing that for real very soon.

"I don't want your money."

"What do you want, then?" He looked petrified, and I reveled in his fear, the adrenaline coursing through me thick and hot.

"Your life."

TWENTY-FIVE

Ryder

TIME SLOWED.

My eyes bored into his, waiting for the moment when he realized the only thing I wanted to rob from him was the beat of his heart.

"Oh my God," he gasped. "Roman."

The evilest grin spread across my face before I gripped his throat and shoved him backward. To say I was surprised he'd recognized me was an understatement; the last time he saw me I was only seven years old. But maybe since he knew exactly who I was, he'd realize that I would be the last person he saw before he drew his final breath.

Clawing at my hand, he struggled to walk while trying to dislodge my hold. I slammed him against the wall, tightening my grip until his eyes started to pop out of his head. His hands finally fell to his sides and he was seconds from passing out when I withdrew and put some distance between us.

"Please" was all he said while his body revolted against the air rushing into his body. He rubbed at his throat, glancing at me every few seconds as if he was planning some sort of defense in case I made any sudden movements.

Still choosing to remain silent, an unnerving tactic I'd learned a long time ago, I pulled my gun from my waistband and placed it on the arm of the chair. I removed my cut and set it next to my weapon.

"What are you gonna do?" he asked, slowly moving to the side because I had him caged in. "Listen, I'm sorry. I wasn't in my right mind back then. The booze . . . the drugs . . . made me . . . different."

With one stride forward we were chest to chest again, his frail body racked with fear while I stood tall and fierce. The roles were certainly reversed, and I was gonna take full advantage.

I shut my mind off, blocking the memories until he started talking again.

"I'm not the same man I was. I swear."

Balling my fist, I hit him as hard as I could, the cracking of his rib signifying success. He fell to the floor and clutched his side, his breathing quite painful from the look on his aged face. "I paid . . . my . . . debt."

I wanted to remain silent, stoic and deadly, but after he spewed that shit, I snapped. No longer was I a man who held any sort of restraint. I was barely sane when I bent down and snatched him up, pulling his limp body closer.

"Paid your debt?" I roared. "Paid your motherfuckin' *debt*? You killed my mother! Right in front of me!" Hauling my arm back, I focused all of my strength as I let loose and punched him harder than I ever had anyone before. I didn't care that he was more than twice my age, frail and unable to defend himself. He deserved everything I had to give.

"Listen. Please. I'm . . . sorry," he gasped, blood flowing from his nose, dripping down his chin and onto the dingy carpet beneath him. "If I could . . . take it back—" He coughed, holding his side before finishing with, "I would. I didn't know . . . what I was doin' . . . when I . . . I. . . ."

"Fuckin' say it," I demanded, hauling him off his feet and throwing him back against the wall. He stumbled but didn't fall down. "Say it!"

"I wasn't in my right mind when I . . . killed your mother." His breathing was labored, and all of the color had drained from his face. "I'm sorry," he repeated, actually looking somewhat sincere. But it was all an act. It had to be. No way this man wasn't the same guy who murdered my mother. Sure, he was older and weaker, but evil still lurked within him.

Only . . . I hadn't seen the glimmer of darkness when I stared into his eyes. Shaking my head to rid myself of some fucked-up internal debate, I reached behind me and seized my gun from the couch. His eyes followed my movements.

"What do you think I should do to you?" I asked, the cool steel resting at my side. With every fiber of my being, I wanted to eviscerate him from existence.

"What?" Blood continued to drip down his face.

"What do you think I should do with you?" I repeated, enunciating every syllable. "It's not a hard question."

"Let me live," he finally muttered, his breathing continuing to worsen.

"Why?" The gun twitched in my palm.

His eyes flicked to my hand before looking me in the eye once more. "Because I made a mistake, and I've paid for it. For twenty-seven years."

"So I should just turn around and walk back out that door?" My anger pulsated in my veins, the audacity of the bastard in front me making me so desperately want to force my gun in his mouth and pull the trigger. *Why are you hesitating?* "Did you think you'd just come home and live out the rest of your days without consequence?"

"I just wanna . . . live in peace."

"Peace?" I laughed, the eerily dark sound foreign to my ears. "You think I should leave you in peace?" I took a step forward.

"Please . . . Roman."

"Stop saying my name!" The more he talked, the more the past and present swirled together. There were brief moments when I'd first laid eyes on him, where I'd been transported back to that seven-year-old kid. Frightened of the man who beat my mom and me. Terrified of the man who stole my mom's life. Then I'd switch to the man I'd become, someone people didn't fuck with because they knew I'd make them pay, sometimes with their life.

I was strong and fearless, so why was I allowing Richard to confuse me, to draw on some part of me that second-guessed ending him right where he cowered?

For the next ten minutes, I found myself at a crossroads, somewhere I thought I'd never be. I knew, or at least I thought I did, that I was coming to his house to kill him. No question. But something was stopping me, and I had no idea what.

Richard deserved to die, yet I still found myself hesitating. And it was during one of those weaker moments that he decided to plead for his life once more.

"Please," he appealed, trying to stand tall, but due to his injuries, it was a half-assed attempt. "I'm begging you not to kill me. I'll do anything. Anything you want. Just let me live."

I hated that I was even considering it. It showed weakness. Doubt. It went against every notion I'd ever had about seeking justice for my mother.

Then I had an idea. Along with the information about where he'd lived, I'd also been told he had a daughter, Ann. She lived somewhere nearby, and while I had no idea whether or not they were close, especially after he'd been away for almost three decades, I decided to test him. To see if he was indeed a changed man.

"I'll tell ya what. I'll let you live, but first you have to decide."

The prospective of him not having a bullet in his brain made him perk up a bit.

"Decide what?"

"You have to choose. Your life . . . or Ann's."

His mouth hung open in surprise, his thin lips trembling while he tried to form words. I could see the proverbial wheels spinning in his head. Was he contemplating giving up his daughter, or was he trying to somehow negotiate for them both to live?

"Five seconds."

A tear fell down his cheek, the sight definitely unexpected. "I don't need five seconds. Kill me. Don't hurt my daughter."

TWENTY-SIX

Braylen

I AWOKE TO A NOTE from Ryder, telling me he had club business to deal with and that he'd be back the following day. He also left instructions for me to wait for Hawke so that he could follow me to work. Rolling my eyes, picturing the look on Ryder's face as I did so, I knew better than to not follow his wish. Besides, I was still very much shaken up over the attack.

I had to admit, I never thought Ryder and I would ever get to the point in our relationship where he'd finally open up to me. Yes, the road to get there had been riddled with obstacles, frustrating and even hurtful at times, but we finally made it. That wasn't to say it'd be easy from here on out, of course; if I knew anything about that man, the word "easy" should never be used.

But it was a start for sure.

Everyone was allowed to leave the clubhouse the same day Hawke and Ryder returned. After hours of glorious sex, Ryder took me back to his house, insisting I stay with him for the next week, just to be safe. I told him I couldn't, that I was worried about Kena, but he assured me that Jagger was going to stay with her at our place. Once I'd confirmed with my sister, I gave Ryder my acceptance.

There was only one simple rule, and that was that I was to sleep in his room while he took the couch. Afraid he'd hurt me again while he slept, he said it was the only way until he could figure something else out.

———◆———

HOW ARE THINGS WITH RYDER going? Kena asked, looking from me to the stage where our friend Kevin was performing. He was the lead guitarist for the local band Breakers. They'd built up quite the following, so much that he'd quit working at our family's restaurant to pursue his music full time. We had no doubt he'd make it, he was that good.

Kevin had casually chased my sister but she'd never accepted, not wanting to deal with groupies. She'd come to find that she still had to deal with brazen women throwing themselves at her man, although the situation wasn't as bad with Jagger. Especially since he never paid attention to any woman at his fights other than Kena.

"Better than before. He still drives me nuts, giving me crap about flirting with my male clients, but he's calmed down some. I think now that he's comfortable enough to let me in, he's more relaxed." I took a sip of my drink. "With life in general, you know?"

Yeah, I do, she signed.

Ryder was supposed to have been back earlier that day, but since I hadn't yet spoken to him, Hawke giving me some excuse about him being out of range or some crap, I'd decided to take Kena up on her offer to get together. We hadn't been able to spend much time hanging out recently. If we weren't working, we were both spending time with our guys; there simply wasn't much time left over for anything else. That was why, when she insisted we go out, just the two of us, I jumped all over the invitation.

I really thought Jagger would've shown up at some point during the evening, if not to check on her to make sure she was okay, then to make sure Kevin didn't try to move in on his woman. What Jagger failed to remember sometimes was that he was it for my sister. Whatever interest she'd held toward Kevin was but a speck of what she felt toward Jagger. No comparison whatsoever.

"I'm having a lot of fun tonight, sis." I raised my glass and she clinked hers to mine. "We need to do this more often for sure."

She smiled and nodded, both of us taking a drink before chitchatting about the latest fashion trends and movies we both wanted to see. We settled in afterward to fully enjoy the band's set, which lasted for another hour.

On my way back from the bathroom, I stopped off at the bar to grab another soda since I was the designated driver. When I turned around, I saw Kena frantically waving to me from our booth. She looked worried, so I hurried over as fast as I could.

"What's the matter?" I asked, looking all around to try and figure out if there was some sort of danger present. I unfortunately had some sort of idea what that would actually look like now.

Your phone keeps ringing. She'd just finished signing when my phone lit up again. "Unknown" flashed across my screen. I didn't pick it up because I had no idea who was calling. While I was in the middle of my internal reasoning for ignoring the calls, my cell flashed again. Whoever was calling wasn't gonna give up. Not until I answered.

Swiping the screen, I answered, "Hello."

"Jesus Christ, Braylen. What the hell?" It was Jagger.

"What's the matter?" His tone unnerved me, put me on alert, yet I had no idea why. "Are you looking for Kena? Why didn't you just text her?"

"I have. A million times. She's not answering."

Holding the phone away from my mouth, I said, "It's Jagger. He said he's been texting you, but you're not responding."

Kena picked up her phone but she couldn't turn it on. The battery had died.

What does he want?

Positioning the phone back to my mouth, I asked, "What's so important that you're blowing up my phone?"

I chuckled but stopped as soon as he said, "You need to get over here. Ryder is flipping the fuck out."

"So you're not calling for Ke—"

"No! You need to get over here. *Now!*" he shouted. I heard people screaming in the background, and one of those voices was Ryder's. From what I could decipher over the phone, his speech sounded slurred.

"What's goin' on?"

"We don't know. All we can tell is that he got his hands on some hard liquor and now he's out of his damn mind." Jagger must've pulled the phone away as he shouted to someone as I couldn't make it out.

"What can *I* do?" I was clueless as to what good he thought I'd be to an out-of-control Ryder. If anything he'd probably scare me. I thought it best to let them handle him, calm him down until he eventually passed out. "Jagger, I don't think—"

"Listen, Braylen. Hear me now. I don't care what you think. I don't care if you're arguing or whatever. You need to put all that aside and get your ass to the club. Right. Now."

"We're not arguing."

He cursed into the phone before hanging up on me. I understood he was concerned about the welfare of his friend, but that didn't give him an excuse to yell at me and then hang up.

"Your boyfriend is a bit of a dick." I reached for my purse and flung it over my shoulder.

He can be. She smiled but stopped when she saw I wasn't joking. *What's going on?*

"I don't know, but I guess we're gonna go find out."

Braylen

AS SOON AS KENA AND I walked in, fear made my heart slam against my chest, and I still had no idea what was going on. A few of the guys were surrounding someone, shouting for him to let go of something or else he was going to be taken down. It wasn't until we took a few more steps forward that Jagger saw us and came running over.

"Oh thank God you're here. You need to try and talk some sense into him." He grabbed my hand and dragged me across the room. I tried to break away from him but the guy was too damn strong.

"Jagger, I don't know what you want me to do. What's wrong with him?"

"He got into that shit. That's the problem." He released me, flicking back the strand of hair that had fallen over his eye. He had a darkening bruise forming high on his cheekbone.

"What happened to your face? Was that from your last fight?"

"No, your boyfriend clocked me."

"What? Why would he hit you?"

"Because Ryder is a goddamn psychotic motherfucker when he drinks like this. He hit at least three other guys, and the only way to make him stop is for us to beat the hell out of him. All of us at once. I don't know why, but when that stuff is flowing through his blood, he has the strength of a goddamn gorilla."

That was an awful lot of information for Jagger to vomit at me all at one time. Trying my hardest to wrap my head around everything, I made a move toward Ryder. Tripp turned around and saw me, hesitation flickering across his face before he looked to Jagger.

"I really think she can calm him."

"I don't know. I think it was a bad move calling her here," Marek added, taking a step forward to shield my presence. He blocked my view, and when I tried to walk away from him, he grabbed my upper arm and pulled me back. He didn't hurt me, but his hold was strong. "I think you should leave, Braylen. We got this."

Choosing to ignore him, I asked, "What happened? Why is Ryder freaking out?"

"We don't know," Tripp answered, switching his attention back and forth from me to Ryder and back again. "He yelled something about not being able to do it. That he's weak and pathetic. He's not making any sense." Tripp looked back toward Ryder once more. "He's got blood on his clothes and his knuckles are split. We didn't do that to him." He ran a frustrated hand over his head. "I probably cracked his rib, but that's it."

"Cracked his rib? Why would you do that?"

"Because he came at me." He said it like it was a normal occurrence, like he had no regrets about hurting his friend when he was in an obvious altered state.

"Get away from me!" Ryder roared, throwing a bottle he'd been holding at the crowd of men caging him in.

"Calm the fuck down, man," someone shouted.

"At least he got rid of his drink," Marek said, finally releasing my arm. "But I still think you need to leave."

As if finally sensing I was near, Ryder pushed through the crowd of men and came straight for me. I wasn't gonna lie—he scared me. I'd never seen him like that before, and the fact that he seemed to be a bit out of his mind was unsettling to say the least.

His dark hair was disheveled. His face was cut and bruised, his gray shirt ripped in several places and spattered with blood. His hands were swollen, his knuckles cracked and covered in the red stuff as well.

"Bra . . . Braylen," he slurred, "What are you doin' here?" Before I could answer, he yelled, "Go! You need to go."

Marek and Tripp tried to hold him back, but he pushed them, causing them to lose their footing. Jagger was right, Ryder seemed to have the strength of ten men. Okay, maybe not ten, but definitely superhuman strength.

"What's wrong, baby," I soothed, reaching out to touch him, to try and offer him some sort of solace in his crazed state of mind.

"You can . . . can't be here. You ca . . . can't see me like this." He erased the remaining distance between us and all of the men froze, waiting to see what he'd do. When I looked into his eyes, they were blank, a void shadowing his essence. I'd never seen anything like it, not in all my life.

"Ryder, please tell me how I can help you. Do you want to go somewhere? Just you and me?"

It was like he never heard me, schooling his expression before grabbing me and pulling me impossibly close. The smell of the whiskey on his breath made my eyes water.

"Let her go!" Jagger shouted, trying to pry Ryder's hands off me, but to no avail. My upper arms started to ache, but I needed to make him see that I was right there with him. For him.

"Tell me what happened," I pleaded.

A tear fell from the corner of his eye but he made no move to wipe it away, allowing the trickle of emotion to show his distress. I'd never seen him look so broken before and it tore at my soul. Something had devastated him. Destroyed him.

"I couldn't do it," he whispered, another tear falling as his shoulders started to shake. He was having some sort of breakdown.

I had to try and be strong enough for the both of us. I had to push aside my fear and attempt to reach him, make him tell me what happened.

"You couldn't do what?"

"He stole every . . . everything from me," he slurred, "and I couldn't fu . . . fuckin' do it." His breathing turned labored. "My mom," he garbled, but I'd heard him.

"Who did?" I tried to keep him on point, but he was drifting all over the place.

"I gave him a ch . . . choice and he didn't pick her."

At that point, I had absolutely no idea what he was talking about. Had he really split from reality? Were his nightmares filtering into his consciousness, making it difficult to decipher what was real and what wasn't?

As if finally realizing he was holding me, a look drifted over his face before he shoved me away from him, stronger than I believed he meant to. I lost my footing and fell on my ass, hurting my wrist on the way to the ground because I was trying to break my fall.

"Goddamnit!" Stone yelled, rushing forward with Jagger and Tripp. They tackled him, but not before Ryder threw out a few punches on his way down.

Kena rushed toward me and helped me to my feet, pulling me back toward the other side of the room. Other than my wrist, I wasn't hurt.

Scared.

Shook up.

But physically intact.

"Don't hurt him," I cried, but my pleas fell on deaf ears. It took all three men just to hold him down. "Please, let him go." I cradled my head in my hands. I just couldn't bear to watch them hurt him any longer.

"Hold him still," someone shouted. "I need to get this in his arm before he hurts someone else. Or himself."

Several moments passed before the shouts subsided. I was afraid to look, so I kept my head down until someone tapped my shoulder. When I didn't budge, they smacked my arm. My head shot up.

Kena.

He's out cold. I think they injected him with something. Tears drifted down her face, she was so shaken up. I hated that she'd witnessed Ryder shove me, but I was fine. I had to convince her of that. Besides, the man who pushed me wasn't Ryder at all. That was someone else inhabiting his body. There was a reason, a dark reason he went off the rails, and I needed to find out what it was.

Jagger finally came over to see me. "Are you okay, Braylen? Are you hurt?"

"I'm fine."

"Shit. I'm sorry. I really thought you being here would've calmed him down. Instead I think I made it worse." Jagger looked so distraught. I felt bad for the guy.

"I'm fine," I repeated. "Really. Don't worry about me." I tried to see if Ryder was still in the room with us, but I couldn't find him anywhere. "Where did they take him?"

"They dragged him to his room and cuffed him to the bed."

"They can't do that. Oh my God." I tried to shove past Jagger, but he caught me midstride, pulling me back toward him. "Let go. Please. I need to see him."

"Uh-uh. No way, Braylen. Not a chance in hell. I learned my lesson the first time. You're not going near him until he sobers up. And even then. . . ."

My body tensed as I asked, "Even then what? Finish what you were gonna say."

"When he sobers up, if he remembers you being here and that you hurt yourself because of him, he won't forgive himself."

"It's only my wrist," I said, gingerly holding my arm. "I'll show him I'm okay. That he didn't really hurt me." I pleaded with him to release me so I could at least check on Ryder, but he held firm, ushering me toward the exit.

"Kena, I need you to take your sister home. Now." Looking at me, he said, "For your own good . . . you're not allowed back here to see him. Do you understand me?"

I remained silent because there were no words sufficient to convey my distress.

"Do you understand me?"

Finally I nodded, Kena helping to hold me upright while guiding me outside.

TWENTY-EIGHT

Ryder

THE CLINK OF STEEL RATTLED and drew me out of my haziness. I moved my limb and the noise sounded again, the soreness creeping down my extended arm causing me to flinch. In truth, I felt like I'd been run over by a goddamn Mack truck. Everything pained me, from my temple to my jaw, to my ribs and arms. Hell, even my tailbone hurt, although I couldn't fathom why.

"Fuck," I grunted, not quite sure what the hell was goin' on. Only half opening my eyes, partly because I was beyond exhausted and partly because my head was gonna explode as soon as the light spearing in through the window hit my pupils, I glanced warily around the room. It was mine, at the clubhouse.

Why am I here?

Craning my neck, I looked toward the iron headboard and saw my left wrist cuffed to one of the rungs, my flesh reddened from the pressure of its grip.

"Hey!" I shouted as loud as my lungs would allow, which wasn't much. The effort instantly made my head hurt, thumping so badly I could feel the bile rise in my throat. Still dressed from the night before, I scooted over toward the edge of the bed and placed my foot on the ground, and I stomped with my heavy boot. When minutes passed and still no one came, I searched my immediate area to see if there was something I could use instead. I couldn't find anything, so I clumsily removed one of the boots I'd been wearing, and with as much strength as I could muster I flung it at the door. It thumped against the hollow wood, and within seconds I heard someone walking down the hallway.

"You better be back to normal," a gruff voice said, the door slowly opening. Jagger's face appeared, and when he gave me a quick once-over, deciding I wasn't any kind of threat, he strolled forward. How much of a threat could I be restrained to a bed?

He looked tired, like he'd been through the ringer. When he pushed his hair away from his face, I saw a pretty nasty bruise near his eye. "Did you have a fight last night?"

"Yeah," he scoffed. "With your ragin' ass."

At first I thought he was joking, but then I realized that he was tellin' the truth. Otherwise, why would I have been handcuffed? I could only recall bits and pieces, not enough for me to fully understand what went down.

Shaking his head, and with a pained expression of disappointment, he removed a key from the front pocket of his jeans. "I can't believe you did this again, man." He leaned over me and unlocked the restraint, letting it dangle around the bottom of the bar once I'd freed myself. "You promised us all last time that it was, well, the last time."

"Cut me some slack," I argued, not entirely sure what made me break my promise to my brothers never to get as out of control as I had the last time. "I don't even remember what happened."

"You never do," he retorted.

I'd been good for years, but obviously something had pushed me over the edge. Rubbing my temples, I asked, "What did I do? Where did I get the whiskey from?" I'd always given the guys slack for not allowing me to drink the hard shit when we were together, threatening to sneak some behind their backs. Hell, I could've stopped by the liquor store at any time and bought some, but I'd made a promise. To them and myself.

Whenever I had mentioned needing something stronger than beer, they'd shout for Trigger to keep an eye on me, or tell Carla to make sure to serve me only beer whenever we swung by Indulge to check things out. To be honest, I loved that they looked out for me, as I would for any one of them.

"You're askin' me?"

His humorless laugh irritated me, but not because I was pissed at him. I was upset with myself. Disappointed even, that I allowed something to affect me so greatly that I threw all caution to the wind and said goodbye to any restraint I'd been holding onto.

"How did I get here?"

"You just showed up, already annihilated as you stumbled through the door."

"Did I say anything?" Stretching my neck, careful not to jostle my head too much for fear the pounding in my brain would increase, I prayed Jagger could give me some kind of answer.

"You were shouting something about not being able to do it. That someone stole something from you and that he made the wrong choice. . . ." Jagger's voice drifted off, his words jumbling together as I desperately tried to recall just what the hell he was talking about.

Then a splintered memory rushed in, an image of an older man lying on the ground with blood running down on his face. Who was he? Clutching strands of my hair, I closed my eyes and willed more images to come forth, but there was nothing. Not until a flash of Braylen popped up, the look of worry and helplessness laced in her eyes . . . for me.

"Braylen." I opened my eyes and found Jagger sitting on the edge of the bed. "Was she here last night?" My body tensed with the thought that she'd witnessed me at my lowest. My worst.

"Yeah," he whispered, knowing his answer would send me back into a tailspin. Not nearly of the same caliber as the prior night, but enough to break me further.

"No, no, no," I repeated, pacing while trying to calm myself. I knew in my gut that whatever had caused me to freak out was bad, and for Braylen to see me like that, after all she's already been through, was unforgivable.

"It gets worse," he confessed, standing before tentatively approaching.

My lungs refused to work. My legs locked into place and I braced myself for what he was gonna say next.

"You shoved her."

"Who?" I knew who he was referring to, but I asked the question anyway.

"Braylen. You grabbed her when she was trying to help you. Then you pushed her away from you and she fell. I think she hurt her wrist even though she said she was fine. She begged me to see you after we carted you off, but for obvious reasons I told her no."

Shaking my head, ignoring the pain radiating behind my eyes, all I could do was stand there in disbelief. Not only had my outburst brought chaos to the club, but I'd injured my woman in the process. She had to know that wasn't me. I would never hurt her. Not even if my life depended on it.

Right before I stormed out of the room to go look for Braylen, every muscle in my body still tender and aching, I stalked toward Jagger. His eyes averted from mine briefly before reconnecting.

"Why was Braylen even here last night?" I had my suspicions; I just needed him to confirm them.

"Uh . . . 'cause I called her."

I didn't even let him continue before I was on him, shoving him against the wall, my forearm pinning him in place. Under normal circumstances, Jagger could give me a run for my money, probably even best me given the right opportunity. The guy was twelve years my junior and was a champion fighter. But right then he knew not to move a fuckin' muscle. He knew he was wrong for calling Braylen to the club while I was out of my mind.

"Why would you do that? Why would you let her see me like that?" I was more hurt than I was embarrassed.

"Because," he scowled, "you were the worst I've ever see you. Whatever happened seemed to have sucked the life out of you, and I needed to do something."

I pulled him forward a few inches before slamming him against the wall again.

"So you put her in danger?" I was livid. *How stupid can he be?*

"I thought she could help you. I really did," he said when I glared at him in disbelief. "I see the way you are when you're around her. You're . . . calmer. I can't explain it, but I see it."

I knew exactly what he was talking about because it was the truth. Braylen soothed me in ways I myself couldn't explain.

"You still shouldn't've called her."

"I know that now," he admitted.

I stepped back but remained close.

"Is there a problem here?" Stone asked, waltzing into my room and frowning at Jagger and me.

I didn't answer right away because I wasn't sure which emotion to claim. I was angry Jagger had called Braylen to come and see me, thinking she could help in some way. Even though I knew his intentions were driven from concern for me, she ended up getting hurt.

"Is there a problem?" our VP repeated. "Because I can get in on this too." Stone glared at me, completely ignoring Jagger because he knew the issue resided with me.

"No," I finally answered, taking a few more steps away from Jagger. Looking more closely at Stone, I pointed at his face and asked, "Did I do that?" His bottom lip was split, and there was a small bruise on his jaw.

"Yeah, ya bastard. You're lucky I didn't feel it, or I would've fucked you up." His smirk told me he'd already forgiven me. "But it gets me some extra lovin' from Addy, so I'm not really complaining."

Stone had a condition called congenital insensitivity to pain. *Lucky bastard.* And I knew Adelaide. Any mark on her man and she was driven to care for him, make him feel better even though she knew he wasn't affected by it. I figured it was the nurse in her.

"So what now?" I asked, plopping down on the edge of my bed.

"You take a shower 'cause you still smell like a brewery, grab something to eat and go make sure your woman is okay," Jagger said so matter-of-factly, as if I would've argued with him.

"Sounds good to me." Normally, before Braylen had come into my life, I would've escaped to my house for the better part of a week, ignoring everyone because of the guilt of my freak-out. But everything was different now. Not only did I have to make sure she was okay, I had to make sure she continued to be safe. It was my job, and for once in a very long time I had a purpose, other than my part in the club.

As I washed away the prior evening, all I could think about was how I hoped Braylen had some sort of insight as to what I'd been rambling about. My gut told me she'd be able to clue me in, but maybe that was simply desperation talking.

Braylen

TOSSING AND TURNING BECAUSE I'D hardly gotten any sleep, I was startled when Kena threw open my bedroom door and barged in. Her long dark hair was piled high on top of her head, sticking out in all different directions and making her look like a crazy person.

"My God, woman. You scared me," I cried out, clutching my chest while being careful of my sore wrist. With everything that'd happened, I knew it could've been worse. Never having seen Ryder in such a way truly scared me, but I'd been more worried than frightened. I'd witnessed him drunk before but never violent. His eyes had never been vacant, and I'd never seen him so . . . lost.

Someone is here to see you. He looks pretty desperate, so go easy on him. Kena knew I would shoot first, then ask questions later, so she was right to give me her warning. What she didn't realize was that I wasn't angry with Ryder. All of my thoughts were consumed by what had happened to him. Jagger mentioned the guys cuffing him to his bed. Had he fought against the restraint and hurt himself?

My whirlwind thoughts flipped from being worried about the man to realizing that he softened me, so to speak. My temper still existed, my protective side over those I loved still fueling my mouth when need be, but I knew I was changing. Whether or not I embraced it was another story.

Flinging off the covers, I didn't even have my feet planted on the carpet before Ryder strode into my room. The sight of him made me feel helpless all over again, his flesh torn apart in places and bruised from fighting with his friends, and from whatever happened that had driven him to lose himself to the evils of the amber liquid he poured down his throat.

"What are you doing here?" Surprised he was even standing in front of me, especially after Jagger had indicated that Ryder would probably not want to see me anytime soon due to guilt, I leaned back on the bed, as if the small amount of distance would save me from a plethora of questions and emotions.

He didn't utter a word as he stalked toward me, reaching me with a few long strides. His hand shot out and wrapped around my waist, hoisting me off the bed and into his arms before I could say anything else. Kena closed the door behind her as she left to give us some privacy.

"Jagger told me what happened to you. I'm so sorry, Bray. Please forgive me."

The warmth from his body relaxed me, the all-too-familiar scent of him enveloping me until all I wanted to do was exist in his embrace. But I knew we had to have a serious talk, so I prepared myself to be strong enough to accept whatever he chose to reveal.

Pulling back so he could see my face, he said, "I would never intentionally hurt you, you know that, right?" He feared I viewed him as a violent man. In some aspects I knew he was, but never with me. I knew in my heart that he would never physically hurt me.

Emotionally . . . that was yet to be determined. He was a man, after all, and men were stupid when it came to affairs of the heart, especially one who'd never truly given himself to anyone before.

One thing at a time, though.

"I know," I answered, leaning back into him to try and soothe the both of us. "I know," I repeated.

A shiver shot through his body, his shoulders twitching before he kissed the top of my head. We stood locked together for countless moments, remaining silent, reveling in the comfort of the other.

The tall, muscular, tough and conflicted man holding me close had so many dimensions, some of which I'd borne witness to and some he guarded with his life, too afraid to let others see. But we were making progress. I believed Ryder was almost ready to let me all the way in, his being there with me a sign he truly cared.

Finally separating, he guided me back to the edge of the bed, sitting beside me and reaching for my hands. I winced when he touched my right wrist.

"Let me see."

I pulled my arm back because I didn't want him to focus on the fact that I'd hurt myself, not badly, but he'd see it as a failure on his part, as if he was completely to blame for what happened to me.

He was and he wasn't. I chose to approach him while I knew he wasn't in his right mind. I thought I could get through to him, but he'd been too far gone to truly see me. Besides, it wasn't like he ran at me and knocked me on my ass. I knew it was an accident. I just had to make sure he never allowed himself to get into such a state ever again.

"I'm fine."

"Again with that word." A half smile graced his mouth before his expression fell back into a serious one. "I wanna see your wrist." He held out his palm and patiently waited for me to place my hand in his. Finally, I gave in. The sooner he inspected me, the sooner we could move on.

Gently handling me, he turned my wrist from side to side, feeling all around by gingerly pressing the pads of his fingers along the area. "There's some minor swelling, but I don't think you broke anything. You really should have this wrapped. Do you have any bandages?"

"In the cupboard, under the sink in the bathroom," I replied, pointing toward the hallway. He rose from the bed, and right before he left, he turned back to look at me. He opened his mouth to speak but no words came out. Thinking better of whatever he was going to say, he clamped his lips shut before disappearing, only to reenter my room two minutes later.

"You have a lot of crap under the sink." The mattress dipped as he sat back down next to me.

"That's not all mine. Some of it is Kena's." A mundane topic, but just the kind of normality I needed in order to soak up my nervousness. Not from Ryder bandaging my wrist but from discovering what was going to happen in the next several minutes. Heck, hours, even weeks.

I watched as he carefully wrapped my wrist, cautious not to tighten the cloth too much for fear of hurting me, applying just the right amount of pressure for the bandage to effectively do its job.

His focus was laser sharp, and in any other situation, I would've found it rather comical. The narrowing of his brows. The way the tip of his tongue peeked out from behind his full lips. The twitch in his jaw when I flinched ever so slightly. Gone was the brooding, sometimes arrogant and infuriating man, replaced with someone who was concerned about the smallest injury, his carefulness not to injure me further mixed with regret and worry that I'd distance myself from him because of what happened. He never spoke those exact words, but he didn't have to. He had very expressive eyes, and I hadn't seen his tell until right then.

As he finished up, placing a piece of tape around the end of the bandage, he inspected his work before resting my hand back on my lap.

"There. That should hold for a bit. Just try not to use it too much." His eyes found mine. "I'm really sorry."

"Stop apologizing. I told you I'm okay."

"I thought you said you were *fine*."

"I'm that too." I smiled. I reached for his hand, lacing the fingers of my good hand with his before scooting closer. Our thighs touched and, although we were fully clothed—him more than me—an electric current coursed through my body. Without realizing, a moan escaped from me as I leaned into him, his mouth mere inches from my own when he interrupted the moment.

"I don't think we should."

"Why?" I hadn't meant to come across as insensitive, knowing he was still dealing with a lot.

"Because my head is still all fucked up. I'm gonna go crazy if I don't start remembering something soon." He held my hand a bit tighter before hanging his head, inhaling deeply while a hush surrounded us.

I wanted to offer him some sort of escape by offering myself to him, but clearly he needed something else.

To remember.

And I'd do my best to help him.

Lifting his head, he slowly brought his eyes to mine, his stare locking me firmly in place. The fear behind his browns gutted me. "Did I say anything to you, ya know, before. . . ." He glanced down at my wrapped wrist.

"You were mumbling a lot of things. Something about how you couldn't do it, and that someone stole everything from you." I wasn't making any sense, but then initially neither had he. Suddenly, I remembered something else. "You mentioned your mom."

He frowned and I could see the wheels turning in his head, urgently trying to connect the dots. Before I knew it, it appeared as if a lightbulb went off. He pulled his hand from mine and shot off the bed, rushing halfway across the room before stopping.

"I remember standing over an old man. He was bleeding and pleading with me not to kill him."

I couldn't help it. I gasped, holding my hand in front of my mouth, which only added to Ryder's anxiousness. I knew something bad had happened, and I knew there was a possibility he'd hurt someone, but I think I refused to believe he could've killed someone. Denial and ignorance worked in most cases, but apparently not when that shit slapped you in the face. But I couldn't focus on that. I had to be there for him so he could try and remember and hopefully move past it. If at all possible. I'd worry about how I felt afterward.

Thankfully he ignored my reaction, raking his fingers through his hair, shaking his head before saying, "I told him to choose. I'd either kill him or his daughter." Ryder still looked like he was piecing together a scattered puzzle. "He begged me not to touch her. He told me to kill him." His expression froze, as if he'd finally remembered. "It was Richard. He was the man I went to see."

"Richard? The man who . . . ?" I couldn't even finish my question.

"Yeah, the man who killed my mother," he finished, sadness and anger twirling together to create a whole other kind of emotion.

"Did you . . . ?" Again, I was at a loss for completion.

He was silent for a few moments, locking eyes with me but looking right through me. I knew he needed to work up to telling me the truth, probably running through all the different reactions I'd surely have if his response was what I thought it might be. Finally, he whispered his answer.

"No."

My lungs deflated as a rush of relieved air pushed from my lips. I believed I would've understood if his answer had been *yes*, but I was thankful it wasn't. Without allowing one more second to pass, I deleted the small space between us and wrapped my arms around his waist, resting my head on his chest.

"No," he repeated, holding on to me as if he feared I'd disappear. "I couldn't do it. I hate myself for allowing him to live, but I just couldn't do it." Ryder was in pure confession mode, and I allowed him to unburden his soul by continuing to remain silent. "He said he was sorry, that he was a different man back then. That he hadn't been in his right mind. I didn't believe him, not until he chose his daughter over himself."

His arms fell from me and he retreated until his back hit the wall with a small thud. Shoving his hands in his pockets, he looked down at the floor.

"Ryder."

No response.

"Ryder," I called out again, that time with more force in my voice. "Look at me." I drew near while still giving him the space he needed. "Please."

"Don't," he finally responded. "I should've snatched his life without a second thought. I should've made him pay for what he did." He shrugged in defeat. "But I didn't. I'm pathetic. I'm weak," he muttered.

"No, you're not. You made a choice. The right one." When we stood toe-to-toe, my bare feet touching the tips of his boots, I placed my hand on his chest. I could feel his heart ramming against his ribcage. "I think you recognized a difference between the man he was and the man he'd become. He chose his daughter, Ryder. He chose her life over his. He was clearly willing to die to protect someone he loved."

I couldn't even begin to understand what he'd gone through, coming face-to-face with the person who stole his mother's life, and right in front of him when he was just seven years of age. But I was with him now, and I wanted to help him. To do whatever I could to make him see that he wasn't weak and pathetic. That he was the exact opposite.

He was strong.

He was brave.

He was complicated.

He was unlike any man I'd ever met.

THIRTY

Ryder

EVERYTHING CAME RUSHING BACK TO me as soon as Braylen told me that I'd mentioned my mother while in the midst of my delirium. Images of holding Richard's address in my hand for hours as I drove to Oregon. Memories of pushing past his front door before beating him flooded my brain, only to end with the recollection that I'd left him cowering in his house as I walked away, my gun resting in the waistband of my jeans, never having been fired.

I heard her words, but I still couldn't shake the feeling that I'd been weak in my decision to allow that bastard to live.

Who am I turning into? What is happening to me?

In my heart I knew what Braylen had said was true, and I believed the reason I didn't shoot Richard in the head *was* because he'd chosen his daughter over himself, but it didn't take away the remorse that I hadn't been able to exact revenge for my mother.

"I need to forget," I said, tugging Braylen closer. "Help me do it."

Without warning, I captured her lips, breathing in her warmth like it was the only thing that kept me grounded. Kept me sane. I lifted her up my body, and she wrapped her legs around me, kissing me back with such need that I knew she was exactly who I needed to lose myself in.

"Are you sure?" she asked, pulling back long enough to look deep into my eyes. "I'm here for you, no matter what, but if you're not up to this, we can just lie together."

"And what? Cuddle?"

"Whatever you need."

"I just need you. Naked and spread for me."

Her hands interlocked behind my neck, but when she tightened her hold, she winced.

"Watch your hand," I instructed. "I feel bad enough, I don't want you to make it any worse."

"I'll be—"

"Fine?"

"Smartass." She laughed before giving me a quick kiss. "Now put me down and do with me what you will." She unhooked her legs from around my waist and slid down my body, every bit of her rubbing against me until she found her footing.

Braylen was wearing a pair of white cotton panties, half of her left ass cheek exposed because I'd had my hands all over her just moments before. A matching cami rode halfway up her belly, exposing her delectable skin. My eyes feasted on her, my hunger increasing the more she looked like she wanted me to devour her.

Jerking my head toward the mattress, she shuffled backward until the backs of her legs hit the edge. Without breaking eye contact, she shimmied her top up and off, tossing the material to the floor. Then she proceeded to lower her panties, the expanse of her creamy flesh driving me insane with the need to claim her. Only when she was completely naked did she lower herself onto the bed, reaching out to pull me close.

Removing my clothes faster than I ever had before, even with all my injuries, I finally covered her body with mine. The heat from our skin mashing together created a fire I prayed would never burn out.

"I need you so much right now," I proclaimed, nipping her throat while spreading her legs with my hand. "I don't know if I'll ever get over what happened, but for now, I wanna forget." My desperation was apparent, but instead of pushing Braylen away, it only drew her closer. The look in her eyes wasn't one of pity but of love.

We hadn't told each other how we felt, and I didn't think I was ready to do it right then, but this woman meant everything to me.

"Then use me however you want. However you need." She squirmed beneath me, her hands coming up to tangle in the thick of my hair.

"Raise your arms above your head and don't move them." Not only did I want to dominate Braylen, I wanted to make sure she wasn't putting any strain on her wrist. Every time I glanced at the bandage, which was every other second, a pang of guilt ate at me. I knew it wasn't a serious injury, but it cut me just the same.

"So bossy," she teased, licking her lips in anticipation of what I would do. A flush spread from her neck to her cheeks, making her look so god-damn sexy. She wanted me, and I wasn't gonna keep either of us waiting much longer.

"You have no idea." Completely pushing aside any thoughts other than the woman lying beneath me, I claimed her mouth while my fingers trailed over her skin. First over her collarbone, then down to her nipple, pinching the erect bud and making her moan. When I moved over her ribcage to her hipbone, her back arched off the bed, knowing where my fingers were headed next.

I lightly tapped her pussy, the air in her lungs catching midbreath before I stroked between her folds. She was drenched, her body trembling when my thumb finally circled her clit. Her moans drove me crazy, the way her body went limp seconds before tensing again, then relaxing once more. Back and forth I played with her, teasing and tormenting her just how I knew she loved.

Inserting two fingers inside her while continuing to play with her clit, I slowly pumped them in and out, the rhythm bringing her closer to release. Before she tipped over, though, I removed my hand.

"What are you doing?" she groaned, annoyed that I'd stolen her pleasure.

"I wanna taste you." Bringing my fingers to my mouth, I deliberately sucked on each one, making sure to keep my eyes on her to see her reaction. "You always taste so sweet." Her eyes widened and her lips parted, but she said nothing. Instead, her breaths came out short and choppy, the flush painting her skin deepening. "Do you want me to lick your pussy now?"

"Please," she begged, keeping her arms above her head while thrusting her hips toward me. I wanted to take my time, draw out her pleasure, but I was anxious to bury myself inside her. The quicker she came on my tongue, the sooner I could fuck her, so I spread her legs farther apart and trailed my finger down the inside of her thigh. Goose bumps covered her skin the closer my mouth moved toward her pussy. Kissing beneath her navel, I moved lower still, blowing over her wetness before licking her juices. "So fuckin' wet," I murmured.

"Please," she repeated, her body rocking against my mouth as I lapped up her sweetness like a starving man.

"I think I'm addicted to you," I confessed, pressing on her clit with my thumb while I fucked her with my tongue.

"Don't stop. Oh . . . I'm so close already," she whimpered. "Oh my

God, yeah, keep doin' that."

Within moments, Braylen found her rhythm, crying out as she hovered on the verge. I'd come to know her body almost as well as I knew my own, knew just what she needed to finally come undone.

Flattening my tongue, I licked the length of her, pinching her clit before wrapping my lips around the overly sensitive bud. I pumped two fingers inside her, hitting her sweet spot until she cried out my name over and over again.

With my face still buried between her legs, I waited until her breathing evened out. Giving her one final kiss on the inside of each of her thighs, I moved up the bed and almost lost it when I came face-to-face with the woman who was slowly changing me.

As cliché as it sounded, she made me wanna be a better man. She called me out on my shit, showing me boundaries when I'd never paid attention to such things before. Even though I continued to struggle with my decision not to end Richard, Braylen made me feel somewhat okay with it—as okay as any man could feel with not killing his mother's murderer, anyway. The entire situation was fucked up beyond belief, but at least I had someone by my side to help me through it. I knew I wasn't an easy man to love, but I truly believed she was destined to be mine.

She better learn to love my ornery ways, or else I'll strap her to my bed until she changes her mind.

The thought of restraining Braylen made my dick twitch. I fisted myself and rubbed back and forth between her velvet lips. "Is this what you want?"

A simple nod from her was all it took for me to bury myself to the hilt.

It was like coming home.

———◆———

I RAVAGED HER FOR HOURS, my stamina even impressing me. I'd flipped her into various positions, always careful of her wrist. I thought for sure after round three I would've slowed down, but I needed to lose myself for as long as possible. And she wasn't complaining.

When we were finally sated—or I should say when I had finally exhausted myself—I fell onto my back beside her. She snuggled close, resting her head on my chest. Careful of the bruises coating parts of my torso, she drew countless circles on my skin. The action was so soothing I'd almost drifted off to sleep, but I knew she wanted to ask me something.

"Ask me what you want," I blurted, waiting for her to deny that she had anything to inquire about. Instead, she surprised me by apologizing, for what I wasn't sure.

"Sorry."

"No need to apologize. Trust me, I've done it enough for the both of us. Just ask me what you want." My breathing remained even, hopefully letting her know I was becoming more comfortable with opening up.

"What was in the needle they shoved in your arm?"

"A mild sedative."

"They just happen to have that stuff lying around?"

"Yeah, for various reasons."

"Like what?"

I should've known she'd push for more.

"Like for whatever reasons they need it for." My last response was a hint for her to move on. I wasn't about to divulge any club business, no matter how much she pestered me. Some topics were just off-limits.

I'd been resting my arm across my chest, a slight welt marking my skin, along with two small tears where the metal had cut into me, no doubt struggling against the cuffs as soon as they'd restrained me.

Braylen gently ran her fingers over my wrist. "Did they really cuff you to your bed?"

"Sure did," I said, almost proudly. "And they had every right to."

"Does it hurt?"

"Not anymore. But don't worry, when I use the handcuffs on you, I'll make sure they're the fur ones."

And just like that, I turned the tables on her, making her squirm with thoughts of more sex.

THIRTY-ONE

Braylen

I HEARD SHOUTING COMING FROM the living room, and although I was extremely tired and wanted nothing more than to fall asleep, I had to find out what was causing Ryder to argue so loudly.

For the past several weeks, his mood would switch on a dime. Stress from the club or thoughts of Richard would do it easily enough. Oh, and I couldn't forget jealousy whenever he stopped by the salon to see me and witnessed me working on some of my male clients—George being his least favorite, of course.

"Yeah? Well I'm tellin' you. . . ." Silence "No, I'm not signing off on that. I don't care. Absolutely not."

I shuffled my bare feet along the hardwood floor until I came to the entrance of the living room. Clenching the sheet tightly around my naked body, I leaned against the wall and waited for him to see me. Some would say I was eavesdropping, but I chose to think I was giving him time to finish his conversation before having to deal with my intrusion.

"I don't care how many assurances you give me, Rose. Zoe's my daughter too, and I'm not comfortable with it." Turning around, he finally spotted me standing there. "I'll call you back. No, I'll call you back," he said through clenched teeth. Ending the call, he threw his phone on the couch. "Ask me again if I get along with Rose?" He snagged his half-full bottle of beer off the counter and chugged down the rest of the contents.

"What happened? Why are you so upset?" I trudged forward and sat on the arm of the sofa. "Do you mind me asking?"

"No, I don't mind." He grabbed another beer from the fridge and drank half of it before answering. "She wants to let Zoe go to Ireland with a group of kids from her school."

"Like a field trip or something?"

"Yeah, somethin' like that."

"And why don't you want her to go?" I knew I was treading a fine line, but I was curious why he was so upset.

"Why?" he shouted, furrowing his brows at me like I was some kind of alien. "Because it's a foreign fuckin' country and neither of her parents will be with her." Okay, that kinda made some sense. "She's a beautiful girl. Someone's gonna snatch her up and sell her. The sex trade is alive and booming all over the world." He paced, trying to regain some semblance of control.

I didn't know what to say. I'd watched enough shows and read enough books to understand where he was coming from.

"Did you tell Rose those things?"

"She wouldn't let me get a word in edgewise. Ramblin' and arguin'," he mumbled.

I wanted to comfort him, to offer him advice, but what did I know about raising kids and what was best for them? What was safe?

Before I knew it, Ryder was standing directly in front of me, his hands resting on my shoulders, his fingers stroking back and forth over my naked skin. "Why don't you lose the sheet?" I knew what he was doing, distracting himself with the prospect of sex.

"Why don't you deal with the issue with Zoe before it escalates and causes you to have a stroke?" I arched a brow, enticing him to disagree, but he remained silent. The only indication he was considering it was the slight tick of his jaw.

"I'd rather deal with you." He tried to tug the sheet from me, but I moved back, falling onto the couch before I could right myself. Ryder laughed, which was a welcome sound indeed, plopped down on the cushion beside me and positioned me on top of him.

Before we started anything, me still shielded and straddling Ryder's lap, Brutus waddled up next to us and sat at Ryder's feet. He was still too little to jump onto the couch, although he definitely tried enough times. The only thing the little pup would accomplish was falling on his butt, only to try again. I had to give it to him—he was persistent, much like his owner.

Brutus was one lucky dog, thriving in his new home, his missing limb never slowing him down. I hated thinking what would've happened to him had Ryder not followed his gut instinct and trailed the bastard who so carelessly tossed the three-legged puppy from a moving vehicle.

"What's up, buddy?" Ryder asked, moving me slightly to the side so he could lean over and see him. "Tell Mommy she needs to give me some lovin'."

"Mommy? Since when am I Mommy?" To say I was shocked was putting it mildly.

"Well . . . I've been meaning to talk to you about something." He hesitated, and I had no idea what he was gonna bring up. Was him calling me Mommy his subtle way of telling me he wanted to have a baby? Because I was nowhere ready for something like that. Besides, we were still working on our relationship, and some days it was really hard. I tried to move off his lap but he held me in place.

"Stop freakin' out, babe. You have no idea what I want, so stop overthinking it." The bastard smiled as I continued to try and stand up. But it was useless. He was too strong and if he didn't want me going anywhere, I simply wasn't moving.

"What did you want to talk about?" *If he says "baby" I'm gonna throw myself backward and hope Brutus moves out of the way in time.*

"I think you should move in with me. You're here all the time anyway." He shrugged. "It just makes sense."

The words came out of my mouth before I could stop them. "Oh, so you don't want a baby?" Closing my eyes briefly, I could've kicked myself.

"What?" He laughed, making the entire scene much more humiliating. "What made you think I wanted a kid?" He continued to chuckle while loosening his grip on me, so I seized the opportunity and swung my leg over his so I could finally plant my feet on the ground. "Hey," he rumbled, "where do you think you're goin'? We're not done talkin'."

"Then stop laughing at me," I snapped, unexpectedly irritated with the turn of our conversation. Brutus barked behind me, sticking his nose into our business, and I found myself outnumbered all of a sudden.

I had no time to escape before Ryder hopped off the couch and grabbed my hand. "I'm not laughing at you," he snickered.

"You still are," I pointed out.

He finally composed himself. "Let's try this again. What made you think I wanted a kid?"

"Because you called me Mommy." Even saying the word made me feel somewhat awkward.

"I said that in reference to Brutus. I wasn't even thinkin' about it when I said it." He crowded my personal space. "It just fit. Besides, I think he likes you better than me." He looked down at the puppy and feigned annoyance.

"No, he doesn't." The words weren't even fully out of my mouth before Brutus grabbed hold of the bottom of the sheet and tugged. I hadn't been expecting it, and before I could gather the material to my body, he ran off with it, leaving me completely naked.

"You're right. He just might like me better after all."

THIRTY-TWO

Braylen

SITTING ON MY COUCH, I became antsy waiting for Kena to come home. Flipping through the channels, I couldn't settle on any one show. Reality, comedy, drama . . . nothing. Even a *Law & Order* episode did nothing to hold my attention because my mind was elsewhere.

Looking down at my phone, I saw I didn't have any new messages. I'd texted my sister earlier and told her I had something I wanted to discuss, and I wanted to do it sooner rather than later. After convincing her that it wasn't anything terrible, she agreed to stop by the house and talk to me before she met up with Jagger. He had a fight later that evening, but I wasn't going. Between late nights with Ryder and working crazy hours at the salon, I was utterly exhausted. And being boxed in at an overly crowded, loud and smelly room was the last place I wanted to spend my evening. Thankfully the next day was Sunday and I didn't have work, so I could rest as much as I needed to.

Finally, at half past six in the evening, Kena strolled through the door, but Jagger and Ryder were hot on her heels.

They showed up outside, she signed. *I can kick them out if you want.* She smiled, but I knew she was serious. Kena would have no reservations about telling the guys to step back outside until we finished our conversation.

My sister looked tired, much how I felt, although she still had a rosy glow to her. Her dark hair was styled in a loose ponytail, and she was wearing her typical work attire, jeans and a T-shirt. Kena always looked nice, even wearing something so simple. Then again, there was no need for her to get all dressed up, because her job was taking care of the finances at our family's restaurant. Her office was in the back of the building, so it wasn't like she socialized a lot, not unless my parents were desperate for her to fill in for the waitstaff due to call offs.

Most of the customers were regulars so they were aware of her challenge, as we liked to refer to it. Disability or handicap didn't fit, because nothing held my sister back from living a full life. Not since Jagger, anyway.

I was happy she had someone, and although he was a bit questionable in the beginning and hadn't always earned my approval, he turned out to be a great guy. Loyal, fierce and protective.

Not that my disapproval would change Kena's mind—she was head over heels for him, and he returned her love tenfold—but having her sister on board just made it easier.

"Why you gonna kick me out?" Jagger teased, pulling his woman in for a kiss as if they were the only ones in the room. "I didn't do anything wrong." He gave her two more pecks before releasing her, his eyes following her every movement. Then he finally looked my way and gave me a wink. "Are you kicking me out?"

"Who's getting kicked out?" Ryder asked, moving to stand next to me.

"No one's getting kicked out," I rebuffed, my voice lower than normal. It appeared my energy was draining with each passing second.

"Are you okay? You look tired." Ryder focused all his attention on me and completely forgot about the possibility of being asked to leave.

"I'm fine."

"Uh-huh," he grunted.

Deciding to ignore his grunted response because I had other pressing matters to attend to, I said, "You guys stay here while Kena and I talk."

They took a seat on the couch and flipped through the channels while they waited.

As soon as we sat on the edge of my bed, side by side, I turned to Kena and blurted, "Ryder wants me to move in with him." No point in beating around the bush. I waited for her reaction. Worry. Sadness. Confusion. These were some of the examples of emotions I'd expected, but I certainly didn't anticipate that she'd be smiling. "What's so funny?"

I thought you were going to tell me you're pregnant.

"Oh my God! No!" I gasped, yelling louder than I meant to. "Don't even say that." I couldn't even imagine if that was true. Instead of bringing bad karma my way, I redirected the conversation back to my original statement, but it took me several seconds to relax my face from a horrified expression.

"So how do you feel about me moving out?" I braced myself to deal with whatever happened. If she didn't want me to leave, I wouldn't.

Well, now that you brought it up, Jagger wants to move in here. We were waiting to tell you until we found the right time, but it looks like you found it for us.

"Oh, well, yeah. It looks like it'll all work out for the best, then." Why, after finding out that our situations were perfectly synced up, did I start crying?

Kena hugged me tightly before asking, *Why are you upset?*

There was no hesitation before I started rambling uncontrollably. "Because we won't be living together anymore. Because we won't be able to just hang out in our pajamas, stuff our faces with junk food and watch corny horror movies. Because—" I sniffed. "—I won't have anywhere to go when Ryder drives me nuts." We both laughed at my last reason, and although Kena never made a sound, the grin on her beautiful face was huge and her chest shook in amusement.

Then we'll kick the men out when one of us has an argument and we'll hang out. Sisters before misters. Kena often found ways to make me feel better, even though that was rightly my job because I was her big sis. Regardless, we hashed out a few minor details, like when the moving was all going to take place, what furniture would be staying and which pieces would be moved. Kena had to make room for Jagger's things just like Ryder did for mine.

After about a half hour, we joined the men. They were in the same exact position, leaning back on the sofa with their legs spread. The typical way men sit.

As soon as Ryder saw me approach, his expression changed. Apparently, I looked drained. "Wait here," he instructed, pushing me to sit down. Moments later he had my overnight bag in his hand.

"You stayin' here?" he asked Jagger.

"Yeah, man."

"Okay, we're going home, then."

Home. What a strange but wonderful thought that Ryder had not only accepted me in his life but that we were going to be living together. Apparently starting right away.

After throwing my bag on the back of his bike, he handed me a helmet. "I don't think I can ride on that tonight." I must've really been out of it since I'd never even heard him pull up. Normally I'd heard the roar of his engine a mile away.

"Yeah, what was I thinkin'? You look like hell."

"Gee, thanks," I said sarcastically. "You sure know how to kick a woman when she's down." I didn't even possess enough energy to be angry at him.

"Sorry, that's not what I meant at all. I just meant. . . ."

"Go get Jagger's keys," I instructed, halfheartedly pointing toward the house.

He jogged off, returning soon after and helping me into Jagger's truck. A half hour later he was practically carrying me into his house, shooing Brutus out of the way so he didn't trip over him.

As soon as Ryder undressed me and tucked me into bed, I closed my eyes, but before he could leave the room, I asked him to stay. "Please lie with me."

A brief silence ensued before he asked, "What if I fall asleep?" At some point we had to try and sleep in the same bed again.

"Please stay."

The bed dipped beside me as I drifted off to sleep.

Ryder

I HAD AN IDEA WHY Marek had called the impromptu meeting, but I wouldn't be 100 percent sure until he started talking. I glanced around the room and saw every man present looked tense, ready to blow if we had to continue to wait and exact our revenge on the rest of the Reapers.

Two less Reapers in the world, the ones we'd most recently dealt with, helped to ease my mind, a sentiment shared by every single member sitting around our wooden meeting table, but the annihilation of the entire club would feel much better.

"Tell us we're not gonna wait one second longer," Hawke barked, leaning forward and staring at Marek. "Because that'll be bullshit. We need to do something, Prez."

I'd watched Hawke transform from someone who used to fuck about, not really caring about much else other than the club and his woman, to a man who'd become harder, not so quick with the jokes.

He'd remained faithful to Edana, trying to help her through the aftermath of the attack, but nothing seemed to work. She'd packed up and left to stay with her sister, so all he had now was his laser focus on taking out as many Reapers as he could.

"And we're gonna." Marek turned to look at Stone. "We still got a signal on the trackers?"

"Yeah," our VP answered. "Last I checked they're all in the same place."

"Then we move out tonight."

"Isn't that kind of a sloppy move?" I asked, hearing my words only after they'd left my mouth. I had essentially told the leader of the Knights Corruption that he wasn't thinking clearly. Quickly backpedaling, especially seeing the angry look on Marek's face, I added, "What I meant to say was, don't you find it odd that all the trackers are still live? After all these weeks? And that they're all in the same place? Together? Call me crazy but I think we might be walking into a trap."

A few of the men contemplated what I'd said and some of them nodded. Marek surveyed the room, leaned over and whispered something to Stone. I had the utmost faith that Marek would take my questions into consideration before he made another move. It was why he was so effective in leading the club. He accepted ideas and suggestions, valuing each member's insight. Maybe he didn't take kindly to anyone blurting out shit like "Isn't that kind of a sloppy move," but he'd allow people to redeem themselves instead of being pissed and writing them off.

"Okay." He looked directly at me when he said, "We act like it's a trap."

"Why now?" Tripp asked. "Not that I'm complaining."

"Because I had to put a few things into play before we went after them." Elaborating, he added, "Salzar and the rest of the men are gonna watch over the women and children for a few days. They just got back and are ready to go."

Salzar was the head of our Laredo chapter. He was a good man, and I had no doubt he'd take good care of our families while we were gone.

Marek reclined in his seat, already knowing our ol' ladies were gonna give us a hard time. For as difficult as Braylen was gonna be, at least she'd have her sister with her. I could only imagine the fight Adelaide was gonna give Stone. Not only would she not want to stay with a bunch of strangers, but she wouldn't want their daughter around them either. I knew Stone didn't want to do it just as much as I didn't, but we had no other choice. If it was indeed a trap, the Reapers would have a game plan in place to come after everyone close to us.

No, we couldn't risk it.

Question was, how the hell did I break the news to Braylen?

———— ✦ ————

"I'M NOT GOING," SHE HUFFED, crossing her arms over her chest and givin' me her most defiant stance. Normally, I'd challenge her until she gave in, but I knew damn well this scenario was entirely different. I was askin' her to go somewhere I didn't completely want to send her. Not because I didn't trust my brothers in Laredo, but because they had a few new members I didn't know, and shoving Braylen under their noses for God knew how long was certainly gonna fuck with me.

"You have to."

"I don't have to do anything I don't want to. That's the beauty of it."

I moved toward her but she backed away, sure to keep her voice low so no one could hear us. I'd surprised her at her job, knowing if I tried to break the news to her at home, she'd rain holy hell on me. I was dealin' with enough; I didn't need to add anything else to my list.

"Bray," I warned, "don't argue with me about this. You have to go."

"Why? Why can't I just stay home? We have a top-of-the-line security system. Besides, Brutus will be with me."

"Really?" I had to laugh at that one. "Brutus is no guard dog, sweetheart. Besides, he's still a puppy. What is he gonna do? Maul someone's ankles? Nice try, though." Speaking of which, I had to find someone to take the little guy while everyone was away. Maybe Braylen's parents could watch him for us. They'd fallen for him almost as fast as I had, so I knew he'd be in good hands.

"Then Kena and I will stay with our parents."

I didn't want to get into too much detail, informing her that her parents would also be in danger if she went that route.

"No."

"Yes," she argued.

I couldn't help it. My voice rose. "I said no!" Her eyes widened before she tried to shove past me, but I caught her by the arm. "Uh-uh, you're not goin' anywhere but out the door with me. So don't make a scene. Or do, I don't care." I dragged her out of the breakroom and past the front desk, her friend slash boss staring at us as I approached the door. "Braylen needs the next week off," I shouted over my shoulder right before I hauled her outside.

"I can't believe you just did that. You had no right." She stood next to my bike, staring at me, stunned I'd done what I had.

Wanting to shield her from the actual reason I needed her to comply, I shook my head and closed my eyes for a brief moment. Taking a few deep breaths, I opened my eyes, reached for her and pulled her to me.

"Look." She parted her lips to interrupt me so I slapped my hand over her mouth to keep her quiet. *God, this woman.* "You're in danger. We all are. We have to take care of something, and when it's all over with, I'll bring you home. Safe and sound. But until then, be quiet and do as I say. Got it?" I didn't want to come off as mean and uncaring, but I was trying to shield her from our enemy. Trying to keep her safe. But all she wanted to do was give me a hard time.

Only able to see her nose and up because my hand was covering half of her face, she shot me a death glare, but I ignored her. Finally, after a solid minute, when I thought she had calmed down some, I removed my hand. She instantly started mumbling. Something about me being an asshole, and I'd pay for this shit and a few other things I couldn't understand.

But the important thing was she hopped on the back of my bike and wrapped her arms around my waist. She could say whatever she wanted as long as she didn't fight me on leaving.

THIRTY-FOUR

Braylen

ANGRILY THROWING CLOTHES INTO MY suitcase, I stomped around the bedroom like a child having a tantrum. But I couldn't help it. I was pissed off. Ryder showed up at my job and told me I had to stay with their charter in Texas. He'd given me no warning whatsoever, spewing some bullshit about the decision being last minute. Maybe if he'd fully explained just what the problem was, I would find myself more on board with the sudden plans, but all he would tell me was that it was club business. Oh wait, he did tell me I was in danger. That was more than he usually gave me.

"We gotta leave soon," he announced, popping into the bedroom and leaning against the doorframe. He watched me for a few minutes before speaking again. "You can be as mad at me as you want, but this is happening."

"You see me packing, don't you?" He smirked, which only served to infuriate me even more. "You can go back to waiting in the living room."

He threw up his hands in mock surrender, turned around and left without another word.

The entire ride to the clubhouse was in silence. I wasn't happy about my life being uprooted over something Ryder wouldn't even fill me in on; I sure as hell wasn't about to make idle chitchat just to pass the time.

There was more than one reason why I was so upset, though. Not only was he shipping me off to Texas, but I knew in my gut that Ryder was putting himself in harm's way, only he wouldn't tell me why. *Club business.* If I heard those two words one more time, I was gonna scream bloody murder.

We eventually pulled into the clubhouse lot and parked. I saw a group of women gathered together and a separate group of men off to the side, reminding me of recess during elementary school. Only this wasn't a break from school—it was more like a break from our everyday lives. And not the good kind.

Slamming the truck's door behind me, I headed toward my sister and the other women she was speaking with. "Hi," I greeted, hugging Kena before smiling at Adelaide, Sully, and Reece. If I thought I'd been upset about having to leave, I could only imagine how Adelaide and Reece felt. Both of them were pregnant, and Adelaide had an infant on her hip as well. Kaden, the baby Sully and Marek had been caring for, was in Sully's arms, tugging on a strand of her long black hair. Knowing these women had more to worry about than I did, I calmed my anger to a simmering boil.

"Don't be too worried," Reece comforted me, placing her hand on my forearm. Seeing my obvious displeasure, she said, "I know I'm pretty new to all this, but I have every faith the men are doing this as a last resort. I know Tripp's torn up about it." She flashed me a sympathetic smile, making me realize everyone standing around me was affected. I needed to get on board and lose the crappy attitude.

We chatted for close to twenty minutes, trying to keep the topics off the next few days and on lighter subjects like children.

Eventually, Ryder came to stand behind me, cautiously putting his hand on the small of my back. My white tank top was split in the back, just above my skirt's waistband, so when he touched me, he stroked his thumb over my bare skin. When I didn't yell at him or pull away, he leaned down and kissed my temple.

"You ladies ready to go?" Jagger asked, pulling Kena in for a kiss. She seemed to be handling the situation much better than I was, and I had no idea why.

On our brief walk toward one of the two black SUVs that were taking us to Texas, I stopped her. "Aren't you upset?"

I'm more scared than upset. Not for us, but for the guys. But my emotions will do nothing except distract Jagger, and I need him focused. For whatever they have to do.

Damnit! I hadn't even thought of it like that, thinking that my mood might inadvertently be a distraction for Ryder. And if he was worried about dealing with my surly ass, then maybe he might get hurt. I couldn't have that on my conscience.

"Thanks, sis." I hugged her again before taking off to search for Ryder.

It didn't take me long to find him, seeing as how he was helping to load the suitcases into the back of one of the vehicles.

"I don't wanna argue," he said as I approached. "I can't deal with that right now."

"I know. I'm sorry. I should have been more sensitive to what you're going through. Sorry for acting like such a brat."

He stopped midthrow and turned to look at me.

"Is this some sort of trick?" He was serious, which made me feel even worse.

"No, it's not." I moved toward him until I could wrap my arms around his neck. Pulling him down, I covered his mouth with mine. When I tried to break away, he grabbed the back of my head and deepened the kiss, swirling his tongue with mine until I completely lost myself to him.

"Get a room," Tripp teased, moving in front of Ryder to help finish the job he'd started. We finally parted and Ryder ushered me toward the side of the truck, where we had some privacy from everyone else standing around.

"I'm sorry we have to do this, but it's necessary. I don't know what I'd do if something happened to you."

"But what if something happens to you? What will I do?" The question rattled me because I knew there was a possibility Ryder could be harmed. In what way and by whom I had no clue, but it didn't matter. The simple fact that he could be scared me.

"Nothin' is gonna happen to me." He wrapped his arm around my waist and stroked the exposed skin on my lower back once more. "But somethin' is gonna happen to someone if they even look at you the wrong way."

I smiled because it was his way of telling me we were all good. And that was the thing with Ryder. He didn't hold grudges.

I could certainly learn a thing or two from him.

———◆———

LAREDO WAS APPROXIMATELY A TWENTY-FIVE-HOUR trip, and because we couldn't afford to waste any time, the guys took turns driving. We stopped every six hours so we could stretch our legs, grab something to eat, use the restroom and top off the gas tanks.

Both SUVs made the same stops. Ryder, Jagger, and Tripp were "in charge," as they called it, of our vehicle, while Marek, Stone, Sully, Kaden,

Addy and Riley rode in the other one. Thank goodness both trucks had third-row seating or we'd all be sitting on each other's laps.

When we weren't talking to our men, Kena, Reece and I chatted about the latest Hollywood gossip, doing our best to pass the long stints on the road. A few times I'd drifted off to sleep, then woke up only to find out that a measly twenty minutes had passed.

"Why didn't we fly?" I asked fifteen hours into the drive, growing more agitated with each passing mile.

Jagger was driving, taking his turn at the wheel while Kena sat beside him in the passenger seat. Every time we got back in the vehicle after stopping, we were sitting next to someone new. Right then Ryder sat next to me, stroking my bare knee with his middle finger.

"Because we don't want anyone knowing," Tripp answered from behind me. He sat next to a sleeping Reece in the third row. I had no idea what he meant and I knew if I asked, one of them would only give me a vaguer answer. It simply wasn't worth getting aggravated over. I was annoyed enough as it was. Tired and miserable, to be more precise.

"You know," Ryder said, leaning close to whisper in my ear, "I would love to fingerfuck you right now." His comment completely came out of left field, but I should've expected something, especially this long into the trip. Besides, he'd been rubbing my knee for the past fifteen minutes. "What do ya think?"

"Are you serious?" I whispered back, keeping my eyes forward so as not to draw attention from any of the other passengers.

"Why not?" His gripped my knee and tried to pull my legs apart. "I'll make you come. Take your mind off being miserable."

"I'm not—"

"Yeah you are, and I don't blame ya." He kissed my neck. "Let me do this for you," he tempted, his fingers moving up the inside of my thigh. I clamped my legs closed before he reached the edge of my panties.

"Remove. Your. Hand." I turned to face him and gave him a tight smile. "You're not shoving your fingers inside me with Tripp and Jagger right next to us. Never mind that my sister is right there," I said, pointing toward the passenger seat.

"Are you sure?" He smirked, but when my expression didn't change, he removed his hand. "Fine, but I'm gonna fuck you so hard when we get to the club." He didn't say the last part quietly, both of his friends laughing out loud when they heard it, Kena turning around and smiling.

"Oh my God, Ryder!" I exclaimed. "How embarrassing."

"Don't worry about it, Braylen. I plan on putting one on your sister as well."

"Ewwww."

Kena at least had the decency to slap his arm, even though she kept the smile on her face.

"Yeah, Reece isn't gonna be able to walk for a few days after I get done with her." Tripp laughed, clasping Ryder's shoulder in amusement. Good thing his woman was asleep; otherwise, she would've joined me in being mortified.

"Oh, please stop talking. All of you. Especially you, Jagger. Just . . . no."

All three of them laughed harder. At least my humiliation helped to ease the rest of the trip for them.

THIRTY-FIVE

Ryder

WE PULLED INTO THE SECLUDED clubhouse compound of our Laredo chapter, closing in on nine in the evening. After spending time with our women, we gathered with our brothers, everyone present and accounted for.

"So if any of you want to come back with us, we'd sure appreciate it," Marek announced, sitting next to Salzar at the head of their meeting table. Jagger, Tripp, and Stone leaned against the nearest wall, next to me.

Salzar was one of the original members of this charter, a full head of white hair and a clean-shaven face making him look innocent. But anyone who knew the man knew the opposite was true. He was loyal as hell but as mean as they come, when driven to be so. He kind of reminded me of Cutter.

"I'll go," a man named Etch said, his long shaggy hair tied back into a low ponytail. He was older, probably mid-fifties. I'd known the guy for many years, and while he may be close to twenty years my senior, his reflexes were on point, especially with a blade.

"Count me in," another said.

"Me too, Marek. Whatever you need."

The last two were new to the charter, at least newer than two years, but I had no doubt Salzar wouldn't have patched them in if they weren't good men.

"I'm in as well," Salzar offered, nodding toward Marek. "We've dealt with the Reapers here too, although this charter has nothing on Psych's.

"Well, it's a good thing we ain't gotta deal with Psych anymore, isn't it?" Stone asked, cocking his head to the side while a ghost of a smile lifted the corners of his mouth.

Marek grinned. It'd been a sweet victory for our president to finally end the life of the man who'd put his wife through hell her entire life. Every once in a while, when he'd mention a nightmare that Sully had—which weren't as frequent anymore—or him not being able to completely push down his rage when he saw the scars that littered her skin, he said he wished that Psych was still tied up in our safe house's basement so he could torture him all over again.

I was thankful the evil fucker was dead, though. Marek was being dragged down a dark path, and we all feared he was gonna lose it once and for all. The small splinter of sanity remaining would have surely unraveled if he hadn't seen his way out of that hell.

"I'm gonna have to ask that you stay here and look after our families," Marek said, turning toward Salzar. "I know you won't let anything happen to them. They'll be safe with you here, and I'll be on my game not having to worry about them."

"Whatever you want is good with me, brother." Salzar was fierce, but the look he shared with Marek was laced with understanding, compassion and something else I couldn't quite decipher.

When the room grew quiet, I felt as if I had to make a declaration, some new faces forcing me to speak my mind. I cleared my throat. "I just wanna throw out there that if one hair is touched on any one of our ol' ladies' heads, you'll deal with us." I waved my hand toward Marek, Stone, Jagger and Tripp. "And it won't be pretty." I looked at every man around the room but focused more on the unfamiliar guys.

Salzar chuckled, easing some of the building tension. "Don't worry, Ryder. No one is gonna touch your women. Look at them? Now that's a different story, my friend." I whipped my head to glare at him. "Calm down." He laughed harder. "I'm just fuckin' with you. We'll treat them like family. You have my word."

A quick nod from me and the conversation was over. I trusted Salzar, and I had every faith he'd keep everyone in line . . . and our women, Riley, and Kaden safe.

———— • ————

AFTER A FEW BEERS, I said my goodbyes and staggered back toward the room they'd given us. My exhaustion mixed with the alcohol flowing through me was enough to make me wanna pass out, but as soon as I opened the door and saw Braylen lying on top of the covers, naked and exposed, I quickly had other ideas. But I didn't want to wake her. She'd been through a lot the past couple days—hell, since the day she'd met me—so if I could give her a few more hours of peace, I would do just that.

Adjusting my dick, trying to lessen the hard-on that had popped up as soon as my eyes landed on her, I proceeded to undress before pulling back the covers and climbing underneath.

Braylen didn't budge, her breathing so slow I knew she wasn't gonna wake up anytime soon. So I lay there, thinking about everything that had happened in my life since the day I met her strong-willed ass in the park, giving Jagger a hard time for something that didn't even involve her.

I found out that day that Braylen Prescott was fierce, loyal and had a mouth I wanted to sometimes silence with my cock. She drew me in all while making me throw up stone walls to protect myself.

She pushed.

I pulled.

She gave me shit.

I demanded things from her.

But when we came together, figuratively and literally, it was out of this world. I wasn't saying our relationship was easy—it definitely wasn't—but I knew I wanted to spend my life with her. I could only hope she reciprocated those feelings.

While Braylen was a challenge to deal with sometimes, I was even more difficult. I was man enough to admit it. I was severely protective, possessive of her time and jealous. It was exactly why I needed her to push when all I wanted was to pull her under. She showed me the error of my ways, and if I didn't acknowledge them, she gave me the cold shoulder. Some days I welcomed the silence, but other days the quiet drove me borderline insane.

Braylen brought light into my world, and after everything I just described, I knew that made me sound crazy, but it sure as hell made perfect sense to me.

It wasn't until she relentlessly pushed me to tell her that I finally divulged everything that happened to my mother. And I swore afterward, even though I was still a little angry that she made me talk about it, I felt lighter. Like I could finally relinquish the past and look forward to the future. Something a lot of the men in the club never did, mainly because we didn't know if we'd be alive long enough to make any long-term plans.

Marek had taken care of those concerns a while back, though, first by breaking with Los Zappas cartel, then steering the club legit. Funny thing was, even though the Knights straddled the right side of the law, our hands were certainly not clean.

Sure, we didn't deal in drugs any longer, but snatching people's lives just happened to still be a necessary evil.

Braylen stirred, lazily rolling over on her side and throwing her arm and leg over me. The warmth from her skin had my dick coming back for a full salute in seconds. Moments passed in stillness, and then her hand slowly slid down my body until she cupped me. I was completely naked, the clubhouse on the warmer side, so when she realized she was touching my cock, she gripped me tighter before releasing a moan. She moved closer and rested her head in the crook of my neck, working her fingers up and down my hardened shaft, all without saying a word.

I'd planned on letting her sleep, but clearly she had a different idea. And who was I to deny her what she wanted? I wasn't selfish, after all.

Shifting her so she was flat on her back, her hand slipping away from me, I spread her legs and thrust inside her. Her sleepy moans thickened my blood, the need to spill myself inside her more potent than ever before.

Because I had no idea what was gonna happen once we returned home, I reveled in the feel of her, imprinting the memory so I'd never forget.

Positioning her leg over my hip opened her up, and I took full advantage, driving home how much I'd miss her with every stroke of my body.

"Look at me," I demanded, slowing my rhythm until she opened her beautiful brown eyes. Once her attention was on me, I took a deep breath, counted to five, and then released the air. "I love you."

I wasn't sure what I expected, but tears and her trying to push me off her were not it.

"Get off me," she cried out, pushing against my hips to dislodge my body from hers.

"Stop it, Bray. What's the matter?" I remained inside her, refusing to budge until she told me why my telling her I loved her made her so angry.

"You just told me you loved me," she blubbered, tears falling down her cheeks while she desperately tried to catch her breath.

"So." I'd never been so confused.

"Why would you tell me that now?"

"What do you mean? It's how I feel."

"But why now?" she repeated, whispering her question as if she didn't fully understand her reaction either. Her fingers continued to dig into my hips, which was more annoying than anything. Leaning back on my haunches and pulling her with me, still careful not to slip from her body, I grabbed her hands in mine and pinned them to the bed.

"Tell me right now what's wrong?" She stared at me, continued to cry, but didn't say a damn word. "So help me God, woman," I threatened. "If you don't tell me why you're so upset, I'm gonna. . . ." My words trailed off because I had no idea *what* the hell I was gonna do. I was stunned by her reaction, and as that feeling waned, I became angry.

Definitely not how I saw the scene playing out in my head.

"You're only telling me you love me because you don't think you're comin' back," she finally confessed. "You know something bad is gonna happen and that's . . . that's why you said it." More tears. More short and choppy breaths. More anguish shrouding her because I knew in my heart she loved me too.

But she was terrified that I wouldn't make it back to her.

THIRTY-SIX

Braylen

MY IMAGINATION RAN WILD WITH thoughts of Ryder lying on the ground. Dead. Shot. Stabbed. And nothing he could say would wipe the images from my brain. I didn't want him to leave. I had a bad feeling, had it ever since we left California, but I tried to be strong. Brave.

But him telling me he loved me, and for the first time, was like a knife to my heart when it should have made me feel elated.

"Get off me."

"No."

"Ryder, please," I begged. "I can't breathe."

"I'm not doing anything to you. The only thing I'm holding down is your hands." His body was still connected with mine, and whenever I felt him twitch inside me, he stole my breath. I knew it didn't make any sense, but I needed him to let me up. I needed distance to come to terms with what was gonna happen in a few short hours.

Ryder was gonna leave me, and there was a strong possibility he wouldn't return.

"Please," I repeated, closing my eyes briefly as my tears continued to fall. "Please."

I heard him grunt before he fell from my body, his weight disappearing altogether as he moved off the bed and stood a few feet away. The heat from his stare bored into me, and I knew there was no way he was gonna leave until I divulged everything.

A month ago he would've walked away, but not now. Not after everything we'd been through. What *he'd* been through. He needed me just as much as I needed him, and that was why hearing those three precious words cut me so deeply.

As the seconds passed with my growing vulnerability, I covered myself with the bedsheet, an action which apparently infuriated Ryder.

"Don't hide from me." Whipping off the fabric, he grabbed my ankles and pulled me toward the edge of the bed.

"What are you doing?" I shouted, struggling to move back up the mattress before my ass hit the ground.

"Come on," he urged, reaching out to grab me again. I avoided his touch.

"Just go." The words surprised me, because I didn't want him to leave. Not then. Not ever.

"You want me to go?" His voice rose a level, his face scrunching in anger. "I tell you I love you, you freak the fuck out, and now you're telling me you want me to go?" I didn't answer. "Well?" he roared. "Is that what's happenin' right now?"

"I don't know." I was scared, petrified even, but I couldn't put any of my emotions into words that would make him understand my reaction.

Running his hands down his face to try and calm himself, he finally looked at me again. There was sadness behind his eyes I hadn't seen earlier. "I do love you, Braylen. I should've told you before but I was too scared. You make me feel things I've never experienced before and that terrifies me, but I know I can't live without you." He took a step. "I'll come back. I promise."

"Don't," I said, holding up my hand to stop him from advancing. "Don't make promises you might not be able to keep."

"I'll do everything in my power to come back to you. There, is that better?" His question was sarcastic but also serious.

"What happens to me if you don't?" I cringed after the words left my mouth. I couldn't imagine not having Ryder in my life, and the mere thought I'd never see him after that day ripped me apart inside. How did the other women deal with this? I could barely handle it one time, let alone time and time again.

"Just don't go out with George. Promise me?" The corners of his lips curved up the slightest bit.

"You're an ass."

"I know. But I'm an ass who loves you." He held out his hand, and I finally accepted, taking hold and allowing him to pull me up to stand in front of him.

I cupped his cheek, then slowly trailed my fingers over his neck and down his chest, coming to rest my hand over his heart. The man was it for me, and I'd regret never telling him in case something did happen.

"I love you too. I fought against it at first because I refused to fall for you when you were so guarded, but my heart won out in the end." There was so much more I wanted to tell him, but I didn't even know where to begin.

Instead of choosing to keep it serious, an uncharacteristic trait of Ryder's that was slowly becoming more frequent, he tried to make light of my freak-out. "By the way, I knew you loved me." A cocky look took hold before he continued. "I mean, come on, how could you not?"

———— ♦ ————

AS WE ALL TOOK TIME saying goodbye to our men, I couldn't help the emotions which flowed freely once more. Only that time I wasn't the only one.

Kena hugged Jagger extra tight, breaking away briefly to sign that she loved him, and that she'd kill him if he got hurt. She smiled through her anguish before he pulled her back toward him, kissing her over and over before whispering something in her ear.

Tripp and Reece huddled near one of the trucks, talking low amongst themselves before embracing for long moments. Tripp was turned toward me, and I could see how sad and worried he looked leaving his woman.

Stone and Adelaide, along with their daughter, Riley, were having a family moment when Marek, Sully, and Kaden joined them. Anyone looking at the small group could tell they were close, closer than anyone else in the club. Other than my sister and me, of course. Both children must have sensed the sadness of the moment, because they broke out in cries simultaneously. Adelaide and Sully rocked them, trying their best to soothe them while they themselves were distraught.

Right or wrong, I took comfort in not being the only one who was visibly upset.

Ryder wrapped his arm around my waist. "It's gonna be okay, babe. You'll see." He leaned down and gave me a kiss, and just before he pulled away, I latched on to him for dear life. Lacing my fingers in his hair, I pulled him as close as I could and kissed him like I never have before. As we tasted each other, I poured every bit of love I could inside him, stealing his breath for my own to keep until he came back.

Only then could I breathe again.

THIRTY-SEVEN

Ryder

TWO DAYS HAD PASSED SINCE we'd left, and every second away from Braylen was agonizing. Even though the rest of the guys were bothered by the departure, they seemed used to it. I didn't think I'd ever become accustomed to leaving her behind, crying and worried out of her mind that she was never gonna see me again. Christ! Every tear she shed tore away a piece of me, and there wasn't a damn thing I could do to comfort her, other than tell her how I felt and promise to come back.

Neither of which she initially took very well.

I talked to Braylen every time we stopped, and her voice gutted me. I knew she was going through it, but so was I. Something I had to remind her of. During our last call, she told me she loved me and not to worry about her. Truth be told, my jealous streak spiked with the thought that she was spending time with one of the guys at the club, taking her mind off her worry for me. When I voiced as much, she called me crazy, then reminded me that she didn't want to be a distraction for whatever I had to do. She just wanted me back safe and sound, and in one piece.

As planned, Etch, Smiley, and Miles joined us, taking turns with the rest of us driving back to California. I learned that Smiley—who was constantly grinning, hence the name—was twenty-six, had two baby mamas and a whole lot of drama. Minus the kids, he reminded me a lot of Hawke, or at least who Hawke was a year back. Personality-wise only. Physically, he was the exact opposite with his bright blond hair and heavy facial scruff. He seemed to be a good guy, telling us that he was honored to wear the KC cut.

Miles had a serious look plastered on his face at all times. He was older than Smiley, closer to my thirty-four years, although he seemed like he might even be older. Hard life. That was what I thought of when I looked at him, and in some ways, he kind of reminded me of myself. Before Braylen.

His light brown hair came to his shoulders, thick and wavy. I overheard Adelaide and Sully whispering about how lucky he was to have such hair, a conversation I definitely wouldn't be mentioning to either Marek or Stone.

———◆———

"YOU GUYS CAN SET UP in these rooms." Marek showed our Texas brothers to some of the empty rooms at the club, since we wouldn't be needing them during their visit. He'd contemplated setting them up at Zip's house, where Reece had initially stayed before moving in with Tripp, because it was so close to the clubhouse, but decided against it at the last minute.

Zip was one of our fallen brothers. He was a good kid, loyal as hell. Unfortunately he'd been killed when some of the Reapers had run his vehicle off the road, snatching Adelaide and Kena per Psych's request. We paid him homage by burying him on the compound since our club meant everything to him.

"Get situated, then meet us in Chambers," Stone announced, checking to see if they needed anything before joining the rest of us.

Before long we were all gathered around the wooden table, our guests leaning against the wall much like we'd done when at their place.

"Okay," Marek started, "the trackers are still live, and it looks like they're are at the docks."

"No doubt waiting on some sort of shipment," Trigger offered. "We ambush them there. Quick and unexpected."

The ol' man was anxious to move on our enemy, just like the rest of us, but we had to be cautious. Like I'd mentioned before . . . it could be a trap.

"All of 'em?" Stone asked, frowning at how easy this all seemed.

"Enough of 'em."

"You all know what I think," I said, leaning back in my chair and crossing my arms over my chest. Everyone remained quiet, too busy processing all of the what-ifs, I was sure.

"What seems to be the problem?" Etch inquired after several moments passed without another word from any of us.

"The trackers were placed on some of the Reapers bikes a while ago. They shouldn't still be active, but they are. It might be some sort of trap,"

Marek gritted, obviously annoyed it was taking us so long to figure out what to do.

"Then why don't we hunt them?" Smiley asked, grinning like he'd just asked the most obvious question.

"What?" Breck chimed in, seemingly annoyed that Smiley even put in his two cents.

Even though Breck looked pissed off, it didn't stop Smiley from explaining. "Scope 'em out. Take a couple trips to where you think they are and watch 'em. See if they're even there. If they are, probably not a trap. If there's no sign of life, then figure something else out." He nodded before adding, "Oh and by the way, I've used a tracker on one of my exes, and the fucker lasted for two months. Just sayin'."

Funny how it took someone new to point out the obvious. The majority of us were dealing with our own personal issues, and because the Reapers had threatened us through our women, we weren't seeing things the way we should've. Blinded with the need for revenge, we ignored what could've essentially been right in front of our faces.

If we indeed weren't walking into a trap, we could've taken care of business much sooner. The thought alone angered me; the war with our enemy could've been over by now.

"Anyone opposed to what Smiley suggested, raise your hand," Marek said. I looked around the room and not one man raised his arm. We were all on the same page in that we wanted to do something . . . anything. "Okay, then." He slammed down the gavel before pushing away from the table.

I was one of the last to leave Chambers, too distracted thinking about Braylen to realize only Jagger remained.

"You okay, man?"

"I guess. It's just . . . there are so many things that can go wrong. And now that I. . . ."

"Have something to lose?" he finished for me. He slid out a chair and took a seat next to me. "Listen, every time I step into that ring, there's always a chance someone is gonna get the best of me."

"I'm not talkin' about losing a fuckin' cage fight," I seethed. "This is so much more than that."

"Let me finish." Jagger was only silent for a moment. "If you remember, I killed someone in that ring." *That fact had slipped my mind.* "All I did was hit him in the wrong spot."

"Wasn't that guy a drug addict? Somethin' was gonna get him sooner or later," I mumbled, growing impatient with our conversation.

"That's not the point."

"Then what is?"

"That I take risks every time I fight. We, as a club, take risks every time we leave this compound, our reputation preceding us, angering our enemies. And we take risks when we fall in love with someone. All of a sudden nothing else matters but the woman holding our heart. It's like the thought of something happening to Kena physically hurts, so I try not to let those images in, but sometimes I can't help it." Jagger took a deep breath, reclining in his seat to give me the time to digest his words.

"When did you get so damn philosophical?"

"I'm an old soul." He laughed, slapping the table and rising to his feet. "Now let's go find out when we're leavin'."

THIRTY-EIGHT

Braylen

SALZAR HAS BEEN EXTREMELY ACCOMMODATING to all of us. He's not much for words but has made sure we're comfortable and have everything we need. Marek left strict instructions that we're not allowed off the compound, even with some of the men accompanying us.

"It's been four days," Reece complained. "When are they coming back for us? I'm going out of my mind, thinking the worst." She sat on the edge of the bed, biting her lower lip in nervousness, a sentiment all of us shared. Her long chestnut-colored hair flowed down her back, her blue-gray eyes rather stunning. She'd been a stripper at Indulge, but not for long, not after Tripp had met her. He'd saved her from being attacked by one of the customers, and the rest, as they say, was history. They seemed to be smitten with each other, and although I was still getting to know Reece, I knew Tripp even less. In fact, the only men of the club I really knew were Jagger and Ryder. I'd been around the rest of them at gatherings here and there, but they were still a bit of a mystery to me. Although they all seemed to have things in common, such as loyalty and being overbearing—"protective," as Ryder would often correct.

"Someone will call soon, sweetie," Adelaide promised. "They're just not done yet." She seemed so sure everything was going to work out, I couldn't help but think she had some sort of inside information. Or maybe she just didn't want all of us to freak out at the same time. Lord knew, she had her hands full with Riley and her unborn little one.

After putting her daughter in the playpen next to Kaden, Adelaide took a seat next to Reece. "Listen, you need to calm down and focus on your baby," she instructed, gently rubbing Reece's belly.

"I know. I just can't help it." Adelaide gave her a sympathetic look before turning her attention to me. "So, Braylen"—she smirked—"things seem to be going much better with Ryder. He finally wise up?"

"For the most part." I smiled, thinking how far Ryder had come in such a short span of time. Don't get me wrong, he fought the majority of the time to let me in, but thankfully he'd come to his senses. Thinking about him just then sent a shiver of unease through me. If I dwelled on it too long, I'd start to become even more depressed about our current situation than I already was. "Hey, why don't we go out to the bar and have a drink. We can pretend like it's a girls' night out and that we're not really stuck inside this place."

"Sounds good to me," Reece agreed, swooping all of her hair to one side and adjusting her shirt once she stood. "Although I'm just having soda."

"Same here." Adelaide laughed. "Christ! I never thought I'd be pregnant *and* breastfeeding at the same time."

Sully and Kena came into the room, laughing and signing to each other, completely engaged in their conversation. I was thrilled Kena had finally opened up after all these years. Before she met Jagger, I was the only one she hung out with, but since him, she'd really blossomed, coming into her own and not being such an introvert. Sully was the one who taught Jagger how to sign so he could communicate with my sister, so I figured I owed her one as well for Kena's social successes.

"What you are two laughing at?" Reece asked, looking into the mirror to glance at her reflection. Tucking a strand of hair behind her ear, she turned to the two women who'd just joined us.

"I think Kena has an admirer," Sully teased, bumping her shoulder into Kena's.

My sister shook her head. *Sully's crazy. All he did was offer me some of his pizza.*

"Oh yeah? Who?" I asked after translating for Reece and Adelaide, who knew some sign language but not enough to keep up with the flowing conversation.

Kena tried to playfully cover Sully's mouth, but she sidestepped my sister and blurted, "Nash."

I knew exactly who they were referring to because Salzar had briefly introduced us to everyone, Nash being the one who stuck out from the rest. He was certainly handsome with his long black hair and dark blue eyes. He was tall and broad shouldered, slender but muscular. The shirt he wore left little to the imagination, fitting him like a glove.

I know, I know. I'm not supposed to notice other men, but I'm not dead. None of us were interested in anyone but the men who held our hearts, but we also knew a handsome bastard when we saw one. But we weren't stupid either—girl talk stayed between us. Besides, causing tension between any of the guys just for looking was the last thing we wanted to do.

"I'm sure he was just being polite." I gave Kena a wink. "We're gonna grab a drink and try to forget for a little while. Wanna come?"

Please.

We all filed out and headed toward the small bar. It wasn't anywhere near the size the guys had back home at their clubhouse, but I counted five seats. *Yep, it'll do.*

Nash had been standing around talking to a few of the other guys, but as soon as he saw us take a seat, he rushed over and walked behind the bar.

"What can I get you, ladies?" He looked at all of us and smiled, but afterward his attention moved to Kena. He tried not to be obvious, taking all of our orders, but his eyes kept drifting back to my little sister. Maybe he did have a little crush on her.

Over the course of the next two hours, I'd been able to relax a little, doing my best to focus on bonding with the incredible women stuck in the same position as me. For the most part, they seemed to be handling it well, but how much of that was a façade? If I had to guess, I'd say the majority.

Salazar checked in on us a few times, at one point even pulling Nash aside to talk to him before disappearing to his room. He'd been staying in one of the back bedrooms, seemingly taking his promise to keep us safe very seriously.

"WELL, THAT'S IT FOR ME." Sully stretched her arms above her head, her white tank top exposing a small amount of skin, enough to where I saw a scar above the waistband of her shorts. My eyes flicked to hers and I prayed she hadn't noticed. The last thing I wanted to do was make her feel uncomfortable.

Ryder had told me a few things about her past, enough for me to realize what a strong woman Sully actually was to have gone through what she had and come out the survivor she was today.

"Me too," Reece yawned, finishing her soda before hopping off her barstool. "You coming?" she asked Kena, squeezing her shoulder.

My sister took another sip and placed her glass on the bar, pushing it toward Nash who was beaming at her. *Jagger better not get wind of this.*

Someone must've filled Nash in on the fact that Kena wasn't deaf, that she just couldn't speak, because a few times he asked her a question, then passed her a notepad and pen. His attention toward her wasn't pushy, but I definitely picked up that he was interested, even though I knew he wasn't stupid enough to make an actual move on her. He knew better. In fact, Ryder had mentioned that he warned everyone. What exactly that meant, I had no idea, but I could take a guess, especially if it came out of Ryder's mouth.

I'm ready too, Kena signed, smiling politely at Nash before standing.

"Yep, I'm ready for bed," Adelaide announced, stifling a yawn as she rose to her feet.

"I guess I am as well," I agreed, walking behind Kena and whispering in her ear. "You *definitely* have an admirer." She looked at the man behind the bar, then back to me.

You're gonna get me in trouble.

"Not me, lil' sis. Not me."

"Good night, ladies," Nash called out as we disappeared down the hallway.

We'd been assigned two of the bedrooms. Sully and Adelaide shared one with the children, and Reece, Kena and I shared the other, my sister and I sharing a bed while Reece occupied the spare one. Grateful not to have to sleep alone, lost in thoughts of what Ryder was doing at that exact moment, I found solace falling asleep next to Kena. Just like when we were kids and one of us had a nightmare.

THIRTY-NINE

Ryder

TWO DAYS AFTER WE'D ARRIVED back in California, we finally decided to take a drive out to where we believed some of the Reapers were gathered. An hour away from our stomping ground. We planned on exacting a few recon missions, so to speak, before doing anything, but lo and behold, the very first ride we took, we saw a few of our enemy unloading crates from a secluded and otherwise abandoned shipyard.

Maybe Smiley was right after all. Maybe the devices we'd placed on some of their bikes were still active, and they had no clue they were even being tracked. However, extremely cautious and aware it could still be a trap, we never made a move. Not that first time. Instead we returned to the clubhouse to discuss exactly how we wanted to proceed.

Most of the Reapers weren't the smartest tools in the shed, which had always worked to our advantage when dealing with them, but we did a thorough sweep of our rides, as well as the cages, just to make sure they hadn't returned the favor and popped some of their own trackers on our vehicles.

When we were satisfied we still had the upper hand, we strapped as many weapons to our bodies as we could, as well as filling up the backs of the cages with enough artillery and ammo to end a war. Which was exactly what we planned to do.

We wanted the other bastard who'd threatened some of the women, but more than that, we needed to take out as many of the Reapers as we could, setting our sights on Rabid more than anyone else. We had to take out the new man in charge before he even had a chance to rally his men. And if Koritz just happened to be there, then we'd make sure he got his as well.

Two days after the first secret visit we'd made, we decided to finally make our move. Marek, Stone, Breck and Jagger rode out in one of the cages, while Tripp, Etch, Smiley, Miles and I occupied the second one. The rest of the guys stayed back at the club per request of our fearless leader. Cutter wanted to go with his son, but in the end he followed orders, remaining on standby along with Trigger and Hawke.

By the time we'd arrived, the sun had long since dipped behind the horizon. Darkness shielded us as we parked half a mile away from the shipyard, the various dilapidated buildings offering us shelter while we cautiously snuck closer to some of the men hanging around the back of one of their trucks. There looked to be six of them, but there could've been more inside the building they were extracting the wooden boxes from.

"Too bad we aren't still in the business," Etch whispered. "Can you imagine how much fuckin' money is in those crates?"

"You don't even know what's in them," Tripp replied, pressing his back against a concrete wall when one of the Reapers passed by fifty feet ahead of where we were all huddled.

"Still," Etch finished, shrugging before following Marek around the corner, disappearing so fast we almost lost both of them.

"Fuck, it's dark out here," I mumbled, resting my hand on the handle of my gun just in case anything popped off unexpectedly. Turning a few more corners and hurrying across the yard, hiding now and again to ensure our attack was truly a surprise, we finally came to a place where we could see all the action. Action we were gonna be a part of soon enough.

When my eyes landed on the sight in front of me, I smiled. A two-birds-one-stone kind of smile. Not only had Rabid just exited the building, but Koritz followed directly behind him. They were still too far away to hear their conversation, but whatever they were talking about, neither of them looked too happy. The only light provided came from the full moon and the building, but it was enough for us to see how many people we had to contend with whenever we decided to show ourselves. The desolation of the area couldn't have been more perfect for executing these bastards and then hiding their bodies in any number of places.

Finally, Koritz threw up his hands, said something incoherent, then walked away. My eyes flicked to Rabid, and with the little I could make out of him, he looked pleased, clasping his hands together one time before walking back toward the building with a cocky gait. As if he'd just been told something he'd wanted to hear.

"You guys ready?" Marek asked, looking at each of us before continuing. "Be fuckin' careful and watch your back." I took a step forward, but he stopped me, shaking his head. "Ryder, you go with Jagger, Etch, and Tripp. That way." He pointed to our right. "Get behind that building as fast as you can." Turning to look at Breck, Miles, and Smiley, he instructed, "You guys come with Stone and me. We're gonna surround them on the other side."

With a lift of his hand, we began to move into position, creeping around the sides of the crumbling structures to get to the one we needed, when a shrill sound rang out, making us all stop dead in our tracks.

"What the fuck was that?" we heard one of the Reapers shout, looking all around until a few of them started yelling to each other. I closed my eyes and took a deep breath, knowing our plan was goin' right down the shitter because someone left their goddamn phone on. Some asinine song that just put us all in more danger.

"Fuck!" I heard Smiley whisper-shout, trying to silence his cell through his cut, but it kept ringing. The shouting in front of us increased, and we knew we had to make a decision to attack head-on or scatter to the sides like Marek had originally planned. Either way, our enemy knew they had company.

"Shut that thing off," Stone demanded, grabbing Smiley and pulling him behind the rest of us. Slamming him against the wall of the building, Stone reached into Smiley's vest, pulled out the device and threw it to the ground, stomping it to pieces at the exact moment it started ringing again. It was probably the first time since I'd met Smiley where he didn't have a grin kicking up the corners of his mouth.

"Sorry," Smiley apologized, keeping his distance from the rest of us because he knew he'd just fucked up. Royally. I thought for sure Stone was gonna knock him out, but instead, our VP walked back toward Marek, mumbling something under his breath.

As we took a step to disband, I heard Koritz shout, "Knights!"

FORTY

Ryder

A SPRAY OF BULLETS SLICED through the air the closer we moved toward the men scrambling to hide behind whatever was in front of them, seeking cover anywhere they could find. Although they were just putting off the inevitable. There was a lot of shouting, from us and from them, instructions becoming jumbled until I barely knew who was speaking.

Moving slightly to the left to peer around the corner of the building I was hidden behind, a bullet struck the concrete beside my head, missing me by millimeters. I knew there was a good chance I wasn't gonna make it out of there alive, so I decided to push fate's hand and retaliate.

Just as I was about to move into the open, a hand shoved me to the ground, dirt going up my nose I'd been so surprised by the attack. Only it wasn't an attack at all—it was Marek. Before I could say a word, though, I saw him spin around and fire off two rounds, followed by a thump. Someone falling to the ground not twenty feet behind us.

"Thanks, man" was all I could say. What other response was appropriate?

"Tripp and Jagger made it around back. When I tell you to, I want you to stand and fire. There are three men in front of us, another two off to the left." How he could see a damn thing with the clouds passing in front of the moon was beyond me, but I had to trust him. And I did. Wholeheartedly.

"Ready?"

"Yeah." My heart crashed into my chest as a bead of sweat trickled down the side of my face.

"Go!" he yelled, pushing past my body as he barreled forth and fired shot after shot into the night air. With all of the commotion and bullets whizzing past my head, my adrenaline kicked into overdrive, pushing my feet with every step I hadn't even realized I was taking. "Behind the building. Your left!" Marek shouted before disappearing.

When I'd finally made it to the building, I indeed found Tripp and Jagger. The light from inside the warehouse allowed me to see much more than I could moments before.

"Where're the rest of the guys?"

"Fuck if I know," Tripp griped, carefully peering through the window to check things out.

"Anyone in there?" Jagger asked. When he turned to face me, I saw a streak of blood on his neck.

"You get hit?" I moved closer to try and inspect it, but he shook his head.

"Just grazed my skin. Nothing serious."

"Jesus, what the fuck is goin' on?" I asked to no one in particular. It seemed like I was drifting through a nightmare, one where all of our lives could be snuffed out in a split second. Only it wasn't a nightmare at all.

I saw movement to my left and when I turned, gun locked and loaded with my arm outstretched, index finger playing with the trigger, I was two seconds away from firing. Then I saw it was Marek running at us.

"I almost fuckin' shot you."

"Good thing you didn't." Marek was calm, calmer than he should've been in those circumstances. Then again, if he freaked out, where would that leave the rest of us?

"Hey, look who just snuck inside," Jagger interrupted, glancing from the window to us and back again. When we all turned to look at who he was referring to, we saw Koritz rifling around inside the back of some ol' truck, seemingly oblivious that there were four of us watching his every movement. All he had to do was look up and he'd see us, but like always, the crooked DEA agent was only worried about himself.

As I pried my eyes away from that bastard, I caught a glimpse of Stone hovering close to the side of the building. He appeared to be hurrying in our direction, but then he stopped, his feet seemingly frozen in place. The popping sounds of guns being fired were still prevalent, so I was baffled as to why he wasn't seeking cover.

Is he looking for us?

Why isn't he moving?

I swore the man had no fear, even when he should, and I was sure it all stemmed back to him not being able to feel pain. He could still be killed, however, and the sight of him just standing there pissed me off. Not only for him, but for us in case we bore witness to a sight that would haunt us forever.

Him being taken out.

"What the hell is he doin'?" Marek asked, shouting a barrage of obscenities before moving past us and toward his best friend.

But he was too late.

My mouth wouldn't open to warn him. I couldn't move, frozen in place much like Stone. Time slowed but didn't allow me the ability to do a goddamn thing other than watch. My heart skipped a beat and my vision blurred.

A man came out of the brush and walked up behind Stone, standing a few feet from him and pointing the gun at the back of his head. He was unaware that our leader was rushing toward him, and right before Marek tackled him, the light from the gun flashed brightly.

Stone's head jerked forward before he was thrown to the ground, his lifeless body sprawled out in front of us. As soon as Marek saw what happened, he went crazy, jamming his gun into the man's mouth and pulling the trigger. When he finally rose to his feet, his right shoulder jerked backward, his feet stumbling to keep him upright.

At that point, I'd come unglued and raced past Jagger and Tripp, intent on running right into the crosshairs of the bullets still relentlessly being fired.

I was feet from Marek when a pain sliced through my thigh, my leg locking up and suddenly becoming dead weight. I lurched forward, my arms reaching out to find something solid to brace me, but there was nothing. I'd made it to the edge of the building and unfortunately had a clear view of the scene continuing to unfold in front of me.

Another bullet pierced Marek, that time in the chest. He was thrown backward, his gun falling to his side and not in front of him to ward off another attack.

As my legs gave out and I fell to the ground, Tripp and Jagger were next to me. Jagger threw off his cut, ripped off his shirt and made quick work of tying it around my thigh, instinctively knowing where I'd been hit. Did they see it happen?

"Did you really think you'd win, you piece of shit," Koritz shouted, stepping from the building with his weapon raised to finish off our president. He spit on the ground near Marek's head. "You made a big mistake making Carrillo cut off all ties with the Reapers. That decision affected me too, ya know." Koritz's foot connected with Marek's wounded shoulder. "Now you'll finally get what you deserve." Laughing, he turned and looked toward Stone's body. "Looks like you'll be joining your VP soon enough," he threatened, stepping forward to snatch Marek's life.

"I don't think so," a gruff voice said, walking up behind the DEA agent and shoving a gun into his back. Whoever it was remained in the shadows, hiding so I couldn't get a good look at him. His voice sounded familiar, though.

Koritz whipped around, lowering his gun because he obviously knew the man; otherwise, he would've fired on him. It was then that Tripp made a move toward Marek, but before he got too far, I grabbed his leg. If he had any chance of not getting shot himself, he needed to assess the situation.

Thankfully Koritz was engaged at the moment, but how long would that last? Who was he even talking to?

"Be careful," I urged, releasing him and wincing as Jagger tied the material tighter around my wound. Seconds later my vision started to tunnel, but I fought like hell to stay alert.

"What are you doin'? We're on the same side," Koritz said, lifting his weapon back in front of him.

The mystery man laughed. "No we aren't."

Koritz wasted no time in pulling his trigger, but nothing happened. Two more clicks sounded before he tossed his weapon to the ground at the man's feet. He knew he was out of ammo and there wasn't a damn thing he could do to defend himself, so he started spouting off at the mouth instead.

My attention flicked to Tripp, who'd been able to sneak up next to Marek, but as soon as he looked toward the two men in front of him, he froze.

"Oh, so now that I gave you my contact's name, you're gonna kill me?" When the man remained silent, it was clear that was exactly what was goin' down. Koritz started bargaining for his life the split second he realized he was expendable. "I'll give ya whatever you want. Half of my take. What do ya say?"

The shadowed man finally stepped forward.

It was Rabid.

The Savage Reaper's VP himself.

"I'm gonna have to decline," he said before putting a bullet through Koritz's head. The agent was dead before his body hit the ground.

The last thing I saw before I blacked out was Rabid walking toward Tripp and Marek, muttering something as he raised his gun toward them.

FORTY-ONE

Braylen

ASTONISHINGLY, I WAS LOST TO the deepest realms of sleep when a loud bang woke me. Then I heard shouting followed by a bright light. Kena stirred beside me.

"What the hell?" I grumbled, disoriented and annoyed that someone woke me up in such a way. Covering my face with my pillow, it took me several seconds to remember where I was, although I'd been in the same place for days. Hearing a distressed voice, I unshielded my eyes and saw Adelaide rushing toward me.

"Get up," she yelled. "We have to go." She was frantic as she glanced around the room, the wild look in her eyes frightening me. I had no idea what she was doing because she wasn't looking at either of us, or Reece, who'd also shot up in her bed in a panic.

Then just as swiftly as Adelaide had arrived, she left.

"What's going on?" I'd already hopped out of bed and run behind her out into the hallway when it dawned on me that maybe the club was under attack. Catching up to her before she entered the large common space, I grabbed her arm and spun her around. "What's happening? Are we in danger?"

She shook her head before tears fell and painted her cheeks. "He's dead," she wailed, pulling her hair as she retreated, hitting the wall which finally kept her in place.

I had no idea who she was referring to, but it had to be one of our men.

Before I could get any answers, I joined in her anguish, crying right along with her. Kena hurried toward us, signing to me while terror stole her reserve.

What's wrong?

"I don . . . don't know," I blubbered, wiping my face with the back of my hand. "Adelaide said 'He's dead,' but I don't know who she's talking about." My lungs worked feverishly, pulling in air faster than I could expel it.

Just when I thought I was going to hyperventilate, Salzar ran toward us.

"We gotta go," he urged, moving quickly but seemingly calmer than the three of us. A flurry of bodies passed, men spouting out instructions while I stood there in the midst of the tornado. I saw Reece and Sully carrying Riley and Kaden, followed by Nash and a few others holding our suitcases.

Next thing I knew we were all loaded into two vehicles and speeding out of the clubhouse lot as if someone had been chasing us.

Apparently, time had been the culprit.

———— ✦ ————

I KEPT HEARING ADELAIDE SAYING "He's dead," but who was she talking about? Furthermore, who had given her the news? She never mentioned that someone had called her. Did one of the guys at the club we were staying at tell her something? If so, why had they chosen to keep the rest of us in the dark?

We'd been driving for three hours when my cell abruptly rang. I'd made sure it was charged, waiting for the moment when Ryder would call me. *Praying* he would call me.

Fumbling with the phone and almost dropping it, I managed to swipe the screen before the ringing ceased. "Hello," I hurriedly answered. "Ryder?"

"No, it's me." Jagger's voice sounded strained.

"Where's Ryder?"

"He can't. . . ." He trailed off, short spurts of air hitting my ear as I listened to him trying to control his breathing. "I don't even know what to say. It's so bad. So bad," he repeated. I swore he was crying, but I couldn't be sure. Either way, something terrible happened, and if I thought I was gonna lose my mind before, I was surely gonna go mental if Jagger didn't start talking.

"You need to tell me what happened, Jagger. Please." Kena whipped her head toward me, and the look on her face was priceless. Like she'd been given the best gift, and in a sense she had. At least she knew her man was alive, well enough to make a phone call.

I remained on the line, the seconds passing in silence until I heard the first syllable of his first word.

"They didn't make it."

I swore my heart stopped beating right before the line went dead. I immediately dialed Jagger's number back, but it went straight to voice mail. I tried five more times, but each time I heard his automated message telling me to leave a message after the beep. Clutching my phone tightly, I willed it to ring, my internal voice screaming at the top of her lungs for the damn thing to burst out in sound.

I hadn't even realized that I'd been crying until Kena unbuckled her seat belt and crawled next to me, pulling me into her embrace. She tried to comfort me, and I loved her dearly for her attempt, but nothing in the world would make me feel better except for Ryder's voice.

Right before I was about to lose it, my screams bubbling inside my throat, I heard one of the men's phones ring. Nash was driving our SUV while one of his buddies sat next to him—I believed his name was Cass.

"Yeah," Nash answered in a hurry. "Fuck. Okay. Yeah. I know. I'm drivin' as fast as I can." Nothing else was said before he hung up, tossing his phone into the center console.

"Who was that?" Reece asked from behind us. I'd completely forgotten she was in the vehicle with us, she'd been so quiet. When Nash didn't answer, she leaned forward in her seat. "Who was that?" That time her voice was louder, and there was no way our driver didn't hear her.

"No one."

"No one?" she screeched, followed by the click of her seat belt coming undone as she tried to crawl over the seat to where Kena and I were sitting, all the while careful of her small pregnant belly. It seemed as if Reece had finally snapped, joining the rest of us in our fear. When she'd managed to clear the seat, she lunged toward the front, hitting Nash on his arm so frantically I feared he was going to veer off the road and crash.

"What the hell? Sit down," he demanded, the gravel in his voice leaving no doubt that he was serious. And extremely angry. But Reece ignored him, her hair flying wildly around her as she continued to slap him. He tried to dodge her hits but he was trapped, trying to keep his eyes on the road while attempting to get away from her flailing arms.

"You need to calm down, sweetheart," Cass coaxed, grabbing her hands and holding them together in front of her, cautious not to injure her. His voice was eerily calm, especially after having witnessed her break with reality. "We're following orders. We're not to give you ladies any info until we know for sure what we're dealin' with, so no amount of yelling and hitting will make us talk." Cass faced not only Reece but Kena and me as well, his dark green eyes flicking to each of us to drive home his point. "Now go back and sit down," he instructed.

He released Reece's hands and turned back around to face front, not even waiting for her to comply, which she did almost right away. Kena and I moved so she could sit between us.

"Can you at least tell us where we're going?" I asked, waiting not so patiently for his answer.

"California," Nash replied. He took a breath. "We're takin' you back home."

FORTY-TWO

Ryder

A FLURRY OF ACTIVITY DREW me back into consciousness, albeit briefly. My eyes were heavy, lifting them a feat I wanted to give up, but the incessant talking around me increased in volume. After raising my arm toward my face, another task I found rather difficult, I managed to open my eyes, my sight hampered by a bright light. When my pupils had finally adjusted, my vision contorted. Blurry. I saw shapes and witnessed movement, but that was all. Before long, I drifted back into the darkness, Braylen's face greeting me as I relished the comfort of the unknown.

AN INTENSE BURNING SENSATION TRAVELED up my thigh and shoved me from sleep, scrambling toward awareness so rapidly I barely had any time to decipher where I was or who was around me.

"Uhhh," I groaned, trying to move my leg. I clutched the table I was lying on just so I had somewhere to focus my energy; otherwise, I feared I'd tear at my flesh just to try and stop the pain.

"He's awake," I heard someone say. My eyes fluttered open, then closed. Open. Closed. Open. I slowly looked around the room but still didn't know where I was.

"Ryder," the rough voice greeted. "Can you hear me?" Whoever stood over me shook my arm before waving his hand in front of my face. "Ryder!" he shouted. "Look at me."

"Fuck, man," I grated. "Shut up." It was then I recognized the voice. Jagger. "What is that awful smell?" A pungent aroma wafted up my nose until I could barely catch my breath. I turned my head to the side and the smell lessened, although I swore it was trapped inside my nostrils.

"Smelling salts," Jagger answered. "Gotta get you up and back in the land of the living."

"You wait till I get up," I threatened, knowing damn well it would be quite some time before my body would finally decide to cooperate with my brain.

"He's fine," Jagger shouted to someone, walking away from me as my eyes drifted shut once more. Slow and steady breaths calmed me as I rode back into unconsciousness. I didn't make it, however, that god-awful, borderline-painful smell filling my nose again. "Nope. You gotta get up, Ryder."

I swatted the air in front of my face, thankful to have mobility of my arm. It was a start. Now all I had to do was move my leg, enough to chop off the goddamn thing so I could rid myself of the excruciating agony.

"What happened?" I tried to sit up but found the effort laughable.

"Don't move. I need you awake, but don't try and get up. Not until he sees you." Jagger stood by my head, prepared to shove me back down if I made another attempt.

"Who? Until who sees me?"

"The guy Rabid brought in to tend to you guys." His words were so matter of fact, I almost missed the name he'd spoken.

Rabid.

The Savage Reaper's VP.

Memories hit me like a sledgehammer, assaulting my brain until all I could do was live through the horrific events all over again, as if it was the very first time.

My next attempt to get up was successful, albeit strained and half-assed. At least I'd managed to swing my good leg over the table and grip the sides of the metal slab I'd been lying on, essentially anchoring myself in place.

"Whoa," a new voice said that time. When I looked up, my vision swiftly crystal clear, I saw Tripp walking toward me. He looked larger than life, his big form striding with ease until he stood by my side. His shirt was covered in blood, but it didn't appear as if any of it was his.

As I continued to stare at the blood on him, scattered images flashed through my brain, pictures forming to piece together a forgotten story. One of Tripp standing near me after a bullet ripped through my leg. Then one of our nomad hovering over Marek. He'd gone to save him after our prez had been shot. Twice. Then my memory flipped to one of watching Stone. Witnessing the way his head jerked forward right before he fell to the ground.

"Fuck!" My eyes found Tripp's before my vision blurred once more, that time filled with unbelievable grief. "Are they dead?"

"Yeah, they are." Tripp's eyes were red-rimmed, indicating he'd already begun to deal with the catastrophe that had landed at our feet, ripping apart all who'd known them.

"I can't believe it. I just can't. . . ." Shaking my head, a tear fell down my cheek for the loss of my friends.

My brothers.

My family.

FORTY-THREE

Ryder

"I CAN'T BELIEVE THEY'RE DEAD." I threw my hands over my face, shielding my anguish from Tripp as best I could, although I knew he shared in my grief. Still, there was something about hiding my emotions that allowed me a private moment of sorts to deal with the news.

"I'm upset too, but I didn't know you'd take it *this* hard," Tripp grumbled. "Didn't even think you liked them all that much."

Drawing my hands back, I stared at him in confusion. "What the hell does that mean?" I tried to move, but the pain radiating through my leg stopped me. "Marek and Stone were like my family. I know I was an asshole sometimes, but they saw past my fuckups and accepted me for who I was." My tears built, but I needed to man up and accept what had happened. I had to learn to move on; otherwise, I'd allow the sadness to fester and rot me from the inside out.

"What are *you* talking about?" Before I could respond, Tripp blurted, "Marek and Stone aren't dead. Yeah, it was a close call, for both of them, but they're alive. They're gonna have some scars, for sure, but they're still breathin'."

After my astonishment finally subsided, Tripp filled me in on what happened after I'd passed out from my own gunshot wound. Apparently, when Marek tackled the Reaper who'd shot Stone, he'd managed to change the trajectory of the bullet intended for our VP. Stone had been shot but the bullet had pierced his ear, tearing off the tip of it. I'd seen him fall forward and it'd appeared as if he was dead, but Tripp explained that the force of the bullet had pushed him forward and when Stone hit the ground, he'd been knocked unconscious. Although Stone hadn't experienced any pain when he awoke, he was pissed he was missing a piece of his ear.

I smiled at the thought of Stone's reaction, but then my thoughts went right to Marek. Whereas Stone's injury ended up not to be life-threatening, our leader's wounds were just that. Not necessarily the one to his shoulder, but the bullet that'd pierced his chest had caused a part of his breastbone to slice a section of his lung before exiting his body.

It was touch and go for a while, but thankfully Marek had pulled through, although he definitely had to take it easy and allow his body to heal properly. I had no doubt Sully would chain him to their bed if he caused too much trouble.

I'd been so lost in the news of my brothers that I'd completely forgotten Jagger had mentioned Rabid.

Psych's right-hand bastard.

As if sensing my impending barrage of questions, Jagger appeared behind Tripp. And when they both moved to the side, Rabid walked up next to me, staring down at me with a look of worry.

What the fuck is goin' on?

Anticipating my struggle, Jagger and Tripp moved to stand on either side of me, holding me down so I didn't further injure myself.

"Calm down," Jagger instructed, putting more pressure on my shoulder until he felt some of the fight leave my overly tired body. Seconds ticked by before anyone spoke, and that time it was the enemy.

Or so I thought.

"I'm not who you think I am," Rabid confessed, running his hands over his bald head in what appeared to be uncertainty. The last time I saw him, other than a couple nights prior, he'd showed up with Kortiz at our club, threatening to rain down holy hell on our club if we didn't tell him where Psych was.

I parted my lips to speak but fell silent when I couldn't decide what to ask first. Rabid saw my hesitancy and took the lead instead. "I won't tell you my real name, but I'm sure at some point you'll find out. I have no doubt you men are resourceful. But until then, I can tell you that I've been undercover, investigating the Savage Reapers. Sam Koritz ended up being icing on the cake."

As he talked about ties with not only the Los Zappas cartel, but links to terrorist groups, sex trafficking and gun running, my mind tried to comprehend everything, pinging back and forth between memories and trying to understand what he was telling us.

"... he up and vanished."

"What?" I asked, doing my best to focus.

Rabid, or whatever his name was, stepped closer to repeat himself, my mind temporarily blanking on what he'd just said.

"Just as I was about to take down Psych, he up and disappeared."

Tripp shoved his hands in his jeans pockets. "Yeah, we heard about that." Our nomad smiled, even though it was brief.

"Yeah, I'm sure you did."

"Don't worry, you won't ever find anything." Tripp took a moment before finishing his thought. "Tying us to it." His smirk reappeared, essentially telling the man Psych was indeed dead.

"Well, if we ever find him, just know I'll be payin' your club a little visit. I do have a job to do, after all."

"Like I said. . . ." Tripp rocked back and forth on his heels as he entered a visual showdown with the guy.

An image pushed its way to the forefront of my memory, and before I could think better of it, I blurted, "But I saw you shoot Koritz."

"He finally gave me the name I was after, the one in charge." He was so matter of fact, it was unexpected.

"Who are you undercover with that would legally allow you to shoot someone?" Jagger asked the question that time, his confusion rivaling my own.

"Doesn't matter," he replied. "Maybe I was under too long, the darkness the Reapers existing in affecting me more than I care to acknowledge." Shrugging, he said, "Or maybe I shot him in self-defense." He smirked, and I knew right then he wasn't sorry for killing that sonofabitch, and would probably do it again if given the chance. Koritz certainly wouldn't be missed, and I was only too happy that he'd finally been dealt with. And who better than from the man Koritz most likely thought was on his side the entire time.

"Why help us, though?" I asked, looking to Tripp and Jagger and then back to the essential stranger standing next to all of us.

"Because even though your club was on our radar, you guys weren't even in the same league as the Reapers. And once I found out your president had cut all ties with the cartel, I focused all of my time, energy and resources on the group I'd infiltrated all those years ago. We have enough to dismantle the club and put away the rest of 'em for a very long time."

He moved aside as I saw several strangers approach—two men and a woman dressed in scrubs. Apparently, they were who'd been called in to help. As they made quick work in checking on my leg, I couldn't help but be thankful the war was finally over between the Knights Corruption and the Savage Reapers.

FORTY-FOUR

Braylen

AT SOME POINT DURING THE trip home, I'd fallen asleep dreaming of Ryder. The images conjured from my subconscious helped keep me locked in my slumber. The man I loved smiled at me, his gentle touch trying to rouse me from sleep, but I refused to open my eyes even though I could hear him calling my name. Then everything changed, the sudden urgency in his voice alarming me. His mouth opened and his lips were moving, but I couldn't hear anything. Even though my lids were squeezed shut, I could see him. A worried expression pained his features. Then I saw blood. So much blood. The next thing I knew, his face morphed into a blank slate before his body turned into a whirlwind of dust circling above me.

"Braylen. Wake up."

My eyes flew open and I clutched my chest, my lungs on fire due to lack of oxygen. Apparently I'd been holding my breath while locked in my dream. No, my nightmare. My vision blurred as I tried to adjust my sight. The first person I saw was Nash, confusion wrapping its ugly arms around me and squeezing the remnants of sleep from me.

"We're here," he announced, cocking his head before shifting back into the driver seat.

"Where?"

"Home. Well, not home exactly, but close enough, I suppose." He was facing front now, fiddling with his phone while I tried to come to grips with my new reality. I still hadn't talked to Ryder, my conversation with Jagger cut short during the only phone call I'd received.

Looking out the window, I saw the sun shining brightly, although the tint on the vehicle helped to dull the effect. As I glanced around, however, I became confused. Nothing looked familiar.

"Where are we?"

Without answering me, Nash opened his door and disappeared outside. I turned my head to the side and noticed I was all alone.

Where are Kena and Reece? Where is Cass?

Where the hell are we?

Slowly opening my door, I tentatively stepped outside the SUV, closing the door behind me when I realized I wasn't in any sort of danger. Up ahead I saw Kena talking to Jagger, her hands frantically signing before he crushed her to him. Only when I shuffled my feet across the dirt separating us did they look in my direction. Jagger released my sister and she ran toward me, drawing me into a tight hug before stepping back. Jagger was slow to approach, the sight of him causing me to tremble. He looked like he'd been through hell, but from what I could tell he wasn't physically injured, other than a scrape on the side of his neck.

"Hi," he greeted, squeezing my hand briefly before releasing it. "Sorry my phone went dead, but I had other things I had to deal with." He kept his eyes on me, his stare starting to freak me out. Before I lost it, though, he lifted his chin toward the building behind him, flashing me a tight smile. "Let's go. Someone wants to see you."

I reached for his arm to stop his retreat. "Wait." A deep inhalation of air coated my lungs. "He's alive?"

"Yeah, and he's waiting to see you."

"Why didn't you tell me that as soon as you came up to me?" All of my fear morphed into anger, everything hitting me like a goddamn freight train. "I thought he was dead," I screamed, hitting his chest. "Do you have any idea what I've been through?" I raised my hands to strike him again but Jagger caught them and pulled me close.

"I'm sorry." Looking a little guilty, he said, "So much shit happened. I'm still trying to deal with everything." We stared at each other while I calmed down, his hold lessening until he finally released me. "Now let's go." He grabbed Kena's hand and pulled her behind him as he walked away.

Once inside the building, still unaware as to where exactly we were, I followed Jagger and my sister as he led us through two empty rooms, down a short flight of steps and down a narrowed hallway. When Jagger pushed open a door and I saw what was inside, I knew we'd reached our destination.

To my left, there were two bodies lying on the ground with leather vests covering their faces. Their clothes were soaked with blood, the image of who that could be instantly causing a rush of panic. Then I remembered that Ryder was alive and my heart slowed to its normal beat. Barely.

Taking one more glance at the dead bodies, I couldn't help but wonder who they'd lost.

"Braylen," Jagger called. "Let's go." He pulled me away from the carnage, knowing I was about to lose it even though my man was still alive, although I had no idea what condition I'd find him in.

Walking farther into the large space, I saw Tripp leaning over a table talking to someone, their voices hushed. It wasn't until he moved to the side that I recognized the man laying down.

Ryder.

I rushed forward, shoving Tripp to the side and launching myself into Ryder's arms, my body partly covering his.

"Uhhh," he groaned. "Careful, baby," he warned, a pained look telling me he was injured. Before I could pull back, his lips found mine and he poured everything into our brief kiss. Our joined fear and uncertainty disappeared as our breaths mingled, a piece of our souls joining and relishing in the moment. "I love you so much," he whispered, breaking the kiss to look into my eyes.

"I love you," I replied, giving him another quick kiss before standing up to look at him. His shirt was ripped and bloody, but it was his left leg that was bandaged—his thigh, to be more exact. When my eyes found his to ask what happened, I saw the distress. Whatever happened had rocked him, and I vowed right then and there to do whatever I needed—what *he* needed—to help him through it.

Gingerly touching his leg, careful not to put any pressure on the bandage, I asked, "What happened?" Tears fell down my cheeks before I could stop them, my body finally releasing the shock I'd been trapped in and starting to tremble.

Instead of answering me, Ryder clutched my hand in his and pulled me close. He tried to sit up, and when Tripp saw him struggling, he rushed over and helped him. Swinging his legs over the edge of the table, Ryder spread them and tugged me between them, my chest hitting his as he took my face in his hands.

"I got shot." Before I started to break down even more, he said, "Don't." He wiped my tears as they continued to fall. "I'm fine. Nothing that won't heal. Trust me." His mouth covered mine, the kiss soft and light, his lips lingering without urgency. I savored his comfort even though

I was the one who should've been soothing him.

After several minutes, I sat next to him on top of the metal table, our fingers linked and resting in my lap. "Can you tell me what happened?" Reservation painted his rugged face, his fingers squeezing mine tighter before he shook his head. "I have a right to know," I whispered, not wanting to upset him but still trying to urge him to fill me in on what had transpired.

"I'm sorry, but I can't really get into it. One day maybe, but not now." He grimaced when he shifted his weight, his free hand gently moving his injured leg.

"Can I at least ask who died?" The breath in my lungs froze while I waited to see if he'd answer. I swore time stood still while I witnessed a plethora of emotions contorting his expression.

"Breck and Smiley."

FORTY-FIVE

Ryder

I REFUSED TO RELIVE THE brief moment in time when I believed that my prez and VP were dead. So instead of delaying my answer to Braylen's simple yet devastating question, I answered. Her face fell because she knew what a blow to all of us Breck's death had been.

Smiley, on the other hand, while upsetting that he'd died during the fight because he was a Knight, wasn't as devastating to me. Not only because we didn't really know the guy, but because I harbored a lot of anger toward him, even in his death. It was because of him and his phone that our initial plan of action had been ripped apart in the first place. Although, when I found out he'd jumped in front of Breck to try and save him being shot, a feat which ultimately hadn't worked, my anger subsided a little.

We all knew the risks, each of us signing up to defend our club against all costs. Unfortunately, two members of Knights Corruption wouldn't make it back to see their loved ones. Tripp called Cutter to tell him that his son had died, and he promised to bring his body back home for a proper burial. The nomad had filled me in on their phone call, although it'd been brief. Cutter hadn't said much, but that wasn't uncommon. He was a man of few words, but we all knew he loved his son and was undoubtedly shredded by the news.

———— ♦ ————

"ARE YOU READY TO GO?" Jagger asked, helping me to stand before I even uttered a reply. "We gotta get back and take care of everything." He mumbled something else before propping me up with his shoulder under my arm, moving slowly toward the edge of the room we'd been staying in for the past two days. Braylen shrouded my other side, ready to assist me if I needed her help as well. Kena followed behind all of us.

As we walked, I was able to finally lay eyes on the rest of the guys. Stone was leaning against the wall, fiddling with the bandage wrapped around his ear. Adelaide was beside him, slapping his hand away and yelling at him not to touch it. A few feet to the left, I saw Marek lying on a steel table, much like the one I'd been resting on. As I hobbled along, I saw Sully hunching over him and crying.

"Are we sure he's gonna be okay?" I asked Jagger, pointing toward Marek.

"Yeah. The doc Rabid, or whoever he is, brought in said he's gonna need some time to heal but he'll pull through."

Still walking slowly, we rounded the corner and down a hallway too narrow for the three of us to walk side by side, so Braylen stayed close behind, walking with her sister. A short flight of steps and two empty rooms later, we finally hit the outdoors, the California sun doing its best to offer some warmth.

"Where the fuck are we?"

"A twenty-minute ride from where all hell broke loose. Rabid had us load everyone up and come here. I don't know whose it is or what the place is used for, but it did the job, so I'm not complaining."

The guy who'd essentially saved our lives had taken off shortly after he'd revealed who he was, sort of. He never said another word to any of us before he disappeared. Months later, we'd come to find out that Michael Chase, aka Rabid, was an undercover NSA agent assigned to dismantle what was later referred to as one of the biggest cases the organization had ever been involved in.

Hey, what can I say? They had their informants and we had ours.

Up ahead, Tripp and Reece were leaning inside one of the other vehicles. As we passed by, I saw they were keeping watch over Riley and Kaden. No doubt Reece had volunteered for the job, and I knew there was no way Tripp would leave her side, not after everything that had happened. When he backed out, holding a crying Riley in his arms, he saw me and shrugged. Sully and Adelaide were still in the basement of the building, but they wouldn't leave their children for long, so I had no doubt they'd be appearing soon enough. Until then, Reece tried to soothe Kaden, who had also started to fuss.

When we finally made it to the SUV I'd be traveling back home in, Kena opened the back door while Jagger propped me against the side of it. Braylen took over and helped to brace me so I wouldn't fall. I put all of my weight on my good leg because I had no doubt my woman wouldn't be able to hold me up otherwise. I'd crush her.

As I was trying to carefully situate myself in the back seat, I saw Salzar, Etch, and Stone carrying Marek the best they could. Sully was right behind them being comforted by Adelaide. That poor woman had been through enough, we all had, and I prayed this was the end of the fuckin' danger surrounding all of us. After the men had laid Marek across the back seat of another SUV, Sully said something to Miles before walking toward Tripp and Reece.

Once Kaden was placed in Sully's arms, he calmed, and she seemed to do the same. Miles had apparently been asked to grab one of the car seats and transfer it to the truck that her husband had been placed in. And because Stone refused to leave his best friend's side, Miles made another trip back to grab the other car seat for Riley, Adelaide refusing to leave her fiancé's side.

Nash and Cass, two of Salzar's other men, the ones who had driven Braylen, Kena, and Reece to us, helped carry Breck's and Smiley's bodies. Even though the men were dead, they made sure to treat them both with the utmost respect as they carefully laid them in the back of the vehicle they'd be riding in. It was their job to transport the fallen Knights back with us.

Everyone was en route back to our clubhouse, which thankfully wasn't too far away. Our Laredo brothers would only be staying with us until the morning, making sure to get the rest they needed before making the long drive back to Texas, transporting Smiley back with them and taking care of his burial.

Cutter had been the first one in the lot as we all pulled in. As I managed to climb out of our truck, I watched everything unfold as Nash opened the back of the SUV where Breck's body was lain, stepping aside to allow Cutter the space he needed to see his son. Trigger and Hawke exited the building and gathered around Cutter, offering him solace as they helped him carry Breck toward a patch of land behind the clubhouse, the same place where we ended up burying Zip. Cutter had already arranged for a coffin while he waited for us to return, and he laid his son to rest that evening. Whoever was well enough to attend, which was everyone except Marek, paid their respects before Cutter put him in the ground.

Over the course of the following week, Adelaide checked on Marek, who had been set up in the room designated for him whenever he had to stay at the club. She watched over him to ensure he was healing properly and staving off any sort of infection. And because his woman was keeping close watch over the Knights' leader, Stone set up in his room, caring for Riley whenever Adelaide's attentions were otherwise diverted.

I'd chosen to stay with my brothers, not completely convinced we were out of harm's way. But after countless nights passed without retaliation or the police knocking down our gates, I'd made the decision to recoup back at my house with my woman.

Finally putting the last piece of the puzzle into place, completing the picture of the future I wanted.

No . . . the future Braylen deserved.

EPILOGUE

Ryder

One year later

"DAD, I DON'T WANNA GO," I heard as I rounded the corner into our guest bedroom. Zoe was standing in the middle of the room, fidgeting with her dress. "Dad . . . ," she whined, throwing her hands on her hips and entering a stare-down with me.

"Zoe," I countered, leaning against the doorframe. "What's wrong? You look beautiful."

"You know I hate dresses." She continued to fiddle with the white and black polka-dotted material. "And my hair won't go the right way," she complained. Oh Lord, I could only imagine how she'd be once she became a teenager the following year. Puberty was gonna be the death of me, I already knew it. And boys . . . I wasn't gonna do well with boys lurking around my little girl. Zoe was already a looker, and I feared for my sanity as she grew up.

Now that the threat toward our club had finally been eliminated, Rose and I had agreed on increased visitation with Zoe. While they still lived in Illinois, we both made the effort so that my daughter and I could get to know each other more. I also wanted to test the waters between Braylen and Zoe as well, seeing how well they got along before I revealed that I was thinking about having another kid. Thing was, Braylen had told me she wasn't ready for a baby, but maybe if I put the thought in her head, she'd come around sooner rather than later.

"Here, honey, let me help you with that," Braylen said, bouncing into the room to save the day. "Do you want your hair up or down?" She pulled Zoe's shoulder-length red hair off her shoulders, then released it, giving my daughter a visual of different hairdos. I honestly had no idea where Zoe inherited the red hair from; both Rose and I have dark brown. I believe my ex mentioned someone on her mother's side being a redhead, but I couldn't really remember. Other than the color of her strands, there was no mistaking Zoe was mine, although she was looking more like her mother as the years passed.

Zoe smiled, looking at Braylen's reflection in the mirror. "Um . . . how about up?"

"Up it is." Braylen described everything she was doing while she set up her tools, Zoe enthralled with the fact that Braylen was a hair stylist. And a very talented one at that. She'd mentioned that one day she wanted to start her own salon, but she just wasn't ready yet. Little did she know I had a surprise waiting for her, whenever she decided to make the leap.

Money wasn't an issue for me. I never had to think about it because I had plenty of it stocked away—mostly from the club's activities before Marek turned us legit. And because of my smart investments, I was set for ten lifetimes. Braylen knew I was wealthy, but she never asked for a figure. She didn't care, wanted to make her own way, and I respected her more for it, even though I showered her with gifts as often as I could.

Upgrading her car, for one. The day I'd picked her up in a shiny new Mercedes, her dream car, she'd thrown herself into my arms, accepting the vehicle without an issue. She'd known I'd only force it on her anyway. Besides, she'd given me the best head of my life later that evening as thanks.

Win-win for the both of us.

"Sweetheart, you need to get ready yourself or we're gonna be late," I urged, pulling Braylen close the second she finished Zoe's hair.

Furrowing her brows, she turned my wrist toward her and looked at my watch.

"But we still have two hours before it starts."

Retreating to the other side of the room so Zoe wouldn't hear me, I leaned in and nipped her lobe before whispering, "But I need some time to fuck you first."

A pink flush tickled her skin, and I knew she wanted me almost as much as I wanted her.

"Gross, Dad," Zoe admonished.

There was no way she heard what I just said. "What?" I feigned ignorance.

"I know you just said something about sex." She casually toyed with her dress, smiling now that she liked her hair.

Braylen laughed, but there wasn't a goddamn thing funny about what Zoe said. I cleared my throat to get her attention. "What do you know about sex?" I probably should've corrected her assumption, but I was too caught up with the fact that she knew anything at all about the topic. She was only twelve, for Christ's sake.

"I've heard about it." She rolled her eyes, and I thought I was gonna lose it for sure. Every muscle in my body locked up tight, but thankfully Braylen stepped in before I gave myself a heart attack.

"I'll talk to her, find out what she really knows," Braylen said quietly. "Sometimes kids say things but have no idea what they mean." I relaxed, if only slightly. "Now why don't you go wait for us in the living room?

"But. . . ." I swore I pouted like a little bitch. "I thought . . . you know." I waved my index finger back and forth between us.

She leaned up on her tippy toes and pressed her lips to mine. "I'm not letting you ruin my hair." She playfully slapped my chest. "Now go get ready, and I'll do the same." Braylen tapped her foot while she pointed toward the doorway. Unfortunately, I knew I'd have to wait to ravage my woman, but I hoped she knew she was in for it once the opportunity presented itself.

As she shut the door behind me, I saw her say something to Zoe, and they both laughed, the sound making me extremely happy. She might just be more receptive to the idea of having my kid after all.

Brutus came barreling toward me as I entered the living room, hopping up on me as soon as I sat down. It wouldn't take me long to get dressed, so I decided to spend some time with my buddy. I loved that damn dog, more than I thought I'd love any animal.

"She knows what she's missin'," I mumbled, patting Brutus's head as if he had any clue what I was talkin' about. He wagged his tail and gave me a sloppy kiss, licking the side of my face when I made a move to roughhouse with him. Jumping off the couch, Brutus ran toward the door, letting me know that while he wanted to play, he needed to go to the bathroom.

It was rather kismet if I did say so myself. Watching after my three-legged friend as he circled the same patch of grass before taking care of business, I realized that we had both been discarded during the early years of our life. Sure, no one had thrown me out of a moving vehicle, but I'd been tossed around from foster home to foster home until I aged out at eighteen, finding my real family when I became a member of the

Knights Corruption years later. I'd been working at a garage when Marek had swung by to pick up a part for a bike he'd been working on. We got to talking and within an hour he'd offered me a job at the club's garage. The rest was history.

Both Brutus and I had reaped a sliver of justice for the wrongs done in our lives as well. About a month prior, I'd been out for a drive when I'd spotted a familiar lookin' piece-of-shit car: an Oldsmobile Cutlass with faded blue paint peeling everywhere on the body and a bumper held on by duct tape.

The vehicle was parked outside a liquor store, and when a man emerged and walked toward the Oldsmobile, I made my move. With his hand resting on the handle of the driver side, I walked up behind him and spun him around. When I'd asked if he was the fucker who tossed a puppy from the car, wanting to make sure I had the right person, he smirked and asked me what business it was of mine. In other words, he was the offender. Breaking his nose didn't satisfy my need for revenge, so I shattered his arm, the one used to discard Brutus like he meant nothing at all.

Much like the payback I'd sought for my dog, fate had done the same with Richard. Although I wanted to put that chapter of my life behind me and remember my mother as she was before her death, wonderful and loving, I still chose to keep tabs on her murderer. It was close to four months after I'd gone to his house that I learned he'd had too much to drink one night and ended up crashing his car into a tree, killing only himself in the accident.

His death brought the final closure to a life of misery, Braylen helping to heal the rest of me with her unconditional love and support. I was one lucky bastard, something she was sure to remind me of whenever she found the opportunity.

Braylen

ON THE RIDE OVER, I couldn't stop staring at the man who'd flipped my world upside down, in more ways than one. Everything from his occasional arrogance to his infuriating protectiveness, to the sweet words he whispered while he buried himself inside me. Ryder was the man of my dreams. It'd been a bumpy road, and there were still some potholes in our future, I was sure, but I knew we could get through anything as long as we loved each other.

And we did.

Fiercely.

For the occasion, he'd chosen to dress up. Not in a complete suit, because that just wasn't him, but a crisp white button-up, sans tie, and a pair of dark blue dress pants, brown shoes completing his dressy yet casual look.

As we sat at a stoplight, Zoe in the back seat with her earbuds in, singing along to whatever pop song was on, Ryder unbuttoned his sleeves and rolled them repeatedly until his entire forearms were exposed, the muscles jumping with each movement he made. He caught me looking and said, "I have another muscle you can stare at. Taste, even."

My eyes widened as I glanced back at his daughter, but she hadn't heard a thing he'd said. The rest of the trip was done so in silence, other than the radio, for fear that I'd lose control and jump over the console and into his lap. Which would be highly inappropriate with a child present. So instead, I chose to keep my eyes away from all things Ryder and stare out the window as the world passed us by.

After we arrived and took our seats under the tent that had been erected on the lawn behind the clubhouse, Ryder on my right and Zoe on my left, I couldn't help but be extremely grateful for all the gifts I'd been given. My thankful thoughts were interrupted, however, when my sex-on-a-stick of a man leaned closer and started saying things in my ear that got me all hot and bothered, all sorts of sordid images flashing through my brain and causing me to twitch in my seat.

"Since you wouldn't let me do it at home, I'm gonna get my way we leave here. I'm gonna hike up your dress and bury my face between your legs. You know I'm addicted to that pussy, baby," Ryder professed, kissing my cheek like he hadn't just threatened me with a good fucking. I kept my eyes straight ahead and smiled, not wanting Zoe to think her father was whispering about sex again.

After Ryder had left the bedroom, allowing me to have a talk with Zoe, I'd discovered that she had indeed learned about sex, although some of it was still confusing. I told her it only got worse, to which she gave me the funniest look. After answering a few basic questions, I told her that if she had any more, she should really talk to her mother about them. I'd also warned her not to ask her father, not until she was much older, like around thirty. We both laughed at that one, although she thought I was joking. I wasn't.

Ryder's daughter had been staying at our house for the past week, scheduled to leave the next morning, and while our time together had been short, we'd bonded rather quickly. She thought I had a cool job, and I thought she was a pretty amazing kid. I definitely looked forward to her next visit, which was only a few months away.

As we waited for everyone to arrive, my thoughts drifted to the people who'd become like family, the tragedy bringing us all closer together. When I wasn't working, or hanging out with Kena or Sia, I was shopping with Adelaide, Sully or Reece, or hitting the town for a girls' night out, although one of the guys always attended. They said it was for our safety, but since there was no more viable threat to their club, I'd chalked up their hovering as just being overprotective.

I shifted in my seat, trying to see who'd just pulled into the lot, when Ryder's fingertips trailed up my leg, my blue dress riding up my thigh when I'd turned around. Zoe's head was turned the other way so she hadn't noticed, but I needed to nip his advance in the bud before he became really brave. Under normal circumstances, I knew he had no qualms about throwing me over his shoulder and disappearing somewhere more private. And while he might be more reserved because of why we were there that day, I still didn't completely trust him not to act . . . like himself.

"What are you doing?" I whispered, turning my head more toward him so as not to draw the attention of his daughter. His fingers were still ghosting over the top of my leg, the heat from his touch driving me insane.

Keep it together.

"Just touching you." He smirked, knowing he was playing a dirty game.

"Well, stop it," I gritted. When his hand trailed farther up my leg, my body shifted completely toward him so only I knew what he was doing.

He gripped my thigh and leaned in. "Meet me inside the clubhouse. I'm gonna fuck you quick before they get started." He hurriedly rose from his seat, then cursed when he saw Kena and Jagger walking toward us. No way in hell we were going anywhere now, and we both knew it. A few more expletives fell from his mouth, but he'd been sure to keep his voice low so as not to have Zoe hear everything. He'd learned to curb his language whenever she was around, although right then he was certainly struggling.

I laughed as I rose to my feet, hugging my sister and then Jagger before engaging them in small talk.

"It's not funny," Ryder growled in my ear, briefly interrupting my conversation.

"It kind of is," I retorted, reaching for his hand which he readily accepted, squeezing a little too hard before I slapped his arm to loosen his grip. A smug grin spread across his face as he continued to hold onto me.

"Can you believe this is finally happening?" Jagger asked, looking first at Ryder and then shooting a glance at Kena, and not his usual smitten expression either. The silent communication was something more, but I didn't have time to dissect it because Zoe was unexpectedly behind us.

"Dad, I have to go to the bathroom," she announced, tugging on his free hand while hopping from one foot to the next.

"I'll take her," I offered, yanking my hand from Ryder's. Or should I say tried to? "You have to let me go."

He leaned down and nipped my bottom lip before swiping his tongue through my mouth. The kiss was quick yet it made my heart race.

"Never," he whispered before pulling back.

"Gross, Dad." Zoe made a face but smiled when I did. Then her expression was back to one of annoyance. "I have to pee. Hello?" She walked off toward the clubhouse and Ryder finally released my hand.

"Should I come with you?" He took a step forward and I stopped him with a hand on his chest. His very muscular, chiseled, hard chest. I lost myself in the moment until I felt his heart thumping harder against my fingertips. Breaking the brief spell of lust, I gave him a quick kiss before taking a step back.

"Later."

He caught on to my meaning and laughed, shaking his head before turning his attentions back to Jagger. The two of them chatted as I caught up with Zoe. Once I stood beside her, we walked in perfect rhythm, her hand reaching out to connect with mine. I looked down at her and she smiled as she wrapped her fingers around my hand, the gesture signifying she'd accepted me, telling me I was welcome in her world without words.

The way her pale green eyes smiled at me made my womb hurt with longing, something I hadn't experienced until right then. She was a part of the man I loved, and I wanted nothing more than to give him back a piece of myself.

A little one that was half of me and half of Ryder.

A baby.

The only thing to do now was decide when to let him in on my plans.

———·———

Marek

"I CAN'T FIND IT," I shouted, searching under the couch, then all over the living room. "Where did you say it was?" My frustration level increased as I continued to look for the goddamn stuffed animal Kaden had apparently thrown somewhere and was now causing a fit over because he didn't have it.

Silence greeted me. Either my wife was ignoring me or she hadn't heard me. My bet was the first option, so I flipped over cushions until I found the bunny wedged in the back of the couch. "Ha!" I yelled, shaking the toy back and forth in the air as if I'd just found lost treasure. But anyone who had small children knew what a win the find was for me.

Reflecting back on where I'd been a couple years before and where I found myself right then, my life couldn't have been more different. Yes, I was still the president of my club, my vote the deciding one on most topics, although I always took the men's concerns and comments into deep consideration. We weren't only a club—we were family. A unit that had seen the worst in life, but a group that had also reveled in the gifts life had to offer.

I'd been staring off into space when Sully appeared in the doorway. "Did you find it?" she asked, cradling a very sleepy Kaden in her arms. Apparently his freak-out had worn him out.

The boy was attached to my wife, and normally I found it sweet. Then there were other times when he was a little cock-blocker. Plain and simple. I called it like I saw it. But I loved the little guy, more than I thought I ever would any child. Don't get me wrong, I had a special place in my heart for my goddaughter, Riley, and would protect her until my last breath, but it was small in comparison to the way my heart swelled watching Kaden smile when he saw me.

I'd finally come to understand why Stone turned into a pile of mush when he held his baby girl, ignoring the razzing from his brothers and focusing on the little one who'd turned him from a hotheaded pain in the ass to a doting father. Wait, never mind. He was still a hotheaded pain in the ass, only now there was another, softer side to him we were able to witness.

Much like I'd become whenever Kaden was around.

"Yeah." I passed her the stuffed animal, and in exchange she handed me the little boy, his hand resting on the side of my face as his blue eyes fluttered open for a moment before closing them and essentially passing out. "Did he go to sleep late? Why is he so tired?"

"I don't know," she answered, shrugging before walking out of the room. Sully was frustrated, and I didn't have a clue as to why. I followed her, careful not to wake Kaden because I had a feeling whatever was bothering her wasn't gonna be a quick fix.

After putting him down in his own room, I continued to our bedroom, finding my wife rifling through the closet. I didn't say a word as I wrapped my arms around her and unknotted the silk belt of her robe, parting the material before my hands roamed over her naked body. Her long, jet-black hair was fixed in a fancy updo of sorts, so I made sure not to mess up the style because I knew she'd be pissed at me if I made her redo it.

Spinning her around to face me, I kissed her as I backed her against the wall, my teeth latching on to her bottom lip before she opened for me. Sully wasn't gonna tell me what was wrong, but if I fucked her senseless, maybe that would help relieve some of the tension and uncertainty trapping her.

It wasn't that long ago when the thought of touching Sully killed me because there was a possibility that she was my half-sister. A parting gift from her evil father, Psych, right before I destroyed what was left of him, stealing his last breath as I sent him to hell. It felt like the longest span of time before I found out the truth, but in the meantime, I'd also done my share of damage by pushing my wife away.

Ignoring her.

Choosing to stay at the clubhouse instead of at home.

Keeping her in the dark as to why I'd detached myself.

Treating her badly just so I could gain the emotional distance I needed in case the results proved to be true.

But they weren't true. I'd allowed Psych to fuck with me one last time, and instead of letting Sully know what was going on I chose a different path, one that hurt her immensely. Thankfully, she'd forgiven me, but it had taken some time. There was a part of me that still believed she was guarded when it came to me, but I had no problem proving to her just how much I loved her, and promising her I would never hurt her like that ever again.

"Lie on the bed," I ordered, pushing the robe off her shoulders until it puddled at her feet.

"I can't."

"Why?"

"Because I'm going to mess up my hair." She laughed when I gave her an annoyed look, then stopped smiling as soon as I pinched her nipple, parting her lips and moaning as she threw her head back.

"Fine. Then you're gonna ride me." I walked backward, pulling her with me until I sat in the chair in the corner, positioning her legs on either side of mine so she was straddling me. I'd showered earlier but hadn't gotten dressed yet, so the only thing between me and my wife was the thin material of my boxer briefs. Tugging down the waistband, I pulled out my cock and rubbed it between her folds. Always so wet and ready for me. She arched her back, and as her tits pushed forward, I latched on, my teeth grazing the puckered bud while my thumb pressed against her clit, rubbing slow circles and driving her insane.

"Please, Cole," she pleaded, running her fingers through my still-damp hair and clutching me to her breast. While holding me close, she rose onto her tippy toes, replaced my fingers with hers and circled my thickness. "I need you to make love to me now." Sully positioned me at her entrance then slowly took me inside her.

Fuck! The feeling was still out of this world, her warmth and tightness clenching around me and pushing me toward the edge. As my mouth found hers once more, I poured every bit of myself into her.

What had begun as a 'fuck you' to the Reapers, kidnapping the president's daughter, had turned out to be my greatest gift.

My wife was the bravest person I knew, and although she always wanted to remind me that I was the one who saved her, I believed the opposite was true.

She'd saved me.

She'd given me purpose.

She'd wrapped me in love and bathed me in light when all I'd ever known was darkness.

—◆—

Sully

AFTER MY HUSBAND MADE LOVE to me, gentle and slow, a change of pace from the sometimes-aggressive sex we both rather enjoyed, we sat together in silence. He jerked inside me a few times before softening, but I didn't break the connection of our bodies.

I knew he was mine, forever and ever, but there was always a small piece of me that believed he'd be ripped from my life. So whenever I could, I stayed as close to him as possible.

Cole's fingers drifted over my skin, slowing when he reached the scars on my lower back. Burn marks my father had inflicted on me when he thought I'd talked to the cops who had raided our club. Cole's muscles stiffened as they often did whenever he felt the remnants of my previous life. I didn't think he'd ever stop becoming angry whenever he was reminded of what had happened to me before he saved me, whether by sight or by touch. I'd let it go, and hopefully one day soon he would as well.

Thankfully we were still chest to chest; otherwise, he'd undoubtedly trace the jagged scars on my lower belly, and the one higher up between my ribs, both courtesy of Vex. The demented man who'd claimed me from my father when I'd stayed at the Reapers' club. My old home. Although harsh, they were all distant memories, and I refused to linger on them for too long. Besides, every touch from my husband erased the past, for me more so than for him.

Pulling me in for another kiss, he said, "We should probably get dressed now. Otherwise we're gonna be late, and the last thing I need to deal with is Stone's mouth."

"Don't you mean Adelaide's mouth?" I stood, and he slipped from my body.

"True enough." Before I made it to the bathroom, Cole grabbed my waist. "I love you," he professed, kissing the side of my neck before slapping my ass. I shrieked in surprise, which only made him smile. I loved it when he was happy. There was an air of peace surrounding him when he lived in the moment.

Our bubble of contentment shattered when we heard the doorbell, then directly afterward an incessant pounding rattling the thick wooden door.

"What the hell?" Cole grumbled, that peace disappearing as he threw on a pair of jeans.

Even though the intrusion wasn't welcome, I couldn't help but admire my handsome, sexy man. His ass was perfection, even in the baggy jeans hanging off his hips. Intricate designs covered both of his muscled arms, drifting over his shoulders and disappearing behind his strong back, his sun-kissed skin a perfect backdrop for the designs littering his body. His club's emblem was inked in the center of his chest, the artwork shredded apart from the gunshot wound he'd endured. He had a matching wound puckering the skin on his right shoulder. I knew how lucky he was not to have died that day, and before I drove myself crazy with the what-ifs, I took a breath and pushed all thoughts of that time aside.

When Cole's piercing blue eyes met mine, he smirked, knowing damn well I'd just been ogling him. Eye-fucking him was probably a better description.

The rapping on the door crushed the moment, and as Kaden's cries joined the noise, Cole cursed before disappearing from our bedroom.

Tying my robe's belt tightly around my waist, I entered Kaden's room, finding him standing in his crib and crying. The noise had obviously startled him, but as soon as he saw me, he seemed to calm down. The tears were still spilling down his little cheeks, but his crying had all but ceased, his chest rapidly expanding to pull in air.

"It's okay, baby," I soothed, picking him up and cradling him close. He rested his head on my chest and snuggled into me. I kissed the top of his precious little head, inhaling his scent and wishing he'd stay this small forever. It was hard to believe he was already a year and a half.

"Sully. Come here," Cole shouted, the tone of his voice urgent.

With Kaden still nuzzled close, I descended the steps and soon came face-to-face with our guest. Tripp stood beside Cole, talking quietly until he saw me. My husband's eyes raked over my body. I knew he was displeased that another man was seeing me in only a robe, but I also knew Cole wouldn't say anything. He didn't have to, though, his annoyance written all over his face. If he could dress me in a potato sack, he would. He'd even admitted as much.

"What's goin' on?" The way Tripp's eyes bounced back and forth between Kaden and me raised an alarm, but I wasn't gonna freak out until he told me the reason for his visit.

"You guys know I've been looking for Rachel ever since she left, right?"

Cole and I both nodded at the same time, neither of us taking our eyes off Tripp. Rachel was Kaden's mother—well, the woman who gave birth to him. I'd managed to convince my husband to allow us to care for the little one until she could be found.

It appeared the day had unfortunately arrived.

My heart picked up its beat. I tried to prepare myself for Kaden to be ripped from my arms, but no amount of planning would make it any easier. So I remained silent.

"Well, I got word." Tripp took a few steps toward me, and when he was near he rested his hand on the top of Kaden's head. I swore I couldn't breathe, a tear streaking my cheek in preparation. Cole saw me start to unravel and rushed to my side, his arm circling my waist to hold me steady.

"Out with it," my husband seethed, his patience for the entire situation rapidly unfolding. "Where is she?"

No more hesitation from Tripp. "She's dead. An apparent overdose. I can't say I'm shocked."

"What? Are you sure?" I knew it was wrong to feel elation at such news, but I couldn't help it. "Does that mean he's ours?" I looked at Cole, then to Tripp. "Does that mean Kaden is ours?" I repeated.

A slow smile spread across Tripp's face. "It does. He was your son the first time you held him, Sully. And now it's final. No one will take him from you." He glanced at Cole. "Either of you," he confirmed.

As soon as Cole closed the door behind Tripp, he strode toward our son and me with more purpose than I'd ever seen, a huge smile on his face as he wrapped us both in his embrace.

Pride beamed from him as he affirmed my inner thoughts.

"Finally."

<hr>

"SO, HOW ARE THEY?" REECE asked, greeting me at the door with our son, Luke, on her hip. My boy was the spittin' image of me, and Reece couldn't be happier. She said it was like I was always with her, even when I wasn't.

"Pretty damn happy." My assessment was surely an understatement.

"I wish I could've been there with you when you told them," she pouted, her attention drawn back to Luke. He was fussy, had been for a few weeks. When we took him to see his pediatrician, she'd informed us that Luke had begun teething a few weeks prior, which was right within the average timeframe for a baby of seven months.

"Where's his teething ring?"

"I think it's on the counter," she answered, trying her best to calm him down. He wasn't full-on crying—not yet, at least.

Our lives had been flipped upside down the day Luke was born, but I wouldn't change a thing. The little boy was truly a gift, and I hated to think what my life would've been like without the both of them.

Even though I hated the thought of her ex-husband, Rick, and what he'd put her through, if she hadn't run away from him, I would've never met her. Her tragedy brought her into my life, and thankfully she'd been able to open her heart and trust me. She had no reason to at first—I was a stranger, after all—but I'd been able to show her that I could protect her. Love her.

"I'm going to put him in his room while I shower. Unless you want to take him."

For as much as I loved my son, I wanted to join my woman. Picturing her as she soaped her body was enough to make me explode where I stood, and even though Reece was self-conscious about the faint stretch marks she'd gained during the pregnancy, I saw her as perfect. I told her so all the time.

"I'd rather join you," I revealed, arching a brow and stalking toward her. She handed me our son, thinking he was gonna save her delectable ass. Once I took him into my arms, she quickly kissed me, then practically ran out of the room.

Taking my time walking up the steps, I talked to Luke as if he understood me. "I'm gonna put you in your room, buddy. Daddy needs to convince Mommy to give him some." Placing a kiss on his head, I lowered him into his crib and surrounded him with some of his favorite stuffed animals. He seemed content so I hurried toward our bedroom, stripping off my clothes and walking into the bathroom. Reece was already finished washing her hair. Fuck, she was fast. When I glanced at the clock by the bed, I understood why. Time was ticking by, and our presence at the clubhouse would be required shortly.

When I opened the door to the shower she turned to face me, flashing me a smile before glancing down at my dick. I took a step toward her, but she shook her head. I thought for a moment she wasn't gonna let me have her. She hadn't been in the mood for the past two weeks, between taking care of Luke and her having just gotten over a pretty nasty cold.

What I thought had been a denial turned out to be the opposite. Reece sank to her knees before I could open my mouth to say anything, the sexy gleam in her eye enough to keep me quiet and frozen in place. I slid past her lips and she worked my shaft with the perfect blend of tongue, teeth, and fingers. The closer she brought me, the harder I pumped into her mouth, anchoring her to me with the grip of her hair. She placed a hand on my stomach to steady herself and took me all the way to the back of her throat, which was quite a feat considering my size. But practice made perfect, right?

After she'd sucked every last drop from me, she pulled back, and I slipped from between her lips. "You're welcome." She chuckled, reaching out her hand so I could help her stand.

"I'm gonna be sayin' that to you in a few minutes," I promised, capturing her mouth and tasting the remnants of my release with the swipe of my tongue.

"I want to talk to you about something," she said, breaking our kiss and placing her hands on my chest, the pads of her fingers grazing over the scars from my bullet wounds, a sign she was deep in thought.

"Can't we talk after I make you scream my name?" I reached down and cupped her pussy, my finger slipping between her folds to tease her.

She groaned but stopped me, grabbing my wrist and pulling back.

"No, I need to talk to you now before you make up some excuse as to why you can't discuss it."

"This better not be about you going back to work at Indulge, because it ain't gonna happen." Reece had finally quit when she was five months along—longer than I'd wanted, her employment there having been a bone of contention between us until she'd finally left. Even though she hadn't been stripping, instead helping Carla with management duties as well as filling in to bartend, I hated the thought of her being surrounded by all of those drunk and horny men. The club had hired top-of-the-line security, and either I or one of my brothers was always present whenever she was there, but I still hated when she worked a shift.

A rush of air flew past Reece's lips and she looked angry all of a sudden, telling me Indulge was exactly what she wanted to talk to me about. I narrowed my eyes, the slight tick in my jaw indicating my stubbornness was coming out to say hello. In turn, my woman shut down, clamped her lips shut and tried to shove past me to exit the shower.

I grabbed her arm before she opened the door. "Where do you think you're goin'?" I pulled her toward me, her back resting against my chest.

"Let go, *James*." She always used my real name when she was upset with me. Although I liked my given name just fine, I hated when it came off her tongue in anger.

"No, not until you tell me what's the matter." I spun her around, reached down and grabbed her under her ass, lifting her up my body before pinning her against the wet shower wall. "Wrap your legs around me," I growled.

"No."

"Yes."

She pursed her lips and I took the invitation, although I didn't think she meant it as such. I fucked her mouth with my tongue, our mouths dueling in a heated passion only she could incite from me. Her breathy moans proved she wanted me to continue my assault, so I did.

My dick was so fucking hard, it hurt. I needed relief, and soon, so I lined myself up and gently pushed inside her, making sure to take my time. Even though we'd had sex countless times, I was rather endowed, and it took Reece's body a bit to accommodate my thickness.

Once I was fully sheathed, I broke away from her mouth. "I love you, baby. But I don't want you at that place. I'm sorry." *Thrust.* "And that's final." *Thrust. Rotate.*

"But I wanna—" Her words were clipped as soon as my thumb pressed against her clit. "Yeah," she moaned, all thoughts of arguing with me vanishing into thin air. Her fingernails dug into my shoulders as I continued to fuck her. Slow and then fast, rotating speeds until she unraveled and came on my cock.

After I quickly followed and our breathing had regulated, she unhooked her legs and slid down my body. Reece was still upset about my denial.

Several minutes later, after we finished washing up, I shut off the water and handed Reece a towel that was slung over the top of the door. I hated the despondent look on her beautiful face, her blue-gray eyes telling me everything without uttering a single word.

"Reece." She ignored me and walked out of the shower. "Babe." Wrapping a towel around my waist, I hurried after her. "Hey," I called, snagging her hand and stopping her from moving forward. "Don't be like that. I don't wanna argue. I'm doing it to keep you safe. Please understand that."

Her shoulders slumped before she turned around to face me.

"I know," she acknowledged. "I just need something to do. I love Luke with all my heart, but I need to get out of this house."

"And there's nothin' wrong with that. I have the club, so I get it."

"I have to get ready," she said, switching the topic and slowly withdrawing her hand from mine. She chose a light yellow sundress, complete with short sweater and a pair of nude sandals. Placing the items on the bed, she went to work picking out my clothes.

"What are you doing?"

"You're not wearing jeans to this." She was completely serious, and I found it adorable that she felt like she had to dress me. In all fairness, jeans had initially been on my list of attire, until I decided I'd dress up a bit for the occasion, wearing black dress pants paired with a crisp white button-down. It was a day to be celebrated, especially seeing as how close to death a few of my brothers had come.

I smiled, waving my hand and giving her a subtle nod to continue.

"I love you, baby."

"You should," she replied before flashing me a smile.

"Is that right?"

"Uh-huh."

Reece moved toward the corner of the room and sat at her vanity. I watched as she flipped her head over and dried her long locks. She'd chosen to wear her hair down and wavy, a simple yet sexy hairstyle on her.

As she was busy getting ready, a sudden thought occurred to me, a suggestion which would turn everything around. I could ensure her safety and make her happy all at the same time. I'd work out the details later with Ryder, but my idea was as good as golden.

"Hey." I caught her eyes in the reflection of the mirror. "How about this? Braylen is gonna open her own salon soon, compliments of a gift from Ryder. Why don't you work with her? I'm sure she's gonna need help setting up, then running the business. You could help manage and take care of the books."

Reece's mouth fell open. "Are you serious?"

"Yeah. It could be a little bit before everything is up and runnin', but it's definitely a viable option for you. I'm sure Braylen would love your help." As far as I knew, the two of them got on well, and I was sure it wouldn't take much at all to convince her she needed my woman's help in her new endeavor.

"Oh my God. Thank you," Reece exclaimed, jumping into my arms and kissin' the hell outta me. I took advantage of her gratitude and ravaged her mouth, my dick at full salute by the time we broke apart.

"I don't have a problem with you wanting to do something with your time," I reiterated. "Even though you don't have to. I just don't want you in that club."

"I understand. I do." Reece was happy, and I'd managed to turn things around and give her what she wanted.

But she'd given me even more.

Reece had given me her heart, a son, and an anchor I'd been missing for so long.

----◆----

Reece

WE WERE EN ROUTE TO the clubhouse when Tripp blurted, "I want to tell you something." I turned around to make sure Luke was content before shifting in my seat to face him.

"What's that?" I slowed my breathing, preparing to hear something I wouldn't like. I never knew what was gonna come flyin' out of his mouth, so better to brace myself for impact.

"It not official yet, but—"He glanced at me, then back to the road ahead of him, a smile curving the corners of his full lips.

"You better tell me," I warned, mirroring his happy expression.

"I'm giving up my nomad patch for a permanent one. I'm staying around for good." Tripp being a nomad, not belonging to any one charter, had always made me uneasy. Because he had no roots tying him down, he could've disappeared at any time, even though he promised he'd never leave me. Then after the birth of our son, he'd look at me as if I had three heads whenever I voiced my fears.

I knew they were ridiculous, but my life hadn't always gone as planned, so I never fully allowed myself to feel anything except apprehension. It lessened as the time passed, but the feeling still existed.

Until right then.

I was sure I had a ridiculous grin on my face, but I couldn't help it.

"Are you happy?" he asked, looking my way when I still hadn't said anything. "You look happy, but you're quiet."

"If you weren't driving, and Luke wasn't with us, I'd show you just how happy you've made me." Clasping my hands in my lap to keep them to myself, I bit my bottom lip in giddiness.

"Don't tell me that, woman." Several seconds passed. "Damnit! Now I'm gonna be sportin' a hard-on when we pull up." His faux-annoyed expression didn't fool me.

"Then slow down. I don't need any of the other women there staring at what's clearly mine."

I wasn't a jealous woman by nature, but when it came to Tripp, all bets were off. Did it bother me when he had business to take care of at Indulge or Flings, the club's two strip clubs? Yes. Did I trust my man around those women? Yes. Did I count the minutes until he came back home? Hell yes.

Tripp had told me on several occasions that he liked when I showed my jealous side, probably because it didn't happen too often. Not because what he did warranted a reaction, but because it made him feel wanted. Desired. The reverse was not true when the roles were switched, however. My man was typically easygoing, joking around with the best of them, but if he thought someone was hitting on me, his temper would boil over. And sometimes, although not often, he'd gotten physical. It didn't take much for Tripp to get his point across to other men, because, well . . . he was huge, towering over most people at six four.

Pulling into the lot, Tripp found a parking space readily enough, turned off the engine and exited the truck. He came around to my side first and took my hand to help me down. We opened the back door and together gathered our son, along with all of the things we'd need to keep him happy for the duration.

Up ahead, I saw Hawke, Tripp's brother, talking to a woman. It wasn't until she turned that I recognized her from a picture Hawke had shown me when he was a little more than tipsy. He was upset over her leaving him to go and stay with her sister. I'd never officially met the woman, but my heart went out to her for what she'd been through.

"I didn't know Edana was back," I blurted, holding Luke close as Tripp and I walked side by side toward the others. The sun hit her hair just so, making me a little envious of her deep red locks.

"Yeah," he answered. "He told me there was a possibility she'd show up today, that she might be moving back here." Tripp slung the baby bag over his shoulder, looking quite the specimen regardless of what he was carrying. Actually, I thought it made him even sexier, but hey, that was just me.

"Well good. I'm happy for him," I said, threading my arm through Tripp's as he led us toward our friends.

"Are we early?" Tripp asked as we walked up behind his brother and Edana, giving her a hug and kiss on the cheek before he approached his brother, doing that man-hug thingy that guys do.

"Yeah, but not by much." Hawke turned his attention to me, giving me a quick kiss before backing up. He glanced toward Edana to see her reaction, but all she did was smile. "Reece, this is Edana. Edana, this is Tripp's ol' lady, Reece."

"Ol' lady? We're still doin' that?" I laughed as I shook hands with Hawke's woman. Tripp had referred to me as such a few times, and each time I told him I didn't care for the phrasing. It made me sound . . . old. He'd shrugged off my protest as if I was being ridiculous. In the grand scheme of things, if that was the worst issue we dealt with, I really had nothing to complain about.

Lost in my thoughts, I was startled when Jagger snuck up behind us, kissing my cheek before slapping Tripp on the back. Holding out his hands, he wiggled his fingers.

"Let me see this guy," he instructed. I passed him Luke, smiling over his enthusiasm over seeing our son. "He's getting so big." He jostled him a bit until he'd positioned him just so, causing my heart to skip a beat in fear that'd he'd drop him.

"You drop my kid and I'll kick your ass. Don't care how undefeated you are."

Jagger laughed at the threat, turning his attentions away from Tripp and back on Luke.

"You wanna be a fighter like me when you grow up? Don't be like your dad. He can't throw a punch to save his life."

Jagger with my son was representative of how most of these men were. Big, tough and loud, yet they all turned into big softies whenever a baby was around.

Making funny faces at Luke, ignoring the jests of his friends, Jagger's demeanor changed as soon as Kena joined the group. The way she watched his interaction with our son was borderline hypnotic, and I could only wonder what kinds of thoughts were running through her head. When she caught me staring at her, she smiled.

He's so adorable. Jagger's eyes were glued to hers.

"Me or Luke?" he teased, moving in to give her a kiss. "Wanna hold him?" A sudden nervousness made her shake her head. "He won't bite." Still, she only stood there, extending her hand to caress the side of Luke's head. "Ya gotta get used to it sometime, babe."

Why.

"Because I'm gonna want one soon, so you might as well get some practice." He laughed but Kena found his comment anything but funny. In fact, she looked petrified. She dropped her hand to her side and took a step back, giving me a pathetic smile before she turned around and walked away.

Jagger looked puzzled, confused as to what he'd said wrong. "Here," he said, handing Luke back to me before he took off after her.

I laughed. One odd expression from her and he was practically tripping over his feet to find out why.

"Where's he goin'?" Tripp asked, and I just shrugged. When I didn't answer, he added, "Looks like he probably stuck his foot in his mouth." He leaned down and planted a loving kiss on my lips. "Been there . . . done that."

"You can say that again," I laughed.

As I turned back around to watch Jagger chase after his future, I knew mine had already arrived.

Gifting me with every possible dream I hadn't even known I'd wanted.

------◆------

"BABE, STOP." *DAMN, SHE'S QUICK.* "Kena!" I finally caught up to her right before she disappeared into one of the bedrooms in the back of the clubhouse. Spinning her around, I asked, "What's the matter? What did I say?" I tried to pull her close, but she pushed me back, her hands resting on my chest to give her some space.

When I finally retreated, she dropped her hands to her sides, looking at the ground as if she feared looking at my face. Paranoia and uncertainty swirled inside me, and instead of blowing off her odd reaction to my joke a few moments before, I continued to press her for a response.

"Are you ever going to answer me?"

She picked her head up, her beautiful eyes looking lost. The longer we stood in silence, the worse I felt, a bead of nervous sweat appearing on my brow. "If you don't answer me, I'm gonna start to think the worst, and considering I have no idea why you're upset, my mind is gonna create some off-the-wall scenarios." I tried to laugh but the sound fell short.

She lifted her hands and signed, *You want to have a baby?*

"Is that what this is all about?" Another failed laugh fell from my mouth. We'd talked about having kids in passing, more so over the past few months, but nothing serious had ever been decided. I wasn't even twenty-five yet, so there was no rush. But eventually, I'd want to start my own family, especially after seeing how happy my brothers were with their kids.

I see the way your eyes light up whenever one of our friend's kids are around.
"So?"

So, I don't want to feel rushed to get knocked up. Her expression morphed into anger, the reason for her sudden change in mood rather confusing.

"Jagger!" I turned my head to the side and saw Tripp enter the clubhouse. When he caught my eye, he said, "We're startin' in like fifteen." He jerked his head toward Kena who was standing across from me in the hallway, a frown on his face as if to ask if everything was all right. I nodded.

Grabbing her hand, I pulled her toward a bedroom, kicking the door closed behind me. I knew if I didn't get her out of her own head, whatever story she was concocting was gonna fester and turn a simple joking statement into something a lot more serious, and unnecessarily so. Advancing toward her left her no option but to back away from me, the backs of her thighs hitting a short dresser against the wall. Nothing except a few motorcycle magazines laid on top, so with a quick swipe of my hand I cleared the items, grabbed her waist and set her on top of it. Spreading her legs, her black and white striped dress riding up her thighs, I moved in between.

"Don't do this. I don't wanna fight with you, so stop overthinkin' shit."
I rested my hand on the side of her neck, her pulse thrumming under my
fingertips. She licked her lips, and I did something I probably shouldn't
have, considering where we were and that I had limited amount of time
alone with my woman. Running my free hand up the inside of her leg, she
fidgeted briefly before I pushed aside her white satin panties and teased
her with my finger. Even annoyed with me, she was always wet and ready.

Kena attempted to stop me, her hand grabbing mine under her dress,
but her efforts were feeble at best. When she knew I wasn't gonna give
up, she leaned back on the dresser, braced herself and spread her legs
farther apart.

"Let's get these off you," I coaxed, helping her to rise off the dresser
before drawing her panties down her legs and tossing them to the ground.
"We only have a few minutes so we have to be quick, and we need to be
quiet." She looked at me and just shook her head before pointing to her
throat. "Okay," I corrected. "*I* have to be quiet."

Fumbling with my belt, I unzipped my pants and pushed them down
my legs, pulling her toward the edge of the dresser. The moment I thrust
inside her was perfection, and seconds later her short pants of air told me
she was already well on her way to exploding. Her fingers tangled in my
hair as I tried to show her how much I loved her.

"I know you don't want to talk about it, but I do want kids with you."
Not the sexiest of talk, but I needed her to hear me, and I knew that while
Kena was in the throes of passion, she wouldn't be locked up inside her
head. Her body stilled as she stared at me, her pussy clenching down
on me while I tried to keep some semblance of composure. "It's gonna
happen. Not today, not tomorrow. Maybe not even next year, but you
will have my babies." She opened her mouth, the action pointless since
she couldn't speak. When she realized what she'd done, she raised her
hands in front of her, but before she could sign a single word, I grabbed
them and held them to my chest. "I would never rush you," I affirmed,
needing her to know that while my mind was made up, she could take
the time she needed to come around to the idea.

She struggled for me to release her hands, and when I did, she signed
something I hadn't expected. *I'm scared.*

"What are you scared of?"

That our child will have my 'challenge'. She used air quotes on the last
word.

"You know what happened to you isn't hereditary, right?" She gave me a slow nod. "Then what's really bothering you?"

She took a moment before raising her hands.

I want to be married before I have children, Jagger. And I know we're nowhere ready for that step yet, so when you make comments about having kids, I think you just want to skip right over that part altogether.

Okay, I could honestly say I didn't expect that either.

I was still buried inside her, although we'd stopped moving in order to have our little conversation. But after what she'd just said, I knew it was as good a time as any to let her in on what I'd been thinking about for the past month. Perfect timing and all.

Pulling her hips toward me, I surprised her with the sudden movement, her hands flying to my shoulders to steady herself.

"Marry me, then. Agree to be my wife."

She looked shocked, and I couldn't say I blamed her. I hadn't planned on proposing so soon, but after what she'd said, I had no idea why I'd been waiting.

Are you asking only because of what I just told you?

"Of course not. I love you and don't want to wait anymore to start the rest of our life together."

I could tell she was thinking about my response, and for a moment I thought she was gonna turn me down. I wouldn't lie; my heart fell into my stomach waiting for her answer. But when she cradled my face in her hands and brought my mouth to hers, kissing my lips in the most tender of moments, I knew her answer in an instant.

I pulled back so I could see her beautiful face. "Was that a yes?"

Her face lit up with the biggest smile I think I'd ever seen. She mouthed "yes" at the same time she signed her answer.

It was in that moment that I knew my life would never be the same again. Yes, I knew Kena was mine, that she was the woman I couldn't live without, but her agreeing to be my wife shoved our love toward a whole other realm of happiness.

———◆———

WHAT JUST HAPPENED? JUST MOMENTS ago, I'd been upset with

Jagger's jokes about having kids. While I knew I'd blown the situation all out of proportion, the thought of having children with him without being married was something that bothered me. I realized I seemed old-fashioned, knowing people didn't worry about getting hitched these days in order to have kids, but it was something I wanted for me. To have babies with my husband, not my boyfriend.

I wasn't sure why my feelings on the subject were so steadfast. Maybe it had something to do with the fact that if we were married, he couldn't walk away as easily as if we weren't.

Or maybe I was scared about the whole idea in general and I was making stuff up to justify my walking away from him in front of Tripp and Reece.

Everything had changed, though.

Jagger had just asked me to marry him.

To be his wife.

And I accepted.

He started to move inside me again, his lips finding the area below my ear that he knew drove me crazy. He cradled my neck in one hand, the other grabbing my ass and pulling me toward him every time he thrust forward.

"Baby," he moaned. "You've made me so fuckin' happy." He pulled back so he could see my face. Sometimes I wished I had the ability to speak, to hear my voice say his name, or to tell him that what he did to my body drove me to the heavens and back. But all I had were facial expressions, body language and the flutter of my hands.

I love you. Those three words summed up everything for me, and I hoped they were enough.

Jagger's mouth covered mine, his tongue sweeping past my lips, the urgency in his kiss telling me his body was building toward release. The soft moans that escaped him sent my desire for him so high I feared I'd never come back down. He was certainly talented, although seeing as how he was the only man I'd ever been with I didn't have anything to compare it to. But I couldn't imagine anyone else treating me so tenderly yet laying claim to me at the same time.

Each thrust of his hips sparked a fire, my body trembling the closer I came to pure bliss. When his thumb found my clit, I rocked my hips toward him with more urgency, the bubble of ecstasy spiraling through my entire body. I wanted him to see what he did to me, to make sure he witnessed my unraveling. Twisting strands of his dark blond hair around my fingers, I stared into his beautiful amber-colored eyes, his pupils darkening the harder he fucked me, the back of the dresser banging against the wall with each twitch of his hips.

My lips parted as the all-too-familiar tingling threatened to split me apart, short pants of air fanning his face as I desperately tried to catch my breath.

"Are you gonna come?"

I was barely able to nod before my orgasm hit me with such force I threw my head back and pulled him with me, still holding onto him for dear life. He buried his face in the crook of my neck, biting my skin as he took me with wild abandon, his cock thickening and stretching me even wider. He grunted out his release, the sound amplified in the barely furnished room.

It took a few moments before Jagger composed himself enough to back away, slowly uncurling my fingers from his hair. I hadn't even realized I was still holding him.

"Damn, woman, I think you may still have some of my hair in your hands." He rubbed the sides of his head, teasing me when he made a pained expression. Gifting me another kiss, he took a step back and looked around the room for something to use to wipe away our sex. There was nothing, so he picked up my panties, wiped me clean and tucked the material inside his pants pocket.

Once he helped me to my feet, I signed, *I thought you were supposed to be quiet.*

He laughed, the tiny dimple in his cheek appearing and making me melt all over again.

"Seems like I can't control myself around you," he admitted. He took a breath to say something else but a knock at the door interrupted him.

"Kena? Jagger? You in there?" My sister. The handle jiggled but thankfully the door was locked. "Hello?"

I smoothed down my dress before opening the door. Jagger was busy tucking himself back into his pants when I came face-to-face with Braylen.

As soon as she saw me, she smiled. "They're here," she announced, briefly looking down the hallway before turning her attention back to me. She tried to look past me into the room, but I blocked her view. "Don't let Ryder find out that you guys escaped to have sex or I'll never hear the end of it."

"The end of what?" Ryder asked, appearing out of nowhere. He pushed the door open with ease, not a care that maybe his friend wasn't dressed, but somehow I doubted he cared.

"What the fuck?" Ryder shouted, shooting my sister an annoyed look. She thought the situation was rather amusing. Her laughter seemed to irritate him, although I suspected he was playing it up more than anything. "Oh, you think that's funny? That he gets to have sex while we're waitin' but I can't?"

She laughed harder, leaning up on her tippy toes to kiss him.

"Poor baby," she cooed. "I'll make it up to you later."

"You're damn right you will." Looking back toward us, more so at Jagger than at me, he said, "Let's go, brother. Time to get started." Then just as quickly as they'd appeared, they left, leaving us to assemble ourselves enough to be seen back in public. I was sure my face was flushed, but thankfully Jagger hadn't messed up my hair, the long dark strands still in perfect curls down my back.

Are you ready?

He grabbed my hand and ran the pad of his finger over the area near my knuckle. "I'll get a ring and make it official."

I don't need a ring to make it official.

"But I want you to have one. Besides, I want you to make all the other women jealous." He gave me the sweetest kiss. "And hopefully it'll spur things along with your sister and that bastard she likes to call her man."

My thoughts instantly flew to Braylen and me being engaged at the same time. How fun would that be to run ideas past each other? To go dress shopping together and drive our men nuts about the tiniest details?

Pulling me from the room, Jagger laced his fingers with mine and led me back outside to join everyone. Up ahead, I saw Sully talking to Reece and Braylen, and all of a sudden I had the sudden urge to share my news. Turning toward Jagger, I tried to tug my hand from his, but he held on tighter. It wasn't until the third try that he realized I wanted to tell him something.

"Bad habit," he admitted, flashing me the sexiest grin.

Should I tell them about the engagement?

He looked uncertain, and for a moment I thought maybe he was having second thoughts. I knew it was stupid to think that way, especially seeing as how he just told me he wanted to buy me a ring to make it official, but sometimes I couldn't help but be a woman, second-guessing and overthinking things too much.

"I would love nothing more, but how about we wait until afterward? I just don't want to steal anyone's thunder. You understand, right?"

Of course.

And I did understand. I understood that while Jagger wanted to shout from the rooftops that we were going to be man and wife, he didn't want to overshadow his friends' big day. He was always thinking about others, aware of how his friends felt. Jagger didn't look like a big softie, his tough exterior exuding the exact opposite, but the man had a heart of gold.

He'd never viewed my inability to speak as a hindrance, instead finding ways to communicate with me. Texting was the easiest, but when he'd wanted to explain himself, for me to hear the sincerity in his voice, he'd called me and asked me to press the keys on my phone so I could answer his yes or no questions.

One for yes and two for no.

The biggest sign of his interest, however, had been when he asked Sully to teach him sign language.

I never dreamed I would ever find someone like Jagger. Every day with him was special, fate's sweetest gift, and soon the world would officially know we belonged to each other.

———•◆•———

Stone

GODDAMN, MY SOON-TO-BE WIFE LOOKED gorgeous. The way her cream-colored dress hugged her in all the right places, her sun-kissed blonde hair styled casually in loose waves. I told her not to even bother with some fancy hairstyle because I was only gonna mess it up as soon as we had a moment of privacy.

I knew people said it was bad luck to see the bride before the ceremony, but we'd already had our fair share of shitty circumstances since we'd been together.

I'd been shot while helping Marek rescue Sully from Vex, her crazy ex.

I'd been run off the road, ending up in Addy's ER so she could patch me up.

Her uncle, Trigger, had shot me in the leg when he found out we'd not only been seeing each other behind his back, but that I got her pregnant.

And most recently, I'd been shot in the head during our final battle with the Reapers. Well, the tip of my ear had been taken off, but it could've been a lot worse if Marek hadn't tackled the fucker who fired at me.

Come to think of it, I'd been shot quite a few times, but none of my close calls even compared to what Addy had dealt with when she was pregnant with Riley. Ovarian cancer. I'd almost lost her. Could've lost them both.

Shoving aside thoughts of the past and what could've happened, I turned in my seat to stare at the woman who loved me beyond reason, who I would gladly die for if the circumstance ever called for it.

"Don't even think about it, mister," Addy warned, a small smile curving her delectable lips.

"What are you talking about?" I reached over and caressed the side of her face before snaking my hand under her hair to lightly grip her neck, her rapid pulse telling me she was more than ready to give me what I wanted. What we both needed. I pulled her close but she placed her hand on my chest, my frenzied heartbeat giving away what my eyes tried to shield.

"You know what I'm talking about. Don't start something we can't finish right now."

Before I could even think of something witty and convincing to say, a rap sounded against my driver-side window. Grunting in annoyance, I turned toward the intrusion and saw Jagger's face staring back at me. The way he looked at me, as if I was the one holding him up, told me it was time to greet everyone who'd gathered to share in our day.

Our wedding day.

I'd wanted to marry Addy the day I found out she was pregnant with Riley, but she'd refused, telling me that having a child was no reason to rush into marriage. So I'd allowed her the time she needed, finally proposing at our daughter's baptism. Then when she was pregnant with our second child, our son, Lincoln, I wanted to get hitched soon after, but she wanted to wait until after she gave birth so she could fit into her dress the way she wanted. I reluctantly agreed.

It didn't take much on my part to convince her to name him after me, his need for his mother only rivaled by my need for my woman. The little one was attached to her, whereas Riley was Daddy's little girl. Don't get me wrong, she still preferred her mother for certain things—reading bedtime stories, for one—but whenever she hurt herself, it was me she came running to, crawling into my lap and resting her head on my chest.

"I guess that's our cue." Addy laughed. Once she'd exited, she popped her head back inside the SUV, that time in the back seat as she fiddled with Lincoln's car seat. Our son was sleeping, but he started to stir once Addy lifted him into her arms. He nuzzled into her and fell back asleep. *Don't blame ya, buddy.* The nine months since he'd been born flew by in a blur. I only hoped the clock ticked by slowly today so I could cherish the moments.

I got to work helping Riley from her seat, her eyes intently watching me, waiting for me to do what I always did whenever I was near her— make a funny face. Twisting my lips and sticking out my tongue, I made a noise before tickling her.

"Daddy." She giggled, her two-year-old face lighting up as she tried to wriggle away from me. Her laughter filled my ears, and I swore it was like the sun shone all day long.

"If she has an accident, you're gonna be the one to change her. And seeing as how I had a hell of a time getting her in that outfit," Addy said, pointing to Riley's purple and white flowered dress, "it's not gonna be a walk in the park." She smiled before shaking her head, knowing damn well her stern words wouldn't deter me from making my little girl laugh once more.

That was until Riley told me she had to pee. Then I withdrew my hands and finally picked her up.

Kissing her cheek a few times, she placed her tiny hand on my face. "Daddy, you hairs tickawin me."

"Your mommy likes them." I winked at Addy as she sidled up next to me, tightly holding Lincoln. She gave me a kiss before going to find our friends.

"Give me my goddaughter," Sully said, reaching for Riley before I even realized she was near. Since I had to grab a few of the kids' bags from the back seat, I handed the little girl over, Sully kissing Riley before giving her a big hug.

"Where's Kaden?" Looking around, I didn't see the little boy. Though I was certain if she was here, so was he.

"Cole has him." She pointed across the lot to where her husband was standing behind Tripp, his large body shielding parts of my best friend. "Did you hear?"

"Hear what?"

The biggest smile appeared on her face. "Kaden is ours, for good. Tripp stopped by earlier and told us." My confusion prompted her to finish, her smile briefly disappearing. "He said Rachel was found dead. Overdose."

"That's great." Sully's eyes widened at my bluntness. "Look, I'm not saying it's great that she's dead, but come on, Sully. From what Tripp told me about her, she was a train wreck. No way she could've been a good mother to Kaden." Reaching out and touching her arm, I said, "That was always your job." Unshed tears filled her brown eyes. "Oh God. Don't cry or your husband is gonna have my head." I smiled, and she laughed, wiping away the lone tear that fell down her cheek.

As we turned around, Marek approached and pulled me in for a quick hug, slapping my back in greeting. He kissed his wife before she went off to join the others, Riley's sweet laughter carrying behind them.

"You ready to do this, brother?" He looked me up and down from head to toe. "I see you pulled out all the stops today." Marek was referring to the black Armani I'd chosen for the occasion. No way was I showin' up half-assed dressed to marry the love of my life.

"I look good," I joked, laughing as I took in the scene around us. All of our friends were present, with the exception of the brothers of the club who'd passed on, Zip and Breck. Two loyal men who were ripped from this world too soon. Although the threat had finally been eliminated, it didn't take away the sting from the loss.

Seeing Cutter talking to two people I'd never seen before, I lifted my chin in his direction, Marek turning to see.

"How's he doin'?"

"As well as he can be, I suppose."

"Who's he talkin' to?"

Marek folded his arms across his chest, a satisfied grin swiftly appearing. "That's his daughter, Kalista."

"What? I thought he wasn't in contact with her." I'd heard bits and pieces about Cutter's daughter, and how he refused to have a relationship with her, but his reasons were much like the excuses we'd all used as to why we didn't want to get attached to anyone outside the club. Safety.

We'd all failed, giving in to loving our women, all the while driving ourselves insane trying to make sure no harm came to them. Unfortunately, we weren't able to stop some of the things that happened, but we were able to move on from the guilt. Mostly.

"I think Breck's death made him realize how short life really is. Besides, there's no more threat, so he's out of reasons why he should continue to keep her out of his life."

"I guess you're right." Looking back toward them, I asked, "Who's the guy?"

"Her husband, Eli. He's the lawyer I met up with a couple years ago, the one who gave me some legal advice about setting up the strip clubs. Stuff I had to know to run the businesses."

"Oh yeah. I remember you telling me about him. Did you know he was married to Cutter's daughter?"

"Not a clue. Besides, I don't think they were married when I met him. And get this—they have a son. Holden, I think his name is. Anyway, that means Cutter's a grandfather."

I made a face. "That's just weird."

"I know," Marek agreed. Although Cutter looked like he could be a sweet old grandpa, his clean-shaven face and short gray hair styled perfectly in place, he was anything but. He was ruthless when he needed to be. I'd seen that man do some shit that made me queasy. I couldn't imagine him tossing around the ball with his grandkid.

"What a small world," I said, shaking my head at the coincidence. Before we were interrupted by Jagger and Ryder who were headed our way, I bumped Marek's shoulder with mine. "I just found out about Kaden. Congrats, man."

"Yeah." A brightness shone behind my friend's blue eyes. "You should've seen Sully's face when Tripp told us. I was kinda jealous that I'd never made her heart soar like that." He laughed. "But I get it. Besides, I really shouldn't be jealous of my son, right?"

"Why not? I'm jealous of my kids. The way Addy dotes on them, ignoring me sometimes." I winked. I wasn't serious. Not completely.

"I wouldn't change a thing, though. Kaden can have all of Sully's attention as long as she continues to smile like she has been."

"When we gonna start this shindig?" Ryder interjected, fast approaching and pulling me into a half hug once he was near.

"Yeah, let's go, brother. What's the matter? You got cold feet?" Jagger was only joking. If anyone besides Marek knew that Addy was my fuckin' life, it was him.

"Funny," I responded, giving him a half hug as well. Slinging the diaper bag over my shoulder, I clapped my hands together. "Let's get me married, boys."

As I walked toward the grounds behind the clubhouse that had been set up for the ceremony, I couldn't help but think of how lucky I'd been to finally convince Addy to be mine. There were times I was sure she'd second-guessed her decision, but I couldn't've been happier that she stuck it out, giving me two healthy and beautiful children to boot.

The woman was absolutely amazing, and in no time at all, she'd legally belong to me.

To cherish and love for the rest of my undeserving life.

———◆———

Adelaide

LOOKING FROM PERSON TO PERSON as my father walked me down the makeshift aisle, I smiled, my heart overflowing with happiness that everyone had made it to celebrate with Stone and me.

"You sure you want to marry him?" my father asked. At first, I thought he was serious. I turned to him to ask him why he'd said such a thing, but then I caught the gleam in his eyes. "Lincoln is a good man, honey." He refused to call him Stone, always using his given name. "I know I didn't want to see it at first, but that was only because I wanted to keep you safe. But he's proven to me that he can take care of you, and my grandchildren. I'm proud to call him my son-in-law." He smiled. "Just don't tell him."

I laughed, tears welling in my eyes as I leaned into him. "You're gonna make me ruin my makeup, Dad." He kissed my temple, neither of us breaking our stride. Catching a glance of my new stepmother, who was holding the baby, I whispered, "Camille looks beautiful. How did you get so lucky?"

"I have no idea," he confessed, a wide smile on his face as their eyes connected. My father had remarried six months before, and I couldn't be happier. She was a lovely woman who'd brought happiness back into his life, so I'd accepted her right away. She never cringed or shied away whenever my father and I spoke of my mother, instead encouraging us to share our memories of her.

I made sure to take my time walking to meet my future husband, partly because I loved to make the man sweat, but also because I wanted to take the time to appreciate the group of people who'd become so intricate in my life.

Cutter sat next to who I'd learned was his daughter, Kalista, and her husband, Eli. From what I understood, their relationship had been nonexistent. Because of the danger that had surrounded the club, he'd chosen to keep her out of his life, only coming to reveal that he was her father when she'd mistakenly walked into the club's bar, The Underground, years back. Out of all the men of the Knights Corruption, I knew the least about Cutter. He kept to himself, a quiet man, but I knew he'd suffered a great loss when Breck was killed. So the fact that he'd chosen to open up communication with his daughter made me happy.

Another two steps closer to my man and I saw Hawke and Edana cuddled close to each other, her head resting on his shoulder as he whispered something in her ear, turning his eyes back on me right afterward. He winked, and the smile that lit up his face was one I hadn't seen before. He'd been depressed over the breakdown in their relationship, the dynamics drastically changing after her attack, but now that she was back, they both looked happier.

Next was Ryder and Braylen. The two of them were made for each other. In fact, they reminded me a bit of Stone and me. He was a pain in the ass most times, and she made sure to tell him about himself. There was a great love between them, though. One that anyone could see as soon as they saw them together. His daughter, Zoe, sat at the end of the aisle, the cutest girl I'd ever seen—next to Riley, of course. I wondered if he and Braylen would have one of their own soon, the way he watched her holding Kaden for Sully making me think the answer would be yes. Then again, maybe I simply had baby fever, so in love with my own children that I wanted everyone to be blessed with them.

Smiling at my thoughts, my eyes connected with Jagger and Kena. I really liked him, and she was his perfect match. She wasn't as ballsy as her sister, but she still didn't take any crap from him. Then again, he didn't give her much to worry about. I'd been the one responsible for him learning sign language. Okay, I hadn't taught him myself, but I'd orchestrated the training to occur between him and Sully, essentially threatening Marek so he'd let it happen. I wasn't delusional; I knew if the leader of the Knights Corruption refused, the only thing I could've done was pester Stone so badly he would've had to convince Marek otherwise. The two of them smiled lovingly toward me, and it wasn't until I was closer that I noticed

Jagger rubbing her left hand. Her ring finger, to be exact. When I looked up, he widened his eyes and grinned.

A few more steps and I saw Tripp and Reece, their adorable son, Luke, cuddled close to his mother. When Tripp's gaze met mine, he flashed me the biggest grin. What could I say? The man had a special place in my heart. I'd been the one who nursed him back to health after he'd been shot and left for dead in front of the club's gates. We'd formed a friendship, a special bond during that time. And although we never had any feelings toward each other, he loved to give Stone a hard time, pretending he was hitting on me. My man had finally calmed down some when Tripp met Reece, and he saw how hard his brother fell for the woman. Reece had escaped an abusive relationship, and I was beyond happy that'd she'd met someone who could love and protect her as fiercely as Tripp could.

My uncle, Trigger, was busy bouncing Riley on his lap when he turned his head to watch my father and me walking toward him. Just the sight of him made me miss my mother more so than normal, the resemblance between them uncanny. They'd shared the same almond-shaped eyes and full cheeks, along with the same shade of brown hair, although my uncle's was mostly gray these days.

Thankfully, my father and uncle had ended whatever feud had kept them apart over the years and started talking again, right after Riley was born. My mother's brother was ferociously protective over me, even going so far as shooting Stone when he'd first found out about our relationship. It took me a little while to forgive him for that, but I knew his actions had been driven by his love for me, as well as some unspoken code amongst the men of the club, a code Stone trampled all over in order to be with me. My uncle had only started to accept Stone after the birth of our daughter, although he continued to give my man a hard time every now and then.

When we'd finally made it to the front of everyone gathered, I passed my bouquet of red roses to Sully, who'd readily agreed to be my matron of honor, her husband standing next to Stone, clasping him on the shoulder while giving me a slight nod and a smile.

My soon-to-be husband took a step toward me and reached for my hand, my father kissing my cheek before releasing me. Two of the most important men in my life shook hands, mutual respect emanating from them both.

"I can't wait to get you naked," Stone whispered in my ear before ushering me to stand in front of Father Houston, the priest who'd come to marry us, the same one who'd performed Riley's baptism.

The flush of my cheeks made Stone laugh. No one had heard what he'd said to me, but one look at my face and they could surely guess.

As I faced the love of my life, barely listening to the priest as he talked, autopilot kicking in as we repeated our vows to each other, I lost myself to Stone's piercing gaze.

So much had happened during our relationship, both good and bad, but we'd persevered.

Fate could've dealt us a different hand altogether.

Cancer could've stolen my life.

Stone could've been killed, multiple times over the course of the past couple years.

But none of that happened. Instead, I was given my happily ever after—the man of my dreams, and two wonderful children I loved more than life itself.

Well, soon to be three. I had yet to tell Stone my little secret.

———◆———

Kaden

Fifteen years later

"COME ON, RILEY," I GROANED, chasing after her while she ran toward the back of the clubhouse. "I didn't kiss her. I swear." *Damn, she's fast.* Increasing my stride, I caught her by the wrist, spinning her around before she could fight me. A gust of wind kicked up, strands of her blonde hair shielding her angry gray eyes from me. Until she swiped them away, glaring at me in the process.

"Let go, Kaden," she whisper-shouted, trying to tug free from my hold. But I wasn't gonna let her go until she heard me out. I wanted to shout that I didn't do anything wrong, that I'd been the one who was caught off guard when Tracy Flemming planted one on me after school the day before, but I had to make sure to keep my voice low enough so no one heard me.

We were at our fathers' club. Everyone had gathered earlier for a barbecue, and the last thing I needed was for Riley's dad to catch us. The man was seriously scary when he wanted to be. I overheard him telling her that he'd shoot any boy who dared to put his hands on her.

I was too young to die.

I'd been able to convince my dad's best friend that I'd watch out for his daughter, that I would make sure no guys came near her. Little did he know I had an ulterior motive for promising such things, that I was the guy staking a claim on his daughter, albeit privately for the time being.

"Not until you let me explain. It wasn't what it looked like." The fire in her eyes turned me on, my almost seventeen-year-old hormones wreaking havoc inside my body. I risked a step closer, which only pushed her to retreat until her back was flush with the concrete wall behind her.

"I know what I saw." She threw her hands on her hips and rolled her eyes. Riley Crosswell was so damn spirited . . . and I loved it.

I loved her, and it was time I reminded her of my feelings.

I moved swiftly, slamming my mouth over hers before my tongue begged for entrance. Moments later, she groaned into the kiss, and I knew I had my opportunity to make her see the truth for what it was.

I only had eyes for her.

My heart belonged to her. Always had, ever since we were kids.

Unexpectedly, she tore her mouth from me and shoved me backward, her hands in front of her in case I tried to come too close again. "Did you sleep with her?"

"No!" I lowered my voice before I drew any unnecessary attention. "I would *never* do that. She kissed *me*, baby. I didn't kiss her back. I swear."

"Well, obviously she thought she could. Seeing as how no one even knows we're together."

"You know how your dad will react," I reminded her, feeling the anger start to bubble inside me, pissed I couldn't openly claim Riley for my own.

"I know," she conceded, looking away from me before chewing on her bottom lip, something she did right before she was about to cry.

"Don't be upset. We'll figure something out," I promised, lifting her face to mine before I kissed her once more.

LIFE WASN'T FAIR. KADEN MAREK was the boy I'd loved my entire life, yet I couldn't tell anyone. My dad would seriously freak if he found out we'd been secretly seeing each other, and he was so damn stubborn—something my mom often complained about—that there would be no convincing him to allow the relationship.

Not only did I have my dad to contend with, but every other man in the club. I swore they made it their personal mission to make sure I grew old alone. The only exception was Kaden's dad, the president of the Knights Corruption. He smiled whenever he saw Kaden and me together. Sometimes I wondered if he suspected something, although he never said anything if he did.

"I love you," Kaden whispered into the kiss. Pulling back, he stared into my eyes, his the most expressive blues I'd ever seen. So much so I was surprised we hadn't been found out yet. Whenever we were around our families, like that day, he would stare after me, and when I'd catch him, he'd give me a sexy smirk before looking away.

"I love you more."

"Not possible," he argued, his hands going from my waist to underneath my ass, lifting me until I wrapped my legs around his waist. He used the wall behind me as an anchor.

His biceps flexed as he held me, the corded muscles of his chest surely contracting beneath his blue T-shirt. I'd seen Kaden naked a handful of times, his body like a work of art, but it was only last month that we'd decided to finally have sex. At first it'd been a little painful, but the six times we'd been together since then were nothing short of electrifying.

Lost to teasing touches, heavy breaths and soul-scorching kisses, neither of us heard him approach.

"Whoa!" he shouted. "What the hell is goin' on here?"

I broke the kiss, unhooking my legs and planting my feet on the ground before pushing Kaden back so I could turn and face the intruder.

"Uncle Trigger," I pleaded, my eyes practically bugging out of my head. "Please don't tell my dad. I. . . . We just. . . ." I clamped my mouth shut because I couldn't think of what to say to persuade him not to rat us out.

Within moments, his expression changed from shock to amusement.

"I won't say a thing, sweetie. On one condition." His smirk made me wary.

"Anything," I promised. Kaden reached for my hand, but I batted it away, not wanting to add fuel to the fire. Although the damage had already been done; he'd seen us groping each other, practically dry humping against the back of the clubhouse.

"You have to promise that whenever you do tell your father, that I'm there to see it." He laughed, and I wasn't quite sure if he was serious or not.

"Why?" Kaden asked the question, just as baffled as I was.

"Let's just say it'll be the sweetest karma."

THE END ... OR IS IT?

NOTE TO READER

IF YOU ARE A NEW reader of my work, thank you so much for taking a chance on me. If I'm old news to you, thank you for continuing to support me. It truly means the world to me.

If you've enjoyed this book, or any of my other stories, please consider leaving a review. It doesn't have to be long at all. A sentence or two will do just fine. Of course, if you wish to elaborate, feel free to write as much as you want. ☺

Also, I mentioned Cutter's daughter, Kalista, and her husband, Eli, in this book. But did you know that they have a story of their own? *Torn* came out in December of 2015.

If you would like to be notified of my upcoming releases, cover reveals, giveaways, etc, be sure to sign up for my newsletter.

ABOUT THE AUTHOR

S. NELSON GREW UP WITH a love of reading and a very active imagination, never putting pen to paper, or fingers to keyboard until 2013.

Her passion to create was overwhelming, and within a few months she'd written her first novel, Stolen Fate. When she isn't engrossed in creating one of the many stories rattling around inside her head, she loves to read and travel as much as she can.

She lives in the Northeast with her husband and two dogs, enjoying the ever changing seasons.

If you would like to follow or contact her please do so at the following:

Website:
www.snelsonauthor.com

Email Address:
snelsonauthor8@gmail.com

Also on Facebook, Goodreads, Amazon, Instagram and Twitter

OTHER BOOKS BY S. NELSON

STANDALONES

Stolen Fate

Redemption

Torn

Blind Devotion

THE ADDICTED TRILOGY

Addicted (Addicted Trilogy, Book 1)

Shattered (Addicted Trilogy, Book 2)

Wanted (Addicted Trilogy, Book 3)

THE KNIGHTS CORRUPTION MC SERIES

Marek

Stone

Jagger

Tripp

Ryder